A NOTE FROM THE TRANSLATOR

The best way of handling a translation is about as slippery a business as the best way of organizing a society, the best way of living a life, or, for that matter, the best way of writing. In dealing with a piece of literature a translator must hear its tone, judge its language, appreciate its style, and understand its subtleties of meaning, and then as if such passive appreciation were not hard enough, he must recreate all these features as closely as possible in a tongue foreign to the original.

In trying to convey the essence of a literary work in another language, he is in the position of a conductor of an orchestra of outlandish instruments asked to perform a classical symphony. He must first adapt the piece to the unfamiliar instruments and then guide his barbarous musicians through it. If he is tone-deaf in the language into which he translates, the effect may be like playing the "Moonlight Sonata" on a tin can.

—Andrew R. MacAndrew

THE BROTHERS KARAMAZOV

FYODOR DOSTOEVSKY

A NEW TRANSLATION BY ANDREW R. MacANDREW

INTRODUCTORY ESSAY BY KONSTANTIN MOCHULSKY

BANTAM BOOKS

TORONTO · NEW YORK · LONDON

THE BROTHERS KARAMAZOV

Bantam Classic edition / August 1970
Bantam edition / October 1972
3rd printing .... October 1973   4th printing .... January 1976
5th printing .... January 1978

ISBN 0-553-11787-4

Published simultaneously in the United States and Canada

Bantam Books are published by Bantam Books, Inc. Its trade-
mark, consisting of the words "Bantam Books" and the por-
trayal of a bantam, is registered in the United States Patent
Office and in other countries. Marca Registrada. Bantam
Books, Inc., 666 Fifth Avenue, New York, New York 10019.

PART ONE

BOOK I: A Peculiar Family History

BOOK II: An Incongruous Gathering

BOOK III: The Sensualists

PART TWO

BOOK IV: Torment

BOOK V: Pro and Contra

BOOK VI: A Russian Monk

PART THREE

BOOK VII: Alyosha

BOOK VIII: Mitya

BOOK IX: Preliminary Investigation

PART FOUR

BOOK X: The Boys

BOOK XI: Ivan

BOOK XII: Miscarriage of Justice

EPILOGUE

DOSTOEVSKY AND
THE BROTHERS KARAMAZOV

Konstantin Mochulsky

In 1839 the eighteen-year-old youth Dostoevsky wrote to his brother: "Man is a mystery: if you spend your entire life trying to puzzle it out, then do not say that you have wasted your time. I occupy myself with this mystery, because I want to be a man."

The great psychologist had a presentiment of his vocation: all his creative work is devoted to the mystery of man. In Dostoevsky's novels there are no landscapes and pictures of nature. He portrays only man and man's world; his heroes are people from contemporary urban civilization, fallen out of the natural world-order and torn away from "living life." The writer prided himself on his *realism;* he was describing not the abstract "universal man," contrived by J. J. Rousseau, but the real European of the 19th century with all the endless contradictions of his "sick consciousness." The Russian novelist first discovered the real face of the hero of our "troubled time"—the "man from underground": this new Hamlet is struck by the infirmity of doubt, poisoned by reflection, doomed to a lack of will and inertia. He is tragically alone and divided in two; he has the consciousness of an "harassed mouse."

Dostoevsky's psychological art is famous throughout the world. Long before Freud and before the school of psychoanalysts he plunged into the depths of the subconscious and investigated the inner life of children and adolescents; he studied the psychics of the insane, maniacs, fanatics, criminals, suicides. Special commentaries exist on Dostoevsky, the psychopathologist and criminalist. But his analysis was not

From *Dostoevsky: His Life and Work,* by Konstantin Mochulsky, translated by Michael A. Minihan (Copyright © 1967 by Princeton University Press): pp. 649-652 and 596-601. Reprinted by permission of Princeton University Press.

limited to individual psychology; he penetrated the collective psychology of the family, of society, of the people. His greatest insights concern the soul of the people, the metapsychic "unity" of mankind.

Psychology is only the surface of Dostoevsky's art. It was for him not an end, but a means. The province of the inner life is only the vestibule of the kingdom of the spirit. Behind the psychologist stands the *pneumatologist*—the brilliant investigator of the human spirit. In one of his notebooks we find the following remark: "I am called a psychologist, it's not true, I am only a realist in the highest sense, i.e., I depict all the depths of the human soul." Dostoevsky had his own doctrine of man—and in this is his great historical importance. He devoted all his creative forces to struggling for the spiritual nature of man, to defending his dignity, personality, and freedom.

In his own personal experience, the author of *Crime and Punishment* lived through the tragic epoch of the *shattering of humanism*. Before his eyes humanism tore itself away from its Christian roots and was transformed into a struggle with God. Having begun with the emancipation of man from "theology" and "metaphysics," it ended by enslaving him to the "laws of nature" and "necessity." Man was conceived as a natural being, subject to the principles of profit and rational egoism: his metaphysical depth was taken away from him, his third dimension—the image of God. Humanism wanted to exalt man and shamefully degraded him. Dostoevsky himself was a humanist, passed through its seductions and was infected by its poison. The romantic idealist of the years of *Poor People* was captivated by utopian socialism and passed through the whole dialectical course of its development: he "passionately accepted" Belinsky's atheistic faith and entered Durov's secret revolutionary society. Starting out from Christian humanism, he came to atheistic communism. In the year 1849, sentenced to capital punishment, the writer stood on the scaffold. During these terrible minutes the "old man" in him died. In penal servitude a "new man" was born; there began a cruel judgment of himself and the "regeneration of his convictions." In Siberia, two events took place in the life of the exiled writer which decided his whole subsequent fate: his meeting with Christ and his acquaintance with the Russian people. Amidst inhuman sufferings, in a struggle with doubt and negation, faith in God was won. Apropos of the *Legend of the Grand*

Inquisitor Dostoevsky wrote in his notebook: "Even in Europe there are not and have not been atheistic expressions of such force; consequently, it is not as a boy that I believe in Christ and confess Him, but *my hosanna has passed through a great furnace of doubts.* . . ."

After penal servitude, the religious theme formed the spiritual center of his work. The question of faith and disbelief was posed in all the great novels. In 1870 he wrote to Maikov: "The main question, which has tormented me consciously or unconsciously throughout my entire life— the existence of God."

"God torments" all of Dostoevsky's heroes; all of them decide the question of God's existence; their fate is wholly determined by the religious consciousness.

Dostoevsky lived through a period of crisis in Christian culture and experienced it as his personal tragedy. Shortly after the Franco-Prussian War and the Parisian Commune, the hero of the novel *A Raw Youth* went abroad. Never had he traveled to Europe with such sadness and with such love. "In those days, especially, one seemed to hear the tolling of a funeral bell over Europe." The great idea of Christian culture was dying; it was being escorted out with catcalls and the flinging of mud; atheism was celebrating its first victories. "I wept," confesses Versilov, "wept for them, I wept for the old idea and, perhaps, I wept real tears."

The Russian Dostoevsky, at the end of the 19th century, felt himself the only European who understood the significance of the world tragedy, which was being experienced by mankind. He alone "wept real tears." And now the "old idea" was gone and mankind was left on earth without God. The writer's "novel-tragedies" are devoted to depicting the fate of *mankind abandoned by God.* He prophetically indicated two paths: man-godhood and the herd.

Kirilov in *The Devils* declares: "If God doesn't exist, then I am God." In place of the God-man appears the man-god, the "strong personality," who stands beyond morality, "beyond the confines of good and evil," to whom "everything is permitted" and who can "transgress" all laws (Raskolnikov, Rogozhin, Kirilov, Stavrogin, Ivan Karamazov). Dostoevsky made one of his greatest discoveries: *the nature of man is correlative to the nature of God;* if there is no God, there is also no man. In the man-god, the new demonic being, everything human must disappear. The Russian writer predicts the appearance of Nietzsche: the superman of the author of *Zarathustra* also signifies in his presence the destruction of man: "the human, the too human" is eradicated in him as shame and disgrace.

The other path of atheistic mankind leads to the herd. The culmination of Dostoevsky's work is the *Legend of the Grand Inquisitor*. If men are only natural beings, if their souls are not immortal, then it is fitting that they be established on earth with the greatest possible well-being. And since by their nature they are "impotent rebels," then one must enslave and transform them into a submissive herd. The Grand Inquisitor will tend them with an iron rod. Then at last, an enormous anthill will be built up, the Babylonian tower will be erected, and now forever. Both ways—man-godhood and the herd—lead to one and the same result: the suppression of man.

Dostoevsky saw history in the light of the Apocalypse; he predicted unheard-of world catastrophes. "The end of the world is coming," he wrote. "The end of the century will be marked by a calamity, the likes of which has never yet occurred." The tragic world-outlook of the author of *The Devils* was inaccessible to the positivists of the 19th century: he was a man of our catastrophic epoch. But God's abandonment is not the last word of Dostoevsky's work; he depicted the "dark night," but had presentiments of the dawn. He believed that the tragedy of history would be culminated in the transfiguration of the world, that after the Golgotha of mankind would follow the Second Advent of Christ and "there would resound the hymn of the new and last resurrection."

———————

Dostoevsky worked for three years on his last novel. For three years the concluding stage of the labor—its artistic embodiment—continued. But spiritually he had worked on it his entire life. *The Brothers Karamazov* is the summit, from which we see the organic unity of the writer's whole creative work disclosed. Everything that he experienced, thought, and created finds its place in this vast synthesis. The complex human world of *Karamazov* grew up naturally, over the course of a decade, absorbing the philosophical and artistic elements of the preceding works: the *Diary of a Writer* is the laboratory in which the ideology of the final novel is given its definitive form; in *A Raw Youth* there is established the structure of the family chronicle and the tragedy of "fathers and children" is delineated; in *The Devils,* the atheist Stavrogin's clash with the prelate Tikhon anticipates the tragic conflict of faith and disbelief (the Elder Zosima—Ivan Karamazov); in *The Idiot* the subject schema, similar to *Karamazov,* is worked out: at the center of the action stands a major crime; the wronged beauty Nastasya Filippovna calls Grushenka to mind, the proud Aglaya—Katerina Ivanovna; the motif of a dramatic meeting between the rivals is repeated in both novels.

The "passionate" Rogozhin is just as engulfed by eros as is Mitya Karamazov; the "positively beautiful individual"—Prince Myshkin—is Alyosha's spiritual brother. In *Crime and Punishment* Raskolnikov steps beyond the moral law, declaring that "everything is permitted," and becomes a theoretician-murderer: his fate determines the fate of Ivan; the struggle between the prosecutor Porfiry Petrovich and the criminal develops in *Karamazov* into the "preliminary investigation" of Dmitry's case. But Dostoevsky's last and greatest creation is genetically linked not only with the "great novels." Mitya's erotic possession had already been delineated in the portrayal of the hero's passion for the fatal woman Polina in *The Gambler;* Ivan's "disease of consciousness" and Fyodor Pavlovich's "underground philosophy" had been outlined in *Works from Underground.* Prince Volkovsky in *The Humiliated and Wronged* already possesses the Karamazov element—sensuality; in *The Village of Stepanchikovo* appears the first draft of the figure of Smerdyakov (the lackey Vidoplyasov). Even the tales of the period before penal servitude are related by countless threads with the last novel: the theme of "romantic dreaming" and the "solitary consciousness" is culminated in Ivan's "abstractness" and uprootedness; Schiller's romanticism finds its poetic expression in Dmitry's "hymn"; the idea of the *Grand Inquisitor* grows out of the tragedy of the "faint heart" *(The Landlady).* Finally, the motif of the personality's duality (Ivan Karamazov's devil) rises from his youthful work *The Double.*

The Brothers Karamazov is not only a synthesis of Dostoevsky's creative work, but also the culmination of his life. In the very topography of the novel his memories of childhood are united with the impressions of his final years: the city ·in which the novel's action is placed reflects the features of Staraya Russa, but the villages surrounding it (Darovoye, Chermashnya, Mokroye) are related to his father's estate in Tula province. Fyodor Pavlovich inherits several traits of the writer's father, and his violent death corresponds to Mikhail Andreyevich's tragic end. Dmitry, Ivan, and Alyosha are three aspects of Dostoevsky's personality, three stages of his spiritual way. Fiery and noble Dmitry, declaiming the *Hymn to Joy,* embodies the *romantic period* of the author's life; his tragic fate, the charge of parricide and exile to Siberia, was inspired by the story of the innocent criminal Ilyinsky and by this is connected with memories of the years of penal servitude. Ivan, the atheist and creator of a social utopia, reflects the *epoch of his friendship with* Belinsky and captivation by atheistic socialism; Alyosha is a symbol of the writer after the period of his penal servitude, when a "regeneration of his convictions" took place within him, when he discovered the Russian people and the Russian Christ.

The novel *Brothers Karamazov* opens before us as its author's *spiritual biography* and his *artistic confession.* But, having once been transformed into a work of art, the story of Dostoevsky's personality becomes the history of man's personality in general. The accidental and individual disappears, what is ecumenical and universal to mankind grows up. In the fate of the brothers Karamazov each of us recognizes his own fate. The writer portrays the three brothers as a *spiritual unity.* This is an organically collective personality in its triple structure: the principle of reason is embodied in Ivan: he is a logician and rationalist, an innate skeptic and negator; the principle of feeling is represented by Dmitry: in him is the "sensuality of insects" and the inspiration of eros; the principle of will, realizing itself in active love as an ideal, is presented in Alyosha. The brothers are joined to one another by ties of blood, grow up from one familial root: the biological given—the Karamazov element —is shown in the father Fyodor Pavlovich. Every human personality bears in itself a fatal dichotomy: the legitimate Karamazov brothers have an illegitimate brother Smerdyakov: he is their embodied temptation and personified sin.

Thus in the novel's artistic symbols the author expounded his own *teaching about personality.* The conflicts of consciousness are converted into a struggle of the passions and into "whirlwinds of events."

The conception of the *organically collective personality* determines the novel's structure. All of Dostoevsky's works are personalistic: their action is always concentrated around the personality of the main hero (Raskolnikov, Prince Myshkin, Stavrogin, Versilov). The main hero of *Karamazov* is the three brothers in their spiritual unity. Three personal themes are developed parallel, but on the spiritual plane the three parallel lines converge: the brothers, each in his own way, experience a single tragedy, they share a common guilt and a common redemption. Not only Ivan with his idea "everything is permitted," not only Dmitry in the impetuosity of his passions, but also the "quiet boy" Alyosha—all are responsible for their father's murder. All of them consciously or semi-consciously desired his death: and their desire impelled Smerdyakov to the crime: he was their docile instrument. Ivan's *murderous thought* was transformed into Dmitry's *destructive passion* and into Smerdyakov's *criminal act*. They are guilty actively, Alyosha passively. He knew and permitted it, *could have* saved his father and did not. The brothers' common crime also involves a common punishment: Dmitry atones for his guilt by exile to penal servitude, Ivan—by the dissolution of his personality and the appearance of the devil, Alyosha by his terrible spiritual crisis. All of them are purified in suffering and attain a new life.

The architectonics of *Karamazov* are distinguished by their unusual rigidity: the law of balance, of symmetry, of proportionality is observed by the author systematically. It is possible to conjecture that Vladimir Solovyov's harmonious philosophical schema influenced the technique of the novel's structure. This is the most "constructed" and ideologically complete of all Dostoevsky's works. The human world of the novel is disposed in a symbolic order: at the center of the plot appears Dmitry—he is the promoter of the action and the source of dramatic energy. His passion for Grushenka, rivalry with his father, his romance with Katerina Ivanovna, the apparent crime, the trial and exile constitute the external content of the novel. On both sides of him stand Ivan and Alyosha; the first prepares the parricide by his ideas and by this influences Dmitry's fate: he is his ideational adversary and spiritual antipode, but is joined to him by blood, by their common hatred for their father and their common guilt. Alyosha sets his "quietness" in opposition to Dmitry's violence, his purity—to his sensuousness; but even in his modest chastity lives the "Karamazov element," he also knows the gnawing of sensuality. They are different and alike: the ecstatic sense of life mysteriously unites them. Therefore, Dmitry's sin is Alyosha's sin.

Behind the group of legitimate sons, set on the first plane, in the distance, in half-illumination, stands the figure of the illegitimate brother, the lackey Smerdyakov. He is separated from them by origin, descent, social position, character; the spiritual unity of the family is rent by his wanton isolation. But nonetheless how mysteriously profound is his tie with his brothers: as a medium, he executes their subconscious suggestion; Ivan determines Smerdyakov's destiny by his ideas, Dmitry by his passions, Alyosha by his squeamish indifference. The theme of "children" in its four ideational aspects is developed by the four brothers; the theme of "fathers" is represented only by Fyodor Pavlovich. It is unique and simple: the impersonal, innate element of life, the terrible force of the earth and sex.

A tragic struggle takes place between the father and his children. Only the men contend, masculine ideas clash together. Dostoevsky's women do not have their own personal history—they enter the heroes' biography, constitute part of their fate. Each of the brothers Karamazov has his own complement in a female image: beside Ivan stands Katerina Ivanovna, beside Dmitry—Grushenka, by Alyosha—Liza Khokhlakova; even Smerdyakov has his own "lady of his heart"—the maidservant Marya Kondratyevna. The brothers' indivisible unity comes forward on the "amorous" plane with special precision. The threads, uniting them with their loves, cross and intertwine. Ivan loves Katerina Ivanovna, Dmitry's fiancée; Alyosha for an instant becomes his rival, feeling himself stung with passion for Grushenka: Katerina Ivanovna is a fatal woman both for Ivan and for Dmitry; Grushenka unites in her love Dmitry and Alyosha. Finally, the unity of the Karamazov family is symbolically shown in Fyodor Pavlovich's and Dmitry's passion for one woman —Grushenka. The remaining dramatis personae are disposed around this central group. Fyodor Pavlovich is surrounded by his own "world" of boon-companions and dissolute women; Grushenka brings with her her admirers and a company of Poles; Mitya bursts in with gypsies, chance friends and creditors. Richest of all is Alyosha's world: the "young lover of mankind" introduces two aspects of human communality into the novel: the monastic communal life and the "brotherhood of children." He connects the dark Karamazov kingdom with the world of the Elder Zosima and Ilyusha Snegiryov. Only Ivan does not have his own world: he does not accept God's creation, that which is human is alien to him, he is disembodied. His sole companion is a phantom, the spirit of nonbeing, the devil.

The story of the Karamazov brothers' collective personality is depicted in a *novel-tragedy*. Everything is tragic in this artistic myth about man, both the enmity of the children toward the father, and the brothers' struggle among themselves, and the inner strife of each brother individually. The disclosure of the metaphysical significance of human fate belongs to Dmitry. In his experience of the passions he came to understand that "the devil struggles with God, and the field of battle is the human heart." Before him are revealed two abysses—above and below. But he is powerless to make a choice and in this lies his personal tragedy. Among the brothers he occupies a middle, neutral position. Ivan and Alyosha, standing on his left and on his right side, already have made this choice. Ivan is irresistibly drawn to the lower abyss, Alyosha reaches for the higher. The one says "no," the other "yes." Fyodor Pavlovich, sitting over his "little cognac," asks Ivan: "Is there a God or not?" The latter answers: "No, there is no God." He appeals to Alyosha: "Alyosha, does God exist?" Alyosha answers: "God does exist." Ivan's personal tragedy is in that "his mind is not in harmony with his heart": with his feelings he loves God's world, although with his reason he cannot accept it.

Of the three brothers the most in harmony is Alyosha, but even in his integral nature there is a split: he knows the temptations of Karamazov sensuality and his faith passes through a "furnace of doubt." The religious idea of the novel —the struggle of faith with disbelief—emerges beyond the limits of the Karamazov household. Ivan's negation begets the ominous figure of the inquisitor; Alyosha's affirmation is mystically deepened in the Elder Zosima's image. Human hearts are only the field of battle, and God and the devil struggle. Under the psychological exterior of the personality, Dostoevsky unveils its ontology and metaphysics. The history of the Karamazov family is an artistic myth which encompasses a *religious mystery:* here is why the *Legend of the Grand Inquisitor* stands at its center.

Dostoevsky was writing not a philosophical treatise or a theological system, he was composing a novel. Religious-philosophical material was introduced into the framework of the novel genre and treated according to its laws. A tense dramatic plot is constructed, at the center of which stands an enigmatic crime; the ideological masses are drawn into the whirlwind of the action, and clashing together, produce effective outbursts. In *The Brothers Karamazov*, the religious mystery-play is paradoxically joined with a crime novel. Notwithstanding all its depth, this is one of the most captivating and popular works of Russian literature.

> Verily, verily I say unto you,
> except a corn of wheat fall into
> the ground and die, it abideth
> alone: but if it die, it bringeth
> forth much fruit.
>
> John XII.24

AUTHOR'S PREFACE

In starting out on the life of my hero, Alexei Fyodorovich Karamazov, I feel somewhat at a loss. By this I mean that, although I refer to Alexei (Alyosha) as my hero, I am well aware that he is by no means a great man, and this leads me to anticipate such obvious questions as: "What is so remarkable about your Alexei Karamazov that you should choose him as your hero? What exactly did he accomplish? Who has heard of him and what is he famous for? And why should I, the reader, spend time learning the facts of his life?"

The last question is the fateful one because all I can answer is: "You may find that out for yourself from the novel." But what if they read the novel and are still unconvinced that my Alexei is a remarkable man? I say this because I sadly anticipate it. To me, he *is* remarkable, but I very much doubt I will succeed in proving it to the reader. The trouble is that, although I suppose he may be described as "a man of good works," he is still indeterminate, not fully recognizable as such. But then, would it not be rather strange to expect to find clear-cut characters in times like ours? One thing, though, is beyond doubt: he is a strange person, we might even say an eccentric. And peculiarity and eccentricity are more likely to create prejudice against a man than make people listen to him, especially nowadays when everyone tries to lump all the special cases together and to read some general meaning into the general meaninglessness. Isn't that so?

Now, if you don't agree with this, if you believe that it is not true, or at least not necessarily true, it will give me hope that my hero may be of some interest to you. For an eccentric is not necessarily an exception or an isolated phenomenon; indeed, it often happens that it is he who embodies the very essence of his time while his contem-

1

poraries somehow seem to have been cut loose from it by gusts of an alien wind.

Had it not been for one more difficulty, I would not have ventured into these boring and unclear explanations. I would have started the novel directly without any introduction, reasoning that a reader will finish the book anyway, if he is enjoying it. The additional difficulty is that, although I have only one life story to tell, there are really two novels here. The main novel is the second one, which describes the life of my hero in our time, at this very moment.* As to the first novel, it takes place thirteen years ago and is perhaps not even really a novel but just the description of an important phase of the early youth of my hero. However, I cannot dispense with this first novel because much of the second one would be incomprehensible without it. And this complicates my original difficulty even further: if I, the biographer, feel that even one novel may be too much for a modest and obscure hero like mine, how can I come forward with two novels about him? How can I justify such presumptuousness?

Being unable to puzzle out these questions, I have decided to leave them unanswered. No doubt, a perspicacious reader will have guessed from the outset that this was what I was driving at and will be all the more irritated with me for spouting useless phrases and wasting his precious time. Well, I'll answer that precisely: I have been spouting useless phrases and wasting precious time, first of all, out of politeness and, secondly, out of slyness, to be able to say later: "Well, I more or less warned you, didn't I?" Besides, I am really quite glad that my novel split into two stories, while the essential unity of the whole was preserved. Once he has acquainted himself with the first story, the reader will be able to decide for himself whether it is worth his while to start the second. Of course, no one is bound in any way, and the book can be put aside after a couple of pages of the first story, too, and never picked up again. However, there are always some scrupulous readers who are determined to read to the end, no matter what, so that they can pass a fair and impartial judgment. Such, for instance, are all the Russian literary critics. And so I will feel less guilty toward these people if, scrupulous and

---

* The second novel, completing the image of Alyosha as a "hero," was never written. [A. MacA.]

thorough as they are, I give them a legitimate excuse for putting my story down in the middle of the very first episode.

So this is all my introduction. I fully agree that it is quite unnecessary, but since it is already written, I shall let it stand.

And now let's get down to business.

PART ONE

———

BOOK I

A PECULIAR FAMILY HISTORY

CHAPTER 1

Fyodor Pavlovich Karamazov

Alexei Fyodorovich Karamazov was the third son of Fyodor Pavlovich Karamazov, a landowner in our district who became a celebrity (and is remembered to this day) because of the tragic and mysterious end he met exactly thirteen years ago, which will be described in its proper place. For the moment, I will only say of this "landowner" (as they referred to him here, although he spent hardly any time on his land) that he belonged to a peculiar though widespread human type, the sort of man who is not only wretched and depraved but also muddle-headed—muddle-headed in a way that allows him to pull off all sorts of shady little financial deals and not much else.

Fyodor Karamazov, for instance, started with next to nothing; he was just about the lowliest landowner among us, a man who would dash off to dine at other people's tables whenever he was given a chance and who sponged off people as much as he could. Yet, at his death, they found that he had a hundred thousand rubles in hard cash. And with all that, throughout his life he remained one of the most muddle-headed eccentrics in our entire district. Let me repeat: it was not stupidity, for most such eccentrics are really quite intelligent and cunning, and their lack of common sense is of a special kind, a national variety.

He had been married twice and had three sons—the eldest, Dmitry, by his first wife, and the other two, Ivan and Alexei, by the second.

Fyodor Karamazov's first wife came from a fairly wealthy family of landed gentry—the Miusovs—also from our district. Why should a girl with a dowry, a beautiful girl moreover, one of those bright, clever young things who in this generation are no longer rare and who even cropped up occasionally in the last—why should she marry such a worthless

7

"freak," as they called him? I will not really attempt to explain. But, then, I once knew a young lady of the old, "romantic" generation who, after several years of secret love for a gentleman whom, please note, she could have peacefully married at any moment she chose, invented insurmountable obstacles for herself and, one stormy night, jumped from a steep, rather cliff-like bank into a fairly deep, rapid river and drowned, all because she fancied herself an Ophelia out of Shakespeare. Indeed, if the bank, on which she had had her eye for a long time, had been less picturesque or had there simply been a flat bank, it is conceivable that the suicide would never have taken place at all. This is a true story, and it must be assumed that in the past two or three generations quite a few similar incidents have occurred. In the same way, what Adelaida Miusov did was undoubtedly an echo of outside influences and also the act of exasperation of a captive mind. Perhaps she was trying to display feminine independence, to rebel against social conventions, against the despotism of her family and relatives, while her ready imagination convinced her, if only for a moment, that Fyodor Karamazov, despite his reputation as a sponger, was nevertheless one of the boldest and most caustic men of that "period of transition toward better things," whereas in reality he was nothing but a nasty buffoon. The fact that the marriage plans included elopement added piquancy to it, making it more exciting for Adelaida. Fyodor, at that time, would, of course, have done anything to improve his lowly position, and the opportunity to latch on to a good family and to pocket a dowry was extremely tempting to him. As for love, there does not seem to have been any, either on the bride's part or, despite her beauty, on Karamazov's. This was perhaps a unique case in Fyodor Karamazov's life, for he was as sensual as a man can be, one who throughout his life was always prepared, at the slightest encouragement, to chase any skirt. But his wife just happened to be the one woman who did not appeal to him sensually in the least.

Right after the elopement, Adelaida realized that she felt nothing but scorn for her husband. It quickly became obvious what married life was to be. Despite the fact that her family accepted the situation quite soon and gave the runaway bride her dowry, relations between husband and wife became an everlasting succession of quarrels. It was rumored that, in these quarrels, the young wife displayed incomparably more dignity and generosity than her husband, who, it was found out later, soon wheedled out of her every kopek of the twenty-five thousand rubles she had received, so that, as far as she was concerned, those thousands were sunk in deep waters never to be salvaged again. As to the little country estate and the quite decent town house that were also part of her dowry, he kept trying desperately to have them transferred to his name by some suitable deed; he probably would have succeeded because of the loathing and disgust his constant pleading and begging inspired in his wife, because she would do anything to have peace, sick and tired as she was of him; but luckily Adelaida's family intervened in time to put a stop to his greed.

People knew that husband and wife often came to actual blows and rumor had it that it was she who beat him, rather than he her. Indeed, Adelaida was a hot-tempered, bold, dark, and impatient lady endowed with remarkable physical strength.

Finally she eloped with a half-starved tutor, a former divinity student, leaving her husband with their three-year-old boy, Mitya.

Fyodor Karamazov immediately installed a regular harem in the house and indulged in the most scandalous drunken debauchery. But between one orgy and the next, he would drive all over the province complaining tearfully to all and sundry of Adelaida's desertion, and revealing on these occasions certain unsavory intimate details of their conjugal life that any other husband would have been ashamed to mention. He even seemed to enjoy—indeed, to feel flattered by—his ridiculous role as a cuckolded husband, for he insisted on describing his own disgrace in minute detail, even embellishing on it. "Why, Fyodor Pavlovich," people remarked, "you act as if an honor had been bestowed upon you. You seem pleased despite your sorrow." Many even added that he was delighted to have the role of clown thrust upon him, that he only pretended to be unaware of his ridiculous position in order to make it even funnier. But who can really tell? Possibly he was quite ingenuous about it all.

He finally succeeded in getting on the track of his runaway wife. It led to Petersburg where the poor thing had moved with her divinity student and where she had abandoned herself to a life of complete emancipation. Fyodor Karamazov immediately busied himself with preparations for the journey to Petersburg, and perhaps he would have gone, although he certainly had no idea what he would do there. But once he had decided to go, he felt that he had a special reason for plunging into a bout of unrestrained drunkenness—to fortify himself for the journey. And just at that time his in-laws received word that Adelaida had died in Petersburg. She died suddenly, in a garret, of typhus according to some, of starvation according to others. Karamazov was drunk when he learned of his wife's death, and some say he exclaimed joyfully, raising his hands to heaven: "Lord, now let Your servant depart in peace." But according to others, he wept, sobbing like a little boy so that people felt sorry for him despite the disgust he aroused in them. It is quite possible that they all were right, that he rejoiced in his regained freedom and wept for the woman from whom he had been freed, both at once. In most cases, people, even the most vicious, are much more naive and simple-minded than we assume them to be. And this is true of ourselves too.

CHAPTER 2

He Gets Rid of His Eldest Son

It is, of course, easy to imagine what sort of a father such a man would be, how he would bring up his children. And he lived up to expectation: he completely and thoroughly neglected his child by Adelaida. He did not do so out of any deliberate malice or resentment toward the child's mother, but simply because he forgot all about the little boy. And while he was pestering people with his tears and self-pitying stories, while he was turning his home into a house of debauchery, a faithful servant of the household, Gregory, took the three-year-old Mitya into his care. If it hadn't been for Gregory, there would have been no one to change the boy's shirt. Moreover, it so happened that the child's relations on his mother's side had also, at first, forgotten his existence. Mitya's grandfather, that is, Adelaida's father, Mr. Miusov, was no longer alive; his widow, Mitya's grandmother, had moved to Moscow and was in very poor health; and, in the meantime, Adelaida's sisters had married and moved away. So Mitya spent almost a year in Gregory's little house in the servants' quarters. And, even if his father had occasionally remembered him (he could not, after all, have been completely unaware of the child's existence), Karamazov would have sent his son back to the servants' quarters anyway, because a child would have been in the way during the orgies.

But one day a first cousin of Adelaida's returned from Paris. Peter Miusov, who was later to settle abroad permanently, was at that time still a young man, but he was already an exception among the Miusovs: he was an enlightened, big-city gentleman, glittering with foreign polish, a European through and through who, later in life, was to become a typical liberal of the 1840's and 1850's. In the course of his life, he came in contact with some of the most liberal minds of his era, both in Russia and abroad. He met Proudhon personally, as well as Bakunin, and, toward the end of his wanderings, liked best to tell of his experiences during the three days of the February Revolution of 1848 which he had witnessed in Paris, implying that he himself had taken part in it, just short, perhaps, of manning the barricades. This was one of the most gratifying recollections of his youth. He was a man of independent means, with an income from an estate of a thousand-odd souls, as property was evaluated in the old days. That splendid estate was located just outside our town and bordered on the lands of our famous monastery. No sooner had young Peter Miusov taken possession of his estate than he started an endless lawsuit against the monastery. It was something about fishing privileges or wood-cutting rights, I'm not sure which, but he felt that in suing "clericals" he was doing his duty as a citizen and an enlightened man.

When Miusov heard what had happened to Adelaida, whom he, of course, remembered, having even, at one time, taken a special interest in her, and when he learned of Mitya's plight, he decided to intervene, although that involved approaching Karamazov, whom Miusov loathed and despised with all the ardor of youth. This was the first time that he met Fyodor Karamazov; he told him point blank that he wished to take the boy and be responsible for his education. Later, he liked to tell at length what had happened at that meeting, because he felt it revealed a great deal about Karamazov's character. When Miusov first broached the subject of Mitya, the fellow stared at him blankly, as though he could not understand what child Miusov was talking about, and he seemed positively taken aback when reminded that he had a young son. And although Miusov's story may have been exaggerated, there was certainly an element of truth in it. It is a fact that all his life Karamazov liked to act the fool and assume all sorts of surprising roles; he would do so even when he had nothing to gain, indeed, even when it could be positively to his disadvantage, as in this instance. This is a quirk found in many people, even very clever ones, let alone the likes of Fyodor Karamazov.

Miusov at first went about the matter with some zest, and was even appointed Mitya's guardian (jointly with Karamazov), since the boy had, after all, the small estate and the town house coming to him as his inheritance from his mother. And he moved the boy to his house. But, not being tied down by a family of his own, just as soon as he had wound up his business in our town, which consisted of collecting the revenue from his estate, he went dashing off to Paris for a long stay. He left the boy in the care of a relative of his, a lady who lived in Moscow. Miusov settled in Paris for good and lost sight of Mitya, his interest in the boy petering out completely after the February Revolution, which made such an ineradicable impression on him. In the meantime, the Moscow lady died and Mitya passed into the care of one of her married daughters. I believe he had to change homes for a fourth time soon afterward. I won't expand on this topic here since I will have a great deal to say later about this first-born son of Fyodor Karamazov's, but I must supply a few facts right away, without which I could not even begin my novel.

First of all, Mitya—that is, Dmitry Fyodorovich Karamazov—was the only one of Fyodor Pavlovich Karamazov's sons who grew up under the impression that, however hard up he might be, he would, when he came of age, come into his inheritance from his mother and that he would then be financially independent. He was unruly as a boy and as a young man. He dropped out of the classical secondary school, but later was admitted to military school. From there he was sent on active duty with an army unit in the Caucasus, where he was given an officer's commission in the field. He was soon demoted to the ranks for fighting a duel, only to be restored to his rank again for gallantry. After this he led a wild, gay life that cost a good deal of money. Since, until he came of age, he never received a single kopek from his father, he was deep in debt by the time that day arrived. He only met and got to know the old man when he came to our town to demand an accounting of the estate left him by his mother. It would appear that, even then, Dmitry took a dislike to his father. He stayed at the paternal house only a short time, leaving as soon as he had managed to get a very small sum from the old man, together with some vague agreement about sending him the revenue from his estate. It must be noted here that on this occasion Dmitry failed to find out from his father what the total worth of his estate was or what income it yielded. Karamazov discovered right away (and this must be noted too) that his son had an erroneous and exaggerated notion of his inheritance, and this discovery pleased him for it fitted in with his own schemes. He realized that the young man was irresponsible, violent, passionate, unruly, impatient, and that he couldn't wait to satisfy all his whims and impulses. And Karamazov now knew how to handle Dmitry: the fellow could always be placated, at least temporarily, with small handouts. Karamazov proceeded immediately to exploit his son's weakness, putting him off with small sums. This went on for four years until, finally, Dmitry lost patience. He made a second appearance in town, this time to force on his father a final settlement of their accounts. He was quite stunned to hear from Karamazov that he had already received, in the many installments, a sum amounting to the value of his estate, that, if anything, it was he who was now in debt to his father, and that, moreover, in view of such and such an agreement which he himself had insisted upon at one point, he had renounced all further claims, etc., etc. The young man was dumbfounded, accused his father of cheating him, and acted as if he would go out of his mind.

It was this confrontation between Karamazov and his eldest son that led to the catastrophe which is the subject (or at least the external plot) of my first, preliminary novel. But before I start on that narrative, I'll have to say a few words about Karamazov's other two sons and explain their origins.

CHAPTER 3

The Second Marriage and the Second Family

Shortly after getting the four-year-old Mitya off his hands, Fyodor Karamazov married a second time. His second marriage lasted eight years. He brought back his second wife, Sofia, who was a very young girl, from another province, where he had gone to transact some small business affair with a Jew who was his partner in the deal. Drunkard and lecher though he was, Karamazov was constantly on the lookout for a profitable opportunity to invest some of his capital and, since he was unencumbered by scruples, these ventures were usually quite successful.

Sofia was the daughter of an obscure deacon. She lost her parents in early childhood and, having no other relatives, was brought up by a wealthy old lady, the widow of General Vorokhov. The old woman was her benefactress and her tormentor. I don't know the details, but I heard that one day the meek and uncomplaining creature had to be cut down from a rope she had tied to a nail in the storeroom. This shows how hard it was for her to submit to the whims and the constant nagging of the old woman who, although not really wicked, had been made tyrannical and eccentric by sheer idleness.

When Fyodor Karamazov asked for Sofia's hand, Mrs. Vorokhov made inquiries about him and, consequently, when he reappeared, had him thrown out. So, as with his first marriage, he asked the girl to elope with him. Had Sofia known a bit more about his past, she might have turned him down, even in her situation; but everything had taken place in another province and, besides, what judgment could a sixteen-year-old girl make, when all she felt was that she would rather jump in the river than stay with her benefactress? This is how the poor thing came to exchange a benefactress for a benefactor.

This time, Fyodor Karamazov didn't get any dowry. The general's widow was outraged and refused to give her charge a single kopek, laying a curse on them both instead. But then, on this occasion, collecting a dowry had not been Karamazov's main motive. Although up till then he had been aroused exclusively by the coarser types of feminine good looks, the lecher's imagination was caught now by the striking beauty of this innocent creature and, indeed, by her child-like innocence itself. As he used to say himself later, with a nasty snicker: "Those innocent eyes of hers slit my soul open like a razor."

In a lecher like Fyodor Karamazov, of course, it only added new spice to his sensual desires. He felt that, since he had accepted this wife without dowry, he had every right to treat her without any consideration whatever—she was, he said, "indebted" to him since he had "practically cut her down from a rope." He took advantage of her phenomenal humility to trample underfoot the most ordinary decencies of marriage, even to the point of bringing loose women into the house and holding orgies in her presence. To indicate how far he went, I will mention that Gregory, the dour, stupid, argumentative old servant, who had hated his former mistress Adelaida, now took Sofia's side, stood up for her, and swore back at his master in a manner that was quite intolerable from a servant; once he even broke up a party and drove the guests and the women out of the house.

After a while the wretched girl, who had been terrorized since early childhood, broke down, afflicted with a nervous disorder sometimes found in peasant women, who are then called "shriekers." Her sickness brought on attacks of hysteria so violent that at times she completely lost her reason. But this did not prevent her from bearing Fyodor Karamazov two sons—Ivan, in the first year of marriage, and Alexei, three years later. When she died Alexei was only just over three, but I know for sure that he remembered his mother all his life, though, of course, as in a dream.

After their mother's death, the fate of the two little boys was a repetition of their older brother Mitya's. Their father seemed to forget them immediately and they were so completely neglected that, like Mitya before them, they ended up in Gregory's cottage. And it was in the servants' quarters that the boys were found by the rich and eccentric widow of General Vorokhov, their mother's former benefactress. For the entire eight years of the marriage, she had seethed under the insult she had received, but she had kept herself constantly informed about Sofia and knew all about her sad plight, her sickness, and the outrageous situation in which she was caught. When she heard these things, she would comment to her lady companions: "It serves her right. God is making her pay for her ingratitude."

Exactly three months after Sofia's death, the General's widow suddenly appeared in our town, going straight to Mr. Karamazov's house. Altogether, she spent only half an hour in town, but the amount she accomplished in that short time was amazing. When she arrived late in the afternoon, Fyodor Karamazov, whom she had not seen for eight years, came out to meet her in a rather besotted state. Without a word of explanation, she stepped up to him and slapped him, landing two mighty, resounding smacks on his face; then she caught him by the forelock, pulling it hard three times. Then, still without explanation, she went to Gregory's cottage where she found the two little boys. Noticing right away that they were unwashed and that their shirts were dirty, she turned on Gregory and slapped his face too. She announced that she was taking the boys away with her and, leading them out just as they were, in their dirty shirts, sat them in her carriage, wrapped them in carriage rugs, and drove away to her own town.

Gregory took the slap slavishly, without a word of recrimination, and as he saw the lady off to her carriage, he bowed deeply from the waist, solemnly pronouncing that the Lord would reward her for taking the orphans.

"And you're a blockhead all the same," the old lady shouted at him as the carriage drove off.

Later, after he had thought it over, Karamazov decided that it was all in his best interest and he made no difficulties when the General's widow asked his formal consent to her taking charge of the boys' education. As to the slaps he had received, he dashed all around the town, telling everyone about the incident himself.

When the General's widow died not long after, she bequeathed a thousand rubles to each boy "to be spent exclusively on his education," but sparingly, so that it should last until their coming of age. She added that this sum was "more than adequate for children of such a background," but that if anyone felt it was not, "let him untie his own purse strings," and so on and so forth. I didn't read her will myself, but I understand that it was something along these lines, eccentric and very strangely worded. However, the old woman's principal heir, the Marshal of Nobility of the province, Efim Petrovich Polenov, turned out to be an extremely honorable man. He informed Fyodor Karamazov of the will but realized immediately that such a man would never contribute a kopek to the education of his own children (although Karamazov never refused directly, he always found reasons for delaying his contribution, occasionally even spouting sentimentalities). So Polenov decided to take care of the abandoned boys himself, and he grew quite fond of them, particularly of the younger, Alexei, who lived for a long time in his house as one of the family. It must be noted right here that if the young Karamazovs were indebted to anyone for their upbringing and education, it was above all to this Mr. Polenov, one of the most generous and honorable men to be found. He kept intact the original thousand left to each boy by the General's widow so that, when they came of age, each of them would receive two thousand rubles, thanks to the accumulated interest. Polenov paid for their upkeep and education out of his own pocket, spending, incidentally, considerably more than a thousand rubles on each boy. Again, I won't give a lengthy account of their childhood and school years, but will only outline the most important facts.

Of the elder, Ivan, I will only say that he grew into a sullen and secretive boy, although by no means a timorous one. I gather that by the time he was ten or so he had become aware that he and his brother were not being brought up in their own home but were, in fact, living on other people's charity, and that there was something about their father that made the very mention of his name a cause for embarrassment. Very early in life, almost in infancy (at least so some people claimed), the boy started to display an uncanny aptitude for learning. I don't know exactly how it came to pass, but when he was barely thirteen he left Polenov's family, being sent to a secondary school in Moscow, where he boarded at the house of a celebrated and experienced educator, a boyhood friend of Polenov's. Later, Ivan Karamazov liked to say that he had been sent to Moscow thanks to "Mr. Polenov's zeal for good works," because Polenov had been carried away by the idea that a boy endowed with a genius for learning should be taught by a teacher of genius.

However, neither Mr. Polenov nor the brilliant educator was alive by the time Ivan entered the university. And since Polenov had somehow neglected to make the proper arrangements to cut through the usual Russian red tape and make the bequests (now worth more than two thousand rubles each) quickly available to the boys, Ivan could not get the money and had to earn his own living during his first two years at the university. It must be pointed out that, on this occasion, he made no attempt whatsoever to ask his father for assistance. It is uncertain whether he acted out of pride, out of contempt for his father, or simply because he reasoned in a cold and detached way that he would never get any substantial help from him anyway. In any case, the young man did not despair and quickly found work—first tutoring at a few kopeks an hour, then making the rounds of the editorial offices of newspapers, peddling ten-line news items on street incidents or the like that he signed "Eyewitness." I gather that these items were so originally and strikingly presented that the newspapers were glad to run them. This in itself goes to show the young man's superiority in practical and intellectual matters over the crowd of needy students of both sexes, who night and day swarm through the offices of the Moscow and Petersburg newspapers and magazines, unable to think up anything more original than to beg for translations from the French or for odd copying jobs. Once Ivan Karamazov got to know people on the editorial staffs, he kept in touch with them, so that during his last years at the university he was able to publish reviews of books on a variety of specialized subjects, in which he showed considerable talent; thus he gradually gained a good reputation in literary circles. However, it was not until quite recently that he succeeded in attracting the attention of a wider circle of readers, and it was one particular incident that made them notice and remember him—and a rather curious incident at that. Ivan Karamazov had been graduated from the university, had collected his two thousand rubles, and was planning to take a trip abroad, when one of the major newspapers carried a very strange article of his that caught the interest even of non-specialists. The most remarkable thing about it was that the topic seemed to be quite outside Ivan's field, since he had specialized in the natural sciences. The article was devoted to a problem much discussed at the time—the ecclesiastical courts. After examining various opinions that had already been expressed on the subject, Ivan presented his own views. The impact was due mostly to the tone and to the unexpectedness of the conclusions. First, many clerics greeted the author as one of their camp. Then, not only secularists but even outright atheists joined in the applause. Finally, however, some perspicacious persons decided that the whole article was a hoax, an insolent joke he had played on them all.

I have mentioned this incident because the article and the argument it stirred up even reached our famous monastery, where the matter of the ecclesiastical courts elicited great interest. They were perplexed by it, and when they noticed the signature under it, their interest increased even further, since the author happened to be a native of our part of the country and "a son of *that* Fyodor Karamazov." Then, in the midst of it all, the author himself suddenly appeared in our town.

Why did Ivan choose to come to our town just then? I remember the uneasiness that question stirred in me at the time. This fateful visit of his, which was to trigger off a whole chain of events, remained unclear to me almost to the end. In general, it was strange that such a cultured, proud, and apparently prudent young man as Ivan should come to that scandalous house to join a father who had ignored him all his life, who didn't know him, indeed, hardly remembered that he existed, a father who would most certainly have refused to give him money under any circumstances and who lived in constant dread lest either of his younger sons, Ivan or Alexei, should one day come and ask him for help. Yet the young man came and installed himself in his father's house. He spent one month there, then another, and the two of them seemed to live in perfect agreement. I was not the only one who was surprised; many others wondered about it too. Peter Miusov, the cousin of Karamazov's first wife whom I mentioned earlier, happened to have returned just then from Paris, where he had settled for good, and was staying on his estate just outside our town. I remember that he was the most puzzled of all, once he had made the acquaintance of the young man, who interested him a great deal and with whom he used to exchange sophisticated barbs, although his feelings were often secretly hurt when he was bested in these confrontations.

"He is proud," he said of Ivan then. "A man like that will always find money to live on. Why, even now he has enough to go abroad. So what can be his motive for coming here? He certainly didn't come in the hope of getting money out of his father, for it is obvious that nothing in the world would make his father give him any. Nor does he go in for wine and debauchery, and yet old Karamazov seems unable to take a step without him. In fact, I've never seen two men get along so famously!"

And they did. Moreover, the young man exercised an obvious influence on his father, who sometimes almost seemed as if he would heed his advice. Although he was often his nasty, unbridled self still, his behavior began to improve slightly. It was only later that we learned that Ivan had come, at least partly, at the request of his older brother Dmitry, whom he also met and got to know for the first time during this visit to our town. The two brothers had been corresponding before on an important matter that concerned Dmitry more than Ivan. What it was the reader will learn at great length in good time. However, even when I learned about that matter, Ivan Karamazov remained a mystery to me and I still did not understand why he had come.

Let me add that Ivan seemed to act as a mediator between his father and his brother Dmitry, who by then had completely broken off relations, Dmitry even instituting legal proceedings against the old man.

I must emphasize here that this was the very first meeting of the Karamazovs, the first time that some members of that strange family had set eyes on each other. Now, Karamazov's youngest son, Alexei, had been living among us for the past year and we had met him before his brothers. It is of this brother, Alexei, that I find it the most difficult to speak in this introductory part of my narrative, although it is indispensable to do so before I bring him out onto the stage of my novel. I must write an introductory piece about him too, if only to explain a point that may strike my readers as very strange, namely, that my future hero will have to wear the cassock of a novice at his very first appearance. Yes, he had been living at our monastery for a year or so and, indeed, it looked as if he were preparing to spend the rest of his life within its walls.

CHAPTER 4

The Third Son—Alyosha

He was then only twenty (his brother Ivan was twenty-three and their older brother, Dmitry, twenty-seven). First, I want to make it clear that young Alyosha was in no sense a fanatic. In my opinion at least, he was not even a mystic. Let me tell you my opinion of him right from the start: he was just a boy who very early in life had come to love his fellow men and if he chose to enter a monastery, it was simply because at one point that course had caught his imagination and he had become convinced that it was the ideal way to escape from the darkness of the wicked world, a way that would lead him toward light and love. This particular way had caught his attention only because he had happened to meet a man who made an overwhelming impression on him— the famous Zosima, the elder of our monastery, to whom he had become attached with all the ardor of the first love kindled in his insatiable heart. I will not deny, however, that he was already rather strange even then, because he had been strange from the cradle. As I have already mentioned, he was just three when he lost his mother, yet he always remembered how she looked and how she caressed him—"just as if she were standing alive before me," he would say. Such memories can be preserved (as everyone knows) from an even earlier age, even in a two-year-old, but they are like bright spots standing out in the darkness, a tiny lighted fragment of a huge canvas, while the rest of the painting remains faded and dark. So it was with Alyosha. He remembered a certain evening—a quiet, summer evening, an open window, the slanting rays of the setting sun (the slanting rays were the clearest part of his recollection), an icon with a lighted lamp in a corner of the room, and, kneeling before the icon, his mother, sobbing hysterically, screaming and shrieking, clutching him with both hands so tightly that it hurt, praying to the Mother of God for him, then holding him away from her toward the icon, as if putting him under the protection of the Mother of God . . . Then, all of a sudden a nanny rushes into the room and snatches him away from his mother in alarm. Ah, that picture! Alyosha always remembered the way his mother's face had looked at that second; he described it as both frenzied and beautiful. But he rarely confided this recollection, and to very few people. As a child and as a boy, Alyosha was rather reserved, one might even say uncommunicative. He was not distrustful, however, or shy and unsociable, just the opposite, in fact. His apparently distant behavior was due to a constant inner preoccupation with something strictly personal, something which had nothing to do with other people, but which was so supremely important to him that it made him forget the rest of the world. But he certainly loved people: throughout his life he seemed to believe in people and trust them, and yet no one ever thought him simpleminded or naive. There was something in him (and it stayed with him all his life) that made people realize that he refused to sit in judgment on others, that he felt he had no right to, and that, whatever happened, he would never condemn anyone. He gave the impression that he could witness anything without feeling in the least outraged, although he might be deeply saddened. Indeed, even when he was still very young, he reached a point where nothing either shocked or horrified him. So when, at the age of nineteen, chaste and pure, he was faced with the shocking debauchery in his father's house, he would walk away in silence when things became too revolting, but never show the slightest sign of scorn or condemnation.

His father, because earlier in life he had scrounged off other people, had developed a special sensitivity to people's attitudes and was prepared to interpret anything as a personal slur. So at first he viewed Alyosha with gruff distrust ("The fellow doesn't say much, but he is thinking all kinds of things underneath"). Within two weeks, however, he was constantly hugging and kissing his son. True, the tears that rolled down his cheeks at these times were drunken tears and the outpourings that punctuated his embraces were those of a besotted sentimentality. Yet it was obvious that the old man had come to love his son deeply and sincerely; in fact, his feelings for Alyosha were such as a man like him could never have expected to have for anyone.

But then, everybody liked the boy, wherever he went, from his early childhood on. When he found himself in the house of Mr. Polenov, his guardian and benefactor, the whole household became attached to him as if he were one of the family. And it must be remembered that when Alyosha was first brought there, he was very young and cannot have set out to gain their affection calculatingly, by trying to please or by cunning flattery. The gift of making people love him was inherent in him; he gained people's affection directly and effortlessly; it was part of his nature. And it was the same at school, although one would have thought him the kind of boy to provoke distrust in his comrades, to become the target of their jokes and sometimes even of their hatred. For instance, he would often become absorbed in his thoughts and, as it were, withdraw from the world. Even as a very small boy, he would go off into a quiet corner and read a book. And yet his schoolfellows liked him so much that it can be said that he was the most popular boy in the school all the time he was there. He was seldom playful or, for that matter, even merry, but a look at him was sufficient to see that there was nothing sullen about him, that on the contrary he was a bright, good-tempered boy. And he never tried to show off to the other boys, perhaps because he was never afraid of anyone. Yet the boys felt right away that he was in no way proud of his fearlessness, that it never even occurred to him that he was fearless or bold. He also never held a grudge when someone offended him. An hour later, he would answer the offender or speak to him himself, with a trustful, friendly look, as if nothing had happened. And it wasn't that he had forgotten or, having thought it over, had decided to forgive the insult; it was simply that he no longer felt offended. It was this trait that won all the boys over to him and made them love him. He had, however, one peculiarity that, throughout his school years, incited his comrades to tease him, not because they were mean but just because they found it funny: this was a fierce, frantic modesty and chastity. He could not bear to hear dirty words or a certain type of talk about women. Unfortunately, though, such words and such talk are inevitable at school. Boys pure at heart, mere children, often whisper in class or even say certain things aloud and describe certain scenes that even soldiers would hesitate to mention. For one thing, there is much that soldiers do not know or understand that is quite familiar to very young boys in our intellectual and upper classes. In this there can hardly be moral depravity or perverted inner cynicism as yet, but there is that outward cynicism which they consider truly refined and subtle, something daring and worthy of emulation. When the other boys realized that Alyosha Karamazov stopped up his ears as soon as they started talking about "those things," they would crowd around him, tear his hands away, and scream obscenities into his ears, while Alyosha tried to break away, throwing himself onto the ground, trying desperately to cover his ears with his hands, struggling without a word, bearing it all in complete silence. In the end, however, they left him in peace and stopped calling him "little girl," at most feeling a little sorry for him for being so peculiar in that respect.

I must mention, by the way, that although academically Alyosha was always among the top students, he was never actually the first in his class.

When Polenov died, Alyosha still had two years to go at the secondary school of our province. Very shortly after losing her husband, the inconsolable widow took all her daughters (they had no sons) on a long trip to Italy, sending Alyosha to live with two ladies who were distant relatives of Mr. Polenov's. Alyosha, who had never seen them before, did not know what the financial arrangements were. This was another trait that was very characteristic of him—he never cared whose money he lived on. In this respect, he was a striking contrast to his brother Ivan, who worked hard to support himself during his first two years at the university rather than ask for help, and who had been painfully aware, ever since his childhood, of living on the charity of strangers. I do not think Alyosha should be judged too severely on this account, however, for he was quite obviously one of those child-like, saintly creatures, who, if he were suddenly to come into a large fortune, would think nothing of giving it all away to some good cause, or simply to the first clever rascal who asked for it. In general, he did not seem to know the value of money. I do not mean that literally of course, but when he was given pocket money (for which he never asked), he either kept it for weeks on end without knowing what to do with it, or spent it at once on anything. After observing Alyosha for some time, Peter Miusov, who set great store by bourgeois respectability and was very punctilious in money matters, passed the following somewhat paradoxical judgment on him:

"Alyosha," Miusov declared, "may be the only man in the world who, if left all by himself in the middle of a strange city inhabited by a million unknown people, would never suffer from cold or hunger. For he would immediately be offered food and shelter; and if no one offered him anything, he would find everything he needed right away himself, and it would cost him no effort, nor make him feel in the least humiliated, nor, for that matter, would he be imposing himself on others; just the contrary, they would all be only too happy to do things for him."

Alyosha did not finish school. When he was still a year away from graduation he told the ladies he lived with that he had to go and see his father to discuss an idea that had occurred to him. The two ladies, who were sorry to lose him, tried in vain to persuade him to stay. Since it was not an expensive journey, he planned to pay for it by pawning his watch, a parting gift from Mrs. Polenov, but the two ladies wouldn't hear of it. They gave him a goodly sum of money and, in addition, bought him a complete wardrobe. Alyosha, however, returned half the money, assuring them that he preferred to travel third class.

When he first arrived in our town, his father questioned him suspiciously, trying to find out just what had brought him here before he had finished school. Instead of answering, Alyosha plunged into his private thoughts, as he so often did. It soon became clear that he was seeking his mother's grave, and he himself practically confirmed that this had been his real reason for coming. But it can hardly have been the only reason. Most likely, at that time he did not really know himself why he had come, not being quite sure what it was that was driving him: a peculiar yearning had arisen in his heart, drawing him irresistibly into a new, unknown, but by then inevitable course.

Mr. Karamazov was unable to show his son where he had buried his second wife for, once the coffin had been lowered into the earth, he had never returned to visit her grave and, since that had been many years before, he had entirely forgotten where the grave was. Moreover, Mr. Karamazov had been away from our town for a long time. Three or four years after his second wife's death, he had gone to the south of Russia, ending up in Odessa where he stayed for several years. There he came across "lots of Yids of all shapes and sizes," as he put it, and even got to know "not only Yids but respectable Jews as well." It was probably during this period of his life that he developed a special knack for making money and holding on to it. He had returned to our town to stay only about three years before Alyosha came. Those who had known him before found him terribly aged, although he was still by no means an old man. His behavior was somehow different, too: it wasn't that he'd become more dignified, but he was more self-assured, even insolent. This former buffoon, for instance, now took an impudent delight in making buffoons of others. But his depravity with women was as bad as ever, if anything, worse. Within a short time he opened a number of new taverns in the district. It looked as if he was worth a hundred thousand rubles or close to it. Many people in town and throughout the district started borrowing money from him, on good security, of course. Of late, however, he had looked rather bloated and seemed to be losing his hold on himself. He had even slipped into a sort of light-headedness. He was unable to keep his mind on any one thing, but would skip off onto something else. He would become confused, and more and more often he drank himself into a stupor. If it hadn't been for that same servant Gregory, who looked after him almost like a nanny, and who had also aged considerably, Karamazov might not even have survived. Alyosha's arrival seemed to restore some of his mental vigor, and even to stir up a scrap of decency that had been buried somewhere in this prematurely aged man.

"You know what?" he would often say, examining Alyosha's face closely. "You're just like her, just like the Crazy Woman." That was his way of referring to Alyosha's mother, his late second wife.

It was Gregory who finally showed Alyosha where the "Crazy Woman" was buried. He took Alyosha to a far corner of our cemetery where he pointed out a cheap but decently kept grave with an iron headstone bearing the name of the deceased, the dates of her birth and death, and even an ancient four-line verse such as is often found on the tombs of lower middle-class folk. Strange as it may seem, the gravestone turned out to be Gregory's doing. He had it placed on the poor "Crazy Woman's" grave at his own expense after Mr. Karamazov, whom he had repeatedly plagued about it, finally left for Odessa without doing anything, turning his back not only on his wife's grave but on all his memories as well.

Alyosha showed no particular emotion at the sight of his mother's grave. After listening attentively to Gregory's dignified and precise account of the erection of the gravestone, he stood there for a while, his head bowed, then walked away without a word. And it was perhaps a whole year before he visited the grave again.

But when Mr. Karamazov heard about the episode, his reaction was quite unexpected: he all of a sudden donated a thousand rubles to our monastery for requiem masses to be said for the soul of his wife, not for his second wife, though, not for Alyosha's mother, the poor "Crazy Woman," but for his first wife Adelaida, the one who used to beat him. Then, later that night, he got drunk and started abusing the monks to Alyosha. Mr. Karamazov had never been a religious man and it may be that until then he had never even placed a five-kopek candle before an icon. But then such characters are sometimes swept up in some unexpected idea or impulse.

As I mentioned earlier, Karamazov's face had grown bloated and showed unmistakable traces of the life he led. Besides the heavy, fleshy bags under his eternally insolent, suspicious, mocking little eyes, besides the multitude of tiny wrinkles on his small flabby face, his large, meaty Adam's apple hung under his sharp chin shaped like a purse, and this somehow gave him a repulsively sensual air. Add to this a long, carnivorous mouth with puffy lips and the black stumps of almost completely decayed teeth, from which saliva sprayed every time he opened his mouth to speak. He often made fun of his appearance himself, although, on the whole, he seemed quite satisfied with it. He particularly liked to point to his nose which, though not very long, was remarkably narrow and beaked. "It is a genuine Roman nose," he would say, "and, with my Adam's apple, it makes me look like a Roman patrician of the decadent period." He seemed very proud of this.

Shortly after he had been shown his mother's grave, Alyosha suddenly announced to his father that he wanted to enter the monastery and that the monks were willing to accept him as a novice. He explained that this was his fervent desire and that he was asking for paternal consent. Mr.

Karamazov was already aware of the impression made by the elder, Zosima, who was living in the monastery's hermitage, on his "gentle boy."

"Old Zosima is certainly the most honest among the monks," he said, after listening to Alyosha's request in thoughtful silence. He seemed hardly surprised. "Hm . . . so that's what you want, my gentle boy!" He had been drinking and suddenly his face dissolved into a wide, half-drunken smile, in which there was a spark of besotted cunning. "Hm . . . you may not believe it, but I've had a feeling for a long time that you'd come up with something like this in the end. Well, if that's what you want, I have no objections. You have those two thousand rubles of your own, for dowry if you need it, and, for my part, you can be sure I'll never let you down. I'll even pay for your admission if they ask for it. Of course, if they don't ask for it, there's no reason for us to force it on them, is there? Why, you're no more expensive to keep than a canary—two grains a week—that's all you need . . . Hm-hm . . . now let me tell you that I know of a monastery with a nice little settlement nearby inhabited only by women, the monastery wives—that's what the people of the district call them, for everyone knows about it. I'd say there are thirty of those 'wives' in the settlement. I've been there, and it was very interesting—in its own way, of course, just as a change. It's a bit spoilt by Russian nationalism, though: there's still not a single Frenchwoman there, although they could easily afford some—it's a very prosperous monastery indeed. But French girls will soon hear of it and they'll come of their own accord. But there's nothing like that in our monastery—no monastery wives although there are two hundred monks. It's all honest. They keep their fasts. Well, I must say . . . hm . . . So you want to be a monk? I'm certainly sorry you want to leave, Alyosha—it's surprising how attached to you I've become . . . It will have one advantage, though: you can pray for us sinners, for we may have gone too far in our sinning. Yes, sir, I've wondered for a long time whether anyone would ever pray for me, whether there was a man in the world who would want to. Ah, my dear boy, you wouldn't believe how stupid I am on that point. Awfully stupid. But stupid as I am about these things, I do think of them now and then—for you wouldn't expect me to think of them all the time, would you? Well then, sometimes I reason like this: 'As soon as I die, the devils are sure to drag me down to their place with their hooks.' But then I think: 'What hooks? What are they made of? Are they iron hooks? If so, where were they forged? Do they have some kind of ironworks down there, or what?' Why, I'm sure the monks in the monastery take it for granted that hell has, for instance, a ceiling. But it would be easier for me to imagine a hell without a ceiling—that would be more refined, more enlightened, more Lutheran, that is. And what difference does it make whether hell has a ceiling or not? Oh no, it damn well makes all the difference in the world, because if there's no ceiling, there aren't any hooks either, and if there aren't any hooks, then the whole idea goes to pieces. And that too is hard to believe because, if they're not going to drag me down to hell, what justice is there in the world? No, even if they didn't exist, those hooks, *il faudrait les inventer*, even especially for me, because you can't even begin to imagine, my boy, all the disgraceful things I've done."

"But there are no hooks there," Alyosha said quietly and seriously, looking attentively at his father.

"I know, I know, just the shadows of hooks. I've heard the story. It's like that Frenchman's description of hell: *'J'ai vu l'ombre d'un cocher, qui avec l'ombre d'une brosse frottait l'ombre d'une carrosse.'* And how do you know, my dear boy, that there are no hooks? We'll see what tune you sing after you've spent a while with those monks. Still, while you're there, try to find out the truth, and when you do, come and tell me what's what. It will be easier to leave for the other world if I know what to expect there. Besides, it will be more seemly for you to live in the monastery than to stay here with an old drunkard like me, and with all these sluts, though nothing could sully you, clean angel that you are. Well, I trust there'll be nothing to sully you there either and that's why I'm letting you go. Why, devils haven't eaten your brains, after all, and if you're all afire to go there now, it'll burn off in good time, cool off. You'll get over it and come back to me. And I'll be waiting for you here, because I know you're the only person on earth who hasn't condemned me—I feel it. I can't help feeling it!"

And he even wept. He was sentimental. He was wicked and sentimental.

CHAPTER 5

Elders

The reader may imagine, perhaps, that my young man was sickly, exalted, a poor physical specimen, an undersized, puny, pale, and consumptive dreamer. Just the opposite was true: Alyosha was then the picture of health, a sturdy, red-cheeked, clear-eyed nineteen-year-old boy. He was very handsome, too, and slender, above average height, with dark-brown hair, a regular although rather long face, and shiny dark-gray wide-set eyes, which gave him a thoughtful and serene look. Of course, nothing prevents a mystic or a fanatic from having red cheeks. But be that as it may, I think Alyosha was more of a realist than anyone I know. Of course, when he was in the monastery he believed entirely in miracles, but I don't think that miracles ever confound a realist. Nor is it miracles that bring a realist to religion. If he is an unbeliever, a true realist will always find the strength and ability not to believe in a miracle, and if he is confronted with a miracle as an irrefutable fact, he will rather disbelieve his own senses than accept that fact. Or he may concede the fact and explain it away as a natural phenomenon until then unknown. In a realist, it is not miracles that generate faith, but faith that generates miracles. Once a realist becomes a believer, however, his very realism will make him accept the existence of miracles. The apostle Thomas said he would not believe until he saw, and when he saw, he said: "My Lord and my God!" Was it a miracle that made him believe? Most likely not. He believed only because he wanted to believe, and possibly he already believed in the secret recesses of his being while he was saying, "Except I shall see, I will not believe."

Some may say that Alyosha was not too bright, rather uneducated, had not even finished school, and so on. It is true that he had not finished school, but it would be doing him a great injustice to say that he was obtuse or stupid. I shall simply repeat here what I have said before: he chose the course he did only because it struck him at that particular moment as the ideal course for his soul, which longed to escape from darkness into light. It must be added that, in a way, he was indeed a member of our younger generation, which means that he was honest, that he believed in, demanded, and searched for truth; that, because he believed in it, he yearned to serve it and give it his whole strength; he was spoiling for immediate action, was prepared to sacrifice everything, his life itself, in an act of supreme devotion. Unfortunately, these young men often fail to understand that the sacrifice of their lives may be the easiest of all sacrifices, much easier, for instance, than giving up five or six years of their seething youth to hard study, to the acquisition of knowledge which would increase their strength tenfold in the service of that same cause, and in the performance of the great works they aspire to. But to sacrifice those few years to study often proves too much for them. Alyosha chose a course opposite to that of the majority, although he felt the same yearning for action and sacrifice as the others. Once, having given it serious thought, he had become convinced of the existence of God and immortality, it was natural for him to say to himself: "I want to live to achieve immortality and will accept no compromise." If by chance he had become convinced that God and immortality did not exist, he would immediately have joined the ranks of the atheists and socialists (for socialism is not just a question of labor organization; it is above all an atheistic phenomenon, the modern manifestation of atheism, one more tower of Babel built without God, not in order to reach out toward heaven from earth, but to bring heaven down to earth). Once he had decided, Alyosha would have felt it strange, even impossible, to go on living as he had been.

It is written: "If thou wouldst be perfect, go and give up all that thou hast and come and follow me." So Alyosha said to himself: "I cannot very well just give up a couple of rubles, instead of all that I have, or, instead of obeying the Lord's 'Follow me,' just attend church." Perhaps there lingered in his mind some early memory of our monastery, to which his mother may have taken him to attend mass. Or perhaps his decision was somehow connected with the slanting rays of the setting sun on the icon before which his crazy mother had held him. When he first arrived, Alyosha had seemed to be pondering deeply about something, perhaps trying to decide whether he would be able to give up "all" or only a couple of rubles. Then he met the elder at the monastery.

This was the elder Zosima whom I mentioned earlier. But before I proceed, I should try to explain what an "elder" in our monasteries is. I regret that I am not fully versed in these matters, but I will do my best to give a rough idea of that institution. First of all, according to the experts, the institution of elder came into existence in our Russian monasteries only quite recently, less than a hundred years ago, although it has existed for well over a thousand years throughout the Orthodox East, particularly in Sinai and on Mount Athos. As I understand it, in olden times there were probably elders in Russia too, but as the country went through a series of calamities—the Tartar invasion, civil wars, and isolation from the Orthodox East after the fall of Constantinople—the institution fell into disuse and the elders vanished from our monasteries. They were reintroduced in Russia toward the end of the eighteenth century by the great ascetic (as he was called) Paisii Velichkovsky and his followers, but to this day, almost a hundred years later, elders are found in only a very few monasteries and they have occasionally been subjected to persecution as an un-Russian innovation. The institution of elder especially flourished in the famous Kozelskaya Optina Monastery. Who introduced it into our monastery and when I cannot say. I only know that there had already been three elders, Zosima being the third. But he was weak and sick and obviously did not have long to live, and no one knew where another would be found to take his place. This was a crucial problem for our monastery because it had not previously been renowned for anything in particular: it had no saints' relics, no miracle-working icons, nor even any glorious traditions connected with the history of Russia. Nor were there any records of special services it had rendered the country. It was only thanks to its elders that it had flourished and its fame spread all over Russia; it was to see and hear our elders that pilgrims from every corner of the country traveled thousands of miles to flock to the monastery.

What precisely is an elder, then? An elder is a man who takes your soul and your will into his soul and his will. Once you have chosen your elder, you renounce your own will, you yield it to him in total submission and self-renunciation. A man who consents to this ordeal, to this terrible apprenticeship, is willing to bear it in the hope that, after a long period of trial, he will conquer himself and achieve a self-mastery that will enable him to finally attain, through a whole life of obedience, complete freedom (that is, freedom from himself) and thus avoid the fate of those who reach the end of their lives without ever having found themselves within themselves.

The institution of elder is not an invention based on theory but evolved in the East in more than a thousand years of practice. The obligations a man contracts toward an elder are quite different from the usual "obedience," such as has always existed in Russian monasteries. Once accepted by an elder, a disciple must live a life of continual confession, and the bond between the two is indissoluble. Once in the early days of Christianity, according to legend, a novice failed to carry out a command imposed on him by his elder and, instead, left his monastery in Syria and went to Egypt. There, after many heroic acts of self-abnegation, he underwent torture and died a martyr for his faith. Yet when before burial his coffin stood in a church where he was already venerated as a saint, a strange thing happened: as soon as the deacon began to intone, "Depart, all ye possessed by the devil," the coffin rose into the air and was hurled out of the church. And this was repeated three times. It was only then that they learned that this saint had broken his vow of obedience to his elder and so, despite his great exploits, had to be pardoned by his elder before he could receive Christian burial. Of course, that is only an old legend, but let me tell you a true story, of something that happened not long ago. One of our Russian monks, seeking salvation on Mount Athos, was suddenly ordered by his elder to leave Mount Athos, a holy place which he loved and where he had found a peaceful haven for his soul, and first to go on a pilgrimage to Jerusalem to worship at the holy shrines, then to return to Russia and go north to Siberia, "because," the elder told him, "your place is there and not here." Stunned and filled with despair, the monk went to Constantinople, where he begged the Ecumenical Patriarch to release him from his vow of obedience; but the Patriarch explained that neither he nor any power on earth could ever release him from his vow of obedience, and that only the elder who had imposed the command had the power to rescind it. Thus, in some ways, elders exercise an authority that is boundless beyond understanding. That is why the institution of elder was at first opposed, even condemned, in Russian monasteries. The common people, however, showed tremendous respect for the elders right away. And soon the uneducated and the humble, the rich and the mighty, were flocking from all over Russia to see the elders of our monastery, to throw themselves at their feet, to confess their sins, to confide their doubts and torments, to seek guidance and advice. This caused the opponents of the elders to accuse them, among other things, of arbitrarily and irresponsibly degrading the sacrament of confession, although the continual baring of a novice's or a layman's soul before his elder was quite different from that sacrament. The institution survived, however, and it is now gradually becoming more common in Russian monasteries. It is also true, though, that this well-tested, thousand-year-old method of spiritual regeneration from slavery to freedom and moral perfection may prove to be a double-edged weapon, for some men, instead of gaining humility and ultimate self-mastery, may acquire the most satanic pride, so that they are fettered rather than free.

The elder, Zosima, was about sixty-five. He came from a family of landed gentry, and as a very young man he had been in the army, serving as an officer in the Caucasus. There was a special spiritual quality about him that must have struck Alyosha. For his part, the elder also grew very fond of the boy and allowed him to share his cell. It must be pointed out that, when he was living at the monastery, Alyosha was not yet bound by any vow, so that he could come and go as he pleased; indeed, he could stay away for days on end whenever he wished, and if he wore a cassock it was by his own choice, so as not to stand out among the others—though he obviously also liked wearing a cassock. It is also quite possible that Alyosha's youthful imagination was greatly stirred by Zosima's spiritual power and the fame that surrounded him. Many said of the elder that, in accepting all those who had come throughout the years to entrust their souls to him, to seek his guidance and solace, he had heard so many confessions, secrets, and tales of human despair that he had finally acquired an insight so keen that he could guess, from the very first glance at a newcomer, what he would say, what he would ask him, and even what was really tormenting his conscience. Often the visitor was surprised, confounded, and even frightened on finding that the elder knew his secret before he had even uttered a word. Alyosha also noticed that almost all who came to Zosima for the first time were filled with fear and apprehension as they entered the cell to face him alone, but that almost without exception they left smiling and serene; even the gloomiest faces emerged beaming with joy. Alyosha noted with particular interest that the elder Zosima was in no way severe, but, if anything, was always rather cheerful. The monks said that he was particularly warm toward the worst sinners and that the greater a man's sins the greater was the elder's love for him. Even toward the end of Zosima's life, there were monks who hated and envied him, but there were fewer and fewer of them, and they kept their feelings to themselves, although some occupied important positions in the monastery. Such was one of the oldest monks, a man famous for the strictness of his fasts and for his long periods of silence. But without doubt the overwhelming majority of the monks were on Zosima's side, and many of them loved him deeply and sincerely. Some were almost fanatically devoted to him and said, although not quite openly, that Zosima was a saint, that there could be no doubt about it. And, as his end was drawing near, they expected it to be followed almost at once by miracles that would shortly bring even greater glory to the monastery. Alyosha was one of those who had unquestioning faith in Zosima's miraculous powers, as unquestioning as his acceptance of the story about the coffin that flew out of church by itself. He saw many who came with sick children or relatives to beg the elder to lay his hands on them and pray for them, and who returned, some the very next day, and, the tears running down their cheeks, prostrated themselves before the elder, thanking him for healing the sick. The question of whether this was miraculous healing or natural recovery never even occurred to Alyosha, for he had complete faith in the spiritual power of his teacher, whose glory he felt as his own personal triumph. He felt a special tremor in his heart and he radiated joy when the elder went out to the gates of the monastery to meet a group of humble folk who had flocked there from all over Russia to see him and ask for his blessing. They prostrated themselves before him, wept, kissed his feet and the earth on which he stood; wailing peasant women held up their children and led sick and hysterical village girls to him. The elder spoke to them, said a short prayer, blessed them, and sent them away in peace. Later, though, he was so weak after his bouts of illness that he hardly had the strength to leave his cell, and there were times when pilgrims had to wait several days for him to appear. Alyosha never felt the least surprise that all these people should love the elder, that they should prostrate themselves before him, weeping with emotion at the mere sight of his face. Oh, he understood very well that for the meek soul of a simple Russian, exhausted by grief and hardship and, above all, by constant injustice and sin, his own or the world's, there was no stronger need than to find a holy shrine or a saint to prostrate himself before and to worship. "Even though sin and injustice and temptation are all around us, we know that there is on this earth a holy man, a saint who is just and knows the truth, and this means that truth and justice have not vanished from the earth and so will come to us too and rule over all the world, as has been promised." Alyosha knew that this was what the humble folk felt, that this was how they thought. This, he knew with his reason, but that Zosima was such a saint, a guardian of divine justice—that was something Alyosha never doubted, something that he felt spontaneously, like all the weeping peasants and the sick women who held their children up to the elder. And the conviction that, after his death, Zosima would confer great glory on the monastery was, perhaps, stronger in Alyosha than in anyone else at the monastery. Indeed, a strange, profound, overwhelming ecstasy had burned in him more and more powerfully of late. He was not in the least troubled by the fact that Zosima stood before him an isolated phenomenon: "It makes no difference, he is a saint, and his heart knows the secret of regeneration for all, the power that will finally establish the rule of truth on earth. Then all men will be saints and will love one another, and there will be no poor and no rich, no mighty and no humiliated—all will be the children of God and the true kingdom of Christ will come." This is what Alyosha felt in his heart.

The arrival of his brothers, whom, before this, he had not known at all, seemed to make a tremendous impression on Alyosha. He got to know his half brother Dmitry more quickly than his brother Ivan and felt closer to him, although Dmitry arrived later. Alyosha was very eager to get to know Ivan, but although his brother had been in town for two whole months and they saw each other quite often, they still seemed unable to really make friends. Alyosha himself was silent and reserved; he seemed a little embarrassed and as if he were expecting something from his brother, and Ivan, although at first Alyosha felt his long and scrutinizing looks resting upon him, soon appeared to lose all interest in him. Alyosha, who was rather taken aback by this change, ascribed his brother's distant attitude to the difference in their ages and, above all, in their education. But at times he also suspected that Ivan's lack of interest and sympathy might be due to other causes about which he knew nothing. He somehow felt that Ivan was absorbed in something within himself, something very important, that he was pursuing some goal, perhaps a very difficult goal, which simply left no room for Alyosha in his thoughts, and that this explained why he looked at him so absentmindedly. Alyosha also wondered whether the cultured atheist might not feel some contempt for a silly novice. He knew very well that his brother was an atheist and could not possibly take offense at his brother's contempt, if contempt there was; yet he was in a state of acute discomfort, for which he himself could not account, as he waited for his brother to deign to come closer to him.

Dmitry, the oldest brother, showed tremendous respect for Ivan and spoke of him with strange emotion. It was from Dmitry that Alyosha learned the details of the important matters that had linked the two older brothers so closely and so strangely. Dmitry's enthusiastic admiration for Ivan struck Alyosha even more forcefully since, compared with Ivan, he was almost entirely uneducated, and the two offered such a remarkable contrast in character and personality that it was hard to imagine two men more unlike.

It was at this time that a meeting, or shall we call it a gathering, of the members of this ill-assorted family took place in the elder's cell, a gathering that was to deeply affect Alyosha. Actually, the meeting was held under a false pretext. By then, the dispute between Dmitry Karamazov and his father over the inheritance and their financial dealings had reached an impasse, and their relations had become untenable. Mr. Karamazov seems to have first suggested, and that in a jocular tone, that all the Karamazovs gather in the elder's cell; without asking for Zosima's direct arbitration, he felt, they could still discuss the matter more decently in the venerable presence of the elder, which might inspire respect and have a reconciliatory effect on them. Dmitry, who had never visited the elder, indeed had never set eyes on him, thought that Zosima was being used to intimidate him; but, since he secretly felt a little guilty about some of the things he had said to his father during their arguments, he accepted the challenge. (It must be noted that, unlike Ivan, Dmitry was not living with his father, but was staying in a house at the opposite end of town.) Peter Miusov, who was in town, turned out to be particularly eager that Mr. Karamazov's suggestion should be taken up. A typical liberal of the 1840's and 1850's, this free-thinker and atheist took a very active interest in the business, perhaps out of boredom or perhaps just to have a little light-hearted fun. He was suddenly eager to have a look at the monastery and at "that holy man." His lawsuit against the monastery was still dragging on and his claims over the property boundaries and the fishing and wood-cutting rights were still unsettled, so he announced that he wished to see the Father Superior to try and reach an amicable settlement with him. He obviously felt that a man visiting the monastery with such laudable intentions would be received and treated with much greater consideration than an ordinary visitor who had come out of mere curiosity. He thought all these considerations might bring pressure to bear upon the elder from within the monastery. Because of his sickness, the elder had hardly left his cell at all of late and he had been unable to see even his regular visitors. In the end, however, he consented to receive them, and the day was fixed. "I wonder who has set me up as judge over them," was all he said, smiling at Alyosha.

When Alyosha first heard of the planned gathering, he was very perturbed. He realized that, of all the contending parties, only Dmitry would take the whole thing seriously, while the others would come to the meeting out of motives that were frivolous and perhaps insulting out of the elder. Ivan and Miusov would come out of curiosity, perhaps of the crudest sort, and his father might very easily be planning some piece of buffoonery which would turn the whole thing into a farce. Oh, although he did not talk much, Alyosha knew his father well, for, I must repeat, he was not at all the uncomplicated lad that many people supposed. So it was with a heavy heart that he awaited the day. He was, of course, very anxious that the quarrels within his family should be brought to an end, but he was even more concerned about the elder. He was full of anxiety for him, for his reputation, and, as he imagined the meeting to himself beforehand, he particularly feared Miusov's subtle and urbane sarcasms and the learned Ivan's haughty insinuations. He even thought of warning the elder about these visitors, but he decided not to and kept silent. He only sent Dmitry word the day before, through a friend, that he was very fond of him and expected him to keep his promise. Dmitry was puzzled, for he could not think what he had promised Alyosha, but he answered by letter that he would do his best not to lose his temper in the event of "some despicable trick" and that, although he had great respect for the elder and for Ivan, he felt certain that some trap was being laid for him or that the whole thing was a farce. "Nevertheless, I'll swallow my tongue rather than offend the venerable old man whom you respect so highly," he said in concluding the letter. Alyosha hardly found this reassuring.

BOOK II

AN INCONGRUOUS GATHERING

CHAPTER 1

They Arrive at the Monastery

It was a beautiful, clear, warm day in late August. The elder was to receive them at about half-past eleven, immediately after late mass. Our visitors did not attend the service, but arrived just as it was over. They drove up in two carriages. The first, an elegant barouche drawn by two fine horses, brought Peter Miusov and a distant relative, Peter Kalganov. He was a young man of twenty or so, who was preparing to enter the university, but Miusov, with whom, for some reason, he was living for the moment, was trying to persuade him to accompany him abroad, to attend the university in either Zurich or Jena and obtain his degree there. Kalganov had not yet made up his mind. He seemed absorbed in his thoughts and rather absentminded. He had a pleasant face, was well built and quite tall. At times, there was a strange fixity in his gaze: like all absent-minded people, he would often stare at you for a long time without seeing you. He was silent and rather awkward, but sometimes when he was alone with another person, he would suddenly become talkative, effusive, and was liable to burst out laughing quite unaccountably. He always dressed well, indeed with studied elegance. He had an independent income even then, and had even more sizable expectations. He and Alyosha were good friends.

The second carriage, a jolting but roomy old hired carriage, which was drawn by a pair of sedate, pinkish-gray horses and which kept falling behind Miusov's barouche, brought Mr. Karamazov and his son Ivan.

As to Dmitry, he was late, although he had been informed in advance of the day and the time they were to meet.

The visitors left their carriages outside the monastery wall, near an inn, and entered the gates on foot. I do not believe any of them, except Mr. Karamazov, had ever been in a

39

monastery before, and, as to Miusov, it is unlikely that he
had seen the inside even of a church for a good thirty years.
He looked around him with a certain curiosity, trying nevertheless to appear quite casual about it all. But there was
nothing there to interest a man of his mentality, except perhaps the architecture of the church and the buildings where
the monks lived, though even they were quite ordinary. The
last of the worshippers were coming out of church, bare-
headed and crossing themselves. Among the simple people
there were a few better-class people—two or three ladies
and a very old general, all of whom were staying at the
nearby inn. Beggars surrounded our visitors as soon as they
appeared, but nobody gave them anything, except for young
Kalganov who dug a ten-kopek piece out of his purse and,
for some reason looking very embarrassed, pushed it hurriedly into one woman's hand, muttering something like
"to share among you." None of his companions commented
on his act, so there seemed no reason for further embarrassment, but when he became aware of it, he grew even
more confused.

It was rather strange, though; there really should have
been someone to receive them, and perhaps even with some
esteem: one of them had just recently donated a thousand
rubles to the monastery and another was one of the wealthi-
est landowners in the district; he was considered one of
the best-educated of men, and his decision about the fishing
rights on the river could determine the whole course of the
litigation. But none of the monastery officials came out to
meet them. Miusov gazed abstractedly at the graves in the
churchyard and was about to remark that the dead had to
pay a very high price for the privilege of being buried in this
"holy place," but he let it pass, for his usual ironic "liberal"
tone was turning into something like anger.

"Damn it, isn't there anyone to direct us in this chaos?"
he muttered as if talking to himself. "We must find out because it will soon be time for us to go back . . ."

Then, all of a sudden a middle-aged, balding gentleman in
a loose summer coat walked up to them. He raised his hat
and, looking at them ingratiatingly, introduced himself to the
whole party in a mellifluous voice. He was a landowner
named Maximov from near Tula. He immediately did his
best to be helpful to them:

"The elder Zosima lives in the hermitage," he lisped. "He
lives in complete seclusion, you know . . . It's about four

hundred yards from the monastery on the other side of that little wood over there . . ."

"I know it's on the other side of the wood," Mr. Karamazov told him. "The only trouble is, we don't quite remember the way—we haven't been here for a long time."

"Well, you can go through that gate over there and then straight through the wood, straight through. Wouldn't you like me . . . I'll be glad to show you. You see, I myself have to . . . It's this way, please . . ."

They went through the gate and crossed the little wood with Maximov, a man of about sixty, trotting along beside them and examining them with an almost morbid curiosity, his eyes almost starting from his head.

"You see, we've come here on private business," Miusov said sternly. "We have been granted what we may call 'an audience' by the person in question and, therefore, grateful though we are to you for showing us the way, we won't be able to invite you to come in with us."

"I've already been there, seen him . . . *un chevalier parfait!*" Maximov said, raising his hand and snapping his fingers.

"Who is a *chevalier?*" Miusov asked.

"The elder . . . He is admirable . . . That elder is the pride and glory of the monastery. An elder such as Zosima . . ."

But his incoherent speech was cut short by a small, cowled monk, pale and haggard, who just then caught up with them. As Mr. Karamazov and Mr. Miusov stopped, the monk bowed almost from the waist and said in a most courteous tone:

"After your visit to the hermitage, gentlemen, the Father Superior invites you to dinner, if possible no later than one o'clock." And then, turning to Maximov, he added: "And you too, sir."

"I will certainly be there!" exclaimed Mr. Karamazov, delighted at the invitation. "I wouldn't miss it for anything. And let me say, we have all promised to behave properly while we're here . . . What about you, Mr. Miusov, are you coming too?"

"Of course I will come. I came here primarily to study monastery customs, after all. The only thing that troubles me is that I'm here with you, Mr. Karamazov . . ."

"But where's Dmitry? He hasn't shown up yet," Mr. Karamazov remarked.

"I wouldn't mind if he didn't come at all," Miusov said. "Do you really think I relish all these squabbles between you two? Your presence alone is bad enough. Please thank the Father Superior for his invitation, then," he said to the monk. "We will be there for dinner."

"Yes, sir, but first I have been told to take you to the elder," the monk said.

"And I," Maximov lisped, "will go straight to the Father Superior's since we've been invited."

"The Father Superior is rather busy just now," the monk said hesitatingly, "but, of course, it's up to you, sir."

"What an awful bore that old man is," Mr. Miusov said as Maximov trotted off, back toward the monastery.

"He reminds me of von Sohn," Mr. Karamazov announced unexpectedly.

"What makes you say that? In what way is he like von Sohn? Have you ever set eyes on von Sohn?"

"I've seen his picture. But I didn't say they looked alike —it's difficult to explain. This man is just another von Sohn. I can tell simply by looking at him."

"Well, I suppose you're an expert in these matters. But let me remind you of one thing, Mr. Karamazov: you said yourself a moment ago that we had promised to behave decently while we are here, and I'd like you to remember it. I warn you—restrain yourself, for if you start playing the fool, I have absolutely no intention of allowing it to reflect on me. You see what kind of a man he is," Miusov said, turning to the monk. "I'm quite afraid to visit respectable people with him."

A suspicion of a smile appeared on the wan, bloodless lips of the monk, a hint of sly amusement. But he kept silent, obviously feeling that it would not be dignified for him to say anything. This only deepened Miusov's frown as he thought to himself: "And to hell with the lot of them—it has taken them centuries to learn to keep that imperturbable face, and underneath they're nothing but a bunch of charlatans."

"Here is the hermitage at last," Mr. Karamazov announced, "but the gates are shut . . ."

And he proceeded to cross himself vigorously before the saints' images painted above and beside the gates.

"When in Rome, do as the Romans," he remarked. "Altogether there are twenty-five saints busy saving their souls in this hermitage, staring at one another, and eating cabbage.

And the most remarkable thing about it is that not a single woman is allowed through these gates. And that's the truth . . . But then how can that be, since I've heard that the elder receives ladies?" he asked suddenly, addressing the monk.

"There are women here right now, sir—peasant women," the monk replied. "See, over there, sitting and waiting under that wooden gallery. And above the gallery, but beyond the walls, where those windows are, there are two special rooms for ladies. When he's well enough to receive them, the elder reaches those rooms by an inside passage, for they are outside the hermitage wall, sir. At this moment, for instance, there's a lady waiting for him there with her sick daughter. She's a landowner from Kharkov Province, Mrs. Khokhlakov is her name. I expect he must have promised to come out to her, although recently he has been so weak that he has hardly shown himself even to the poor people."

"Well, so there is a secret passage from the hermitage to the ladies after all! But please, Holy Father, you mustn't think for one moment that I'm implying anything—I was just wondering . . . But on Mount Athos, you may know perhaps, they keep out not only women but all creatures of the female sex—like hens, turkey hens, cows . . ."

"Mr. Karamazov, please!" Miusov said. "If you go on like this, I'll walk out on you, and once I've left they'll turn you out too, that I can promise you."

"I don't see why what I say should affect you, Mr. Miusov . . . But look at that!" Karamazov suddenly exclaimed, stepping through the gate onto the hermitage grounds. "These people live in a regular rose garden!"

Although there were no roses in the hermitage garden, there were many rare and beautiful autumn flowers that had been planted wherever there was room for them, and it was clear that they were tended by a skillful hand. There were also flowerbeds all around the church and between the graves in the churchyard. The elder's cell was in a small wooden one-story house with a porch before the entrance, which was also surrounded by flowers.

"I wonder if it was like this under the previous elder, the elder Varsonofy?" Mr. Karamazov asked as he walked up the front steps. "I understand he didn't go in for refinement and that he even had a propensity for suddenly leaping up and using his stick on persons of the female sex."

"The elder Varsonofy did at times seem a little strange,"

the monk said, "but many of the stories that are told about him are nonsense. In any case, he certainly never used a stick on anybody. And now, gentlemen, I beg you to wait here a minute while I announce you."

"For the last time, Mr. Karamazov," Miusov warned him again hurriedly in a threatening whisper, "remember your promise to behave—or I'll make you pay for it!"

"I really cannot see why you should be so excited," Karamazov replied sarcastically, "unless you're worrying about your sins at last? Why, they say he can tell just by a man's eyes what's troubling him! And anyway, why should the opinion of these people be so important to you, a Parisian and an enlightened gentleman? You really amaze me!"

But before Miusov could answer this sarcasm, they were asked to come in. He entered feeling rather irritated.

"Ah, I know myself. I'm irritated now and I'll start arguing and lose my temper. I will discredit both myself and my ideas," he thought.

CHAPTER 2

The Old Buffoon

Just as they entered the cell, the elder appeared, emerging from his bedroom. Two monks from the hermitage were already waiting, the Father Librarian and Father Paisii, a sickly man who, although he was not very advanced in years, had a reputation as a great scholar. Besides them, a young man of about twenty-two wearing ordinary clothes stood waiting in a corner (where he remained standing all the time). He was a divinity student who, for some reason, was a protégé of the monks. He was fairly tall, had a fair complexion, prominent cheekbones, and narrow brown eyes that were intelligent and observant. His bearing was deferential but dignified, without the least subservience. As if conscious of his subordinate and dependent position, of not being their equal, he did not greet the visitors.

The elder Zosima entered accompanied by a novice and by Alyosha. The monks rose, greeted him with bows so deep that their fingers touched the floor, and went up to him, to kiss his hand and receive his blessing. After he had blessed them, Zosima in turn bowed just as deeply, also touching the floor with his fingers, and asked each of them for his blessing. The whole ceremony was performed very seriously, not like some daily rite but with a real show of feeling. Miusov, however, was convinced that it was all put on to impress the visitors. He stood in front of the party deliberating (he had been wondering about it since the day before) whether he should, despite his ideas, just out of courtesy (since it was the custom here), step forward and ask the elder for his blessing, although he certainly would not kiss his hand. Now, seeing all the bowing and hand-kissing of the monks, he made up his mind. Serious and dignified, he went up to the elder, bowed rather deeply by ordinary standards, and moved over to a chair. Mr. Karamazov went through exactly the same motions, but exaggerated them, making them seem ridiculous. Ivan also bowed politely and gravely, his hands stiffly at his sides, while Kalganov was so embarrassed that he didn't bow at all. The elder dropped his hand, which he had raised to bless them, bowed to them once more, and invited them to sit down. Alyosha's worst forebodings were coming true; he was ashamed and the blood rushed to his cheeks.

The elder sat down on a leather-covered mahogany sofa of antique design, while inviting his four visitors to sit on four mahogany chairs covered with badly worn black leather ranged along the opposite wall. The two monks took chairs on either side of the room—one by the window and the other by the door—while the divinity student, Alyosha, and the novice remained standing. The whole cell was rather small and drab-looking. It had only the most indispensable furniture, and even that was poor and crude. There were two pots of flowers on the window sill and, in a corner, many icons, one of them a large picture of the Mother of God probably painted long before the Schism. A lamp burned in front of it. Next to it were two icons in shiny settings, and beyond them some carved cherubs, little china eggs, an ivory Catholic cross with a *Mater Dolorosa* with her arms around it, and a few foreign engravings, copies of the great Italian masters of bygone times. Beside these costly, graceful foreign engravings were some rather crude native Russian lithographs of saints and martyrs, the kind that could be bought at any local fair for a few kopeks. On the other walls hung a few portraits of Russian bishops, past and present.

Miusov made a cursory inspection of all this "conventional rubbish," then turned to look intently at the elder. He rated his own powers of judgment rather highly, a weakness which was excusable in him, since he was already past fifty, an age at which an intelligent, cultured man of the world of independent means acquires an exaggerated opinion of his own judgment, sometimes despite himself.

He disliked the elder at first glance. Indeed, there was something in Zosima's face that many besides Miusov would have disliked. He was a short, stooped little man with very weak legs who, because of ill-health, looked at least ten years older than his sixty-five years. His very thin face was covered with tiny wrinkles, especially around his eyes. His eyes, small, quick, and shiny, made two bright dots in his face. He was bald except for some thin gray hair around the temples; his wedge-shaped beard was very small and scanty, and he had thin, thread-like lips, which formed readily into a smile. His nose, although it was not really long, was sharp, like the beak of a small bird.

"All the signs of a wicked, pettily supercilious nature . . ." flashed through Miusov's head. He was still very annoyed with himself.

A small, cheap wall clock with weights hurriedly struck twelve times, and this helped to get the conversation started.

"Noon on the dot!" Mr. Karamazov cried out. "And still no sign of my son Dmitry! I apologize for him, Holy Elder!"

The "Holy Elder" actually made Alyosha shudder.

"I, on the other hand," Karamazov went on, "am always punctual. I always arrive exactly on time, knowing that punctuality is the courtesy of kings."

"Well, whatever else you may be, you're certainly no king," Miusov muttered, unable to contain his irritation.

"Yes, that's true, I'm no king. Believe it or not, Mr. Miusov, I was aware of that myself. I'll even swear to it! I don't know why, but I always say the wrong thing! Ah, Your Reverence!" he exclaimed with a sudden pathos. "You have before you a buffoon, a true buffoon—that's how I will introduce myself. Alas, it's an old habit with me! And if I sometimes talk nonsense, it is actually intentional, to make people laugh, to please them. One must try to please, mustn't one? For instance, about seven years ago, I arrived in a small town where I was trying to set up a little business deal in partnership with some small local businessmen. Of

course, we had to see the local *ispravnik** first to ask a
favor of him—you know what I mean—and invite him to
dinner. So we go there, and the *ispravnik* appears, and he
turns out to be a big, fat fellow with blondish hair and an
unsmiling face—the most dangerous type in such cases—
it's their livers, you see, their livers . . . Well, I turn to him
and, with the self-assurance of a man of the world, I say,
'Mr. *Ispravnik*, we've come to beg you to be our Napravnik,
if I may say so.' 'How's that, your Napravnik? What do you
mean by that?' I could see right away that it hadn't gone over.
He just stood there staring at me and looking solemn. 'I was
just trying to make a pun,' I said, 'trying to cheer up the
company a little. That Mr. Napravnik I was referring to
is one of the greatest Russian conductors, and it's a sort
of conductor that we need for the harmony of our little
enterprise.' I thought I had given him a reasonable explanation, and the comparison was to the point too, but he just
said, 'I'm an *ispravnik* and I will not tolerate puns with
reference to my official capacity.' And he started to walk out
on us. 'Wait,' I call out to him. 'You're right, absolutely right.
You're an *ispravnik* and not Mr. Napravnik.' 'No,' he says,
'you cannot take it back now—I am Napravnik.' And, of
course, our business deal fell through. It's always the same
with me—I get myself into trouble by being too friendly!
Once—it was many, many years ago—I said to a very
important man: 'Your wife, sir,' I said, 'is a very ticklish
lady,' meaning in the sense of honor, of moral qualities, you
know, and I never expected him to ask me: 'What do you
know about it? Have you ever tickled her?' Well, I thought
it was an opening for some amiable chit-chat, so I said,
'Why, yes, sir, I must say I have.' Well, the fellow gave me
quite a tickling then, too! I can tell it now without shame
because it happened so long ago but, in general, I always
manage to do myself some harm that way."

"Like right now, for instance," Miusov muttered disgustedly.

The elder was looking at the two of them in silence.

"You don't say! Well, will you believe me, Mr. Miusov, if
I tell you I was aware of that too and, what's more, as
soon as I started to speak, I knew, I somehow felt, that
you'd be the first to make some remark? Whenever I realize,
Your Reverence, that my joke isn't succeeding, my cheeks

---

* Police inspector. [A. MacA.]

begin to stick to my lower gums, like a sort of cramp. It's happened ever since my youth when I used to be a hanger-on to the local landed gentry, earning my living by being a parasite. I'm a thorough-going buffoon, a born buffoon, which is like being one of God's fools, Your Reverence. I won't deny, though, that there may be an unholy spirit in me, too, but it must be one of minor rank—if it were more important it would surely have chosen better quarters—but certainly not you, Mr. Miusov. You'd offer it pretty shabby quarters, let me tell you. I, at least, believe in God. And if I've had some doubts of late, they're gone now as I sit here, expecting to hear words of great wisdom. I, Reverend Father, am like the philosopher Diderot. You may have heard, Holy Father, how Diderot went to see the Metropolitan Platon, in the time of the Empress Catherine. He marched in and immediately announced: 'There is no God!' The holy patriarch raised his finger and replied: 'The fool has said in his heart, There is no God!' And the next thing, Diderot was lying at his feet and wailing: 'I believe. I want to be baptized!' And so he was baptized then and there, and Princess Dashkov acted as his godmother and Potemkin as his godfather."

"This is outrageous! You know very well you're talking nonsense and that stupid anecdote is quite untrue. Why must you carry on like this?" Miusov said in a shaking voice, feeling that he was losing control over himself.

"All my life, I've suspected it wasn't true!" Karamazov cried excitedly. "And now let me tell you the whole truth, gentlemen! Forgive me, oh great elder—I made up that last bit about Diderot's being baptized as I was telling the story. It had never even occurred to me till then. I invented it to spice things up a bit. That's why I'm carrying on, Mr. Miusov, to be good company, you know, although there are times when I don't really know myself why I do it. As to the Diderot story, I heard the patriarch's reply to him at least twenty times from the landowners in whose houses I spent my youth and, by the way, from your Auntie Mavra, among others, Mr. Miusov. To this day, they are all convinced that the atheist Diderot went to see the Metropolitan Platon to argue with him about God."

Miusov was on his feet now. He had not only lost patience —he didn't seem to know what he was doing. He was seething with rage and was conscious that that made him ridiculous too. Indeed, something quite incredible was taking place in the cell. Until then, for forty or fifty years, the people who had been received there by the elder and his predecessors had come with a feeling of deep reverence. Everyone admitted was conscious of having been granted a great favor; many knelt the moment they entered and remained kneeling throughout the visit. Even the most learned and prominent people, including free-thinkers who came out of curiosity or for some such reason, all felt bound to behave with tact and respect as long as they were in the elder's presence, whether they were received with other visitors or privately. This was especially so because there was no question of money here, but only of love and kindness, on the one hand, and, on the other, penitence or the longing to solve some spiritual problem or resolve a difficult personal crisis. Consequently, Karamazov's buffoonery, so disrespectful and out of place, surprised and bewildered at least some of the witnesses to the scene. The monks, although their expressions did not change, waited tensely to hear what the elder would say, and seemed ready to leap to their feet like Miusov. Alyosha stood with his head bowed, looking as if he were about to burst into tears. He was surprised, too, that his brother Ivan, the only person there on whom he had relied, and the only person in the world who had an influence on his father and could have stopped him, sat motionless in his chair, his eyes lowered, apparently waiting curiously to see how it would all end, as if he himself were a complete outsider and could not possibly be affected. As to the divinity student, Rakitin, whom he knew well, almost intimately, Alyosha didn't even dare look at him, for he knew his thoughts (he was, indeed, the only man in the monastery to know them).

"Please forgive me," Miusov said, addressing the elder. "I am afraid you may think that I too have a part in this ridiculous farce. I made a mistake in thinking that even a man like Fyodor Karamazov would understand his obligations when received by a highly respectable person . . . It never occurred to me that I would have to apologize merely for having come in his company and . . ."

Miusov, too embarrassed to go on, was about to walk out of the room.

"Please don't worry," the elder said. He stood up abruptly on his weak legs, took Miusov by both hands, and made him sit down again. "Think nothing of it. Believe me, I particularly appreciate having you as my guest," Zosima added, bowing to Miusov and returning to his own seat on the sofa.

"Oh, great elder! I await your verdict: am I insulting you with my exuberant behavior or not?" Karamazov cried, gripping the arms of his chair with his hands as though he would jump up if he received an unfavorable answer.

"You too, sir, please be at ease and rest assured that there is nothing to worry about," the elder said in a firm tone. "I want you to feel completely at home and, above all, not to be ashamed of yourself, for that is what causes all the trouble."

"Completely at home? You mean be my natural self? Oh, that is too kind, much too kind, but I am deeply moved and I accept your invitation! But let me warn you, Blessed Father, do not encourage me to be my natural self. Don't take the chance. Even I wouldn't dare to let myself go entirely. I tell you that for your own good. As for the rest, it is still shrouded in darkness, although there are those who are only too anxious to tell all sorts of stories about me. Yes, I'm referring to you, Mr. Miusov. As for you, most holy man, allow me only to express my profound admiration!" He stood up and, raising his hands toward the ceiling, declaimed: " 'Blessed be the womb that bore thee and the paps that gave thee suck'— particularly the paps! Your remark just now that I mustn't be ashamed because 'that is what causes all the trouble' showed that you could see right through me and decipher all that's going on inside me. Just as you said, I do feel ashamed when I meet people—that I am the lowest of the low and that they take me for a buffoon. 'All right,' I say to myself, 'so I'll act like a buffoon.' I don't care what they think of me because I really believe that every one of them is even lower than I. Yes, that's why I'm a buffoon—it's out of shame, as you said, great elder, out of sheer shame! It's a fact that I misbehave this way because I'm oversensitive. If I could only feel that all the people I met considered me a nice, intelligent fellow, I'm sure I'd be the kindest of men!"

All of a sudden he knelt down, exclaiming:

"Oh teacher, what should I do to gain eternal life?"

It was hard to tell whether he was still fooling or was now really deeply moved. The elder looked at him smilingly and said:

"You have known for a long time what to do—you are intelligent enough to see it yourself: stop indulging in drunkenness and incontinence of speech, do not give way to sensual lust and particularly to your passion for money. Also, close down your taverns; if you cannot close them all, close at least two or three. And, above all, stop lying."

"You mean that story I told about Diderot?"

"No, I didn't really mean that. The important thing is to stop lying to yourself. A man who lies to himself, and believes his own lies, becomes unable to recognize truth, either in himself or in anyone else, and he ends up losing respect for himself as well as for others. When he has no respect for anyone, he can no longer love and, in order to divert himself, having no love in him, he yields to his impulses, indulges in the lowest forms of pleasure, and behaves in the end like an animal, in satisfying his vices. And it all comes from lying—lying to others and to yourself. A man who lies to himself, for instance, can take offense whenever he wishes, for there are times when it is rather pleasant to feel wronged—don't you agree? So a man may know very well that no one has offended him, and may invent an offense, lie just for the beauty of it, or exaggerate what someone said to create a situation, making a mountain out of a molehill. And although he is well aware of it himself, he nevertheless does feel offended because he enjoys doing so, derives great pleasure from it, and so he comes to feel real hostility toward the imaginary offender . . . But, please, get up off your knees and sit down. You know very well that your kneeling is also an insincere gesture, a lie . . ."

"Blessed man, allow me to kiss your hand!" Karamazov exclaimed, leaping to his feet, snatching the elder's wizened hand, and hurriedly planting a loud kiss on it. "You're right, so very right! It is very pleasant to feel wronged! I've never heard it put so well before. I have, indeed, been taking offense all my life because I enjoyed it and felt it was beautiful. It is not only pleasurable, it is also esthetically satisfying to feel offended. Yes, that is something you left out, great elder—the beauty of it. I must make a note of it! It is a fact that I have lied all my life, every day and every hour. In truth, I am a living lie, the father of lies . . . No, wait a minute, not the father of lies—I always get my quotations mixed up—well, let's say the son, and that's good enough. But don't you think, angelic man, one can tell lies like the one about Diderot now and then? Diderot can do no harm, but sometimes a word can cause a lot of trouble . . . Ah, I almost forgot, great elder—for two years I've been determined to come here to consult you about something special . . . But first, perhaps you'd better warn Mr. Miusov not to interrupt me. Here's what I wanted to ask you: is it true, Holy Father, as it says somewhere in the *Lives of the Saints,* that one holy miracle worker who suffered martyrdom for his faith stood up, after they had beheaded him, picked up his head, 'kissed it affectionately,' and walked for a long time, carrying it in his hands and 'kissing it affectionately.' Is that story true? I'm addressing the question to all of you, reverend fathers!"

"No, it isn't true," the elder said.

"There's nothing of the sort in the *Lives of the Saints*," said the Father Librarian. "About which saint is it supposed to be written?"

"I don't know myself. Haven't the slightest idea. I was just told the story, misled. And shall I tell you who told me? All right—it was Mr. Miusov here, who just now was so furious about Diderot. It was he who told it to me."

"I never told you anything of the sort. To begin with, I never speak to you at all."

"Right, you didn't tell it to me, but you did tell it to others in my presence, about three years ago. I bring it up now because, by telling that ridiculous story, you undermined my faith. Although you didn't know it, Mr. Miusov, I returned home that day with my faith shaken, and it has been getting shakier and shakier ever since. Yes, Mr. Miusov, you were the cause of my terrible fall. And that's much worse than my telling the Diderot story."

Karamazov's tone was brimming with pathos, although it was perfectly clear to everyone that he was acting again. Yet Miusov was still stung to the quick:

"Nonsense, utter nonsense . . ." he muttered angrily. "I may have said something of the sort, but I didn't tell it to you, I'm sure of that. I was also told the story. When I was in Paris, a Frenchman told me it was from the *Lives of the Saints* and that they read it in Russia in the mass . . . He was a very learned man who was making a statistical study of Russia. He had spent a long time in this country. As for me, I've never read the *Lives of the Saints*, nor do I intend to . . . Anyway, one says all sorts of things at a dinner party and it was at one that I told the story."

"So you ate your dinner and, as a result, I lost my faith that day," Karamazov said, still taunting him.

"Much I care about your faith!" Miusov was ready to shout at him but then, containing himself, he said scornfully: "You defile everything you touch."

The elder rose abruptly from his sofa:

"I hope you will excuse me, gentlemen, if I leave you—just for a few minutes," he said, addressing everyone present.

"Some people who were here even before you arrived are waiting for me. And you," he said, looking cheerfully at Karamazov, "see if you can manage without lying."

As he started out of the cell, Alyosha and the novice hurried over to help him down the steps. Alyosha, who had been standing holding his breath, was very glad to be out of there, but he was also relieved that the elder didn't seem at all offended and was cheerful as usual. The elder was about to leave the cell to bless those who were waiting for him, but Karamazov stopped him in the doorway:

"Blessed man!" he cried out emotionally. "Allow me to kiss your hand once more! I see I can talk to you, I can get along with you. Perhaps you think I always lie like this and play the clown? Well, I want you to know that I was deliberately testing you—I wanted to find out if it was possible to get along with you, whether there was room for my humility next to your pride. So let me give you a certificate of good character: it is indeed possible to get along with you! And now I'll remain silent the rest of the time. I'll sit in my chair and I won't say one word. It's your turn to have the floor now, Mr. Miusov. You will be the most important person here for the next ten minutes . . ."

CHAPTER 3

Women of Great Faith

A score of visitors, this time all peasant women, were waiting below by the gallery built outside the hermitage wall. They had been told that the elder would eventually come out and so had gathered there. Mrs. Khokhlakov and her daughter had also come out into the gallery to wait for the elder, but in the part reserved for ladies. Mrs. Khokhlakov, a wealthy woman, always tastefully dressed, was still young and very pretty; she was rather pale, with very lively, almost black eyes. She was no more than thirty-three and had been a widow for five years. Her fourteen-year-old daughter, whose legs were paralyzed, had been unable to walk for six months and had to be pushed around in a wheel-chair. She had a charming face, a little emaciated by sickness, but cheerful. There was a mischievous sparkle in the big dark eyes behind her long lashes. Her mother had planned to take her abroad in the spring, but they had been detained throughout the

summer by urgent business on the estate. They had been in
our town for a week already, having come on business rather
than for devotions. Nevertheless, they had already been to see
Zosima three days before. And now, although they knew that
the elder could receive hardly any visitors, they had come
back, begging for one more chance to see "the great healer."

The mother sat in a chair next to her daughter's wheel-
chair and near her stood an old monk. He came from a little-
known monastery somewhere in the far North and was also
a visitor. He also sought the elder's blessing.

But when the elder appeared in the gallery, he didn't stop
but went straight down to the peasant women crowded around
the three steps by the entrance. The elder stood on the top
step, put on his stole, and began blessing the women as they
pressed close to him. A crazy village girl was dragged toward
him by both hands. As soon as she saw the elder, she let out
strange shrieks, was seized by violent hiccoughs, and shook as
if in convulsions. Zosima, placing the stole on her head, said
a brief prayer, and the girl immediately quieted down.

I do not know what it is like now, but when I was a boy
I often saw and heard such crazy, wailing women, in the
villages or at monasteries. When they were brought to mass,
they shrieked, or barked like dogs, their cries filling the
church. But as soon as the Host was elevated and they were
led up to it, their "devilry" stopped and they calmed down
for a while. As a child, I was greatly surprised by this. But
then the neighboring gentry and especially my teachers, who
came from town, told me the women were malingering to
avoid work, and that proper firmness would cure them once
and for all. They told me a number of stories to prove the
point. Later, however, specialists told me that it was not a
sham at all, that it was a terrible female disease, particularly widespread in Russia (which shows what a hard life
Russian peasant women have), a sickness resulting from
exhausting work following too soon upon a difficult, abnormal
labor without medical help, and from an intensely unhappy
life, full of brutality and ill-treatment, which, although common enough, is beyond the powers of endurance of some
women. The strange and immediate healing effect of the Host
on these crazy women, which was dismissed as shamming or
even as a trick of the "clerics," can probably be explained
quite simply by the fact that the women who lead such a
woman forward, and above all the sick woman herself, are
absolutely convinced that the evil spirit that has entered her

will have to leave her body when she is led to the Host and made to bow down before it. And so the overwrought and mentally sick woman always experiences (and cannot help experiencing) a violent shock throughout her entire body at the moment when she bends over the Host, a shock produced by her complete faith in the forthcoming miraculous cure. And the miraculous cure is certain to occur, even if it lasts for only a moment. That is what happened now, as soon as the elder covered the hysterical girl with his stole.

Many of the women standing near him wept in ecstasy and exultation, some pressed forward to kiss the hem of his robe, others intoned prayers. He blessed each one of them, speaking to some. He already knew the sick girl—she came from a village only five miles from the monastery and had been brought to him on several previous occasions.

"Here's one from far away!" he said, indicating a woman who, though still young, was thin and haggard, and whose face seemed more blackened than suntanned. She was kneeling, her eyes fixed on Zosima. There was something frenzied in her look.

"From far away, Holy Father, from far away," she answered in a sing-song, her head swaying rhythmically from side to side, her face in her hands. "Five hundred miles away, Holy Father, far, far away . . ."

It sounded like an incantation. There is among peasants a dumb and long-suffering grief that is bottled up inside them and stifled. But there is also a grief that bursts out, first in sobs, then in wailing—fits of wailing. This happens mostly to women. But it is no easier to bear than the silent grief. The wailing only assuages by further lacerating and exasperating the heart. Such grief does not seek consolation but feeds on an awareness of its hopelessness. The wailing simply satisfies the constant need to irritate the wound.

"You come from tradespeople, don't you?" the elder asked, looking at her curiously.

"We live in town now, Father. We used to live on the land, but we moved to town . . . I came to see you, Father, because we'd heard so much about you, so much. I buried my baby son and then I set out—to pray for him. I went to three monasteries and they told me, 'Go there too, Nastya, go and pray there too,' meaning this monastery, that is. I arrived yesterday and I went to church, and today I've come to see you."

"And why, exactly, are you weeping?"

"I'm sad about my little boy, Father . . . He would have been three in two months. I miss my little son, my sweet baby, my last. We had four, Nikita and I, but we can't seem to keep them, our little ones, they just won't stay, dear Father, they just won't . . . When I buried the three older ones, I didn't grieve too much for them, but this last one—I can't get him out of my head. It's just like he's standing here, right in front of my eyes, and never leaves me. My heart has shriveled up. Just looking at his little shirt or his tiny shoes starts me wailing. I put out his things that are left, all of them, and I look at them and wail. So I say to my husband: 'Let me go, Nikita, let me go on a pilgrimage to pray, to God.' He is a coachman, my Nikita, and we aren't poor, Father, we own the carriage and the horses ourselves. But what's the good of it all now? And I'm sure my Nikita has taken to drink without me. I know he has, because even before he'd indulge whenever I turned my back. But I can't even think about him now. I've been away from home more than two months. I've forgotten everything. I don't want to remember, for how will I be able to live with my Nikita now? No, I'm through with him, through with everybody. I don't want to set eyes on our house anymore or on our things, I don't want to see any of it again . . ."

"Let me tell you something, mother," the elder said. "Once, in ancient times, in a church, a great saint saw a woman just like you, weeping for her baby, her only one, whom God had also taken. 'Don't you know,' the saint said to the woman, 'how bold these little ones are before the throne of the Lord? No one in the kingdom of heaven is bolder than they are. "You gave us the gift of life," they say to the Lord, "but as soon as we beheld it You took it back from us." And they ask and demand so boldly that the Lord at once gives them the rank of angel. And so,' the saint told the woman, 'you must rejoice instead of weeping, mother, because your little one is now with the Lord among the angels.' That's what the saint told the weeping woman, long, long ago. And he was a great saint and cannot have told her an untruth. So you too must know that your child stands before the throne of the Lord, rejoicing and happy, and prays to God for you. And so you, too, weep but rejoice."

The woman listened to him, her eyes cast down, one cheek resting on her hand. She sighed deeply.

"That's just what my Nikita tried to tell me—word for word what you have said, Father: 'Why are you crying, you fool? Our little boy must be with the Lord now, singing with the angels.' But as he says it, I see he's crying himself. 'I know that, Nikita,' I say to him. 'Where else would he be, if not with the Lord? But then he's not here with us anymore. He's not by my side as he used to be.' If only I could see him just once more! I wouldn't even go up to him, or say a word to him. I'd just stay quiet in my corner. If only I could see him and hear him playing, just for a minute, outside in the yard—and then come into the house as he used to and call out in his little voice: 'Ma! Where are you, ma?' If only I could hear his little feet walking across the room, if only once more, his tiny, tiny steps—pitter patter, pitter patter. Ah, I remember how often he used to run up to me, squealing and laughing—if only I could hear his little footsteps, I'd recognize them right away! But he's gone, Father, I'll never hear his steps again. Here's his little belt, but he isn't here, and I'll never see him or hear him again."

She pulled out of her bosom a small embroidered belt, looked at it, and at once began shaking with sobs, the tears flowing from her eyes, which she covered with her fingers.

"Now," the elder said, "you are like Rachel in the Bible, weeping for her children and refusing to be comforted because they were no more. Such is the lot of mothers on earth. So do not be comforted—there is no need. Weep, but every time you do, remember that your little son is one of God's angels, that he is looking down on you from where he is now, that he sees you and rejoices in your tears and shows them to God. You will shed a mother's tears for a long time to come, but in the end your weeping will turn into quiet joy, and your bitter tears will become tears of quiet tenderness which will cleanse your heart of sin. And I shall pray for the peace of your boy's soul. What was his name?"

"Alexei, Father."

"That is a sweet name. Was he named for Alexei the man of God?"

"For the man of God, Father, for Alexei the man of God."

"A great saint, he was! I will certainly remember your son in my prayers. I will remember your sorrow too and I will also pray for your husband, that the Lord may grant him health and happiness. And now, go back to your husband and look after him. If your little boy sees from up there that you have abandoned his father, he will weep over both of you. Why must you disturb his bliss? For he is alive, very much alive, since the soul lives forever. Although you cannot see him in the house with you, he is there, invisible, by your side. But how can he come home to you when you say that you hate your home now? To whom will he come if he cannot find his father and mother together? Now he comes to you in your dreams and torments you, but if you go back he will send you sweet dreams. Go back to your husband, mother, go back to him this very day."

"I'll go, Father, I'll do as you say. You've seen into my heart! Ah, Nikita, my Nikita, you're waiting for me, my good husband!" the woman started in a wailing cadence, but the elder had turned away from her to a very old woman. This one was not dressed like a pilgrim but wore ordinary town clothes. It was obvious from her expression that she had come on business, that she had something to tell him. She said she was the widow of an army sergeant. She had not had to travel a long way, since she was from our town. Her son Vasya, who was in the civil service, had been transferred to Irkutsk in Siberia. She had received two letters from him at first, but now there had been no word from him for over a year. She had tried to make inquiries about him, but she really didn't even know where to inquire.

"The other day, Mrs. Bedryagin—she's the wife of a rich merchant—she says to me, 'Why don't you go to church, Prokhorovna, and put your son's name down for a requiem mass, just like he was dead. That will make his soul feel uneasy,' she says, 'and he'll write you a letter. It's a sure thing,' Mrs. Bedryagin tells me, 'it has worked time and again.' But I don't know, somehow it doesn't feel right . . . Enlighten me, Father. Is she telling the truth? Would it be the right thing to do, Father?"

"Don't even think of it! You ought to be ashamed of yourself for asking. How can anyone ask for a requiem mass for someone who is still alive, and you, his mother of all people! That would be a mortal sin, akin to sorcery, and it is forgiven you only because of your ignorance. Instead, you'd better pray to the Mother of God to intercede for your son, that the Lord may grant him health, and for you, that He may forgive you for the error of your ways. And let me tell you this, Prokhorovna: your son will come back to you soon or at least he will certainly send you a letter. You can count on it. Go now and stop worrying—your son is alive, I promise you."

"May God reward you, O beloved benefactor, who prays for us all, that all our sins may be forgiven . . ."

But the elder's attention had already been caught by two burning eyes in the haggard, consumptive face of a young peasant woman. She looked at him in silence, her eyes imploring him, but did not dare to come closer.

"What is it you wish, my dear?"

"Take a load off my soul, dear Father," she said softly and slowly as she went down on her knees and bowed to the ground. "I have sinned, my Father, and I'm afraid of my sin."

The elder sat down on the bottom step, and the woman moved closer to him without rising from her knees.

"I've been a widow for two years," she said in a half whisper, shuddering as she spoke. "It was hard being married to him, he was old and beat me terribly. So when he lay sick, I looked at him and I said to myself: 'If he gets better, he'll get up and then what?' And that is when the thought came to me . . ."

"Wait," the elder said and brought his ear close to her lips. The woman went on, whispering so quietly that it was almost impossible to make out the words. Soon she had finished.

"Over two years ago?" the elder asked.

"Yes. At first I didn't think about it much, but now I've got sick, and it bothers me."

"Have you come from far away?"

"Three hundred miles."

"Have you already confessed this to a priest?"

"I have. Twice I've confessed it."

"Have you been admitted to communion?"

"Yes. But I'm still afraid, Father. I'm afraid to die."

"Don't be afraid of anything, ever. And do not grieve. As long as your repentance does not weaken, God will forgive everything. There is not—there cannot be—a sin on earth that God will not forgive the truly repentant. Why, a man cannot commit a sin so great as to exhaust the infinite love of God. How could there be a sin that would surpass the love of God? Think only of repentance, all the time, and drive away all fear. Have faith that God loves you more than you can ever imagine. He loves you, sinful as you are and, indeed, because of your sin. It was said long ago that there is more joy in heaven over one repentant sinner than over ten righteous men. Go now, and fear nothing. Do not be offended if people treat you badly. Do not hold it against them. And forgive your departed husband all the harm he did you. Become truly reconciled with him. For if you repent, you love, and if you love, you are with God. Love redeems and saves everything. If I, a sinner like yourself, am moved and feel compassion for you, how infinitely much more will God! Love is such an infinite treasure it can buy the whole world and can redeem not only your sins, but the sins of all people. So go and fear no more."

He made the sign of the cross over her three times, took the holy icon from his own neck, and put it around hers. She bowed down to the ground in silence.

He got up from the step where he had been sitting, looking smilingly at a big, strong peasant woman with a baby in her arms.

"I'm from Vyshegorie, beloved Father."

"So you walked five weary miles, carrying the child," he said. "What's your trouble?"

"I just wanted to see you, Father. I've been here before. Don't you recognize me? Your memory can't be too good if you've forgotten me already. People in my village were saying you weren't feeling good, so I think: 'If that's so, I'd better go and see for myself.' But now I'm here, you don't look too sick to me. You'll be around for another twenty years yet, God bless you! Besides, there are enough people to pray for you to keep you from being sick."

"Thank you for everything, my dear."

"While I'm here, I must ask you a small favor too: I have sixty kopeks here, take it and give it to someone poorer than me. On my way here, I says to myself: 'Guess I'd better give him this money. He knows better who needs it most.' "

"Thank you, my dear, thank you, good woman. I love you. I will do as you ask without fail. Is it a girl you have?"

"Yes, dear Father. Her name's Lizaveta."

"May the Lord bless you, both you and baby Lizaveta. You have gladdened my heart, my dear. And now, good-by, my dear, good-by, beloved people."

He blessed all the women and bowed low to them.

CHAPTER 4

A Lady of Little Faith

Watching the elder talking to these humble women and blessing them, Mrs. Khokhlakov kept wiping away her tears with a little handkerchief. She was a sentimental lady with many genuinely kind impulses. When the elder finally approached her, she looked at him ecstatically.

"I've experienced so much, watching this inspiring scene, that . . ." She was too moved to finish. "Oh, I understand why the simple people love you . . . I myself love ordinary people, I want to love them . . . Besides, how can one help loving our wonderful Russian people, so simple in their very greatness?"

"How does your daughter feel? Did you want to talk to me again?"

"Oh, I begged for an interview. I requested it most insistently. I was prepared to go down on my knees, to stay kneeling before your windows for three whole days if I had to, until you received me. We have come to you, great healer, to express our fervent gratitude. Why, you have cured my Lise, cured her completely . . . And how? Just by saying a prayer over her last Thursday and laying your hands on her. We are anxious to kiss those hands, to pour out our feelings and our veneration."

"What do you mean—I healed her? She's still in her wheel-chair, isn't she?"

"But she's had no fever for the past two nights, no fever since Thursday, none at all," the lady rattled on. "Besides, her legs have grown stronger. She felt well when she woke up this morning. She had slept soundly all night, and her cheeks were rosy and her eyes bright . . . She used to cry all the time, but now she is cheerful and keeps laughing. Today she actually demanded to be allowed to get up, to stand on her feet, and she did stand up for a whole minute without any help. She wants to make a wager with me that in a fortnight she'll be dancing the quadrille. I called in the local doctor, Herzenstube, to see her, and he just spread his arms wide in amazement: 'I'm stunned!' he said. 'I just can't explain it.' And you expected us not to disturb you, as though we could keep ourselves from flying over here to thank you. Well, Lise, come, thank the elder!"

Lise's pretty, laughing face suddenly turned grave. She raised herself as far as she could in her wheel-chair and, looking at the elder, clasped her hands as if in prayer. But the next second she lost control of herself and burst out laughing.

"It's his fault. He's the one who makes me laugh!" she cried, pointing at Alyosha, childishly annoyed at herself for not being able to restrain her laughter.

Anyone looking at Alyosha, who was standing one step behind the elder, would have noticed that his cheeks turned bright red; his eyes flashed and he lowered them.

Mrs. Khokhlakov turned toward Alyosha and, giving him her elegantly gloved hand, said: "She has a message for you, Alexei."

The elder turned suddenly to look attentively at Alyosha, who then walked over to Lise and, smiling awkwardly, gave her his hand. Lise put on a serious face.

"Katerina Ivanovna asked me to give you this," she said, handing him a small envelope. "She asks particularly that you come and see her, and she wants you to come soon, without fail, and not to let her down."

"She wants me to go and see her? Me? Why?" Alyosha muttered, extremely surprised. His face took on a very worried look.

"Oh, it's about your brother Dmitry and all that business that happened recently—you know," Lise's mother explained casually. "Katerina has made up her mind on a certain subject, but she absolutely must see you first. Why must she? That I don't know, but she insisted it was very urgent and that you should go as soon as possible. And you must go. I would even say it is your duty as a Christian to go."

"But I've only seen her once," Alyosha said, still bewildered.

"She is such a noble, such an exceptional person! If only because of what she's been through . . . Just imagine how she has suffered, how much she is suffering now, and how much more suffering she has in store for her . . . It's most appalling, most appalling . . ."

"All right, I'll go and see her," Alyosha decided, holding in his hand the brief note, which contained no explanation, only an urgent request that he come.

"It would be so nice, so good of you!" Lise cried out, at once becoming very animated. "I never thought you would. 'He won't go,' I told mother. 'He's too busy saving his soul.' But you're really wonderful! I always thought you were wonderful and I'm very happy to tell you so."

"Lise!" her mother said reproachfully, but she could not suppress a smile and, turning to Alyosha, went on: "You seem to have forgotten us completely, Alexei. You refuse to come and visit us, although Lise has told me twice that you're the only person with whom she feels at ease."

Alyosha raised his downcast eyes, again turned red, and

again grinned rather incongruously. The elder, however, was no longer watching him but was talking to the visiting monk who had been waiting near Lise's chair. He was apparently a very lowly monk, of humble origin, a stubborn man with a narrow, rigid set of beliefs, but with genuine faith. He said he had come from the monastery of St. Sylvester in Obdorsk, somewhere in the far north, a poor little monastery that had only ten monks. The elder blessed him and invited him to come and visit him in his cell whenever he wished.

Suddenly the monk pointed at Lise and asked in a solemn and admonishing tone: "How do you presume to accomplish such feats?" He meant her "miraculous cure."

"Of course, it's still too early to tell—partial relief is by no means a complete recovery, and it could be due to other causes. But if something has been accomplished, it was not brought about by any power other than God's will. Everything comes from God. Come and see me, Father," the elder added, looking at the monk, "although there are moments when I'm in no state to see people. I'm a sick man and my days are numbered."

"Oh, no, that cannot be. God will not take you from us—you will be with us for a long time yet," Mrs. Khokhlakov exclaimed. "Besides, how can you be sick? You look gay, cheerful, and in good health to me!"

"As a matter of fact, I do feel incomparably better today, but I know very well that it cannot last. I've come to understand my illness unerringly now. And if you think I look cheerful, nothing you could say could give me more pleasure. For human beings were created to be happy, and those who are perfectly happy are entitled to say to themselves: 'I have carried out God's will on this earth.' The righteous, the saints, the holy martyrs—they were all happy people."

"Oh, you speak so well. Your words are so bold and so noble!" Mrs. Khokhlakov exclaimed ecstatically. "When you say something, you go right to the essence of things . . . And yet you talk of happiness. Happiness? Where is that happiness? Who can say that he is truly happy? And since you have been so kind as to see us once more, I hope you will allow me to tell you something I didn't finish telling you last time . . . I didn't dare tell you all that has been tormenting me for such a long, long time! I suffer, forgive me, I suffer . . ."

She clasped her hands prayerfully, overwhelmed by emotion.

"What makes you suffer so?"

"I suffer from my lack of faith . . ."

"From not believing in God?"

"Oh no, no! I wouldn't even dare think of that . . . But life after death—it is such a puzzle and no one, no one at all, has the answer! Please listen to me, you who can heal, you who know the human soul so well; of course I don't dare to presume that you will believe everything I say, but I give you my solemn word that I am not talking lightly now, and that the thought of life beyond the grave worries, terrifies, and torments me. And I don't know to whom to turn. I've never dared to speak of it before . . . And now I've told you . . . Oh, my God, what will you think of me now!"

And she threw up her hands in despair.

"Don't worry about my opinion of you," the elder said. "I entirely believe in the sincerity of your anguish."

"Oh, thank you, thank you! You see, I close my eyes and I reason like this: people do have faith, but where does it come from? I've heard it said that it all came originally from fear of menacing natural phenomena, and that there's nothing else to it. So I say to myself: 'What if, after I've been a believer all my life, when I die it suddenly turns out that after life there's nothing at all, nothing but wild grass growing on my grave,' as some writer put it. That's horrible! And how can I regain my faith? I must say, I only really believed when I was a little girl. I took things for granted then, without questioning. What is there to prove it to me now? This is what I have come here for, to throw myself at your feet and ask you. Why, if I miss this opportunity, I will never find the answer in all my life. So how can I prove it to myself, how can I become convinced? Oh, I am so unhappy! When I look around me, I realize that people don't care, hardly anyone does, and I'm the only one who cannot bear it. It is dreadful, just dreadful!"

"I am sure it is dreadful, but nothing can be proved, although one can become convinced."

"How? By what?"

"By acts of love. Try to love your neighbors, love them actively and unceasingly. And as you learn to love them more and more, you will be more and more convinced of the existence of God and of the immortality of your soul. And if you achieve complete self-abnegation in your love for your fellow man, you will certainly gain faith, and there will be no room in your soul for any doubt whatsoever. This has been tested. This is the true way."

"Acts of love? That's another problem, and what a problem! You see, I love mankind so much that, believe it or not, there are moments when I would like to give up everything, abandon Lise, and become a hospital nurse. I close my eyes and let my imagination wander, and during those minutes I feel an irresistible strength within me. No wounds, no infected sores, however terrible, could frighten me away then. I would clean them with my own hands. I would look after those sufferers. I would be ready to kiss their sores . . ."

"It is good that you should think of these things rather than others . . . But it would be very nice if you actually performed some good deed."

"Yes, but how long do you think I could live such a life?" Mrs. Khokhlakov said heatedly, an almost hysterical note creeping into her voice. "That's the crucial point! Yes, that's the question that torments me most. I close my eyes and I ask myself: 'How long do you think you could endure that life? What if a patient, whose sores you were cleaning, instead of being grateful to you, tormented you with his whims and had no appreciation whatsoever for your services to mankind, talked rudely to you, or even complained about you to your superiors, as people who are in pain so often do? What would happen then? Would you go on loving him or not?' And I must tell you that, to my own dismay, I have come to this conclusion: if anything could dampen my 'active love' for mankind, it is ingratitude. In other words, I'm willing to work if I'm paid for it. But I want to be paid at once. I mean I want to be praised and paid for love with love. Otherwise, I'm quite incapable of loving anyone."

She seemed to be in a paroxysm of sincere self-deprecation and, as she finished, there was a challenge to the elder in her eyes.

"That's exactly what a doctor told me quite some time ago," the elder remarked. "He was not a young man and he was certainly intelligent. He was just as sincere as you are, although he spoke in an amused tone, with a sort of bitter humor. 'I love mankind,' he said, 'but I find to my amazement that the more I love mankind as a whole, the less I love individual people. In my thoughts,' the doctor told me, 'I often visualize ecstatically the sacrifices I could make for mankind and, indeed, I might even accept martyrdom for my fellow men if circumstances suddenly demanded it of me. In actual fact, however, I cannot bear to spend two days in the same room with another person. And this I know from personal experience. Whenever someone is too close to me, I feel my personal dignity and freedom are being infringed upon. Within twenty-four hours I can come to hate the best of men, perhaps because he eats too slowly or because he has a cold and keeps blowing his nose. I become a man's enemy,' he said, 'as soon as he touches me. But to make up for it, the more I hate individual people, the more ardent is my general love for mankind.' "

"But what's the answer then? What's to be done in such a case? Is it completely hopeless?"

"No, because the very fact that it worries you is enough in itself. Do the best you can and it will stand you in good stead. As it is, you have done a great deal, for you have come to know yourself deeply and sincerely. However, if you have spoken to me so frankly only to make me praise you for your sincerity, then, of course, you will fail to accomplish true acts of love; all your good intentions will remain mere daydreams, and your whole life will slip by like a shadow. In that case, you will certainly forget all about the future life as well, and in the end you will somehow or other stop worrying altogether."

"I feel completely crushed! This very second I realize that, just as you say, I was expecting you to praise me for my sincerity when I told you that I would not be able to bear ingratitude. You have brought out what was within me. You saw it and you have shown it to me!"

"Do you really mean what you say now? If so, after what you have admitted, I am sure that you are sincere and that you have a good heart. Even if it is not given to you to achieve happiness, you must always remember that you are on the right path and you must try not to stray from it. Above all, avoid lying, especially lying to yourself. Keep watching out for your lies, watch for them every hour, every minute. Also avoid disgust, both for others and for yourself: whatever strikes you as disgusting within yourself is cleansed by the mere fact that you notice it. Avoid fear too, although fear is really only a consequence of lies. Never be afraid of your petty selfishness when you try to achieve love, and don't be too alarmed if you act badly on occasion. I'm sorry I cannot tell you anything more reassuring. A true act of love, unlike imaginary love, is hard and forbidding. Imaginary love yearns for an immediate heroic act that is achieved quickly and seen by everyone. People may actually reach a point where they are willing to sacrifice their lives, as long as the ordeal doesn't last too long, is quickly over—just like on the stage, with the public watching and admiring. A true act of love, on the other hand, requires hard work and patience, and, for some, it is a whole way of life. But I predict that at the very moment when you see despairingly that, despite all your efforts, you have not only failed to come closer to your goal but, indeed, seem even farther from it than ever—at that very moment, you will have achieved your goal and will recognize the miraculous power of our Lord, who has always loved you and has secretly guided you all along. And now, please forgive me—I cannot stay with you any longer. Some people are waiting for me. Good-by."

Mrs. Khokhlakov was weeping.

"Lise, Lise. Won't you bless her? Please bless her!" she cried suddenly, as if emerging from a trance.

"She doesn't even deserve to be loved," the elder said jokingly. "She's been misbehaving. I've been watching her . . . Why have you been laughing at Alexei all this time?"

And it was true. Lise had been doing just this. She had realized, ever since she had seen Alyosha on the previous occasion, that he seemed embarrassed in her presence and avoided looking at her. She found this very funny and amused herself by trying to catch his eye. Feeling her intense gaze constantly following him, Alyosha felt impelled by some irresistible force and was unable to prevent himself from quickly glancing at her from time to time. And whenever he did so, their eyes met and she smiled triumphantly, right in his face, and Alyosha became even more embarrassed and angry with himself. So finally he turned away from her completely and hid behind the elder's back. After a few minutes, again acting on the same uncontrollable impulse, Alyosha turned to see whether she was still looking at him, and saw Lise, leaning over so far that she was almost hanging out of her chair, looking at him from the side and waiting intently for him to glance at her. This time, when she caught his eye, she laughed aloud, so that the elder turned to her and said:

"You are a bad girl! Why are you trying to embarrass him?"

Lise unexpectedly turned very red. Her eyes flashed, her face became grave, and she spoke heatedly and nervously, as though complaining indignantly about Alyosha:

"And why has he forgotten everything? When I was little, he used to carry me around and we used to play together. You know he taught me to read? And when he was leaving two years ago, he told me he'd never forget me and that we'd always be friends, always, always, he said. And now he seems to be afraid of me, as though I were going to eat him or something. Why won't he come over and talk to me? Why doesn't he want to come to our house? Is it you who won't allow him to come and visit us? But we know that he goes where he pleases. It wasn't right for me to have to invite him. He should have thought of it himself if he really hadn't forgotten me. But I see that he's too busy saving his soul now! But why do you make him wear that cassock? It's too long, and he'll fall down if he tries to run . . ."

And suddenly, unable to restrain herself, she covered her face with both hands and burst into nervous, violent, but muted laughter.

The elder listened to her with a smile and then blessed her with great gentleness. As she was about to kiss his hand, she suddenly pressed it against her eyes and began to cry.

"Please don't be angry with me," she said. "I'm a fool and I'm really not worth bothering about . . . And I think Alyosha is right, quite right, not to come and see a ridiculous person like me."

"I'll see to it that he comes to see you," the elder said.

CHAPTER 5

So It Shall Be and So Be It!

The elder had been away from his cell for about twenty-five minutes. It was after twelve-thirty and Dmitry Karamazov, who was the main reason for the gathering, had still not arrived. They seemed almost to have forgotten about him, however, and when the elder returned to his cell his guests were engaged in a very animated conversation. The principals were Ivan Karamazov and the two monks. Miusov kept trying —apparently very anxiously—to join in the argument, but again he had no luck. He was obviously not taken seriously, the others hardly even bothering to answer him, and this seemed to increase his irritability even further. The trouble was that even before this he and Ivan had needled each other on various learned subjects and he could not bear Ivan's condescendingly casual air toward him. "Up till now I've always been abreast of the latest developments in European thinking, yet this new Russian generation is just determined to ignore us," he thought. As to Fyodor Karamazov, who had promised to remain silent, he did indeed stay quiet for a while. He sat in his chair and watched his neighbor Miusov with a sarcastic little smile, obviously delighting in his frustration. For a long time he had been planning to get even with Miusov for certain things and now he did not want to miss the opportunity to do so. Finally, unable to contain himself any longer, he bent toward his neighbor's ear and said in an undertone, taunting him:

"How is it that you didn't leave right after the kissing ceremony, but consented to stay in such disreputable company? Shall I tell you why? It was because you felt humbled and insulted and decided to stay to get your own back and show them all how brilliant you are. And now you won't leave until you've succeeded in showing them."

"There you go again! Well, you're wrong, I'll leave now . . ."

"You'll leave after all the others!" Karamazov said, needling him again.

It was at this point that the elder came back into the room. The conversation came to a halt for a moment, but as the elder resumed his seat, he looked around at the others, apparently inviting them to continue their discussion. Alyosha, who had come to know every expression on the elder's face, saw clearly that he was exhausted and that it cost him a great effort to remain there. In the latest phase of his sickness, Zosima often suffered fainting fits which were caused by physical weakness. Now he was almost as pale as just before such a fit, and his lips had turned white. But he obviously did not want to send the visitors away yet. He seemed to have something on his mind—but what could it be? Alyosha watched him intently.

"We've been talking about the very interesting article this gentleman wrote," the monastery librarian said, gesturing toward Ivan. "It is full of original ideas, but I think it cuts both ways. It is about the jurisdiction of the ecclesiastical courts and was written in answer to a whole book by a prominent churchman on that subject . . ."

"Unfortunately I haven't read your article, but I have heard about it," the elder said, looking intently at Ivan.

"He has a very curious approach to the problem," the

monastery librarian explained. "He seems to reject completely the separation of Church and State when dealing with the jurisdiction of the ecclesiastical courts."

"That is curious . . . But in what sense?" the elder asked Ivan.

When Ivan answered him, he did not do so condescendingly, as Alyosha had feared he would, but spoke quietly, self-effacingly, with great courtesy and apparently complete frankness.

"I start from the premise that, although they are doomed to failure, attempts will always be made to combine the essential elements of Church and State, considered as separate entities, but these attempts can never succeed in producing a workable solution because they are based on a complete fallacy. Thus, the conciliation of claims between Church and State on such matters as the administration of justice is, in my opinion, quite impossible by its very nature. The churchman against whom I argue contends that the Church has a clearly defined place within the State. I answer that, on the contrary, instead of occupying some little corner within the State, the Church should contain the State, and if it cannot do so immediately, it ought to make that a prime goal in the development of a Christian society."

"Very true," Father Paisii, a learned and taciturn monk, assented in a tense, decisive tone.

"That's sheer Ultramontanism!" Miusov said, impatiently recrossing his legs.

"Eh, we don't even have any mountains here," the monastery librarian remarked and turned back to Zosima. "The author of this article answers, among other things, the following fundamental contentions of his opponent, who is, be it remembered, an ecclesiastic: first, that no social organization should claim or be allowed to usurp the civilian and political rights of its members; second, that the criminal and civil courts cannot be controlled by the Church because that would be incompatible with the nature of an institution vested with divine authority, or of an association of men formed for religious purposes; and third, that 'the Church is a kingdom not of this world.' "

"That is playing on words in a way quite unworthy of an ecclesiastic!" Paisii interrupted again indignantly. "I have read the book against which you argue in your article," he said, turning to Ivan, "and I was quite taken aback by the words 'the Church is a kingdom not of this world' coming from an ecclesiastic. If it is not 'of this world,' how can it be on earth at all? The words 'not of this world' are used in a completely different context in the Holy Gospels, and no one should trifle with them. The very purpose of the coming of our Lord Jesus Christ to earth was to establish the Church here. Obviously, the kingdom of heaven is not of this world, since it is in heaven, but the only way to enter it is through the Church that has been set up on this earth. And, therefore, any interpretation or sophisticated play on words is impermissible and unworthy of a churchman. Indeed, the Church is a kingdom, ordained to reign, and ultimately it will become a kingdom of all the earth, as was preordained by our Lord . . ."

He suddenly fell silent, making an obvious effort to restrain himself. Ivan, who had listened to him with respectful attention, spoke again with perfect composure. His tone was frank and unaffected as he addressed the elder.

"My whole article is based on the idea that, during its first three centuries, Christianity existed on earth as a church. But when the pagan Roman Empire decided to become Christian, it was inevitable that, in turning Christian, it simply incorporated the Church while, in fact, remaining essentially pagan. Indeed, it was bound to be that way. But in Rome too much was left of her pagan wisdom and civilization—among other things, the very goals and foundations of the State. On the other hand, in entering the State, Christ's Church certainly could not renounce any of its principles, the rock on which it was built, and could only pursue the goals set for it by our Lord Himself. Among these goals is the integration of the whole world—including, therefore, the pagan State—into the Church. Thus, in view of these long-range goals, it is not up to the Church to seek a proper place for itself within the State, like any other public agency or 'association of men for religious purposes,' as the author of the book against which I argue puts its. Since ultimately every secular state is to be integrated into the Church and become nothing but the Church, it is the State that must discard all goals that are incompatible with those of the Church. And this would involve no humiliation, no slur on the honor and glory of a great state, or loss of prestige to its rulers. It would simply transfer the concept of the State from the wrong premises to the correct ones, to the only true way of achieving the eternal goals. For this reason, the author of the *Foundations of the Ecclesiastical Courts* would have been right if, in searching for and defining those foundations, he had considered them as a temporary compromise for our sinful and transitory era, but nothing more than that. But when the author dares to declare that the foundations he mentions—some of which were noted by Father Joseph a few moments ago—are natural, immutable, and eternal, he thereby goes directly against the Church and its sacred mission, preordained from time immemorial. And that is the gist of my article."

"Which means, to sum up briefly," said Father Paisii, stressing every word, "that, according to certain theories of which the point has become only too clear in our nineteenth century, the Church is to evolve into a state, the way a lower order of life evolves into a higher one, and eventually is to disappear altogether as a religious institution, being superseded by science, technical progress, and secularism. And if the Church refuses to accept that fate and resists, it is to be rewarded for its pains by being allotted a corner in the preserve of the State, and even that would be under the supervision of the State. This is the situation today in every European country. But, according to the Russian idea and hope, it is not the Church that is to be transformed into the State, as an inferior form into a superior one; it is rather the State that must eventually become part of the Church. So it shall be and so be it!"

"Well, I must say, I feel somewhat reassured!" Miusov snorted, again recrossing his legs. "As far as I can make out, you seem to be talking about the realization of some ideal in the distant future, perhaps at the second coming of Christ. In that case, I have no objection. It is a beautiful, utopian dream of a world without wars, diplomats, banks, and so on. In a way, it resembles socialism . . . For a moment I thought you were talking seriously about the Church doing such things as prosecuting criminals and sentencing people to floggings, detention, and even, I suppose, death."

"Hardly so," Ivan said without batting an eye. "Even if all justice today were administered by ecclesiastical courts, the Church would not sentence anyone either to forced labor or to death. The whole concept of crime, and how to deal with it, would be different. Of course, it would not change suddenly, all at once, but would evolve gradually. But still, it wouldn't take very long . . ."

"Can you possibly mean what you say?" Miusov asked, looking closely at Ivan.

"If everything were integrated into the Church, the Church would excommunicate the criminal and the subversive, instead of chopping off their heads," Ivan went on. "Just think—where could the excommunicate go? Why, he would be cut off not only from men but also from Christ, since his crime would be a crime not only against his fellow men but also against Christ's Church. Strictly speaking, of course, this is true now. But it has not been officially proclaimed, and our criminals today often compromise with their consciences in a number of ways. 'I steal,' one may say, for instance, 'but I wouldn't do anything against the Church, because I am not an enemy of Christ.' But while criminals often justify themselves in this way today, the moment the Church superseded the State, they could no longer appease their consciences unless they said: 'Everyone else is wrong; they have all lost God, and their Church is a false church. It is we, the thieves and murderers, who alone represent the true Church of Christ.' But it would be rather difficult for a man to say that to himself, unless he was living under exceptional circumstances, during world-shaking events, and such situations do not occur very often. Now let us look at the Church's approach to crime: isn't it bound to differ from the State's approach today, which is an almost pagan approach—the mechanical amputation of the diseased limb for the protection of society? The Church would aim at the total, true regeneration of man, his spiritual rebirth, and the salvation of his . . ."

"What are you saying? I've lost you again," Miusov interrupted him. "It's some sort of dream again, something formless . . . I can't even follow you. What is this about excommunication? What excommunication? I suspect you're just having fun at other people's expense, Ivan."

"But this is just as true today," the elder suddenly spoke out, and they all immediately turned to him. "If Christ's Church did not exist today, there would be nothing to restrain a man from committing crimes, for there would be no real punishment . . . I'm not talking of 'mechanical' punishment, such as was described a moment ago, which in most cases only hardens a criminal, but of real punishment, the only effective one, that people fear and that can bring peace—the awareness of one's own conscience."

"But what do you mean by that?" Miusov asked, filled with lively curiosity.

"What I mean," the elder went on, "is that all this business of sentencing people to hard labor, with or without flogging, does not reform criminals and, more to the point, does not deter them from committing crimes. So the number of crimes not only does not diminish—it keeps increasing. Why, you must concede that at least. It turns out, consequently, that society is not really protected by this method because, even if a dangerous member is cut off and put far away out of sight, immediately another criminal will appear in his place, and sometimes even two. If anything protects society in our time, if anything can reform the criminal and make a new man out of him, it is only the law of Christ, which manifests itself in the awareness of a man's own conscience. It is only after a man has recognized his guilt as a son of Christ's society, that is, of the Church, that he will become conscious of his guilt toward society, that is, toward the Church. Consequently, today's criminal can recognize his guilt only toward the Church, and not toward the State. So if the administration of justice were in the hands of society as represented by the Church, it would know whom it should absolve from excommunication and receive again as its son. But as things stand today, the Church has no legal authority, only the power of moral condemnation. And so she refuses to take part in the punishment of a criminal. She does not excommunicate him, she only offers him maternal advice. Indeed, she tries to abide by the pledge made by Christ's Church to the criminal: to admit him to church services and to the holy sacrament, to give him alms and treat him as a captive rather than as a convict. And what would become of the criminal, O Lord, if the Christian community, that is, the Church, rejected him and cut him off as the law of the State does? What would happen if every time a man was punished by the State, the Church followed suit by excommunicating him? The answer is that there could be no deeper despair, at least for a Russian criminal, because Russian criminals are still believers. And who knows, perhaps the result would be truly tragic—in his despair the criminal might lose his faith. And what would be gained by that?

"And so the Church, acting like a tender and loving mother, will take no part in meting out punishment because, even without the Church, a man condemned by the state courts is sufficiently punished, and there should be someone, after all, to take pity on him. But the main reason for the Church's keeping aloof is that the law of the Church is the only true law and it cannot, therefore, make the slightest concession to any other law or even accept a temporary compromise.

"But a non-Russian criminal, I have been told, rarely

repents, since many modern theories confirm him in his belief
that a crime is not really a crime but only a gesture of protest
against an unjust and oppressive force. Society cuts him off,
as a matter of course, because it is stronger than he, and
accompanies its ostracism of him with hatred (so, at least,
Europeans themselves describe it); then it shows no interest
whatever in the further fate of that human being and soon
forgets all about him. And as all this takes place, there is no
one to take pity on the condemned man, because in many
countries there is no church any longer; all they have left is
the clergy and magnificent buildings that used to be churches.
For their churches have long been evolving from the lower
form of church into the higher form of state, in which they
will be completely dissolved and vanish. This is what happens
at least in Lutheran countries, I believe. As to Rome, they
proclaimed a state instead of a church a full thousand years
ago. Hence, a criminal there cannot consider himself a member of the Church. He is excommunicated and sinks into
despair. And if he does return to society, he is so full of
hatred that it is he, as it were, who excommunicates society
from himself.

"How it will end, I leave to your imagination. At various
times it has seemed as though Russia would follow the same
course. But the difference lies in the very fact that, in addition
to the civil courts of justice, we also have a church that
never loses contact with the criminal and treats him like a
dear and still beloved son; and also the Church in Russia
does play a role in upholding the law, even if only in people's
minds; for, although the Church does not actually sit in
judgment over criminals, they fear her condemnation and
thus acknowledge her authority.

"It is also true, as has been contended here, that if the
Church were given full control of the administration of justice,
that is, if the whole community were integrated into the
Church, then not only would the ecclesiastical courts work
for the regeneration of criminals as no courts of justice can
today, but also the number of crimes might be tremendously
reduced. And there is no doubt that the Church herself would,
in many cases, look upon criminals and crime quite differently, and she would succeed in bringing back the outcasts,
in preventing crimes from being committed, and in regenerat-
ing the fallen. It is true, though," the elder said with a faint
smile, "that Christian society itself is not yet ready for this, as
it still rests precariously on seven righteous men. But as long

as these men exist, society will stand firm, waiting for total transformation from a pagan community into one universal sovereign church. And even if this should not happen till the end of time, happen it will because it has been so ordained. So it shall be and so be it! Nor should we worry about the length of time it will take or the day when it will come to pass, because the secret of the time and the day lies in God's wisdom, His vision of the future, and His love. And what to a man may appear infinitely remote may in God's design be very near, already within reach. So it shall be and so be it!"

"So it shall be and so be it!" Father Paisii echoed with stern solemnity.

"All this is very, very strange," Miusov said. He sounded somehow more personally offended than angry.

"What exactly strikes you as so strange?" the monastery librarian asked him quietly.

"What is it all about finally?" Miusov shouted, as though no longer able to bear it. "What is this about the State being eliminated and the Church raised to the status of a state! This is no longer Ultramontanism, this is Arch-Ultramontanism! This is something that Pope Gregory VII himself could not have dreamed up!"

"You have completely misunderstood, sir," Father Paisii said sternly. "It is not the Church that is to be turned into the State. That is Rome and its dream. It is the third temptation of the devil! Just the opposite is true—it is the State that will be transformed into the Church. It will rise to the status of a church and become the universal Church. It is just the opposite of Ultramontanism, of Rome, and of your interpretation, and it is the great mission and destination of the Orthodox Church on earth. The star will rise in the East!"

Miusov maintained a dignified silence. His entire person contrived to convey his tremendous respect for himself. A condescending smile twisted his lips. Alyosha's heart pounded as he watched them all. What had been said had shaken him to his very foundations. For a second his glance rested on Rakitin. Rakitin was still standing by the door, motionless, listening, following intently, although he kept his eyes lowered. From his flushed cheeks, Alyosha could see that Rakitin was no less excited than he himself, and he guessed what the cause of his excitement was.

Suddenly Miusov broke his silence, speaking with overbearing condescension.

"I wonder," he said, "if you gentlemen would allow me to

tell you a little story. When I was in Paris a few years ago—
it was soon after the December *coup d'état*—I went to see an
acquaintance of mine who at that time held a very important
position in the government, and during my visit I met an
extremely interesting gentleman. This character was not only
a secret agent—he was in charge of a whole team of secret
agents which, in its way, made him a man of considerable
influence. I took advantage of the opportunity to make him
talk, as I was quite intrigued. Now, since he was there as a
subordinate, to make some sort of report to my acquaintance,
whereas I was received as a personal friend—a fact which he
realized very well—he answered my questions with a certain
degree of frankness—or at least he was extremely courteous
rather than frank, the way Frenchmen can be courteous, especially to foreigners. But I understood him perfectly. The main
topic of our conversation was the socialist revolutionaries
who, incidentally, were at that time being persecuted. I will
spare you the brunt of the conversation and repeat only a
curious remark that the gentleman made quite inadvertently:
'We aren't really too worried about all these socialists, anar-
chists, atheists, revolutionaries, and the like. We keep our eye
on them and we know what they're likely to try next. But
there are among them some, though not many, peculiar types
who believe in God—Christians who are at the same time
socialists. They are the ones who worry us most. They are
the most dangerous! A Christian socialist is much more dangerous than an atheistic socialist.' I was struck by these words
at the time and now they come back to me . . ."

"You mean that you apply them to us and that you regard
us as socialists?" Father Paisii asked him point blank.

But before Miusov could answer, the door opened and
Dmitry Karamazov made his very late appearance. Apparently
they had all given up hope of seeing him, since his sudden
arrival seemed to cause a certain surprise.

CHAPTER 6

Why Should Such a Man Live?

At twenty-eight, Dmitry Karamazov looked much older
than he was. He was of medium height, powerfully muscled,
and obviously endowed with great physical strength, but his
thin, sallow, hollow-cheeked face left an impression of ill-

health. And there was something vague·about the otherwise
determined look in his rather large, dark, somewhat bulging
eyes. Even when he grew excited and spoke irritatedly, his
eyes seemed disconnected from his inner state and to express
something quite unrelated to what he was saying. "Hard to
know what he's thinking," was the general impression he produced on people who talked to him. At times, he would look
at people with a dreamy, melancholy gaze and then suddenly
surprise them by bursting into gay laughter, which probably
reflected gay and playful thoughts that had been churning in
his head all the while.

It must be said that anyone could think of many good
reasons for Dmitry's drawn and haggard features; everyone
had heard of the irregular and dissipated life he had been
leading, particularly of late, and they also knew how upset
and irritated he was by his arguments with his father over
money. Several stories on the subject were going around
town. It is true, though, that Dmitry had by nature a temper
that he found hard to control. "An unbalanced and unpredictable spirit," as our justice of the peace, Semyon Kachalni-
kov, once aptly described him at a public gathering.

Dmitry arrived impeccably dressed in the latest fashion,
wearing a black coat buttoned all the way down and black
gloves, and carrying a top-hat in his hand. Having recently
retired from the army, he still wore an officer's moustache.
His dark-brown hair was short and combed forward at the
temples. He walked with the long, firm stride of a military
man. He stopped for a second by the door as he came in,
glanced quickly around, and then went straight over to the
elder, guessing him to be the host. He bowed deeply to him
and asked for his blessing. The elder half rose from his seat
and blessed him. Dmitry kissed his hand with great reverence and then, sounding very agitated, almost angry, said:

"Please forgive me for being so late. My father's servant,
Smerdyakov, who was sent to inform me of this meeting,
repeated twice with the utmost assurance, when I asked him
about the time, that it was set for one p.m. . . . And now
suddenly I'm told that it was for . . ."

"Please think nothing of it. Don't let it worry you," the
elder interrupted him. "Even if you are a little late, no harm
has been done at all . . ."

"Thank you very much. I could not have expected less
from a man of your kindness," Dmitry said, interrupting him
in his turn. He bowed once more to the elder, and then, turn-

ing abruptly toward his father, unexpectedly bowed to him just as deeply and respectfully. It was quite evident that he had planned that bow well in advance, sincerely feeling that it was his duty to register his good intentions and his respect for his father.

Although Mr. Karamazov was caught unawares by his son's gesture, he managed to cope with the situation in his own style: he answered Dmitry's bow by leaping up from his chair and bowing back to him just as solemnly and respectfully. His face took on a grave and solemn expression, and this somehow made him look positively evil.

Dmitry looked around the room, bowed once more, this time generally to all the other people there, and walked in his long, firm soldier's stride toward the window where, near Father Paisii, stood the last unoccupied chair. He sat down, leaning forward, ready to listen to the conversation he had interrupted by his arrival.

All this had taken no more than a couple of minutes, and the conversation was resumed as a matter of course. Miusov, however, did not find it necessary to answer Father Paisii's pressing and almost angry question.

"Allow me to decline to discuss this subject any further," he said with urbane casualness. "It is a rather intricate matter, you know . . . But I see that Ivan Karamazov is smiling at us: I suppose he has some interesting comment to make. Why don't you ask him?"

"I'd just like to share a small observation with you," Ivan answered immediately, "namely, that for a long time European liberals and even our native Russian liberal dilettantes have frequently confused the final results of socialism and of Christianity. Such an absurd idea is, of course, characteristic of these people. Actually the liberals and the dilettantes are not the only ones to lump socialism and Christianity together. In some cases the security police do so too—I mean abroad, of course. And your Paris story, Mr. Miusov, is quite typical."

"I must ask you once more, gentlemen, to excuse me if I refuse to discuss this subject any further," Miusov repeated. "Let me, instead, tell you another little story, this one about Mr. Ivan Karamazov himself, an extremely interesting and characteristic story, I think. Well, not more than five days ago, in a company consisting mostly of ladies of our town, he solemnly declared, in the course of a discussion, that there was nothing on earth to force men to love their fellow men, that there was no law of nature that a man should love mankind, and that if there was love on earth it did not stem from any natural law but rather from man's belief in immortality. And here he added parenthetically that if there was any natural law, it was precisely this: Destroy a man's belief in immortality and not only will his ability to love wither away within him but, along with it, the force that impels him to continue his existence on earth. Moreover, nothing would be immoral then, everything would be permitted, even cannibalism. He went even further, finally asserting that, for every individual—people like us now, for instance—who does not believe in God or immortality, the natural moral law immediately becomes the opposite of religious law and that absolute egotism, even carried to the extent of crime, must not only be tolerated but even recognized as the wisest and perhaps the noblest course. From this paradox you may draw your own conclusions, gentlemen, as to what other declarations may be expected from our dear eccentric and lover of paradoxes, Ivan Karamazov."

"Just a minute!" Dmitry shouted unexpectedly. "I want to get it straight: crime must be considered not only as admissible but even as the logical and inevitable consequence of an atheist's position. Did I get it right?"

"You've got it right," Father Paisii said.

"Good, I'll remember that."

Having said this, Dmitry lapsed into silence just as abruptly as he had butted into the conversation. They all looked curiously at him.

"Is this really your conviction about what would happen if men lost their faith in the immortality of the soul?" the elder asked, looking at Ivan.

"Yes, I did argue that there is no virtue if there is no immortality."

"If you believe that, you must be either blissfully happy or desperately unhappy."

"Why unhappy?" Ivan asked, smiling.

"Because it is extremely unlikely that you yourself believe either in the immortality of your soul or even in what you wrote about the Church and the problems of Church and State."

"You may be right. But I wasn't simply joking when I said all that," Ivan admitted quite unexpectedly, albeit blushing slightly.

"True, you weren't just joking: you haven't quite solved that problem in your heart and it still torments you. But a man who suffers also sometimes likes to divert himself with his own despair, and that also out of despair, we may say. For the moment, your despair is driving you, too, to divert yourself, either by writing magazine articles or by expressing daring, sophisticated opinions in cultured company, while you do not believe in your dialectics yourself and laugh at them inwardly, although it hurts you . . . Within you, that problem has not been solved and yours is a great unhappiness, because the problem demands an answer."

"But is it possible that there is an answer for me? I mean, could there be an affirmative answer?" Ivan said in a strange questioning tone, looking at the elder with a quizzical little smile.

"If the answer cannot be affirmative, it can never be negative either, for, as you know very well yourself, that is a peculiarity of your nature and the source of your suffering. But you must thank your Creator for having given you a heart so noble that it can experience this torment: 'to mind high things and to seek high things forasmuch as our dwelling is in heaven.' May God grant that your heart find the answer while you are still on this earth, and may He bless you on your journey through life!"

The elder raised his hand and was about to make the sign of the cross toward Ivan, when Ivan suddenly got up, walked over to him, received his blessing, kissed his hand, and went back to his seat—all without uttering a sound. He looked grave and determined. Ivan's unexpected action, and his dialogue with the elder, puzzled everyone in the room, and they were all struck by his almost solemn air. They remained silent for a moment, Alyosha looking quite alarmed. Then Miusov shrugged his shoulders, and at that very moment old Karamazov leaped up from his chair.

"O divine and saintly elder!" he cried, addressing the elder and pointing to Ivan. "This is my son, flesh of my flesh, the dearest of my flesh and blood. He is, I may say, my most dutiful Karl Moor, while this other son of mine, the one who just came in, Dmitry, against whom I am seeking justice from you, is my most undutiful Franz Moor—both from Schiller's *The Robbers*—and in that case I myself am the Regierender Graf von Moor! Judge us and save us! We ask not only your prayers but also your prophetic insights."

"Try to speak simply, without playing the clown, and don't start by being offensive to your children," the elder said in an exhausted voice. He was visibly tiring, the strength draining from him.

"A disgraceful farce! Just as I expected on my way here!" Dmitry shouted, also jumping to his feet. "Please forgive me, Reverend Father," he said, turning to the elder. "I am an ignorant man who doesn't even know how to address you . . . You have been deceived and you have been much too kind in allowing us to meet here. All my father wants is a disgraceful public scene, which he somehow calculates is in his interest. He's always calculating. But I think I know now, why . . ."

"They all keep accusing me, every single one of them!" Old Karamazov was shouting now too. "Take Miusov, for instance. You accused me, Mr. Miusov, didn't you?" He suddenly turned on Miusov, although the man was not even thinking of interrupting. "They accuse me of tucking my children's money away in my boots and swindling them all. But tell me, isn't there such a thing as legal action? The judges will help you to reckon up that money if you're really interested, Dmitry. They will add up the sums mentioned on your own receipts, your letters, and the agreements you signed, and it will be clear how much you had, how much you have spent, and how much there is still coming to you! Why does Mr. Miusov refuse to act as arbitrator? Dmitry is no stranger to him. It's because, while they all make accusations against me, in actual fact, it is Dmitry who owes me money, and not just a small sum, but several thousand rubles. I have the documents to prove it! And besides, the whole town is in an uproar about his wild revelries! And before, while he was still in the army, he thought nothing of spending a thousand or two on seducing respectable young ladies; that's something I'm very well informed about, Dmitry, in every detail, and I'll prove it when the time comes . . . Believe me, Holy Father, he gained the affections of a most honorable young lady, from a good and wealthy family, the daughter of his former superior officer, a brave and gallant colonel, a bearer of the Order of St. Anne with palms. He compromised the young lady. He offered to marry her. And now that his poor, orphaned fiancée has come to our town, he is running after a certain local beauty in front of her very eyes. And although that local beauty is, as they say, living in sin with a most respectable man, she is a very independent character, an unassailable fortress to other men, just as if she were lawfully married, because she's a virtuous woman—yes, holy fathers," he said, looking in turn at each of the monks, "a virtuous woman, just as I say! But Dmitry wants to break into that fortress, to unlock it with a golden key, and if he's trying to bully me now, it's to get money out of me for that purpose. Indeed, he has already wasted a good thousand rubles on the beauty, and that's why he keeps borrowing money . . . And where do you think he's borrowing it? Shall I tell them, Mitya, my boy?"

"Be quiet!" Dmitry screamed. "Don't you dare besmirch the name of that most honorable girl in my presence! Wait at least until I've left the room . . . The very fact that you've dared to mention her at all is a disgrace to her . . . I won't allow it!"

He was gasping for breath.

"Mitya, Mitya!" Karamazov exclaimed hysterically, forcing tears from his eyes. "Does your father's blessing mean nothing to you? What if I should put a curse on you? What would you do then?"

"You shameless hypocrite!" Dmitry roared furiously.

"That's the way he talks to his father, his father, mind you! So imagine how he treats other people. Listen, gentlemen, there is in our town a poor but honorable man, a former army captain; he had some bad luck and was forced to resign his commission, but it was done quietly. There was no court martial, and no slur on his honor. He is the head of a large family . . . Well, three weeks ago, this son of mine, Dmitry, met him in a tavern, grabbed him by the beard, pulled him out into the street, and gave him a brutal beating in public. And his only reason for doing it was that the man had been running occasional errands for me, in connection with a certain business of mine."

"You liar, you liar!" Dmitry roared, shaking with rage. "Superficially it's true, but deep down it's a lie! I'm not trying to justify what I did, father. Yes, I admit publicly that I acted like a wild beast toward that captain, and now I'm sorry. I loathe myself for losing my temper and behaving like a brute. But that captain, acting on your behalf, went to see the lady whom you describe as the 'local beauty,' offered to give her promissory notes of mine that you have in your possession, and told her that if I continued to pester you she could demand that I pay up at once. Then, if I insisted too rigorously on settling the matter of my inheritance, she could have me thrown into debtor's prison. Now you talk disapprovingly of my weakness for that woman, but it was you yourself who prompted her to lure me! Why, she told me that quite plainly and laughed at you! As to having me locked up, you only want it done because you're jealous of me, because you've been chasing after that woman yourself. I found out about that too, and again she laughed—do you hear me?—laughed at you, as she repeated it all to me. So, holy men, you can see what kind of a father he is—whether he has the right to accuse his son of disorderly behavior! Gentlemen, please forgive me for losing my temper again, but it's just as I anticipated: the old hypocrite has lured us all here to take part in a disgraceful public scene. I came here intending to forgive him if he would just offer me his hand; I was prepared to ask his forgiveness and to forgive him. But now that he has insulted not only me but also one whose name I venerate too highly to pronounce here, I've decided to expose his schemes for everyone to see, even though he is my father."

He could not go on. His eyes flashed. He could hardly catch his breath. But everybody in the cell seemed perturbed. They all, except the elder, rose nervously from their seats. The two monks watched what was happening with stern expressions, looking at the elder to see what to do next. The elder, however, remained seated, looking very pale, but from sheer physical exhaustion rather than from emotional tension. A wan, imploring smile twisted his lips and from time to time he would raise one of his hands, as though begging the two raving men to stop. Of course, he could have put an end to the scene if he had wished, but he himself seemed to be waiting for something, watching attentively, as though he were trying to make up his mind about something that was still unclear to him . . .

In the end it was Miusov who, feeling himself humiliated and disgraced, decided he could not stand it any longer.

"We are all to blame for this disgraceful scene!" he said angrily. "But I must say I didn't anticipate anything of this sort, although I knew the man with whom I came here. We must put an end to it at once! Please believe me, Your Reverence, I was quite unaware of certain details that have come to light here; I refused to believe the rumors I heard and this is the first time I have learned . . . A father jealous of his son because of a disreputable woman and plotting with the creature to have his son locked up . . . And it was in such company that I had to come here! My trust has been abused and I want to make it clear that I am as much a victim of deception as all the others . . ."

"Dmitry Karamazov!" old Karamazov shrieked suddenly in a voice that was not his own. "If you were not my son, I'd challenge you to a duel this very second—pistols . . . at three paces . . . across a handkerchief!" He stood there, stamping his feet.

There are moments when old fakes who have been play-acting all their lives become so involved in the role they have assumed that they actually shake and weep with emotion, even though at that very moment (or perhaps a second later) they may whisper to themselves: "Why, you shameless old fake, you're putting it all on even now; all your holy indignation and outraged wrath is nothing but a sham!"

Dmitry frowned deeply, looking at his father with unutterable contempt.

"I somehow . . . somehow imagined," he said in a quiet, controlled voice, "that I'd come home with the girl I loved, my future wife, and that we'd look after my father in his old age . . . Instead, I find nothing but a depraved, despicable old buffoon!"

"I challenge you to a duel!" the old man, gasping for breath, shrieked again, every word accompanied by a shower of spittle. "As to you, Mr. Miusov, let me tell you, that I don't believe there is, or ever has been, in your entire family history, a woman as honorable as the one whom you have dared refer to as a 'creature'! And you, Dmitry, you're only too eager to exchange your fiancée for that 'creature' and so admit that your fiancée is not worth the 'creature's' little toe even!"

Father Joseph could not refrain from murmuring, "Shame, shame . . ."

"A shame and a disgrace!" Kalganov, who until then had not uttered a sound, cried out in his boyish voice, the blood rushing to his face.

"Why should such a man live?" Dmitry growled, almost frantic with rage, his shoulders so bent that he looked like a hunchback. "You tell me," he said slowly and deliberately, looking at everyone in the room in turn, and pointing at his father. "Should he be allowed to go on defiling the earth with his existence?"

"You heard him, you heard him, you monks! You heard the parricide!" Fyodor Karamazov turned suddenly on Father Joseph. "That may answer your 'shame' perhaps. What should I be ashamed of anyway? That 'creature,' that 'disorderly woman,' may actually be more holy than you, you gentlemanly monks who are so busy saving your souls! Even if, depraved by her environment, she succumbed to sin in her youth, she has since loved much, and Christ Himself forgave her who loved much . . ."

"It wasn't for that kind of love that Christ forgave . . ." Father Joseph, the gentle librarian, replied quickly and impatiently.

"You're wrong, monk, it was for just that kind of love! You sit here, eat cabbage, and think that you're saving your souls, that you're righteous men! You eat carp, a carp a day, and you are convinced that you can bribe God by eating carp, aren't you?"

"It's too much! It's unbearable! It's intolerable!" Voices came from all sides of the cell.

Then the outrageous scene came to an abrupt and most unexpected end. The elder rose from his seat. Alyosha, who was almost out of his mind with anxiety for him and for the rest of them, managed nevertheless to support him by the arm. The elder moved toward Dmitry and, when he was close to him, he went down on his knees before him. Alyosha at first thought he had fallen from sheer exhaustion, but it was not so. Once on his knees, the elder bowed to the ground before Dmitry—a deliberate, complete bow so that his forehead actually touched the ground. Alyosha was so surprised that he could not collect himself in time to assist the elder as he got to his feet again. A faint smile was playing on the elder's lips.

"Forgive me! Forgive me, all of you!" he said, bowing to each visitor in turn.

For a few seconds Dmitry stood there like a man stunned by a blow. The elder bowing to the ground before him—what was this? Suddenly he cried, "Oh, my God," covered his face with his hands, and rushed out of the cell.

The other visitors followed him out, in their confusion even forgetting to take leave of the elder. Only the two monks went over to him and asked his blessing once more.

As the visitors were leaving the hermitage, Mr. Karamazov, who had quieted down for the moment, made an attempt to resume the conversation.

"Why did he have to prostrate himself like that?" he said, without daring to address anyone in particular. "Was it symbolic of something, or what?"

"I cannot understand what goes on in a madhouse and what makes madmen act as they do," Miusov replied irritatedly. "But one thing I can tell you, Mr. Karamazov—I'm going to rid myself of your company once and for all . . . Ah, where's that other monk?"

"That monk," that is, the one who had earlier brought them the invitation to lunch at the Father Superior's, did not keep them waiting. He was right there to meet them as they came down the steps from the elder's cell, as if he had been waiting for them all the time.

"Do me a great favor, Venerable Father," Miusov said to him in an irritated tone. "Convey my deepest respects to the Father Superior and apologize to him for me—Miusov—personally and tell him that, much as I would have liked to, I am unable to attend his lunch, because of unforeseen circumstances."

"And to think that the 'unforeseen circumstance' is me!" Karamazov butted in. "You understand, Father, Mr. Miusov refuses to accept the Father Superior's invitation because he doesn't wish to be seen in my company—otherwise, he would have accepted it. And you will accept it, Mr. Miusov. Please go to lunch with the Father Superior, and I wish you *bon appetit!* It is I who will decline the invitation, not you. I'll go home and eat there, for I don't feel I could do so here, Mr. Miusov, my dear kinsman!"

"I'm no kinsman of yours and never have been, and I despise you!"

"I said that just to enrage you, because you deny that we are relatives, although we are—you may say what you wish, but I can prove it. As to you, Ivan, you may stay if you wish. I'll send the carriage to pick you up later. Well, Mr. Miusov, even simple courtesy obliges you to accept the Father Superior's invitation now, if only to apologize for your bad behavior and mine in his monastery."

"Are you really leaving? This isn't just another trick of yours?"

"How could I dare to trick you now, after what has just happened? I got carried away, gentlemen, a little carried away, and, besides, I received quite a shock in there! And I am ashamed, too. You know, gentlemen, one person will have a heart like Alexander the Great's, and another one like a lap-dog's. Mine is like a lap-dog's. And so I lost my nerve! Well then, how, after that escapade, could I go to a luncheon and fill myself with a variety of monastery sauces and specialties? No, gentlemen, I am too embarrassed to do so, so you'll just have to excuse me!"

As Karamazov walked off, Miusov followed him with his eye, wondering: "What if the old clown is trying to trick me again? Who can tell with him?" Karamazov looked back and, seeing that he was watching him, blew him a kiss.

"What about you, Ivan?" Miusov asked gruffly. "Are you going to the lunch?"

"Why not? Especially since the Father Superior sent me a personal invitation yesterday."

"Unfortunately," Miusov said in the same bitter, irritated tone, paying no attention to the presence of the monk, who could hear everything, "I really feel obliged to go to this confounded luncheon . . . We should at least apologize for what happened at the elder's and explain that it was really none of our doing, don't you think?"

"Yes, we ought to make clear that it was not our fault," Ivan said, "and besides, my father won't be there."

"I certainly hope he won't—that would really be the last straw! Ah, damn the lunch!"

And yet they all went. The little monk listened to their conversation in silence. Only once, as they were crossing the little wood that separated the hermitage from the rest of the monastery, did he remark that the Father Superior must have been long expecting them, since they were already half an hour late. No one answered him. At one point Miusov glanced at Ivan with hatred in his eyes.

"He's going to the luncheon as if nothing had happened," he thought. "He is brazen-faced and has the conscience of a Karamazov."

CHAPTER 7

A Career-conscious Divinity Student

Alyosha helped his elder to the bedroom and sat him down on the bed. It was a tiny room containing only the most indispensable furniture. The very narrow iron bed had a strip of felt for a mattress. In a corner by the icons, there was a lectern with a cross and a Bible lying on it. The elder lowered himself onto the bed, completely exhausted; his eyes shone and he breathed with great difficulty. Once seated, he looked at Alyosha very intently, as if deliberating about something.

"Go on, my boy, be off. Porfiry will take care of me," he

said. "They need you over there, so go to the Father Superior's and help them out during lunch."

"Allow me to stay here," Alyosha murmured beseechingly.

"They need you more than I do. There's no peace there. So you help them out, be really useful to them. And if the devil stirs them up again, say a prayer. And you know, son" (the elder liked to call him that), "the monastery is really no place for you. Remember that, my boy. When God decides the time has come for me to die, you must leave the monastery, leave it for good."

Alyosha gasped.

"What's the matter? No, this isn't the place for you, at least not yet. I am sending you out into the world with my blessings, and you will be of great service there. There's still a long, long road ahead of you. And you'll take a wife, too. Yes, you will. You'll have to go through many, many things before you return. And there is a great deal for you to do. But I have no doubts about you. That is why I am sending you. Christ is with you. Do not abandon Him and He will not abandon you. You will know great sorrow and in that sorrow you will find happiness. This is my last message to you: Seek happiness through sorrow. Work and work without rest. And from now on, remember my words for, although we shall talk again, not only my days but my hours are numbered."

Alyosha's face again showed great emotion. The corners of his lips quivered.

"There you go again," the elder said, smiling gently. "Let the worldly shed tears for their dead. We here are happy for a father who is departing. We rejoice with him and pray for him. So go now—it is time for me to pray. And hurry. Stay close to your brothers—not just one of them, but both."

The elder raised his hand to bless him. Alyosha could not protest, although he longed to stay. He also wanted to ask the elder—the question almost slipped off his tongue—what he had meant by bowing to the ground before Dmitry, but he didn't dare. He knew that Father Zosima would, if it had been possible, have explained it to him without being asked. But apparently the elder did not think it was. That bow, however, had made a staggering impression upon Alyosha, who was absolutely convinced that it had some mysterious meaning. Mysterious and perhaps also frightening.

As Alyosha left the hermitage, hurrying to get to the monastery (where he was, of course, simply to wait on table) in time for lunch, his heart suddenly contracted painfully and he stopped dead: the elder's words announcing his own impending end came back to him. Whatever the elder predicted, especially with such precision, was bound to happen. Alyosha believed that implicitly. But what would Alyosha do without him? How could he live without ever seeing him again, without hearing him? And where would he go? The elder had ordered him not to weep, and to leave the monastery. Oh, Lord! It was long since Alyosha had felt so miserable. He started walking again, crossing the little wood between the hermitage and the monastery very quickly. Unable to bear his own thoughts, so much did they oppress him, he started to look at the ancient pines on either side of the path. He didn't have far to go, five hundred yards or so, and at this hour of the day it was unlikely that he would meet anyone. Yet, as he rounded the first bend in the path, his eyes suddenly fell on Rakitin, who seemed to be waiting for someone.

"Are you waiting for me, by any chance?" Alyosha asked him as he came up to him.

"Yes, precisely for you," Rakitin said with a grin. "You're hurrying over to the Father Superior's. I know—that meal. He hasn't given a meal like this since he had the Bishop and General Pakhatov at his table. I won't be there, but you'd better go and pass around the sauces. But first, tell me, Alexei, what did that gesture mean? That's what I wanted to ask you."

"What gesture?"

"I mean that bow before your brother Dmitry. He even banged his forehead on the floor!"

"Are you speaking of Father Zosima?"

"That's right—Father Zosima."

"He banged his forehead?"

"What's the matter? Didn't I express myself respectfully enough? Well, never mind, respectfully or not, what does it mean?"

"I don't know what it means, Misha."

"Just as I thought—he didn't explain it to you. Well, there's really nothing so very complicated about it, just his usual holy mumbo-jumbo. But it was a well-planned trick. And now all those sanctimonious people will be going around the town and the province asking one another what that gesture could possibly have meant. Well, I believe the old man has a pretty keen nose: he's caught the scent of crime. Your house stinks of crime, Alyosha."

"What crime? What are you talking about?"

Rakitin was obviously anxious to talk.

"The crime in your nice little family, between your dear brothers and your rich papa. So Father Zosima decided to bang his forehead on the floor, just in case. And later, if anything does happen, people will say: 'Ah, that saintly elder prophesied it!' Although, come to think of it, what kind of prophesying is it to bang one's head on the floor? No, they will say, it was symbolic, allegorical, or heaven knows what! They'll sing his praises and remember it forever: he anticipated the crime and pointed out the perpetrator of it. That's the way it always is with God's fools: they're liable to cross themselves at the sight of a tavern and then hurl stones at a church. And that's how your elder is, too: he'll drive a righteous man out with a stick and then prostrate himself before a murderer."

"What crime? What murderer? What's the matter with you?"

Alyosha stopped dead. Rakitin also stopped.

"What murderer? As though you didn't know yourself. I'd bet anything that it's occurred to you before this. I'm curious, though, Alyosha: I know you always tell the truth, even though you never like to say what you think. So tell me then, has it ever occurred to you before or not? Answer me."

"It has," Alyosha said, and even Rakitin was taken aback.

"Do you mean that? Is it possible that even you have thought of it, Alyosha!" he exclaimed.

"Well, I . . . I didn't actually think of it," Alyosha murmured, "but just now, when you said it so strangely, it seemed to me that it had occurred to me too."

"So then—and I like the way you put it—you see perfectly well what I mean. Today, when you looked at your papa and at your big brother Mitya, the idea of a crime occurred to you, didn't it? I wasn't just imagining things, was I?"

"Wait, wait," Alyosha interrupted him anxiously. "What makes you see it that way? . . . And why does it preoccupy you so much?"

"You've asked me two separate questions, but natural ones; I'll answer them one at a time. Why do I see it that way? Well, I wouldn't have seen anything at all if, today, I hadn't suddenly understood your brother Dmitry completely. I can see right through him now. I understood the whole man through one particular trait in his character. There is a certain line that no one is allowed to cross in dealing with a man like that, who is scrupulously honest, but sensuous and passionate. Otherwise, a man like him could easily slash his dear papa's throat. Especially when his dear papa is a drunken and unscrupulous lecher who never knows just how far he can go. They'll neither of them be able to control themselves and the next thing you know, they'll both land in the ditch . . ."

"No, Misha, if that's all there is to it, I feel rather reassured. It'll never reach that point."

"Then why are you shaking? You know what? Even if your brother Mitya is an honest man—which he is, stupid and honest—he is also sensuous and passionate. That's the definition of his character, his very essence. He inherited his animal sensuality from his father. As a matter of fact, what puzzles me no end is how you, Alyosha, have managed to remain virgin to this day—you, a Karamazov! Why, sensuality runs through your family like a feverish obsession . . . Here, these three sensualists are stalking one another now, each one of them with a knife hidden in the leg of his boot. The three of them have met head-on, and you may be the fourth . . ."

"You mean about that woman? You're wrong, Dmitry despises her . . ." Alyosha said, his whole body shuddering strangely.

"Despise Grushenka? No, my friend, Dmitry doesn't despise her. How can he, when he obviously prefers her to the woman he's promised to marry? This is something you can't understand yet, my friend. A man, you know, may fall in love with physical beauty, with a woman's body, maybe even with just a bit of that body. Any sensualist can understand that. And then, for her sake, he'll willingly give up his children, betray his father and mother and his native country; he may be honest, but he'll steal; he may be gentle, but he'll kill; he may be faithful, but he'll deceive. Pushkin was a bard of women's legs. He celebrated women's legs in his poems. Others do not devote poems to them, but they can't look at them without inner commotion . . . But in this case it's not just the legs. In this case scorn wouldn't help; even if Dmitry did despise Grushenka, he still couldn't tear himself away from her."

"I understand that very well," Alyosha blurted out quite unexpectedly.

"Really? Well, maybe you do understand it, at that—the way you blurted that out," Rakitin said, with malicious enjoyment. "You didn't mean to say that. It just slipped out. And that makes the admission so much the more valuable. It goes to show the subject is already familiar to you, that you've given it some thought—sensuality, that is. Ah, you virgin boy! You're a quiet one, Alyosha—a regular little saint, it's true, but a quiet one, and who knows all the things you know and think about! You're virgin, but what depths you've already explored. I've been observing you for a long time. You're a Karamazov, as much a Karamazov as the rest; your breed and natural selection must count for something. You're a sensualist like your father and one of God's fools like your mother. Why are you trembling? Isn't it true what I say? Shall I tell you what Grushenka asked me to do? 'Bring him here,' she said, meaning you. 'I'll pull that cassock off his back.' You should have heard her insist: 'Bring him here, bring him, see that he comes!' I really wonder why she should be so curious about you. She's no ordinary woman herself."

"Give her my regards and tell her that I won't come," Alyosha said with a twisted smile. "And now finish what you wanted to tell me, Mikhail, then I'll tell you what I think of it all."

"I've really nothing more to say—it all seems pretty clear now. The rest falls into place by itself. If even a boy like you is a sensualist underneath, that leaves very little doubt about Ivan, who was born of the same mother and is a Karamazov too. That's your family's problem: you are all sensualists, money-grubbers, and God's fools. For the time being, Ivan writes theological articles, although he is an atheist and admits that he does not seriously mean what he says in them, and he does it all for some strange, idiotic reasons. On top of that, Ivan is trying to take his brother Mitya's fiancée away from him, and he seems to be succeeding. As a matter of fact, he's doing it with Dmitry's consent, since Dmitry is only too eager to disentangle himself from her so that he can rush off to Grushenka. And through it all, Dmitry remains highly honorable and disinterested; I want you to note that, because men like him are the most dangerous of all. Who the hell can explain you Karamazovs! How can a man realize that he has acted despicably, admit it, and then continue acting in the same way?

"And now listen to this: there's someone still in Mitya's way: the old man, his own father. He's crazy about Grushenka, too. He positively drools when he looks at her. It was because of her that he made that disgraceful scene in the elder's cell—just because Miusov referred to her as a 'creature' or something. He's like an amorous tomcat now. At first, she was only a paid employee in some of his shady dealing over his chain of taverns. Then one day when he took a good look at her, he suddenly became frantic and started pestering her with all sorts of propositions, none of them honorable, as you can well imagine. Well, they'll clash head-on, father and son, this way. For the moment, Grushenka doesn't allow either of them to come too close; she's teasing them both and studying the situation to see which one will be more profitable. She could, of course, get quite a lot of money out of your father, but then he wouldn't marry her and eventually he's likely to turn tight-fisted and hide his purse away. And that's where Dmitry has his value: he has no money, but he at least is quite capable of marrying her. Yes, sir, he'd marry her all right! He'd leave his Katerina, a girl of great beauty, a lady, a colonel's daughter, for the sake of that Grushenka, the former mistress of the merchant Samsonov, that debauched peasant who is our mayor! So there's enough there for a clash of passions and a crime. And that's just what your brother Ivan is waiting for. It would suit him in every respect: he'd get Katerina, for whom he's pining, and along with her a dowry of sixty thousand rubles. Not a bad start for a fellow like him without money or position. And I want you to note that he wouldn't be hurting Mitya; indeed, Mitya would be indebted to him for as long as he lived. I know for a fact that, only a week ago, in a tavern with some gypsy girls, Mitya was drunk and was holding forth about how he wasn't good enough for his fiancée Katerina whereas his brother Ivan was indeed worthy of her. As to Katerina herself, it's not very likely that she would turn down a charmer like Ivan in the end, since even today she seems to be hesitating between the two of them. Speaking of Ivan, I really can't understand how he's won you all over, so that you all admire him so much, while he sits there comfortably, having a good laugh at your expense."

"What makes you think that you know so much about these things? How can you be so sure of what you say?" Alyosha suddenly asked, frowning.

"Tell me why, having asked that, you're afraid beforehand of my answer? Doesn't that mean that you admit the truth of what I've said?"

"You just don't like Ivan. Ivan wouldn't do anything like that for money."

"Wouldn't he? And what about the beautiful Katerina? It's not just for money, although I must say, sixty thousand rubles is something to think about."

"Ivan is aiming at higher things. He wouldn't be tempted even by thousands of rubles. He's not looking for money or for security. What he's looking for is perhaps . . . perhaps it's suffering and torment that he's after."

"What's this—another wild dream? Ah you . . . you gentlemen!"

"No, Misha, his is a soul in turmoil. His mind is entirely preoccupied with one thing: a great, unresolved idea. He's one who has no use for millions; all he wants is to find an answer to the problem."

"Now you're guilty of literary plagiarism, Alyosha, my boy. You're just paraphrasing your elder. He has certainly befuddled you all, that brother of yours!" Rakitin cried maliciously, his mouth twisting so that his whole face changed. "Besides, the riddle he offers is just plain stupid. In fact it's not worth deciphering. His article is ridiculous, absurd. And I also heard his idiotic theory that if there is no immortality of the soul, there can be no virtue and therefore everything is permissible. (By the way, do you remember how your big brother Mitya cried out, 'I'll remember that!'?) Of course, it's a very attractive theory for villains . . . Ah, it is stupid of me to use such strong words. I should have said, not villains, but rather schoolboys showing off, pretending they're oppressed by profound and insoluble problems. He's just a miserable little braggart and all he says just amounts to: 'On the one hand, we cannot but admit and, on the other, we must confess.' His whole theory is vile! Mankind can find enough strength within itself to live for virtue's sake, even without believing in the immortality of the soul. In the love of freedom, of equality and the brotherhood of man, it will find it . . ."

Rakitin had so worked himself up that he could hardly control himself. Then suddenly he seemed to remember something and stopped.

"Well, I've talked enough," he said, his smile more twisted than ever. "Why are you laughing? You think I'm a vulgar boor?"

"No, I've never thought you were a boor. You're an intelligent person, but . . . Don't pay any attention to me. I really don't know why I felt like laughing. I understand why you got a bit carried away, Misha—from your heated tone I guess you're not quite indifferent to Katerina yourself. I've suspected as much for a long time, you know. That's why you dislike Ivan. You're jealous of him, aren't you?"

"And I suppose I'm also jealous because of her money, no? Go on, why don't you say that too?"

"No, I've nothing to say about the money—I have no wish to offend you, Misha."

"I believe it, since you say so, but again, as far as your brother Ivan is concerned, you can go to hell! You, none of you understand that one might thoroughly dislike him, quite apart from being jealous of Katerina. And why should I like him, damn it all? Since he does me the honor of abusing me, why shouldn't I abuse him?"

"I've never heard him say anything either good or bad about you. He's never mentioned you at all as far as I know."

"Well, I was told that two days ago he was belaboring me for all he was worth at Katerina's. Doesn't that prove that he's very much interested in yours truly? Can you be so sure who's jealous of whom? He was pleased to predict on that occasion that, if I decided in the near future that the career of an archimandrite was not for me, and that I would not be tonsured, I would be sure to go off to Petersburg, that I would get myself onto the staff of some thick magazine, in the literary section, of course. He said I'd write for it for about ten years, by which time I'd have managed to get the whole magazine under my own name. Then, according to him, I'd be sure to make it toe a liberal, atheistic line, with socialist overtones, a slight varnish of socialism that is, but very carefully handled, keeping an ear to the ground. That is, pleasing everyone and hoodwinking the fools. The crowning glory of my career, according to your dear brother, would come when, despite my socialist varnish, I had accumulated a solid bank account from the subscriptions to the magazine, which I would swell by investing at every good opportunity, through the intermediary of some Jew, until I had enough to buy myself a large apartment building in Petersburg. Then I would transfer my editorial offices there and rent the rest of the apartments. He even decided on a location for the house—near the Newstone Bridge that is to be built across the Neva between Liteinaya and Vyborg Streets . . ."

"Ah, Misha, you know, that's how it will really happen,

word for word!" Alyosha cried out, unable to suppress a cheerful grin.

"Now you're being sarcastic too, Mr. Alexei Karamazov."

"No, no, I was joking. Don't be angry with me. I have something altogether different on my mind. But tell me— who could possibly have repeated what he said to you in such detail? Surely, you can't have been at Katerina's when he said all that about you . . . ?"

"I wasn't there, of course, but your brother Dmitry was and I heard it from him with my own ears. As a matter of fact, though, he did not tell me; I overheard him—accidentally, it goes without saying—because I was sitting in Grushenka's bedroom and I couldn't get out of there as long as Dmitry was in the next room."

"That's right! I had completely forgotten—she's a relative of yours."

"Grushenka, a relative of mine!" Rakitin shouted loudly, turning red. "You're out of your mind! Your brains must be turning soft!"

"Why, isn't she related to you? I'd heard she was."

"Where could you possibly have heard that? Oh, you Karamazovs! You give yourselves airs as though you came from an ancient line of distinguished gentry, whereas in fact your father used to act the clown, scrounging meals in other people's houses, depending on their charity. And even if I am only the son of a lowly priest and a mere louse compared with you members of the landed gentry, you shouldn't keep insulting me so light-heartedly and with such zest. For I also have a sense of dignity, Alexei Karamazov, and I'd like you to get it through your head that I could not possibly be related to a prostitute like Grushenka."

Rakitin was in a state of great agitation.

"Please forgive me. I'm terribly sorry . . . It never occurred to me . . . Besides, why is she a prostitute? Is she really?" Alyosha suddenly turned beet-red. "I repeat, I heard someone say she was related to you. You do often go to see her, and you told me yourself that you'd never been her lover . . . I had no idea that you felt such profound scorn for her. Do you really think she deserves it?"

"I might have special reasons for visiting her and that should be good enough for you. As for being related to her, you have a much better chance than I have of winding up as a relative of hers, courtesy of your brother, or perhaps even of your father. Well, here we are. You'd better hurry in to the kitchen. But what's going on? Are we late? Why, they can't possibly have finished eating their lunch so quickly! Perhaps the Karamazovs have been up to something again? It looks like it. There's your father over there. And look, Ivan is following him. They've left the Father Superior's. Look, Father Isidore is shouting something to them from the doorstep. And your father is shouting too, and waving his hands in the air—I'm sure he must be swearing. And there's Miusov, driving off in his carriage. And now I see Maximov, the landowner, running—there must have been a real explosion. The luncheon can't have even taken place! They can't have beaten up the Father Superior! Or perhaps they got beaten? I wish I could have seen it . . ."

Rakitin had good reason for shrieking with excitement: something scandalous, unheard of, and completely unexpected had just taken place. And it had all happened as the result of an "inspired" idea.

CHAPTER 8

A Scandalous Scene

Being a well-bred and sincerely decent man, Miusov underwent a rapid process of self-examination, as he entered the Father Superior's rooms with Ivan, as a result of which he grew ashamed of having lost his temper. He felt that he should have sufficiently despised that old wretch Karamazov not to have lost his own composure in the elder's cell as he had done. In any case, he decided as he crossed the threshold of the Father Superior's rooms, the monks were not to blame for anything, and if, here too, they were such respectable men ("I believe Father Superior Nikolai himself comes from the gentry"), why not be courteous and polite with them? "I won't get involved in any arguments," he promised himself. "In fact, I'll try to agree with them. I'll overwhelm them with graciousness, and . . . and I'll prove to them that I have nothing in common with that Aesop, that clown, that ridiculous *pierrot,* that I was in his company by sheer bad luck, just as everyone else was . . ."

As to the contested wood-cutting and fishing rights (he wasn't actually too sure which streams and woods were involved), he decided to concede them to the monastery once and for all, that very day, especially since it would cost

at the Father Superior's lunch as if nothing at all had happened. This was not really because he was too embarrassed or too angry with himself—quite the contrary, perhaps—but still, he felt it would not be appropriate for him to attend the party. When his ramshackle carriage drove up to the doorway of the inn to pick him up, however, and he was already climbing into it, he suddenly stopped. He remembered what he himself had said in the elder's cell: that whenever he appeared among people, he always felt they considered him the most despicable of men and that his usual reaction at those moments was to say to himself, "Well, if that's so, I'll act like the fool they think I am and show them that in reality they are stupider and more despicable than I am." And he felt an urge to punish the others for his own disgusting display. He also remembered that when someone had once asked him, "Why do you hate so-and-so so much?" he had answered in a fit of shameless buffoonery: "True, the fellow has never wronged me, but I have wronged him in the most disgusting, unscrupulous manner, and I have hated him ever since." He grew thoughtful for a second. He snorted wickedly, his eyes flashed, his lips quivered. "Well, once I've started something, I might as well finish it," he decided. His state of mind at that moment could be described as follows: Since it was not in his power to regain their respect, why shouldn't he go on and disgrace himself altogether, to show them that he could not care less what they thought of him?

Ordering his driver to wait for him, he hurried back to the monastery, and went straight to the Father Superior's rooms. He still did not know exactly what he was going to do, but he did know that he was no longer in full control of himself and that the least provocation could push him to the very limit, to some unspeakable abomination—although he knew he would not do anything for which he could be held legally punishable and that he would never commit a crime. He could always stop himself before breaking the law and, at times, he wondered at that himself.

And so he appeared in the dining room at the very moment the Father Superior finished saying grace and everyone started to move toward the table to sit down. He stood in the doorway, staring at them. Then he let out a long, arrogant, spiteful chuckle and, with a challenging glare in his eyes, shouted:

"So you people thought I was gone, but here I am!"

They all gaped at him in silence, sensing that something disgraceful was about to happen, something absurd that would end in a disgusting public exhibition. Within a second, Miusov's mood switched from the utmost benignity to fury. The fire that had been subdued within him exploded and burst forth.

"No, no!" he cried. "I can't stand it, I can't, I won't! . . ."

The blood rushed to his head. Feeling confused and unable to utter a word, he seized his hat.

"What is it he can't and won't stand? Tell me, Your Reverence, may I come in or not? Will you receive a fellow diner?"

"You are most welcome!" the Father Superior said. "Gentlemen," he added suddenly, addressing the rest of the company, "may I beg you to forget your past quarrels and to be reunited in love and harmony as befits relatives, and we will pray to God at our humble table . . ."

"No, no, it is quite out of the question!" Miusov cried, still beside himself.

"Well, if he feels it's out of the question, then it's out of the question for me too—I won't stay either. I decided on my way here that now Mr. Miusov and I will be inseparable—if he leaves, I'll leave; if he stays, I'll stay. You know, Father Superior, you hurt his feelings by mentioning family harmony: he refuses to acknowledge the fact that we're related. Isn't that so, von Sohn? It is von Sohn standing here, isn't it? Good afternoon, von Sohn, how are you?"

"Are you addressing me, sir?" Maximov muttered in amazement.

"Of course, I am. Who else? You don't think I'd address the Father Superior as von Sohn, do you?"

"But I'm not von Sohn either, sir. My name is Maximov."

"It isn't. It's von Sohn. By the way, Your Reverence, do you know who von Sohn really was? Well, there was a criminal proceeding: he was murdered in a house of ill-fame—I believe that is how you refer to those establishments—he was murdered and robbed, and despite his venerable years, he was packed into a crate, which was nailed, labeled, and dispatched from Petersburg to Moscow in a freight train. While they were nailing up the crate, by the way, the harlots sang and played the psaltery, or was it the piano? That's who von Sohn is. So you've come back from the dead, have you, von Sohn?"

"What's he talking about?" "What does this mean?" came the voices of the monks.

"Come on, we're leaving!" Miusov called out to Kalganov.

"Ah no! Just a moment!" Karamazov cried shrilly, moving a step closer. "First you must let me finish. Back in the cell I was reproached for disrespectful behavior, for yelling something about carp. My kinsman Peter Miusov would rather speeches contained *plus de noblesse que de sincérité,* whereas I prefer mine to have *plus de sincérité que de noblesse,* because I don't give a damn about *noblesse!* Am I right, von Sohn? Forgive me, Father Superior—I may be a buffoon and act like one, but I have a courtly idea of honor and must be allowed to speak my mind. Yes, sir, and while I'm filled with chivalry, Mr. Miusov here is just a case of frustrated sensitivity. Perhaps I came to the monastery today to have a look around and then express my opinion. One of my sons—Alexei—is seeking salvation here and, being his father, it is my duty to concern myself about his future. All the time I was playing the fool I was secretly listening and observing, and now it's time for me to give you the last act of my performance. Well, what's going on here? It looks as if when something falls here it stays fallen—once down, it will lie there to all eternity. I don't accept that: I want to rise again! I am outraged by you, holy fathers! A confession is a confession—a holy sacrament—I revere it and prostrate myself before it. But what did I find in that cell? I found all sorts of people kneeling and confessing aloud. Do you think it is really right to confess publicly? The Church Fathers decreed that confession should be whispered into the priest's ear, that only then would it be a sacrament. And so it has been since ancient times . . . How could you expect me, for instance, to explain to him in front of a whole audience that I . . . that I have . . . well, done certain things—you can imagine what. Why, some of those things are not even mentionable, as you know. No, really, the whole thing is scandalous! The next thing you know, holy fathers, they'll be practicing flagellation in your monastery . . . I'll write and complain to the Holy Synod at the very first opportunity, and I'll have to take my son Alexei back home . . ."

It must be noted here that Karamazov had heard some things. All sorts of wicked rumors had been circulating about the goings-on in the monastery, and some of these stories (not only about our monastery but also about others where the institution of elders had been introduced) had reached the Bishop himself. They claimed that the elders were venerated at the expense of the father superiors, that they abused the sacrament of confession, and so on. These accusations were quite absurd and they were gradually dropped in our part of the country, just as they were everywhere else. But some stupid devil, by manipulating his victim's nerves, was pushing Karamazov deeper and deeper into the pit of disgrace and making him formulate these discarded accusations, about which he did not understand the first thing. He had even failed to set them forth intelligently. After all, when he was in the cell no one had knelt and confessed aloud, so he could not have seen anything of the sort and was just repeating old gossip that he somehow remembered. But having said it and feeling that he had made a stupid blunder, he was suddenly filled with an uncontrollable urge to prove to his audience, and even more to himself, that he had not really blundered, that what he had said was indeed very much to the point. And although he was conscious of sliding deeper and deeper into absurdity with every word he said, he was quite incapable of stopping and felt like someone slipping faster and faster down the side of a mountain.

"Disgraceful!" Miusov cried.

"Allow me," the Father Superior interjected. "It was said long ago: 'Many have spoken out against me, saying evil things, and hearing them I said to myself: it is the healing of the Lord and He has sent it to cure my vain soul!' Therefore we thank you humbly, dear guest."

He bowed waist-deep to Karamazov.

"Tut-tut-tut, the same old phrases, the same old hypocrisy! A pack of old lies, the old bowing that has become meaningless! We all know what it is worth: 'a kiss on the lips and a dagger in the heart,' as in Schiller's *Robbers*. I don't like sham, fathers. What I'm after is truth, and it's not in carp that you're likely to find truth! I have said so before. Why do you keep fasting, fathers? Because you expect it to be credited to you in heaven? Why, for a reward, I would fast too! Now, fathers, try to be virtuous in life instead of confining yourselves inside the walls of a monastery with your meals assured and expecting a reward up there—that'll be more difficult. You see, Father Superior, I too can express myself nicely . . . Now, let's see what we have here . . ." He moved toward the table. "Why, but this is some nice old port, and that's good Médoc bottled by the Yeliseyev Brothers . . . Well done, fathers. That's no carp for you! Look at those lovely bottles, fathers! And who provided you with all that? It is the same hard-working old Russian *muzhik*, laboring with his calloused hands, who brings his copper kopek to you instead of giving it to his poor family or to the State! Why, holy fathers, don't you realize that you suck the blood of the poor!"

"Now that's really an improper thing to say," Father Joseph, the monastery's librarian, remarked. Father Paisii remained stubbornly silent. Miusov leaped up and rushed out of the room, followed by Kalganov.

"Well, fathers, I must keep up with Mr. Miusov. Good-by now. I won't come back to pay you another visit even if you beg me on bended knee. Since I sent you that thousand rubles, you've been eyeing me so sweetly, hoping perhaps for more, ha-ha-ha! But you're wasting your efforts—you won't get another ruble. I've paid you back now for my lost youth, for all the humiliations I had to suffer!" He banged the table with his fist, carried away by his own playacting. "This little monastery, though, meant so much to me!" he went on. "How many bitter tears I have shed because of it! It was you who set my poor crazy wife against me. You anathematized me in the seven cathedrals. You spread evil rumors about me all over the countryside! But it is finished, fathers; now we live in an age of liberalism, railroads, and steamboats, and you'll never get another thousand rubles from me, or a hundred rubles, or even a single kopek!"

It must be noted again that our monastery had never played an important role in his life and that Karamazov had never shed any tears because of it. But he was so carried away by his false misery that for a second he almost believed himself and was so moved that he actually did shed a few sentimental tears. But he also knew that the time had come to leave.

When Karamazov stopped spouting his stream of malicious slander, the Father Superior bowed his head and once more said solemnly:

"It is also written: 'Bear with patience and fortitude the dishonor that befalleth thee and hate not him who dishonoreth thee.' We shall obey."

"Tut-tut—'befalleth,' 'dishonoreth,' all that verbiage and claptrap! But while you 'dishonoreth thyself' I'll be off and I'll use my parental authority to remove my son Alexei from here once and for all. And you too, Ivan, my respectful son, hear that I command thee to follow me from this place! And what about you, von Sohn, there's no point your staying around. Come back to town with me and pay me a visit. We'll have a bit of fun at my house. It's just a mile or so from here and, instead of their lenten diet, you'll get a suck-

ling pig for dinner and I'll bring out some brandy for you
and then some liqueur too—I have, for instance, a certain
raspberry liqueur . . . So what do you say, von Sohn? You
wouldn't want to miss such an opportunity, would you?"

He left, shouting and gesticulating.

That was the moment when Rakitin caught sight of him
and pointed him out to Alyosha. And when Karamazov saw
his son, he called out to him:

"Alexei! I want you to move back home for good! Today!
Bring your pillow and mattress too, and don't you ever dare
set foot here again!"

Alyosha stood motionless, watching in silence. Mr. Karamazov got into his carriage and Ivan, grim and silent, was
about to follow him without even turning to Alyosha to say
good-by. But at that moment something almost unbelievably
absurd took place, a worthy finale to the whole preposterous
episode.

The little landowner Maximov suddenly appeared at the
step of the carriage. He was panting—he had run all the way
to catch up with Karamazov before he drove off. Rakitin and
Alyosha had seen him running. He was so anxious to get into
the carriage that he put his foot on the step although Ivan
still had his left foot on it. Maximov nevertheless continued
to pull himself up by the strap, trying to jump in, Ivan notwithstanding.

"I'm coming too!" he shouted, wriggling and chuckling
with delight. "Take me with you!"

"Wasn't I right?" Mr. Karamazov shouted delightedly.
"Wasn't I right when I said this fellow was von Sohn! He's
the true von Sohn risen from the dead! But how did you
manage to escape? What von Sohnish trick did you play on
them? How could you leave the table? One needs the skin of
an elephant to do that! I know mine is like that, but I'm surprised at you! Come on, jump in, friend, hurry! Let him in,
Vanya, my son. We'll have great fun with him and in the
meantime he can lie somewhere between our feet. Or shall
we put him on the box with the coachman? Jump up on the
box, von Sohn!"

But Ivan, who had silently taken his seat, suddenly swung
around, put his hands on Maximov's chest, and shoved him
so violently that he landed a good three yards away, only by
miracle remaining on his feet.

"Drive on!" Ivan shouted angrily to the coachman.

"Why did you do that, Vanya? What's come over you?" Karamazov protested, but Ivan didn't answer.

"Can't make you out!" Karamazov said again after a two-minute silence. "This whole visit to the monastery was your idea," he said, looking angrily at Ivan. "You suggested it, you insisted on it, so what's the matter with you now?"

"Haven't you had enough nonsense yet?" Ivan said grimly. "Why don't you give yourself a rest for a while?"

Old Karamazov remained silent for another two minutes.

"Wouldn't it be nice to have a swig of brandy now?" he asked conversationally. As Ivan didn't answer, he added: "When we get home, we'll both have a drink."

Ivan still ignored him. Karamazov waited two more minutes.

"But however much you may disapprove, my dear Karl von Moor, I'm still determined to take Alyosha out of the monastery," he announced.

Ivan glanced at him scornfully, shrugged, and turned away to look at the road. Not another word was uttered until they got home.

BOOK III

THE SENSUALISTS

CHAPTER 1

In the Servants' Quarters

Although it was far from the center, Fyodor Karamazov's house was not altogether on the outskirts of town. Rather old and weather-beaten, but still pleasant looking, it was a two-story gray house with a red iron roof. Old as it was, it seemed solid enough to last many years, and the inside was spacious and comfortable. It had many closets, snug little corners, unexpected little stairways and passages. It had some rats too, but Karamazov didn't really mind them: "You don't feel quite so lonely in the evenings with them around," he used to say. He was usually alone at night, since he sent the servants off to their quarters in a cottage on the grounds, locking himself in until morning.

The servants' cottage was in the yard and it, too, was solidly built and quite roomy. It was in the kitchen of the cottage that Karamazov's meals were prepared. There was a kitchen in the main house, but he disliked the smell of cooking, so his food had to be carried across the yard all year around, summer and winter.

The house must have been built for a very large family, for it could easily have accommodated five times as many people, masters and servants, as it ever had since Karamazov had owned it. And now the main house was occupied only by Fyodor Karamazov and his son Ivan, and the cottage by only three servants: old Gregory, his wife Martha, and another, younger man-servant called Smerdyakov.

At this point it is necessary to say a few words about these three servants. We have already met old Gregory. He was a steadfast, resolute man, who would stubbornly and unwaveringly follow a course once, for some reason (often extremely illogical), he had decided it was incontrovertibly right. On the whole, he was an honest and incorruptible man. His wife Martha, although she always submitted to her husband's decisions in the end, often nagged him mercilessly. For instance, after the emancipation of the serfs, she tried to persuade Gregory to leave Mr. Karamazov, move to Moscow, and open a little store with their savings. But Gregory decided then and there that his wife was talking nonsense, "because all women are dishonest," that it would be improper to leave the master whose serf he had been, whether that master was a good or a bad man, that it was their duty to stay with him now.

"Don't you know what duty means, woman?"

"I know what duty means, Gregory, but I don't see why it's our duty to stay here; that don't make sense to me," Martha objected firmly.

"So it don't make sense to you—we're still staying here. And don't bring it up again."

And that's the way it was. They stayed. Mr. Karamazov named the wages he'd pay, and paid them regularly. Besides, Gregory knew that he had a certain influence over his master; he gauged quite correctly that, although his clownish master was a very strong and obstinate man in some respects, in others he was surprisingly weak. Karamazov himself was aware of his weak points. There were many things that frightened him, and he worried constantly—and this would have made it hard if he had not had someone who was loyal to him—and Gregory was as loyal a man as anyone could hope to have. In the course of Karamazov's life there had been many occasions when he had been in danger of being beaten, sometimes quite badly, but every time Gregory came to his rescue, although afterward the old servant would always admonish him at great length. But Gregory meant much more to Karamazov than a means of avoiding beatings; there were moments when, for some complex and subtle reasons that he himself could not explain, he felt an urgent and pressing need to have someone loyal and trustworthy by him. Some of these times were of a rather morbid nature: debauched in his sensuality and often cruel, like some vicious insect, Karamazov was occasionally, especially when drunk, subject to moments of mental anguish, of torment arising from a feeling of guilt that made him feel his soul was hurting him physically, so to speak. "It feels as if my soul had got caught in my throat and was quivering there," was the way he sometimes described it. It was at such moments as these that he wanted somewhere close to him—not necessarily in the same room, in the servants' quarters was good enough—someone firm and faithful, someone quite unlike his dissipated self, someone who, aware of all his goings-on and knowing all his secrets, would still tolerate it all out of sheer loyalty, would not try to stop him, and would make neither reproaches nor, above all, threats by bringing up all the horrible retributions to come in this world or the next. And again, in case of need, he wanted someone to protect him from something unknown but terrifying. What Karamazov actually needed was to have near him *another* human being, someone he had known for a long time, someone friendly, someone he could call on in a painful moment just to look into his face, perhaps exchange a few words, sometimes completely extraneous words. Then he would be relieved to see that the faithful man was not angry, or, if he was angry, well, then he would feel a little sad about it. Sometimes, though very seldom, Karamazov would even go over to the servants' cottage, wake Gregory up, and ask him to come over to the house for a few minutes. Then he would just talk to him about complete trifles and let him go, perhaps even with a sarcastic remark or a sneer, after which he would shrug, go to bed, and sink into the sleep of the just.

When Alyosha came to live with his father, Mr. Karamazov felt rather the same way about him. Alyosha "touched his very heart by being there, seeing everything, condemning nothing." Moreover, Alyosha offered his father something that he had never had before—a complete absence of contempt for him. Indeed, Alyosha treated him with invariable kindness and a completely genuine and sincere affection, which Karamazov little deserved. All this came as a complete surprise to the old profligate who led a bachelor's life and who, until then, had known only "wicked" joys. And when Alyosha left his house, his father understood and admitted to himself something he had refused to understand before.

I have already mentioned at the beginning of my story that, while Gregory had hated Fyodor Karamazov's first wife, Dmitry's mother, Adelaida, he had sided with Sofia, "the crazy one," his master's second wife, against the master himself or against anybody who said anything deprecating or slighting about her. His sympathy for that unhappy woman had turned into a sort of sacred cause for him so that, even twenty years after her death, he would not let a disparaging remark about her go unchallenged. Outwardly, Gregory appeared to be a cold, grave man whose words were few but weighty and trenchant. And it would have been hard to tell

faith. His reading of "godly things" lent his face an even graver expression.

It is possible that Gregory was naturally inclined toward mysticism so that the birth of his six-fingered son, followed by the boy's death and another strange and unexpected event, "left a mark" on him, as he put it himself. On the night after the child's funeral, Martha was awakened by what she took to be the crying of a newborn baby. She was frightened and awakened her husband. He listened and thought it sounded more like moaning—"could be a woman." He got up and pulled on some clothes. It was a warm May night and, as he stepped out onto the porch to listen, he heard clearly that the moans were coming from the garden. Yet he knew that the gate between the garden and the yard—the only way into the garden—had been padlocked for the night and that no one could have climbed over the solid, very tall fence. He returned to his cottage to get a lantern and the key to the padlock. Ignoring his wife's frightened and hysterical protests that they were the cries of her little baby calling her, Gregory went into the garden. Once there, he realized that the moans were coming from the bath-house near the garden gate and that it was a woman moaning. He opened the door of the bath-house and was stunned by what he saw: the local God's fool, known throughout the area as Reeking Lizaveta, had hidden herself in the Karamazovs' garden bath-house where she had just given birth to a baby boy. And now she lay dying beside her newborn baby. She did not say anything since she had never been able to speak.

But all this needs further explanation.

CHAPTER 2

Reeking Lizaveta

The circumstances of this childbirth confirmed an unsavory and revolting suspicion that Gregory had had ever since a certain incident. Reeking Lizaveta was a tiny creature, "just a teeny-weeny thing of four-and-a-half feet," as many of the old women around the church tearfully described her after her death. At twenty, she had a round, rosy, healthy face, but it was the face of an idiot; her eyes, although gentle enough, had a peculiar, heavy stare that made an unpleasant impression. Winter and summer, she went around barefoot,

wearing only a hemp smock. Her hair, which was very thick,
almost black, and curly as lamb's wool, looked like some
huge strange hat sitting on her head, a dusty, muddy hat,
with leaves, small twigs, and wood shavings sticking out of it,
for she often slept on the ground. Her father was a former
shopkeeper who had lost all his money, and, homeless and
sickly, had taken to drink. His name was Ilya and for many
years he lived with a family of well-to-do shopkeepers, working for them as a sort of handyman. As for Lizaveta's mother,
she had been dead for quite some time. Always in poor health
and irritable, Ilya would beat Lizaveta mercilessly whenever
she came home. And so she went home very seldom; she slept
outside and the townsfolk fed her, believing her to be a holy
fool. Ilya himself, his employers, and various kind-hearted
townspeople, mostly local merchants, often tried to make
Lizaveta dress more decently. They gave her other clothes and
in winter they would dress her in a sheepskin coat and a pair
of boots. But, after meekly allowing them to put these clothes
on her without a word of protest, she would usually go to a
particular corner somewhere behind the cathedral, pull off all
the things that had been given her, leave them there in a
heap, and walk away barefoot in just her smock as before.

Once, when the newly appointed governor of our province
was making a tour of inspection, he paid a surprise visit to
our town and was quite outraged when he caught sight of
Lizaveta, although they explained to him that she was a holy
fool. God's fool or not, he declared, a young girl going
around in nothing but a smock was a violation of the standards of decency, and he issued a warning that it must happen
no more. But after the governor was gone, Lizaveta was again
to be seen around town wearing nothing but her smock, just
as before.

After her father died, the pious people of the church
became even more sentimental about her, since she was now
officially an orphan. Indeed, everyone in town seemed to like
her and no one bullied or annoyed her, not even the schoolboys—and our schoolboys are a mischievous lot. She could
enter strange houses and no one would chase her away. Indeed, people always received her kindly and gave her a kopek
or two. But she would take the coin and go straight to an
alms-box in the church or outside the prison and drop it in.
If she was given a bun or a roll, she never failed to give it
away to the first child she met, or she would stop some
wealthy lady and offer it to her. And, strangely enough, the

rich ladies would accept it with great joy. She herself lived on black bread and water—nothing else. She could walk into any big store and wander around amidst expensive things. Even if they had money lying there, the owners never bothered to keep an eye on her, for they knew that they could have left a thousand rubles in cash and forgotten all about it, and she would not have taken a single kopek.

She seldom went inside a church and either spent her nights on a church porch or climbed over some wattle fence (we still have many wattle fences in town) into a vegetable garden.

About once a week she went home, that is, to the house of her late father's employers, and in cold winters she went there to sleep almost every night, either in the entrance hall or in the cowshed. People looking at her wondered how she survived, but she was used to living as she did and, although she was so short, she was very strongly built. Some of our respectable people claimed she lived the way she did out of sheer pride, but that didn't seem to make much sense: she could not pronounce even one word—now and then she would move her tongue about and produce only a mooing sound—so where was there room for pride in her?

Once, quite long ago, on a warm September night, when there was a full moon and it was late by our provincial standards, half a dozen of our gentlemen, who had left the club in a rather inebriated state, were making their way home through the back gardens. They were walking along a lane bordered by wattle fences behind which lay the kitchen gardens of the nearby houses. The lane itself led to a little bridge over the long, stinking puddle that is often referred to, in these parts, as a river. And by one of the wattle fences the merry gang found Lizaveta asleep among the weeds and nettles. The sight of her made the gentlemen laugh uproariously and elicited some extremely crude remarks. Then one of them asked a rather outlandish question: "Could anyone regard this animal as a woman? For instance, at this moment, could . . ." etc. With haughty disdain, the others decided that it was quite unthinkable. But one disagreed—Fyodor Karamazov, who happened to be among them. He stepped forward and declared that she could very easily be regarded as a woman, that, indeed, she had a certain spice to her, and so on and so forth. It is true that at that time he was particularly anxious to be an amusing companion to the local gentlemen, and while he pretended to be one of them, felt they

considered him a flunkey. This was soon after he had received
the news from Petersburg of his first wife Adelaida's death
and, wearing mourning crape on his hat, he was drinking
and misbehaving scandalously enough to outrage even the
most unprincipled rogues in our town. The gentlemen burst
into loud laughter at Karamazov's surprising statement and
one of them even challenged him to back his words with
deeds while the others went on elaborating on their horror
and disgust, although with extraordinary exhilaration. Finally,
however, they tired of it and walked off.

Later, Karamazov swore he had left with the rest of the
gang, and it may have been quite true: no one has ever
known for sure. But five or six months later, the town discovered with shock and horror that Lizaveta was pregnant.
Who could possibly be the offender? Then suddenly the
rumor spread that it was Fyodor Karamazov. Where did that
rumor originate? Of the merry gang of gentlemen, only one
was still in town by then, a middle-aged and respectable state
councillor, the father of grown-up daughters, who certainly
would not have spread such a rumor even if there had been
something to it. The other five had moved out of our area.
But the rumor pointed at Karamazov, and persistently so.
Karamazov, of course, did not seem bothered by it all. Had
the allegations against him been made only by some local
shopkeepers or tradesmen, he would hardly have bothered to
acknowledge them. For at that time he was proud and kept
company only with gentlemen and civil servants, whom he
felt obliged to amuse. This was one of the occasions on which
Gregory fiercely defended his master, not only trying to dis-
prove the allegations against him, but openly upbràiding the
accusers until he succeeded in making many of them change
their minds. "Whatever happened to her was her own fault,"
he claimed with great assurance, and her seducer, he said, was
none other than Karp the Wrench—a dangerous escaped convict, who at that time was living in hiding in our town. This
seemed quite a plausible conjecture because people remembered Karp well and especially that around that time, in the
fall, he had been roaming the streets at night and had robbed
three people. But all these rumors and arguments did not in
the least change the general sympathy for the poor holy fool;
in fact, the opposite was true—people showed even more
kindness and concern for her. Mrs. Kondratiev, a well-to-
do merchant's widow, took Lizaveta to her house early in
April and tried to keep her there at least until the baby was

born. Lizaveta was watched night and day, but on the very last day she managed to slip away, ending up in Fyodor Karamazov's garden. How she managed to get over the tall fence, especially in the last stages of pregnancy, remains a mystery. Some claim that she was helped over it, others that it was a case of levitation. Complicated though it may be, the true explanation probably does not involve any supernatural intervention—having spent many nights in people's vegetable gardens, Lizaveta had become an expert climber of wattle fences and could conceivably, pregnant as she was, have somehow managed to climb over the tall wooden fence and jump down into Fyodor Karamazov's garden, perhaps hurting herself in the process.

Gregory rushed back, sent Martha to help Lizaveta, and himself went to fetch an old midwife who, very conveniently, lived nearby. The baby was saved, but Lizaveta died at dawn. Gregory took the baby boy home, told his wife to sit down, put the little boy into her lap, right against her breast, and said to her: "This is a child of God, an orphan; he is everybody's kin, and ours more than anyone else's. Our little departed one has sent us this baby born of the son of the devil and of a holy woman. Feed him and weep no more." And Martha brought up the boy. They christened him Paul and registered his patronymic as Fyodorovich as a matter of course, without asking anyone's permission. Fyodor Karamazov did not object to this; in fact, he found it rather amusing. And later he called him Smerdyakov—the Reeking One—from his mother's nickname—Lizaveta Smerdyashchaya, Reeking Lizaveta. And now this same Smerdyakov was Karamazov's cook, and at the beginning of our narrative he lived in the servants' cottage with Gregory and Martha.

I should really say more about him, but I am ashamed to impose any more stories of common servants on my readers. So I will resume my story, trusting that, as it develops, Smerdyakov will become sufficiently understandable to the reader.

CHAPTER 3

The Confession of an Ardent Heart in Verse

After he had heard Mr. Karamazov's command, shouted at him from the carriage as it was pulling away from the monastery, Alyosha stood for a while looking quite lost. Not that he stood there brooding for long—that would not have been like him at all. Despite his great uneasiness, he went to the Father Superior's kitchen and found out what had happened. Then he set out for town, hoping that on the way he'd somehow manage to settle the problem that was now weighing on him. He was not really worried by his father's order that he move back home, "mattress, pillow, and all"—he understood very well that a command shouted out like that was just his father's way of showing off and enjoying the sheer "beauty" of the gesture. Alyosha felt that his father was a bit like a certain tradesman in the town. A few days earlier, in front of his guests at his own birthday celebration, this man had started smashing his own crockery and tearing his and his wife's clothes, because he was not offered enough vodka; then he went on to break every stick of furniture in his house and smash all the windows, and he did it all for the "beauty" of the gesture, as Mr. Karamazov had just now. Obviously, the next day, when he had calmed down, the tradesman regretted his smashed furniture, broken crockery, and all the rest; and Alyosha was convinced that tomorrow, perhaps even today, his father might very well allow him to return to the monastery. Besides, he was sure that, whomever else his father might want to hurt, he would never hurt him. As a matter of fact, Alyosha was convinced that there was not a man in the whole world who would wish to offend him or, for that matter, who could offend him. He had accepted that once and for all as a self-evident truth, and so he had no misgivings now on his way to his father's house.

He was filled, however, with a vague, entirely different sort of apprehension. It was tantalizingly painful because he could not quite put his finger on it. It was an uneasy feeling about the woman—Katerina—who had begged him so insistently to come and see her, in the note transmitted to him by Mrs. Khokhlakov. He had no idea what it was about and the urgency of her demand had immediately filled his heart with an anguish that had grown stronger with every hour, throughout all the incidents and scenes that had taken place in the monastery, including his father's latest performance at the Father Superior's. It was not because he had no idea what she wanted to say to him or what he would answer her that he was worried. Nor was it because she was a woman for, although he knew very little about women, he had lived among them from his early childhood until the day he had entered the monastery. No, he was uneasy about this particular woman—he was afraid of Katerina and he had been afraid of her ever since he had first seen her. He had seen her only once or twice, at the most three times, and on one occasion he had exchanged a few words with her. The impression she had left on him was that of a beautiful, haughty, and domineering young woman. Yet it was not her beauty that troubled him; it was something else. And it was the indefinable origin of his anxiety that was causing it to increase in him now. He knew her aims were of the noblest; he had no doubt about that. She was trying to save his brother Dmitry, who had wronged her, and she was doing it out of sheer generosity. But although he understood this and acknowledged her noble and generous intentions, the nearer he came to her house, the more strongly he felt cold shivers running down his spine.

He knew that his brother Ivan, who was a very close friend of hers, would not be there, since he was at that moment with their father. He was even more sure that Dmitry would not be with her either, and he even felt the reason for Dmitry's absence. So he would have to face her all alone. He would have very much liked to see Dmitry before having this frightening talk with her. He wanted to stop off at his place first and find out a few things from him, without, of course, showing him the note. But Dmitry lived far away and very likely was not even at home now. He stopped and then, after a minute's deliberation, made up his mind. He hurriedly crossed himself in a familiar gesture and, suddenly smiling over something, set out for the frightening woman's house.

He knew which house she lived in. If he went there by Bolshaya Street and then crossed the square, it would be quite a distance. Our small town is spread out and it takes quite a while to get from one end to the other. Besides, his father was expecting him: he might not have calmed down yet and might still be thinking of what he had told Alyosha and have another fit of temper—so Alyosha had to hurry if he wanted to get to both places quickly. He decided to take every possible short cut since he knew the town like the palm of his hand. So he went the back way, ignoring the streets, following deserted paths, climbing over fences, walking across other people's yards, but since he was well known and liked in town no one objected—people simply waved to him. In this way he could get to Bolshaya Street twice as fast. At one point he passed very close to his father's house, as he crossed the yard of a little old house with four windows that stood

next to Karamazov's property. The house belonged to a legless old woman. She lived there with her daughter, a former
chambermaid, who had worked for a succession of upper-
class Petersburg families until a year before, when she had
been forced to come home to look after her invalid mother,
and who liked to go about town in her elegant Petersburg
dresses. The old woman and her daughter, however, had
gradually spent all their savings and were now completely
indigent; every day they came to Mr. Karamazov's kitchen
for bread and soup, which Martha very readily gave them.
But though she came for her plate of soup, the daughter
never sold any of her dresses, one of which even had a long
train. Alyosha had learned this quite accidentally from his
friend Rakitin, who knew absolutely everything that went on
in town. Of course, no sooner had Alyosha learned that fact
than he immediately proceeded to forget it. But now, as he
came up to the old woman's garden, the thought of the dress
with the train came back to him. He raised his lowered head
and, to his immense surprise, saw someone he had never
expected to find there.

From behind the wattle fence giving onto the next garden
emerged the head and shoulders of his brother Dmitry, who
obviously was standing on something. Dmitry was making
violent gestures with his hands, beckoning to Alyosha to come
closer and obviously not wanting to call out to him or even to
utter a word for fear of being heard. Alyosha ran over to
the fence.

"Thank God you turned this way—I could hardly prevent
myself from calling out to you," Dmitry said in a hurried,
joyful whisper. "Come, climb over here. Hurry! It's so lucky
you came by! I was just thinking about you . . ."

Alyosha was also pleased and was only concerned about
how to get over the wattle fence. He tucked up his cassock
and, as he leaped with the agility of a street urchin, his
brother's powerful paw caught him by the elbow and helped
him over the fence.

"All right, let's get going now!" Mitya whispered excitedly.

"Where to?" Alyosha whispered back, glancing around him.
They were alone in a smallish garden. The house was at
least fifty yards away.

"Why do you have to whisper?" Alyosha asked. "There
doesn't seem to be anyone around."

"Whisper? Yes, you're damned right," Dmitry suddenly cried

in a loud voice. "Why am I whispering? As you can see, I'm all mixed up: I'm here secretly in order to protect a secret. I'll explain it to you later but, with all this secrecy weighing on me, I even started speaking like a conspirator and, like an idiot, whispering when there's no need for it at all. Let's go. But keep your mouth shut until we get there. Oh, I'd like to give you a bear hug, man!

> Glory to the Highest in the World!
> Glory to the Highest in me . . .

I was repeating that over and over again just before you came . . ."

The garden covered about three acres. There were trees planted only along the four sides—maples, birches, lime trees, and apple trees—while the center was a grass meadow that produced several hundredweight of hay in the summer. The owner of the garden leased it out for a few rubles every spring. Along the fences, there were also beds of raspberries, gooseberries, and black currants and there were vegetable patches close to the house, but these had obviously been planted not long before.

Dmitry led Alyosha to the corner of the garden farthest from the house. There, in a clump of lime trees, amidst old black currant, elder, and lilac bushes, was an old, tumble-down summer house, its latticed walls blackened and sagging, but with a roof that still offered some protection from the rain. God knows how old the summer house was, although some people said it had been built fifty years before by a retired lieutenant colonel named Alexander von Schmidt, who had owned the house. In any case, by now it was in a state of decay. The floor was rotting, the floorboards loose, and the woodwork musty. In the middle of the summer house was a round green table fixed to the ground and surrounded by green wooden benches on which it was still possible to sit.

Alyosha, who had previously noticed his brother's excited state, now saw on the table a glass and a half-empty bottle of brandy.

"Yes—it's brandy!" Dmitry said, bursting into a peal of laughter. "I can hear you thinking: 'He's on a binge again!' But you mustn't trust appearances, you know:

> Heed not deceitful, shallow crowds
> And cast aside your doubts . . .

I'm not on a binge. I've just been 'indulging' a little, as that piggish friend of yours, Rakitin, puts it, and will still put it even when he becomes a state councillor. Sit down. You know, Alyosha, I'd like to press you to my heart hard enough to crush you, because you're the only person—do you understand me—you're the only one I'm really fond of . . ." Dmitry said in strange exaltation.

"Yes, I only care for you and for some slut I've fallen in love with, who will drive me to my perdition. But falling in love with someone doesn't mean loving that person. It's possible to fall in love and to hate at the same time—I want you to remember that. But now, while I'm feeling good, I'd like to talk to you. So sit down here at the table and I'll sit next to you, look at you, and talk. You just keep quiet and I'll do all the talking, because the time has come for me to say what I have to say. But I've decided that we really should talk quietly because . . . you never know, there may be some . . . some indiscreet ears around, after all. I'll explain everything to you: the continuation will follow. Why do you think I was so anxious to see you just now and these few past days? For I've been anchored in this spot for five days now. Because you happen to be the one person to whom I want to tell everything, because I must tell it, because I need you, because tomorrow I'm going to leap down from my cloud, because tomorrow my life will end and begin anew. Have you ever dreamt of falling from a mountain straight into a deep hole? Well, I'm about to experience that, and not in a dream. But I'm not afraid and I don't want you to worry either. Actually, I am afraid, but I sort of enjoy it too. No, enjoy isn't the right word—I'm sort of enthusiastic about it, you understand? Well, the hell with it—strength of spirit or weakness of spirit or spirits of a female—be that as it may! Let's glorify nature: look how bright the sun is, and the sky so clear and the leaves so green. It's still summer and three in the afternoon and it's so still and quiet . . . Where were you going, Alyosha?"

"I was on my way to father's . . . But I wanted to see Katerina first . . ."

"Her and father! Good God, what a coincidence! Why do you think I was waiting for you? Why did I want to see you so badly? Why did I yearn, thirst, and hunger to meet you in every recess of my soul and even with every one of my ribs? It was precisely to send you on my behalf to father and Katerina, so that I could have done with both of them. I wanted to send an angel to them. I could send anyone, but I wanted an angel as my messenger. And now it turns out that you're on your way to see her and father."

"Did you really want to send me?" Alyosha cried with a pained expression.

"Wait a minute! You knew it—I can see from your face that you understood everything right away. No, don't say anything just now. Don't be sorry for me and don't weep!"

Dmitry stood up, held a finger to his forehead, and for a moment stood there deep in thought.

"It was she who asked you to come," he said. "She must have sent you a note or something . . . Why would you go to see her otherwise?"

"Here it is," Alyosha said, taking Katerina's note out of his pocket.

Mitya read it quickly.

"And you decided to take the short cut! Ah, good God, what a coincidence! And, like a pretty goldfish, you've landed in the net of an old good-for-nothing fisherman. In that case, Alyosha, I'll make a clean breast of everything, for there must be someone who knows the whole truth. I've already told it to the angel in heaven and now I'll tell it to the angel on earth. Because you are an angel on earth, Alyosha. You'll hear me out, you'll understand, and you'll forgive. And that is just what I need—for someone who is better than me to forgive me. Listen, what if two human beings suddenly sever all their ties with the earth and take off for another, extraordinary world—or at least one of the two does—and if, before taking off, he asks another man to do something for him that people usually only ask on their deathbed—could the other man refuse him, especially if he is a friend and a brother?"

"I'll do whatever you want me to, but please tell me what it is. What is it?"

"What's the hurry, Alyosha? There's plenty of time now— the whole world has turned a corner and started on a new course. Ah, Alyosha, it's such a pity you don't really know what exaltation is! But what am I talking about? How can I tell *you* that *you* don't know what exaltation is? How stupid of me! 'Be generous, O man!' Who wrote that?"

Alyosha decided to wait as long as necessary. He realized that it was here that he was needed the most. Mitya was lost in his thoughts, his elbows on the table and his head resting on one hand. They both remained silent for a while.

"Alyosha," Mitya said after a while, "you're the only per-

son in the world who won't laugh at me . . . I would like to
start my confession with Schiller's 'Hymn to Joy,' but I don't
know it in German, except that it's called *An die Freude*.
Now don't go imagining that I'm talking like this just because
I'm drunk. That's not so. Brandy is brandy, but it would
take two bottles to make me drunk—

> A ruddy-faced Silenus
> On his stumbling donkey.

But as it is, I'm no Silenus. I haven't even drunk a quarter of
a bottle. But I'm strong and silent because I've made a final
and irrevocable decision. You must forgive the bad pun, since
you'll have to forgive me many other things much worse than
that today. Don't worry, I'm not just talking nonsense. I'm
getting to the point now and you won't have to pull words
out of me . . ."

He raised his head, thought a second, then started to recite
with great emotion:

> Shivering naked in a cave
> Hid a frightened troglodyte.
> Like a devastating wave,
> Roamed the nomads through the night.
> Armed with spear, the hunter crept,
> Stalking tirelessly a boar.
> In despair, poor strangers wept,
> Washed up on this barren shore.
>
> Down Olympia's great height,
> On her kidnapped daughter's trail,
> Wandered Ceres and caught sight
> Of the world in grim travail,
> Where men offer gods no haven
> No respect for things divine,
> Selfish, wicked, mean, and craven,
> Fail to worship at their shrine.
>
> From the fields no flowers gay,
> From the grapes no gen'rous flood,
> Only smoldering corpses lay
> On the altars stained with blood . . .
> And wherever the sad stare
> Of the goddess still did light,
> It met sorrow, wild despair,
> Man's humiliating plight.

Mitya suddenly burst into sobs and seized Alyosha by the hand.

"Yes, my friend, yes—humiliating plight, humiliation, to this very day! Man's fate on earth is terrifying—there's so much trouble everywhere! I don't want you to take me for an unthinking brute with an army officer's commission, who spends his time soaking up cognac and sleeping with loose women. No, sir, I hardly ever stop thinking about man's humiliation unless . . . unless I'm deluding myself now. But I hope to God I'm not deluding myself and, believe me, I'm not trying to make myself out better than I really am. And the reason I think so much about man's humiliation is that I'm such a humiliated man myself, you know . . .

> Raising up his soul from vileness
> Reaching for his human worth,
> Man must enter an alliance
> With eternal Mother Earth . . .

But what makes it hard for me is that I don't know how I could possibly enter that eternal alliance with Mother Earth. I don't kiss Mother Earth, I don't plow her soil . . . Should I, then, become a peasant, a shepherd, or what? I go on and on, and I don't know where I'll find myself next—in stench and disgrace or in light and joy. And that's where the main trouble lies: everything in this world is a puzzle. Whenever I've sunk into the deepest shame of depravity—and that has happened to me more often than anything else—I've always recited that poem about the goddess Ceres and man's fate. But has it reformed me? No—because I'm a Karamazov, because if I must plunge into the abyss, I'll go head first, feet in air. I'll even find a certain pleasure in falling in such a humiliating way. I'll even think that it's a beautiful exit for a man like me. And so, in the very midst of my degradation, I suddenly intone a hymn. Even if I must be damned, even if I am low and despicable, I must still be allowed to kiss the hem of the veil in which my God is shrouded; and even if I may be following in the devil's footsteps, I am still Your son, O Lord, and I love You, and feel the joy without which the world cannot be.

> Joy eternal pours its fires
> In the soul of God's creation,
> And its sparkle then inspires
> Life's mysterious fermentation.

Joy fills with light the plants' green faces,
Regulates the planets' runs,
Fills immeasurable spaces
With innumerable suns.

All things drink with great elation
Mother Nature's milk of joy,
Plant and beast and man and nation
Sweetness of her breast enjoy.
To man prostrated in the dust,
Joy brings friends and cheering wine;
Gives the insects sensual lust,
Angels—happiness divine.

"But that's enough poetry! The tears are pouring from my
eyes, so let me weep. Maybe people would laugh at me for
being so stupid and ridiculous if they saw me now, but I
know you won't laugh. In fact, I see your eyes are glistening . . . So enough poetry. Now I'd like to tell you something
about insects—the ones endowed with sensuality by God's
eternal joy:

Gives the insects sensual lust . . .

"I'm just such an insect, Alyosha, and that verse applies
specifically to me. All we Karamazovs are such insects and one
lives in you too, my angel brother, and it will stir up storms
in your blood too. Storms, because sensuality is a storm, even
more than a storm. Beauty is a terrifying thing! It's so frightening because it's indefinable and it's indefinable because God
has surrounded us with nothing but riddles. Here the shores
of a river meet, incompatibilities coexist. I am not an educated man, brother, but I have been thinking about this a
great deal. There are so many mysteries; so many riddles that
weigh man down to the ground. He is expected to solve them
somehow or other and to climb dry out of the water. It's
beautiful, isn't it? What I really can't bear, though, is that a
man with a noble heart and a superior intelligence may start
out with the Madonna as his ideal and end up with Sodom
as his ideal. It is even worse for one already striving for his
Sodom ideal, who has not renounced his Madonna ideal,
which still sets his heart ablaze, as it did when he was young
and innocent. Yes, sir, a man's range of feelings is wide, too
wide even, and if I had my way, I'd narrow it quite a bit.
It's a hell of a situation, you know: what the head brands as

shameful may appear as sheer beauty to the heart. But can there be beauty in Sodom? Yes and, believe me, it is precisely there that beauty lies for most men. Weren't you aware of that secret? The terrible thing is that beauty is not only frightening but a mystery as well. That's where God and the devil join battle, and their battlefield is the heart of man. But actually, everyone always talks about his own particular trouble. Now I'm getting to the point, listen to me."

CHAPTER 4

The Confession of an Ardent Heart in Prose

"I led a wild and drunken life," Dmitry went on. "You heard father say this morning that I thought nothing of spending a few thousand rubles on seducing some innocent girl. That's a disgusting lie, absolutely unfounded. Those things never required any money at all, anyway. To me money is only an accessory. It is a means to satisfy the impulses of the moment, to create the right atmosphere. Today, it may be a lady, but tomorrow a whore may take her place. And I want them each to have a great time, and so I throw money around by the handful. I want them to have music, glitter, gypsies, everything . . . And if I have to, I'll give them money too, for some women take money and take it with passion too; I admit that pleases them and makes them thankful . . . But some ladies liked me too, not all of course, but some did . . . However, I preferred the little backstreets and dark alleys to the large lighted squares, because all kinds of unexpected things happen there, because in the filthy gutters I felt I could find natural human gems. Of course, I'm speaking figuratively. In reality there were no such alleys and gutters in that town, but there were moral gutters all right. If you were like me, you'd understand right away what I mean: I liked debauchery and I liked the shame it brought down on me. And I enjoyed cruelty. So am I not just a bedbug, a vicious insect? Well—I'm a Karamazov.

"Once, in winter, they had a big picnic outside town. All our society people drove out there in seven troikas. Sitting in a dark corner of a sleigh, I started pressing the hand of the girl who sat next to me and I forced her to accept my kisses. She was a sweet child, gentle and helpless, the daughter of a local official. She let me . . . let me do pretty much as I pleased in the darkness. The poor child imagined that I'd come to the house the next morning and propose to her (I was somehow considered an eligible bachelor). But, for five months after that, I never said one word to her. I noticed, though, at various dances—we had a lot of dancing parties— that her eyes would flash a look of helpless anger at me. That game aroused the insect sensuality that I was nurturing within me. Well, five months later she married a civil servant and left the town, still angry, perhaps still in love with me. Anyway, she's happily married now.

"I want you to note, though, that I never mentioned it to anyone or did anything that could have injured her reputation because, beastly though I may be in my desires and much though I love to do vicious things, I am not dishonorable . . . I see you're blushing and your eyes are flashing. I suppose you've had enough of listening to all this filth. But what you've heard so far is no more than Paul de Kock's little flowers, although the nasty insect was already growing in my soul. I have a whole collection of such reminiscences, my boy, and may God bless them all. I've always wanted to stay on good terms with a woman after breaking off with her. I never betrayed any of them, never ruined a single reputation. But enough of that, because, as I suppose you imagine, I didn't call you in here just to tell you all this nonsense. No, Alyosha, I'm about to tell you something much more interesting. Don't be surprised, however, if you find me quite unashamed in telling you my story; indeed, I somehow enjoy telling it to you."

"You're saying that because I blushed?" Alyosha said suddenly. "But it was not anything you said or have done that made me blush—it was the fact that I'm just the same as you are."

"What, you? Aren't you going a bit far now?"

"No, not too far," Alyosha said with an excitement which showed that the thought had been with him for quite a while already. "We're on the same ladder. I'm on the bottom rung while you're much higher up, perhaps on the thirteenth rung. That's how I picture it. But it doesn't make much difference, it's the same sort of thing. And once a man has stepped onto the bottom rung, he is sure to climb to the top."

"So it would be best not to step onto the ladder at all, wouldn't it?"

"Well, certainly, if one could help it . . ."

"But can't you help it?"

"It doesn't look as if I can."

"Be quiet, Alyosha, be quiet, my dear boy. I'm so moved I feel like kissing your hand. That bitch Grushenka, who understands so much about men, told me once that she'd eat you up one of these days . . . But I don't want to go on about that. Let's leave that field befouled by fly droppings and go on to my private tragedy, that is, back again to another field befouled by fly droppings. The trouble is, although our nasty old man lied about my way of seducing innocent girls, something of that sort did actually happen in my tragedy, but only once and even then it didn't come off. The old man was telling that cockeyed tale about me, but he knows nothing about this. You'll be the first person I've told it to, except, of course, for Ivan, for he knows everything and knew it all long before you. But Ivan is silent as the grave."

"Ivan—silent as the grave?"

"Yes, he certainly is."

Alyosha looked at Dmitry with great concentration.

"Although I held a second lieutenant's rank in that battalion of the line regiment, I was under a sort of permanent surveillance, like a former convict or something. Yet the town received me very nicely. I threw money around, people thought I was rich, and I ended up believing it myself. There must have been something else about me that pleased them though and, even if they sometimes shook their heads, they liked me all right.

"Not so my commanding officer, an old lieutenant colonel. He had it in for me and kept trying to get me in trouble, but it wasn't all that easy for him because I had some highly placed friends and, besides, the whole town was on my side. It was partly my own fault because I deliberately refused to treat him with proper respect—I was too proud to. That stubborn old fellow, who was really a kind, decent, generous man, had been married twice and both his wives had died. His first wife had been a woman of humble origin and had left him a daughter who looked rather common too. When I was there she was already old-maidish at twenty-four; she lived with her father and an aunt, her mother's sister. The aunt was a common woman who never said a word, while the niece was a common woman full of words and fire. I like to say a kind word about people when I'm reminiscing about them, so let me tell you, my boy, I've never met a woman with a more charming character than this Agafia. She wasn't bad-looking either, to the Russian taste: tall, strong, with a

full figure and beautiful eyes, although her face was somewhat coarse. Two fellows had asked her hand in marriage,
but she had turned them down and remained a spinster. Yet
she was always gay and cheerful. We became good friends—
no, not the way you may think. It was all clean this time and
aboveboard, just friendly. Why, I've often been good friends
with women without there being anything else to it. I would
talk to her frankly about all kinds of shocking things, but it
was all right with her—she just laughed. There are many
women who like us to talk to them frankly—I want you to
note that—but this one was still a virgin, and it amused me
to see her listening to it all. And one more thing: it was
somehow quite impossible to refer to her as a young lady.
Perhaps it was partly because she and her aunt, although
they lived in the house, did not behave like the members of
the family they were, but rather like inferiors, as if they did
not belong to our society. Everyone loved Agafia, though, and
they needed her because she was a marvelous dressmaker.
She had a real talent for it, and she would make dresses for
the ladies just to help them out, never asking them for anything in exchange, although if they really insisted on giving
her things or money as presents, she would accept them.

"But her father, the Lieutenant Colonel, was quite a different matter. He was one of the prominent personalities of our
town. He lived on a grand scale, entertained lavishly, gave
dinners and balls. When I joined his battalion, the whole
town was talking about the imminent arrival of the Lieutenant
Colonel's second daughter, a staggering young beauty who
had just graduated from one of the most elegant Petersburg
boarding schools. This was Katerina, his daughter by his
second wife. Unlike the first, the second wife came from an
old and distinguished family and was the daughter of a
general, although, as far as I know, she did not bring the
Lieutenant Colonel any money either. So Katerina had nothing
but a distinguished background to recommend her and, except
for some vague possibility of inheriting something from some
relative or other, she had no money to her name at all.

"Nevertheless, when she arrived—and she had just come to
spend some time with her family, not to stay—our whole
town seemed to come to life. Our most distinguished ladies
—two of them the wives of generals and one of a full colonel
—and all the others behind them at once displayed great
eagerness to entertain her, vying with one another to invite

her to balls and picnics; they even managed to organize a gala evening with *tableaux vivants* for the benefit of some distressed governesses, and always Katerina was the queen of the event.

"But that was none of my concern and I went right on drinking and having a wild time. In fact, just at that time, I pulled off something so wild that the whole town resounded with it. I remember I saw her for the first time at my battery commander's one evening. Out of the corner of my eye I saw her looking me over, but I didn't go over to introduce myself: 'Let her know,' I thought, 'that there's someone here who's not interested in her.' It was not until another party some time later that I actually spoke to her. And then, she hardly glanced at me and the corners of her mouth turned down in scorn. 'So that's how she feels,' I thought. 'All right, my girl, I'll teach you a lesson.' I often acted like a terrible heel at that time, and I was well aware of it myself. And I was also instinctively aware that this little Katya was no innocent schoolgirl but a person with a strong character, a truly honorable young lady, and, above all, someone with both a good education and an acute intelligence, whereas I had neither. You may think that I was about to propose to her, Alyosha, but I had no such intention—all I wanted was to make her pay for not properly appreciating the dashing young gentleman that I was. And in the meantime I went on drinking and painting the town red.

"Finally the Lieutenant Colonel put me under house arrest for three days. It was just then that I received six thousand rubles from father, after sending him an officially signed document renouncing all my rights and stating that I'd received everything that was due to me and that I would not ask him for anything anymore. The thing is, Alyosha, I understood nothing in my financial dealings with father at that time, or until very recently, perhaps even till today. But to hell with that—we'll get to it later . . . The day I received the six thousand, I also received a letter from a friend of mine containing a very curious piece of information—namely, that my lieutenant colonel's superiors were displeased with him. He was suspected of irregularities—in brief, his enemies were preparing a nice surprise for him. And sure enough, soon the general in charge of our division arrived and gave him hell. A little later the Lieutenant Colonel was asked to hand in his resignation. I won't go into all the details here—

how it came about, etc.—but his enemies in town certainly had something to do with it. In any case, people suddenly became very cool toward him and all the members of his family and even his friends turned their backs on him. And this was the moment I chose to play my first trick. I met Agafia, with whom I had remained on friendly terms. 'I hear,' I said to her, 'that your papa is short four thousand five hundred rubles of government money.' 'What are you talking about?' she said. 'The General was just here and every ruble was there . . .' 'It was there then, but today it's all gone.' She looked terribly upset. 'Don't frighten me, please . . . Where did you hear that?' 'Don't worry,' I told her, 'I won't tell anyone. I'll be as silent as the grave about it. What I actually want to tell you was that in case of—let's call it an emergency—I mean when they ask your papa to produce those four-and-a-half thousand that he doesn't have, well, rather than let him be court-martialed and demoted to the ranks in his old age, I suggest you secretly send me your learned little sister, because I've just received some money and I guess I could let her have, say, four thousand. And I promise to keep it secret.' 'You pig,' she said, 'you vicious, nasty pig! How dare you . . .' Yes, that was what she called me—a pig—and she walked off in terrible indignation as I shouted after her once more not to worry, that I'd keep it all strictly confidential and secret.

"Those two women, that is, Agafia and her aunt, proved to be a couple of real angels. They adored Agafia's little sister Katya, spoiled and proud as she was; in fact, they waited on her hand and foot as if they were her servants . . . Nevertheless, as I found out later, Agafia went straight to Katerina and repeated everything I had said. Which, of course, was exactly what I had hoped she would do.

"All of a sudden a new major arrived in town. He had come, it turned out, to take over our battalion. Just as suddenly, the old lieutenant colonel became very sick and was unable to leave the house for two days, so he couldn't hand over the government funds. Our medical officer, Kravchenko, insisted that he really was ill. But there was something I knew confidentially from an unimpeachable source and, indeed, had known for a long time. Namely, that for four years, after the accounts had been checked by the army inspectors, the monies entrusted to the Colonel would disappear for a certain length of time. Our colonel would lend the money to a local merchant, Trifonov, a bearded widower who wore gold-rimmed glasses and was a most reliable man. Trifonov went off to the annual fair, made various financial transactions, and always returned the money to the Colonel, along with presents from the fair and interest on the capital. Only this time, when Trifonov came back from the fair, he had no money to pay back, as I found out accidentally from his slobbering son and heir, the most depraved youth the world has ever seen. The Colonel went dashing over to Trifonov's, but the merchant cut him off: 'I never received any money from you, nor could you possibly have given me any.' That was all he had to say.

"And so our colonel was home, with a towel wrapped around his head and the three women taking turns putting ice in it, when suddenly a messenger appeared with a note demanding that the monies be handed over at once, 'within two hours.' He signed the messenger's book—I saw the signature later myself—got up, saying he was going to put on his uniform, went to his bedroom, took down his double-barreled shotgun, loaded it with an army bullet, removed his right boot, pressed the barrel against his breast, and started feeling for the trigger with his big toe. But Agafia, remembering what I'd told her and suspecting that her father might try something of the sort, stole up to his bedroom door, peeped through a crack, and saw what he was up to. She rushed in, threw herself on him from behind, throwing her arms around him. The gun went off and the bullet hit the ceiling without harming anyone. In the meantime, the others dashed in, took away the shotgun, and held the old man's arms . . .

"I found out all these little details later. But at the time I was at home. It was getting dark and I decided to go out. I dressed, combed my hair, put some eau de cologne on my handkerchief, took my cap, and was about to leave when the door opened and there she was—Katerina, standing in my room.

"Strangely enough, she had met no one she knew on her way and no one saw her enter my lodgings, so no one in town was aware of her visit. I rented my rooms from two aged ladies, both the widows of civil servants, who were very considerate to me, did whatever I asked them, and never breathed a word to anybody about Katerina's visit, as I expressly asked them not to.

"Of course, I realized at once what she wanted. She was staring straight into my face as she came in, and there was a strange determination, even arrogance, in her dark eyes, although around her lips there were signs of wavering.

" 'My sister told me that you'd give me four thousand five hundred rubles if I came in person. Well, here I am. So give me the money . . .' she fired off. But then she couldn't go on; she gasped, her voice failed her, and her lips and the lines around the corners of her lips quivered . . . Hey, Alyosha, my boy, are you still following me or have you fallen asleep?"

"I know you'll tell me the whole truth, Mitya," Alyosha muttered nervously.

"That's just what I'll tell you. It will be the truth and I won't spare myself. Well, the first thought that came to me was the one a Karamazov would be likely to have under such circumstances. You know, I was once bitten by a centipede and was in bed for two weeks with a high fever. So now I felt as if a centipede or some other noxious insect had again stung my heart and contaminated me. I suppose you see what I mean, don't you?

"I looked her over from head to toe. Why, you've seen her. You know how beautiful she is. But there was something else in her then, besides her beauty. She seemed even more beautiful to me at that moment because she was noble and generous while I was a low pig; she was magnanimously sacrificing herself for her father, while I was just a bedbug. And now, I felt, she was at my mercy, me, the pig and the bedbug—the whole of her, body and soul. She was cornered. Let me tell you that this thought I had, a centipede's thought, gripped my heart so violently that it was almost bled white from the pain alone. There seemed to be no room for any inner struggle on my part—I was going to act like a vicious bug, like a tarantula, just go ahead without any restraint . . . It took my breath away.

"I want you to understand, Alyosha, that of course I'd have gone over to their house afterward and asked for her hand in marriage, finishing it all decently, if I may call it that, and no one would or could have known anything about it because, for all my beastly desires, I am, after all, an honorable man. But then it was as though someone whispered into my ear: 'You can be sure, if you go to ask for her hand tomorrow, that with a character like hers she'll refuse to receive you and order her flunkey to throw you out of the house, as if challenging you to go ahead and cry it from the roof-tops, to show you that she isn't afraid of you.' I looked at her and saw that the voice in my ear wasn't lying. I knew

that was exactly the way it would be—they'd kick me out—
I could tell it from her expression at that moment. I felt my
blood seething with anger within me and I wanted to play a
filthy, piggish trick on her, to treat her the way some vulgar
shopkeeper would have under the circumstances. I thought
I'd look at her scornfully as she stood there in front of me
and say in that special tone that shop-assistants use when
they're being insolent: 'You mean you'd really expect me to
give you four thousand rubles for that? Don't you see, ma'am,
it was a joke—I never really meant it. It was rather gullible
of you to believe that I'd pay you so much. I suppose I'd
let you have a couple of hundred. Indeed, I'd be glad to pay
you that, but four thousand, that's quite a different matter.
I wouldn't think of wasting a sum like that so thoughtlessly.
I'm afraid you took all this trouble for nothing.'

"Of course, I realized I would lose everything, for she
would run away, but it would have been an infernally clever
revenge that would have been worth all the rest. Even if it
meant I'd suffer remorse all the rest of my life, it was terribly
tempting to go through with that trick now! Believe me, never
before had I looked at any woman with hatred at such a
moment, but, this once, I just stood there and for maybe
three, maybe five, seconds stared at her with a terrifying
hatred, with the kind of hatred that is only a hair's breadth
from the maddest, most desperate love.

"I walked over to the window and put my forehead against
the ice-cold pane. I remember the ice burning my forehead
like a flame. Don't worry, I didn't keep her waiting long. I
turned back to the room, went to the desk, pulled out the
drawer, and took the five per cent letter of credit for five
thousand rubles, which I had put in the French dictionary,
and showed it to her. Then I folded it, handed it to her,
opened the door leading to the entrance, stepped back, and
bowed to the waist, with the deepest and most sincere reverence—and I mean reverence!

"Her whole body shuddered. She looked at me intently for
a second, turned terribly pale, as pale as a sheet, and all of
a sudden knelt down and bowed to the ground to me, like a
simple Russian woman and certainly not like a finishing-
school graduate. Then she jumped up and ran out.

"When she ran out, I drew my saber (I was wearing it,
because I was about to go out when she came in) and was
going to thrust it into my chest. I'm not sure why I wanted
to do that. I realize how stupid it would have been, but I

suppose it was the sheer ecstasy of the moment. Can you understand, Alyosha, that there are moments of ecstasy in which we could kill ourselves? But I didn't stab myself. I kissed the blade and sheathed it—something, by the way, that I didn't have to mention to you. Actually, I believe that, in telling you all about the struggle that took place in me, I twisted things a little, to make myself look a bit better. But I don't care if I did. The hell with all this spying on the human heart! Well, that's what happened between Katerina and myself. Now you and Ivan know about it—and no one else."

Dmitry stood up. He was tense. He took a handkerchief out of his pocket and wiped the sweat from his forehead. Then he sat down again, not in the same place as before but on a bench that stood by the opposite wall so that to see him Alyosha had to turn completely around.

CHAPTER 5

The Confession of an Ardent Heart: Head over Heels

"Now," Alyosha said, "I know the first part of this business."

"Yes, you know the first part. It was quite dramatic and it took place in that other town. But the second part will end tragically and it will take place right here, in this town."

"I still don't understand a thing about the second part," Alyosha said.

"What makes you think I understand it? I don't either."

"Just a minute, Dmitry, there's one word that puzzles me in this whole business: engagement—tell me, are you still engaged to marry her?"

"We didn't get engaged right away, not for three months after her visit. The next day I told myself that the incident was closed, over and done with, and that there must be no sequel to it. To propose to her now, I felt, would be rather despicable. And as to her, for the whole of the six weeks that she stayed in town after that, I never heard a single word from her. Except for one thing, it's true: the day after her visit, her maid appeared stealthily and, without explanation, handed me an envelope addressed to me. When I opened it, I found it contained the change from the five thousand rubles. They needed four and a half thousand and, in addition, they lost about two hundred rubles in cashing the letter of credit. So she sent me only two hundred and sixty rubles, I believe, and I remember very well that it was just the money without an explanatory note or anything. I examined the envelope hoping to find some penciled note, some sign, but found nothing.

"Well, what could I do? I went on a spree to use up what money I had left, and I went so wild that finally the new major was forced to reprimand me. As to the Lieutenant Colonel, to everyone's surprise he handed over the battalion monies in time—to everyone's surprise since no one thought he had the full amount. But after he had turned it over, he fell sick and took to his bed. After three weeks, softening of the brain set in and he died five days later. He was buried with military honors since his resignation had not had time to go through. About ten days after the funeral, Katerina, Agafia, and Agafia's aunt left for Moscow. And it was only on the very day of their departure (I had not seen them and didn't go to see them off) that I received a tiny envelope containing a one-line message on dainty blue notepaper: 'I'll write to you later. Wait. K.' That was all.

"Now I'll tell you the rest of the story very briefly. In Moscow, their fortunes suddenly changed, as unexpectedly as in a story from the *Arabian Nights*. Katerina's richest relative, the widow of a general, lost her two nieces, who were her heiresses, within a few days; they both died of smallpox during the same week. The grief-stricken old woman received Katerina, who had just arrived in Moscow, as if she were a long lost daughter, immediately changing her will in her favor and thus taking care of her future. And, for the meantime, she transferred eighty thousand rubles to Katerina's name 'as a dowry or to be used as she saw fit.' She was a somewhat hysterical old lady—I saw quite a bit of her later in Moscow.

"Well, then, I suddenly receive in the mail four-and-a-half thousand rubles. Obviously, I am very surprised, indeed, quite stunned. Three days later, the promised letter arrives. I still have that letter. I'll always carry it with me. I'll die with it. Would you like to see it? I want you to read it. She proposes to me herself in that letter. 'I love you,' she writes, 'I love you madly. It's all the same if you don't love me—if only you're willing to marry me. Don't be afraid—I won't interfere with you in any way. I'll be like a piece of your furniture, like the rug under your feet . . . I want to love

you as long as I live. I want to save you from yourself . . .'
Alyosha, I am not even worthy to rephrase those lines in my
own vile words or to repeat them in my vile tone, that
loathsome tone of mine which I have never been able to get
rid of. That letter pierced something very, very deep inside
me and it still hurts me to this day, don't you see?

"I answered her immediately (I couldn't possibly go to
Moscow right away). The tears were running down my
cheeks as I wrote to her. There is one thing I'm ashamed of,
though: I mentioned in my letter that she now was a rich heiress
with a dowry, while I was still a penniless and uneducated
oaf. I dragged money into it that way. I should have kept
quiet about money then, but somehow I wrote it without
realizing what it would mean to her at first. By the same
mail, I wrote to Ivan too, explaining everything to him. He
was also in Moscow then, and I wrote him a six-page letter,
explaining it to him as best I could. Why are you gaping at
me like that? Well, sure, Ivan fell in love with her and he
still loves her, and now I realize it was a blunder on my part,
a blunder, that is, in the worldly, conventional sense, but
perhaps that blunder will save us all yet! Why, can't you see
that she likes him and respects him tremendously? Do you
imagine that, after comparing the two of us, she could go
on loving a man like me, especially after what happened?"

"I am certain that she can love only a man like you and
not a man like him."

"What she loves is not me but her own virtue," Dmitry
blurted out almost spitefully. His eyes flashed, he laughed
awkwardly, and his face turned deep red. Then he banged
his fist on the table.

"I swear, Alyosha," he cried, sounding furious at himself,
"and you are free to believe me or not, but it is as true as
that God is holy and that Christ is our Lord, I swear that,
though I just laughed at her noble feelings, I know she's a
million times better than I am, infinitely superior to me, and
that those noble feelings of hers are perfectly sincere, as
sincere as an angel's! And what makes it so tragic is that I
know it. What's wrong with indulging in dramatic gestures?
Why, I make dramatic gestures myself, but I know that I'm
sincere, completely sincere. As to Ivan, I can well imagine how
he must be cursing human nature now, especially a man of
his intelligence! Who is given preference over him? A freak
who, while already engaged to her, is quite unable to abstain

from debauchery in full view of everybody, including her! And a creature like that is accepted, while he is rejected! And why? For no other reason than that, out of sheer gratitude, a woman has decided to do violence to herself and to throw away her life. It makes no sense! Of course, I've never talked about that side of it to Ivan and he's never even hinted at it to me. But I'm sure that life will follow its proper course in the end: the worthy man will occupy his rightful place and the unworthy one will vanish in some dark alley and never be heard of again. And there, in that dark and filthy alley, which is so dear to him, where he feels so much at home, amidst the stench and the dirt, he'll perish happily, because that's what he really wants . . . But I guess I've talked myself dry and my words have lost much of their meaning. I'm just slapping them together any old way. But it will happen just as I say: I'll drown in the mud in my back alley and she'll marry Ivan."

"But wait a minute, Mitya," Alyosha said very nervously. "There's still a point that you haven't cleared up for me: you're still engaged to her, aren't you? So how can you break the engagement if she doesn't want it broken?"

"Yes, I am officially and solemnly engaged to marry her. We became engaged when I got to Moscow and it was done in grand style with all due ceremony, icons and all. And that relative of hers, the rich general's widow, not only gave Katya her blessing, but even went so far as to congratulate her, believe it or not. 'You have chosen the right man,' she told her. 'I can see that right away.' She didn't like Ivan, though, and was cool toward him. You know, in Moscow I talked to Katya a great deal and told her a lot about myself; I did so honestly and was completely frank, completely sincere. She heard me out and, of course,

> There was sweet embarrassment,
> There were tender words . . .

Although there were some proud words too. Anyhow, she made me promise to reform, so I did promise, and now . . ."

"And now what?"

"And now I called to you and pulled you over the fence into this garden in order to send you today—I want you to remember this date—to see Katerina for me, and it must be today, and tell her that . . ."

"That what?"

"That I'm not coming to see her. Ever. And to give her my regards."

"How can you do that?"

"That's just why I'm sending you instead of going myself: because I can't do it."

"But you, where will you go?"

"To that back alley."

"So you'll go to Grushenka!" Alyosha cried in pain, throwing up his hands in despair. "I couldn't believe it, when Rakitin told me. I thought you just went to see her a few times and that was the end of that."

"You mean, how can a man engaged to a girl like Katerina go and see someone like that, especially when the whole town knows about it? Now, Alyosha, despite everything, I do have a sense of honor. At the very moment I started seeing Grushenka, I stopped being Katerina's fiancé and stopped being an honorable man. Why, I'm very well aware of that. Why do you look at me like that? The first time I went to her place it was to give her a beating. I had learned—and I know it's the absolute truth—that that retired captain, acting on father's behalf, had given her one of my IOU's, so she could threaten to sue me and thus make me behave. They thought that they could scare me that way. So I went to Grushenka's to give her a good thrashing. I only vaguely remembered having seen her before. There's nothing so striking about her at first glance. I knew about the old merchant who kept her. He is sick now and bedridden, but nevertheless, he is pretty sure to see that she lacks nothing, whatever happens. I also knew that she was greedy for money and satisfied her greed by lending money at exorbitant rates of interest, that she was a sharp and merciless bitch. So I went there to give her that beating, but then I just stayed. It was as if all hell had broken loose, like an epidemic of the plague . . . Well, I got infected and am still infected today, and I know now it will never be any different. I am doomed to go around in that circle for all time. So that's where I stand, Alyosha.

"And it so happened that on the day I went to her place I had three thousand rubles in my pocket—fancy that, a beggar with three thousand rubles in his pocket! So we took a little trip to Mokroye, which is twenty miles away, paid for gypsies and champagne, made all the local peasants drunk on champagne, and tossed hundreds and hundreds of rubles to the women who were there. Three days later I felt marvelous and

was completely broke. You may think I was feeling so marvelous because I'd achieved what I was after. No, sir, she
wouldn't even let me look at it from a distance. I tell you,
Alyosha, it's that curve she has. Grushenka's whole body has
a particular curve that can be recognized even in her foot,
even in the little toe of her left foot. Well, that I saw and I
kissed it, but that's as far as I went, believe me. 'Why should
I marry you?' she told me. 'You haven't a kopek to your
name. But if you promise never to beat me and to let me do
whatever I please, then I may marry you yet.' She laughed
when she said that and still laughs when I bring it up . . ."

Dmitry got up in a fury. All of a sudden he looked very
drunk. His eyes were bloodshot.

"Do you really want to marry her, Mitya?"

"If she wants me, I will—right away. And if she doesn't,
I'll go on as I am now—try to hang around her, be the janitor in her yard, if I can. Hey, Alyosha!" Dmitry suddenly
stopped, seized his brother by the shoulders, and shook him
with tremendous force. "Hey, you innocent little boy, don't
you understand that all this is just raving, just the impossible
raving of a madman, that it is all fated to end tragically? I
assume you know, Alyosha, that although I am a man of
despicable and depraved passions, I'll never become a petty
thief, that nothing will ever turn Dmitry Karamazov into a
pickpocket. Well, for your information, Alexei, my brother,
I *am* a petty thief who steals from people's pockets or wherever else he can find money. Just before I went to Grushenka's that first time, when I intended to beat her up, Katerina
had sent for me to ask me to go to another town and mail
three thousand rubles to her sister Agafia in Moscow for her,
because, for some reason or other, she didn't want people
here to learn about it. And that was the three thousand rubles
that I had in my pocket when I got to Grushenka's and it
was that money that I spent in Mokroye . . . I told Katerina
that I had gone to the town and sent the money and that I'd
give her the post office receipt later because I hadn't brought
it with me, and of course I've never given it to her to this
day. Now, imagine: you go to her place today and tell her
that I sent you to give her my regards and say good-by, and
she asks you, 'And what about the money?' If it hadn't been
for that, you could still have said: 'My brother is a despicable
sensualist who cannot control his passions. He did not send
the money you gave him because he is like a primitive animal
and had to follow his instincts.' Now, if I hadn't stolen her

money, you still could have told her: 'But whatever else he is, he is not a thief, so here is your three thousand rubles—he sends it back to you. He suggests you mail the money to your sister yourself, and he sends you his best regards.' But as things stand now, what could you answer her if she suddenly asked you about that money?"

"Oh, Mitya, you feel so terribly miserable. But please don't torture yourself, don't despair like this—it's not quite as bad as you imagine . . ."

"Are you saying that because you're worried that I may shoot myself if I can't give her back the three thousand? You needn't worry. I won't kill myself, and that's the trouble. I don't have the strength to do it now. Later, perhaps—I don't know—but now the only thing I want to do is to go to Grushenka's. I don't care about anything else."

"And what will you do with Grushenka?"

"I'll be her husband and I'll be worthy of her. And when a lover comes to visit her, I'll step out of the room and wait outside, clean the mud off the galoshes of her gentlemen friends, light the samovar, run errands . . ."

"Katerina will understand everything," Alyosha said in an unexpectedly solemn tone. "She'll understand how deeply unhappy you are and she'll resign herself. She's a woman of superior intelligence and she will see that it's impossible to be unhappier than you are."

"She won't forgive me at all," Mitya said with a bitter grin. "This is something, my boy, that no woman would accept. But do you know what would be best?"

"What?"

"To pay her back the three thousand."

"Where can you get it, though . . . But wait, I have two thousand myself and Ivan will give you a thousand. That will make up the three. So take the money and give it back to her."

"Yes, but how long do you think it will take to get hold of that three thousand rubles? Besides, you're not legally of age yet and cannot dispose of your money . . . No, it must be today and no later that you give her my regards, with or without the three thousand, because it has reached a point where I cannot stand it any longer—tomorrow will already be too late. I want you to go to father's for me . . ."

"Father's?"

"Yes, stop at father's before you go to see her and ask him for the three thousand."

"But Mitya, he'll never give it to me."

"Of course he won't, I know it only too well. Do you know, Alexei, what it means to be desperate?"

"Yes, I do."

"So listen then: legally he doesn't owe me a thing. But morally he owes me something, doesn't he? Why, it was by using my mother's twenty-eight thousand that he managed to make a hundred thousand for himself. So let him give me just three thousand for the twenty-eight, only three, and take my soul out of a living hell—he'll have many of his sins forgiven him if he does that. And I give you my solemn word that the three thousand will be the end of it. He'll never hear of me again. For the last time I'm giving him a chance to act as a father. Tell him that God Himself has sent him this opportunity."

"He'll never give it to you, Mitya."

"I know it, I know it perfectly well, especially under the present circumstances. Moreover, there's something else I know: very recently, perhaps only yesterday, he found out that there was a *serious* possibility—I say *serious*—that Grushenka meant it when she said she might take the plunge and marry me after all. He knows that hell cat's character. So how could he possibly even consider giving me money which would, if anything, strengthen the possibility, when he's crazy about her himself? And even that's not the whole story. There's more to it: I know that at least five days ago he drew three thousand rubles out of the bank in hundred-ruble bills, put them in a large envelope, sealed it with five seals, and tied it up with a red ribbon. Then he inscribed the envelope: 'To my angel Grushenka, if she comes to me.' He did all that in great secrecy. No one except his flunkey Smerdyakov knows about the money, but then father trusts him as he does himself. And so he's been waiting for Grushenka for three or four days now; he hopes she'll come to pick up the envelope, for he sent her word about it and she answered that she 'might' come. But if she does go to the old man, how can I marry her after that? So you understand now why I'm here, sitting as though in ambush, lying in wait for . . ."

"For her?"

"That's right, for her. There's a fellow called Foma who lives in this house with those sluts. Foma was a private in my battalion. He does odd jobs for them, acts as their watchman at night, and shoots grouse during the day. That's how he lives. So here I am in Foma's place, but neither Foma nor the women know my secret—that I'm lying in wait here."

"Is Smerdyakov the only one who knows about Grushenka and father?"

"Right, the only one. And he'll let me know if she comes to the old man's."

"Was it he who told you about the envelope?"

"That's right. In utmost secrecy. Even Ivan knows nothing about the money or about the rest. As a matter of fact, the old man wants Ivan out of his way for a few days, so he's sending him to Chermashnya. Someone there has been offering eight thousand rubles for the wood-cutting rights to the forest. So father asked Ivan: 'Help me out. Go over there for two or three days and see what it's all about.' What he really wants is to have Ivan out of the way when Grushenka comes."

"So he's expecting Grushenka even today?"

"No, she won't come today. There are indications of that . . . She certainly isn't coming today!" Mitya suddenly shouted. "That's what Smerdyakov says. Father is drunk and is sitting at table with Ivan. Go there, Alexei, and ask him for three thousand."

"But wait, Mitya, what's the matter with you?"

Alyosha jumped up from his seat, looking intently at Dmitry. For a moment he thought his brother had gone mad.

"Don't worry, I'm not crazy. I know what I'm doing," Dmitry said emphatically and in a peculiar, solemn tone, "and I did ask you to go and see father. I know what I'm saying: I believe in miracles."

"What miracle?"

"In the miracle of God's providence. God knows what's in my heart. He can see my despair. He sees the whole thing, so surely He won't allow something horrible to happen? I do believe in miracles, Alyosha. Go on then."

"All right, I'm going. Will you wait for me here?"

"Yes, I will. And I understand that you won't be back too soon, that you won't be able to just walk in and ask him for it! Besides, he's drunk now. So I'll wait for you three or four or five or six hours or even seven hours, but I want you to know that today, even if it's at midnight, you must go to Katerina's, *with or without* the money, and tell her that I send her my best regards. I want you actually to use those words: 'He told me to give you his best regards.' "

"But Mitya, listen—what if Grushenka comes today, and if not today, tomorrow or the day after?"

"Grushenka? I'll find out about it, break in, and stop them."

"And what if . . ."

"And if . . . Then I'll kill . . . I won't be able to stand it."

"Kill whom?"

"The old man. I won't kill her."

"How can you say that, Mitya!"

"I don't know, I don't know . . . Perhaps I won't kill him. But maybe I will. I'm afraid I'll hate the sight of him too much at that moment. I hate his Adam's apple, his nose, his eyes, his shameless sneer . . . It's a direct, spontaneous loathing. That's what I'm afraid of. I feel I won't be able to resist the temptation."

"I'll go now, Mitya. I trust that God will take good care of everything and see to it that nothing terrible happens."

"And I'll sit here and wait for that miracle. But if it doesn't happen, then . . ."

Alyosha went his way to his father's house deep in thought.

CHAPTER 6

Smerdyakov

Just as expected, Alyosha found his father sitting at table. The table was laid as usual in the living room, although there was a proper dining room in the house. The living room, the largest room in the house, was furnished with a sort of old-fashioned pretentiousness. The furniture was white, very old, upholstered in a red silky material, which was worn and faded. On the walls between the windows hung mirrors in overelaborate frames, also white, with gilt. The walls, covered with white wallpaper which was cracking in places, were adorned with two large portraits, one representing some prince who had been the Governor General of the province thirty or so years before and the other of some bishop long deceased. In one corner there were several icons, in front of which a lamp was lighted every night, not for religious reasons so much as to light the room.

Mr. Karamazov usually went to bed late—at three or four in the morning—and until then he would pace the room or sit in an armchair and meditate. This had become a habit with him. Sometimes he would send the servants off to their cottage and spend the night in the house all alone, but more often than not the servant Smerdyakov stayed with him all night, sleeping on a cot in the entrance hall.

They had finished eating when Alyosha arrived. Fruit preserves and coffee had been served—Mr. Karamazov liked sweet things with brandy after his meal. Ivan was sipping his coffee. The servants, Gregory and Smerdyakov, stood by. Apparently all of them—masters and servants—were in high spirits. Mr. Karamazov was laughing very loudly. Alyosha heard the shrill laughter he knew so well while he was still in the hall, and realized from the sound of it that his father was still in the blissful state preceding drunkenness, but not yet drunk.

"Ah, here he is, here he is!" Karamazov shouted, obviously greatly pleased at Alyosha's arrival. "Come, join us, sit down, have some coffee—it's lenten, for sure, but it's nice and hot! I won't offer you any brandy since you're fasting, although perhaps . . . you're sure you won't have a drop after all? No, wait, have a little liqueur instead—it's marvelous stuff, you know. Hey, Smerdyakov, go and get it. It's in the cupboard, on the second shelf on the right. Here are the keys. Hurry!"

Alyosha tried to protest that he didn't want any liqueur.

"It'll be served anyway, and if you don't want any, we'll have some," his father said, beaming happily. "Ah, but wait—have you had lunch?"

"I have," Alyosha said, although actually he had only had a piece of bread and a glass of kvass in the Father Superior's kitchen. "But I would love some hot coffee."

"Good boy! Have some coffee then. Shall I have it heated up? No, it's boiling hot as it is. It's the famous Smerdyakov coffee. When it comes to coffee, pies, and fish soups—my Smerdyakov is a real artist. Come and have fish soup whenever you like—only let us know in advance when . . . No, wait, didn't I tell you today to move back here, mattress, pillow, and all? Have you brought your mattress with you, hee-hee-hee?"

"No, I haven't brought my mattress," Alyosha said smilingly.

"But it gave you a fright, didn't it, when I said that? Ah, my sweet boy, how could you think I would ever want to hurt you! Listen, Ivan, I can't resist it when he looks into my eyes and laughs like that—all my innards begin to laugh too, looking at him . . . Ah, how I love this boy! Wait, Alyosha, I must give you my parental blessing right now."

But as Alyosha stood up, Mr. Karamazov changed his mind.

"Never mind that—let me just cross you. That'll do for now. Sit down. And now I'll tell you something that will give you great pleasure, something that's just your kind of thing. It's certain to make you laugh: Balaam's ass here has started talking, and you should hear him talk! It's really something!"

By Balaam's ass Mr. Karamazov meant the twenty-four-year-old servant Smerdyakov—an utterly taciturn and unsociable young man. It was not that he was shy or easily embarrassed. In fact, he was a rather arrogant fellow who seemed to despise everybody. But at this point we really must devote a few more words to him. He had been brought up by Martha and Gregory, but as he grew he felt no gratitude for what was done for him, as Gregory often pointed out, and turned into a wild and solitary boy who seemed to look out on the world from a lonely corner. In his childhood he loved to hang cats and then bury them with great ceremony. On those occasions he would wrap himself in a sheet, pretending it was a surplice, and chant over the dead cat, waving something over its head like a censer. And all this was done in great secrecy. Once, however, Gregory surprised him during such a ceremony and gave him a sound whipping. After that, young Smerdyakov crept into his corner and sat glowering from it for a whole week. "That little freak doesn't like us," Gregory remarked to Martha. "He doesn't like anyone." Then, suddenly addressing Smerdyakov directly, he said: "You aren't a human being—you're made of the slime of the bath-house—that's what you are." And, as it turned out later, Smerdyakov never forgave him for those words. Gregory taught him to read, and when Smerdyakov was twelve he began to teach him the Scriptures, but nothing came of it. When they were on the second or third lesson, Smerdyakov suddenly snorted scornfully.

"What's the matter with you?" Gregory asked, looking at him threateningly over his glasses.

"Nothing. But if God created the world on the first day and the sun, the moon, and the stars only on the fourth day, where did the light come from on the first day?"

Gregory was horrified. The boy was looking at him and grinning. There was scorn in his look. Gregory lost all control.

"This is where it came from!" he yelled, furiously slapping the boy's face. The boy took the slap without protest, and stayed in his corner for the next few days. And it so happened that a week after that he had his first fit of the falling sickness, an ailment that was to afflict him for the rest of his life.

When Mr. Karamazov found out about it, his attitude toward the boy underwent an abrupt change. Until then he had showed very little concern for the boy, although he never scolded him, occasionally gave him a kopek, and when in a good mood, sent him something sweet from his table. But when he heard that the boy was afflicted with the falling sickness, he showed a great deal of concern, and called in a doctor, in the hope that the child could be cured. It turned out, however, that the disease was incurable. The fits occurred irregularly, about once a month. Their severity varied—some were quite mild, others very violent. Karamazov forbade Gregory to raise a hand to the boy to punish him and started to allow young Smerdyakov into the upstairs rooms of his house. He also forbade Gregory to try to teach the boy anything at all. But then one day, when Smerdyakov was fifteen, Karamazov noticed that he was reading the titles of the books through the glass of the bookcase. Karamazov had quite a number of books, a hundred or more, although no one had ever seen him reading one. He at once gave Smerdyakov the key to the bookcase, telling him: "Here, go ahead, read if you feel like it. You'll be the librarian. That's better than running around in the yard. Sit down, then, and read this one." Karamazov handed him Gogol's *Evening on a Farm near Dikanka*. Smerdyakov read it, but he didn't like it; he never smiled once, and when he had finished it, he screwed up his nose in disapproval.

"What's the matter? You don't think it's funny?"

Smerdyakov remained silent.

"Answer me, you fool."

"It's all about a lot of things that aren't true," Smerdyakov mumbled with a smirk.

"All right, the hell with you—you have a flunkey's spirit. No, wait, here's Smaragdov's *Universal History*. It's all about true things. Read it then."

But Smerdyakov could not get through more than ten pages of it: it was too boring. And so, as a result, the bookcase was locked again.

Soon after this Gregory and Martha reported to their master that Smerdyakov had suddenly become peculiarly fastidious. He would, for instance, sit in front of his plate and feel around in his soup with his spoon, as if searching for something, leaning over it, holding up spoonfuls to the light and examining them.

"What have you found there, a cockroach?" Gregory would ask him.

"A fly?" Martha would inquire.

The fussy young man never answered. And it was the same with the bread and the meat and whatever else he ate: he would spear a piece of meat with his fork and then lift it in the air to examine it minutely in the light, giving it a microscopic examination, thoroughly and at great length before finally deciding to put it in his mouth. "Who is this young gentleman we're saddled with?" Gregory and Martha muttered, watching him. But when Karamazov learned of this new development in Smerdyakov, he at once decided that he was destined to be a cook and sent him off to Moscow to be trained.

Smerdyakov spent several years as an apprentice-cook, and when he came back, his appearance had changed a great deal. He had aged tremendously and now looked much older than he was: wrinkled, shriveled, and yellow-faced, he reminded one of a eunuch. But his character was the same as before he had left for Moscow: he was still as unsociable as ever and seemed to have no need whatever for anyone's company. And it was learned later that even in Moscow Smerdyakov had been his usual silent self. The city itself had aroused very little interest in him and, although he learned something there, he paid little attention to the rest. He went to the theater once, but came back bored and displeased. He returned from Moscow wearing good, neat clothes with a clean shirt and underwear. He brushed his suit with great care twice a day. But most of all he loved his beautiful boots, which he took great joy in polishing with English boot polish until they shone like mirrors.

He proved to be an excellent cook. Mr. Karamazov decided to pay him regular wages, which Smerdyakov spent almost entirely on clothes, hair pomades, perfumes, and so on. However, he seemed to despise women as much as he despised men and was cool and distant with them.

Now Karamazov started to look at him again with different eyes. Smerdyakov's epileptic fits became worse and on those days Martha had to cook for the master. Karamazov did not like that at all.

"Why should your fits occur more often now?" he would

mutter sometimes, glaring at his Moscow-trained cook and studying Smerdyakov's face intently. "What about getting married? Would you like me to get you a wife?"

Such suggestions only made Smerdyakov turn pale with indignation, although he never answered anything. Karamazov would throw up his hands helplessly and turn away.

A very important fact is that Karamazov was completely and unshakably convinced that Smerdyakov was honest and would never steal or take anything that wasn't his. Once, when he was drunk, Karamazov dropped three hundred-ruble bills, which he had just received, into the mud of his own courtyard. He only remembered about them the next morning, and then, as he started feverishly searching through his pockets, he saw the three bills lying on his dining table. How had they gotten there? Smerdyakov had picked them out of the mud and put them there. "Well," Karamazov liked to conclude, "I've never known a servant like that!" He gave Smerdyakov ten rubles as a reward. It should be added that Karamazov was not only convinced of Smerdyakov's honesty —he was even fond of him somehow, although Smerdyakov made no exception for him, looking at him with the same jaundiced eye as he looked at the rest of the world and seldom saying anything to him. If at that time anyone had looked at Smerdyakov, he could not possibly have told what he was interested in or what he was thinking about. And yet, sometimes, even in the house, and more often in the yard or as he was walking along the street, he would suddenly stop and stand stock still, deep in thought, for ten minutes or so. A physiognomist might have said that there were no ideas, no thoughts in his head, that it was a sort of contemplation. The painter Kramsky has a remarkable painting called "The Contemplator": a road with a wintry forest in the background and on the road, wearing a ragged coat and felt shoes, stands a lonely, forlorn peasant who has lost his way, and who seems to be thinking hard about something, but is actually not thinking at all, but just "contemplating." If you pushed him, he would give a start and stare at you uncomprehendingly as if you had just awakened him. True, he would collect his wits right away, but if you asked him what he'd been thinking about as he stood there, he would be quite unable to remember. He certainly would remember, however, the inexpressible sensations he experienced during his contemplation. And these sensations would be dear to him and he would treasure them without realizing it himself, indeed, without knowing why or what he would ever do with them. Perhaps, having accumulated in the course of the years a great many such sensations, he would suddenly leave everything behind and go off on a pilgrimage to Jerusalem to seek salvation, or he might just as likely set fire to his own village, or possibly both. There are many contemplators among the simple people. Probably Smerdyakov was one of them; most likely he, too, was eagerly collecting the sensations he experienced, although hardly aware of it himself.

CHAPTER 7

The Debate

But Balaam's ass suddenly spoke up. And the subject was a rather strange one. That morning Gregory had gone in Lukyanov's shop to buy something, and the owner had told him a story about a Russian soldier who, while serving somewhere far away, on the frontier, had been taken prisoner by Asian tribesmen. Under threat of torture, he was ordered to renounce the Christian religion and be converted to the Muslim faith. He refused and underwent the ordeal. They flayed him alive and he died a martyr's death, praising and glorifying Christ. His act of heroism had also been reported that day in the newspapers. It was this that Gregory had mentioned when Mr. Karamazov and Ivan were sitting at table. Mr. Karamazov had always liked to exchange a few words and a joke or two at the end of the meal, while he was having dessert, even with Gregory. And today he was in a gay, exuberant mood. He listened to the story, sipping his brandy, and remarked that the soldier in question ought to be immediately promoted to sainthood and the skin that had been peeled off him sent to some monastery: "You can just imagine all the people who'd go running, and all the money they'd make." When Gregory saw that Karamazov was not in the least moved by his story, and was making the usual irreverent comments, he frowned in disapproval. But Smerdyakov, who was standing by the door, twisted his lips in a sneer. Smerdyakov was often allowed to stand by the table, at the end of the meal, and always took advantage of the privilege when Ivan was there.

"What's the matter with you?" Mr. Karamazov asked,

noticing the sneer and realizing at once that it was directed at Gregory.

"It's about that soldier, sir," Smerdyakov said in an unexpectedly loud, brisk voice. "Even if his act was very brave, I still think he would not have sinned if he had renounced Christ on that occasion, as well as his own baptismal vows, so as to save his life for good works, which in time would have made up for his moment of weakness."

"What do you mean, would not have sinned? You're saying wicked things and you'll go straight to hell for it. They'll roast you there like mutton," Mr. Karamazov declared.

It was just at this moment that Alyosha walked in. As we have seen, Mr. Karamazov was overjoyed at the arrival of his youngest son.

"This is just your subject, your subject exactly," he chuckled gleefully, inviting Alyosha to sit down and listen.

"As for the mutton, sir, that's not so. I won't get into trouble for it there. I couldn't if there's true justice," Smerdyakov declared sententiously.

"What do you mean 'if there's true justice'?" Mr. Karamazov said, gaily egging him on and nudging Alyosha with his knee.

"He's just no good, that's what!" Gregory suddenly blurted out, glaring at Smerdyakov.

"Don't you be in such a hurry to call me names, Mr. Gregory," Smerdyakov parried with quiet self-assurance. "You'd better try to work it out for yourself. If I happen to be in the hands of Christ's enemies and they demand that I curse the name of God and renounce my holy baptism, my reason tells me that I have the right to do it, and that there would be no sin in doing so."

"You've already said that. Don't just keep repeating it again and again—prove it!" Mr. Karamazov said challengingly.

"Just listen to the miserable cook!" Gregory hissed scornfully.

"Again, don't be in too much of a hurry to call me names instead of trying to reason things out, Mr. Gregory, because the moment I say to my captors, 'No, I'm no Christian and I curse my God,' I at once become anathema by God's highest judgment and am banned from the Church, just as if I was a heathen—all that not within a second of when I say it, but the moment I think it; before a quarter of a second has passed after I've thought it, I'm already excommunicated from the Church. Isn't that right, Mr. Gregory?"

He obviously enjoyed addressing old Gregory, although he was really answering Mr. Karamazov's questions. He was very well aware of this, but he pretended it was Gregory who had asked them.

"Ivan!" Mr. Karamazov shouted. "Lean over—I want to whisper something in your ear. It's for your benefit that he's putting all this on," he whispered. "He wants your appreciation, so tell him you appreciate it."

Ivan listened expressionlessly to his father's excited whisper.

"Wait, Smerdyakov, hold your tongue a moment," Mr. Karamazov shouted loudly again. "Lean close to me once again, Ivan."

Ivan bent toward him again, looking perfectly serious.

"I love you as much as Alyosha, you know. Don't think I don't love you. Have some brandy?"

"All right," Ivan said and, looking closely at his father, he thought: "Well, you have quite a load on now." But all the time he watched Smerdyakov with great curiosity.

"You're anathema and you're damned already!" Gregory exploded suddenly again. "And how dare you argue after that, you scum, when . . ."

"Stop that, Gregory, don't keep abusing him like that," Mr. Karamazov interrupted him.

"Why don't you wait a short moment, Mr. Gregory, and hear what I have to say, because I haven't finished yet. Because at the very moment when God damns me, at that exact, precise moment, it's just the same as if I'd become a heathen and my baptism is taken away from me and no longer counts. Don't you agree at least with that?"

"Come, my boy, get to the point quickly," Mr. Karamazov urged, sipping his brandy with relish.

"Well then, if I'm no longer a Christian, it's not a lie I told my torturers when they asked me whether I was a Christian or not. Because by that time God Himself had stripped me of my Christianity, just for having thought it, before I even said one word to them. And if I was already stripped of it, how could they accuse me in the other world of renouncing Christ since, before I could renounce Him, I had already been deprived of my baptism? It's the same as for a pagan Tartar: who could hold him responsible, even in heaven, Mr. Gregory, for not having been born a Christian, and who would want to punish him for that,

since no one can strip two hides off the same ox? Besides,
God Almighty Himself, even if He decides to punish the
Tartar after he dies (since it's impossible not to punish him
at all), would give him only a very small punishment, considering that a Tartar cannot be blamed for having been
brought into this world by infidel parents. For how could
God Almighty treat a Tartar, who was brought before Him,
like a Christian? That would be just like God Almighty
telling an untruth. And how could the ruler of heaven and
earth tell a lie, even one single lie?"

Gregory stood there dumbfounded, staring at the speaker
with his eyes popping out of his head. He had not followed
very well what Smerdyakov was saying, but then he suddenly
grasped what it was all about and stood there, looking like a
man who had butted his forehead against a wall in the dark.
Mr. Karamazov took the last sip of his brandy and burst into
a shrill laugh.

"Alyosha, Alyosha, my boy, what do you say to that? Ah,
what a casuist he has turned out to be! Ivan, I bet he picked
it up from the Jesuits somehow. Ah, it smacks of the Jesuits,
Smerdyakov. Who taught you all that? But you're talking
nonsense, you casuist. It's all false, false, false! Don't weep,
Gregory—we will at once annihilate his argument, reduce it
to dust and ashes. Now, you tell me, Balaam's ass—let's
assume then that you're in the hands of your captors and,
whichever way you put it, you do renounce your faith at a
given point, whether in words or in thought, and just as you
said yourself, at that very instant you become anathema.
Surely you don't expect them to pat you on the back in the
other world for being anathema, or do you? What do you say
to that, my beautiful Jesuit? Let's hear it!"

"Within myself I've renounced my faith—that's for sure.
But I still say there's no special sin in it, or if there is it can
only be a very ordinary sin."

"But why is it only a 'very ordinary sin'?"

"You're lying, you . . . damn you!" Gregory hissed.

"Try to reason it out for yourself, Mr. Gregory," Smerdyakov went on solemnly and imperturbably, the magnanimous
winner of a debate lecturing his routed opponent. "It says in
the Scriptures that if you have as much as a grain of faith
and if you ask a mountain to move into the sea, it will do so
at once and without delay, the second you ask it. So, Mr.
Gregory, since you're a believer and I'm an unbeliever—for
which you keep reproaching me—why don't you try asking

the mountain to slide not even all the way into the sea (because there's no sea anywhere near here) but just down into our stinking little river, the one that runs behind our garden. If you do, you'll see for yourself that nothing will move, that everything will remain where it is, even though you shout all you want, and that should prove that you too, Mr. Gregory, do not have the true faith, which you like to reproach others for lacking. And again, if we remember that in our times, not just you but absolutely everybody is without faith, everybody from the most important people down to the lowliest peasants, and that there is no one who could make the mountain slide into the sea, except perhaps one or at the most two men, seeking salvation secretly somewhere in the Egyptian desert where we couldn't even find them—well then, if nobody has faith, does it follow that God will damn the whole population of our earth, except maybe those two men in the desert, and that with all His infinite mercy He will forgive no one? And, therefore, I too hope that, even after having doubted once, I will be forgiven when I shed tears of repentance."

"Wait, wait!" Mr. Karamazov shrieked in a transport of delight. "So, after all, you do believe there are two fellows who can move mountains, right? I want you to take note of that, Ivan, to write it down: it's so typically Russian!"

"You're quite right that it's typical of the national character," Ivan said with an approving smile.

"Good, you agree then! It must be true if you agree! What about you, Alyosha my boy? You agree too, don't you? This is typical of the way Russian people believe, isn't it?"

"No, Smerdyakov's faith isn't Russian," Alyosha answered quietly and firmly.

"I wasn't talking about faith in general, but about that particular trait, about those two hermits, about just that small detail which is so completely Russian—it's typically Russian, isn't it?"

"Yes, that detail is very Russian," Alyosha said, and smiled.

"Those words of yours, Balaam's ass, are worth their weight in gold, and I'll see to it that you get a gold piece today. But as for the rest, you're full of wind and nonsense. For your information, you fool, the reason we generally lack faith is that we refuse to give it serious thought. We're much too busy. First of all, we're too much involved in our personal affairs; and secondly, God hasn't given us enough time for it: with twenty-four hours in the day we can't even get enough sleep, let alone repent our sins. But when you give up your faith under torture, you do it at a time when you have nothing else to do but think about that faith of yours, and that is just the proper time to stand up for it! And so it does constitute a sin, doesn't it, my good man?"

"It does, Mr. Gregory, it does," Smerdyakov said, again addressing Gregory instead of Mr. Karamazov, "but if you look at it, you'll find that that only makes it easier on you. Why, if I truly believed at that moment, it would be a real sin for me to renounce my faith and to accept the faith of the infidel Muslims. But then it would never even come to torture, because I'd only have to say to that mountain, you know, 'Move, come over here and crush my captors,' and it would come at once and crush them like cockroaches, and I'd just walk off unharmed, praising and glorifying my God. But what if I'd already tried all that and called out to the mountain to come and crush my captors and the mountain hadn't even budged? Tell me, please, how could I have helped doubting, especially at a moment of such deadly danger? Even without that, I know I won't be admitted straight into the kingdom of heaven (the mountain not moving when I ask it to shows that they don't believe very much in my faith up there, and so I can't expect too great a reward when I get there), and so what good would it do me if, on top of that, I allowed those people to flay me alive without getting anything in return for my pains? Because, even if I called out to the mountain to move when the infidels were already half way through skinning me, even then it wouldn't budge an inch. Besides, at a moment like that, a person could not only begin doubting, but might very well lose his reason as well and be completely unable to think after that. So if I can't win either way, who can blame me too much for at least trying to keep my hide on my back? And therefore, trusting in our Lord's mercy, I hope I'll be entirely forgiven . . ."

CHAPTER 8

Over Brandy

The debate ended suddenly. Mr. Karamazov, who had been in such a happy mood, frowned strangely. He frowned and gulped down his glass of brandy. And that was one glass too much.

"Ah, get out of here, you bunch of Jesuits!" he shouted at the servants. "On your way, Smerdyakov! I'll send you the gold piece I promised you, but I want you out of here now. And you, Gregory, don't whimper. Go to Martha—she'll make you feel better and put you to bed. These animals won't give one a chance to relax in peace after dinner."

Now Mr. Karamazov's voice became peevish and irritated. The servants left the room at once.

"Smerdyakov comes and hangs around every day after meals now," he added, turning to Ivan. "I think it's you he's so interested in—what did you do to impress him so much?"

"I didn't do anything at all," Ivan said, "and I don't know why he should think so highly of me. As for me, I think he's a flunkey and a yokel, but also a forerunner of progress, raw material for the coming era."

"Forerunner of progress?"

"Eventually there'll be better material too, but some of it will be of this quality. First there will be the likes of him, then there'll be better ones."

"And when will that be?"

"When the fuse is lighted. But perhaps it will fizzle out before anything happens. For the moment, the masses are none too eager to listen to what cooks like him have to say."

"That's just it, my boy. Balaam's ass broods in silence and then, all of a sudden, he comes out with God knows what."

"He just stores up ideas," Ivan said with a crooked grin.

"You see, I know very well he hates me, just as he hates everybody, including you, even though you have the impression that he thinks highly of you. And he certainly despises our poor Alyosha here. But the good thing about him is that he won't steal, doesn't talk much, and won't gossip about what goes on in this house, and he bakes a good meat pie. But why should we bother to talk about him—the hell with him."

"Yes, he's certainly not worth it."

"And as to the ideas he may get into his head—well, I've always been of the opinion that the best way of handling the ordinary Russian is to flog him: he's a scoundrel and there's no need to be sorry for him. Thank God he still gets his birching occasionally. Russia is rich in birch. If the Russian forests were destroyed, it would be the end of Russia. I'm all for clever people. Now we've stopped flogging them, our peasants who have sense enough have started flogging themselves. And they're doing the right thing. For whatever you sow, you shall reap, or however the saying goes . . . In any case—you shall reap. Russia is just a nasty mess. Ah, my friend, if only you knew how I hate Russia . . . That is, not Russia, but all these birchings, floggings, although, yes, I must say I loathe Russia too. *Tout cela c'est de la cochonnerie.* You know what I like? I like wit."

"You've just emptied another glass. I think you've had enough to drink."

"Not yet: one more and then another one and that will be all. But I was trying to say something when you interrupted me. Once, passing through Mokroye, I asked an old peasant about flogging. 'What we like best of all,' he told me, 'is to have girls sentenced to be flogged and then to flog them. We let our lads do the flogging. For the girl the lad flogs today he'll marry tomorrow. So,' he said, 'it suits the girls too.' Talk of the Marquis de Sade! But whatever you say, it *is* witty! Wouldn't it be nice if we all went to have a look too? Well, what do you say, Alyosha, my pet? Why, you're blushing! Don't be so bashful, my child. What a shame I didn't stay for lunch at your father superior's—I could have told them about those Mokroye girls being flogged. All right, Alyosha, don't be angry with me because I offended your father superior. It makes me furious, though, when I think of it: if God exists, then no doubt I've sinned and I'll answer for it; but if there is no God, I didn't offend them nearly enough, those holy fathers of yours. If there's no God, chopping off their heads wouldn't be sufficient, for they're holding up progress. Will you believe me, Ivan, if I tell you I take it as a personal offense? No, I can see by your eyes that you don't believe me. You believe those who say I'm nothing but a buffoon. What about you, Alyosha, do you believe I'm more than just a buffoon?"

"Yes, I believe you are not just a buffoon."

"And I believe you believe it and that you're sincere. You look sincere and you talk sincerely. But not Ivan. Ivan is proud and condescending . . . Nevertheless, I'd do away with your lousy monastery; I'd like to take all that mystical stuff and sweep it out of Russia altogether and finally bring all those fools to their senses. And think of all the gold and silver the government could recover for the mint!"

"But there's no need to do away with it all," Ivan said.

"No need? But that would bring the hour of truth closer."

"But the moment truth triumphs, you'll be the first to be robbed and then . . . then eliminated altogether."

"You don't say! Well, I believe you may be right at that: I'm a real fool, I see!" Mr. Karamazov cried, tapping himself on the forehead. "All right then, let the monastery stand, Alyosha, if that's how it is. But that shouldn't prevent us, the clever people, from sitting in a warm house and putting brandy to good use. You know what, Ivan, everything must have been arranged this way by God Himself. I'm sure of it. Tell me, Ivan, is there a God or not? Seriously, tell me. Why are you laughing now?"

"I'm thinking of your witty remark about Smerdyakov's faith in the existence of the two saints who could move mountains."

"Why, is there any connection between that and what I just said?"

"A considerable connection."

"Well, so I'm a Russian too, and I have that Russian trait. Even in you, philosopher that you are, it must be possible to discover it, too, if one catches you unawares. Do you want me to try to catch you? But first I want you to answer my question: Is there a God or not? But I want you to be serious. I want your serious opinion."

"No, there is no God."

"What about you, Alyosha—is there a God?"

"Yes, there is."

"And what about immortality, Ivan? I mean, isn't there any immortality at all? Not even a tiny little bit?"

"No, there's no immortality either."

"None at all?"

"None whatsoever."

"You mean there's just nothing, just a vacuum? Perhaps there's something or other? Not nothing . . ."

"No, there's absolutely nothing."

"Now you, Alyosha. Is there immortality?"

"Yes."

"There is God and there is immortality then?"

"Yes, both God and immortality. And immortality is in God."

"Hm. Most likely it's Ivan who's right. Think how much faith and energy men have devoted to that dream, how much strength has been wasted on it, and for thousands of years! Once more, for the last time: Is there or isn't there a God? I want a final, definite answer."

"For the last time—there is no God."

"Well, who can be playing that joke on men, then, Ivan?"

"The devil, probably," Ivan said with a vague smile.

"The devil exists then?"

"No, the devil doesn't exist either."

"Now that's a real shame. Ah hell, I can't even think what I would do to whoever it was who first invented God. Hanging would be too good for him."

"If they hadn't invented God, there would have been no civilization today."

"No civilization without God? Why?"

"Nor would there be any brandy. I must take that brandy away from you."

"Wait, wait, my boy, just one more little glass. I think I've offended Alyosha. Are you angry with me, Alexei? Ah, my sweet little Alyosha!"

"No, father, I'm not angry—I know your ideas. But your heart is better than your head."

"*My* heart is better than my head? Good God, look who's talking. Tell me, Ivan, do you like Alyosha?"

"I do."

"I want you to like him," Mr. Karamazov said, now visibly drunk. "Listen, Alyosha, I was rude to your elder. I was excited then . . . But I can see now that the elder has wit. What do you say, Ivan, does he have wit?"

"I suppose he has. You might call it that."

"He has, I'm sure: *il y a du Piron là-dedans.** That is— he's a Russian Jesuit. Being a man of noble feelings, he must hide his anger at being forced to playact, to wrap himself in a veil of saintliness."

"I don't see why—he, for one, does believe in God."

"He doesn't believe a bit. Didn't you know? He admits it to everybody—that is, not to everybody, but to every intelligent visitor who comes to see him. Once he even said to Governor Schultz: '*Credo,* but I'm not sure in what.'"

"Did he really say that?"

"Yes, that's just what he said. I respect him for it. There's something of a Mephistopheles in him, or rather something of that character in Lermontov's *Hero of Our Times,* Arbenin —or whatever his name was. I mean, he's a sensualist, such a sensualist that I would worry about my daughter or

* Alexis Piron (1689–1773), French poet with a certain reputation for bawdiness, author of *La Métromanie.* [A. MacA.]

my wife if she went to him to confess. You know, when he begins telling his stories . . . Two years ago, he invited us to tea. He served some liqueur too—the liqueur those rich ladies send him. And then he started telling us things. We thought we'd burst our insides laughing . . . There was one story especially, about how he'd cured a paralyzed lady: 'If my legs didn't ache so,' he says, 'I'd show you a dance you've never seen before.' What do you say to that? 'I've pulled a lot of tricks in my life,' he says. Why he even told us he'd managed to relieve Demidov—the merchant, you know—of sixty thousand rubles . . ."

"What do you mean by relieve him of it? Did he steal the money?"

"Well, Demidov brought it to him, as an honest man: 'There will be a search of my place tomorrow,' Demidov told him. 'Would you keep it for me?' Well, he kept it all right. 'Why,' he told the merchant later, 'you gave it to the Church.' 'You're a lousy crook,' Demidov told him. 'No,' he answered, 'I'm not a crook—I'm a generous man . . .' But it wasn't really the elder, it was someone else. I've got a bit mixed up. Well, one more glass and that'll be all. You can take the bottle away, Ivan. I was talking nonsense just now. Why didn't you stop me, Ivan, why didn't you tell me I was talking nonsense?"

"I knew you'd stop by yourself."

"You're lying. You didn't stop me because you hate me. That was the only reason. You despise me. You've come to see me and you despise me in my own house."

"Well, I'm leaving soon. But in the meantime you've had too much brandy."

"I've begged you, in the name of Christ, to go to Chermashnya for me for a day or two, but you won't go."

"I'll go tomorrow if you really insist."

"I don't believe you will. What you really want is to keep an eye on me here all the time, you spiteful son, and that's why you don't want to go."

Nothing would calm the old man now—he had reached the dangerous line of drunkenness beyond which some drinkers, peaceful until then, deliberately try to lose their tempers and to assert themselves.

"Why are you looking at me with those eyes? Those eyes of yours, they're looking at me and saying 'Ah, you lousy, drunken swine!' They're sly and full of contempt, your eyes.

I don't trust them . . . You must've had some scheme when you came here. You're not at all like my Alyosha—when *he* looks at me, his eyes beam. He doesn't despise me. You mustn't like Ivan, Alexei, you mustn't . . ."

"There's no reason for you to be angry with Ivan," Alyosha said with a strange insistence. "Stop saying insulting things to him. Leave him in peace."

"Oh, all right, all right . . . Ugh, I have a headache. Take that brandy away, Ivan. That's the third time I've told you . . ." He suddenly lapsed into dreaminess, then, grinning broadly and slyly, said: "Don't be angry with a senile old man, Ivan. I'm well aware that you don't like me, but still, don't be angry with me. Besides, there's no reason at all why you should love me. Go to Chermashnya for me and I'll soon follow you there myself and bring you some presents. I'll show you a girl there I've had my eye on for quite a while. She goes around barefoot still, but there's no reason why that should frighten you; don't turn up your nose at barefoot beggar girls. They're real pearls!"

And smacking his lips noisily, he kissed the tips of his fingers.

"To me," he said, suddenly snapping out of his drunken torpor as he stumbled onto his favorite topic, "to me—there's no such thing as a repulsive woman. That's my motto, children, my own dear little suckling pigs. In all my life I've never met a woman who was repulsive to me! Do you understand? But how can you understand, though: you have milk instead of blood in your veins. You're not mature yet! According to my idea, you can find something devilishly interesting in every woman, something you won't find in any other. But then, you need to know how to find it and that takes talent! No woman is to be sneezed at. The mere fact that she's a woman is already half of it . . . But how could you understand that? Even in an old maid you sometimes stumble across such a treasure that you're amazed that so many fools can have allowed her to grow old without ever noticing her! Barefoot beggar girls and ugly women must first be taken by surprise—that's how you get them. Why, didn't you know that? Yes, you must amaze her, bewilder her, make her feel utterly befuddled and embarrassed by the fact that a fine gentleman like you could ever take a fancy to such a rough, coarse creature. It is really a marvelous arrangement in this world that there are gentlefolk and common people. There will always be some lovely scullery maid for her master, and that's all that's needed to make one happy! Wait, Alyosha, my boy, listen to this now: I always used to surprise your late mother, but that was different. For long periods I'd stay without touching her, without saying a kind word to her, and then, at the right moment, all of a sudden I'd sort of melt before her, go down on my knees, kiss her feet, and in the end I always succeeded in getting her into such a state that she would let out that nervous little tinkling, cracked laugh of hers. Only she had a laugh like that, and I knew that was how her fits always started. The next day she'd go into her hysterical screaming like a village girl. And that little laugh of hers wasn't an indication of pleasure, but still, even though I knew all that, it was just as if it did indicate rapture. So you see what it means to be able to find the unique trait in everybody! There was that fellow Belyavsky, rich, good-looking, and all, who took a fancy to her and would hang around here all the time. Well, one day he suddenly slapped me in her presence. You should have seen that meek lamb pounce on me! I thought she was going to attack me herself for that slap. 'You had your face slapped, slapped,' she kept repeating. 'You were trying to sell me to him and he slapped your face! How did he dare slap your face, and in my presence too! Don't you ever come near me again! Never, never, never! Go on, get out, run after him and challenge him at once to a duel!' I had to take her to the monastery that day and have the holy fathers lecture her on meekness and calm her down. But I swear to you by God Almighty, Alyosha—I never did anything to hurt my hysterical wife. Well, once perhaps . . . It was during the first year of our marriage still. She really did a lot of praying then, especially during the holidays of our Lady, when she used to drive me away from her and make me sleep in my study. So I decided to try to beat that mystic stuff out of her. 'Look,' I said to her, 'see this icon of yours? I know you think it works miracles, but you watch: I'm about to spit on it and you'll see that nothing will happen to me.' The way she looked at me, I thought she'd kill me, but she only jumped up, threw up her hands in despair, then, covering her face with them, started to shake, and fell to the floor . . . Alyosha, Alyosha! What's the matter?"

Karamazov leapt up from his seat in a fright. From the moment he had started talking about his mother, a gradual change had come over Alyosha's face. The blood rushed to his cheeks, his eyes glowed, his lips quivered . . . But the drunken old man went on spluttering, noticing nothing, until something very strange happened to Alyosha—an exact repetition of what had happened to the boy's mother on the occasion which he had just recounted. Alyosha suddenly leapt up from his seat, just as his mother had, threw up his hands, covered his face with them, then collapsed back into his chair as though his legs had been pulled out from under him, and suddenly started shaking in a succession of hysterical, violent, soundless sobs. The boy's uncanny resemblance to his mother at that moment amazed the old man.

"Ivan, Ivan, quick—get some water . . . He's just like her, exactly, just like his mother! Spit some water out at him from your mouth—I used to do that to her. It's because he feels for her, for his mother, he feels sorry for her . . ." Karamazov kept muttering.

"As far as I understand, his mother happens to have been my mother too, or wasn't she?" Ivan said. There was cold contempt and a note of anger in his voice. The old man looked at him and shuddered before the strange glare in his son's eye. And then something very strange happened, although it lasted for only one second: it somehow really escaped Karamazov's mind that Alyosha's mother was also Ivan's mother.

"What are you saying—your mother? . . ." he muttered uncomprehendingly. "What are you talking about? Whose mother? Why, was she . . . Ah, damn it, of course! Yes, of course, she was your mother too! It was like an eclipse, a blackout—I've never experienced that before. Forgive me, please, I was under the impression, Ivan, that—ha-ha-ha!" He stopped short. A broad, drunken, almost meaningless grin appeared on his face.

At that very second all hell seemed to have broken loose in the entrance hall. There was a terrible din, loud banging and frantic shouting. The door opened and Dmitry burst into the room.

The old man rushed to Ivan in terror.

"He'll kill me! He'll kill me! You mustn't let him, you mustn't!" he screamed, clutching at Ivan's jacket.

CHAPTER 9

The Sensualists

Gregory and Smerdyakov rushed in right behind Dmitry. Obeying instructions their master had given them a few days earlier, they had tried to stop him by force, to bar him from entering the house. As Dmitry, after bursting into the room, stopped for a second to look around, Gregory dashed around the table to the opposite side of the room, closed the double doors leading to the interior of the house, spread his arms crosswise, and stood there barring the entrance with his body, looking determined to defend this passage, as they say, with the last drop of his blood. When Dmitry saw his maneuver, he let out a cry, or rather an animal snarl, and pounced on Gregory.

"So she's in there! She must be in there! You've hidden her! Get out of my way, you scum!"

He clutched at Gregory to pull him away, but Gregory pushed him off. Beside himself with fury, Dmitry swung his fist and hit Gregory with all his strength. The old servant went down as if felled by an axe. Dmitry jumped over the prostrate body and pushed the doors open. During all this time, Smerdyakov, pale and trembling, had stayed in the opposite corner of the room, huddling close to Mr. Karamazov.

"She's here!" Dmitry yelled. "I saw her just now, coming this way. I couldn't catch her . . . Where is she, where?"

Dmitry's yell, "She's here!" had an unexpected effect on the older Karamazov—all fear suddenly left him.

"Hold him, hold him!" he screamed and rushed in pursuit of Dmitry.

In the meantime Gregory had struggled back to his feet, but he still seemed badly shaken. Ivan and Alyosha ran after their father. Two rooms away, something fell to the floor with a crash and broke: in his wild rush, Dmitry had upset a large but not particularly expensive glass vase that stood on a marble table.

"Get him, get him, help!" Mr. Karamazov kept shouting.

Ivan and Alyosha caught up with the old man and brought him back forcibly to the living room.

"What are you doing?" Ivan shouted angrily at his father.

"Going after him like that, you're just asking for it—he'll really kill you!"

"Vanya, Alyosha, my dear boys, does that mean that Grushenka came? Why, he said himself that he saw her coming this way . . ."

He was out of breath. He had not expected her to come that night, and now the idea that she might have come was driving him out of his mind. He was shivering all over; he looked quite insane.

"But you know she's not here. You'd have seen her come in!" Ivan shouted in his ear.

"What about the back entrance? She could . . ."

"You know it's locked and you have the key."

At that moment, Dmitry reappeared in the living room. He had, of course, found the back entrance locked and, as Ivan had remarked, the key was in their father's pocket. All the windows in every room were also closed, locked from the inside. There was, therefore, no way that Grushenka could have come in or got out.

"Grab him!" Karamazov shrieked at the sight of Dmitry. "He has stolen the money from my bedroom!"

With a sudden jerk, he broke loose from Ivan's grip and rushed at Dmitry. Dmitry raised his hands, seized the few remaining tufts of hair on either side of the old man's head, pulled him off his feet, and hurled him down on the floor with a great crash. Then, before his brothers could stop him, he managed twice to ram his heel into his father's face. A piercing moan escaped from the old man. Ivan, although less strong than his older brother, grabbed him by the waist from behind and pulled him away from his father, while Alyosha from the front pushed him back with all his strength.

"You're crazy!" Ivan shouted. "You've killed him, you madman!"

"Serve him right!" Dmitry snarled breathlessly. "And if I haven't killed him this time, I'll come back. You won't stop me!"

"Get out of here, Dmitry, at once!" Alyosha cried in a commanding voice. "Go."

"Alexei! You tell me, for you're the only one I'll believe: was she here just now or not? I just saw her myself turning in here from a backstreet and slipping along the fence . . . I called out to her and she ran . . ."

"You have my word that she wasn't here and that no one here was even expecting her!"

"But I saw her . . . That means that she . . . I'll find out where she is right away . . . Good-by, Alexei. It's not the moment, of course, to ask the old ape for the money—so don't. But go at once to Katerina's, give her my regards, and say farewell to her for me. Yes, my best regards, just like that. And describe this scene to her too."

Ivan and Gregory had raised the old man from the floor and sat him in an armchair. His face was covered with blood, but he had regained consciousness and was listening intently to what Dmitry was saying. He was still under the impression that Grushenka was really there, hiding somewhere in the house.

As he was leaving, Dmitry glared at him with loathing.

"I'm not sorry to see you covered with blood like that!" he shouted. "Watch out, old man, you'd better be careful with your plans because I have some plans of my own! I disown you as my father from now on, and I wish you damned!" And he rushed out.

"I'm sure she's here, I'm sure!" the old man whispered hoarsely and hardly audibly. "Smerdyakov, come here, Smerdyakov . . ." and he beckoned to his servant with his finger.

"She's not here," Ivan said irritatedly. "You're really a crazy old man! Hey, he's fainted again . . . Smerdyakov, get me some water and a towel. Move!"

Smerdyakov hurried out to get some water.

Finally they undressed the old man, carried him to his bedroom, and put him to bed, wrapping his head in a wet towel. With all the brandy inside him and after the violent emotion and the blows he had received, Karamazov fell asleep as soon as his head touched the pillow. Ivan and Alyosha then went back to the living room. Smerdyakov was carrying out the pieces of broken glass. Gregory stood by the table, looking gloomily at his feet.

"Shouldn't you put a wet towel around your head too, Gregory?" Alyosha said to him. "Don't worry, we'll look after father . . . You know, Dmitry gave you a pretty bad whack . . ."

"He dared to lift his hand to me!" Gregory said grimly and clearly.

"He dared rather more than that—he did the same thing to his own father," Ivan said with a crooked grin.

"I used to bathe him in a trough and he dared to do that to me," Gregory repeated.

"Hell, if I hadn't pulled him off, I suppose he'd have killed him—how much more could the old fool take . . ." Ivan whispered.

"God forbid," Alyosha said.

"Why God forbid?" Ivan continued in the same whisper, his mouth crooked with spite. "If one wild beast devours another, it's good riddance to both of them."

Alyosha shuddered.

"It goes without saying that I'll try to prevent the murder, just as I did now . . . Say, Alyosha, would you stay here for a bit while I go out and get some fresh air? I've got a headache from all this."

Alyosha went into his father's bedroom and sat by the old man's bed behind the screen for an hour or so. Mr. Karamazov suddenly opened his eyes and stared at Alyosha for a long time, apparently trying to remember exactly what had happened. Abruptly the expression on his face changed and he became very agitated.

"Alyosha," he whispered, looking around fearfully, "where's Ivan gone?"

"He had a headache and went outside. He's here. He's keeping an eye out for anything that might happen."

"Give me that mirror over there."

Alyosha handed him a small, round folding mirror that stood on the chest of drawers. The old man looked in the mirror: his nose was very swollen and over his left eyebrow was a large purplish bruise.

"What did Ivan say, Alyosha? You know, you're my only true son: I'm afraid of Ivan, even more than of the other one. You're the only one I'm not afraid of."

"You mustn't be afraid of Ivan. He's angry with you, but he'll protect you."

"And what about the other one, Alyosha? He ran to Grushenka's, didn't he? Now tell me the truth, my dear boy, was Grushenka here when all that happened?"

"No one saw her. You're wrong—she never came here."

"Did you know that that no-good Dmitry wants to marry her?"

"She won't marry him."

"Right: she won't, she won't, she won't!" old Karamazov cried in joyful agitation. There was apparently nothing he wanted to hear more than that assurance. He was so moved that he seized Alyosha's hand and pressed it to his heart, tears filling his eyes.

"Alyosha," he said, "that icon of the Mother of God, your

mother's, you know, the one I was telling you about this evening—well, take it and keep it . . . And I allow you to go back to your monastery . . . I didn't mean what I said then seriously. It was just a joke. Forgive me. My head is awfully sore, Alyosha . . . Be a real angel, my dear boy, put my heart at rest, tell me the truth . . ."

"What again—whether she's been here or not?" Alyosha said sadly.

"No, no, not that. I believe what you told me before. What I want you to do is to go over to Grushenka's, or meet her somehow or other—but as soon as possible, because there's a great, great hurry—and ask her, or somehow find out the truth, whom she really intends to take—him or me? What do you say? Will you do it or not?"

"I'll ask her if I see her . . ." Alyosha mumbled, visibly embarrassed.

"No, that's not good enough—she won't tell you," the old man interrupted him. "She's a fickle thing, quite unpredictable—she may start kissing you and tell you it's really you she wants. She's a liar and quite shameless. No, you really mustn't go to her place."

"Yes, father, it wouldn't be right for me to go to see her, it wouldn't be right at all."

"But where was Dmitry sending you when he was shouting, 'Go and see her!' just before he left?"

"It was Katerina he wanted me to see."

"Did he send you there to get money from her, to ask her to give him some money?"

"No. It was not to get money from her."

"But I know he hasn't got any money. I know for sure he hasn't a penny. You know what, Alyosha—I'll sleep on it, and in the meantime you can go. Who knows, perhaps you'll run into her. But be sure to come and see me tomorrow morning. I'll tell you something very important then. Will you come?"

"I will."

"If you come, make it seem as though you came on your own, just to find out how I feel. Don't tell anyone I asked you specially to be here. And don't tell Ivan either."

"All right."

"Good-by, my dear boy, I'll never forget that you came to my defense tonight. I'll remember that as long as I live. And I'll tell you something tomorrow. But I must do some thinking first . . ."

"How do you feel now?"

"I'll be up and about tomorrow. I'm quite all right really. I feel fine, perfectly fine!"

As Alyosha crossed the courtyard, he saw Ivan. He was sitting on a bench and writing something in a notebook with a pencil. Alyosha told him that their father had woken up, that his head had cleared completely, and that he had said Alyosha could return to the monastery.

"I'd very much like to see you tomorrow morning, Alyosha, if you can make it," Ivan said.

He had risen when he saw his brother and his voice sounded warm and friendly; indeed, its warmth rather surprised Alyosha.

"Tomorrow . . ." Alyosha said. "Tomorrow I must go and see the Khokhlakovs, and probably I'll have to go to Katerina's as well, unless I can still see her this evening."

"So you're off to Katerina's now, after all," Ivan said with a smile. "I suppose it's to give her those 'best regards' and say good-by, isn't it?"

Alyosha was very embarrassed.

"I believe I have the whole picture now," Ivan went on, "thanks to those instructions shouted to you, together with some other indications. I assume that Dmitry has asked you to go to her place and tell her from him . . . well, to let her understand that he is . . . so to speak bowing out. Do I have it right?"

"Vanya, how will all this horrible business end between father and Mitya?" Alyosha asked despairingly.

"It's impossible to say for sure. Perhaps nothing will come of it, and it will just peter out by itself. The woman between them is a wild animal. In any case, the old man must be kept inside the house and Dmitry mustn't be allowed to get in."

"There's something else I want to ask you, Vanya: Do you really believe that any man has the right to decide, when he looks at other people, which of them deserves to live and which no longer deserves to?"

"Why bring in this business of deserving? Men usually answer that question without worrying about merit; their answer is determined by much more natural reasons. But a man certainly has the right to wish for whatever he likes, and no one can deprive him of that right."

"Even to wish the death of another man?"

"Well, why shouldn't he wish another man to die? What would be the point of lying to ourselves when that's just how things are in life and, I suppose, it's the only possible way they can be. Are you asking me all this because of what I said about two beasts devouring each other? If so, let me ask you this: Do you think that I'm like Dmitry—capable of smashing the head of . . . well, capable of killing that old fool —do you?"

"How can you ask, Ivan! Nothing of the sort ever entered my mind . . . Besides, I don't think Dmitry's capable of it either, he . . ."

"Well, thank you for that, anyway," Ivan said with a short laugh. "You can count on me to protect him whenever I can. Nevertheless, I reserve to myself complete freedom to wish for whatever I think fit, in this instance as well. So, see you tomorrow. And please don't judge me too harshly, don't consider me a criminal," he added with a smile.

They parted with a warm handshake, warmer than ever before. Alyosha felt that Ivan had, on his own initiative, taken the first step to come closer to him and that he had some reason, some purpose, in taking that step.

CHAPTER 10

Two Women Meet

Alyosha left his father's house even sadder and more depressed than when he had entered it. His thoughts were splintered and scattered and he realized that he was afraid to bring all the fragments together to get a total picture of all the painful and conflicting feelings he had experienced in the course of that day. He was bordering on despair, something that had never happened to him before. Above all his preoccupations, like a mountain, loomed the fateful and unanswerable question: How would it end between his father and his brother Dmitry with that sinister woman between them? Now he had witnessed it himself. He had been there and had seen them facing each other. And Alyosha felt that the one who was likely to be most hurt, hurt horribly in this affair, was Dmitry and that a terrible catastrophe was awaiting his brother. There were other people involved in this affair too, involved much more deeply than Alyosha could have imagined before. There was something puzzling, something mysterious about it all. For instance, his other brother, Ivan, had made a warm gesture toward him, something

Alyosha had been hoping for all this time; but now, for some reason or other, that friendly gesture frightened him. Then, those two women. When, a few hours earlier, he had set out to see Katerina—one of the two—he had been in a state of great embarrassment, but now, on his way to her house, he felt completely at ease. In fact, he was impatient to see her, as though hoping to obtain from her some indication of what he should do next. He realized, though, that it would be even more difficult to transmit Dmitry's message to her now that Dmitry had given up all hope of paying her back the three thousand rubles. Since Dmitry felt disgraced and had no prospects of getting any money, Alyosha knew that his brother would do nothing to prevent himself from slipping lower and lower. And on top of it all, Dmitry had asked him to tell Katerina about the disgraceful scene in their father's house.

It was seven o'clock and just getting dark when Alyosha entered the spacious, comfortable house on Bolshaya Street. He knew that Katerina lived with two aunts—that is, one of these women was actually her sister Agafia's quiet, self-effacing aunt who had lived in her father's house and had looked after Katerina with such devotion when she had come home after her graduation from school. The other, Katerina's real aunt, was an elegant Moscow lady, albeit impoverished. It was said in town that the two aunts did exactly what Katerina wanted and only lived with her as her chaperones for the sake of appearances. As to Katerina, she only listened to the old general's widow, to whom she owed everything she had; the old lady had been kept in Moscow by her sickness and Katerina had to write to her twice a week, to keep her up to date on all the latest developments.

Alyosha entered the house, giving his name to the parlormaid who had opened the door for him. But apparently the ladies in the drawing room already knew of his arrival (they might have seen him from the window). He heard women's hurried footsteps, the rustling of skirts—it sounded to him as if two, or perhaps three, women had hurried out of the drawing room. It struck him as strange that his arrival should cause such a commotion. He was, however, immediately shown into the drawing room.

It was a very large room, elegantly and lavishly furnished, not at all the sort of drawing room one would expect to find in a small provincial town. There were many sofas, settees, armchairs, large and small tables of all kinds with a variety

of vases and lamps on them; there were flowers in the vases
and paintings on the walls, and also an aquarium near one
of the windows. As the day was fading, the room was rather
dark. Looking around him, Alyosha saw on a sofa someone's
silk shawl and on the table next to it two half-empty cups of
chocolate, a plate of cookies, a china dish of raisins and
another of candy. Obviously, people had been sitting there
a moment before. Alyosha frowned, realizing that he had
stumbled on some other visitors, but at that moment the
portiere was raised and Katerina came in. She held out both
hands to him, looking at him with a radiant, happy smile.
Behind her came the maid carrying two candles that she put
on the table.

"Ah, here you are. I'm so glad you came! I've been praying all day that you would come. Do sit down, please."

Katerina's beauty struck Alyosha again, as it had three
weeks or so before, when Dmitry had brought him to introduce him to her, on her insistence that she wanted to meet
his youngest brother. On that occasion, however, they had
not talked to each other very much. Feeling that Alyosha
was very shy of her and wanting to spare him, she had
hardly said anything to him and had talked almost all the
time to Dmitry. But although he had not said much on that
occasion, Alyosha had seen and understood a good deal. He
had been struck by Katerina's domineering ways and by her
casual, easy, self-assured manner. And Alyosha had been certain that she really was as he saw her and that he had not
exaggerated these traits in her. He had thought that her big,
very dark, sparkling eyes, magnificent in themselves, looked
even more impressive in her pale, slightly yellowish, oval
face. But he had also detected in those eyes and in the line
of her lips something that explained not only why Dmitry
had fallen madly in love with her but also what made it
impossible for him to remain in love with her for long.
He had almost told his brother about this when they left
Katerina's the first time, for Dmitry had insisted that Alyosha
tell him what impression his fiancée had made on him.

"You'll be happy with her, but perhaps not . . . perhaps
you won't find peace with her . . ."

"Well, that's how it is, brother! That kind of woman never
changes, never gives in . . . So you don't think I'll always be
in love with her?"

"Why, I didn't say that. Perhaps you'll always be in love
with her, but perhaps you won't always be happy . . ."

As he said this, Alyosha felt that he had turned very red and was furious with himself for having yielded to Dmitry's insistent demand that he say what he thought of Katerina, and for being forced to give such stupid answers. Besides, he felt it was quite ridiculous that he should offer his opinion about a woman, as though he were an expert in such matters.

Now, when he saw her coming toward him, he immediately realized that he might have been wrong about her before. This time, she radiated great warmth and kindness, and complete, uncompromising sincerity. Her arrogant, haughty, domineering airs had vanished; but he saw that her drive, her generosity, and her impressive self-reliance were still there. From the very first words she said, Alyosha realized that her tragic predicament with the man she loved was no mystery to her, that possibly she already knew everything, absolutely everything. Yet, despite all that, there was so much light in her face, so much faith in the future, that Alyosha felt guilty before her; he felt he had done her serious and deliberate harm. She had won him over and captured him in one fell swoop. And with all that, he also realized that she was terribly tense and that her tension had perhaps reached the extreme limits of endurance, causing her to act as though she were in a trance.

"I was so anxious to see you—you're the only one from whom I can learn the whole truth. No one else will tell it to me."

"I've come," Alyosha muttered, feeling he was getting mixed up, "I came . . . he sent me . . ."

"So he sent you—I had a feeling he would . . . All right, now I understand everything!" Her eyes flashed and she suddenly raised her voice. "But let me tell you first, Alexei, why I wanted to see you so badly. You see, perhaps I know much more, as it is, than you do yourself; it's not information I need from you. What I want to hear is your own, personal impression: How did he seem to you when you saw him last? I want you to give me a plain, unadorned, even rude, answer (oh, you may be as rude as you wish!); I want you to tell me what you thought of him and of the situation he's in, after you saw him today. That would be more useful—since he doesn't wish to see me anymore—than if I went and asked him directly. Do you understand now what I want of you? Now tell me why he sent you to me (as I told you, I knew he would send you). Tell me frankly and plainly, without hiding anything from me."

"He asked me to . . . he told me to say good-by to you for him, that he won't come to see you anymore and that . . . that he sends you his regards . . ."

"His regards? That's what he said? Those are his words?"

"Yes."

"Perhaps it was a slip of the tongue? Perhaps he meant to use some other word instead . . ."

"No, he insisted that I give you his regards. He reminded me several times to tell you he sent you his regards. Just that—regards."

The blood rushed to Katerina's cheeks.

"You must help me then, Alyosha. I can't do without your help: I'll tell you what I think and I want you to tell me whether I'm right or not. Listen, if he'd just told you vaguely to say good-by to me on his behalf and to give me his best regards, if he hadn't insisted as he did on the word 'regards'—that would have really been the end of everything. But since he insisted on that word, made you promise not to forget it, then he must have been agitated, not himself—don't you agree? Perhaps he made up his mind, and then was frightened by his own decision. Maybe he didn't walk away from me with a cool, determined step, but took a headlong plunge as though over a precipice? His insistence on one particular word could be simply bravado, couldn't it?"

"Right, right, I think so myself now!" Alyosha agreed with great eagerness.

"And if I'm really right, then he's not lost yet! He's simply in deep despair, and I think I can pull him out of it. Wait now—did he mention anything to you about money, about a certain three thousand rubles?"

"Not only did he mention it, but that was perhaps what worried him most. He told me that, as things stand now, he's dishonored and he doesn't care about anything anymore," Alyosha said, speaking with great heat, with the hope pouring back into him that perhaps there really was a way out, that his brother could still be saved. But then a thought stopped him short and he asked in a different, hesitating tone: "But . . . but, how is it that *you* . . . that you know about the money?"

"I've known about it for a long time, and for certain. I checked by wiring to Moscow to find out whether the money had been received. I knew he hadn't sent it, but I never said anything to him. And last week I found out that he needed more money . . . My only desire in all this is that he should

know who is his true friend and to whom he can turn for
help. But no, he refuses to believe that I am his most loyal
friend. He doesn't want to get to know me really—because
I'm only a woman to him. For a whole week I worried
terribly, for fear he would feel embarrassed in front of me
for having kept and spent that three thousand. I mean, let
him be ashamed before other people, before himself even, but
not before me. Why can't he understand, even to this day,
just how much I can bear for him? Why, why doesn't he
know me yet? How dare he not know me after all that has
happened between us? I want to save him once and for all.
He can forget that we were engaged, if he wishes! But how
can he be afraid of being dishonored in my eyes! After all, he
wasn't afraid to admit that to you, was he, Alexei? Haven't
I deserved, by this time, to be treated as you are?"

Tears filled her eyes as she uttered these last words. And
now they were running down her cheeks.

"He also wanted me to tell you something else," Alyosha
said, his voice quivering. "He wanted me to tell you what
happened between him and his father today."

And he told her everything: how he had been sent to their
father's to get the money from him, how Dmitry had broken
into the house, how he had given his father a brutal beating,
and how, after that, he had again reminded Alyosha to go to
see her—Katerina—and give her his regards.

". . . and then he went to see that woman," Alyosha muttered finally.

"Why, do you suppose I couldn't put up with that woman?
Does he imagine that I wouldn't be able to put up with her?
Besides, he won't marry her, for how could a Karamazov be
eternally consumed by such a passion? And it is passion, not
love, that he feels for her." She let out a nervous laugh.
"Besides, he won't marry her because she will never marry
him," Katerina added with a strange smile.

"He may marry her, though," Alyosha said sadly, looking
down at the floor.

"No, he won't. You can take my word for it. That girl . . .
she's an angel," Katerina cried, her tone suddenly acquiring
extraordinary warmth. "She's a fantastic creature, without
peer! I'm well aware of the fact that she's quite irresistibly
fascinating, but I also know that she's kind and strong and
generous. Why are you staring at me like that, Alexei? Perhaps it surprises you that I should say this; perhaps you
don't believe me? Grushenka, my dear!" Katerina called sud-

denly, looking toward the portiere that separated the drawing room from the room next door. "Please come and join us. I have a very nice visitor here—Alexei Karamazov—he knows all about our affairs. Come in and meet him, my dear."

"I was waiting—I thought you'd call me."

Alyosha heard a tender, almost too caressing voice. The portiere was raised and Grushenka made her entrance. She laughed gaily as she walked over to them. Something snapped inside Alyosha. He knew he was staring, but he could not take his eyes off her. So here she was, that frightful woman, that animal, as Ivan had called her half an hour before. But the woman Alyosha was looking at appeared at first glance to be a quite ordinary, pleasant, kindly person. True, she was beautiful, but beautiful though she was, she looked much like many other "ordinary" beautiful women. But then, in all fairness, it must be said, she was very, very beautiful and her beauty was that typical Russian beauty that inspires passion in so many men. Grushenka was not quite so tall as Katerina, who was very tall indeed. Her body was strong and full and, when she moved, her movements were so light that they seemed inaudible. And, as in her voice, there was perhaps something too provokingly tender, perhaps a touch of deliberate seductiveness, in her movements. Unlike Katerina, whose step was quick and energetic, Grushenka walked noiselessly: her feet touched the floor without a sound. She slid smoothly into an armchair with a soft rustle of her sumptuous black silk dress, drawing an expensive black cashmere shawl delicately around her strong white neck and wide shoulders. She was twenty-two and she looked exactly her age. Her complexion was very fair and her cheeks delicately rosy. Her face was rather broad at the temples and her lower jaw protruded, although only very slightly. Her upper lip was much thinner than the lower, which was quite full. But her magnificent, abundant, dark-brown hair, her sable eyebrows, and her beautiful blue-gray eyes with their long lashes were certain to stop even the least interested, most absentminded man who met her in the street or saw her in a crowd, even if he was in a hurry—he would not be able to help staring at her and remembering her for a long time. What struck Alyosha most about her face was its child-like, trusting expression. She looked like a child who is delighted about something and, as she came toward the table, she looked just that—*delighted*, as though she expected something nice to happen and was full of curiosity and trusting anticipation.

Her gaiety was contagious and Alyosha felt its effect. And there was something else in her too that Alyosha could not have described but that he felt, although perhaps unconsciously—a lightness and softness of movement, a strange, cat-like noiselessness, which was in curious contrast to her large, powerful body. For under the cashmere shawl, he could see her broad shoulders and her full, young bosom. The curves under her dress suggested the proportions of a Venus de Milo, although already somewhat exaggerated. Those who know the beauty of Russian women could have told by looking at Grushenka that, by the time this young beauty was thirty, her body would lose its harmony, her face would grow flabby, wrinkles would appear around her eyes and forehead, her complexion would coarsen, perhaps turn ruddy—in a word, Grushenka had the "beauty of an hour," a fleeting beauty that one so often meets among Russian women.

Of course, this is not what Alyosha was thinking when he saw her. Although he was fascinated by her, he wondered at the same time, with a touch of irritation, why she had to drawl as she did, instead of speaking naturally. Evidently she thought that drawing out certain vowels and modulating certain syllables exaggeratedly made her voice beautiful and attractive. Of course, it was her humble background and lack of education that were to blame; her way of talking was the result of a childhood misconception about proper speech. To Alyosha, however, her accent and her intonations seemed incongruous, incompatible with her happy, child-like expression and the radiant purity of her eyes.

After kissing her warmly several times on her laughing lips, Katerina asked her to sit down in an armchair directly in front of Alyosha. Katerina acted as though she were in love with Grushenka.

"This is the first time the two of us have met," Katerina announced to Alyosha in an excited tone. "It was I who wanted to meet her, to get to know her. I was prepared to go to her place but, as soon as she learned of my wish, she came here herself instead. And I was sure beforehand that we could settle everything between the two of us! I just had a feeling it would be this way . . . Some people tried to convince me not to do it, but I followed my own hunch and I was right! Grushenka has explained everything and told me her plans—like a good angel, she descended and brought peace of mind and joy . . ."

"And you didn't feel you were too good for me, dear, sweet Miss Katerina," Grushenka drawled in her sing-song voice, still radiating her warm, cheerful smile.

"You mustn't say that. You know very well what a bewitching, irresistible charmer you are! How could I possibly have felt I was too good for you? Here, let me kiss once more that lower lip of yours—it's so full, it looks almost swollen, and I'd like to make it even more swollen, again, and again . . . Ah, Alexei, that laughter of hers—it gladdens one's heart to look at this angel."

Alyosha blushed, shaken by tiny, imperceptible shivers.

"You're certainly very sweet to me, Miss Katerina, but you may find that I don't really deserve your kindness."

"How can you say that? How can you not deserve it? I want you to know, Alexei, that Grushenka here is very whimsical, that she can be eccentric, and that she's very, very proud! And she's also generous and magnanimous, Alexei, did you know that? The only trouble was that she was unhappy; she was too willing to sacrifice everything for an unworthy and irresponsible person. There was someone once, also an army officer—she fell in love with him and gave herself to him. That was long ago—five years or so. But he forgot her and married someone else. Now he is a widower and has written that he's on his way here. And you know what? He's the only man she has ever loved, whom she still loves, and whom she will always love. So he will come back and Grushenka will be happy again. During these past five years she has been desperately unhappy. But who can say anything against her? Who can boast of having enjoyed her special favors? There was only one man who was close to her—the bedridden old merchant, but then he was much more of a father, a guardian, to her than anything else. He appeared on the scene when she was in deep despair, when she was disconsolate after having been deserted by the man she loved . . . And, you know, she would have drowned herself if that old merchant hadn't stopped her then . . ."

"You're really defending me too much, dear Miss Katerina. Aren't you a bit quick to draw conclusions?" Grushenka said, still in her drawling voice.

"I—defend you? Who am I to defend you? I would never have the presumption to do that, Grushenka, my dear angel! Give me your hand, Grushenka—look at this tender, plump, charming hand, Alexei! And since the owner of this hand has brought me back to life and made me happy, I will kiss it now, kiss the back of it and the palm, see, and here, and here, and here again." Katerina eagerly kissed Grushenka's really beautiful, although perhaps rather plump hand three times. Grushenka, although she offered her hand quite willingly, watched Katerina with a charming, nervous little laugh, obviously enjoying having her hand kissed by the lady she addressed as Miss Katerina.

Alyosha turned red. "Perhaps," the thought flashed through his head, "she's overdoing her enthusiasm a bit." He felt somehow tense and nervous.

"You know, Miss Katerina, you won't make me feel embarrassed by kissing my hand like this in front of young Mr. Karamazov here," Grushenka said.

"But . . . but I wasn't trying to embarrass you, Grushenka," Katerina said, slightly taken aback. "Ah, how little you understand me, my dear!"

"And perhaps you don't quite understand me either, dear Miss Katerina; perhaps you'll find that I'm not nearly as nice as I seem. I'm headstrong and my heart is wicked. It was just to have a good laugh that I made poor Mr. Dmitry Karamazov so crazy about me."

"Yes, but now you're going to save him. You'll talk reason to him and explain to him that you love another man, that you've loved that other man for a long time, and that now he has asked you to marry him . . ."

"No, no, I never promised you anything of the sort. It was you who said all those things, but I never promised."

"Well, then I must indeed have misunderstood you," Katerina said very quietly, turning slightly paler. "You did promise, though . . ."

"No, my angel, Miss Katerina, I promised you nothing at all," Grushenka interrupted, looking at her with the same cheerful, innocent expression. "You see for yourself, my worthy young lady, how wicked and headstrong I really am, for I'll do whatever I feel like at the particular moment. I may have promised you something before, but just now I thought to myself: 'And what if I take a fancy to him again, that Mitya fellow, since I took a fancy to him once and it lasted nearly a whole hour? I may even go right now and tell him to come and stay with me' . . . That's how fickle I am."

"That's not at all what you said a little while ago," Katerina whispered barely audibly, "not at all . . ."

"Ah, that was a little while ago! But, you see, I'm a bit

soft-hearted and silly. Just think what he's been through because of me, so what if I suddenly feel sorry for him when I get back home? What then?"

"I never expected . . ."

"Well, dear Miss Katerina, I make you look very good—you're so kind and generous compared with me. And I suppose you'll stop loving poor silly me once you've got to know me better. So give me your sweet little hand, Miss Katerina, my angel," Grushenka said in a tender voice, in a tone of great reverence, taking Katerina's hand in hers, "and I will kiss it just as you kissed mine, dear miss. You kissed my hand three times so, to make things even, I should kiss yours three hundred times. Well, that's how it is, and after this, let it be according to God's will. Perhaps I'll end up as your slave and do everything to please you, as a slave must. So let it be just as God decides for us all. There's no need for any arrangements, agreements, or promises between us. Ah, what a pretty hand you have, a sweet, sweet hand. Ah, my dear miss, you're so beautiful it's just impossible!"

Slowly Grushenka raised Katerina's hand to her lips with the strange intention of getting even with her in hand-kissing. Katerina made no effort to pull her hand away. She had listened with still flickering hope to Grushenka's words about the possibility of doing everything to please her one day, like "a slave"; she looked intently into Grushenka's eyes and saw in them still the same cheerful, innocent trustfulness as before. "She may be a little too naive," Katerina thought with a spark of hope, as Grushenka was still slowly raising her hand toward her lips . . .

But when her lips were almost touching Katerina's hand, Grushenka stopped as if something had suddenly occurred to her.

"You know what, Miss Katerina, my angel," she announced in a voice even more sweet and tender than before, "I think I may still decide not to kiss your hand, after all," and she broke into a very cheerful tinkling laughter.

"Please yourself . . ." Katerina said with a shudder, "but why are you doing this?"

"I simply want you to remember that you kissed my hand and I didn't kiss yours." Something suddenly flashed in her eyes and she looked at Katerina with terrible intensity.

"You're an insolent creature!" Katerina flared up. She seemed to have suddenly understood. She leapt up from her chair.

Grushenka stood up too, but unhurriedly.

"And now I'll be able to tell Mitya about you kissing my hand while I wouldn't kiss yours. I can just imagine how he'll laugh! . . ."

"Get out, you filthy slut! Get out of here!"

"Oh, you should be ashamed of yourself, talking like that, dear young lady; you shouldn't use words like that, sweetie."

"Get out, you whore!" Katerina was screaming now, every part of her face quivering and distorted by rage.

"You're a fine one to call me a whore! And what about you, going to visit gentlemen after dark to try and peddle your charms for money? Why, I know all about that."

Katerina let out a wild yell and would have thrown herself on Grushenka if Alyosha had not seized her and held her back with all his strength.

"Don't move," he was saying. "Don't say anything. Don't answer her. She'll go. She'll leave now . . ."

Katerina's two aunts and the maid came running into the drawing room and the three hurried to her.

"Yes, I'm leaving," Grushenka said, picking up her shawl from the sofa. "Please, Alyosha, won't you see me off?"

"Hurry, go, please go," Alyosha said, clasping his hands beseechingly.

"But I want you to see me off, my sweet boy. I promise to tell you something that'll please you very much. It was for your sake, Alyosha, that I put on all this show. See me off now. Later you'll be glad you did."

Alyosha turned away from her, nervously clasping and unclasping his hands. Grushenka, letting out peals of laughter, ran from the room.

Katerina had some kind of fit: she sobbed, shook convulsively, gasped for breath. The women fussed around her.

"I warned you," the older aunt said. "I tried to stop you from doing this . . . You're much too rash. How could you allow this to happen? You know nothing about women of that type, and I've heard that this one is the worst of them all . . . I think you're much too impulsive, Katerina."

"She's a wild beast, that's what she is!" Katerina screamed. "I wish you hadn't held me back, Alexei. I'd have given her such a beating. I'd have beaten her mercilessly!" She could not restrain herself in front of Alyosha, perhaps she did not even want to. "She must be flogged in public . . ."

Alyosha started backing toward the door.

"But, my God!" Katerina cried out in a different voice

now, throwing up her arms in despair. "How could *he* be so dishonorable, so inhuman! He told that creature what happened on that terrible, fateful, accursed day when I was, as she put it, 'trying to peddle my charms for money'—so she knows. Well, for your information, Alexei, your dear brother is a low, despicable man."

Alyosha wanted to say something, but words would not come to him. His heart contracted painfully.

"Go now, Alexei. I feel ashamed, terribly ashamed . . . But please come back tomorrow. I beg you on my knees to come. And I beg you not to judge me too harshly. I still don't know what I'll do with myself!"

Alyosha almost staggered out into the street. He was on the verge of tears himself. The maid came running after him:

"Miss Katerina forgot to give you this letter, sir . . . It's from Mrs. Khokhlakov and she received it at lunch time."

Alyosha took the small pink envelope and put it in his pocket, hardly realizing what he was doing.

CHAPTER 11

One More Reputation Ruined

It was just about a mile from the town to the monastery. Alyosha hurried along the road, which was deserted at that hour. It was almost night and so dark that it was hard to make out anything thirty yards away. About half way, at a crossroads, Alyosha discerned a human shape under a willow tree. When he reached the crossroads, the figure leaped toward him, shouting in a fierce, threatening voice:

"Your money or your life!"

"Why, you . . . Mitya!" Alyosha cried, startled and surprised.

"Ha-ha-ha! You didn't expect me, did you? I said to myself: 'Where should I wait for him?' Near her house? But from there you could have gone three different ways and I might have missed you. So I decided to wait for you here: you were bound to come this way, since there's no other way to get to the monastery. Go on then—tell me the truth and let it crush me like a cockroach! But what's the matter with you?"

"Nothing, nothing, you just frightened me. Oh, Dmitry,

that blood on father . . ." Alyosha began to weep. He had
been on the verge of tears for a long time and now the sobs
finally broke through. "You almost killed him . . . you cursed
him . . . and now you're fooling around . . . 'Your money or
your life' . . ."

"Why, do you think it's unbecoming, doesn't fit the situation, or what?"

"It's not that, I just wanted to say . . ."

"Wait a moment. Just look at this cold, bleak night, at
those big clouds, the wind coming up. So I hid under this
willow here to wait for you. Then I suddenly thought (I swear
I did): 'Why should I have to go on like this? What do I have
to wait for? Here's a tree; I can tie my handkerchief and my
shirt together and use them as a rope, and if that's not
enough, I have my suspenders too. There's no reason why I
should burden the earth and impose my vile presence on
men.' Just at that moment I heard you coming, and something dawned on me: 'Why, there is, after all, a human being
I love, and here he is, this little brother of mine, whom I
love more than anything in the world and who is really the
only person in the world I love!' And I loved you so much,
so much at that second, that I said to myself, 'I must hug
him at once, I must!' But then I had that stupid idea: 'Let me
scare him first, for fun, to amuse him,' and so I hollered like
an idiot, 'Your money or your life.' Well, forgive my horseplay—it was just a stupid idea, that's all. Inside me, though,
I'm quite a mess, you know . . . But the hell with it. Tell me,
then, what happened there? What did she say? Go on, let me
hear it, all of it, don't spare me: was she mad, did she have
a fit?"

"It didn't happen the way you expected, Mitya—it was
different. You see, I saw . . . they were both there, Mitya. I
found both of them there."

"Both of whom?"

"Both Grushenka and Katerina."

Dmitry was stunned.

"You must be raving . . . It couldn't be . . . Grushenka in
her house?"

Alyosha told him all he had seen and heard from the
moment he had stepped into Katerina's house. It took him
ten minutes to tell it all, and it cannot be said that he told it
very smoothly or in the best order. But he gave his brother
an accurate enough picture, repeating the principal words

exchanged, the key gestures, indicating his own reactions by some simple detail. Dmitry listened in complete silence, staring at him in terrible immobility, but Alyosha realized that his brother had already grasped what had happened and understood everything. As Alyosha continued his account, Mitya's face became not only more dejected but also more threatening. He knit his brows and clenched his teeth, and his fixed glare became even more fixed and frightening. This made it all the more unexpected when Dmitry's face, up to that second fierce and angry, underwent a sudden and total transformation: the tightly compressed lips relaxed and he burst into uncontrollable laughter. He literally rolled with laughter and could not talk for quite a while.

"So she wouldn't kiss her hand! You say she got out of there without kissing it!" he yelled with a strange delight, a delight that might have seemed spiteful had it not been so sincere and unaffected. "So the other one called her a wild beast! Well, that's exactly what she is . . . So she said she ought to be flogged in public? That's absolutely true. I've been of that opinion myself all along, and I think a flogging is long overdue! You see, little brother, I don't object to her being flogged, but I'd like first to get cured of her, to get her out of my system. I know her so well, that queen of arrogance, and that hand-kissing incident—that's her all over, the hell cat! She's really the queen of all the world's imaginable she-devils! She's really absolutely marvelous in her own way! And you say she went home from there? Well, I guess I'll be going . . . I'll run over and see her. Don't judge me too harshly, Alyosha, my friend. I can't help it really and, besides, I agree that hanging is too good for her . . ."

"But what about Katerina?" Alyosha asked sadly.

"I see right through that one too, and more clearly than ever now! I have now discovered the four—or is it five—continents of the world! Just think what a move she tried! It seems hard to imagine, doesn't it, that this is the same schoolgirl who wasn't afraid to go to the house of an absurd, uncouth army officer, exposing herself to terrible humiliation, in order to save her father's honor! But her pride, her need to expose herself, to challenge everything and everybody, is just an endless defiance of the world. You told me her aunt said she'd tried to stop her. Well, that aunt is herself a pretty headstrong woman. She's the sister of that general's widow from Moscow and she used to be even more high-and-mighty than her sister until her husband got caught misappropriating government monies and lost everything he had. After that the proud lady quieted down somewhat, and she's stayed pretty quiet . . . So you say she tried to stop Katya, but Katya wouldn't listen to her? Well, she must've thought to herself: 'There's nothing I can't manage, nothing I can't cope with, and if I try, I'll put my spell on Grushenka too, like anyone else.' And she really believed it. If she had such delusions about her powers, who's to blame but herself? But you may think that when she kissed Grushenka's hand it was part of a stratagem, a cunning move to obtain something from her opponent? Well, it was nothing of the sort—she really fell in love with Grushenka, at least, not actually with Grushenka, but with her own idea, her own delusion, because it was *her* idea, *her* delusion. Oh, my dear boy, I can't imagine how you managed to escape unscathed from those two women. I guess you just tucked up your cassock and ran away. Right? Ha-ha-ha!"

"I don't think you even realize, Mitya, how much you hurt Katerina by telling Grushenka about her coming to your place. It was awful when Grushenka hit back at her by saying: 'You're a fine one to talk after trying to peddle your charms.' How could you have insulted Katerina in a worse way than by telling Grushenka that?"

Alyosha was terribly bothered by his brother's apparent delight in Katerina's humiliation, even though he couldn't quite believe it was genuine.

"Wait a minute!"

Dmitry frowned fiercely and slapped his forehead. Only now had his mind registered Katerina's scorn and indignation at his indiscretion, although Alyosha had told him about her remark along with the rest.

"Yes," Dmitry said, "I may very well have told Grushenka about that fateful day, as Katya likes to call it. Yes, yes, I remember now—I told her about it all right! It was that time in Mokroye. I was very drunk and the gypsies were singing . . . But I was sobbing myself as I told her. I was kneeling, holding Katya's little icon before me and praying, and Grushenka understood . . . Yes, at that time she did understand and—I remember now—she cried herself . . . Ah, hell, but how could it be otherwise now? Then she wept and now she plunges the knife into Katya's heart. Well, that's women for you!"

He lowered his eyes and remained deep in thought for a moment.

"But I am a despicable creature, no doubt about it," he announced in mournful tones. "Whether I was sobbing at the time or not changes nothing—I'm low and despicable! Tell her I agree with her, that I deserve the names she calls me, if that makes her feel any better. But enough of this, there's no use wagging our tongues about it. It's not a very cheerful subject anyway. You take your way and I'll take mine. And I don't want to see you again, except as a last resort. Good-by, Alexei."

He squeezed Alyosha's hand hard, still looking down. Then, without raising his eyes, he turned away, walking rapidly toward town. Alyosha followed him for a while with his eyes, unable to believe that his brother would leave him like that. And suddenly Dmitry turned back.

"Wait, Alexei! I must make one more confession, but to you alone!" Dmitry said. "Look at me, look hard: you see, here, here, something terribly dishonorable is being concocted!" And he struck his chest with his fist, as if the dishonorable thing were kept somewhere there, perhaps in a pocket or perhaps around his neck. "You already know what a low, despicable person I am, but I want you to know that, whatever I've done so far, it is nothing compared with the disgrace I am carrying inside my breast this very moment, here, right here, a disgrace that I could stop, for I want you to note, I am completely in control of the situation and could stop it if I so chose. But I won't stop myself and I'll do that dishonorable, disgraceful thing. I told you everything before, everything, but not that, because even I wasn't brazen enough to talk about it. I can still stop myself and, if I did, I would still regain at least part of my honor. But I'm not going to stop. I'll go through with my vile and dishonorable scheme, and I want you to be a witness to my ignominy in advance, to know that I'm acting with the full knowledge of what I'm doing. Death and loneliness! There's nothing more to explain —you'll find the rest out for yourself. There's nothing for me but a stinking alley and that she-cat! Good-by then and don't bother to pray for me—I'm not worth it and, anyway, there's no need, no need at all. The hell with it all!"

And he walked off, this time for good. Alyosha set off for the monastery. "What did he mean when he said he wouldn't see me again? What did he mean by that?" he wondered. The whole thing struck him as absolutely mad. "I'll see him. By tomorrow at the very latest, I must find him . . . Ah, what is he talking about?"

Alyosha skirted the monastery, reaching the hermitage directly by going through the little pine wood. They let him in, although as a rule they didn't open for anyone at that hour of the night. His heart was quivering as he entered the elder's cell. Why did he, Alyosha, have to leave the monastery? Why had the elder told him to go back into the world? Here in the hermitage there was peace and holiness, while outside all was confusion and darkness, in which Alyosha was afraid to lose his way.

The novice Porfiry was in the cell when Alyosha arrived, and also Father Paisii, who had been coming in every hour throughout the day to inquire about Elder Zosima. Alyosha learned with consternation that the elder was getting worse and worse. He had not even been able to hold his regular evening meeting with the monks. As a rule, the monks gathered in the elder's cell in the evening just before they separated for the night, and each monk confessed aloud the sins he had committed that day, his sinful desires, his thoughts and temptations, and also his quarrels with his brother monks, if there had been any. Some of them knelt as they made their confessions, and the elder advised, guided, exhorted, imposed penances, reconciled, gave his blessing, and dismissed them. It was to these informal confessions that the opponents of the institution of elder objected, claiming that they were a profanation of the sacrament of confession and a sacrilege, although they were entirely different from the usual confession. They had even pleaded with the diocesan authorities that such "confessions" not only failed to serve any useful purpose but, indeed, led directly to sin and temptation. They claimed that many monks did not like to go to the evening meetings at the elder's but went, nevertheless, to avoid being accused of pride and disobedience. It was said that some of the monks went to these evening meetings after agreeing among themselves what they would "confess" to the elder. One, for instance, would suggest to another: "I'll tell him I lost my temper with you this morning, and you confirm it"—and this, just to have something to tell, just to satisfy the elder. Alyosha knew that sometimes this was exactly what happened. He also knew that some monks were quite outraged by the custom in the hermitage of first bringing all letters received, even those from relatives, to the elder, who unsealed and read them before handing them over to the recipient. The assumption was, of course, that all this was an act of freely and sincerely accepted obedience and voluntary submission to salutary guidance. Often, however, it was quite insincere and, at times, even contrived and hypocritical. But the older and more experienced monks stood their ground and maintained that those who entered the monastery walls in a sincere search for salvation would find the acts of obedience and self-denial salutary and tremendously rewarding, and that those on whom it weighed and who recriminated against it were not real monks anyway and were just wasting their time in the monastery when they should be outside in the world. Since, they said, it is just as impossible to escape sin and the devil in the church as in the outside world, there was no point in coddling sinners.

Father Paisii blessed Alyosha and told him in a whisper: "He has grown weaker. He sleeps all the time. It's hard to wake him, and it's better not to. He was awake for five minutes, asked me to send his blessings to the monks and to ask them to pray for him during the night. He wants to take the sacrament again in the morning. He asked about you, Alexei, whether you'd left, and we told him you were in town. 'That's where he ought to be,' he said, 'not here—he went with my blessing.' He spoke of you with love and concern. Do you realize what a great honor that is for you? But what made him decide that you should go out into the world now? That means he foresees something in your destiny. You must understand, Alexei, that even if you return to the world, it will be to carry out the task assigned to you by the elder and not for vain pursuits and worldly pleasures."

Father Paisii left. Alyosha was sure now that the elder was dying, although he might still live a day or two. So he firmly and ardently determined to disregard his promises to go and see his father, his brother, the Khokhlakovs, and Katerina, and to stay with his elder in the monastery until the end. His heart was burning with love for the elder and he reproached himself bitterly for having forgotten about the old man, whom he venerated more than anyone in the world, dying in the monastery while he himself had spent the day in town. Alyosha went down on his knees and bowed to the ground before the sleeping elder. The elder lay quite motionless in his sleep, breathing evenly and almost inaudibly; his face was serene.

Alyosha left the elder's bedroom and went into the cell

where Zosima had received his visitors earlier that day. Taking off his boots, he lay down without undressing on the hard narrow leather sofa on which he had slept every night for a long time now, bringing only his pillow with him. As to the mattress his father had mentioned, he had long since forgotten about it and had not bothered to put it on the hard sofa. He would simply remove his cassock and cover himself with that in place of a blanket.

But before he went to sleep, he threw himself down on his knees and prayed for a long time. In his fervent prayer, he did not ask God to clear up his confusion, but only sought the rapture he always experienced in the glorification of God, of which his nightly prayers consisted.

As he was praying now, he chanced to feel in his pocket the little envelope that the maid had given him after he had left Katerina's house. Alyosha was disturbed by this discovery, but he completed his prayers and then, after a moment's hesitation, opened the pink envelope. It contained a note signed by Lise, Mrs. Khokhlakov's daughter, who had made fun of him that morning in front of the elder.

"Dear Alexei," she wrote.

No one knows about this letter. Even mother is not in on the secret. I know it isn't right. But I simply cannot go on living if I don't tell you about something that has arisen in my heart, and that no one must know of for the time being, except the two of us. But how can I tell you what I so long to tell you? They say that paper cannot blush, but that isn't true. It does blush, just as I am blushing myself at this moment. My sweet Alyosha, I love you, and I have loved you ever since I was a little girl in Moscow, when you were not at all the same as you are now, and I will love you all my life. My heart has chosen you—I want to be united with you and I want us to live out our lives together. Of course, provided you leave the monastery. As to being too young to marry, we will just have to wait as long as the law prescribes. And by that time I will certainly be completely cured and will be able to walk around, dance, and all; there's no doubt about that.

You see, I've thought of everything—that is, everything but one thing that I cannot imagine: What will you think of me when you read this? I always seem to be laughing and being naughty, and I think you were annoyed with me this morning. But believe me, before I started writing this, I prayed before the icon of the Mother of God. I am praying even now, and I am almost in tears.

So now you know my secret and I don't know how I'll be able to look you in the eye when you come tomorrow. Ah, Alexei, what will happen if I again cannot control myself and begin to laugh like a fool when I see you, as I did today? Then you may think I am just a nasty scoffer, trying to make fun of you, and you won't believe my letter. And so I beg you, my dear Alyosha, if you have any compassion, don't look directly into my eyes when you come tomorrow, for if our eyes meet, I'm afraid I will indeed burst out laughing, especially since you'll be wearing those long skirts of yours . . . Even at this moment, I feel the cold creeping over me as I think of it. So when you come in, you'd better not even look at me for a while—look at mother or out of the window instead.

Here I've written you a love letter. My God, what have I done! Alyosha, please don't despise me for this, and if it is really an awful thing to do and if it annoys you very much, forgive me please. Now my secret is in your hands and my good reputation may be lost forever.

I'm afraid I will cry today. So, until we meet, until that *terrifying* moment,

Lise

P.S. Alyosha, be sure to come without, without, without fail! Lise.

Alyosha read it all, greatly surprised. He reread it twice, thought for a while, and suddenly began to laugh, quietly and sweetly. Then the sound of his own laughter made him shudder—he felt it might be sinful. But a second later he was laughing again, just as quietly and happily. He slowly put the letter back into the envelope, crossed himself, and stretched out on the sofa. All that had been weighing on him was gone. "Have mercy upon them all, O Lord. Save them, the unhappy and the tormented. Guide them onto the path that is right for each one of them, according to Your wisdom. You are love. You will bring joy and happiness to all . . ." Alyosha muttered, crossing himself and drifting into peaceful sleep.

PART TWO

PART TWO

BOOK IV

TORMENT

CHAPTER 1

Father Ferapont

Alyosha was roused before dawn. The elder had awakened and, although he felt extremely weak, had asked to be moved from his bed to the armchair. His mind was entirely clear and, tired though he looked, his expression was serene, almost happy, and there was a cheerful, warm glow in his eyes. "I may not live through the day," he told Alyosha, adding that he wished to confess and receive the sacrament right away. Father Paisii, his regular confessor, complied. When he had received the two sacraments, there was a gathering in the cell. Monks started to come in and the cell gradually filled with the inmates of the hermitage. As it grew lighter, monks from the monastery began arriving too. After the prayers, the elder expressed the wish to take leave of everyone and, as he did so, he kissed each of them. Because the cell was overcrowded, those who had come earlier left to make room for others. Alyosha stood by the elder's chair. Zosima spoke and preached to them, his voice weak but firm.

"I have been preaching to you for a great many years, my dear fathers and brethren, and, of course, all the time I have been doing the talking. It has become such a habit with me to talk all the time and give you advice that, finally, I find it almost harder to keep quiet than to talk, even in my present weak state."

Making this light remark, he looked with warm affection on those crowding around him.

Some of what Zosima said that day was to remain engraved in Alyosha's memory forever. But, although the elder spoke distinctly and in a firm voice, his speech was somewhat incoherent. He spoke of many things and seemed to want, before dying, to say all that he had left unsaid during his lifetime. And it was not just for their edification that he wanted to say it all—it was more like a yearning to convey

195

the joy and rapture he felt, a yearning to share it with everyone, to pour forth his heart once more while he was still alive.

This is what Alyosha later remembered of his words:

"Love one another, fathers. Love God's people. We are no holier than those outside, just because we have shut ourselves up behind these walls. Just the opposite, by coming here, each of us has acknowledged to himself that he is worse than those who remain outside, worse than anyone in the world. The longer a monk lives within the monastery walls, the more acutely must he be aware of this. Otherwise there was no reason for him to come here. It is only when it is revealed to him that not only is he worse than all those outside these walls, but also that he is responsible to all men for everyone and everything, for all human sins, universal and individual—only then will he have achieved the purpose of his seclusion. For I want you to know, my beloved ones, that every one of us is responsible for all men and for everything on earth, not only responsible through the universal responsibility of mankind, but responsible personally—every man for all people and for each individual man who lives on earth. Such an awareness is the crown of a monk's life and, indeed, the crown of any human life on earth. For monks are no different from other men, and they must be what other men ought to strive to become. Only then will our hearts be moved by a love that is infinite and universal, and knows no surfeit. Then every one of you will be able to gain the whole world by his love and wash away the world's sins with his tears . . . Each of you must keep constant watch over his heart and constantly confess to himself. Do not be afraid of sin, even if you recognize it as such, as long as there is repentance, but do not try to bargain with God. And, above all, remember—do not be proud! Do not be proud before the weak or before the mighty. Do not hate those who reject you, those who dishonor you, those who abuse you and slander you. Do not hate atheists, or teachers of evil, or materialists, whether they are wicked or good—for many among them are good people, especially in our time. Remember them in your prayers thus: 'Save all those, O Lord, who have no one to pray for them, and all who refuse to pray.' And you must add this to that prayer: 'I do not pray for them out of pride, O Lord, for I myself am the most loathsome creature of all' . . . Love God's people and do not let strangers drive your flock from you. For if you lose interest out of idleness, supercilious pride, or, worst of all, greed, others will come from all directions and snatch your flock from you. Never cease to explain the Gospels to the people . . . Do not be avaricious, do not love gold and silver. Do not hoard . . . Have faith and defend its banner. Raise it, raise it high."

Actually Zosima's speech was less smooth than it appears here, or than Alyosha noted it down afterward. At times his voice would break off. He seemed to gasp for breath, but he was in a state of ecstasy. Most of those listening to him were very moved, although some were rather bewildered by his words and found them obscure. Later, those words were remembered and discussed.

When Alyosha had to leave the cell for a moment, he was struck by the general atmosphere of anxiety and suspense among the monks, both in and outside the cell. Some looked worried, others wore solemn expressions. All of them were expecting something immensely significant to happen immediately after the elder's death. Such an expectation seemed in a sense frivolous, but even the oldest and sternest monks succumbed to it. The severest face of all was Father Paisii's.

A monk whispered into Alyosha's ear that Rakitin had just arrived from town and wanted to see him. Rakitin had a letter from Mrs. Khokhlakov for him. It contained a strange and very timely message. She wrote that, among the women who had come to see the elder the day before, to receive his blessing, there was an old sergeant's widow from town, one Prokhorovna. It was she who had asked the elder whether she could have prayers said for her son Vasya's soul as if he were dead, because she hadn't had any news from him for more than a year and didn't know whether he was still alive in Irkutsk, in faraway Siberia. The elder had told her sternly that she could not have prayers said for the soul of a living person, that it would be witchcraft, but he then had forgiven her because she didn't know any better and added, "as though reading out of the Book of the Future," as Mrs. Khokhlakov put it in her letter, that her son Vasya was indeed alive and that he would soon either come back to her or send her a letter, and that she should go home and wait. "And what do you think?" Mrs. Khokhlakov wrote ecstatically. "This prophecy has been fulfilled, indeed more than that!" When the old woman arrived home, she was handed a letter from Siberia that had come during her absence. But that was not all. In the letter, mailed in Ekaterinburg, Vasya informed his mother that he was on his way home, traveling in the company of a government official, and that he hoped "to embrace his mother within three weeks." Mrs. Khokhlakov begged Alyosha to report this "miraculous prophecy" to the Father Superior and to the monks—for "everyone should know about it!" she exclaimed at the end of her letter. The letter was written hurriedly and the excitement of the writer was evident in every line.

But Alyosha had nothing new to tell the monks for they already knew all about it: when Rakitin had sent the monk to call Alyosha, he had also asked him "to most respectfully request His Reverence Father Paisii" to receive him, because he had "a message of such great urgency" to deliver that he didn't dare to "delay one minute." He begged Father Paisii "to forgive his presumption." Since the monk had spoken to Father Paisii before speaking to Alyosha, all Alyosha had left to do, after reading the letter, was to give it to Father Paisii as further evidence of the "miracle." And now that stern, severe man, having read the letter with a frown, could not prevent himself from showing his feelings a little. A glint appeared in his eye and his lips stretched into a grave and solemn smile.

"We may see even greater things yet," he said, the words barely escaping his lips.

"We may see greater things, see greater things yet!" the surrounding monks repeated, but Father Paisii frowned again and asked them not to tell anyone, for the time being, what had happened. "Not until there is further confirmation, for there is a great deal of irresponsibility among laymen and, besides, the whole thing may have a natural explanation," he added prudently, to satisfy his conscience, although he himself did not really believe the reservation was necessary, as those around him realized very well. Within the hour, everyone in the monastery had heard about the "miracle," even the outsiders who came to attend mass. But the person most impressed by it was the visiting monk from St. Sylvester of Obdorsk, a small monastery in the far north. He was the monk who had stood next to Mrs. Khokhlakov the day before and who, indicating that lady's "cured" daughter, had asked Elder Zosima how he "dared" to tamper with such things.

This monk was already somewhat at a loss and was not sure what he should believe. Later the same day, he had gone to see Father Ferapont in his isolated cell behind the apiary, and the visit had made a tremendous and terrifying impression on him. Father Ferapont was a very old monk who was famous for his fasting and his vow of silence and who was a staunch opponent of the institution of elders in general and of Elder Zosima in particular. He considered the institution a harmful and irresponsible new fad. He was a very dangerous opponent, even though, because of his vow of silence, he hardly ever spoke to anyone. He was dangerous mainly because many monks were in sympathy with him and also because so many lay visitors considered him a great ascetic and a saint, although they did not doubt that he was one of God's fools. His being a holy fool only moved and impressed them.

Father Ferapont never went to see Father Zosima. Although he lived within the confines of the hermitage, he was not subject to its rules, again mainly because he behaved like a holy fool. He was at least seventy-five years old and he lived behind the hermitage apiary, by the wall, in a dilapidated wooden shack that had been built long before, back in the eighteenth century, for another famous observer of fasts and silence, one Father Jonas, who had lived to the age of a hundred and five and about whose acts of devotion many curious stories were told in the monastery and in the surrounding countryside. Father Ferapont had obtained permission to move into this isolated cell, or rather shack, about seven years before. It looked like a chapel because of its tremendous number of icons with lamps perpetually burning before them, all brought by visitors to the monastery. And Father Ferapont was supposed to act as keeper of these holy icons. It was said—and it was quite true—that he lived on only two pounds of bread every three days. The bread was brought to him every fourth day by the monk bee-keeper, but even with him Father Ferapont seldom exchanged a word. So his weekly fare consisted of four pounds of bread and the communion wafer sent to him regularly by the Father Superior after the late mass on Sundays. The water in his jug was changed every day. He rarely appeared at mass. His visiting admirers watched him kneeling in prayer throughout the day, never once standing up or looking around. And even when he did, on occasion, talk to them, he was always brief, abrupt, and peculiar, and often rude. On very rare occasions, he would hold a whole conversation with his visitors, but mostly he would just utter some strange word that would puzzle them, after which, even if he was beseeched to say more, he would not give any explanation at all. He was just a simple monk with no priestly rank. There was a strange rumor circulating—only among the less educated people, it is true—that Father Ferapont was in direct communication with celestial spirits and that this was the reason for his silence with men.

The visitor from remote Obdorsk reached the apiary and from there followed the directions of the bee-keeper, also a very glum and taciturn monk, who explained to him how to find Father Ferapont's shack and warned him:

"He may talk to you or you may not get a single word out of him."

As the visiting monk recounted later, he approached the shack with immense apprehension. It was already late in the day. Father Ferapont was sitting on a very low bench outside the door of his cabin. A huge elm rustled faintly overhead. The evening freshness could be felt in the air. The visitor prostrated himself before the holy man and asked for his blessing.

"Do you want me, too, to prostrate myself before you, monk?" Father Ferapont said. "Get up."

The visitor got up.

"It is by blessing that one is blessed. Sit down here, next to me. Where do you come from?"

What surprised the visitor most was that, despite his known fasting and his advanced years, Father Ferapont was such a strong old man—tall, erect, with a fresh complexion and a healthy albeit drawn look. He was powerfully built and it was quite obvious that he still had considerable physical strength. Despite his great age, he was not even completely white-headed and there were still black strands in his hair and his beard. His eyes were large, gray, luminous, and amazingly prominent. He spoke with a strong regional accent. He wore a long rust-colored coat of a coarse material called at the time "prison cloth," and had a rope tied around his waist. Under his coat, his rough cotton shirt was almost black with dirt since he did not take it off for months at a time. It was open at the neck, leaving his chest bare. It was said that he wore thirty-pound chains under his coat. His sockless feet were thrust into dilapidated shoes with gaping holes in them.

"I come from a small monastery, St. Sylvester in Obdorsk," the visiting monk said in a humble tone, watching the hermit out of quick, curious, and somewhat frightened eyes.

"I've been at your Sylvester's. Stayed with him. So how is Sylvester? Is he all right?"

The monk looked at him, taken aback.

"You muddle-headed people! How do you keep your fasts?"

"Since ancient times, in our monastery, we have had no meals on Mondays, Wednesdays, and Fridays during Lent. On Tuesdays and Thursdays we receive white bread, stewed fruit with honey, wild berries or pickled cabbage, and oatmeal porridge. On Saturdays, cabbage soup, peas, noodles, and porridge—everything with vegetable oil. During the week we get dried fish with gruel as well as cabbage soup. During Holy Week, from Monday through Saturday, for those six days, no food is cooked at all and we get only bread and water, and very little of that; and we abstain from eating at all on some days, as is prescribed for the first week of Lent. We eat and drink nothing on Good Friday and nothing on Holy Saturday until three o'clock in the afternoon, and then only a little bread and one glass of wine. On Holy Thursday, we have something cooked without oil and drink wine with some dry food, because the Laodicean Council says of Holy Thursday: 'It is wrong to break your fast on the Thursday of the last week of Lent and thus dishonor the whole of Lent.' That's how it is in our monastery. But that's nothing compared with your own fasting, Reverend Father," the visiting monk added in a bolder tone, "for you live on nothing but bread and water throughout the whole year, even during Easter, and the bread we eat in two days lasts you a whole week. Your fasting is, indeed, wondrous to behold!"

"And what about mushrooms?"

"Mushrooms?" repeated the puzzled visitor.

"That's right. I could easily do without their bread—I don't need it at all: I could go into the forest and live on mushrooms and berries, while here they can't leave, for they can't do without the bread they're given. That shows they're tied to the devil. And nowadays some of these heathens say there's no need to fast all that much; that's insolent, heathen talk, that's what it is!"

"Very true."

"And did you see devils there, among them?"

"Where? Among whom?" the monk inquired timidly.

"I went to see the Father Superior last year on Trinity Sunday, and I've never been back since. I saw devils hiding under the cassocks of some of those monks, close to their bosoms, with just their horns showing. Others had devils peeping out of their pockets; they had those quick, shifty little eyes, the unholy ones, and they were certainly frightened of me. And one of them went to live inside the unclean belly of a monk; another hung around a monk's neck, and the monk carried him everywhere he went without ever seeing him."

"And you . . . you saw them?"

"I'm telling you I saw them—I can see through things, that's why. As I was leaving the Father Superior's, I looked and saw one of them trying to hide from me behind the door. That was a big one, more than three feet tall, and you should have seen the tail he had: it was thick and long and brown! Well, the end of that tail of his was in the crack of the door and, as I had a sharp eye open, I quickly slammed it shut and caught his tail in it. Ah, the way he squealed then and started pulling and jumping! But I made the sign of the cross over him, three times I made it, and that got him—he was dead as a stepped-on spider! And now I'm sure he's rotting away in that corner and reeking, but they can't see or smell him . . . Well, I haven't been back there for over a year, and I've only told this to you because you're a visitor from other parts."

"It's frightening what you tell me, Blessed and Reverend Father. But tell me now, are the wonderful things they say about you true? Do you really converse with the Holy Ghost as you are reputed to even in the most distant lands?"

"Sometimes. He comes down to see me."

"How does he come down to you, in what shape?" the monk asked, becoming bolder and bolder.

"As a bird."

"The Holy Ghost in the shape of a dove?"

"That's the Holy Ghost. I'm talking about the Holy Spirit and the Holy Spirit can come down in the shape of some other bird—a swallow, a goldfinch, or sometimes a tom-tit."

"And how do you recognize him in a tom-tit?"

"He talks to me."

"In what tongue does he talk?"

"In human tongue."

"And what does he say to you?"

"Well, today, for instance, he warned me that a fool would visit me and ask me stupid questions. You want to know too much, monk."

"Your words are frightening, Blessed and Reverend Father," the visitor said, shaking his head. But in his frightened little eyes there was a suggestion of disbelief.

"Do you see that tree there?" Father Ferapont asked him after a brief silence.

"I do, Blessed Father."

"And you think it's an elm, don't you? But I see it differently."

After waiting in vain for Father Ferapont to tell him what the tree looked like to him, the monk asked:

"And what is it to you, Reverend Father?"

"See those two branches? Sometimes at night they are Christ's arms. He stretches His arms out toward me, searching for me with those arms. I see it clearly and I tremble: it's frightening, too frightening!"

"But why is it frightening since it is Christ Himself?"

"And what if he grabs me and carries me off to heaven?"

"What do you mean? Carries you off to heaven alive?"

"Why, haven't you heard about Elijah? He'll just put those arms around me and carry me off . . ."

Even though the visiting monk from Obdorsk was rather taken aback by this conversation, when he returned to the cell assigned to him, which he shared with another monk, his sympathies were still with Father Ferapont rather than with Father Zosima. The visitor considered fasting of the utmost importance and he thought it quite natural that a man famous for his observance of fasts should have miraculous visions. Of course, certain things Father Ferapont had said sounded rather incongruous, but our Lord knows the meaning of those words and, besides, all the holy fools whom Christ loves say and do far stranger things than Ferapont. As to the story about the devil's tail being caught in the door, the Obdorsk monk was not only prepared to accept it in a metaphorical and symbolic sense—he was eager to believe it literally. On the other hand, before he had even come to our monastery, he had been very strongly prejudiced against the institution of elders, an institution which he knew only from hearsay and which, subscribing to the opinion of many others, he viewed as an extremely undesirable and harmful innovation. Moreover, in our monastery, he had found considerable resentment against the institution of elders among some irresponsible and dissenting monks. On top of this, the visitor was very curious by nature. He was a very energetic and inquisitive man; and the news about the great "miracle" performed by Father Zosima puzzled him. Later, Alyosha remembered that, among the monks who crowded around Zosima and stayed constantly in the vicinity of the cell, there was always the smallish figure of the inquisitive visiting monk, darting from one group to another, listening to conversations, asking everybody questions. At the time, though, he paid little attention to him; it was only later that he remembered it.

Alyosha had other more important things to worry about right then. Zosima, who again felt very tired and had been transferred back to his bed from the armchair, was just dozing off when he remembered Alyosha and asked for him. Alyosha came running at once. Near the elder were only Father Paisii, Father Joseph, and the novice Porfiry. The elder opened his tired eyes, looked intently at Alyosha, and asked:

"Aren't people expecting you, my dear son?"

Alyosha mumbled something hesitatingly.

"Doesn't someone need you? Didn't you promise someone yesterday that you'd come to see them today?"

"I did promise . . . I promised my father . . . and my brothers . . . others too . . ."

"So you see. You must go without fail. And don't be sad. Know that I won't die without saying my last words on earth in your presence. I'll say those words to you, my dear son, and I'll bequeath them to you. To you, my sweet son, because you love me. But now you must go to see those you promised."

Alyosha obeyed immediately, although he found it very painful to leave. But the elder's promise that he would hear his last words on earth and, above all, that those words would be bequeathed to him—Alyosha—filled him with elation. He hurried to town so that he could attend as quickly as possible to everything he had to do there and get back as soon as he could. Before he left, Father Paisii also said something to him that made a strong and unexpected impression on him. As they stepped out of the elder's cell, Father Paisii spoke suddenly and without preliminaries:

"Secular science, which has grown into a great force, has investigated, particularly during the past century, everything that has been handed down to us in the sacred books. That is something you must always remember, young man. After their thorough, merciless analysis, there was nothing sacred left in the hands of those secular scholars. That was because they analyzed only the parts and failed to study the whole, showing thereby a truly astonishing blindness. And the whole still stands today, firm and unassailable before their eyes, and the gates of hell shall not prevail against it. Hasn't it survived nineteen centuries and isn't its existence apparent today in the spiritual emotions experienced equally by individual men and by masses of people? And in the hearts of the very atheists who are trying to destroy everything, that spiritual emotion lives on to this day. This is so because even those who have renounced Christianity, even those who rebel against it—even they, in their essence, were created in the image of Christ and have remained in His image. Their combined wisdom and their desperate efforts to create a nobler man with greater dignity, the ideal set by Christ, have come to naught. From all their attempts, only freaks have resulted. I want you to remember that, young man, because your dying elder has decided that you shall live in the secular world. And perhaps, remembering this day, you will also think of my words of guidance uttered from the bottom of my heart, because you are still young and the world is full of great temptations beyond your endurance. Well, you must go now, my bereaved boy." And Father Paisii blessed Alyosha.

As he left the monastery gates, thinking of Father Paisii's unexpected speech, Alyosha suddenly understood that, in that severe and unsmiling monk who had until now always treated him sternly, he had suddenly found a new friend and guide, just as if Father Zosima had bequeathed Father Paisii to him as he was dying. "Perhaps that's exactly what happened between them," Alyosha suddenly thought. The fact that Father Paisii had started directly with a philosophical discourse rather than with some other approach testified to the impulsiveness of his heart: he was anxious to arm Alyosha's young mind for the forthcoming struggle against temptations and to provide the young soul that was now entrusted to him with the strongest defenses he could conceive of.

CHAPTER 2

Alyosha in His Father's House

Alyosha went to his father's house first. Just before reaching it, he remembered his father's insistence that he slip into the house unseen by Ivan. This struck him suddenly as very strange. "Why?" he wondered. "Even if father wishes to tell me a secret, there's still no reason why Ivan shouldn't see me come in. It's true, though, that father wanted to tell me something else yesterday, but somehow couldn't in his excitement . . ." He was nevertheless very pleased when Martha opened the gate for him (Gregory, it turned out, was sick in bed in the cottage) and, in answer to his question about Ivan, told him that his brother had left two hours before.

"And what is father doing?"

"He's up and having his coffee," Martha replied, rather drily it seemed to Alyosha.

When he entered, the old man was sitting alone at the table. He wore bedroom slippers and an old overcoat and was looking distractedly through some accounts. Mr. Karamazov was entirely alone in the house, as Smerdyakov had gone out to do some shopping for dinner. His thoughts had obviously wandered away from the accounts he had before him. And although he had been up since early morning and had tried to convince himself that he felt fine, he looked weak and tired. Huge purplish bruises had come out on his forehead during the night and he had tied a red scarf around his head. His nose was also considerably swollen and displayed smaller dark bruises that somehow gave him an impatient and irritated expression. The old man was aware of this himself as he greeted Alyosha with an unfriendly look.

"The coffee's cold. I won't offer you any," he shouted abruptly. "What can I do for you?"

"I came to find out how you were."

"I see, and besides I told you to come here myself yesterday. But that was all a lot of nonsense and I wish you hadn't bothered to come. I was pretty sure, though, that you'd be hanging around here today."

He said this in the sourest possible tone, got up and looked at his nose in the mirror—for about the fortieth time that morning. Then he adjusted the red kerchief more becomingly around his head.

"I prefer something red around my head—white would remind me too much of a hospital. Well, how are things with you, over there? How's your elder?"

"He's very weak; he may die today," Alyosha answered, but his father wasn't listening and appeared even to have forgotten his question.

"Ivan has gone out," Mr. Karamazov announced. "He's trying as hard as he can to take that good-for-nothing Dmitry's fiancée away from him. That's actually the only reason he's staying here," he added spitefully.

"Did he really tell you that?"

"He certainly did, and not just now—he told me three weeks ago. What other reason could he have had for coming here? I don't expect it was to cut my throat secretly, or was it? He certainly must have had some reason for coming."

"But why? How can you say things like that?"

"True, he never asks me for money, but it would be all the same if he did. For your information, my good son Alexei, I plan to stay in this world as long as possible, so I need every kopek I have, and the longer I manage to live, the more I'll need it."

Mr. Karamazov paced the room from corner to corner, his hands thrust into the pockets of his soiled, loose yellow summer topcoat.

"I'm only fifty-five," he went on. "I'm a man in my prime and I intend to live like a man, in the full sense of the word, for another twenty years or so, when I'll have become repulsive and they won't come to me of their own free will. Well, then I'll need all my money. So now I'm trying to put as much aside as I can, and just for my personal, private use, my dear son Alexei Karamazov—I want everyone to know that. A sinful life is sweet, you know, and although they all say they disapprove, every one of them lives sinfully. Only they all do it in secret, whereas I do it openly. And it's because of my frankness that all those sinners have pounced on me. As for reaching your paradise, Alexei, my son, I don't even want to reach it—I want you to understand that. Even if there is such a paradise somewhere, I don't think it's a suitable place for a self-respecting man. But the way I picture it is this: A man goes to sleep and never wakes up, and there's nothing left of him. Now if you wish to have prayers said for my soul, you're welcome to, and if you don't wish to, you can go to hell yourself for all I care—and that's my whole philosophy. Yesterday Ivan talked sense about these things, although we were all pretty drunk. But otherwise Ivan is just a little braggart, and he's not at all the great scholar he fancies he is. He's not even that well educated, I dare say; all he does is look at you and grin, without saying much. And that's how he gets away with it."

Alyosha listened to him in silence.

"Why won't he talk to me? And when he does, it's just to give himself airs. No, he's no good, your Ivan, a low schemer —that's all he is! As for me, if I decide to marry that Grushenka woman today, no one can stop me. For if a man has money, all he has to do is to wish for something and he'll get it. And that's something Ivan is afraid of and that's why he's here watching me. He wants to stop me from marrying her, and he is encouraging that good-for-nothing to marry her. You see, he's trying to guard me from her, as though I'd leave him some money in my will if I didn't marry her! Besides, if that miserable Mitya married Gru-shenka, Ivan could help himself to his rich fiancée. So you see what he's reckoning on! What a low scheming crook, that Ivan of yours!"

"You're upset because of what happened yesterday," Alyosha said. "I think you ought to go back to bed and get some more rest."

"Just now, for instance," Mr. Karamazov said, looking as if he had suddenly understood something for the first time, "I don't feel angry with you at all for saying that, but if Ivan had said exactly the same thing, I'd have been furious. With you alone I feel like a decent person at certain moments, for I'm really a wicked man."

"You're not wicked," Alyosha said with a smile. "You're just twisted."

"Listen to me: I thought today I'd have that bandit Dmitry locked up, but I still haven't decided what to do. I know that nowadays respect for one's father and mother is considered an old-fashioned and unnecessary convention; however, it seems to me that even today there's a law forbidding people to pick up their elderly fathers by the hair and then, when they're lying on the floor, to kick them in the face, and to do all that in their own house and then stand around and boast about coming back to kill them altogether. And in front of witnesses, too. If I felt like it, I could make him suffer for all that. To start with, I could have him put under lock and key for what he did yesterday."

"So you're not planning to lodge a complaint against him?"

"Ivan has talked me out of it. Of course, I'd have sent Ivan to hell, but something else stopped me . . ." He leaned toward Alyosha, then went on in a confidential whisper: "If I had the vicious lout locked up, she would hear about it and would rush to him right away. But if she hears that he beat me, a poor feeble old man, half to death, she may very well drop him and come here to pay me a visit . . . Because that's how she is: she'll always do the opposite of what one would expect —but I know her through and through! Say, how about a little glass of brandy? Or pour yourself some of this cold coffee here and I'll put some brandy in it, just a quarter of a glass? What do you say? Just for the taste?"

"No, father, thanks very much. But if you don't mind, I'll take a roll with me." Alyosha took a three-kopek French roll and put it in the pocket of his cassock. "And you shouldn't be drinking brandy either, father," Alyosha said, worriedly examining the old man's face.

"You're right, my boy, that stuff just irritates one instead of putting one at ease . . . But one glass can't do any harm . . . Wait, I'll get it out of the cupboard."

He unlocked the cupboard, filled himself a glass, emptied it, put the bottle back, and locked the cupboard.

"That'll be all. I don't suppose one little glass will kill me."

"You know, you're much nicer now," Alyosha said with a smile.

"Hm . . . Well, I like you even without brandy, but with wicked schemers I'm a wicked schemer myself. And why doesn't that wretch Ivan go to Chermashnya for me when I ask him to? It's because he has to spy on me. He's afraid I'll give too much of my money to Grushenka, if she comes here. They're none of them any good, and I certainly have no time for Ivan. Where does he come from, anyway? He's completely different from us, you know. How could he ever imagine I was going to leave him anything? Besides, I won't leave any will when I die, and you may all just as well know it in advance. As to Dmitry—I'll squash him like a cockroach. I often squash cockroaches at night and hear them crunch under my slipper. And your Mitya will crunch too. I say *your* Mitya because I know you love him, but that doesn't worry me. Now, if Ivan loved him too, I'd be afraid for my life. Ivan doesn't love anyone, though; Ivan is not like us. He's different. He's like a cloud of dust: the wind will blow and he'll be gone . . . Yesterday a stupid thought came to me, you know, when I asked you to come over today: I wanted to find out something about Mitya from you. What if I let him have a thousand or maybe two right now, would that brutish beggar consider clearing out of here altogether for, say, five years, or better yet thirty-five years, and leaving Grushenka behind, giving her up for good? What do you say, do you think he would?"

"I . . . I'll ask him," Alyosha mumbled. "Perhaps if you could give him the whole three thousand, perhaps then he . . ."

"Oh no, you'll ask him nothing of the sort! I've thought

better of it. It was just a stupid idea that crossed my mind
yesterday when my brain wasn't working too well. I'll give
him nothing, exactly nothing, because I can use the money
for myself, myself," the old man said, waving his hands.
"I'll crush him like a cockroach anyway, without giving him
anything. So don't tell him anything, or he'll get his hopes up.
And you, too, you have nothing to do here, so you can be
on your way. But tell me first, that fiancée of his, that
Katerina, whom he's been hiding from me all this time,
will she marry him or not? I understand you went to see her
at her house yesterday."

"She doesn't seem to want to give him up for anything."

"Well, that sort of tender, refined young lady is likely to
go for wild, irresponsible scoundrels like him! Those pale
young ladies are worth nothing, not a thing; you should have
seen how I handled them when *I* was twenty-eight. And I
looked better at his age than he does today. Ah, the animal!
But whatever he does, he won't get Grushenka—I'll turn him
into dirt before he gets her. I'll turn him into dirt!"

He was working himself up into a rage with his own words.

"Go on then—there's nothing for you to do here today,"
he snapped harshly. Alyosha went up to take leave of him,
kissing his father on the shoulder.

"Why did you do that?" the old man asked, slightly surprised. "I'll see you again, won't I? Or don't you expect ever
to see me again?"

"No, no, I wasn't thinking. I did it mechanically."

"All right, all right, I didn't mean anything either . . ."
the old man said, staring at Alyosha. "Hey, listen, hey!" he
shouted after his son. "Come back soon, very soon. We'll have
fish soup—a special, fresh one, not today's heated up. Be
sure to come! What about tomorrow?"

As soon as Alyosha had left, he walked to the cupboard,
poured himself half a glass, and emptied it.

"That's all, no more!" he muttered, clearing his throat. He
locked the cupboard, put the key in his pocket, went into the
bedroom, lay down exhausted on his bed, and at once fell
asleep.

CHAPTER 3

Alyosha Gets Involved with Schoolboys

"Thank God he didn't ask me anything about Grushenka," Alyosha thought to himself as, leaving his father's house, he set out for Mrs. Khokhlakov's. "If he had, I suppose I would have been forced to tell him about meeting her yesterday."

He felt unhappily that, during the night, the opposing forces had recovered their strength and that, with the daylight, their hearts had again become as hard as stones.

"Father is angry and full of resentment. He's got an idea into his head and has taken a stand on it. And Dmitry? Probably he has grown even more desperately determined during the night too, and is also angry and irritated, and so he's sure to have thought up something for his next move . . . I absolutely must find him today. I must get to him, whatever else I do."

But Alyosha did not have a chance to pursue his thoughts. He became involved in an incident, which, although apparently unimportant, made a very strong impression on him. When, after crossing the square, he turned into a sidestreet that leads toward Mikhailovskaya Street, which is parallel to Bolshaya Street and separated from it only by a narrow canal (there is a whole network of such narrow canals throughout our town), he saw down by the footbridge a small group of schoolboys ranging in age from about nine to twelve. The children were on their way home from school, some with their satchels on their backs, others with leather bags slung over their shoulders, some wearing just their jackets, others in overcoats; some wore soft leather kneeboots which formed accordion-like folds around their ankles, the type that the small boys of well-off fathers like to show off to other children.

The children were discussing something very animatedly, as though they were taking counsel together. Alyosha had never been able to walk past children indifferently, even back in Moscow. And although his favorites were three-year-olds or thereabouts, he was also fond of schoolchildren of ten or eleven. So, despite all his present preoccupations, he felt a sudden urge to stop and talk to these children. As he drew closer to the group, admiring their pink-cheeked, animated

faces, he noticed with surprise that they held stones in their
hands; some had one stone, others two. Then he noticed
another schoolboy with a bag at his side, standing by a fence
about thirty yards away, across the canal. Judging by his size,
he was about ten, or even less, a pale, delicate boy. He was
watching the group of children intently, with dark, flashing
eyes. They were probably his classmates—they must have left
school together, and he must have quarreled with them.
Alyosha walked up to the group and, looking at a blond,
curly-haired boy with rosy cheeks who wore a short black
jacket, said to him:

"When I was a schoolboy and had a bag like yours, I
always carried it on my left side—that way it's easier to
reach it with your right hand. Don't you find it awkward to
reach it, carrying it on your right side?"

Alyosha had started with that matter-of-fact remark quite
spontaneously; he had not planned it as a strategic opening
move with which to approach the children, although without
an approach of that sort an adult can never gain the confidence of a child, let alone a whole group of children. An
adult must always start with a serious, business-like statement
and put himself on an equal footing with the child. Alyosha
felt that instinctively.

"But he's left-handed," another boy answered at once for
the one Alyosha had addressed. This one was a sturdy, spirited
eleven-year-old. The other five boys now had their eyes
riveted on Alyosha.

"He throws stones left-handed too," a third boy said.

At that moment a stone whistled by the group, brushing
the left-handed boy's shoulder. The stone had been thrown
hard and expertly by the boy beyond the canal.

"Let's get 'im! Go after him, Smurov!" the boys shouted.

But Smurov, the southpaw, needed no instructions. He
hurled a stone at the boy, but it hit the ground too soon and
missed him. The other boy responded at once from beyond
the canal, and his next stone, aimed at the group, hit Alyosha
quite painfully on the shoulder. The boy had his overcoat
pockets filled with stones ready to throw; one could see his
pockets bulging with them thirty yards away.

"He was aiming at you! He did it deliberately! Because
your name is Karamazov, isn't it? Yes, you're a Karamazov,
aren't you?" the boys shouted laughingly. "All right, all at
the same time—fire!"

Six stones flew all at once. One of them hit the boy on the

head. He fell down but immediately jumped up again and started fiercely firing stones back at the gang. Stones were now flying uninterruptedly in both directions, for, it turned out, the other boys also had some ready in their pockets.

"What do you think you're doing? Aren't you ashamed of yourselves—six against one! You could kill him that way . . ."

Stepping forward, Alyosha used his body to bar the path of the stones aimed at the boy beyond the canal. That seemed to calm three or four of the boys.

"But he started it all!" a red-shirted boy shouted, his young voice shrill with excitement. "He's mean! Just now, in class, he slashed Krasotkin with his penknife so that he even bled. Krasotkin didn't want to complain, but that one certainly deserves a good beating."

"I'm sure, though, that you've been teasing him."

"See what I mean! Now he hit you again, in the back this time! He knows you and now he's aiming at you, not at us! All right, ready, everybody, fire! Don't miss him, Smurov!"

And the battle of stones was resumed, this time very viciously. The boy beyond the canal was hit in the chest. He cried out, started to sob, and ran uphill toward Mikhailov-skaya Street. The boys in the gang shouted after him: "Coward! Back-scrubber! There goes the back-scrubber!"

"You have no idea, Mr. Karamazov, how nasty he is! Killing wouldn't be good enough for him," said the black-jacketed boy with the shining eyes, who seemed to be the oldest of the group.

"Why is he so nasty? Does he squeal on others, or what?"

The boys exchanged glances and Alyosha had the impression that they were smiling understandingly at each other.

"If you're going toward Mikhailovskaya Street, why don't you catch up with him? Look, there, he's stopped and is looking back at you."

"Yes, yes, he's looking at you, at you!" the other boys chimed in.

"And ask him whether he likes bath-house back-scrubbers, tousled ones. Remember, ask him that—don't forget."

They all laughed aloud. Alyosha looked at them and they at him.

"Don't go, you may get hurt," Smurov warned Alyosha.

"I certainly won't ask him about back-scrubbers. I imagine it's something you tease him about, but I will ask him why you all hate him so."

"Go on, go on, find out!" the boys said, laughing.

Alyosha crossed the bridge and climbed uphill along the fence, straight toward the ostracized boy.

"Watch out," the other boys shouted after him, "he may hurt you. He won't hesitate to stick a knife into you just as he did to Krasotkin."

The boy stood still, waiting. When he reached him, Alyosha saw that he could not be more than nine and was rather small for his age, a thin, puny boy with a narrow face and large dark eyes which glared angrily at Alyosha. He wore an old, threadbare overcoat which he had grown out of and which now looked ridiculous on him, for his bare arms stuck out of the sleeves. There was a large patch on the right knee of his trousers and a gaping hole in his left shoe on the side of the big toe, which was thickly painted over with ink from inside in an effort to make it invisible. Both the side pockets of his overcoat were bulging with stones.

Alyosha stopped a couple of steps away from him, looking at him in surprise. From that look the boy understood that Alyosha had no intention of attacking him; he dropped his defiant attitude and spoke first:

"I'm on my own while there are six of them." Then his eyes flashed and he added: "But I'll get them all, one by one!"

"One of their stones hurt you pretty badly, I believe," Alyosha said.

"Yes, but I hit Smurov in the head!" the boy cried nervously.

"They told me that you know me and that you had your reasons for aiming at me. Is that true?" Alyosha asked the boy, who only looked at him morosely without answering. "But I don't know you at all," Alyosha insisted. "How is it possible that you know me?"

"Leave me alone!" the boy shouted irritatedly, his eyes flaring up again, but he still did not move, as though he was waiting for something.

"All right, I'll go away," Alyosha said, "but I want you to understand that I don't know you and that I'm not taunting you. They told me what they call you to tease you, but I have no wish to tease you at all. Good-by, now."

"Monk in fancy trousers, monk in fancy trousers!" the boy cried out challengingly, still glaring at Alyosha angrily and defiantly, but taking a defensive stance as he obviously expected Alyosha to pounce on him now after this last provocation. Alyosha looked at him helplessly and walked off. But when he was only a few steps away, a rock hit him painfully in the back: the boy had thrown the largest stone he had in his pocket.

"So you attack people from behind? They were right, then, when they told me you always do things like that when people aren't looking!"

As Alyosha was turning away again, the boy, enraged, hurled another stone at him, this time aimed straight at his face. Alyosha just managed to ward it off by raising his arm, and the stone hit his elbow.

"You ought to be ashamed of yourself," Alyosha cried. "What have I done to you?"

Full of defiance, the boy waited. He felt sure that now Alyosha would attack him. But when he saw that Alyosha was still not going to do anything, he grew vicious, like a little wild animal, and himself attacked. Before Alyosha even had time to move, the boy lowered his head, grabbed Alyosha's left hand with both his hands, and bit the middle finger painfully. He sank his teeth into it and didn't let go for ten seconds. Alyosha yelled in pain, trying to pull his finger away. Finally the boy let his finger go, jumped back to a safe distance as before, and waited. The finger was bitten to the bone, close to the nail, the blood spurting out of it. Alyosha took out his handkerchief and tied it tightly around the wound. It took him a good minute, and all that time the brat stood there watching. When he had finished attending to his finger, Alyosha raised his gentle eyes to the boy and said:

"Well, all right, now that you've bitten me pretty badly, as you can see, I suppose you must be satisfied, so perhaps you could tell me at last what I've done to you?"

The boy looked at him in surprise.

"Although I don't know you and this is the first time I have set eyes on you," Alyosha went on in the same quiet voice, "I must have done something somehow to make you feel this way—otherwise you wouldn't have hurt me like this for no reason. So tell me, what have I done to you? How have I wronged you?"

Instead of answering, the boy burst into loud sobs and suddenly started to run away. Alyosha walked slowly after him, toward Mikhailovskaya Street, watching the boy as he ran ahead of him without slowing down, without turning around, and probably still crying aloud. Alyosha decided that, as soon as he had time, he would try to discover the reason for the boy's mysterious and puzzling resentment of him. But he certainly had no time for it right now.

CHAPTER 4

At the Khokhlakovs

Soon he reached Mrs. Khokhlakov's beautiful, two-story stone house, one of the best houses in our town. Although Mrs. Khokhlakov spent most of her time elsewhere—either at a country estate she had in another province or in Moscow where she also had a house—the house in our town had belonged to her family for several generations and the estate was the largest of the three estates she owned. And yet she came here to our province very seldom.

When Alyosha arrived, she ran out to the hall to meet him herself.

"You did get my letter about the new miracle, didn't you?" she said, speaking quickly and nervously.

"Yes, I did," Alyosha said.

"Did you show it to everybody? Did you spread the word? He gave that mother back her son!"

"He'll die today," Alyosha said.

"Yes, I know, I've heard . . . Oh, I was so anxious to talk to you about it, to you or someone . . . No, to you, to you. I'm so sorry I can't go and see him. The whole town is in great excitement. Everybody is expecting things to happen. But . . . do you know that Katerina is here right now?"

"What a lucky coincidence!" Alyosha cried. "I'll be able to talk to her now, for yesterday she insisted that I come and see her today."

"Oh, I know, I know all about it. I've heard everything, down to the smallest detail, about what happened at her house yesterday, about the terrible trick that unspeakable creature played on her. C'est tragique, and if I were in her place I . . . Well, I don't even know what I'd do. But I must say, I don't think too highly of your brother Dmitry either. Oh, good Lord, Alexei, I'm getting all mixed up. Now your brother is sitting there talking to her . . . no, no, not the horrible one who did all those dreadful things yesterday, your other brother—Ivan. He's sitting in there with her and they're having a very important talk. Oh, if you only knew what's going on between the two of them at this very moment—it's heartbreaking, a terrible story, something unbelievable: they're both throwing away their lives for no good reason; they are both perfectly aware of it and actually enjoying it . . . Ah, I've been waiting so impatiently for you to come—I needed you here so badly! I cannot bear what's going on. I'll tell you everything in a moment, but first there's something else, the most important of all—my goodness, I'd almost forgotten the most important thing . . . Tell me, why is Lise in hysterics? The moment she heard you coming she became hysterical!"

"It is you, *maman*, who is hysterical, not I!" Lise's voice trilled suddenly through the crack of a door to a side room. The crack was tiny and Lise's voice had a catch in it—it sounded as if she were making a desperate effort to keep from bursting into laughter. Alyosha saw the crack and thought that Lise might be watching him from her wheel-chair, but he himself could not see her.

"And that wouldn't be so surprising either, Lise—you may very well drive me to hysterics with these whims of yours! But I must say, Alexei, she's very sick, all night she was so sick; she was feverish and moaning . . . I could hardly wait for morning and for Dr. Herzenstube to come. He said he couldn't diagnose it yet, that we would just have to wait and see. That Herzenstube always comes and starts by saying that he can't understand. Well, when Lise saw you approaching the house, she let out a cry, became hysterical, and had her wheel-chair moved to that room there . . ."

"But, mother, I had no idea Alyosha was coming, and it was not because of him that I wanted to be moved to this room."

"Now, Lise, that's not true at all. Julia rushed in to tell you that Alexei was on his way. You made her watch out for him."

"My dearest mother, what you are saying is not at all amusing! Now if you want to make up for it and say something witty, why don't you, my dear mamma, tell that kindly gentleman, Mr. Alexei Karamazov, that, just by coming here today, after what happened yesterday, he has shown that he isn't too sharp and doesn't realize that he's the laughing stock of the town."

"Now you're going a bit far, Lise! I'm afraid you really need to be taken in hand, and I'll have to do it. Who is laughing at Alexei? I'm absolutely delighted to see him—I needed him. It was absolutely indispensable for me to see him. Ah, Alexei, I am so miserable . . ."

"But what is it, mother dear? What's the matter with you?"

"Ah, you're so capricious, Lise, so unpredictable; you're

sick and that terrible night, with the fever and all, and then that impossible Herzenstube, always, always the same, unchanging Herzenstube! And all the rest of it, and even that miracle—oh, Alexei, my dear, I can hardly tell you the tremendous impression that miracle made on me! And on top of it all, the tragedy taking place up there, in my drawing room —I can't bear it. I warn you—it's too much for me! And yet, it may be a comedy rather than a tragedy. Tell me, you don't think Father Zosima will last until tomorrow? Oh, my Lord, what's happening to me? I keep closing my eyes and everything appears completely unimportant to me, sheer rubbish . . ."

"I wonder whether you could spare me a clean piece of rag or something to bind my finger," Alyosha interrupted her suddenly. "I hurt it and now it's rather painful."

Alyosha unbound his bitten finger. The handkerchief was soaked with blood. Mrs. Khokhlakov let out a little scream and half closed her eyes.

"My God, what a horrible wound! It's awful!"

Through the crack Lise, too, saw Alyosha's finger and she flung open the door.

"Come here, come right in here!" she ordered in a tone that brooked no objection. "Now let's forget all that nonsense. My God, why did you just stand there without saying anything? He could have bled to death, mother! How did you manage to do it? First of all, I want some water, quick! We must wash the wound—you must put your finger in cold water and hold it there until the pain ceases. Water, mother, get some water in a basin. Do hurry, for heaven's sake!" Lise shouted impatiently. She was very upset and frightened by Alyosha's wound.

"Shouldn't I send for Herzenstube?" Mrs. Khokhlakov suggested, but Lise interrupted her.

"You'll be the death of me yet, mother! All your Herzenstube will say is that he can't make out what it is. We need water, mother, water, at once! For heaven's sake, go and see that Julia hurries! What's happened to her, anyway? Has she got lost or something? Well, go on, mother, hurry up! You're driving me crazy!"

"But it's nothing, really," Alyosha said, becoming frightened himself—their fright rubbing off on him.

Julia brought a bowl of water and Alyosha put his finger into it.

"Get me some bandages, mother, some gauze . . . And get

that opaque disinfectant stuff for cuts, I forget what it's called . . . Yes, I'm sure we have some—in the medicine chest; you know, it's in a large glass jar, and the gauze and bandages are there too . . ."

"I'll get everything, Lise, right away, but relax and don't shout like that. Look at Alexei—how firmly he is facing his misfortune. Wherever can you have done that to yourself, Alexei?"

Mrs. Khokhlakov hurried out. It looked as if Lise had been waiting for her to do so.

"First of all, tell me at once: how did you manage to hurt yourself like this? And then we'll talk about something else quite different. Well?"

Feeling that Lise did not want to waste the time that her mother was out of the room, he told her briefly and with many omissions, but quite clearly and matter-of-factly, about his strange adventure with the schoolboys. When he had finished, Lise threw up her hands in despair:

"But how, how can you have got yourself involved with those boys, especially wearing that garb of yours," she said indignantly, as if she had the right to tell him off. "You're no better than a brat yourself; indeed, you're as bad as the youngest of those urchins! But be sure to find out all about that horrible child and then tell me, because I'm sure there must be some mystery there. Now, for the other thing—but before we go into it, I want you to tell me this: can you, despite your pain, talk about something that's quite unimportant, yet still talk sensibly about it?"

"I can easily. Besides, it doesn't hurt that much at all now."

"It only doesn't because you're holding your finger in the cold water. It should be changed soon because it gets warm very quickly. Julia, hurry, go to the cellar and get me a piece of ice, and also another bowl of water. Now that she's gone, let's get down to business. Quickly, Alexei, give me back the letter I sent you yesterday—hurry, because mother will be back any moment now and I don't want . . ."

"I'm afraid I don't have it with me."

"That's not true. You do have it with you. I expected you to say that, though. It's right there, in your pocket. I'm so sorry I played that silly trick on you. It kept me awake all night. Give me back the letter right away. Give it to me!"

"I left it behind there."

"But you mustn't consider me a little girl because of that

silly prank. I'm not a silly little girl and I ask you to forgive me for writing it. I want you to give me back that letter, though. If you don't have it with you now, please, please go and get it. I want it today, today without fail!"

"I can't possibly do it today, I'm sorry. I have to go back to the monastery and I don't expect to leave it for two, three, or maybe four days, because Father Zosima . . ."

"Four days! Nonsense. Listen, did you laugh at me very much when you read it?"

"I didn't laugh at all."

"Why not?"

"Because I fully believed what you wrote."

"Now you're being insulting."

"Not at all. When I read it, I thought, that's exactly what's going to happen. As soon as Father Zosima dies, I'll have to leave the monastery and go on with my studies. By the time I've passed all my exams, we will be legally old enough and we'll get married. And I will love you. Although I haven't had time to think of it, I don't believe I'd ever be able to find a better wife than you, and also Father Zosima told me I should get married."

"But I'm a cripple. I have to be pushed around in a wheel-chair!" Lise cried, laughing nervously, her cheeks turning bright pink.

"If need be, I'll wheel you around myself. But I'm sure you'll be well by that time."

"You're crazy," Lise said nervously. "It was just a joke, and here you go and make such nonsense out of it! . . . But here's my mother coming back and, I must say, she's just in time! You're so slow, mother. How could it take you so long! And here's Julia bringing us the ice!"

"Ah, Lise, don't scream like that. You drive me frantic with your fussing and screaming. How could I help it when you hadn't put the bandages back in the proper place? I looked and looked for them, and I almost suspect you did it on purpose."

"What are you talking about? How could I possibly have known that he'd come here with his finger half bitten off? Otherwise, really I might have hidden them, just as you say. I see that you have at last come up with a clever remark today."

"Clever or not, I'm a little taken aback by the fuss you're making about poor dear Alexei's finger . . . Ah, Alexei, what upsets me is not just one particular thing. It's everything together—Herzenstube and all the rest put together. It's more than I can bear!"

"Why don't you forget Dr. Herzenstube, mother, and just give me that gauze," Lise said laughingly. "Hurry, mother, give me the gauze and water. This is simply a solution of zinc, Alexei. I remember now what it is. It's very good stuff . . . You know what happened to him, mother? Well, on the way here, he simply got into a fight with some schoolboys and one of those streetboys bit him like that. Doesn't that prove, mother, that he's only a little boy himself and that it's absolutely impossible for him to get married yet? Because, guess what, mother—he's planning to get married! Just imagine him as a married man! Wouldn't that be funny, terribly funny?"

And Lise went on giggling nervously, casting sly, sidelong glances at Alyosha.

"What are you talking about, Lise? Who's going to marry? Why? How can you talk such nonsense when the boy who bit Alexei may have had rabies . . ."

"Is there really such a thing as rabid little boys, mother?"

"Why not? Don't look at me as if I'd said something idiotic. Suppose the boy was bitten by a rabid dog and then goes around biting other people . . . I must say you have bandaged Alexei's finger beautifully—I could never have done such a good job of it. Does it still hurt you?"

"Very little now."

"And you're not worried about rabies, are you?"

"That's enough, Lise. Perhaps I was a bit hasty when I mentioned the possibility of the boy having rabies. You know, Alexei, when Katerina heard you were here, she rushed to me and asked me to tell you that she is very, very anxious to see you."

"You go and join her yourself, mother. Alyosha can't go yet, his finger still hurts too much."

"It doesn't hurt me at all," Alyosha said. "I could go and see her right now."

"What? You're leaving me now? So that's the way you are!"

"What do you mean? As soon as I'm through there, I'll be back and we can talk as long as you like. And I'd like to see Katerina right away because I want to get back to the monastery as soon as possible today."

"So take him away, mother. And you know, Alexei, there's no need for you to bother to come back; when you've finished with Katerina, you may as well go straight to the monastery, because that's where you really belong. Besides, you know I didn't sleep properly last night and I'm very sleepy now."

"Ah, Lise, I know you're just saying that, but I think it would be very good if you really did have a little sleep," Mrs. Khokhlakov said.

"I really don't know what I've . . ." Alyosha muttered. "I could stay with you three more minutes . . . or perhaps five, if you wish."

"Five whole minutes! That would be much too kind of you, really! Take him away, mother, take the monster away with you!"

"What's the matter, Lise, have you gone quite mad? Let's go, Alexei. She's really impossible today, and I'm afraid she'll only get more irritated if we stay. It's really very hard to deal with a nervous woman. And yet, perhaps she really felt sleepy while you were with her. How did you manage to make her sleepy so soon—and it's so fortunate!"

"I love the way you talk, mother. I'd like to kiss you for saying all those sweet things!"

"And I'd like to kiss you too, Lise," Mrs. Khokhlakov said, and as soon as she and Alyosha had left the room, she started whispering to him in an important and business-like manner: "I don't want to influence you in any way, nor do I wish to tell you anything beforehand. Go in and see for yourself what's going on in there. It's a real heartbreak, a fantastic farce: she's in love with your brother Ivan but is trying very hard to convince herself that she's really in love with your brother Dmitry. I suppose I'll come in with you and I'll stay to the end unless they throw me out."

CHAPTER 5

Heartbreak in the Drawing Room

But by that time they had almost finished talking in the drawing room. Katerina seemed very agitated, and yet determined. When Mrs. Khokhlakov and Alyosha entered, Ivan was already on his feet, about to leave. He seemed rather pale and Alyosha gave him a worried look. At that moment Alyosha found the answer to something that had been puzzling him, to one of the doubts that had been tormenting him for some time. For more than a month he had been hearing from various sources that Ivan was in love with Katerina and, above all, that he was trying to take her away from Mitya. Until very recently Alyosha had felt that this was a quite inconceivable slander, but it had nevertheless worried him a great deal. He loved both his brothers and the possibility of such a rivalry frightened him. But then Dmitry himself had told him the day before that he welcomed Ivan's interest in Katerina, that it was very helpful to him in many respects. How could it be helpful to him, though? By enabling him to marry Grushenka? But such a marriage, Alyosha felt, would be a final gesture of despair. Until the day before, Alyosha had had no doubt whatever that Katerina was deeply and passionately in love with Dmitry. Moreover, he had felt that Katerina could not love a man like Ivan, that she could only love Dmitry, and love him just the way he was, however monstrous the circumstances surrounding her passion. The day before, however, during the scene between Katerina and Grushenka, Alyosha had received a somewhat different impression. The word "heartbreak" that Mrs. Khokhlakov had just used had almost made him shudder because, when he had awakened before daybreak that morning, he had muttered twice, "Heartbreak, heartbreak," apparently in connection with his dream. And he had been dreaming all night about the scene he had witnessed between the two women. And now Alyosha found a new meaning in Mrs. Khokhlakov's assertion that Katerina was really in love with Ivan but that she was denying it, playing some sort of a game with herself, trying to "break her own heart" by pretending to herself that she was in love with Dmitry, out of some sort of gratitude. "Yes," he thought, "what she said may be the real truth." But then what about Ivan? Alyosha felt instinctively that a woman like Katerina had to dominate and, while she could dominate Dmitry, she could not possibly dominate a man of Ivan's character. Eventually (it would take some time, though), Dmitry would calm down and accept her domination "for his own good" (Alyosha hoped for that), but Ivan would never be able to submit to her; besides, submission would never bring him happiness. This was, for some reason, the way Alyosha imagined Ivan. And now, as he entered the drawing room, all these feelings and impressions again flitted through his mind, along with a new thought: "And what if she doesn't really love either of them?" It must be noted, though, that Alyosha was rather ashamed of such ideas and when they had kept cropping up during the past month, he had told himself reproachfully: "Much I know about love and women to qualify me to draw such conclusions!" But he could not prevent himself from thinking. He felt that this rivalry was much too crucial a point in his brothers' lives and that too much depended on it. "One wild beast will devour the other," Ivan had said irritatedly the day before, referring to their father and their brother Dmitry. So then, Dmitry was a wild beast to him and had been for a long time. Perhaps ever since Ivan had come to know Katerina? Of course, those words had escaped Ivan involuntarily, when he was irritated. But didn't that make them even more significant? And if that was the truth, what peace could there be between them? Wasn't this only a new cause for feuds and hatred within their family? And, above all, for whom should he, Alyosha, be sorry? What should he wish for each of them? He loved both Dmitry and Ivan, but what could he hope for each in the face of all these violent and conflicting passions? A man could get completely lost in all these complications and Alyosha could not bear the unknown because his love was an active one. He was unable to love passively: as soon as he came to love someone, he had to help that person. And in order to help, he had to set himself a goal. He had to be sure what was good for each person, what it was he needed, and then when he was sure of what was best for everyone, he got to work. But now, instead of a clear picture, he saw only confusion. "Heartbreak"—the word he had heard—kept turning in his mind, but what could he understand about "heartbreak," even in this particular case? He felt he could not understand the first thing in all this twisted business.

Katerina seemed very pleased to see Alyosha.

"Wait a moment," she said quickly to Ivan, who was ready to leave. "First, I'd like to hear the opinion of one whom I trust with my whole being. And you, too, Mrs. Khokhlakov, please stay."

Katerina made Alyosha sit down next to her, while Mrs. Khokhlakov installed herself next to Ivan, facing them.

"You are all my friends here, the only friends I have in the world," she began in a voice vibrating with deep and genuine pain and verging on sincere tears, a voice that made Alyosha's heart go out to her once more. "You, Alexei, you witnessed that nightmare yesterday and . . . and you saw me for what I am. You, Ivan, you didn't see it, but he did. What he thought of me I don't know, but I do know that if the same circumstances were repeated today, I would react in exactly the same way, show the same emotions, use the same words, make the same gestures, the same movements . . . You remember my movements, Alexei, since you yourself intercepted one of them and held me back," she said, reddening, her eyes flashing. "I'll tell you this, Alexei: I am not one who just accepts things and resigns myself. Listen, I'm not even so sure that I still love *him* now. I'm *sorry* for him, and that doesn't go well with love. If I were still in love with him, I don't suppose I'd be sorry for him. I think, rather, that I'd hate him, if anything . . ."

Her voice quivered and tears appeared on her eyelashes. Alyosha shuddered inwardly: "She is truthful and sincere," he thought, "and . . . and she no longer loves Dmitry."

"Right, right!" Mrs. Khokhlakov cried approvingly.

"Wait, my dear Mrs. Khokhlakov, I haven't yet said the most important thing. I haven't told you yet the final decision I came to last night. I suspect it may be an awful decision, but I feel I will stick by it as long as I live and nothing will make me change it. My dear, kind, and generous adviser, my only friend in the world, Ivan Karamazov, who possesses a profound knowledge of the human heart, approves that decision and has praised me for making it. He knows what it is."

"Yes, and I think you're right," Ivan said in a quiet but firm voice.

"But I would also like Alyosha—I hope you will forgive me, Alexei, if I call you Alyosha—to tell me now, in front of my friends here, whether he thinks I am right or not. Somehow I feel instinctively, Alyosha, my sweet little brother—for that's what you are, my sweet brother," she said, ecstatically seizing his cold hand in her burning one, "I feel that your judgment, your approval, will calm my torments. I feel that I will find peace in your words and will be able to accept my fate. I feel it!"

"I have no idea what you're about to ask me," Alyosha said, his cheeks glowing. "I only know that I like you and that, at this particular moment, I'm more concerned about your happiness than about my own! You must understand, however, that I'm not much of an expert in this kind of thing," he somehow felt obliged to add.

"In those things, my dear Alexei, what counts most is honor and duty and something else, something perhaps more important. My heart tells me about that irresistible feeling and I'm irresistibly drawn to it. But let me tell it all in just two words: my mind is made up, and even if he should marry that creature, whom I'll never, never forgive, *I shall still never abandon him,"* she announced slowly and solemnly. "Yes, as of today, I shall never abandon him!" she repeated with a sort of twisted ecstasy and a strange break in her voice, her face turning pale. "I don't mean that I'll always be trailing after him, getting in his way every moment, making his life miserable. No, I may even move to some other town, anywhere, but as long as I live I'll never stop watching over him. And when that woman makes him unhappy—which is bound to happen soon—he can come to me and he'll find in me a friend and a sister . . . Yes, just a sister, of course, and it must always be that way, but he will realize then that this sister really loves him and has sacrificed her life for him. And I will finally succeed in making him understand what sort of person I am and then he will trust me and tell me everything without being ashamed!" she exclaimed ecstatically. "I shall be the god to whom he will pray—and that is the least he owes me to make up for his betrayal and for the calvary I suffered yesterday through his fault. And let him see, as long as he lives, that I stay true to him and to the promise I have given him once and for all, even though he himself has been untrue and has betrayed me. I will be . . . I will become just a means to his happiness, or, should I say, an instrument, a machine, to help him achieve happiness, and that until the end of my life. And I want him to see it and be aware of it as long as he lives. So that is my decision, and Ivan is in full agreement."

She was almost out of breath. Perhaps she had planned to explain her idea in a more dignified, skillful, and natural way and felt she had done so too hurriedly, too openly. Indeed, there was much that was callow in her words, much that reflected her irritation at what had happened the day before and her need to make a proud gesture—she was well aware of it herself. Her face darkened and her eyes took on a hostile look. Alyosha noticed it and compassion stirred in his heart. Just at that moment Ivan said:

"I've only said how I felt about your plan. Coming from another woman, the whole idea would have sounded twisted and contrived, but in your case that isn't so. For another woman it would be wrong, but for you it is right. I don't know how to explain that, but I can see you are absolutely sincere, and that's why your decision is right."

"Yes, but perhaps it is right only now, at this particular moment . . ." Mrs. Khokhlakov said, "because of what happened yesterday, because of the insult. Perhaps that's what makes it right now, but only for now . . ."

She had been trying not to interfere, but could not restrain herself, for she knew she had stumbled on the truth.

"Certainly, certainly," Ivan said heatedly, as though resenting her interruption, "that might be true for any other woman whose feelings at such a moment would be determined merely by her reaction to what happened the day before, but for a person of Katerina's character that moment can last a lifetime. What to another person would be just a promise, to Katerina, is a life-long, grim, painful, and perhaps unrelenting duty. And what will keep her going is just that feeling of fulfilled duty. Your life, Katerina, will unroll now in painful contemplation of your own feelings, of your own devotion to duty, of your own grief. Later, however, your suffering will be alleviated and your life will turn into a sweet contemplation of the complete fulfillment of your firm and proud design. Yes, in a sense it is proud and, in any case, it is a madly bold design, but you will have accomplished it against all odds, and the consciousness of that accomplishment will, in the end, give you the most complete satisfaction and reconcile you to all the rest."

He spoke resolutely with an overtone of impatience, which he apparently did not try to conceal—indeed, perhaps he wanted the others to understand that he didn't really mean what he was saying and was being derisive.

"Oh, dear, it's all so wrong!" Mrs. Khokhlakov exclaimed.

"Well, speak, Alexei—what is *your* opinion? It is terribly important for me to know what *you* think," Katerina said, suddenly bursting into tears as Alyosha rose from the sofa. "Please, please, pay no attention to this," she went on, as the tears rolled down her cheeks. "I am most upset after the night I had . . . But with friends such as you and Ivan, I feel secure, for I know . . . I know that neither of you will ever leave me."

"Unfortunately," Ivan said, "I'm off to Moscow tomorrow, so I'll have to leave you, and for a long time too . . . Much as I may want to, I can do nothing about it."

"You are going to Moscow tomorrow!" Katerina cried, her face suddenly becoming contorted. "But, but that's just wonderful!"

In a flash her expression changed and her tears vanished without trace. The sudden change in her took place literally in a flash and it completely stunned Alyosha. The weeping, humiliated, heartbroken girl had suddenly turned into a strong, self-possessed woman, in full control of the situation and pleased with the news she had just heard.

"Oh, it isn't parting from you that makes me so pleased," she said half apologetically, with a charming, worldly smile, "but I know that a real friend like you cannot have thought that for one moment, of course not! In fact, I'm terribly sad to lose you."

She rushed up to Ivan, seized his hands, and shook them with great warmth.

"I'm so pleased," she went on, "because now you will be able to explain my situation personally to my aunt and to Agafia, to tell them all about the horror of my present predicament, concealing nothing from Agafia, but sparing my aunt certain details, which I can leave to your own judgment. You can hardly imagine how miserable I was yesterday and this morning, wondering how I would write them about these unspeakable things! I'd have been quite incapable of conveying it all to them in a letter . . . Now it will be easy for me to write, because you will have explained the circumstances to them beforehand. Oh, I'm so pleased that you're going! But only for the reason I've told you, you must believe me! You yourself, of course, are quite irreplaceable . . . But I must run off and write that letter," she concluded abruptly, even starting to walk toward the door.

"But what about Alyosha?" Mrs. Khokhlakov cried. "What about his opinion that you were so terribly anxious to hear?"

An irritated and sarcastic note could be detected in her voice.

"I haven't forgotten it at all," Katerina said, stopping short. "Besides, why should you be so unfriendly to me at a moment such as this, dear Mrs. Khokhlakov?" she said in deep reproach. "What I've said, I'll say again: I must have his opinion, or even more than that, what I want is for him to decide for me. Whatever he decides—I will abide by. That should show you, Alexei, how anxious I am to hear what you have to say . . . But what's the matter with you?"

"I never expected it, I never imagined it . . ." Alyosha said bitterly.

"Imagined what? What are you trying to say?"

"When Ivan said he was leaving for Moscow, you actually exclaimed with delight and then started explaining that, of course, it wasn't his departure that made you so happy, that, on the contrary, you were sorry he was leaving, that you were losing a friend . . . But you were just saying those words for the effect. You didn't mean them. You were acting, acting as if you were in a comedy, on the stage . . ."

"Comedy? On the stage? What are you talking about?" Katerina cried out in amazement. She knit her brows and her face reddened darkly.

"Yes, you may have assured him that you were sorry to lose a friend, but you still insisted on telling him to his face that you were happy he was leaving," Alyosha said, breathing with difficulty. He was standing by the table and did not sit down again.

"I really don't understand you—what actually do you mean?"

"I don't know too well myself . . . It's as if I had suddenly seen something. I know I can't express it properly, but I'll say it all the same," Alyosha went on in the same trembling, faltering voice. "What I suddenly saw . . . I saw that perhaps you never loved Dmitry . . . not even at the beginning . . . And he, Dmitry, he may never have loved you either . . . also not even at the beginning . . . he may have just respected you. I really don't know how I dare tell you all this, but somebody ought to tell you the truth . . . because no one here wants to tell the truth . . ."

"What truth?" Katerina shouted, on the verge of hysterics.

"This truth," Alyosha said, feeling that he was jumping off a roof. "Call Dmitry here at once—I'll get him for you if you're willing—and when he gets here, allow him to take your hand and Ivan's and to join your hands together. Because you're tormenting Ivan simply because it's he you really love, and the reason you're making him suffer is that your feeling for Dmitry is unhealthy and twisted, it's a false love . . . you've simply talked yourself into it . . ."

Alyosha broke off and fell silent.

"You . . . you . . . you're a holy little fool! That's all you are," Katerina cut him off, her face turning ashen and her lips twisting in rage.

Suddenly Ivan began to laugh and stood up, hat in hand.

"You're mistaken, Alyosha, my dear boy," he said, looking at his brother with an expression that Alyosha had never seen on his face before: there was a youthful sincerity in it and a feeling too strong to conceal. "Katerina has never loved me. She's known all along that I loved her, although I never told her. But she never loved me. Nor have I ever been her friend, not for one single day: she's a proud woman who has no need of my friendship. She has kept me by her side to use me as an instrument of continuous revenge. She has avenged herself by making me pay for all the insults she has borne from Dmitry all this time, ever since their first meeting, for even their very first encounter weighed on her heart like an insult. And that is the kind of person she is. All I did was listen to her tell me about her love for him. So now I'm leaving, but I want you to know, Katerina, that the truth is that you love him, and only him. And the more he insults you, the more you'll love him. That's where your twist really lies. You love him just the way he is, you love his insulting you. And if he changed and treated you decently, you'd grow cool toward him at once and stop loving him. But you need him in order to constantly admire your heroic loyalty to him while you reproach him for his unfaithfulness. And all this because you're so proud! I'm still young and I've loved you too much . . . I know I really should not have told you all this, that it would have been much more dignified for me just to get out of your life. And it would have been less humiliating for you. But, anyway, I'm going far away and I won't come back. And it's for good. I have no wish to sit and watch you perversely enjoying your heart-breaking predicament. I don't know what more I can say to you. Good-by then, Katerina. You mustn't be angry with me because I am punished a hundred times more severely than you, punished by the simple fact that I'll never see you again. Good luck to you. I don't want your hand. You knew too well what you were doing when you were tormenting me for me to forgive you at this moment. Eventually I shall forgive you, but right now I don't want to shake your hand. And *'den Dank, Dame, begehr' ich nicht,'*" he added with his crooked grin, thus quite unexpectedly revealing the fact that he too had read and reread Schiller often enough to remember passages by heart, something that, before this, his brother Alyosha would never have believed. Ivan walked out of the room without even taking leave of Mrs. Khokhlakov, the mistress of the house. Alyosha threw up his hands in despair.

"Ivan!" he called after his brother like a lost child. "Come back, Ivan! No, no, I know he'll never come back now! Nothing, nothing will bring him back now, I know it," he cried sorrowfully. "It's all my fault. I started it all! Ivan spoke wickedly, in anger. It was ugly, unfair, and unkind . . . He must come back here . . ." Alyosha kept crying out, like one demented.

Katerina walked out of the room.

"You have nothing to reproach yourself for, Alyosha. You were absolutely marvelous and quite angelic," Mrs. Khokhlakov whispered enthusiastically into the ear of a very dejected Alyosha. "I shall do everything in my power to prevent your brother Ivan from leaving town . . ."

To Alyosha's great distress, her face was beaming with joy. Katerina suddenly reappeared. She held two rainbow-colored hundred-ruble notes in her hand.

"I'd like to ask you a great favor, Alexei," she said in a calm, even voice, as though nothing had happened. "About a week ago—yes, I believe it was just a week ago—in a fit of temper, Dmitry did something that was very unfair and very ugly. There's a rather disreputable tavern in this town where Dmitry met that retired army captain whom your father was using for some business errands. Dmitry lost his temper for some reason or other and seized the man by the beard, dragging him outside in front of everybody. Then for a long time he pulled him along the street in that humiliating manner. I am told that the captain's son, a boy who attends the local school, still a child, saw it and, running alongside them, cried aloud, begging Dmitry to let go of his father, asking people in the street to interfere. But they only laughed. Forgive me, Alexei, but I cannot help getting very angry when I think of such disgraceful behavior . . . It is one of those things that only a man like Dmitry Karamazov could do . . . in a fit of anger, or carried away by his passions. I can't even describe it properly. I can't find the right words. Well, I made inquiries about the victim of the offense and I found out that he's very poor and that his name is Snegirev. He got into some trouble in the army and was forced to resign his commission. I'm afraid I don't know any more about it, but I do know that, burdened by an unhappy family, sick children, and, I believe, a mad wife, he has slipped into dire misery. He has been living in this town for a long time now, working at odd jobs. Lately he worked as a copying clerk somewhere, but they didn't pay him. When I saw you . . . I mean, I wonder whether you . . . Forgive me, I find it so hard to express myself. What I'm trying to say is that I wanted to ask you, dear, kind Alexei, to go to the house where Captain Snegirev lives, I mean, to see him under some pretext—oh, it's so difficult to say it—well, very tactfully, very delicately, as you and you only can do" (Alyosha turned very red at this point), "and try to give him these two hundred rubles. I'm sure he'll accept, I mean, that you'll succeed in persuading him to accept it . . . Or perhaps we could put it this way: it's not an attempt to conciliate him, to stop him from lodging a complaint—I understand he was thinking of suing Dmitry—it's simply out of sympathy, out of a desire to help him. It's from the woman to whom Dmitry is engaged to be married, not from Dmitry himself . . . I'm sure you'll find a much better way of giving it to him than I could myself. He lives in Kalmykov's house on Lake Street . . . Do me this favor, Alexei, I beseech you . . . And now, now I feel—I feel rather tired. Good-by."

She turned and again vanished behind the heavy curtain, so quickly that Alyosha didn't even have time to answer her, although he had things to say to her. He wanted to ask her to forgive him, to tell her that it was he who was to blame for everything, to say anything, whatever came to mind, because his heart was full to the brim and he felt he could not leave without saying something. But Mrs. Khokhlakov seized him by the hand and it was she who led him out. And just as she had before, she stopped him in the hall.

"She's proud—doing violence to herself . . . But she's kind and wonderful and generous," she said in a half whisper. "I like her so much, especially at certain moments. And now I am once again happy with the way things are. You don't know about it, my dear Alexei, but we've had a whole plot hatched here, all of us—both her aunts, myself, and even Lise—and for a whole month we've been doing our utmost and praying that she should break with your favorite brother Dmitry, who doesn't love her and doesn't even want to have anything to do with her. We want her to marry Ivan instead, a cultured and responsible young man who is deeply in love with her. Yes, we hatched a real plot, and that's perhaps the reason I haven't left town."

"But she was crying," Alyosha said. "She's suffered one more humiliation here."

"Pay no attention to women's tears, Alexei; when it comes to that, I'm always against women, always for men."

"Mother, you're spoiling him, ruining him," Lise's thin little voice came from behind the door.

"No, no, it is I who am to blame for everything. I feel dreadfully guilty," Alyosha repeated disconsolately, feeling so infinitely ashamed of what he had told Katerina that he hid his face in his hands.

"Just the opposite, you acted like an angel, yes, like an

angel, and if I have to repeat it a thousand times to convince you, I will."

"Mother, how did he act like an angel?" Lise's voice was heard again.

"Watching what was going on, I somehow suddenly thought it was Ivan she loved, so I said those stupid things. And I don't know what will happen to her now . . ." Alyosha said, apparently without having heard Lise.

"Happen to whom? To whom?" Lise cried. "Mother, what are you trying to do, to kill me? I'm asking you something and you won't even answer me!"

At that moment a maid rushed in.

"Miss Katerina is not well . . . She's crying, ma'am . . . hysterics . . ."

"What's happening?" Lise shouted now in real alarm. "If someone is going to have hysterics, it will be me, not her!"

"For heaven's sake, Lise, don't carry on like that or it'll really be the end of me. You're still too young to know everything that grown-ups know, but I'll be back and I'll tell you as much of it as possible . . . Hysterics is a good sign, Alexei. I'm delighted that she has hysterics. That's just what she needed. On these occasions I'm always against women, against their tears and hysterical outbursts. Julia, run along and tell her I'm coming at once. As to Ivan's walking away as he did, she has only herself to blame. But he won't leave town. Lise, for heaven's sake, stop that screaming! I'm sorry, you're right, it wasn't you, it was I who was screaming. Please forgive your poor mother—she's been rather carried away! Did you notice, Alexei, how young Ivan looked when he walked out of the room just now, when he said what he had to say and just strolled out? I used to think of him as the learned, scholarly type, but this time he acted so impulsively, so youthfully, displaying such a lack of experience, and all that is so good, so marvelous, so wonderful! Yes, he was wonderful, he reminded me of you . . . And that German line he quoted—it was so much like you! But I must run along now, Alexei, I really must. And you, please hurry and do that errand for her and come back as quickly as possible. You need anything, Lise? And please don't hold up Alexei. He'll see you a little later, when he gets back."

Finally Mrs. Khokhlakov ran out. Before leaving, Alyosha wanted to open wide the door that separated him from Lise.

"No, don't do that now! Never! It's too late now!" Lise shouted. "Talk to me through the door. And tell me, what did you do to be suddenly promoted to angel? That's the only thing I want to know."

"I did something utterly idiotic. Good-by, Lise."

"Don't you dare walk out on me just like that!"

"There's something that makes me very unhappy, Lise, terribly unhappy, but I'll be back anyway."

And he rushed out.

CHAPTER 6

Heartbreak in a Hovel

Alyosha really had something to make him seriously unhappy, unhappy as he had seldom been before. He had pushed himself forward, and he had blundered—blundered in a matter involving love and the emotions connected with it. "But what do I really understand about these things, what kind of judge am I in these affairs?" he repeated to himself for the hundredth time, the very thought making him blush. "Oh, I'm so ashamed . . . but that's nothing—being ashamed is only the punishment I deserve—the real trouble is that I'll cause others new unhappiness . . . And when I think that the elder sent me out to reconcile and unite people! Is that the way to unite them?" He remembered his idea of Dmitry uniting Ivan's and Katerina's hands, and again he felt ashamed. "Although I was sincere in what I said, I'll have to be a bit more intelligent in the future," he concluded, and his conclusion did not even make him smile.

To carry out Katerina's errand, Alyosha had to go to Lake Street and it so happened that Dmitry lived nearby, in a sidestreet that gave onto Lake Street. Alyosha decided to stop at his brother's first, although he didn't expect to find Dmitry at home. He suspected Dmitry would avoid him now, but he felt he had to find him at any cost. Time was running out, and the thought of the dying elder had never left him for a minute, not even a second, since he had left the monastery.

There was something in Katerina's errand that aroused Alyosha's curiosity: when she had mentioned the captain's young son who had run behind his humbled father crying, it had suddenly occurred to Alyosha that it might be the same child who had later bitten his finger when Alyosha was trying to find out how he could possibly have wronged him. Now Alyosha was almost sure that it must be the same boy, although he did not know why he was so sure. Distracted by this thought, he decided not to think of the "mess" he had made of things and, instead of torturing himself with remorse, to try and do what he had to do now as best he could and just hope that things would take care of themselves. This thought cheered him up completely. As he was turning into Dmitry's street, he suddenly realized that he was hungry. He took out of his pocket the French roll he had taken at his father's and ate it as he walked. That made him feel even stronger.

Dmitry was not in. The owner of the small house—an old carpenter, who lived there with his wife and son—examined Alyosha suspiciously.

"He's been out for two days—hasn't even come home to sleep," the old man told him. "He's out of town, perhaps," was all he would answer to Alyosha's insistent questioning, and Alyosha understood that the man was answering according to instructions he had received.

"Isn't he at Grushenka's, or perhaps hiding at Foma's again?" he asked, deliberately showing them he knew of these confidential matters, but the landlord only stared at him in alarm. "They must like him," Alyosha thought. "They're trying to help him. That's good."

It took Alyosha a while to find Kalmykov's house on Lake Street, where Captain Snegirev lived. It was a ramshackle, sagging little house that had only three windows giving onto the street and a grimy courtyard in the back, in the middle of which stood a lonely cow. The entrance was from the yard and it led into a passage. In a room on the left of the passage lived the very ancient landlady, Mrs. Kalmykov, and her daughter, who was also already an old woman, both of them apparently deaf. He had to ask them several times about Captain Snegirev before one of them understood that he was asking for their tenants and pointed out to him a quite clean little wooden hut in the yard. It was, indeed, nothing more than a hut. Alyosha took hold of the iron latch to open the door but stopped: he was suddenly struck by the complete silence inside. From Katerina's words, he had gathered that Snegirev lived here with his whole family. "They may all be asleep just now," he thought, "or perhaps they heard me coming and are waiting for me to knock. I'd better knock before I go in." He knocked and received an answer but not right away. Indeed, it took perhaps as much as ten seconds.

"Who's there?" someone asked in a loud, harsh voice.

Alyosha opened the door and stepped in. He found himself in a wooden cabin, quite spacious but terribly crowded with both people and all sorts of household junk. To the left was a big Russian stove. A clothes line, tied across the room between the stove and the window on the left, was hung with all sorts of ragged washing. Along two of the walls were beds covered with knitted blankets. On the bed on the left was a heap of pillows in black calico cases, each smaller than the next. On the bed on the right, there was only one little pillow. The far corner was screened off by a curtain, or rather a sheet, hanging on another clothes line that stretched across the angle formed by the walls. Behind that screen could be seen another bed, made of a bench and a chair tied together. A square wooden peasant table had been moved out of that corner and was now under the middle window. The three windows, each divided into four small panes which were greenish with mildew, let in little light and, since they were tightly closed, there was no air and the room was dark and stuffy. On the table was a frying pan with the remains of some fried eggs in it, a half-eaten slice of bread, and a half bottle with only the dregs of the joy-giving stuff it had contained.

A woman, who wore a cheap calico dress but who looked as if she might be a lady, sat on a chair by the bed on Alyosha's left. Her face was very thin and her skin had a yellowish tinge. Her cheeks were so sunken that one could see at first glance that she was very sick. But what struck Alyosha most was the look the poor lady gave him—it was questioning and at the same time immensely scornful. And, till the moment she spoke herself, during the whole time that Alyosha was talking to the captain, her large brown eyes kept shifting from Alyosha to her husband and back with the same questioning, scornful look in them. By the window, next to the woman, stood a rather plain-looking girl with thinnish red hair, poorly but quite neatly dressed. When Alyosha entered, she too gave him a look of unconcealed disgust. On his right, also sitting beside a bed, was another girl—a pitiful creature of about twenty. She was a hunchback and, as Alyosha learned later, her legs were withered. Her crutches leaned against the wall behind her bed. The extraordinarily beautiful, gentle eyes of the crippled girl looked at Alyosha with infinite serenity.

At the table was the man who had been eating the fried eggs. He was about forty-five, small and puny, with reddish hair and a thin reddish goatee that looked very much like a bast back-scrubber; the comparison, and particularly the word "back-scrubber," flashed across Alyosha's mind as soon as he saw the Captain. This, apparently, was the man who had shouted, "Who's there?" when Alyosha had knocked at the door, since there was no other man in the room.

As soon as Alyosha walked in, the man literally leapt up from his chair and, hurriedly wiping his mouth with a tattered napkin, flew across the room up to Alyosha.

"Some monk taking up a collection for his monastery," the red-haired girl standing in the corner said in a loud voice, but the man who had rushed up to Alyosha turned sharply on his heels toward her and said emotionally in a strangely faltering voice:

"No, Barbara, you're all wrong, completely off the mark!" Then, turning just as abruptly back to Alyosha, he said: "Now perhaps you would be kind enough to explain what brings you to these lower depths?"

Alyosha was watching him closely. It was the first time he had ever seen the man. There was something awkward about him. He looked as if he was very irritable, as if he was always in too much of a hurry. Although it was obvious that he had had something to drink recently, he was by no means drunk. His face wore an extremely arrogant look and yet, at the same time, was unmistakably full of fear. He looked like a man who had been persecuted for a long time but was still capable of jumping up at any moment to assert himself. Or, even more, like a man who would love to hit you but was terribly afraid that you might decide to hit him. In his words and in the inflections of his rather strident voice could be detected a sort of cracked, fool's humor, now wicked, now timorous, never maintaining the same tone and constantly breaking off. He asked Alyosha the question about coming to the "lower depths" trembling and with his eyes popping, and he stepped up so close to him that Alyosha instinctively took a step back. This gentleman wore a thin topcoat, stained and patched. His trousers were of a very light checkered material such as no one wore anymore, and they were so crumpled below the knees that they didn't reach his shoes, so that it looked as if he had grown out of them, like a growing boy.

"I am . . . my name is Alexei Karamazov," Alyosha said in answer to his question, but the man interrupted him at once.

"I am aware of that already," the man snapped, anxious to let Alyosha know unmistakably that he knew who he was. "Well, I am Captain Snegirev. But I would still like to know exactly what it was that inspired you to . . ."

"I just thought I'd like to come and see you . . . I would actually like to talk to you but, of course, only if you will allow me . . ."

"In that case here's a chair, please be seated, sir. That's how they invite people to sit down in good old-fashioned plays: 'Please be seated,' they say," and the captain quickly grabbed an empty wooden chair (a plain wooden peasant chair without upholstery), put it almost in the middle of the room, then took another such chair for himself, and sat down on it facing Alyosha, again so close that their knees almost touched.

"So, I am Nikolai Ilyich Snegirev, former captain in the Russian infantry, and still a former army captain, all my disgraces notwithstanding. Actually, perhaps I should have introduced myself as Captain Downtrodden rather than Captain Snegirev because I have come to sound very much like a downtrodden man, which is something that we acquire when we're down on our luck, a tone acquired through humiliation . . ."

"I suppose that's true," Alyosha said with a smile, "but I'm not too sure whether one acquires it involuntarily or deliberately. What do you think?"

"As God is my witness, I acquired it involuntarily. I never sounded like a downtrodden man before and suddenly, lo and behold, that's just what I started sounding like. This should be decided, I would say, by some higher authority. I see that you're interested in such worldly questions. But I still wonder how I could possibly arouse your curiosity, for, after all, I live in an environment that is hardly suitable for receiving visits."

"I wanted to talk to you about . . . about that other business."

"What 'other' business?" Snegirev interrupted impatiently.

"About your incident with my brother Dmitry," Alyosha said in an embarrassed tone.

"What incident do you have in mind? Are you referring to the incident involving my back-scrubber, by any chance?" he said, jerking his chair forward so that this time their knees actually bumped.

"What back-scrubber?" Alyosha muttered.

"He's come to complain about me, papa," Alyosha heard the already familiar voice of the boy coming from behind the screened-off corner, "because it was his finger I bit today." The sheet was pushed aside and Alyosha saw his recent enemy lying on the chair and bench tied together in the corner under the icons. The little boy lay there under an old quilt and the overcoat he had worn earlier that day. He was sick and was running a temperature, as could be seen from the feverish brilliance of his eyes. Unlike in the street, he now glared fearlessly at Alyosha, as if challenging him: "You can't do anything to me here because this is my home!"

"What finger? Whose finger did he bite? You mean he bit your finger," Snegirev said, jumping up from his chair, "your finger, sir?"

"That's right. He was having a battle with some other boys —they were throwing stones at him and he at them. There were six of them against him and he was all alone. I walked over to him, but he threw a stone at me too and then another one, aimed at my head. When I asked him why, he suddenly rushed at me and bit my finger rather badly. I still don't know why."

"I'll give him a good whipping right away, sir, right away!" The captain looked as if he was about to put his words into action.

"But I wasn't complaining at all. I just told you what happened . . . I don't want you to whip him. Besides, I think he's sick now . . ."

"Did you really think I was going to do it? That I'd take my little Ilyusha and whip him just to please you? Must I do it at once or could you wait a little, my good sir?" The captain suddenly turned toward Alyosha as though he were about to attack him. "I'm awfully sorry about your precious finger, my dear sir. Perhaps you'd like me, before I start whipping Ilyusha, to cut off these four fingers of mine with this knife, to satisfy your sense of justice? I do hope, though, that you'll be satisfied with four of my fingers and not demand the fifth as well . . ."

He stopped abruptly. He seemed to be gasping for breath. His every feature was jerking and twitching as he glared at Alyosha with the utmost defiance. He was beside himself.

"I think I understand everything now," Alyosha said quietly and sadly, without getting up. "I see now that your little boy is a good son. He loves you, and he attacked me because I am the brother of the man who offended his father. Yes, it all makes sense to me now," Alyosha repeated musingly. "May I say that I know my brother, Dmitry Karamazov, is now very sorry for what he did and that, if you would allow him to come and see you or, if you prefer, to meet you in the same public place and apologize to you before everybody, he would do so . . ."

"You mean he can pull my beard, then say he's sorry, and everything is fine and no damage done? Is that what you're suggesting?"

"No, no, not at all. He'll do anything you want, whatever you ask him to . . ."

"You mean if I asked his highness to get down on his knees before me in that same inn—by the way, it's called the Capital City Inn—or, say, in the middle of the square, he'd do it?"

"Yes, he'd kneel too, if you demanded it."

"I'm moved to the core, sir, moved to the core and moved to tears. Or am I being a bit overappreciative of your brother's magnanimity? Allow me to finish introducing myself, that is, to introduce my family, my two daughters and my son—I mean my litter, dear sir. If I should die, who would care for them? And as long as I'm alive, who except them gives a damn for a repulsive old man like me? A family is a great arrangement that God has provided for men like myself, because even a man like me must have someone in the world to love him . . ."

"You're absolutely right!" Alyosha cried approvingly.

"Stop making a fool of yourself, will you!" the girl who stood by the window suddenly cried out, looking at her father with scorn and distaste. "An idiot comes and you at once feel obliged to disgrace yourself before him!"

"Give me time, Barbara, give me a chance to make my point," the captain shouted at her commandingly, although he gave her a very approving look nevertheless. "That's just the way she is, sir. You know the type:

> In all creation there was nothing
> To which his blessing he would give.

It should, of course, be 'she' instead of 'he': she certainly wouldn't give her blessing to anything . . . And now allow me to introduce my wife, Arina, a lady of about forty-three, who has no legs to speak of—what legs she has cannot carry her far. She comes of humble folk. Arina, my dear, relax your features. Get up, Mr. Karamazov!" The captain seized Alyosha by the hand and pulled him up with a strength that no one would have suspected in him. "Come, ladies, come and introduce yourselves. You must stand up for that, remember . . . No, no, mother, this isn't the same Karamazov who . . . well, you know who. This is his brother, famous for his meekness and his virtue. Please allow him, Arina, allow me first to kiss your hand."

And the captain bent down and, with great courtesy, kissed his wife's hand. The girl standing by the window turned her back on them in disgust, but the puzzled and disdainful expression on Mrs. Snegirev's face suddenly vanished.

"Please sit down, Mr. Chernomazov," she said, great warmth radiating from her eyes.

"His name is Karamazov, mother," the captain corrected her. "She's of humble origin, you know," he reminded Alyosha in a whisper.

"All right, let it be Karamazov, but somehow I always say Chernomazov instead . . . Sit down then, please. I don't really know why he had to get you up . . . He said I'm a lady without legs, but in fact I have huge legs, like barrels. That's because they're swollen, while the rest of me has dried out. Once upon a time I was quite a big woman, but today it's as if I'd swallowed a worm . . ."

"We're humble, ordinary people, please keep that in mind," the captain said again.

"Ah, father, father!" the hunchbacked girl, who until then had sat silent in her chair, said suddenly, covering her eyes with a handkerchief.

"Clown!" the girl standing by the window said.

"You see how things are with us," the mother said, indicating both her daughters at once with a sweeping gesture. "It's just like clouds passing over us . . . But the clouds will pass and the music will play for us again. In the old days, when we were with the army, we had many guests coming to visit us. I make no comparisons, sir, if someone likes someone—that's his own business. Once the deacon's wife comes to see me and she says to me, 'Alexander is the sweetest man on earth, but Natalia,' she says, 'she's an emanation from hell.' 'Well,' I say to her, 'that depends on people's taste and, as to you,' I say, 'you aren't big, but you stink.' 'And you,' she says, 'you ought to be taught a lesson.' 'Ah, you ignorant creature,' I say, 'do you think you're going to teach me or what?' 'I breathe clean air,' she says, 'and you breathe foul air.' So I say to that woman: 'Go and ask the officers around here whether the air in me is pure or foul, ask them.' And ever since then, that woman has weighed on my heart. So some time later, I was sitting just as I'm sitting now when that general comes in, the same general, you know, who came here during Holy Week. 'Tell me, Your Excellency,' I asked him, 'is it possible for a true lady to breathe fresh air into herself?' 'It is indeed,' he answered, 'and it would be nice if you opened a window or a door, because it's rather stuffy in here.' So they're all the same and I wonder why they all speak like that about my air? Dead people smell even worse. Then I said to him: 'I'm not spoiling your air, but I'll leave as soon as I get myself a new pair of shoes.' Ah, my lovely ones, don't blame your own mother! Ah, Nikolai, my husband, how have I displeased you? All I have is my little Ilyusha—he loves me when he comes back home from school. Yesterday he brought me an apple. Forgive me, my dear ones, forgive me, a poor, lonely, abandoned woman . . . And why is it that my smell has become so repulsive to you?"

Tears gushed from the eyes of the poor madwoman. The captain rushed toward her.

"Mother, mother, darling, stop, please stop! You aren't lonely or abandoned, we all love you, adore you."

He kissed both her hands again and gently stroked her cheeks; then he took the napkin from the table and wiped away her tears with it. Alyosha felt tears in his own eyes too.

"Well, now you've seen, now you've heard for yourself!" the captain shouted suddenly, turning toward Alyosha and pointing his finger at the madwoman.

"I've seen and heard," Alyosha mumbled.

"Papa, papa, you aren't trying to plead with him, are you? Don't bother with him, papa. Let him go!" the boy shouted, sitting up in bed and looking at his father with burning eyes.

"Perhaps it's time you stopped acting like a fool at last and showing your stupid tricks, which never achieve anything anyway!" Barbara cried from her corner. She was really furious now and even stamped her foot.

"This time you're absolutely right to be angry, my dear Barbara, and I'll comply with your wishes at once. Here, Mr. Karamazov, here's your hat; let me get my own cap, and let us be on our way. I have something pretty serious to say to you, but I would like to say it outside these walls. This other daughter of mine, Nina—I believe I forgot to introduce her to you—is an angel of God in the flesh, sent down among mortals . . . if you understand what I mean . . ."

"You're shaking all over as if you were having a fit," Barbara said with indignant disgust.

"And the one who stamped her foot at me and called me a clown, she, too, is an angel incarnate, and she was right to say what she said about me. So let us be on our way, Mr. Karamazov. It's high time we put an end to this, sir."

And grabbing Alyosha by the arm, the captain led him out of the room and into the street.

CHAPTER 7

Heartbreak Outdoors

"At least the air is fresh here, and I'm afraid I can't say the same of the air in my house—I mean that in every sense. Let's take a little walk, my good sir, because I have something to tell you that I hope will interest you."

"I, too, have a very important matter to discuss with you, only I don't know how to begin," Alyosha said.

"I gathered that much, you know, for if you hadn't had some important matter to discuss with me, you'd never have come here in the first place. Unless you really wanted to complain about my boy, but that's extremely unlikely. And speaking of the boy, now I can describe the whole scene to you, for I couldn't possibly do so inside. You see, my back-scrubber used to be thicker before, I mean, no more than a week ago—I'm referring, of course, to my beard, which the schoolboys have nicknamed a back-scrubber. Well, then, it was by this beard of mine that your dear brother Dmitry decided to pull me out of the inn. Oh, for no particular reason, just because he felt in the mood for it and I happened to be at hand. So he dragged me out into the street just when the boys were walking home from school, and among them was my Ilyusha. When he saw me in that state, he rushed up to me shouting, 'Papa, papa!' flung his arms round me, trying to pull me away, shouting at my assailant, 'Let go of him, he's my papa, please let him go, forgive him!' Yes, he said just that, 'Forgive him,' and he caught the hand that was clutching my beard and even kissed that hand . . . I can still see his little face at that moment—I'll never forget it as long as I live, you know . . ."

"I swear to you," Alyosha cried, "my brother will apologize to you completely sincerely and, if he must, he will kneel on that same square . . . I will make him kneel, for if he refuses, he will no longer be a brother to me!"

"Ah, it is all still in the planning stage, I see. Indeed, it doesn't even come from him but from your own warm heart. I wish you had said so in the first place, sir. In that case, allow me to tell you more of your brother's sense of the honor and chivalry of an officer and a gentleman. When he had had enough of pulling me by the beard, he let go and said: 'You're an officer and I'm an officer, so if you can find yourself an acceptable second, send him to me and I'll give you satisfaction, although you're nothing but a dog.' That's exactly what he said. A real knight in shining armor! Well, we walked off, Ilyusha and I, and I'm afraid the picture of our family honor was changed once and for all in my boy's mind. No, sir, we can't afford to remain gentlemen in our circumstances. Anyway, you can judge for yourself since you've been inside our castle and seen the three ladies sitting there—one legless and simple-minded, the second legless and hunchbacked, and the third one with legs but, alas, too intelligent for her own good. She has a degree and is impatient to return to Petersburg and fight for women's rights on the banks of the Neva. And, of course, there's Ilyusha, who's only nine. Well, I'm their sole support in the world and just think what would happen to them if I were to die! And since that is the situation, how can I challenge him to a duel? Suppose he kills me—what will they all do without me? And even worse, if, instead of killing me outright, he only crippled me, made it impossible for me to work, made me into just one more mouth to feed—well, who would there be to feed all those mouths then? Of course, we might take Ilyusha out of school and send him begging. So that's what his offer to accept my challenge means to me—just stupid words and nothing else."

"He will beg you to forgive him. He will kneel before you and bow to the ground before you in the middle of the square," Alyosha said again, his eyes afire.

"I thought of suing him, but if you take a look at the laws on our books, you'll see there is very little I could claim for a personal insult. Besides, when she heard about it, Grushenka warned me: 'Don't you ever dare sue him, because if you do, I'll see to it that everyone finds out that he gave you that beating because of your own crooked dealing, and you'll wind up being tried yourself!' But as God is my witness, if I got involved in that crooked deal at all, I was just an insignificant worm, acting on her and Mr. Karamazov's—your father's— behalf. 'And on top of that,' she told me, 'if you sue him, I won't have anything to do with you and you'll never earn one kopek from me, and my merchant will kick you out.' Yes, sir, 'my merchant,' that's how she refers to him. 'Well,' I said to myself, 'if her merchant kicks me out too, where will I be able to earn anything at all?' Those two are now the only sources of income I have left, since your father not only doesn't trust me anymore for another, quite unrelated, reason, but also wants to drag me into court himself, making use of papers in his possession with my signature on them. Well, in view of all this, I decided to keep quiet and do nothing, and you yourself have now had the opportunity of seeing my home. And now allow me to ask you this: How badly did my Ilyusha bite your finger? I didn't want to go into these details in the house."

"Pretty badly, for he was quite exasperated at the time. But everything is clear now—he did it to avenge you, because I'm a Karamazov. But I wish you had seen him in that rock-throwing battle with the other boys. That's very dangerous— he could get killed. They're just silly children, but a rock could very well break somebody's skull."

"Certainly, and he has already been hit, not in the head but in the chest, just above the heart. He has a bruise there today, from a stone. He came in moaning and crying, and now he's ill."

"But, you know, he attacks first . . . They told me that he had slashed a boy, Krasotkin, with his penknife."

"I heard about that too, and it's a bad business. His father is a local government official and that may cause us quite a bit of trouble."

"If I were you, I'd keep him at home for a while, until he quiets down a bit, until his anger passes . . ."

"Anger, sir! That's just the right word! There's great anger in that little boy. And you still don't know all of it. Allow me to explain the following point to you. After that incident, the schoolboys started taunting him by shouting, 'Back-scrub-ber.' Schoolboys are a merciless breed. Taken individually, they may be little angels, but in a crowd they're completely without pity. So they started taunting him and it aroused his sense of honor. Another boy with less character would have resigned himself and just become ashamed of his father, but this one decided to stand up for his father, one against the world. He wants to defend his father and uphold truth and justice. What he went through while he was kissing your brother's hand and begging him to let go of his papa, only God and I know, no one else. And that's the way our children —I mean, not your children, but the children of the likes of me, honorable but despised men—learn the truth about life by the time they're nine. Rich people may never find out about these things as long as they live, but my Ilyusha knew the truth the second he kissed that hand on the square. And at the very moment it was revealed to him, the truth maimed him in such a way that he'll never recover . . ."

The captain spoke heatedly and again as if in a fever, striking the open palm of his left hand with his right fist, as if trying to illustrate how the truth had hit his boy.

"That night he became feverish and delirious," he went on, "and the following day he hardly spoke to me. I noticed that he looked at me now and then out of the corner of his eye, but mostly he looked out of the window and pretended to be busy with his schoolwork, although I knew very well he did not have his mind on his lessons. The next day I drank quite a bit in my misery and, I confess, there are many things I don't remember. My wife, too, started crying that day—I must say that I love my wife very much—so I drank up the last kopeks we had in the house. You mustn't despise me for that, my dear sir, because in Russia drunks are the kindest people and the kindest people are drunks. So I lay there, pretty drunk, and I don't remember much of what Ilyusha was like that day, but that was the day when the schoolboys started taunting him from the early morning on: 'Back-scrubber,' they shouted, 'your father was dragged out of the inn by his back-scrubber and you ran along behind begging for him.' Next day he came back from school looking terrible, all pale in the face. 'What's the matter, Ilyusha?' I asked him. He wouldn't answer. Anyway, it was impossible to do much talking in my house because my wife and daughters would always interfere, especially since the girls had found out everything the very first day, and Barbara was already making remarks like, 'What else could one expect to happen to a clown and a buffoon? Nothing sensible, for sure.' 'How right you are, Barbara, my daughter, you can't expect anything sensible from such people,' I told her, and for that time I got out of it that way.

"Well, in the evening I took my son out for a walk. I must tell you at this point that the two of us had been going out for a walk every evening before that, following roughly the path that you and I are taking now; from our gate to that big rock over there, see the one by the fence where the town pasture begins. It's a deserted spot and very nice. So I was walking hand in hand with Ilyusha, as we usually did, me holding his tiny hand with his fingers so thin and cold—because, you know, his chest is weak. 'Papa,' he says, 'papa . . .' 'What is it, my boy?' 'The things he did to you, papa,' he says, and I saw how his eyes flashed. 'It can't be helped,' I said. 'Don't make up with him, papa, don't. The boys at school say that he gave you ten rubles to make it up to you.' 'No, Ilyusha,' I told him, 'I'll never accept money from him now, not for anything.' He began to tremble all over then, and the next thing I knew, there he was kissing my hand again. 'Papa,' he said, 'I want you to challenge him to a duel, papa, because the boys at school are teasing me—they say you're a coward and won't dare to challenge him to a duel and, instead, will accept ten rubles from him.' 'I can't challenge him to a duel, Ilyusha,' I told him, and I explained to him briefly why I couldn't, just as I've told you. He heard me out. 'Papa,' he said then, 'still, you mustn't make up with him. When I grow up, I'll challenge him to a duel myself, and I'll kill him!' His eyes sparkled and flashed when he said that. Well, whatever the facts, I felt that being his father, it was my duty to tell him what I thought was right: 'It's a sin, you must remember,' I said, 'to kill people, even in a duel.' 'Then, papa,' he said, 'when I grow up and fight him, I'll knock his sword out of his hand with my sword, throw myself at him, knock him down, raise my sword over him, and tell him that I could kill him if I wanted, but that I forgive him.'

"So you see, my good sir, how he'd worked it all out in his little head in those two days; he must have been thinking up that scene of revenge, sword in hand, for two days and nights and I suppose that was what he was raving about when he was feverish. But the trouble is, he has started coming back from school badly beaten up. I learned about it all the day before yesterday . . . As a matter of fact, I think you're right, I won't send him to school anymore. I learned then that he was at war with the rest of his class, that he provokes them because he has become bitter against them and his heart is afire. I've become really frightened for him. Well, we walked on for a while and then suddenly he says, 'Isn't it true, papa, that the rich are the most powerful people on earth?' 'Right, Ilyusha, there's nothing in this world more powerful than the rich.' 'You know what, papa, I will get rich, become an officer, and rout all enemies. The Tsar will decorate me, and when I come here no one will dare to . . .' He didn't say what no one would dare to do, didn't finish, and his lips were still quivering as before. 'Our town, papa,' he said, 'is a bad town, isn't it, papa?' 'It's none too good,' I said to him, 'it's none too good.' 'So let's move to another town, papa, a good one, where people know nothing about us.' 'We'll do that, Ilyusha, we'll move as soon as we have saved up a bit of money.' I was glad to find something to take his thoughts off those painful things. So we began talking about that other town where we would move and about buying ourselves a horse and buggy. We'd put mother and the girls in the buggy and cover them with blankets, and the two of us would walk alongside; now and then he would climb into the carriage too, for a ride and a rest, while I would have to walk all the way, because we had to think of the horse. And that was how we'd move, we decided. He loved the idea, especially that we'd have our own horse and he could drive it. It's a fact that every Russian boy comes into the world thinking about a horse . . . So we chatted for a long time and I was sure that I had distracted him. That was two days ago.

"But last night it was something else again. He had left for school in the morning and had come back looking very, very gloomy. In the evening I took his hand and we went out for our walk. He kept silent, wouldn't talk to me. A wind came up, clouds came over the sun, it smelled of autumn, and it was getting rather dark. We walked in silence, feeling very sad, both of us. 'Well, what about discussing that trip of ours a bit?' I said, hoping to resume our previous night's talk. He didn't answer and I only felt his fingers giving a little jerk in my hand. It looked bad. 'Something else must have happened,' I thought. So we reached the big rock—we were just at the point where we are now, as a matter of fact. I sat down here on this rock. And over us kites were flying; they were rustling and crackling in the air, lots of them, maybe as many as thirty. It's the season for kite-flying now, it so happens. 'It's time we flew our last year's kite, Ilyusha, don't you think? I'll fix it up if you'll tell me where it is.' Still no answer from him. And he stands sideways to me, looking away . . .

"Just then, there was a burst of wind and sand started flying in all directions. Suddenly my Ilyusha flew to me and threw his arms around my neck, hugging me as hard as he could. You know how it is with children who are proud and silent and who have been holding back their tears for a long time—if something happens that's too much for the child to bear and the tears finally break through, they don't simply flow, they pour from their eyes in streams. And my whole face was wet from those warm tears. He sobbed and shivered and clung to me desperately as I sat on this stone. 'Papa, my papa, ah, the way he treated you!' I couldn't stand it and burst into sobs too and we sat there, the two of us, hugging one another and sobbing. 'Ilyusha,' I kept saying, 'oh, my Ilyusha . . .' And no one saw us then, no one except God, and I only hope that He will put it into my service record; if so, you can thank your dear brother for me, Mr. Alexei Karamazov, but I'm afraid I won't give my boy a whipping even to satisfy you."

At the end, he had slipped back into his bitter tone with its clownish twist. But Alyosha felt that the captain trusted him now and that he would not have told anyone else what he had just told him. This encouraged Alyosha, who was himself on the verge of tears.

"Ah, I would like so much to make friends with your boy," he said, "if only you could help me . . ."

"Why, yes, just as you wish . . ." the captain muttered.

"But now I want to talk to you about something else. Please listen to me," Alyosha went on excitedly. "I have a message for you. That same brother of mine, Dmitry, has also insulted his fiancée, a highly respectable girl of whom you may have heard . . . I have the right to tell you about the humiliation he inflicted on her, indeed, it is my duty to do so, because, when she learned about what he had done to you and about your difficult circumstances, she asked me today, just an hour or so ago in fact, to . . . well, she wanted me to give you this from her, from her personally, not from Dmitry, who has broken with her. Nor is it from me, his brother, or from anyone but her, her alone. She beseeches you to accept it—both you and she have been harmed by the same man; indeed, she thought of you only after she had been insulted just as badly—I mean hurt as deeply—as you were . . . She is like a sister trying to help her brother . . . She asked me to persuade you to accept this two hundred rubles as coming from a sister who knows how hard up her brother is. And no one will ever learn of it, there'll be no wicked gossip . . . So here is the two hundred rubles, and, believe me, you must take it, for otherwise . . . otherwise it would mean that everyone has to be everyone else's enemy in the world. But you know that all men must be brothers. You're a magnanimous man, you must understand these things, you must . . ."

And Alyosha handed the captain the two brand new, rainbow-colored hundred-ruble bills. They were standing by the big rock, near the wattle fence, and there was no one else near. The sight of the bills seemed to affect the captain very strangely. He shuddered, taken completely by surprise. The possibility of such an outcome had never occurred to him. He hadn't expected financial assistance from any quarter, and such a substantial sum was beyond his wildest dreams. He took the bills and held them in his hand for almost a whole minute without saying a word, and a completely new expression appeared on his face.

"Is this for me? Two hundred rubles? My God—I haven't seen so much money in four years! And she says she feels a sister to me? Good Lord! But is it true, is it?"

"I swear that everything I've told you is the truth," Alyosha said emotionally.

The captain turned deep red.

"But tell me, my dear friend, tell me this: wouldn't you despise me yourself, Mr. Karamazov, if I accepted this money? No, wait, please, listen to me . . ." he rattled on hurriedly, touching Alyosha with one hand and then the other, "listen to me . . . you were saying, in order to persuade me, that it was like a sister sending it to a brother, but inside, you yourself . . . wouldn't you feel disgusted if I accepted?"

"Of course I wouldn't! I swear by my salvation! And no one else will ever hear about it. We'll be the only ones to know, the three of us, and one more lady who is a very close friend . . ."

"Never mind the lady, I want you to listen to me, Alexei Karamazov. The time has come when you must hear what I have to tell you, because otherwise you won't even be able to understand what this two hundred rubles means to me," the poor man went on, gradually working himself up into a state of wild exuberance. He seemed to be completely overwhelmed and spoke in a great hurry as if afraid he wouldn't have time to say everything he had on his mind.

"Besides the fact that this money would be honestly acquired from a highly respected and saintly sister, I would be able to get medical treatment for my wife and Nina—you know, my hunchback daughter. Once Dr. Herzenstube came and examined them both, just out of sheer kindness; he examined them for a whole hour and then said: 'You know, I can make no sense out of it.' Nevertheless, he prescribed some mineral water that they have in the pharmacy here for my wife, and I'm sure it would do her good. He also prescribed medicinal foot baths for her. Now, a bottle of mineral water costs thirty kopeks and she'd have to drink perhaps as many as forty bottles. So I took the prescription and put it on the shelf where the icons are and just left it lying there. And for Nina, he prescribed hot baths with a special solution in them, twice a day—morning and evening—but how could I possibly provide her with such a treatment in my mansion, without a maid, without help, without a bathtub, and without even water? And my Nina suffers from rheumatic pains, which I haven't told you about yet; at night her whole right side aches so badly she can't help moaning, although the angel tries very hard not to wake us up . . . We eat whatever we can get, but even so she insists on taking only what is left over, something that one would throw to a dog otherwise, as if she felt, 'I'm not worthy to receive even that much and to deprive you of it, because I'm a useless cripple and a burden to you all.' But she is wrong. We need her badly because it is thanks to her meekness that God tolerates us and, without her constant angelic kindness, our house would have become a real hell; she makes us all gentler, even Barbara. But please don't misjudge Barbara either, because she, too, is an angel in her own way and because she, too, has a hard life. She came home in the summer with sixteen rubles that she had earned by giving lessons. She had put that money aside to pay for her return trip to Petersburg in September. But then we took her money and spent it, so she couldn't go back to Petersburg. Besides, she cannot go away because she does all the work for us at home—we have harnessed her and saddled her and she pulls us like a draft horse: she looks after us all, mends the clothes, does the laundry, sweeps the floors, puts her mother to bed, which is very hard, because mother is very whimsical, tearful—because mother is crazy!

"But now if I take this two hundred rubles, I can hire a servant, and you must understand, Mr. Karamazov, that it would make medical treatment for my loved ones possible, that I'd be able to send my learned daughter back to Petersburg, that I'd buy us some meat and we'd have a new diet . . . My God, but it'd be just like in a dream!"

Alyosha was elated to see the poor man happy and willing to accept what made that happiness possible.

"Wait, Alexei, wait!" the captain cried, as if snatching another daydream out of thin air, and once more he went rattling on excitedly and at great speed. "You know what? Perhaps it would be possible now for Ilyusha and me to make our dream really come true: perhaps we could really buy a horse and buggy—it must be a black horse, though, he especially insisted on that point—and we could leave just as we planned to do a couple of days ago. I know a lawyer in Kursk Province—I knew him when we were boys—and I have been assured by a reliable person that if I could get there, he would take me on as a clerk in his office. Well, who can tell, perhaps he'd really take me on . . . Ah, it would be wonderful to seat mother and Nina in the buggy, put Ilyusha on the driver's box, and I would run along beside it, watching my family ride . . . Ah, dear God, if only I could collect a little debt that someone owes me as well, there would be enough money even for that too!"

"There will be enough, there will be!" Alyosha assured him enthusiastically. "I'm sure Katerina will send you more. She'll send you all you need . . . And then I, too, I have some money of my own, and I'd like you to take as much as you need, accept it as from a friend, a brother. You'll pay me back some day . . . Because I'm sure you'll get rich, I'm sure of it . . . And you know, you could think of nothing better than moving to another province! That would be salvation for you, and especially for your little boy. And, believe me, you should do it soon, before the winter sets in, before it starts to freeze. I hope you'll write me from there and that we'll always be like brothers . . . No, no, this is no daydream!"

Alyosha was so pleased and so full of enthusiasm that he felt like hugging the captain, but as he looked at him again, he stopped dead. Snegirev stood with his neck stretched forward, his lips pursed, and a frenzied expression on his pale face. His lips were moving in an effort to say something, but no sound came out. It was a frightening sight.

"What's the matter?" Alyosha said with a shudder.

"Mr. Ka-Karamaz-ov . . . I . . . you . . ." Snegirev muttered, staring strangely and wildly straight into Alyosha's eyes with the look of a man who has suddenly decided to jump off a mountain peak, while at the same time he forced his lips into a smile, "I, sir . . . wouldn't you like me, sir, to

show you a little trick?" he managed to whisper quickly, his
speech suddenly no longer faltering.

"What trick?"

"A hocus-pocus trick," the captain whispered, his mouth
twisting to the left and his left eye narrowing as he stared at
Alyosha as though his gaze were riveted on him.

"What are you talking about, what trick?" Alyosha asked
in alarm.

"Here, look at this!" the captain shrieked.

For a second he waved before Alyosha's eyes the two
hundred-ruble bills that, throughout their conversation, he
had been holding by a corner between thumb and forefinger.
Then he snatched at them with his other hand, crumpled
them, and squeezed them tightly in his fist.

"Did you see it? Did you see it?" he screeched, pale and
beside himself. He lifted his fist in the air and with all his
might threw the crumpled bills into the sand. "Did you see?
Well, so now you know!"

He raised his foot and trampled the bills under his heel,
furiously, breathing hard, shouting each time he brought his
heel down:

"Here's your money! Here's your money! Here it is, see!"
Then suddenly he jumped back and stood erect, facing
Alyosha, his whole figure striving to express his unquench-
able pride.

"Kindly transmit to those who sent you that the back-
scrubber's honor is not for sale!" he cried, waving his finger
in the air.

Then, abruptly turning away, he started to run. But a few
steps away, he stopped, turned toward Alyosha, and blew
him a kiss. Then he ran a few steps farther, stopped again,
and for the last time looked back at Alyosha. This time his
features were no longer twisted and his clownish expression
had vanished. Instead, tears were running down his cheeks
and he was shaken by sobs. In a tearful, choking, faltering
voice, he shouted:

"And how could I explain to my boy why I accepted your
money for having been disgraced!"

He ran off again and this time did not turn back.

Alyosha watched him disappear, feeling infinitely sad. He
knew that, until the very last moment, Snegirev had not
known himself that he would crumple up the bills and throw
them away. Also, as he watched Snegirev, he knew the man

would not look back now. Alyosha did not want to call him or try to catch him, for he knew it would be to no avail.

When Snegirev was out of sight, Alyosha picked up the two bills. They were very crumpled, crushed, and pressed deep into the sand, but otherwise they were quite undamaged. They even crackled like new bills as he smoothed them out. Having done so, he folded them neatly, put them in his pocket, and went to report to Katerina on the results of the errand.

BOOK V

PRO AND CONTRA

CHAPTER 1

An Engagement

It was again Mrs. Khokhlakov who came out to meet Alyosha. She was in a great hurry. Something grave had happened—Katerina's hysterics had ended in her fainting, after which, Mrs. Khokhlakov said, "she felt terribly weak and lay down; her eyes rolled back and she became delirious. She's feverish now and I've sent for Herzenstube and the aunts. The aunts have already arrived, but Herzenstube isn't here yet. They're all sitting by her bedside, waiting. I'm very worried—she's still unconscious. What if it should turn out to be brain fever? . . ."

Mrs. Khokhlakov looked really frightened as she told Alyosha about it, and she kept adding, "This is very, very serious," to everything she said, as if all that had happened before had not been serious. Alyosha listened to her sadly, then tried to tell her about his own adventure, but after the very first words she interrupted him: she had no time to listen to that now, and she would appreciate it if he would go in to see Lise and keep her company for a while, and could he please wait for her there?

"My dear Alexei," she whispered in Alyosha's ear, "Lise really amazed me just now, but she also moved me and for that I'm forced to forgive her for everything. Just after you left, she suddenly became very sorry for having laughed at you yesterday and again today. Of course, I know she wasn't really laughing at you. She was just teasing you, just joking. But she was so deeply sorry, almost in tears over it, that I was quite surprised. She has never been so sincerely sorry after laughing at me. She has always turned it into another joke. As you know, she's constantly making fun of me. But now she's serious. Everything is serious now. Your opinion is serious now. She values your opinion so tremendously, my dear Alexei, so if you can, please don't be offended at her remarks, don't hold them against her. I myself keep forgiving her, because she's such a clever little girl. You wouldn't believe how clever she is! Just now she told me that you were her childhood friend, 'the closest childhood friend I ever had,' as she put it—just imagine that, the closest—and what about me? Where do I come in? She feels very strongly about this and remembers many things very clearly. She says things that again and again take me completely by surprise. Recently, for instance, about a pine tree—we had a pine tree in our garden when she was very little. Well, possibly that pine is still there, so there's no need to talk about it in the past tense, for pines are not people—they don't change so quickly. 'Mother,' she said, 'I remember so clearly now that pine I've been pining for.' You understand, 'pine' and 'to pine'—although actually she said it somewhat differently—I'm a bit confused. The word 'pine' by itself is just a silly word, but she said something extremely original, something that I can't seem to repeat. Besides, I've forgotten exactly what she said. Well, I'll see you in a few minutes, Alexei. I'm sorry I'm in such an awful state. I think I'm about to lose my mind. You know, Alexei, twice before in my life I began to go mad and had to be put under medical care. Please go to Lise and cheer her up, as you always do so well. Lise!" Mrs. Khokhlakov called, as they approached the door of Lise's room. "Here, I've brought you Alexei Karamazov, whom you offended so badly, and I assure you he's not in the least angry with you. Indeed, he's quite surprised that you should have thought he would be!"

"*Merci, maman.* Do come in, Alexei."

Alyosha went in. Lise looked at him in embarrassment and suddenly blushed red. She was obviously ashamed of something and, as always happens in such cases, she started talking instead about something completely unrelated, as though that extraneous topic was the only thing she was interested in at that particular moment.

"Mother just told me about the two hundred rubles and the errand you were given . . . for that poor ex-army officer . . . She told me how horribly he'd been insulted and, you know, despite my mother's quite hopeless way of telling anything—she interrupts herself constantly and keeps skipping from one idea to another—the story made me weep. Well, how did it go? Did you give him the money? And what is the wretched man doing now?"

"That's the trouble—I couldn't give it to him. It's a whole

story," Alyosha said, as if he, too, were exclusively pre-occupied with his failure to get Snegirev to accept the money, although Lise could see that he, too, was looking away and trying not to broach a certain subject.

Alyosha sat down at the table and started to tell his story. From the very first words, he completely forgot his embarrassment, and soon Lise became absorbed too. He spoke under the influence of a strong emotion and of the stark impression the scene had made on him; he reconstructed the incident powerfully and in great detail. Even back in Moscow, when Lise was still a child, he had liked to tell her about things that had impressed him, whether it was something he had read or had experienced, recently or in his childhood. Sometimes the two of them would dream up whole stories together, but these were usually cheerful, funny stories. And now, suddenly, they both felt as if they had been transported back to the old days in Moscow, two years before.

Lise was tremendously moved by the story. Alyosha had drawn a very warm, vivid portrait of little Ilyusha Snegirev for her. And when he had finished his complete account of the scene in which the hapless captain trampled the hundred-ruble bills underfoot, Lise threw up her hands in despair and cried with unrestrained feeling:

"So you didn't manage to get him to keep the money! And then you let him run away! Good God, you should at least have tried to run after him, to catch him, and . . ."

"You're wrong, Lise. I'm glad I didn't run after him. It's better this way."

He got up and paced the room, looking worried.

"Why is it better this way? They have no money even for bread now. They face real starvation."

"No, they won't starve, because they'll get that two hundred rubles, whatever happens. He'll accept it tomorrow anyhow. I'm pretty sure he'll take it tomorrow," Alyosha said, pacing the room, his face concentrated in thought. "You see, Lise," he went on after a while, stopping in front of her, "I made one mistake, but even that mistake turned out to be all for the best in the end."

"What mistake? And why was it for the best?"

"Well, because that man is weak and frightened. He's been terribly harassed, and he's very kind. So I've been wondering what it was that could have infuriated him enough to make him trample that money underfoot, for, believe me, he had no idea himself until the very last second that he'd throw it down and stamp on it. Well, I see now that much of what I said to him could have offended him, in fact was bound to offend a man in his position. To start with, he was angry at himself for having shown too openly how glad he was to get the two hundred rubles, for not having hidden his joy from me. If he had been a bit less excited when I handed him the bills, if he hadn't shown how pleased he was, if he had pretended to be offended and acted at first as if he would refuse it, that is, if he had gone through all the routines customary under such circumstances, he could have taken the money in the end. However, because he had allowed himself to show his joy sincerely, he felt insulted. Ah, Lise, he's a kind, sincere man, and that makes it all the more difficult in such cases! When he decided to reject the money, his voice was so terribly weak, so faltering; the words came out so quickly and he was sort of chuckling all the time, or was he weeping even then? . . . Yes, he was weeping even before that, when he talked of his daughters with such infinite admiration and when he told me he hoped to get that job in the town in Kursk Province. And then, having bared his soul before me, he became ashamed of himself, and the next second he hated me. For he's one of those poor people who are painfully sensitive about their poverty. But what offended him most was that he had accepted me too quickly as his friend and had been in too much of a hurry to lower his guard. Before that, he had made threatening movements and it even looked as if he were about to attack me, but the moment he saw the money he wanted to embrace me. He really felt like hugging me. He kept touching me all the time. I think that's why he felt so humiliated when he thought of it, and it was at that moment that I made my mistake: I suddenly blurted out that if this two hundred rubles wasn't enough to enable him to move to another town, he'd be given more, and that, in fact, I had some money of my own and he could have as much of it as he needed. That was what suddenly offended him: who was I to push myself forward like that and offer him help? You know, Lise, it's horribly painful for a man down on his luck when every person he meets looks at him as if he were his benefactor. The elder explained that to me. I don't know how to put it, but I've observed it myself. Besides, I'd feel exactly the same way, too. And the most important fact is that, although until the last moment he didn't know he would trample those bills underfoot, he certainly had a foreboding of it. That's why his joy and elation were so great, because he had that foreboding . . . And yet, although it is so sad, it's all for the best. I don't think it could have turned out any better."

"Why, why couldn't it have turned out any better?" Lise cried, looking at Alyosha in amazement.

"Because if he hadn't trampled on the money but had taken it, one hour later, at home, he would have wept bitterly at this new humiliation. He would have wept and probably tomorrow he'd have come to see me, thrown down the bills, and trampled on them in front of me, just as he did today. Instead, as things are now, he has walked away with his head erect, feeling infinitely proud, although conscious of the fact that, by that gesture, he has sealed his doom. So there's nothing easier now than to make him accept the two hundred rubles no later than tomorrow, since he's already proved to himself that he's a man of honor by throwing away the money offered to him and trampling it underfoot. After all, how could he know, when he was trampling the bills, that I'd bring them back to him again the next day? And he did it despite the fact that he needs that money desperately. Proud though he may feel today, he cannot help but think sadly of the assistance he rejected. Tonight he'll think of it even more, he'll dream of it, and by morning perhaps he'll be ready to hurry to me and beg me to forgive him. But instead of his having to do that, I'll go to him and tell him something to the effect that now he has proved his pride and I beg him to forgive us for our presumption, but insist that he must accept . . . And this time he will."

Alyosha said the words "And this time he will" in a sort of rapture. Lise clapped her hands.

"It's true, so true, I see it so clearly now! You're so young, but yet you understand so well how people feel—I'd never have thought of all that!"

"The most important thing now is to convince him that he's on an equal footing with us even though he has accepted money from us," Alyosha went on hopefully. "Indeed, he is not only on an equal, but even on a sort of superior, footing . . ."

"A superior footing? A charming idea—please go on, Alexei!"

"Well, maybe I didn't put it quite right when I said 'superior footing,' but it doesn't make any difference, because . . ."

"Of course, of course, it makes no difference . . . You

know, Alyosha dear, until now I had very little respect for you, I mean, I respected you only on an equal footing, but from now on I'll respect you on a superior footing . . . Please, my sweet Alyosha, don't be angry, I'm just trying to be witty. I'm just a ridiculous little girl, while you . . ." Strong emotion could now be detected in her voice. "Listen, Alexei Karamazov, isn't there in all this analysis of ours—I mean yours, no, better say *ours*—isn't there a certain contempt for that unhappy man, just in the way we allow ourselves to examine his soul as if from somewhere high above, in our deciding that now he can't fail to accept the money?"

"No, Lise, there's no contempt for him," Alyosha said firmly, as if he'd been expecting that question. "I was thinking about that on my way here. What sort of contempt could there be when we're all just like him, for we are—we are not his betters. And even if we were his betters, in his position we would have acted just as he did . . . I don't know about you, Lise, but I consider myself a quite despicable person in many respects. But he isn't despicable; on the contrary, he's a very sensitive, vulnerable man . . . No, no, Lise, there's no contempt for him whatsoever! You know, my elder once said that we should always treat people as if they were children and sometimes we should treat them as if they were patients in a hospital . . ."

"Good, Alexei, my dear boy, from now on let's treat people like hospital patients!"

"Let's, Lise, I'm quite willing, although I don't always feel up to it yet, because I lack patience and my judgment is often poor. But for you, it's quite different."

"I can't believe it! I'm so happy, Alexei!"

"It's so good that you should say that!"

"You're an amazingly nice person, Alexei, but there are times when you sound rather smug. Then I take a good look at you and I know you're not smug at all. Please go to the door, open it a little, and see if mother isn't eavesdropping," Lise suddenly whispered nervously.

Alyosha got up, walked over to the door, and reported that no one was listening to them.

"Now, come over here, Alexei," Lise said, blushing more and more. "Give me your hand. Good. There's something I must confess to you: that letter I wrote you yesterday, it wasn't really a joke—I meant it."

She covered her eyes with her other hand and it was obvious that she was very ashamed of making this confession.

All of a sudden she drew Alyosha's hand to her lips and kissed it three times in quick succession.

"Ah, Lise, it's all right! Anyway, I was quite sure you meant it seriously."

"Imagine that—he was sure!" She quickly removed his hand from her lips without letting go of it and giggled happily. "What a man: here I am kissing his hand and all he has to say is 'all right.'"

Her reproach was unfair, though, because Alyosha, too, was very embarrassed.

"I wish I knew how to make you like me always," he muttered, blushing too.

"My dear Alyosha, you're a very cold and conceited man. You have done me the honor of accepting me as your wife and now you feel you've done enough for me. And you took it for granted that I meant what I wrote seriously. Well, what is that if not the utmost conceit!"

"But why is it so wrong if I was sure you were serious?" he said, suddenly beginning to laugh.

"There's nothing wrong with it; on the contrary, it's wonderful." She looked at him tenderly and happily, still holding his hand. Suddenly Alyosha bent down and kissed her right on the lips.

"And what's that now? What's come over you!" Lise cried. Alyosha felt completely at a loss.

"Well, forgive me if I've done the wrong thing . . . Perhaps it was very stupid of me . . . You said I was cold, so I kissed you. But now I see it looks rather stupid . . ."

Lise laughed, covering her face with her hands.

"And wearing that cassock, too!" she managed to say amidst her laughter. But she suddenly stopped laughing and grew serious, almost severe. "Well, Alyosha, we'd better postpone kissing for a while, because neither of us is very good at these things yet and, anyway, we have still a very long time to wait. Instead, wouldn't it be better if you tried to explain to me why an intelligent and thoughtful man like you should choose a silly thing like me, and a cripple to boot? Oh, Alyosha, I'm awfully happy, but I know I'm not worthy of you!"

"Wait, Lise. In a few days I'll be leaving the monastery for good, and once I'm out in the world, I know I *must* get married: *he* said so. And where could I find a better wife than you? And, also, who besides you would consider marrying me? I've already thought it all over. In the first place, we've known each other since we were children and, in the second place, you have many talents that I lack completely. You're a much gayer person than I am, and you're also much more innocent than I, for I've already seen quite a lot . . . Ah, you don't know what it means, but I'm a Karamazov! And I don't mind at all if you poke fun at me; indeed, it pleases me, so go ahead and laugh. But while you laugh like a little girl, you think like a martyr."

"Me, a martyr? What do you mean by that?"

"Take, for instance, the question you asked me earlier, Lise —whether we weren't showing scorn for poor Captain Snegirev by trying to dissect his soul that way. Well, that's something a martyr would ask . . . I don't know how to express it, but a person to whom such questions occur is himself capable of suffering. While sitting in your wheel-chair all this time, I'm sure you've given much thought to these things . . ."

"Give me your hand, Alyosha! Why do you keep trying to pull it away?" Lise said in a voice made strangely weak by happiness. "Tell me, what are you going to wear when you leave the monastery? What sort of suit? Don't laugh and don't be angry; it's very important to me."

"I hadn't thought about it, Lise, but I'll wear whatever you want me to."

"I want you to wear a navy-blue velvet jacket, a white piqué waistcoat, and a soft gray felt hat . . . Tell me, did you really think I didn't love you when I told you that my yesterday's letter was a joke?"

"No, I didn't believe you."

"Oh, that unbearable, incorrigible conceit!"

"You see, I knew that . . . that you seemed to love me, but I pretended to believe you to make it easier for you."

"But that's even worse! The worst and the best of it is that I'm so terribly in love with you, Alyosha. Yesterday, before you came in, I said to myself: 'I'll ask him to give me back my letter and if he takes it out and calmly returns it to me— which is to be expected of him—that'll show that he doesn't love me in the least, that he's just an unfeeling, stupid, unworthy boy, and that this is the end of me.' But you'd left the letter in your cell at the monastery and that gave me hope. Tell me now, did you leave it there because you knew I'd ask for it and you didn't want to give it back to me? It's true, isn't it?"

"Ah, you're completely wrong, Lise: I have the letter here and when you asked for it earlier, it was right here, in this pocket." Laughingly, he took the letter out of his pocket and showed it to her from a distance. "But I'm not going to give it back to you. You may just look at it from there."

"What? You lied to me then? You, a monk!"

"I suppose I did," Alyosha said, still laughing. "I lied so that I wouldn't have to give it to you. It's very dear to me," he added with sudden emotion, turning crimson again, "and I'll never give it up to anyone!"

Lise looked at him ecstatically.

"Alyosha," she whispered breathlessly, "go and make sure mother isn't listening behind the door."

"I'll look, Lise, but don't you think it would be better if I didn't? Why do you have to assume that your mother would do anything so low?"

"Why would it be so low on her part? If she was trying to find out what her daughter was up to, it would be her right and there'd be nothing low about it!" Lise said, flushing. "And you may be quite sure, my dear Alexei, that when I'm a mother myself, and if I must have a daughter like me, I will certainly eavesdrop on her!"

"Will you, Lise? But I don't think it's right."

"But why would it be wrong, for goodness sake? Of course, if it was just some ordinary polite conversation, and I eavesdropped, that would be wrong, but if one's own daughter shut herself in with a young man . . . Do you know, Alyosha, as soon as we get married, I'll start keeping my eye on you too. I'll open all your letters and read them—I might as well warn you now."

"Why, of course, if you must . . . But that still doesn't make it right," Alyosha muttered.

"Oh, how reproachful! Alyosha dear, let's not quarrel from the very beginning. I'd better tell you the whole truth: of course it's very bad to eavesdrop, and certainly you are right, and not I, but nevertheless, I *will* eavesdrop."

"Do so then. But there will be nothing to catch me at," Alyosha said, laughing.

"And another thing, Alyosha, you'll have to do what I tell you, do you agree to that? That must be settled in advance."

"Willingly, Lise, certainly I will, except for the thing that matters to me the most. In that most important thing, I will do what I feel is my duty, whether you agree or not."

"And that's just as it should be. Now, as for me, I'm prepared to give in to you not only on that most important point but on every point and in everything, and I swear right now that that's the way it will be as long as I live!" Lise cried ardently. "I'll yield to you joyfully, and I'll be happy to! I also swear to you now that I'll never spy on you, that I'll never read a single letter addressed to you, because you are right about that and I'm wrong. And although I'm sure there'll be times when I'll desperately want to eavesdrop on you, I'll never do so, because you think eavesdropping is low. From now on, you will be like my Providence. Tell me, Alexei, why were you so sad both yesterday and today? I know you have worries, but I see that you're also feeling some special sorrow. Perhaps it's a secret, though?"

"Yes, Lise, there is something, and it is a secret," Alyosha said sadly, "but I know you love me since you guessed it."

"What can be making you so sad? I wish I could ask you . . ." Lise said with a look of timid entreaty.

"I'll tell you some day, later," Alyosha said awkwardly. "I don't suppose you'd understand now if I did tell you. Besides, I wouldn't know how to say it."

"I know that, on top of everything, you're unhappy about your brothers and your father."

"Yes, my brothers too," Alyosha said, with some hesitation.

"I don't like your brother Ivan, Alyosha," Lise said unexpectedly.

Alyosha seemed a little surprised at her remark but he did not comment on it.

"My brothers are bent on destroying themselves and so is my father. And they're dragging others down to destruction with them. The other day Father Paisii described 'the Karamazov drive' as 'earthy, frantic, and primitive,' and I don't even know whether there's an awareness of the divine spirit beyond that drive. All I know is that I, too, am a Karamazov —I, a monk, a monk . . . Am I a monk, Lise? A moment ago you said I was a monk, didn't you?"

"Yes, I did."

"But what would you say if I told you that perhaps I don't even believe in God?"

"You, not believe in God? What are you saying?" Lise said guardedly in a very quiet voice.

But Alyosha didn't answer her. There was something too intimate and mysterious in his unexpected statement, something that was, perhaps, unclear even to him, but that had certainly been tormenting him for some time.

"And on top of everything, my friend is leaving me. He's the best man in the world and he's leaving it. If only you knew, Lise, how attached I am to this man, how closely tied I am to him! And now I'll be left all by myself. I'll come to you, Lise, and then we'll always be together."

"Yes, yes, we'll be together as long as we live. Here, kiss me now, I want you to."

Alyosha kissed her.

"And now go, and may Christ be with you," she said, making the sign of the cross over him. "Hurry back to *him* while he's still alive. I realize it was cruel of me to keep you here. I'll pray for you today. We shall be happy, Alyosha, don't you think?"

"It looks as if we shall."

When he left Lise, Alyosha did not feel like seeing Mrs. Khokhlakov and was about to leave the house without saying good-by to her. But no sooner had he opened the door of Lise's room and come out to the top of the stairs than Mrs. Khokhlakov suddenly appeared out of nowhere. From her very first words, Alyosha realized that she had been waiting for him there.

"It's absolutely impossible, Alexei. It's sheer childishness. I hope you don't take it seriously. It's utter, utter nonsense!" she fired at him point blank.

"The only thing I ask of you is not to say that to her— you'll upset her and that's very bad for her now."

"I'm glad to hear a sensible word from a sensible young man. Should I conclude, then, that you only pretended to go along with her because you didn't wish to hurt her by contradicting, out of compassion for her physical condition?"

"Oh, no, not at all. I meant everything I said to her quite seriously," Alyosha told her firmly.

"It's all absolutely out of the question. For a start, I'll never receive you again in my house, and then I'll leave this town and take her away with me. So now you know."

"Why, what would be the point of that, since it won't take place for a long time yet? In any case we'll have to wait for at least eighteen months or so."

"Well, that's true, of course, and in eighteen months you two will have time to quarrel and break up at least a thousand times. But I feel terribly depressed by it, even if it is just a bit of foolishness. I feel like Famusov in the last scene of that Griboedov play—you're Chatsky, of course, and she's Sofia . . . And just think of it, I had to hurry here to intercept you on the stairs, and that crucial scene in the play also takes place on the landing of a staircase, remember?

I heard everything and I could hardly control myself. So this is what accounts for the horrible night she had and all her recent fits of hysteria! What is love to a daughter is death to a mother, and I might just as well be in my grave. And now I want to ask you about something else, something more important: What is this letter she wrote you? I want to see it. Show it to me, at once!"

"No, you don't really want it . . . Tell me, rather, how Katerina is. I must know."

"She's still delirious. She hasn't regained consciousness. Her aunts are here and all they do is moan and snub me. Herzenstube finally arrived but he was so frightened by what he saw that he almost fainted himself. I didn't know what to do with him and wanted to send for another doctor for him, but in the end I had him taken home in my carriage . . . And now, on top of all this commotion, you have to come along and worry me with that letter. I know that I still have eighteen months; nevertheless, I beseech you, in the name of the dying elder, in the name of that great and holy man, to show me, her mother, that letter, Alexei! If it will make you feel any better, you can hold it in your hand while I read it, but please show it to me!"

"No, Mrs. Khokhlakov, I wouldn't show it to you, even if she gave me permission to do so. If you want, I'll come and see you tomorrow, for there are many things for us to talk about, but for now, good-by."

And Alyosha ran downstairs and out into the street.

CHAPTER 2

Smerdyakov and His Guitar

Alyosha was in a great hurry. While taking leave of Lise, he had suddenly conceived a very cunning plan to catch his brother Dmitry, who was evidently hiding from him. It was already after two o'clock and he was anxious to get back to the monastery as soon as possible, to be with his dying elder, but he absolutely had to see Dmitry first. With every hour, Alyosha's foreboding of an approaching catastrophe had been growing stronger, although he probably could not have explained exactly what catastrophe or even what he wanted to say to his brother at that moment. "If it must be, let the man to whom I owe everything die without me; at least I won't have to reproach myself for the rest of my life because I might have staved off disaster but didn't because I was in a hurry to get back to what I feel is my home. I shall act, now, the way he wants me to act."

Alyosha's plan was to catch Dmitry unawares: he would climb over the fence, as he had the day before, hide himself in the summer house, and wait for his brother there. "And if he's not there, I'll wait until evening if I must, without letting either Foma or the landladies know of my presence . . . But if he's still watching out for Grushenka, he may very well come to the summer house sometime or other." Alyosha didn't think out the details of his plan very thoroughly. He simply decided to carry it out even if it meant not going back to the monastery at all that day.

He reached the place without incident. He climbed over the fence at the same spot as the day before and hid himself in the summer house without being seen. He was very anxious to avoid being seen by the landladies or Foma, if the man happened to be around, for they were in league with Dmitry and might either prevent Alyosha from entering their garden or warn Dmitry that someone was there, waiting for him. The summer house was empty. Alyosha sat down on the bench where he had sat the day before, and waited. He glanced around the deserted summer house and today it struck him as older and more dilapidated than it had yesterday. It looked terribly shabby, although the weather was just as clear and sunny as the day before. On the green table there was a round mark left, probably, by yesterday's glass from which some of the brandy had spilled. Useless and unrelated thoughts kept drifting into Alyosha's head, as often happens during a time of idle waiting. He started wondering, for instance, why it was that when he had come into the summer house now, he had sat down without thinking in exactly the same spot as the day before, rather than anywhere else. Gradually the uncertainty of the situation began to weigh on him and he became very despondent. But he had not been there for a quarter of an hour before he suddenly heard the strumming of a guitar somewhere quite nearby. Someone must be sitting in the bushes no more than twenty yards away. Alyosha suddenly remembered that, as he was leaving the summer house the day before, he had noticed a low, green garden bench by the fence, half concealed under the bushes. Someone must be sitting there now.

But who could it be? Then a male voice started singing in a
sentimental falsetto to the accompaniment of a guitar:

> A force irresistible
> Ties me to my darling.
> Lord have mercy
> On both of us,
> On both of us,
> On both of us.

The voice stopped. This high-pitched tenor was a lackey's,
and the manner of singing and dragging out the words was
a lackey's manner. Then Alyosha heard a woman's voice,
caressing, coy, and blatantly affected.

"Why haven't you been to see us for so long? Is our company too dull for you?"

"Not at all," the man said politely but with marked dignity.

It was obvious that he was in a strong position and the
woman was making a play for him.

"Sounds like Smerdyakov," Alyosha thought, "and she
must be the landlady's daughter, the one who came back
from Moscow and who has a dress with a train and goes
to father's house to get a bowl of soup from Martha."

"I love verses, especially nice ones like those," the woman
said. "But why have you stopped? Please go on."

The voice started to sing again:

> By the crown of the Tsar,
> May my darling prosper.
> Lord have mercy
> On both of us,
> On both of us,
> On both of us.

"Last time, it came out even better: you sang it 'May my
dearest keep well,' and that made it kind of warmer, more
tender; you must have forgotten it today."

"Poetry is rubbish anyway," Smerdyakov snapped.

"Oh no, I don't go along with you there. I like a nice
verse."

"As long as it's verse, it's nonsense. Think for yourself:
have you ever heard people talking to each other in verse?
And if we tried to talk to one another in verse all the time,
even if the higher authorities ordered us to, how much do

you think we'd be able to say? No, poetry, that's not a serious thing."

"You're so clever about everything," the woman's voice said with even more ingratiating tenderness. "How do you manage to think about all those things?"

"That's nothing compared with what I might have known if it hadn't been for the bad luck that's haunted me ever since my birth. I would have liked to kill in a duel the man who called me a bastard just because I was born fatherless to Reeking Lizaveta. And there were so many who threw that in my face in Moscow. I guess they must have learned of it from Gregory. He reproaches me for having rebelled against my birth. 'You,' he says, 'tore her open when you came out.' Well, I don't know about tearing her open, but I certainly would rather have been killed in her womb than been brought into this world. I've heard in the market place, and your mother, most inconsiderate of my feelings, also told me, that Lizaveta went around with her hair standing on end and that she was just a *wee bit* over four feet; she dragged out those words, although she could perfectly well have said a wee bit in the ordinary way. I guess she was trying to move me to tears, imagining that a peasant could be stirred to tears by it because it is, so to speak, a peasant's way of feeling. Can a Russian peasant resent an educated person? No, he can't, because he's too ignorant to have any feelings at all. But ever since I was a small child, whenever I heard people say a *wee bit* like that, I felt like smashing my head against a wall. I hate Russia and everything about it, Maria."

"If you'd been a young army officer, a dashing hussar, or something of that sort, you'd have drawn your sword and rushed off to fight for Russia."

"I not only have no wish to be an army officer, Maria, I'd like to do away with soldiers altogether."

"But what would happen if the enemy attacked us? Who'd defend us then?"

"There's no need to. In 1812 Napoleon I, the French emperor, the father of the present Napoleon, invaded Russia, and it would have been better if he'd conquered us right then, because those French are a clever nation and it would have been a good thing if they'd annexed our stupid country. Things would have been quite different around here today, believe me!"

"As if they were so much better over there in those countries than we are here! Let me tell you, I wouldn't exchange

some of our handsome Russian men for three young English-
men even," the woman said, probably accompanying these
words with a languorous look.

"Well, that's a matter of personal preference."

"But you yourself, you look like a foreigner. You look
like a regular foreign gentleman. I have to tell you that, even
if it makes me blush."

"If you want to know the truth, I can tell you, when
it comes to vice, people are the same all over, whether
in this country or over there. They're all low scoundrels; the
only difference is that over there they swagger around in
shiny patent leather boots, while our native scoundrels are
poor and filthy and stink, and it doesn't bother them in
the least. What the Russian people need is flogging, as Mr.
Karamazov said yesterday, and he was right, crazy as he is
with those sons of his."

"But you told me you had great respect for his son Ivan,
didn't you?"

"But he said I'm a stinking flunkey. He thinks I might
rise up against the way things are, but he's dead wrong
there: if only I had a bit of ready cash, I'd clear out of
here right away. And take the other son, Dmitry: that one
behaves much worse than any flunkey I've ever seen, and
he doesn't have any more brains or any more money than
a flunkey, and he isn't any good at anything, but that
doesn't prevent everybody around from treating him like a
gentleman and respecting him. I'm just a cook, of course,
but with some luck I could perhaps get myself a restaurant
in Moscow, in the Petrovka district, or somewhere around
there, because I know something special about cooking that
none of them in Moscow knows, except for the foreigners.
Now again, Dmitry, who doesn't have a kopek to his name,
can challenge the son of the most important count in all
Russia to a duel, if he wants, and the fellow would accept
his challenge. But why is he better than me? Is it because
he's stupider than I am and has managed to pour lots of
money down the drain with nothing to show for it?"

"I think duels are very nice," the woman remarked surprisingly.

"In what way are they nice?"

"It's brave and frightening, especially if they're young
officers firing at one another with their pistols because of
some lady. It's a lovely picture! I wish they'd let ladies come
and watch those duels. I'd love to see one!"

"It's all right as long as it's you who's aiming the pistol, but when it's the other fellow who's taking good aim at your mug, you feel pretty stupid, you know. You wouldn't stay and watch, Maria, you'd be in a big hurry to get out of there."

"And what about you? Would you run away too? I can't believe it!"

Smerdyakov ignored this. After a minute of silence, the guitar resounded again and the falsetto drawled the final verse of the song:

> Cost me what it may,
> I shall get away,
> Be merry and gay.
> For the capital I'll leave,
> Never again grieve,
> Have no cause to grieve.

At that moment something quite unforeseen happened: Alyosha suddenly sneezed. The two on the bench fell silent. Alyosha got up and went over to them. There was Smerdyakov, with his hair pomaded, perhaps even curled, wearing a pair of glittering patent leather shoes. The guitar lay on the bench beside him. Maria, the daughter of the landlady, was wearing a light blue dress with a six-foot train. She was still quite young and might have been described as pretty if her face had not been so very round and so terribly freckled.

"Do you know whether my brother Dmitry will be back soon?" Alyosha asked in as casual a tone as he could muster.

Smerdyakov rose slowly from the bench. Maria, too, got up.

"I am not informed as to the whereabouts of Mr. Dmitry," Smerdyakov said quietly, in a measured, scornful tone. "I am not employed to look after him, am I?"

"I simply asked in case you happened to know," Alyosha explained.

"I know nothing of Mr. Dmitry's whereabouts, nor do I want to know."

"But he told me that it was you who kept him informed of what was going on in my father's house and that you'd promised to let him know when Miss Grushenka came."

Smerdyakov, slowly raising his eyes, looked imperturbably at Alyosha.

"But what about you, Mr. Alexei? How did you get in

here? I know the gate was locked more than an hour ago," he said, looking intently at Alyosha.

"I climbed over the fence in the sidestreet and came directly to the summer house. I hope you'll forgive me," he said, addressing Maria, "I was trying to catch my brother. I must see him urgently."

"Oh, we don't mind at all. How could we!" she said, flattered by Alyosha's politeness. "Anyway, that's how Mr. Dmitry gets in when he comes here—sometimes we don't even know it and he's already sitting in the summer house."

"It's terribly important that I see him now—I had hoped to find him here or to find out from you where he was. It is extremely important for him."

"I'm afraid he doesn't tell us of his comings and goings, sir," Maria murmured.

"And even though I was here as a guest," Smerdyakov said, "Mr. Dmitry kept pestering me even here, asking me questions all the time about my master, like what's going on in the house, who comes, who leaves, and whether I haven't anything else to report. Twice he even threatened to kill me."

"What do you mean, to kill you?"

"Why, that's nothing so special for a man of Mr. Dmitry's character. You saw for yourself yesterday the sort of a man he is. 'If,' he said to me, 'you let Miss Grushenka into the house and she spends the night there, you'll be the first I'll kill.' I'm very scared of him, and if I wasn't even more scared of complaining to the police, I'd have done it long ago. One can never tell what a man like Mr. Dmitry might do."

" 'I'll pound you in a mortar'—that's what Mr. Dmitry said to him the other day," Maria chimed in.

"Well, if he said in a mortar, then it must have been just talk," Alyosha said. "But I'll speak to him about that too, if I manage to find him now."

"This is what I can tell you, Mr. Alexei, but no more than this," Smerdyakov said, apparently having made up his mind. "I come to visit my neighbors here and there's no reason I shouldn't, is there? On the other hand, your other brother, Mr. Ivan, sent me very early this morning to Mr. Dmitry's place on Lake Street, to tell Mr. Dmitry—he gave me no letter to deliver—to be at the inn on the square today without fail and that they'd eat lunch together there. I got to Mr. Dmitry's place at eight in the morning, but his landlord told me he'd already left. 'He was here but he's left now'—that's exactly what they told me. Looks to me like there's some kind of plot between them. But perhaps Mr. Dmitry is at the inn by now with his brother, because Mr. Ivan didn't come home for lunch today and so your father, Mr. Karamazov, had lunch all by himself and is having his nap now. But I beg you never to mention me or what I've just told you to Mr. Dmitry, because he'd kill me for much less, I'm sure."

"Ivan asked Dmitry to meet him at the inn for lunch today?" Alyosha asked quickly.

"Yes, sir, just as I said."

"The Capital City Inn?"

"That's right."

"That's very probable," Alyosha cried excitedly. "Thank you very much, Smerdyakov. I think I'll go over there right away."

"But please don't give me away, Mr. Alexei, remember."

"Don't worry, I'll pretend to have gone there by chance."

"Wait, I'll unlock the gate for you," Maria cried.

"Don't bother, it's quicker this way. I'll climb over the fence again."

Alyosha was quite shocked by the news and hurried off to the inn. He felt it would be awkward to go into the inn in his cassock, but he could inquire downstairs whether his brothers were there and ask them to come down to see him. But as he approached the inn, a window opened and Ivan himself called out to him: "Alyosha, could you come in here please. I'd very much appreciate it if you would."

"I'd like to very much . . . But what about the way I'm dressed?"

"That's all right, I'm in a private room. Come in and I'll come downstairs to meet you."

A minute later Alyosha was sitting at the table with Ivan. Ivan was alone. He was having lunch.

CHAPTER 3

The Brothers Get Acquainted

Ivan was not really in a private room, however. He had merely been given a table by a window that was screened off from the rest of the dining room so that they could not be seen by the other customers. This was the first dining room off the entrance and it had a bar along one wall. The waiters kept dashing back and forth to the bar. There was only one other customer, an old retired army officer who was having tea at a table in a corner. But the usual tavern noises could be heard clearly from the other rooms: calls for the waiters, the opening of beer bottles, the clinking of billiard balls, the droning of an organ . . . Alyosha knew that Ivan hardly ever came to this inn, that in general he had no liking for such places, and that, consequently, he must have come especially to meet Dmitry. But Dmitry was not there.

"Let me order some fish soup for you, or anything you like," Ivan said, apparently extremely pleased that Alyosha was there. "You can't possibly subsist on tea alone," he added.

He himself had finished eating and was drinking tea.

"All right, order me some fish soup and then tea. I'm quite hungry," Alyosha said cheerfully.

"And what about some cherry jam? They have some here. Remember how much you liked it when you were little and we lived at Polenov's?"

"How can you remember that? Good, get me cherry jam too. I still like it."

Ivan rang for the waiter and ordered fish soup, tea, and jam.

"I remember everything, Alyosha. I remember you up to the age of eleven. I was fifteen then. Fifteen and eleven—that much difference in age makes it impossible for two brothers to be very close. I'm not even sure whether I had any affection for you then. When I left for Moscow, I don't believe I ever thought of you during the first few years. Then, when you came to Moscow yourself, I remember meeting you only once and I can't even recall on what occasion. And now I've been living here for more than three months and we've hardly spoken two words to each other. Well, I'm leaving tomorrow and I was just thinking that I'd like to see you before I went, to say good-by to you, when all of a sudden I saw you walking along."

"Did you really want to see me very much?"

"Very much. I wanted to get to know you properly and I wanted you to get to know me, and once that was done, for us to say good-by to each other. I think the best time to get to know people is just before parting from them. I noticed how you looked at me with a sort of expectation during these three months, and that was just why I didn't make a move toward you—I couldn't bear that expectant look of yours. But lately I've acquired considerable respect for you—'This boy,' I said to myself, 'certainly has pretty definite views about life.' Please understand—although I'm laughing now, I mean exactly what I say: you do have quite definite views about things, don't you? I like people with such strong beliefs, even if they happen to be just young boys like you. So lately your expectant look has stopped repelling me; indeed, I've come to like it finally. I'm under the impression that you rather like me, don't you, Alyosha?"

"I do, Ivan. Dmitry says you're silent as the grave, but I say you're an enigma. Even at this moment you're an enigma to me, although I caught a glimpse of something in you just this morning."

"What precisely did you see?" Ivan asked with a laugh.

"You're sure you won't be angry if I tell you?" Alyosha said, laughing too.

"Go ahead."

"That you're just a young man of twenty-three like any other, that you're really a nice, very young, unspoiled . . . well, an inexperienced twenty-three-year-old. I hope I haven't offended you, have I?"

"No, no, not in the least. In fact, this is a very strange coincidence!" Ivan said gaily and warmly. "Will you believe me if I tell you that, after I left you this morning, after that scene there, I was thinking to myself that, after all, I'm just a callow twenty-three-year-old, and you, you saw it right away and it's from that that you start. I was sitting here, before you came, and do you know what I was thinking about? I was thinking that even if I believed that life was pointless, lost faith in the woman I loved, lost faith in the order of things, or even became convinced that I was surrounded by a disorderly, evil, perhaps devil-made chaos, even if I were completely overcome by the horrors of human despair—I would still want to live on; once I have started drinking from this cup, I won't put it down until I have emptied it to the last drop. It's quite possible, though, that by the time I'm thirty I will have tossed away the cup without really having finished it, and I will go off in who knows what direction. I know for sure that until then my youth will have overcome everything—every disappointment, every disgust caused by life. Many times I've asked myself whether there is anything in the world that could crush my frantic, indecent appetite for life, and have decided that it looks as though nothing of the sort exists. But, of course, that may be true only until I reach the age of thirty, for then I may lose interest in life altogether, at least so it seems to me. This appetite for life is often branded as despicable by various spluttering moralists and even more so by poets. It, of course, is the outstanding feature in us Karamazovs— and you, too, you have this inordinate appetite for life, I'm certain of it—but what is there so despicable about it? There's still an enormous amount of centripetal force left in our planet, Alyosha, my boy, so I want to live and go on living, even if it's contrary to the rules of logic. Even if I do not believe in the divine order of things, the sticky young leaves emerging from their buds in the spring are dear to my heart; so is the blue sky and so are some human beings, even though I often don't know why I like them; I may still even admire an act of heroism with my whole heart, perhaps out of habit, although I may have long since stopped believing in heroism.

"Here's your fish soup, Alyosha. They make a good fish soup here. Go ahead, eat it, enjoy it. You know, I've been wanting to go to Western Europe and that's where I'll go from here. Oh, I know that going there is like going to a graveyard, but it's a glorious graveyard, I tell you! The dead who lie under the stones there are dear to me, and every gravestone speaks of their ardent lives, of human achievements, of their passionate faith in the purpose of life, the truth they believed in, the learning they defended—and I know in advance that I'll prostrate myself and kiss those stones and shed tears on them, although the whole time I'll be fully aware that it's only a graveyard and nothing more. And I will not be weeping out of despair, but simply because I'll be happy shedding those tears. I'll get drunk on my own emotion. I love those sticky little leaves in the spring and the blue sky, that's what! You don't love those things with reason, with logic, you love them with your innards, with your belly, and that's also how you love your own first youthful strength. Well, do you understand anything in all this ranting, Alyosha, my boy, or are you completely at a loss?" Ivan asked, suddenly beginning to laugh.

"I understand it only too well: it's the innards and the belly that long to love. You put it wonderfully and I'm terribly glad that you have such an appetite for life!" Alyosha cried. "I've always thought that, before anything else, people should learn to love life in this world."

"To love life more than the meaning of life?"

"Yes, that's right. That's the way it should be—love should come before logic, just as you said. Only then will man be able to understand the meaning of life. You know what I think, Ivan—half your work is already done; you love life. Now you must concentrate on the second half and you'll be saved."

"So you're saving me already! Wait a bit, I don't think I'm lost yet. But what does that second half involve?"

"Bringing back to life those dead of yours, who, perhaps, may never even have died. All right, pour me some tea now. I'm so glad we're having this talk, Ivan."

"I can see that you're in a kind of ecstasy—I love such *professions de foi* from you novices. You're a very determined man, Alexei. Is it a fact that you're leaving the monastery?"

"Yes. My elder is sending me out into the world."

"Well, then I suppose we shall meet again—in the world. Before I'm thirty, that is, when I begin tearing the cup from my lips . . . But our father has no wish to tear the cup from his lips. He plans to go on drinking from it until he's seventy or even eighty; that's what he says at least, and although he's a buffoon otherwise, he sounds as if he meant it seriously. He's planted himself on the pleasures of the flesh as if they were a solid rock. But then, once you're over thirty, there doesn't seem to be anything much else to stand on. Yet to carry on like that until seventy is disgusting. Until thirty, though, it's all right. One can even retain an air of dignity by feigning high-mindedness . . . By the way, Alyosha, you haven't seen Dmitry today, have you?"

"No, I haven't . . . But I saw Smerdyakov." And Alyosha told Ivan every detail of his meeting with Smerdyakov. A worried look suddenly appeared on Ivan's face; he listened intently, even asking Alyosha to repeat certain things.

"But Smerdyakov asked me not to repeat what he'd told me to Dmitry," Alyosha added.

Ivan frowned and grew very thoughtful.

"Are you frowning over Smerdyakov?" Alyosha asked him.

"Yes, it's because of Smerdyakov—to hell with him! I really did want to see Dmitry, but now there's no need anymore," Ivan said reluctantly.

"Are you really leaving town very soon?"

"Yes."

"But what about Dmitry and father? How will it end between them?" Alyosha asked in a worried voice.

"Ah, there you go again with that nonsense! Anyway, where do I come into it? I'm not my brother Dmitry's keeper, you know," Ivan snapped irritatedly, but then he suddenly smiled crookedly and added with bitterness: "Does that sound to you like Cain's answer to God about his murdered brother? Isn't that what you were thinking just this second? But what the hell, I really can't stay here and be their keeper. I've completed my business here and I'm leaving. I hope you don't imagine that I'm jealous of Dmitry and that during these three months I've been trying to take his beautiful Katerina away from him? Oh no, my boy, I had my own affairs to take care of, and now that I've dealt with them, I'm leaving. You were present when I finished with the last business that was holding me here, remember?"

"You mean with Katerina earlier today?"

"Right, I've finished with everything there. And now, why should I worry about what happens to Dmitry? That's no concern of mine. I had my own accounts to settle with Katerina. Besides, you know very well that Dmitry behaved as if we'd planned it all secretly, the two of us. I never asked him for anything. It was on his own initiative that he solemnly handed her over to me and gave us his blessing. It is all ridiculous. Ah, Alyosha, I wish you knew how freely I can breathe now! You know, as I sat here eating my lunch, I thought of ordering champagne to celebrate my first hour of freedom. Ah, hell, after almost half a year, I've suddenly managed to throw it off! Why, even yesterday I never suspected that if we decided to put an end to it we could do so, just like that!"

"Are you talking about your love for her?"

"You can call it love if you want. Well, yes, I did fall in love with that educated young lady. I suffered because of her, and she did her best to torment me. I sat with her and brooded . . . But now it's all evaporated! When we were there today, you know, I made those eloquent speeches, remember, but no sooner was I outside than I burst out laughing. Yes, laughing—I mean that exactly."

"Even now you look so pleased when you say that," Alyosha said, looking at his brother's face, which had indeed taken on a relaxed, merry look.

"But how could I know that I didn't really love her in the

least? Ha-ha-ha! But that's exactly how it turned out. I found her very attractive, even this morning when I was holding forth. As a matter of fact, I still feel attracted to her at this moment, very strongly, and yet it's so easy for me to leave her for good. You don't think this is just bravado on my part, do you?"

"No, but I think perhaps it wasn't love that you felt for her."

"For heaven's sake, little Alyosha, don't start making dissertations on love! It doesn't become you very well," Ivan said, laughing. "Ah, when I think how you came out with that opinion of yours! You were so sweet, I'd like to give you a big hug for it now! . . . But the fact is, she really did make me suffer. I was involved in a terrible mixture of twisted emotions and heartbreak. She certainly knew I loved her, and she loved me, not Dmitry," Ivan said cheerfully, "but she needed Dmitry to provide her with a broken heart. Everything I told her today is absolutely true. But the trouble is, it may take her fifteen or even twenty years to find out for herself that she doesn't really love Dmitry, that she loves only me, whom she torments. As a matter of fact, she may never understand it, despite the lecture I gave her today. Well, so much the better. As for me, I just got up and walked out on her once and for all. By the way, how is she now? What happened after I left?"

Alyosha told him about Katerina's hysterics and that she had still been delirious when he had last heard.

"Mightn't it be all Mrs. Khokhlakov's invention?"

"I shouldn't think so."

"I suppose I ought to inquire . . . But, after all, no one has ever died of hysterics. So let her have hysterics, for hysteria is a loving gift God has sent to women. I don't think I'll go there at all anymore. I don't want to get mixed up in it again."

"Tell me—why did you say in front of her that she had never loved you?"

"I said it without meaning it. Listen, Alyosha boy, I'll order some champagne and we'll drink to my freedom. Ah, I wish you knew how happy I am."

"No, Ivan, I'd rather not drink now," Alyosha said suddenly; "besides, I feel somehow sad."

"Yes, I know you're feeling sad. I've noticed it all along."

"So you have definitely made up your mind to leave tomorrow morning?"

"In the morning? I never said I was leaving in the morning . . . I don't know, though, it may be in the morning after all. You know, I came here to eat lunch today just to avoid eating with the old man—that's how sick I am of him. If I could have, I'd have left town just to get away from him. But why should it worry you so much that I'm leaving? You and I still have plenty of time to spend together before I leave, a whole eternity."

"What kind of eternity is it if you're leaving tomorrow?"

"But why should that concern us," Ivan said with a laugh, "as long as we have time to settle all the matters we've met to discuss? Well, why do you look so surprised? Tell me yourself, then, why we met here. Was it to talk about my love for Katerina, about the old man and Dmitry? Life abroad? Russia's fateful position? The Emperor Napoleon? Was that the purpose of our meeting?"

"No, I don't think so."

"So you know yourself what the purpose was. It's different with other people, but we callow youths, we have first of all to settle the eternal verities that worry us. All young Russia is talking of nothing but those eternal questions, just at the moment when the old generation has suddenly turned its attention to practical problems. And why do you think you've been looking at me so expectantly for the past three months? I'll tell you—you wanted to ask me, 'What do you believe in, or don't you believe in anything at all?' That was what all your questioning glances boiled down to, Alexei Karamazov, wasn't it?"

"I guess you're right," Alyosha said with a smile, "and I only hope you're not making fun of me now, Ivan."

"I—poke fun at you? How could I disappoint my little brother who's been looking at me with such intense expectation for three whole months? Look at me, Alyosha, don't you see that I'm nothing but a young boy, just like you, except perhaps for the fact that I'm not a novice. And what have Russian boys, some of them at least, been doing all this time? Take, for instance, that stinking local tavern: they gather there in a corner. They've never set eyes on each other before in their lives and they'll never see each other again for the next forty years after they step out of the tavern, but what do you think they talk about during those fleeting moments in the tavern? You can bet what you like that they'll go right to those eternal verities, such as the existence of God and the immortality of the soul. And those who do not believe in God will bring in socialism, anarchy, and the re-organization of society according to a new scheme. But, as you realize, it really boils down to the same damned thing—they're all the same old questions, they're just approached from a different angle. And there are many, many extremely original, clever boys who spend their whole time nowadays debating these eternal questions. Isn't that the truth?"

"Yes, and for true Russian people, problems such as the existence of God and the immortality of the soul, or those other questions that approach these matters from another angle, as you put it, are the most important, and that's exactly what they should be," Alyosha said, looking intently at his brother with his gently probing smile.

"Well, Alyosha, I don't see anything so wonderful about being a Russian, and it's really hard to imagine a more stupid occupation than the one in which Russian boys are so immersed these days. Nevertheless, I'm extremely fond of one of those Russian boys."

"You managed to bring that in very cleverly," Alyosha said, laughing.

"All right, then, place your order. Where shall I begin? You decide. What about starting with God? Does God exist or not—shall I start there?"

"Start wherever you like, attack the question 'from another angle,' if you wish, since yesterday at father's you flatly stated there was no God," Alyosha said, looking at his brother.

"I said that at the table yesterday just to tease you, and I saw how your eyes were shining. But now I don't at all mind discussing it with you, and I'm quite serious. I'd like us to get to know each other better. I have no friends and I'm curious to see what it's like to have one. Well then, just imagine, perhaps I, too, accept God," Ivan said laughingly. "Why, does that surprise you?"

"It does, indeed—unless you're joking."

"Joking! That's what they said to me at the elder's yesterday—'You're joking,' they said. You know that old sinner of the eighteenth century who said that if God didn't exist He would have to be invented—*s'il n'existait pas Dieu il faudrait l'inventer*. And true enough, man has invented God. What is so strange and extraordinary is not that God really exists but that such a thought—the very idea of the necessity of God—should have occurred to a vicious wild animal like man, for that concept is so holy, so touching, and so wise

that it does man too much honor. For my part, I've long
since stopped worrying about who invented whom—God man
or man God. I won't, of course, bother to repeat to you all
the fashionable axioms accepted by our Russian boys—all of
them derived from hypotheses formulated by Europeans—
because what to a European is a mere hypothesis is at once
accepted as an axiom by a Russian boy; and, alas, not only
by the boy, but also often by his professor, because a Russian
professor nowadays is very often just another Russian boy.
And so, I'll ignore all those hypotheses for the time being.
For what is the purpose of this conversation between us? Its
purpose, as I understand it, is for me to explain to you, as
briefly as possible, what I am—that is, what sort of a man
I am, what I believe in, and what I hope for. And so I will
just state here plainly and briefly that I accept God. But I
must point out one thing: if God does exist and if He really
created the world, then, as we well know, He created it
according to the principles of Euclidean geometry and made
the human brain capable of grasping only three dimensions
of space. Yet there have been and still are mathematicians
and philosophers—among them some of the most outstanding—who doubt that the whole universe or, to put it more
generally, all existence was created to fit Euclidean geometry;
they even dare to conceive that two parallel lines that, according to Euclid, never meet on earth do, in fact, meet somewhere in infinity. And so, my dear boy, I've decided that
since I'm incapable of understanding even that much, I cannot possibly understand about God. I humbly admit that I
have no special talent for coping with such problems, that
my brain is an earthly, Euclidean brain, and that therefore
I'm not properly equipped to deal with matters that are not
of this world. And I would advise you too, Alyosha, never
to worry about these matters, least of all about God—
whether He exists or not. All such problems are quite un-
suitable for a mind created to conceive only three dimensions. And so not only do I readily accept God, but I also
accept His wisdom and His purpose, of which we really know
absolutely nothing, the divine order of things, the meaning
of life, and the eternal harmony into which we are all to be
fused. I believe in His Word, toward which the universe is
striving, the Word that itself was 'with God' and that, indeed,
is God—well, and so on and so on and on, to eternity; so
much has been said on that subject. Well then, it looks as if
I were on the right path, doesn't it? Well, let me tell you this:

in the final analysis, I do not accept this God-made world and, although I know it exists, I absolutely refuse to admit its existence. I want you to understand that it is not God that I refuse to accept, but the world that He has created—what I do not accept and cannot accept is the God-created world. However, let me make it clear that, like a babe, I trust that the wounds will heal, the scars will vanish, that the sorry and ridiculous spectacle of man's disagreements and clashes will disappear like a pitiful mirage, like the sordid invention of a puny, microscopic, Euclidean, human brain, and that, in the end, in the universal finale, at the moment universal harmony is achieved, something so magnificent will take place that it will satisfy every human heart, allay all indignation, pay for all human crimes, for all the blood shed by men, and enable everyone not only to forgive everything but also to justify everything that has happened to men. Well, that day may come; all this may come to pass—but I personally still do not accept this world. I refuse to accept it! Even if I see the parallel lines meet myself, I'll look at them and say they have met, but I still won't accept it. That's the way I am, Alyosha, this is where I stand. And this time, I mean what I say seriously. I deliberately started this conversation as stupidly as I could, but I've ended up by making a clean breast of my opinions, because that was what you really wanted of me. You didn't want to hear about God from me. You simply wanted to find out what your dear brother lives by, and now I've told you."

Ivan finished his long explanation with strange emotion.

"But why did you have to start as stupidly as you could, as you put it?" Alyosha asked, looking thoughtfully at his brother.

"First of all, to make it sound really Russian: Russian discussions of this subject are conducted in the most stupid manner conceivable. And secondly, because the more stupidly we talk about these things, the closer we come to the point. The stupider, the clearer. Stupidity is brief and straightforward, while intelligence is tortuous and sneaky. Intelligence is crooked, while stupidity is honest. I've carried my argument to the point of despair, and the more stupidly I present it, the more to my advantage that will be."

"Will you explain to me why you won't accept the world?"

"Of course I will. It's no secret. I was coming to that. Ah, my dear little brother, I'm not trying to corrupt you, to destroy the foundations on which your beliefs are based.

Rather, I'm trying to make use of you as a way of healing myself."

Ivan smiled. He suddenly looked like a gentle little boy. Alyosha had never seen that sort of child-like smile on his face before.

CHAPTER 4

Rebellion

"I must admit," Ivan began, "I have never been able to understand how it was possible to love one's neighbors. And I mean precisely one's neighbors, because I can conceive of the possibility of loving those who are far away. I read somewhere about a saint, John the Merciful, who, when a hungry, frozen beggar came to him and asked him to warm him, lay down with him, put his arms around him, and breathed into the man's reeking mouth that was festering with the sores of some horrible disease. I'm convinced that he did so in a state of frenzy, that it was a false gesture, that this act of love was dictated by some self-imposed penance. If I must love my fellow man, he had better hide himself, for no sooner do I see his face than there's an end to my love for him."

"Elder Zosima has often discussed that," Alyosha remarked. "He also said that a man's face often prevents those inexperienced in love from loving him. But then there is much love in men, almost Christ-like love, I know that myself, Ivan . . ."

"Well, I for one know nothing about it yet. I cannot understand it, and there are masses of people just like me. The question is, then, whether this is because people are bad or because that is their nature. In my opinion, Christ's love for human beings was an impossible miracle on earth. But He was God. And we are no gods. Suppose, for instance, that I am in great pain. Someone else cannot possibly know how much it hurts me, because he is someone else and not me. Besides, a man is seldom willing to acknowledge another's suffering, as if suffering placed one in a superior position. And why won't he acknowledge it? Perhaps because the other fellow doesn't smell right, or because he has a stupid face, or because once upon a time he may have stepped on his toe. Moreover, there are many kinds of suffering. There are humiliating ways of suffering, such as hunger, with which a benefactor may still be able to credit the man he feeds, but very rarely will a man accept a slightly more refined form, such as, say, suffering for an ideal, in another man, because he may take a look at his face and declare that it's not the face of one suffering for that particular ideal, or, at least, it's not the way he imagines such a face should look. So he'll deprive him of his sympathy and help, and not necessarily because he's evil. Beggars, particularly well-born beggars, should never show themselves in person, but should do their begging exclusively through newspaper advertisements. The idea of loving one's neighbor is possible only as an abstraction: it may be conceivable to love one's fellow man at a distance, but it is almost never possible to love him at close quarters. If life were like the theater, the ballet, where the beggars come out in silken rags and beg while they perform the graceful steps of a ballet, then I suppose we could enjoy looking at them. But even then, to enjoy looking at someone is still not the same thing as loving him. But enough of that for now. I was simply trying to make you look at things from where I stand. And, although I had originally thought of talking to you about human suffering in general, I have now decided to talk to you only about the suffering of children.

"It will reduce the scope of my argument to about a tenth of the total, but I still prefer to restrict myself to the subject of children. Not that that restriction is to my advantage. But, in the first place, it *is* possible to love children, at close quarters, even if they are dirty, even if they have ugly faces, although to me a child's face is never really ugly. In the second place, I also will not speak of adults at the moment, because, besides being disgusting and undeserving of love, they have something to compensate them for their suffering: they have eaten their apple of knowledge, they know about good and evil and are like gods themselves. And they keep eating the apple. But little children haven't eaten it. They're not yet guilty of anything. Do you like small children, Alyosha? I know you do and that you'll understand why I have chosen to speak exclusively of them. Well then, if they suffer here in this world, it's because they're paying for the sins of their fathers who ate the apple. But that is the reasoning of another world and it's incomprehensible to the human heart here on earth. No innocent should be made to suffer for another man's sins, especially innocents such as these!

Doesn't it surprise you, Alyosha, that I, too, love children? I want you to note, by the way, that cruel, carnivorous, sensual people like the Karamazovs are sometimes very fond of children. Children, as long as they are young, say seven years old, for instance, are very different from adults— entirely different creatures, totally unlike adults in their very essence. In prison I once met a bandit who had often broken into people's houses at night to rob them, and who had killed entire families, and sometimes children too. But in prison he showed a strange love for children. For instance, he would stand for hours at the window of his cell and watch the children playing in the prison yard. He succeeded somehow in communicating with a little boy, who thereafter would often come and stand under the man's window, and the two of them became great friends . . . Do you know why I'm telling you all this, Alyosha? I have a sort of headache and I'm feeling sad."

"You look strange," Alyosha said worriedly. "You don't look yourself."

"By the way, in Moscow not long ago, a Bulgarian told me," Ivan went on, ignoring Alyosha's remark, "of the atrocities committed all over his country by Turks and Circassians, who, fearing a general uprising of the Slav population, set villages afire, rape women and children, nail their prisoners to fences by the ears and leave them in that state until morning, when they hang them, and who commit other atrocities that are difficult even to imagine. People often describe such human cruelty as 'bestial,' but that's, of course, unfair to animals, for no beast could ever be as cruel as man, I mean as refinedly and artistically cruel. The tiger simply gnaws and tears his victim to pieces because that's all he knows. It would never occur to a tiger to nail people to fences by their ears, even if he were able to do it. Those Turks, by the way, seem to derive a voluptuous pleasure from torturing children—they do everything from cutting unborn babes out of their mothers' wombs with their daggers to tossing infants into the air and catching them on the points of their bayonets as the mothers watch. It's doing this in front of the mothers that particularly arouses their senses. But, of the things the Bulgarian told me, the following scene particularly caught my attention. Imagine a baby in the arms of his trembling mother, with Turks all around them. The Turks are having a little game: they laugh and tickle the baby to make it laugh too. Finally they succeed and the baby begins to laugh. Then one of the Turks points his pistol at the baby, holding it four inches from the child's face. The little boy chuckles delightedly and tries to catch the shiny pistol in his tiny hands. Suddenly the artist presses the trigger and fires into the baby's face, splitting his little head in half . . . Pure art, isn't it? Incidentally, I understand that Turks are very fond of sweet things."

"Why are you telling me all this, Ivan?" Alyosha asked.

"I think that if the devil doesn't exist and is therefore man's creation, man has made him in his own image."

"Just as he has created God, in that case."

"Oh, you're really very good at 'cracking the wind of the poor phrase,' as Polonius says in *Hamlet*," Ivan said, laughing. "You caught me up on my 'poor phrase.' Good, I'm glad you did. But I don't think much of your God, if man has created Him in his image. You asked me a few seconds ago why I was telling you all this. Well, it's because I'm a collector of certain little facts; I even write them down. I collect them from news items, from stories people tell me, wherever I happen to find them, and I already have quite a respectable collection. These Turks, of course, are part of my collection, but they're just foreigners. I have quite a few home-grown facts that are even better than the Turkish ones. You know, we go in more for beating, flogging, whipping—that's more to our national taste. To us, nailing people by their ears is unthinkable because, despite everything, we *are* Europeans. But birch and lash, they're different—they're something that's really ours and cannot be taken away from us. I hear that they have stopped flogging in Europe altogether, whether because their habits have become milder or because they've passed new laws forbidding it, so that a man no longer dares to beat another, I don't know. What I do know is that they have made up for it with something else, something that is as native to them as flogging is to us. Indeed, it is so peculiar to those countries that it seems impossible here, although actually it is spreading in Russia too, along with a certain religious movement prevalent among our upper classes.

"I have a charming little pamphlet translated from French. It's about the execution in Geneva, not more than five years ago, of a twenty-three-year-old convicted murderer called Richard. The man repented and was converted to the Christian faith just before the execution. He was an illegitimate child and when he was only six years old his parents gave him as a present to some shepherds in the Swiss mountains, who took him to make him work for them. He grew up among them like a little wild animal. They taught him nothing. When he was only seven, they sent him out in the cold and rain to take the cattle to graze, without giving him any warm clothes and without even feeding him properly. And it goes without saying that they never questioned their right to treat him like that or felt guilty about it, because, after all, Richard had been given them as a present, like an inanimate object, and they didn't imagine they could have any obligations even to feed him. In his testimony, Richard himself recounted that during those years he was like the prodigal son, longing to eat the slops given to the pigs to fatten them up for market, but even that was not for him and he was beaten whenever they caught him stealing the pigs' feed. And so passed his whole childhood and his early youth, until he became big and strong enough to go out and steal on his own. The young savage would go to Geneva, hire himself out as a day laborer, and then drink the money he earned. He lived like a brute and ended up by robbing and killing some old man. He was caught, tried, and sentenced to death. They're not exactly sentimental over there. But once in prison, he was immediately surrounded by pastors of various Christian sects, lady philanthropists, and such people. In prison they taught him to read and write, explained the Gospels to him, preached to him, exhorted him, worked on him, nagged him, put pressure on him, until at last he himself solemnly admitted his crime. He was converted and wrote to the court that he had been a monster but that finally God had made him see the light and had granted him grace. Everyone in town was greatly moved, all of philanthropic and pious Geneva was tremendously excited. All the well-bred, important people of the city hurried to the prison to embrace and kiss Richard, exclaiming, 'You are our brother, grace has descended upon you!' to which Richard, himself in tears, answered, 'Yes, grace has descended upon me! When I was a small child and a youth, I was glad when I got pigs' feed, whereas now grace has descended upon me and I'm dying in the Lord!' 'Yes, yes, Richard,' they said, 'die in the Lord. You have shed blood and must die in the Lord. Although it was through no fault of your own that you knew nothing about the Lord when you were a small boy and, envying the pigs their feed, you stole some of it, for which you were beaten, because stealing is very wicked, now you have shed blood and must die.' And so Richard's last day arrived. In his weak, emotional state, Richard kept tearfully repeating again and again: 'This is the best day of my life, for I am joining the Lord!' 'Yes!' cried the pastors and the philanthropic ladies. 'It is indeed your happiest day, for you are joining the Lord!' And all these people, afoot or in their carriages, followed Richard as he was taken to the scaffold in his ignominious cart. Finally they reached the scaffold. 'Die, brother!' they called out to him, 'die in the Lord, because His grace has descended upon you too!' And the next thing, brother Richard, covered with the kisses of all his brothers and sisters, was dragged up onto the scaffold, placed under the knife of the guillotine, had his head chopped off in the most brotherly fashion, and gained eternal bliss.

"Well, that is a quite typical story. The pamphlet about Richard was translated into Russian by some high-society Russian do-gooders of the Lutheran persuasion, and it was distributed free as a newspaper supplement, for the enlightenment of the Russian masses. The story is a good one because it reveals so much about a national mentality. While in Russia it may seem absurd to chop off one's brother's head just because he has become one's brother and grace has descended upon him, I repeat once again that we have our native tricks that are hardly any better. Our traditional and most widespread national passion is inflicting pain through direct beating. Nekrasov has a poem in which a peasant whips his horse, aiming at the animal's eyes—'the horse's gentle eyes.' Is there anyone among us who hasn't witnessed something of the sort? Well, it's just typically Russian! Nekrasov describes the poor, feeble nag, trying in vain to pull an over-loaded cart which is stuck in the mud. The peasant whips the nag, whips it savagely, and in the end, no longer knowing what he's doing, continues to hit it, the act itself intoxicating him, hitting, whipping, on and on, frantically, as if saying, 'Even if you can't do it, pull! Die, but pull!' The poor nag strains and strains in vain, and that's when he lashes out at the defenseless creature's tearful and 'gentle eyes.' The nag then makes a desperate effort, pulls the cart out of the mud, and moves forward, its whole body trembling, unable to breathe, walking somehow sideways, skipping in a strange, unnatural, horrible way. Nekrasov's description is terrifying. But that was just a horse, after all, and God Himself gave us horses so we could whip them. We were taught that by the Tartars, who left us the whip to remember them by . . .

"But when one comes to think of it, people can be beaten too. I have noted down a detailed account of a well-educated, cultured gentleman and his wife flogging their own seven-year-old daughter. The papa is delighted that the twigs he uses to flog the child have knots in them. 'That'll add to the stinging effect,' he declares and proceeds to use them on the little girl. I know for a fact that there are people who get more and more excited with every blow when they beat someone, until they experience a sensual joy, a real, voluptuous pleasure, stronger and stronger as they go on . . . They flog the girl for one minute . . . five minutes, they go on to ten, harder, faster, more stingingly. The child screams. Then the child can no longer scream, she's gasping for air . . . 'Ah, papa, papa, papa dear' . . .

"Somehow, after one such frantic, diabolical, disgusting performance, the parents are brought to court. They engage a counsel, 'a conscience for hire,' as our peasants call lawyers. The counsel screams in his clients' defense: 'This concerns no one but the family! All right, so a father flogged his daughter, what of it? It only proves what strange times we are living in that this should be brought to court!' The conscientious jury go out and come back with a verdict of 'not guilty.' The spectators roar with joy because the child torturer has been acquitted. Ah, if only I'd been present in that court-room, I'd have gotten up and proposed at the top of my voice that a special scholarship grant should be named for this torturer. Yes, it was a charming picture.

"But I have even better stories about children than that, Alyosha. I have a quite impressive collection of such stories about our Russian children. There's one about a little five-year-old girl, hated by her parents, who are described as 'most respectable and socially prominent people, cultured and well educated.' You see, I repeat, there is no doubt whatsoever that many people share this trait: a passion for inflicting pain on children, but just on children. These people may be kind and even behave with gentleness toward other adults of the human species, as any normal, humane, educated European would, but they love torturing children. In fact, in a sense, they even love the children because of the tortures they inflict upon them. What excites them is the utter helplessness of the little creatures, the angelic trustfulness of the child who has nowhere to turn for help—yes, that's what sets the vicious blood of the torturer afire. Of course, we know that there are wild beasts lurking in every human being —the beast of explosive fury, the beast of sensuous intoxication that grows with the cries of the tortured victim, the unrestrained beast let off the chain, and the beast of sickness contracted in debauchery—diseased liver, gout, and all.

"And so these refined parents subjected their five-year-old girl to all kinds of torture. They beat her, kicked her, flogged her, for no reason that they themselves knew of. The child's whole body was covered with bruises. Eventually they devised a new refinement. Under the pretext that the child dirtied her bed (as though a five-year-old deep in angelic sleep could be punished for that), they forced her to eat excrement, smearing it all over her face. And it was the mother who did it! And then that woman would lock her little daughter up in the outhouse until morning and she did so even on the coldest nights, when it was freezing. Just imagine the woman being able to sleep with the child's cries coming from that infamous outhouse! Imagine the little creature, unable even to understand what is happening to her, beating her sore little chest with her tiny fist, weeping hot, unresentful, meek tears, and begging 'gentle Jesus' to help her, and all this happening in that icy, dark, stinking place! Do you understand this nonsensical thing, my dear friend, my brother, you gentle novice who is so eager to spend his life in the service of God? Tell me, do you understand the purpose of that absurdity? Who needs it and why was it created? They say that man could not do without it on earth, for otherwise he would not be able to learn the difference between good and evil. But I say I'd rather not know about their damned good and evil than pay such a terrible price for it. I feel that all universal knowledge is not worth that child's tears when she was begging 'gentle Jesus' to help her! I'm not even talking about the sufferings of adults: they, at least, have eaten their apple of knowledge, so the hell with them. But it's different when it comes to children. It seems I'm hurting you, Alyosha, my boy. You don't look very well. I won't go on if you don't want me to."

"Never mind. I want to suffer too," Alyosha mumbled.

"One more little sketch then, the last, and that only because it's a rather curious little story and a very typical one, and, above all, because I read it very recently in one of our anthologies, I believe it was in the *Archives of the Old Times*. I must check on that. See, I've even forgotten where I read it. Well, this happened early in our nineteenth century, during the darkest days of serfdom—and, by the way, long live our Tsar Alexander II, the Liberator of the People! Well then, at the turn of this century, there lived a retired general, a man with the highest connections, a big landowner, one of those, you know (although even at that time there were only a few such left), who, upon retiring from the service of their country, feel sure that they have earned the right of life and death over those subjected to them. Yes, there used to be such people then. This general lived on his estate, which had two thousand serfs. He strutted around, feeling immensely important, and bullying his lesser neighbors as if they were hangers-on and clowns obliged to amuse him. He had hundreds of hounds and just about as many kennel attendants, all dressed in special livery and every one of them mounted.

"It so happened that one day an eight-year-old boy, playing in the courtyard, threw a stone and inadvertently hit the General's favorite hound in the leg, injuring it. 'Why is my favorite hound limping?' the General demanded, and he was informed that the boy had hit it with a stone. 'So it was you,' the General said, looking the boy up and down. 'Lock him up.' They took the boy away from his mother and locked him up in the guardroom for the whole night. The next day, at dawn, the General rode out to the hunt in full dress, surrounded by his obsequious neighbors, hounds, kennel attendants, huntsmen, every one of them on horseback. All the serfs of the estate were summoned too, for their edification, and so was the boy's mother. They brought the boy out of the guardroom. It was a bleak, foggy, raw day— an ideal day for hunting. The General ordered the boy stripped naked. The boy was shivering. He seemed paralyzed with fear. He didn't dare utter a sound. 'Off with him now, chase him!' 'Hey, you, run, run!' a flunkey yelled, and the boy started to run. 'Sic 'im!' the General roared. The whole pack was set on the boy and the hounds tore him to pieces before his mother's eyes. I believe that, as a result of this, the General was later declared incompetent to administer his own estates without an appointed supervisory body . . . But perhaps you could tell me what should have been done in this case? Perhaps he ought to have been shot, to satisfy the moral indignation that such an act arouses in us? Well, speak up, my boy, go on!"

"Yes, shot . . ." Alyosha murmured, raising his eyes to his brother with a strange, faint, twisted grin.

"Good!" Ivan cried with affected delight. "Now, if you say so, it really shows that . . . Ah, you little novice, so there is that devil lurking in your heart too, you wicked Alyosha Karamazov, you!"

"What I said was pretty stupid, but . . ."

"Yes, that 'but' is just the thing!" Ivan cried. "I want you to know, novice, that absurdity is very much needed on this earth of ours. Indeed, the whole universe is founded on absurdity, and, perhaps, without absurdity there would be nothing at all. There are a few things we do know, after all."

"And what do you know?"

"I don't understand anything," Ivan said, like a man in delirium, "and I don't wish to understand anything. The moment I start wanting to understand something, I distort the true picture, when what I really want is to stick to the facts."

"Why are you trying to test me like this?" Alyosha cried frenziedly. "Will you at least tell me that finally?"

"Of course I'll tell you. That's just what I've been leading up to. You're dear to me and I have no intention of letting you go and giving you up to that Zosima of yours."

Ivan remained silent for a moment and suddenly his face grew very sad.

"I want you to understand me," he said. "I spoke only of small children to make my point more obvious. I didn't mention the other human tears with which our earth is soaked from crust to core, because I was deliberately narrowing the subject. I'm nothing but a bug and I most humbly admit that it's quite beyond me why things are arranged the way they are. I suppose that men themselves are to blame for it: they were given a paradise on earth, but they wanted freedom and they stole fire from heaven, although they knew that it would bring them unhappiness. So there's no reason to be sorry for them. All that my puny, Euclidean, earthling's mind can grasp is that there is such a thing as suffering, that no one can be blamed for it, that quite uncomplicatedly cause precedes effect, that everything that flows finds its proper level—but then all that is just Euclidean gibberish, and, being aware of that fact, I cannot agree to live by it! What good does it do me to know that no one is to blame, that every effect is determined by a cause, which itself is an effect of some other cause, and so on, and that, therefore, no one should ever be blamed for anything? For, even though I may know it, I still need retribution. Without it I'd rather destroy myself. And I must have that retribution not somewhere far off in infinity but here, on earth. I want to see it myself. I believe in justice and I want to see justice done with my own eyes; if I should be dead by that time, I want to be brought back to life, because the idea that, when justice finally does triumph, I won't even be there to witness it is too abhorrent to me. Why, I certainly haven't borne it all so that my crimes and my sufferings would be used as manure to nurture the harmony that will appear in some remote future to be enjoyed by some unknown creatures. No, I want to see with my own eyes the lamb lie down with the lion and the resurrected victim rise and embrace his murderer. I want to be here when everyone understands why the world has been arranged the way it is. It is on that craving for understanding that all human religions are founded, so I am a believer. But then, what about the children? How will we ever account for their sufferings? For the hundredth time I repeat, there are many questions that could be asked, but I ask you only one—about the children—because I believe it conveys fully and clearly what I am trying to tell you. Listen, even if we assume that every person must suffer because his suffering is necessary to pay for eternal harmony, still do tell me, for God's sake, where the children come in. I can understand the concept of solidarity in sin and also solidarity in retribution. But how can there be solidarity in sin with small children? And if it is true that children share the responsibility for the sins committed by their fathers, then that concept must be true in some different world from the world I know, and it is quite beyond my grasp. Some joker may say that the child will grow up and have time to sin later, but, for instance, the eight-year-old boy who was torn to pieces by the hounds was never given a chance to grow up and sin. This is no blasphemy, Alyosha, I assure you! I can imagine what a universal upheaval there will be when everything up in heaven and down in the entrails of the earth comes together to sing one single hymn of praise and when every creature who has ever lived joins in, intoning, 'You were right, O Lord, for Your way has now been revealed to us!' The day the mother embraces the man who had her son torn to pieces by the hounds, the day those three stand side by side and say, 'You were right, O Lord,' that day we will at last have attained the supreme knowledge and everything will be explained and accounted for. But that's just the hurdle I can't get over, because I cannot agree that it makes everything right. And while I am on this earth, I must act in my own way. You see, it's quite possible, if I'm still alive or am resurrected on the day the mother embraces her child's murderer, that I may join them all in their praises and shout with them, 'You were right'; but as of now, I do not want to join them. And while there is still time, I want to dissociate myself from it all; I have no wish to be a part of their eternal harmony. It's not worth one single tear of the martyred little girl who beat her breast with her tiny fist, shedding her innocent tears and praying to 'sweet Jesus' to rescue her in the stinking outhouse. It's not worth it, because that tear will have remained unatoned for. And those tears must be atoned for; otherwise there can be no harmony. But what could atone for those tears? How is it possible to atone for them? By avenging them perhaps? But whom would vengeance help? What good would it do to send the monsters to hell after they have finished inflicting their suffering on children? How can their being in hell put things right? Besides, what sort of harmony can there be as long as there is a hell? To me, harmony means forgiving and embracing everybody, and I don't want anyone to suffer anymore. And if the suffering of little children is needed to complete the sum total of suffering required to pay for the truth, I don't want that truth, and I declare in advance that all the truth in the world is not worth the price! And finally, I don't really want to see the mother of the little boy embrace the man who set the hounds on him to tear him apart! She won't be able to forgive him. If she wants to, she may forgive him for herself, for having caused her, the mother, infinite suffering. But she has no right to forgive him for her child torn to pieces. She may not forgive him, even if the child chooses to forgive him himself. And if I am right, if they cannot forgive, what harmony can there be? Is there one single creature in the whole world who could forgive or would have the right to do so? No, I want no part of any harmony; I don't want it, out of love for mankind. I prefer to remain with my unavenged suffering and my unappeased anger—*even if I happen to be wrong.* I feel, moreover, that such harmony is rather overpriced. We cannot afford to pay so much for a ticket. And so I hasten to return the ticket I've been sent. If I'm honest, it is my duty to return it as long as possible before the show. And that's just what I'm trying to do, Alyosha. It isn't that I reject God; I am simply returning Him most respectfully the ticket that would entitle me to a seat."

"That's rebellion," Alyosha said softly, lowering his eyes.

"Rebellion? I wish you hadn't used that word," Ivan said feelingly. "I don't believe it's possible to live in rebellion, and I want to live! Tell me yourself—I challenge you: let's assume that you were called upon to build the edifice of human destiny so that men would finally be happy and would find peace and tranquility. If you knew that, in order to attain this, you would have to torture just one single creature, let's say the little girl who beat her chest so desperately in the outhouse, and that on her unavenged tears you could build that edifice, would you agree to do it? Tell me and don't lie!"

"No, I would not," Alyosha said softly.

"And do you find acceptable the idea that those for whom you are building that edifice should gratefully receive a happiness that rests on the blood of a tortured child and, having received it, should continue to enjoy it eternally?"

"No, I do not find that acceptable," Alyosha said and his eyes suddenly flared up. "But a moment ago you asked whether there was in the world 'a single creature who could forgive.' Well, there is. And He can forgive everyone for everything, because He Himself gave His innocent blood for everyone's sins and for everyone's sake. You forgot to mention Him, although it is on Him that the edifice must be founded, it is to Him that they will sing, 'You were right, O Lord, for Your ways have now been revealed to us!' "

"You mean 'the one without sin' and His blood! No, Alyosha, I hadn't forgotten about Him. Indeed, I was wondering how long it would take you to bring Him into our discussion, because the people on your side usually make use of Him above all else in their arguments. You know—well, don't laugh now—about a year or so ago I composed a sort of poem and, if you're willing to waste, say, another ten minutes with me, I could recite it to you."

"You? You wrote a poem?"

"No, no, I didn't write it," Ivan said, laughing, "I've never written two verses in my whole life. But I did think it up and I've memorized it. I composed it in a moment of real inspiration. Well, you'll be my first reader, I mean, audience.

Why should an author forego even one listener, after all?"
Ivan said with a grin. "So, are you willing to hear it?"

"I'm listening attentively."

"My poem is called 'The Grand Inquisitor.' It's a ridiculous
piece really, but I'd like you to hear it."

CHAPTER 5

The Grand Inquisitor

"But now that I think of it, I can't just start without some
preliminary remarks. I mean it needs a sort of literary introduction . . . Ah, hell," Ivan laughed, "what kind of an author
am I? Well, I want you to understand that the action takes
place in the sixteenth century, and in those days, as you
may remember from school, it was usual to bring heavenly
powers down to earth—in poetical writing, that is. Not to
even mention Dante, in France the clerks and the monks in
monasteries staged plays in which the Virgin, angels, saints,
Christ, and even God Himself were brought out onto the
stage. It was done very naturally then. Victor Hugo's *Notre
Dame de Paris* has a passage about such a play—*Le bon
jugement de la très sainte et gracieuse Vierge Marie*—performed under Louis XI in the city hall of Paris on the
Dauphin's birthday. It was considered an edifying play and
admission was free. In the course of the performance, the
Virgin comes out on stage and announces her *bon jugement*
in person. We, too, occasionally had plays like that performed
in Moscow in the old days, before the rule of Peter the
Great, plays based mostly on Old Testament stories . . . But,
besides plays, many stories and 'poems' circulated all over
the world at that time, in which saints, angels, and even the
supreme heavenly powers appeared whenever their presence
was required. In our monasteries, too, monks copied, translated, and even composed such poems, back at the time of
the Tartar invasion. One of these monastery-written poems,
for instance, is called *The Virgin's Journey Through Hell*, and
it contains some scenes and descriptions as bold as Dante's.
In the play, which is obviously influenced by the Greeks, the
Mother of God visits hell, where the Archangel Michael is
her guide. She sees the sinners being tortured. Incidentally,
there is one very interesting category of sinners there: they
float on a lake of fire, trying to swim out, but in vain, because

'God has forgotten about them'—extremely powerful and meaningful words, I think. Shocked and weeping, the Holy Virgin kneels before the throne of God and beseeches Him to forgive all those she has seen in hell, every one of them, without exception. Her dialogue with God is absolutely fascinating. She pleads, she refuses to give up. God points to the wounds left by the nails on her son's hands and feet and asks, 'How can I forgive His tormentors?' She then summons all the saints, all the martyrs, and all the angels and archangels to kneel with her before Him and pray for the pardon of all the sinners without exception. In the end, she obtains from God a yearly suspension of all torture between Good Friday and Trinity Sunday, and the sinners in hell thank the Lord and cry out: 'You are just in Your judgment, O Lord!'

"Well, what I'm trying to tell you is that my own little piece is a bit along such lines, as if it had been written in those days. In my piece, He comes on the scene, although He doesn't say a word; He just appears and vanishes again.

"Fifteen centuries have passed since He promised to come in His glory, fifteen centuries since His prophet wrote, 'Behold, I come quickly.' 'Of that day and hour knoweth no man, neither the Son, but the Father,' as He Himself announced when He was still on earth. But men still wait for Him with the same faith, with the same love. Nay, with even greater faith, for fifteen centuries have passed without a sign from heaven to mankind.

> Trust to what your heart will tell you,
> For from heaven no sign comes.

"And there is nothing but the faith still alive in the heart! It is true, though, that many miracles happened in those days. There were saints who worked miraculous cures. To some holy men, according to the stories of their lives, the Mother of God came down in person. But the devil was not idle and, among men, some started questioning the truth of these miracles. Just then there appeared a deadly new heresy in the North, in Germany. 'A huge star bright as a luminary'—i.e., the Church—'fell upon the sources of the waters and they became bitter.' The heretics blasphemously dismissed miracles. But that only made the faith of those who still believed more ardent. And, as of old, human tears rose up to Him; people still awaited His coming and loved Him; and men still placed their hopes in Him and were prepared to suffer and die for

Him. For centuries, men had beseeched Him with faith and fervor: 'O Lord, our God, hasten Your coming.' And He, in His infinite mercy, had come down to them. He had visited saints, martyrs, and holy hermits while they were still on earth, just as it says in their *Lives*. In Russia our poet Tyuchev, believing deeply in the truth of his words, wrote:

> Through our mother earth entire
> Wandering, His cross He bore,
> The Heavenly King in slave's attire,
> Blessing all He came before.

And that is just what happened, believe me. He decided to show Himself, if only for a moment, to His people, long-suffering, tormented, sinful people who loved Him with a child-like love. My story takes place in Spain, in Seville, during the grimmest days of the Inquisition, when throughout the country fires were burning endlessly to the greater glory of God and

> In autos-da-fé resplendent
> Wicked heretics were burned.

"Of course, this was not the coming in which He had promised to appear in all His heavenly glory at the end of time and which would be as sudden as a bolt of lightning cutting the sky from east to west. No, He wanted to come only for a moment to visit His children and He chose to appear where the fires were crackling under the heretics.

"In His infinite mercy He came among men in human form, just as He had walked among them fifteen centuries before. He came down to that sun-baked Southern city the day after nearly a hundred heretics had been burned all at once *ad majorem gloriam Dei*, in a resplendent auto-da-fé by the order of the Cardinal, the Grand Inquisitor, and in the presence of the King, the royal court, knights, beautiful ladies-in-waiting, and the entire population of Seville.

"He came unobserved and moved about silently but, strangely enough, those who saw Him recognized Him at once. This might, perhaps, be the best part of my poem—I mean if I could explain what made them recognize Him . . . People are drawn to Him by an irresistible force, they gather around Him, follow Him, and soon there is a crowd. He walks among them in silence, a gentle smile of infinite compassion on His lips. The sun of love burns in His heart; light, understanding, and spiritual power flow from His eyes and set people's hearts vibrating with love for Him. He holds His hands out to them, blesses them, and just from touching Him, or even His clothes, comes a healing power. An old man who has been blind from childhood suddenly cries out to Him: 'Cure me, O Lord, so that I may see You too!' And it is as if scales had fallen from his eyes, and the blind man sees Him. People weep and kiss the ground on which He walks. Children scatter flowers in His path and cry out to Him, 'Hosannah!' 'It is He, He Himself!' people keep saying. 'Who else could it be!' He stops on the steps of the cathedral of Seville at a moment when a small white coffin is carried into the church by weeping bearers. In it lies a girl of seven, the only daughter of a prominent man. She lies there amidst flowers. 'He will raise your child from the dead!' people shout to the weeping mother. The priest, who has come out of the cathedral to meet the procession, looks perplexed and frowns. But now the mother of the dead child throws herself at His feet, wailing, 'If it is truly You, give me back my child!' and she stretches out her hands to Him. The procession stops. They put the coffin down at His feet. He looks down with compassion, His lips form the words *'Talitha cumi'*—arise, maiden—and the maiden arises. The little girl sits up in her coffin, opens her little eyes, looks around in surprise, and smiles. She holds the white roses that had been placed in her hand when they had laid her in the coffin. There is confusion among the people, shouting and weeping . . .

"Just at that moment, the Cardinal, the Grand Inquisitor himself, crosses the cathedral square. He is a man of almost ninety, tall and erect. His face is drawn, his eyes are sunken, but they still glow as though a spark smoldered in them. Oh, now he is not wearing his magnificent cardinal's robes in which he paraded before the crowds the day before, when they were burning the enemies of the Roman Church; no, today he is wearing just the coarse cassock of an ordinary monk. He is followed by his grisly assistants, his slaves, his 'holy guard.' He sees the crowd gathered, stops, and watches from a distance. He sees everything: the placing of the coffin at His feet and the girl rising from it. His face darkens. He knits his thick white brows; his eyes flash with an ominous fire. He points his finger and orders his guards to seize Him.

"The Grand Inquisitor's power is so great and the people are so submissive and tremblingly obedient to him that they immediately open up a passage for the guards. A death-like silence descends upon the square and in that silence the guards lay hands on Him and lead Him away.

"Then everyone in the crowd, to a man, prostrates himself before the Grand Inquisitor. The old man blesses them in silence and passes on.

"The guards take their prisoner to an old building of the Holy Inquisition and lock Him up there in a dark, narrow, vaulted prison cell. The day declines and is replaced by the stifling, black Southern night of Seville. The air is fragrant with laurel and lemon.

"Suddenly, in the complete darkness, the iron gate of the cell opens and there stands the Grand Inquisitor himself, holding a light in his hand. The old man enters the cell alone and, when he is inside, the door closes behind him. He stops and for a long time—one or even two minutes—he looks at Him. At last he sets the light down on the table and says: 'You? Is it really You?' Receiving no answer, he continues in great haste:

"'You need not answer me. Say nothing. I know only too well what You could tell me now. Besides, You have no right to add anything to what You said before. Why did You come here, to interfere and make things difficult for us? For You came to interefere—You know it. But shall I tell You what will happen tomorrow? Well, I do not know who You really are, nor do I want to know whether You are really He or just a likeness of Him, but no later than tomorrow I shall pronounce You the wickedest of all heretics and sentence You to be burned at the stake, and the very people who today were kissing Your feet will tomorrow, at a sign of my hand, hasten to Your stake to rake the coals. Don't You know it? Oh yes, I suppose You do,' he added, deeply immersed in thought, his eyes fixed for a moment on his prisoner."

"I don't quite understand what you're trying to say, Ivan," Alyosha said with a smile. Until then he had listened in silence. "Is it just some wild fantasy or is there a mistake in identity, a *quid pro quo,* by your grand inquisitor?"

"Why, you may assume the latter if you wish," Ivan said laughingly, "since, as I see, you have been so spoiled by our contemporary brand of realism that you cannot accept anything that is a bit fantastic. If you wish to call it an error of identity, all right, so be it! It is a fact though," he said, starting to laugh again, "that the Inquisitor is ninety years old, so he has had plenty of time to have been driven completely out of his mind by his *idée fixe.* As to his prisoner, he may

have been struck by the man's looks. Or perhaps he was just
having hallucinations, which can easily happen to a ninety-
year-old man close to death, and what's more, excited by the
previous day's burning at the stake of a hundred heretics.
But, really, why should we care whether it is a wild fantasy
or a *quid pro quo?* What matters is that the old man must
speak his mind. At ninety this is the first time that he is
saying aloud something about which he has kept silent all
those ninety years."

"And the prisoner—He just looks at him and says nothing?"

"Why, yes," Ivan laughed once more, "and that's as it
should be in any case. Besides, the old man himself reminds
Him that He may not add a single word to what He has said
before. I might add that this may be the most crucial feature
of Roman Catholicism, at least the way I see it. It's as if the
Grand Inquisitor said to Him: 'You have transmitted all Your
authority to the Pope and now he wields it. As to You, You
had better stay away or, at any rate, not interefere with
us for the time being.' They don't just say that, they even
have it in writing, at least the Jesuits have. I've read it
myself in the works of their theologians.

" 'Do You think You have the right to reveal even a single
mystery of the world from which You come?' the Grand Inquisitor asks Him and then answers himself: 'No, You do
not, for You may not add anything to what has been said
before and You may not deprive men of the freedom You
defended so strongly when You were on earth. Anything new
that You might reveal to them now would encroach upon the
freedom of their faith, for it would come to them as a miracle, and fifteen centuries ago it was freely given faith that
was most important to You. Didn't You often tell them then
that You wanted to make them free. Well, then,' the old man
adds with a grin, 'so now You have seen *free* men. Yes, that
business cost us a great deal,' he continues, looking sternly at
Him, 'but at last, in Your name, we saw it through. For fifteen hundred years we were pestered by that notion of freedom, but in the end we succeeded in getting rid of it, and
now we are rid of it for good. You don't believe that we got
rid of it, do You? You look at me so gently, and You do
not even consider me worthy of Your anger? I want You to
know, though, that on this very day men are convinced that
they are freer than they have ever been, although they themselves brought us their freedom and put it meekly at our

feet. This is what we have achieved, but was it really what You wanted, was this the freedom that You wanted to bring them?' "

"I'm afraid I'm lost again," Alyosha interrupted Ivan, "is he being sarcastic? Is he laughing at Him?"

"He certainly is not. Indeed, he is claiming for himself and his church the credit for having done away with freedom and having thus given happiness to mankind.

" 'It is only now,' he says, obviously thinking of the Inquisition, 'that it has become possible, for the first time, to think of men's happiness. Man is a rebel by nature and how can a rebel be happy? You were warned,' he says to Him. 'There was no lack of warnings and signs, but You chose to ignore them. You spurned the only way that could have brought happiness to men. Fortunately, though, You allowed us to take over from You when You left. You made commitments to us, You sealed them with Your word, You gave us the right to loosen and to bind their shackles, and, of course, You cannot think of depriving us of that right now. Why, then, have You come to interfere with us now?' "

"What does that mean—there was no lack of warnings and signs?" Alyosha said.

"Well, that's precisely the most important point the old man must make.

" 'The wise and dreaded spirit of self-destruction and non-existence,' the old man went on, 'spoke to You in the desert and we learn from the books that he tried to tempt You. Was he really trying to *tempt* You, though? Could anything be truer than what he revealed to You in his three questions that You rejected, questions that were called "temptations" in the books? And yet, if a truly blinding miracle has ever happened on this earth, it happened on that day in the form of those three temptations. And it was precisely in those three questions that the miracle lay. If, for instance, those three questions asked by the dread spirit had been lost and we had had to rediscover and reinvent them, we would have had to assemble for that purpose all the world's wise men— rulers, high priests, scholars, philosophers, and poets—and to ask them to formulate three questions that would not only fit the magnitude of the occasion but also express in a few words, in three brief human sentences, the whole future history of the world and of mankind. Do You really believe that the combined wisdom of the earth could produce anything comparable in strength and depth to those three questions that the wise and powerful spirit asked You that day in the desert? From those questions alone, from the miracle of their formulation, it must be clear that it is not a matter of a transient human mind, but of something absolute and outside time. For those three questions contain the entire future history of man and they offer three symbols that reconcile all the irreconcilable strivings on earth which derive from the contradictions of human nature. It was not as clear at that time, because the future was still unknown. But now, fifteen centuries later, we can see that in those questions everything was perfectly foreseen and predicted and has proved so true that there is nothing we can add or subtract anymore.

" 'Judge for Yourself, then: who was right, You or the one who questioned You? Do You remember the first question? It was worded differently, but this is its purport: "You wanted to come into the world and You came empty-handed, with nothing but some vague promise of freedom, which, in their simple-mindedness and innate irresponsibility, men cannot even conceive and which they fear and dread, for there has never been anything more difficult for man and for human society to bear than freedom! And now, do You see those stones in this parched and barren desert? Turn them into loaves of bread and men will follow You like cattle, grateful and docile, although constantly fearful lest You withdraw Your hand and they lose Your loaves." But You did not want to deprive man of freedom and You rejected this suggestion, for, You thought, what sort of freedom would they have if their obedience was bought with bread? You replied that man does not live by bread alone, but do You know that for the sake of that earthly bread, the spirit of the earth will rise up against You, will confront and conquer You, and they will all follow him, shouting, "Who is there to match the beast who has brought us fire from heaven?" Do You know that more centuries will pass and men of wisdom and learning will proclaim that there is no such thing as crime, that there is therefore no sin either, that there are only hungry people. "Feed us first, then ask for virtue"—that will be the motto on the banners of those who will oppose You, of those who will raze Your temple and build in its place a new, terrifying tower of Babel. And although they will never complete it, any more than they did the last one, nevertheless You could have prevented men from making this second attempt to build the tower and thus have shortened their sufferings by a thousand years, for in the end it is to us that they will come, after this unnecessary thousand years of torment! They will find us hiding somewhere underground, hiding again in the catacombs —for we shall again be persecuted and tortured—and they will beg us: "Give us food, for those who promised us fire from heaven have not given it to us!" And that will be the day when we shall finish building their tower for them, for the one who feeds them will be the one who finishes building it, and we will be the only ones capable of feeding them. And we shall give them bread in Your name and lie, telling them that it is in Your name. Oh, never, never would they be able to feed themselves without us! There is no knowledge that could supply them with bread as long as they remain free. So, in the end, they will lay their freedom at our feet and say to us: "Enslave us, but feed us!" And they will finally understand that freedom and the assurance of daily bread for everyone are two incompatible notions that could never co-exist! They will also discover that men can never be free because they are weak, corrupt, worthless, and restless. You promised them heavenly bread but, I repeat, how can that bread compete against earthly bread in dealing with the weak, ungrateful, permanently corrupt human species? And even if hundreds or thousands of men follow You for the sake of heavenly bread, what will happen to the millions who are too weak to forego their earthly bread? Or is it only the thousands of the strong and mighty who are dear to Your heart, while the millions of others, the weak ones, who love You too, weak as they are, and who are as numerous as the grains of sand on the beach, are to serve as material for the strong and mighty? But we are concerned with the weak too! They are corrupt and undisciplined, but in the end they will be the obedient ones! They will marvel at us and worship us like gods, because, by becoming their masters, we have accepted the burden of freedom that they were too frightened to face, just because we have agreed to rule over them—that is how terrifying freedom will have become to them finally! We shall tell them, though, that we are loyal to You and that we rule over them in Your name. We shall be lying, because we do not intend to allow You to come back. And it is in this deception that our suffering will consist, because we will have to lie! So this is the meaning of the first question You were asked in the desert, and this is what You rejected in the name of the freedom that You put above all else. And yet that question contains one of the great mysteries on

which our world is founded. Had You been willing to give
them bread, You would have satisfied the eternal craving of
both individual man and human society as a whole—to have
someone to worship. There is nothing a free man is so anxious
to do as to find something to worship. But it must be something unquestionable, that all men can agree to worship com-
munally. For the great concern of these miserable creatures
is not that every individual should find something to worship
that he personally considers worthy of worship, but that they
should find something in which they can *all* believe and
which they can all worship *in common;* it is essential that it
should be in common. And it is precisely that requirement of
shared worship that has been the principal source of suffering for individual man and the human race since the beginning of history. In their efforts to impose universal worship,
men have unsheathed their swords and killed one another.
They have invented gods and challenged each other: "Discard
your gods and worship mine or I will destroy both your
gods and you!" And this is how it will be until the end of
time, even after gods have vanished from the earth—for they
are bound, in the end, to yield to idols. You knew, You
couldn't help knowing, this fundamental mystery of human
nature and, knowing it, You nevertheless spurned the only
banner that was offered You, that would have made them follow You and worship You without a murmur—the banner of
earthly bread. But You chose to reject it in the name of
freedom, in the name of spiritual bread! And look what You
did after that, again in the name of freedom. I tell You once
more that man has no more pressing, agonizing need than
the need to find someone to whom he can hand over as
quickly as possible the gift of freedom with which the poor
wretch comes into the world. But only one who can appease
a man's conscience can take his freedom from him. In bread,
You were offered something that could have brought You
indisputable loyalty: You would give man bread and man
would bow down to You, because there is nothing more indisputable than bread. But if, at the same time, someone else
succeeded in capturing his conscience, then man might even
spurn Your bread and follow the one who ensnared his conscience. This is something about which You were right. For
the mystery of human existence lies not in just staying alive,
but in finding something to live for. Without a concrete idea
of what he is living for, man would refuse to live, would rath-

er exterminate himself than remain on this earth, even if bread were scattered all around him.

" 'That is so, but what came of it? Instead of seizing men's freedom, You gave them even more of it! Have You forgotten that peace, and even death, is more attractive to man than the freedom of choice that derives from the knowledge of good and evil? There is nothing more alluring to man than freedom of conscience, but neither is there anything more agonizing. And yet, instead of giving them something tangible to calm their consciences forever, You came to them with words that were unfamiliar, vague, and indefinite; You offered them something that was quite beyond them; it even looked as if You didn't love them, You who came to give them Your life! Instead of ridding men of their freedom, You increased their freedom, and You imposed everlasting torment on man's soul. You wanted to gain man's love so that he would follow You of his own free will, fascinated and captivated by You. In place of the clear and rigid ancient law, You made man decide about good and evil for himself, with no other guidance than Your example. But did it never occur to You that man would disregard Your example, even question it, as well as Your truth, when he was subjected to so fearful a burden as freedom of choice? In the end they will shout that You did not bring them the truth, because it is impossible to have left them in greater confusion and misery than You did, leaving them with so many anxieties and unsolved problems. You see, then, You Yourself sowed the seeds of destruction for Your own kingdom, and no one else is to blame. And think now, was this the best that You could offer them?

" 'There are three forces, only three, on this earth that can overcome and capture once and for all the conscience of these feeble, undisciplined creatures, so as to give them happiness. These forces are miracle, mystery, and authority. But You rejected the first, the second, and the third of these forces and set up Your rejection as an example to men. When the wise and dreaded spirit placed You on the pinnacle of the temple and said, "If You would know whether You are the Son of God then cast Yourself down, for it is written: The angels shall hold Him up lest He fall and bruise Himself; and You shall know then whether You are the Son of God and shall prove how great is Your faith in Your Father," You heard him out, then rejected his advice, withstood the temptation, and did not plunge from the pinnacle. Oh, of course, You acted proudly and magnificently; indeed, You acted like God, but can You expect as much of men, of that weak, undisciplined, and wretched tribe, who are certainly no gods? Oh, You knew very well at that moment that if You had made the slightest move to jump, You would have tempted God, proving You had lost Your faith in Him, and You would have been smashed against the earth that You had come to save, and would thus have gladdened the wise spirit who was tempting You. But again, how many are there like You? Could You possibly imagine, even for one second, that men would be able to withstand such temptation? Is human nature such that it can reject a miracle when confronted with the most frightening choices, the most heartbreaking dilemmas, and remain facing them with nothing but freedom of choice? And You knew only too well that Your act would be recorded in books, that it would reach the remotest corners of the earth and be passed on down to the end of time. Did You really expect that man would follow Your example and remain with God without recourse to miracles? Didn't You know that whenever man rejects miracles he rejects God, because he seeks not so much God as miracles? And since man cannot live without miracles, he will provide himself with miracles of his own making. He will believe in witchcraft and sorcery, even though he may otherwise be a heretic, an atheist, and a rebel.

" 'You did not come down from the cross when they shouted, taunting and challenging You, "Come down from the cross and we will believe that You are He." You did not come down, again because You did not want to bring man to You by miracles, because You wanted their freely given love rather than the servile rapture of slaves subdued forever by a display of power. And, here again, You overestimated men, for they are certainly nothing but slaves, although they were created rebels by nature. Look around and judge for Yourself. Fifteen centuries have passed. Examine them. Whom have You raised up to Yourself? I swear that man is weaker and viler than You thought! How could he possibly do what You did? By paying him such respect, You acted as if You lacked compassion for him, because You demanded too much of him—and that from You, who love him more than Yourself! Had You respected him less, You would have demanded less of him and that would have been more like love, for the burden You placed on him would not have been so heavy. Man is weak and despicable. What if, today, he rebels everywhere against our authority and is proud of his rebellion? It is a childish pride, the pride of a schoolboy, of little children rioting in their classroom and driving out their teacher. But the end will come soon and they will have to pay dearly for their fun. They will raze churches and flood the earth with blood, but the stupid children will finally realize themselves that, although they are rebels, they are weak and are unable to bear their own rebellion. Shedding their silly tears, they will finally admit that He who created them rebels intended to mock them and no more. They will say it in despair and it will be blasphemy, and then they will be even more unhappy, because human nature cannot bear blasphemy and in the end always punishes itself for it. And so man's lot is nothing but unrest, confusion, and unhappiness —after all the suffering You bore for their freedom! Your great prophet had a vision and told us in an allegory that he had seen all those who were in the first resurrection and that there were twelve thousand of them from each tribe. But if there were so many, they must have been gods rather than men. They bore Your cross, they endured years and years of hunger in a barren wilderness, living on roots and locusts— and, of course, You can point proudly at these children of freedom, at their freely given love, and at their magnificent suffering for Your sake. Remember, though, there were only a few thousand of them and even these were gods rather than men. But what about the rest? Why should the rest of mankind, the weak ones, suffer because they are unable to stand what the strong ones can? Why is it the fault of a weak soul if he cannot live up to such terrifying gifts? Can it really be true that You came only for the chosen few? If that is so, it is a mystery that we cannot understand; and if it is a mystery, we have the right to preach to man that what matters is not freedom of choice or love, but a mystery that he must worship blindly, even at the expense of his conscience. And that is exactly what we have done. We have corrected Your work and have now founded it on *miracle, mystery,* and *authority.* And men rejoice at being led like cattle again, with the terrible gift of freedom that brought them so much suffering removed from them. Tell me, were we right in preaching and acting as we did? Was it not our love for men that made us resign ourselves to the idea of their impotence and lovingly try to lighten the burden of their responsibility, even allowing their weak nature to sin, but with our permission? Why have You come to interfere with our work? And why do

You look at me silently with those gentle eyes of Yours? Be angry with me. I do not want Your love, because I do not love You myself. Why should I go on pretending that I do not know to whom I am speaking? Everything I have to say You already know—I can read it in Your eyes. How could I expect to hide our secret from You? But perhaps You want to hear it from my own lips. Listen then: we are not with You, we are with *him*—and that is our secret, our mystery! We have been with *him* and not with You for a long time, for eight centuries already. Exactly eight centuries ago we accepted from him what You had rejected with indignation, the last gift he offered You—all the kingdom of earth. We accepted Rome and Caesar's sword from *him,* and we proclaimed ourselves the sole rulers of the earth, although to this day we have not yet succeeded in bringing our work to final completion. But You know who is to blame for that. Our work is only beginning, but at least it has begun. And, although its completion is still a long way off and the earth will have to face much suffering until then, in the end we shall prevail, we will be Caesars, and then we shall devise a plan for universal happiness. But You, You could have taken Caesar's sword when You came the first time. Why did You reject that last gift? Had You accepted the third offering of the mighty spirit, You would have fulfilled man's greatest need on earth. That is, the need to find someone to worship, someone who can relieve him of the burden of his conscience, thus enabling him finally to unite into a harmonious ant-hill where there are no dissenting voices, for the unquenchable thirst for universal unity is the third and last ordeal of man. Men have always striven to be organized into a universal whole. There have been many great nations with a glorious past history, but the higher the stage of development they reached, the greater was their discontent, because they became more and more obsessed with the need for universal unification. The great conquerors, the Tamerlanes and the Genghis Khans, who swept like whirlwinds across the earth, striving to subdue the whole world, were also, even if they were unaware of it themselves, obeying that eternal human craving for universal union. Had You accepted Caesar's purple, You would have founded a universal empire and given men everlasting peace. For who can rule men if not one who holds both their consciences and their bread? So we took Caesar's sword and, by taking it, we rejected You and followed *him.* Oh, there will still be centuries of chaos, in which men will be guided by their own unbridled thinking, by their science, and by their cannibal instincts, for, since they started building their tower of Babel without us, they will end up devouring each other. But it will be just at that moment that the beast will crawl to us, lick our feet, and spatter them with tears of blood. And we shall saddle and mount the beast and raise the cup on which the word "mystery" is engraved. Then, and only then, will the reign of peace and happiness come to men. You pride Yourself on Your chosen ones, but You have only the chosen, while we will bring peace of mind to all men. And that is not all: how many of those strong enough to be among the chosen have already or will in the future take their mighty minds and ardent hearts away from You and give them to some other cause, in the end raising their *free* banner against You? Yet You were the one who gave them that banner.

"'Under us it will be different. Under us they will all be happy and they will not rise in rebellion and kill one another all the world over, as they are doing now with the freedom You gave them. Oh, we will convince them that they will only be free when they have surrendered their freedom and submitted to us. And that will be the truth, will it not? Or do You think we will be deceiving them? They will find out for themselves that we are right, for they will remember the horrors of chaos and enslavement that Your freedom brought them. Freedom, free-thinking, and science will lead men into such confusion and confront them with such dilemmas and insoluble riddles that the fierce and rebellious will destroy one another; others who are rebellious but weaker will destroy themselves, while the weakest and most miserable will crawl to our feet and cry out to us: "Yes, you were right. You alone possessed His secret, and we have come back to you. Save us from ourselves!" And when they receive bread from us, they will be clearly aware that it is bread they have earned with their own hands, the same bread we took away from them, that we perform no miracles by turning stones into bread, and yet the fact that they receive it from our hands will make them happier than the bread itself! For they will remember only too well that, without us, this same bread that they earned turned to stones in their hands, whereas, after they came to us, the stones in their hands were turned back into bread. Ah, they will value all too highly the advantages to be derived from submitting to us once and for all. And as long as men do not understand this, they will be unhappy. Now tell me, who is most to blame for their failure to understand? Who was it who broke up the human herd and sent men along innumerable unexplored paths? The herd will be gathered together and tamed again, however, and this time for good. And then we shall give them tranquil, humble happiness, suitable for such weak creatures. Oh, we shall have to convince them, finally, that they must not be proud, for, by overestimating them, You instilled pride in them. We shall prove to them that they are nothing but weak, pathetic children, but that a child's happiness is the sweetest of all. They will grow timid and cling to us in fear, like chicks to a hen. They will admire us, be terrified of us, and be proud of the strength and wisdom that enabled us to subdue a turbulent herd of many millions. They will tremble abjectly before our wrath; they will become timorous; their eyes will fill with tears as readily as those of women and children; but at the slightest sign from us, they will just as readily change to mirth, laughter, and untarnished joy, and they will burst into a happy children's song. Yes, we shall force them to work but, in their leisure hours, we shall organize their lives into a children's game in which they will sing children's songs together and perform innocent dances. Oh, we shall allow them to sin too, for, weak and defenseless as they are, they will love us like children if we allow them to sin. We shall tell them that every sin they commit with our permission can be expiated, that we allow them to sin because we love them, and that we shall take upon ourselves the punishment for their acts. And we shall indeed take their sins upon ourselves, and they will adore us as their saviors, who will answer to God for the sins they, the weak, commit. And they will have no secrets from us. We shall allow them or forbid them to live with their wives or mistresses, to have or not have children—all according to the degree of their obedience to us—and they will submit to us with cheerfulness and joy. They will tell us the secrets that most torment their consciences, they will tell us everything, and we shall solve all their problems, and they will trust to our solutions completely, because they will be rid of the terrible worry and the frightening torment they know today when they have to decide for themselves how to act.

" 'And everyone will be happy, all the millions of beings, with the exception of the hundred thousand men who are called upon to rule over them. For only we, the keepers of the secret, will be unhappy. There will be millions upon millions of happy babes and one hundred thousand sufferers who have accepted the burden of the knowledge of good and evil. They will die peacefully with Your name on their lips, but beyond the grave they will find nothing but death. But we shall keep the secret and, for their own happiness, we shall dangle before them the reward of eternal, heavenly bliss. For we know that, even if there is something in the other world, it is certainly not for such as they. They say and prophesy that You will come again with Your proud, strong chosen ones and that You will be triumphant. But our answer will be that those around You have saved only themselves, whereas we have saved all mankind. It is said that the whore who rides the beast and holds the *mystery* in her hands will be put to shame, that the weak will rise and rend her royal robes and expose her vile naked body. But I will rise then and show You the millions upon millions of happy babes who have known no sin. And we, who have taken their sins upon us to give them happiness, will stand up and say to You: "Judge us if You can and if You dare!" Know that I am not afraid of You; know that I, too, lived in the wilderness, fed upon roots and locusts, that I, too, blessed the freedom which You bestowed upon men, and that I, too, was prepared to take my place among the strong chosen ones, aspiring to be counted among them. But I came to my senses and refused to serve a mad cause. I turned away and joined those who were endeavoring to *correct Your work*. I left the proud and turned to the meek, for the happiness of the meek. What I have told You will happen and our kingdom will come. I repeat, tomorrow You will see obedient herds, at the first sign from me, hurry to heap coals on the fire beneath the stake at which I shall have You burned, because, by coming here, You have made our task more difficult. For if anyone has ever deserved our fire, it is You, and I shall have You burned tomorrow. *Dixi!* "

Ivan stopped. His emotion had gradually increased as he spoke, reaching its highest point at the end. But when he stopped, he suddenly smiled.

Alyosha, who at first had listened in silence, had also become very agitated toward the end; he looked as if he wanted to interrupt his brother and was restraining himself with great difficulty. Now, when Ivan stopped, words gushed from him, as if he could no longer hold them back.

"But it makes no sense!" he cried, turning red. "Your poem is no disparagement of Jesus, as you intended—it is in praise of Him! And who will accept what you say of freedom in the way you want it to be understood? Is that the way the Russian Orthodox Church interprets it? That is the reasoning of a Roman Catholic, but it doesn't even give a fair picture of their views either. It represents only the worst there is in Catholicism—its inquisitors and Jesuits! Besides, your inquisitor is too fantastic; such a character is quite impossible. And what sort of sins of others do these people take upon themselves? And also, who are these keepers of the secret—of the *mystery*—who are willing to bear some peculiar curse for the sake of the happiness of mankind? Who has ever heard of them? We know there are Jesuits with a pretty bad reputation, but they are nothing like what you describe. They are nothing, nothing, like that; in fact, they're simply the Pope's army, preparing the way for the establishment of their future empire on earth, with the Roman pontiff at its head. That is their actual goal and there is no *mystery* or sad, noble resignation in it: theirs is a plain and simple lust for power, low, despicable material advantages, enslavement of the people—something like Russian serfdom used to be, with them as the landowners . . . That's all they are after. They may not even believe in God for all I know. No, your tormented inquisitor is nothing but a figment of your fantasy."

"Wait a minute, don't get so excited," Ivan laughed. "You say it is a fantasy. Very good, I concede, it most certainly is a fantasy. Tell me one thing, though: Do you really believe that, during these centuries, the Catholics have directed all their efforts merely at seizing power in order to gain what you call low, despicable material advantages? Did you get that, by any chance, from that Father Paisii of yours?"

"No, no, not at all . . . In fact, once Father Paisii said something that resembles a bit what you were saying . . . But, no, of course it wasn't the same thing at all!" Alyosha added hurriedly, as if as an afterthought.

"I'm delighted to hear it, although you say it wasn't the same thing at all. What I'm asking you is this: Do you really think that the Jesuits and inquisitors would plot like that for the sake of mere despicable material advantages? Why couldn't there be among them one martyr, a man filled with great sadness and love for his fellow men? Just assume that, among all those interested only in material gain, there is one, only one, man like my grand inquisitor, who has lived on roots by himself in the wilderness, who has writhed in agony to overcome the needs of the flesh, in his efforts to gain freedom and perfection. Then that man, who has always loved his fellow men, suddenly realizes how puny is the moral satisfaction of achieving a triumph of will when he is convinced that millions of other children of God have been created as a sort of mockery, that they will never be able to cope with the freedom that has been forced upon them, that these wretched rebels will never grow into giants who will complete the construction of the tower of Babel. It was not geese such as these that our great idealist visualized joining in the final harmony. And so, having understood that, he turns around and joins the . . . well, the intelligent people. Why can't you imagine that something like that could happen?"

"Whom did he join, did you say? Who are these intelligent people?" Alyosha cried, almost angrily. "There's nothing so very intelligent about them, nor do they have any secrets or mysteries . . . Their only secret is their godlessness, and your inquisitor's only secret is that he doesn't believe in God, that's all!"

"Fine! Let's assume you are right. You've guessed it at last! And it's true—that is the only secret he has. But wouldn't a man who had spent his whole life in the wilderness performing acts of self-sacrifice and devotion without curing himself of his love and concern for mankind, wouldn't such a man suffer? In the last years that are left to him, it becomes clear to him that only the guidance of the great, wise, and dreaded spirit would make it possible to organize feeble and undisciplined men in such a way as to make their lives bearable, for they are just unfinished, ridiculous attempts, created in mockery. He becomes convinced that his duty is to follow the instructions of the wise spirit of death and destruction. And so he is willing to use lies and deception to lead men consciously to their death and destruction, while at the same time deceiving them, so that they will not see where they are being led, so that, at least on the way, these wretched, blind creatures may think they are happy. And I want you to note that the old inquisitor will be deceiving them in the name of the one in whom he believed so ardently for most of his life! Isn't that suffering, tell me? And if even just one man like that finds himself at the head of the whole army of those who crave nothing but power and despicable material gains, even so, wouldn't one such man be enough to make it a tragedy? I'll go even further: I say that, with one such man at their head, they would be a true, guiding ideal for the whole Roman Church with its armies and its Jesuits. I am also absolutely convinced that there has never been any lack of such individuals among those who head their movement; possibly even some of the popes themselves were such exceptional individuals. And who knows, perhaps a tormented old man who loves mankind as stubbornly as my inquisitor exists today, perhaps there is even a whole army of such individuals, and perhaps they exist not by mere chance but as the result of combined efforts to form an alliance whose aim is to keep the secret from the weak and the wretched, in order to make them happy. This, I am sure, is true, because it is bound to be. I even have the impression that the Freemasons are founded on a mystery of that sort, which would explain why the Catholics hate them, seeing in them competitors threatening to split their unifying idea; for they believe that there must be only one shepherd and one herd . . . But, in defending my idea this way, I sound like an author who cannot bear criticism. So we might as well talk about something else."

"Perhaps you're a Mason yourself!" Alyosha blurted out angrily, but then added at once with great sadness: "You don't really believe in God." He had the impression that his brother was looking at him sarcastically; he lowered his eyes and asked: "Does it have an ending, your poem, or is that how it ends?"

"Here's how I propose to end it," Ivan said, continuing.

"The Grand Inquisitor falls silent and waits for some time for the prisoner to answer. The prisoner's silence has weighed on him. He has watched Him; He listened to him intently, looking gently into his eyes, and apparently unwilling to speak. The old man longs for Him to say something, however painful and terrifying. But instead, He suddenly goes over to the old man and kisses him gently on his old, bloodless lips. And that is His only answer. The old man is startled and shudders. The corners of his lips seem to quiver slightly. He walks to the door, opens it, and says to Him, 'Go now, and do not come back . . . ever. You must never, never come again!' And he lets the prisoner out into the dark streets of the city. The prisoner leaves."

"And what about the old man?"

'The kiss glows in his heart . . . But the old man sticks to his old idea."

"And you too, you stick to it?" Alyosha cried out bitterly. Ivan laughed.

"You know what," he said, "it's all nonsense really, a meaningless poem by a scatter-brained student who's never written two lines of poetry in his life. Why must you take it so seriously? Or do you expect me to rush off at once and join the crowd of Jesuits devising corrections of His work? Don't you understand that I really don't give a damn about anything, that, as I told you before, I'm only interested in lasting out until I'm thirty, because by then I'll be willing to throw down the cup of life."

"And what about your sticky little leaves and the graves that are so dear to you and the blue sky and the woman you love?" Alyosha said bitterly. "How will you be able to live until then and love all those things with the hell that is in your heart and in your head? No, you *are* going to join them now or else you will kill yourself, because you won't be able to stand it!"

"There is a drive in me that can withstand anything," Ivan said coldly, with a twisted grin.

"What drive?"

"The Karamazov drive—the vile, earthly drive."

"You mean you plan to drown yourself in debauchery, to disintegrate your soul by rotting it? Is that what you want?"

"Something like that . . . I guess, though, I'll avoid it until I'm thirty, but after that, well yes . . ."

"And how do you intend to avoid it until then? How will you manage it, with those ideas of yours?"

"There again, I'll act like a Karamazov."

"By that you mean you'll act as if 'everything is permitted'? For you feel that's true—whatever you do is all right?"

Ivan frowned and suddenly turned very pale.

"Now you've picked up the phrase that shocked Miusov so much yesterday and that Dmitry picked up and repeated rather naively," Ivan said, smiling crookedly. "Well, since you've brought it up—I suppose everything is permitted, just as I said; I don't take it back. And I don't dislike our dear Mitya's formulation either."

Alyosha stared at him in silence.

"Ah, my little Alyosha, I thought that when I left this town you would be the only friend I had in the world," Ivan said with sudden feeling, "but now I realize that there is no room for me even in your heart, my dear recluse. Well, I won't go back on my idea that everything is permitted, but then, will you, too, turn your back on me?"

Alyosha stood up, walked over to him, and, without a word, kissed him on the lips.

"That's plagiarism!" Ivan shouted, suddenly beaming with

delight. "You stole it from my poem! But it's time we were on our way, Alyosha. We've got things to do, both of us."

They went downstairs, but stopped outside the inn.

"Know what, Alyosha?" Ivan said with deliberation. "If I last long enough to get around to the sticky little leaves, I will love them only thinking of you. The thought that you are somewhere here will be enough for me not to lose all desire to live. Is that good enough for you? If you want, you may take this as a declaration of my affection for you. But for now, you're turning right and I'm turning left, and that's that, understand? I mean that if I'm still in town tomorrow (which is extremely unlikely, for I expect to leave today) and if we happen to meet, I don't want to even mention any of these topics, not a word. Please, remember that. And also I'd like you never to mention our brother Dmitry to me, never!" he added irritatedly. "So now we've exhausted all possible topics, discussed everything. But I promise you this: when I'm close to thirty and decide to throw down my cup of life, I'll come especially to have one more talk with you—wherever I may be, even if I'm in America, I'll come all the way back to see you. Besides, I'll be very curious to have a look at you and see what you're like then. This is a rather solemn promise, as you can see, but then, we may be parting now for as long as seven, perhaps even ten, years. Well, go and join your Pater Seraphicus then, since he's dying, and if he happens to have died without you, you may be angry with me for having held you up. Good-by then, kiss me once more. Good. Now be off."

Ivan turned away abruptly and walked off. He did not once look back. It was a bit the way Dmitry had left Alyosha the day before, but it was also somehow quite different. That impression flashed like a red streak among the painful, sorrowful thoughts that were churning in Alyosha's head. He stood for a while, following Ivan with his eyes. Suddenly it struck him that Ivan rolled slightly as he walked, listing to the right, so that from behind it seemed to Alyosha that his right shoulder was lower than his left. Alyosha had never noticed that Ivan walked like that before. Then, all of a sudden Alyosha turned in the opposite direction, hurrying off toward the monastery. The day was already fading and he suddenly felt a strange fear creeping over him. Some new, unknown shadow was rising before him and he could not find an answer to it. As on the previous evening, a strong wind was rising and the ageless pine trees rustled gloomily on either side of him as he crossed the little wood between the monastery and the hermitage. He was almost running. "Where did he get that Pater Seraphicus from?" flashed through his head. "Ah, poor, poor Ivan, when will I see you again? Here's the hermitage. Oh, God! Yes, yes, he *is* Pater Seraphicus, he'll save me . . . he'll save me from him, save me forever . . ."

Later in his life, Alyosha often wondered how he could have forgotten so completely about Dmitry after he left Ivan —Dmitry, whom that very morning he had been determined to find at all costs, even if it made it impossible for him to return to the monastery that night.

CHAPTER 6

Still Unclear

As to Ivan, a strange and violent anxiety descended upon him as he left Alyosha, setting out for his father's house. And the closer he came to the house the more intense the anxiety became. It was not the anxiety in itself that was so strange but the fact that, hard though he tried, Ivan was quite unable to explain what it consisted of. He had often before known moments of anxiety and depression and there was nothing surprising in his feeling this way at a moment when he was about to break with everything that had brought him here and start on a completely new and unknown course—a course that he would follow all alone as before, full of hope without knowing what he actually hoped for, and expecting a great deal, perhaps too much, from life without being able to define what he expected or even what he wished for. But now, although he was worried about the unknown new life that lay ahead of him, that was not what filled him with this strange anxiety. "Can it be the revulsion I feel for father's house?" he thought. "Perhaps, for although I know that this will be the last time I enter that revolting place, I cannot help feeling sick . . ." But no, it wasn't that either. Could it possibly be his conversation with Alyosha and their parting just now? "After all these years of silence, when I wouldn't talk to anyone about those things, I suddenly let myself go and rattled off all that stupid nonsense . . ." Perhaps it was his irritation at himself, at his callowness and immature vanity, his annoyance at having failed to express himself properly, especially to such a one as Alyosha, who certainly figured importantly in Ivan's view of his future. Of course that was part of it—his annoyance with himself—but that still was not really *it*. "This anguish makes me feel physically sick, but I'm entirely unable to say what I want. Perhaps I ought to try not to think about it at all . . ."

He tried not to think of it, but that did not help either. The most irritating thing about it was that the anxiety seemed completely accidental, external, as if it had nothing to do with him. Something was disturbing his conscience, just as some object may irritate a person, when he is absorbed in work or a heated argument, without his being aware of it. The irritation grows and grows and becomes really painful before he manages to remove the offending object, which often turns out to be some insignificant thing like a handkerchief that has fallen on the floor or a book that has not been replaced in the bookcase.

By the time Ivan reached his father's house, he was really in the worst possible mood. Then suddenly, when he was only fifty feet or so from the gate, he finally succeeded in identifying the object that had caused him to feel such acute anxiety.

Smerdyakov sat on the bench by the garden gate, enjoying the cool evening air, and Ivan at once realized that it was this man who had been weighing on his mind, that he could not bear the very idea that this creature existed. He suddenly understood this with perfect clarity. When, in the restaurant, Alyosha had told him about his encounter with Smerdyakov, it had been as though something sinister and slimy had slipped into Ivan's heart and he had immediately reacted angrily. Later, as they had talked on, he had forgotten Smerdyakov for the time being, but he had kept weighing on Ivan's heart, and no sooner had he left Alyosha and started walking toward his father's than the half-buried, unpleasant sensation started working up to the surface again. "Why on earth," Ivan thought furiously, "should that miserable wretch weigh on me like this?"

Recently Ivan had taken a strong dislike to Smerdyakov and this antipathy had increased considerably during the last few days. He had become aware that his growing dislike was actually turning into something akin to real hatred. It is quite possible that his hatred was growing so intensely now just because, when he had first arrived, Ivan had felt quite differently. Then, if anything, he had shown some sympathy for Smerdyakov and, indeed, had found him a rather original fellow. He had encouraged Smerdyakov to talk to him, although he was somewhat taken aback by the confusion, or rather the restlessness, of the lackey's thoughts, and wondered what it was that so constantly and persistently disturbed that "contemplative mind." They even touched upon philosophical matters and discussed such puzzles as how there could have been light on the first day of creation, when the sun, the moon, and the stars were created only on the fourth day. Soon enough, however, Ivan realized that, although Smerdyakov was curious about the sun, the moon, and the stars, they were only of secondary interest to him, that he was really after something quite different. In a variety of ways, Smerdyakov's vanity became evident, and Ivan saw that it was an inordinate vanity and, what's more, a vanity wounded by frustration. Ivan did not like what he discovered and, out of this discovery, his revulsion grew. Later, when trouble began in the house, when Grushenka appeared on the scene and the tension between his father and his brother Dmitry increased, Ivan and Smerdyakov discussed these matters too. But, although Smerdyakov was obviously very concerned about the matter, Ivan could not make out what he felt about it all or how he thought it ought to be resolved. Indeed, Ivan was very surprised at the inconsistency and confusion of Smerdyakov's aspirations, aspirations that he would blurt out involuntarily and that were always rather obscure. Smerdyakov always seemed to be trying to ferret some information out of him, asking him indirect and obviously carefully thought out questions, but he never pursued them to the end and usually fell silent or changed the subject just when his questioning was at its most intense. But what irritated Ivan most about the man and gave him a strong feeling of revulsion for him was a certain unpleasant familiarity that Smerdyakov began to display toward him, which increased every time they talked. It was not that Smerdyakov let himself go or used improper language in his presence; on the contrary, he always addressed Ivan with the utmost respect. In their relations, however, it became apparent that Smerdyakov was beginning, God knew why, to behave as if there were some implicit understanding between them, and he spoke as though once upon a time they had agreed on something, something that only the two of them knew about and understood and that was quite beyond the grasp of the other mortals crawling in the dust around them. Ivan, however, still did not understand for a long time the true reason for the violence of his growing revulsion; it was only quite recently that he had realized what caused it.

Now, filled with disgust and irritation, he thought he would pass by Smerdyakov, ignoring him. But the man rose from the bench and, from the way he did so, Ivan understood that Smerdyakov had something special to say to him. Ivan stopped and faced him, and the fact that he had stopped instead of walking right by made him tremble with rage. He stood, looking with anger and revulsion at the eunuch-like, hollow-cheeked face, with the hair neatly combed back at the temples and flattened out and a curled strand of hair in the middle of the forehead carefully fluffed up. Smerdyakov's left eye was slightly narrowed in a half wink and looked at Ivan slyly as if to say: "What are you trying to do? You can't pass by me like that; you must know there's something that we two clever people have to discuss." Ivan, trembling violently, was about to shout: "Out of my way, you dog! There's nothing in common between us, you idiot!" But instead, to his amazement, his lips started shaping completely different words.

"Is father still asleep or is he up?" he said quietly and resignedly, listening in surprise to his own voice, and then, completely unexpectedly, he sat down on the bench.

As he remembered it later, he sat there quite terrified during that first second, while Smerdyakov stood in front of him, his hands behind his back, looking at him with complete self-assurance, indeed with a certain sternness.

"Master is still resting," he answered in an unhurried tone, as if pointing out to Ivan that it was he and not Smerdyakov who had spoken first. Then, after a short pause, he brought his right foot forward, wriggling his toes inside his patent leather boot, lowered his eyes demurely, and said: "I'm surprised at you, sir."

"Why are you surprised at me?" Ivan asked gruffly in a stern voice, trying hard to keep himself under control and suddenly realizing with enormous self-disgust that he was immediately curious to know how he could have displeased this flunkey and that he would not move away before he had satisfied his curiosity.

"Why haven't you left for Chermashnya, sir?" Smerdyakov said suddenly, lifting his little eyes from the ground and smiling familiarly at Ivan, while the narrowed left eye seemed to be saying: "An intelligent man like you must understand perfectly well why I'm smiling."

"Why should I go to Chermashnya?" Ivan asked in surprise.

Smerdyakov remained silent for a moment.

"Why, your father himself begged you to go, sir," he said indifferently, as if to convey to Ivan that he had answered so irrelevantly, giving a very insignificant reason why he should have gone to Chermashnya, just not to leave his question unanswered.

"Damn you, man, why don't you say plainly what you want?" Ivan said rudely, dropping his restraint.

Smerdyakov pulled back his right foot until it was level with the left one and drew himself up. But he was still grinning and looked at Ivan with the same composure.

"I don't want anything, sir, nothing important; we were just talking, sir . . ."

There was a long silence lasting almost a whole minute. Ivan knew that he ought to get up and tell the man off; he had the impression that Smerdyakov, who was standing in front of him, was waiting and thinking: "Let's see whether he'll dare to tell me off, dare to lose his temper, or not." Finally Ivan stirred, ready to get up. Smerdyakov noticed the movement.

"I'm in a terrible position, sir, and I don't even know what to do about it," he said, this time very clearly and distinctly, and sighed.

Ivan remained seated, listening.

"They are completely mad, sir. They're behaving like little boys," Smerdyakov went on. "I mean Mr. Karamazov, your father, sir, and your brother, Mr. Dmitry. As soon as he gets up now, the master will start asking me every minute, over and over again: 'Has she come? Why hasn't she come?' On and on like that until after midnight. And if Miss Grushenka doesn't come—and I don't think she even intends to, ever—he'll be after me again tomorrow, first thing in the morning. 'Why didn't she come? When is she coming?'—as if it was my fault or something. On the other hand, sir, as soon as it gets dark, and even before, your brother comes in from the yard next door, armed and all, and says to me, 'You'd better remember, you lousy cook, if you miss her and don't let me know at once when she comes, you'll be the first I kill.' And when the night is over, Mr. Dmitry starts pestering me, just like the master: 'She didn't come, ha? You sure? When will she show up?' And it's as if I'd wronged him too somehow, because I haven't seen his lady love. And with every day and every hour each of them gets more and more furious about it. Why, I'm so frightened I've even thought of taking my life. I can't trust what either of them will do, Mr. Ivan."

"Well, why did you get mixed up in it? Why did you have to spy for Dmitry in the first place?" Ivan asked irritatedly.

"I couldn't help it, sir; in fact, I tried very hard to stay out of it, if you want to know the truth. I kept my mouth shut at first. But I didn't dare argue with Mr. Dmitry, who decided for some reason to make me his watchdog, so to speak. And since then all he says to me is, 'I'll kill you, you dog, if she comes and you don't let me know.' It's got to the point where I'm sure I'll have a long fit of the falling sickness tomorrow."

"What's a long fit of the falling sickness?"

"A long fit is a fit that lasts for a very, very long time. It may last several hours, sometimes a whole day, or even longer. Once I had a fit that went on for three days. That was the time I fell from the attic. I'll stop shaking for a while and then it'll start again. I never regained my senses during those three days. That time the master sent for Dr. Herzenstube, the doctor here, and he put some ice on my head and tried some other remedy too. It almost killed me that time."

"But I understand that an epileptic can never predict when he'll have a fit, so how can you tell in advance that you'll have one tomorrow?" Ivan asked, exasperated but at the same time full of a strange curiosity.

"That's right. It's impossible to tell in advance when one is going to have a fit."

"Besides, as you said, you fell from the attic that time."

"But since I climb up to the attic every day, why shouldn't I fall from the attic again tomorrow? And if I don't fall from the attic, I could very well slip and fall down into the cellar, where I also go every day."

Ivan gave him a long, long look.

"Now you're just talking nonsense and I don't know what you mean by it," he said quietly but threateningly. "Are you trying perhaps to tell me that you're planning to simulate a fit tomorrow, a fit that'll go on for three days, is that it?"

Smerdyakov, who had been looking at the toe of his right foot, which he had thrust out in front of him, pulled it back, put the left foot in front instead, raised his head, smiled, and said:

"Even if I was able to do what you say, sir—and it isn't very difficult for an experienced man to pretend—I'd have every right to do it, if it would save my life from the danger that's threatening me. For if I was laid out with a fit and

Miss Grushenka did come to Mr. Karamazov, even Mr. Dmitry couldn't possibly demand of a sick man who was unconscious why he hadn't come and reported it to him. Even he would be ashamed to do that."

"Ah, to hell with you!" Ivan said, his face contorted with anger. "Why must you worry about your damned safety all the time? Dmitry's threats are just words he lets out when he gets carried away. He won't kill you. If he does kill someone, it won't be you."

"He'd kill a man without even blinking an eye and he'll start by killing me. But what I'm most afraid of is that, later, they'll say I was his accomplice if he tries to do something stupid of that sort to his father."

"Why should they think you were his accomplice?"

"They'll think it because I gave away the big secret about the signals."

"What signals? Whom did you tell? God damn it, man, can't you try to talk so that I can understand you?"

"I must first of all admit to you, sir," Smerdyakov started, drawling his words smugly and ponderously, "that there's a certain secret agreement between me and Mr. Karamazov, your father, sir. As you may or may not be aware, sir, your father has locked himself in for several nights now, and sometimes he locks the gate early in the evening. Now I've noticed that you, Mr. Ivan, have been going up to your room pretty early these days, and yesterday you never left your room at all. That's why, I believe, you don't really realize how thoroughly Mr. Karamazov has been locking himself in at night. Even if Gregory himself came to the door, the master would only let him in when he recognized his voice. But Gregory never comes in the evening now and I'm the only one to serve him in the house. It's been arranged this way ever since he started this business of waiting for Miss Grushenka. But even now, at night, I go back to the servants' cottage, the agreement being that until midnight I'm not to go to bed, but must make the rounds of the yard every so often, watching out for Miss Grushenka, for whom he's been waiting the last few days just as if he'd gone mad. This is how he sees the situation: she, he says, is afraid of him—meaning Mr. Dmitry, to whom he refers as 'that damned dog, Mitya'—and so she'll come late at night by the back alleys. So he wants me to keep a look-out for her until after midnight. And if she comes, he says, I must knock on his door or window from the garden: first two slow knocks like this—one, two—and then three quick ones—bang-bang-bang. And then, he says, he'll know she's come and he'll open the door quietly and let her in. Then he told me to use another signal in case something unforeseen happens: first two quick light knocks and then, after a second, one more, much harder knock. Then he'll understand that something has happened and that I must see him urgently, and he'll let me in so that I can tell him what it is. That is in case Miss Grushenka can't come herself but sends him a message. He also wants me to warn him if Mr. Dmitry is around, because he's very much afraid of Mr. Dmitry. So, even if he and Miss Grushenka are already locked inside the house and Mr. Dmitry comes around, I'm still to warn him by knocking three times. So the first signal—five knocks altogether—means 'Miss Grushenka has arrived,' the second signal—three knocks—'Something urgent to report.' That's what he taught me himself, and he made me repeat it over and over again. And since he and I are the only ones in the whole world to know about these signals, it's absolutely certain that the master will open the door as soon as he hears the knocks, without asking, 'Who's there?'—because he's very much afraid to raise his voice. And it is these signals that have become known to Mr. Dmitry now."

"How have they become known to him? Did you tell him? What made you do that?"

"As I told you, sir, I was too afraid of him. I didn't dare keep the secret from him. And Mr. Dmitry pushed me around a bit and kept repeating: 'You aren't hiding anything from me, are you? If you are, I'll break both your legs for you.' Well, when he said that, I told him about those secret signals, to show him how loyal I was to him and that I wouldn't deceive him for anything, and that I'd report whatever I found out to him."

"So if he comes and tries to make use of those signals, just don't let him in. That's all there is to it."

"But what if I'm laid up with a fit of the falling sickness? How could I refuse to let him in, even if I dared refuse otherwise, knowing what a desperate person Mr. Dmitry is?"

"But, damn it, what the hell is there to make you so sure that you'll have an epileptic fit just then? You aren't trying to make fun of me, by any chance, are you?"

"I'd never dare try to make fun of you, sir, and, besides, I don't at all feel like making fun of anyone, frightened as I am. I feel I'm about to have a fit. I have that feeling, and I could have it just from being so afraid."

"Oh, hell, if you're laid up, Gregory will be watching out instead of you. So warn him about it all and he's sure not to let Dmitry in."

"I'd never dare tell Gregory about the signals unless the master ordered me to. As for stopping Mr. Dmitry from getting in when he hears him come, Gregory, I must tell you, has been sick since yesterday and Martha is planning to give him her treatment tomorrow. That treatment is a very curious one: it's an infusion of certain herbs that Martha prepares according to some secret recipe. It's very powerful and she always has some on hand, ready to use. She gives him that strong stuff perhaps three times a year or so, when he gets those pains around the waist and then gets like paralyzed from the waist down, which happens to him, as I said, about three times a year. Then Martha takes a towel, dips it in the solution, and rubs it all over his back for maybe half an hour, until the towel is completely dry, and usually her face is all red by the time she's through. Then she pours some of the stuff into a glass and makes him drink it, and says a certain prayer. But she's careful not to give him all of it. She always leaves some, which she drinks herself. And let me tell you, sir, that those two, who would never take a drink otherwise, as soon as they taste that stuff, they drop off to sleep and they keep sleeping soundly for a very long time. And when Gregory wakes up after that sleep, he's almost always recovered, while Martha always has a headache. So if she's planning to give him that treatment tomorrow, it's not very likely that either of them will hear when Mr. Dmitry comes, and there'll be no one to stop him. They'll be fast asleep when he comes."

"It sounds as if you were raving, with all these incredible coincidences, all these things happening exactly at the same time: you laid up with your epileptic fit and both Gregory and his wife lying unconscious after drinking their medicine! Unless . . . unless you're planning to help things happen yourself that way . . ."

These last words escaped him unwittingly and he knit his brows menacingly.

"How could I be planning it, sir, and why should I help things happen when everything is in Mr. Dmitry's hands and everything depends on what comes into his head? If he decides to do something, he'll do it; if not, he won't; and I certainly won't be the one to bring him over here and push him into his father's house."

"But why should he try to get into the house at all, if Miss Grushenka, as you told me yourself, doesn't even intend to come?" Ivan went on, turning pale with anger. "You said so yourself and I myself, since I've been living here, have become convinced that the old man is just fooling himself and that the creature will never come to him. So why should Dmitry try to break into the house when she's not there? Speak up—I want you to explain what is really in your mind."

"You know very well yourself why he'll come here, so what's in my mind really has nothing to do with it. He'll come here because he'll be raving mad or because he'll be afraid that I've failed to let him know because of my illness, or he may just lose patience, become suspicious, and want to search the house, as he did yesterday when you were here yourself, to make sure that she hasn't slipped in unnoticed somehow. He also knows that his father has an envelope in the house with three thousand rubles in it, which he sealed with three seals, tied with a ribbon, and addressed in his own hand 'to my darling Grushenka if she comes to me,' to which, three days later, he added, 'To my little chick.' Well, all this worries me, Mr. Ivan."

"Rot!" Ivan shouted, almost in a frenzy. "Dmitry will never break in to steal money, or kill his father in order to do so! He could have killed him yesterday over Grushenka, enraged, maddened fool that he is, but he would never stoop to theft!"

"Mr. Dmitry happens to need money very badly just now, very, very badly. You have no idea how much he needs it," Smerdyakov said with great composure and the utmost clarity. "Besides, Mr. Dmitry feels that that three thousand is in a way his by right, as he told me himself: 'I still have three thousand rubles of my money coming to me from my father.' And whatever we may say, it's the truth, Mr. Ivan—you can work it out for yourself—that if Miss Grushenka should so decide, she could surely make him marry her, I mean my master, Mr. Karamazov himself, and, after all, it's pretty likely that she'll end up by deciding to do so. For I wasn't all that sure really when I told you that she wouldn't come here. She may very well feel like becoming a lady just like that, right away. I know myself that her merchant friend, Samsonov, told her quite frankly that it would not be at all stupid of her to do it, and he even laughed when he told her that. And Miss Grushenka is certainly not stupid. She's not likely to marry a fellow who doesn't have a thing to his name, like Mr. Dmitry. So if you take that into account, then you must real-

ize that there will be not one single ruble coming to you after
Mr. Karamazov passes on, neither to you, Mr. Ivan, nor to
Mr. Dmitry, nor to your brother, Mr. Alexei, because once
she marries him, Miss Grushenka will see to it that everything
is transferred to her, and whatever capital there is will be in
her name. On the other hand, if your father dies right now before anything of that sort happens, each of the three of you
is sure to get forty thousand right away, even Mr. Dmitry,
whom Mr. Karamazov hates so much, because there happens
to be no will . . . Well, Mr. Dmitry is well aware of all this."

Ivan's face twitched in a peculiar way. Then the blood
rushed to his cheeks.

"If that's the way it is," he interrupted Smerdyakov, "why
would you want me to leave town and go to Chermashnya?
What are you trying to tell me? Is it that if I leave, that's
what will happen here?" He was breathing with difficulty.

"That's right, sir," Smerdyakov said in a quiet, reasonable
tone, but his eyes remained riveted on Ivan.

"What is right?"

Ivan could hardly control himself. His eyes flashed threateningly.

"I spoke out of concern for you, sir. If I were you and
happened to be here at this time, I'd just drop everything and
leave . . . I wouldn't sit around here, considering all the things
that may happen," Smerdyakov said suddenly, with the utmost
candor, looking straight into Ivan's flashing eyes.

"I believe you're an awful idiot," Ivan said, rising abruptly
from the bench, "and certainly a terrible, crooked monster . . ."
He walked to the gate and was about to pass through it into
the garden when he stopped, turned back, and looked at
Smerdyakov. Then something strange happened. Ivan's face
twitched spasmodically; he bit his lips, clenched his fists, and
in another moment would have pounced on Smerdyakov.
Smerdyakov realized it at once; he shuddered and his whole
body pulled back. But after one alarming second, Smerdyakov
was out of danger. Ivan suddenly looked at him in bewilderment, turned silently away, and entered the gate.

"If you must know," Smerdyakov suddenly heard Ivan say
in a loud, clear voice, "I'm leaving for Moscow tomorrow
morning, early. And that's all."

Later Ivan often wondered why he had had to tell Smerdyakov that.

"That's the best thing to do, sir," Smerdyakov said at once
approvingly, as though he had expected Ivan to say just that.

"Only, of course, sir, they may call you back by telegram if anything should happen here when you're gone."

Again Ivan stopped and again he turned his head to look at Smerdyakov. But something seemed to have happened to Smerdyakov. There was nothing left of his familiarity and his faintly arrogant air. His face was tense and expectant, but now he looked at Ivan with servile timidity. "Is there anything else you would care to order, sir," his fixed, unblinking look seemed to be asking Ivan.

"Why would it be any different if I were in Chermashnya? Wouldn't they summon me from there too?" Ivan unaccountably shouted at the top of his voice.

"That's right, sir, they'd bother you just the same in Chermashnya . . ." Smerdyakov said almost in a whisper, taken aback a bit but still looking very intently into Ivan's eyes.

"So, since the only difference is that Moscow is farther away than Chermashnya," Ivan said, "you must want me to save the train fare. Unless you think that it would be too tiring for me to do all that extra traveling?"

"That's right, sir . . ." Smerdyakov murmured now in a faltering voice, smiling abjectly, prepared to draw back at any second before Ivan's anger. But, to his surprise, Ivan suddenly began to laugh, and he went on laughing as he passed through the gate and walked across the garden. Anyone seeing his face would have understood that he was not laughing because he felt in a laughing mood. He himself could not have explained what was going on inside him at that moment—it was as if all his movements were determined by some sort of spasmodic muscular contraction beyond his control.

CHAPTER 7

It's Always Rewarding
to Talk to a Clever Man

Ivan's speech was spasmodic too. Entering the house and seeing his father in the living room, he shouted to him, gesticulating: "I'm going right upstairs to my room. I'm not coming in. Good-night," and he walked on, not even looking at his father. It is quite possible that the sight of the old man was more than he could bear at that moment, but such an overt display of hostility surprised even Mr. Karamazov. Indeed, it seemed the old man was anxious to tell his son

something and he had come out into the living room especially to meet him. But after such a greeting, he stopped and with
sly amusement watched Ivan dash upstairs and disappear
from sight.

"What's the matter with him?" he asked Smerdyakov, who
had followed Ivan into the house.

"Seems to be angry at something . . . One can never tell
with Mr. Ivan," Smerdyakov muttered evasively.

"So let him be angry, the hell with him! Bring in the samovar, and then clear out, you too. There's nothing new, is
there?"

And he started peppering Smerdyakov with the kind of
questions the man had just complained about to Ivan—all
about the lady visitor he was waiting for—questions that we
will omit here. Half an hour later the house was locked up
and the obsessed old man was walking back and forth through
the deserted rooms, quivering with anxiety, expecting to hear
at any moment the five prearranged knocks, now and then
looking out of the dark window, beyond which he could see
nothing but the night.

It was very late, but Ivan had still not gone to bed. He was
thinking. He went to sleep very late that night, at two o'clock
or so. But we will not describe the train of his thoughts, especially as the time has not come yet for us to look into
his soul—we shall do that in due course. Besides, even if we
wanted to describe what was going on inside him, it would be
very difficult, because it was not exactly thought but something hard to define, and something extremely troubled. Ivan
felt he had lost his bearings. He was also tormented by all
sorts of strange, almost unaccountable desires. When it was
already well past midnight, for instance, he suddenly felt an
almost irresistible urge to run downstairs, unlock the door, go
over to the servants' cottage, and give Smerdyakov a beating.
But if he had been asked why, he would have been quite unable to give a single exact reason, except perhaps that Smerdyakov had become unbearably loathsome to him and he felt
as if he had offended him more than anyone ever had before.
On the other hand, during that night, he was submerged by
waves of a peculiar and degrading fear which, he felt, drained
him of his physical strength. His head ached and he felt dizzy. An inexplicable feeling of hatred seized him again and
again, as though he were about to wreak a terrible revenge
on someone. He even hated Alyosha, remembering their conversation that day, and at certain moments he hated himself.

But he hardly, if at all, thought of Katerina. Later this fact surprised him, especially since he clearly remembered that when, the previous morning, he had so dramatically announced to her that he was leaving for Moscow the next day, an inner voice whispered: "You won't go and you know it. It won't be that easy to tear yourself away from her—you're just showing off now!" Much later, when Ivan thought of that night, he remembered, with a particularly sickening feeling, getting up several times from his bed, tiptoeing very quietly to the door as if afraid to be caught, letting himself out onto the landing, and listening to his father moving about downstairs. Ivan would stand there for a long time, maybe five minutes, filled with a strange curiosity, holding his breath, his heart pounding wildly, but why he was doing this and what he was trying to overhear he had no idea himself. But throughout his later life he considered it loathsome that he had listened like that and, deep down in the mysterious recesses of his soul, he knew it was the most despicable thing he had ever done in his life. He felt no hatred for his father during those minutes; he was just somehow irresistibly curious about him, walking about down there, and, wondering what he was doing at that moment, imagined him staring out of the window into the night, pacing the floor again, stopping abruptly in the middle of the room, and listening to hear whether someone was knocking . . . Ivan went out onto the landing a couple of times to listen in that way. Only when his father went to bed at about two in the morning and everything became quiet did he, too, finally go to bed. He was completely exhausted and was determined to go to sleep right away. And he did fall asleep at once, slept deeply and dreamlessly, but he awoke early, at seven.

When he opened his eyes and saw that it was already light, Ivan, to his own surprise, felt an extraordinary surge of energy within him. He jumped out of bed, dressed quickly, pulled out his suitcase, and without wasting a minute hurriedly started packing. His laundry had been brought to him the day before and Ivan grinned at the thought of how everything was working out nicely so that there would be nothing to delay his sudden departure. And his departure was indeed sudden. For, despite the fact that he had announced it the previous day to Katerina and Alyosha, and later to Smerdyakov as well, he remembered clearly that when he had gone to bed he had not even thought of leaving the next day and it certainly had never occurred to him that the very first thing in the morning he would start packing. About nine, when his suitcase and his small bag were packed, Martha came in and asked him the usual question: Where would he like to have his tea, in his room or downstairs? Ivan said he'd have it downstairs that day and went down looking almost cheerful, although there was something hurried and absent-minded in his gestures and the way he spoke. He greeted his father warmly, even inquired after his health, but then, without giving the old man a chance to finish answering him, Ivan blurted out that he was leaving for Moscow in an hour, that he was leaving for good, and that he would appreciate it if his father would order the carriage, to take him to the station. The old man heard the announcement without any visible surprise, forgetting quite unashamedly to show any chagrin over his son's departure. Instead, he suddenly remembered something that concerned him directly and became quite agitated.

"Ah, you! What a way to do things! You might have told me yesterday at least. Well, never mind, let's settle it now. Do me this favor, my boy, stop at Chermashnya on your way. It's only about nine miles from the Volovya railroad station—the road turns to the left there, and you can be in Chermashnya in no time."

"But I can't, father: you know it's about fifty miles from here to the railroad station and the Moscow train leaves at seven p.m. I can barely make it as is."

"You'll make it tomorrow then. And if you don't make it tomorrow, you'll make it the day after tomorrow. But today you'll just have to take that little side trip to Chermashnya. If I weren't tied down here with all this business, I would dash off there myself, because it's really important, very urgent. But with the way things are here . . . well, you know, I can't leave now . . . You know, I have that wood there on two lots—one in Begichev and the other in Dyachkina . . . It's wasteland. Now the Maslovs—father and son—they're offering me eight thousand rubles for the lumber, while last year a fellow offered me twelve thousand for it. But then, he didn't come from around here. No local merchant can sell anything in the district. You see, with those Maslovs, who are worth more than a hundred thousand—it's as if they had a monopoly on selling lumber: whatever price they name, people just have to take it, for no one dares to compete with them. But here the Ilyinskoye priest wrote me last Thursday that a merchant called Gorstkin had come to town. I know the fellow and there's nothing so wonderful about him, except that he comes from Pogrebov and therefore is not a local man and is not afraid of the Maslovs. He said he'd pay eleven thousand for the lumber, hear me? But the priest tells me he'll only be here for a week. So I'd like you to go there and close the deal with him."

"You could write the priest and ask him to close the deal for you."

"He couldn't do it—that's just it. He doesn't even know what to look out for. Aside from that, he's worth his weight in gold and I wouldn't hesitate to trust him with twenty thousand rubles without a receipt, but he doesn't know a thing about business. It's as if he'd never grown up, in that respect; a crow could trick him, although he's a very learned man otherwise. As to Gorstkin, he looks like a peasant, goes around dressed in a peasant's blue coat, but really he's a downright fraud and that's where we're bound to have a lot of trouble, especially with his lies. Sometimes he'll tell such lies that you wonder why he's doing it. A couple of years ago he told me a whole story about his wife dying and him remarrying another woman, but there wasn't a word of truth in it; his wife had never thought of dying. She's still alive to this day, and she gives him a beating every third day. So now we must first find out if he really means to buy the lumber and pay eleven thousand rubles for it or if it's just one of his lies . . ."

"But I wouldn't be of any use; I have no eye for business either, you know."

"Wait, listen to me: you'll manage, because I'll explain all his tricks to you beforehand. I've been dealing with Gorstkin for a long time, you know. You have to keep watching his beard. It's a miserable, thin, reddish beard. Now if that beard quivers as he talks and he himself gets angry—then he's telling the truth and he's really serious about the deal. But if he strokes his beard with his left hand and grins as he does it, then he's just trying to take you in. Never look into his eyes, you won't learn anything from them—it's like looking into a murky pond. He's too crooked to let you see anything in his eyes. No, just look at his beard. I'll give you a note for him that you'll show him. His name is Gorstkin, but that's not what they call him: he's known as 'the Hound' in the district. But you mustn't call him that; he may resent it. If you have a talk with him and see that all's well, write me at once, something like: 'He's not lying this time.' And wait, if you must, you may reduce the price from eleven thousand to ten, but no lower than that. Just bear in mind that the difference between eight and eleven thousand is three thousand. It would be just like finding three thousand. And how soon could I get another buyer, for I need the money badly, right away! As soon as I get word from you, I'll somehow snatch a moment and dash over there to close the deal. But as it is, why should I go rushing off when the whole thing may be just in the fellow's imagination? So will you do it for me or not?"

"But I really have no time. Spare me that, please."

"Couldn't you do it for your father? I'll see that you don't regret it! What difference can a day or two make to you? Where are you off to now, anyway? To Venice? Well, it won't fall apart in two days, your Venice, I promise you! I'd send Alyosha, but what good would he be in this kind of business? The only reason I'm asking you to do it is that you're a clever man, and I'm very well aware of it, too. I know you're not a lumber merchant, but I'm sure you have a good eye for business. All you have to do is see whether he really means what he says. As I said, just keep your eye on his beard: if it trembles, the beard, it means he's in earnest."

"So you're pushing me out of the house yourself, to go to your damned Chermashnya, right?" Ivan said, grinning wickedly.

Mr. Karamazov either did not see or did not want to see the wickedness, but responded in kind, grinning back.

"So you'll go, won't you? Wait, I'll write you the note."

"I don't know yet whether I'll go. I'll decide on the way."

"Why must you decide on the way? Decide right now. Come, decide, my dear fellow! Talk to him, scribble me a couple of lines, give the note to the priest, and he'll see to it that I get your message in no time. After that, I won't detain you—you can be off to your Venice. The priest will have you driven in his own carriage to the Volovya station."

The old man was absolutely delighted now. He quickly wrote his note, ordered the horses, and had some brandy and a snack served. When he was pleased about something, Mr. Karamazov almost always became exuberant, but this time he seemed to be restraining himself. For one thing, he never even mentioned Dmitry's name. The prospect of parting with Ivan did not seem to move him in the least; indeed, he did not have much to say to Ivan now. Ivan was acutely aware of this and thought: "He must have grown pretty tired of my company." Only when he came to the door to see his son off did the old man become a little agitated and even make a gesture to embrace him. But, to stave off any further effusions,

Ivan quickly offered him his hand. The old man at once took the hint and stopped in his tracks.

"Well, God speed, God speed to you," he repeated from the doorway. "I suppose you'll turn up again some time. Come, I'll always be glad to see you. May Christ bless you!"

Ivan climbed into the carriage.

"Good-by, Ivan, and don't curse me too much when you think of me," his father shouted after him for the last time.

All the members of the household came out to see him off —Smerdyakov, Martha, and Gregory—and Ivan gave them ten rubles each. When he was already sitting in the carriage, Smerdyakov hurried over to arrange the rug on Ivan's knees.

"So you see, I'm going to Chermashnya . . ."

Again, as on the day before, the words seemed to have escaped from Ivan's lips by themselves and, what is more, they were accompanied by a nervous little chuckle. He remembered it long afterward.

"So it's true then, as they say, that it's always rewarding to talk to a clever man," Smerdyakov said with deliberation, looking meaningfully at Ivan.

The carriage drove off, gradually gaining speed. Ivan felt as if there were a sort of thick fog inside him, but he looked eagerly at the fields stretched out around him, at the hilly countryside, at the trees, at a flock of geese flying high overhead across the clear sky. And suddenly he felt fine. He tried to start a conversation with the driver and became extremely curious about something the man said in answer to him, but the next moment he realized he was not taking in what the other said and that he had not really understood his answer in the first place. So he lapsed into silence, which he also enjoyed: the air was clean, fresh, and cool, and the sky was clear. The images of Alyosha and Katerina flashed across his mind; he smiled quietly, blowing gently on these sweet ghosts, and they flew away. "Their time will come," he thought.

They reached the first post station, changed horses, then drove on to Volovya. "What did he mean when he said it's always rewarding to talk to a clever man?" he thought, suddenly feeling breathless. "And why did I have to announce to him that I was going to Chermashnya?"

When they reached the Volovya station, Ivan stepped out of the carriage and was at once surrounded by coachmen vying with one another to take him to Chermashnya—a nine-mile ride by a small country road. He ordered one of them to harness the horses. He stepped into the station house, glanced around, looked at the station master's wife, and suddenly walked out again and said:

"I don't think I'll go to Chermashnya, after all. Is there still time for me to make the seven o'clock train?"

"If we hurry, sir. Shall we harness up?"

"All right, be quick. Tell me, is anyone among you going to town tomorrow?"

"Why, yes, sir. Mitry here will be going."

"You're Mitry? Well, could you do something for me, then? Would you go to see my father—Mr. Karamazov—and tell him that I couldn't go to Chermashnya? Could you do that for me?"

"Why, of course, I'll do it, sir. We've all known Mr. Karamazov for a long, long time."

"Well, here's a tip for you, because he may not give you one," Ivan said, laughing gaily.

"You're right there, sir. He certainly won't," Mitry said, laughing too. "Thank you, sir, I'll be sure to do it."

At seven o'clock in the evening Ivan boarded the train and was on his way to Moscow. "I'm through with the past now, through with it once and for all, and I don't want to hear of it ever again, not a word, not an echo. I'm moving into a new world. I'll see new places and never look back." But instead of exultation, everything inside him grew suddenly dark and a deep despair, such as he had never known before, enveloped his heart. He sat up all night, thinking as the train rumbled on, and only toward daybreak, as they were entering the Moscow suburbs, did he suddenly feel as if he were emerging from a haze. "I'm a despicable beast," he whispered.

In the meantime Mr. Karamazov, having seen his son off, felt very pleased. For two whole hours he felt almost happy and kept sipping his brandy. But then something very annoying and unpleasant happened in the house, making Mr. Karamazov terribly anxious and distraught. Smerdyakov, who had gone to fetch something or other in the cellar, slipped on the first step and fell all the way down the stairs. It was lucky that Martha, at least, happened to be in the yard at the time and heard him. She did not see him fall, but she heard him cry out. It was a very strange cry, quite unique, but familiar to her—it was the cry of an epileptic falling in a fit. It was impossible to establish whether Smerdyakov had suffered the attack while he was going down to the cellar, which of course would have resulted in the unconscious man's falling headlong, or whether it was the fall that had triggered the epileptic attack, to which, as everyone knew, Smerdyakov was prone. When they reached him, he was already writhing on the cellar floor at the foot of the steps, his body twisted by convulsions, his mouth frothing. At first they were sure he had broken bones, but it turned out that "God had preserved him," as Martha put it, and nothing so disastrous had happened. It was very difficult to get him up the steep cellar steps, but neighbors were asked to give a hand and somehow Smerdyakov was brought out. Mr. Karamazov was present during these rescue operations and even helped a bit, looking very frightened and bewildered.

The patient did not regain consciousness. The spasms would stop for a while, but they kept returning again and again and everyone surmised that this would be a repetition of what had happened the year before, when Smerdyakov had fallen from the attic. They remembered that, then, they had put ice on his head and, since there was still some ice in the cellar, Martha did the same now. In the evening Mr. Karamazov sent for Dr. Herzenstube, who came right away, examined the patient very thoroughly (for he was the most thorough and attentive doctor in the whole province, an elderly and respectable gentleman), and diagnosed it as an "exceptionally severe attack." He said it "could be dangerous," that for the moment he did not understand completely what it was, but that if the remedies he prescribed now proved useless, he would prescribe others when he returned the next morning. They then carried Smerdyakov to the servants' cottage and put him to bed in the room next to the one occupied by Gregory and Martha.

And after that, all day long, it was disaster after disaster for Mr. Karamazov. Martha cooked the dinner and, compared with Smerdyakov's soups, her master complained, her soup tasted like slops, and, he said, the chicken was so tough he couldn't chew it. Martha answered these bitter, albeit justified, reproaches by pointing out that the hen had been an old hen and that she herself was not a trained chef like Smerdyakov. The next blow to Mr. Karamazov came when he learned in the evening that Gregory, who had been suffering pains for the past two days, was now completely laid up with severe pains in his back. Mr. Karamazov finished his tea in a great hurry and locked himself in earlier than usual. He was in a state of terrible suspense and anxiety. This was because, this night, he really expected Grushenka to come. At least, Smerdyakov had assured him that very morning that "tonight Miss Grushenka promised almost certainly to come." The heart of the restless old man pounded unevenly in his chest as he wandered through his deserted rooms, listening to every sound. He really had to keep his ears open now. Dmitry might be lying in wait for her somewhere, so as soon as she knocked on the window (Smerdyakov had told him two days ago that he had explained to her where and how to knock) he would have to let her in at once, without wasting a second, for who knew what might happen otherwise? And what if she became frightened and ran away without waiting? . . . Mr. Karamazov was tense and worried, but never before had his heart basked in sweeter expectations: why, it was almost certain now that this time, at last, she would come!

BOOK VI

A RUSSIAN MONK

CHAPTER 1

The Elder Zosima and His Guests

When, full of fear and anxiety, Alyosha entered the elder's cell, he stopped, somewhat amazed: instead of the sick, dying man, perhaps already unconscious, he had expected, he found the elder sitting up in a chair. Although he looked weak and exhausted, he seemed gay and cheerful and was engaged in a quiet conversation with the guests who sat around him. In fact, he had left his bed a quarter of an hour before Alyosha's arrival. The visitors had gathered in his cell earlier, waiting for him to awaken, for Father Paisii had positively assured them that "the teacher will get up once more to talk to those dear to his heart, as he promised he would this morning." In this promise, as in any other the dying elder had ever made, Father Paisii believed so completely that, had he seen Father Zosima unconscious and no longer breathing after he had promised to get up and say good-by to him, he would have distrusted even death itself and expected the dying man to regain consciousness and carry out his promise. That morning, before lapsing into sleep, the elder had told him: "I shall not die before enjoying one more talk with you, my dear ones, before once more looking at your dear faces and once more pouring out my soul to you." Those who had come to hear this last talk of the elder's were his oldest, most devoted friends. There were four of them, including the senior monks Father Joseph, Father Paisii, and Father Mikhail, who was the prior of the hermitage. Mikhail was neither very old nor very learned; he was a man of humble origin but of strong character and simple, unshakable faith; his exterior was forbidding, concealing the great tenderness of his heart as if he were ashamed of it. The fourth was Brother Anfim, a simple monk, very old and almost illiterate, who came from a very poor peasant family; he was a quiet, gentle man, who seldom spoke to anyone, the meekest of the meek, who always looked as if he had been frightened by something great and awesome that was too much for his intelligence to grasp. The elder loved this constantly trembling man and always treated him with great respect, but it is possible that he knew no one with whom he had exchanged fewer words, despite the fact that once upon a time the two of them had wandered all over holy Russia together. That had been very long before, perhaps as much as forty years, when Zosima had just started his hard monastic life in a poor and little-known monastery near Kostroma, and when, shortly afterward, he had accompanied Brother Anfim on his wanderings to collect alms for their poor monastery.

All of them, the host and the guests, were sitting in the elder's second room, the narrow little cell where his bed was, so there was hardly enough room for the four chairs (the novice Porfiry was also present, but he remained standing). It was beginning to grow dark and the light in the room came from the lamps and wax candles burning before the icons. When Father Zosima saw Alyosha, who had stopped with an embarrassed look in the doorway, he smiled joyfully and stretched out his hand to him.

"Good evening, quiet one. I'm glad to see you have come, my dear boy; I knew you would come."

Alyosha went over to him, bowed very low, and began to weep. Something tore at his heart—he felt his soul quivering within him and he could hardly control his sobs.

"Come, come, it's a little soon to weep for me," the elder said, smiling and placing his right hand on Alyosha's head. "Look, I'm sitting here talking to my friends and I may live for another twenty years yet, as that nice kind woman wished for me yesterday—the one from Vyshegorie with the baby girl, Lizaveta, in her arms. May God bless them both, the mother and little Lizaveta." Zosima crossed himself. "Porfiry," he said, turning to the novice, "did you take her offering where I told you?"

He was thinking of the sixty kopeks the cheerful woman had given him for someone who was even poorer than herself. Such donations are usually a self-imposed penance and are always paid out of money earned by the person's own labor. The elder had sent Porfiry that same day to a widow with many children, whose house had recently been destroyed by fire and who had been forced to go out and beg to keep her family alive. Porfiry answered quickly that he had done as he had been told and had handed the widow the money from "an anonymous well-wisher."

"Come, get up, my sweet boy," the elder said to Alyosha. "Let me look at you. Have you been at home with your family, and did you see your brother?"

It struck Alyosha as very strange that the elder should ask him in such a matter-of-fact way about one particular brother. But which brother did he mean? It must have been for the sake of that brother that the elder had sent him away both that day and the day before.

"I saw one of my brothers," Alyosha said.

"I mean the one who was here yesterday, the oldest one, the one before whom I bowed to the ground yesterday."

"That one—I saw him yesterday, but I couldn't find him today."

"You must find him tomorrow. It is urgent. Leave everything else and find him. If you do, you may still be able to prevent something horrible from happening. It was to his future great ordeal that I bowed yesterday."

He stopped and seemed to be deliberating about something. Father Joseph, who had witnessed the elder bowing to Dmitry the day before, exchanged glances with Father Paisii. Alyosha could not hold back a question.

"Father and teacher," he said in great agitation, "your words are so obscure. What is the ordeal that is awaiting him?"

"Do not try to know . . . Yesterday I glimpsed something very frightening—I read his whole future in a look in his eye . . . Yes, at one moment he looked at me and my heart was filled with horror at what that man was preparing for himself. In the course of my life, I have seen that expression once or twice before on men's faces; it was an expression that seemed to foreshadow the doom awaiting them, a doom that, alas, came to pass. If I sent you to him, Alexei, it was because I thought that your face, the face of his brother, could perhaps save him. But everything and all our destinies are in the hands of God. 'Except a corn of wheat fall into the ground and die, it abideth alone: but if it die, it bringeth forth much fruit.' You must remember that. As to you, Alexei, many a time in my life have I blessed you for your face— know that." The elder smiled gently. "This is what I think your life will be: you will leave these walls, but in the world outside you will still be like a monk. There will be many who will oppose you, but even your enemies will love you. Life will bring you many hurts and pains, but it is in them that you will find happiness, and you will bless your life and make other men bless their lives, which is the most important thing. Well, that's how I see you.

"Fathers and teachers," the elder then said, turning to his visitors with a warm smile, "never until this day, not even to him, have I revealed why the face of this youth is so dear to my heart. But I will tell you now. His face is like a reminder and a prophecy to me. At the dawn of my life, when I was still a very small boy, I had an older brother who died in his youth, before my eyes, when he was only seventeen. And later, in the course of my life, I realized that this brother was like a sign to me, like a message from above, for if he had not come into my life, if he had not existed, I do not believe I would ever have taken monastic orders and followed a path that is so precious to me. And now the face that first appeared to me in my childhood has made a second appearance as I near the end of my life, as if it were a reminder. It is strange, fathers and teachers—although Alexei's face bears only a limited resemblance to my brother's, I have felt the resemblance in spirit to be so great that to me he has often been that other boy, my brother, coming to me mysteriously as I reach the end of my journey, to remind me of the past and to inspire me. I have even been surprised at this strange, dreamy feeling in me.

"Did you hear, Porfiry?" The elder addressed himself now to the novice who attended him. "Many times I have seen a hurt look in your eyes because you felt I loved Alexei more than you. So now you know the explanation. But I want you to know that I love you, too, and that many times I have felt deeply unhappy because you were hurt. To you now, my dear guests, I would like to talk about that youth, my brother, because nothing in my life has been more important, more prophetic, and more touching . . . I feel deeply moved now, and at this minute I can see in a glance my whole life, as though I were living it all over again . . ."

It must be pointed out here that this last talk of the elder's with those who came to see him on the last day of his life has been partly recorded and preserved. It was written down from memory by Alexei Fyodorovich Karamazov a few days after the elder's death. However, it cannot be vouchsafed that this is an exact record of what the elder said on that occasion, for it is impossible to ascertain whether Alexei did not add elements from his previous conversations with his teacher. Moreover, in this record, the elder seems to be talking without interruption, as if presenting his life to his friends in the form of a story, while, according to other, later accounts, this is not quite the way it happened, since the conversation that evening was general and, although the guests did not interrupt the elder very often, they did occasionally make comments and even told of their own experiences. And finally, in the state he was in, the elder could not possibly have carried on such a long monologue, for he breathed with difficulty, his voice faltered, and he even had to lie down and rest several times, although he never actually went to sleep and his guests never left their seats. Once or twice the conversation was interrupted by readings from the New Testament. Father Paisii did the reading.

It is remarkable also that none of the visitors expected the elder to die that night, especially because, on that last evening of his life, he had emerged from the deep sleep into which he had fallen during the day looking full of new and unexpected vigor that sustained him through his long talk with his friends. This last burst of fervor kept him in a state of great animation. But it did not last, for his life was suddenly cut off. But we will come to that later.

For now, I must warn the reader that I have decided to omit the details of the conversation and to limit myself to the elder's story as written down by Alexei Karamazov. That will make it shorter and less tiresome, although, I repeat, Alyosha must have expanded it somewhat with things the elder had told him in their previous conversations.

CHAPTER 2

From the Life of the Deceased Monk and Priest, the Elder Zosima, as Taken Down from His Own Words by Alexei Fyodorovich Karamazov

Biographical Notes

A. The Youth Who Was Elder Zosima's Brother

Beloved fathers and teachers, I was born in a faraway Northern province, in the town of V. My father was a gentleman by birth, but he was neither wealthy nor socially prominent. He died when I was only two and I do not remember him at all. He left my mother a small, wooden house and some money, not very much, but enough for her and her children to live on without privation. There were only two of us: my older brother Markel and myself, Zinovy. Markel was eight years older than I. He was impulsive and short-tempered. But he was really very kind and he never teased me. He was a strangely silent boy, especially at home with mother, me, and the servants. He was a good student, but at school always kept aloof from the other boys, although he did not quarrel with them or, at least, that is how our mother remembered it. About six months before he was to die (he was already seventeen at the time) he started visiting a man who led a very isolated life in our town, a man who had been exiled from Moscow for what amounted to free-thinking. This exile was a quite well-known scholar and he had once taught philosophy at the university. Somehow he got to like Markel and received him in his house. The boy spent whole evenings there throughout the winter, until the exile was summoned back to Petersburg, to take an appointment for which he had petitioned and, since he had some protectors, had now received. In the meantime Lent had begun, but Markel refused to fast. He made fun of it and even became rude. "All that is delirium," he said, "because there is no such thing as God." He really horrified our mother and the servants, and me too, for, even though I was just nine years old, I was very frightened when I heard him say that. Our servants were serfs—there were four of them—and they had been bought in the name of a landowner we knew. I still remember my mother selling one of the four, our cook Afimya, a lame elderly woman. Mother received sixty rubles for her and hired a free woman in her place . . .

Well, in the sixth week of Lent, my brother became seriously ill. His health had always been very poor; he was weak in the chest, had a frail constitution, and was predisposed to consumption. He was rather tall, very thin and frail, but his face was extremely handsome. He may have caught cold, but whatever it was, the doctor told mother that he now had galloping consumption and would not live through the spring. Mother wept all the time and then, very gradually, so as not to alarm him, she started to beg my brother to fast and to take holy communion, for he was still on his feet. He became very angry and said rude things about the Church. But then he thought about it and understood it all: he was dangerously

ill and his mother was asking him to fast and to confess and
to take the sacrament while he still had some strength left in
him. He had known all along that his health was very bad
and, the year before, he had even told our mother and me:
"I'm not here for long. I don't think I'll last out another
year." And now it was as if he had prophesied it himself.
Three days later Holy Week began, and on the Tuesday
morning my brother started fasting and went to church.
"Actually, I'm only doing it for your sake," he told our
mother. "I want you to be happy and to stop worrying."
Mother wept from joy then and also from grief, because she
said to herself that his end must be near, to have brought
about such a change in him. And it was not many times that
he went to church. He soon had to take to his bed, so he
confessed and took the sacrament at home.

Easter was late that year, and the days grew long and clear
and bright and full of the fragrance of spring. I remember
he spent restless nights, coughing all the time, but in the
morning he would insist on getting dressed and trying to sit
up in an armchair. And I can still see him now, sitting in
that armchair, gentle, smiling, and always looking cheerful
despite his illness. He was completely changed; it was really
an unbelievable change that took place in him. When, for
instance, our old nanny entered his room and asked him,
"Would it be all right, my dear, if I lighted the lamp before
your icon"—something he used not to allow her to do; he
would even blow the lamp out if he found it lighted—this
time he said to her: "Go ahead, dear nanny, light it. I was a
monster before not to let you light it. For that's your way of
praying to God, and watching you makes me happy and in
my happiness I pray for you too, which means that both of
us are praying to the same God."

These words seemed very strange to us, and mother cried
all the time except when she went into Markel's room; then
she'd dry her eyes and try to look cheerful. "Don't cry,
mother, don't," he'd tell her. "I still have a long time to live
and have a good time, for life is so good and so full of joy!"

"How can it be such a joy to you, my darling, when you
are so feverish at night and cough so that it sounds as if
your chest is about to burst . . ."

"Mother," he would answer, "don't be sad. Life is paradise;
we all live in paradise, although we don't want to see it. As
soon as we are willing to recognize it, the whole world will
become a paradise; it could happen tomorrow, any time."

Everyone was surprised at his words and at the assurance with which he said these things; we were all moved and it made us cry. When friends came to see him, he would say to them: "It's so nice of you to come, for I don't know what I've done to earn your love and I can't begin to understand how you can love someone like me, nor can I understand how I could have failed to appreciate it until now." To the servants who entered his room, he kept saying, "Why must you wait on me like this, my dear friends? Do you really think I deserve to be waited on by you? If God spares me for now and I go on living, I'll wait on you too, for we should all wait on each other."

Mother listened to him, shaking her head. "It's your illness that makes you talk like this, my dear."

"My dearest, beloved mother," he said, "since it is impossible to do without masters and servants in the world, let me also be a servant to my servants, just as they are to me. And I'll tell you also, mother dear—we are all guilty toward others and I am the guiltiest of all."

That made even mother laugh. "I would like to know," she said, laughing and crying at the same time, "how you can be the guiltiest of all? With all the thieves and murderers, what have you done to accuse yourself like this?"

"Mother, my own dear blood"—he sometimes used the most peculiar endearments—"my own dear blood, my sweet joy, know that this is the truth and that every one of us is answerable for everyone else and for everything. I don't know how to explain it to you, but I feel it so strongly that it hurts. And now, the way we used to live before seems strange to me, how we got annoyed at one another, and how we knew nothing then."

And he would awaken in this state every morning, becoming more and more touching and more and more elated, literally trembling with love.

When the doctor came—an old German called Eisenschmidt—Markel would ask him: "Tell me, doctor, will I be one more day in this world?" He always joked with the doctor, who would answer: "It's not a question of a day, or even many days. You'll be here for many months and years yet . . ."

"There's no need for years or even months, days are enough; a single day is sufficient for a man to discover what happiness is. Why must we quarrel, brag, and remember offenses against us? Why shouldn't we go into the garden right now and love, kiss, praise, and enjoy one another, and bless our lives?" When mother saw the doctor off, he said to her: "I'm afraid your son is not long for this world—his illness has affected his brain now."

The windows of my brother's room gave onto our garden, which was full of shady old trees in which the young spring buds were swelling and the first spring birds were chirruping and singing. And as he watched and admired the little birds, he suddenly started to ask them, too, to forgive him: "God's little birds, please forgive me, for I have sinned before you, too." Now that was something nobody could really understand. But Markel lay there with tears of joy rolling down his cheeks. "Yes," he explained, "I used to be surrounded by the glory of God—the birds and the trees and the fields and the sky—and I alone lived in degradation. I was the only one who was an insult to everything, and I didn't even notice all the beauty and the glory of the world."

"Aren't you taking too many sins upon yourself?" mother would ask him sometimes.

"Mother, my life's delight, why, don't you see that it's not out of sorrow that I am crying? I am crying from joy, mother. Why, I want to stand guilty before everybody and everything, although I can't explain to you why, because I don't even know how to love them. But if I have sinned before everyone, they will all forgive me now, and then we will have heaven on earth. Don't you think I am living in heaven now?"

And there was much more of this that I cannot remember or describe. I recall coming into his room once when no one else was there. It was a clear evening, the sun was setting, and the whole room was lighted by its slanting rays. He beckoned me to him when he saw me. I walked over to him and he put his hands on my shoulders. He looked tenderly and lovingly into my eyes and continued to look at me in that manner for a whole minute perhaps, without saying anything. "All right," he said in the end, "now go and play and live some of life for me." So I left him and went out to play. But later I often remembered with tears in my eyes how he had asked me to live for him. Yes, he said many more inspired and beautiful things that at the time, however, I could not understand. He died in the third week after Easter. He was fully conscious until the very end, although he could no longer talk by then. Still, up to the very last moment he did not change. He looked happy and there was a spark of joy in his eyes. He smiled at us, seeking each one of us out, as if speaking to us. Even in town, people talked of his death for a long time. It was all a shock to me, but not a very violent one, although I cried a lot when they buried him. I was still too young, a mere child, but it all remained in my heart, ineffaceable, but dormant for a while. In good time, though, it was bound to come to life again and make itself known. And that's just what happened.

B. The Holy Bible in Father Zosima's Life

I was all my mother had left then, but soon some good friends persuaded her that, since I was now her only son and she was not really poor, she ought to follow the example of so many other parents and send me to Petersburg, so as not to deprive me of a brilliant career. And they convinced her to send me to the Petersburg Cadet Corps School so that eventually I could become an officer in the Imperial Guards. Mother hesitated for a long time, as it was very hard for her to part with her remaining son, but finally, after much weeping, she made up her mind to do it, because she felt it was the best for my future happiness. So she took me to Petersburg and entered me in the Cadet Corps School. And that was the last I ever saw of her, for she died three years later, having spent the time in between missing her two sons and being wretched without them.

I have nothing but happy memories of my mother's home. There is nothing a man cherishes more than the memories of his early childhood in his parents' home; this is always true as long as there was at least a little love and harmony in his family. Even if a man's childhood was spent in a very bad home, he may still have some happy memories, as long as his mind can seek out the patches of happiness. Among memories of my childhood, I must also include my memories of the story of Jesus, about which I was very curious when I was still quite small. I had at that time a book with beautiful pictures in it called *A Hundred and Four Stories from the Old and New Testaments;* indeed, it was the book from which I learned to read. That book is still on my shelf here; I have treasured it as a reminder of my childhood. But I remember that, before I was eight and before I had learned to read properly, I had a sort of spiritual experience. That year my mother took me to morning mass on the Monday before Easter. I don't remember where my brother was that day, but there were only the two of us—my mother and I. It was a bright, sunny day and I remember clearly the incense rising from the censer and wafting slowly upward, while from a little window in the cupola sunbeams streamed down into the church, and it looked as if the incense, rising in waves, was melting in the sunlight. I looked at it, feeling somehow deeply moved, and it was then that, for the first time in my life, I felt I had glimpsed the meaning of the Word of God and was open to receive its seeds. Then a boy came out and stood in the middle of the church. He was holding a big book, so big, indeed, that it seemed to me that he had difficulty carrying it. He placed the book on the lectern, opened it, and started to read from it. And all of a sudden I understood something of what was being read in the house of God . . .

There was a man in the land of Uz, a righteous and pious man, and he had so much wealth, so many camels, so many sheep, and so many donkeys; his children were happy and he cherished them and prayed for them, in case they sinned as they enjoyed themselves. But when the sons of God came before the Lord, Satan came among them and said to Him that he had been everywhere, all over the earth and beneath it. "And have you seen My servant Job?" God asked him and with pride pointed out to Satan His great and holy servant. Satan smiled at God's words and said: "Give him over to me and You will see that Your servant will deny You and curse Your name." And God gave over to Satan the righteous man whom He so loved, and Satan smote his children, killed his cattle, and scattered his wealth, bringing all this down upon him at the same time, as if it were caused by divine lightning. And Job tore his clothes and threw himself on the ground and said: "Naked came I out of my mother's womb, and naked shall I return into the earth: the Lord gave, and the Lord hath taken away; blessed be the name of the Lord now and forever!"

Fathers and teachers, please forgive my tears now—it is as if my whole childhood were rising up before me and I breathe now as I breathed then, as an eight-year-old boy, and I feel just as I felt then—surprised and awed and happy. Everything struck my imagination then: the camels, Satan talking to God in that way, God giving His servant over to Satan who sought his perdition, and the servant of God exclaiming, "Blessed be Your name though You chastise me," followed by the soft, sweet singing of "Harken unto my prayer" in the church, and again the incense rising from the priest's censer and everyone kneeling in prayer. And ever since then I have been unable to read that holy story without my eyes filling with tears—I know, for I read it only yesterday! There is so much in it that is great, mysterious, inconceivable!

Later I was to hear sarcastic and blasphemous remarks about it, words full of conceit: Why should God give the most beloved of His saints to Satan so that he could play games with him, take away his children, smite him with sores and boils from which he would scrape the pus with a potsherd? Was it simply to enable Him to boast to Satan later and say to him something like, "See how My saint can suffer for My sake!" But then the very greatness of the story lies precisely in its mystery—here fleeting, earthly reality confronts eternal truth. Just as in the first days of creation when the Creator, at the end of each day, paused to admire His work with the words, "That which I have created is good!"— so in this story He looks at Job and again praises His creation. And Job, when he praises the Lord, serves not only Him but His whole creation, for generations and generations, forever and ever, for that is what he was foreordained to do.

Oh, what a great book it is and how much we learn from it! What a miraculous book is the Holy Bible and what strength it gives to man! It is like a sculpted model of the world, of mankind, and of the characters of men; everything is there and it contains guidance for us for all ages. How many mysteries are solved in it, how many revealed!

And so God raises Job up and gives him back his wealth, and many years pass. Job again has children, new children, whom he loves. But how can he possibly love these new children of his when the others are no longer there, when he has lost them? Can he be completely happy when he remembers his dead children, however dear to his heart his new children may be? But he can be happy, he can know happiness again, because a mysterious process gradually transforms an old grief into a quiet happiness; seething youth is replaced by gentle and serene old age. Every day I bless the rising sun and my heart sings to it as it did before; but now I love the sunset even more, and its long, slanting rays bring back to me quiet, touching, tender memories, dear faces, and images from my long and blessed life. Over everything there hovers the Lord's truth and justice that moves our hearts, reconciles everything, and is all-forgiving!

My life is coming to an end—I know it, hear it. But with every day that is left to me I feel that my earthly life is already blending into a new, infinite, unknown, future life, anticipation of which sets my soul atremble with ecstasy, makes my mind glow and my heart weep with joy.

Friends and teachers, I have often heard, and of late more than ever, that our clergy, particularly our rural clergy, complain bitterly over their lowly status and the low stipends they receive. They go so far as to declare in print—I have read such statements myself—that they can no longer interpret the Holy Scriptures to people because they are so poor and that if Lutherans or heretics come to take their flocks away from them—then, let them, for "we are not properly paid." I think to myself, may the Lord grant them the higher stipend that is so important to them (because their complaint is justified), but the truth is that, if someone is to blame, we must share in that blame ourselves. For even a priest who is short of time and overburdened with work and church services can still snatch at least an hour a week to remember God. Besides, he does not work all the time, all year round. He could start by inviting a group of children to his house once a week in the evening, for instance, and perhaps, when their parents heard about it, they might come and join their little ones. And there is no need to build palaces to do that; let him invite them to his hut and not worry that they may make it dirty, for he'll only have them there for one hour a week. He could open the Book and read to them out of it; there would be no need for him to spout wisdom to them, to give himself airs, and to feel himself superior to them. He need only read with feeling and humility and be gratified if they listen to him and understand him; he himself should enjoy the words he reads, only stopping now and then to explain some expression or phrase that an uneducated person might not know—and let him not worry: the heart of a Russian Christian will, in the end, understand everything!

He should read to them about Abraham and Sarah, about Isaac and Rebecca, about Jacob going to Laban, wrestling with the Lord in his dream, and saying, "This is a frightening place," and these stories will impress the devout minds of the simple people. He could read, especially to the children, the story of how Joseph's brothers sold him into bondage, their own brother, the tender boy who dreamt prophetic dreams and was a great seer, and they later told their father that Joseph had been devoured by a wild beast and showed him the boy's bloodstained clothes. He could read to them how the brothers later went to buy grain in Egypt, where, by that time, Joseph had become a powerful man at the court; and, unrecognized by them, he tormented and accused them, and kept his youngest brother Benjamin as a hostage, although all the time he loved them—"I love you and, loving you, I torment you"—but had never forgotten how one day, somewhere in the parched plain, by a well, they had sold him to some passing merchants and he had wept, wringing his hands and begging his brothers not to make him a slave in a foreign land . . . And then, seeing them after many, many years, he again loved them beyond measure, although he tormented them and made them suffer as he loved them. And finally he himself could stand it no longer and threw himself on his couch and wept; then wiping away his tears, he went out to them and joyfully announced: "Look at me, I am your brother Joseph!" Then let the priest read to the children about the joy of the old patriarch Jacob when he learns that his beloved son is alive, about his leaving his native land for Egypt and later dying there and announcing before his death the great prophecy that he had concealed throughout his life in his gentle, timid heart—the prophecy that, from his stock, from the Hebrews, would come the great hope of the world, who would bring it peace and salvation.

Fathers and teachers, forgive me and bear with me for telling you now, like a little child, about things long familiar to you, things, indeed, that you could tell me a hundred times better and more skillfully. I have talked of these things for sheer joy, and I beg you to forgive my tears, for I dearly love that book. Let the priest, who is here to spread the word of God, weep too, and he will find that the hearts of those who listen to him will respond and be touched. All he needs is a small seed, a tiny seed; once he has dropped it into the heart of a simple man, it will never die; it will live there as long as he lives; it will be hidden there like a bright spark, like a great reminder amidst the darkness that surrounds the man in the stench of his sins. And there is no need for many explanations and much teaching—he will understand everything by himself. Or do you think that a simple, uneducated man is unable to understand? Just try reading him the moving story of the fair Esther and the haughty Vashti or the marvelous legend about the prophet Jonah in the belly of the whale. And you must not forget the parables of our Lord, taken mostly from St. Luke (which I used), then the conversion of Saul from the Acts of the Apostles (absolutely without fail), and, finally, the *Lives of the Saints:* for instance, the life of Alexei, the man of God, and the life of Mary of Egypt, the greatest of

the great, the blessed martyr who saw God, and the bearer of
Christ. The priest will reach people's hearts with these simple
tales. It will only take him one hour a week, and that he can
do despite his low stipend. He will find out that our people
are generous, that they will be grateful to him and reward
him a hundredfold. They will respond to the priest's zeal and
the moving words they hear from him. They will be eager to
help him in his field and in his house, and they will respect
him more than they did before—that is how his stipend will
be increased. It is so simple that one might hesitate to say it
for fear that people might laugh, although it is the absolute
truth! He who does not believe in God will not believe in
God's people either. But he who has come to believe in God's
people will have his eyes opened to the glory of God, even
if he was unable to see it before. Only the masses of simple,
humble people and their growing spiritual power will be able
to convert the atheists, who have been uprooted from our
native soil. And what good is the Word of Christ without an
example? A nation is lost without the Word of God, for every
human soul thirsts for His Word and for the good and the
beautiful.

Almost forty years ago, when I was still young, Father
Anfim and I wandered all over Russia, collecting alms for our
monastery. Once we spent the night with some fishermen on
the bank of a large river. A handsome peasant lad of eighteen
joined us. He was on his way to a place where the next day
he was to join a team of men to tow a merchant's barge. I
was struck by the brightness and warmth in that boy's eyes.
It was a clear, still, warm night in July. A cool mist was
rising from the broad river. The birds had quieted down and
now and then a fish would splash in the water. Everything
was hushed and beautiful, praying to God as it were. Only
the two of us, the boy and I, were not asleep, and we talked
about the beauty of this world of God's and of the great
mystery in it. Every blade of grass, every bug, every ant, every
golden bee, knowing so amazingly what to do, without intelligence, reveals the existence of God's mystery and continuously
demonstrates it to us. I saw that the boy was glowing with
fervor and he told me that he loved the forest and the forest
birds; he used to be a bird catcher; he could recognize and
imitate the calls of all the birds and knew how to make them
come to him. "I know nothing better than the forest," he told
me, "although I think everything is good."

"That's true," I said, "everything is good and beautiful

because everything is truth. Take, for instance, the horse," I said to him, "it is a great animal and it is so close to man; or take the ox, that sad and dreamy beast that feeds man and works for him. Look at these animals—what meekness, what devotion to man, who often beats them mercilessly, what gentleness and trustfulness there is in them—and that is so beautiful! It is so moving to think that these creatures are free of sin, because all but man are sinless and Christ was with them even before He came to us."

"Do you mean," the boy asked, "that Christ is with them too?"

"How could it be otherwise," I said, "since the Word is for all creation, and every creature and every little leaf obeys the Word, singing the praises of God, weeping to Christ and, all unaware, accomplishing it all by the mystery of its sinless existence. Take, for instance, the fierce, formidable, frightening bear, roaming through the forest. He is not in the least responsible for what he is . . ." And I went on to tell him about the bear which once came to the hut of a great saint who was seeking salvation in the forest. The saint, feeling great tenderness for the beast, came out fearlessly, gave it a loaf of bread, and said: "There, go along now, and may Christ be with you." And the fierce bear went off obediently and meekly without hurting the saint.

The boy was deeply moved by the story, because the beast had not hurt the saint and because Christ was with him, too. "Ah," he said, "how wonderful it is, how everything of God's is good and beautiful!" And he sat there deep in quiet, sweet thoughts. I saw then that he understood. Then, by my side, he slipped into an easy, sinless sleep. May God bless the young! Before I went to sleep myself, I prayed for him. O Lord, send peace and light to Your people!

C. Reminiscences of Elder Zosima's Worldly Youth. The Duel

I spent a long time, almost eight years, at the Petersburg Cadet Corps School, and my new environment stifled many of my childhood impressions, although I forgot nothing. I picked up enough new habits and even new opinions there to turn me into a cruel, absurd, almost wild creature. While I acquired a varnish of good manners and some French, I also learned to look upon the soldiers who waited on us at the school as cattle. And I, inclined as I was to carry everything to an extreme, treated them perhaps worse than anybody. By the time we graduated from the school and received our officers' commissions, we were prepared, at a moment's notice, to shed our blood for the honor of our regiment, although hardly one of us had any idea of the true meaning of the word "honor," and if any of us had known, he would have been the first to ridicule it. Drunkenness, debauchery, and rowdyism were almost matters for pride. And although I cannot say that we were evil—nice young men that we were—we certainly behaved badly, and I worst of all. The main trouble was that I came into some money and started spending it in the pursuit of pleasure with the total recklessness and abandon of youth. Strangely enough, though, at the same time, I read books, and quite avidly at that. The only book I never opened then was my Bible, from which I had never parted and which always accompanied me in all my travels; I was keeping it, without realizing it myself, "for an hour and a day, a month and a year."

After I had lived four years of this life in the army, my regiment was moved to K. The social life in that town was varied and gay; there were many rich people and we were invited to their homes and entertained. I was welcomed everywhere, being of a gay disposition and also having a reputation as being rather well off, which does count for something in social relations.

And then something happened that was to change the course of my life. I became interested in a pretty young girl. She was intelligent, well bred, bright, and generous, and her parents were highly respected in town. They occupied a rather prominent social position, were wealthy, and had good connections. They received me warmly and well. Then somehow I got the impression that their daughter had romantic feelings for me and at once my imagination was fired. Later, however, I realized that it was no passionate love that I felt for her. I simply admired her intelligence and the nobility of her character, which no one could help admiring. Besides, selfishness prevented me from asking for her hand, because I could not face giving up the freedom and joys of my debauched bachelor life when I was still so young and had money to spend. And so I decided at least to postpone for the time being the final step, although I did drop a few hints about my feelings for her.

Then I was suddenly sent on duty to another district and

when I returned two months later, I learned to my surprise that during my absence the girl had married a wealthy local landowner. He was somewhat older than I, but still young, and he had connections in Petersburg high society, which I did not have. He was also very kind and, what is more, a man of high culture, such as I myself did not have at all.

I was so shocked by the news that I lost all sense of reality. But the most painful part of it for me was when I learned that the young landowner had been engaged to the girl for a long time, for, although I had met him at her house, I had never suspected there could be anything between the two of them, deluded as I was by what I thought were my own irresistible charms. And this is what actually hurt me most: how could it be that everyone else knew about it except me? It made me blush just to think how close I had come, on so many occasions, to blurting out a declaration of my love! And since she had never said anything to me, had never told me of her engagement, she was, I decided, mocking me. Thinking about it later, I realized that she certainly was not trying to make fun of me, for, whenever I had started to speak to her about my feelings, she had invariably warded me off with a joke and talked of something else. But at the time I was quite unable to see it that way and was filled with an overwhelming desire to avenge myself. It amazes me now when I think of it—this anger and desire for revenge quite pained and sickened me, for, being by nature rather easy-going, I could not be angry with anyone for long and so I had to kindle these feelings artificially, which made me quite unbearable and absurd.

I bided my time, until, at a large gathering, I found an opportunity to insult the man I somehow considered my rival. I picked an unrelated pretext, trying to ridicule his opinion on an important political event—this was in 1826. People said that I succeeded in making fun of him bitingly and wittily. I maneuvered him into a position in which he had to ask me for an explanation and, in the course of that explanation, I was so rude to him that he at once challenged me, despite the great difference in our social positions—not only was I younger than he, but I was a man of no consequence and of low rank. Later I found out that he responded to my provocation because he, too, somehow felt jealous of me: he had rather resented my past friendship with his wife—his fiancée at the time—and now he feared that if she learned I had insulted him and he had not challenged me to a duel, she might come to despise him and then would not love him as before.

I found a second right away—a lieutenant from my regiment. At that time, although dueling had been outlawed and was severely punished, it was very much in fashion in the army, for wild and stupid customs have a way of taking root and becoming firmly established.

It was the end of June and we were to meet outside of town at seven in the morning. At this point something fateful happened to me. On the evening before, I returned home in a nasty, ugly mood, lost my temper with my orderly Afanasy, and rammed my fist into his face twice, bloodying it. He had not been with me for very long and, although I had hit him a few times before, I had never indulged in such unrestrained brutality. And please believe me, my dear friends, although all this happened more than forty years ago, I still feel pain and shame when I think of it.

I went to bed, slept for three hours or so, and awakened to find the day already breaking. I could not go back to sleep so I got up, went to the window, and opened it. My window, which gave onto the garden, faced the rising sun. It was a warm and beautiful morning and the twittering of the birds was beginning to fill the air. But what this shameful and distasteful feeling within me was, I could not explain. Was it because I was about to shed blood? No, that didn't seem to be what was bothering me. Was I afraid of being killed, afraid to die? No, that was certainly not it, that couldn't be . . . And then, all of a sudden, I found it! It was because I had struck Afanasy the night before. I relived the whole scene: there he was in front of me. I swung my fist back and slammed it in his face . . . He was still facing forward; his arms stiffly at his sides, he stood to attention, not even dreaming of lifting his hand to ward off my blows, which only made his head jerk back. And this is what a man can be driven to do—to beat another man! I knew it was a crime and the realization was like a long, sharp needle piercing my heart. So I stood there like a lost soul while the sun shone, the little leaves shimmered gaily in the light, and the birds praised the Lord. I covered my face with my hands, threw myself on my bed, and wept aloud like a child. Suddenly the words of my brother Markel came back to me, the words he had spoken before his death, when he had asked the servants why they were so kind to him and waited on him, and had wondered if he deserved their services. And I asked myself: "Do I deserve to be waited on? Why should another man, made in the image of the Lord, just like me, be my servant?" It was the first time this question had arisen in my mind. And I remembered my brother Markel saying, "Mother, my own dear blood, every one of us is answerable for everyone else, but we don't know it; if we did, we would at once have heaven on earth!" Might that not be true? I felt tears come to my eyes and I thought: "Perhaps I am really guilty before everyone; indeed, I must be guiltier and worse than anybody else in the world." And suddenly I saw my whole situation in its true light: What was I about to do now? Wasn't I planning to kill a kind, intelligent, and honorable man, who had never done me any harm? Would that not also bring to an end his wife's happiness, make her miserable, and perhaps even kill her?

I lay thinking such thoughts, with my face buried in the pillow for I don't know how long. Then my fellow officer, the lieutenant who was to act as my second, came in with the pistols.

"It's a good thing you're awake," he said, "because it's time for us to leave. Let's go."

I became very excited and was not sure what I was doing. Nevertheless we went downstairs but then, as I was about to climb into the carriage, I said to him: "Wait for me a minute. I've left my purse behind. I must get it—it won't take me a second."

So I rushed back upstairs and straight to Afanasy's tiny, partitioned-off room. "Afanasy," I said, "last night I hit you twice in the face. Please forgive me," I said to him. He started as if frightened and stared at me. I saw then that I had to do more, and the next thing, just as I was, in dress uniform with epaulets and all, I threw myself down at his feet, touching the floor with my forehead. "Please forgive me!" I begged him.

This time he was completely dumbfounded. "Sir . . . Please, sir . . . how can you . . . who am I for you to do that . . . please . . ." And, just as I had done earlier that morning, he covered his face with his hands and started to sob; he turned away from me, facing the window, his whole body shaking with his weeping, while I rushed out of the room, tore downstairs to my second, and jumped into the carriage.

"Drive on!" I shouted. "Have you ever seen a conqueror? No? Well, look here—here's one!" I was so happy and excited that I never stopped talking as we drove to the meeting place;

I cannot even imagine all the things I said then. My comrade-in-arms kept looking at me and saying approvingly: "That's the spirit. That's the way to take it. I'm sure you won't let your regiment down."

The others were already waiting for us when we arrived. They placed my opponent and me twelve paces apart, and it was he who had the first shot. I stood there, feeling very gay and happy, looking straight into his face, never batting an eye. And it was with love that I looked at him—I am certain of it, for I knew now what to do. He fired and the bullet just grazed my cheek, scratching my ear slightly. "Thank God," I cried to my adversary, "you haven't killed a man!" Then I turned my back on him and tossed my pistol far away, shouting: "Begone, I have no further need of you!" I turned back and said to my opponent: "Can you please forgive me, sir, stupid young man that I am, for having offended you deliberately and having forced you to take a shot at me. You are by ten times a better man than I am. Please tell that to the person whose opinion is the most important to you."

When they heard that, all three of them—he and the two seconds—began to shout at me. My opponent was very indignant at what I had said.

"But if you had no intention of fighting, why did you bother me at all?"

"Yesterday I was stupid," I told him cheerfully, "but today I'm a bit wiser."

"I agree with you about yesterday, but I cannot concur with your opinion about today."

"Very well taken!" I cried, clapping my hands. "I agree with you—I deserve that!"

"Are you or are you not going to fire the shot to which you are entitled, sir?"

"No," I said, "I am not going to. But you can go ahead and shoot at me again, although I believe it would be better for you if you didn't."

The seconds were protesting noisily, especially my second:

"What do you mean by begging your opponent for forgiveness in the middle of a duel! You're a disgrace to the regiment! If I had suspected anything like this!"

I stood there facing them and now I addressed them all seriously: "Gentlemen," I said, "is it really so surprising these days to meet a man who can admit he has done something stupid and apologize publicly for the wrong he has done?"

"But you cannot apologize in the course of the duel," my second shouted at me angrily.

"That's just it," I said. "I agree that I really should have apologized as soon as I arrived, before the gentleman fired his shot, so as not to expose him to a mortal sin. But we have things so stupidly twisted in our conventions that it was almost impossible for me to do that: only when I had allowed him to shoot at me from a distance of twelve paces could my word have any weight at all for you, for if I had apologized before that shot, you would have simply dismissed me as a coward and not even listened to me . . .

"Gentlemen!" I cried in a burst of passion, "look around you and see all the things God has given us: look at the clear sky, at the air that is so transparent, at the tender grass and at the birds, at the beauty of immaculate and sinless nature, in which we are the only stupid, godless creatures who do not understand that life is a heaven. As soon as we understand that, we shall have that heaven here in all its beauty and we shall embrace one another and weep with joy . . ."

I wanted to say more but could not go on because I was so moved it took my breath away; everything looked so lovely and enchanting and I was filled with a joy such as I had never before experienced.

"That all sounds quite reasonable and very pious," my opponent said. "Whatever else, you are certainly a rather original person."

"You can laugh at me now and I'll laugh with you, but I'm sure that some day you will approve of what I am doing now."

"Why," he said, "I'm prepared to approve of it right now—here's my hand—because I believe you are really sincere."

"No," I said, "it's too early for that; wait until I make myself into a better person, who deserves your respect, and then you will give me your hand."

As we drove back, my second kept berating me, while I kept embracing him. That very day, my fellow officers all heard the story and met to discuss what I had done and to decide what to do about it. "He has disgraced the uniform," some said, "so let him hand in his resignation." "But he did stand there while his opponent fired at him," my defenders argued. "Yes, but he was too afraid to expose himself to more shots and begged for mercy under fire." "If he had been afraid of facing more shots, he would have fired at his opponent when his turn came, instead of tossing his loaded pistol away . . . No, there's obviously something else to it, something quite original."

It amused me to watch them and listen to them. "Dear friends and comrades," I said to them, "please don't bother to argue over whether I should or should not resign my commission—I have already sent in my resignation, today. As soon as it comes through, I will enter a monastery, since that's why I want to leave the army."

They roared with laughter at that, every single one of them. "Why didn't you say so from the start? Now it's all clear; we would certainly never have sat in judgment on a monk . . ." They kept laughing for a long time. They couldn't stop, but there was nothing sarcastic in their laughter. It was just gay and friendly and, indeed, they all suddenly became very fond of me, even those who had been fiercest in accusing me. For the whole of the following month, while my resignation was being processed, they fussed over me lovingly. "Our monk," they called me, and each of them would try to say something nice to me; some were even so sorry to see me go that they tried to convince me to cancel my resignation: "Why must he do that to himself?" they said. "He's brave; we all know that he stood there while his opponent fired at him, and he would have shot him then but for the dream he had had the night before, which made him decide to become a monk. That's the whole explanation."

And it was the same with local society. Before the duel, although I had been received warmly in various houses, I had never made any great impression. But now I was in great demand everywhere: people would invite me to visit them, and they would laugh at me, but love me at the same time. I should note here that, although everyone talked openly about the duel, the military authorities declared the whole affair closed, because my opponent happened to be closely related to the General and, since the whole thing had ended bloodlessly and almost like a joke, they treated it as such, especially since I had handed in my resignation.

I spoke my mind fearlessly despite their laughter, for it was kind, not wicked laughter. It was mostly in the evenings, in the presence of the ladies, that I had an opportunity to voice my beliefs, for the women came to like listening to me and made their men listen too.

"But how can you possibly be responsible for everyone?" people would say, laughing at me openly. "How could you be responsible for our acts, for instance?"

"How can you understand," I told them, "when the whole world has been running on false ideas for so long, when we accept unmitigated lies as truth and demand lies of others. Now that, for the first time in my life, I have acted sincerely, you all look upon me as if I were one of God's fools and, although you like me, you still laugh at me."

"How could anybody help liking you?" my hostess said, laughing openly in front of the many guests gathered in her house.

A lady stood up abruptly then, and I recognized the young woman who had been the cause of the duel and whom, so recently, I had almost considered my future bride. I had not seen her arrive. She came over to me and gave me her hand.

"Allow me to assure you," she said, "that I for one am not laughing at you. In fact, I want to thank you with tears in my eyes and tell you how deeply I respect you for the way you behaved on that occasion."

Her husband came up to me too and then they all surrounded me, almost hugging and kissing me. I felt elated, but I was particularly struck by a middle-aged gentleman who also came up to me. I knew his name, but I had never really been acquainted with him before and I had never even exchanged a word with him until that evening.

D. The Mysterious Visitor

He had come to that town long before and he occupied a very important position there. He was highly respected, extremely wealthy, and famous for his philanthropy, having donated large sums to the old people's home and the orphanage. It was to be discovered after his death that he had made many other donations secretly, shunning publicity. He was in his fifties, had an almost stern look about him, and was a man of few words. He had been married then for only ten years; his wife was much younger than he was and they had three young children.

Well, the next day, while I was sitting at home, the door opened and this man walked in.

I should note here that by this time I had moved to another house. I had left my old quarters after handing in my resignation. I now rented a room in the house of a civil servant's widow, the rent including the services of her own servants. I had moved like this because that same day, when I returned from the duel, I sent my orderly Afanasy back to his company; I was ashamed to look him in the face after the apologies of the morning—an immature young man of the world is often most ashamed of his noblest acts.

"I have listened to you with great interest several times when you have spoken in various houses in town," the gentleman said to me, "and now I am very anxious to get to know you personally and talk at length with you. You would oblige me very much if you would consent to talk to me."

"Why, certainly, with the greatest pleasure; I'd consider it a special honor," I said to him, but as I spoke I felt almost frightened, because I was very impressed by this man. For, although many people had listened to me with interest, no one had ever aproached me looking so stern and intense and, besides, this man had come especially to my house. He sat down.

"I see great will power in you," he said, "for you were not afraid to do what you considered right in a matter in which you risked making yourself the victim of general contempt."

"I think you have an exaggerated opinion of me."

"No," he said, "it is not exaggerated. Believe me, it's much harder than you think to do what you did. Actually, that is precisely what amazed me and why I have come here," he went on. "I would like you to describe to me—that is, if you don't think my curiosity impertinent—exactly what you felt in that second during the duel when you decided to ask your opponent to forgive you. Can you remember? And please don't think this is just idle curiosity on my part; on the contrary, in asking you this, I am pursuing a certain secret goal that I will explain to you later if it is God's design to bring us closer together."

I looked him straight in the face as he spoke and I felt I could trust him completely. I also felt very curious, for I guessed that there was a secret weighing on him.

"You want to know what I felt as I asked my opponent for forgiveness," I said, "but allow me first to tell you something I have never told anyone else." And I went on to tell him about hitting Afanasy and then throwing myself at his feet. "And so," I concluded, "as I suppose you'll understand now, it was much easier for me to do what I did during the duel, because I had already started out on a new life before even leaving my house. Indeed, after that, everything was not only easy but even pleasant and exhilarating."

He looked at me very warmly as I was speaking.

"This is all so fascinating," he said. "If I may I'll come back to see you again and again."

And after that, he came to see me almost every evening. We would have become very close friends if he had spoken to me about himself, but he practically never said a word about his private affairs; he only seemed interested in talking about me. Despite that, I grew very fond of him and confided all my thoughts and feelings to him, for even without knowing his secret I knew that he was a righteous man. Moreover, I was flattered that such a serious man so many years my senior was not too proud to come and talk to a young fellow like me. I learned a lot from him, for he was a highly intelligent person.

"I have been thinking myself, for a long time, about life being heaven," he told me once. "Indeed, I've been thinking of nothing else," he added quickly. "And you know, I'm even more firmly convinced of it than you are, and one day you'll find out why."

As he spoke he looked at me and smiled, and I thought he was about to reveal something to me.

"Heaven is within reach of every one of us, and now it is within my reach too; if I chose I could have it tomorrow, real heaven, for all my life."

He spoke with fervor and looked at me mysteriously, as if asking something of me.

"As to every man being answerable for everybody and everything, not just for his own sins," he went on, "you are absolutely right about it, and the way you succeeded in grasping that idea so fully, all at once, is really remarkable. It is true that when men understand that idea, the kingdom of God will no longer be a dream but a reality."

"But when do you expect that to happen?" I cried bitterly. "When will it come about, if ever? Perhaps it's just a dream and nothing more."

"So you don't believe yourself," he answered, "in the things you preach to others. Let me tell you, then, that this dream, as you call it, will most certainly come true. You may rest assured of that, but it will not happen immediately, because everything that happens in the world is controlled by its own set of laws. In this case, it is a psychological matter, a state of mind. In order to change the world, man's way of thinking must be changed. Thus, there can be no brotherhood of men before all men become each other's brothers. There is no science, no order based on the pursuit of material gain, that will enable men to share their goods fairly and to respect each other's rights. There will never be enough to satisfy everyone;

men will always be envious of their neighbors and will always destroy one another. So to your question when heaven on earth will come about, I can only promise you that it will come without fail, but first the period of man's isolation must come to an end."

"What isolation?" I asked him.

"The isolation that you find everywhere, particularly in our age. But it won't come to an end right now, because the time has not yet come. Today everyone asserts his own personality and strives to live a full life as an individual. But these efforts lead not to a full life but to suicide, because, instead of realizing his personality, man only slips into total isolation. For in our age mankind has been broken up into self-contained individuals, each of whom retreats into his lair, trying to stay away from the rest, hiding himself and his belongings from the rest of mankind, and finally isolating himself from people and people from him. And, while he accumulates material wealth in his isolation, he thinks with satisfaction how mighty and secure he has become, because he is mad and cannot see that the more goods he accumulates, the deeper he sinks into suicidal impotence. The reason for this is that he has become accustomed to relying only on himself; he has split off from the whole and become an isolated unit; he has trained his soul not to rely on human help, not to believe in men and mankind, and only to worry that the wealth and privileges he has accumulated may get lost. Everywhere men today are turning scornfully away from the truth that the security of the individual cannot be achieved by his isolated efforts but only by mankind as a whole.

"But an end to this fearful isolation is bound to come and all men will understand how unnatural it was for them to have isolated themselves from one another. This will be the spirit of the new era and people will look back in amazement at the past, when they sat in darkness and refused to see the light. And it is then that the sign of the Son of Man will appear in the heavens . . . But until that day we must keep hope alive, and now and then a man must set an example, if only an isolated one, by trying to lift his soul out of its isolation and offering it up in an act of brotherly communion, even if he is taken for one of God's fools. This is necessary, to keep the great idea alive."

It was in such intense discussions that we spent our evenings, one after another. I even gave up a great deal of my social life and stayed mostly at home. Besides, I was no longer as much in fashion as I had been. I say that without bitterness, because people still treated me with cheerful warmth, but it is a fact that fashion is quite a queen in society. As to my mysterious and constant visitor, I was filled with tremendous admiration for him, for, beyond being enthralled by his intellectual powers, I vaguely felt that he was nurturing certain plans within him and that he was preparing something very important. Possibly he also appreciated the fact that I never asked him about his secret, never made hints about it. In the end, however, I felt that he himself was longing to tell me something. This became quite apparent about a month after he had started visiting me.

"Do you know," he said to me, "people in town are getting quite curious about us, particularly about my coming to visit you so often. But never mind, they'll have an explanation soon enough now."

There were times when he would suddenly become visibly agitated and, in those instances, he would almost always just get up and leave. At other times, he would look at me penetratingly at great length and I was certain that he was about to announce something very important but, instead, his expression would suddenly change and he would start discussing something that was not secret and that we had discussed before. He also started complaining of frequent headaches. And once, after he had talked at great length and with great feeling, he suddenly turned very pale, his face became twisted, and he stared at me fixedly.

"What's the matter?" I asked him. "You're not feeling well?" He had told me earlier that he had a headache.

"I . . . I want you to know . . . I have killed someone."

He smiled as he said it, but his face was pale as chalk. Why did he have to smile like that? That was the first thought that flashed through my head, even before I had fully taken in what he was saying. Then I felt myself turning pale.

"What are you saying?" I cried.

"You see," he answered, a faint smile still playing on his lips, "how hard it was for me to utter that first word. But now that I've torn myself loose, I think I'll be able to go on . . ."

I did not believe him at first. In fact, when he left me that day, I still didn't believe him; it was only after he had come to see me three days in a row and told me all about it in great detail that I finally came to believe him. I thought at first that he was mad and imagining it all, but in the end, with great amazement and great chagrin, I became convinced.

He had committed a great and horrible crime fourteen years before. He had murdered the rich widow of a landowner, a young and beautiful woman who had a house in town. He fell deeply in love with her, told her of his love, and tried to persuade her to marry him. But she already loved another man, a distinguished, high-ranking army officer; he was away at the time on active service, but she expected him back soon. So she rejected his proposal and asked him not to visit her. He stopped visiting her house, but then one night, taking advantage of his familiarity with the layout of the place, he entered the house through the garden and by the roof, with reckless disregard for the risk of being caught. But the most daring crimes are often the most successful. He entered the attic through a skylight and made his way down the attic stairs, knowing that the servants, through carelessness, often left the door at the bottom of the stairs unlocked. And that night they had. From there, he made his way in darkness to the lady's bedroom, where a lamp was burning before the icon. By sheer chance, her two maids had slipped unnoticed out of the house, without permission, to attend some birthday party down the street. As for the rest of the servants, they slept in the servants' quarters in the basement, near the kitchen.

When he saw her sleeping, his passion for her flared up. But at once it was superseded by a frantic, vengeful, jealous rage. Without knowing what he was doing, as if drunk, he went up to the bed and plunged a knife straight into her heart. She never even made a sound. Then, with cold and diabolical deliberation, he arranged things so that suspicion should fall on the servants. He was not too squeamish to take her purse, to open her chest of drawers with the keys he found under her pillow, and to take things an ignorant servant would be likely to take—ready cash and the larger gold articles—while leaving untouched infinitely more valuable securities and smaller but ten times more costly jewelry. He also took something of personal, sentimental value to him, but we will come to that later.

The sinister scheme completed, he left the house just as he had entered it, and neither on the following day when they found the victim, nor at any time after that, did anyone have the slightest suspicion as to who the real murderer was. Nor did anyone know about his love for the victim, for he had always been a taciturn and uncommunicative man and had never had a close friend to whom he might have confided his passion. People thought he was just an acquaintance of the victim, and not even a very close acquaintance, for he had not visited her during the last two weeks she was alive.

Suspicion fell at once on a servant named Peter, a serf of hers, whom, it was known (for she had said so herself), she had intended to send into the army to meet the recruitment quota for her serfs. She had picked him because he was single and also because she had been dissatisfied with his behavior, and he was aware of this. People in the tavern had heard him, when drunk, declare angrily that one day he would kill her. Then, for a couple of days before the murder, he had been away from the house without permission, and no one knew where he had been during that time. And on the day after the murder, they found him dead drunk outside town. His knife was in his pocket and somehow the palm of his right hand was smeared with blood. He said he had had a nosebleed, but they did not believe him. The two maids admitted that they had gone out to a party and left the entrance door unlocked while they were out. There were quite a few more such clues, which led to the arrest and trial of the innocent servant. However, a few days after the trial had started, the accused became ill with a fever and died in the prison hospital without regaining consciousness. And that closed the case, since the judges, the police authorities, and the public all agreed that the murderer was the dead serf. So the rest was left to the will of God, and that is when the punishment began.

My mysterious visitor, now my friend, admitted to me that, at first, his conscience had not bothered him in the least. He suffered, though, for having killed the woman he loved, simply because she was not there anymore and, by killing her, he had killed his love while his passion still ran in his veins. But he never gave a thought at the time to the fact that he had shed innocent blood and taken the life of a human being. The thought that his victim would have become the wife of another man was unbearable to him, so for a long time he felt that, in conscience, he could not have acted differently. True, the arrest of the servant weighed on him heavily, but the man's illness and sudden death released his conscience from that burden, for, he reasoned at the time, the man did not die from shock or fright caused by his arrest but from a cold he had contracted, probably on the night of the murder, after which he had been found sprawled dead drunk on the damp ground. As to the things he had taken from her room, he was not in the least bothered by them since he had not intended to steal them but had taken them only to divert suspicion from himself. Besides, the value of the items he had taken did not amount to much and, in order to allay his conscience completely in this respect, he soon afterward donated first an equivalent and then a considerably larger sum to the alms house that had just been founded in town. He did this just to appease his conscience and, strangely enough, he found that it was, indeed, appeased, and for quite some time.

At the same time he gave himself over feverishly to his work, took upon himself a particularly difficult and time-consuming assignment, to which he devoted all his time for a couple of years, and, being a man of strong will, he almost succeeded in forgetting what had happened, for, whenever he was somehow reminded of it, he made an effort to drive it from his mind. Then he went in for philanthropy on a large scale, donated an immense amount of money to charities in our town, became known in the capitals, and was elected to national charity committees in Moscow and in Petersburg.

In the end, however, he started brooding; he gradually became aware of the burden weighing on his conscience and then realized he was not strong enough to bear that burden. About that time he met a beautiful and sensible girl; he was attracted to her and soon married her, hoping that her company would put an end to his lonely brooding. He hoped that devoting himself to his new obligations toward his wife and future children would lift the old anxiety from him once and for all. But the marriage had just about the opposite effect. During the very first month, he became bothered by the thought of what would happen if his wife, who loved him, knew the truth. And, when she told him of her first pregnancy, he became very upset. "Giving a life after having taken a life," flashed through his mind. The child was born, and then more children. "How can I," he wondered, "love them, bring them up, and teach them about good and evil, when I have shed blood?" The children were beautiful, he longed to fondle them, but was prevented by the thought: "I have no right even to look into their innocent eyes because of what I am." And finally he became haunted by his victim, by the young life he had destroyed, by the blood crying out for justice. Dreadful dreams started to torment him. But, being a man of strong character, he bore his ordeal in silence for a long time. "I shall atone for my crime with my secret suffering," he thought hopefully. But his hope was vain, for the longer it lasted, the more excruciating was his ordeal. Although people were rather intimidated by him because of his stern and forbidding appearance, they respected him highly for his charitable work. Yet the more they respected him, the more painful it was for him. He told me that he often thought of killing himself. Then, instead, he conceived another idea, an idea that at first seemed quite impossible to him but that little by little became such an obsession that he could no longer dismiss it. What he wanted to do was to come out, face the people of the town, and announce publicly that he was a murderer. For three years he carried that idea within him, and carried it in many different ways in his dreams and musings. Finally, he became convinced that, by confessing his crime publicly, he would heal the wound in his soul and find peace forever. But at the same time he was gripped by terror: how could he make himself do it? Then something happened that, he felt, made it possible for him. That something was my duel.

"Looking at you, I decided to go through with it."

I stared at him in surprise.

"Why? How could a minor incident like that make you decide to take such a fateful step?" I cried, throwing up my hands in bewilderment.

"My decision has been ripening within me for three years," he told me, "and your duel has only provided the final impetus. Looking at you, I became envious," he added grimly.

"They may not even believe you," I said; "it's been fourteen years, after all."

"I have irrefutable proof," he said, "which I will present."

I wept then and put my arms around him and kissed him.

"Tell me, tell me," he said then, as if everything were suddenly up to me, "what about my wife and children? My wife may die of grief and the children, although they will not lose their birthright and their estate, will always be the children of a convict serving a life sentence. What a picture of their father they will have to carry in their hearts forever!"

I had nothing to say to that.

"And leaving them forever? Because I'll never come back, of course."

I sat there and whispered a prayer under my breath. I got up. I was frightened.

"So what do you say?" he asked, looking at me.

"Go," I said to him, "tell people what you did. Everything will pass and the truth alone will remain. Your children will understand when they grow up; they will appreciate the nobility of your great resolution."

He left, and he seemed to have really made up his mind then. But he came back to me; and for two weeks after that, he kept coming back every evening, still preparing himself, still unable to make himself go through with it. It was terribly hard on me too. One day, for instance, he came in and said with great fervor:

"I know it will be heaven for me the moment I confess. For fourteen years it has been hell. I want to suffer for what I have done. I will accept that suffering and I will begin to live. In the world you can go far under false pretenses, but lies will never bring you back to the fold. For, as things are now, I don't dare love my own children, let alone my fellow men. O Lord, I so hope that my children will understand the price I have paid in suffering for what I have done, and will not condemn me. God lies not in strength but in truth."

"Everybody will understand your act of expiation," I said, "and if they don't do so right away, they will understand later, because you are obeying not man-made laws but supreme truth and justice."

He left me then, looking reassured and calm, but the next day he appeared pale and irritated again and said sarcastically:

"Each time I come here, you stare at me with great curiosity and I can almost hear you thinking: 'He still hasn't done it!' Wait, don't be in such a hurry to despise me; it's not as easy as you imagine. In fact, I may still decide not to do it at all. For I am pretty sure that you won't denounce me in any case, or will you?"

I had never stared at him with curiosity; indeed, if anything, I was rather afraid to look into his face at all. I was in a state verging on exhaustion myself and my heart was full of sorrow. I did not sleep well, thinking of him at night.

"I have just left my wife," he went on. "Do you have any idea what the word 'wife' means? As I was leaving, my children called out to me: 'Come back soon, papa, and read us more from the *Children's Magazine!*' No, I see that you cannot begin to imagine what it all feels like. We learn nothing from our neighbor's afflictions."

His eyes flashed, the corners of his lips quivered. He brought his fist down on the table so hard that the things on it jumped. It was the first time I had seen this self-controlled man let himself go like this.

"Must I really do it?" he cried. "Is it really indispensable? Why, no one has been condemned for my crime, no one has been sentenced to hard labor because of me. You know it was of natural causes that the servant died. And I have already paid with my suffering for the blood I shed. Besides, they won't believe me, despite all the proofs I bring them. Must I really give myself up, even if I am willing to go on suffering all my life for the life I took? Can't I avoid hurting my wife and children? Would it be fair to them to drag them to their perdition along with me? Perhaps we have been wrong, both of us? What is the right course? And if there is a right course, do people know which it is? Will they recognize it? Will they respect it?"

I thought to myself: "My God—here he is, at such a moment, worrying about whether people will respect him . . ." And I suddenly felt such infinite pity for him that I believe I would willingly have shared his predicament if only it could have made things a bit easier for him. I saw that he was on the brink of madness. I was horrified by what I saw, because now it was no longer with my reason alone that I realized what his decision meant to him, but with my whole living being.

"Go on, you decide!" he shouted.

"Tell them," I whispered. My voice failed me, but I whispered the words firmly. I took the New Testament and made him read the Gospel of St. John, Chapter XII, Verse 24, which I had read just before he had come in: "Verily, verily I say unto you, except a corn of wheat fall into the ground and die, it abideth alone: but if it die, it bringeth forth much fruit."

"That's true," he said with a smile, a bitter smile, though. "It's quite incredible all the things that one comes across in that book. That makes it very convenient for thrusting under people's noses on all sorts of occasions. I wonder who really wrote all those things? Were they written by men?"

"The Holy Spirit wrote them," I said.

"It doesn't cost you much to pay lip service."

He smiled again, but now almost with hatred in his look.

I took the book out of his hand and opened it at another place: the Epistle to the Hebrews, Chapter X, Verse 31. I handed it to him.

"It is a fearful thing to fall into the hands of the living

God," he read and flung the book violently away. I saw that he was trembling.

"A frightening verse . . . Well, you certainly know how to pick them!" He got up.

"Good-by, then. Perhaps I won't be back again—see you in heaven. So, fourteen years ago I fell 'into the hands of the living God'—that's how those fourteen years are to be described. And tomorrow I'll beg those 'hands of the living God' to let me go . . ."

I felt like hugging and kissing him, but I didn't dare—his face was all twisted and his gaze was somber.

He walked out of the room. "My God," I thought, "the things this man will have to face now!" I hurried to the icon, went down on my knees, and wept before the image of the Mother of God, who so readily intercedes for us and comes to our rescue. I was still there, kneeling and praying, the tears rolling down my cheeks, when suddenly the door opened and there he was again. I was stunned to see him.

"Where have you been?" I asked him.

"I . . . I think I forgot something here," he said, "my handkerchief or something . . . But even if I didn't forget anything, let me sit down for a minute."

He took a chair and sat down. "You sit down too," he said, as I was standing in front of him. I did. So we sat there, both of us, for perhaps two whole minutes, he looking at me fixedly all the time. Suddenly, and I can still see the way he looked at that moment, half smiling, he got up, hugged me hard, and kissed me.

"Remember this, Zinovy," he said, "my coming back to you for a second time. I want you to remember this; do you hear, Zinovy?"

It was the first time he had ever called me by my Christian name.

He left. "Tomorrow . . ." I thought.

And so it was. I did not know then that the next day was his birthday. I had not been out at all recently, so no one could have told me. Every year on that day there was a great reception at his house attended by practically the whole town. This year too, it was the same.

And then he did it. Immediately after dinner, he stepped into the middle of the room with a sheet of paper in his hand. He explained that it was an official statement addressed to the highest local authorities and that, since those highest authorities were present there in his house, he would read the document aloud for everyone to hear. And, as everybody listened, he read a full account of his crime, without omitting a single detail.

"I cast myself out from the company of men, for I am a monster. But God has visited me now and I want to suffer for what I have done," were the final words of his statement.

Then he went and fetched all the evidence he had to prove his crime. He laid out on the table all the items he had preserved during those fourteen years: the gold ornaments he had taken from his victim's drawer to avert suspicion from himself, her cross and the locket he had removed from her neck after he had killed her, with the portrait of the man she loved inside it, her notebook and two letters—one from that man to her, announcing his imminent return, and the other her unfinished answer to it, which she had left on her desk, obviously intending to finish it and mail it the next morning. But why had he kept these two letters for fourteen years, instead of destroying them as incriminating evidence?

Although everyone present was entirely bewildered and horrified by his story, listening to it with immense curiosity, they all absolutely refused to accept what he said as true, and they looked at him as though he were a sick man. And, in a few days, almost everyone in town had decided that, indeed, the poor man had gone mad. Of course, the police and the legal authorities could not ignore the confession altogether and had to start a criminal investigation, but it was soon dropped on the grounds that even if the evidence presented—the letters and other articles—could be proved authentic, it would still not be sufficient for a conviction. She could simply have entrusted him with those things herself, since it was known that they had been acquainted.

Later I heard that the items presented as evidence were identified by the victim's friends and relatives and that there could be no doubt about their authenticity. But, again, nothing came of it for, five days later, the whole town learned that the wretched man had become seriously ill and that his life was in danger. What his sickness was I still cannot explain very well; some claimed that it was his heart, but then it was announced that, on his wife's insistence, a group of doctors had examined him and had discovered early symptoms of mental disorder.

I did not tell anything of what I knew to anybody, although many people were quick to question me; but when I tried to go and visit my friend, they would not let me near him. His wife especially was adamant.

"It is you who brought it on," she said. "He was always gloomy, but recently everybody noticed his strange excitement and the peculiarities in his behavior. The things you have been saying to him must have had something to do with it— he practically never left your house during the past month."

And it was not just his wife; soon everyone in town was blaming me for the whole business. "It's all your fault," they said to me. I did not answer them. In fact, I rejoiced inwardly, because I felt that God had taken mercy on that man, who had risen up against himself and had asked for the punishment he deserved. I did not believe at all in his insanity. Eventually they did let me in to see him. He had asked for me himself, insisting that he wanted to say good-by to me. When I saw him, I realized immediately that it was not a matter of days, but of hours. He was weak, his face was yellow, his hands trembled, and he breathed with difficulty. But there was joy in his eyes and deep serenity in his expression.

"It's done!" he told me. "I've been longing to see you all this time, Zinovy. Why didn't you come before?"

I did not want to tell him that they had not let me come near him.

"God has taken pity on me and is calling me. I know I am dying, but I feel happy and at peace with the world for the first time in many years. As soon as I had done what I had to do, it was heaven. I feel I have the right now to love and to kiss my children. No one believed me—my wife, the judges—no one. Nor will my children ever believe what I did. I see in this a sign of God's mercy to my children. When I die, my name will remain without stain for them. Now I feel the presence of God and my heart rejoices. I have done my duty."

He could not speak anymore; he was gasping for breath. He just pressed my hand and looked at me with radiant eyes. We were not allowed long together anyway, for his wife kept looking in every minute. Still, he did manage to whisper to me:

"Do you remember my coming back for the second time that night, around midnight, when I told you to remember my second visit? Shall I tell you why I came back? I came back to kill you."

I shuddered.

"After I left you the first time, I went out into the darkness and roamed the streets, a battle raging within me. And all of a sudden I hated you, hated you so much I couldn't stand it. 'He's the only one in my way,' I thought. 'He is my judge and, since he knows everything, I cannot avoid my ordeal as long as he exists.' It was not that I was afraid that you would denounce me to the authorities—that never even occurred to me. 'But how,' I thought, 'can I ever face him if I don't confess publicly now?' Even if you had been at the other end of the earth, the mere thought that you were alive and judging me would have been absolutely unbearable. I hated you as though you were the cause of it all, as though everything had happened through your fault. I went back to your house, remembering that I had seen a dagger lying on your table. I sat down and asked you to sit down and then, for more than a minute, I deliberated. If I had killed you, that murder would have doomed me anyway, even if I had not confessed my other crime. But that was not what I was thinking during that minute; it didn't even interest me. I only hated you so that every fiber in me yearned for vengeance. But God vanquished the devil in my heart. I want you to know, though, that you have never been so close to death."

A week later, he died. The whole town accompanied his coffin to the grave, where the Bishop delivered a moving oration. People spoke with deep sympathy of the terrible sickness that had cut short his life. And after the funeral everyone in town turned against me. People stopped receiving me altogether. Eventually, though, at first a few individuals and then more and more people came to believe that the confession he had made was true. Then they started coming to me and questioning me with great eagerness and curiosity, for people enjoy witnessing the fall and disgrace of the upright. But I would not answer them, and soon afterward, I left the town for good.

Five months later, by the grace of God, I embarked upon the true and righteous life and I bless the invisible finger that showed it to me. To this day I always mention in my prayers Mikhail, the servant of God, who suffered so much.

CHAPTER 3

Some Thoughts and Teachings
of the Elder Zosima

E. A Few Thoughts on the Russian Monk
and His Potential Role

Fathers and teachers, what is a monk? Nowadays this word is often pronounced with a sort of derision by the educated, and some even use it as a term of abuse. This attitude is growing worse all the time. It is, alas, absolutely true that, among monks, there are many parasites, gluttons, voluptuaries, and shameless beggars. And it is at them that educated people point when they say: "You are lazy, useless members of society, shameless beggars living off other people's labor." Yet there are so many meek, humble monks who yearn only for solitude and quietness, where they can abandon themselves to their ardent prayers. People seldom point out these monks; they mostly ignore them altogether, and they would be very surprised to hear that it is perhaps on these meek and humble monks, yearning for solitude and prayer, that the salvation of Russia may depend! For, indeed, they have been prepared in their quiet retreat "for an hour and a day, a month and a year." In their retreat, they faithfully preserve for us the pure and undefiled image of Christ, the purity of the divine truth as they have received it from the fathers of old, the apostles, and the martyrs. And when mankind's faith is shaken, the monks will hold up the image before the wavering world. That is a great thought. The star will rise in the East.

Is this that I think of the monk untrue and presumptuous? Look at the worldly, at those who set themselves above the people of God—have they not distorted the image of God and His truth? They have science, but science contains nothing that does not come through the senses. The spiritual world, the nobler side of man's being, has been rejected altogether, banned as it were triumphantly, perhaps even with hatred. The world has proclaimed freedom, now more loudly than ever; but what do we find in that freedom of theirs? Nothing but enslavement and suicide! The world says: "You have needs—satisfy them. You have as much right as the rich and the mighty. Don't hesitate to satisfy your needs; indeed, expand your needs and demand more." This is the worldly doctrine of today. And they believe that this is freedom. The result for the rich is isolation and suicide, for the poor, envy and murder; for while the poor have been handed all these rights, they have not been given the means to enjoy them. Some claim that the world is gradually becoming united, that it will grow into a brotherly community as distances shrink and ideas are transmitted through the air. Alas, you must not believe that men can be united in this way. To consider freedom as directly dependent on the number of man's requirements and the extent of their immediate satisfaction shows a twisted understanding of human nature, for such an interpretation only breeds in men a multitude of senseless, stupid desires and habits and endless preposterous inventions. People are more and more moved by envy now, by the desire to satisfy their material greed, and by vanity. Giving dinners, riding in private carriages, occupying high social positions, and having myriads of servants—these are considered so important by some that they devote their whole lives to acquiring them and sacrifice for their sake their love of their fellow men, and sometimes even kill themselves if they cannot obtain what they believe they must have. It is the same with those who are not rich. And, as to the poor, who cannot satisfy their needs at all, they just drown their envy of others in alcohol. But the way they are being aroused now, it will soon be blood rather than liquor on which they will get drunk. Now let me ask you: Do you really think that such men are free? One "champion of freedom" told me himself that when he was arrested and deprived of tobacco, the privation was so painful to him that he was on the verge of betraying his "cause," just to get something to smoke. And this was a man who said: "I am fighting for mankind!" What can such a man do, though—what is he good for, unless he acts on some sudden impulse? He will never be able to endure pain for the sake of his "cause." So it is not surprising that, instead of freedom, they lapse into slavery, that, instead of promoting unity and brotherhood, they encourage division and isolation, as my mysterious guest and teacher explained to me in my youth. That is why the idea of service to mankind and brotherly love has been dying out in the world; indeed, now it is often sneered at, for what can a man do who has become the slave of the innumerable needs and habits he has invented for himself? He lives in his separate little world and does not care about the great world outside. The result of all this is that, today, when more material goods have been accumulated than ever, there is less joy.

Now, the monastic life is quite a different matter. People may ridicule the vows of obedience, fasting, and prayer, yet these are the only way to attain true freedom. It is by discarding cumbersome and unnecessary demands, by subduing and disciplining selfish and conceited aspirations, by obedience, that the monk, with God's help, achieves spiritual freedom and thereby finds spiritual happiness. Who is more likely to conceive a great idea and serve it: the isolated rich man or the man *freed* from the tyranny of habits and material goods? The monk is sometimes reproached for his "isolation": "You have," they tell him, "isolated yourself behind the walls of your monastery; you are preoccupied only with saving yourself and forget the duty of serving mankind." It remains to be seen, however, who serves mankind better. For, in fact, it is not we who are isolated, but they. Besides, since ancient times, great leaders of men have come from our midst, and there is no reason why this cannot happen today. One day these meek and humble monks who fast and keep their vows of silence may go out and work for the great cause. For it is by her people that Russia will be saved. And if the common people live in isolation, we too should live in isolation. The people share our faith, and a leader without faith will never achieve anything in Russia, even if his feelings are sincere and he has the mind of a genius. That, you must remember. The people will rise up against the atheist and subdue him, and a unified Christian Russia will appear under the Russian Orthodox Church. So always think of the people and preserve the purity of their hearts. And educate them in your quiet retreats. That is your duty as monks, for the Russian people are a God-bearing people.

F. Of Masters and Servants and of Whether They Can Become Brothers in Spirit

Of course, there is sin among the common people too. Corruption is spreading visibly; every hour it is working its way down the social scale. Even among the people now, individuals become isolated more and more often, turn into greedy thrifty peasants and village usurers. Uncouth merchants, today, are full of social ambition and, ignorant as they are, try to appear educated by rudely scorning ancient traditions and turning in shame from the faith of their fathers. A merchant may be received by princes today, but he is really nothing but a corrupted peasant. People are rotted by liquor, but they cannot give it up. And there is so much cruelty within the family today—cruelty to women and children—and that, too, comes from drunkenness. I have seen the marks of this cruelty on the children working in factories. Some of them, hardly more than nine years old, are weak, sickly, round-shouldered, and already depraved. Stuffy workshops, clanging machines, day-long drudgery, foul language, and liquor and more liquor. Is that what this creature, still only a little child, needs? A child needs sunshine, he needs to play with other children, he needs someone to set him a good example, and above all he needs love, even if it is only a tiny drop of love . . . So let there be no more of this, monks, let there be no more brutalized children; rise up against it, preach against it, hasten to do so! But God will save Russia, for even if the uneducated man of the people is depraved and cannot abstain from his foul sins, he knows that his sins are cursed by God and that he is doing wrong when he sins. So our humble people still believe unwaveringly in the truth, still acknowledge God, and still shed fervent tears.

But this is not true of the upper classes. They want to organize themselves scientifically, to devise a system of justice based on pure reason, not on Christ, as before, and they have already declared that there is no such thing as crime and that there is no sin. And, from their point of view, they are right —for how can there be crime if God does not exist? In Europe, the masses are rising against the rich; their leaders are inciting them to blood and violence and are teaching them that theirs is a righteous anger. But "cursed be their anger because it is cruel." And God will save Russia as He has saved her many a time before. And her salvation will come from the common people, from their faith and their humility.

Fathers and teachers, preserve the faith of the common people! For this is not something I have imagined: I have been impressed throughout my life by the profound and genuine dignity inherent in our great people. I have seen it. I have witnessed it myself, and I have recognized it in the stench of sin, amidst the degradation caused by destitution.

Our people are not servile, despite two centuries of serfdom. They are free and independent in their ways, but without arrogance. They are neither vengeful nor envious. "You are important, rich, clever, and talented—so may God bless you. I honor you, but I remember that I, too, am a man. And by honoring you without envy, I show you my human dignity." Even if they do not actually say that (because they cannot yet express it), this is exactly how they behave, as I can bear witness, having seen and experienced it. And would you believe it?—the poorer and humbler a Russian man of the people is, the greater is that true grandeur in him, for the better-off among them, the avaricious peasants and the money-lenders, have already become corrupted. Much of the blame for this must be laid at our door, because we have neglected them and failed to see the danger. But God will save His people, because Russia is great in her humility! I dream of our future destiny and it seems to me that I can really see it already: it will come to pass that even the rich will be ashamed of their wealth before the poor, while the poor, seeing this humility, will understand it and grant them their advantages and respond with joy and love to the dignified shame of the rich. Believe me, that is where we are heading and that is how it will be in the end. Equality lies only in human moral dignity, and this will be understood only in our country. Let there be brothers first, then there will be brotherhood, and only then will there be a fair sharing of goods among brothers. We are preserving the image of Christ —may that image shine like a precious diamond over the world. It will be so and so be it!

Fathers and teachers, I would like now to tell you of a touching incident. During my wanderings I met my former orderly Afanasy, in the provincial town of K. I had not seen him for eight years. We met by chance on the market place. He recognized me and hurried over to me. It seemed he was so pleased that he almost embraced me.

"Is it really you, sir, is it? I can't believe my eyes!"

He took me home with him. He had been discharged from the army by that time, was married, and had two small children. He and his wife had a little stall at the market and that was how they made their living. They lived in a small room, but it was clean and sunny. He made me sit down, lighted the samovar, and sent someone to call his wife, as my visit apparently called for a special celebration. He brought his children to me.

"Bless them, Father," he said.

"Who am I to bless them?" I said. "I am just an ordinary,

humble monk, you know. But I will pray for them, I promise. And you, Afanasy, I have prayed for you every day ever since that time. It was thanks to you that it all turned out the way it did."

And I explained to him as best I could how it had all happened. And how do you think this simple man felt about it? He kept looking at me and could not imagine how I, a gentleman, his former officer, could be sitting with him in that attire. The very thought even made him cry.

"Why are you crying?" I said. "You should be happy for me. I will never forget you, because of what I have gained thanks to you, for my life is bright and happy now."

He did not say much, but just kept shaking his head, sighing, and looking at me tenderly.

"But what happened to the money you had?" he asked me at one point.

"I gave it to the monastery," I said. "We all live together there and share what we have."

When we had finished our tea, I got up and was about to say good-by to him, when he suddenly produced a half-ruble piece, saying: "This is for your monastery." And then he was pushing a second half ruble into my hand: "This one is for you, sir. It may come in useful sometime in your wanderings . . ."

I took that half ruble too, bowed to him and to his wife, and left, filled with gladness, and thinking as I went: "Here we are, the two of us, he in his home and I on the road, both probably sighing over our memories, yet smiling joyfully at the way God brought us together again, and both of us happy because of this meeting."

I have never seen him since. Once I had been his master and he my servant, but after we had exchanged that loving, brotherly embrace, our hearts were filled with a deep fervor, and a true communion of souls came into being. I have thought about it a great deal and have come to this conclusion: Why should it be so inconceivable for such a true and simple communion to exist some day among all Russian people? I myself believe that it will come to pass and that the time is near at hand.

And I will say this of servants too. When I was young, I often grew angry when the cook served me a meal that was too hot or my orderly brought me my boots not properly polished. But the words I had heard from my brother as a child came back to me. "What have I done to deserve to be

waited on? Why should another man serve me just because
he is poor and ignorant?" And I was very puzzled: why is it
that such simple, self-evident ideas take so long to occur to
us? Since the world cannot exist without servants, you must
see to it that your servant feels freer in spirit than if he were
not a servant. And why shouldn't I be my servant's servant?
Let him feel it. Let there be no pride on my part or distrust
on his. Why shouldn't my servant be like one of the family?
Why shouldn't I accept him as a member of it and rejoice
in doing so? This could be achieved even now, but it would
be only the beginning of the future great communion among
men when, instead of wanting to turn other human beings
into servants, a man will strive to become the servant of
others, as the Gospels teach us. Or do you think it is a vain
hope that one day man will find joy in noble deeds of light
and mercy, rather than in the coarse pleasures he indulges
in today—gluttony, fornication, ostentation, boasting, and envious vying with his neighbor? I am certain this is not a vain
hope and that the day will come soon. Some may laugh and
ask: "But when will it happen? Does it really look as though
it ever will?" I believe we shall achieve it with the help of
Christ. Why, there have been so many ideas in the history of
man, ideas that would have seemed inconceivable ten years
before, but that suddenly took root and flourished when, by
some mysterious process, the time was ripe for them—and
they quickly swept the earth. So it will be in Russia; our
nation will be like a star shining over the world and people
will say: "The stone that was rejected has now become the
cornerstone of our edifice."

And we in turn could ask those who scoff at us: "If we are
the victims of a delusion, what about you? When will you
build your own edifice and organize your life justly by
reason alone and without Christ?" For when they claim that
it is they who are working for the union of men, only the
credulous among them really believe it and, indeed, it is
surprising that they can be so credulous. The truth is that
they indulge in wishful thinking much more than we do. In
trying to bring about a just society without Christ, they will
end up by flooding the world with blood, for blood cries out
for more blood and he who lives by the sword shall perish
by the sword. And if it were not for Christ's solemn promise,
they would annihilate one another down to the last two men
on earth. Then, in their pride, even these two would be

unable to restrain each other and the last man would destroy the last but one, and then kill himself. That is how it would end were it not for Christ's solemn promise that, for the sake of the meek and the humble, it will never happen.

Soon after my duel, still wearing my officer's uniform, I spoke in various houses in town about my views on servants. I remember the surprise my words caused among the society people. "What do you expect us to do—have the butler relax in an armchair while we serve him his tea?" And I remember answering them: "Well, why not? You could at least do it from time to time." They all laughed. Their question had not been serious, of course, and the answer I gave was rather vague, but I still believe there was some truth in it.

G. Of Prayer, Love, and Ties with Other Worlds

Do not forget to pray, my boy. If your prayers are truly sincere, every day a new fervor will appear, a new thought of which you were unaware before, and that will give you new strength. You will understand then that prayer is education. Remember this, too. Repeat to yourself every day and as often as you can: "O Lord, have mercy on all those who will appear before You today." For every hour, every second, thousands of men leave this world and their souls appear before the Lord, and no one knows how many of them leave this earth in isolation, sadness, and anguish, with no one to take pity on them or even care whether they live or die. And so your prayer for such a man will rise to the Lord from the other end of the earth, although he may never have heard of you or you of him. But his soul, as it stands trembling before the Lord, will be cheered and gladdened to learn that there is someone on earth who loves him. And the Lord's mercy will be even greater to both of you, for, however great your pity for the man, God's pity will be much greater, for He is infinitely more merciful and more loving than you are. And God will forgive him for your sake.

Brothers, do not fear man's sins. Love man in his sin too, for such love resembles God's love, the highest possible form of love on earth. Love God's creation, love every atom of it separately, and love it also as a whole; love every green leaf, every ray of God's light; love the animals and the plants and love every inanimate object. If you come to love all things, you will perceive God's mystery inherent in all things; once you have perceived it, you will understand it better and better every day. And finally you will love the whole world with a total, universal love.

Love the animals: God has given them the beginnings of thought and untroubled joy. So do not disturb their joy, do not torment them, do not deprive them of their well-being, do not work against God's intent. Man, do not pride yourself on your superiority to the animals, for they are without sin, while you, with all your greatness, you defile the earth wherever you appear and leave an ignoble trail behind you— and that is true, alas, for almost every one of us!

Above all, love little children, for they are sinless, like little angels, and they are there to arouse our tenderness, to purify our hearts, and in a sense to guide us. Woe to the man who offends a small child! It was Father Anfim who taught me to love children. During our wanderings, this dear, silent man would buy gingerbread and candy with the coppers he received as alms, and give them to the children we came across, for he could not pass a child without his heart trembling with tenderness—that is the sort of man he is.

There will be moments when you will feel perplexed, especially in the presence of human sin. You will ask yourself: "Must I combat it by force or try to overcome it by humble love?" Always choose humble love, always. Once you have chosen it, you will always have what you need to conquer the whole world. Loving humility is a powerful force, the most powerful, and there is nothing in the world to approach it.

Every day, every hour, every moment, examine yourself closely and see that your appearance is seemly. You may, for instance, pass a small child; your face may be angry, you may be uttering wicked words, and there may be rage in your heart; you may not even notice the child, but as long as the child sees you in that state, that unseemly and ugly picture may become engraved in his innocent little heart. So, without knowing it yourself, you may thus have sown an evil seed, which perhaps will sprout within the child, and all simply because you failed to control yourself before the child, because you failed to cultivate within yourself a considerate and active love for others. Brothers, love is a teacher, but a hard one to obtain: learning to love is hard and we pay dearly for it. It takes hard work and a long apprenticeship, for it is not just for a moment that we must learn to love, but forever. In anyone, even the wicked, love can be kindled by chance.

My brother, a dying youth, asked the birds to forgive him. That may sound absurd, but when you think of it, it makes sense. For everything is like the ocean, all things flow and are indirectly linked together, and if you push here, something will move at the other end of the world. It may be madness to beg the birds for forgiveness, but things would be easier for the birds, for the child, and for every animal if you were nobler than you are—yes, they would be easier, even if only by a little. Understand that everything is like the ocean. Then, consumed by eternal love, you will pray to the birds, too. In a state of fervor you will pray them to forgive you your sins. And you must treasure that fervor, absurd though it may seem to others.

My friends, pray to God for joy. Be joyful like children, like the birds. Do not be discouraged in your efforts by men's sins; do not fear that they will obliterate your work and prevent its fulfillment; do not say, "Sin, wickedness, and bad environment are too much for us—we are alone and helpless against them, and the surrounding evil will not allow us to accomplish our good works." Rid yourselves of that despair, children! There is one way for you to overcome these obstacles: take firm hold of yourselves and make yourselves answerable for all men's sins. This is also the truth, friends! For as soon as a man sincerely accepts the idea that he is answerable for the sins of all men, he will realize that that is, indeed, the truth, that he is answerable for everybody and everything. But if you seek excuses for your idleness and impotence by blaming other people, you will end up bloated with Satan's pride and murmuring against God. And this is what I think of Satan's pride: it is difficult for us on earth to perceive it and so we readily slip into error, become contaminated by it, and then delude ourselves that we are performing great and admirable deeds. Besides, there are many human emotions and twists in human nature that men on earth are still unable to understand. But do not be tempted and do not try to use this ignorance as an excuse for yourself, for the Eternal Judge will only call you to account for what you can understand, not for what you cannot, and by then you will see everything in the true light and you will not protest.

But while we are on earth, we grope almost as though in the dark and, but for the precious image of Christ before us, we would lose our way completely and perish, just as men did during the flood. Much is hidden from us on earth but, as compensation, we have been given a mysterious, sacred sense of a living bond with another world, with a lofty and superior world; and, indeed, the roots of our thoughts and feelings are not in the earth but in other worlds. That is why the philosophers say it is impossible for us on earth to grasp the essence of things. God took the seeds of other worlds and sowed them on this earth and they sprouted in His garden; everything that could grow, did. And all that has grown remains alive and lives by its awareness of its ties to other, mysterious worlds, and if that awareness weakens or dies in you, then all that has grown within you will also die. And you will become indifferent to life, will even come to hate it. That is what I believe.

H. Can a Man Judge His Fellow Men? Of Faith to the End

Above all, remember that you cannot be anyone's judge. No man on earth can judge a criminal until he understands that he himself is just as guilty as the man standing before him and that he may be more responsible than anyone else for the crime. Only when he has understood this can he become a judge. Absurd though it may sound, this is the truth. For it is possible that, if I myself had been upright, this man would not be standing before me accused of a crime. If you can accept the responsibility for the crime committed by the man standing before you, whom you are judging in your heart, then take the crime upon yourself and pay for it with your suffering and let the accused walk away without reproach. And even if the law itself makes you his judge, you must still endeavor to act in that spirit, for when he leaves he will condemn himself more severely than you could have. Even if he walks away unmoved by your embrace, laughing at you, do not let it deter you; it only means that his time has not yet come—and it will come in due course. And if it does not come, it is no matter either, for if not he, then someone else will understand and answer for him, condemn himself and suffer in his place. And justice will be done. Believe that, never doubt it, for therein lies the hope and the faith of the saints.

Attend tirelessly to good works. If, before going to sleep at night, you remember something you have not done, rise at once and do it. If you are surrounded by wicked, ruthless people who will not listen to you, go down on your knees and beg them to forgive you, for if they do not listen to you, it is through your own fault. And if these evil men still refuse to hear your words, serve them in silence and humility and never abandon hope. And if they should all turn against you and drive you away by force, prostrate yourself on the ground when you are all alone, kiss it, and wet it with your tears, and the earth will bring forth fruit from your tears, even if no one sees or hears you in your solitary retreat.

Have faith to the end. Even if everyone else on earth goes astray, give your life to your faith and keep praising the Lord, even if you are the last of the faithful left on earth. And if you find another being who has preserved his faith, there will be a world of living love, for you will fall into each other's arms and praise the name of the Lord with fervor. For in the two of you, His truth will have been fulfilled.

If you should sin yourself and be weighed down until death by your sins or by a single sinful act committed spontaneously, rejoice for the righteous and be happy, for, although you have sinned, they have not.

If the evil deeds of men sadden you too greatly and arouse in you an anger you cannot overcome and fill you with the desire to wreak vengeance on the evil-doers—fear this feeling most of all, and at once go and seek suffering for yourself, because you too are responsible for the evil deeds of all men. Bear that ordeal and your desire for revenge will be quenched when you understand that you were guilty yourself for having failed to show the light to the wicked, as a man without sin could. For if you had done so, you would have lighted the path for the sinful, and the criminal might not have committed his crime. And even if you lighted his way but still did not manage to save the evil-doer, keep the faith, never doubt the power of the heavenly light, and have faith that if they are not saved now, they will be saved later. And if they are not saved later either, their children will be saved, for, although you yourself may be dead by then, the light you shed will remain. The righteous man passes away, but his light remains. Men are always saved, even if only after the death of the one who saves them. The human race does not accept its prophets and its prophets are slain, but men love their martyrs and honor those who have been slain.

What you do, do for the whole world, and work for its future. Never seek reward, for you have been greatly rewarded already on this earth with the spiritual joy that is reserved for the righteous.

Fear not the mighty and the rich, but be always wise and dignified. Learn how to know the right measure and recognize the right time. When you find yourself alone, pray. Learn to enjoy prostrating yourself and kissing the earth. Kiss it tirelessly, love it insatiably, love all men and all things, seek that fervor and ecstasy of love. Water the earth with tears of joy and love those tears. And do not be ashamed of these raptures, treasure them: they are a special gift of God that He has not given to many—only to the elect few.

I. Of Hell and Hell Fire, a Mystical Discourse

Fathers and teachers, what is hell? I think it is the suffering of one who can no longer love. Once, in the infinity of existence unmeasurable by time or space, a spiritual creature, upon its appearance on earth, is given the power to say: "I am and I love." Once, and only for a moment, is that creature given the knowledge of active, *living* love, and this is why that creature was given life on earth, and with it, time and space. And what happens? The privileged creature rejects that priceless gift, fails to appreciate it, does not even like it, sneers at it, and remains unmoved. When such a creature leaves the earth, sees Abraham, and talks with him as in the parable about Lazarus and the rich man—when he is already in sight of heaven and is allowed into the presence of the Lord, he is filled with suffering at the thought that he will appear before the Lord never having loved and will be brought into the presence of those who have loved him but whose love he has scorned. For now he sees clearly and says to himself: "I now have the knowledge and I am yearning for love; but now that my earthly life is over, there can be no self-abnegation, no sacrifice in love, and Abraham will not come to me again and bring me even a tiny drop of living water (that is, the gift of life on earth, the active life I possessed before); since I will never again be given life and time, I will never be able to quench the fiery thirst for love that burns in me, because I scorned love while I was on earth. I would be glad to give my life for the love of others, but it is too late now because I no longer have the life to sacrifice, and there is a chasm between that life and this existence."

Men speak of hell fire as a physical fire. I will not look into this mystery, for I am afraid. But I believe that if the fire was physical, sinners would be glad, for if they were subjected to a physical ordeal, they would forget for a brief moment the infinitely more fearful spiritual torment. But it is impossible for them to escape that spiritual torment because it is within, not outside, them. And even if they could escape it, they would, I believe, become even more wretched. For even if the righteous in heaven forgave them at the sight of their sufferings and, in their infinite love, called them to join them in heaven, they would only further exasperate their suffering, for that would simply intensify their burning thirst to give the responsive, active, and grateful love which was now beyond their power forever. And here I would like to suggest, in all humility, that perhaps this very awareness of the impossibility of loving might lead to an eventual alleviation of the sinners' torments, for, by accepting the love of the righteous along with the impossibility of their responding to it, through the resignation and humility which would result from that acceptance, they might come to experience a feeling resembling the active love they neglected on earth . . . I am sorry, my friends and brothers, that I cannot express this more clearly.

But woe unto those who have laid hands upon themselves on earth, woe betide the suicides! For I do not believe there can be anyone more wretched than they. They say that it is a sin to pray to God for them and the Church appears to deny them. But, deep down, in the secret recesses of my heart, I feel that for them, too, we may pray. Christ will never hold it against us if we act out of love. I have prayed for them inwardly all my life; I confess to you, fathers and teachers, that I prayed for them today, too.

Oh, even in hell there are some who remain proud and fierce, even though they have acquired knowledge beyond doubt and have seen the truth that cannot be rejected. Some frightening ones surrender themselves entirely to Satan and his spirit of pride. For them, hell is voluntary and unending. These have chosen by their own free will to suffer. For they have cursed themselves by cursing God and life. They feed on their evil pride, which is the same as if a starving man in the desert were to start sucking the blood from his own veins. But they will never be satisfied until the end of time, for they refuse to be forgiven and they curse God, when He calls them to Him. They cannot behold the living God without hatred. They wish God did not exist. They demand of God that He destroy Himself as well as all His creation. And they shall burn in the fire of their own rage forever and ever, always yearning for death and non-existence. But they shall not find death . . .

Here Alexei Karamazov's manuscript ends. I repeat, it is incomplete and fragmentary. For instance, the biographical information covers only the elder's early youth. His views and teachings, uttered at different times and prompted by different circumstances, are gathered and arranged into what is, perhaps, a meaningful whole. It is impossible to determine how much of this the elder actually said in the last hours of his life, but the spirit of what he said can be gleaned from those earlier pronouncements of his which Alexei Karamazov mentions in his manuscript.

The elder's death came quite unexpectedly. For, although those who had gathered around him that evening knew that death was near, they never thought it would be so sudden. Indeed, as I mentioned earlier, seeing him so cheerful and talkative, they felt there was a noticeable improvement in his health, even if it was only for a short time. Even five minutes before the end, as they later reported with wonderment, none of them suspected anything. He suddenly felt an acute pain in his chest, turned pale, and pressed his hand to his heart. They all rose from their seats and rushed to him. Although in pain, he was still smiling at them. He slipped slowly from his arm-chair to the floor, knelt, bowed his head to the ground, spread his arms, and, apparently in a state of ecstasy, praying and kissing the ground—as he had taught others to do—quietly and joyfully, he gave up his soul to God.

The news of Zosima's death immediately spread through the hermitage and reached the monastery. The departed's closest friends, as well as those whose position and monastic rank made it their duty, began to lay out the body according to the ancient rites, and all the monks gathered in the monastery church. Before daybreak, it was said later, the news of the death had reached town. By morning, the whole town was talking of it and throngs of townspeople flowed toward the monastery. We shall say more of this in the next book, but for now we shall only warn the reader in advance that, before that day was over, something completely unexpected happened. It made such a strange, bewildering, and puzzling impression, both in the monastery and in town, that many people still remember it to this day.

PART THREE

BOOK VII

ALYOSHA

CHAPTER 1

The Smell of Decay

The body of the deceased monk-priest Father Zosima was prepared for burial in conformity with the established ritual. As is well known, the bodies of monks and hermits are not washed after death. The *Great Prayer Book* says: "Whenever a monk departs in the Lord, a specially designated monk must make the sign of the cross with a sponge on the forehead, the chest, the hands, the feet, and the knees of the deceased, rinse the body with warm water, and do nothing more."

Father Paisii performed these rituals and, after sponging the body, clothed it in monastic garb and wrapped it in a cloak which, as prescribed, he slit slightly so as to wrap it crosswise around the body. On the head, he put a cowl bearing an orthodox cross. The cowl was left open, but the face was covered by a black veil. An icon of the Saviour was placed in the dead man's hands. Thus arrayed, the body was placed toward morning in a coffin that had been prepared long in advance. The coffin was to be left in the elder's cell— the larger room where he used to receive his visitors. In accordance with the rule, the deceased being a monk-priest and an ascetic, the Gospel rather than the Psalter was to be read over his body by monks who were ordained priests like himself.

After the requiem service, Father Joseph began the reading. Father Paisii, who wished to follow him and to continue reading over the body all day and throughout the following night, was greatly agitated, just then, and was conferring feverishly with the prior of the hermitage. For a strange, unheard of—one might even say unseemly—excitement and impatient expectation were increasingly evident among the monks, among the laymen in the inns around the monastery, and among the throngs of people arriving from town. The prior and Father Paisii tried hard to calm the fidgety crowds.

By the time the sun had fully risen, some townspeople had arrived, bringing with them the sick, in particular, sick children. They had obviously been waiting for just that moment in the belief that the healing powers of the dead man would at once become effective. Now it became apparent how certain everyone in town had been that Father Zosima was a great and indisputable saint. And it was not, by any means, only the uneducated who believed it.

This great expectation sweeping the faithful, displayed with such haste, so openly, with even a suggestion of demanding impatience about it, struck Father Paisii as a clear temptation to sin. He had foreseen that something of the sort would happen after Zosima's death, but this exceeded all his anticipations. He now started to rebuke those of the monks who shared the general excitement:

"Your impatient expectation of something miraculous," he told them, "is a mark of levity, which may be excusable in a layman but is most unseemly in a monk."

But his words had little effect on them. Father Paisii was aware of this and it worried him, although deep down he himself—if we are to be completely truthful about it—despite all his indignation at the impatient expectations of others, which he considered vain and irresponsible, was waiting for something, just as the excited monks were, as he had to admit to himself. Nevertheless, some of those he came across that day made a very unpleasant impression on him and filled him with uneasy forebodings.

Among the crowd in the dead man's cell, he noticed with a shudder of revulsion—for which he at once rebuked himself—such people as Rakitin and the visiting monk from distant Obdorsk, who was still at the monastery. Somehow Father Paisii was particularly suspicious of these two men, although they were not, by any means, the only ones he looked upon with distrust. The Obdorsk monk's excitement stood out even amidst the excited crowd. He scampered about, asking questions, eavesdropping on conversations, whispering mysteriously. He looked impatient, annoyed as it were, as if something that was about to happen was being unduly delayed. As to Rakitin, it turned out later that he was in the hermitage at the special request of Mrs. Khokhlakov. That kindly but distracted lady, hearing of the elder's death upon awakening that morning, had been seized by such violent curiosity that she had at once delegated Rakitin to observe everything for her at the hermitage (since she could not be admitted herself) and to send her a "complete" written report every half hour or so. She considered Rakitin a devout and deeply religious young man, for he was very good at creating whatever impression he wanted in people, if he thought it was to his advantage.

It was a bright, clear day and many of the visitors crowded in among the hermitage graves, which were scattered all over the grounds, although more thickly concentrated around the church. Walking around the hermitage, it suddenly occurred to Father Paisii that he had not seen Alyosha since the night before. At the moment he thought of him, however, he caught sight of him in a faraway corner of the hermitage, sitting on the ancient gravestone of a monk who had been renowned for his devotion. Alyosha sat facing the wall. He seemed to be making himself as inconspicuous as possible behind the gravestone. Father Paisii went over to him and saw that Alyosha was weeping bitterly, his hands covering his face. He was weeping noiselessly, but his sobs shook his whole body. Father Paisii stood over him in silence for a while.

"Come, son, that's enough, my boy," he said sympathetically. "Why, you should be glad instead of crying. Don't you know that this is the greatest of his days? Just remember where he is at this very moment, just think of it!"

Alyosha uncovered his face, which was swollen from crying, like a child's face, and looked up at Father Paisii. But he at once turned away and, without saying a word, quickly put his hands over his face again.

"Well, I suppose that's how it is," Paisii said thoughtfully. "All right, go ahead, weep if you must. Christ has sent you these tears . . ."

As he walked away, feeling a great tenderness for the boy, he thought: "Your warm tears will bring you peace and will gladden the soul of your dear departed." In fact, he had left Alyosha so abruptly because he had felt that he would be unable to control his own tears much longer if he stayed with him.

Meanwhile the requiem mass and the monastery service for the departed were performed in due course. Father Joseph again read the Gospels by the coffin and Father Paisii once more took over from him. But then, just before 3 p.m., something happened. This was the completely unexpected thing to which I alluded at the end of the preceding chapter. It was so contrary to the general hopes and expectations that, as I said before, every last detail of it is remembered to this day by everyone in our town and throughout our district. At this point I would like to say for myself personally that it makes me quite sick when I think of all the commotion caused by that phenomenon, which, though it was unpleasant and unsavory, was at the same time unimportant and quite natural. I would have left it out of my narrative altogether had it not strongly affected my principal hero—or rather my future principal hero—Alyosha, bringing him to a turning point and giving him a violent shock, but as a final result strengthening his resolution to pursue his goal to the end.

But now, back to the story. When before daybreak the elder's body had been made ready for burial, laid out in the coffin, and taken into what used to be his reception room, someone had wondered aloud whether the windows should not be opened. The question, asked in a casual tone, remained unanswered and would have passed unnoticed had not some of the people present been struck by the very absurdity of its implication—that the body of such a saint might give off a smell of decay. Such thoughtlessness, such a flagrant lack of faith, was felt to be pitiful, not to say ridiculous. Indeed, everyone expected just the opposite to happen.

But shortly after midday, those going in and out became silently aware of something. They were obviously afraid to remark upon it aloud to others. By three in the afternoon, though, it became so clear and unmistakable that the news spread at once through the hermitage, was caught up by all the visitors there, reached the monastery, causing great amazement among the monks, and finally swept the town, stirring tremendous excitement among believers and unbelievers alike. The unbelievers, of course, were delighted, although some of the believers were even more delighted than the unbelievers themselves, because "men enjoy witnessing the fall and disgrace of the upright," as the elder himself had said in one of his discourses.

The fact was that a slight whiff of decay from the coffin became more and more perceptible and by three in the afternoon the smell had become quite distinct, and it continued to increase. Not in the living memory of our monastery had there been such a disgraceful display of sinful and unrestrained behavior among the monks as there was immediately after this fact had become known. Later, the most reasonable of our monks could not remember the events of that day without horror and amazement, wondering how the public scandal could have reached such incredible proportions. For, of course, monks of well-established righteousness and God-fearing elders had died before and the smell of decomposition had come from their humble coffins too, just as it comes from all corpses. But that had never provoked any such disgraceful display or, for that matter, had it ever stirred up any undue excitement. Of course, there had also been some monks whose memory had been preserved in our monastery and whose remains, according to belief, had never been touched by decay. This fact was treasured with sacred fervor by the monks as a beautiful and miraculous pledge of an even greater sanctity for the monastery's tombs in the future, if, by the grace of God, that time should come. One such monk, Father Job, a celebrated ascetic, famous for his feats of fasting and his long unbroken silences, whose memory was greatly cherished, had died at the beginning of the nineteenth century at the age of a hundred and five. His grave was always shown with great veneration to visitors and mysterious hints were made about certain great hopes the monastery nurtured in connection with it (this, by the way, was the grave on which Father Paisii had found Alyosha sitting that morning). As well as this saint of long ago, the monks also greatly revered the memory of another famed priest-monk, who had died much more recently. This was Father Varsonofy, whom Father Zosima had succeeded as the monastery's elder and whom all the visiting monks and pilgrims had considered almost a holy fool. These two saintly men, tradition had it, had lain in their coffins just as though they were alive and had been buried without showing any signs of decay whatever. Indeed, they had smiled in their coffins. Some even insisted that their bodies had given off a fragrance of flowers.

However, even such glorious memories still hardly account for the thoughtless, preposterous, and spiteful demonstrations that took place by Father Zosima's coffin. For my part, I think that there was much more to it and that there were other reasons for what happened—among these, the ancient, deep-rooted hostility toward the institution of elders, which was openly considered a harmful innovation by many outside the monastery, and also secretly thought to be so by a number of monks inside. There was also, it goes without saying, envy of the saintliness that had been so insistently attributed to Zosima during his lifetime that, indeed, one was not even allowed to question it. For, although Father Zosima had won over followers by his love rather than by miracles and had surrounded himself with what became a sort of world of love and affec-

tion, that very fact also made some people envious of him
and many of these eventually became his bitter enemies, both
openly and secretly, both within the monastery and without.
He had never harmed anyone, but people nevertheless somehow felt resentful and asked: "Why should this man be considered such a saint?" And because it was repeated again and
again, this question eventually generated an insatiable hatred
for him. That is why, I believe, when many people noticed
the smell of decay coming from his dead body, so soon moreover (less than a day) after his death, they were delighted
beyond all measure. And this is also why some of the elder's
most devoted and still loyal disciples felt almost personally
offended by this occurrence.

The whole affair developed as follows.

Once the decay had been noticed, monks kept hurrying in
and out of the cell, and it was quite obvious why they came.
They would come in, stand about for a moment, then leave
again, to confirm the news to a group of others waiting outside. Of these, some would just gloomily shake their heads,
while others did not even bother to hide the joy that gleamed
in their malevolent eyes. It was strange that no one felt outraged by their attitude, that no one protested against it, for,
after all, most of the monks had been devoted to the elder.
It was apparently the will of God that, this time, the minority
should prevail for a while. And soon lay observers, mostly
educated people, also came to find out what was happening.
Of the common people, very few came into the cell, although
many gathered at the gates of the hermitage. It is a fact that
the flow of lay visitors visibly increased after 3 p.m. and
there is no doubt that this increase was due to the shocking
news. People who would never have come that day, who,
indeed, had not planned to come at all, were now there,
among them some extremely important and highly placed
people. Decorum was still maintained, however, and Father
Paisii, with a stern expression on his face, kept reading from
the Gospels in a firm, clear voice, as if he noticed nothing,
although he had been perfectly aware from the beginning
that something was going on. In the end, however, these
people's words reached his ears too, words uttered at first in
hushed tones, then gradually louder as the visitors grew
bolder.

"It just goes to show that God's judgment is different from
that of men," Father Paisii suddenly heard someone say.

The man who was the first to say this aloud was a middle-aged civil servant from the town, a pious man by reputation. And he had only stated aloud an idea that the monks had been whispering into each other's ears for quite some time. These words of condemnation had long been in the air and the worst of it was that every minute the note of triumph in the tone in which they were uttered became more and more obvious. And soon even decorum began to give way, for many evidently felt that there was no longer any need for discretion now.

"It's strange, though, that *this* should have happened to him," some monks said, at first pretending to be sad about it. "Why, he was so small and thin—nothing but skin and bones —it's even hard to imagine where the smell could be coming from."

"It must be a special sign from heaven then," others chimed in eagerly, and their opinion was accepted unquestionably when they explained that even an ordinary sinner's body does not usually start to decay until about twenty-four hours after death, whereas in this case it had started uncannily soon, and that was also against the laws of nature and therefore must be seen as the finger of God! "God wants to warn us," they said, and to many this argument seemed irrefutable. Father Joseph, the gentle monk-librarian and one of the closest friends of the deceased, tried to argue with some of these ill-wishers. He told them that the basis of their judgment was not necessarily true, that it was not a dogma of the Orthodox Church that the body of the righteous never decays, that it was only a belief held by some, that, indeed, in the most strictly Orthodox countries, on Mount Athos, for example, they attached no particular importance to decay and, to them, an absence of decay was not as important a sign of the deceased's saintliness as, for instance, the color of his bones after the body had been buried for several years and had rotted in its grave.

"If the bones are yellow, like wax, it is a most important sign that the Lord has glorified the deceased; if they are black instead, it shows that the Lord has deemed him unworthy of glory," Father Joseph explained, adding: "That is what they believe on Mount Athos, a famed and holy place where Orthodox teachings have been preserved in the greatest purity since the most ancient times."

But the gentle Father Joseph's words were wasted on them and even met with sarcastic rejoinders. "That's all hair-splitting and innovation," the monks came back at him. "Our own

ancient ways are good enough for us," some said. "Why must
we pick up innovations? There are too many of them," others
answered Father Joseph. "No use listening to him!" chimed
in still others. "We have at least as many holy fathers as they
do. Besides, they are sitting there under the Turks and have
lost touch with many things, even their orthodoxy is no longer
pure: they have even given up church bells nowadays," the
most sarcastic of them all concluded.

Father Joseph walked away from them filled with a sadness
that was the greater because he felt he had not defended his
views strongly enough, as if he himself had not been entirely
convinced of what he had said. He felt that something unseemly was afoot and that disobedience itself loomed behind
it. Gradually all the reasonable voices were silenced, as Father
Joseph's had been. And somehow it happened that all those
who had loved the departed elder and had obediently and
devotedly accepted the institution of elders now seemed terribly afraid of something. When they met they only dared
exchange timid and fleeting glances. At the same time, the
enemies of that institution walked about with their heads
raised proudly.

"When Father Varsonofy died, not only was there no smell
of decay, there was even a decided aroma of flowers from his
body," they repeated with malicious insistence, "but it was
not because he had been an elder that he deserved it, but
because he was a righteous man."

Then some began to criticize openly the recently deceased
elder, and even to make accusations against him.

"His teachings were false," some confused monks said.
"He taught that life was a great joy and not tearful resignation."

"His interpretation was too modern," others, even more
confused, joined in. "He didn't believe in actual physical fire
in hell."

"He didn't observe the fasts very strictly," some of the
envious said. "He indulged in sweet things; he liked to have
his tea with the cherry jam that was sent him by rich ladies.
Is that right for an ascetic?"

"He sat in pride and fancied himself a saint," the most
spiteful said cruelly; "people knelt and prostrated themselves
before him and he accepted it as normal, as his due."

"He abused the sacrament of confession," came the accusing angry whispers of the most hardened opponents of the
institution of elders, who counted among them some of the

oldest monks, the strictest in their devotions, great fasters, famed for their long periods of silence, some of whom, indeed, had not spoken since long before Father Zosima's death and who had now suddenly unsealed their lips. And that made even greater the effect of their words upon the younger monks, whose ideas were not yet settled.

The visiting monk from the St. Sylvester Monastery of Obdorsk listened intently to all this talk and kept sighing and repeating to himself: "Well, I see now how right Father Ferapont was in what he said yesterday." Then he saw Father Ferapont approaching.

It was as though Father Ferapont had left his retreat just in order to increase the confusion.

As I noted earlier, Father Ferapont left his wooden hut behind the apiary only on very rare occasions. He even appeared very rarely in church, and this was tolerated in his case because he was considered a simple holy fool, not bound by the monastery rules. In actual fact, they had no choice but to grant him this dispensation because they could not very well impose their rules on a monk who fasted constantly, kept his vow of silence, and often prayed day and night without rest (he would even fall asleep on his knees). "Why should a monk who is holier than any of us and who imposes even stricter rules upon himself be subject to the official regulations?" the monks would have objected. "As to his church attendance, well, he knows best himself when he should attend services." It was probably to avoid such remarks and comments that Father Ferapont was allowed to do as he pleased. Everyone in the monastery was aware that Father Ferapont bore no love whatever for Father Zosima. And now the news had reached him in his hut that "God's judgment proved to be different from that of men," and "God has even overruled natural law to stress it." It must be assumed that one of the first to announce the news to him was the Obdorsk monk, who had been to see him the day before and then had left in such a state of terror. As was also mentioned earlier, although Father Paisii remained constantly by the coffin reading the Gospels and so could not see or hear what was going on, he was nevertheless fully aware of the essentials, for he knew the monastery all too well. He was not worried. He was prepared to face whatever might happen, and to face it fearlessly, as he watched the general agitation, already anticipating the outcome.

Suddenly there was a loud noise that could not be ignored. The door of the cell was flung open wide and Father Ferapont appeared. Behind him could be seen a whole crowd of monks who had accompanied him, and even some laymen too. The others, however, did not enter the cell. They remained outside, waiting for Father Ferapont to say or do something, for they suspected, and, indeed, despite their irreverent behavior, with some apprehension, that Father Ferapont had not come there for nothing.

As Father Ferapont stopped in the doorway and raised his hands, there appeared, under his right arm, the curious little eyes of the Obdorsk visitor, who at the last moment had not been able to resist the temptation and had followed Father Ferapont into the cell, while the others, on the contrary, had pressed back in sudden fear when the door was so brutally flung open.

Raising his arms over his head, Father Ferapont roared: "Casting out, I cast out!"

Then, describing a full circle, he made the sign of the cross eight times in succession, once on each wall and once in each corner. Those who had followed him understood his gesture at once, for they knew that he always did this whenever he entered a room and that he would never sit down anywhere or utter one word until he had driven out the unholy spirits.

"Satan, get thee hence; Satan, get thee hence," he said each time he made the sign of the cross. "Casting out, I cast out!" he roared again when he had finished his ritual.

He wore his coarse cassock with a rope around the waist. His hemp shirt was open at the neck, showing his chest covered with gray hair. He was barefoot. When he waved his arms, the heavy chains he wore under his cassock clanked.

Father Paisii interrupted his reading, stepped forward, faced him, and waited.

"What do you want here, worthy father?" he asked after a while, looking sternly at Father Ferapont. "Why do you disrupt peace and order and lead astray the meek flock?"

"What do I want here? Is that what you are asking me, you whose faith is so weak?" Father Ferapont shouted in the sing-song tone of a holy fool. "I am here to drive out your guests—the unholy devils that are here with you. I have come to see how many of them you have gathered here while my back was turned. I have come now to sweep them out with a broom . . ."

"You say that you want to cast out the unholy spirit, but

it looks rather as if you were serving him yourself," Father Paisii said fearlessly. "Who is the man who can say of himself, 'I am holy'? Are you that man, Father?"

"I'm unclean, not holy, and I will not sit in an armchair and demand that people worship me like an idol!" Father Ferapont thundered again. "Nowadays people destroy faith—that saint of yours, the deceased," he shouted, pointing at the coffin, "he denied devils, he gave you castor oil to keep them away, and now this whole place is teeming with them. They are breeding in every corner like spiders. And now he stinks himself, and that is a great sign from God."

Father Ferapont was referring to something that had really happened. One of the monks, who dreamt constantly of devils, had started seeing them when he was awake as well. Trembling with fear, he had told this to the elder, who had advised continual prayer and strenuous fasting. But when that failed to help, Father Zosima had advised him, without giving up his prayers and fasting, to take a certain medicine. When they heard about this, the monks were scandalized and discussed it excitedly, shaking their heads. And the most shocked of all was Father Ferapont, who had been quickly informed by Father Zosima's enemies about the elder's "peculiar" remedy for such a complaint.

"Go away, Father!" Father Paisii said imperiously. "It is for God to judge, not men. Perhaps there is a 'sign' here that neither you nor I nor anybody is able to interpret. Go away, Father, and do not confuse the flock."

"He did not keep the fasts according to the rules of his order—that is why the sign is here. That is quite clear and it is a sin to try to hide it!" the fanatic screamed, quite impervious to reason in his zeal for denunciation. "He indulged in the sweet things those rich ladies brought him in their pockets, didn't he? He liked to fill himself with tea. He was a slave to his belly, which he stuffed with sweetmeats, while his mind became stuffed with pride and irreverent thoughts—that is why he has been put to shame now!"

"These are thoughtless words, Father!" Paisii said, raising his voice. "I admire your fasting and your ascetic life, but your words are as thoughtless as if they were spoken by some vain and callow youth from the outside world. So go now, Father—I order you to leave!"

Father Paisii's voice had also grown to a roar.

"I'll go," Ferapont said, looking somewhat taken aback but still full of anger. "Ah, you learned ones! Your learning

makes you look down on me because I came here hardly
able to read and write and then forgot what little I knew,
which goes to show that God Almighty Himself has sheltered
his humble servant from that learning of yours . . ."

Father Paisii stood facing him, looking determined. Father
Ferapont remained silent for a moment; then, with a sorrowful expression, he covered one cheek with the palm of his
right hand, fixed his eyes on the coffin, and said in a whining,
self-pitying sing-song voice:

"Over him, tomorrow, they'll sing the glorious anthem
'Our Helper and Our Defender.' But over me, when I die,
they'll just reel off the little canticle 'What Earthly Joy.' "*

All of a sudden, Ferapont's countenance changed completely.

"You have grown rotten with pride and think yourselves
almighty!" he screamed like a madman. "This is an unholy,
unholy place!" And, with a sweeping gesture of condemnation,
he turned around, walked out of the cell, and went quickly
down the few steps into the yard.

The crowd waiting for him outside stirred hesitantly. Some
followed him right away, others waited, for the door of the
cell had been left open, and Father Paisii, who had followed
Ferapont to the top of the steps, stood there, watching. But
the infuriated old man had not said his last word yet. After
taking a few steps, he suddenly faced the setting sun, raised
both arms, and, just as if someone had cut him down, hurled
himself to the ground, yelling crazily:

"My Lord has conquered! Christ has overcome the setting
sun!"

His voice was frantic, his hands were raised toward the
sun, his face was pressed against the earth. Then he began to
sob, crying aloud like a little child, his body shaking convulsively, his arms now spread out crosswise on the ground.

The whole crowd was around him now, shouting excitedly,
some beginning to sob with him. They were all gripped by a
strange frenzy.

"Here's the one who is really a saint!" "Here's a truly
righteous man!" was shouted from the crowd. The monks

---

* When the body of a monk is carried from his cell to the
church and from there to the graveyard, the canticle "What
Earthly Joy" is sung; if, however, the deceased was an ordained
priest as well as a monk, "Our Helper and Our Defender" is
sung instead. [A. MacA.]

were no longer afraid, and some even cried out spitefully: "He's the one who should be an elder!"

"He wouldn't want to be an elder!" others replied at once. "He would refuse it if it was offered to him. He would have no part of that accursed innovation. He's not one to imitate their ridiculous clowning . . ."

It is hard to say how all this would have ended had it not been for the bell that rang just then to summon the monks to church. They all started crossing themselves. Father Ferapont, too, got up and, repeatedly making the sign of the cross around him as though fencing himself off from the world, he made his way to his hut, muttering some incoherent phrases, and never once turning his head. A few monks followed him, but most of them dispersed, hurrying to church.

Father Paisii turned the reading over to Father Joseph and went out into the yard. Of course he had not been shaken by the crazy shouting of the fanatics, but there was something he could not define that disturbed him a great deal, something that made him very sad. He stopped and asked himself: "Why do I feel so depressed?" Suddenly, to his own great surprise, he realized that the cause of his depression was rather strange and, on the whole, quite insignificant.

In the excited crowd that had gathered outside the cell, Father Paisii now remembered, he had seen Alyosha and the sight of him had caused a feeling of pain. "Why should this boy be so important to me?" he asked himself, suddenly feeling very surprised. And just at that moment Alyosha passed quite close by him, apparently hurrying somewhere, although he was not going toward the church. Their eyes met. Alyosha turned quickly away, keeping his eyes on the ground. From Alyosha's very appearance, Father Paisii could tell that a violent upheaval was taking place within the youth.

"Do you, too, feel like the others?" Father Paisii said to him at last. "Have you joined these men who have so little faith?" he added bitterly.

Alyosha stopped, lifted his eyes, gave Father Paisii a strangely vague glance, and looked down again. He was standing at an angle to Father Paisii and he did not turn to face him fully. Paisii watched him intently.

"Where are you off to in such a hurry? Didn't you hear the bell announcing the service?" he asked again, but again Alyosha did not answer. "Or are you leaving the hermitage?" Paisii went on. "But if so, why without taking leave and without a blessing?"

A strange twisted grin then appeared on Alyosha's face. He looked in a very strange way at the man to whose guidance he had been entrusted by his dying elder, who had such great influence on his mind and heart. Then he shrugged and, still without answering, walked quickly to the gate and out of the hermitage.

"You'll be back yet!" Father Paisii whispered as he watched him in sad surprise.

CHAPTER 2

The Crucial Moment

Father Paisii was, of course, quite right in anticipating that "the sweet boy" would come back, and he may even have guessed fairly accurately (although not entirely) the true nature of Alyosha's inner feelings. But I must admit that I myself would find it very hard to describe clearly the exact nature of that strange and unclear moment in the life of the youthful hero of my narrative, for whom I feel such deep affection. I could, however, have answered Paisii's bitter question as to whether Alyosha had joined those of "little faith." No, Alyosha had not joined them. Actually, just the opposite was true: Alyosha's inner upheaval arose from the very intensity of his faith. And yet he had received a shock and felt bewildered, so deeply bewildered, in fact, that, long after, he was to remember that day as one of the most fateful and painful in his life. Now if I were asked directly, "Is it really possible that all his anxiety and distress stemmed entirely from the fact that, instead of at once acquiring healing powers, the elder's body started almost immediately to decay?"—I would answer without hesitation, "Yes, that is correct." I would like, though, to ask my readers not to be in too great a hurry to laugh at my hero's naivety. That does not mean that I feel I must apologize for him and find excuses for the simplicity of his faith by bringing in his youth, his limited understanding of the sciences he had studied at school, and so on and so forth. Indeed, I state here and now that I have a tremendous respect for Alyosha's kind of heart.

There is no doubt in my mind that some other young man, who responded more cautiously to the impulses of his heart, who had learned to love tepidly rather than hotly, whose judgment was correct, even though a bit too dispassionate (and therefore cheap) for his age—that that young man would certainly have avoided the pitfall of my young hero. I submit, however, that there are cases when there is more honor in allowing ourselves to be swayed even by unreasonable passion, as long as it stems from a great love, than in not being subjected to it at all. And that is particularly true in youth, for there is something suspect about a young person who is always very reasonable, and I do not rate such a person very highly. So now you know my personal opinion! I suspect that some reasonable people may declare that every youth, after all, cannot expect to believe in such a superstition and that my young man certainly would not be a very good example for others to follow. To that, I would answer once more that my young man had faith, a sacred and unshakable faith, and that I still refuse to apologize for him.

But now I realize I may have been a bit hasty in declaring that I will not apologize for my hero or try to explain his behavior, for I may, after all, have to explain a few things that are indispensable for the further understanding of my story. Let me say at this point that it was not an irresponsible impatience for miracles that was the cause of Alyosha's trouble. It was not to prove to himself that his convictions were true that he wanted miracles (he certainly did not need that), nor was it because he wanted to see some preconceived idea of his triumph over some other idea. No, it was nothing like that. What concerned him above all was the image of his beloved elder, the image of the righteous man whom he had venerated to the point of adoration. The truth of the matter was that all the love contained in that pure young heart, a love sufficient to extend to "everyone and everything," had then, as it had during the whole preceding year, been concentrated, perhaps wrongly, on one single person. And that person, Alyosha's beloved elder, was now dead. It is true that the elder had been his unquestionable ideal for so long that all his aspirations and youthful energies could not help but follow that ideal to the exclusion of all others, even to the point of forgetting everything and everyone else at certain moments. (Alyosha later remembered himself that on that terrible day he forgot completely about his brother Dmitry, although earlier he had been so worried about him; he also forgot to take the two hundred rubles back to Ilyusha's father, although he had been so anxious to do so the day before.) What he needed after Father Zosima's death was not miracles but "higher justice," and he felt it had been violated. It was this that had wounded him so deeply and cruelly. And what does it matter if that "justice" had, in Alyosha's thoughts, gradually assumed the form of miracles expected at once from the remains of his beloved teacher? Didn't everyone in the monastery expect it, even men whose intelligence Alyosha admired so greatly, such as Father Paisii? And so, untroubled by doubts, Alyosha's belief came to be expressed in the same hopes as those of everyone around him. Besides, these hopes had been building up within him during the whole year of his life in the monastery and had become a habit with him. But it was not miracles, it was justice that he craved above all! And now the one whom he had expected to be glorified above all others, instead of receiving the glory that was his due, was being cast down and disgraced! Why? By whose judgment? What could have determined that judgment? These were the questions that arose at once in his inexperienced young heart and made it writhe in pain. He felt it an insult, and it was with bitterness that he watched the most righteous of men exposed to the derision and spite of a mindless crowd made up of creatures so infinitely inferior to him. If it had been only that the expected miracles had not happened immediately after the elder's death, that would have been all right —let there be no miraculous manifestations at all—but what was the point of inflicting that indignity upon him? Why was he allowed to be disgraced by having his body decay so quickly that, according to some spiteful tongues, even "the laws of nature" were violated? What was the reason for this "sign" which they, like Father Ferapont, had now seized upon so eagerly? And why should they think they had the right to interpret it that way? Where was Providence, then, and its guiding finger? Why, Alyosha wondered, had Providence made that finger invisible at "the crucial moment" as if it were deliberately submitting itself to the blind, deaf, and merciless laws of nature?

All this made Alyosha's heart bleed and obviously, as I mentioned before, what hurt him most was that the one he had loved more than anybody in the world now stood "dishonored" and "disgraced." Even if this rebellion on the part of this young man was callow and unreasonable, I repeat for the third time (and I admit that I, too, am perhaps being unreasonable) that I am very pleased to find that this young man did not turn out to be too reasonable at this juncture, for everyone, unless he is very stupid, acquires sufficient reason in time, but if a young heart shows a lack of love at such a critical moment, when will it know love? I must not, however, pass over in silence another strange feeling that arose, although only briefly, at that fateful and confusing moment in Alyosha's life. This fleeting new feeling was due to a lingering, nagging impression left from his conversation of the day before with Ivan, which now kept coming back to him. Oh, it was not that any of Alyosha's fundamental beliefs, beliefs that were an integral part of him, so to speak, had been shaken: he loved God and unwaveringly believed in Him, even though he murmured against Him now. And yet some vague, painful, evil residue from his conversation with Ivan kept stirring deep within him, striving to come to the surface.

It was growing dark when Rakitin, crossing the small wood separating the hermitage from the monastery, caught sight of Alyosha lying face downward under a tree. Alyosha lay motionless and seemed to be asleep. Rakitin walked over to him.

"Alexei," he called out, "is that you, Alexei? Is it really possible that . . ." He was about to say "that you should have come to this?" Although Alyosha did not answer, Rakitin knew by a slight jerk of his body that he had heard him.

"But what's the matter with you, after all?" he asked in surprise. But soon the surprised expression on his face changed to a smile which grew increasingly sarcastic.

"Listen," he said, "I've been looking for you for more than two hours—you seemed to have suddenly vanished. Anyway, what are you doing here? What's all this stupid nonsense? You might at least look at me now!"

Alyosha raised his head from the ground and sat up, leaning against a tree. His eyes were dry, but his face was ravaged by pain and there was an irritated look in his eyes, although he was not actually looking at Rakitin but somewhere off to the side.

"Why, you look completely different—there's not a trace of that famous gentleness of yours in your face! Are you angry with someone? Have they offended you or something?"

"Leave me alone," Alyosha said, with a weary gesture of his hand, still without looking at him.

"Aha, that's how it is! You're snapping at people now, just like the rest of us mortals. So you're not an angel anymore! Well, Alyosha, my boy, this is really a surprise, and I mean it! And you know, with all that goes on here, I haven't been surprised at anything for a long time. It's amazing, though—I used to consider you an educated man . . ."

Alyosha looked at him at last, but absentmindedly, as if he still hardly understood him.

"Are you really in this state just because that old man of yours has begun to rot? You didn't really believe he'd start performing miraculous tricks the moment he died, did you?" Rakitin cried, again genuinely surprised.

"I did believe, I still believe, and I want to believe—and now what more do you want to know?" Alyosha cried irritably.

"Nothing, nothing at all . . . But, listen, no . . . after all, a thirteen-year-old schoolboy doesn't believe in these things. Still, the hell with it, it's up to you. But what it really amounts to is that you're angry with your God today—it's as though there had been unfair discrimination and the right man had not got his promotion or his name was left off the New Year's list of honors. Ah, what a bunch, the lot of you!"

Alyosha gave Rakitin a long look, his eyes narrowed, and then an angry flash appeared in them. But it was not against Rakitin that his anger was directed.

"I'm not angry with my God—I just cannot accept His world," Alyosha said with a twisted grin.

"What does that mean—you cannot accept His world?" Rakitin paused for a second and thought. "What sort of nonsense is that?" he said after a while.

Alyosha didn't answer.

"Well, we've wasted enough time on these imbecilities," Rakitin said. "Let's talk about important things: have you had anything to eat today?"

"I'm not sure . . . I suppose so."

"I can tell by your face that you could do with some nourishment. You're a heartbreaking sight, you know. Besides, you must have been up all night, for I understand you had a meeting in there, and with all that fuss and bustle I bet you haven't had anything more substantial to chew on than a little piece of holy bread. You know what, I have some salami in my pocket, which I picked up in town just in case I got hungry on my way here . . . I don't suppose you'll eat salami under the circumstances, will you?"

"Salami would be fine."

"I see—that's the way it is now! You're in open rebellion then, ready to man the barricades! In that case, why not come to my place? Such an opportunity should not be allowed to slip by . . . In fact, I myself wouldn't at all mind having a swig or two of vodka. I feel pretty tired and it would give me a lift. Now, what about you, would it be going too far for you to have a drink with me?"

"Fine, let's have some vodka too."

"Look at that! This *is* a real miracle!" Rakitin cried, staring unbelievingly at Alyosha. "Well, whatever it is, vodka or salami, this is great and we mustn't let the opportunity slip! So let's get going!"

Alyosha stood up and followed Rakitin.

"I wish your dear brother Vanya could see this. I can just imagine how surprised he'd be! And, by the way, that sweet brother of yours left for Moscow today. Did you know that?"

"Yes, I knew," Alyosha said apathetically.

Suddenly the picture of his other brother, Dmitry, flashed through his head. It just came and vanished in a flash, vaguely reminding him that he had something terribly urgent to do, something that could not be delayed another minute, some duty to perform, some obligation . . . But even that awareness left him indifferent, did not go to his heart, and within a minute he had forgotten about it altogether. But later Alyosha was to remember about this for a very, very long time.

"Vanya, that charming brother of yours, once described me as a 'talentless windbag of a liberal.' And once you, too, were unable to resist the pleasure of making me understand how 'dishonest' I was . . ." Rakitin said, and then added under his breath: "I don't care, but I'll soon find out how talented and honest you people are yourselves." "Oh hell!" he said aloud. "You know what—let's take this path, avoid the monastery, and go straight to town, because, now that I come to think of it, I ought to drop in on Mrs. Khokhlakov. Imagine what happened: I sent her a complete written account of everything and she at once answered me with a penciled note (the lady loves writing notes!) that she 'never expected such *behavior* from a venerable elder like Father Zosima.' Yes, that's exactly the way she put it—'such *behavior*'! You see, she too was furious—you're really all the same! Wait!" he suddenly shouted, stopping and seizing Alyosha by the shoulder. "You know, Alyosha," he said at last, looking searchingly into Alyosha's eyes. Rakitin seemed full of enthusiasm over a new idea that had suddenly descended upon him, and yet, although it made him laugh, he was afraid to mention the scheme that had suddenly become possible because of the peculiar and surprising mood in which he had found Alyosha. "You know where we really ought to go now, Alyosha?" he said in the hesitant voice of a man groping in the dark.

"I don't care. Let's go wherever you want."

"What about Grushenka's? Will you come there?" Rakitin said, after hesitating painfully. He was even trembling in his anxiety.

"Fine, let's go to Grushenka's," Alyosha answered right away in a completely indifferent tone. This tone and the casual way in which Alyosha had accepted came as such a surprise to Rakitin that he almost jumped back upon hearing it.

"Really? You mean it?" Rakitin shouted in amazement. Then, suddenly seizing Alyosha's arm, he hurriedly pulled him along the path, still fearing that Alyosha might change his mind. They walked in silence now. Rakitin was afraid to say the wrong thing.

"You can't begin to imagine how glad she'll be . . ." he muttered at one point, but immediately fell silent again.

Besides, it was not to please Grushenka that Rakitin was taking Alyosha to her place, for he was a serious man and never did anything which didn't have some personal advantage for him. And now, taking Alyosha to Grushenka's, he was pursuing a double goal. First, this was a way to get even with Alyosha—that is, to witness "the fall of the upright," Alyosha's transformation from a saint to a sinner—and he was savoring that in advance. Second, there was a certain material advantage for him in it, and a quite substantial one, but we shall come back to that later.

"Well, I suppose this just happened to be the right moment," he thought with spiteful joy, "and I certainly mean to squeeze every drop of advantage out of this welcome opportunity!"

CHAPTER 3

One Onion

Grushenka lived near Cathedral Square, in the busiest section of town. She rented a wooden cottage in the yard behind the house belonging to Mrs. Morozov, a merchant's widow. Mrs. Morozov's own house was a rather large two-story stone building, old and unprepossessing. The landlady, a very old woman, lived there with two nieces, themselves already elderly spinsters. She was well off and did not really have to rent out the cottage in her yard, but everyone in town knew that she did so to please her relative, the merchant Samsonov, who was Grushenka's avowed protector. Some claimed that the jealous old man had originally installed his "protégée" there to have her under Mrs. Morozov's "sharp eye." Soon it became quite evident, however, that Grushenka required no "sharp eye" to watch over her behavior. And the old woman not only did not pester her with any surveillance but hardly ever saw her.

It is true, though, that four years had passed since the old merchant had installed her in that cottage, after bringing her back with him from the capital of the province, and much had changed since then. When she had first arrived, she was a slender, shy, eighteen-year-old girl, dreamy, brooding, and timid. People in town knew very little of her past history and what they did know was vague and uncertain. And they didn't get to know much more as time passed, not even after four years during which Miss Grushenka Svetlov had attracted considerable interest by becoming the town's acknowledged "great beauty." It was rumored only that when she was seventeen, she had been seduced and abandoned by some army officer, who had moved elsewhere and married another woman, leaving Grushenka disgraced and dishonored. It was also rumored that, although the old merchant Samsonov had saved her from dire poverty, she originally came from a respectable family, that her father was a deacon or something of that sort. And so in four years the brooding, sensitive, abandoned girl had grown into a blooming, rosy-cheeked, full-bodied Russian beauty, a woman with a strong and determined character, proud, arrogant, with a sharp eye for business, acquisitive, avaricious, and cunning, who by fair means or foul had succeeded, it was rumored, in accumulating a tidy little sum for herself. On one thing, however, everybody seemed in agreement—that in all those four years Grushenka had never been easy to approach and no one except old Samsonov could boast of her favors. This was a perfectly well-established fact, for there had always been many candidates for those favors, particularly in the past year or two. But all their aspirations came to nothing; some of those who sought her favors had to beat an undignified retreat and became the butt of general jokes, for she had a special firm and mocking way of rejecting unwanted advances.

It was also common knowledge that for a year or two the young lady had been engaged in all sorts of "financial operations," that she had displayed great talents in that field, so that in the end many said she was as sharp as any Jew. Although she didn't actually go in for usury, she was known, for instance, to go in for buying IOU's at nominal prices, along with Mr. Fyodor Karamazov, paying something around ten kopeks for a ruble's worth of debts, and eventually getting back ten times the value of her original investment.

Samsonov was a sick man and during the past year he had lost the use of his swollen legs. This rich, greedy, and implacable widower, who still bullied his grown-up sons, had at first treated Grushenka with a heavy hand and kept her on "short rations," so the gossip had it. Grushenka had, however, succeeded in emancipating herself from him while instilling in him a limitless trust in her loyalty. The old man, a most astute businessman, was (he has been dead for some time now) quite a personality himself. He was hard as flint and so stingy that, despite his passion for Grushenka, without whom he could not live (and this was especially so in the last two years), he still would not give her any substantial capital; even when she threatened to leave him unless he gave her a large sum, he still never yielded. He, nevertheless, did let her have a small sum and even that fact, when it became known in town, greatly surprised many people.

"You're quite a business woman yourself," he told her, giving her eight thousand rubles or so, "so why don't you operate with it on your own. I warn you, though," he added, "you won't get another kopek out of me, except, of course, your regular living allowance, which will be paid to you as long as I live."

And he kept his word: he died and left everything he had to his sons—whom, during his lifetime, he had treated as if they and their wives were his servants—while Grushenka was not even mentioned in his will. None of this became known until later, but while he was alive Samsonov did help Grushenka with advice on how to run her own "operations" and he would now and then throw some "good thing" her way. When Mr. Karamazov had become Grushenka's partner in one particular deal and then, to his own great surprise, had found himself head over heels in love with her, Samsonov, who already had one foot in the grave at the time, was vastly amused. It is remarkable that, throughout their entire relationship, Grushenka was apparently always completely frank with her old protector; indeed, he was perhaps the only person in the world whom she ever trusted. But when Dmitry Karamazov fell in love with Grushenka, Samsonov no longer laughed. In fact, he told Grushenka:

"If you really have to choose between those two, you'd better pick the father over the son. But then you must absolutely insist that the old crook marry you and, even before that, make him transfer at least some capital to your name. But, above all, stay away from the Captain, no good will ever come of that."

These were the very words of the old lecher, who knew he was dying and who, indeed, did die within five months. I would like to mention in passing here that, although many people in our town knew about the monstrous rivalry over Grushenka between the father Karamazov and his son, no one really understood much about the nature of her relations with either of them. Even Grushenka's two servants testified at the trial (after the catastrophic events we shall describe later) that their mistress received "the younger Mr. Karamazov" for fear that otherwise he might kill her, for, they said, "he did threaten to kill her." Her two servants were an old cook, a sick, deaf woman who had once worked in the house of Grushenka's parents, and the old cook's granddaughter, a lively girl of twenty or so, who was the maid. Otherwise Grushenka lived very frugally and her place was anything but luxurious. The three-room cottage she lived in was rented furnished, and the furniture was of old, red mahogany in the unfashionable style of the 1820's.

When Alyosha and Rakitin arrived, it was already almost night, but there was still no light in Grushenka's rooms.

Grushenka herself was lying on a large, cumbersome, mahogany-backed sofa in her drawing room. It was hard and

was covered with worn, cracked leather. Her head rested on
two white pillows from her bed. She lay quite motionless,
stretched out on her back, her hands under her head. She
wore a black silk dress and a light lace cap that was very
becoming; a lace shawl pinned with a massive gold brooch
was thrown over her shoulders. From the way she was dressed
she appeared to be expecting visitors.

And, indeed, she was waiting for someone; she seemed
tense and impatient. Her face was rather paler than usual,
her lips and eyes were burning, and she nervously tapped
the wooden arm-rest of the sofa with her foot. The arrival
of Rakitin and Alyosha caused a slight commotion, and
from the passage they heard Grushenka jump up and ask,
"Who is it?" in a frightened voice. But the young maid, who
had let them in, reassured her mistress at once:

"It's all right, ma'am, it's not him—it's someone else."

"I wonder what's going on here?" Rakitin mumbled,
pushing Alyosha ahead of him into the drawing room.

Grushenka stood by the sofa, still looking frightened. A
thick coil of dark brown hair suddenly escaped from under
her cap and slipped onto her shoulder, but she paid no
attention to it and made no attempt to put it back in place;
she gazed intently at her visitors until she made out who
they were.

"Ah, so it's you, Rakitin! You gave me a scare! And who's
this with you? Ah, just look who he's brought along with
him!" she cried in surprise when she recognized Alyosha.

"Why don't you have some candles brought in?" Rakitin
said in a familiar tone that suggested he could even give
orders to the servants here.

"Candles . . . yes, right . . . Here, Fenya, get him a
candle . . . But what a time to choose to bring guests!" she
cried again, glancing at Alyosha, and then, turning toward
the mirror, she quickly started to tuck the escaped coil
of hair in under her cap with both hands. She seemed displeased about something.

"Why, have I inconvenienced you by any chance?" Rakitin
asked, immediately feeling offended.

"You frightened me, that's what you did, Rakitin," Grushenka said, and then looked smilingly at Alyosha. "But
please, don't you be afraid of me, Alyosha dear, for I'm terribly pleased to see you, my unexpected guest! Rakitin frightened me because I thought it was Mitya breaking into the

house. You see, I lied to him today. I gave my word and he believed me, but it was a lie. I told him that I was going to my old man Samsonov's house for the whole evening and would stay there very late counting money. For, you see, I go to his house every week and we work together on the accounts. We lock ourselves in and he bangs the abacus beads about while I write down the figures in the books, for I'm the only one he trusts. So Mitya believed me when I said I was going there, but instead I locked myself in here. I'm waiting for a message, you know. I don't understand really why Fenya let you in. Fenya, Fenya! Run out to the gate and have a good look around to make sure that the Captain isn't there. Perhaps he's hidden somewhere, watching. I'm terribly afraid of him!"

"There's no one around, ma'am—I just looked. I keep peering through the crack every minute. I'm frightened myself, ma'am."

"Are the shutters bolted, Fenya? And I want you to draw the heavy curtains too. Here, that's better!" and she herself closed the heavy curtains. "For if he sees light in the windows, he'll want to come in. You know, Alyosha, I'm particularly afraid of your brother Mitya today," Grushenka said.

She was talking loudly, and although she really seemed alarmed, there was also a certain excited challenge in her voice.

"Why do you say you're so particularly frightened of that charmer Mitya?" Rakitin asked her. "You don't usually seem all that afraid of him. In fact, you make him dance to your tune whenever it pleases you."

"I told you—I'm expecting a message, a most alluring and promising little message, and dear Mitya would be very much in my way just now. Besides, I feel he didn't really believe me when I told him I was going to Samsonov's house. I'm sure he's sitting right now in his hiding place behind his father's house watching for me. But then, if he's sitting and waiting for me there, at least he won't come here and that's good. I did go to Samsonov's house. Mitya himself escorted me there, and that was when I told him I'd stay until midnight and he should come and escort me back home at that time. After he left, I stayed for ten minutes and then hurried home as fast as I could, running all the way, and I was terribly afraid of bumping into him on the way."

"And why are you dressed as if you were going out somewhere? Just look at that curious bonnet you've got on!"

"Oh, how inquisitive you are yourself, Rakitin. But anyway I've already told you I'm waiting for a certain message and, as soon as it arrives, I'll have to fly off somewhere, and I mean fly off—you'll see me vanish. Well, now you know why I'm all dressed up—I want to be ready as soon as I get the word."

"And where do you plan to fly?"

"You want to know too much, Rakitin, and too much knowledge will make you old before your time."

"Look at her! She's all happy and excited . . . I've never seen you like this before. And all dressed up as if for a ball . . ." Rakitin kept muttering, examining Grushenka from various angles.

"What can a fellow like you know about balls?" Grushenka said.

"And you, how much do you know about them?"

"I've seen a ball. Two years ago, my Samsonov married off one of his sons and I watched the ball from the gallery. Besides, why should I waste my time talking to you, Rakitin, when I have this prince charming standing before me. What a visitor I have tonight! Alyosha, my pet, I look at you and I can hardly believe you are here, in my house! To tell you the truth, I didn't expect to see you here, for I never thought you'd be willing to come. And although this is not the best moment, I'm madly pleased you have come! Sit down, my dear, here, right here, on the sofa. Good, that's the way, my young knight in shining armor! I simply cannot believe it—I'm still in a fog . . . Ah, Rakitin, if only you'd brought him yesterday or the day before! . . . I'm awfully glad, though, and perhaps it's even better that he's come at this moment and not two days ago . . ."

Playfully she sat down on the sofa very close to Alyosha, looking at him in undisguised delight. And she was not putting this on. She was obviously sincerely happy that he was there: her eyes were afire, her lips were smiling, but smiling with great warmth and joy. Alyosha was surprised, never having expected that this face could glow with such sincere warmth. When he had met her before, this woman had always left him with the uneasy impression that she held a threat; and the last time he had been terribly shaken by her malicious, wicked behavior toward Katerina . . . But now he was looking at a completely different person. And despite his own deep, private grief, his gaze involuntarily rested attentively on her. Grushenka's manner, too, had changed radically since Alyosha had last seen her: there were no traces of that genteel affectation in her pronunciation, no artificially tender inflections in her voice, no annoying mannerisms in her gestures—everything about her was natural and straightforward; her movements were quick, unaffected, and relaxed, even though she was obviously tense.

"My God, all the things that are happening to me today!" she kept saying. "And why on earth should I be so pleased to see you, Alyosha? I really have no idea. I couldn't explain it if you asked me."

"So now you no longer know why you wanted him here," Rakitin snorted. "Why did you have to pester me that way, then, for such a long time? I'm sure when you kept nagging me, 'Bring him here, Rakitin, just get him here,' I'm sure you had something in mind."

"Yes, I had something in mind before, but things are changed; it's quite different now. But I must receive you properly and offer you something. Yes, that's what I'll do. You know, Rakitin, I've suddenly become a kinder person. Come—why don't you get yourself a chair; there's no reason to stand up . . . But you do have a chair, I see. Good. Actually I should have known that Rakitin would never forget to take good care of himself! Look at him, Alyosha: he's sitting on that chair now feeling offended because I invited you to sit down first. Ah, you wouldn't believe how touchy this Rakitin is!" Grushenka laughed. "All right, don't be angry, Rakitin—I feel kind today . . . But you, Alyosha darling, why do you look so sad? You aren't afraid of me, by any chance, are you, my pet?"

And she peered laughingly into Alyosha's eyes.

"He's been disappointed—the promotion was denied."

"What promotion? What are you talking about?"

"It turned out that his elder stinks."

"Stinks? How? Sounds like a lot of nonsense. Or are you trying to say something nasty? Why don't you keep quiet, you idiot! . . . Say, Alyosha, won't you let me sit in your lap for a while? Like this!"

She suddenly got up and laughingly jumped onto Alyosha's knees—like an affectionate cat—winding her right arm tenderly around the boy's neck. "Let me cheer you up then, my pious little boy! But is it all right if I stay like this, sitting on your lap, for a while? I'll get off whenever you say."

But Alyosha said nothing. He sat there, afraid to move. He heard her promise to get off if he asked her to, but instead of answering her, he sat there as though paralyzed. But it was not at all what one might have thought and what Rakitin, for one, was imagining now as he watched rapaciously from his corner. The great grief inside Alyosha had completely blunted any other possible sensations, and if he could have analyzed what was going on inside him at that moment, he would have understood that in his present state he was perfectly immune to any temptation or seduction. And yet, despite his confused state and his oppressive grief, he was lucid enough to be surprised at the strange way he was reacting to this woman. He was not afraid of this "frightening" woman; he did not even have the fear he always felt whenever his thoughts wandered onto the subject of women. Indeed, this woman, whom he had feared more than any other, who was now sitting in his lap with her arm around his neck, aroused in him a singular and quite unexpected feeling—an immense human interest, a sincere curiosity in which there was no trace of his previous terror. And he was himself surprised that he should feel this way now.

"Ah, enough of all this nonsense!" Rakitin cried, finally losing patience. "What about serving us some champagne—you must remember our deal!"

"That's right, I owe it to you. For you know, Alyosha, I promised him champagne if he could get you to come over here. Good, I wouldn't mind champagne myself. Fenya! Go and get the bottle that Mitya left behind. Hurry! Stingy though I am, I'll open that bottle. But it's not because of you, Rakitin—you're just a mushroom. It's for him, for my prince charming! And although I have other things on my mind just now, I'll drink with you, for I feel like having a bit of a good time!"

"But what's all this talk about this not being the right moment, and what's the message you're expecting? Can't you explain, or is it all so terribly secret?"

"It's not all that secret and, besides, you know already," Grushenka said, turning toward Rakitin with a worried air and leaning slightly away from Alyosha, although she still remained seated in his lap. "My officer is arriving, Rakitin. He's on his way here."

"I heard he was on his way, but isn't he still pretty far away?"

"He's in Mokroye at this moment. He's supposed to send me a messenger from there. That's what he wrote me himself. I got the letter today. So I'm sitting here and waiting for his messenger."

"So that's it! But what's he doing in Mokroye?"

"That's a long story. And, anyway, you know enough for now."

"I can just imagine dear Mitya when he finds that out! Does he know about it already or not?"

"Why should he? Of course he doesn't. If he knew, he'd kill me. But I'm not afraid of that now. I have no fear of his knife. Shut up, Rakitin! Don't remind me again of Dmitry Karamazov, for he's entirely shattered my heart. Besides, I don't want to think about all that just now. I want to think only of sweet Alyosha, while I look at him. Smile at me, my pet; cheer up, my darling; laugh at my joy and at my silliness, but laugh . . . Look at that, he's really smiling now! Ah, what a nice, friendly way you have of looking at people! You know, Alyosha, I thought you were furious with me for what I did the other day to that young lady . . . I was a bitch that day, but, you know, I'm still glad I did it—it was good." Grushenka had become strangely thoughtful and there was suddenly a suggestion of cruelty in the curve of her lip. "Mitya told me she was screaming that I ought to be whipped. I did offend her quite badly. And she was so nice, invited me to dinner, thought she'd disarm me with her chocolate . . . Now I'm glad it ended the way it did," she said again with the same smile. "I was only afraid you were angry with me . . ."

"And she really was afraid of that," Rakitin put in, as if suddenly surprised at something he'd just discovered. "I'm beginning to believe she's really afraid of you, Alyosha, you poor chicken!"

"He may be a chicken to you, Rakitin, but that's only because you're a man without a conscience—that's what. But I love Alyosha with my whole soul, do you hear me? Do you believe that I love you with my whole soul, Alyosha?"

"You're really the most shameless creature I've ever seen! Don't you understand, Alexei, this is her way of making you a declaration of love?"

"And why not? I love him."

"But what about that officer of yours? What about the message you're supposed to be waiting for from Mokroye?"

"That has nothing to do with it."

"Ah, women! I wish I could understand how you worked that one out!"

"You're beginning to get on my nerves, Rakitin! One thing has nothing to do with the other, as I've told you. I love Alyosha in a different way. It's true I did have designs on him before. But that's because I'm a low, violent creature . . . But you know, Alyosha, at other moments I've looked on you as my conscience and thought: 'How much he must despise a bad woman like me!' And that's what I was thinking on my way here from that young lady's the other day. I noticed you a long time ago, Alyosha, and Mitya knows about it; I told him. Mitya understands exactly how I feel. Would you believe it, Alyosha, sometimes I look at you and I'm ashamed of myself and of everything about me . . . And so I started thinking of you, I can't even tell you exactly when, I don't remember . . ."

Fenya came in with the uncorked bottle of champagne and three glasses on a tray.

"Here comes the champagne at last!" Rakitin exclaimed. "Ah, Grushenka, you're in quite a state tonight, not at all your usual self. Perhaps once you've had a glass of this stuff, you'll start the dance, though. My God, they couldn't even do that properly!" he said, examining the bottle. "The old woman uncorked it without cooling it. It's quite warm . . . Well, never mind, I'll have it the way it is."

He went up to the table, filled a glass, emptied it and filled it again.

"One doesn't get a chance to have champagne too often," he said, licking his lips. "Here, Alyosha, take this glass and show us your mettle. What shall we drink to, then? To the gates of heaven, all right? You too, Grushenka, here, drink with us to the gates of heaven!"

"What gates of heaven?" she said, taking her glass.

Alyosha took his, took a few sips, and put it back on the table.

"I think I'd better not have any more," he said with an apologetic smile.

"Why did you tell me you'd drink then?" Rakitin cried.

"Well, if that's how it is, I won't drink either," Grushenka said. "Besides, I don't really feel like drinking now. You go ahead, Rakitin—finish the whole bottle. I'll only have some if Alyosha does."

"Oh, how very touching!" Rakitin taunted her. "Why, just keep sitting on his lap! What's the matter with you, Grushenka, after all? He, at least, has something to be sad about: he has revolted against his God and was even getting ready to devour some salami . . ."

"Why, what happened?" Grushenka asked.

"His saintly elder died today, you know, the holy Father Zosima."

"Oh! So Father Zosima did die!" Grushenka cried, and crossed herself devoutly. "My God, and here I am sitting on his lap!" She started as though frightened, quickly got off Alyosha's knees, and sat down on the sofa.

Alyosha looked at her intently. Gradually the surprise on his face turned into bright warmth.

"Rakitin," Alyosha said suddenly in a loud, firm voice, "stop teasing me by saying that I've rebelled against my God. I don't want to be unkind to you and that's why I would like you not to be so unkind either. I've lost something that was more precious to me than anything has ever been to you, so you really cannot judge me now. Did you notice just now how kind Grushenka was and what respect she showed for my loss? I expected to find a wicked soul here and I was attracted because I myself was wicked and despicable . . . But instead I have found a true sister, a treasure, a loving soul . . . She has spared me . . . I mean you, Grushenka, you helped me to recover my soul just now . . ."

Alyosha's lips quivered. He was out of breath, and fell silent.

"So now it turns out that she's been doing all this to save you!" Rakitin laughed sneeringly. "Well, for your information, my boy, what she was trying to do was to eat you up! Take it from me."

"Wait, Rakitin!" Grushenka cried, leaping to her feet. "Keep quiet, both of you. I'll tell everything now. I want you to keep quiet, Alyosha, because you've made me feel ashamed with what you said about me. I'm bad. I'm not good as you said I was, and that's the truth. And you, Rakitin, shut up, because you're lying. Although I did once have the wicked idea of eating him up, as you put it, it's completely different now, not the same thing at all . . . And I don't want to hear another squeak out of you, do you hear?" Grushenka said in great agitation.

"They're crazy, both of them," Rakitin hissed, staring at Alyosha and Grushenka in amazement. "I feel as if I were in a madhouse. They're so moved and so touched, they look as if they're about to burst into tears!"

"And I may very well burst into tears at that," Grushenka said. "He called me his sister and I'll never, never forget it. You know what, Rakitin, I may be a wicked woman but still I gave away one onion."

"What onion? What are you talking about? Damn it, you've really gone out of your mind!"

Rakitin was puzzled by their emotional state and he felt offended and angry, although it might have occurred to him that circumstances had combined to plunge both Grushenka and Alyosha into an emotional crisis such as people seldom experience in their lives. But Rakitin, who was very sensitive to things that touched him directly, was quite unreceptive to the feelings and emotions of others, partly because he was young and inexperienced, and partly out of plain egotism.

"You see, Alyosha dear," Grushenka said with a nervous giggle, "I was bragging to Rakitin about giving away one onion. I don't want to brag to you, but I'll tell you about it for another reason. It is just a fairy-tale, but a good fairy-tale, and I heard it from Matryona (who's my cook now) when I was a little girl. This is how it goes. Once upon a time there lived a very nasty, horrible old woman. When she died, she didn't leave behind her one single good deed. So the devils got hold of her and tossed her into the flaming lake. Meantime, her guardian angel stood there, trying hard to think of one good deed of hers that he could mention to God in order to save her. Then he remembered and said to God: 'Once,' he said, 'she pulled up an onion in her garden and gave it to a beggar woman.' So God said to him: 'Take that onion, hold it out to her over the lake, let her hold on to it, and try to pull herself out. If she does, let her enter heaven; if the onion breaks, the old woman will just have to stay where she is.' So the angel hurried to the woman, held out the onion to her, and told her to take hold of it and pull. Then he himself began to pull her out very carefully and she was almost entirely out of the lake when the other sinners saw she was being pulled out and grabbed on to her so that they'd be pulled out of the flames too. But when she saw them, that wicked, horrible woman started kicking them, saying: 'I'm being pulled out, not you, for it's my onion, not yours!' As soon she said that, the onion snapped and the woman fell back into the flaming lake, where she's still burning to this day. And her guardian angel wept and walked away.

"So that's the fairy-tale, Alyosha, and I remember it by heart because I am that wicked, horrible woman. When I said to Rakitin now that I had given away an onion, I was being proud and boastful. But to you I'll put it this way: in my whole life I've never done anything more than give away an onion; I have no other good deeds to my credit, and you mustn't say kind things about me and insist that I'm good, because I'm wicked and horrible. If you praise me, you only make me ashamed of myself . . . No, let me make a clean breast of it now. Listen, Alyosha, I was so eager to get you here, all to myself, that I promised Rakitin twenty-five rubles if he would bring you to me. Well, Rakitin, here it is!"

Grushenka walked quickly over to her desk, opened a drawer, took out a purse, fished out a twenty-five-ruble bill, and handed it to Rakitin.

"What's that? What's going on here? I don't understand!" Rakitin cried out, not knowing what to do.

"Take it, Rakitin. I'm sure you won't refuse to collect a debt," she said and threw him the bill.

"I wouldn't think of refusing it, not for one moment," Rakitin said in a hoarse voice. Although he tried to hide it, he was obviously embarrassed. "I can certainly use the money. Besides, why shouldn't a clever man take advantage of the stupidity of others?"

"All right, Rakitin, now I want you to keep out of it and not butt in, for what I'm going to say now is not for your ears. Just sit in your corner and keep quiet. I know you don't like us and that's fine with me. Just shut up."

"Why the hell should I like you?" Rakitin snapped back, no longer bothering to hide his fury. He thrust the twenty-five-ruble bill into his pocket, feeling terribly awkward in front of Alyosha. He had expected her to settle with him later and was furious now, because he had been put in such an embarrassing position. Up till then, he had diplomatically restrained himself from irritating Grushenka too much and had ignored many of her biting snubs; it was obvious that she had some advantage over him that enabled her to treat him this way. But now he no longer cared.

"People love people for something," he said, "but what has either of you two ever done for me?"

"So you must learn to love for nothing, like Alyosha."

"What makes you think he loves you so much? And anyway, what do you see in him that you should make all this fuss over him?"

Grushenka stood in the middle of the room. She seemed very excited and a hysterical note had crept into her voice.

"Shut up, Rakitin! You don't understand a thing . . . And don't you ever dare address me so familiarly again. I forbid you to, once and for all. Go and sit in the corner and wait there like the flunkey you are! And you, Alyosha, listen now. I'll tell you the whole truth, because I want you to know what a horrible creature I am. And I'm saying this because I want *you* to hear it and I don't care whether Rakitin hears or not. I wanted to ruin you, Alyosha, that's the real truth. I wanted to so badly that I promised Rakitin I'd give him money if he brought you here. And why did I want to so badly? You never even noticed how I looked at you every time we met, for you always turned away, lowered your eyes, and walked past me. And I asked everyone questions about you. I couldn't get your face out of my mind. 'He despises me,' I thought, 'he doesn't even want to look at me.' And that feeling took such a hold on me, I was surprised at myself, worrying about what a mere boy thought of me. 'Why,' I thought, 'I'll take him and eat him alive. And then I'll laugh.' I became really furious. Believe me, no one dares come near me with any ideas, you know. No one would even think of it. I have only my old Kuzma Samsonov. I was sold to him and I'm tied to him, since we were married by the devil, and there has never been any other man. But looking at you, I decided: 'This one, I'll eat up and when I've swallowed him, I'll have a good laugh.' So you see what a bitch I am, I whom you called your sister!

"Now that seducer of mine has arrived. And I sit here waiting for a word from him. And do you know what that seducer meant to me? Well, it's almost five years now since Kuzma brought me here. I used to sit here, hiding myself from people. I didn't want them to see or hear me, I was so ashamed. I was a thin, silly girl, sitting there and crying all day, staying awake at night and thinking: 'Where is he now, my seducer? He must be with another woman, laughing at me! Ah,' I thought, 'if only I could see him again, I'd pay him back for everything, everything' . . . At night, in the darkness, I'd sob into my pillow, thinking of it all the time, trying to calm myself by repeating again and again: 'I'll pay him back, I'll pay him back, for everything, everything' . . .

Sometimes I'd even cry out in the darkness. But then it would dawn on me that I couldn't do anything to him, and he must be laughing at me now, unless he had already forgotten me altogether. I would get out of bed, throw myself on the floor, and writhe there, weeping in helpless fury, until daybreak. And in the morning I'd get up feeling as wicked as a snarling dog, ready to tear the whole world to shreds. So what do you think I did? I started accumulating some capital. I became hard and callous, and I put on weight. But do you think I grew any wiser for all that? Well, I didn't. And although no one in the whole world knows it, every night I lie there in the dark and gnash my teeth and cry with rage, just as I did five years ago, when I was just a girl, and I still keep repeating: 'I'll show him, I'll show him, for what he did to me!' . . .

"Well, now that you've heard all that, Alyosha, tell me what you think of this: about a month ago I got a letter from him, in which he writes that he's a widower now and wishes to see me. It took my breath away when I read it. 'My God,' I thought, 'if he comes now and just whistles for me, I'll crawl to him, cringing like a beaten dog.' I thought that, but I refused to believe it of myself. 'Do I have pride or don't I? Will I run to him or won't I?' I kept thinking, and all this month I've been even more furious with myself than I was five years ago. So now, Alyosha, that you know the whole truth, you can see what a frantic, violent creature I am! And I've been playing around with your brother Mitya to stop myself from running to that other man . . . Don't say anything, Rakitin, you have no right to judge me, nor did I tell this to you. Just now, before the two of you came in, I was lying here thinking, deciding my future, and you'll never be able to understand what I felt . . . I want you, Alyosha, to ask that young lady whom I offended not to be angry with me . . . No one in the whole world can possibly know what I'm going through . . . for I may take a knife with me when I go there, I haven't decided yet . . ."

Unable to go on, Grushenka covered her face with her hands and threw herself onto the sofa, sobbing aloud like a small child. Alyosha stood up and walked over to Rakitin.

"Don't be angry, Misha," he said. "She's offended you, but you mustn't be angry. You heard what she said just now, didn't you? We cannot demand so much of a human heart— we must be more merciful . . ."

In saying this, Alyosha had followed an irresistible impulse. He had felt he had to give expression to his feelings, and he had addressed himself to Rakitin. If Rakitin had not been there, he would have cried out those words to himself. But Alyosha suddenly realized that Rakitin was looking at him mockingly and he stopped short.

"They've loaded you with that elder of yours over there and now you're firing your elder at me, Alexei, you little man of God," Rakitin said with a hate-filled grin.

"Don't laugh, Rakitin, don't talk about the elder—he was better than any man on earth!" Alyosha cried with tears in his voice. "When I came over to you now, I was not speaking as a judge, for I myself am the lowest of the accused. What am I beside her? When I came here, I was walking to my perdition and I kept saying, 'Fine, let it be, I don't care' —all out of cowardice. But she, on the other hand, after five years of suffering, as soon as he uttered one sincere word to her, she forgave him for everything, forgot all that she had suffered because of him, and is now weeping tenderly. The man who offended her is back and is calling her; she is hurrying happily to him and she will not take a knife with her! But I'm not like that. I don't know whether you are, Misha, but I certainly am not. I've learned a great lesson today. She is our superior in love. Had you heard the things she was telling us now before? I'm sure you hadn't, for if you had you'd have understood it all long ago . . . And Katerina, whom she has also offended, must forgive her too. She will forgive her when she comes to know her, and she will come to know her . . . Hers is a soul that has not yet found peace, and it must be treated gently, because there may be a treasure in it."

Alyosha could not go on. His breath failed him. Angry as he was, Rakitin gaped at him in surprise. He had never expected to hear such a long speech from Alyosha, who was usually so quiet.

"She's certainly got herself an eloquent counsel for the defense!" he exclaimed with an aggressive chuckle. "Why, have you finally fallen for her too? Look Grushenka, our little ascetic has fallen in love with you. You've won!"

Grushenka lifted her head from the pillow and looked at Alyosha tenderly. A smile lighted up her face which was swollen with crying.

"Pay no attention to him, Alyosha, my little cherub. You know how he is. Your words are only wasted on him. And you, Rakitin, I was about to apologize to you for having insulted you the way I did, but now I don't feel like doing so. Alyosha, come over here—sit down," she said, beckoning him with a radiant smile. "That's right, here . . . good . . . Now, I want you to tell me this." She took him by the hand and looked intently into his eyes. "Tell me, do I still love that man, or don't I? That's what I kept asking myself as I lay here in the dark before you arrived: 'Do I love him or don't I?' Answer that question for me, Alyosha, and whatever you say, so it will be. Shall I forgive him or not?"

"But you've already forgiven him," Alyosha said with a smile.

"That's right, I have," she said dreamily. "That's just the kind of unproud heart I have. So let's drink—to a heart without pride!" She seized the champagne glass from the table, downed it, raised it in the air, and hurled it violently on the floor. The glass exploded with a ring. There was a hint of cruelty in her slightly twisted smile.

"Although perhaps I haven't really forgiven him yet," she said, an indefinable menace in her voice, her eyes fixed on the floor; she sounded as if she were talking to herself. "Perhaps this heart is only considering forgiveness. I'll still have to argue with it and see how it comes out . . . You see, Alyosha, I've come to love my tears in those five years, to love them terribly . . . It's possible that what I love is only the suffering he caused me, and that I really don't care about him at all."

"I must say, I wouldn't want to be in his shoes now," Rakitin hissed.

"No need to worry, Rakitin, you'll never be in his shoes. But you'll clean my shoes for me—that's something I may use you for. Otherwise, a woman like me wouldn't have anything to do with someone like you . . . Nor perhaps with someone like him either, for that matter."

"Not even with someone like him? So why are you all dressed up then?"

"Don't keep taunting me about being dressed up, Rakitin. You still don't know what's going on inside me. If I choose, I'll tear off my dress this very minute!" she cried in a ringing voice. "You don't understand why I'm wearing this dress. Maybe I want to appear in it before him and say: 'Have you ever had a good look at me before?' Why, when he saw me last I was just a thin, anemic, tearful seventeen-year-old. And I'll get close to him, set him afire, make him crazy. 'Well,' I'll tell him, 'so now you've seen what I look like and that's enough for you. Content yourself with that, my dear

man, for there's many a slip twixt cup and lip!' So, you see,
that may be the reason I'm dressed up now, my poor Rakitin,"
Grushenka concluded with a wicked chuckle. "I'm crazy,
Alyosha. Nothing can hold me back at times: I may rip off
my dress, maim myself with a knife, burn my beautiful face,
and go begging for alms. But I may also decide not to go
anywhere, not to see anyone, to send Kuzma Samsonov back
all the money and things he's given me, and myself become a
cleaning woman. You think I wouldn't dare do it, Rakitin?
You're wrong. I could do it right now if I decided to. So stop
annoying me. As to that other man, I'll tell him what he can
do with himself and he'll see that I'm not for him either!"

These last words she cried out hysterically. She broke down,
covered her face with her hands again, and threw herself on
the sofa, her whole body shaken with sobs. Rakitin stood up.

"We must be on our way," he said. "It's getting late. We
won't be able to get back into the monastery."

Grushenka leapt up at once.

"And you, Alyosha, do you really want to leave? Do you?"
she cried in pained surprise. "What are you doing to me,
Alyosha? Now that you've put me into this state, put all my
emotions in a turmoil, you want to leave me to live through
this night all alone."

"You don't expect him to spend the night here alone with
you, do you? But it's up to you, really. I'm leaving," Rakitin
said sarcastically.

"Shut up, you vicious creature!" Grushenka shouted angrily
at him. "You've never spoken to me as he has tonight."

"What did he say to you that pleased you so much?" Rakitin said irritably.

"I can't tell you what it was. I wouldn't know. He just
spoke straight to my heart and turned it upside down . . .
Perhaps he was the first one, perhaps the only one, to take
pity on me—yes, that may be it! Why didn't you come to me
sooner, Alyosha, my cherub?"

All of a sudden she was kneeling before him as if in a
frenzy.

"I've waited all my life for someone like you," she said. "I
knew he'd come one day and forgive me. I believed he'd love
me, unclean as I am, love me truly, not just like an animal . . ."

"Why, what have I done?" Alyosha said with a shy smile.
He bent down and took her tenderly by the hand. "Perhaps

it's just an onion," he said. "I gave you just one tiny little onion, no more . . ." And he himself burst into tears.

There was a sudden noise at the entrance door. Someone entered the house. Grushenka got up quickly, looking terribly frightened.

"Madam, oh, dear, dear me, the messenger is here!" Fenya shouted, bursting gaily into the room. "There's a carriage from Mokroye waiting for you, ma'am—Timofei the coachman told me that they're changing the horses now . . . And here's a letter for you, ma'am!"

The letter was in Fenya's hand. She had been waving it in the air all the time. Grushenka snatched the letter from her and held it close to the candle. It was just a short note, only a few lines, which she read in one second.

"So he's whistled for me!" she cried, a painful grimace contorting her pale face. "He's whistled: Come on doggie, crawl back to me!"

But a second later, the blood rushed to her head and set her cheeks on fire.

"I'm going!" she shouted. "Five years of my life! Finished now—good-by to everything! Farewell, Alyosha. My fate is sealed now! Go away, leave me, all of you, and I hope I never see you again . . . Grushenka is off to a new life! Well, don't think too badly of me, Rakitin, my boy, for who can tell, I may be going to my death! Ah, I feel as if I were drunk! . . ."

She left them and ran into her bedroom.

"She has other things on her mind now," Rakitin grumbled. "Let's clear out of here, Alexei, or there'll be more of those woman's shrieks . . . I'm pretty sick of those tearful shrieks as it is."

Alyosha absent-mindedly followed Rakitin out of the house. A carriage was standing in the yard. The horses were being unharnessed. People were hurrying about with lanterns. Three fresh horses were being led through the open gates. But as Alyosha and Rakitin stepped into the yard, the window of Grushenka's bedroom flew open and she cried out in her ringing voice:

Alyosha absentmindedly followed Rakitin out of the house. and ask him for me not to think too badly of me, wicked woman that I am. And tell him this, yes, in these words: 'A despicable scoundrel got Grushenka in the end and not an honorable man like you!' And tell him, too, that Grushenka did love him for an hour, but just for an hour. Tell him to remember that hour all his life, tell him, 'Grushenka wants you to remember it always.' "

There were sobs in her voice as she finished. The window closed with a bang.

"Ha, that's really something!" Rakitin chuckled. "She's all but cut dear Mitya's throat and now she wants him to remember it all his life. Never seen anyone so bloodthirsty!"

Alyosha did not answer. Perhaps he had not even heard him. He was walking very fast, as though hurrying somewhere. His mind seemed to be elsewhere. Rakitin suddenly felt as though someone had poked a finger into a fresh wound. Things had not worked out at all the way he had expected when he had delivered Alyosha to Grushenka. The result was quite different from what he had hoped for.

"That officer of hers is a Pole," he said, restraining his rage. "Besides, he's no longer an army officer—he's been working for the customs office in Siberia lately, somewhere on the Chinese border, I believe, just a lousy little Polack customs official. I bet he lost his job and learned somehow that Grushenka had money and that that's behind this miraculous return."

Again Alyosha did not appear to hear him. Rakitin lost patience.

"So now what? You feel you've converted a sinner?" he said with a spiteful laugh. "Is the harlot back on the righteous path? Are the seven devils cast out? Are these the miracles we've been waiting for so eagerly? So the expectations have come true, after all!"

"Stop it, Rakitin," Alyosha said, pained.

"Perhaps you despise me so much now because of those twenty-five rubles? Perhaps you think I sold my trusting friend? But please remember, at least, that you are no Christ and I am no Judas."

"I assure you, Rakitin, I'd completely forgotten about that. I wouldn't even have thought of it if you hadn't reminded me now."

That made Rakitin lose his temper altogether.

"Ah, the hell with you all, with every single one of you!" he screamed, beside himself. "Damned if I know why I had to get involved with you! Listen, from now on, I don't know you anymore. Go, get out of my sight, off with you!"

And he turned abruptly into a sidestreet, leaving Alyosha alone in the darkness. Alyosha made his way out of town, toward the monastery.

CHAPTER 4

Cana of Galilee

Alyosha reached the hermitage too late by the monastery rules and the gatekeeper let him in through a special entrance. Nine o'clock had struck. It was time for general rest after a day that had been very tiring and tormenting for everyone. Alyosha quietly opened the door to the elder's cell, where his coffin now was. There was no one there except Father Paisii, who was reading the Gospels by the coffin, and the young novice Porfiry, who, exhausted by the vigil of the previous nights and the distressing events of the past day, was now deep in youthful sleep on the floor of the adjoining cell that had been the elder's bedroom.

Although Father Paisii heard Alyosha come in, he did not even look in his direction. When he entered, Alyosha went to a corner, knelt down, and began to pray. His heart was full to overflowing, but no one feeling stood out clearly from the others. Indeed, his feelings kept displacing one another, but smoothly in a sort of quiet, harmonious rotation. Somehow, a sweet feeling pervaded Alyosha and, strangely, he was not surprised by it. Again he had before him the coffin enclosing the man who had been so dear to him, but now the acutely painful feeling of pity that had gnawed at his heart in the morning was gone. Now he knelt before the coffin as before a holy shrine, and gladness filled his heart and his mind. One of the windows was open and fresh, cold air flowed into the cell. "The smell of decay must have increased since they decided to open the window," Alyosha thought, but this idea, which had seemed so horrible and disgraceful to him earlier, aroused no indignation in him now, nor did it sadden him. He prayed on quietly, but soon realized that he was doing so almost mechanically. Fragments of thoughts flashed through his mind like little sparks, were at once extinguished, and were replaced by other sparks. But they were part of something continuous, of a greater whole, of something solid and very satisfying. Again and again he started to pray in his yearning to express his gratitude and his love . . . But once he had started, his thoughts soon shifted to something else. He became immersed in these thoughts, forgot his prayer, and finally gave it up altogether. He also tried to listen to the Gospels Father Paisii was reading. Gradually, though, feeling very tired, he began to doze . . .

" 'And the third day there was a marriage in Cana of Galilee,' " Father Paisii read, " 'and the mother of Jesus was there: and both Jesus was called, and His disciples, to the marriage.' "

"Marriage . . . What marriage? . . ." The words whirled through Alyosha's head. "There is happiness for her too . . . she has gone to the ball . . . No, she didn't, she didn't take the knife . . . she just said that . . . People must always be forgiven for saying such emotional things . . . emotional words make people feel better . . . Sometimes the pain would be unbearable if they couldn't say those things . . . Rakitin turned into a back alley and walked away . . . As long as he thinks of the offenses he has suffered, he will always be turning off into back alleys . . . But there is a bright, wide open road, a straight road, shining like crystal, leading to the sun . . . Ah, what is he reading? . . ."

" 'And when they wanted wine, the mother of Jesus saith unto Him, They have no wine' . . ." Alyosha heard the voice reading.

"Ah, yes, I missed a passage there . . . That's a shame—I didn't want to miss it—I love that passage—it's Cana of Galilee, the first miracle . . . Ah, that miracle, what a lovely miracle! It wasn't sorrow, it was human happiness that Christ extolled, and the first miracle He worked was to bring men happiness . . . 'He who loves men loves their happiness,' Father Zosima used to repeat so often—that was one of his guiding ideas . . . And Mitya says it's impossible to live without happiness . . . Yes, Mitya . . . Whatever is true and beautiful is always full of forgiveness—the elder used to say that too . . ."

" 'Jesus saith unto her, Woman, what have I to do with thee? Mine hour is not yet come.

" 'His mother saith unto the servants, Whatsoever He saith unto you, do it.' "

"Do it . . . Give happiness to some poor people . . . very poor, since they hadn't even enough wine for the wedding . . . Historians say that the people around the lake of Gennesaret and in that whole region were as poor as can be imagined . . . Another great heart belonging to another great being—the heart of His mother—knew that He had not come down only for His great sacrifice but that His heart was open to the simple and artless joys of the plain, uneducated people who had warmly invited Him to a humble wedding. 'Mine hour is not yet come,' He says with a meek smile (yes, that's very important—he smiles at her meekly) . . . Certainly, though, He had not come down on earth to increase the supply of wine at the weddings of the poor . . . And yet He did as she asked Him and went . . ."

" 'Jesus saith unto them, Fill the waterpots with water. And they filled them up to the brim.

" 'And He saith unto them, Draw out now, and bear unto the governor of the feast. And they bare it.

" 'When the ruler of the feast had tasted the water that was made wine, and knew not whence it was: (but the servants which drew the water knew); the governor of the feast called the bridegroom.

" 'And saith unto him, Every man at the beginning doth set forth good wine; and when men have well drunk, then that which is worse; but thou hast kept the good wine until now.' "

"But what is happening? Why is the room growing? Ah, yes, it's that wedding, that marriage, of course. Here are the wedding guests, the bride and the bridegroom are sitting over there, and there's the merry crowd and . . . where's the wise governor of the feast? But who is this? Who? The room has grown larger again . . . Who is that getting up from the long table over there? What? . . . So he is here too! But he's in the coffin now . . . Yes, but he's here too. He has risen from the table because he has seen me, and he's coming over here . . . Ah, Lord!"

Yes, the dried-up little old man with his fine network of wrinkles and his gentle, radiant smile came up to Alyosha. The coffin was no longer there and he wore the clothes he had worn on the night when they had all gathered in his room. His face was uncovered, his eyes shone. How was it that he too had been invited to the wedding at Cana of Galilee?

"Yes, my dear boy, I was invited. I was called. I was bidden," a soft voice said over Alyosha. "But why are you hiding here where no one can see you? Come and join us too."

It was his voice, the voice of the elder Zosima . . . Besides, who else could it be, since he had invited Alyosha to join him? The elder took Alyosha by the hand and raised him from his knees.

"Let us enjoy ourselves," said the dried-up little man. "Let us drink new wine, the wine of great, new happiness. Look at all the guests, and look, there are the bridegroom and the bride. And now the wise governor of the feast will taste the new wine. Why are you looking at me with such surprise? Once I gave an onion away and here I am. Many others here have also given away only one onion, one single little onion each . . . What do you think our deeds were? Why, you too, my quiet, gentle boy, you too knew how to give an onion to a needy woman today. So start out, my sweet, gentle boy, do your work . . . Can you see our sun now? Can you see Him?"

"I am afraid . . . I don't dare look," Alyosha whispered.

"Don't be frightened of Him. Though He is frightening in His greatness, terrifying in His majesty, He is also infinitely merciful and, out of love, He has made Himself like one of us and shares our joy and turns our water into wine, so that the joy of the guests shall not cease, and He invites more and more guests, unceasingly, more new guests forever and ever. Look, see, they are bringing new vessels in . . ."

A bright flame burned in Alyosha's heart. His heart was full to the brim and even pained him. Tears of rapture welled up from his soul. He stretched out his arms and awoke . . .

The coffin was back, and the open window and the measured voice reading the Gospels. But Alyosha no longer listened to the words. It was strange: he had fallen asleep kneeling down, but now he was on his feet. Suddenly, as if tearing himself from the ground, he took three determined steps that brought him so close to the coffin that his shoulder brushed against Father Paisii without his noticing it. Father Paisii raised his eyes from the Gospels and glanced at Alyosha, but then he quickly lowered them to his book again, realizing that something strange was happening to the youth. For half a minute Alyosha gazed at the coffin, at the covered, motionless body with the icon on his chest and the cowl on his head with the eight-cornered cross on it. He had just heard the dead elder's voice and that voice was still resounding in his ears. Alyosha was listening, still hoping to hear . . . Suddenly he turned abruptly away and walked out of the room.

He did not stop outside the door, but walked quickly into the yard. His soul was overflowing with emotion and he felt he needed lots of room to move freely. Over his head was the vast vault of the sky, studded with shining, silent stars. The still-dim Milky Way was split in two from the zenith to the horizon. A cool, completely still night enfolded the earth. The white towers and the golden domes gleamed in the sapphire sky. The gorgeous autumnal flowers in the flowerbeds by the buildings were asleep until morning. The silence of the earth seemed to merge with the silence of the sky and the mystery of the earth was one with the mystery of the stars . . . Alyosha stood and gazed for a while; then, like a blade of grass cut by a scythe, he fell to the ground.

He did not know why he was hugging the earth, why he could not kiss it enough, why he longed to kiss it all . . . He kissed it again and again, drenching it with his tears, vowing to love it always, always. "Water the earth with the tears of your joy and love those tears," a voice rang out in his soul. What was he weeping about? Oh, he was weeping with ecstasy, weeping, even, over those stars that shone down upon him from infinite distances, and he was "unashamed of his ecstasy." It was as if the threads of all those innumerable worlds of God had met in his soul and his soul was vibrating from its contact with "different worlds." He craved to forgive everyone and everything and to beg for forgiveness—oh, not forgiveness just for himself, but for everyone and everything. "Others will ask forgiveness of me too," the voice rang out in his soul again. Every moment he felt clearly, almost physically, something real and indestructible, like the vault of the sky over his head, entering his soul. Something, a kind of idea, had taken over his soul forever and ever. He was a weak youth when he fell on the ground and he rose a strong and determined fighter. He knew it. He felt it during that moment of rapture. And never, never thereafter would Alyosha forget that moment. "Someone visited my soul then," he would say later, with firm faith in his words.

Three days later, he left the monastery in accordance with the wish of his late elder, who had directed him to "go out into the world."

BOOK VIII

MITYA

CHAPTER 1

Kuzma Samsonov

While Grushenka, before starting out on her new life, was sending Dmitry Karamazov her regards and bidding him to remember forever the "short hour" during which she had loved him, Dmitry himself was having a hectic time, although he knew nothing of what was happening to her. For the previous two days he had been in such an unimaginable state that he could very well have contracted brain fever, as he said himself later. On the previous morning, Alyosha had not been able to find him anywhere and he had never turned up to meet Ivan at the inn. His landlady would not reveal his whereabouts, on his express orders. "I was fighting my fate, trying to escape it," he said later about those two days. Terrified as he was to take his eye off Grushenka even for a second, he nevertheless made a hurried trip out of town for a few hours on urgent business. All these details came out later and were thoroughly documented, but for now we shall confine ourselves to the essential events of these two nightmarish days that preceded the horrible catastrophe that was suddenly to engulf him.

Although it was true that Grushenka had loved him "for an hour," truly and sincerely, this had never prevented her from treating him cruelly, and at times with complete ruthlessness. The worst of it was that he could never make out what she really wanted. Neither his passionate tenderness nor his fits of violence were of any use: he felt that she would never yield to him either way and that he only risked making her angry, making her turn her back on him for good. He suspected then—and rightly as it turned out—that she herself was passing through a profound crisis, that she was desperately trying to decide something, and that she could not make the decision; he suspected, with good reason, that there were moments in which she actually loathed him, his passion

for her, and everything about him. But with all that, he still
never understood what was actually causing Grushenka's torment. To him the whole business had only two possible out-
comes: it would be either he, Mitya, or his father. It must
be clearly noted here that he was certain his father would
propose to Grushenka—if he had not done so already—for
he never believed that the old lecher could get her for a mere
three thousand rubles. Mitya knew Grushenka and her character too well for that. And this was why he was under the
impression, much of the time, that Grushenka's tenseness
and torment came from the tantalizing choice before her:
she could not decide which of the two to choose, which would
be the more profitable choice. As to the imminent return of
"the officer," the man who had played such a fateful role
in Grushenka's life, Dmitry somehow did not even give it
much thought during those days. It is true that Grushenka
had not mentioned the matter to him recently, although she
had told him about the letter from her seducer a month before and had even shown him some passages in it. Grushenka
had done so to torment him, in one of her wicked moments,
but, to her considerable surprise, Dmitry had shown very little
interest in it. It would be difficult to explain why he had been
so indifferent. Perhaps it was because he was so disgusted by
the monstrousness and the horror of his rivalry with his own
father over this woman that, at the time, he could not imagine anything worse or more threatening. Indeed, he somehow
could not envisage this man who had suddenly come to life
after vanishing for five years, and he did not believe in the
man's imminent appearance on the scene. Besides, in this
first letter that Dmitry had seen, the man's arrival was only
hinted at and the whole letter seemed very vague and high-
flown, and was filled with sentimental clichés. Actually,
Grushenka had not let him see the closing lines, in which the
sender's forthcoming arrival was mentioned more definitely.
Dmitry had also sensed Grushenka's scorn for the message
in that letter from Siberia, her contempt having escaped her
in an unguarded moment. And since then, Grushenka had not
mentioned her further communications with the new rival.
So eventually Dmitry forgot about him altogether. In general,
Dmitry felt that, whatever happened later, whichever way
things turned out, he had to face the imminent clash with
his father first. So, holding his breath, he waited for Grushenka's decision, which he expected her to make without warning, on the spur of the moment. She might, for instance, say

to him without any preamble: "Take me, I'm yours forever." And that would be that: he would take her and they would leave at once for the edge of the world. Ah, yes, he would take her away at once, if not to the edge of the world, then at least as far as possible, to the edge of Russia, where he would marry her and live with her, knowing no one, here or there, or anywhere. Then a completely new life would start for them! Of that new, "virtuous" life (it absolutely had to be "virtuous"), he would dream and daydream constantly, obsessively. He craved that renewal and regeneration. The foul quagmire in which he was sinking of his own volition made him sick and, like so many others under such circumstances, he believed in the magic of a change of place—just to get away from this spot, to be surrounded by different people, to be in a different situation, where everything would be new and different! That is what Dmitry believed in and yearned for.

But all this would come about only if the whole business had a happy outcome. There was another possible outcome, though, a tragic one. She might suddenly say: "Go away. I've come to an agreement with your father and have decided to marry him. I don't need you anymore." Well, in that case . . . Actually, Mitya was none too sure what would happen then, and, up till the very last moment, he still didn't know. That much must be said for him. He had no definite ideas and was not contemplating committing a crime. He watched, spied, and suffered all that time, but he expected the first, the happy, outcome to the fateful dilemma. He deliberately refused to envisage any other possibility.

There was something else, though, that also tormented him, a new and unrelated trouble, but one that was also fateful and that he could not resolve. If things did turn out well, if she did say to him, "I'm yours, take me away," how would he take her away? Where would he get the necessary money? His resources, which for many years had consisted solely of the sums he received from his father, had now run dry. Grushenka, of course, had money, but Mitya's pride would keep him from touching it: he had to pay for their journey himself and then earn their living by his own efforts; he could not live on her capital. The mere thought of accepting money from her made him physically sick.

I don't want to dwell here on this attitude of his; I don't wish to analyze it and will only state that this is how he felt at that particular moment. This feeling may have stemmed indirectly, unconsciously perhaps, from the guilt he felt over having dishonestly spent Katerina's money. "Isn't it enough to have acted despicably with the other one? Must I act like a despicable wretch with this one too?" he thought, as he was to admit later. Besides, he was worried that "if Grushenka should ever learn about that matter, she wouldn't want to have anything to do with a wretch like me!" But where was he to get the money he needed so desperately? "Is it possible that the opportunity will be wasted and nothing will come of it, just because I have no money?" he ranted on in despair. "Ah, what a disgrace!"

I must say here, in anticipation, that he may have known where he could get hold of the money he needed and perhaps he knew exactly where it was hidden. I won't go into the details for the time being, for it will become clear later on, but I will say that Dmitry's situation was aggravated by his conviction that, before he could take the money, before he could consider himself "entitled" to it, he would first have to pay back the three thousand rubles he owed Katerina. "Otherwise," he reasoned, "I'm nothing but a wretched, petty thief and I have no desire to start out on my new life as a petty thief." And so he decided to turn the whole world upside down if he had to, in order to get three thousand rubles to pay back Katerina, *before anything else*. This decision had taken shape on the road to the monastery. That day, when Grushenka had insulted Katerina and Mitya had heard of it from Alyosha, he had admitted his despicable act to Alyosha and asked him to tell Katerina about it, "if that would make her feel any better." And, after leaving his young brother that night, Mitya had felt, in his wound-up state, that he would murder and rob someone if that were the only way he could get the money to pay back Katerina. "I'd rather be condemned as a thief and a murderer before my victim and before all other men, and be sent to Siberia," he thought that night, "than give Katya the right to say that, after having betrayed her, I stole her money and used it to run away with Grushenka and start a new, 'virtuous' life with her. No, that is one thing I could not do!"

This is what Mitya, gnashing his teeth, was saying to himself, and so it is hardly surprising that he thought he might end up with brain fever. But, meantime, he tried desperately to do whatever he could.

It may seem that, having come to such a decision, there was nothing left for Dmitry but despair, for where could a penniless man like him find such a large sum of money? But, strangely enough, up until the very last moment, he kept hoping to find the three thousand, to get hold of it somehow or other, to see it drop from the sky, as it were. But that is the way people like Dmitry Karamazov usually are about money: they only know how to spend it, how to throw around whatever they inherit, and have not the slightest notion of how money is earned. After he had left Alyosha, a most fantastic whirlwind started in his head, leaving his thoughts in utter confusion. And he started his search for money, on a wild hunch, in the most improbable place imaginable. But, then, perhaps the least likely and most fantastic undertakings come most naturally to such men.

It was the merchant Samsonov, Grushenka's protector, whom Dmitry chose to approach first. He decided to ask him for the entire sum he needed and to propose a certain "plan" to him. Dmitry had no doubts about the business side of the deal he was going to offer Samsonov; he was only worried about how Samsonov would regard the deal from a non-commercial point of view. Mitya knew Samsonov only by sight. They had never spoken to each other, but somehow he had long felt that the old seducer, now a dying man, would not object to Grushenka's settling down to an honest life and marrying a "reliable man." In fact, Dmitry thought that, far from objecting, this was what Samsonov wanted and that he would be glad to promote it if the opportunity presented itself. In any case, whether he had heard it from other people or perhaps had gathered it from Grushenka herself, he was under the impression that Samsonov would prefer her to marry him rather than his father.

Some readers may possibly find Dmitry's reliance on the help of his fiancée's protector and his willingness to, as it were, accept her from his hands, rather coarse and even unsavory. To that I can only reply that he now viewed Grushenka's past as non-existent. He was filled with infinite compassion for her and had decided with passionate enthusiasm that, as soon as she told him she loved him and would marry him, she would become a different Grushenka and he would become a new Dmitry Karamazov—one without vices, with only virtues—and they would forgive each other and from then on live a different life. As to Kuzma Samsonov, Dmitry looked upon him as a shadow from Grushenka's vanished past, a man who had played a fateful part in her life but whom she had never loved, who had now been left behind and was no longer there. Mitya could not even consider him as a man now, for everyone in town knew that Samsonov was a wreck, whose relations with Grushenka could only be those of a father with his daughter—not at all what they had been before—and that it had been that way for quite some time already, almost a whole year. In any case, there was a great deal of child-like simplicity in Mitya's way of thinking. For all his debauchery and his vices, he was really a very naive, child-like person. And this same child-like simplicity also led Mitya to believe that, since old Kuzma was about to depart for the other world, he must sincerely repent his past relations with Grushenka and that now she could not find a better friend or protector than that harmless old man.

After his conversation with Alyosha on the road to the monastery, Mitya stayed awake almost all night, and at ten o'clock the next morning he walked into Samsonov's house and asked the servant to announce him. It was a bleak old two-story house, very large, surrounded by a courtyard, a cottage, and several sheds and barns. On the ground floor lived Samsonov's two married sons with their families, his elderly sister, and an unmarried daughter. In the cottage lived two of his shipping clerks, one of them with his family. Samsonov's children and his clerks were rather crowded in their quarters, while the old man had the entire upper floor of the house all to himself; he would not even allow his daughter to live there, although she looked after him and had to run upstairs whenever he called her, at any hour of the day or night, despite her chronic asthma.

The top floor consisted of a succession of large living rooms furnished in the old style of Russian merchants' houses, with endless rows of heavy, cumbersome mahogany chairs and armchairs lined up along the walls, with cut-glass chandeliers in dust-covers, with somber mirrors between the windows. All these rooms seemed deserted, for the sick old man lived mostly in one room, his smallish bedroom at the far end of the house, where he was waited on by an old woman-servant with a kerchief on her head and a young valet who spent most of his time sitting on a chest in the corridor. Because of his swollen legs, the old man could hardly walk; he seldom left his big leather armchair and when he did was usually supported by the old maid-servant who led him around the room. He hardly even spoke to this old woman and was very stern with her.

When they announced that "Captain Karamazov" was there to see him, he at once declared he would not receive him. But Mitya insisted, sending the servant back to the old man. Samsonov then asked his valet what the Captain looked like, whether he didn't seem drunk, and whether he was behaving decently. When he was told that the visitor was sober but that he would not leave, the old man sent once more to tell Dmitry that he would not receive him. Having anticipated the old man's refusal, Dmitry had brought with him a piece of paper and a pencil. Now he wrote hurriedly on it: "I am here on very important business concerning Miss Grushenka Svetlov," and sent it up to the old man. The old man deliberated for a while, then sent the valet to show the visitor into the main living room and ordered the old woman to get his younger son and bring him upstairs.

This younger son was a huge man of well over six foot and exceptionally strong. He was clean-shaven and dressed in European style, unlike Samsonov himself who was bearded and wore a kaftan. He came at once and waited in silence for, like all the rest of them, he lived in awe of his father. Samsonov had sent for this giant not because he was really afraid of Dmitry—he was not one to be easily frightened— but because he thought it would be better to have a witness and, well, just in case . . . And so, supported by his son and his valet, Samsonov finally hobbled into the living room, prob-ably rather curious about the man he would find there.

The living room where Mitya waited was vast, bleak, and depressing. It had two big windows, a gallery around it, imitation marble wallpaper, and three huge cut-glass chan-deliers in covers. Mitya sat on a straight chair by the door. He was obviously waiting with nervous impatience. When the old man appeared at the opposite end of the room, about sixty feet away from him, Mitya stood up at once and walked toward the old man with his long, firm military stride. He was dressed very correctly that morning—a frock-coat buttoned up all the way and black gloves, and with a top-hat in his hands, exactly the same clothes as he had worn three days earlier at the elder's, when he had met with his father and brothers at the monastery. The old man, dignified and stern, stood waiting for him and, as he walked toward him, Mitya felt that Samsonov had thoroughly appraised him. Mitya was very struck by Samsonov's face, the lower part of which had lately become so swollen that his lower lip, always naturally thick, now protruded like a saucer. Samsonov bowed

to him in dignified silence and, gesturing him to an armchair
by the sofa, started slowly installing himself on the sofa
facing Mitya, groaning and leaning heavily on his son's arm
as he did so. Watching this obviously painful effort, Mitya
now felt sorry for having imposed such exertions on this
venerable and important man and, at the same time, felt
ashamed of his own insignificance.

"What can I do for you, sir?" the old man said when he
was finally installed. He spoke slowly, articulating his words
clearly, but without rudeness.

Mitya gave a start, jumped up without thinking, and sat
down again. Then he spoke hurriedly and nervously, in a
loud voice, gesticulating in his excitement, becoming more
and more agitated . . . It was obvious that this was a man
on the brink of disaster, looking desperately for a way out,
without which there would be nothing left for him but to
plunge into the abyss. Kuzma Samsonov must have seen all
this within a minute, although his face remained cold and
expressionless, like the face of an idol.

"I suppose you must have heard, sir, about my disagreements with my father, Fyodor Karamazov, who has cheated
me out of my inheritance from my mother . . . It has been
the talk of the town for quite a while now . . . for people
here like to talk about things that are really none of their business. Besides, Grushenka—I'm sorry, I mean Miss Svetlov—
may have told you about it . . ." Mitya started out, interrupting
himself all the time. We will not bother to reproduce his
speech verbatim, however, but will just report the gist of it.
What he wanted to say was that three months earlier he
had gone on purpose to see (he deliberately avoided the
word "consult") a lawyer in the provincial capital ("Pavel
Korneplodov—I'm sure you must have heard of him, sir. A
tremendous mind, the intelligence of a statesman almost . . .
he knows you . . . thinks very highly of you"). Mitya became
sidetracked again but these diversions did not stop him. He
just skipped back from them to his story. Well, then, that
great lawyer, after having questioned Mitya thoroughly and
studied the documents (Mitya was rather vague about these
documents and seemed in a hurry to get this part of his
story over with), declared that Chermashnya should really
be Mitya's as it was part of his mother's estate and that Mitya
could claim it by legal action, which would make things very
unpleasant for "my unbearable old father," because, Mitya

said, "he has not established his rights to it very firmly and
a good lawyer would soon find a loophole." In brief, there
was a good chance of getting another six or perhaps even
seven thousand out of the old man, for Chermashnya was
worth "at least twenty-five, I mean, twenty-eight thousand . . .
no, no, it's worth all of thirty thousand, sir, while, I—would
you believe it?—I haven't even had seventeen thousand rubles
for it out of that stone-hearted man!" And Mitya went on
to say that, while he was away, he had dropped the matter
"because I'm no good at these legal matters," but now, having
come back, he was dumbfounded by his father's counter-
claim. At this point he got mixed up again and, instead of
pursuing this subject, concluded his speech with his proposition: Wouldn't "the highly esteemed Mr. Samsonov" be interested in acquiring Mitya's rights to Chermashnya for just
three thousand rubles? "I give you my word of honor, you
won't lose anything on the deal. Indeed, I'm absolutely certain,
I swear on my honor, that you'll get back six or seven thousand for these three . . ." What Mitya wanted, though, was
"to settle this whole thing no later than today."

"We could meet at a notary's, or wherever you say . . .
In short, I'll hand over all the papers to you, everything,
whatever you want. I'll sign anything . . . And then we can
draw up a legal agreement and . . . if it is possible . . . if
you think it is feasible, I'd like to have . . . the three thousand . . . this morning. For no one but you in this town has
such a large sum at his disposal . . . And you'd save me
from . . . I mean you'd save my poor head, so that I could
act like an honorable man, I dare say—for I have very honorable feelings toward someone you know very well and in
whom you take a fatherly interest . . . For I wouldn't be
here if I were not aware that your interest in her was fatherly,
sir. If I may put it this way, sir, three men have collided
head-on—that's fate for you, Mr. Samsonov, a horrible fate!
But that's realism, sir, sheer realism! Well, since you haven't
been involved in it for a long time now, that leaves two
heads . . . Perhaps I'm not expressing it very clearly, but
then I have no literary talent. What I was trying to say was
that my head is there and also the head of that monster . . .
And so you choose—who is it to be—the monster or me?
Everything is in your hands now—three men and two lots
to draw . . . forgive me, I am a bit mixed up, but I can see
by your highly esteemed eyes that you are following me . . .

And if you are not, I'll have to jump in the lake this very day. So that's it."

And with this "So that's it," Mitya rested his absurd plea. Jumping up from his seat, he waited for Samsonov's answer to his preposterous proposition. As he was uttering his closing phrase, it suddenly dawned on him that it had not worked and that he had been talking utter nonsense. "That's strange," the thought flashed through his head. "It all seemed so reasonable when I was on my way here, and now it makes no sense . . ." While he had been talking, the old man had kept an icy, immobile gaze fixed on him, and once Mitya had finished, Samsonov waited for a minute or so and then said in a firm tone that left no room for hope:

"I'm sorry, sir, but I don't go in for that sort of business."

Mitya felt his legs giving way under him.

"But, sir . . ." he said with a wan, helpless smile, "that means, then . . . means that I'm lost now, don't you think so?"

"I am sorry, sir."

Mitya was still standing there, gaping straight into the old man's face, when suddenly he thought he saw something move in it. He gave a violent start.

"You see, that is really not our line of business at all," the old man said very slowly. "Getting involved with lawyers, hearings, all that, is too much trouble . . . But I know a man who might be interested. Perhaps you should address yourself to him."

"Oh! . . ." Mitya felt life returning to him. "What's his name? Oh, Mr. Samsonov, you've given me a new lease on life!"

"He's not a local man and he's not in town at the moment. He sells lumber to peasants and they call him 'the Hound.' He's been trying to buy that Chermashnya wood of yours from your father for a year, but they have not been able to agree on the price. You may have heard about it. Now he's in Chermashnya again and is staying at the priest's house in Ilyinskoye village, about eight miles from the Volovya railroad station. He wrote me too about that business. I mean, he wanted my advice on it. I believe your father is planning to go and see him himself. So I suppose if you got there before him and made the Hound the same offer you've just made me, who knows, he might possibly consider it . . ."

"What an inspired idea!" Mitya interrupted him enthusiastically. "Yes, right, that would suit him fine! He's interested in buying it, the price he's been asked for it is too high and here, all of a sudden, he'll have a document showing his ownership! Ha-ha-ha!" Mitya suddenly burst into wooden laughter that was so unexpected that Samsonov started.

"I don't even know how to thank you, sir," Mitya muttered excitedly.

"Please don't mention it," Samsonov said, slightly lowering his head.

"You don't realize what you've done for me—you've actually saved me! Oh, I had a feeling you'd help me! . . . So I'm off to the priest's now!"

"There's really nothing to thank me for."

"I'll hurry over there right away! I'm sorry to have imposed on you when you were not feeling well, and I'll never forget what you've done for me. You have my word for that, the word of a *Russian* man."

"I see, I see."

Mitya was about to seize the old man's hand and shake it, but a hostile glint appeared in Samsonov's eye and Mitya hurriedly pulled his hand back, and then at once reproached himself for being overly suspicious: "He's just tired," he thought.

"It's for her, Mr. Samsonov! You understand, I'm doing all this for her!" he suddenly roared so that his voice resounded through the huge room. Then he turned about face and marched off toward the door with the same long soldier's stride. He was wound up and trembling. "Everything seemed lost and then, all of a sudden, my guardian angel saved me." Thoughts whirled around in his head. "But if a big business-man like him—ah, what a dignified figure of a man!—advises me to do it this way, I'm sure the deal is as good as settled . . . unless . . . no, surely he couldn't be pulling my leg, could he? . . ." And Mitya kept exclaiming under his breath all the way to his lodgings; and, indeed, there were only these two alternatives: either this was sound business advice from a solid businessman, who knew all the facts of the business at hand, moreover, and also that man, the Hound—what a peculiar name!—or the old man was sending him on a fool's errand.

Alas, it turned out that the second alternative was the right one. Much later, after the catastrophe, old Samsonov admitted laughingly that he had deliberately played a trick on "the Captain." For Samsonov was a cold, cruel, mocking man, who sometimes took violent dislikes to people. It could have been the enthusiastic look on Mitya's face, or perhaps "that useless spendthrift's" notion that he, Samsonov, could be taken in by such idiotic ravings as Mitya's "plan," or he may even have felt jealous over Grushenka, in whose name this "good-for-nothing" had come to him with a cock and bull story about needing money—it's hard to say exactly what made Samsonov do it, but at the moment that Mitya's legs had given way under him in despair and he had explained that he was lost, the old man had glanced at him with immense hatred and had decided to play a cruel trick on him.

When Mitya had left, Samsonov, pale with rage, told his son to see to it that that "good-for-nothing" was never allowed into the house again, otherwise . . .

He did not say what would happen otherwise, but even his son, who had often seen him angry, shuddered in fear. And for a whole hour after that, the old man shook with rage. In the evening he felt ill and sent for a doctor.

CHAPTER 2

The Hound

And so Mitya rushed off "at a gallop." But he did not have even enough money to pay for horses. Altogether he had forty kopeks, the remains of his years of prosperity! Ah yes, he also had an old silver watch that had stopped long before. He dashed off to a Jewish watchmaker who had a little shop on the market place, and got six rubles for it. "I never expected to get that much!" Mitya cried enthusiastically (he was still in the same exhilarated state) and ran back home. There he increased the sum by borrowing three rubles from his landlord and his wife, who gave it to him gladly, although it was all they had, because they had such great affection for their lodger. In his excitement, Mitya revealed to them that his fate was being decided and told them—to be sure, in a tremendous hurry—just about everything, including the "plan" he had offered Samsonov and the advice Samsonov had given him; he explained to them his hopes for the future, and so on. Mitya had confided many of his secrets to these people before, and for that very reason they felt as if he were one of them rather than a haughty gentleman.

Having collected nine rubles, Mitya ordered post-horses to take him to Volovya station. And thus it was later to be established and recorded that "at noon, on the day preceding the event, Dmitry Karamazov had no money at all and, in order to get some, had to sell his watch and borrow three rubles from his landlord—both of which facts are confirmed by witnesses."

I mention this beforehand and later it will become clear why I do so.

On his way to Volovya, Mitya was beaming in joyful anticipation of "getting all this business over and done with," although shivers ran up and down his spine when he imagined all the things that might happen to Grushenka in his absence. What if, just that day, she decided to go to his father's? That was why he had left without telling anyone, except the people in his house, whom he had asked expressly not to tell anyone of his whereabouts, whoever asked for him. "I must be back tonight without fail and, if I have to, I'll drag that fellow the Hound back by force with me to complete the deal here," Mitya repeated to himself, as he jogged along in the carriage, hoping breathlessly that everything would turn out well. But alas, his hopes were not destined to be fulfilled according to his "plan."

To start with, it took him much longer to get to the village from the Volovya station than he had expected, for, instead of eight miles of narrow country road, it turned out to be a good twelve miles. Then, when he finally got to Ilyinskoye, he found that the priest was away—he had gone off to another village. Mitya had to drive on to that village with the same tired horses, and by the time he succeeded in finding the priest, it was almost night. The priest, a shy and apparently kindly little man, told Mitya that, although the Hound had at first stayed at his house, he was now staying at the forester's hut in the Sukhoi settlement, because he sold lumber there too. Mitya started to plead with the priest to accompany him and help him get hold of the Hound—"You'll save my life if you will, Father"—and, after some hesitation, the priest finally agreed to go with Mitya to Sukhoi, probably because he was curious about the whole business. Unfortunately, though, he suggested they go on foot, for, he assured Mitya, it was only a mile's walk "or just a wee bit more." Mitya readily agreed and set out with his long, fast strides, so that the poor priest had to almost trot behind him. On the way, Mitya told him, too, about his plans, speaking heatedly and nervously and asking him for advice about how to handle the Hound. The priest, who was not yet an old man, turned out to be very cautious and answered Mitya's questions with "I

wouldn't know really," "I'm sorry, I'm not sure about that,"
and other such evasive answers. And when Mitya brought up
his disputes with his father, the priest actually became frightened, for he was in some way or other in a position of
dependence on Mr. Karamazov. He asked with unconcealed
surprise why Mitya kept referring to the man in question as
the Hound, explaining that, although the Hound was indeed
the fellow's nickname, he resented it very much. He advised
Mitya to be sure to call him by his proper name—Gorstkin—
otherwise "he won't make that deal with you. In fact, he won't
even want to listen to you." Mitya was surprised in his turn
and told the priest that that was how Samsonov had referred
to the man. When he heard that, the priest changed the
subject, though it might have been kinder of him to have
imparted to Dmitry his suspicion—namely, that if Samsonov
had recommended the man to him only as the Hound, either
he must have done so as a joke or there must be something
wrong somewhere. But Mitya had no time to stop and examine such "details." He was in a hurry, walking fast with his
long strides, and it was only when they finally got to Sukhoi
that it occurred to him that they had not walked just one mile,
nor even a mile and a half, but a good two miles. The realization angered him, but he controlled himself and they entered
the hut.

The forester, whom the priest knew, had allowed Gorstkin
to occupy the better of the two rooms in his hut. They entered
this room and lighted a tallow candle. The room was overheated. On a pine table in the middle of it was a samovar
with the flame beneath it out, a tray with some cups, an empty
rum bottle, a not quite empty bottle of vodka, and the remains
of a loaf of white bread. Gorstkin himself lay stretched out
on the bench, with his coat rolled up under his head for a
pillow, snoring heavily. Mitya stood there for a moment,
perplexed.

"Of course, I must wake him up," he said worriedly. "My
business is too important. I was in a great hurry to get here
and ought to be on my way back as soon as possible . . ."

The priest and the forester would not express an opinion;
they just stood there in silence and waited.

Mitya walked over to the sleeping man and started to
shake him, but the fellow just would not wake up.

"My God, he's dead drunk. What shall I do?"

Now, losing patience, Mitya pulled the man violently by
the arms and legs, lifted his head, picked him up, sat him on

the bench, and finally, after long and stubborn efforts, succeeded in getting the drunken man to produce an inarticulate
bovine lowing, which was followed by slurred cursing.

"I suppose you'd be better off if you waited a bit," the
priest finally decided to advise him. "He doesn't seem to be
in much of a state to discuss business right now."

"He's been drinking all day," the forester put in.

"Oh God!" Mitya cried dejectedly. "If only you people
knew how important it is to me—I'm really getting desperate!"

"I would still advise you to wait until morning," the priest
said.

"Until morning! But don't you understand that that's absolutely out of the question!" In his despair he was about to
rush over to the drunken man and shake him some more, but
he suddenly realized the futility of it.

The priest said nothing; the sleepy forester was gloomy.

"What terrible tragedies people suffer through realism!"
Mitya said incongruously, overwhelmed by utter despair.
Sweat was running down his face.

Taking advantage of the pause, the priest quickly and very
reasonably called to his attention the fact that, even if he
succeeded in waking Gorstkin up, he would still be too drunk
even to talk, let alone to discuss "an important business matter such as you have in mind. No, sir, I really think you
ought to postpone it until the morning now."

Mitya, throwing up his hands in despair, decided to take
his advice.

"I'll stay here with the candle, Father," Mitya said. "I'll
bide my time, and the moment he wakes up, I'll start . . . I'll
pay you for the candle," he said, turning to the forester, "and
also for spending the night in your hut. Don't worry, you
won't regret what you do for Dmitry Karamazov . . . But
what about you, Father? Where could you make yourself
comfortable, I wonder?"

"Oh, please don't worry about me. I'll be on my way home.
He'll lend me his mare," the priest said, indicating the forester. "Well, good-night now, and I wish you every success."

And that is how it was to be. The priest borrowed the mare
and rode home, only too glad to be out of it all, though shaking his head worriedly and wondering whether he should not
inform his benefactor, Mr. Karamazov, in the morning, for,
"Who can tell—he may be furious at not being told and stop
doing me all those little favors." The forester scratched himself and silently departed to his half of the hut. And Mitya

sat down on the bench next to the drunk "to bide his time," as he had put it. A deep anguish enveloped his soul like a heavy fog, a deep, frightening anguish. He sat there sunk in thought, but he could not find an answer. The candle guttered. A cricket chirped. The overheated room was becoming unbearably stuffy. He suddenly visualized his father's garden, the passageway in the back of it, the door of the house opening quietly and Grushenka dashing inside . . . He jumped up from the bench.

"What a tragedy . . ." he muttered, gnashing his teeth, and without knowing what he was doing, he went up to the sleeping man and stood there staring into his face. He was a middle-aged peasant, spare, with a longish face, curly, light-brown hair, and a long, sparse, reddish beard. He wore a blue cotton shirt and a black waistcoat with a silver watch sticking out of the pocket. Mitya examined the face with immense hatred. Somehow, it was the man's curly hair that he found most revolting. What enraged him was that he, Mitya, who had such urgent business for the sake of which he had rushed here, leaving everything in a mess, now had to sit and wait while "this parasite, on whom my whole future now depends, is snoring as if nothing had happened, as if he'd just arrived from some other planet . . ."

"Oh, the irony of fate!" he shouted suddenly and, losing patience, again started shaking the drunken peasant. He shook him in a rage now, banged at him, pulled him, even hit him a few times, but, after he had been at it for five minutes, he realized the complete futility of it and sat down once more on the bench, feeling utterly hopeless.

"How stupid, how stupid," he kept exclaiming. "How dishonorable!" he suddenly added for no apparent reason. He was getting a bad headache. "Shall I give up and leave?" the thought flashed through his head. "Oh no, since I'm here, I may as well stay until morning. Why should I have come all this way otherwise? Besides, where will I get the money to go back? Oh, the stupidity of it all!"

His headache was getting worse and worse. Now he sat motionless and he did not notice when he dozed off; then he fell asleep as he sat there. He must have slept like that for at least two hours before he was awakened by an unbearable headache—bad enough to make him moan. His temples were throbbing, the top of his head was terribly painful. After he woke up, it took him a long time to understand where he was and what was happening. Finally he realized that the overheated room was filled with charcoal fumes and that he could have been asphyxiated, poisoned. The drunken peasant was still lying there, snoring. The candle was guttering and was about to go out. Mitya let out a yell and ran into the forester's room across the passage. The forester woke up quickly enough, but, when told that the other room was full of deadly fumes, took the news with such peculiar equanimity that Mitya felt both surprised and offended.

"But what if he dies?" Mitya cried. "What'll happen if he dies? What will I do then?" he kept repeating frantically.

They opened the window and the flue. Mitya brought a bucket of water from the passage, first wet his own head, then picked up a rag, dipped it in the water, and put it on the Hound's head. The forester still treated the whole thing almost with scorn and, after he had opened the window, he just mumbled sullenly, "It's good enough like this," and went back to sleep, leaving Mitya a lighted iron lantern. After he had left, Mitya kept working on the half-asphyxiated drunkard for half an hour, constantly wetting the man's head, and he was quite determined to keep at it the rest of the night. But when he grew too tired and sat down for one minute to catch his breath, his eyes closed instantly and, without knowing it, he stretched out on the bench and slept like a log.

He awoke very late in the morning—nine o'clock or so. Sunshine was pouring in through the two little windows. Last night's curly-haired, drunken peasant was sitting up with his coat on. A freshly lighted samovar and another bottle of vodka stood on the table before him. He had finished what was left of the bottle that had been there at night and had drunk more than half the new one. Mitya abruptly realized that the damned fellow was again utterly and irretrievably drunk. He leaped to his feet and stared at the peasant, his eyes almost popping out. The peasant, for his part, kept throwing sly glances at Mitya, appearing irritatingly unperturbed, even contemptuously insolent—or at least so it seemed to Mitya.

Mitya rushed up to him.

"Excuse me . . . you see, I'm . . . I suppose the forester must have told you—I'm Lieutenant Dmitry Karamazov, the son of old Fyodor Karamazov, whose wood you are interested in buying . . ."

"You're lying there," the peasant declared in an unexpectedly calm, firm voice.

"What do you mean, I'm lying? You do know Mr. Karamazov, don't you?"

"I don't know no Mr. Karamazov," the peasant said, manipulating his heavy tongue with an effort.

"But you're trying to buy the wood from him—the wood!
Wake up, please, wake up! The Ilyinskoye priest, Father
Pavel, brought me here . . . You wrote to Samsonov and it
was he who sent me to you . . ." Mitya insisted breathlessly.

"It's nothing but lies," the Hound declared emphatically,
and Mitya felt his legs go weak and cold under him.

"For God's sake, man, this is no joke, understand! I know
you're a bit under the weather . . . But surely you can talk.
You must understand what's going on . . . or . . . or I don't
understand anything myself . . ."

"You're that house painter!"

"What are you talking about? I'm Karamazov, Dmitry
Karamazov, and I want to make you an offer—a profitable
one—a great offer . . . It's about that wood, you know."

The peasant stroked his beard with a dignified air.

"No, you're the one who contracted for that job, and you
bungled it. You're a son of a bitch!"

"I assure you, you're mistaken!" Mitya cried, wringing his
hands.

The peasant was still stroking his beard. Suddenly he
screwed up his eyes and gave Mitya a crafty look.

"First of all," he said, "I want you to show me what law
allows you to play filthy tricks on people, do you hear? And
I tell you—you're a son of a bitch, understand?"

Mitya stepped back in despair. Then, as he explained afterward, "It was as if something had hit me on the head." In
the twinkling of an eye, the hopelessness of his position
dawned on him. "A kind of light went on and I saw everything clearly," he was to say later. He stood there dumbfounded: how could he, a supposedly intelligent man, have
allowed himself to be sent on such a fool's errand, to get
entangled in all this poppycock and bother with this Hound
man all night, wetting his head and all? "Well, the man is
drunk, drunk as a pig, and he'll go on drinking for another
week maybe, so what good will it do me to wait? And, besides, what if Samsonov sent me here just to make a fool of
me and in the meantime she . . . Oh, my God, what a mess
I've got myself into!"

The Hound was looking at him and grinning. On another
day Mitya might have killed the fool in a fit of rage, but now

he felt as weak as a child. He went quietly to the bench, picked up his overcoat, put it on, and walked out of the room without saying a word. The other room across the passage was empty: the forester had left. He took fifty kopeks out of his pocket and put them on the table to pay for the night spent in the hut, for the candle, and for the trouble he'd caused.

He stepped outside. There was nothing but the forest all around him. He walked off at random, having no idea whether he should go right or left. He had been in such a hurry when he had come there with the priest the night before that he had paid no attention to the road. There was no anger in him now, not even against Samsonov. His mind was blank as he walked along the narrow forest trail, all hopes shattered; he no longer cared where he was going. A child, meeting him at that moment, could have attacked him with impunity, so weak did he feel in body and in spirit.

Somehow, though, he eventually got out of the forest and started across bare, harvested fields stretching all the way to the horizon. "Death and despair all around," Mitya kept muttering in rhythm with his steps, as he walked on and on.

He was lucky. An old merchant, who was being driven in a hired carriage along the small rural road, passed him. Mitya asked the way and it turned out that they were also going to Volovya station; after some discussion, they agreed to take Mitya with them. It took about three hours to get to Volovya, where Mitya at once ordered post-horses for the drive back to town. Then he suddenly realized that he was terribly hungry. While the horses were being harnessed, they prepared him an omelet, which he ate with a thick slice of bread and some salami that they happened to have, downing at the same time three small glasses of vodka. When he had eaten, he felt better; a beam of sunlight broke through his gloom and he cheered up somewhat.

They drove fast toward town, but that didn't keep Mitya from urging on the coachman. Suddenly he conceived a new "plan"—one he felt sure "cannot fail to get me that damned money."

"And just to think, just to imagine," he mumbled scornfully under his breath, "that a human life was almost ruined for lack of a miserable three thousand rubles! But that's enough—I'll settle it all today!"

Perhaps if it had not been for his continuous worrying about Grushenka and all the things that might have happened to her, he would have felt perfectly gay and cheerful. The thought of Grushenka, however, kept stabbing him like a sharp blade. At last they reached town, and Mitya immediately dashed off to her house.

CHAPTER 3

The Gold Mines

This was the visit which had frightened Grushenka so much and of which she had told Rakitin. She was waiting for her "message" at the time and, as Mitya had not come over either that day or the day before, she was hoping that with luck he might not come at all before she left. But suddenly he burst in on her. We already know what happened then: she quickly convinced him to accompany her to Samsonov's house, where she was supposed to help the old man "count his money." And when Mitya had seen her to the door, she made him promise he would come back and pick her up at midnight, to see her back to her house. Mitya was rather pleased with this arrangement—"If she sits there with Samsonov, at least she won't be rushing off to father's . . . Unless, of course, she's lying to me," he added at once. But he did not think she was lying to him. He was the type of jealous man who, when he is away from his beloved, immediately thinks of God knows what horrors about her deceiving him, but once back with her, shaken and crushed, furious and convinced that *this* time she has certainly betrayed him, he regains his confidence as soon as he sees her gay, laughing, tender face and forgets all his suspicions, is ashamed of his jealousy, and joyfully berates himself for it.

Having seen Grushenka off, Dmitry hurried home, for there were still many, many things he had to do that day! But now, at least, the weight was lifted from his heart. "I must find out from Smerdyakov, though, whether anything happened last night, whether she didn't by any chance go and see father while I was away . . ." The thought flashed through his head, and even before he had reached home, jealousy had again taken hold of his restless heart.

Jealousy! "Othello was not jealous; he was trusting," Pushkin said. This remark in itself attests to that great poet's uncanny insight. Othello's heart was broken and his whole understanding of the world was dimmed because *his ideal had been shattered.* But Othello would not hide, spy, or sneak, for he was a trusting man. Indeed, it took tremendous efforts to lead him on, arouse his suspicions, and fire his imagination so that the thought of betrayal should occur to him. This is not what the truly jealous man is like. It is hard to imagine what shameful and morally degrading acts a jealous man will not commit, and without the least pang of conscience. And it is not at all that men afflicted with jealousy are necessarily mean and dirty-minded. Indeed, men of noble character, whose love is pure and who would sacrifice anything for the woman they love, can very easily hide under tables, bribe unspeakable people, and indulge in such vile acts as spying and eavesdropping. Othello could never have reconciled himself to infidelity—he might have been able to forgive it, but he would never have been able to reconcile himself to it, though he was unwicked and as innocent as a babe. But a truly jealous man is quite a different matter. It is difficult to think of anything a jealous man will not put up with, reconcile himself to, and forgive! In fact, jealous men are the first to forgive—all women know that. A jealous man is willing and able to forgive (after, of course, making a violent scene) an infidelity that has almost been proven to him, even after he has caught his beloved in the arms of another man, kissing him, as long as he can somehow convince himself that it has happened "for the last time," that the other man will now disappear, leave for the other end of the earth, or if he himself can take her to a place where the dangerous rival can never follow them. It goes without saying that the reconciliation is only temporary, for, even if the rival in question really does disappear, the jealous man will at once find someone new to be jealous of. And one may wonder what good there is in a love that must be watched all the time, what joy there is in such a love. But this is precisely what jealous men cannot see, although many of them happen to be men of admirable character. But then these admirable men, even though they understand with their admirable hearts, while they are spying and eavesdropping in some little hiding place, how much they have been willing to degrade themselves, still feel no compunction whatsoever as they stand there spying.

And so it was with Mitya. As soon as he saw Grushenka, his jealousy vanished and he became temporarily trusting and considerate and even despised himself for his evil suspicions. But that only goes to show that his love for this woman included something higher than he knew himself, something more than carnal passion, something much deeper than "curves," about which he had tried to tell Alyosha. On the other hand, no sooner was Grushenka out of his sight than Mitya once more began to suspect her of perfidy and think her capable of every vile trick to deceive him, and at these moments he felt no pangs of conscience at all.

And so jealousy surged up in him once more. Whatever else, he had to hurry. First, he had to raise a little money for his immediate needs. Almost all of yesterday's nine rubles had been spent on his traveling, and without some money, of course, he could not move at all. But along with the "new plan" he had conceived the day before, he had also thought up a way of getting some money for his immediate needs. He owned a couple of good dueling pistols and their cartridges, which he had not yet pawned because he happened to prize them above all his other belongings. In the Capital City Inn he had become acquainted some time ago with a young government official, a rather well-off bachelor who had a passion for weapons and who liked to buy pistols, revolvers, and daggers to hang on his walls, so that he could show off his familiarity with these arms and his ability to explain the different loading systems, the variety of designs of pistols, and so on, to his acquaintances. Without further thought, Mitya went to this man and offered to pawn his pistols to him for ten rubles. The fellow tried to convince Mitya to sell him the pistols outright, but Mitya refused and the man gave him the ten rubles he had asked for, refusing, of course, to accept any interest on that sum. They parted good friends. From there Mitya dashed off to his hiding place—the summer house at the bottom of his father's garden—and sent for Smerdyakov to come to him as soon as possible . . .

These actions made it possible later to establish that, just three or four hours before a certain event took place, of which much more will be said later, Mitya had to pawn his most treasured possession because he was almost without a kopek—and then, three hours later, he had thousands of rubles in his hands . . . But I am getting ahead of my story . . .

It was from his father's neighbor, Maria Kondratiev, that Mitya heard, with surprise and consternation, of Smerdyakov's sickness. They told him about Smerdyakov's fall down the cellar steps, and the epileptic seizure that followed, about the doctor's visit and Mr. Karamazov's concern; and he also learned with surprise that his brother Ivan had left for Moscow earlier that day. "He must have passed through Volovya just before me," Dmitry thought. But what bothered him most was Smerdyakov. "What will happen now? Who will keep a look-out for me and let me know?"

He eagerly questioned the women about whether they had noticed anything special the evening before. They knew very well what he was driving at and reassured him: no one had spent the night in Mr. Karamazov's house, except for Mr. Ivan, and everything was all right. Mitya was perplexed: of course, he would have to keep watch himself now, but he wasn't sure where he should post himself—right here or at Samsonov's gate? He finally decided that he would have to take care of both places "as circumstances demanded," but in the meantime, in the meantime . . . In the meantime he had to carry out his "new plan that could not fail," the one he had conceived while driving back to town. He could not put off the execution of that plan. He would devote one hour to it. "Within an hour I'll settle it all and then I'll know where I stand. Then I'll go to Samsonov's house, inquire whether Grushenka is there, rush back, stay here until eleven, then back to Samsonov's to pick her up and see her home," Mitya decided.

He ran home, washed, combed his hair, brushed his clothes, dressed, and went to Mrs. Khokhlakov's, for she, alas, figured in that new plan of his. He was to ask the lady to lend him three thousand rubles. Somehow he had suddenly become absolutely convinced that she could not refuse him. It may seem rather surprising that, if he was so convinced of this, he had not gone to her in the first place and thus remained, so to speak, within his own social circle, instead of going to a man from a different background, such as Samsonov, to whom he did not even know how to talk. The explanation is that Dmitry and Mrs. Khokhlakov had all but broken off relations during the past month, that they had never been very closely acquainted even before, and that he was very well aware of the fact that she had never been able to stand him anyway. The lady had detested him from the very beginning, simply because he was engaged to Katerina, who, she had for some reason decided, should break off with him and marry his brother Ivan instead, "such a nice, chivalrous, cultured man" with "such charming manners." Dmitry's manners, on the other hand, she detested. Mitya found all this very amusing and once quipped that "the lady is as forceful and uninhibited as she is ignorant." And so, while driving back to town earlier that day, a brilliant idea had suddenly occurred to him: "If she is really so much against my marrying Katerina and feels so strongly about it" (he knew she was almost hysterical on the subject), "why should she refuse me the three thousand rubles that would enable me to finish with Katya and leave, never to come back? These spoiled society ladies, when they get an idea into their heads, won't spare a thing to see their whims realized. Besides, this one is so damned rich," Mitya's reasoning went. As to the practical aspect, this "plan" was very much the same as the previous one; that is, he would offer as a guarantee to transfer his rights to Chermashnya to her, but, of course, he would not bring in the incentive of profit he had tried to use with Samsonov the day before, for she certainly would not be interested in the possibility of getting back six or even seven thousand rubles for the three she would lend him; no, with her, Chermashnya would simply be a gentleman's security for his debt. The more he thought of this new idea of his, the more enthusiastic Mitya became, but then that is the way he always was when he embarked on anything. He always gave himself over passionately to every new idea he had.

Nevertheless, as he was going up the front steps of Mrs. Khokhlakov's house, an icy shiver of fear chilled his spine, for he realized in a flash that this was his last hope, that if he failed now, there would be nothing left for him, "unless it is to cut someone's throat and rob him, and all that for a miserable three thousand . . ."

It was seven-thirty when he rang the bell. At first the business seemed quite hopeful. No sooner had he announced himself than he was shown in with the utmost promptness. "It's as if she'd been waiting for me," the thought flashed through his head. And hardly a second after he had been ushered into Mrs. Khokhlakov's drawing room, she herself came in, almost running, and told him openly that she had been expecting him.

"Yes, yes, I was expecting you to come! I was, although, you must agree, there was no reason at all for it even to occur to me that you'd come and see me—I have the most extraordinary instinct, don't you think? I have known that you'd come ever since the morning."

"That is really amazing, madam, I must say," Mitya said, sitting down awkwardly. "I've come, you see, on very im-

portant business . . . I mean, it's most important to me, just
to me, and I'm in a terrible hurry . . ."

"I know how important it is, Mr. Karamazov. I'm well
aware of it. It is not a matter of premonition or primitive,
superstitious belief in miraculous insight—did you hear, by
the way, about the elder Zosima?—in this case it is purely a
matter of mathematics: you could not *not* come to see me
after what has happened with Katerina—you simply could
not stay away. It's sheer mathematics."

"It's the realism of true life, madam, that's how I'd describe it . . . But please allow me to . . ."

"You've hit the nail on the head, Mr. Karamazov, realism
is just the word for it. As of now, I am all for realism! For
I've been taught a good lesson about miracles. You've heard,
haven't you, that the elder Zosima died?"

"No, madam, this is the first I've heard of it," Mitya said,
slightly surprised, and the thought of Alyosha flashed through
his mind.

"He died last night, and imagine . . ."

"Madam," Mitya interrupted her, "the only thing I can
imagine just now is the desperate situation in which I happen
to be. And if you don't help me, it will be the end of
everything, and first of all the end of me, for I am at the
end of my tether. Please forgive me for expressing myself so
banally, but I feel feverish, I feel as if I were on fire . . ."

"I know, I know you're feverish, because you could not
possibly not be. Besides, I know in advance everything you
have on your mind even before you say it. I've been watching
you for a long time, Mr. Karamazov; I've been studying
your behavior for a long time, you know . . . Oh, Mr. Karamazov, I'm a very experienced doctor of human souls, believe me!"

"Good, madam, for if you are an experienced doctor, I
myself am an experienced patient," Dmitry said, making an
effort to sound amiable, "and I feel that, since you've been
watching over my life with such interest, you will not allow
me to ruin it and will let me take the liberty of telling you
about the plan I have in mind . . . and then about the favor
I have come to ask of you . . . I've come, madam . . ."

"Don't bother to tell me about it—it's only of secondary
importance! As to helping people out, you won't be the first
person to receive my help, Mr. Karamazov, you may rest
assured of that! I'm sure you must have heard of my cousin,
Mrs. Belmesov, whose husband was a lost man, at the end

of his tether, as you put it so characteristically. And what do you think—I advised him to go in for horse-breeding on a large scale and now he's prospering. Do you know anything about horse-breeding, by the way, Mr. Karamazov?"

"Nothing, madam, absolutely nothing, I'm sorry to say!" Mitya cried with nervous impatience, getting up from his chair. "Please madam, I beg you, let me tell you what I've come to tell you! It won't take me more than two minutes if you will only let me talk, and I'll explain the whole plan I wanted to present to you. Besides, I have terribly little time! . . ." he almost shouted, sensing that she was about to interrupt him again and hoping to drown her out. "I've come here because I'm desperate. I've reached the limits of my endurance . . . I want to ask you to lend me some money, to lend me three thousand rubles . . . But I have a perfect security . . . please allow me to explain to you, madam . . ."

"Later, you can do that later, later." Mrs. Khokhlakov waved her hands at him in a hushing gesture. "Besides, I know in advance everything you're going to say to me, as I told you before. You're asking me for a certain sum, you say you need three thousand rubles, but I'll give you infinitely more than that, my dear Mr. Karamazov, incomparably more—I'll save you. But for that you'll have to listen to what I have to say."

Mitya almost leaped into the air.

"Would you really be so awfully kind, madam!" he exclaimed with tremendous feeling. "My God, madam, you've saved my life! You have just saved a man from violent death, from a bullet . . . I'll be eternally grateful to you!"

"Yes, I'll give you infinitely more than three thousand!" Mrs. Khokhlakov cried in her turn, smiling as she saw Mitya's exultation.

"Infinitely more? But I don't even need that much. All I need is the three terrible thousand rubles. And for my part, I can guarantee that sum, for which I am so infinitely grateful to you, and I would like to offer you the following plan, which . . ."

"Enough, Mr. Karamazov—I've said it and I'll do it!" Mrs. Khokhlakov cut him short with a modesty worthy of her generosity. "I've promised to save you and save you I shall. I'll save you just as I saved my cousin Belmesov. Have you ever thought of gold mines, Mr. Karamazov?"

"Gold mines, madam? No, I've never given a thought to gold mines."

"You haven't, but I've been thinking for you. I've been thinking and thinking and that is what has made me watch you during this past month. I watched you walking by in the street a hundred times and I kept repeating to myself: 'There's an energetic young man who ought to go out to the gold mines.' I even studied your way of walking and I decided that here was a man who would discover many gold mines."

"You decided that from my way of walking, madam?" Mitya asked with a smile.

"And what's so strange about that? Do you really refuse to recognize that one can tell a man's character by the way he walks? Why, that's been established by natural science, Mr. Karamazov. And from today on, after that terrible thing that happened in the monastery, I have become an out-and-out realist and have decided to go in for practical endeavors. I have been cured once and for all, I assure you. 'Enough of that!' as Turgenev said."

"But, madam, the three thousand, which you so generously offered to lend me . . ."

"It won't escape you, Mr. Karamazov," Mrs. Khokhlakov cut him off at once. "You can consider the three thousand as in your pocket, and not just three thousand, but three million, Mr. Karamazov, in no time at all! Now let me tell you your idea: you will find the mines and make millions, and then return and become a businessman. And you will run our lives, too, directing us to good deeds. Does it all have to be left to the Jews? You will construct buildings and various enterprises. You will help the poor, and they will bless you for it. This is the age of railroads, Mr. Karamazov. You will become famous and indispensable to the Ministry of Finances, which is now in such need. The fall in value of the paper ruble keeps me awake at night, Mr. Karamazov—this side of me is little known . . ."

"Madam, madam . . ." Dmitry interrupted her, somehow beginning to worry again, "I may . . . I may very well take your advice, your excellent advice, madam . . . I may indeed go there, to those mines . . . And, if I may, I'd like to come back sometime and talk to you about it some more . . . many times . . . But now, what about the three thousand you so generously promised me? That would untie my hands . . . If you could do it today . . . That is, you understand, I haven't a minute, not a minute to spare . . ."

"Enough of that, Mr. Karamazov," Mrs. Khokhlakov in-

terrupted him imperiously. "The question is now: Are you or
are you not going gold mining? Have you made up your
mind? I want a mathematically precise answer."

"I'm going, madam, but not just now . . . I'll go wherever
you wish, madam, but now . . ."

"Wait a second then," Mrs. Khokhlakov cried. She hurried
over to her magnificent desk with its innumerable little
drawers that she proceeded to pull out in turn, obviously
looking for something which she was tremendously impatient
to find.

Mitya's heart came almost to a standstill—"Three thousand . . . and right away, without even having to sign any
documents, without even drawing up an IOU, a true gentlemen's agreement . . . What a wonderful woman! If only she
talked a little less . . ."

"Here!" Mrs. Khokhlakov cried joyfully, coming back from
her desk. "I've found what I was looking for!"

She was holding a tiny silver icon, the kind some people
wear around their necks on a chain with a cross.

"This comes from Kiev, dear Mr. Karamazov," she said
reverently, "from the relics of the holy martyr Barbara. Allow
me to put it around your neck myself and to give you my
blessing for your new life and new exploits."

And she actually put the icon around his neck and even
started to push it inside his shirt. Mitya, feeling very embarrassed, bent down, and tried to help her, and finally,
between the two of them, they managed to slip the icon
under his tie and shirt onto his chest.

"And now you are ready to leave!" Mrs. Khokhlakov
announced solemnly, resuming her seat.

"I'm greatly touched, madam. I don't even know how to
thank you for such kindness . . . But you cannot imagine
how short of time I am now . . . and that sum I'm waiting
for . . . that you so generously . . . Oh, madam, you are so
kind, so touching, so generous to me, that I hope you will
allow me to confess to you," Mitya suddenly cried in exaltation, "allow me to confess to you, although you must have
known it for a long time, that . . . that I am in love with a
woman here . . . I have betrayed Katya, I mean Katerina . . .
Oh, I know I have behaved cruelly and dishonorably toward
her . . . But I fell in love with another woman here, someone
you may despise—for you know everything already—but still
I cannot give her up anymore. I just can't, and that's why . . .
the three thousand rubles . . ."

"Forget all that, Mr. Karamazov," Mrs. Khokhlakov said in a tone that brooked no contradiction, "and, above all, forget women, for from now on your goal in life is the gold mines and there's no need to take women with you there. Later, when you return, rich and famous, I'm sure you will find a life-companion among the girls of our highest society. And she will be a modern girl, well educated, without any of the old prejudices and superstitions. By that time the emancipation of women will have become a reality and the new woman will have come into existence . . ."

"Yes, yes, madam, but that's not . . . that's not the point now . . ." Mitya pressed his hands together prayerfully.

"It is very much the point, Mr. Karamazov. It's just what you need. It's just what you are yearning for, although you may be unaware of it yourself. I am not at all unfavorably disposed toward the emancipation of women as things stand now, Mr. Karamazov. Higher education for women and even a role for women in politics in the near future—I believe in this ideal, my dear sir. I have a daughter myself, and people know very little of that side of me. I wrote to Saltykov-Shchedrin about it. That writer has revealed so very much to me about the role of women that a year or so ago I sent him an anonymous two-line letter: 'I embrace you, I kiss you, you are a writer after my heart and the champion of contemporary woman. Please continue,' and I signed it, 'A mother.' I thought of signing it, 'A contemporary mother,' but after long hesitation I decided to leave it just, 'A mother.' I thought it had greater moral impact and beauty that way. Besides, the word 'contemporary' would have reminded Saltykov-Shchedrin of his magazine *The Contemporary,* a rather painful reminder in view of the difficulties they are having with our present censors . . . But, good gracious, what's the matter with you?"

"Madam!" Mitya had been unable to stand it any longer. He was now standing with his clasped hands stretched out toward her in a gesture of impotent supplication. "You will make me weep, madam, if you postpone any longer your generous promise . . ."

"And what's so terrible about weeping a little! That is a very fine way to feel, for you have a very, very long journey ahead of you. Tears will make your ordeal easier and there'll be time enough for joy when you're back. Indeed, you'll come hurrying all the way from Siberia to see me, to share some of your happiness with me!"

"But please listen to me too!" Dmitry shouted suddenly. "For the last time, madam, I beseech you, answer me plainly: Will you give me, today, the sum you have promised me or won't you? If you can't let me have it right away, tell me, when may I come for it?"

"What exactly do you have in mind, Mr. Karamazov?"

"The three thousand that you promised . . . that you so generously . . ."

"Three thousand? What do you mean—three thousand rubles? My goodness, I certainly don't have three thousand rubles," Mrs. Khokhlakov said, sounding mildly surprised.

Mitya was stupefied.

"How can you? Why, you just said . . . the way you put it, it was as if I had the three thousand in my pocket . . ."

"Oh no, Mr. Karamazov, you didn't understand me properly; in fact, you have misunderstood me completely. I was thinking of the gold mines . . . I remember now that I promised you much more, infinitely more, than three thousand, but I was thinking of the mines when I said that."

"And what about the money? What about the three thousand rubles?" Dmitry cried incongruously.

"Oh well, if you were thinking of borrowing that sum from me—I just don't have it. I am entirely without money just now, Mr. Karamazov; I have to fight for it constantly with the manager of my estates. In fact, the other day, I had to borrow five hundred rubles from Mr. Miusov myself. No, I just don't have any money at all! Besides, you know, Mr. Karamazov, even if I had the money, I still wouldn't give it to you. In the first place, I never lend money, because lending money to people means quarreling with them. Moreover, you are the very last person I'd lend money to, because I like you and I feel I must save you, and the only place for you is the gold mines, the gold mines, and the gold mines . . ."

"Ah, the hell with . . . !" Mitya roared, slamming his fist down on the table.

"Help!" cried Mrs. Khokhlakov in alarm, retreating hastily to the other end of her drawing room.

Mitya shrugged in disgust and walked quickly out of the room, out of the house, into the street, into the darkness. He looked like a madman, beating his breast as he walked, striking the same spot he had struck the last time he had spoken to Alyosha on the dark road. What Dmitry's beating his breast meant—striking *that spot*—and what he was trying to show by it was still a secret, a secret that no one in the world knew and that he had not told Alyosha either. That secret meant more to Mitya than disgrace, it meant death and suicide. For that is what he had decided on, if he failed to find three thousand rubles to pay back Katerina and thus remove *from that spot on his breast* the disgrace which was lodged there, weighing on his conscience. The reader will understand this fully later, but now, after the last hope of getting the money had vanished, this strong man, having walked only a few steps away from Mrs. Khokhlakov's house, burst into tears like a small child. He walked on, unaware of anything, wiping away his tears with his hand. As he turned into the square, he suddenly bumped hard into someone. An old woman's squeaky voice protested violently. He had almost knocked her over.

"Lord! He almost killed me! Can't you look where you're walking, you hooligan!"

"Oh, it's you!" Mitya cried, recognizing in the darkness Samsonov's old maid-servant, whom he remembered very clearly from the previous day.

"But who are you, sir?" the old woman said in a completely different voice now. "I don't recognize you in the dark, sir."

"You live and work at Mr. Samsonov's, don't you?"

"That's right, sir. I've just been out to see Prokhorovich . . . But how is it I still don't recognize you, sir?"

"Just tell me this, mother, is Miss Svetlov still at the house? I brought her there earlier."

"She was there, sir, stayed for a while, and then left."

"What? She left? When did she leave?"

"She left right after she came—she stayed in the house for just a minute, told Mr. Samsonov something that made him laugh, and then ran off."

"You're lying, you damned old hag!" Mitya roared.

"Help, help!"

But Mitya had vanished. He was galloping at full speed toward Mrs. Morozov's house. Just about fifteen minutes earlier, Grushenka had left for Mokroye. Fenya, the maid, and the old cook, Matryona, her grandmother, were sitting in the kitchen when Dmitry suddenly broke in. At the sight of him, Fenya started to call for help.

"Why are you yelling?" Dmitry roared. "Where is she?" And before the girl, paralyzed with terror, could answer him, he threw himself down at her feet.

"Fenya, in the name of Christ our Lord, where is she? Please, Fenya, tell me . . ."

"But I don't know, sir, I don't know, Mr. Karamazov. I swear to God I don't know; may I die here and now if I have any idea," Fenya started to assure him. "You yourself went out with her . . ."

"But she came back after that, didn't she?"

"No, sir, she didn't. I swear to God she didn't!"

"You're lying. I can see that just by the way you were frightened. So where is she?"

He rushed out again. The terrified Fenya was only too glad to get off so easily, but she realized that he did not have time to argue with her then and that otherwise she might have paid dearly for her lies. But as he was rushing out, he did something that surprised her: he had already opened the door with one hand when he suddenly paused for a second, snatched the pestle out of the mortar with his other hand, and slipped it into the side pocket of his coat.

"My God, he'll end up murdering somebody!" Fenya cried, flinging up her hands in despair when he had gone.

CHAPTER 4

In the Dark

Where was he off to? He had no hesitation: "The only place she can be now is at father's . . . She must have rushed straight there from Samsonov's. Everything's clear now . . . Her whole scheme of deception is obvious . . ." These fragments of thought whirled around in his head. He didn't stop at Maria Kondratievna's yard. "I mustn't show myself there, I mustn't . . . I don't want them to be warned . . . Otherwise, someone will warn them . . . Maria Kondratievna must be in on it with them . . . And so is Smerdyakov . . . They've all been bribed . . ."

He changed his plan of action. He gave his father's house a wide berth, taking first a sidestreet, then Dmitrievsky Avenue, crossed the bridge, and entered the small lane at the back of the house. It was a deserted lane: no one lived there. On one side was a wattle fence with vegetable patches behind it and on the other was the tall, strong fence around his father's garden. There, he picked the spot where, according to what he'd heard people say, Reeking Lizaveta had once

climbed over the fence. "If she could do it," the thought
somehow flashed through his head, "why can't I?" And sure
enough, he jumped up and caught hold of the top of the
fence; then, making a great effort, he pulled himself up and
was astride the fence. The bath-house was right there by
the fence. Beyond it, he saw the lighted windows of the main
house. "That's it, that light's in the old man's bedroom window—she's there!" He jumped down from the wall into the
garden. And although he knew that Gregory was ill, that
Smerdyakov, too, was probably sick in bed, and that there
was no one who could hear him, he instinctively stood still,
holding his breath and listening. Silence lay all around him.
It so happened that the night was completely still, without
a breath of wind.

"Only the stillness whispering . . ." Somehow the line of a
poem flashed through Mitya's head. "I hope no one heard
me jump down . . . I don't think anyone did." He waited
quietly for a minute and then walked stealthily across the
lawn, keeping close to the trees and bushes, muffling each
step and constantly listening to make sure he made no noise.
It took him five minutes to reach the lighted window. He
remembered that there were several tall, thick elder and
guelder-rose bushes growing right under the windows. As
he went past it, he carefully noted that the door leading to the
garden on the left side of the house was locked. When he
reached the bushes, he hid there for a while. He tried
not to breathe. "I must wait—if they heard my footsteps,
they'll be listening now. I want them to be reassured . . .
Above all, I mustn't cough or sneeze . . ."

He waited there for two minutes. His heart was pounding
wildly. At moments he felt he was suffocating. "It doesn't
seem as if my heart will ever stop palpitating—I can't
wait any longer." He was standing in the dark shadow of
the bushes, the top branches of which were bathed in the
light from the window. "The guelder-rose berries—they're so
red!" he whispered for God knows what reason. In a few
measured, noiseless strides, he reached the window and
raised himself on tiptoe. He could see into his father's bedroom clearly now. It was a rather small room divided in
half by a red screen. " 'Chinese' screen, the old man calls
it," flashed through Mitya's head, "and Grushenka must be
behind it." He looked intently at his father. The old man
was wearing a new, striped silk dressing gown, tied at the
waist with a tasseled cord. Mitya had never seen that dress-

ing gown before. An immaculate white linen shirt with gold studs showed under the dressing gown. On his head Mr. Karamazov had the same red bandage that he had worn when Alyosha had seen him last. "All dressed up," Mitya thought. His father was standing near the window, apparently lost in thought; suddenly he raised his head as if listening for something but then, hearing nothing, gave up, walked to the table, poured himself half a glass of brandy, drank it down, and took a deep breath. After that he stood still for a while, then went over to the mirror by the window, pushed his red bandage aside slightly, and examined the bruises and scratches that were still clearly visible. "He's all by himself," Mitya decided, "he must be." The old man took his eyes off the mirror, walked to the window, and suddenly looked out. Mitya quickly jumped back into the shadow.

"Perhaps she's behind the screen, asleep already." The thought stabbed at Mitya's heart. Mr. Karamazov left the window. "No, he's still waiting for her to come. Why else would he be looking out of the window into the darkness? He's dying of impatience . . ." Mitya went back to the window and looked in again. The old man was sitting at the table, looking disappointed, his elbow on the table and his cheek resting on the palm of his right hand. Mitya watched him intently.

"He's all by himself, all by himself . . ." he kept muttering under his breath. "He wouldn't have that look on his face if she were there with him." And, strange as it may seem, he suddenly felt cheated somehow, because she was not there. The absurdity of this must have struck him for he at once gave himself an explanation for his strange feeling: "It's not because she isn't here. It's because I can't be sure whether she is or not."

Later Mitya remembered that at that moment his brain worked with the utmost lucidity and that he took in every minute detail. At the same time, however, an acute anguish from the uncertainty of the situation mounted within him. "Is she there or isn't she, after all!" His impatience boiled up in him and suddenly he made up his mind. He lifted his hand and knocked on the window pane. He gave the signal the old man and Smerdyakov had agreed on: first—two spaced knocks, then—three knocks closer together, indicating that Grushenka had arrived. The old man started violently, jerked his head back, and rushed over to the window. Mitya leaped sideways into the shadow. Mr. Karamazov opened the window and stuck his head out.

"Grushenka?" he called out in a strange quivering whisper. "Is that you, Grushenka? Where are you, my beauty? Where are you, my angel?"

He was terribly agitated and could hardly control his breathing.

"So there's no one in there," Mitya decided.

"Where are you then?" the old man called again, sticking his head farther out of the window and then his shoulders, as he looked into the darkness in all directions, right and left. "Come here, I've got a present for you. Come in, I'll show it to you . . ."

"Must be that envelope with the three thousand rubles," flashed through Mitya's head.

"But where are you? Are you by the door? Wait, I'll let you in . . ."

The old man almost climbed out of the window in an effort to make out Grushenka there in the darkness by the door. One more second and he certainly would have run to unlock the door without waiting for Grushenka's answer. Mitya watched him from the side without stirring a muscle. He had a full view of the old man's profile that was so loathsome to him, with his protuberant Adam's apple, his hooked nose, his lips grinning in lecherous anticipation, all sharply outlined by the light of the lamp on the old man's left. A horrible, frantic fury surged up in Mitya: "So this is my rival! This is the man who's made such a hell, such a nightmare, of my life!" This was the sudden tidal wave of hatred and vengeful fury that Mitya, as if in anticipation, had described to Alyosha when they had met in the summer house and he had told his young brother that he might kill their father. "How can you say that, Mitya?" Alyosha had asked him then in disbelief, to which he had replied: "I don't know, I don't know . . . Perhaps I won't kill him. But maybe I will. *I'm afraid I'll hate the sight of him too much at that moment.* I hate his Adam's apple, his nose, his eyes, his shameless sneer . . . It's a direct, spontaneous loathing. That's what I'm afraid of. I feel I won't be able to resist the temptation."

And now, as he had foreseen, that spontaneous loathing was overwhelming him. He no longer knew what he was doing. The brass pestle that had been in his pocket was now in his hand . . .

But, as Mitya was to put it later, "God was watching over me that night . . ."

At that very second Gregory, who was laid up in bed, awoke. Earlier that evening he had undergone the treatment Smerdyakov had described to Ivan: with the assistance of his wife, he had rubbed himself all over with a mixture of vodka and a certain potent infusion, had drunk what was left of it as his wife whispered a certain prayer over him, and then had gone to sleep. Martha had drunk some of the potion too and, since she was not used to spirits, had fallen into a deep sleep beside her husband.

But, quite unaccountably, Gregory awoke late at night and, after thinking for a while, despite the persistent pain in the small of his back, sat up in bed, deliberated for another minute or so, got up, and hurriedly dressed. He may have been worried that all the time he was lying in bed the house was unguarded, and "at such a dangerous time," too. Laid low by his epileptic seizure, Smerdyakov was lying immobile in his little room. Martha was as motionless as a log. "The woman had a bit too much of it this time," Gregory thought, glancing at her, and stepped out onto the porch of the servants' cottage. He thought he would just look around from the porch, for walking was too strenuous for him in his weak state and, besides, the pain in the small of his back and in his right leg was becoming unbearable. But he suddenly remembered that that evening he had forgotten to lock the gate between the yard and the garden. Being a man of order and a meticulous observer of established ways and routines, Gregory, limping and twisted with pain, went down from the porch into the yard. And, just as he had feared, the gate leading into the garden was wide open. Without thinking about it, he stepped into the garden. He thought he heard something, glanced to the left, and saw the open window of his master's bedroom, which was empty now, with no one looking out of it. "Why is that window open—it's not summer . . ." Gregory wondered, and while he was wondering he caught sight of something quite unexpected. Something that could have been the shadow of a running man flashed no more than forty yards in front of him, moving very fast. "Good Lord," Gregory muttered and, forgetting the pain in his lower back, he dashed forward, trying to cut off the fast-moving shadow. Gregory obviously was more familiar with the garden than the stranger and, realizing that the other man was dashing toward the bathhouse, took a short cut. The man rushed toward the fence. Gregory followed the intruder without ever losing sight of him and, just as the man was pulling himself up onto the fence, Gregory reached him, succeeded in catching one of his feet and clutching it with both hands.

Yes, Gregory's foreboding had not deceived him; he had somehow known that this was the "monster," the "father-killer."

"You father-killer!" old Gregory roared in a deafening voice.

But that was all that he had time to say before he fell to the ground as if struck by lightning. Mitya jumped down into the garden and leaned over the prostrate figure. The brass pestle was in Mitya's hand and he tossed it away without even noticing what he was doing. The pestle fell a couple of steps from Gregory on the gravel path, where it was certain to attract attention. For several seconds Mitya stared at the old man. Gregory's head was splattered with blood. Mitya put his hand out and touched it. Later, he remembered clearly that he had felt a terrible need to find out whether he had broken the old man's skull or whether the blow of the pestle had just stunned him. But blood was still gushing out and Mitya's trembling fingers were immediately splashed by the hot stream. He also remembered that he took out of his pocket a new white handkerchief, which he had carefully taken before going to see Mrs. Khokhlakov, and tried senselessly to wipe the blood off Gregory's forehead and cheeks. But, of course, within a few seconds, the handkerchief, too, was completely soaked with blood. "My God, what am I doing that for?" Mitya suddenly came to his senses. "If I have broken his skull—how could I find it out now? Ah, and what difference could it make now?" he added in complete hopelessness. "If I've killed him, I've killed him. It's just too bad, old man—can't be helped now!" He said this aloud and all of a sudden dashed to the fence, climbed over it, and started to run. He had been holding the blood-soaked handkerchief in his hand and now thrust it into the right-hand pocket of his coat. Mitya ran at full speed, and the few people he passed were to testify later that they had seen him galloping madly through the streets on that particular night. He was hurrying now to Mrs. Morozov's house.

Earlier that evening, as soon as he had left, Fenya had gone to the head janitor and beseeched him, "in the name of Christ our Lord, not to let the Captain in, either tonight or tomorrow." The janitor had promised but, unfortunately, at one point he was summoned upstairs by the old lady who owned the house. On his way, he met his twenty-year-old nephew, who had only recently come to town from his village, and told him to stay in the courtyard while he was away, forgetting, however, to say anything about "the Captain." Soon Mitya came running up and knocked at the gate. The nephew recognized Mitya right away, for Mitya had often tipped him, and he opened the gate with a cheerful smile. He also hastened to inform him that Miss Svetlov was not at home.

"Where is she then?" Mitya stopped short.

"She left for Mokroye, sir. Timofei drove her there a couple of hours ago."

"Why?" Mitya shouted.

"That I can't say, sir, but I think she's gone to join some officer who sent for her from there . . ."

Mitya left him and dashed upstairs like a madman to see Fenya.

CHAPTER 5

A Sudden Resolution

Fenya and her grandmother were sitting in the kitchen. They were about to go to bed. Relying on the janitor's promise, Fenya had not bothered to lock the cottage door. Mitya rushed in and seized Fenya by the throat.

"Tell me at once, where is she now and with whom is she, in Mokroye?" Mitya roared at her.

Both women squealed in terror.

"I'll tell you, sir. I'll tell you, Mr. Karamazov. I'll tell you everything I know. I won't hide anything," Fenya muttered hurriedly, in terror. "She's gone to Mokroye, sir, to that officer of hers . . ."

"What officer?" Mitya screamed.

"That same officer she used to know five years ago, the one who left her and went away," Fenya rattled off as fast as she could.

Dmitry dropped the hands that had been squeezing her

throat. He was pale as a corpse and speechless, but it could be seen from his eyes that he now understood everything, that the situation had suddenly become clear to him. Of course, poor Fenya was in no condition at that moment to observe whether he had grasped the facts or not. She was still sitting on the trunk, as she had been when he burst into the room. She sat there trembling, her hands still stretched out in front of her defensively, as if they were frozen in that position, and stared at Dmitry, her pupils dilated with fear. On top of everything, both his hands were caked with blood. And he must have touched his face, as he was running over there, to wipe the sweat from it perhaps, for there were spots of dried blood on his forehead and his right cheek. Fenya was on the verge of hysterics. The old cook stood there, looking around like a madwoman, almost unconscious.

Dmitry remained standing for a minute or so. Then, without knowing what he was doing, he sank into a chair next to Fenya. He was trying to think about what he had just understood, but he just sat there in a state of benumbed stupor. Everything was clear anyway: so it was that officer, and Mitya had known about him all along from Grushenka herself, who had even told Mitya that she had received a letter from him a month ago . . . So for a month, a whole month, she had been preparing all this in absolute secrecy, planning everything, even the appearance of this new man on the scene today! And he, he had never even given him a serious thought! How, how could he have just dismissed him from his mind? What had made him forget the very existence of that officer almost as soon as he had first heard about him? This question loomed before him like a monstrous ghost and he stared at that ghost, feeling his flesh freeze in terror.

Then he spoke to Fenya. He spoke to her like a gentle and affectionate little boy. He seemed to have completely forgotten that a few moments earlier he had terrified, insulted, and hurt her. He asked Fenya many questions, very precise questions which one would never have expected from a man in his state. And Fenya, although she stared wildly at his bloodstained hands, answered him with an unaccountable willingness and eagerness, as if it were very important to her personally to tell him "the whole truth." She even seemed to enjoy providing him with all the minute details, but not because she savored his pain. No, she was simply anxious to help him. She gave him a complete account of that day, of Rakitin's and Alyosha's visit, of herself having to keep a look-out, of Grushenka's departure, and of her shouting to Alyosha from the window, asking him to give her regards to him, Mitya, and to tell him that she had loved him even if "only for an hour."

Mitya's pale cheeks flushed and he smiled when he heard about Grushenka's last message, and just then Fenya said to him, without the slightest fear that her curiosity might provoke his anger:

"Look, Mr. Karamazov, your hands are covered with blood!"

"Yes, that's right," Mitya said, glancing absentmindedly at his hands.

But the next second he had completely forgotten about them, and about Fenya's remark. He again sank into silence. Twenty minutes had passed since he'd burst in on Fenya. His erstwhile frightened stupor was gone. Instead, he now seemed to be strangely and unshakably resolved. He stood up, smiling pensively.

"Sir . . . What happened to you, sir?" Fenya again pointed to his hands. There was sincere concern in her voice, as if she were the closest person in the world to him and was now sharing his grief.

"It's blood, Fenya," he said, gazing at her with a strange expression. "It's human blood, and, God knows, there was no reason for it to be shed! But . . . you see, Fenya . . . there's a fence, a tall fence . . ." he looked at her as if he were setting her a riddle, "terrible to look at, but . . . tomorrow at dawn, when the sun rises, Mitya Karamazov will jump over that fence . . . Never mind, Fenya, you'll hear of it tomorrow anyway and then you'll understand. And now, good-by! . . . I won't stand in her way. I know how to take myself out of the way, how to stand aside . . . Since she loved me for an hour, she'll always remember her Mitya-boy . . . Remember, Fenya, that's what she used to call me—Mitya-boy . . ."

With these words, he abruptly walked out of the kitchen, and Fenya was almost more frightened by his departure than she had been by his earlier intrusion and attack.

Ten minutes later Dmitry entered the house of Peter Perkhotin, the young government official to whom he had pawned his dueling pistols the day before. It was eight-thirty. Perkhotin had just finished a glass of tea, had put on his coat,

and was about to leave for the Capital City Inn for a game
of billiards. Mitya caught him just as he was going out. Seeing
Mitya's bloodstained face, Perkhotin cried in surprise:

"My God, what's happened to you!"

"I've come for my pistols," Mitya said quickly. "I've
brought the money. I'm very grateful to you for having lent
it to me, but I'm in a terrible hurry right now, and I'd
appreciate it very much if I could have my pistols right
away."

Perkhotin's surprise grew when he saw a whole wad of
bills in Dmitry's hand. But the strangest thing of all was
the way Dmitry was holding the money. No one else would
hold money like that: he held all the bills in his outstretched
right hand, as if exhibiting them. Perkhotin's young valet,
who had let Dmitry in, said later that this was how he had
entered the house—carrying the money out in front of him—
so it would seem that in the street, too, he had carried the
bills in his outstretched right hand. They were all rainbow-
colored hundred-ruble bills and he held them in his bloodstained fingers. Later, when asked to give an estimate of the
sum Dmitry was carrying with him then, Mr. Perkhotin
said that it was hard to tell at a glance but that he would
not be surprised if there was as much as two or even three
thousand rubles, for what he saw was certainly "a pretty
thick wad of bills." As to Dmitry, Perkhotin later also
testified, "he was not quite himself. I don't mean he was
drunk, but he was in an exalted sort of state. He seemed
both absentminded and, at the same time, very tense, as
if he were trying hard to work something out, looking for
an answer he couldn't find. He was in a great hurry, answered
abruptly and very strangely, but at certain moments did not
sound at all like an unhappy man; indeed, he seemed rather
gay."

"But what's happened to you, what's the matter?" Perkhotin cried again, gazing wildly at Dmitry. "How did you
manage to get all covered with blood like that! Did you
fall, or what? Just look at yourself!" And seizing Dmitry
by the elbow, he dragged him to a mirror.

Mitya saw his bloodstained face, shuddered, and frowned
angrily.

"Hell, that's all I needed now," he muttered in annoyance.

He hurriedly transferred the money from his right hand
to his left, and with his right hand nervously pulled out
his handkerchief. But, since it was the handkerchief he had

used to wipe the blood off Gregory's head, it was so thoroughly soaked with blood that there wasn't a single white spot left on it and it now had stiffened into a hard, crumpled ball, which was difficult to unfold. Mitya threw it impatiently on the floor.

"Ah, damn it! Don't you have a rag or something, so I could wipe it off a bit?"

"You've just got blood on you, and you're not wounded, then? Well, in that case you'd better wash it off," Perkhotin said. "There's the washbowl. I'll go and get you some water."

"A washbowl? Good. But what will I do with this?"

Peculiarly perplexed, Mitya indicated the wad of hundred-ruble bills. He was looking questioningly at Perkhotin, as though waiting for him to decide what Mitya was to do with his own money.

"Put it in your pocket or put it on the table. What's the difference? It won't get lost here."

"In my pocket? Right, in my pocket. Good . . . No, it's really too absurd!" he cried, as if he had suddenly come out of his daze. "Listen, I think we'd better attend to our business right away: here's your money and you give me back my pistols . . . because I need them very badly . . . and . . . I'm in a terrible hurry. I haven't got a minute to lose."

Mitya peeled off the top hundred-ruble bill and handed it to Perkhotin.

"I'm afraid I don't have change for this. Don't you have anything smaller?"

"No," Mitya said, glancing at the bundle and fingering the top two or three bills as if to make sure. "No, I don't. They're all the same," he added, looking questioningly at Perkhotin.

"Where did you get all that?" Perkhotin asked. "Wait a second. I'll send the boy to the Plotnikov store—they stay open late. They may give us some change. Hey, Misha!" he called to the valet out in the passage.

"The Plotnikov store? That's great!" Mitya exclaimed, as if some brilliant idea had just occurred to him. "Misha," he said to the young valet, who had just come in, "here, see this? Run to Plotnikov's and tell them that Dmitry Karamazov sends them his regards and that he'll be there soon . . . And tell them to prepare champagne for him, three dozen bottles, say, and have them pack it just the way they did the time I went to Mokroye . . . I took four dozen bottles then," he said, turning for a second to Perkhotin. "Don't

worry, they know me. And Misha," he said, turning to the
valet again, "tell them to pack some cheese too, some Strasbourg pies, smoked whitefish, ham, caviar, and . . . well,
whatever else they have, about a hundred or, say, a hundred
and twenty rubles worth, just like the other time . . . Yes,
and let them not forget the sweet things either: candy, pears,
two, three, no, four, watermelons . . . no, I suppose one
watermelon should do, but I also want chocolate, fruit-drops,
toffee, caramel—well, everything they packed for me the
time I went to Mokroye. It came to about three hundred
rubles, including the champagne, then, so make it the same
thing this time too. Can you remember all that, Misha? That
is, if you are Misha . . . isn't his name Misha?" he asked,
turning to Perkhotin again.

"But wait a minute," Perkhotin said in a worried tone,
watching Dmitry uneasily. "Perhaps it would be better if you
did your ordering yourself. I'm sure he won't get everything
right."

"Yes, I can see he won't get it right! Ah Misha, I was just
going to kiss you for doing this errand for me . . . But now, if
you get everything right, there'll be ten rubles for you here.
So hurry! The main thing is the champagne—see that they
bring some up from the cellar . . . And while they're at it, let
them also bring up some brandy and red and white wine—just
like that other time. They know what I want."

"But listen to me, for heaven's sake," Perkhotin said, with
marked impatience now. "Let him just run over there, get
the change, and warn them that you're coming so they won't
close the store, and when you get there you'll tell them what
you want yourself . . . Give me that bill, then. All right, off
with you, Misha, and be quick about it."

Perkhotin was probably anxious to get the young valet out
of the room as quickly as possible, for the lad was staring at
the visitor's bloody face and the bloodstained hands that held
all those bills between trembling fingers—gaping in fear and
amazement, and apparently taking in very little of what Mitya
was saying.

"And now, come and wash," Perkhotin said sternly. "Put
your money on the table or in your pocket . . . That's right.
Now take off your coat." Perkhotin had started to help Dmitry
to take his coat off, when he suddenly cried: "Look at that—
your coat is soaked with blood too!"

"It's . . . it's not the coat . . . It's only a little dirty here,
by the sleeve . . . Yes, and here too, around the pocket where

the handkerchief was. The blood soaked through when I sat on it at Fenya's," Mitya explained with a strange, boundless trustfulness.

Perkhotin frowned.

"You've really got yourself into a mess. Did you have a fight with someone, or what?" he muttered.

The washing operations began. Perkhotin held the jug and kept pouring more water. Mitya was in such a hurry that he could not manage to soap his hands properly (his hands were trembling—Perkhotin noticed that) and his host had to insist that he soap them more and wash them more energetically. He seemed to be taking command more and more; it should be noted that he was a young man who was not easily intimidated.

"Look, you didn't get it out from under your nails properly; and now rub your face—right here . . . on the temple . . . just under your ear now . . . How can you go anywhere in this shirt? Where are you going, anyway? Can't you see that the cuff of your right sleeve is all covered with blood?"

"Yes, that's blood," Mitya said, looking absentmindedly at the cuff of his shirt.

"You must change your shirt then."

"I have no time. I know what I'll do. I'll turn that cuff up, like this," Mitya said with the same trusting air. He dried his face and put on his coat. "See," he said, "it doesn't show at all!"

"And now tell me what happened. Did you get into a fight? Perhaps in the inn, like the other day? Was it that captain again—the one you beat up and dragged out by his beard?" Perkhotin reminded Dmitry disapprovingly. "Or did you beat up somebody else this time, or perhaps you even killed somebody?"

"Nonsense," Dmitry said.

"What's nonsense?"

"Forget it," Mitya said, suddenly smiling. "I just ran down an old woman on the square, that's all."

"You ran down an old woman?"

"An old man, it was!" Mitya shouted very loudly, as if Perkhotin were deaf, looking straight into his face and laughing unrestrainedly.

"What the hell are you talking about? Old woman, old man . . . Have you killed someone by any chance?"

"No, we made it up. We had a fight and then made it up. We parted good friends. He was a fool . . . he forgave me . . .

yes, I'm sure he's forgiven me now . . . If he'd gotten up, though, he wouldn't have forgiven me!" Mitya said with a sly, incongruous wink. "But the hell with him. I don't want to hear about him now, not just now, at least, do you understand?" Dmitry declared determinedly.

"What I'm trying to say is that you so often get involved with all kinds of people, like that other time, with that captain . . . You get yourself into a fight and then you go off on a spree. That's the kind of man you are. So it's three dozen bottles of champagne now—what will you do with all that?"

"Bravo! Just let me have my pistols now. You know, I'd love to stay and have a long chat with you, my friend, but I'm afraid I haven't got a minute to spare. Besides, it's too late for that now. But where's the money? Where did I put it?" and Mitya began rummaging through his pockets in a panic.

"You put your money on the table. It's over there, see? You forgot, didn't you? You treat money as if it were garbage or water. Here are your guns. It's pretty strange, though. You pawned them sometime between five and six o'clock for just ten rubles and now I don't know how many thousands you have. I bet there must be two or three thousand rubles here?"

"Three, I guess," Mitya said, laughing, as he stuffed the wad into the side pocket of his coat.

"Be careful, you'll lose it that way. But then, I suppose you have a gold mine or something."

"Gold mines, gold mines, that's right!" Mitya shouted at the top of his voice, roaring with laughter. "Tell me, Perkhotin, would you be interested in gold mining? Because there's a lady here who will let you have three thousand without batting an eye the moment you agree to go gold mining. She gave it to me because that's how much she loves those gold mines! Tell me, have you met Mrs. Khokhlakov?"

"No, I haven't been introduced to her, but I've heard of her and I've seen her. So she was the one, then, who gave you the three thousand rubles? She counted them off, just like that, and gave them to you?" Perkhotin asked incredulously.

"Why, you can check for yourself first thing tomorrow morning, as soon as young Phoebus the sun arises. Just praise the glory of God and go to Mrs. Khokhlakov and ask her whether she did or did not peel off three thousand rubles and give them to me. Go and find out."

"I have no idea of your relations with her, but since you tell me so positively that she gave you the money, she must have given it to you . . . And now I see that, instead of leaving for the Siberian gold mines, you're trying very hard to get rid of it right here . . . But tell me, where are you really off to now?"

"Mokroye."

"Mokroye! At this late hour?"

"From riches to rags!" Mitya said suddenly.

"What do you mean to rags? With all that money?"

"I'm not talking of the thousands—the hell with them! I'm speaking of the ways of women. 'Gullible, fickle, corrupt is the heart of a woman,' Ulysses said, and I fully agree with him."

"I'm afraid I don't quite follow you."

"Why, do I sound drunk to you?"

"No, not drunk—worse."

"I'm drunk in spirit, Perkhotin, drunk in spirit . . . But enough of this . . ."

"Why are you loading that pistol?"

"Just loading it."

Mitya had opened the pistol case, untied the powder horn, carefully poured out some powder, rammed the charge into the pistol, picked up a bullet, and, before inserting it, was holding it between his thumb and finger, examining it in the light of the candle.

"Why are you examining the bullet like that?" Perkhotin asked, curious and worried at the same time.

"For no special reason. I'm just trying to imagine what it would be like . . . Suppose you decided to fire this bullet into your brain, wouldn't you have a good look at it first while loading your gun?"

"What would be the use of looking at it?"

"Well, since it will be lodged in my brain, I'm rather curious to see what it's really like . . . No, that's really all nonsense, just a crazy notion that lasted a moment only! All right, so that's done now," he announced, putting the bullet in and ramming some tow stuffing on top of it. "Yes, Perkhotin, my dear fellow, that's all nonsense. Everything is nonsense, such nonsense you can't even imagine! And now, please give me a scrap of paper."

"There's a scrap of paper."

"No, I mean a clean sheet of paper, to write on. That's good enough, fine!"

Mitya grabbed a pen from Perkhotin's desk, quickly scrawled two lines, folded the paper in four, and thrust it into his waistcoat pocket. Then he replaced the pistols in the case, locked the case with a little key, and picked it up. Then he gave Perkhotin a long, dreamy look, smiling at him.

"And now let's go," he said.

"Go where?" Perkhotin said, sounding really worried now. "You'd better wait a minute . . . You may have really decided to put that bullet into your brain . . ."

"The bullet? What nonsense! I love life and I want to live! I want you to know this: I love golden-haired Phoebus and his warm world! Tell me, Perkhotin, my dear friend, tell me, do you know how one gets out of people's way?"

"What do you mean, get out of the way?"

"I mean to yield the way—yield the way to the creature you love and to the creature you hate. And to do it so that you come to love the hated one as well? That's what I mean by getting out of the way . . . And I'll say to them, God bless you, go ahead, don't worry about me, because I . . ."

"Because you what?"

"That's enough now. Let's get going."

"I swear I'll have to have you stopped—you must be prevented from going there," Perkhotin said, looking intently at Dmitry. "Why do you have to go to Mokroye now?"

"The woman, the woman is there, see. But that's enough for you, Perkhotin. That's all you'll get out of me. That's enough."

"Listen, I know you're a wild man, but—and I really don't know why—I've always liked you, and that's why I'm worried for you now."

"Thank you, brother . . . So I'm a wild man, am I? Ah, savages, savages! Yes, that's what I've been saying all along— there's nothing but wild savages . . . Ah, here's Misha coming back. I'd almost forgotten him!"

Misha came in with his hands full of change and reported that "everybody was rushing around" now at Plotnikov's store, that they were getting the bottles and fish and everything ready. Mitya picked out two ten-ruble bills. He gave one to Perkhotin and handed the other to Misha.

"Don't do that! Not in my house. I don't believe in spoiling them that way. Put away your money. Here, put it in this pocket. You've no need to be in such a rush to get rid of it all. It may still be useful to you tomorrow, and you'll be coming here again to ask me to lend you another ten rubles.

Why do you keep stuffing your money into your side pocket? That's the best way to lose it, you know."

"Listen, dear fellow, what about coming to Mokroye with me?"

"What would I do there?"

"Look, shall I open a bottle right now, to drink to life? I'm longing to have a drink, especially to have a drink with you. I don't think we've ever drunk together, have we?"

"I suppose we can have a drink at the inn. I was going there anyway when you came in."

"No, there won't be enough time for us to go to the inn, but we'll drink a bottle at Plotnikov's. But let me ask you a riddle first, all right?"

"Go ahead."

Mitya took the piece of paper out of his waistcoat pocket, unfolded it, and showed it to Perkhotin. In a large, legible hand he had written on it: "I condemn myself for my past life and I sentence myself to suffer for the rest of my life."

"I really must go and report you. You must be stopped," Perkhotin said.

"You won't have time, now, my friend. So let's go ahead and have that drink. Forward march!"

The Plotnikov store was only two houses away from Perkhotin's, right on the corner of the block. It was the largest grocery store in our town and belonged to a wealthy merchant family, a pretty good store by any standard. It had just about everything that could be found in a large store in the capital, all sorts of delicacies, all the wines "bottled by Yeliseyev Brothers & Co."; it carried all kinds of fruit, cigars, and, of course, tea, coffee, sugar, and such things. There were always three attendants at the counters and a couple of messenger boys constantly dashing about. And, although our part of the country was not as prosperous as it had been, and many of the rich local landowners had left, and trade was a bit slack, the grocery business was flourishing as before, in fact, more and more so with every year, for there was no shortage of buyers for such goods.

They had been waiting eagerly for Mitya in the store. They remembered very well that three or four weeks before he had ordered at one time, as now, a quantity of wines and delicacies, for which he had paid several hundred rubles in cash (they would never, of course, have given it to him on credit), and they remembered, also, that on that other occasion he had held in his hand a whole wad of hundred-ruble bills, just as now; that he had thrown the bills about without bothering to count them, never even trying to figure out how much wine or food he really wanted. Afterward everyone in town said that, when he had gone to Mokroye with Grushenka that time, he had managed, in one night and the following day, to go through the whole of the three thousand rubles he had had and that he had come back "as naked as the day he was born." He had picked up a whole gypsy camp that was in the vicinity and for two days had treated them to the most expensive wines, while they kept stealing bills out of his pockets when he was drunk. People said, making fun of Mitya, that during his Mokroye spree he had made illiterate laborers drunk on champagne and had gorged peasant women on Strasbourg pies and delicate bonbons. And at the inn people also laughed at him (of course, not to his face; that would have been much too dangerous) when he admitted simpleheartedly that all he had got for his extravagance was Grushenka's permission to kiss her foot, and nothing more.

When Dmitry and Perkhotin reached the store, they saw a cart harnessed with three horses standing at the entrance. The cart was covered with a rug and there were bells on the horses' harnesses. Andrei, the coachman, was waiting there for Mitya. And in the store almost everything had been packed in a crate and they only needed Mitya's final approval before they put the crate into the cart. Perkhotin was very surprised.

"How did you manage to get this cart ready so quickly?" he asked Mitya.

"I met Andrei on my way to your house and I told him to drive here to the store and wait for me. There was no time to waste, you know. The last time, it was Timofei who took me to Mokroye, but this time he's gone there with the enchantress . . . Tell me, Andrei, will we get there much after them?"

"One hour, sir. They won't get there more than an hour before us. I helped Timofei harness and I know which way he went. And they can't go as fast as we can, sir, nowhere near. So they won't be there even an hour before us," Andrei, a lean, youngish, red-haired man, assured Dmitry eagerly. The coachman wore a long-skirted peasant's coat and had a heavy overcoat rolled up over his left shoulder.

"You'll earn yourself a fifty-ruble tip if we get there no more than an hour behind them."

"I can swear to that, Mr. Karamazov, sir. Perhaps they won't beat us to Mokroye by even as much as half an hour!"

Although Mitya took care of everything and saw to all the arrangements, he gave his orders in a strange, disconnected way, starting on one thing, leaving it unfinished, and skipping to something else. Finally Perkhotin felt he had to interfere.

"I want it to come to four hundred rubles—it must be the four hundred, make no mistake about that—just like the other time," Mitya ordered. "Four dozen bottles of champagne—not one less."

"What do you need so much for? Hey, stop!" Perkhotin shouted. "What's in this crate? Is there really four hundred rubles worth of goods there?"

The bustling shop attendants hurriedly reassured him in sugary tones that the crate in question contained only half a dozen bottles of champagne and "a few items of immediate necessity," such as cold snacks and pastry, as well as some sweets, candy, etc. But that the main supply would be packed and sent off in a special cart as soon as it was ready, just as on the other occasion. It would also go in a fast cart drawn by three horses and it would reach its destination no more than an hour after Mr. Karamazov.

"No more than one hour, no more, and put in as much toffee as possible—the girls love it," Mitya demanded insistently.

"All right, get all the toffee you want, but why must you absolutely have four dozen bottles of champagne? I say one dozen will be plenty!" Perkhotin said angrily. He demanded a bill of an attendant, disputed some of the figures, but managed to save no more than a hundred rubles. It was finally agreed that the supplies to be sent to Mokroye would come to only three hundred rubles.

"Ah, to hell with it after all!" Perkhotin cried, suddenly sick of it all. "If you want to throw your money away, go ahead. Why should I worry about it?"

"Come here, come here, my money-saving friend! Don't be angry with me," Mitya said, dragging Perkhotin off with him into the back room of the store. "Let's drink that bottle here. They'll serve it to us. Ah, Perkhotin, you must come with me to Mokroye. I like fellows like you!"

Mitya sat down on a wicker chair at a tiny table which was covered with a stained cloth. Perkhotin installed himself on the chair opposite him and the champagne was on the table in no time.

An attendant appeared and asked them whether they would also like to have some oysters, "the very best, from the latest shipment."

"To hell with the oysters," Perkhotin snapped almost spitefully. "I won't have any. In fact, we don't need anything."

"No time for oysters," Mitya remarked, "and, besides, I'm not hungry. You know what, Perkhotin?" he said suddenly. "I really hate this lack of order . . ."

"Who likes it? Why, it's ridiculous—three dozen bottles of champagne wasted on uncouth peasants . . . It's enough to make anyone sick."

"I didn't mean that. I was talking about a higher order. There's no order in me, you see. And so everything is hell. My life has been one continual mess and disorder, but now I'm going to try and put some order into it. Do you think I'm making puns?"

"That's not punning—it's raving."

> Glory to the highest in the world,
> Glory to the highest in me,

Mitya declaimed. "Once those lines burst from my soul, and they're not poetry so much as a moan . . . I thought up those lines myself, but not while I was pulling that captain by his beard . . ."

"What made you think of him all of a sudden?"

"All of a sudden? Nonsense! Everything comes to an end. Everything must eventually be paid for. One day you have to draw a line and add it all up."

"Listen, I can't forget about those pistols. I'm worried about them."

"The pistols are nonsense too! Here, drink, and stop imagining things. I love life, you know. I've come to love it so much, in fact, that it's really quite disgusting. Enough! Here's to life! Drink up. Why am I so pleased with myself? I know I'm vile, but still I like being what I am. I bless God's creation and I am prepared to bless God, but . . . but I feel I must crush a certain stinking insect that is crawling about and spoiling life for others . . . So let's drink to life, brother, for what can be more precious than life? Nothing, nothing! So here's to life and to the queen of queens!"

"So let's drink to life . . . All right, I suppose we can drink to your queen too."

They emptied their glasses. Excited and impatient though

he was, Mitya's sadness was becoming apparent, a heavy anxiety was weighing on him visibly.

"Look," he cried, "your Misha's here. Hey, Misha, my boy, come here. I want you to drink this glass to golden-haired Phoebus, who in the morning . . ."

"Leave him be!" Perkhotin said irritably.

"Why, I want him to drink it. Please let me . . ."

"Ah, you . . ."

Misha emptied the glass, bowed, and hurried away.

"He'll remember a bit longer now," Mitya remarked. "Listen, Perkhotin, I love a woman. What is a woman? She is the queen of the earth. I feel sad, Perkhotin, very sad. Do you remember Hamlet saying, 'Alas, poor Yorick'? So perhaps I'm Yorick. Yes, that's what I am now, and later I'll be the skull."

Perkhotin was listening in silence. Mitya fell silent too.

"What dog is this?" he suddenly asked a shop assistant, pointing to a neat little black-eyed lap-dog in a corner of the room.

"It belongs to Mrs. Plotnikov, our boss's wife. She brought it in here earlier and then forgot to pick it up. Someone will have to take it back home to her."

"I saw a lap-dog just like this one when I was in the army," Mitya said dreamily, "only one of its hind legs had been broken . . . By the way, Perkhotin, tell me, have you ever stolen anything in your life?"

"What kind of a question is that?"

"I just wondered. Have you ever picked anyone's pocket, for instance? Of course, I'm not talking about government funds. Anybody who could get his hands on them would steal them, of course, and that goes for you too."

"Go to hell."

"I mean, have you ever stolen someone else's money straight out of his pocket or purse. See what I mean?"

"I once stole a twenty-kopek piece my mother had left on the table. I put my hand quietly on top of it, closed my hand, and kept it in my fist. I think I was nine years old at the time."

"And what happened?"

"Nothing. I kept it for three days, but grew too ashamed of myself, gave the coin back, and admitted what I'd done."

"And what happened then?"

"Obviously, I got a good spanking. But why are you asking me all this? Have you stolen something, by any chance?"

"Yes, I have," Mitya said with a sly wink.

"What?" Perkhotin wanted to know.

"Twenty kopeks from my mother when I was nine, but I gave it back three days later," Mitya said and abruptly stood up.

"Mr. Karamazov, sir, shouldn't we be getting under way?" Andrei called from the door of the shop.

"Is everything ready? Good, let's go!" Mitya said, again becoming hurried and agitated. " 'One last tale to end my chronicle . . .' and one glass of vodka for Andrei . . . for the road. And now a glass of brandy on top of the vodka. Here, this case, see?" He pointed at the case with the pistols. "Put it under my seat. Good-by then, Perkhotin, don't remember me too unkindly after I've gone."

"Why, you'll be back tomorrow, won't you?"

"I most certainly will."

"Would you like to settle your bill now, sir?" An attendant hurried up to Dmitry.

"Ah yes, the bill, of course."

Again he produced the whole wad of bills, counted off three of them, tossed them onto the counter, and hurriedly left the store, accompanied by the shop assistants and errand boys, all of them bowing to him and wishing him a good time. Andrei cleared his throat after swallowing his brandy and jumped up onto the driver's box. But just as Mitya was installing himself in the cart, to his great surprise, Fenya appeared. She was running, completely out of breath, and as soon as she reached him, she let out a cry and threw herself down at his feet.

"Mr. Karamazov, sir, dear, don't kill my mistress, please! It'd be my fault, because it was me who told you everything! And don't kill him either, sir. He was there before you. He's her man, Mr. Karamazov. He's come especially, all the way from Siberia, to marry my mistress. Please, Mr. Karamazov, sir, you mustn't take human lives . . ."

"Aha, I see, so that's what he's up to," Perkhotin muttered under his breath. "You'll get yourself into a real mess over there. All right, Karamazov, let's have those pistols now! Give them to me at once! Come, act like a decent man, Dmitry, do you hear me?"

"The pistols? No need to worry about them. I'll throw them into some puddle on the way. And you, Fenya, why are you lying there like that? Don't worry, Mitya won't kill anyone anymore. The stupid man is through harming people

now. And Fenya," he called out to her when he was already
seated in the cart, "I offended you today, so I beg you to forgive me, dog that I am . . . But if you don't forgive me, it
won't really make much difference now, because nothing really makes any difference anymore. Drive on, Andrei, and be
quick about it!"

Andrei drove off. The bells jingled.

"Farewell, Peter Perkhotin, my last tear is for you!"

When the cart was gone, Perkhotin thought: "I know he
isn't drunk, so why is he raving like that?" At first he
thought he would stay to supervise the loading of the supplies
that were to follow Dmitry to Mokroye, for he was sure
that they would try to cheat Mitya and not give him his
money's worth in food and wine. But suddenly he grew
angry with himself, shrugged, and went off to the inn to play
billiards.

"What a fool, but what a nice fellow," Perkhotin muttered
to himself on his way to the inn. "Yes, I heard something
about that retired army officer of Grushenka's. Well if he's
back for her . . . But those pistols! Ah, hell, what am I—his
nurse? Let them all fend for themselves. Besides, I'm sure
nothing much will happen. They just like to holler and that's
all: they'll get drunk, have a fight, make it up, and get drunk
again. They're not serious people. And what was all that
rubbish about his 'getting out of the way' and about 'punishing himself'? No, nothing terrible will happen. I've heard him
hold forth like that a thousand times before—when he was
drunk at the inn. But he wasn't drunk now. 'Drunk in spirit,'
he said. Ah, they love fancy phrases, these people! I'm not
his nurse, after all! And he couldn't miss picking a fight
today—all his face covered with blood. I wonder who the
other fellow was? I'll inquire in the inn. And that handkerchief soaked in blood . . . Damn it, it must still be on the
floor in my bedroom."

He got to the inn in a foul mood and immediately joined
a game. Playing billiards relaxed him. He started another game
and suddenly told one of his partners that Dmitry Karamazov
seemed to be in the money again, that he had perhaps as
much as three thousand rubles on him, that he himself had
seen the bills, and that now Dmitry had gone off to Mokroye
to have a spree with Grushenka. His words provoked an interest quite beyond his expectations. But nobody laughed. On
the contrary, they all looked very grave. They even stopped
playing.

"Three thousand, did you say? Where could he get three thousand?"

They questioned him further, but did not take seriously what he told them about Mrs. Khokhlakov.

"Isn't it more likely that he robbed the old man?"

"Three thousand, eh? Something fishy about that."

"Why, he's shouted around here often enough that he'd kill his father. Everybody has heard him. And several times he also specifically mentioned the figure three thousand!"

Perkhotin, listening to them, suddenly started answering their questions curtly and evasively. He did not say a word about the blood on Mitya's hands and face, although, on his way to the inn, he had planned to tell them about it . . . Eventually, the topic of Mitya was exhausted and they started on a third game. But Perkhotin did not feel like playing anymore; he put down his cue and dropped out of the game. And, without having supper as he had planned, he left the inn. In the square outside, he stopped, not knowing what to do, surprised at himself. Then it suddenly dawned on him that where he really wanted to go was to old Karamazov's house, to find out whether anything had happened there. "It's all nonsense, I'm sure, and if I go there I'll just wake everyone up and cause a whole commotion! Besides, I'm not a nanny to look after them all!"

In a foul mood again, he decided to go home to bed. Then he suddenly remembered Fenya. "Why the hell didn't I question her when I saw her?" he thought in annoyance. "I would know everything now if I had." And he was suddenly seized by such an irresistible urge to speak to Fenya, to find out as much as he could from her, that he abruptly turned around and walked quickly toward the house of Mrs. Morozov, Grushenka's former landlady. When he got there and knocked on the gate, the sound of his knocking resounding loudly in the still night suddenly sobered him up and made him furious with himself. Besides, no one seemed to have heard him—everybody appeared to be asleep. "I could cause a commotion here too!" he decided, feeling really sick now; but instead of walking away, he began to bang wildly on the gate. The noise echoed up and down the street.

"Hell, happen what happen may, I'll knock until someone hears me!" he muttered, becoming more and more furious with himself with every knock, but only knocking harder and harder, just the same.

CHAPTER 6

I'm Coming!

In the meantime Dmitry was speeding along the road. It was just about fifteen miles to Mokroye, but at the rate Andrei was driving his three horses they seemed likely to get there within an hour and a quarter. The fast drive seemed to revive Mitya completely. The air was fresh and cool, large stars twinkled in the clear sky. This was the same night, perhaps even the very same hour, that Alyosha threw himself down on the ground and ecstatically vowed to love the earth forever and ever. But Mitya was troubled, deeply troubled, and many claws lacerated his heart. And yet, at this moment, his whole being yearned only for her, for his queen, to whom he was flying for the last time. One thing is certain: his heart did not waver, not for one second. I don't know whether I'll be believed, but I insist that this jealous man felt not the slightest trace of jealousy toward this new rival who had sprung up from nowhere, for that "army officer." Had it been any other man, jealousy would have overwhelmed him at once, and perhaps those terrifying hands of his would have again been covered with blood. But toward this man, "her first love," Dmitry felt no jealous hatred whatsoever, nor even any hostility for that matter, as he streaked toward them in his troika. It's true, though, he had not yet seen the man.

"There's no doubt she has a right to him and he to her. He's her first love and she hasn't forgotten that love for five years, and he's really the only man she's ever loved. So where do I come in here? What claims can I possibly have? Out of their way, Mitya! Besides, the way things are now, it's all over for me anyway; even without that officer, it would have been the end . . ." These words would have roughly expressed Mitya's feelings had he been able to analyze them. But he was no longer capable of such clear thought. His present determination was not thought out; it was spontaneous; it had come to him all at once, the second Fenya had spoken to him; and he had accepted it in its entirety, with all its consequences. And yet, despite his resolution, he felt deeply confused, so deeply that he was filled with anguish. Even his inner determination to accept the situation gave him no peace. Too much had already happened, and it weighed upon him. And this seemed strange to him at moments, for hadn't he already pronounced himself guilty and sentenced himself to suffer for the rest of his life? Wasn't the piece of paper he had written it on in his waistcoat pocket and wasn't the pistol loaded and ready for use? Hadn't he already decided how he would greet the first warm rays of golden-haired Phoebus tomorrow? Yes, he had, but he still could not get rid of the past—it was still there, tormenting him; apparently he could not atone for the past just like that. This realization pierced his soul with a shaft of despair. At one point, he wanted to order Andrei to stop, and then to take the loaded pistol, jump down from the cart, and finish the business at once, without waiting for dawn. But the impulse came, then died out like a spark in the night. Besides, the three horses were steadily eradicating the distance that separated him from his immediate goal and, as he came closer to it, the thought of her, of her alone, gripped him more and more strongly, displacing the horrible ghosts that peopled his mind. He yearned desperately to see her, even if only for a second and from a distance: "She's with *him* now . . . so I'll see them together, her and her first love . . . I ask for nothing else." Never before had he so loved this woman who had played such a fateful role in his life; never before had he been filled with this unknown tenderness for her, a feeling that surprised him, a tenderness that merged into prayer, into self-immolation before her. "I will make myself disappear!" he said aloud in hysterical rapture.

They had been on the way for almost an hour. Mitya was silent and so was the usually talkative Andrei, who seemed afraid to say a word and only kept urging on his rather thin but lively bays. Suddenly Mitya shouted, sounding terribly worried:

"Hey, Andrei, what if they're asleep?"

The possibility had never occurred to him before.

"It's likely that they've gone to bed by now, sir."

Mitya frowned painfully. That would be awful—if he arrived there in a rush . . . feeling the way he did . . . and they were asleep . . . and she was there, asleep by his side . . . A current of wickedness shot through him.

"Whip them up, Andrei. Get moving!" he shouted frantically.

"They may still be up, though," Andrei remarked after a while. "Timofei told me today that there were lots of people there, sir."

"Where, at the station?"

"No, sir, not at the station, at Plastunov's guest house. They have a private posting station, Mr. Karamazov. They hire out horses there too."

"I know that. But who are all the people? Where are there lots of people? What people?"

Mitya became very agitated over this unexpected information.

"From what Timofei said, they're all gentry. Two are from our town, but I don't know who they are—Timofei didn't say—and the two others are from somewhere else. They're like travelers, I guess. There may be even more of them. I didn't ask really. They've started a card game, Timofei said."

"Card game?"

"Right, sir, so I reckon they may still be up if they're playing cards. It's not late. It's not eleven yet, I'm sure."

"Faster, Andrei, move!" Mitya urged him on nervously.

"May I ask you something, sir—only I'm afraid you'll get angry at me," Andrei said after a silence.

"What?"

"Just now, Fenya threw herself at your feet, sir, and asked you not to kill her mistress and someone else too . . . And now, sir, I'm driving you right there to them . . . Forgive me, sir, it's my conscience that's kind of bothering me . . . sounds stupid, sir . . ."

Mitya grabbed him from behind by the shoulders.

"You're a coachman, aren't you?" he started excitedly.

"Yes, sir . . ."

"If you're a coachman, you must know that there are times when you must yield the right of way. No coachman can just drive on regardless of what's there, running over people as he goes by. No, you can't do that. You aren't allowed to run over people, to mess up people's lives—and if you do, you must condemn yourself, punish yourself, and take yourself out of the way."

Mitya seemed quite hysterical as he said this. Andrei, surprised as he was by the outburst, kept up the conversation.

"You're sure right, Mr. Karamazov, sir. No one can run over people and hurt them, like no one can hurt no creature, because every creature has been created by God. Take a horse, for instance, sir, some people whip and whip a horse for no reason, even coachmen just like me, and there's nothing to hold them back. They just whip it and drive the poor beast on . . ."

"To hell?" Dmitry interrupted him, bursting into a short,

dry laugh. "Tell me, Andrei, you simple soul, will Dmitry Karamazov go straight to hell, wherever that may be? What do you think?" Mitya again grabbed the coachman by the shoulders.

"I wouldn't know, sir. It depends on you, because you are . . . You see, Mr. Karamazov, when the Son of God was crucified and died, He came down from the cross and went straight to hell to set free all the sinners that were being tortured there. So the devils in hell started moaning and crying because they thought they wouldn't get no more sinners after that. But then the Lord said to them: 'Don't moan because from now on you'll get the important people. You'll get governors and judges and the rich, and hell will be as full as it was before, until I come again.' And that's true. Those were His very words, sir."

"What a beautiful story! And now, Andrei, whip up that left bay!"

"So that's who hell is for, sir," Andrei said, whipping the left horse, "but you, Mr. Karamazov, you're just like a little child—that's what we all think of you, sir, and God will forgive you everything for that, although I must say you're pretty hot-tempered too."

"And what about you, Andrei, will you forgive me too?"

"I have nothing to forgive you for, sir. You've never harmed me."

"No, I mean, will you forgive me for all the others? Answer me now, on this road: Will you, you alone, forgive me for all other men? Tell me that, you simple soul, you man of the people!"

"Oh, sir, it's scary to drive you . . . you talk so strangely, sir."

Mitya didn't hear him. He was praying fervently, whispering wildly to himself:

"O Lord, accept me, lawless as I am, and do not judge me. Let me pass without Your judgment. Do not judge me because I have already condemned myself. Do not judge me because I love You, O Lord—vile as I am, I love You. Even if You send me to hell, I will love You there too, and I'll cry out from there that I will love You forever and ever . . . But while I am on earth, let me love her to the end, O Lord; grant me five more hours to love her, just until the first bright rays of Your sun . . . for I love the queen of my heart and I cannot stop loving her. You know me, O Lord. I will go to her, throw myself at her feet, and say to her: 'You were right when you passed me by. Farewell, forget me, whom you have made suffer, and never let the thought of me come to haunt you again.'"

"Mokroye!" Andrei shouted, pointing ahead with his whip.

A widely scattered mass of completely black houses was emerging from the paler darkness of the night. It looked as if almost all the two thousand inhabitants of Mokroye were asleep, for there were very few lights to be seen.

"Hurry, Andrei! I'm coming. Hurry!" Mitya kept repeating like a man in a fever.

"So they aren't asleep!" Andrei said, pointing with his whip at the Plastunov guest house at the entrance to the village. The six windows giving onto the street were brightly lighted.

"That's right, they're not asleep!" Mitya repeated joyfully. "Make the horses gallop, Andrei, make the bells jingle and the cart rattle—I want lots of noise so they will know I'm coming. Yes, I'm coming!" he cried in exultation.

Andrei whipped his tired horses into a gallop and managed to produce a considerable rattling as he rolled up to the steep front steps of the inn and brought his steaming, choking horses to a sudden stop. Mitya jumped down from the cart, and just at that moment the landlord, who had been about to go to bed, appeared on the front steps to see who had pulled up in such a dashing style.

"Is that you, Trifon?"

The landlord looked at him and then ran down the steps, greeting his visitor obsequiously:

"How good to see you again, Mr. Karamazov, sir. I'm so happy to see you!"

Trifon Plastunov was a solidly built man of medium height, with a rather fleshy face and an expression that was stern and forbidding, especially when he was dealing with the local villagers, but he had the gift of making himself most ingratiating when he felt there was some advantage to be derived from it. He dressed in a Russian shirt with the collar buttoned on one side and a long-skirted peasant coat; he had considerable savings, but constantly dreamed of still better things. He had half the local inhabitants in his clutches, for almost everyone around Mokroye owed him something. He rented land from landowners in the area, and even bought some himself, and set the villagers who owed him money to work on it in order to pay off their debts, which they could never do. He was a widower with four grown-up daughters, one of whom was already a widow herself; she lived at her father's inn with her little children (who were his grandchildren, of course), where she had to work like a servant. Another of the daughters of this former peasant was married to some pen-pusher who had worked his way up to become a petty government official; and now, in one of the rooms of the guest house, one could see among the family photographs exhibited on the wall a picture of the official in his dress uniform, epaulets and all. The two youngest daughters, who went to church in blue and green dresses fashionably tight-fitting with three-foot trains, got up at dawn on ordinary mornings and, arming themselves with twig brooms, swept out the rooms of the guest house and emptied the slops left by the travelers who had spent the night. Although by now Trifon had quite a few thousand rubles put aside, he was still as eager as ever to fleece a guest when he had the chance and he certainly had not forgotten that less than a month before he had relieved Dmitry Karamazov of well over two—indeed, almost three—hundred rubles during his wild spree in Mokroye with Grushenka. And that was why he welcomed him so enthusiastically now, feeling that, just from the way he had pulled up to the entrance of the inn, Dmitry would be a good person to fleece again.

"Have you come to stay with us again, Mr. Karamazov, sir?"

"Wait a minute, Trifon, first tell me—where is she?"

"You mean Miss Svetlov, sir?" the landlord said, guessing at once whom Mitya meant. "Yes, Mr. Karamazov, she's here too. She's here all right."

"Who is she with?"

"I don't know them, sir, some strangers . . . One of them is a government official, must be a Pole judging by the way he talks, the one who sent the horses for her from here. The other gentleman is a friend of his, or perhaps just a fellow traveler—I can't tell. He is wearing civilian clothes."

"They're having a great time, aren't they? Lots of money, I bet?"

"What great time, sir! They don't amount to much, these people, sir, I can see that."

"So they don't amount to much, don't they? And what about the others?"

"The other two gentlemen are from town, sir. They're on their way back from Chermy and stopped here for the night. One of them is a young gentleman, a relative of Mr. Miusov's

I believe, but I've forgotten his name. And I think you must know the other one too, sir. He's a landowner by the name of Maximov, and he says he met that young relative of Mr Miusov's at the monastery when he went on a pilgrimage there. And now they're traveling together . . ."

"And that's all the people there are?"

"That's all, sir."

"Wait, tell me—I must know, Trifon: How is she? How does she look?"

"She just arrived a short while ago and now she's sitting in there with them."

"Does she seem gay? Is she laughing?"

"She doesn't seem to be laughing much. In fact, she looks rather sad, if anything, sitting there and combing that young gentleman's hair."

"You mean that Pole's hair, the officer's?"

"I said the young gentleman. The Pole is not young, sir. And he's no officer either. No, Mr. Karamazov, it's Mr. Miusov's relative, the young one . . . I can't remember his name."

"Is it Kalganov?"

"Yes, sir, that's exactly what it is—Mr. Kalganov."

"All right, I'll see for myself. Are they playing cards?"

"They were playing, but they aren't any longer. They've finished their tea and the official has ordered some liqueurs."

"Wait, Trifon, wait, my friend. I'll decide about it myself. Now tell me the most important thing—are there any gypsies nearby?"

"I'm afraid I haven't seen any gypsies lately, Mr. Karamazov. The authorities chased them away. But there are some Jews who play cymbals and fiddles in Roshdestvenskaya. If you say the word, I'll send for them right away, sir."

"Yes, send for them at once!" Mitya shouted. "And the girls—you could get them out of bed, like the other time. I want Maria above all, and Stepanida, and also Arina. There will be two hundred rubles for the singers."

"For that money, sir, I'll raise the whole village. I'll pull every single one of them out of bed! I don't believe, though, Mr. Karamazov, that all the villagers here are worth so much kindness on your part, or the girls either for that matter. That's much too large a sum to waste on such an ugly, ignorant lot! It's not right that peasants should smoke those expensive cigars you gave them the last time. Why, sir, they stink, the wretches. And the girls—every one of them has lice, believe me, sir. Why, I'll get my daughters up for you, sir, and won't charge you anything for it, let alone a sum like the one you mentioned. I don't care if they're asleep. I'll kick their backsides and make them sing for you. Ah, it breaks my heart when I think of the way you made the peasants drink champagne! It just breaks my heart, sir."

Trifon was not really concerned about Mitya, for on that last visit he had managed to pinch half a dozen of the bottles of champagne himself, after picking up a hundred-ruble bill under Mitya's chair and concealing it in his clenched fist, where it stayed.

"Remember, Trifon, I went through at least a thousand rubles here that time."

"How could I not remember it, sir? In fact, you went through three thousand that time."

"And it will be the same thing now. See this?" And Dmitry took his wad of bills out of his pocket and almost touched the landlord's nose with it.

"Now listen carefully: in one hour, the wine, the pies, all the food, and the sweet things will be here. I want everything brought up and opened as soon as it arrives, and I want the champagne served immediately . . . And above all, the girls, and on no account forget Maria."

He turned back to the cart and pulled out the case with the pistols.

"Now let's settle our accounts, Andrei. Here's fifteen rubles for the cart and the horses; and here's fifty rubles for your zeal and your affection . . . and to remember your fare, Dmitry Karamazov."

"I'm afraid, sir," Andrei said hesitatingly, "I can't accept all that. If you wish, sir, you can tip me five rubles, but I won't accept more. Let Mr. Plastunov here be my witness, I mean no offense, sir."

"What are you afraid of?" Dmitry said, looking him up and down. "But if that's the way you feel, the hell with you," he cried, tossing Andrei five rubles. "And now, Trifon, I want you to take me in quietly so I can first have a little look at them all without being seen. Where are they now—in your blue room?"

Plastunov glanced worriedly at Dmitry but obeyed at once. He led him cautiously inside, went alone into the first large room next to the one where the guests were sitting, and brought out the candle. Then he quietly led Mitya in, placed him in a dark corner from which he could clearly see the whole party in the other room without being seen by them. But Mitya did not watch for long. Indeed, he was in no state to stand and observe. As soon as he saw her, his heart began to pound wildly and everything became blurred before his eyes. She was sitting in an armchair, sideways to the table. Next to her, on a settee, was Kalganov, a very nice looking young man, still almost a boy. She was holding his hand and seemed to be laughing, while he was saying something in a very loud voice, without looking at her, to Maximov, who sat across the table from him. Kalganov seemed irritated at something, while Maximov was laughing. *He* was sitting on a sofa, and next to him, on a chair, sat another stranger. The one on the sofa was sprawled out, smoking a pipe, a smallish, pudgy, broad-faced man, disapproving of something or other —that was Mitya's fleeting impression of him. His companion, the other stranger, struck Mitya as an exceptionally tall man, but that was all he was able to notice about him. Mitya's excitement made him breathless. He could not bear to stand in the corner for more than a minute. He put his pistol case on a chest next to him and, feeling a cold tingling in his spine, his heart missing beats, he marched straight into the blue room and up to the party.

Grushenka was the first to see him.

"Ah . . ." she shrieked.

CHAPTER 7

The First and Rightful One

With his long, rapid stride Mitya walked up to the table.

"Gentlemen," he said in a loud voice, almost shouting, "please don't mind me . . . don't be afraid. Why, I'm not going to do anything," he said, suddenly addressing Grushenka, who had pulled back toward Kalganov and was tightly clutching his hand. "I'm going away too, you see. I'm only staying until morning . . . May I then . . . may I join you, please, as one passing traveler joins other travelers? Only till morning, and for the last time in this room?"

At the end he was addressing the pudgy little man with the pipe, who was sprawled on the sofa. The man removed his pipe from his lips and said sternly with a strong Polish accent:

"This is a private party, sir. I'm sure there are other rooms in this inn."

"Why, Mr. Karamazov, it's you!" Kalganov said, suddenly recognizing him. "Why, do join us. Please, sit down! How are you?"

"Hello, my dear friend!" Mitya said happily, reacting at once to his friendliness and shaking his hand across the table. "You know, I've always liked you."

"Ouch!" Kalganov cried with a laugh. "What a handshake —you almost broke my fingers!"

"That's just his normal way of shaking hands," Grushenka said, smiling but still looking apprehensively at Dmitry. She had gathered just from looking at him that he would not turn suddenly violent right now, but there was still a good deal of alarm mixed with a tremendous curiosity in the way she looked at him. There was something about him that struck her as uncanny; she would never have expected him to behave and speak as he was doing in those circumstances.

"How do you do, sir," Maximov said in a honeyed voice, following suit, and Mitya responded most eagerly to this overture too.

"I'm so glad you're here too," he said to him. "But, gentlemen, gentlemen . . ." Mitya again turned to the pipe-smoking Pole, apparently considering him the most important person in the party. "As I was hurrying here . . . I was so anxious to spend my last night and my last hour in this room . . . in the room where I once worshipped my queen! Forgive me, sir," he cried, becoming agitated, "as I was speeding here, I swore . . . I promised . . . Oh, please, don't be afraid of me— this is my very last night! Let us drink to our reconciliation, sir! They will bring in the wine right away . . . I've brought this, see . . ." and he suddenly produced his wad of bills. "Allow me, my good sir—I want music and noise, just like that other time . . . The useless worm will crawl on the earth for the last time, and disappear! Let me relive my happiest hour on my last night!"

He was almost choking. There was much more he wanted to say, but only inarticulate exclamations escaped his lips. The Pole stared fixedly at the wad of bills in Mitya's hands; then he threw Grushenka a quick glance, indicating his bewilderment.

"If my queen permits . . ." he began slowly in his Polish accent, but Grushenka impatiently interrupted him.

"You pronounce everything so funnily—I suppose you

mean 'queen' but it sounded more like 'quin' or something. I can't help laughing, listening to you two . . . Sit down, Mitya, and tell me what you've been trying to say. And don't frighten me anymore. Tell me—you won't try to frighten me, will you? For if you won't, I'm glad you're here."

"Me frighten you?" Mitya cried, throwing up his hands. "Oh no, you and he, you can go right ahead, and I'll step out of your way so as not to disturb you!" And to everyone's complete surprise, even his own, he flung himself astride a chair and burst into abundant tears, turning his head away from them, toward the opposite wall, and hugging the back of the chair.

"Ah, come on, Mitya, stop it, you crazy man," Grushenka said reproachfully. "That's the way it was with him when he used to come and see me: he would talk and talk and say all sorts of things, and I wouldn't understand a word. And once he burst into tears, just like now—a real shame! Tell me, what are you weeping about? *I would understand if you had some good reason at least,*" she added rather enigmatically, irritatedly stressing every word.

"I . . . I'm not weeping . . ." Mitya turned around, turning his chair with him, and began to laugh, but not in his abrupt, wooden way; this was a nervous, convulsive laughter.

"Oh, this is no good, not like this," Grushenka said, trying to calm him. "Come, Mitya, cheer up, cheer up now. You know, I'm awfully pleased that you've come, terribly pleased! I want him to sit here, with us," she said imperiously, addressing no one in particular, although she looked at the man on the sofa. "I want him here. Do you understand me, all of you? For if he leaves, I leave too!" she added with flashing eyes.

"Whatever my tsarina says is law to me," the Pole said gallantly, raising Grushenka's hand and kissing it. "Please, sir, join our company!" he said, inviting Mitya with a gracious gesture.

Mitya leaped up again and was obviously about to deliver himself of another of his speeches, but instead he just said:

"Let's drink to it, Mr. Pole."

This made them all laugh.

"Thank heaven! I thought he was going to make another speech," Grushenka cried nervously. "Listen, Mitya," she said firmly, "I don't want you to keep jumping up like that. But it's nice of you to have brought champagne with you. I'm going to have some myself, for I loathe liqueurs. The best part of it, though, is that you've come yourself. It was deadly boring here . . . But tell me, have you come to have another wild spree here? Put that money back in your pocket, for heaven's sake, Mitya! Where did you get all that?"

Mitya, who was still holding the crumpled bills in his hand —bills that had attracted everyone's attention, particularly the two Polish gentlemen's—looked at her in sheepish embarrassment and quickly thrust the money into his pocket. He turned red. At that moment, the landlord brought in an opened bottle of champagne and glasses. Mitya grabbed the bottle, but a lost look appeared in his eyes and he seemed to have forgotten what to do with it. Kalganov took it out of his hand and poured the champagne into the glasses.

"Get us another bottle, and still another!" Mitya shouted to the landlord and, forgetting to clink glasses with the Pole whom he had formally invited to drink to their reconciliation with him, he emptied his glass without waiting for the others. A sudden change came over him: instead of the solemn, tragic look he had worn when he came in, his expression became that of a small child. He became meek and subdued, looked at the others shyly and cheerfully, tittering nervously and politely, behaving like a grateful little dog who has misbehaved but has now been forgiven and allowed back into the room, and is petted on the head. He seemed to have forgotten everything and was looking at his companions admiringly, a child-like smile on his face. He kept looking at Grushenka and laughing and gradually moving his chair closer to hers.

At the same time he observed the two Poles with curiosity, still unable to quite make them out. Mitya was impressed by the dignified bearing of the one on the sofa, by his Polish accent, and above all his pipe. "Well, why shouldn't he smoke that pipe of his if he enjoys it?" Mitya mused contemplatively. So far, Mitya had no misgivings about the Polish gentleman's rather bloated, almost middle-aged face, with its very short nose and the stringy, dyed, arrogant moustache beneath it. Mitya didn't even particularly object to his very poor-quality, Siberian-made wig with the hair absurdly combed forward at the temples. "I suppose that's how wigs are supposed to be," Mitya simply concluded. As to the other Pole, who sat by the wall at some distance and looked at the company with scorn and defiance as he listened to the general conversation, Mitya noticed only that he was a little younger than the one on the sofa. He was struck by the huge size of the man, which was especially impressive in contrast with his fellow Pole. "I bet that fellow must be over six foot nine," Mitya thought; and it somehow occurred to him that the big Pole was probably a friend of the little Pole's in a somewhat subordinate position, "a kind of bodyguard," flashed through Mitya's head; but in any case, he decided, it was the little pipe-smoking Pole who was in charge. But that didn't strike Mitya as at all strange either—it was perfectly proper and just as it should be. Having turned into a little dog, there was no sense of rivalry left in Mitya. As to Grushenka's strange attitude and her rather enigmatic remarks, he had not yet made anything out of them; he felt only that she was warm and friendly toward him, that she had "forgiven" him and allowed him to sit next to her, and this made his heart throb with joy. He watched her with boundless admiration as she sipped champagne from her glass.

At one point, however, he suddenly became aware of a general silence and his surprised and expectant look, wandering from one face to another, seemed to ask them: "What are we waiting for, isn't it time to begin?"

Kalganov seemed to have guessed what Mitya felt.

"Before you came in, he kept telling all kinds of crazy stories and making us laugh," he said, indicating Maximov with his head.

Mitya quickly glanced first at Kalganov, then at Maximov.

"Crazy stories? Ha-ha-ha," he said with a short, wooden laugh, as if pleased at something.

"He claims, for one thing, that in the 1820's, our cavalry all got themselves Polish wives. Can anything beat that for nonsense?"

"Polish wives, ha!" Mitya exclaimed with great delight.

Kalganov was aware of Mitya's relations with Grushenka; he probably also had a good idea of what the Pole meant to her, but he was not much concerned with all that. The person who interested him now was Maximov. He and Maximov had just happened by chance to stop at the guest house and there he had met the two Poles for the first time in his life. He had met Grushenka before and once had even gone to her place with someone or other, but on that occasion she had rather disliked him. Here, however, before Mitya's arrival, she had looked at him rather warmly and even flirted with him, although Kalganov seemed quite insensitive to her attentions. This most elegantly dressed young gentleman was hardly more than twenty, had an extremely pleasant face, a fine complexion, and thick, light-brown hair. But in that charming face of his there was a pair of very light-blue eyes that shone with intelligence and sometimes revealed a depth of thought strange in a boy of his age. This, however, did not prevent him from sometimes behaving and talking like a child, a fact of which he was quite aware himself but about which he was completely unconcerned. In general, he was eccentric, even whimsical, although always pleasant and warm. At times, though, there was an absent, obstinate look about him: he could listen to you without taking his eyes off you, while thinking of something completely different. He was also somewhat unpredictable—at times appearing lazy, almost listless, and at others, becoming extremely excited at the slightest provocation.

"Imagine, I've been dragging Maximov around with me for four days," Kalganov said in his lazy, elegant drawl, which, nevertheless, was completely unaffected. "Do you know, I became interested in him the day your brother Ivan pushed him out of your father's carriage so violently and he went flying through the air. I was so curious about him that I took him with me to my place in the country. But he talked such a collection of nonsense and lies all the time that I became quite ashamed to be seen with him and now I'm taking him back to town."

"The gentleman can never even have seen a Polish lady in his life," the pipe-smoking Pole remarked, "for what he claims is impossible."

Obviously the Pole spoke Russian much better than he pretended and deliberately tried to pronounce Russian words in such a way as to make them sound Polish.

"Except that I was married to a Polish lady myself," Maximov countered with a chuckle.

"Why, did you serve in the cavalry then, since it was the Russian cavalry that you were talking about? Are you a cavalryman then?" Kalganov quickly asked him.

"Yes, quite—is he a cavalryman then? Ha, ha!" Mitya cried, listening eagerly and quickly shifting his questioning glance to each one who started to speak, as if he were expecting to hear God knows what from each of them.

"N-no, not really," Maximov said, turning to him. "What I was trying to say was that those pretty Polish ladies—some of them are very pretty, by the way—when they dance a mazurka with our Uhlans . . . Well, as soon as the mazurka is over, she immediately sits herself on his lap, just like a little white kitten . . . while her gentlemanly Polish papa and her lady-like Polish mamma watch her without objecting. And then, the next day, the Russian Uhlan comes to the house and asks for the girl's hand, see? He-he-he!" Maximov ended in a chuckle.

"The useless windbag . . ." the big Pole growled, crossing one leg over the other, and Mitya was struck by the size of his boot with its thick, muddy sole. In general, he noted, the clothes of the two Polish gentlemen could have done with some cleaning.

"Windbag?" Grushenka said angrily. "What does this fellow mean by calling people names like that?"

"What the other gentleman saw in Poland was peasant girls, not ladies," the pipe-smoking Pole explained to her.

"You can bet on that!" the big Pole put in scornfully.

"That's what you think," Grushenka snapped back. "He says it's different. Why try to stop people from talking? It's more fun if they say what they want."

"I'm not stopping him," the Pole with the hairpiece said, giving Grushenka a long, scrutinizing look. Then, with a most dignified air, he went back to puffing at his pipe.

"No, no, no, the Polish gentleman is right." Kalganov suddenly became agitated as if a matter of the utmost importance were at stake. "As far as I know, Maximov has never even been to Poland, so how can he speak about it? You didn't get married in Poland, did you, Maximov?"

"No, as a matter of fact, I got married in Smolensk Province. But then it was an Uhlan who brought my future wife from Poland with him, along with her mamma, her auntie, and some other lady relative of hers who had a grown-up son. So he found her in Poland, brought her fresh from there, and it was only after that that he handed her over to me. He was a young lieutenant from our town, a very nice young man indeed. At first he was going to marry her himself, but he decided not to because she turned out to be lame."

"So you married a lame lady?" Kalganov asked, surprised.

"That's right. Well, between the two of them, they managed to conceal it from me at the time . . . I saw that she sort of skipped a bit when she walked, but I thought she was doing it out of sheer joy."

"Out of joy? Because she was getting married to you!" Kalganov cried loudly like a young boy hearing something very funny.

"That's right, I thought it was out of joy. But then later I learned the real reason. After the wedding she explained to me that, when she was a little girl, she'd jumped over a puddle and damaged her leg. She apologized profusely about it, very movingly too, he-he!"

Kalganov rolled about with laughter, that boyish laughter of his, so violently that he almost fell onto the sofa. Grushenka laughed too. Mitya simply beamed with delight.

"And this time it's the truth. He's not lying this time," Kalganov said, leaning toward Mitya. "And you know, he's been married twice. That was his first wife he just told us about. The second one ran away from him and she's still alive—did you know that?"

"Is that true?" Mitya said, turning to Maximov with an expression of infinite amazement. "Did she run away?"

"Yes, sir, I had that unpleasant experience," Maximov said, modestly confirming the fact. "She left me for a certain Frenchie *monsieur*. The worst thing about it, though, is that before she left she neatly managed to transfer my little property to her name. 'You,' she said to me, 'are an educated man. You'll always be able to make enough to live on.' And that's all I have to show for that marriage. Once a very venerable bishop remarked to me in that connection: 'Your first wife was lame, but the second was too light-footed.' He-he-he-he!" Maximov chuckled.

"Just listen to him!" Kalganov cried in excited amusement. "Even assuming he makes up his stories—and I'm sure he often does invent them—he does it only to give pleasure to his listeners and I say there's nothing so evil or despicable about that! You know, I like him very much at times. I realize he's very much a toady, but that's just his nature. Another man may fawn on you and clown for you when he thinks he can get something out of you for his pains, but not Maximov. He acts like that because it's his natural way of behaving . . . Yesterday, for instance, he got it into his head, arguing it throughout the entire trip, that Gogol had used him as a prototype when he wrote *Dead Souls*. Do you remember, there's a character, a landowner, called Maximov? Nozdryov gives him a thrashing and is arrested and tried for 'inflicting personal injury on the landowner Maximov by flogging him while in an inebriated state.' Well, he claims that he is that very same Maximov and that he was actually flogged, imagine that! Now, since Chichikov's travels date from the 'twenties at the latest, it obviously couldn't be him, if only for chronological reasons. So he couldn't possibly have been flogged then, could he?"

It was hard to imagine why Kalganov should be so excited about it, but somehow he really was, and Mitya was eager to show his interest in the matter.

"But suppose he was really flogged!" he shouted with a loud laugh.

"I wasn't really flogged . . . Well, that . . . you know," Maximov suddenly said.

"Were you flogged or weren't you?"

"What time is it?" the Pole with the pipe asked his huge fellow countryman in Polish. The little Pole looked very bored.

The big Pole just shrugged. Neither of them had a watch.

"What's the matter? Can't people talk anymore?" Grushenka said aggressively, as if trying to pick a quarrel. "Can't people have a conversation, just because you happen to be bored?"

Now, finally, it occurred to Mitya that things might not be quite the way he had imagined them. This time the pipe-smoking Polish gentleman answered with obvious irritation:

"I haven't objected to anything as far as I know."

"So go on, tell us more," Grushenka cried to Maximov. "Why have you all become so quiet all of a sudden?"

"Oh, there's nothing much to tell really. It's all nonsense really," Maximov answered with obvious pleasure, although pretending to be a little coy. "In Gogol, too, you understand, it's all meant allegorically, for all the names he gives his characters are allegorical too. Nozdryov is not really Noz-dryov but Nosov, and the real Kuvshinnikov's name is alto-gether different—Shkornev. And Fenardi—for there really was a man like Fenardi—was a Russian in real life, not an Italian, and his name was Petrov. And Mademoiselle Fenardi was very pretty; she had very fine legs and she wore tights and a very short skirt with spangles on it, and she did spin around and around in real life, but not for four hours as Gogol has it—only for four minutes, although she still man-aged to turn everyone's head . . ."

"No, you tell us why you were flogged!" Kalganov shouted.

"Because of Piron."

"What Piron?" Mitya yelled.

"The French Piron, the famous French writer. There was quite a large party drinking in a tavern, at this fair, you know. They invited me to join them and I at once started making epigrams: 'Why, you Boileau, I so admire, Where are you off to in that attire?' And Boileau answers that he's going to a masquerade, that is, to the bath-house. Hee, hee. They took it personally, though, so I quickly recited another epigram that every educated person knows:

> I am Phaon, you are Sappho,
> But what good is that to me,
> If you don't know your way to the sea.

"That offended them even more and they started applying all sorts of unseemly words to me. So, in order to save the situation, I told them then and there a very cultured anecdote about Piron. It was when they had refused to make him a member of the French Academy; to avenge himself, he wrote his own epitaph, that goes:

> *Ci-gît Piron qui ne fut rien,*
> *Pas même académicien.*

"So they got hold of me and flogged me."

"I still don't see why."

"Because of my education. Since when do people need special reasons to flog a person?" Maximov offered this conclusion as if it were a profound lesson in a nut shell.

"Ah, enough of that. I don't want to listen to that stuff anymore, I thought you'd tell us something funny," Grushenka suddenly cut him off.

Mitya gave a start and at once stopped laughing. The tall Pole stood up and, with the bored and disdainful air of a man who is forced to put up with people with whom he ordinarily would not consort, began pacing the room from corner to corner, his hands behind his back.

"Look at the way he's walking up and down," Grushenka said, looking at him scornfully.

Mitya became worried. Moreover, he noticed that the other Pole was watching him from the sofa with an annoyed look.

"Hey, *pane*," Mitya called out to him, "let's have a drink together. And the other *pane*, too—let's drink, gentlemen!" And he quickly filled three glasses.

"To Poland, gentlemen—let us drink to your Poland!" Mitya said.

"I accept your invitation with pleasure, sir," the Pole with the pipe said, condescendingly accepting a glass from Mitya.

"And the other Polish gentleman, too. Hey, you, most honorable sir—what's your name?—here's your glass!" Mitya called out.

"His name is Pan Wrublewski," the little Pole told Mitya. Pan Wrublewski walked with a rolling gait to the table and took the glass Mitya was holding out to him.

"So here's to Poland, gentlemen. Hurray!" Mitya announced.

The three of them emptied their glasses. As soon as they had done so, Mitya took the bottle and refilled the three glasses.

"Now, to Russia, gentlemen, and to our friendship!"

"Pour some for us, too," Grushenka said. "I want to drink to Russia myself."

"So do I," said Kalganov.

"I, too, would like to drink to sweet old Russia, our grandmother," Maximov chimed in with a titter.

"Let's all drink, all of us! Innkeeper, bring some more bottles!"

The bottles were brought in and Mitya poured out the champagne.

"Here's to Russia. Hurray!" Mitya announced again.

Everyone except the Poles drank, and Grushenka emptied her glass in one gulp. The Poles did not even touch theirs.

"What do you mean by this, my Polish friends? Why didn't you drink?" Mitya cried in surprise.

Pan Wrublewski took his glass, lifted it, and announced in a resounding voice: "To Russia within her borders of 1772!"

"That way, it's all right," the other Pole said and the two of them emptied their glasses.

"You're a couple of damned fools, gentlemen," Mitya blurted out without thinking.

"Sir!" the two Poles cried, indignantly glaring at Mitya like two fighting cocks. Wrublewski looked particularly menacing.

"Are we not allowed to love our country?" he asked.

"Quiet! I don't want any quarrels here, do you hear me?" Grushenka cried, imperiously stamping her foot on the floor. Her cheeks and eyes were afire. Perhaps the glass of champagne she had just drunk was having its effect. Mitya became terribly frightened.

"Forgive me, gentlemen. It was all my fault. Forgive me, Pan Wrublewski, it won't happen again!"

"Be quiet at least, you silly thing. Sit down, for heaven's sake," Grushenka snapped at him impatiently.

They all sat down, looking at one another in silence.

"It's all my fault," Mitya started, having again misunderstood Grushenka's rebuke. "Why are we all sitting here like this? What shall we do to have some fun? How can we have some fun?"

"I must say, we're not having a very wild time right now," Kalganov drawled lazily.

"So why not have another little game of faro as we had before?" Maximov suggested with a chuckle.

"Faro?" Mitya cried. "Excellent idea! And if our Polish friends are agreeable . . ."

"It's rather late," the little Pole said reluctantly.

"That's right," Wrublewski agreed.

"It's always late for them. It's always, 'Don't do this, don't do that!' " Grushenka cried almost shrilly in her irritation. "They sit there with bored faces and they're determined that everyone shall be bored too. Before you came, Mitya, they hardly said a word, just scowled at the world . . ."

"My goddess," the Pole on the sofa said, "if I am sad, it is because I see that I displease you. I am ready to play, sir," he announced, turning toward Mitya.

"You start then," Mitya said, pulling his wad of bills out of his pocket. He peeled off two one-hundred-ruble bills and put them on the table. "I'd be glad to lose a lot of money to you, my Polish friend. Here, take these cards and deal."

"We'll ask the innkeeper for a pack of cards, sir," the little Pole said emphatically.

"Yes, that's the proper way," Wrublewski backed him.

"Ask the innkeeper? Fine. Good idea, gentlemen . . . A pack of cards!" Mitya shouted to the landlord.

Trifon brought a new, sealed deck and reported to Mitya that some of the girls had already arrived, that the Jews with the cymbals would be there soon, but that the cart with the provisions had not yet arrived. Mitya jumped up and dashed out of the room to give the necessary instructions. Only three girls had arrived and Maria was not among them. Actually, Mitya himself was none too sure what instructions he was supposed to give and why, actually, he had hurried out like that. He simply told the landlord to take the sweets out of the box and let the girls have what they wanted.

"Ah, yes, I want you to serve Andrei some vodka. I think I offended him!" he ordered hurriedly.

At that moment someone touched his shoulder. It was Maximov, who had come out after him.

"Could you let me have five rubles?" he whispered. "I wouldn't mind having a go at faro too, he-he-he!"

"Good idea! Here, take ten." Mitya pulled all the bills out of his pocket again and found a ten-ruble bill among them. "And if you lose, come back for more."

"I will. Thank you very much," Maximov whispered happily, trotting back to the blue room.

Mitya returned too and apologized for having kept them waiting. The Poles were already seated. They had unsealed the pack of cards. They seemed much more amiable now, almost friendly. The little Pole lighted his pipe again and prepared to deal. He looked like a man about to perform a solemn ritual.

"Take your seats, gentlemen!" Pan Wrublewski called out.

"I don't think I'll play anymore," Kalganov said. "I already lost fifty rubles to them earlier."

"You had a streak of bad luck, Pan Kalganov," the little Pole remarked. "You may be lucky now, though."

"How much is there in the bank?" Mitya asked. "Does this cover it?"

"Whatever you say, sir—one hundred, two hundred, whatever you wish to stake."

"One million!" Mitya shouted and roared with laughter.

"Have you, sir, heard the story about Pan Podwysocki?"

"Who is this Podwysocki?"

"The way we play in Warsaw, anyone can come and stake against the bank. So Podwysocki comes in, sees there is a thousand zlotys in the bank, and says, 'Banco.' The banker says, 'Pan Podwysocki, are you putting up cash or your word of honor?' 'My word of honor.' 'Good, I like that best.' So the banker deals and Podwysocki wins what he thinks is one thousand zlotys. 'Just a minute, sir,' the banker says to him and hands him a box containing one million zlotys. It was a million zloty bank. 'You won it, Pan Podwysocki, we trust your word of honor and we keep ours.' So Podwysocki took the million and left."

"That's not true," Kalganov said.

"That's no way to talk in decent company, Pan Kalganov."

"I can just imagine a Polish gambler giving away a million like that!" Mitya said, but at once checked himself. "I'm sorry, gentlemen, I'm wrong again. I'm sure he would give away a million, because of his Polish sense of honor—honor Polska—ha-ha-ha! You see, I can even speak Polish! So now, see, I stake ten rubles. The knave leads."

"And I'll stake one little ruble on this pretty little lady, the queen of hearts, the nice damsel," Maximov said, gingerly pushing his card forward as though hoping no one would see it. He pulled his chair up as close to the table as he could and made a quick sign of the cross under the table.

"A corner!" Mitya cried. Both he and Maximov won.

"I'll risk another little ruble now, one more single little ruble," Maximov muttered blissfully, delighted that he had already won one ruble.

"Lost!" Mitya cried out. "A double on the seven!"

The double was lost too.

"Don't. Stop it!" Kalganov said suddenly.

"Double, double!" Mitya kept doubling his stakes and every time he doubled, he lost. But Maximov's single rubles kept winning.

"Double!" Mitya shouted furiously.

"You have lost two hundred, sir," the little Pole informed him. "Do you wish to stake another two hundred?"

"What, I've lost two hundred already? All right, I'll stake another two hundred and everything on the double!" Mitya pulled out two more one-hundred-ruble bills and tossed them on the queen.

But Kalganov covered the money with his hand.

"That's enough!" he said in his ringing young voice.

"What's the matter with you?" Mitya asked, staring at him.

"I won't let you play anymore."

"But why?"

"Just take my word. The hell with it—let it go at that. I simply won't let you go on like this."

Mitya gaped at him, completely dumbfounded.

"Give it up, Mitya. He may be right—you've lost enough as is," Grushenka said with a peculiar intonation in her voice.

The two Poles suddenly stood up. They looked extremely offended.

"You must be joking, sir," the little Pole said to Kalganov sternly, looking him up and down.

"How dare you!" Pan Wrublewski barked at Kalganov.

"What do you mean by shouting like that," Grushenka burst out angrily, "you big turkey!"

Mitya looked at them all in turn. Something in Grushenka's expression struck him, and a strange new notion flashed through his mind.

"Please, madam!" the little Pole began, turning to Grushenka, his face crimson with anger.

Mitya suddenly went up to him and tapped him on the shoulder.

"I would like to have a couple of words with you, honored sir," he said.

"What is it you wish, sir?"

"Come into the other room with me. I'll tell you something you'll just love to hear. Come on."

The little Pole seemed taken aback and looked at Mitya distrustfully. But he agreed at once, on condition, though, that Pan Wrublewski go with them.

"You want to have your bodyguard with you? Fine, let him come along. Besides, I want him, too. I even insist on it!" Mitya said. "Come on, my Polish friends, let's go."

"Where are you off to?" Grushenka asked with alarm.

"We'll be back in a minute," Mitya said. There was something self-confident and unexpectedly cheerful about him, and his face was quite different from what it had been when he first arrived. He led the Poles, not to the room where the girls were getting ready and the table was being set, but to another one, at the opposite end of the blue room. It was a bedroom with trunks and suitcases next to two large beds, which were piled high with pillows in cotton calico covers.

There was a small deal table in a corner with a lighted candle on it. Mitya and the little Pole sat at the table opposite each other while the huge Pan Wrublewski stood nearby, his hands clasped behind his back. The two Poles looked grim, but they were also obviously curious about what was to come.

"What can I do for you, sir?" the little Pole murmured when he was seated.

"I'll tell you. I don't want to make a long speech. Here's three thousand rubles. Take it and go wherever you like, as long as you get out of here." Mitya pulled the bundle of money out of his pocket.

The little Pole looked at Mitya with tremendous intensity, as if his eyes were trying to penetrate inside him.

"Three thousand?" he asked finally, exchanging a quick look with Wrublewski.

"Three thousand, that's right—I said three. Listen to me: I can see you're a reasonable man, so take the three thousand and get the hell out of here and take your Wrublewski along with you. But I want you to get out now, this very minute, and never come back. You'll go right through this door. What do you have here? A coat, a fur coat? Wait, I'll get it for you myself. I'll order horses harnessed for you, and then good-by forever, my Polish friends! Well?"

Mitya waited calmly. He did not doubt that his offer would be taken up.

Something flashed in the Pole's eyes and it looked as if he had made his decision.

"When do I receive the money, sir?"

"This is how we'll do it: you get five hundred rubles right now—that will pay for the horses and you'll keep what's left as an advance. The remaining two-and-a-half thousand you'll receive tomorrow in town, and I give you my word of honor that I'll get it to you whatever happens!"

The Poles exchanged glances again. The little Pole's face hardened.

"You can have seven hundred rubles instead of five right now," Mitya said, raising his offer, as he sensed that something had gone wrong. "What's the matter—don't you trust me? You don't really expect me to give you the whole three thousand right away, do you? If I gave it to you now, what would prevent you from going back to her tomorrow? Besides, I don't have three thousand on me right now, but I swear I have the money hidden at home, in town . . ."

The face of the little Pole immediately assumed an expression of immense personal dignity.

"Is that all you wanted to tell me?" he asked sarcastically. "You should be ashamed of yourself . . . pfft!"

He spat in disgust. Wrublewski spat too.

"You're spitting now, you Pole," Mitya said in despair, realizing that he had failed, "because you reckon that you'll be able to get more out of Grushenka—you're a couple of capons, that's what you are!"

"You're being insulting now." The little Pole turned red in the face, got up, and rushed out of the room with the air of a man who can no longer bear such indignity.

Wrublewski followed him in his rolling gait and the disheartened and confused Mitya brought up the rear. Mitya was now very frightened of Grushenka, anticipating that the Pole would make a scene. And he was quite right. The little Pole walked in and stopped in front of Grushenka in a theatrical pose.

"Pani . . ." he started, but she interrupted him.

"My name is Grushenka Svetlov, and if you want me to listen to you, you'll just have to speak Russian," she cried, losing her temper, as if he had touched a very sore spot in her. "I don't want to hear one single Polish word. You used to speak Russian once upon a time, and I don't believe you can have forgotten it in these five years . . ."

"Miss Svetlov . . . I . . . come from far to forget past and forgive . . . that was until today," he said with an air of outraged dignity, in deliberately broken Russian.

"You have come to forgive *me?"*

Grushenka leapt to her feet.

"That's right, *pani*. I am not petty. I am a generous man. But I was surprised when I see all your lovers. Pan Mitya offered me three thousand rubles to go away. I spat in Pan Mitya's face."

"What! He offered you money for me? Is that right, Mitya? So you think I can be bought, do you!"

"Gentlemen, gentlemen!" Mitya shouted. "She is pure and chaste and I have never, never been her lover! You lied, you, you . . ."

"Don't you dare defend me before that man!" Grushenka cried. "If I stayed chaste it was not out of virtue or because I was afraid of Kuzma, but to be able to face this miserable wretch proudly when we met again and tell him to his face that I loathe him. In fact, I can hardly believe that he didn't accept the money you offered him!"

"He wanted to take it, all right. He did," Mitya cried. "Only he wanted me to give him the whole three thousand at once, and I insisted on giving him seven hundred down and the rest tomorrow."

"Why, I know he somehow found out I had some money and so came rushing here to marry me."

"Pani!" the little Pole shouted angrily. "I am a gentleman, a nobleman, not a good-for-nothing parasite. I came here to make you my wife, but I find here not the woman I know before, but a different woman, a woman who behaves bad and has lost all shame."

"So go back where you came from!" Grushenka screamed, beside herself. "If I demand that they throw you out now, they will do it. You can be sure of that! How stupid I was to have tormented myself for five years the way I have. But it was not because I missed you that I suffered. No, it was my rage that tormented me. I don't even think you are the same man! He couldn't possibly have looked like this! You might be his father or something. Well, tell me, where did you order that hairpiece you're wearing? No, that other man looked like a hawk to me and you look like a half-plucked drake. The other one laughed and sang to me . . . Ah, what fool I am to have shed so many tears during these five years, a shameless fool . . ."

She sank into the armchair and covered her face with her hands.

At that moment the singing of the Mokroye girls resounded in the room next door. They had all been assembled at last and now they started with a fast dance song.

"What is this Sodom?" Wrublewski roared indignantly. "Innkeeper, throw those shameless women out!"

Trifon, who had been peeking curiously into the room for quite some time, had realized that his guests had quarreled. So now he hurried in.

"What are you hollering like that for?" he addressed Wrublewski with quite surprising rudeness.

"You pig!" Wrublewski roared at him.

"Who's a pig?" the landlord shouted back. "Why don't you tell them what cards you were using just now? For you hid the deck of cards I brought you, didn't you? And the cards you played with were marked. I could have you packed off to Siberia for that, because it's just as bad as forged bills. You know that?"

Trifon walked over to the sofa where the little Pole had been sitting, thrust his fingers between the back of the sofa and the cushions, and pulled out a sealed pack of cards.

"Here, this is my deck, and it hasn't been opened!" he said, holding it up for everyone to see. "I saw him from the door shoving my deck in there and replacing it with his own . . . No, this gentleman is a common card sharp!"

"Ah, how disgraceful, how disgusting! How could a man turn into that!" Grushenka cried, throwing her hands up and actually turning red with shame.

"And I saw the other one changing a card," Kalganov said. "He did it twice, in fact."

"I thought so too . . ." Mitya was going to say something else, but before he could go on, Wrublewski, mad with rage at being so thoroughly exposed, turned to Grushenka and, threatening her with his fist, shouted:

"You dirty whore!"

But he had hardly uttered the words before Mitya was on top of him. He grabbed the Pole with both hands, lifted him off the floor, and in an instant had carried him into the room where he had been with the two Poles before.

"I've put him down on the floor in there," he announced

breathlessly, returning almost at once. "He's thrashing about, the animal, but I don't expect he'll come back." Then, closing one half of the double door and holding the other half open, he turned to the little Pole: "Now, you noble Polish gentleman, would you be so kind as to join your friend in there?"

"Mr. Karamazov, sir," the landlord said, "why don't you take your money back from them? It's just as if they'd stolen it from you!"

"As far as I'm concerned, they can keep my fifty rubles," Kalganov said.

"And I don't want my two hundred back either," Mitya cried. "Let them keep it as a consolation."

"That's the right thing, Mitya. Good boy!" Grushenka shouted loudly and there was a note of wicked anger in her voice.

The little Pole, beet red with fury but still maintaining his supercilious air, walked slowly toward the door.

But before reaching it, he stopped and said, looking at Grushenka:

"*Pani*, if you still wish to follow me, come; if you do not, good-by!"

And breathing heavily with indignation and offended pride, he walked through the half of the double door that Dmitry had left open. He was indeed a man of character and great conceit, for, after all that had happened, he still hoped Grushenka would choose him, so highly did he value himself.

Mitya closed the door behind him.

"Lock them in," Kalganov suggested, but just as he said it, the lock clicked from the inside: the two Poles had thought of locking themselves in first.

"Wonderful!" Grushenka said with implacable hatred. "Great! Good riddance!"

CHAPTER 8

Delirium

Then a big party began, a free-for-all, almost an orgy. Grushenka was the first to call for champagne:

"I want to drink. I want to get completely drunk, just like the time we got to know each other, Mitya, remember?"

Mitya was in a sort of delirium. Happiness was within

his reach. Right now, though, Grushenka kept sending him off to join the others.

"Go, Mitya, have a good time. I want everybody to have a wild time! Make them dance 'Round goes the stove, round goes the house,' just like the other time, remember?" she kept shouting to him.

She was terribly excited. Mitya dashed about giving orders. The singers had gathered in the room next door. The blue room, in which they had been sitting until then, was rather stuffy, since a section of it was divided off from the rest by a cotton curtain which concealed a huge bed covered with a puffy eiderdown and the usual pile of pillows in bright cotton covers (there were beds in all four of the "living rooms" of the guest house).

Grushenka wanted to sit by the very door, in the very spot she had sat "that other time," and Mitya put an armchair there for her. It was from that spot that she had watched the singers and the dancers. The girls were the same as the last time. Soon the Jews arrived with their cymbals and fiddles. Then finally the long-awaited cart with the champagne and food also arrived. Mitya was very busy. Villagers, men and women who had already gone to bed, had got up again for fear of missing another sumptuous party like the one they had witnessed before, or heard of, and were now peering into the room. Mitya greeted those he already knew with a hug, trying hard to remember whether he had seen some of the faces before. He uncorked bottles and poured out wine for anyone who happened to be there. It was the women who eyed the champagne the most eagerly; the men really preferred brandy, rum, and particularly hot punch. Mitya also saw to it that there was hot chocolate for every girl, and he insisted that three samovars be kept boiling throughout the night so that anyone arriving at any time should be able to get himself hot punch or tea. In short, a most chaotic and absurd party was under way. But Mitya seemed in his natural element, and the more absurd things became, the happier he felt. If some villager had had the inspiration to ask him for money, he would have pulled out his bundle of bills immediately and proceeded to hand them out right and left without restraint. Probably sensing this, Trifon the innkeeper kept making circles around him. He had apparently given up completely the idea of going to bed that night. He drank little (he "indulged" in a glass of punch only), for he felt it was in his interest to keep a sharp eye on Mitya's money. Whenever he had a chance, he would try gently and fawningly to prevent Mitya from distributing cigars to the peasants or from making them drunk on Rhine wine, "like that other time, sir," and "God forbid that you should give them money, sir." It broke his heart, as it was, to watch the village girls devouring caramels and sipping liqueurs: "They're crawling with lice, Mr. Karamazov. They're the kind you can kick in the backside and you'd still be doing them too great an honor." Mitya again remembered Andrei and ordered that a glass of punch be sent to him. "I offended him," he kept repeating sadly.

At first, Kalganov said that he did not want to drink and that he did not like the village singers. But after downing a couple of glasses of champagne, he became terribly gay, and kept making the rounds, praising everything and everybody, singers, dancers, musicians. Maximov, quietly and blissfully drunk, followed Kalganov wherever he went. Grushenka, who was also beginning to feel the effects of the champagne, kept pointing to Kalganov and saying to Mitya, "Isn't he sweet? What a sweet boy!" And Mitya would at once rush over and hug Kalganov and Maximov. Oh, it was all just a feeling he had! Grushenka hadn't said anything special to him and, in fact, she deliberately refrained from saying anything to him. But occasionally he saw her glancing at him, not just with warm affection, but with something like ardor.

At last she caught him by the arm and pulled him violently to her. She was sitting in her armchair by the door.

"Ah, the way you looked when you first came in! What a face you had! I was so scared, you know . . . But why were you prepared to give me up and let him have me? For that's what you were going to do, wasn't it?"

"I didn't want to spoil your happiness," Mitya mumbled blissfully, but she didn't need him to tell her that.

"All right, go away—enjoy yourself," she said, chasing him away. "And don't start crying—I'll call you back soon."

And when he had left, she again listened to the singing and watched the dancers, though always keeping an eye on Mitya. Then, after a quarter of an hour or so, she called him back.

"Now sit down here, next to me, and tell me how you found out yesterday about my leaving. And how did you know I would come here?"

And Mitya told her, disconnectedly, incoherently, feverishly. And then, suddenly, in the middle of it, he unexpectedly stopped and knitted his brows.

"Why are you frowning like that?" she asked him.

"Nothing . . . it's just that I left someone behind in a pretty bad state . . . I'd give ten years of my life for him to get well."

"What can you do about it? He's sick, so he's sick! Tell me, am I right that you were planning to shoot yourself in the morning, you silly, you! Whatever for? Why, you know I only like the crazy ones like you!" she muttered as her tongue grew thicker. "So you'll do anything for me, won't you? You were going to shoot yourself, you crazy, silly man! No, you'd better wait. There's something I'll tell you tomorrow . . . not today, tomorrow, although I bet you'd like to hear it today . . . No, I don't feel like telling you today . . . Now go and have a good time . . ."

At one point, however, when she called him back, she looked at him in alarm.

"Why are you so sad, Mitya? I know you're sad . . . Don't say no, I can see it," she said looking into his eyes. "Yes, you may be shouting over there with the villagers and hugging them, but I can see that something is troubling you. That's not what I want—I feel gay and I want you to be gay . . . You know, there's someone here I love, and guess who it is? Now look at that! That sweet boy has had enough to drink and has passed out, the poor darling!"

She pointed to Kalganov, who had had quite a bit to drink and had dozed off sitting on the sofa. But it was not the wine that had put him to sleep; he had suddenly felt depressed or, as he would have put it, "bored." In the end he felt sickened by the girls' songs which, as they became more and more drunk, gradually became more and more outspoken and dirty. And the dances, too, displeased him. There was a dance in which two girls impersonated bears while Stepanida, a pert girl, played the part of bear trainer, making them "perform."

"Move livelier, Maria!" she shouted, "or you'll get a taste of my stick!"

At the end the bears rolled on the floor with no semblance of decency any longer, and this provoked delighted roars of laughter from the packed audience of villagers, men and women alike.

"So let them, let them all enjoy themselves," Grushenka kept repeating sententiously, looking blissfully at the performers. "Why shouldn't people have a good time when they're given a chance!"

Kalganov, though, felt as if he had been dirtied:

"It's filthy, disgusting!" he muttered, moving away from

the crowd. "What a sickening sight, this peasant feast! These are their spring rituals, when they keep watch for the sun throughout midsummer's night."

But he especially disliked a certain "new" song sung to a lively dance tune. It started with a landowner trying to find out whether the girls from his village loved him:

> Master's curiosity was hot:
> Do girls love me? Do they not?

The girls didn't think they could love their master:

> Master'll beat me with a rope,
> For such love I do not hope.

Then came the gypsy, who also wanted to know whether the girls loved him:

> Gipsy's curiosity was hot:
> Do girls love me? Do they not?

It turned out the girls couldn't love him either because:

> Gypsy, he will always steal,
> Wretched all my life I'll feel.

And many other people wondered about the girls' love, including the soldier:

> Soldier's curiosity was hot:
> Do girls love me? Do they not?

But the soldier was rejected with contempt:

> Soldier will be rough and blunt
> Always chasing after ————.

This unprintable verse, sung with complete frankness, created a real furor among the audience.

Finally it was the turn of the merchant:

> Merchant's curiosity was hot:
> Do girls love me? Do they not?

And it turned out that they did because:

Merchant will make pots of gold,
He my love will win and hold.

Kalganov actually became angry:

"That song is already out of date," he said aloud. "I wonder who composes these things for them? They could have completed it by adding a railwayman and a Jew—they'd certainly take the jackpot!"

He took the song almost as a personal insult, announced that he was bored, sat down on the sofa, and dozed off. His pretty face turned slightly paler and his head fell back on the cushions.

"Look how pretty he is," Grushenka said, taking Mitya to him. "I was combing his hair earlier this evening. It's just like flax, and so thick!"

She leaned tenderly over the boy and kissed him on the forehead. Kalganov at once opened his eyes, sat up, and, looking very worried, asked:

"Where's Maximov?"

"So that's who he wants!" Grushenka laughed. "But couldn't you sit here with me for a minute while Mitya finds your Maximov? Will you, Mitya?"

It turned out that Maximov had not left the girls except to dash off a few times to refill his glass with liqueur. He had also helped himself to two cups of chocolate. His face was red, his nose was purple, his eyes were moist and amorous. He came at a trot and announced that he was going "to dance a *sabotière* to a certain tune," because, he explained, "I was taught all these society dances when I was a little boy, you know."

"All right, go ahead. Go with him, Mitya. I'll watch him dancing from here."

"But I want to go too," Kalganov cried, thus most innocently spurning Grushenka's offer to keep him company. So they all went. Maximov performed his dance but, except for Mitya, it did not gain him any admirers. His dancing consisted of leaps into the air, during which he would turn one foot sideways and slap the sole of his boot with the palm of his hand. Kalganov thought nothing of the dance, whereas Mitya was so enthusiastic that he even kissed Maximov.

"That was great, great!" Mitya said. "I see you looking over there—what would you like? Some candy? A cigar perhaps?"

"I think I'd like a little cigaret, please."

"And what about a drink?"

"I wouldn't mind a drop of liqueur . . . And is there some of that nice chocolate candy left?"

"You can see there's a whole heap of it on the table, so you'd better go and pick what you like, you angel face!"

"No, but I want one with vanilla, you know—it's specially good for little old men, he-he-he . . ."

"I'm afraid those are all gone, brother."

"Listen!" Maximov suddenly whispered right into Mitya's ear. "What about that girl Maria? Do you think it would be possible for me to become better acquainted with her? Through your kindness, I mean . . ."

"So that's what you're after! Sorry, brother, I can't help you there."

"I didn't mean any harm . . ." Maximov mumbled dejectedly.

"I know, I know, but you see, these girls have only come to sing and dance . . . Although, wait . . . Ah, hell . . . Eat, drink, enjoy yourself for now . . . Tell me, do you need a little money?"

"I don't know—maybe later." Maximov was smiling again. "Fine, good . . ."

Mitya's head was burning hot. He went out into the hall and from there onto the long wooden balcony that skirted the side of the house overlooking the inside courtyard. The fresh air revived him somewhat. He stood there for a while, all alone in the darkness, and then clutched his head between his hands. Suddenly his scattered thoughts and his disconnected sensations merged into a whole that became phosphorescent . . . And in that sinister, horrible light, he saw it! "If I'm going to shoot myself, this is the best moment," the words formed in his mind. "Shouldn't I go and get my pistol, bring it here, and put an end to everything right here in this dark corner, facing this grimy yard?" For almost a whole minute he stood there wavering. Driving here a few hours ago, he had been a completely disgraced man—he had committed a plain, outright theft and . . . and that blood, that blood . . . Yet it was so much easier then, oh, incomparably easier! Then he had felt everything was finished: she was gone, gone with another man; he had lost her, lost her irretrievably . . . The death sentence he had passed on himself seemed much lighter then, because he had felt it was logical and inevitable —there was no reason for him to remain alive. But now it was not at all the same. Now, at least, that horrible ghost of the past had been destroyed; her "first, unchallengeable love" had dissolved into thin air; the man who had played such a fateful part in her life had turned into a wretched caricature and was now locked in a bedroom. And never again would that phantom come back to haunt her! Indeed, she was ashamed of her former illusions, and he could see in her eyes who she really loved now. So it was now that he wanted to be alive! But he was not allowed to live now, he could not stay alive, and that was the hell of it!

"O God, please bring back to life the man I struck down by the garden fence! Spare me this horrible tribulation! O Lord, have you not performed miracles to save sinners as bad as me before? . . . But even if Gregory is alive, even so . . . No, no, if he is alive, I will atone for the other disgrace. I will wipe it out. I'll pay back the money I have stolen. Even if I must sweat it out in blood, I'll get it! There will be no trace of my disgrace left anywhere, except in my heart, where the scars will remain forever . . . No, no, these are just impossible, cowardly dreams . . . Ah, hell!"

Nevertheless, a strange ray of hope flashed in the darkness surrounding Mitya. He rushed back inside the house. He wanted to see her now, quickly, to be with the one who was his queen forever. "Why, isn't one hour, one minute of her love worth spending the rest of my life in torture and agony?" That wild question clutched at his heart. "To her, quickly! All I want is to be with her alone, look at her, listen to her voice, not think of anything else, forget all the rest if only for one night, one hour, one second . . ."

Just as he was about to step from the balcony into the hall, Mitya ran into Trifon. The man looked worried and concerned, and Mitya thought he was looking for him.

"What's the matter, Trifon? Looking for me?"

"No, no, not you, Mr. Karamazov," Trifon said, apparently taken aback. "Why should I be looking for you? But where have you been, sir?"

"Why are you looking so dismal, Trifon. Are you angry or something? Don't worry, soon you'll be able to go to bed and get some sleep. What time is it, by the way?"

"It must be at least three, or even later . . ."

"We'll be ending soon, don't worry."

"Good Lord, sir, please . . . You just go on as long as you feel like it."

"There's something the matter with him, though," Mitya thought as he went into the room where the girls were danc-

ing. Grushenka wasn't there. Nor was she in the blue room—
Kalganov was all alone there, dozing on the sofa. Mitya
glanced behind the curtain—and there she was. She was
sitting in a corner on a trunk, leaning forward, her hands
and her head resting on the edge of the bed. She was weeping
violently, trying hard to restrain her sobs so as not to attract
attention. She saw Mitya and beckoned to him. He hastened
to her. She took his hand and grasped it tightly.

"Mitya, Mitya," she whispered, "you know, I did love
him. I loved him all those five years, all that time . . . Was
it him I loved or was it just my own spite? Oh, it was him,
all right! I'm lying to myself when I say that what I loved was
just my anger. You must understand, Mitya—I was only
seventeen then and he was so tender to me and he would
sing me those songs . . . Or, at least, that was how he
seemed to me, stupid little girl that I was. But now . . . oh,
he isn't the same. He's a different man altogether. Even his
face is completely different. As I was driving here with
Timofei, I kept wondering what it would be like to see him
again, what I would say to him when I saw him, how we
would look at each other. It took my breath away to think
about it . . . And then it was as if someone had emptied a
bucket of slops on my head . . . He behaved like a school-
teacher, so pompous and important, and he spoke to me so
learnedly, so slowly . . . I was completely lost, didn't know
what to say to him. At first I thought he was embarrassed for
that long-legged friend of his. I sat there with them and
wondered to myself why I didn't even know how to talk to
him now. You know, I think it was his wife who did that
to him, the wife he married after he deserted me then. It was
she, I think, who turned him into what he is today. Ah,
Mitya, I feel so ashamed, so terribly ashamed, ashamed of
my whole life! I loathe the thought of those five years—may
they be damned, damned . . ." And tears gushed from her
eyes as she clung to Mitya's hand, never relaxing her grip.

"Mitya, dear, don't go away yet—there's something I'd like
to tell you," she whispered, and for the first time lifted her
face and looked straight at him. "Listen, you tell me who I
love now. There's someone here I love, and I want you to tell
me who it is. So who is it, Mitya? You tell me!" A smile
lighted up her face that was swollen with crying, and her
eyes glowed in the dim light.

"So, as I sat there with them, suddenly an eagle appeared.
My heart sank when he came in. 'Idiot, this is the man you

love,' it whispered to me, my heart. Everything turned bright the moment you came in. 'But what is he afraid of?' I thought to myself. For you were scared, you were so scared, you were so scared that you couldn't even talk. 'He surely can't be afraid of them?' I said to myself. 'He's never been afraid of anybody. Therefore he can only be afraid of me,' I decided. So Fenya must have repeated to you the silly message I asked Alyosha to give you—that I'd loved you for one hour but that I was leaving now and would always love someone else. Didn't Fenya repeat it to you, my crazy fool? Ah, Mitya, Mitya, how could I ever have imagined that I could love that other one after having loved you! Can you forgive me—can you? Do you still love me, Mitya? Do you love me?"

She stood up quickly, seizing him by the shoulders. He was speechless, just staring in adoration at her smiling eyes, her face . . . Suddenly he threw his arms around her and kissed her madly, desperately.

"And will you forgive me, too, for having deliberately made you suffer? I made you all suffer, just out of sheer spite. It was just out of sheer viciousness that I drove your old man insane . . . Remember, once in my house, you smashed the glass you were drinking out of? Well, that was what I was thinking of when I smashed my glass today as I drank to my vile heart . . . Mitya, my eagle, why don't you kiss me? What is it? You started to kiss me, then stopped in the middle, and now you're just staring at me and listening to me! What is there to listen to? Come, kiss me, kiss me harder . . . like this . . . If it's to be love, let it be love then! I'll be your slave now, your slave as long as I live, and I'll love being your slave . . . Come, Mitya, keep kissing me! You can beat me, hurt me, do what you want to me . . . Yes, I suppose I have really deserved to be made to suffer . . . Wait, stop! I don't want it like this . . ." She suddenly pushed him off. "Go away—leave me, Dmitry Karamazov. I'll go and get myself some wine now. I want to get drunk, and then I'll dance, dance drunk. That's what I want, and that's what I'll do!"

She broke away from him, pulled aside the curtain dividing the blue room, and dashed out. Mitya followed her as though moving in a drunken haze. "I don't care, I don't care," the thought throbbed inside him. "I don't care what happens. I'd give the world for a minute like this one . . ."

Grushenka did as she said: she downed a large glass of

champagne and it went straight to her head. She sat down in the armchair where she had sat earlier. She was smiling happily. Her cheeks were aflame, her lips were hot, her eyes, filled with passion, flashed under her heavy lids. There was an irresistible fascination in her look. Even Kalganov, feeling as if something had stung him, got up and walked over to her.

"Did you feel me kiss you while you were asleep?" she mumbled to him. "The wine has gone to my head now, you see . . . Tell me—what about you? Aren't you drunk too? And why isn't Mitya drinking? Hey, Mitya, why aren't you drinking? I'm drinking and you're not . . ."

"I'm drunk as it is, drunk on you . . . But now, I want to be drunk on wine too." He emptied a glass and had the strange impression that this was the first time that night that he had felt its effect. Until then, he felt, he had been absolutely sober. But from that second on, everything started to turn around him as in delirium. He walked about, laughed, talked to people, no longer conscious of himself. He was only conscious of a persistent, burning sensation that felt "like a burning coal in my soul," as he described it later . . . He kept coming back to Grushenka, sitting down next to her, looking at her, listening to her. She herself was seized by an unrestrainable urge to talk; she kept beckoning to people to come and chat with her; she would suddenly call over a girl from the group of singers and kiss her maybe, or just make the sign of the cross over her . . . There were moments, though, when she seemed on the verge of tears. But then she would be cheered up by Maximov, the "old cutie," as she called him, who kept dashing up to her every moment to kiss her hand and "every single finger thereof," as he put it, and who finally performed one more dance to the tune of an old song that he sang himself. He leapt into the air and stamped his feet with particular zest every time he got to the refrain:

> The little pig says froo-froo-froo,
> The little calf says moo-moo-moo,
> The little duck says dack-dack-dack,
> The little goose says quack-quack-quack,
> The hen wandered through the shed,
> Chuck-chuck-chuck, she said,
> Clack-tack-pack, she said . . .

"Give him something, Mitya," Grushenka kept saying; "you must make him some nice present. He's so poor and

he has to put up with so much ! . . . You know what, Mitya
—I think I'll become a nun. I'm not just saying that, I mean
it—I'll end up in a convent some day. Alyosha said something to me before I came here, something I'll always remember. Tomorrow it'll be the convent, but today I'll dance! I
want to have a wild time today, good people! Now what's
wrong with that? I'm sure God will forgive me. If I were
God, I'd forgive everyone. 'My dear sinners,' I'd say to them,
'as of today, you are all forgiven!' Tomorrow I'll go and
ask people for forgiveness: 'Forgive me, stupid woman that
I am,' I'll beg them. I'm a beast, that's what I am, and I
want to pray. I gave away an onion, though. A vicious
woman like me needs to pray. Mitya, let them dance; don't
interfere. Everyone in the world, without exception, is good.
It's nice to live in the world—even if we are wicked, it's still
nice to be here . . . We're both good and bad, bad and
good . . . Come over here, everybody, come over here! I
want every one of you to tell me why I am so good. Because
I am good, am I not, very, very good? All right then, tell me
why I am so good."

Grushenka went on and on like this, getting more and
more drunk, and in the end declared that she wanted to
dance all by herself. She rose from her armchair, staggering.

"Don't give me any more wine, Mitya," she mumbled,
"don't. Wine won't give me peace. Everything is turning,
turning, the stove is turning . . . I want to dance. I want
everyone to watch me dance. I want everyone to admire how
marvelously I can dance . . ."

She meant it. She pulled a white lawn handkerchief out
of her pocket and held it by one corner in her right hand
to wave as she danced. Mitya made everyone stop dancing
and be quiet. The singers stood ready to burst into a dance
song at the first signal. Hearing that Grushenka was to perform a solo dance, Maximov actually squealed with delight
and started skipping around her, singing:

> With legs trim and hips slim
> And tail in a wiggle . . .

But Grushenka waved him away with her handkerchief.
"Sh-sh-sh . . . quiet! Mitya, where are they all? I want
everybody to come and watch me. Call those fellows locked
up in there too. Why did you have to lock them in? Tell them
I'm about to dance. Let them watch me dance, too . . ."

With a drunken man's enthusiasm, Mitya went to the door and banged on it with his fist.

"Hey, you, Podwysocki fellows, come out. She's dancing and she wants you to watch her!"

"You good-for-nothing!" one of the Poles answered him from behind the door.

"And you're worse than a good-for-nothing. You're a lousy little crook, that's what you are!"

"I wish you'd stop insulting Poland," Kalganov said pompously. He, too, was hopelessly drunk.

"Shut up, boy, I only told him what he is and that doesn't go for Poland as a whole. One crook doesn't make a Poland, you know. Anyway, shut up, pretty boy—better put a candy in your mouth."

"So that's how they feel! They're not even human. Why don't they want to make peace?" Grushenka said and decided to start dancing. The singers burst into a popular folk song. Grushenka tossed her head back, parted her lips, waved the handkerchief over her head, then swaying violently, stopped dead in the middle of the room, looking completely bewildered.

"I feel all weak . . ." she said in an exhausted voice. "I'm sorry, I feel too weak . . . I can't do it . . . I'm sorry . . ."

She bowed to the singers and then bowed in turn in all four directions, repeating "I'm sorry . . . Forgive me."

"The pretty lady's been drinking . . . The beautiful lady's had one too many," voices came from all around.

"Yes, you see, madam is quite full of drink," Maximov explained to the girls with a titter.

"Take me out of here, Mitya. Take me away," Grushenka said weakly.

Mitya hurried to her, picked her up in his arms, and carried his precious booty into the blue room and behind the curtain.

"Now, that does it!" Kalganov muttered under his breath. "This time I'm leaving and I mean it!" And he walked out of the blue room, carefully closing the two half doors behind him.

But in the big room the party went on again, louder than ever.

Mitya laid Grushenka down on the bed and his kiss tore open her lips.

"No, don't . . ." she mumbled imploringly, "don't do it Mitya. I'm not yours yet . . . I've told you that I'm yours,

but you mustn't touch me . . . Please don't—spare me . . .
I can't with these people . . . they're too near. And he's still
here. It's revolting here . . ."

"As you wish . . . I didn't mean it . . . I adore you," Mitya
muttered breathlessly. "Yes, it is revolting here, and it's degrading too . . ."

And, without letting go of her, Mitya slipped from the
bed and knelt beside her on the floor.

"I know, Mitya, I know you're a wild animal, but you're a
noble and generous animal," Grushenka said, pronouncing
the words with difficulty. "I want everything to be proper and
decent, and I want us to be decent, honorable people, good,
nice people, not wild animals . . . I want you to take me
away from here, very, very far away—do you hear me? I
don't want to be here, Mitya. I want to be far, far, away . . ."

"Yes, yes, of course," Mitya said, folding her in his arms.
"I'll take you away. We'll leave forever . . . Oh, I'd be happy
to die if I could live for one single year without knowing
about that blood. I'd be happy to give my whole life for that
year . . ."

"What blood?" Grushenka asked, taken aback.

"Never mind," Mitya mumbled through clenched teeth.
"You said just now, Grusha, that you wanted us to be
honest, decent people, but how can I? I am a thief. I stole
money from Katya, you know. I'm ashamed, ashamed . . ."

"From that Katya damsel? No, you haven't stolen from
her, since you'll give it back to her. I'll give it to you and
you'll pay her back. What are you hollering like that for?
Now everything that's mine is yours. What's money for? We'd
have ourselves a good time and squander it all anyway. Such
people as you and I—how could we hold on to money? I
think we really ought to become peasants and till the soil. I
want to scrape a living from the earth with these hands, see!
I want to work hard. Alyosha said I should. I won't be just
your mistress—I'll be your true and faithful wife, your slave,
and I'll work for you. We'll both go and see that Katya
damsel; we'll both bow low to her and ask her to forgive us,
and then we'll leave. And if she refuses to forgive us, we'll
leave anyway. And you, you'll take the money to her, and
all you have to do is to love me, not her, because if you ever
think of loving her, I'll strangle her. And before that, I'll
gouge out both her eyes for her with a needle."

"It's you I love, you alone, and when I'm in Siberia, I'll
love only you."

"Why Siberia? But if that's where you want to go, it suits me fine. We'll work there together. There's lots of snow in Siberia and I like driving over the snow in a sled. I insist we have bells, though . . . Mitya, do you hear bells jingling? Where are those bells jingling, Mitya? Someone is coming—don't you hear? They've stopped now . . ."

Exhausted, she closed her eyes and seemed to doze off for a minute. But a distant bell had jingled and then stopped, just as she had said. Mitya's head was resting on her breast. He had not noticed that the jingling had stopped, but then neither had he noticed that all of a sudden there was no more singing and, instead of songs and drunken voices, a dead silence had descended on the house. Grushenka opened her eyes.

"What's happening? Did I fall asleep? . . . Yes, yes, I know . . . the bells . . . I was asleep and I dreamt I was riding over the snow . . . the bells jingled and I was dozing. I was driving with the man I love, with you, Mitya. We were going very, very far . . . I was hugging you and kissing you and clinging hard to you, because I was so cold and the snow was glistening . . . You know how it is when the moon is up and the snow glistens. It felt as if I was somewhere else, not on earth . . . And now I have woken up and the man I love is still here with me. It's so good."

"With you . . ." Mitya muttered, kissing her dress, her neck, her hands.

But suddenly it struck him as strange the way she was looking straight in front of her, not at his face but somehow over his head, beyond him, staring intently, her eyes strangely fixed, in surprise and then in fright.

"Mitya, who's that looking at us from over there?" she whispered.

He turned around and saw that the curtain had been pulled aside and that someone was watching them, and apparently not just one person either. Mitya jumped to his feet and walked quickly to the curtain.

"Would you please come in here, sir," a voice said quietly but firmly.

Mitya stepped out from behind the curtain and stopped dead. The rest of the room was packed with people, but they were not the people who had been at the party, but others quite different. An icy chill ran down Mitya's spine and he shuddered. Now he recognized these new arrivals. That tall, heavy-set, elderly man in the long greatcoat and the peaked cap with a badge was Mikhail Makarov, the police inspector. And that consumptive-looking dandy in blindingly shiny boots was the assistant prosecutor—"he has a four-hundred-ruble timepiece—he showed it to me," flashed through Mitya's mind. And that short, rather young fellow with glasses—Mitya couldn't think of his name, but he was sure he had met him; in any case he knew that he was the new examining magistrate—"he hasn't been in town very long." And over there, that, of course, was Mavriky Mavrikevich, whom Mitya knew very well. But what were all those men with shiny buttons doing here? And those other two who looked like peasants? And there by the door was Kalganov, and next to him Trifon, the innkeeper.

"What is it? What's going on, gentlemen?" Mitya asked at first, but a second later he shouted in a strangely loud voice, as though he had been turned into someone else: "I un-der-stand!"

The bespectacled young man stepped toward Mitya and said quickly, albeit in a very dignified tone:

"We have something . . . to make it short, I would appreciate it if you would come over here, to the sofa . . . There are certain questions we'd like you to answer . . ."

"The old man!" Mitya shouted in despair. "The old man . . . his blood! I understand . . ." and he dropped in a heap into a nearby chair.

"Ah, you understand, do you, you father-killer, you parricide monster!" the old police inspector roared suddenly, moving toward Mitya's chair. His face had turned dark purple and he was shaking all over.

"This is quite inadmissible!" cried the short young man. "Please, inspector, this is most improper, absolutely improper! I insist that I be allowed to speak without interference from you. I never expected such an outburst from you!"

"But this is sheer delirium, gentlemen," the police inspector exclaimed. "Just look at him: in the middle of the night with a loose woman, covered with his father's blood . . . Nightmarish delirium, gentlemen, sheer delirium!"

"I must beg you to control yourself, sir, please," the dandified assistant prosecutor whispered quickly into the old inspector's ear, "otherwise, I'll have to take the necessary steps . . ."

But the little examining magistrate did not give him a chance to finish his threat and, turning toward Mitya, he said in a firm, loud, dignified voice:

"Retired Lieutenant Dmitry Karamazov, it is my duty to inform you that you are charged with the murder of your father, Fyodor Pavlovich Karamazov, committed earlier tonight . . ."

He went on to say something else and then the public prosecutor put in a few words of his own, but, although Mitya heard their voices, he could no longer understand what they were saying. He just stared wildly around him.

BOOK IX

PRELIMINARY INVESTIGATION

Peter Perkhotin Starts Out
on His Career as Civil Servant

We left Peter Perkhotin banging wildly on the solid gate of Mrs. Morozov's house. In the end, of course, the gate was opened. Fenya, whose frightening experience of two hours before had left her in such a state of fear and anxiety that she could not make up her mind to go to bed, was now frightened almost into hysterics by the banging at the gate. She was convinced it was Dmitry again (although she had seen him drive away), for she knew of no one else who would bang on the gate like that. She hurried to the janitor, who by then had been awakened and was on his way to the gate, and begged him not to open it. But the janitor asked Perkhotin what he wanted and, upon hearing that he had to see Fenya most urgently, decided to let him in. They all went to Fenya's kitchen, she asking the janitor to come in too, "just in case," and hoping Mr. Perkhotin "wouldn't mind." Perkhotin started to question her at once and within a second had elicited from her a most important piece of information—that, as he was dashing off in search of Grushenka, Dmitry Karamazov had snatched the pestle out of the mortar and that, when he had come back, he did not have the pestle, but his hands were covered with blood. "It was still dripping from them, the blood, dripping, dripping, dripping!" Fenya exclaimed, having obviously conjured up that picture out of her distraught imagination. But then Perkhotin had also seen Dmitry's bloodstained hands and, in fact, had helped him wash them. True, he had not seen blood dripping from them, but the point of interest was not how quickly the blood had dried; rather it was where Dmitry had gone with the pestle, whether it was to his father's house, and what conclusions could be drawn from that fact. It was on this point that Perkhotin dwelt most insistently, and although he did not find out any conclusive facts, he felt pretty certain that Dmitry could not possibly have gone anywhere else but to his father's house and that, therefore, *something* must have happened there.

"And when he came back," Fenya added in great agitation, "and I told him all about my mistress, and then said to him, 'How come, Mr. Karamazov, sir, your hands are all covered with blood?' I think he answered me right away that it was human blood, that he had just killed a man—he admitted it just like that—and then he suddenly rushed out like a madman. So I sat down and I thought: 'Now where can he be rushing to like a madman? What if he goes to Mokroye and kills my mistress?' That's when I ran out to plead with him not to kill Miss Svetlov. I was going to his place, but on my way there I saw him outside the Plotnikov store. He was just about to drive off. I also saw that there was no blood on his hands anymore . . ." (This fact had struck Fenya and she had remembered it.)

Fenya's grandmother confirmed Fenya's statements as far as she could. Perkhotin asked them a few more questions and then left. He was even more worried now, upon leaving this house, than he had been when he had entered it.

The most obvious and direct course seemed to be to go straight to Fyodor Karamazov's house, find out whether anything had happened there and exactly what, and, having ascertained the facts, to pass the information on to the police inspector. And this was exactly what Perkhotin decided to do. But then, it was a dark night, the gate of Mr. Karamazov's house was very solid, so it would again involve a lot of knocking, and, if he was wrong and nothing had really happened there, he was afraid Mr. Karamazov (with whom he was hardly acquainted, but who had the reputation of being a very sarcastic man) would go all over town the next day talking about how Peter Perkhotin had broken into his house in the middle of the night just to find out whether he had not, by any chance, been murdered by someone! It would be a public scandal, and public scandal was something Perkhotin dreaded more than anything.

However, the impulse to go ahead and do something was so strong that Perkhotin at once dashed off again. Instead of going to Mr. Karamazov's house, he went to Mrs. Khokhlakov's. If she denied giving three thousand rubles to Dmitry Karamazov, he decided, then he would go straight to the police inspector without going to old Karamazov's place. If, on the other hand, she confirmed it, he would put off further investigations till the next day and return home.

It may, of course, seem a strange decision—for a young man to go so late at night, at almost eleven o'clock, to the house of a society lady to whom he had not even been introduced, to possibly rouse her out of bed, and then ask her a question that would sound quite strange under the circumstances. All this was even more likely to cause a public scandal than going to Mr. Karamazov's. But even the most cool-headed and efficient people are liable to make very peculiar decisions when faced with such dilemmas, and at that moment Peter Perkhotin was anything but cool-headed. He was to remember for the rest of his life that his restlessness that night became so overwhelmingly painful that it impelled him to act against his own better judgment. He was, in fact, quite furious with himself all the way to the lady's house, but he repeated to himself about ten times: "I'll go through with it, happen what may!" And he did go through with it.

It was exactly eleven o'clock when he entered Mrs. Khokhlakov's house. The porter opened the door quickly enough, but he was unable to tell Perkhotin whether his mistress was still up; he could only say that she usually went to bed at about that time.

"Why don't you go upstairs, sir. The servant will announce you, and if the lady wishes to receive you she will, if not she won't." Perkhotin went upstairs, but there things became more complicated. The butler refused to announce him himself. Finally he summoned a maid, to whom Perkhotin explained politely but firmly that he was a local government official, that he had to see her mistress on urgent business, and that if it had not been so very urgent he would never have dreamt of disturbing her at such an hour. "Please tell her that in exactly those words," he told the maid. She left, and he waited in the hall.

Mrs. Khokhlakov was already in her bedroom but had not yet gone to bed. She had been quite upset by Mitya's visit and felt that she would not escape the migraine from which she usually suffered after a commotion of that kind. The message greatly surprised her and, although her curiosity was considerably aroused by a "government official" visiting her at such an hour, she told the maid irritatedly that she would not receive him. But on this occasion Peter Perkhotin proved to be as stubborn as a mule, and when the maid told him of her mistress's refusal, he demanded that she go back and tell Mrs. Khokhlakov, "in exactly these words," that he had come about something extremely important and that she would be very sorry later if she did not receive him now. "I was desperate," he explained later. "I felt I just had to see her . . ." The maid looked at him in surprise and went back with the message. Mrs. Khokhlakov was amazed, pondered for a while, then asked the maid what the visitor looked like. She was informed that he was well dressed, young, and very polite (we may add parenthetically that Perkhotin was a rather handsome young man and was well aware of it himself). Finally Mrs. Khokhlakov decided to see him. She was already in her dressing gown and slippers, so she threw a black shawl over her shoulders. Perkhotin was ushered into the same drawing room where she had received Mitya a few hours earlier. She entered with a stern and questioning look and, without inviting him to sit down, started right off with a crisp, "What is it?"

"I have taken the liberty of intruding upon you, madam, because of a matter that concerns a mutual acquaintance, Mr. Dmitry Karamazov," Perkhotin began; but as soon as he mentioned that name, the lady's face showed violent irritation and she interrupted him in a voice shrill with fury:

"Why have you come to pester me about that terrible man!" she screamed. "How dare you come to the house of a lady who does not know you at such an hour! And, what's more, to speak to her about a man who only three hours ago came here, to this very drawing room, with the intention of killing me and who, when he walked out of here, was stamping his feet in a way no gentleman ever does when leaving a respectable house! And I warn you, sir, I am not going to allow you to get away with this: I will lodge a complaint against you. You'll hear of it . . . Please leave at once . . . I am a mother, you know, and I will . . . at once . . . I will . . . I . . ."

"Killing you, did you say? So he wanted to kill you, too?" too?"

"Why, has he already killed someone?"

"If you would only listen to me for half a minute, madam, I'd explain everything to you," Perkhotin said firmly. "At five p.m. today, Mr. Karamazov borrowed ten rubles from me, as a friend . . . Well, I know for a fact that at that

time he had no money whatsoever. Then, at nine p.m., he
walked into my apartment with a bundle of hundred-ruble
bills. I'd say he had two or even three thousand rubles.
Now, his face and his hands were covered with blood and
his behavior was not that of a normal man. When I asked
him where he had got all that money, he told me very
clearly that you had just given him three thousand rubles
to go to the gold mines . . ."

Mrs. Khokhlakov suddenly looked incredibly pained and
shocked.

"Oh God! He must have murdered his old father then! I
never gave him any money, never! Oh, run, please run
quickly—save the old man! Run and save old Karamazov!"

"Forgive me, madam, are you quite sure you never gave
him any money? You are absolutely certain?"

"I didn't give him anything. I didn't! I refused to, because I knew he wouldn't appreciate it . . . So he left
stamping his feet. He tried to attack me, but I jumped aside
and escaped . . . And let me tell you—for I don't intend to
hide anything from you now—he even spat at me. Can you
imagine that! But why are we standing here like this? Won't
you sit down? Please forgive me . . . Unless, maybe you
should run over there and save the unfortunate old man from
a horrible death?"

"But since he has already killed him . . ."

"Ah, good Lord, of course, of course! But what are we
going to do now? What do you think our next move should
be?"

Meanwhile she had made Perkhotin sit down and herself
sat facing him. He gave her a concise account of the business, at least of the part of the story of which he himself
had been a witness earlier that day, and also of his visit
to Fenya just before and what he had learned there about
the pestle. All these details were a terrible shock to the
impressionable lady and she kept shrieking and covering
her eyes with her hands.

"The most extraordinary thing is that I had a feeling this
would happen! I have a gift of premonition—I always feel
in advance when something is going to happen and it unfailingly does. You know, many, many times before, I have
looked at that terrible man and I always thought that he
would end up killing me. And now that's exactly what happened . . . I mean, if this time he didn't actually kill me,
but only his father, I see in that a sign of God's interven-

tion . . . Besides, he would have been ashamed to kill me at that moment, because I had just put the icon of St. Barbara, the holy martyr, around his neck . . . Ah, when I think how close I was to death as I stood there within his reach, putting it around his outstretched neck! You know, Mr. Perkhotin—I hope I have your name right. It is Mr. Perkhotin, isn't it?—generally speaking, I do not believe in miracles, but this time, with that icon, it's really amazing! I'm so impressed that I think I'm prepared to believe anything . . . Did you hear, by the way, about Elder Zosima? Now I've forgotten what I was going to say . . . But, imagine, that man actually spat at me while he had the icon I'd given him around his neck! Of course, he just spat at me, instead of murdering me . . . So that's where he rushed off to afterward! What are we going to do now? What is next? What do you think?"

Perkhotin stood up, saying that he was going straight to the police inspector to tell him what he knew and that then it would be up to him.

"Ah, he's such a wonderful man! I have known Mikhail Makarov for a long time. Yes, you must absolutely go and see him right now. You're so clever and so quick-thinking, Mr. Perkhotin. That's really a good idea! You know, I would have never thought of it myself."

"It so happens that I know the police inspector very well myself," Perkhotin said, obviously anxious to escape from the impetuous lady, who would not give him a chance to take his leave.

"And you know what," she prattled on, "you absolutely must come back and tell me what you find out, what happens next, what they decide, what sentence he gets, and where he is to serve it . . . Tell me, we don't have capital punishment anymore, do we? But you must come and tell me, even if it's three in the morning, even four, even half-past four! Tell them to wake me up, and to give me a good shake if I don't get up. Oh, I don't think I'll be able to sleep at all now . . . I have an idea, though—what would you say if I came with you?"

"Hm . . . I really don't think so, madam . . . But, on the other hand, I think it would be helpful if you wrote three lines in your own hand to the effect that you never gave any money to Dmitry Karamazov . . . just in case it should come up."

"I will certainly be very glad to do so!" Mrs. Khokhlakov

cried ecstatically, actually skipping over to her desk. "You know, I am simply flabbergasted and stunned by your ingenuity, by your inventiveness in an affair of this sort . . . Where do you work? Oh, it's so nice to know that you are serving in our town . . ."

And she went on talking, while scribbling in a large, hurried scrawl three lines on a half sheet of notepaper that went: "I have never in my life lent to the unhappy Dmitry Karamazov (because, after all, he is unhappy at this moment) three thousand rubles or any other sum, today, or at any time. I swear this by everything that is holy in this world. Katerina Khokhlakov."

"Here it is!" she said, turning quickly to Perkhotin. "So go and save . . . This is a heroic deed on your part."

She made the sign of the cross over him three times and saw him off to the door.

"I *am* most awfully grateful to you! You cannot imagine how much I appreciate the fact that you came to me first! How is it we never met before? I'll be delighted to receive you in my house in the future and I'm so glad to hear that this town has a civil servant like you, with your resourcefulness and clear thinking . . . But I feel they ought to understand you; in the end they should appreciate your exceptional qualifications . . . Believe me, I would be only too glad to do anything I can . . . Oh, I love young people. I am in love with youth! Young people are the mainstay of our suffering Russia, her only hope . . . Oh, go, go! . . ."

But Perkhotin had already dashed out of the house, for she would not have let him get away so quickly of her own free will. All in all though, she made a rather pleasant impression on him, which somewhat made up for his misgivings about becoming involved in an unsavory affair. As is well known, there is tremendous diversity in tastes, and Perkhotin thought pleasantly, "She's not at all middle-aged really! In fact, I could have taken her for her own daughter."

As to Mrs. Khokhlakov, she had been utterly charmed by the young man. "What amazing competence and clear thinking in such a young man, especially these days! And combined with such a charming manner and such good looks! When I think of those detractors who claim that today's young men cannot do anything properly—well, there's an example for them! . . ." And her thoughts followed these lines, so that she quite forgot about "the dreadful tragedy," and it was only when she was going to bed that she remembered "how close to death" she had been earlier that day and mumbled: "Ah, how dreadful, dreadful! . . ." But this did not prevent her from sliding at once into the sweetest and soundest sleep.

I would not have dwelt at such length on such a trivial episode had that peculiar meeting between the young civil servant and the by-no-means elderly widow not become the foundation of the whole future career of this meticulous and methodical young man, a fact which is still remembered with amazement in our town and of which we may yet have a few words to say in the sequel to our long novel about the brothers Karamazov.

CHAPTER 2

Alarm

Mikhail Makarovich Makarov was a former army lieutenant colonel who had transferred to the civil service with the rank of court counselor and had been appointed police inspector in our town. Although this worthy widower had arrived here only three years before, he had already gained general approval, because he was "one of those men who know how to rally the public behind them." His house was always full of visitors and it seemed he could not live if he did not have people around him constantly. He had guests to dinner every evening, if only one or two, for he never dined alone. He also gave many formal dinner parties under all kinds of pretexts, often quite unusual ones. The food he served, although none too refined, was always plentiful; his meat pies were excellent; and his wine, which was not of a particularly good vintage, made up in quantity for what it lacked in quality. He had a large billiard room with all the proper furnishings, that is, even with black-framed pictures of English race-horses hanging on the walls, the type always found in the billiard room of a single man. Every evening there was a game of cards, for there were always enough card players to fill at least one table. Also, from time to time, the town's high society would gather at Mr. Makarov's house for a dance, the mothers chaperoning their unmarried daughters. Although a widower, the inspector led the life of a family man; his house was run by his widowed daughter, herself the mother of two grown-up daughters, Makarov's granddaughters. They were gay, pretty girls who had recently completed their education, and although it was common knowledge in town that they would have no dowries, their grandfather's house still attracted the young men of our society.

Makarov was not a particularly perspicacious civil servant, but he carried out his duties as well as anyone. To put it bluntly, there were considerable gaps in his education and he had an extremely vague understanding of the range and limitations of his administrative powers. It was not that he was completely incapable of understanding the reforms carried out under the present tsar, but he usually misinterpreted them, sometimes rather grossly, not necessarily out of sheer stupidity, but mostly out of an inherent reluctance to fully think things out, a process he found painful and time consuming. "I'm still more of a soldier at heart than a civilian," he liked to say of himself. He had not even grasped the fundamental ideas underlying the agrarian reforms; he only found out about them gradually as he went along, a little each year, acquiring knowledge willy-nilly, just because he was faced by the hard facts of life—all of which was particularly surprising in view of the fact that he was a landowner himself.

As he walked toward Inspector Makarov's house, Perkhotin was sure he would find guests there and wondered who they would be. They turned out to be the assistant district prosecutor and Dr. Varvinsky, who had quite recently graduated with high honors from the Petersburg Medical Academy and had been sent to our town. Ippolit Kirillovich, the assistant district prosecutor, whom everyone in town called simply the prosecutor, was a rather peculiar man. He was still relatively young, about thirty-five, apparently had a predisposition to consumption, and was married to a very big, childless woman. He was extremely touchy and irritable but at the same time had a good solid brain and, deep down, was a kind man. Perhaps his main fault was his somewhat exaggerated idea of his own abilities. This may explain his constant restlessness. He even claimed to have a certain special intuition, a sort of artistic insight, into the criminal mind, that provided him with a psychological explanation of crimes. Because of his belief in these special talents of his, he felt that his remote superiors had failed to appreciate him fully, that his career had been hampered by secret enemies. He even had moments of depression during which he threatened to resign his post and become a defense counsel. But now the unexpected Karamazov parricide case brought him new hopes for his career: "With a case like this, my name could become famous all over Russia," he thought. But I am anticipating.

Nikolai Nelyudov, the very young examining magistrate who had been assigned to our town only two months previously, was being entertained by the young ladies in another room of Makarov's house.

Later, people in town were to say that it was really amazing that all these people should have been gathered by sheer chance in the police inspector's house on the night of the crime. Actually, though, there were quite simple—we might say, natural—explanations for this. The prosecutor's wife had been suffering from a bad toothache for two days and he had to go somewhere to escape her moaning. The doctor was a man who, by nature, could not imagine spending an evening anywhere but at a card table. The youthful examining magistrate had for three days been planning to pay a surprise visit to the inspector's on that particular night in order to "astound" Makarov's eldest granddaughter Olga with his knowledge that it was her birthday, a fact she had wanted to conceal so as not to have to invite all the people of the town society to a birthday party. He had been looking forward to the opportunity of teasing her about being afraid that people would know she was a year older, and saying that, since he had discovered the secret, he would now tell everybody, and so on and so forth. This nice young man was a naughty tease. As a matter of fact, that is how the ladies often referred to him, as "the naughty tease," and this seemed to delight him. He came from a rather good family and had nice manners, and, although he liked to have a good time, his pleasures were usually quite harmless and highly proper. He was a small, delicate young man, on whose thin fingers two or three rather large rings always glittered. When he acted in his official capacity, however, he immediately became extremely grave as if, at that moment, he considered his duties and his person sacred. He was particularly good, during interrogations, at catching murderers and other criminals off their guard, the uneducated ones especially; and even if this ability did not really instill respect for him in the suspects, it often quite surprised them.

When he entered the police inspector's house, Perkhotin

was completely dumbfounded to find that everybody already knew all about it. They had abandoned the card table and Nelyudov, the young investigating magistrate, had come dashing in at a gallop from the other room, where he had been with the young ladies, and now wore a most determined and bellicose expression. Perkhotin was met with the stunning news that Fyodor Karamazov had really been murdered and robbed that night in his house. They themselves had learned about the crime just before Perkhotin's arrival.

Although she had been deep in her drugged sleep and appeared likely to continue sleeping like that until morning, Gregory's wife Martha suddenly awoke. She had been woken by Smerdyakov's bloodcurdling epileptic scream. He lay unconscious in his little room next to hers. His epileptic fits always began with such a scream. Martha had never been able to get used to them; they always horrified her and gave her a sickening feeling. She jumped up from her bed and, still almost unconscious, rushed to Smerdyakov's room. The room was completely dark and she could only hear the epileptic hoarsely gasping for breath and writhing about. Martha started to scream herself and to call her husband, when it suddenly occurred to her that, when she had awakened, Gregory had not been there in bed beside her. She went back to the bed and felt for him with her hands in the dark, until she was convinced that the bed was really empty. Where could he be, she wondered. She went out on the porch and called him worriedly. There was no answer. But then, in the silence of the night, she suddenly heard distant groans coming from the direction of the garden. She listened intently: the groans came again. Yes, they were coming from the garden, she was sure now. "Good Lord, it's just like that time with Reeking Lizaveta," the thought flashed through her distraught mind. Full of fear, she stepped out into the yard and saw that the gate leading into the garden was open. "He must be there," she decided and went to the gate. When she reached it, she clearly heard Gregory calling her, "Martha, Martha . . ." in a weak, halting, frightening voice. "God save us from trouble," she mumbled and hurried forward into the darkness. And that was how she found him.

She did not find him, however, by the garden fence where he had been struck, but about twenty yards away. Later it turned out that he had tried to crawl back to the house. It must have taken him a long time to get even that far, for he had certainly fainted several times as he crawled, then had regained consciousness and crawled further. Martha realized at once that he was covered with blood and started yelling for help at the top of her voice. Gregory, however, kept mumbling in a weak, hardly audible voice: "He . . . he's killed his father . . . Stop screaming, you fool . . . run and get help . . ." But Martha would not stop screaming. Suddenly noticing the light in Mr. Karamazov's window, she ran over there to call the master. But when she glanced inside, a horrible sight met her eyes. The master lay motionless on his back. His light-colored dressing gown and his white shirt were soaked with blood. In the light of a candle that was burning on the table, she could clearly see the blood and the mask-like face. By now Martha had reached rock bottom in horror. She rushed away from the window, ran to the back gate, which gave onto a backstreet, unbolted it, and ran headlong to Maria Kondratiev's house next door.

Both Maria Kondratiev and her daughter were asleep, but they were awakened soon enough by Martha's shouting and desperate pounding, and opened their shutters. In shrill, almost incoherent screams, Martha managed to give them an idea of what had happened and to ask them for help. Foma happened to be spending the night in the room he had in their house, so he was at once routed out of bed and all three rushed to the scene of the crime. On the way, Maria Kondratiev suddenly remembered that some time between eight and nine in the evening she had heard a terrible, piercing cry from the garden. That, of course, was Gregory's shout, "Father-killer!" as he caught Dmitry's dangling foot, when Dmitry was already sitting astride the fence. "Someone started screaming and then suddenly stopped," she told her companions as they ran.

When they reached Gregory in the garden, the two women and Foma carried him to the cottage. They lighted a candle and saw that Smerdyakov was still writhing in convulsions, his eyes rolled back and frothing at the mouth . . . They washed Gregory's head with water and vinegar, and this brought him back to his senses. The first question he asked was: "Has the master been killed?"

The two women and Foma went to the big house. As they approached it from the garden, they saw that not only the window of Mr. Karamazov's bedroom but also the door leading into the garden was wide open, although they were well aware that for at least a week Mr. Karamazov had locked himself in every night and had forbidden even Gregory to knock on his door for any reason whatever. Seeing the door open now, Foma and the two women were reluctant to go into the house, for, "Who knows what complications it might make later." When they returned to Gregory, he told them to run at once to the police inspector's house and inform him of what had happened. Whereupon Maria Kondratiev hurried to Inspector Makarov's house and alerted everyone there. As a matter of fact, she had arrived only five minutes before Perkhotin, so that, to the officials, he appeared not with just guesses and theories, but as an important witness, whose story corroborated their common assumption as to the murderer's identity. Deep down, however, Perkhotin himself had refused to believe it up to the very last moment.

They decided to act at once and the town's assistant police inspector was dispatched to gather four qualified witnesses with whom to enter Fyodor Karamazov's house in order to draw up an official report according to the legally established procedures, which I shall not describe here. Dr. Varvinsky, the recently appointed district medical officer, was zealous enough and young enough to insist on accompanying the police inspector, the public prosecutor, and the examining magistrate.

I must note here briefly that Fyodor Karamazov was found to be dead, his skull fractured with some object. It could not, however, be ascertained what the object was, although it was most likely the same object with which Gregory had been struck later. And that object was found soon after they had heard Gregory's testimony. Gregory, who was given all possible medical help, managed, although in a very weak and halting voice, to give a quite coherent account of how he had been struck. They searched all along the garden fence with lanterns and finally found the brass pestle lying quite conspicuously on the gravel path. There was no particular disorder in Mr. Karamazov's room. But behind the screen, by his bed, they found a large, thick envelope on the floor of the sort used for business purposes. It bore the inscription, "To my darling Grushenka, this present of three thousand rubles—if she comes to me," and under it were the words "to my little chick," apparently added later by Mr. Karamazov. The envelope, which had been closed with three large, red wax seals, had been torn open and was empty—the money was gone. The narrow pink ribbon that had been tied around the

envelope was found on the floor. One point in Perkhotin's
account particularly impressed both the prosecutor and the
examining magistrate, and that was his insistence that Dmitry
Karamazov would shoot himself at dawn, that Dmitry had
made up his mind, had told Perkhotin about it, had loaded
his pistol in his presence, had written a note that he had put
in his pocket; and when Perkhotin, still refusing to believe
that Dmitry would really shoot himself, had said that he
would get help to prevent him from going through with it,
Dmitry Karamazov had grinned and replied that it would be
too late by then.

Consequently, their course of action was obvious: they had
to hurry to Mokroye and get hold of the murderer before
he really carried out his plan to shoot himself.

"It's all pretty straightforward," the prosecutor repeated
excitedly; "that's exactly the way a desperate man of that
type thinks: 'I'll kill myself tomorrow, but before I die I'll
have a wild time.'"

And when Perkhotin described the way Dmitry had bought
wine and food in the store, the prosecutor became even more
excited:

"Don't you remember the fellow who killed that merchant
Olsufiev? He robbed him of fifteen hundred rubles and then
went straight to have his hair curled and, without even bothering to hide the money, practically carrying it around in
his hand, just like this one, went off to a brothel."

They were delayed, however, by the investigation in the
Karamazov house, the search, and the other formalities. It all
took time and so, two hours before starting out themselves,
they sent ahead to Mokroye the rural police officer, Mavriky
Shmertsov, who had come to town that morning to draw his
salary. Once in Mokroye, Shmertsov was to keep a constant
watch on the criminal without, however, arousing suspicion,
and also to prepare witnesses, police, etc., before the arrival
of the competent authorities. And this is exactly what Shmertsov did; he kept his mission a secret from everyone except his
old acquaintance Trifon Plastunov, whom he took partly
into his confidence. It was just after Trifon had learned about
all this that he met Mitya in the darkness, going back into
the house from the balcony, and that Mitya noticed that something had changed both in Trifon's attitude and in the way
he spoke. Neither Mitya nor anyone else knew then that they
were being watched. And long before that, Trifon had taken
the case with the pistols and hidden it in a safe place.

It was only at about 5 a.m., shortly before dawn, that the authorities arrived. The police inspector, the prosecutor, the examining magistrate, and their assistants arrived in two carriages drawn by teams of three horses. The district medical officer had stayed in Mr. Karamazov's house. His reason for staying was to perform the autopsy on the victim, which had been arranged for the following morning. But what interested him most was the condition of the sick servant Smerdyakov. "Absolutely amazingly long epileptic seizures, recurring constantly for forty-eight hours! This is definitely a matter for scientific investigation," Dr. Varvinsky declared excitedly to his colleagues, who laughingly congratulated him on his discovery. Later, the prosecutor and the examining magistrate remembered clearly that the doctor had declared very definitely that Smerdyakov would not live until morning.

And now, after this long but, I believe, indispensable digression, we shall resume our story at the point where we interrupted it in the last book.

CHAPTER 3

From Ordeal to Ordeal: The First Ordeal

And so Mitya sat staring wildly at the people around him without taking in what they were saying. Then suddenly he stood up, flung up his arms dramatically, and shouted: "Not guilty! Not of that blood! No, I am not guilty of my father's murder . . . I thought of killing him, but I didn't do it . . . No, it wasn't me!"

Mitya had hardly finished when Grushenka rushed out from behind the curtain and threw herself at Inspector Makarov's feet.

"It's me, it's me, it's all my fault!" she cried in a heartrending wail, wringing her hands, as tears filled her eyes. "It was because of me that he killed! . . . I drove him to it by tormenting and baiting him. And the poor dead man—I made him suffer too. Just out of spite, I did it to him! I am the really guilty one. I am the first to blame for everything!"

"Right, you are all that! You are the guiltiest of all, you vicious, depraved whore; it's you who's the chief criminal!" the inspector screamed, shaking his fist at her.

But the others quickly interfered and the prosecutor even threw his arms around Makarov's body as if to block his movements.

"This is absolutely intolerable, inspector," he said. "You're really making things difficult for us . . . It's quite impossible to conduct the investigation under these conditions . . ." The prosecutor could hardly breathe, he was so indignant.

"Something must be done to stop this," Examining Magistrate Nelyudov cried heatedly; "otherwise we just cannot go on!"

"We must be tried together!" Grushenka, who was still kneeling, kept screaming frantically. "Punish us together. I must follow him to the gallows if you send him there!"

"Grusha, my life, my flesh and blood, my only joy!" Mitya knelt beside her on the floor, put his arms around her, and held her tight. "Don't believe her," he shouted to the others. "She had nothing to do with it. There is no blood on her conscience!"

Later, he vaguely recollected several men tearing her from him by force and leading her away . . . He remembered sitting at a table. Men with brass badges sat on either side of him and stood behind him. Across the table from him, Nikolai Nelyudov, the examining magistrate, was trying to convince him to take a sip from a glass of water that stood on the table next to him. "It will refresh and relax you a little," he was insisting very politely. "And please don't worry. Don't be afraid." Mitya also remembered later that he became very interested in Magistrate Nelyudov's large rings—one with an amethyst and the other with a bright yellow, transparent stone that had a wonderful sparkle to it. Thinking of it later, he found it very surprising that he should have been so fascinated by these rings and that, throughout all the grim hours of questioning, he was never able to tear his eyes from those shiny objects that were so completely irrelevant in the whole situation.

On Mitya's left—in the place occupied earlier that evening by Maximov—the prosecutor now sat; on Mitya's right—Grushenka's former place—was a ruddy-cheeked young man in a rather worn hunting jacket with a pad of paper and a pot of ink in front of him. He turned out to be a clerk whom Nelyudov had brought with him from town. Inspector Makarov stood by a window at the opposite end of the room, next to Kalganov who was sitting there on a chair.

"Please take a sip," Magistrate Nelyudov said softly for the tenth time.

"All right, I will, I will . . . But what are you waiting for? Go ahead, crush me, punish me, decide what will happen to me," Mitya said, looking at Nelyudov with fixed, strangely dilated eyes.

"So you definitely assert that you are not guilty of the death of your father?" Nelyudov asked with gentle insistence.

"No, I am not guilty of it! I have the blood of another man on my conscience, but not my father's blood. Yes, and I am sorry I killed that man—I struck him . . . he fell . . . I killed him. But it is too much to answer for that murder by the other one, that terrible murder, of which I am not guilty . . . It is an awful thing you are accusing me of, it's a terrible blow! But who, then, can have killed father? Who killed him, since I didn't do it? That's a mystery . . . It's absurd, impossible!"

"That's just it—who could have killed him?" said the assistant prosecutor (whom we shall call just the prosecutor for short), exchanging glances with the examining magistrate. "But let me reassure you—you have no need to worry about the old servant. Old Gregory is alive. He recovered from the terrible blow which, according to his deposition, you inflicted on him, a fact that has now been confirmed by your own statement. In fact, if we are to take the doctor's word, his life is no longer in danger."

"So he is alive, alive!" Mitya shouted happily, waving his hands, his face beaming with joy. "I thank you, I thank you, O God, for the great miracle You have wrought in answer to the prayers of a miserable sinner! Yes, yes, yes, God has answered my prayer, for I have been praying all through the night!" Dmitry crossed himself three times. He was breathless.

"Good. Now it was from this same Gregory that we received very important evidence concerning you . . ." the prosecutor started, but Mitya interrupted him, leaping up from his chair.

"Just a second, gentlemen, please allow me—I must run over to see her for one second, please . . ."

"Wait! What do you think you're doing!" Nelyudov cried shrilly, also leaping to his feet, while the men with the brass badges grabbed Mitya. But Mitya sat down of his own accord.

"What's the matter? I just wanted to see her for a second—just to tell her that the blood that I thought was splattered all over me has been washed off now, that I am not a murderer! I have the right to tell her that, gentlemen—she is my future wife!" he said ecstatically, looking around him. "Oh,

I am so grateful to you anyway, gentlemen. You have brought me back to life, made a new man of me in one second! Why, old Gregory used to carry me in his arms when I was little. He used to bathe me in a tub when I was three, and no one else cared what happened to me . . . He was a real father to me!"

"And so you . . ." Nelyudov began again.

"Excuse me, one more minute," Mitya interrupted him again, putting his elbows on the table and covering his head with his hands, "give me a second to recover, to regain my senses; all this has been such a shock, such a shock. A man is not a drum, after all, gentlemen!"

"I think you should take another sip of water," Nelyudov said.

Mitya took his hands away from his face and laughed. He looked gay and his entire countenance had changed. He was now a man sitting among his peers. All these people were his acquaintances and he felt just as he would have if they had all gathered on some social occasion the day before, before anything had happened. It should be noted here that, when he had first come to town, Mitya had been received very cordially at Inspector Makarov's house, but that later, particularly during the past month, he had practically stopped going there and recently, when they had met in the street, the inspector had barely acknowledged Mitya's greetings— enough not to be outright rude, but that was all, and this fact Mitya had noticed. He was even less closely acquainted with the prosecutor, although he had occasionally called on his wife, a temperamental, moody lady with whom he had had very proper chats on those occasions. Mitya would have been unable to explain why he had bothered to go there, but she always received him very warmly and somehow took an interest in him up to the very last. As to Examining Magistrate Nelyudov, they had not really had enough time to get properly acquainted, although they had met a few times and even chatted on a couple of occasions, the fair sex being the topic of conversation both times.

"I can see what a skillful investigator you are, Mr. Nelyudov," Mitya said with a relaxed laugh; "still, I think I'll help you and make things even easier for you. You know, gentlemen, I feel like a man risen from the dead, so I beg you not to be offended if I address you informally. Besides, I admit I've had quite a bit to drink. I believe I had the pleasure, Mr. Nelyudov, of meeting you in the house of a relative of mine, Mr. Miusov . . . Oh, don't worry, gentlemen, I make no claim to be treated as an equal under these circumstances. I understand my present position. If Gregory has made accusations against me, I fully appreciate the fact that I am suspected of that horrible crime! It is horrible, revolting —I am fully aware of the horror of it . . . But now let us get down to business, gentlemen. I am ready, and now we can get it over with very quickly because—listen to me—since I now know that I'm not guilty, we can certainly finish it up in a few minutes, can't we? Am I right?"

Mitya spoke quickly, nervously, effusively, as if taking it absolutely for granted that he was among well-wishers and friends.

"So we can note down, for now, that you absolutely deny the accusation," Nelyudov said and, turning to the clerk, directed him what to write down.

"Write it down? Why do you have to write anything down? But if that's what you want, please, gentlemen, you have my whole-hearted consent . . . But wait, you'd better put it down this way: write that he is guilty of disorderly conduct, guilty of violently attacking and badly hurting a poor old man. Yes, and on top of that, deep down in my heart, I am also guilty of . . . But you mustn't write that," he said, looking at the clerk. "That is my private life, gentlemen, and cannot be any of your concern, I mean what goes on deep down inside me . . . But I am not guilty of killing my father, no! The whole idea is absurd, completely absurd! I'll prove it to you! You'll see at once how wrong you were! You'll laugh at your former suspicions, gentlemen!"

"Please, Mr. Karamazov, calm yourself, please," Nelyudov said very quietly, obviously trying to counteract Mitya's agitation with his own cool detachment. "Before we continue, I would like you to tell us, if you are willing to, whether it is correct that you disliked your late father and that you were constantly quarreling with him . . . If I am right, you yourself said here just fifteen minutes ago that you wanted to kill him. You actually said, 'I did not kill him, but I wanted to.' "

"Did I say that? Well, that's very possible, gentlemen! Because I did want to kill him, many, many times; I did, alas I did . . ."

"So you did want to kill him? Now, would you be willing to tell us what actually caused you to hate your father so much?"

"What is there to explain?" Mitya said gloomily, shrugging

his shoulders. "I've never hidden the way I felt about him—
the whole town knows it; I've said it often enough in the
tavern. And not so long ago I talked of how I felt about my
father at Elder Zosima's, in the monastery . . . And later
that day I attacked and almost killed my father and then,
before witnesses, promised to go back and kill him. For a
whole month, I kept repeating it all over town. Oh, there are
a thousand witnesses who will tell you that! That is a fact
and it speaks, it shouts, for itself . . . But when it comes to
inner feelings, that's quite a different matter, gentlemen,"
Mitya said frowning, "and I don't really think you have the
right to ask me about my feelings. Oh, I understand that you
have the official authority to question me, but not about any
intimate thoughts I may have had. But . . . but since I have
never hidden my feelings and have revealed them to anyone
who was interested, I won't make a secret of them now. You
see, I realize very well that there is overwhelming evidence
against me: I went around telling everyone I was going to
kill him and now that he has been killed, who else should be
suspected but me? Ha-ha! I don't blame you for suspecting
me, gentlemen. I don't blame you at all! In fact, I'm completely dumbfounded and bewildered myself, for I cannot
imagine who but me could have killed him! Yes, that's the
truth—if I didn't do it, who did? I want you to tell me—
indeed, I demand that you tell me: Where was he killed? How
was he killed and what weapon was used? Tell me!"

His eyes were darting back and forth from the examining
magistrate to the prosecutor.

"We found him in his room, on the floor, lying on his back,
with his skull broken," the prosecutor said.

"How horrible, horrible!" Mitya shuddered and, leaning
forward, covered his face with his hands.

"So let us continue," Nelyudov said. "What, then, was the
immediate reason for your hatred for your father? You did
say publicly that it was jealousy, didn't you?"

"There was jealousy too, but there were other things as
well."

"Arguments about money?"

"Yes, money came into it too."

"Is it correct that you had an argument specifically about
three thousand rubles that you claimed he still owed you as
part of your inheritance?"

"Three!" Mitya cried indignantly. "Much, much more than
that—more than six, perhaps more than ten thousand rubles!

I have been screaming about that around town, too! But finally I decided to let him off if he would give me only three thousand. So the envelope with the three thousand rubles that he had prepared for Grushenka and was keeping under his pillow, which I knew about, I considered my property; it was just as if he'd stolen it from me—that's exactly how I felt about it!"

The prosecutor and the examining magistrate exchanged significant glances. The prosecutor even winked discreetly.

"We'll come back to that," Magistrate Nelyudov said quickly; "in the meantime, I would like the clerk to write down this point, namely, that you considered the money in that envelope as your rightful property. Is that correct?"

"Go ahead, have it written down. Why, do you imagine that I can't see that it is one more piece of evidence against me? I can, but I'm not afraid of any evidence or of telling you things that will further incriminate me in your eyes. I feel that you have completely misjudged me, gentlemen," Mitya said sadly, sounding bitterly disappointed now. "I am an honorable man. A man who has done many vile, despicable things, but an honorable man nevertheless. I don't know how to explain it to you, but most of the trouble in my life has come precisely from my yearning to be honorable. I have been—if I may put it this way—a martyr for honor, a kind of Diogenes going about with a lantern and looking for honor in the dark . . . But somehow I always ended up doing some terrible, unspeakable thing, just as we all do . . . No, no, I didn't mean that—it's only so for me, for me alone! . . . Gentlemen, I have a terrible headache," he said, knitting his brows in pain. "Let me tell you this: I hated his looks—he looked false, conceited; he always sneered at sacred things; he believed in nothing; he was so horrible, disgusting . . . But now that he is dead, I feel differently."

"In what way differently?"

"No, not really differently, but I'm sorry I hated him the way I did."

"Do you repent it now?"

"No, repent isn't the right word—don't write it down. I'm no good myself, gentlemen. I'm pretty ugly too and so I really had no right to find him so revolting. That, I think, is true and you can write it down."

Great sadness descended on Mitya. For some time a feeling of gloom had gradually been creeping over him as he answered the questions of the examining magistrate. And then, just at this moment, there was another unexpected interruption.

When they had torn Grushenka from his embrace and led her away, they had taken her only two rooms away from the blue room where Mitya was now being interrogated. It was a small room just beyond the largest room of the guest house, where they had been singing and dancing during the night. With her there was only the terribly frightened and bewildered Maximov, who clung to her as if looking to her for protection. A man with a brass badge on his chest stood by the door of their room. Grushenka, who until then had been sitting quietly crying, suddenly felt she could not stand it any longer. She jumped up and, with the shriek of a wounded animal, rushed out of the room so unexpectedly that no one had time to stop her, and dashed straight toward where Mitya was. Her shriek reached him. His whole body shook crazily. He leapt to his feet, and, with a wild responsive howl, not knowing what he was doing, rushed to meet her.

But they were stopped before they reached each other, although they did see each other. Mitya was grabbed by the arms, but he shook himself loose and it finally took three or four men to hold him. He watched helplessly as they dragged her away, crying and stretching out her hands to him. After the incident was over and Mitya was back at the table facing Nelyudov, he heard himself asking him in hoarse barks:

"What do you want with her? Why did you do that to her? She has nothing, nothing, to do with it!"

For ten minutes or so, Nelyudov and the prosecutor tried to calm him, but to no avail. Then Makarov, who had been out of the room for a moment, came back and announced to the prosecutor in a loud and excited voice:

"She's been moved farther away. She's downstairs now . . . But, gentlemen, would you please allow me to say something to this unhappy man? I'll say it here, in your presence, gentlemen."

"Please go ahead, Mr. Makarov; under the circumstances, we have no objection."

"Listen, Dmitry, listen, my friend," Inspector Makarov said, now looking at Mitya with warm, almost paternal compassion. "I took your friend Grushenka downstairs and put her in the care of the innkeeper's daughters . . . And that old fellow Maximov is there with her, too. Listen, I have persuaded her to be quiet and explained to her that you have to clear yourself and that she must give you a chance to do so and not make it harder for you by making you even more miserable and wretched, since that will only cause you to say the wrong things and hurt your case. Well, in short, I explained it to her and she understood. You know, my boy, she's such an intelligent girl and she's really good too. She even wanted to kiss my old hands so that I'd help you, and it was she who asked me to tell you not to worry about her now. I want to be able to go back to her and tell her that you are not worrying about her, that you are all right. I was wrong about her—she is a good, true Christian. Yes, gentlemen, she is a good soul and she is not to blame for anything! So Dmitry, my boy, shall I tell her not to worry, that you'll be calm now?"

The kind-hearted Inspector Makarov had said much more than he was supposed to, but he had been deeply moved by the human sorrow he had seen and he even had tears in his eyes. Mitya jumped up impulsively and moved toward him.

"Excuse me, gentlemen, please, just one second," he cried, turning to Makarov. "Ah, you're such a good, decent man, Mr. Makarov, so kind, a real angel! Thank you, thank you for her! I shall be calm. I shall even be happy now, and I beg you to tell her that. Yes, please tell her that I am gay and feel like laughing now that I know she has a guardian angel like you . . . And, as soon as I get through with this business here, I'll hurry to her right away—she can count on it and she should wait for me! Gentlemen," he said, turning to the prosecutor and the examining magistrate, "now I will open up my whole soul to you, so that we can finish it all in a second, and then we'll all have a good laugh about that absurd suspicion . . . Gentlemen, that woman is the queen of my heart! Please let me tell you this secret of mine . . . because I see I am in the presence here of most honorable men. She is my light, the most sacred thing in my life! Didn't you hear her cry that she would follow me to the gallows? Follow me, a penniless beggar, a clumsy, dishonored brute! How can I have deserved to be loved enough for her to follow me to my doom? She is proud, and completely innocent of everything, and she threw herself at your feet to beg for me! How could I help adoring her, how could I stop myself from shouting the way I just did and hurrying to her? Please forgive me for that, gentlemen. Oh, I feel very much better now."

Dmitry sank into his chair, hid his face in his hands, and sobbed aloud. But these were happy sobs and he recovered quickly. The old inspector seemed pleased and so apparently were the others: they probably felt that the interrogation had entered a new phase. Mitya watched old Makarov leave the room and he seemed actually happy as he addressed his interrogators.

"And now, gentlemen, I am entirely at your disposal. I'm sure that, if it hadn't been for all these little obstacles, we would have already come to an understanding. But I'm drifting off again . . . I'm all yours, gentlemen, but I swear there must be mutual trust between us—you must trust me as I trust you—for otherwise we will never finish with it. I say this for your own sakes—understand that! Now let's get down to brass tacks, gentlemen, and, above all, stop digging into my soul—don't lacerate it with irrelevancies. Ask me about facts and I will answer everything to your satisfaction. And to hell with the irrelevancies!"

And the interrogation was resumed.

CHAPTER 4

The Second Ordeal

"You can hardly imagine how encouraging it is for us to see you so eager to cooperate," Nelyudov said with evident pleasure reflected in his large, protruding, very short-sighted, light-gray eyes, from which a few seconds before he had removed his glasses. "And I think you were right in what you said about mutual trust, without which, sometimes, it is impossible to get anywhere in cases as important as this one, unless the suspect is really eager and able to clear himself. For our part, we will do everything in our power to help you, and I'm sure you must have seen by now how we're handling it. Do you approve of what I say, sir?" he asked, suddenly turning to the prosecutor.

"Certainly," the prosecutor said, although his answer was rather cool compared with the examining magistrate's enthusiasm.

I will note at this point that Nelyudov, who had only recently arrived in our town, had from the outset felt tremendous respect for our assistant public prosecutor and also had become very attached to him. He was perhaps the only man in the world, besides the prosecutor himself, to be convinced of the man's extraordinary psychological endowments and oratorical talents, and he shared his conviction that he had not been properly appreciated by his superiors. He had heard of him while he was himself still in Petersburg.

And, in turn, the young examining magistrate was the only man in the whole world for whom the prosecutor with "unrecognized talents" had a sincere affection. On the way to Mokroye they had discussed the case ahead of them and now, sitting at the table, Nelyudov's keen senses caught and understood every movement on the face of his senior colleague, every wink, every sound he made.

"Gentlemen, give me a chance to tell you everything myself and do not interrupt me to ask irrelevant questions," Mitya said excitedly.

"Very good. I greatly appreciate your willingness to cooperate. Before we hear your statement, however, I would like to go over one more fact. Yesterday, at about five o'clock, you borrowed ten rubles from your friend Mr. Perkhotin, using your pistols as security—is that right?"

"Yes, I did pawn my pistols to him for ten rubles, and so what? As soon as I got back to town, I went and pawned them."

"Did you say you came back? Had you been out of town, then?"

"Yes, about thirty miles away. Why, didn't you know?"

The prosecutor and Nelyudov exchanged glances.

"In general, I would like you to begin your story with a systematic account of all your movements, starting with yesterday morning. I would, for instance, like to know why you went out of town, at what time, exactly, you left, and at what time you came back—that kind of fact, you see . . ."

"You should have asked me that to begin with." Mitya laughed loudly. "Actually, it would be even more useful if I began not with yesterday morning, but with the morning of the day before, for then you would understand where I went and why. So, then, two days ago, I went to see Samsonov, the local merchant, to borrow three thousand rubles against excellent security. I needed the money urgently. Something had come up and I had to have that sum quickly . . ."

"Allow me, just a second," the prosecutor interrupted politely. "Would you tell us now why you urgently had to have precisely that sum: three thousand rubles, that is?"

"Oh, gentlemen, can't you stop worrying about all these unimportant details—all these hows and whens and whys, and how was it I had to have so much money rather than so much and all that kind of ridiculous stuff. It would take three big volumes to write it all down, and even then you'd still have to add an epilogue to it!" Mitya said this with the good-natured, gruff impatience of one eager to cooperate fully in order to get to the whole truth. "Please, gentlemen, please forgive me for my impatience," he added quickly, checking himself, "and once again, believe me, I have the utmost respect for your competence and fully realize the gravity of the situation. And I'm not drunk—I have completely sobered up now. Besides, even if I were drunk, it wouldn't make that much difference. With me, you know, it's like this: when I sober up, I get wise and stupid, and when I'm drunk, I get stupid and wise. Yes, that's how I am, ha-ha! I see, however, that it's not fitting for me to joke with you, gentlemen; that is, not until things are cleared up. I am entitled, however, to my self-respect too. I see very well the present gap between us: I am a criminal in your eyes and so you cannot possibly consider me your equal, and it is your duty to keep me under control. And, of course, I cannot expect you to pat me on the back for what I did to Gregory, for one cannot be allowed to go around breaking old men's heads with impunity. I suppose I will be tried for that and get perhaps six months, perhaps a year; I don't really know what the sentence for something like that is. I only hope it won't entail loss of civil rights, will it, Mr. Prosecutor? You see, gentlemen, I am well aware of the difference that exists between us . . . You, however, must admit, too, that even God himself would be befuddled by questions like 'Where did you turn? Why did you turn that way? How did you turn that way? And what did you step on when you turned?' All right, so I'll get mixed up and contradict myself and you'll quickly write it down. Where will that get you? Nowhere, believe me.

"And now, since you've allowed me to get all that off my chest, I'll go on to the end, hoping only that you, highly educated and honorable gentlemen that you are, will bear with me. And now I want to end, gentlemen, with a plea: Please, gentlemen, try to unlearn once and for all the prescribed methods for conducting interrogations! They've taught you to start with some completely trivial and apparently irrelevant detail—how, for instance, I got up, what I had for breakfast, how and where I spat; and then, 'when the prisoner is off guard,' you are supposed to stun him with, 'Whom did you murder? Whom did you rob?' Isn't that the way you're supposed to operate? Isn't that the trick they teach you? It may work perhaps with some peasant, gentlemen, but I assure you it's wasted on me. Why, I know the ropes. I have some experience, after all! And please do not think this is insolence on my part. You are not really angry with me, are you?" Mitya added, looking at them with a strangely good-humored smile. "Why, coming from that hooligan Mitya Karamazov, it should be excusable! Of course, if any intelligent man talked like that, it would be quite another matter!"

Nelyudov laughed too, as he listened to him. The prosecutor did not laugh. He listened with great interest to everything Mitya said, never taking his eyes off him, as if he were afraid to miss a single word, the slightest movement, the faintest tremor of a facial muscle.

"But you must admit," Nelyudov said, still laughing, "that we didn't start by trying to catch you off your guard, by asking you how you woke up and what you had for breakfast . . . In fact, I dare say we started with pretty substantial matters, didn't we?"

"I understood and appreciated that, just as I also appreciate your present patience, kindness, and generosity. The three of us here, we are honorable men, and I would like everything to be based on the mutual trust of well-bred, educated gentlemen linked by the common bond of honor. In any case, allow me to regard you as my best friends at this moment of my life when I am in this humiliating position. I hope you will not consider this impertinent on my part, gentlemen?"

"Quite the contrary, Mr. Karamazov, you express it very well," Nelyudov assented with approving dignity.

"And so to hell with all those little tricks, gentlemen!" Mitya cried enthusiastically. "Otherwise, God knows where we will wind up."

"I accept your very sensible advice without reservation," the prosecutor suddenly intervened. "I don't think, however, that I will take back my last question, because I do feel it is essential for us to find out why you needed precisely three thousand rubles, why just that figure."

"Why I needed it? For one thing and another . . . all right, to pay back a debt."

"To whom?"

"That I absolutely refuse to answer. And I refuse, not because I cannot answer it, or dare not, or because I'm afraid of something, for it's really completely unimportant. I won't answer it as a matter of principle—it's my private life. That question is irrelevant to the case at hand and, being irrelevant, it becomes my private business. I wanted to pay back a debt, a debt of honor. But I won't tell you to whom."

"Allow me to have this written down," the prosecutor said.

"Please do, by all means, write down that I won't answer it. You may even put down that I would consider it dishonorable to answer, since I see that you have lots of time to waste writing things down."

"Let me remind you once again," the prosecutor said in a rather severe tone, "of your right not to answer any question we ask you now, and, for our part, we have no right whatsoever to extort answers from you if, for any reason whatever, you elect to withhold them. In this, you must follow your own judgment entirely. But we are also duty-bound in a case such as this to warn you of the harm you may do yourself by refusing to answer this or that particular question. And now, please go on."

"I don't really resent your asking me that, gentlemen, I . . ." Mitya muttered, somewhat put off by the admonition. Then he went on with his story. "You see, that Samsonov to whose house I went . . ."

Of course, we shall not repeat here what the reader already knows. Mitya was anxious to tell everything with the utmost accuracy and in all possible detail. But he was also in a tremendous hurry. As his evidence was being taken down, he continually had to be interrupted and asked to wait. He often protested, but still good-humoredly. Now and then, of course, he would let out an exclamation such as, "But, gentlemen, that would make God himself lose patience!" or, "Don't you see that you're just exasperating me this way!" But otherwise, he was still in an effusively friendly mood. And so he got through telling them about Samsonov making such a fool of him (for by now Mitya had no doubt at all that Samsonov had deliberately sent him on a fool's errand). When he came to the sale of his watch for six rubles, of which his interrogators had not even heard, the story elicited great interest and, to Mitya's immense indignation, they insisted on having it written down in great detail, as they felt it would further establish the fact that at that time Mitya had no money whatsoever. Little by little, Mitya grew somber. He went on, however, describing his trip to see the Hound, including the account of the night spent in the forester's smoke-filled hut and all that. Then he described his return to town and, without requiring any prompting, depicted the agonies of jealousy he had gone through because of Grushenka. They listened to him attentively and took special note of the fact that Mitya had, quite some time before, established an "observation post" at the back of Maria Kondratiev's garden, next to his father's house, from which he reckoned to intercept Grushenka. They were also very interested to hear that it was Smerdyakov who kept Mitya informed of what went on inside old Karamazov's house, and the clerk had to write it all down in detail. Of his jealousy, Mitya spoke excitedly and at great length and, although he felt inwardly that it was rather humiliating to expose his intimate feelings to public scrutiny, he overcame his reluctance in order to make his account as true as possible. The stern, detached gaze of the two pairs of eyes fixed on him, particularly the prosecutor's, gradually discouraged him. "Neither Nelyudov, that boy with whom only a few days ago I exchanged those stupid remarks about women, nor that consumptive prosecutor really deserves my trust in telling them all these things," Mitya now thought mournfully. "Resign yourself to your disgrace—this shame and horror you must face!" Mitya somehow summed up his feelings in this rhyme and forced himself to go on with his statement. When he came to his visit to Mrs. Khokhlakov, he became gay again and, laughing, was about to tell them an anecdote concerning that lady which had recently been going around town, although it had no connection with the case. But the examining magistrate politely suggested that Mitya stick to the point. Finally, Mitya told them of his despair upon leaving Mrs. Khokhlakov's and of his thinking: "I must get the three thousand, even if I have to kill someone to get it!" At that point he was stopped and the clerk was told to write down that Mitya was "thinking of killing someone." Mitya allowed them to write it down without saying a word. At the point in the story when Mitya found out that Grushenka had tricked him and left Samsonov's house right after him, although she had told him she would stay there until almost midnight, Mitya blurted out: "If I didn't kill Fenya when she told me that, it was only because I was in too great a hurry." And that was carefully noted down, too. Mitya waited gloomily until the clerk had finished writing and then was about to tell them about his climbing over the fence into his father's garden, when the examining magistrate suddenly opened a large briefcase that lay next to him on the sofa and drew out the brass pestle.

"Do you recognize this object?" he asked Mitya.

"I certainly do," Mitya said with a mournful grin. "Say, let me have a look at it . . . Ah, no, I don't want to really. The hell with it!"

"How is it you forgot to mention it?" Nelyudov inquired.

"What the hell! Do you think I wanted to conceal it from you? I could not have managed to keep it out of my story anyway, as you can well imagine! It just slipped my memory now."

"Would you be so kind as to tell us exactly how you got it?"

"I will be so kind, gentlemen."

And he told him how he had taken the pestle and dashed off.

"But what exactly was your purpose in picking up this implement?"

"Purpose? I didn't have any particular purpose. I just grabbed it and dashed out."

"But why would you take it with you without any purpose?"

Mitya was boiling with resentment. He glared at "that boy Nelyudov" and snorted in gloomy disgust. He felt more and more ashamed of himself for having told "these people" so sincerely and in such soul-searching detail about his pangs of jealousy over Grushenka.

"I don't give a damn about the pestle!" he barked.

"Nevertheless?"

"To keep the dogs away, if you want—anything. It was dark. Who knows what could happen . . ."

"Did you customarily take some such object along with you when you went out after dark?"

"Ah, the hell with you! What's the good of trying to talk to people like you!" Mitya cried. He had reached the last degree of irritation. He turned to the clerk; his face very red with anger, and with a strange, shrill note vibrating in his voice, he said:

"Now write this down at once! 'I grabbed that pestle for the purpose of killing my father, Fyodor Pavlovich Karamazov, by smashing his head with it.' All right, gentlemen, are you satisfied now? Will that put your minds at rest?"

He glared challengingly at his interrogators.

"We understand very well," the prosecutor said drily, "that the statement you have just made is the result of your irritation with us, your exasperation at questions that you consider trivial but that happen to be really quite essential."

"Ah, but what do you expect me to tell you? Let's say I took the pestle . . . Well, sometimes people snatch up an object under such circumstances. I don't know why—I just took it and ran out of the house, and that's all there is to say. You ought to be ashamed of yourselves, gentlemen. Don't go on like this or I swear I won't tell you anything more."

He sat with his elbows on the table, his head resting on his hand. He turned his profile to them, staring at the wall and trying to overcome the despair mounting in him. He was longing to get up and announce that he would not tell them another word, "even if they lead me off to be executed."

"You see, gentlemen," he said suddenly, doing violence to himself, "when I listen to you I get the impression I'm dreaming . . . There's one particular dream I keep having again and again; it haunts me . . . In that dream, someone is pursuing me, someone of whom I am terribly afraid. He is pursuing me at night, searching for me in the dark. I hide from him, behind a door or a cupboard. I feel humiliated at having to hide from him, but the worst of it is that he knows very well where I am and only pretends he doesn't, just so that he can savor my terror a little longer . . . And that's what you're doing now. That's the way it feels to me."

"So that's the sort of dreams you have?" the prosecutor inquired.

"Yes, that's the sort of dreams I have." Mitya smiled wryly. "Wouldn't you like that noted down too?"

"N-no. I don't think that will be necessary. It's interesting, though."

"But now it's not a dream. It's realism, gentlemen, the realism of real life! I am the wolf and you are the hunters, and you're hunting me down."

"I do not believe your comparison is very accurate," Nelyudov said in a very soft voice.

"Oh, it's accurate enough, pretty accurate!" Mitya cut in heatedly. But then, apparently relieved by having released the anger that had been accumulating inside him, he gradually regained his good humor and became friendlier and friendlier as he went on. "You have good grounds, gentlemen, for distrusting a suspected criminal as he tries to ward off your stinging questions. But you have no right to distrust an honorable man or the honorable impulses of his heart—I'm not afraid to speak like this of myself. No, no, gentlemen, you have no right to dismiss that!

> Be quiet my heart,
> Resign yourself and suffer!

Well, shall I go on?" he suddenly interrupted himself, growing gloomy again.

"Please, we would appreciate it very much," the examining magistrate said.

CHAPTER 5

The Third Ordeal

Mitya sounded sullen, but he was visibly trying even harder not to leave out of his account even the minutest detail. He told them how he had climbed over the fence into his father's garden, how he had stood under his father's window, and all that had happened there. Very clearly and precisely, as if carefully choosing the right words, he described the great urge he had had to find out whether Grushenka was in there with his father or not.

Strangely enough, though, both the prosecutor and the examining magistrate now listened to him with apparent indifference, looking at him very coldly and hardly asking him any questions. Mitya looked in surprise at their faces, unable to make out what they were thinking. "They must be offended by something I said, and now they're angry with me. But the hell with them. I don't give a damn," he said to himself. Even when he told them about his knocking on the window, the "signal" that would make his father believe that Grushenka had arrived, neither the examining magistrate nor the prosecutor seemed to pay any attention to the word "signal," as if they didn't understand the importance of it. Mitya was quite struck by this. When, after that, he described the moment when he had seen his father's face peering out of the window and, overwhelmed by loathing, had pulled the pestle out of his pocket, he deliberately cut his story short and sat there staring at the wall, knowing that their eyes were still fixed on him.

"So," Nelyudov said, "you pulled the weapon out of your pocket. What happened after that?"

"After that? After that I killed him . . . I whacked him on the top of the head and split his skull . . . Isn't that what happened according to you?" Mitya looked at him with angrily flashing eyes. His anger, which had all but subsided, flared up with the utmost violence.

"According to us?" Nelyudov said. "Well, tell us what happened according to you."

Mitya lowered his eyes. A long silence followed.

"This is what happened according to me," he said in a very quiet voice. "Perhaps God was moved by the tears of someone praying for me, perhaps the entreaties of my late mother, perhaps a heavenly spirit who came to my rescue— I don't know, but the devil was defeated. I rushed away from the window and started running toward the garden fence . . . My father was alarmed by the noise and must have caught sight of me, for he reeled away from the window—that, I remember clearly. As for me, I ran across the garden and was already sitting astride the fence when Gregory got to me . . ."

At last Mitya looked at his interrogators. They seemed to be listening to him with perfectly serene detachment. A paroxysm of rage seized Mitya.

"I'm sure that at this very minute you're inwardly laughing at me," he said suddenly.

"What makes you think so?" Nelyudov wanted to know.

"You don't believe one word of what I've told you. I appreciate full well that I've reached the crucial point in my story. The old man is now lying there with his skull bashed in, but, having made the dramatic confession of my own urge to kill him and even of pulling the pestle out of my pocket, I'm now asking you to believe that I suddenly decided to run away from the window . . . It must sound like some crazy story to you, like some ballad in prose, and, of course, you're not at all likely to believe a fellow! Ah, gentlemen, I'm sure you're having a great deal of fun at my expense!"

And he swung around in his chair so violently that it cracked.

"Did you notice by any chance," the prosecutor said, appearing to pay no attention to Mitya's agitation, "as you were running away from the window, whether the door at the other end of the house, the one giving onto the garden, I mean, was open or closed?"

"It wasn't open."

"Did you say it wasn't?"

"It was locked. Who could possibly have opened it? Wait, that door . . ." Mitya seemed to remember something. "Why, did you find it open?"

"It was open."

"Who could have opened it then, unless it was you yourselves?" Mitya seemed extremely puzzled all of a sudden.

"The door was open and your father's murderer must most certainly have entered the house through it and, when he had killed him, left by it," the prosecutor said, letting the words roll slowly out of his mouth and pronouncing every syllable carefully. "We are absolutely satisfied that the victim was struck from inside the room and *not from outside the window*. That is obvious from the investigation that was made on the premises; the position of the body, and everything, leads us to this conclusion. There is not the slightest doubt about it."

Mitya seemed amazed by what he was hearing.

"But how is that possible?" he shouted, in confusion. "I . . . I never went in . . . I'm sure of what I said—that door was closed. It was closed all the time I was in the garden, up to the moment I ran away. I only stood under the window, and I only saw him through the window, that's all, that's all . . . I remember everything, up to the very last second. And if I didn't remember seeing the door with my own eyes, I would still know that it was shut, because no one knew those 'signals' except for myself and Smerdyakov, and my father, of course. And you can be sure that my father would never have let anyone in without the signals."

"What signals? What signals are you talking about?" the prosecutor said with sudden, almost hysterical eagerness, his dignified bearing dissolving before Mitya's eyes.

"I see—this is something you didn't know then." Mitya winked at him sarcastically. "And what if I refuse to tell you? How would you ever find out then? Only the dead man, Smerdyakov, and I knew about those signals . . . Oh, God knew of them too, but I'm sure He wouldn't tell you. And there's no doubt about it—it's quite a curious little detail; quite a few theories could be neatly constructed on it. Well, don't despair, gentlemen—I'll let you in on this little secret. I can see that you have all kinds of silly ideas about things. And you have somewhat underestimated the man you're dealing with on this occasion. For you're dealing with a suspect who is perfectly willing to give you evidence that will incriminate him! Simply because, unlike you, I happen to have a true sense of honor!"

The prosecutor swallowed all these bitter pills. He was trembling with impatience to learn about the new fact. So Mitya told them in great detail about the signals his father had devised for Smerdyakov; he explained the meaning of the various sequences of knocks, even demonstrated them by banging on the table. And when Nelyudov asked whether he himself had knocked on his father's window, Mitya said he had used the signal signifying that Grushenka had arrived, and banged it out on the table again.

"So, take that and try to build your tower on it," Mitya said, again turning contemptuously away from them.

"So only you, your late father, and Smerdyakov knew the signals? No one else?" Nelyudov asked again.

"Yes, the servant Smerdyakov and, besides him, only God. I would write down what I just said about God knowing it too. Besides, you will soon need God's help yourselves."

Of course, they wanted that noted down, but while the clerk was writing it, the prosecutor said, as if the thought had just occurred to him:

"Why, since Smerdyakov knew these signals too, and inasmuch as you categorically deny having anything to do with the death of your father, couldn't it have been Smerdyakov who tapped out the agreed signal and, when your father opened the door, perpetrated the crime?"

Mitya gave him a deeply sarcastic look that immediately turned into one of infinite loathing.

"Bravo! Once again you've caught the fox by the tail! Ha-ha-ha! You know, I can hear you thinking, prosecutor! Now, for instance, you thought that I would clutch desperately at the straw you offered me, hold on to it, start shouting at the top of my voice, 'It was Smerdyakov, it was Smerdyakov, he's the murderer!' Admit now, that that's exactly what you expected, and if you do, I will continue."

But the prosecutor would not admit anything; he waited in silence.

"Well, you're wrong anyway. I'm not going to start accusing Smerdyakov."

"And you don't even suspect him?"

"Do you?"

"Suspicion has fallen on him too."

Mitya fixed his eyes on the floor.

"Now let's stop playing games," he said grimly. "Listen to

this. At the very start, indeed, almost the second I ran out from behind that curtain, when you arrived, the thought flashed through my mind, 'It's Smerdyakov!' Then I sat here shouting that I was innocent of my father's murder and thinking, 'Smerdyakov, Smerdyakov.' And I couldn't get Smerdyakov out of my head. And just now I thought again, 'Smerdyakov!' but only for a second, for right after that I thought, 'No, not Smerdyakov.' He's not a man to do a thing like that!"

"Is there someone else you suspect, then?" Nelyudov asked cautiously.

"I don't know who did it or whether it was the work of God or of the devil, but it was not Smerdyakov," Mitya said with conviction.

"What makes you so sure it couldn't be Smerdyakov?"

"It's an inner conviction, the feeling I have about the man. Smerdyakov is a man of the lowest human type and he's a coward. He's not just a coward: he is an essence and combination of all existing forms of cowardice that has been made to walk on two legs. He was born of a hen. Whenever he spoke to me, he trembled for fear I might kill him, although I never even raised my hand to him. He would fall at my feet and weep. You see these boots? Well, he would kiss them, begging me 'not to frighten him'! What kind of talk is that for a man? In fact, all I ever did to him was to offer him money. He's a chicken who suffers from the falling sickness and a weak mind; an eight-year-old boy could give him a beating. No, Smerdyakov is no killer! Besides, he wasn't even interested in money. He wouldn't accept presents from me . . . And why would he kill the old man? In fact, it's very possible he was his illegitimate son. Did you know that, by the way?"

"Yes, we have heard that story. But it proves nothing: you too are your father's son, and that never prevented you from telling everybody that you wanted to kill him."

"Bang! You've scored a direct hit! But what a dirty blow that was! Still, I don't really care. But, gentlemen, doesn't it make you feel a little sick with yourselves to say a thing like that straight to my face? It's despicable of you because I myself told you that in the first place. Well, I not only wanted to kill him, but I could have done it, and I've even volunteered the information that, in fact, I almost did do it. But I did not kill him. I was prevented by my guardian angel and that's something you've forgotten to take into consideration . . . And so your behavior is pretty low and disgusting. For I did not kill him, I did not, I did not! Do you hear me, prosecutor, I did not kill him!"

Mitya was gasping for breath. During all the questioning, he had not reached such a peak of agitation before.

"But what did Smerdyakov say to you?" he asked them after a pause. "Am I allowed to ask you that question?"

"You may ask us anything you wish," the prosecutor answered in a cold, stern tone, "as long as it has a bearing on the facts of the case. As a matter of fact, it is our duty to answer any questions you may ask. Now, we found your father's servant Smerdyakov, about whom you are inquiring, lying unconscious in his bed in the midst of a very violent epileptic seizure, which was perhaps his tenth consecutive attack. The medical officer who accompanied us to your father's house and who examined Smerdyakov while we were there told us that he may not even live till morning."

"In that case it was the devil who killed my father!" Mitya blurted out. Despite everything, he had still, up to that very second, kept asking himself whether it might not be Smerdyakov.

"We shall come back to that later," Nelyudov said after a moment's hesitation, "but wouldn't you like to go on with your statement in the meantime?"

Mitya said he would like a rest. His request was courteously granted. When he had rested, he resumed his statement. But he obviously felt depressed. He was tired and hurt, and felt morally degraded. Besides, the prosecutor, as if deliberately trying to annoy him, started picking on what Mitya considered irrelevancies. After Mitya had described how, sitting astride the fence, he had used the pestle to hit Gregory on the head when the old man had grabbed his left foot, and how, after hitting him, he had jumped back down into the garden to the wounded man, the prosecutor stopped him and asked him to describe the manner in which he had sat on the fence.

"Why, astride, like this . . . one leg here and the other there . . ."

"And what about the pestle?"

"The pestle was in my hand."

"Wasn't it in your pocket? Are you certain of that? Did you swing at him hard then?"

"I suppose it was pretty hard. But what are you getting at?"

"I wonder whether you would sit on your chair just as you sat on the fence and show us how you took your swing and in what direction."

"What is all this? Are you trying to make a joke out of it?" Mitya said, looking scornfully at his interrogator, but the prosecutor did not bat an eye. Mitya then turned abruptly, sat astride his chair, and swung his arm: "Here, that's how I hit him! That's how I struck him down! Now, what else would you like to know?"

"Thank you. But would you be so kind as to explain to us what really prompted you to jump back into the garden? What did you actually have in mind when you did that?"

"Oh, hell . . . I jumped down to look at the man I'd struck. I don't know why."

"And you did so while in a state of tremendous agitation and while trying to escape?"

"Yes, while in a state of agitation and trying to escape."

"Did you want to help him?"

"Who said anything about helping . . . Although, perhaps . . . I don't know really."

"You didn't know very well what you were doing, then? Might we even say that you were acting unconsciously at the time?"

"Oh no, I remember everything very clearly, every scrap. I jumped down, looked at him, and started wiping away the blood with a handkerchief."

"We saw your handkerchief. What did you hope to achieve? Were you hoping to bring the man you had struck back to life?"

"I don't know what I was hoping to do. I simply wanted to find out whether he was dead or alive."

"So you wanted to find out, I see. Well, what did you find out?"

"I'm not a doctor. I couldn't be sure. When I ran away, I thought I'd killed him, but now it turns out that he's recovered."

"Very good," the prosecutor concluded. "I thank you very much; that is all I really wanted to know. And now, kindly proceed."

Alas, it never even occurred to Mitya to tell them—although he remembered it very well—that he had jumped down because he was concerned about the old servant and that, while standing over the prostrate Gregory, he had even muttered something sadly about what a misfortune it was that the poor old fellow had got hurt like that. And, because Mitya passed over this in silence, the prosecutor concluded that, in jumping down "at such a moment and in such a state of agitation," the suspect could have had only one aim—to make sure that the sole witness to his crime had been silenced—which proved the criminal's strength of character, determination, and cool and calculating judgment, even at such a moment . . . etc., etc. The prosecutor was very pleased with himself; by taunting this nervous fellow with "irrelevancies," he had succeeded in exasperating him, throwing him off balance, and now the man had said what he had wanted him to say.

Painful as it was to him now, Mitya went on. He was, however, interrupted almost at once, this time by Nelyudov.

"How could you go and see the maid Fenya with your hands covered with blood? Besides, as was established later, even your face was stained with it."

"I never even noticed I was covered with blood," Mitya said.

"That makes sense," the prosecutor said, giving the examining magistrate a significant look; "that's usually the case."

"Right, I didn't notice it at all. You hit the nail on the head, prosecutor!" Mitya said approvingly.

Then followed an account of Mitya's sudden decision to step out of Grushenka's life and resign himself to the idea that she would be happy with another man. But he could no longer make himself open his heart to these men, as he had done earlier, or try to explain to them how he felt about "the queen of his heart." He felt nauseated by their "cold, fixed eyes clinging like bedbugs" to him, and he answered their repetitive questions curtly.

"So I decided to shoot myself. Why should I go on living? It was only natural that I should ask myself that question. The man who had seduced her, her first love, the one to whom she rightfully belonged, had come back after five years to repair by marriage the harm he had done her. Well, I saw that, for me, all was lost . . . And behind me there was nothing but disgrace and Gregory's blood now . . . So what was the point of staying alive? And that was why I went to redeem the pistols I had pawned. I had to load them in order to be ready to put a bullet through my brain at dawn."

"And in the meantime, during the night, you decided to have a good time—is that right?"

"That's right. But what the hell, gentlemen—how long do

you intend to go on with this? I had definitely decided to shoot myself. I was going to do it not far from here, as a matter of fact, just outside the village. My plan was to dispose of myself at five in the morning. I had a note ready in my pocket: I had written it at Perkhotin's at the time I loaded the pistols. Here it is. You may read it. You know," he said suddenly, with infinite scorn, "it's not for your benefit that I've been telling you all this!" He pulled the folded note from his waistcoat pocket and tossed it on the table.

The interrogators read it with curiosity and, following the regulations, added it to the exhibits.

"But at that point it still had not occurred to you to wash your hands, not even when you went to see Mr. Perkhotin? You weren't afraid to arouse suspicion then, were you?"

"What suspicion? Ah . . . no, I didn't care one way or the other. I'd have come here anyway, and since I was determined to shoot myself at five in the morning, they wouldn't have had time to do anything about me. Oh, this is all the work of the devil: he killed my father and it was he who saw to it that you should find out about me so quickly! Tell me, how did you manage to get here so quickly? It's really amazing!"

"Mr. Perkhotin informed us that when you came to see him you were holding a bundle of money in your hands . . . your bloodstained hands . . . a lot of money, bills of high denomination—a wad of hundred-ruble bills. His young valet saw it too."

"Yes, that's true. I remember."

"One question arises now," Nelyudov said particularly softly; "could you please tell us where you suddenly got hold of all that money, because, from the facts we have established, you cannot possibly have had time even to go home."

The prosecutor screwed up his nose slightly as if he had tasted something bitter; he obviously did not quite approve of his colleague's putting the question so openly. But he did not intervene.

"No, I didn't go home," Mitya said with apparent calm, but still looking persistently at the floor.

"Well, in that case, allow me to repeat my question," Nelyudov said, leaning forward as if trying to get closer and closer to Mitya. "Where can you have gotten such a considerable sum so quickly, since, according to your own admission, only a few hours earlier, at five in the afternoon of that same day, you . . . ."

" 'Needed ten rubles and pawned your pistols to Perkhotin

and then went to ask Mrs. Khokhlakov for three thousand rubles, which she did not give you,' and so on and so forth," Mitya interrupted him impatiently. "Yes, strange, isn't it? 'There he was, without a kopek and the next thing, lo and behold, he had thousands of rubles in his hands!' Surprising, isn't it? I know I've got you both worried now: 'What if he refuses to tell us where he got it?' Well, you're damned right— I won't tell you that!" Mitya declared emphatically.

The questioners were silent for a moment.

"I hope you appreciate, Mr. Karamazov, how essential it is that you answer this question," Nelyudov said suavely.

"I appreciate it, but I still won't tell you."

The prosecutor intervened, repeating once more to Mitya that he did not have to answer any questions if he thought that not answering them would be to his advantage, etc., etc. Considering, however, the damage he could do himself by refusing to answer, especially with questions as important as this one, he should perhaps . . .

"And so on and so forth. Thank you very much for your little speech, but I believe I've heard it somewhere before," Mitya cut him off again. "I do, in fact, understand perfectly well the gravity of the situation and that the point in question is absolutely crucial, but nevertheless I will not answer you."

"You know, though, that it is not us you will harm, but yourself," Nelyudov said a bit nervously.

"Well, let's stop playing games now," Mitya said, raising his eyes and looking determinedly at his interrogators. "I felt from the very outset that this would be the point where we would collide head-on. But at first, when I started making my statement, everything was sort of floating in a fog and I was even simple-minded enough to suggest to you that all the questioning should be based on mutual trust. But now I realize that there never could be any mutual trust between us because, anyway, we would have wound up in front of this damned wall! So here we are now. That's the end. There's no way out now. I must say, though, I can't really blame you, for I understand very well that you can't take my word for everything either."

And he lapsed into gloomy silence.

"But couldn't you, Mr. Karamazov," Nelyudov said, "couldn't you, without altering your determination not to answer this question, just give us an idea of what considerations are powerful enough to make you refuse to clear up a point of such absolutely vital importance?"

A strange, slightly dreamy smile appeared on Mitya's lips.

"I'm much nicer than you think, gentlemen, and I will give you an idea of the powerful considerations I have for refusing to answer the question. I won't answer it because the answer would dishonor me. If I told you where I had got the money, it would be a disgrace that would be even worse for me than killing and robbing my father—if I had done it, I mean. So you see, it's shame that prevents me from talking . . . What's that? You want that written down, too?"

"Yes, we'd better have it written down," Nelyudov mumbled.

"I don't think it's fair of you to write down what I told you about its being a disgrace, you know. I told you that out of sheer kindness. I didn't have to tell you. It was a sort of present I made you, and now you're planning to use it as evidence against me. But go ahead, put it in writing, you can write down anything you wish," Mitya concluded in a scornful, disgusted tone. "I'm not afraid of you and . . . I can still hold up my head before you."

"Couldn't you just tell us the nature of the disgrace you mentioned?" Nelyudov mumbled again.

The prosecutor frowned violently.

"Ha-ha-hee—c'est fini! No, don't waste your breath. Besides, why should I roll myself in the mud just to please you? I feel sufficiently spattered with mud as it is, after talking to you. You don't deserve my trust, neither you two nor anyone else . . . And that's enough now—it's over."

This sounded final. Nelyudov stopped insisting, although when his eyes met the prosecutor's he understood from his colleague's look that all hope was not yet lost.

"What about telling us exactly how much money you had on you when you went to Mr. Perkhotin's? Would you give us a figure? How many rubles?"

"I won't tell you that either."

"I believe you told Mr. Perkhotin then that you had just received three thousand rubles from Mrs. Khokhlakov—is that correct?"

"I may have told him that. But why don't you give this up? I won't tell you anyway."

"All right. In that case would you tell us how you came here and what you did after your arrival?"

"Why don't you ask the people in the guest house? But, all right, I'll tell you if you wish."

He told them. But we shall not repeat it here. He told the story briefly and impersonally. He did not speak of his love and his feelings; he told them only that he was no longer so determined to shoot himself "in view of certain new developments." He did not bother to explain the motives behind his actions anymore, did not go into subtleties. Besides, his interrogators did not interrupt him very often to ask him questions; it was obvious that this was not what interested them most.

"We'll check it all, go over it all again with the other witnesses—in your presence of course," Examining Magistrate Nelyudov said, concluding the session. "There's only one more thing I have to ask you now: Would you please put on the table everything you have on you, particularly all the money you still have on your person."

"Money? Most certainly, gentlemen. I understand perfectly. I was wondering why you hadn't asked me to do so from the beginning. Although obviously I could not have left with it. So here it is: count it, take it. I guess that's all there is . . ."

He pulled all the money he had, including the small change, out of his pockets. Then he found two more twenty-kopek pieces in his waistcoat pocket and tossed them on the table too. When they had counted it all up, there was eight hundred and thirty-six rubles and forty kopeks.

"Is that all there is?" Nelyudov asked.

"That's all."

"In your statement just now you said you had spent three hundred rubles at the Plotnikov store, you paid ten rubles back to Perkhotin, ten to the coachman, you lost two hundred at cards, then . . ."

Nelyudov went over everything, Mitya willingly helping him. They tried to remember and write down every kopek. The examining magistrate quickly added it all up.

"It would appear, then, that, including this eight hundred-odd rubles, you originally had around fifteen hundred, is that right?"

"So it would appear."

"How is it, then, that everybody says there was much more than that?"

"They can say what they want."

"But you said so yourself."

"Did I? Well, so I did."

"We'll check it all against the evidence of the persons who have not yet been examined. In the meantime, please don't worry about your money. It will be safe and will be returned to you in the end . . . that is, if it is established that you have an indisputable claim to it. Well, and now . . ."

Examining Magistrate Nelyudov abruptly got up and in a very firm voice announced to Mitya that he was "duty-bound" to have him searched, "pockets and all."

"All right. Shall I turn out my pockets, then?" Mitya asked and started turning out one pocket after the other.

"I am afraid you will have to undress altogether."

"What? Undress? Damn it, can't you search me like this?"

"It is absolutely out of the question, Mr. Karamazov. I am sorry but you will just have to take everything off."

"As you wish," Mitya said gloomily. "Only I insist that it not be here, but behind that curtain. Who's going to search me?"

"Certainly, behind the curtain is fine," Nelyudov said, inclining his head in assent, his small, boyish face assuming a tremendously solemn expression.

CHAPTER 6

The Prosecutor Catches Mitya

Mitya had never expected what followed and it caught him by surprise. A minute before, he could never have imagined that he, Dmitry Karamazov, would be treated like this. The main thing about it was that it was humiliating for him, whereas they were in a position to treat him with "condescension and contempt." He would not have minded so much if they had asked him to take off just his jacket, but they asked him to undress further. And they didn't actually ask him, they told him—that he plainly understood. Out of pride and to show his contempt for them, he complied without a word of protest. Besides the prosecutor and the examining magistrate, some of the men also followed him behind the curtain. "To use force if necessary," Mitya thought, "and perhaps for some other purpose too."

"What about my shirt? You want me to take it off too?" he asked sharply. But neither the prosecutor nor Nelyudov answered him, for they were both busy examining Mitya's jacket, trousers, waistcoat, and cap. They were completely engrossed in what they were doing. "They've lost all restraint now. They don't even bother to observe the most elementary rules of courtesy," flashed through Mitya's head.

"I'm asking you for the second time: do I have to take my shirt off too, yes or no?" he asked in an even sharper and more irritated tone.

"Don't worry, we'll let you know," Nelyudov answered in what sounded, to Mitya at least, like a superior and supercilious tone.

All that time a lively conference had been going on in hushed tones between the two interrogators. They were examining large bloodstains on the back of the coat, especially down the left side. The blood had dried, but not to the point of becoming hard and crumbling. There were bloodstains on the back of the trousers too. Then Nelyudov, in the presence of the witnesses, ran his fingers along the lapels, the cuffs, and all the seams of the jacket and trousers, as though looking for something—money, of course. They did not even try to conceal from him that they suspected him of sewing money into his clothes. "They're treating me like a petty thief now, not like an officer," Mitya snarled under his breath. And all the time they kept exchanging observations with a surprising lack of concern for whether he could hear them or not. At one point the clerk, who had followed them behind the curtain too, and who was fussing around his superiors, suddenly called Nelyudov's attention to Mitya's cap, which was also being felt and fingered.

"Remember Gridenko, the rural clerk, sir? That fellow who, last summer, went to town to collect the wages for the whole office and later claimed that he had got drunk and lost the money—remember him, sir? Well, where did they find the money in the end? It was in the piping of his cap; all those hundred-ruble bills were tightly rolled up and sewn into the piping . . ."

The prosecutor and the examining magistrate remembered Gridenko's trick very well and it was precisely for that reason that they had put Mitya's cap aside, having decided that they would have to have it and the rest of Mitya's clothes subjected to an even more thorough scrutiny later.

"Excuse me, what's this?" Nelyudov suddenly exclaimed, noticing that the right cuff of Mitya's shirt was turned up and soaked with blood. "What is it? Blood?"

"Certainly," Mitya snapped.

"But what blood is it? And why was the cuff turned back?"

Mitya told him that his cuff had got soaked with blood while he was fussing over Gregory and that later he had decided to turn it back when he was washing at Perkhotin's.

"Then you'll have to take your shirt off too. That's very important material evidence."

The blood rushed to Mitya's head. He turned red with fury.

"Do you want me to stand here naked, then?" he shouted.

"Don't worry, we'll do something about that. But in the meantime we would like you to remove your socks too."

"You must be joking! Is that really necessary?" Mitya's eyes flashed with fury.

"We have other things to do than joke with you," Nelyudov snapped back.

"Well, if it's really indispensable, I suppose . . ."

Mitya sat down on the bed and started pulling off his socks. He felt terribly ill at ease, naked in front of all these dressed men. In a strange way, being undressed somehow made him feel guilty before them and, what was even worse, he felt that now he had become their inferior and they had the right to despise him. "If everyone was undressed, it would be all right, but if it's just me and they're all looking on, it's an insult." These words flashed again and again through his mind. "It's just like a dream—I've often been in this degrading position in dreams . . ." It was even more painful to him to take off his socks, because they were very dirty. So were his under-clothes. And they all noticed it. What made it even more awful was that all his life he had somehow hated the sight of his feet, particularly his big toes, which he found absolutely hideous, and on the big toe of his right foot there was that horrible, rough flat nail that insisted on curling downward . . . And now all these people were going to see it all! The un-bearable embarrassment caused him to become even more defiantly rude. He tore off his shirt impatiently.

"Anything else you would like to search? Please don't let your discretion stop you."

"No thanks. That's all for the time being."

"And, for the time being, am I supposed to wait naked?" Mitya said, his voice quivering with rage.

"Yes, for the moment, you will have to put up with it . . . Please sit down; if you wish, you may take the blanket off the bed and cover yourself with that . . . I'll see what I can do."

All the things were then examined by witnesses, and after that they drew up a report on the search. Finally Nelyudov left and Mitya's clothes were carried out after him. The prosecutor left too. Mitya was now alone with the men guarding him. They stood there silently without taking their eyes off him. Feeling cold, he wrapped himself in the blanket. His bare feet would not stay under the blanket and kept peeping out, despite all Mitya's efforts to keep them inside. It took Nelyudov a terribly long time to come back. "He's doing it deliberately . . . like giving me a whipping . . . he's treating me like a little dog," Mitya muttered, gnashing his teeth. "And that other wretch, the prosecutor—he walked out because he felt it was sickening to look at me without clothes . . ." Mitya still hoped, however, that when they were through examining his clothes they would bring them back to him. But Nelyudov returned with a man who handed Mitya some strange clothes.

"Here are some clothes for you," the examining magistrate said in a casual tone; "this is a suit that Mr. Kalganov is willing to sacrifice on this memorable occasion and he sends you a clean shirt too. By luck he had this change of clothes in his suitcase. And you can have back your own socks and underwear."

Mitya was outraged.

"I don't want someone else's clothes!" he shouted threateningly. "Give me back my own things at once!"

"That's impossible."

"Give me my clothes, do you hear? To hell with Kalganov and his clothes!"

They reasoned with him for a long time and finally succeeded in calming him down. They explained to him at great length that the bloodstains on his clothes made them "material evidence," that they could be presented as an "exhibit," and that, indeed, even if they wanted to, they did not have the right to allow Mitya to keep them, for no one knew yet "what the results of the preliminary investigation will show." Mitya finally accepted their explanations, stopped protesting, and gloomily began to dress. As he huriedly put on the unfamiliar clothes, he commented, however, that they were more expensive than his own clothes and that he did not want to "derive any personal profit" from the substitution. Besides, he found Kalganov's clothes looked "humiliatingly tight" on him and asked whether he was supposed "to clown in them so you two can laugh at me."

Again, they assured him that, although Mr. Kalganov was a little taller and somewhat slighter, he was exaggerating the difference in their builds, that the clothes fitted well enough, except perhaps the trousers, which were a bit too long. However, when Mitya put the jacket on, it was much too narrow in the shoulders.

"God damn it, men! Can't you see that I can't even button it!" Mitya grumbled. "And please go at once and tell Kalganov that it was not my idea to ask him for his clothes and that I look like a clown in them!"

"I'm sure he fully appreciates that and, besides, he asked me to tell you how sorry he is . . . No, not about the clothes not fitting you—he meant about the whole business . . ." Nelyudov said gently.

"He feels sorry for me, ha! You can tell him from me what he can do with his feelings! So where do we go now? Or am I to stay here?"

They asked him to come back "into the other room." Mitya's face was grim when he emerged from behind the curtain; he was shaking with indignation and tried not to look at anyone. In those clothes that did not belong to him, he felt completely disgraced and dishonored and was even ashamed before the uncouth men guarding him and before a vulgar peasant like Trifon, whose face suddenly appeared in the doorway, only to vanish at once. "He just wanted to have a peep at the clown," the thought occurred to Mitya.

He sat down in the same chair that he had occupied before. He now had a strong feeling that everything was absurd and nightmarish and that he had gone insane.

"Why, I suppose the next step will be to order that I be flogged, for what else is there left?" he snarled, glaring at the prosecutor. He turned away from Nelyudov altogether, as if he had decided not even to address him. "He examined my socks so eagerly; the pig even ordered my underwear to be turned inside out for everyone to see how dirty it was—that's too much . . ."

"Well, now we will have to proceed with the examination of the witnesses," Nelyudov said, as though answering the question Mitya had addressed to the prosecutor.

"Hm . . . yes," the prosecutor said, as if trying to work out something.

"You see, Mr. Karamazov," Nelyudov went on, "we've done everything within our power to help you clear yourself. Since, however, you categorically refuse to tell us anything about where you obtained the sum found in your possession, we are now forced . . ."

"What stone is that in your ring?" Mitya asked him dreamily, pointing at one of the large rings on Nelyudov's right hand.

"The ring?" the magistrate asked, surprised.

"This one here, on your middle finger, this stone with the little yellow veins, what's it called?" Mitya insisted in the irritated tone of a child about to have a temper tantrum.

"That's a smoky topaz," Nelyudov said with a smile. "Would you like to have a look at it? Shall I take it off?"

"No, no, don't take it off!" Mitya shouted fiercely, as if suddenly awakened; he was furious with himself. "I don't want your damned ring . . . You know, you have defiled my soul, the two of you! How can you people imagine for a second that, if I had really killed my father, I would have denied it and told all these lies just to get away with it? No, that is not the kind of man Dmitry Karamazov is! If I had killed him, I swear I would not have waited for you to come here, nor would I have waited for sunrise as I was doing—I would have destroyed myself at once, then and there! I can feel it now inside, for I have learned more about life during this horrible night than in the last twenty years. And do you think that I would have behaved this way throughout the night, and right now, at this moment, as I face you, that I would have looked at you as I am doing, at you and at the whole world, if I were really a parricide? Why, the very idea that I had accidentally killed Gregory gave me no rest all night! And, believe me, it was not because I was afraid of your punishment! You should be ashamed! And how can you expect me to reveal another shame and disgrace to blind moles like you, sneering and distrusting moles! No, I would rather be sent to Siberia than let you in on that secret! It was the person who opened the door to the house who killed and robbed my father! Who is he? That question tortures me and torments me, but I can tell you that it was not Dmitry Karamazov, and that is all I can tell you. That's enough now. Don't pester me. Leave me alone . . . Send me wherever you wish, punish me, do anything, but stop pestering me. I won't say anything anymore. Call your witnesses!"

Mitya delivered himself of this tirade, and it looked as if he had definitely decided not to answer any more questions. The prosecutor had been watching him all the time he was talking and when he had finished he remarked in a cold, detached tone, almost casually:

"Now, speaking of that open door you just mentioned, it just so happens that we can now tell you about a very curious

bit of the testimony of old Gregory, whom you wounded—
something that is quite important both for you and for us.
As soon as he recovered and could answer our questions, he
declared most categorically that when he walked out onto the
porch of the servants' cottage, he heard a noise and decided
to enter the garden through the gate, which had been left
unlocked. Entering the garden, even before he caught sight
of you running away from the window through which
you'd seen your father—according to your own testimony—
he glanced to his left and saw that, indeed, the window was
open just as you said. But at the same time he also noticed that
the door, which was much closer to him than the window,
was also wide open. He was, of course, referring to the door
that you insist was closed all the time that you were in the
garden. Now, I see no reason to conceal from you that
Gregory himself says that he concluded that you must have
just come out of that door, although he did not actually see
you do so, since he first caught sight of you when you were
already in the middle of the garden, running toward the
fence . . ."

Mitya was on his feet well before the prosecutor had finished his speech.

"Not true!" he screamed like a madman. "It's a damn lie,
an impudent lie! He couldn't have seen the door open, because
it was closed! He's lying!"

"I must repeat that Gregory testified that he is absolutely
sure about it. He has no doubt on that point whatsoever. He
insists that the door was open. We asked him about it again
and again."

"But it isn't true! It is either deliberate slander or the
hallucination of a madman," Mitya shouted again; "he must
have imagined it—he was bleeding. He had that wound. He
could have been delirious when he came to . . . So he was
raving, that's all . . ."

"But he didn't see the open door when he regained consciousness after being wounded, but before he was struck;
he saw it just after he came out of the cottage . . ."

"But it's not true! It's just not true. It's impossible! He
must be saying it out of spite, because he's angry with me.
He couldn't have seen it . . . I didn't come through that
door . . ."

Mitya was choking.

The prosecutor turned to the examining magistrate and in
a gravely decisive tone told him:

"Show it to him, then."

"Do you recognize this?" Nelyudov placed on the table a large envelope made of thick paper, the kind used in government offices. It still bore three seals. It was, however, empty; the contents must have been removed; it had been torn open at one end. Mitya's eyes almost popped out as he stared at it.

"That's my father's . . . it must be the envelope that he put that three thousand in . . . If it has that thing written on it . . . here it is, 'to my darling . . .' and here it says 'three thousand' . . . See, it says so!"

"Of course, we've seen that. But it was empty when we found it. The money was gone, and the envelope was on the floor by the bed, behind the screen."

For a few seconds Mitya was like a man stunned.

"I know, it's Smerdyakov!" he yelled at the top of his voice. "It's he who killed father and stole the money! He was the only one who knew where father had hidden that envelope . . . Now I know it was he who did it—it's obvious!"

"But, then, you yourself also knew about the envelope and that your father kept it under his pillow, didn't you?"

"No, I didn't know that. I've never seen this envelope before; this is the first time I've set eyes on it. But Smerdyakov told me about it and he knew where father had hidden it, while I didn't . . ."

"So how is it that you testified earlier that you knew your father kept the envelope under his pillow? That's exactly what you told us—under his pillow. So you knew very well where the envelope was hidden."

"Yes, we have it written down," Nelyudov confirmed.

"That's absurd! I had no idea it was under his pillow! Besides, I'm not so sure that it was under the pillow. I must have just said the first thing that came into my head. What does Smerdyakov say? Did you ask him where the envelope was? That is the most important point. I just said it was under the pillow the way I might have said anything . . . A man can blurt out anything . . . No, Smerdyakov is the only one who really knew. So now I'm absolutely certain that he is the murderer; it's as clear as daylight now!" Mitya shouted in tremendous excitement, stubbornly repeating himself, losing patience. "Try to understand! You must arrest him, arrest him right away! . . . He killed father after I'd run away, while Gregory was lying unconscious. I see it all clearly . . . He tapped the signal, father opened the door for him, and . . .

Remember, he was the only one who knew the signals, and without the proper signals father would never have let anybody in . . ."

"But, once again, you disregard the fact that there was no need for anyone to tap any signals since the door was already wide open, even while you were still in the garden," the prosecutor remarked, still quietly but with a note of triumph already detectable in his voice.

"The door . . . the door," Mitya mumbled, staring blankly at the prosecutor, and he sank back into his chair in utter exhaustion. There was a general silence. "The door . . . It was a ghost . . . God is against me!" he cried. His eyes were completely empty of thought now.

"So you see, Mr. Karamazov—judge for yourself," the prosecutor said in an important tone; "on the one hand, there is testimony that the door was open and that you must have come through it, which we feel is damning for you. And, on the other hand, we are faced with your incomprehensible, stubborn, almost obdurate refusal to reveal the source of the money that suddenly appeared in your hands when only three hours earlier you had had to pawn your pistols to obtain ten rubles—by your own admission! In view of these facts, you can judge for yourself what we are likely to believe and what our conclusion may be. And please do not accuse us of being cold, sarcastic cynics, incapable of appreciating the generous impulses of your heart or putting unlimited faith in your truthfulness. Please try instead to understand us, in our position."

Mitya was in a state of unimaginable agitation. He turned white.

"All right," he said, "I will reveal my secret to you and tell you where the money came from; I will expose myself to shame and disgrace so that later I can't accuse either myself or you . . ."

"And believe me, Mr. Karamazov," Nelyudov said in a peculiarly affectionate and joyful voice, "every frank admission you make now, at this critical moment, could be tremendously helpful later in making the outcome much easier, and even, perhaps . . ."

But the prosecutor kicked him lightly under the table and the young examining magistrate stopped just in time. However, it made very little difference really, for Mitya was not listening to him anyway.

CHAPTER 7

Mitya Reveals His Secret and Is Heckled

"Gentlemen," Mitya started, still in the same state of great agitation, "that money, gentlemen—I'll make a clean breast of it—well, that money belonged to *me*."

The faces of the two interrogators dropped—that was not at all what they had expected.

"What do you mean when you say it was your money?" Nelyudov muttered. "Why, then, at five p.m. of that same day, by your own admission, you . . ."

"To hell with five p.m. of that same day and my own admission—that has nothing to do with it! That money was mine. That is, I had stolen it. It was stolen money—about fifteen hundred rubles—and I had it on me all the time."

"Where did you get it?"

"I took it from around my neck, right here! The money was sewn up in a rag and I wore it hanging around my neck. I had been carrying it around for a long time, for a whole month, carrying it around to my terrible shame."

"But from whom did you . . . you take it?"

"You were going to say stole it, weren't you? Don't be squeamish, use the proper words. For it is just the same as if I had stolen it, or, if you wish, misappropriated it. But the right word for it, I think, is stolen. And after last night, it became an unmitigated theft."

"Last night? But you just told us that you got that money a month ago!"

"Yes, but I didn't get it from my father. Don't worry—I didn't steal it from him. I stole it from her. Let me tell you, and don't interrupt me. It is very painful for me to talk about it. Listen—a month ago Katerina Ivanovna Verkhovtsev, to whom I was formerly engaged, sent for me . . . Do you know her, by the way?"

"Of course, of course . . ."

"I know you've met her. Well, she is the most generous and the most honorable person, but she hates me and has hated me for a very long time, and deservedly so . . ."

"Who, Miss Katerina Verkhovtsev?" the examining magistrate asked in great surprise. The prosecutor also looked at him in bewilderment.

"Don't you pronounce her name! I feel like a pig as is, dragging her into this sordid story. Yes, I realized that she hated me, had hated me for a long time, ever since that first time in my lodgings . . . But that's enough on that subject—it has nothing to do with you anyway. All you need to know is that, about a month ago, she sent for me and gave me three thousand rubles that she wanted me to mail to Moscow, to her sister and some other relative of hers . . . As if she couldn't have gone herself and sent it! And it happened just at that fateful moment in my life when I—well, to make a long story short—when I'd just fallen in love with another woman, *her,* the one whom you sent downstairs, Grushenka . . . And so I took Grushenka to Mokroye and we had a party right here, in this very inn, a party that went on for two days and two nights and on which I spent half of that stinking money, that is, about fifteen hundred rubles. And the rest I kept for myself. So the money I had is the balance of that three thousand, and I wore it around my neck like a medallion. But yesterday, I tore open the rag, took out the bills, and spent them. That is, spent all except the eight hundred-odd rubles that I had on me and that you now have. That's what is left of the fifteen hundred rubles, Mr. Nelyudov."

"Just a minute, please. Everybody knows that a month ago you spent not just fifteen hundred rubles, but rather three thousand, here."

"Who knows that? Who counted the money? Whom did I give it to to count?"

"But you yourself went around town telling everyone who would listen to you that you had gone through all of three thousand rubles that time, didn't you?"

"That's right. I told everyone in town that, the whole town repeated it, and everyone in Mokroye thought I had thrown away three thousand here. Nevertheless, the truth is that, in actual fact, I only spent fifteen hundred and I sewed the other fifteen hundred up in that rag. So that's where the money I had yesterday came from, gentleman."

"It sounds almost miraculous," Nelyudov murmured.

"Allow me to ask you this," the prosecutor intervened at last. "Is there anyone at all to whom you have told this fact before? I mean the fact that you kept fifteen hundred rubles and carried them about with you for a month after that?"

"No, I never told anybody."

"Strange. You are sure—no one at all?"

"No one at all, ever."

"But why did you make such a mystery of it? Why all this secrecy? Let me put it this way: you have finally consented to let us in on your secret, which, you told us, would bring disgrace and dishonor down on you once and for all. But I see it turns out to be, relatively speaking, only a minor misappropriation of three thousand rubles, and moreover, probably only a temporary misappropriation, which I suppose could be considered simply an irresponsible act, but certainly not something that would disgrace a man once and for all . . . What I'm trying to say is that, for a month, even without this present confession of yours, many people in town have suspected that you were spending Miss Verkhovtsev's three thousand rubles. I, for one, have heard the story, and I happen to know that Inspector Makarov has too. So finally it was really hardly a suspicion anymore; it was gossip going around town. Besides, if I am not mistaken, you have already told it to other people. So it is quite beyond me why you have made such a mystery of the fifteen hundred rubles that you supposedly put aside from the three thousand you had misappropriated earlier. It is quite unbelievable that it should cause you such profound suffering to reveal a secret of that sort to us! When you were telling us earlier that you would rather be sent to Siberia than reveal that mystery, we were quite puzzled . . ."

The prosecutor fell silent. As he was talking, he had become heated. He had not tried to hide his annoyance, almost spite, and he had given vent to the irritation against Mitya that had accumulated within him. He had even forgotten his elegant formulation and enunciation and sounded almost unclear and inarticulate.

"The disgrace lies not in the fifteen hundred rubles," Mitya said firmly, "but in the fact that I had put them aside from the three thousand."

"Why?" the prosecutor asked, letting out an exasperated laugh. "What makes it so particularly disgraceful to separate fifteen hundred from three thousand that you had anyway appropriated rather shamefully, even disgracefully? The important thing here is the fact that you misappropriated three thousand rubles and not how you decided to spend them later. But while we're at it, would you tell us why you put half the sum aside? What was your purpose? Can you explain now?"

"Ah, gentlemen, don't you understand that precisely the purpose makes the whole difference?" Mitya cried. "I separated the sum into halves because I am a low creature, because I calculated that it would be more to my advantage, and it is the fact that I was calculating under those circumstances that constitutes the baseness of the act . . . And then that unspeakable act was prolonged for a whole month!"

"I don't understand what you're saying."

"I'm surprised at you. But perhaps I didn't express myself well. I'll try again. Now try to follow this: I misappropriate three thousand rubles that she has entrusted to my honor, go and have a wild time with it, spend every kopek of it, and in the morning go and see her and say: 'I'm sorry, Katya, I've just thrown away your three thousand!' Is that a decent way to act? It certainly isn't—it's dishonest and cowardly. It's the act of an animal who is unable to control his animal impulses. Right. But still a man doing that is not necessarily a thief, not a downright thief at least—you must see that! He's spent the money, thrown it all away, but he hasn't stolen it. That was one alternative. Now here's another, even more favorable one. But please follow me closely in case I get mixed up, for I feel a bit dizzy . . . In the second alternative I spend only fifteen hundred of the three thousand rubles—that is only half the sum. The next day I bring her back the remaining half and say: 'Here, Katya, please accept from me, irresponsible scoundrel that I am, these fifteen hundred rubles, for I have spent the other fifteen hundred and I'm afraid I won't be able to prevent myself from spending this as well. Take it back so I won't be tempted!' Well, what do you say about a situation like that? Of course, I'm still a low scoundrel and an outright animal, but in this case, I'm definitely not a thief, because a thief wouldn't have brought her back what was left—he would have kept it. And she would understand, then, that since this time I was bringing back half the sum she had entrusted to me, I would pay her back the rest too—I mean the money I squandered, even if it took me my whole lifetime to earn it or to raise it. In that case, I am not a thief. I'm anything you like, but not a thief . . ."

"Fine, I grant you that there is some difference," the prosecutor said with an icy smile. "But I still find it rather peculiar that the difference should appear so crucial to you."

"But I do feel there is a crucial difference! Anyone can act despicably. I even believe that everyone does so occasionally. But far from everyone is a thief—only a most despicable arch-scoundrel would stoop to stealing. I'm not too good at explaining all these subtleties, but one thing I'm sure of—a thief is viler than an ordinary vile scoundrel. Now, imagine this: Understand that I carry the money on me for a month, and that, if I decide to, I can give it back tomorrow and I will no longer be such a low scoundrel. But that's just it—I cannot make up my mind to do it, although every day I think to myself, 'Go on, do it, you scoundrel!' But a month has gone by and I still haven't decided. Well, what do you think of that—is it nice?"

"I dare say it isn't very nice. I understand perfectly well, and I don't wish to argue the point," the prosecutor answered with great restraint. "But I would like to pass over, for the time being, all this about the subtle differences in the acts of scoundrels and get back to the point. And the point is that you still have not answered our earlier question, namely, why did you divide the money in half, then proceed to squander one half and put the other half aside? Specifically, what was your purpose in hiding the fifteen hundred rubles? I'm afraid I must insist that you answer this question, Mr. Karamazov."

"Why, of course!" Mitya cried, slapping his forehead as if suddenly remembering something. "I don't know why I've been wasting your time like this. I should have explained to you the most important thing first, for then you would have understood at once that it is the motive that determines the degree of disgrace. You see, my father kept trying to persuade Grushenka to come and live with him and I was terribly jealous, for I imagined then that she was hesitating over whom to choose—him or me. And so I thought to myself, 'What if she gets tired of making me miserable and says to me: "You're the one I love, and I want you to take me away to the other end of the world." What would I do, then, with forty kopeks as my entire fortune?' I didn't understand her at all then: I thought she wouldn't come with me unless I had some money, that she would never accept me penniless. And so, on the sly, I counted off half the three thousand and cold-bloodedly picked up a needle and sewed it up in the rag myself; it was only after I had it safely tucked away that I went off to squander the other fifteen hundred on that spree. Well, that's something really unspeakably low—do you understand that now?"

The prosecutor laughed aloud. The examining magistrate followed suit.

"I think it was, if anything, more reasonable and less unethical on your part to abstain from throwing away every single kopek of the money," Nelyudov said with a chuckle. "I really don't see what is so especially bad about it."

"Why, the fact that I stole it, that's what! Good God, I'm completely appalled at your lack of understanding! Every day, every hour, I went about with the fifteen hundred rubles dangling from my chest. I kept repeating to myself, 'I'm a thief, I'm a thief!' And that's why I had all those brawls in taverns during that month. That's the real reason I gave my father that beating—it was all because I felt I was a thief. I didn't even dare tell my brother Alyosha about the fifteen hundred rubles, so horrible did it feel to be a crook and a thief! But I want you to know that all the time I was carrying that money on me, I kept saying to myself, 'No, Dmitry Karamazov, you may still prove that you're not really a thief!' And why? Precisely because all I had to do was to go and see Katya the next day and give her back the fifteen hundred rubles. And it was only yesterday, on my way to Perkhotin's, that I decided to tear the money from around my neck. I hadn't dared to until then, but then I did it and became an out-and-out irredeemable thief, a man dishonored for the rest of his life. In tearing open that rag, I tore up my hope, for now I would never be able to go to Katya and say to her, 'I'm not a thief. I'm just an irresponsible scoundrel.' Now, do you understand? Do you?"

"And what made you decide to take that money yesterday? Why precisely yesterday evening?" Nelyudov asked.

"What a question! Obviously because I had sentenced myself to die at five the following morning. I didn't think it would make much difference at that point whether I died a thief or a man of honor. But then it turned out that it did make a difference! I want you to believe me, gentlemen, that what tormented me most that night was not the thought that I had killed poor old Gregory and that I faced the danger of being sent to Siberia at the very moment when I'd found that my love was requited and heaven had opened up to me! Oh, all that, of course, made me feel wretched, but not as terrible as the horrible realization that I had spent the money and was, therefore, now irredeemably a thief! Oh, gentlemen, I swear to you, I have learned so much about life during this night! And I have also learned that it is not only impossible to live a crook, it is also impossible to die one. No, gentlemen, a man must die honorable."

Mitya was pale. He looked as if he were at the end of his

tether, completely spent, although he was still in a state of great agitation.

"I am beginning to understand you now, Mr. Karamazov," the prosecutor drawled, in a soft, almost sympathetic tone, "but if you don't mind my saying so, I believe your nerves had snapped under the strain and that you were in a state of nervous disorder. Otherwise, for instance, you could have put an end to that terrible torment, which lasted almost a month, by returning the fifteen hundred rubles to the person who had entrusted you with the money, and then, having explained to her the terrible situation you were in, as you described it to us, you could have done the most natural thing, that would occur to anyone—namely, after having acknowledged your mistake, to ask her to lend you that same sum. And I would say it is most unlikely that a person of her generosity, seeing your great distress, would have turned you down. Besides, you could have given her an IOU or, even better, offered her the same security as you offered Mr. Samsonov and Mrs. Khokhlakov. You still consider that security good, don't you?"

Mitya suddenly turned red.

"Do you really consider me that low then! I cannot believe you mean it!" he said in tremendous indignation, looking straight into the prosecutor's eyes as if unable to believe that he had heard him right.

"I assure you I am absolutely serious . . . I don't even see what surprises you so much," the prosecutor said, looking at Mitya with equal surprise.

"But that would be unspeakably low! Don't you realize how you are tormenting me! All right, I will now reveal my bottomless baseness to you. But it will make you feel uneasy when you see to what depth of infamy a man's feelings can drag him. I want you to know, prosecutor, that I thought myself of the scheme you have just suggested to me. Yes, I thought of it during that terrible month: I was about to go and see Katya, tell her about my betrayal and beg her for some money to take care of the expenses that betrayal would incur (yes, I said *beg*, do you hear me?), so that I could run away with her hated rival, a woman who had mortally offended her. You must really be out of your mind, prosecutor, if you think I could have gone through with that!"

"Out of my mind or not, I admit that in the heat of the argument I failed to make allowances for jealousy between women, if there actually can have been jealousy in this case, as you contend. Yes, I suppose you have a point there . . ."

The prosecutor snorted.

"But it would have been such a filthy, disgusting thing to do," Mitya shouted fiercely, slamming his fist down on the table. "It would have been a stinking infamy beyond all imagining . . . And you know, she would most certainly have given me the money. She would have given it to me just to avenge herself, to show me how much she despised me, for she is also a creature of hell, a woman whose hatred is terrible! But I would have taken the money. I would have, I would have, and then . . . then all my life . . . oh, God! Please forgive me for screaming this way, gentlemen; it is because I considered this possibility just recently, only two days ago, the night when I was trying to bring the dead drunk Hound back to life, and then again yesterday throughout the evening. Yes, I remember, until, until . . ."

"Until what?" Nelyudov prompted him curiously, but Mitya did not hear him.

"I have made a terrible confession," he concluded grimly. "Please appreciate that. And it is not enough to appreciate it —you must value it, for if you don't, if you just take it for granted without understanding what it has meant to me to admit all this to you, then, gentlemen, it will show that you have not the slightest respect for me, and I will die of shame at having confessed to people like you. Oh, I will shoot myself! Why, I can see, I can already see that you don't believe me! What? You want that written down too?" he shouted in horror.

"Only what you just said now," Nelyudov said, looking at him in surprise. "So then, until the very last moment you were still thinking of going to see Miss Verkhovtsev and asking her to lend you that sum, is that right? I assure you that this is an extremely important point, Mr. Karamazov, and it is especially important for you, particularly for you."

"Have mercy, gentlemen! Please don't write it down! Please, not that! I have torn my soul in half before you and now you are poking your fingers into both halves . . . God, God, what are they doing to me!"

In despair, he buried his face in his hands.

"Please don't get so excited, Mr. Karamazov," the prosecutor said. "Everything that has been written down will be read back to you and if you don't agree with anything, we will make the necessary changes . . . But now I would like to ask you a certain question, and this is the third time I am asking it: Are you really absolutely certain that no one, not a single person, had ever heard of the money you had sewed up in that rag and were carrying around your neck? That is really very hard to believe."

"No one, no one at all. I've already told you that! Ah, you haven't understood me! Leave me alone, then."

"Suit yourself. But this point will have to be cleared up eventually, and we have all the time in the world. In the meantime, however, consider this: we have perhaps several dozen witnesses to testify that you yourself went around telling people, even shouting from the roof-tops, that you'd gone through three thousand rubles on that spree, and it was always three thousand, never fifteen hundred. And even this time, when you suddenly appeared with money, you managed to tell many people that again you had three thousand rubles . . ."

"You have not dozens but hundreds of witnesses; I'd say two hundred people heard me say that, perhaps even a thousand!" Mitya cried.

"So you see, then, *all* bear witness to it. Doesn't the word 'all' indicate anything to you?"

"Nothing. I lied and they all started repeating my lies."

"But what need was there for you to do that, to lie like that as you put it?"

"Damned if I know. Perhaps it was just pleasant to brag, to say, 'See all the money I threw away.' Or perhaps I was trying to make myself forget about the money sewn up in that rag. Yes, I guess that was the reason. But hell, how many times have you asked me this same question? So I lied once and then didn't want to admit I had lied. Why do you think people usually lie?"

"That is a very difficult question to answer," the prosecutor said sternly. "But tell me this now: how large was that bundle with the bills in it that you had around your neck?"

"Not too big."

"Can't you give me a rough idea?"

"If you fold a hundred-ruble bill in two, it would be about that size."

"Couldn't you show us the scraps of the rag the money was wrapped in? You surely must have them somewhere . . ."

"What nonsense! I don't know where they are now . . ."

"When did you take it off your neck? And where did you

do it, since, according to your own statement, you didn't go home?"

"After I'd left Fenya's and was on my way to Perkhotin's —that's when I tore it off my neck."

"In the dark?"

"I didn't need a candle for that. I opened it with one finger and it took me about a second."

"You did it in the street, without scissors?"

"Not in the street—on the square as a matter of fact; and I didn't need scissors—it was an old rag. It tore easily."

"What did you do with it?"

"With the rag? I just threw it away."

"Whereabouts?"

"On the square, where I happened to be, of course! You don't expect me to tell you the exact spot where I was when I threw away the torn rag, do you? Anyway, I don't see how that could help you."

"It is extremely important, Mr. Karamazov. It could be material evidence to back up your testimony. Can't you see that? And who helped you sew the money up in the rag?"

"No one. I did it myself."

"Do you know how to sew, then?"

"It didn't take much skill. Anyway, a soldier has to know how to sew."

"Where did you find the material? I mean the rag you sewed the money in?"

"You must be making fun of me! I can't believe it!"

"I am not making fun of you at all. I have much more important things on my mind, Mr. Karamazov!"

"I really don't remember where I got the rag. I guess I must have picked it up somewhere or other."

"It's something, it would seem, that you should remember."

"I tell you, I don't remember. I may have torn off a piece of my linen or something."

"That could be very helpful to us. Tell me, is it possible that the piece of linen, perhaps an old shirt or something of that sort, from which you tore the rag is still somewhere in the room where you live? What material was the rag, linen or cotton?"

"Who the hell would pay attention to that! Wait . . . I don't think I tore it off anything. I sewed the money up in my landlady's mob-cap. I think it was made of calico . . ."

"Your landlady's mob-cap?"

"Yes, I pinched it from her."

"What do you mean, you pinched it?"

"You see, I pinched her mob-cap because I needed a rag . . . no, I think I needed it to wipe my pen. I helped myself to it because it was all torn and couldn't possibly have been of any use to her. So after that, the torn cap was lying there in my room and when I wanted to tuck the fifteen hundred rubles away, I just sewed it up in that old calico thing that must have been laundered a thousand times."

"And you now have a clear recollection of all that?"

"I don't know how clear it is, but I think I sewed it up in that cap. But who the hell cares about that!"

"In that case, your landlady might remember missing the article in question, mightn't she?"

"I don't think she'd have missed the damned thing. It was an old rag, I tell you, a worthless old rag!"

"And where did you get the needle and thread from?"

"I've had enough of this. I won't answer any more questions."

"It is strange, though, that you have no recollection at all of where you can have dropped the rag."

"Why don't you order the square swept tomorrow? They may find it for you," Mitya snorted. "And now, why don't you leave me alone?" he said in a tired voice. "I can see you don't believe what I've told you; in fact, you never believed a word I said. It's my fault, not yours, though, I should never have trusted you in the first place. Why, oh why, did I degrade myself by revealing my secret to you? And you, you find it just too funny—I can see that by your eyes, you know! You in particular, prosecutor, have driven me to such extremes. So go and sing yourself a triumphant hymn, if you have the stomach for it. Ah, may you be damned, you torturers!"

He lowered his head and put his hands over his face. His questioners were silent. After a minute, Mitya raised his head and looked unseeing in their direction. He looked like a man already hopelessly doomed. He seemed mute and forlorn.

It was time, though, to conclude the preliminary investigation with the interrogation of the witnesses. By now it was already eight o'clock. The candles had been snuffed out a while before. Inspector Makarov and Kalganov, who during the interrogation had kept coming in and out of the room, got up and walked out again. Both the prosecutor and Examining

Magistrate Nelyudov looked very pale and tired. It was a gray, bleak morning, the sky was overcast, and it was raining hard. Mitya gazed blankly toward the window.

"All right if I go and look out the window?" he asked suddenly.

"Please do—of course," the examining magistrate said.

Mitya got up and went over to the window. The rain was pelting down hard against the greenish panes. The muddy road passed just under the window and farther away in the rainy mist stood the black shapes of the poor, unprepossessing wooden houses, looking even blacker and poorer than usual through the rain. Mitya remembered about "golden-haired Phoebus" and his plans to shoot himself when his first bright ray appeared. "I guess it would be easier to go through with it on a morning like this," he thought. He suddenly smiled, waving his hand at his "torturers."

"Gentlemen," he said, "I am quite aware that it's all over for me. But what about her? Tell me, I beg you—she won't be ruined because of me, will she? For she had nothing to do with it at all; she was crazy last night when she cried that it was all her fault. She has absolutely nothing to do with it, nothing. I've been worrying about it all night while sitting here with you, so won't you please tell me what you intend to do with her?"

"I assure you that you have nothing to worry about on that account," the prosecutor replied quickly. "So far we have no reason whatsoever to bother the lady about whom you are so concerned. And I hope it remains that way as the case develops . . . Indeed, we will do everything within our power in that respect. Please put your mind at rest on that score."

"I thank you for that, gentlemen! Let me tell you that I really knew all along that you were fair and honorable men, despite everything. You've taken a load off my mind! . . . Well, what are we going to do now? I am ready for it, whatever it may be."

"We really must move quickly," the prosecutor said. "We must start right away with the interrogation of the witnesses. And since the interrogation must take place in your presence, you . . ."

"But what about having some tea first?" Nelyudov interrupted him. "Don't you think we've earned it?"

They decided to go downstairs on the chance that there would be tea already made, since, if Inspector Makarov was there, he certainly would be having some. Then they could help themselves to a cup and come back and carry on to the end. As for a proper breakfast "with something to go with it perhaps," that would just have to wait until they could take a much longer break. At first Mitya declined Nelyudov's friendly invitation to have a cup of tea too, but later he asked for some himself and drank it down greedily. He looked incredibly worn out and exhausted. It would seem that a man with a powerful constitution like his should have been able to weather a night of drinking, even one full of violent emotions. But now he could hardly sit up in his chair and at times things in the room started swaying and spinning before his eyes. "If it goes on like this, I'll start talking to myself," he thought.

CHAPTER 8

The Testimony of the Witnesses. The Babe

The interrogation of the witnesses started. We will not, however, continue our account of the proceedings in such great detail as heretofore. We will pass over the little speech the examining magistrate made to each new witness about how it was his duty to tell the truth and nothing but the truth, and that he would have to repeat it all under oath later and, moreover, every witness would have to sign his present deposition. We shall point out, however, that the main interest of the interrogators was again centered on that same matter of the three thousand rubles—that is, whether it was three thousand or one-and-a-half thousand that Mitya had spent during his first spree at Mokroye a month before and, again, whether he had spent three or one-and-a-half thousand rubles the night before. Alas, all the statements of the witnesses clashed with Mitya's contention; not one of them supported him; and some of the witnesses even introduced amazing new facts that all but refuted his recent claim once and for all.

The first witness to be interrogated was the innkeeper, Trifon Plastunov. As he stood before the interrogators he showed not the slightest fear, indeed, he had a grim air of outraged indignation against the accused, which, without any doubt, added weight and credibility to his testimony. He answered briefly, with restraint, waited for the interrogators to complete their questions before answering, and obviously thought out his replies. He testified in a firm voice, without hesitation, that Mitya, on his previous spree a month ago, could not possibly have spent less than three thousand rubles and that any of the villagers would confirm that they had heard Mr. Karamazov mention the figure of three thousand himself.

"You should have seen him tossing money to those gypsy girls! I'd say he threw out a good thousand on the gypsies alone."

"I didn't spend even five hundred on them," Mitya commented gloomily, "although I admit I was too drunk to count the money at the time. I wish I had counted it . . ."

Mitya was now sitting, not at the table, but next to it, his back to the curtain. He listened mournfully to the depositions and his sad, tired expression seemed to say: "You can testify whatever you wish. I don't care anymore."

"I say you spent more than a thousand on them, Mr. Karamazov," Trifon brushed off Mitya's protest with great assurance. "You were just tossing money about for no reason and they were picking it up. You know those gypsies— they're all thievish and crooked, a lot of horse thieves . . . They've been driven out of the district since then, or they could have testified themselves how much money they got out of you. And I myself saw the money in your hands— although it's a fact that you didn't give it to me to count, I could tell just by the size of the bundle that there was much more than fifteen hundred rubles there . . . Fifteen hundred rubles, indeed! I've seen money in my time. I know what it looks like. I can tell."

As to the sum spent the previous night, Trifon testified that the first thing Mitya had done upon his arrival was to announce to him that he had brought three thousand rubles like the last time.

"Come, come, Trifon, are you really so sure I told you I had three thousand with me?" Mitya tried to object.

"That's exactly what you said, Mr. Karamazov, and Andrei was there when you said it. Andrei is still here, so you can ask him and see what he says. And in there, in the other room, when you were going around pouring drinks for the singers and dancers, you even said that it was the sixth thousand you were going through here. You must have meant, I guess, including the three you spent here the time before. I know Stepan heard it, and Semyon did too. And I even remember that Mr. Kalganov was standing next to you when you said it, so perhaps he remembers it too . . ."

The prosecutor and the examining magistrate were very much impressed by this testimony about the sixth thousand. They liked this new formulation very much: three and three makes six, so he'd spent three thousand the first time and three again the second time, adding up to six. Everything seemed perfectly clear now.

Then they verified Trifon's testimony by calling in the men he had mentioned: the two villagers Semyon and Stepan, Andrei the coachman, and Kalganov. The two villagers and Andrei confirmed unhesitatingly what Trifon had said. Andrei also told them how Dmitry had asked him during the drive where Andrei thought he, Dmitry Karamazov, would go after he died, to hell or to heaven, and whether he thought they would forgive him in the other world. The prosecutor, who considered himself a very profound psychologist, listened to this with a subtle little smile and demanded that the transcription of Andrei's testimony, including Mitya's question, be added to "the dossier."

When they called him in, Kalganov complied reluctantly, looked sullen and peevish, and spoke to the prosecutor and the examining magistrate as if he were seeing them for the first time in his life, although in fact they were old acquaintances whom he met almost every day. He began by saying that he neither knew anything "of all this," nor had any wish to know. But he had heard about "the sixth thousand" and admitted that he had been standing next to Mitya when Mitya said it. As to the amount of money Mitya had on him, Kalganov refused to make an estimate: "I don't know how much there was." He confirmed that the Poles had cheated at cards. He also confirmed reluctantly, and only after insistent questioning, that, after the Poles had been turned out, Mitya's standing with Grushenka had improved dramatically and she herself had let him understand that she loved him. Of Grushenka, Kalganov spoke with restraint and considerable respect, as if she were a lady of the best society, and he referred to her all the time as Miss Svetlov. Despite Kalganov's obvious distaste at being interrogated, the prosecutor insisted on questioning him at great length, and it was from him that he obtained all the elements that made up what can be described as Mitya's "romance" during that night. Mitya never once intervened in Kalganov's testimony. When he was at last excused, Kalganov walked away in unconcealed indignation.

The Poles were examined too. Although they had gone to

bed in the little room in which they had locked themselves, they had not gone to sleep and, when they heard the authorities arrive, they quickly got up and dressed, for they expected to be called too. They came in looking dignified, although also rather apprehensive. The leader of the two, that is, the little Pole, turned out to be a retired civil servant of the twelfth class, who had served in Siberia as a veterinarian. His name was Musijalowicz. As to Wrublewski, he turned out to be a dentist in private practice.

Although it was Examining Magistrate Nelyudov who questioned them, the Poles, in their ignorance, assumed from the moment they entered the room that Inspector Makarov was the highest-ranking official and therefore addressed their answers to him, calling him "Pan Colonel." It was only after Makarov himself had told them repeatedly that they must address the official who was interrogating them directly and not him that the Poles finally understood. It turned out that their Russian was quite good, apart, perhaps, from the mispronunciation of certain words, and it was even grammatical. When asked about his relations with Grushenka, past and present, Pan Musijalowicz began to speak in a proud and heated tone, which made Mitya lose his temper at once. He shouted that he was not going to allow "this crook" to speak like that in his presence. The Pole immediately drew attention to the word "crook" and demanded that it be entered in the record. This made Mitya fly into a rage again.

"Yes, that's exactly what you are—a damned crook! Go on, write it down if you want to! Whether you do or not, he is still a crook!" Mitya shouted.

Nelyudov had it put in the record, but he displayed considerable tact in dealing with the unpleasant situation: he reprimanded Mitya sternly for his disorderly conduct, but he did not pursue this line of questioning about the romantic aspects of the evening and instead passed quickly on to the essential matter—Mitya's offer of money to Musijalowicz when they went out to the little room. The interrogators were extremely interested to hear that Mitya had offered the Pole three thousand rubles—seven hundred rubles down, the balance of twenty-three hundred to be paid in town in the morning. Musijalowicz testified that, in promising to pay him the balance, Mitya had sworn, giving him his word of honor, that he did not have the whole sum with him here in Mokroye but that he had the money in town. At first Mitya heatedly denied that he had definitely promised to pay the balance in town, but then Wrublewski confirmed the testimony of his fellow Pole and, after thinking hard for a minute, Mitya frowned and finally agreed that the Poles must be right after all, that he had been very excited at the time and could very well have promised them that sum. The prosecutor literally pounced on that statement. According to him, the preliminary investigation clearly established the possibility (as, indeed, was later accepted) that half or a certain portion of the three thousand rubles that had fallen into Mitya's hands might be hidden somewhere in town, or even perhaps in Mokroye, and this disposed of a fact that had been causing the prosecution some difficulty—namely, that Mitya had only eight hundred rubles in his possession. Up till then this had been the only point, albeit not a very important one, in Mitya's favor, and now it was disposed of too!

The prosecutor immediately asked Mitya where he had expected to get the twenty-three hundred rubles he had promised the Poles on his honor when, according to his present statement, he had only fifteen hundred rubles in the first place. To that Mitya replied, without the slightest hesitation, that, instead of the money, he would have offered "that lousy Pole" a formal deed certifying his rights to the Chermashnya estate that he had previously offered to Mrs. Khokhlakov and Samsonov. The prosecutor merely snorted sarcastically at Mitya's "innocence" if he believed that he "could get away with that."

"And did you expect," the prosecutor asked, "that he would be willing to accept that deed instead of twenty-three hundred rubles in cash?"

"Of course he would!" Mitya cried heatedly. "Don't you understand—that way he'd get, not twenty-three hundred rubles, but four thousand; he might even have made six thousand on the deal! As soon as he had the deed in his hand, he would at once have mobilized a whole army of Polish and Jewish lawyers and they'd have managed to get him not just three thousand—they'd have stripped my father of the whole estate!"

It goes without saying that every detail of Musijalowicz's testimony was carefully recorded.

The Poles were excused and their cheating at cards was not mentioned again. The examining magistrate was much too grateful to them and did not wish to complicate matters with such trifles, especially since the whole thing seemed to be just an ordinary argument between people who were drunk.

Besides, there had been so many other scandalous goings-on that night. So the Poles went off, keeping the two hundred rubles in their pockets.

Maximov was next. He approached shyly, with mincing steps, disheveled, and looking very sad. All that time he had been sitting quietly by Grushenka's side. Later Inspector Makarov said that from time to time Maximov had started whimpering, looking at Grushenka and wiping his eyes with a blue-and-white checked handkerchief, and that she had tried to calm and console him. Maximov at once admitted, with tears in his eyes, that, being "so poor," he had accepted ten rubles from Mr. Karamazov, but, he said, he was prepared to give it back. When Nelyudov asked him directly whether he had noticed how much money Mr. Karamazov had on him, since he had had a better chance than anybody else to see it when Dmitry was giving him the ten rubles, Maximov declared without the slightest hesitation: "There was twenty thousand there, sir."

"Tell me, had you ever seen twenty thousand rubles before?" Nelyudov asked him with a smile.

"I certainly had, sir—when my wife mortgaged my little estate. To be precise, though, it was not actually twenty, but seven. She showed me the money from a distance, even boasting about it. It was a very big bundle of bills, and every one of them a rainbow-colored hundred-ruble bill . . ."

They excused him very quickly, and then it was Grushenka's turn. The interrogators were obviously worried about the effect her appearance would have on Mitya, and Nelyudov even muttered a brief admonition to him, to which Mitya responded by slightly inclining his head, thus reassuring him that he would behave. Inspector Makarov himself went to fetch Grushenka. She entered with a hard and distant expression on her face, looking almost composed, and silently sat down in the chair indicated to her, facing the examining magistrate. She was very pale and seemed to be cold, for she kept her beautiful black shawl tightly wrapped about herself. Indeed, she was having the first chills, which were the beginning of a long illness that started that night. Her severe expression, the straightforward, serious look in her eyes, and her composure impressed everyone present; the examining magistrate was even somewhat taken by her. Later, he would tell his friends that it was only then that he fully realized how beautiful she was, for, although he had seen her a few times before, he had thought of her as just another provincial *femme fatale.* "She has the bearing of a lady of the highest society," he once blurted out in the presence of some ladies. They were quite indignant at his remark and called him "a naughty tease," which pleased him no end.

When she came in, Grushenka threw only a quick glance at Mitya, who was watching her in great alarm. But her appearance at once reassured him. After the admonitions and the first routine questions, Nelyudov, somewhat hesitatingly, trying to be as gentlemanly as possible under the circumstances, asked her to describe her relations "with Retired Army Lieutenant Dmitry Karamazov," to which she replied in a quiet, firm voice:

"He was an acquaintance. And it was as an acquaintance that I received him during the past month."

To further probing questions about their relations, she answered plainly and frankly that, although there were moments when she had felt strongly attracted to him, she had not been in love with him, that she was "teasing" him, just like "that poor old man," out of "vile spite," that she knew how desperately jealous Mitya was of his father but that it just "amused" her. She also said that she had never really intended to go to old Karamazov and was only laughing at him.

"This past month I really had no time to be bothered much about either of them; I was waiting for someone else, someone who had once deserted me . . . But I don't think there is any need for you to go into that any further, or any obligation for me to answer such questions, because it is all my private concern."

And the examining magistrate apparently agreed, for once more he dropped his line of questioning and did not insist on the "romantic aspects" of the case. And so he passed directly to the main point—the three thousand rubles. Grushenka confirmed that a month before Mitya had spent three thousand rubles in Mokroye, according to his own admission, although she pointed out that she had not actually counted the money.

"Did he tell you that when you were alone or in the presence of witnesses? Or perhaps you simply heard him tell it to others?" the prosecutor butted in.

Grushenka said he had told it to her, both in the presence of witnesses and when they were alone.

"When you were alone, did he tell it to you once or many times?" the prosecutor wanted to know further. She told him, many times.

The prosecutor was highly pleased with her answers. From further questioning, it transpired that Grushenka knew Dmitry had taken the money from Katerina.

"Now, did you ever hear, during this past month, that he had actually spent only fifteen hundred rubles of the money and kept the other fifteen hundred to himself?"

"No, I never heard that."

Further it was elicited from her that during the past month Mitya had often told her he did not have a kopek to his name but that he expected to get some money from his father.

"And did he ever mention in your presence, even if only vaguely or when he was irritated, that he . . . that he might make an attempt on his father's life?" Nelyudov suddenly let out.

"Oh . . . yes, he did," Grushenka said with a sigh.

"Did he say it once or several times?"

"Several times, when he was angry."

"And did you believe that he would do it?"

"No, I never believed it," Grushenka said firmly; "I knew he was an honorable man."

"Gentlemen!" Mitya suddenly intervened; "I would like permission to say something to Miss Svetlov, right here in your presence."

"Please go ahead," the examining magistrate consented.

"Grushenka," Mitya said, getting up from his chair, "I am not guilty of my father's murder."

As Mitya sat down, Grushenka stood up, turned toward the icon in the corner of the room, and crossed herself devoutly.

"Thank God!" she said in a voice trembling with emotion and, without resuming her seat, turned toward Nelyudov: "You must believe what he has just said. I know him. He can tell a lie sometimes, just for the fun of it or out of stubbornness, but he would never lie against his conscience. When he says something like that, it is always the truth. Believe it!"

"Thank you, Grushenka, you've restored my faith in myself," Mitya said in a quivering voice.

When questioned about how much money he had had on him the previous night, she said she did not know but that she had heard him tell others that he had brought three thousand with him. And as to where that money had come from, he had told her and her alone that he had "stolen" it from Katerina, to which she had answered that he had not stolen it since he would pay it back the next day. But when the prosecutor asked her to specify which money he had had in mind— what he had that night or the three thousand that had been spent on the previous occasion, a month before, she said that she had understood him to mean the money spent on the first occasion.

Finally Grushenka was excused. Nelyudov impulsively announced to her that she was free to return to town any time she liked, that if he could be of any assistance in getting horses or an escort for her, he would do his utmost; he, for his part . . .

"Thank you very much," Grushenka interrupted him with a bow. "I think I'll take Mr. Maximov with me and drop him off at his house. But I'd like to wait here for a while first and find out what you decide about Mr. Karamazov."

She left the room. For a minute or so Mitya looked calm and almost cheerful. But it didn't last. A strange physical weakness came over him, which increased with every moment. In his fatigue, his eyes kept closing. Finally the interrogation of the witnesses came to an end and they began to work on the final draft of the testimony. Mitya got up from his chair, went over to the corner of the room where there was a large trunk covered with a rug, sprawled out on it, and within a second was asleep. He had a peculiar dream, completely inappropriate to the circumstances, time, and place. In his dream he was crossing the steppe, where he had served once long ago in the army, in a cart drawn by a pair of horses and driven by a peasant. The ground was muddy. Mitya was cold. It was early November; it was snowing and the large flakes melted as soon as they touched the ground. The peasant was driving briskly, waving his whip in the air. He was not really old, maybe fifty or so; he had a long, light-brown beard and wore a gray, homespun peasant coat. They came in sight of a village, and as they drew closer he saw that half the huts had been burnt down and there were only charred beams sticking up into the sky. As they entered the village, they had to drive past a long row of peasant women, all of them thin and haggard, with strangely black faces. One especially, at the end of the row, caught his attention. She was bony and very tall; she looked about forty, although she might have been only twenty; and she was holding a baby in her arms, who was crying, probably because the woman's breasts were completely dried up and did not have a drop of milk in them. The baby was crying and crying and stretching out its tiny bare arms, its little fists quite blue from cold.

"What are they crying about? What's the matter?" Mitya inquired as they drove past.

"The babe," the coachman said to him, and it struck Mitya that he said "babe" instead of "baby." It pleased Mitya that this peasant had said "babe" the way peasants do, because it seemed to him there was more warmth and human pity in it.

"But why is it crying?" Mitya insisted stupidly. "Why are its arms bare? Why doesn't she cover them?"

"Because the babe is frozen through and his clothes are frozen, so they can't give him any more warmth now."

"But why, why?" Mitya stupidly persisted in asking.

"The poor people have been burnt out. They have no bread, and they're going about begging for their poor, burnt-out village . . ."

"No, no," Mitya, who still couldn't understand, insisted. "I want you to explain to me why these burnt-out mothers are standing here, why there have to be poor people, why the poor babe must suffer, why the steppe is barren, why people don't embrace and kiss one another, why they don't sing joyful songs, why they look blackened from that black misfortune, why there is nothing to feed the babe."

And although Mitya realized that it was stupid of him to keep on asking like that and that no good would come of it, he felt he had to ask and he had to ask just that way. He also felt a new, unknown fervor welling up in his heart; he felt like weeping; he longed to do something to stop the baby and its blackened, dried-up mother from crying, to stop all tears forever and ever, and he wanted to do it now, right now, without delay, regardless of everything; he wanted it with all the unrestrained passion of a Karamazov.

"And I'm coming with you. I'll never leave you again. We'll walk together all our lives," he heard Grushenka's voice nearby, full of deep emotion.

And his heart caught fire and turned toward a light; he wanted to live now, to live and to walk on and on toward that unknown light that was beckoning to him; he had to start quickly, quickly, right away!

"What? Where?" Mitya cried, opening his eyes, sitting up on the trunk as if he had come to after a fainting fit, and smiling brightly.

The examining magistrate was standing over him, asking him to listen to the final draft of the testimony and to sign it. Mitya realized that he had been asleep for an hour or more. He did not listen to Nelyudov, though; he was wondering how it happened that there was a pillow under his head. He knew it had not been there when he had sunk exhausted onto the trunk.

"Who put this pillow under my head? Who was so kind as to do that?" he exclaimed in rapt gratitude, his voice quivering, as if some extraordinary favor had been granted him.

The kind person was never to be identified. It might have been one of the witnesses, or perhaps the clerk Nelyudov had brought along, who, out of compassion, had placed the pillow under Mitya's tired head. It was as if Mitya's whole soul was shaken by sobs. He got up, walked over to the table, and told them that he would sign anything they wanted.

"I had a good dream," he said in a strange voice. His face looked changed—it was radiant with joy.

CHAPTER 9

They Take Him Away

After Mitya had signed the deposition, the examining magistrate turned to him and solemnly read out to him the Decision: he, the accused, was to be taken into custody pending trial. The Decision read that at such and such a place, on such and such a date, the examining magistrate of such and such a district court, having examined the accused, who was charged with such and such crimes (all the charges were carefully listed), and taking into account the fact that, although he denied the charges, the accused could offer no evidence in his defense, whereas the witnesses (such and such) and the circumstances (such and such) pointed sufficiently to his guilt (in accordance with articles such and such of the Criminal Code), had decided to confine the accused to such and such a prison, to prevent him from evading further investigation, of which decision the accused was notified, with a copy of the notification to be communicated to the district assistant public prosecutor, etc., etc. In short, Mitya was told that, from then on, he was a prisoner and would be taken at once to town to be locked up in a rather unpleasant establishment. Mitya listened to them attentively, then simply shrugged.

"All right then, gentlemen, I'm sure I cannot blame you for it . . . I'm ready to leave any time; I don't suppose there's anything else you want with me."

Nelyudov told Mitya that he would be taken to prison by the rural police officer, Shmertsov, who happened to be there.

"Just a moment," Mitya suddenly interrupted him. "Gentlemen, we are all cruel. We are monsters. We force people to shed tears, mothers and infants," he said with uncontrollable fervor. "But let it be known once and for all that, of all the people in the world, I am the most despicable, the lowest creature. So be it! Every day of my life I have beaten my breast and promised myself to change, but then every day I have done the same vile things again. I understand now that men like me must be struck down by life; they must be caught as in a lasso and bound by an outside force. Without that, I would never have risen by myself! But lightning has struck and I accept the ordeal of the accusation and my public disgrace; I want to suffer and to cleanse myself by suffering! For I may be cleansed some day, may I not, gentlemen? But I want to tell you for the last time: I am not guilty of my father's murder! I accept punishment, not because I killed him, but because I wanted to kill him, and because perhaps I might have killed him if . . . I intend, however, to fight you—I warn you of that—and I shall fight you to the bitter end; after that it will be up to God. Goodby, gentlemen, and please forgive me for having shouted at you during the interrogation; I was still so stupid then . . . In one minute I will be a prison inmate, but now, for that one more minute, I am still Dmitry Karamazov, and it is as a free man that I hold out my hand to you, as I take leave of you and of everyone!"

Mitya's voice quivered and he really made as if to hold out his hand. But Nelyudov, who stood nearest to him, quickly and nervously hid his hands behind his back. Mitya noticed this and shuddered. He dropped his outstretched hand at once.

"The investigation isn't really over yet," Nelyudov muttered, somewhat embarrassed. "We'll continue with it in town and, as far as I am concerned, I'm prepared to wish you the best of luck . . . I mean in obtaining your acquittal . . . I personally feel, Mr. Karamazov, that you are more the victim of unhappy circumstances than a really bad

man . . . All of us here, if I may take the liberty of speaking
for the others too, are prepared to recognize that you are a
basically honorable man, who, however, has unfortunately
been swayed by rather excessive passions . . ."

By the time he had finished speaking, the little figure of
the examining magistrate had become the personification of
majestic dignity. But Mitya had the feeling that this "boy"
could still now, at any moment, catch him by the arm, walk
off into a corner with him, and resume a conversation they
had once had about women. But then, all kinds of incongruous notions may pass through the head even of a criminal
who is being led off to execution.

"Gentlemen," Mitya said, "you have been so kind and
humane to me that I wonder whether you'd allow me to see
her for the last time, to say good-by?"

"Of course, but it must be in our presence . . . otherwise
it would be impossible . . ."

"By all means, please."

They brought Grushenka in. But the farewells were short.
Only very few words were said, and Nelyudov seemed somehow disappointed. Grushenka bowed low to Mitya.

"I've already told you I'll be yours, and I'll be yours forever, wherever they may send you. Good-by, Mitya, you who
have been ruined through no fault of your own."

Her lips quivered and tears poured from her eyes.

"Forgive me, Grusha, for my love, for ruining you with
my love . . ."

Mitya was about to say something else but suddenly
changed his mind and went out. He was at once surrounded
by people, who never took their eyes off him. Outside, by the
front steps, to which Andrei had driven up so dashingly and
with such a clatter in his three-horse cart the night before,
two carts were already waiting. Mavriky Shmertsov, the rural
police officer, a short, thick-set man with a bloated face,
seemed to be irritated at some unexpected difficulty and was
shouting angrily. With uncalled for brusqueness, he told
Mitya to get into one of the carts. "When I used to pay for
his drinks in the tavern, he had a quite different look," Mitya
thought, as he climbed into the cart. The innkeeper Trifon
appeared at the top of the steps. Coachmen, villagers, men,
and women gathered by the gate, staring at Mitya.

"Forgive me, good people!" Mitya suddenly shouted to
them from the cart.

"You forgive us too!" two or three voices called back.

"You, too, Trifon, forgive me!"

But Trifon did not even look at Mitya. He had his back turned to him. Possibly he was too busy. He was fussing about, shouting something . . .

Apparently everything was not in order in the second cart, in which two men with brass badges were to accompany the rural police officer. The little peasant who had been hired to drive the second cart and was putting on his coat was still arguing that Akim should be the one to drive the cart and not him. Everyone was looking for Akim, but he was nowhere to be found. The little peasant argued, begging them to wait for Akim.

"These people nowadays have no shame, Mr. Shmertsov, no shame at all!" Trifon complained. "Akim gave you twenty-five kopeks two days ago, remember? And what did you do with it? You drank it all, didn't you, and now you're shouting! I'm really surprised at your patience with these people —one can never trust them!"

"But what do we need the second cart for, Mavriky?" Mitya tried to interfere. "Can't we go without them? I assure you I'm not planning to attack you or try to escape. You don't have to have an escort, believe me . . ."

"First learn to address me properly!" Shmertsov cut him off fiercely. "I'm not Mavriky to you, remember! And keep your damned advice to yourself!" He seemed to be glad of the opportunity to vent his irritation on Mitya.

Silenced, Mitya flushed all over. The next second he felt very cold. The rain had stopped, but the sky was still murky and overcast, and a sharp wind was blowing straight into his face. "I must have caught a chill," Mitya thought, his shoulders twitching.

Finally the rural police officer climbed into the cart next to Mitya. He sat down heavily and spread out his legs, pushing against Mitya as he installed himself, without appearing to notice it. It is true that Shmertsov was in a foul mood, for he did not like this assignment at all.

"Good-by, Trifon!" Mitya called out again, feeling that this time he was doing so not out of the warmth of his heart, but out of spite, almost against his own will. But this time, again, Trifon did not answer: he stood proudly, his hands behind his back, staring straight at Mitya with a stern and disapproving expression.

"Good-by, Mr. Karamazov, dear fellow, good-by!" Mitya suddenly heard the voice of Kalganov, who had appeared from nowhere. Hatless, he hurried over to the cart to shake hands.

"Good-by, my dear fellow, I'll never forget your generous gesture!" Mitya cried warmly. But the cart moved off, and their hands were separated. The bells jingled—they took Mitya away.

And Kalganov went back into the house, sat down in a corner of the entrance hall, covered his face with his hands, and wept. He sat there, weeping and weeping as if he were still a little boy and not a young man of twenty. Oh, he was almost convinced that Mitya was guilty. "But what kind of people are they, what kind of people!" he repeated incoherently again and again in bitter desolation, verging on despair. "What can I think of these people after this?" At that moment, he didn't even want to go on living: "What's the point?" the young man kept asking himself in distress.

PART FOUR

BOOK X

THE BOYS

CHAPTER 1

Kolya Krasotkin

It was early November. The temperature was eleven degrees below zero (centigrade) and the ground was crusted with ice. It had snowed lightly during the night and a sharp, dry wind was raising a snowy powder and sweeping it along the town's bleak streets and all across Market Square. Although it was no longer snowing, the morning was gray.

Mrs. Krasotkin's house, which, though not large, was very neat inside as well as out, stood a few doors from Plotnikov's grocery store, quite near the square. Krasotkin, a local government official, had been dead for almost fourteen years and his widow, a good-looking woman in her thirties, lived in the snug little house on an independent income. A prim but cheerful lady, she led a quiet, respectable life. She had lost her husband when she was only eighteen, after only a year or so of marriage and soon after bearing him a son. Since her husband's death, she had devoted herself entirely to bringing up her little Kolya and, although she loved him dearly, she had certainly had far more trouble than joy from him during those fourteen years, trembling with fear almost every day lest he catch cold, fall ill, do something naughty, climb a chair and fall off, and so on. When Kolya went first to elementary school and later to high school, his mother began to study all the subjects along with him in order to help him with his homework and go over his lessons with him; she arranged to meet all his teachers and their wives, and was nice to the boys in Kolya's class in an attempt to gain their favor so they would not tease her Kolya, be rough with him, or push him around. Indeed, she went so far that the boys ended up by teasing Kolya precisely because of her, taunting him with being a "sissy" and a "mummy's boy." But it soon turned out that Kolya could take care of himself very well. He was not easily frightened and quickly acquired a reputation in his class for being "terribly strong." And in fact he was very agile, persevering, daring, and enterprising. He was also a good student and some of the boys went so far as to say that, in arithmetic and world history, he could show up even their teacher, Dardanelov. But, although he seemed to look down on those around him, Kolya was a good friend and never tried to bully the others; he accepted the respect of his comrades as his due, but he was friendly with them. Above all, he had a sound idea of how much he could get away with and when it was time to stop; in his relations with the school authorities, he never went beyond a certain limit, after which an infraction of discipline would be considered disorder, rebellion, and lawlessness, and no longer tolerated. And yet he certainly was always ready to play a mischievous prank like any wild street urchin, and not just a prank but something unbelievably clever, something that would leave everybody gaping open-mouthed, something extra-special, for which he would be particularly admired. In fact, he was extremely vain. He had even succeeded in getting the upper hand over his mother and at times treated her almost despotically. She obeyed him and had done so for quite a while already; there was only one thing that worried her greatly, and that was the idea that the boy did not really love her. The idea kept coming back to her that Kolya was an "unfeeling" boy, and on occasion she would cry hysterically and bitterly reproach him for his coldness. The boy disliked these scenes very much and the shriller her demands for a show of affection became, the less responsive he was. But this was not deliberate on his part; he could not help it—that was just the way he was. And she was wrong about his feelings: he did love his mother and disliked only what he called in his schoolboy lingo "that sickening slobbery stuff."

There was a bookcase in the house containing a number of books left by Kolya's father, and the boy, who was fond of reading, had read a few of these. This did not worry his mother, although she was a little puzzled to see Kolya spending hours and hours at the bookcase, reading some book or other, instead of playing with the other boys. So Kolya had read a few books that, at his age, he should not have been allowed to read.

Lately, it had happened that this boy, who before had always known where to stop, had begun to do things that really worried his mother. It is true there was nothing particularly morally reprehensible about the things Kolya did, but there was something surprisingly wild and reckless in his behavior. During the past summer holidays, for instance, mother and son had spent a week in July with a distant relative who lived in a neighboring district, about fifty miles away. The relative's husband worked at the railway station there. It was the nearest railway station to our town and, incidentally, the one where, a month later, Ivan Karamazov was to catch his train for Moscow. Well, when the Krasotkins arrived there, Kolya began by making a thorough study of the workings of the railway: he visited the station and the tracks, examined the train schedules, etc., expecting that this new knowledge of his would impress the boys tremendously when he went back to school. It so happened that some other boys were also staying in the neighborhood of the railway station and soon they all became acquainted. They ranged in age between twelve and fifteen, six or seven boys altogether, two of them from our town. So the boys played together, showing off to each other, and on the fourth or fifth day of Kolya's visit he—almost the youngest of them and for that reason somewhat looked down upon by the others—made a stupid and incredible two-ruble bet with them. Either out of vanity or because of his complete fearlessness, he bet them that he would lie down at night on the track in the space between the rails and stay there while the 11 p.m. train thundered over him at full speed. First of all, though, they made a thorough investigation and found that it really was possible to flatten oneself out between the rails so that the train would pass over you without touching you; but to actually lie still while the thing rattled deafeningly over your head—that was something else again! Kolya boasted that he could do it. At first they just laughed at him and called him a little liar and a silly braggart, but that only made him all the more determined to go through with it. It had all started, probably, because the fifteen-year-olds looked down on him because he was just "a kid" and would hardly accept him as one of the gang, and this stung his pride quite unbearably.

So they agreed that they would meet in the evening about a mile from the station, to give the train a chance to gather speed. All the boys went. It was a moonless, almost completely black night. As the hour drew close, Kolya lay down between the rails. The other five boys, who were betting with him, waited in the bushes around the embankment, their hearts pounding with apprehension and remorse. At last, in the distance, they heard the rumble of the train leaving the station. Two red lights shone in the darkness and the rattle of the approaching monster increased. "Run! Get off the rails! Hurry!" the boys yelled in terror from under the bushes. But it was too late. The train was already there. And then it was gone. The boys rushed over to Kolya. He lay there motionless. They started pulling him and shaking him, but he suddenly got up by himself and silently walked down from the embankment. He told the boys he had pretended to have fainted just to scare them, although the truth was that he had really fainted, as he admitted to his mother much later. After that exploit, he acquired a reputation as a "desperado" once and for all. He went back to the station and returned home, his face white as a sheet. The next day he was a bit feverish, but otherwise he was very cheerful and pleased with himself.

Eventually the story reached our town and the school principal's office. But Mrs. Krasotkin pleaded with the school authorities not to take any disciplinary action against her son and, in the end, thanks to the teacher Dardanelov, who was highly regarded and respected by his colleagues and the principal, succeeded in having the matter dropped. Dardanelov was a middle-aged bachelor who, by a strange coincidence, had been in love with Mrs. Krasotkin for many years and who, about a year before, had most delicately and with a sinking heart offered her his hand in marriage. She had unhesitatingly turned him down, declaring that it would be a betrayal of her darling son, although from certain mysterious signs Dardanelov might have observed that he was not altogether unattractive to this charming widow, who was such an overdutiful and tender mother. Now Kolya's crazy act seemed to have improved Dardanelov's standing, and, because of his efforts on the boy's behalf, he was made to understand that there might be some hope for him after all, although as yet a very remote hope. But then Dardanelov himself was a paragon of chastity and delicacy in these matters, so this was quite sufficient for the time being to make him a perfectly happy man. He was also very fond of the boy, although he would have considered it undignified, in view of the circumstances, to try and gain his affection and he was always strict and demanding with him in class. But Kolya himself was anxious to keep his distance from the teacher; he always did his homework well, was second in his class, and treated Dardanelov coldly; many boys were still convinced that he was good enough in world history to show up Dardanelov himself. And, indeed, when Kolya once asked the teacher who was the founder of Troy, Dardanelov replied in general terms about the migration of peoples, about the difficulty of discerning facts in such ancient times, about the creation of legends, without giving Kolya a precise answer, i.e., without naming the person or group of persons who had founded Troy. Indeed, for some reason he considered Kolya's question idle and irrelevant. The boys, however, remained convinced that Dardanelov simply did not know who the founder of Troy was. Kolya, on the other hand, had read about the founding of Troy in Smaragdov's book, which he had found in his father's bookshelf. In the end, every boy in the class became terribly anxious to know who had founded Troy, but Kolya would not reveal his secret, and his scholarly reputation was well established.

After the incident on the railroad track, there was a change in Kolya's relations with his mother. When Anna Krasotkin learned about Kolya's exploit, she almost went insane. She had recurring fits of hysterics for days on end. Kolya was very frightened and swore to his mother that he would never do such a thing again. He swore it, as his mother demanded, by the memory of his father, kneeling before an icon, and on that occasion the fearless, "manly" Kolya burst into tears out of "slobbery sentimentality," after which mother and son had several joint sobbing fits, crying in each other's arms. The following day, however, Kolya awoke as "unfeeling" as before, although he was somewhat quieter, graver, less brazen, and rather dreamy. True, six weeks or so later, he again got into trouble and this time his name became known to our justice of the peace. The new prank was, however, of a very different nature; it was quite innocent, indeed, foolish, and besides, as it turned out later, it was not even of Kolya's direct doing; he was only involved in it. But more of this later.

In the meantime Mrs. Krasotkin kept worrying and suffering, and the more she worried, the stronger Dardanelov's hopes grew. It must be noted that Kolya saw and guessed how Dardanelov felt and it goes without saying that he despised him no end for "that sentimental stuff." Once he was even tactless enough to express his scorn to his mother, hinting to her that he, Kolya, was very well aware of what Dardanelov was after. However, after the railroad track adventure, his attitude toward this matter also changed and he no longer made hints of that sort. This his sensitive mother noticed, and she was tremendously grateful. But now, if Dardanelov's name happened to come up in conversation with visitors in Kolya's presence, the poor woman would blush like a rose while Kolya would pointedly look out of the window, or examine his boots to see if they needed repairing, or impatiently call Perezvon, a large, shaggy, mangy dog which he had found somewhere a month before and had kept secretly at home, for some reason not wanting any of his schoolmates to see it. He bullied the animal terribly, teaching it all kinds of tricks, and reducing it to such a state that the poor beast howled for hours on end when Kolya was away at school and, when he came back, squealed crazily with delight, stood on its hind legs, lay down and pretended to be dead, and so on, repeating all the tricks it had been taught without being ordered to, just out of overwhelming gratitude and love for its master.

I believe I have forgotten to mention that Kolya Krasotkin was the one whom Ilyusha Snegirev, the boy we have already met, had stabbed in the side with a penknife when the boys were teasing him by calling his father "back-scrubber."

CHAPTER 2

The Children

And so, on that frosty, windy November morning, Kolya Krasotkin was at home. It was a Sunday and there was no school. It was already past eleven and he had to go out on some "most important business." But it so happened that he was all alone in the house, its only guardian, as it were, since all the grown-ups had been forced, owing to a peculiar combination of circumstances, to leave the house. At the other end of the house were rooms that Mrs. Krasotkin rented to an old friend of hers, a doctor's wife, who lived there with her two small children. The doctor himself had left a year or so before for Orenburg, then he had moved to Tashkent, and now, for more than six months, he had not been heard from at all. Had it not been for her friendship with Kolya's mother, the abandoned woman would have cried herself dry in her misery. And then, to top off everything, Katerina, the only servant of the doctor's wife, had just the night before taken her poor mistress completely by surprise by announcing to her that she was going to have a baby before morning. How it happened that no one had noticed anything before was something of a wonder. The doctor's wife decided to take Katerina, while there was still time, to a certain establishment that was run by a midwife in our town and that dealt with such emergencies. Since she was very attached to her servant, she immediately hired a carriage, drove the girl there, and, moreover, stayed with her to look after her. In the morning, somehow or other, she also had to have the friendly help of Mrs. Krasotkin, who apparently had influence with someone or other who could be of assistance. So the two ladies were out. Mrs. Krasotkin's own maid, Agafia, was shopping at the market, so Kolya had been left alone in the house to look after the two little children, a boy and a girl. Kolya did not mind at all. He ordered Perezvon to lie down in the hall and pretend he was dead; for just that reason he would give two loud, ingratiating taps on the floor with his tail every time Kolya came by while making his rounds, but, alas, there was no releasing whistle. Instead, Kolya glared sternly at the wretched beast, who relapsed obediently into his self-induced paralysis. But what worried Kolya was the "kids." He had, of course, nothing but the utmost scorn for Katerina's unexpected adventure, but he was very fond of the abandoned children and had already taken them a children's book. Nastya, the eight-year-old girl, could read very well, and her seven-year-old brother, Kostya, liked to listen when she read to him. There were many ways, of course, in which Kolya could have amused them more, such as standing them up side by side and making them do soldiers' drill, or hiding from them and making them look for him all over the house. He had often played with them like that before and did not mind doing it at all. In fact, rumors about it had reached his classmates and there was even gossip going around that Krasotkin played "horsey" with his little lodgers, that he galloped around and even held his head sideways as if he were the side-horse of a troika. But Kolya proudly parried this talk by saying that it would have been, indeed, pretty childish of him if he had insisted on playing "horsey" with other thirteen-year-olds like himself—"particularly at our age"—but he obviously did it to amuse the little kids, because he was fond of them, and he did not have to account to anyone for his feelings. For their part, the kids worshipped him.

Now, however, he had other things on his mind than playing with them. He had some very important and even somewhat mysterious business to attend to. But time was running short and Agafia, who was to look after the children as soon as she came in, had not yet returned from market. He had already gone down the hall several times, entered the rooms of the doctor's wife, and glanced worriedly at the children who, still sitting obediently over the book, smiled broadly at him each time he came in, hoping he would do something very funny and fantastic. But Kolya was much too worried to stay and play with them. When it struck eleven, Kolya furiously decided that "if that damned Agafia isn't back in ten minutes, I'll just go out without waiting for her." He thought he would make the kids promise him not to be frightened to be left alone for a short while, not to cry, and not to make a mess. As he was thinking of this, he put on his quilted winter jacket with its fur collar, strapped his schoolbag across his shoulder, and, despite his mother's instructions that "in this cold you must never go out without your overshoes," looked at them with scorn as he passed them by. When Perezvon saw his master all dressed up like that, he began beating his tail excitedly on the floor, his whole body shaking nervously, and he even emitted a tiny plaintive howl. Seeing this great impatience, Kolya thought that he must give Perezvon a lesson in discipline, so, despite his hurry, he stood there for a whole minute with his eyes fixed on the dog. When he finally whistled, the dog jumped up madly, leaping about in front of Kolya in endless delight. Kolya then went out into the hall and opened the door of the room where the children were. They were still sitting at their little table, although instead of reading they were now arguing about something or other. These two often argued with each other about all sorts of problems of everyday life and Nastya, the older of the two, always came up with the clinching argument. When, thus silenced, Kostya still felt his sister was wrong, he would appeal to Kolya, whose verdict was final and could not be appealed further. Kolya was curious to hear what they were arguing about this time, so he stopped by the door for a while to listen to them. Seeing that he was listening, the children went on arguing with even greater zest.

"I'll never, never, never believe it," Nastya lisped heatedly. "It's not true that midwives find babies in vegetable gardens among the cabbages. It's winter now, so there are no cabbage beds at all, and so the old woman couldn't have brought a little girl to Katerina."

"Whew!" Kolya whistled to himself.

"Or perhaps they do bring babies from somewhere, but then only to people who are married."

Kostya stared at his sister. He was thinking hard.

"You're silly," he said in the end, firmly and without any excitement. "What kind of baby can Katerina have since she isn't married?"

Nastya became very angry.

"You don't understand anything," she cut him off irritatedly. "She may have a husband but he's in jail now. So she could have a baby all right."

"Does she really have a husband in jail?" the practical Kostya inquired gravely.

"Or do you know what?" Nastya interrupted him, hurriedly discarding and completely forgetting her original hypothesis. "She doesn't have a husband. You're right. But she does want to get married and she's been thinking and thinking and thinking about a husband, and so she got him in the end . . . I mean not the husband, but the baby."

"Oh, so that's how it is," Kostya said, finally convinced. "Why didn't you tell me that in the first place?"

"Hey, kids," Kolya said, stepping into the room, "what a dangerous lot you are!"

"I see Perezvon is with you," Kostya said with a wide grin, trying to snap his fingers to call the dog.

"Listen, kids, I'm in trouble," Kolya started in a serious tone. "You must help me. It seems pretty clear that Agafia has broken her leg, for I can't think of any reason why she's not back yet, and I absolutely must go out. Will you let me go?"

The children exchanged worried glances. Their grinning faces fell, although they were still not quite sure what Kolya was driving at.

"You won't run wild after I leave, will you? You won't climb on top of the cupboard and break your legs, or start crying because you're frightened to be alone in the house, will you?"

A look of distress appeared on the children's faces.

"And if you promise to be good, I'll show you something very interesting: a little brass cannon that you can fire with real powder."

The children's faces cleared at once.

"Show us the little cannon!" said Kostya, who was now beaming.

Kolya plunged his hand into his bag and came up with a little bronze cannon that he put on the table.

"I knew you would want to see it. Look, it has little wheels, see!" Kolya rolled the toy cannon on the table. "And it can fire too—I could load it with shot and fire it."

"Would it kill somebody?"

"Sure, it'd kill anybody. All you have to do is to train the gun on somebody."

He explained to the children where to put the powder charge and where to roll in the shot. He showed them the little hole for priming and explained to them about the recoil. The children watched and listened with immense curiosity. Somehow, what struck their imagination most was the recoil.

"Do you have any powder?" Nastya asked.

"Yes."

"I want to see it," she said with an imploring smile.

Kolya's hand dove into the satchel once again and emerged with a little vial that contained real powder. And he also had some shot wrapped in a piece of paper. He opened the vial and shook some powder out onto the palm of his hand.

"I only hope there's no fire around, otherwise we'll all be blown up and killed," he said to impress them.

The children now looked at the powder with an awe which increased their fascination still more. Kostya, however, was more interested in the shot.

"The shot doesn't burn, does it?" he asked.

"No, the shot doesn't burn."

"I'd like to have some shot. Please give me some," Kostya said in a tiny, ingratiating voice.

"All right, I'll give you some shot, but you mustn't show it to your mother until I come back, for she may think it's powder and just about die of fright and give you a big spanking."

"Mummy never spanks us," Nastya remarked.

"I know she doesn't. I just said that because it sounded good. And you must never hide things from your mummy, except this time, and only until I come back. And so, kids, is it all right with you if I go now? You won't be afraid to stay alone and you won't start crying, will you?"

"Weeee will . . ." Kostya drawled out, preparing to cry.

"Yes, yes, we will cry. We'll cry for sure," Nastya rattled off quickly and worriedly.

"Ah, children, children, what an impossible age! Well, I suppose I'm doomed to sit with you for God knows how long. And it's getting really late."

"I want you to tell Perezvon to pretend to be dead!" Kostya said.

"Well, I guess I'll have to bring Perezvon into this too. Perezvon, here!" And Kolya proceeded to make the dog do all the tricks he knew. The shaggy, smoky-gray mongrel was blind in the right eye and his left ear was peculiarly split down the middle. He yelped and jumped, begged and walked on his hind legs, lay on his back with his paws pointing at the ceiling, stretched himself out motionless as if he were dead.

As Perezvon was performing his last trick, the door opened and Agafia, a fat, pockmarked woman of forty, appeared. She had returned from market with a sack full of provisions. She stood in the doorway looking at Perezvon. Although he had been waiting for the servant so eagerly, Kolya did not interrupt the performance and kept Perezvon dead until he decided it was long enough. At last Kolya whistled and the dog leapt up and started jumping about, elated at having done his duty so well.

"Look at that dog . . ." Agafia muttered.

"And what happened to you?" Kolya said sternly. "These women, you can never rely on them."

"Women, indeed, you little puppy!"

"Are you calling me a puppy!"

"Yes, puppy! And if I'm late, it's none of your business," Agafia replied gruffly, although she seemed to enjoy an exchange like this with her mistress's lively young son.

"Listen, you irresponsible old woman," Kolya said, getting up, "I want you to swear to me on everything that is sacred to you in this world, plus something else to make it a bit stronger, that you'll keep an eye on these children here while I'm away."

"Why should I swear to you of all people?" Agafia said, laughing. "I'll look after them anyway."

"No, that won't do. I won't leave the house until you swear to me on the eternal salvation of your soul."

"All right, so stay home, what do I care? Besides, it's cold out. You'd be better off staying in."

"Kids," Kolya said, "this woman will look after you until

I come back. Your mummy may be here before me, because it's high time she was back too. Besides, Agafia will feed you. Will you give them something to eat, Agafia?"

"Perhaps."

"Good-by, then, children. I'm leaving you with a clear conscience. And you, woman," he said in an undertone as he passed Agafia, "I just hope you won't stuff their heads with the usual stupid explanations about what happened to Katerina. Try to spare their tender years. Here, Perezvon!"

"Ah, get out of here, you," Agafia snapped at him with real annoyance now. "You're so stupid sometimes—you should get a good hiding for saying things like that."

CHAPTER 3

The Schoolboys

But Kolya wasn't listening to her. He was free to leave at last. He went out of the gate, looked around, twitched his shoulders, mumbled, "Brrr, it's freezing!" and walked quickly down the street. Soon he turned to the right into a narrow lane that led toward Market Square, stopped in front of the last house but one before the square, took a whistle out of his pocket, and blew it as if giving a prearranged signal. In a second a red-cheeked eleven-year old boy, dressed in a smart quilted coat, came dashing out of the gate. It was Smurov, a boy who was still in the lower school, that is, two years behind Kolya. He was the son of a rather well-off civil servant and it seemed that his parents strongly disapproved of his having anything to do with Kolya Krasotkin, whose dangerous escapades were well known in town. So Smurov must have dashed out of the house without the knowledge of his parents. If the reader still remembers, we met this Smurov about two months earlier when, with the other boys, he was throwing stones across the canal at Ilyusha; it was he who told Alyosha Karamazov about Ilyusha.

"I was waiting for you for more than an hour, Krasotkin," Smurov said, as the boys walked toward the square.

"I know I'm late. I was held up. Won't your parents give you a good whipping for coming out with me?"

"What are you talking about? My parents don't whip me! So you've brought Perezvon with you too."

"Right."

"Are you taking him there too, then?"

"Right."

"Ah, I wish it was Juchka instead!"

"What's the point of wishing—it's impossible. Juchka doesn't exist. Juchka has vanished into the darkness of the unknown!"

"But couldn't we pretend . . ." Smurov said, stopping suddenly. "Look, since Ilyusha says that Juchka was shaggy and smoky-gray, just like Perezvon, why can't we say this *is* Juchka? Perhaps he'll believe us."

"Listen, boy, avoid lying, even for a good cause. I hope, by the way, you didn't tell anyone there about my coming, did you?"

"God forbid. I understand, you know. But I still don't think Perezvon will do. His father, the Captain, the back-scrubber, you know, well, he said he'd bring him a pup today, a real mastiff puppy with a black nose. He thinks that will make Ilyusha feel better, but I doubt it."

"And how's Ilyusha feeling?"

"Not well, not at all well. I think it's consumption he has. His head is completely clear, but he can't breathe too well—it sounds terrible. The other day he said he wanted to get up, so they dressed him and put on his shoes, and he tried to walk, but he couldn't even stand up, kept falling over all the time. So he said to his father: 'I told you before I couldn't walk in these shoes. They're no good anymore.' You see, he thought he couldn't walk because of the shoes, but it's simply that he has no strength left. He won't last another week. Dr. Herzenstube comes to see him every day. They are rich now. They have pots of money."

"Ah, the pigs!"

"Who're pigs?"

"The doctors, the whole lousy medical profession in general and every one of them in particular. I just don't believe in medicine—I say it's useless. I'll make a complete study of it later. But what's all this tear-jerking stuff that's going on? I understand your whole class visits him now?"

"It's not the whole class—only about ten of us. Someone visits him every day. It's nothing."

"The one who surprises me in all this is Alexei Karamazov. Why, his brother is going on trial tomorrow for such an awful crime, but he himself seems to be able to spend most of his time playing sentimental games with little boys."

"There's nothing sentimental about it. Anyway, if that's

how you feel, why are you going there yourself to make it up with Ilyusha?"

"Make it up? That's a ridiculous way of putting it. Anyway, I won't allow anyone to analyze my actions."

"But Ilyusha will be very happy to see you! He has no idea you're coming. Tell me—why did you refuse to come until now?" Smurov suddenly asked heatedly.

"Now look here, that's none of your business, my boy. I'm going now because I've decided for myself that I should go, whereas all of you were dragged there by Alexei Karamazov. So you can see there's quite a difference. Besides, perhaps I'm not planning to make it up with him. What makes you so sure of that? What a stupid expression, really."

"It was not Karamazov at all. It was simply that we felt like going. Of course, at first, we went with Karamazov. And there was nothing so stupid about it either. The father was terribly happy when we came. You know, I think he'll go insane when Ilyusha dies. And he can see Ilyusha's dying. But he's very glad that we've become friends with Ilyusha now. Once Ilyusha asked about you, but he never said anything more after that. He just asked and nothing more. I'm sure his father will either go mad or hang himself. Why, even before, he behaved like a madman. You know, he's a good and honorable man and it was all a mistake. The whole thing was really the fault of that terrible father-killer who beat him up."

"Still, Alexei Karamazov is a riddle to me. Oh, I could have made his acquaintance long ago, but there are times when I like to be proud. I also have a certain opinion of him that I must first check out."

Kolya lapsed into dignified silence. Smurov fell silent too. He admired Kolya tremendously and would never have thought of considering himself Kolya's equal. He had been extremely curious when Kolya had told him that he had suddenly decided to go and see Ilyusha precisely today. Why today? There must be some kind of mystery! They crossed Market Square, in which, that day, there were many carts from the surrounding villages and a lot of live fowl. The town women stood in their closed stalls, selling articles ranging from thread to pretzels. Such Sunday markets are referred to rather naively as "fairs" in our town and there are several such "fairs" in the course of a year. Perezvon trotted along in high spirits, constantly zigzagging right and left to take a good sniff at something or other, to say nothing of his sniffing exchanges with other dogs, which he performed according to all the proper rules of courtesy.

"I like to look at things realistically," Kolya suddenly said, breaking the silence. "Tell me, Smurov, have you noticed how dogs sniff each other? It seems to be some law of their nature."

"It's a funny law too."

"You're wrong. There's nothing funny or ridiculous about it or about anything that's natural; it may only look that way to man because of his own prejudiced ideas. If dogs could reason and criticize, I'm sure they'd find as much or even more to laugh at in the social relations of their human masters. And I say that because I'm absolutely convinced that there's much more stupidity among us than among them. That's Rakitin's idea, and a great idea too. I'm a socialist, you know."

"What's a socialist?"

"It's when all people are equal and everything is owned in common, when there's no more marriage and when everyone can choose his own religion and the laws he likes, and all the rest of it. But you're still too young to understand . . . Isn't it cold though?"

"Yes, it is. It's twelve below freezing. My father looked at the thermometer earlier today."

"Tell me, Smurov, have you noticed that when it's, say, fifteen or even eighteen below freezing in the winter it never seems as cold as now when it's only twelve below and there's practically no snow. That shows that people are not used to the cold yet. For human beings, habit is the prime mover . . . Look at that funny peasant!"

Kolya pointed to a tall, kindly-looking peasant in a sheepskin jacket, who stood next to his cart clapping his gloved hands to keep warm. The man's long, light-brown beard was covered with hoar-frost.

"Your beard is frozen!" Kolya said teasingly as he passed near him.

"Many people's beards are," the peasant answered sententiously.

"Don't annoy him," Smurov said.

"Don't worry. He doesn't mind. He's a nice fellow. Good-by, Matthew."

"Good-by, kid."

"Are you really Matthew?"

"That's right—as if you didn't know."

"I didn't. I just guessed."

"You're smart. I bet you're a high-school kid."

"I am."

"Do they flog you?"

"Well, not really . . . Just now and then."

"Does it hurt?"

"It sure does, sometimes."

"That's just the way life is," the peasant said with a deep sigh.

"Good-by, Matthew."

"Good-by, kid. You're a nice kid, you know."

The boys walked on.

"Why did you lie to him and say they flog us?" Smurov asked.

"I wanted to make him feel better."

"Why should it make him feel better?"

"You know, Smurov, it's tiring when people keep asking questions on and on, the way you do. There are things that are hard to explain. Well, according to the peasant's idea, a schoolboy is someone who is flogged and that's the way it should be. 'What kind of a schoolboy is he if he isn't flogged,' he thinks. So if I told him they don't flog us, he would have actually been disappointed. But don't try to understand it—you won't anyway, for one has to know how to talk to the uneducated."

"Only please don't go provoking people or we'll get into trouble, like that time with the goose, remember?"

"Why, are you scared?"

"Don't laugh, Kolya. I swear, I'm really scared. My father was furious that time and he absolutely forbade me to go around with you."

"Stop worrying, then. Nothing will happen this time. Hey, Natasha, how are you?" Kolya called out to a woman who stood under the awning of her stall.

"Why do you call me Natasha? I'm Maria," she said. She was still a youngish woman.

"That's great. I'm glad you're Maria. Good-by then."

"Ah, the little shrimp! He's still wet behind the ears and he's already getting ideas!"

"I'm sorry, I have no time today. You'll tell me about it next Sunday!" Kolya said, waving his arms to keep her off, as if she were pestering him.

"And what is it I'll tell you next Sunday, you saucy kid? It was you who was pestering me, remember!" the woman shouted. "What you need is a good beating, that's what; who do you think you are—going around insulting people, you impudent brat, you?"

Other market women around Maria burst out laughing. Then suddenly an angry man came rushing out from the nearby arcade. He was a merchant's clerk who had come to the fair from another town. He was still quite young, had a pale, pockmarked face and curly, dark-brown hair. He wore a long blue coat and a peaked cap. He seemed to be in a peculiar state of stupid excitement and came toward Kolya threatening him with his fist.

"I know you!" the fellow said angrily; "I know you all right!"

Kolya looked at him closely but could not remember ever having seen the fellow before, let alone having had a row with him. But he had been in so many street rows that he did not really expect to remember every one of them.

"So what do you know about me?" he asked sarcastically.

"I know you!" the clerk kept repeating idiotically; "I know you, I know you!"

"So good for you! Anyway, good-by, I have no time to waste."

"So why are you looking for trouble?" the fellow shouted. "I know you—you're looking for trouble again! I know you!"

"What I'm looking for is none of your business, mister," Kolya said, stopping again and looking the fellow up and down.

"What do you mean, it's none of my business?"

"It just isn't."

"So whose business is it? Whose? Tell me, whose?"

"It's Trifon Nikitich's business, not yours."

"And who is Trifon Nikitich?" the man asked, staring at Krasotkin in idiotic amazement, although he was still shaking with anger. Kolya slowly measured him from head to toe.

"Have you been to the Church of the Ascension?" he asked him severely.

"What church? Why? No, I haven't," the fellow said, slightly taken aback.

"And do you know Sabaneyev?" Kolya asked him even more sternly.

"But who's Sabaneyev?"

"Well, you can go to hell then!" Kolya suddenly cried, abruptly turning away and walking off quickly with an air of disgust, as if he could not stand one second longer the company of a freak who didn't know who Sabaneyev was.

"Hey, wait, you! Who's Sabaneyev?" the clerk shouted, recovering from his surprise and seeming very worried now. "What was he talking about?" he said, turning to the women, who had been watching the scene. The women burst out laughing.

"What a funny brat," a woman said.

"But who is that Sabaneyev he was talking about?" the clerk insisted, still gesticulating angrily.

"That must be the Sabaneyev who used to work for the Kuzmichevs, I guess," one of the women suggested.

The clerk gaped at her.

"Did you say Kuzmichev?" another woman said. "His name is Kuzma, not Trifon. The boy said his name was Trifon Nikitich, didn't he?"

"I say that it was neither Trifon nor Sabaneyev, but Chizhov," said a third woman, who until then had been listening intently in silence. "His full name is Alexei Ivanovich Chizhov."

"That's right, it's Chizhov, all right," a fourth woman said with assurance.

The man kept looking in bewilderment from one woman to another.

"But why did he ask me that? Why?" he cried in despair. "Why did he ask me, 'Do you know Sabaneyev?' And who the hell knows who Sabaneyev is?"

"You're really slow in understanding, fellow!" one of the women cried impatiently. "How many times do we have to tell you that it was not Sabaneyev, it was Chizhov, Alexei Ivanovich Chizhov, that's who it was. Do you get it now?"

"And who's Chizhov? Tell me, if you know so much."

"That tall fellow with the long hair; he had a stall here in the summer."

"But what's Chizhov got to do with me, my good women?"

"And how the hell do you expect us to know what he has to do with you! I thought you'd know what you wanted him for, since you're the one who's doing all the yelling. The boy said it to you, not to us, you fool. Or do you really not know who he is?"

"Who?"

"Chizhov."

"Damn Chizhov, and damn you too! I'll go and give that boy a good hiding! I think he was just pulling my leg!"

"He's going to give a hiding to Chizhov! Perhaps he'll give you a hiding. You're a fool, fellow, that's what you are."

"I didn't say I'd beat up Chizhov, you spiteful woman. I said I'd beat up that saucy brat! I'll teach him to laugh at me."

The women roared with laughter.

By that time, Kolya was already far away, walking jauntily along with an air of triumph. Smurov, walking beside him, kept looking back at the shouting group behind. He, too, felt happily excited, although he was still worried that eventually Kolya would get him into trouble.

"Who's that Sabaneyev you asked him about?" Smurov inquired, foreseeing the answer.

"Do you think I know? They'll be shouting and arguing about him until evening now. I like to stir up fools, whatever social class they belong to. Now, look at that peasant over there—what a lump! You know, they say there's no one stupider than a stupid Frenchman, but I maintain that many Russians could challenge that statement. Look at that pudding face, for instance, isn't it written all over his face that the man's an idiot?"

"Leave him alone, Kolya. Let's go."

"Not on your life, chum, watch me now . . . Hey, you, fellow! Good-morning!"

The thick-set peasant had already passed them. He was walking slowly and it looked as if, early as it was, he already had a few drinks in him. He had a plain round face and a graying beard. He stopped, turned back, and looked at Krasotkin.

"Well, good-morning, if you mean it," he drawled unhurriedly.

"And what if I don't mean it?" Kolya said, laughing.

"If you don't mean it, that's fine too. It's all right with me. There's nothing wrong with having fun."

"I'm sorry, friend, I was just joking."

"That's all right. God bless you, boy."

"But what about you? Do you forgive me?"

"Yes, sure, you're all forgiven, boy. Run along now."

"Why, you are a clever peasant, aren't you?"

"Cleverer than you, boy."

"I don't think so," Kolya said, slightly taken aback.

"Oh, you can bet on it, boy."

"Well, perhaps you're right, after all."

"So you see."

"Good-by, then, peasant."

"Good-by, boy."

"There are all kinds of peasants," Kolya told Smurov when they had walked on in silence for a while, "so I couldn't really know in advance that I'd come across a smart one. But I'm always prepared to acknowledge intelligence when I find it in people."

In the distance, the cathedral clock struck eleven-thirty. The boys walked faster. They still had quite a long way to go to Captain Snegirev's house and they hardly spoke the rest of the way. About twenty yards from the house, Kolya stopped and ordered Smurov to go in and tell Karamazov that Krasotkin wanted to talk to him.

"We must sniff at each other first," he explained.

"There's really no need to call him out," Smurov tried to object. "Why don't you just come in? I'm sure he'll be very glad to see you. Anyway, what's the big idea of making someone's acquaintance out in the cold?"

"I have my own reasons why I want to see him out here in the cold," Kolya answered sharply, and Smurov hurried off to carry out his order.

Kolya immensely enjoyed treating younger boys this way.

CHAPTER 4

Juchka

Kolya stood leaning against the fence and, with a dignified air, waited for Alyosha. He had wanted to meet him for a long time. He had heard a lot about him from the boys, but up till now he had always feigned a contemptuous lack of interest and if he said anything it was only to challenge the praises he heard. But secretly he was very eager to meet Alyosha as there appeared to be something very attractive and interesting about him, to judge from all the stories. Consequently, he considered this moment extremely important. In the first place, Kolya had to save face by demonstrating his independence. "Otherwise he'll treat me just like any other thirteen-year-old, or even like those other little boys," Kolya thought. "Anyway, why does he spend so much time with those little boys? I'll ask him that when I get to know him better. It's a shame, though, that I'm so short—Tuzikov is younger than I, but he's half a head taller. I have an intel-

ligent face, though. I know I'm not good-looking, I have a
nasty face, but it looks intelligent all right. Also, I must be
very reserved with him, for if I just throw myself at him,
he will think . . . Whew! It's just too sickening, what he'd
think! . . ."

And Kolya stood there worrying and trying to look completely casual and detached. What worried him most was his
lack of height. To him this was a much worse handicap
than his "nasty" face. In a corner of his room, there was a
little pencil mark on the wall. Last year he had measured his
height and drawn a line. And since then, every two months,
he had gone to that corner and measured himself again. But,
alas, he grew so slowly! It often drove him to real despair . . .
As to his face, there was really absolutely nothing "nasty"
about it. Indeed, it was a nice-looking, rather pale, freckled
face. His gray eyes, although not very large, were lively and
bold, and constantly sparkling with feeling. His head was
rather wide at the temples, his lips quite thin but very red,
his nose small and turned up, which caused him to mutter,
every time he looked into the mirror, "I'm so horribly snub-
nosed," and indignantly turn away. And sometimes he
doubted, even, whether his face was intelligent. "Doesn't really
look all that intelligent to me," he thought sometimes.

But all this does not necessarily mean that Kolya Krasotkin
was constantly worrying about his height and his face. In
fact, just the opposite was true. However humiliated he may
have felt in front of the mirror, he usually forgot all about it
as soon as he turned his back and never thought of it again
for long periods of time, "giving himself over without reservation to his ideas and to the realities of life," as he liked to
think of his activities.

Alyosha soon emerged from the house and went quickly
up to Kolya. As he approached him, Kolya was struck by
Alyosha's cheerful face. "Why should he be all that glad to
see me?" Kolya thought, feeling pleased.

It must be noted, incidentally, that considerable changes
had taken place in Alyosha since we met him last. In the
first place he had discarded his cassock and now wore instead
a very nicely cut jacket and a round felt hat. Also, his hair
was cut much shorter. All this made him extremely handsome. His charming, smiling face radiated a gentle, quiet
joy. Kolya noticed with surprise that, despite the cold, Alyosha had come out of the house without putting on his overcoat, which showed how anxious he was not to keep Kolya

waiting. And he came up to him now with his hand out-stretched.

"Ah, so here you are, at last! We were all waiting for you!"

"Certain things prevented me from coming earlier. I'll explain it to you later. In any case, I'm very glad to meet you. I've been waiting for an opportunity . . . I've heard so much about you," Kolya rattled off, a bit breathlessly.

"Oh, I'm sure we would have met eventually anyway. I've heard a lot about you, too. I wish you'd come here a little sooner, though."

"How are things in there?"

"Bad. Ilyusha is sure to die."

"It's that bad then, is it? Ah, medicine is such a filthy swindle," Kolya cried heatedly.

"You know, Ilyusha has often mentioned you, even when he was delirious, and in his sleep as well. That shows how important you were to him . . . I mean before that business with the penknife. And there's another reason . . . Tell me, is this your dog?"

"Yes. His name is Perezvon."

"You're sure it isn't Juchka?" Alyosha looked sorrowfully into Kolya's eyes. "So Juchka is definitely lost then?"

"I know, I know, you all wish it was Juchka. I've heard that," Kolya said with a mysterious smile. "Listen, Karamazov, I'll explain the whole thing to you and that's why, in fact, I had you called outside—I wanted to tell you before we went inside. You know it was last spring when Ilyusha entered the lower school, don't you, Karamazov?" Kolya started animatedly. "Well, you must know what kids are like in the lower school—they're just little brats, and they at once started teasing him. Being two classes above them, I just watched what was going on from the side. Well, I saw that this tiny, weak kid wouldn't take it lying down. He'd fight back. You should have seen his eyes—he was so proud. Well, I like kids like that! But the more he fought back, the more they teased him. The worst of it was that he had a horrible old overcoat, his trousers were too short, and there were big holes in his boots. So they teased him about his clothes. They really humiliated him. Well, that was a bit much, I felt, so I stepped in and really gave a few of them a good walloping. You know, Karamazov, it's funny, the more I beat the daylights out of them, the more they like me!" Kolya couldn't help bragging. "But I myself, I like kids. In fact, the reason I was late coming here was that I couldn't leave two small children I was looking after at home . . . Well, so the brats stopped beating him and he became my protégé. He was very proud, but in the end he became devoted to me, obeyed me blindly, listened to me as if I were God Almighty Himself, and even tried to imitate me. During recess he would always come running to me and walk around with me until the bell rang. And it was the same thing on Sundays. I know it's considered funny among schoolboys when a big boy becomes so friendly with a little one, but I think that's just a prejudice. If I care to be friends with someone, it's my own business and I don't have to account to anyone—that's the way I feel about it. So I explained things to him, helped him develop his mind. And why shouldn't I have, since I enjoyed it? I guess it's a bit like you, Karamazov: haven't you made friends with all these kids? I suppose you want to influence the younger generation, help them to grow, and be useful, don't you? In fact, I admit that it was that side of you, of which I've heard so much, that made me so interested in you . . .

"But let me get back to my story. Well, eventually I noticed that the boy was getting more and more sensitive, sort of sentimental . . . And I must tell you right now that, ever since I can remember, if there is one thing I've really loathed, it is slobbery sentimentality. And then there were those contradictions in him: he was proud and at the same time slavishly devoted to me; but despite that slavish devotion he could flare up at any moment and start arguing with me, fly into a rage, and not agree with anything. And it was not that he really disagreed so much with the ideas I was trying to explain to him—it was that he had decided to rebel against me because I was so cool to his sentimental stuff. And so, to toughen him up and make a man of him, the more sloppily sentimental he was, the colder I became; I did it deliberately, and I'm still convinced that it was the right way to treat him. Well, then . . . Oh, I'm sure I don't have to spell it all out for you. I noticed at one point that he was sort of depressed. It went on for a whole day, and the following day and the day after that. I could see it was not for sentimental reasons that he felt that way—there was something else to it, something more important. I wondered what all the tragedy could be about. So I questioned him and here's what I found out.

"Somehow or other, he had made friends with your father's lackey Smerdyakov (your father was still alive at the time), who taught the little boy a stupid trick—I mean the filthy and beastly trick of kneading a piece of soft bread into a ball, sticking a pin into it, tossing it to a hungry dog, and watching what happens. For if a dog is hungry enough, he'll swallow it without chewing it. So they prepared a ball of bread like that and tossed it to Juchka, that shaggy mongrel over which all the fuss is being made now. That dog was never fed and he spent days barking into the wind. (I can't stand that stupid sort of barking, Karamazov, can you?) And so Juchka pounced on the thing, swallowed it, started to squeal and rush around, and darted off whimpering. That's the way Ilyusha himself described it to me. When he told me the story, he was crying and crying and shaking all over. 'He ran and squealed,' he kept repeating. 'He ran and squealed, ran and squealed . . .' He was terribly struck by the scene. He had real pangs of guilt. I thought it was very serious. Well, I decided to give him a lesson for this and for other things he'd done before. So here, I admit, I put on an act. I pretended to be very indignant whereas, in fact, I wasn't all that outraged. 'You've done something disgusting, and you're a mean little beast,' I told him. 'Of course I'm not going to tell on you, but, for the time being at least, I will have nothing to do with you. I'll think it all over and decide whether I'll ever resume my relations with you or whether I'll break with you for good. I'll let you know what I decide through Smurov,' I told him. (Smurov, you know, is the kid who came with me today; he's always been devoted to me.)

"Ilyusha was so completely dumbfounded when he heard that that I thought perhaps I'd overdone it a bit. But I considered that was the proper way to act at that moment. The next day I sent Smurov to inform Ilyusha that I was no longer talking to him, which meant that our relations were broken off. Secretly I was planning to punish him for a few days and then, when he was really sorry for what he'd done, I'd forgive him and we'd be friends again. That was my plan. But when Smurov went to him, his eyes flashed and he shouted: 'Go and tell Krasotkin that now I'll feed bread with pins in it to all the dogs.' 'Well, well,' I thought, 'he's getting out of hand, but I'll tame him!' And so every time he crossed my path, I would either turn away or look at him sarcastically.

"And then there was that story with his father, you know, the back-scrubber. You can understand that, even before that happened, he was already in a state of nervous exasperation. The boys, who realized that I had broken with him, started taunting him again by shouting, 'Back-scrubber, back-scrubber!' whenever he appeared. That was when their battles began, and I'm terribly sorry about it all now, because I understand he got very badly beaten up. On one occasion he attacked a whole bunch of them in the school yard as I stood there, perhaps ten yards away. I'm sure I wasn't laughing at him then, for I remember feeling terribly sorry for him. In fact, I think I was on the point of joining the battle to defend him. But suddenly our eyes met. I don't know what he thought he saw in my look but the next thing I knew he was rushing at me with his penknife open and he jabbed it into my right thigh, right here, see? I didn't even move, for you see, Karamazov, I can be pretty fearless too on occasion, even if I do say so myself. I gave him one of those scornful looks as if to say, 'Here, go on, take another stab at me if you like, since that's your way of showing your appreciation for all I've done for you.' But he didn't stab me again. He got scared of what he'd done, threw the penknife away, and rushed off, crying out loud. Of course I didn't go and squeal on him and I saw to it that no one who had seen what happened did. I didn't even tell my mother until the wound was completely healed. Besides, it was not much of a wound really. It was just a scratch. Now, later that same day, I was told that he rushed at you and bit your finger. Well, I'm sure you understand now what a state he was in that day . . . I admit now that I should have gone to see him when he first got sick and forgiven him . . . I mean made up with him, then. I'm really sorry I didn't. But then I thought up something else. Well, that's the whole story. I'm afraid I've been rather stupid, all in all."

"It's a shame I didn't know anything about your previous relations with Ilyusha," Alyosha said worriedly. "If I had I'd have come to see you long ago and tried to persuade you to come with me to visit him. Do you know, as he lay there in a fever, he kept talking about you? I had no idea that you'd been so close to him. But you really couldn't find Juchka anywhere after that? His father and all the kids have looked for him all over town. Sick as he is, Ilyusha has repeated three times to his father: 'If I'm sick, papa, it's because I've killed Juchka. God is punishing me for it now.' And it's quite impossible to dissuade him. I almost believe that if Juchka was found alive and brought to him and he was convinced that he hadn't killed the dog, the boy would come back to life out of sheer joy. And so we were all hoping that you . . ."

"But what made you hope that I would find Juchka? Why me?" Kolya asked in extreme surprise. "Why didn't you expect that someone else would find Juchka?"

"Rumor had it that you were looking for Juchka and that you'd come with him as soon as you'd found him. Smurov said something to that effect, too. Above all, we've all been trying to convince Ilyusha that Juchka is alive, that someone has seen him. One day the boys brought him a live rabbit, but he just glanced at it, smiled, and asked them to let it loose in the fields, which they did. And just now his father came home with a mastiff puppy. The poor man had thought to console Ilyusha with it, but he only made things worse . . ."

"Another thing, Karamazov—tell me, what sort of a man is his father? I've met him, but I want to hear your opinion. Is he some kind of buffoon, a clown, or what?"

"Oh no, not at all. He's one of those very sensitive people who have been crushed by life. Their clowning is really a show of spite to people whom they don't dare to answer back, after they've been humiliated for a long time and intimidated. Believe me, Krasotkin, that clowning can be terribly sad at times. And now everything on earth that is dear to this man is concentrated in Ilyusha, and if Ilyusha dies, his father will either go mad or kill himself. Whenever I look at him, I'm almost certain that that is what will happen."

"I see what you mean, Karamazov," Kolya said with feeling. "I can see that you really understand the man."

"You know," Alyosha said, "the minute I saw you with this dog, I was sure you'd brought Juchka."

"Wait, we may yet find Juchka, but this is Perezvon. I'll bring him into the room and perhaps Ilyusha will be more pleased with him than he was with the mastiff pup. Wait, Karamazov, perhaps you'll find out something in a moment. But, good God, here I'm keeping you out in this cold and you have no overcoat on!" Kolya suddenly cried. "You see how selfish I am! Oh, we're all such terrible egoists, Karamazov!"

"Don't worry. It's none too warm, but I practically never catch cold. But do let's go in, by all means. What shall I call you, by the way?"

"My full name is Nikolai Ivanovich Krasotkin," Kolya said laughingly and then added quickly: "But, of course, I detest the name Nikolai."

"Why? And why 'of course'?"

"It's so terribly banal and common."

"How old are you? Twelve?"

"No, I'm thirteen. In fact I'll be fourteen pretty soon—in two weeks. Now let me make a confession to you, Karamazov, so that you'll know from the start what kind of a person I am. First of all, I hate it when people ask me how old I am. And then there's a rumor going around about me that I played at robbers with boys from the lower school. Well, I did, but it was not because I enjoyed it myself but to please them. I suppose you must have heard that gossip too, but I want you to believe me—the only reason I did it was that, without me, the brats couldn't think of anything to do with themselves. But in this town there's always so much ridiculous gossip going around!"

"But suppose you did enjoy it yourself—what's so terrible about that?"

"How can you suppose I could enjoy it? Tell me, would you enjoy, for instance, playing 'horsey' with tiny kids?"

"Look, why can't you think of it this way?" Alyosha said with a smile. "Adults, for instance, enjoy going to the theater, don't they? And what are they shown there if not the adventures of all kinds of heroic men. Sometimes there are also robbers and there's some fighting . . . So isn't it in a way the same thing—in a different form, of course? And when young people play at soldiers or at robbers in their free time, it's also a manifestation of the burgeoning need for artistic expression, and those games are often better and more natural than a theatrical performance. Another difference, of course, is that when people go to the theater it's to watch the actors, while in their games the boys are their own actors. And it's all completely natural."

"Do you really sincerely believe that?" Kolya said, looking very intensely at Alyosha. "You have quite an idea there, I believe, and when I get home, I'll have to think it over. I admit, I suspected there might be quite a few things I could learn from you. Yes, I've come to learn from you, Karamazov," Kolya concluded in a confidential tone.

"Thanks, and I've come to learn from you," Alyosha said with a shy smile, shaking Kolya by the hand.

Kolya was absolutely delighted with Alyosha. What pleased him most of all was that Alyosha treated him like an equal and talked to him as if he were "a real adult."

"I'll show you a trick now, Karamazov, a kind of theatrical performance," Kolya said with a nervous laugh.

"Wait, let's first go in there, to the left, to the landlord's place. That's where all the boys leave their coats; otherwise it gets too cluttered in the room. It's so hot and crowded as it is."

"Oh, but I don't expect to stay long. I'll just pop in for a
second and I can simply keep my coat on. Perezvon can stay
in the passage and die for a while. Here, Perezvon, lie down!
Die! See, he's dead now. I'll go in first, get an idea of the
layout, and then, when the time comes, I'll whistle for
Perezvon and you'll see him come flying in like a bullet. As
long as Smurov doesn't forget to open the door for a second
just then. But I'll see to it that it comes off right, don't you
worry!"

CHAPTER 5

At Ilyusha's Bedside

The room, which we already know, where the family of
Captain Snegirev lived was at this moment very stuffy and
very crowded. Several boys from Ilyusha's class were visiting
him and every one of them, like Smurov, would have angrily
denied that it was Alyosha who had made peace between him
and Ilyusha and that, if he was there now, it was because of
Alyosha. This, however, was the truth. Alyosha's great merit
in this matter lay precisely in the way he had succeeded in
tactfully reconciling each boy in turn with Ilyusha, as though
by chance, and without any "slobbery sentimentality." And
this reconciliation brought Ilyusha great relief in his suffering.
He was very touched to see the almost tender concern all
these recent enemies now showed for him.

Only Kolya Krasotkin's absence lay like a heavy stone on
his heart. His stabbing his only true friend and his protector
with a penknife was the bitterest of all the bitter memories of
school that teemed in Ilyusha's head. And Smurov, who was
an intelligent little boy, realized that; he had been the first to
make up with Ilyusha and to visit him. But when Smurov had
vaguely told Krasotkin that Alyosha was planning to come
and see him on "very important business," Kolya had told
him to go and tell "that Karamazov fellow" that Krasotkin
knew what to do himself, that he needed no advice, and that
if he decided to go and see Ilyusha, he would go in his own
good time, and that he had his own reasons for acting the way
he was acting. That was about two weeks before this Sunday.
And that was why Alyosha had not gone to see Kolya as he
had planned. However, although he had waited for Kolya to
act of his own accord, he had sent Smurov to him a couple

more times to ask whether he would not talk to Alyosha after all. To that Kolya had answered with an open threat that if Alyosha ever came to his house he would never go to see Ilyusha whatever happened, and he asked Smurov to tell Alyosha that Kolya did not wish to be pestered by him anymore. And even Smurov only knew of Kolya's plans the day before Kolya had finally decided to come. He had told Smurov the previous evening, just as they were parting, that he would go. Kolya had suddenly told him to be home in the morning and to wait for him to come by, for he wanted them to go together to see Ilyusha. But he had warned Smurov not to say a word to anyone on the subject, for Kolya wanted it to appear as if he had just popped in by chance as he was passing by. Smurov complied. As to the idea that Kolya would appear with Juchka, that had been Smurov's own idea and it had been based on Kolya's statement that "they would be a real bunch of idiots, all of them, if they couldn't find the dog, if the animal was alive." But when, after a long and discreet wait, Smurov finally hinted that he suspected the real identity of Kolya's dog, Kolya flew into a rage and shouted:

"What do you think I am, an idiot like all of them, to waste my time looking all over town for other people's dogs when I have my own Perezvon? And who on earth supposes that a dog who has swallowed a pin can live? That's all just slobbery old sentimental stuff, and I won't have any part of it!"

Ilyusha had not left his bed in the corner under the icon for nearly two weeks. He had not been back to school since the day he had bitten Alyosha's finger. Actually it was on that day that he became seriously ill, although for the first month or so he had still been able to get out of bed and walk around the room and the passage. After that he grew too weak to move at all without his father's help. His father worried about him constantly; he even stopped drinking almost entirely. The thought that the boy might die drove him nearly insane. Often, particularly after he had walked around the room with Ilyusha, supporting him by the arm, and then put him back to bed, the father would rush out into the passage, hide himself in some dark corner, put his forehead against the cold wall, and weep, shaken by violent sobs, which he tried desperately to stifle so that the boy should not hear them. Returning to the room, he would try to distract his Ilyusha by telling him stories and funny anecdotes, and making ridiculous imitations of people or of animal cries and howls. But Ilyusha did not like to see his father clowning and trying to make him laugh. And, although he tried not to show his father how unpleasant it was for him, it made him painfully aware of Snegirev's humiliating position in town and always brought back to him "that terrible day" and then the shouts of "back-scrubber." Nina, Ilyusha's gentle, crippled sister, also disliked it when their father played the fool (the other sister, Barbara, had left for Petersburg to resume her studies), but the half-witted Mrs. Snegirev was always tremendously amused whenever her husband made funny faces or ridiculous gesticulations. Indeed, it was the only thing that made her happy; the rest of the time she whimpered continuously and complained that everyone had forgotten her, that no one showed her any respect, that she was being neglected, etc., etc. In the past few days, however, a sudden change had come over her. More and more often she glanced into Ilyusha's corner and seemed to be thinking hard about something. She stopped complaining, grew very quiet, and even when she whimpered or cried, she tried to do so quietly so that the others would not hear her. Snegirev noticed this change with misgiving. At first, she had not liked the boys' visits. They only irritated her. Later, however, the cheerful din of their voices and the stories they told began to distract her, and eventually she came to enjoy their presence so much that she would really have missed them had they suddenly stopped coming. When the children played at something or told their stories, she would laugh and clap her hands. Now and then she would call a boy over to her and kiss him. And her special favorite was Smurov. As to Captain Snegirev himself, he was immensely grateful that the boys now came to the house to keep Ilyusha company; it filled him with tremendous joy and he even hoped that their presence would put an end to Ilyusha's depression and hasten his recovery. For until the very last moment, he never doubted that his son would recover, despite his continuous anxiety over Ilyusha's illness. He met his young visitors with enthusiastic gratitude, fussed over them, tried to anticipate their wishes; indeed, he would gladly have let them ride on his back, and he actually did so once or twice, until he realized that Ilyusha disliked such horseplay and it was abandoned. But Snegirev did buy the boys candy, nuts, and gingerbread, and he made tea and sandwiches for them.

It must be noted that he never lacked money during all this time. Just as Alyosha had predicted, Snegirev had accepted Katerina's two hundred rubles when they were offered to him a second time. Then, when she learned more about their circumstances and about Ilyusha's sickness, Katerina had gone to the house herself, met the whole family, and even managed to charm the half-witted Mrs. Snegirev. And since that time Katerina's generosity had never failed them, and Snegirev himself was much too worried about his son to be bothered about pride and humbly accepted her gifts. During all this time, Dr. Herzenstube visited Ilyusha regularly every other day, on Katerina's instructions, stuffing him with all sorts of drugs, which, however, did not seem to do the boy any good. But on this Sunday Ilyusha was to be examined by a new doctor, a Moscow celebrity, whom Katerina had invited to come at considerable expense, although not actually for Ilyusha but for another purpose, of which more will be said later. But since he was in town, she had asked him to examine Ilyusha as well and had notified Snegirev in advance.

But Snegirev had no idea that Kolya Krasotkin was also planning to come that day, although he had long been anxious that the boy whom his son seemed to miss so badly should come. Now, as Krasotkin opened the door and stepped into the room, Snegirev and all the young visitors were gathered around Ilyusha's bed examining the tiny mastiff puppy that Snegirev had brought his son in the hope of taking his mind off Juchka, who was probably dead. Snegirev had ordered it a week ago, but the pup had only been born the day before. Ilyusha, however, who had been told three days ago that he was about to receive a puppy, and not just an ordinary puppy but a real mastiff—which, of course, was extremely important—seemed to be only tactfully pretending that he was delighted with the present. His father and the boys could see clearly that the puppy only brought back more strongly the memory of poor Juchka, whom he had killed. And while the puppy wriggled restlessly next to him and he stroked it with his pale, emaciated hand, it was obvious that, although he found the little animal sweet, it could not replace Juchka for him. Ah, if only Juchka could be there too, as well as the puppy, then he would be really happy!

Suddenly one of the boys caught sight of Kolya.

"Krasotkin!"

There was a considerable commotion. The boys spontaneously stepped aside so that Kolya had a full view of Ilyusha. Snegirev hurried over to Kolya.

"Please, do come in, do come in. I'm so glad you've come . . ." he prattled. "Look, Ilyusha, Mr. Krasotkin has come to see you . . ."

But Krasotkin, having hurriedly shaken Snegirev's hand, proceeded to display his perfect command of the social graces. First he had to present his respects to Mrs. Snegirev, so he walked over to the chair where she had been sitting and grumbling because her husband and the boys were screening Ilyusha's bed from her, so that she could not even see the puppy. Kolya greeted her with the utmost courtesy, clicking his heels. Then he turned to Nina and greeted her too with the deference to which a lady was entitled. This display of good manners made a great impression upon Mrs. Snegirev.

"One can tell a well-bred young man at once," she said loudly, spreading out her arms in an appreciative gesture. "It's not like the others, who just rush in, practically on top of one another . . ."

"That's right—on top of one another," Snegirev said to her gently, although he was a little worried about what she might come out with next.

"Yes, that's just what they do. Outside, in the passage, one climbs on another's back and in they ride. Is that the way for guests to behave?"

"But who does that, dear? Who comes riding in here?"

"Why, that boy, see? Well, he came in riding piggyback on top of that one over there . . ."

But Kolya was already standing by Ilyusha's bed. Ilyusha turned even paler. He sat up slightly, looking intently at Krasotkin. Kolya had not seen his young friend for two months and he was shocked. He had not expected the boy's face to have grown so thin and yellow, or his eyes to look so huge and to burn so feverishly, or his hands to seem so brittle. Kolya also noticed sadly how difficult it was for Ilyusha to breathe and how dry his lips were.

Krasotkin took a step forward and, feeling almost at a loss, said:

"Well, old man, how are you getting along?"

But his voice faltered, the casual air he had assumed dissolved, his face twitched, and he felt his lips beginning to quiver. Ilyusha looked at him with a pained smile. He still could not utter a word. Kolya suddenly stretched out his hand and ran it over Ilyusha's hair.

"Well, never mind," Kolya muttered in a whisper, apparently trying to cheer him up, but with no idea why he had uttered those words.

"What's this new puppy you have?" Kolya said after a moment's pause, now sounding completely detached.

"Ye-yes . . ." Ilyusha whispered, gasping for breath.

"Black nose—hm! That means he'll be ferocious and you'll have to keep him chained," Kolya commented expertly, as if he had come especially to examine the pup and its black nose, although in fact he was still trying to overcome the alarming feeling inside him that he might suddenly begin to cry like one of "those little boys." "He'll be a great watchdog, but he'll have to be chained, believe me. I know what I'm talking about."

"And he'll be enormous!" one of the boys exclaimed.

"Sure, mastiffs are enormous. Everyone knows that. It'll be about the size of a calf—like that!" another boy put in.

"Yes, yes, just like a calf," Snegirev said quickly. "And I purposely asked for the fiercest one; you know his parents are terribly fierce and they come up to here . . . But please, Mr. Krasotkin, sit down on Ilyusha's bed, or on this stool if you prefer. Ah, we're all so glad you're here . . . You came with Mr. Karamazov, did you?"

Kolya sat down on the bed at Ilyusha's feet. Although on the way he had prepared things to talk about quite casually with Ilyusha, now he did not know how to start.

"N-no," he said, "I didn't come with Karamazov . . . I came with Perezvon. I have a dog now. His name is Perezvon. It's a good old Slav name. He's waiting for me in the passage. If I whistle, he'll come tearing in. So you see, old man, I have a dog too," he said, turning to Ilyusha, and then all of a sudden he asked him: "Do you remember Juchka?"

"Where . . . where is Juchka?" Ilyusha asked in a breaking voice.

"Ah, that's something I don't know, old man. It looks as if Juchka's vanished!"

Ilyusha said nothing. He just gave Kolya another intent look. Alyosha caught Kolya's eye and started signaling to him vigorously, but Kolya ignored him and looked elsewhere.

"I bet Juchka must have hidden somewhere and then died there, for it seems very unlikely that he could have lived after such a snack," Kolya said mercilessly, although he himself was finding it rather difficult to breathe now. "But, instead, I have my Perezvon. It's a nice Slav name as I said, and I've brought him to meet you."

"I don't want to!" Ilyusha said suddenly.

"Yes, yes, you do. You must have a look at him . . . it'll amuse you. I brought him specially . . . He's just as shaggy as the other . . . Will you allow me, madam, to call my dog in here?" he said, turning suddenly to Mrs. Snegirev, by now in an altogether incomprehensible state of excitement.

"No, no, I don't want to!" Ilyusha cried bitterly, and his eyes looked at Kolya in deep reproach.

"I wonder whether . . . Perhaps some other time . . ." Snegirev suddenly tore himself from the trunk by the wall where he had been sitting. "Please, any other time," he muttered.

But, ignoring him, Kolya suddenly turned to Smurov:

"Now, Smurov, open the door!"

As soon as Smurov did so, Kolya whistled. Perezvon came rushing into the room.

"Here! Jump, jump! Now beg, Perezvon, beg!" Kolya yelled, getting up, and the dog stood on his hind legs right in front of Ilyusha's bed.

Then something quite unexpected happened. Ilyusha started trembling all over and suddenly leaned violently forward toward Perezvon, staring at him as if in a trance.

"But this is . . . this is Juchka!" Ilyusha cried in a voice trembling with pain and joy.

"Sure, who else?" Kolya cried in a resounding, happy voice and, leaning down, he picked up the dog and held him up to Ilyusha.

"See, old man, see this blind eye, and this ear split in two —aren't those the special marks you told me about? It was thanks to those marks that I was able to find him. And it didn't take me long either. You see, this dog didn't belong to anyone really," he explained, looking in turn first at Ilyusha's mother, then at his father, then at Alyosha, and then back at Ilyusha himself. "He lived in the back of the Fedotovs' yard, but he didn't belong to them; I guess he came from some outlying village. The Fedotovs didn't feed him. But anyhow, it was there that I found him. So you see, old man, it turns out that he didn't swallow that snack you gave him, for if he had he certainly wouldn't be here! He must have managed to spit it out somehow or other, without your noticing it. But he still must have pricked his tongue, since you say he squealed as he ran away. He must have squealed an awful lot because the skin inside a dog's mouth is, as you know, extremely tender, in fact, much tenderer than the skin in a human mouth, beyond comparison!"

Kolya was shouting at the top of his voice and beaming with delight.

Ilyusha was speechless. He stared at Kolya. His eyes were

huge and now seemed strangely prominent. His mouth was open. His face was as white as the sheets of his bed. If Kolya Krasotkin had understood how bad, even fatal, such emotion could be for the sick boy, he would never have thought of playing such a trick on him. But of all those present, no one understood it, except possibly Alyosha. As to Snegirev, he seemed to have been suddenly transformed into a little boy himself.

"Juchka! So this is Juchka, then!" he kept exclaiming blissfully. "Look Ilyusha, this is Juchka, your own Juchka! Look, mother, see, Juchka is here!" The man was on the verge of tears.

"I never guessed it!" Smurov cried ruefully. "Ah, that Krasotkin! But I was sure from the very beginning that if anyone could find Juchka, he'd be the one, and you see, he found him all right!"

"He sure did!" a boy shouted.

"That's great, Krasotkin!" another boy put in.

"Great! Marvelous! Good boy, Krasotkin!" other voices resounded.

"Keep quiet, now, that's enough!" Kolya was trying to outshout them all. "Let me tell you how it happened, because that's what's so curious about it. You see, I found him, took him home, and locked him up without letting anyone see him until the last day. Smurov was the only one to find out about him being hidden in my house, but then I managed to convince him that it was Perezvon. In the meantime, I had taught him all those tricks so that Smurov agreed that it couldn't possibly be Juchka. Ah, you should see all the tricks he can perform! And do you know why I trained him, Ilyusha, old man? It was to bring him to you already smart and well-trained, so you could admire how great your Juchka had become. Tell me, don't you have a little piece of meat? Because if so, he could show you a trick that'll make you split your sides laughing! Can't you really find a little piece of meat in the house?"

Snegirev dashed out of the cottage and ran over to the landlord's house, where the meals for the Snegirev family were now prepared. While he was away, Kolya, not wishing to waste a second, suddenly shouted, "Pretend you're dead, Perezvon!" and the dog spun around a few times, then lay on his back with all four paws sticking up in the air. The boys roared with laughter, while Ilyusha watched the animal with the same pained smile. But the most delighted of all was Mrs.

Snegirev; she kept giggling and snapping her fingers and shouting:

"Perezvon, Perezvon!"

"Nothing doing! He won't stir!" Krasotkin cried with well-earned pride. "The whole world can call him, it won't make any difference. But if I tell him, he'll jump up at once. Watch now: 'Here, Perezvon!' "

The dog leaped up squealing with joy, as Snegirev appeared with a piece of meat.

"It's not too hot, I hope?" Kolya inquired in a business-like tone, holding the meat in his hand for a moment. "No, I guess it's fine. You see, dogs don't like hot food. And now, everybody watch this! Hey, watch, Ilyusha, why aren't you watching? I brought him here for you and you won't even watch him perform!"

The new trick consisted in making the dog stand on his hindlegs with his head in the air and his nose stretched forward and then placing the appetizing morsel on the very tip of the poor beast's nose. And Perezvon was supposed to remain like this without moving for any length of time—as long as half an hour, Kolya claimed—until his master ordered him to move.

This time, however, the dog's patience was tested for only a few seconds:

"Catch it!" Kolya cried, and the piece of meat at once flew from the tip of Perezvon's nose right into his mouth. The boys exclaimed in admiration and wonder.

"I can't believe you didn't come all this time just because you wanted to finish training your dog," Alyosha said with a note of reproach in his voice.

"That was exactly the reason, though!" Kolya cried innocently. "I wanted to present Perezvon in all his glory!"

"Perezvon, Perezvon!" Ilyusha suddenly called the dog, snapping his brittle fingers.

"What do you want? You want him to pay you a visit in your bed? Here, Perezvon!" Kolya slapped his hand on the blanket and Perezvon was there beside Ilyusha. The boy threw his arms around the dog's neck and at once his entire cheek was thoroughly licked by the animal. Ilyusha hugged the dog hard, stretched himself out, and buried his face in the shaggy fur.

"Oh, my God, my God!" Snegirev kept repeating.

Kolya sat on the bed beside Ilyusha and said:

"I'd like to show you something else now. I've brought you

a little cannon. Remember, I told you about it before and you said you'd very much like to have a look at it. Well, I've brought it with me."

And Kolya hurriedly pulled his little brass cannon out of his satchel. He was in such a great hurry because he was feeling quite overwhelmed with joy himself. On another occasion he would have waited until the effect produced by Perezvon had worn off. But now he threw his usual self-control to the winds, as if thinking: "Here, people, I'm aware that you're already quite happy, but I have even more for you!" He was delighted with it all himself.

"I saw this thing long ago at Mr. Morozov's, old man, and I got it for you. It was just gathering dust there and I swapped it for a book of my father's, *A Kinsman of Mahomet or Therapeutic Buffoonery.* It was published in Moscow a hundred years ago when there was still no censorship and it's full of that kind of thing, you know . . . Well, Mr. Morozov seems to love that sort of stuff and he was glad to give me the cannon for it. He even thanked me afterward."

Kolya held the cannon up so that they could all see and admire it. Ilyusha raised himself and looked admiringly at the toy with his arm still around Perezvon's neck. The effect Kolya produced reached its highest point when he declared that he had some gunpowder with him and that he could fire the gun if he was certain that it would not inconvenience the ladies. Mrs. Snegirev demanded to be allowed to have a closer look at the cannon and Kolya immediately complied with her wish. She was absolutely delighted with the shiny little gun and started rolling it up and down on her knee. When asked for her permission to fire the cannon, she granted it enthusiastically, although she did not really understand what she had been asked. Captain Snegirev, as a former soldier, was entrusted with the loading of the gun. He took the smallest amount of powder, but asked Kolya to postpone the firing with shot until some other time. The cannon was placed on the floor, the barrel trained away from the spectators. Three grains of powder were placed in the touch hole and a match was put to it. A brilliant report followed. Mrs. Snegirev shuddered but at once recovered and giggled happily. The boys looked on in silent admiration. But the happiest of them all was Snegirev, who looked blissfuly at his son. Kolya then picked up the cannon from the floor and presented it to Ilyusha, together with the supply of powder and the shot.

"This is all yours! I prepared it for you long ago," Kolya repeated, wallowing in his own happiness.

"Oh, why don't you give it to me instead? Yes, you'd better give it to me!" Mrs. Snegirev suddenly cried out. Her face expressed infinite anxiety lest they refuse her the toy. The Captain, looking terribly worried, began to fuss over her.

"Mother, mother dear, please!" he said, hurrying to her. "It is yours, yours, but let Ilyusha have it for a little while, because it was really meant to be a present for him. But you understand that it's just the same as if it were yours, for he'll always let you play with it. Say, what about the two of you owning it in common?"

"No, no, no! I don't want to own it in common with him. I want it all to myself—it cannot be Ilyusha's!" Mrs. Snegirev said, ready to cry.

"Mamma, please, you can have it. It's yours!" Ilyusha suddenly said. "Is it all right with you, Krasotkin, if I give it to my mother?" he said, looking beseechingly at Krasotkin and obviously worried that Kolya might be offended at his giving away his present.

"Of course, it's all right!" Kolya at once agreed. He took the gun from Ilyusha's hands, and handed it to the boy's mother with a graceful bow. The woman burst into tears of sheer joy.

"Ah, Ilyusha, my darling, you're a nice, nice boy who really loves his mamma!" she cried, and began to roll the cannon up and down on her knee.

"Allow me to kiss your hand, mother dear!" her husband said, hurrying to her and doing so.

"And do you know who is the nicest of all? It's that young man over there. He's the kindest of all the boys!" the grateful lady said, pointing to Kolya.

"And I'll be able to bring you as much gunpowder as you want. We're making gunpowder ourselves now. You see, Borovikov has discovered the ingredients that go into it: twenty-four parts of saltpeter, ten of sulphur, and six of birchwood charcoal. You have to pound it all together, add some water so it forms a kind of a paste, and then pass it through a very fine strainer, like sheepskin—and there you have your powder!"

"Smurov told me about it. But my father says it isn't real gunpowder," Ilyusha said.

"What do you mean, it isn't real?" Kolya said, turning very red. "Ours burns all right. But, after all, I don't know . . ."

"No, no, I didn't mean it quite that way," Snegirev said, looking guilty and contrite. "I simply said that that isn't the way they make real gunpowder. But I'm sure this way is fine too."

"Well, I'm sure you know more about it than I do, sir. We burned some of our stuff in a stone jar and it burned beautifully, burned all up, and there was only very little ash left. And that was only the paste, so if we'd strained it properly . . . But I really don't know much about it . . . And did you hear, Ilyusha? Bulkin's father gave him a hiding because of our powder."

"Yes, I heard about it," Ilyusha said, listening to Kolya with endless joy.

"It was because we'd prepared a whole bottle of powder and Bulkin was keeping it under his bed. His father found it. 'You'll blow us all up!' he said to him and gave him a hiding then and there. At first, he wanted to complain to the school principal, but he finally decided not to allow Bulkin to play with me anymore. And you know, Smurov's parents won't allow him to have anything to do with me either. I've really got myself quite a reputation around here! They all say I'm a 'desperado,' " Kolya added with a scornful snort, "and it all dates from that time on the railroad track."

"Oh, we heard about that exploit of yours!" Snegirev cried. "I can just imagine how it must have felt lying there. Wasn't it frightening, though, having that train pass over your head? I bet it must have been!"

Snegirev was trying desperately to please Kolya.

"N-no . . . no, not all that bad, really!" Kolya replied casually. "But you know who really did the most damage to my reputation here?" he said, turning again to Ilyusha. "It was that damned goose!"

Although he tried to assume a careless and casual air, Kolya could not control his excitement and kept slipping out of what seemed to him the right tone.

"Ah, I heard about the goose too!" Ilyusha cried laughing. "But I didn't quite understand—did they really take you to court for it, before a judge?"

"It was really just a stupid little prank, but they managed to make a whole production out of it, as they often do in this town," Kolya started carelessly. "One day I was crossing the square when they were driving some geese into town. So I stopped to look at the geese when all of a sudden a fellow who works at Plotnikov's store as a messenger boy—Vishnyakov is his name—comes over to me and says, 'What are you staring at those geese for?' So I look at him and see that he has one of those stupid round mugs—he must be about twenty or so . . . But I want you to understand that I like common people . . . I think we've lost touch with the people —that's an axiom of mine . . . What's so funny about what I'm saying, Karamazov? Why are you laughing?"

"No, no, I'm not. I'm very interested!" Alyosha said with such a sincere air that Kolya at once felt reassured.

"My theory, Karamazov, is plain and clear," Kolya started off in a hurry again. "I have faith in the common people and am always prepared to render them justice, but that doesn't mean I'm in favor of coddling them, that's *sine qua* . . . But I was talking about that goose. Well, then, I turn to that imbecile and I say to him, 'I'm looking at the geese because I'm trying to figure out what they're thinking about.' So he gives me one of those dumb looks and says: 'And what does a goose think about?' 'See that cart of oats?' I ask him. 'And do you see those oats dropping out of the sack and that goose over there with its neck stretched out right under the wheel, pecking the grain—do you see it?' 'Sure, I see it,' he says. 'Now,' I say, 'suppose someone gave that cart ever so slight a push, what do you say, would the wheel run over the goose's neck or wouldn't it?' 'It sure would,' the fellow says. I see him grinning from cheek to cheek as if he were going to melt with joy. 'So let's go, fellow. Let's do it.' 'All right,' he says, 'let's.' And, believe me, it didn't take us long to manage it. He took hold of the bridle and I stood behind the goose, to kind of direct it. Well, the peasant who had driven the geese into town was busy talking to someone and was paying no attention. I didn't even have to direct that goose. It managed all by itself. It stretched out its neck under the cart, right under the wheel, and I winked to the fellow, he pulled the bridle, and cr-rrack—the wheel rolled over the middle of the goose's neck! But it so happened that, just at that very second, all the peasants looked around and saw what had happened. And they began to yell at him: 'You did it on purpose!' 'No, not on purpose!' 'Yes, on purpose.' And the next thing I hear is shouting, 'Take him to the Justice of the Peace!' And they got hold of me too, shouting, 'You were in it with him. You helped him. Everyone in the market knows you anyway!' And it is a fact—I don't know why, but they all know me," Kolya remarked with a certain pride.

"Well, so we all went in procession to the Justice of the

Peace and they even took the goose along too. The other fellow was getting scared, and suddenly I see he's weeping like an old woman. And the owner of the geese keeps hollering, 'They could have killed lots of geese that way!' Well, with all the witnesses, it didn't take the judge very long to decide. The fellow was told he must pay the peasant one ruble for the goose but that he could keep the goose. The judge also warned him never to play such tricks again. But the fellow was still crying and whimpering like an old woman. 'It wasn't me, it wasn't me,' he kept saying. 'It was he who put me up to it,' and he points at me. So very coolly I say to the judge that I never put him up to anything, that I only formulated the basic idea and that I simply meant it was theoretically feasible. Well, Justice of the Peace Nefedov smiled when I said that, but then became angry with himself for smiling. 'I will report you to your school principal and you'd better see to it that, instead of going about testing your theories, you sit over your books and do your schoolwork!' Actually he didn't report me to the school, but the rumor went around town and the school authorities heard about it soon enough, just because they happen to have pretty long ears. Kolbasnikov, the classics teacher, was outraged, but Dardanelov got me off the hook again. Now Kolbasnikov is furious with all of us, like an incensed donkey . . . By the way, Ilyusha, did you know he just got married to that Miss Mikhailov? He took three thousand rubles of dowry along with his bride, whose face is like the snout of an aging pig. The boys of the third class at once made up the following epigram:

Astounding news has reached the class:
A pig got married to our ass!

There's more of it and it's very funny. I'll bring it to you some time. I can't say anything against Dardanelov—he's a man who knows his stuff. Yes, he's definitely quite a learned man, and I don't say that because he comes to my defense. I simply respect people who are competent."

"But you did show him up when you asked him who founded Troy," Smurov said. He was terribly proud of Krasotkin at that moment. The story about the goose pleased him no end.

"Did you really show him up?" Snegirev put in ingratiatingly. "Yes, that was about who founded Troy—we heard about that. Ilyusha told us at the time . . ."

"He knows more than anyone else on any subject, papa. He's just pretending to be like that; actually he's the top student in every subject," Ilyusha declared, gazing happily at Kolya.

"Oh, that business about Troy is nothing. I myself think my question was pretty unimportant," Kolya said with a conqueror's modesty. He felt he had finally succeeded in adopting the right tone, although something still worried him. He felt that he was still a bit too excited, that he had told the story about the goose with too much sincere excitement, and that, while he was telling it, Alyosha had kept looking at him unsmilingly and never making any comment, so that Kolya, touchy as he was, started wondering whether Alyosha didn't "despise" him. "He must be thinking I'm trying hard to get his approval," Kolya decided. "Well, if he has that conceited notion, I'll . . ."

"Actually, the question was completely irrelevant," Kolya said again.

"But I know who founded Troy," said a boy, who until then had sat in silence by the door. He was a very pretty, obviously shy boy of about eleven, named Kartashov. Kolya, in surprise, gave him a dignified look. The name of the founder of Troy had come to be considered at school as a sort of a secret that could only be answered by reading Smaragdov's book. But no one in town except Kolya had a copy of it. And so one day while Kolya's back was turned, young Kartashov had picked up Smaragdov from among Kolya's other books and had been lucky enough to open it at just the place where it discussed the founding of Troy. This had happened quite a while before, but until then the boy had been too shy to reveal his knowledge publicly. He had also been afraid that Kolya might somehow make a fool of him if he did. But now, for some reason, he could no longer restrain himself and spoke up. He had been longing to do so for quite a while.

"So who was it?" Kolya asked contemptuously, turning toward Kartashov. From the boy's face, he knew at once that he knew and prepared himself to meet the new situation.

A discordant note could be detected in the general mood now.

"Troy was founded by Teucer, Dardanus, Ilius, and Troas," the boy rattled off in one breath, turning so red that it was impossible to look at him without feeling sorry for him. All the boys, however, kept their eyes riveted on him for a whole minute, after which all those eyes, as if at a command, turned to Kolya, who was still glaring with contempt at the impudent little boy.

"What do you mean, actually, when you say they founded Troy?" he finally said, as if doing the boy a tremendous honor just by acknowledging his existence. "Besides, how does one go about founding a city or a state? Do you think each of those fellows came along carrying a brick and put it down there, is that it?"

There was laughter. Poor Kartashov turned from red to purple. He didn't answer and was ready to burst into tears. Kolya kept him in this state for another minute before going on.

"Before you speak of such historical events as the founding of a nation, you should first try to understand what it means," he said in a stern, lecturing tone. "Actually, I don't lay great store in these old wives' tales and I don't have much respect for world history as a whole," he added, now addressing himself to everybody in general.

"You mean world history?" Snegirev asked with a strange note of fear in his voice.

"Yes, world history. It's nothing but the study of a succession of human blunders. The only subjects I respect are mathematics and the natural sciences," Kolya said, showing off. He glanced quickly at Alyosha, who was the only person there about whose opinion he was worried. But Alyosha remained silent and unsmiling. If Alyosha had said something then, that would have ended the matter, but he said nothing and his silence could very well indicate his contempt, Kolya felt, becoming quite irritated.

"Now, take the classical languages—it's sheer madness . . . I don't believe you agree with me, Karamazov?"

"I don't." Alyosha smiled restrainedly.

"If you want my true opinion about Greek and Latin—they're just a way of policing people. That's the only reason they're taught . . ." Kolya noticed that again he was becoming breathless with excitement. "They were introduced in school curriculae to dull the students' intelligence. It was already pretty boring before, but they felt they had to make it even more boring; it was already senseless, so they had to make it still more senseless. And so they dragged in classical languages. That is my sincere opinion and I hope I never change it," Kolya concluded challengingly. A bright red spot appeared on each of his cheeks.

"That's the truth!" Smurov said in a tone ringing with conviction. He had been listening attentively to Kolya's every word.

"He says that, but he's top of his class in Latin," a boy remarked.

"That's right, papa, he says all these things, but no one's as good as he is in Latin," Ilyusha echoed.

"But what does that prove?" Kolya felt he had to ward off this objection, although he was very pleased with it. "The only reason I cram Latin is because I'm made to, because I promised my mother that I'd graduate from the school, and because I believe we must do whatever we do as well as we can. But deep down in my heart I have nothing but contempt for the whole swindle. I'm sure you disagree again, Karamazov?"

"Why do you call it a 'swindle'?" Alyosha said, smiling again.

"Just think: the classics have all been translated into modern languages and so we don't have to study Latin to read them. We study it only because it dulls our senses and makes us more susceptible to police control. So why shouldn't I call it a swindle?"

"But who has put all these ideas into your head?" Alyosha asked him in considerable surprise.

"First of all, I can have ideas without their being put into my head by anyone, and in the second place, what I've just told you about the translations of the classics, Kolbasnikov said publicly in front of his whole class, the third . . ."

"The doctor has arrived!" Nina suddenly announced.

And, indeed, Mrs. Khokhlakov's carriage had driven up to the gate. Snegirev, who had been expecting the doctor since morning, rushed headlong out to meet him. Mrs. Snegirev sat up a little higher in her armchair and assumed a dignified air. Alyosha went over to Ilyusha's bed and straightened the pillows, and Nina worriedly watched him tidy her brother's bed. The boys hurriedly took their leave, some of them saying they'd come back in the evening. Kolya called Perezvon and the dog jumped down from the bed.

"I'm not leaving yet," Kolya quickly said to Ilyusha. "I'll wait in the passage while the doctor is here and then I'll come back with Perezvon."

But the doctor was already on the way in, an important-looking figure of a man in a bearskin coat, with long, dark side-whiskers and a clean-shaven, shining chin. He seemed somewhat taken aback as he stepped into the room and stopped, apparently believing that he'd come to the wrong place. "What is this? Where am I?" he muttered, without removing his bearskin coat or his sealskin cap. The crowd of people, the poverty of the room, the washing hanging on a line in a corner—all this quite confused him.

Snegirev was bowing low before him.

"This is the right place, sir. This is it," he kept mumbling ingratiatingly. "This is my house. This is where the patient is . . ."

"Snegirev?" the doctor asked in a loud, imperious voice. "Are you Mr. Snegirev?"

"Yes, sir."

"I see."

The doctor glanced disgustedly around the room once more and removed his bearskin coat. Everybody noticed an important decoration which flashed on his front for all to see. Snegirev took his coat and the doctor removed his cap.

"So where's the patient?" the doctor asked in a peremptory tone.

CHAPTER 6

Precociousness

"What do you think the doctor will say?" Kolya said nervously and quickly. "What a repulsive mug the man has, don't you think? I loathe medicine!"

"Ilyusha's going to die," Alyosha said sadly. "There doesn't seem to be any doubt about it."

"A bunch of frauds! Ah, medicine is such a fraud. I'm very pleased, though, to have got to know you, Karamazov. I've been wanting to meet you for a long time. It's only a pity we had to meet under such sad circumstances."

Kolya would have liked to say something warmer, more effusive, but something stopped him. Alyosha felt it, smiled, and shook his hand.

"I've long considered you an exceptional person and respected you," Kolya started again, feeling he was about to get mixed up. "I understand you're a mystic and I know you've lived in the monastery. But contact with real life will cure you; it never fails to, with natures such as yours."

"Why do you call me a mystic? And what am I supposed to be cured of?" Alyosha asked him, a little surprised.

"Well, you know, all that stuff about God and the rest . . ."

"Why, don't you believe in God yourself?"

"No, no, don't misunderstand me—I have nothing against God. I know, of course, that God is only a hypothesis, but I recognize the fact that it is a useful hypothesis, to keep order . . . order in the world, and so on, so that if God didn't exist, He would have to be invented."

Kolya was beginning to blush. He was afraid Alyosha would think he was trying to display his knowledge to show him that he was a grown-up. "But I'm not trying to show off my knowledge to him at all," Kolya thought indignantly, and he suddenly became very annoyed.

"I must say, I hate to get into this sort of debate," he said sharply, "because, after all, it's perfectly possible to love mankind even without God, don't you think? Why, Voltaire didn't believe in God, but he loved mankind . . ."

Oh damn, there he went again!

"Voltaire did believe in God, but not very much I think, and if he liked mankind I don't think it was so very much either," Alyosha said quietly and unaffectedly, as if talking to someone of his own age. Kolya was particularly struck by Alyosha's uncertainty about Voltaire's belief, as if he were submitting the matter to him, thirteen-year-old Kolya, to settle. "You have read Voltaire, haven't you?" Alyosha added.

"N-no, not really . . . Although I did read *Candide* in a Russian translation, an old and ridiculous translation, too . . ." Ah, he was showing off again!

"But you did understand it, didn't you?"

"Oh yes, of course, everything . . . What makes you ask? You're thinking about the obscenities in it? . . . But I understood, of course, that it's a philosophical novel and that Voltaire wrote it to prove an idea and . . ." Kolya was getting a little entangled now. "You know, Karamazov, I'm a socialist, an incorrigible socialist," he suddenly declared.

"A socialist!" Alyosha said, beginning to laugh. "You've managed to become a socialist pretty quickly. Why, I believe you told me you were only thirteen!"

Kolya winced.

"First of all, I'm practically fourteen—I'll be fourteen in two weeks," he said, flushing, "and in the second place, I really don't see what my age has to do with it! We were talking about my convictions and not about my age, remember?"

"When you're a few years older, you'll realize yourself what an important role age plays in our beliefs. I have the feeling that these are not really your own opinions that you've been expressing," Alyosha said in as friendly and unassertive a way as he could, but Kolya heatedly interrupted him.

"Wait a minute. You're demanding obedience and mysticism of me. Now, wouldn't you agree, for instance, that the Christian religion has mainly served the interests of the rich and the powerful by enabling them to enslave the lower classes? Isn't that a fact?"

"Oh, I know where you got that from! I was sure someone had put you up to it!" Alyosha cried.

"Why, again you insist that I must have picked this up somewhere or other. No one has put me up to anything! I can think for myself, you know! Now, let me say this: I'm not against Christ, for He was an extremely humane character and if He were alive today, I'm certain He would join the revolutionary movement and might even play a leading role in it . . . As a matter of fact, I'm pretty sure He would."

"But where on earth did you get all this stuff from? What fool have you been talking to all this time?" Alyosha cried.

"Well, since the truth is bound to come out in the end anyway, I can tell you I've talked quite a bit with Mr. Rakitin, with whom I had a certain business . . . But then, of course, I understand that old Belinsky also held similar opinions."

"Belinsky? I don't remember his writing anything of that sort."

"If he didn't write such things, I understand he said them. Someone told me . . . But the hell with it."

"But you yourself, have you read any Belinsky?"

"N-no, not quite . . . but I read something . . . you know that passage about Tatyana—why she refused to leave with Onegin. That I've read."

"Why she refused to leave her husband and go off with Onegin? But how can you possibly understand things like that at your age?"

"I'm beginning to think you take me for a little boy, like Smurov or somebody," Kolya said with an irritated grin. "I don't want you to think, though, that I'm really a revolutionary extremist. There are many things on which I don't see eye to eye with Mr. Rakitin at all. I mentioned Tatyana just now, but that doesn't mean that I'm for the emancipation of women. I'll go along with the idea that woman is a subordinate creature and that she should be obedient. 'Les femmes tricottent,' as Napoleon said once." Kolya for some reason snorted as he said this. "And, on this point at least, I fully share the opinion of that pseudo-great man. I also feel that leaving our country and running away to America is the most despicable thing a man can do, or even worse, it's a mistake! Why should anyone want to go to America when there are so many things to be done in the service of mankind here in Russia? And precisely now, right now! There is so much fruitful work facing us here. Well, that was my answer."

"Your answer to whom? Has anyone invited you to go to America with him?"

"I admit such offers have been made me, but I turned them down. But look, Karamazov, it's understood that you won't repeat a word of this to anyone, isn't it? This is strictly between us. I have absolutely no desire to land in the hands of the Secret Service and then learn lessons by the Chain Bridge. You know the song: 'Remember that Chain Bridge building . . .' You know it, don't you? But what's so funny about it? Why are you laughing? You don't think, by any chance, that I just invented all this to impress you?"

(And what if Alyosha found out that Kolya had read only one single issue of *The Bell* in his father's bookcase and that he hadn't read anything else about all this, Kolya thought with a shudder.)

"Oh no, not at all. I'm not laughing at you and it never even occurred to me that you might have invented it. That's just the trouble, it's all too real. But tell me this: you were just talking about Tatyana. Have you read Pushkin's *Evgeny Onegin,* at least, since you judge Tatyana?"

"No, I haven't read it, but I'm planning to. I'm not prejudiced one way or the other, Karamazov. I intend to give a fair hearing to both sides. But why did you ask me that?"

"For no reason."

"Tell me, Karamazov, do you despise me so very much?" Kolya suddenly straightened up and faced Alyosha, as though ready to fight him. "Do me a favor and tell me frankly what you think."

"Whether I despise you?" Alyosha looked at him in surprise. "Why should I despise you? I'm a bit sad, though, that such a naturally charming boy as you, who hasn't even begun to live, should already be corrupted by all this wicked nonsense."

"You needn't worry about my charms, you know," Kolya cut him off sharply, although he was pleased to hear what Alyosha thought of him. "It's a fact that I'm pretty touchy. And when, just now, you had that smile on your face, I had the impression . . ."

"No, no, I was smiling about something else, about something I read recently. It was about the impression our students made on a German who lived for some time in Russia: 'If you show a celestial map to a Russian schoolboy who has never heard about such things before,' that German wrote, 'the next day he will return your map corrected.' The German was trying to say of Russian youth that they combine infinite conceit with total ignorance."

"But that's perfectly true! What a smart German—he hit the nail right on the head!" Kolya suddenly burst into delighted laughter. "But then the Teuton missed the good side of it, don't you think? Conceit there may be, that comes from youth and it will pass if you really think it should pass. But what about the independent spirit that manifests itself almost from early childhood, the boldness of thought and conviction, which is so different from the cringing servility before authority that is so typical of his Sauerkraut compatriots . . . Nevertheless, that German hit it just right. Bravo for him. Although, as a matter of principle, the best way of handling the Germans is to strangle them. They may be pretty good in science, but they ought to be strangled nevertheless."

"Why strangle them?" Alyosha said with a smile.

"Oh, well, I went a bit overboard there, I agree. There are times when I must sound terribly immature and that's because, when I'm pleased about something and don't restrain myself in time, I'm likely to say heaven knows what . . . But listen, I wonder what that doctor could have been doing in there while we've been talking all this nonsense? He's been in there for quite a while, hasn't he? Although perhaps, while he was at it, he also examined Ilyusha's mother and his sister Nina. You know, I like that Nina. Do you know what she said to me when I was leaving just now? She said: 'Why didn't you come sooner?' And it sounded like a sort of reproach, the way she said it. I have the impression that she's an awfully nice person and I'm terribly sorry for her."

"You're right, and if you come here often enough, you'll find out what a wonderful person she is. It would be good for you to get to know people like her and to learn to appreciate them; yes, and there are so many other things that one can learn from such people," Alyosha said with deep conviction. "That more than anything else will make you reconsider many things."

"You know I'm terribly sorry, in fact I'm furious with myself for not having come here before," Kolya said ruefully.

"Yes, it's an awful shame. You saw what happiness you gave that poor child! And he was so miserable before you came."

"Don't keep telling me that. I feel bad enough as it is. But I guess I deserve to be told. I stayed away out of pride, out of selfish, contemptible, petty pride, of which I've been unable to rid myself, although I've been trying all my life. I can see it all now, Karamazov, and I realize what a despicable creature I am."

"I think you have a wonderful nature, although it's been corrupted a little. You know, I can see very well how you can have had such an influence on that sickly, generous, oversensitive little boy," Alyosha said with sincere warmth.

"It's strange that you of all people should say that, Karamazov, because several times, and even just now, I thought you despised me. You cannot imagine how important your opinion is to me."

"But why should you be so suspicious of people, at your age already! You know, curiously enough, as I was looking at you inside there, while you were telling some story, I suddenly thought you must be overly suspicious and sensitive. Isn't that curious?"

"Did you really think that? You've got quite an eye, you know. Wait, I bet you thought that when I was telling the story about the goose! At one point while I was telling it, I suddenly got the feeling that you despised me because I was trying to impress the others with what a smart fellow I was. I suddenly hated you at that moment and spouted all kinds of nonsense . . . And then I got the same impression out here in the passage, only a few minutes ago, when I was holding forth about God, when I said that if God didn't exist He would have to be invented—I was afraid that you might think I was trying to show off my knowledge to you, especially since I picked up that sentence from some book. But I swear to you that I wasn't saying all these things out of vanity, but just because I felt happy. I swear, it was simply sheer joy that made me talk like that, although I realize perfectly well that it's rather disgraceful for a fellow to throw himself at people like that just because he feels happy. I'm aware of that, too. But now, at least, I know that you don't despise me and that I just imagined it all. You know, Karamazov, I am extremely unhappy. God knows the things I imagine sometimes—that everyone is laughing at me, the whole world, and then I'd like to turn the whole order of things upside down."

"And so you make those around you miserable." Alyosha smiled.

"Yes, and in particular my mother. But tell me, Karamazov, am I being ridiculous at this moment?"

"Why don't you stop carrying on about that? Just forget about it altogether!" Alyosha cried. "Anyway, what does it mean, being ridiculous? There are so many different ways a man may seem funny to someone else. Especially these days when everyone who has any talent seems to be morbidly afraid that he may appear ridiculous. That's why so many gifted people are so unhappy. The only surprising thing is that you've started feeling this way when you're still so young, but I've noticed it in many other young people too. Nowadays, mere children suffer from it. It's almost an obsession. The devil has crept into that insanity—yes, I actually mean it, the devil," Alyosha said unsmilingly, although Kolya, who was watching him closely, had the impression that he grinned. "You're really just like the rest of them. I mean, like very many people today," Alyosha concluded, "but there's no need for you to be like the rest."

"Even if everybody else becomes like that?"

"Yes, even if everybody else is like that. Be the only one who is not like it. Besides, you *are* different, because you weren't ashamed to admit to me things that you consider bad or even ridiculous in yourself. Who else today is willing to admit such things? No one. In fact, they've lost even the need to admit that they're wrong when they know they are. So be different from the others, even if you are the only one who is different from all the rest."

"Great! I was right about you—you know how to make people feel better. Oh, Karamazov, I've been so anxious to meet you for such a long time! Did you really think about me too? You told me you thought of me too, didn't you?"

"Yes, I knew of you by reputation and I did think of you . . . And if it was pride that made you ask that now, there's nothing so wrong about it."

"Do you know, Karamazov, all this sounds a bit like a

declaration of love," Kolya said shyly, with a strange languor. "Do you think it's ridiculous?"

"Not in the least. But even if it were, it wouldn't matter, because it's good," Alyosha said with a bright smile.

"But tell me honestly—aren't you yourself a little ashamed to be with me? I can see it by your eyes . . ." Kolya smiled slyly, but there was almost happiness in his eyes.

"What is there to be ashamed of?"

"Why are you blushing then?"

"It's you who's making me blush," Alyosha laughed. He had really turned very red. "Well, yes, it is a bit embarrassing, but I don't really know why it should be . . ." he muttered, quite confused now.

"Oh, I like you so much right now, this minute, maybe just because you feel ashamed to be with me, because I can see that you feel just the same way I do!" Kolya was in a state of great elation. His cheeks were afire, his eyes were sparkling.

"Listen, Kolya, there will be times in your life when you'll be very unhappy," Alyosha said quite unexpectedly.

"I know, I know. But it's so strange the way you can tell things in advance . . ."

"But, on the whole, you'll be pleased with your life."

"Good! Hurray! You're a prophet! Oh, Karamazov, we'll become very close friends. And shall I tell you what I like most about you? It's that you treat me just like an equal. But we are not equals—you are by very far my superior! But we will become friends. You know, during the past month I kept saying to myself: 'Either we will at once become friends for the rest of our lives or we will turn our backs on each other and be enemies till the grave!'"

"And while you were saying that, you, of course, already liked me." Alyosha laughed gaily.

"Yes, I did, I did, an awful lot, and I was thinking and imagining all kinds of things about you . . . But how could you know that in advance? But look, here's the doctor . . . I wonder what he'll say? Look at his face, oh . . ."

CHAPTER 7

Ilyusha

The doctor had on his bearskin coat again, with his sealskin cap on his head. His wore an almost angry, disgusted expression, as if he were afraid of dirtying himself in this house. He glanced quickly across the passage and sternly measured Alyosha and Kolya with his eyes. Alyosha stepped outside and signaled to the coachman to drive up to the steps. Then Snegirev came rushing out into the passage. Bent almost in two and looking apologetic, he stopped the doctor to hear his final verdict. The poor man's face looked miserable and frightened.

"Doctor, doctor, sir, is it possible? . . ." His hands dropped in despair, although his eyes were still fixed beseechingly on the doctor's face, as if what the doctor said now could alter Ilyusha's fate.

"What can I do? I'm not God," the doctor said casually, although out of habit in a lecturing tone.

"Doctor . . . sir . . . But how soon, how soon?"

"You had better be prepared for anything," the doctor said, pronouncing each syllable distinctly. He was about to step out of the house, to the carriage waiting for him.

"But, doctor, in the name of Christ, tell me," Snegirev muttered in terror, "please, tell me—isn't there anything, anything at all that could save him?"

"It does not depend on me, you understand," the doctor said impatiently. "However . . . hm . . ." he stopped suddenly, "if you could, for instance, send your son . . . er, but then it must be done at once, right away, without delay!" The doctor said the words "at once" and "without delay" so severely, even angrily, that Snegirev started. "Send him then . . . er . . . to Sy-ra-cuse . . . and, as a result of the change and the favorable conditions, he might perhaps . . ."

"Syracuse?" Snegirev cried in bewilderment, as if unable to grasp what the doctor was saying.

"Syracuse is in Sicily," Kolya said in a loud voice. The doctor glanced at him.

"Sicily! Oh, but, sir, you saw yourself . . ." Snegirev made a helpless sweeping gesture, as if to show the doctor the surrounding poverty. "What will I do with my wife and my family?"

"N-no, your family needn't go with you to Sicily. Your family should go to the Caucasus in early spring . . . The Caucasus would be good for your daughter. As to your wife, after she has taken a cure of the waters, for her rheumatism, in the Caucasus, you will have to send her at once to Paris to the psychiatric hospital of Dr. Lepelletier. If you wish, I can give you a letter for him . . . And then there might be a . . . er . . ."

"But, doctor, doctor, you can see for yourself . . ." Snegirev again pointed in despair at the bare wooden walls in the passage.

"Well, that's something I can do nothing about," the doctor said with a grin. "I've only told you what science could do as a last resort . . . For the rest, I'm sorry to say it isn't up to me."

"Don't worry, doc, my dog won't bite you," Kolya said loudly and angrily, noticing the worried way the doctor kept glancing at Perezvon. He had, as he explained later, called him "doc" to "insult him."

"What's that?" The doctor glared at Kolya in surprise. "Who's he?" the doctor somehow asked Alyosha, as if he considered him responsible.

"I am Perezvon's master, doc, and beyond that you needn't worry about my identity," Kolya said loudly again.

"Perez—what?" the doctor repeated, not realizing that was the dog's name.

"Perez yourself! Good-by, doc, see you in Syracuse!"

"But who is he? Who?" the doctor inquired angrily.

"He's just a schoolboy, a bit cocky. Don't pay any attention to him," Alyosha said quickly, frowning. "Keep quiet, Kolya! You needn't pay any attention, doctor," Alyosha added, an impatient note creeping into his voice.

"That brat should get a good hiding, a good hiding!" the doctor said, stamping his foot and becoming really angry.

"You know, doc, perhaps Perezvon does bite, after all!" Kolya said in a quivering voice. He had turned pale and his eyes were glowing. "Here, Perezvon!"

"Kolya, if you say one more word, I will never have anything to do with you again!" Alyosha cried peremptorily.

"You know, doc, there's only one person in the world who can tell Kolya Krasotkin what to do, and it happens to be him." He pointed to Alyosha. "So, all right, I'm leaving. Good-by!"

Kolya walked quickly to the door leading inside and opened it. Perezvon rushed after him and they both disappeared. The doctor stood there for five seconds more, staring at Alyosha as if in a stupor. Then he made a spitting sound and went toward his carriage, repeating, "Well, I'll be—I'll be—I'll be . . ." Snegirev hurried to help him into the carriage and Alyosha followed Kolya into the room. Kolya was standing by Ilyusha's bed. Ilyusha held his hand and was calling for his father. Within a minute Snegirev returned.

"Papa, papa, come here," Ilyusha muttered in great excitement, but he was too weak to go on. He suddenly threw his emaciated arms forward, one around his father's neck, the other around Kolya's, and hugged them as hard as he could. Snegirev shook all over in soundless sobs and Kolya's chin and lips began to quiver.

"Papa, papa, I'm so, so sorry for you," Ilyusha moaned.

"Ilyusha, darling . . . Why, the new doctor said you'd get better . . . We'll all be so happy then . . . The doctor said . . ."

"Ah, papa, I know what the new doctor said about me . . . I could see it," Ilyusha said, and again hugged both his father and Kolya as hard as he could.

"Don't cry, papa . . . When I die, get another boy, a good one . . . Choose the best one of them all, call him Ilyusha too, and love him instead of me . . ."

"Stop talking nonsense, old man. You'll get better soon," Kolya said angrily.

"But you must never forget me, papa," Ilyusha said. "I want you to come to my grave . . . And you know what—you can bury me by our big stone, where we used to go for our walks. Come and visit me there in the evening with Krasotkin . . . And I want Perezvon to come too. I'll be waiting for you in the evenings . . . Papa, papa . . ."

His voice failed him and the three of them remained for a while in their silent embrace. Nina was crying quietly in her chair too. And seeing them all weeping, Mrs. Snegirev also burst into tears.

"Ilyusha, Ilyusha!" she called out.

Kolya suddenly freed himself from Ilyusha's embrace.

"I must go now, old man. My mother is waiting for me for lunch," he said very quickly. "I wish I'd warned her I'd be late. She must be terribly worried by now . . . But I'll be

back later in the afternoon and I'll stay with you all evening,
for I have thousands of things to tell you about. I'll bring
Perezvon with me too, but for now I think I'll take him
along, because he'd be howling all the time I was away and
that would disturb you. So good-by for now."

And he rushed out into the passage. He was trying hard not
to cry, but once out in the passage he could not hold back
his tears. And it was in that state that Alyosha found him.

"Kolya, you absolutely must do as you promised and come
back here, or he'll be terribly miserable."

"Oh, I'll be here without fail. I hate myself so for not
having come much sooner," Kolya said, no longer ashamed
of his tears.

Snegirev suddenly appeared in the passage, quickly closing
the door behind him. His face was painfully contorted and his
lips were trembling. He stopped in front of Alyosha and
Kolya and flung up his arms in despair.

"I don't want a good boy! I don't need any other boy!" he
whispered, wildly gnashing his teeth. " 'If I forget thee, Jerusalem, may my tongue . . .' "

The words died on his lips and he sank helplessly to his
knees beside the wooden bench. Clutching his head between
his fists, he sobbed, now and then incongruously whimpering
in his attempts to suppress the sounds, so that they wouldn't
hear him inside. Kolya rushed out into the street.

"See you, Karamazov. By the way, will you be here tonight?" he asked abruptly, almost angrily.

"Yes, I'll be here in the evening without fail."

"What was it he said about Jerusalem?"

"It's from the Bible. 'If I forget thee, Jerusalem'—meaning
if I forget what is most precious to me, if I exchange it for
something else, then . . ."

"I understand! No need to go on. So don't forget to come
too. Here, Perezvon!" he called the dog with real fierceness
now and set out for home at a very fast pace.

BOOK XI

IVAN

At Grushenka's

Alyosha was walking toward Cathedral Square. He was on his way to Mrs. Morozov's house, where Grushenka lived. Early that morning she had sent Fenya to him with an urgent message, asking him to come and see her. From Fenya, Alyosha had found out that her mistress had been in particular distress since the day before.

Since Mitya's arrest, two months earlier, Alyosha had often been to see Grushenka, either of his own accord or to transmit messages to and from Mitya. On the third day after the arrest, Grushenka had been taken ill, and she was very ill for almost five weeks. For a whole week she had been unconscious. She was much changed now: she was thinner and paler, although for the past couple of weeks she had been well enough to leave the house. To Alyosha, however, her face seemed even more attractive than before and it was a joy to him to look at her when he went to see her. She had a new air of firmness and intelligent purpose about her. There were signs of a spiritual transformation in her: an unshakable determination filled her with both resignation and peace of mind. A little vertical line had appeared between her eyebrows, which gave her beautiful face a look of thoughtful concentration and, at first glance, made it appear almost austere. In any case there was nothing left now of her former frivolity. Alyosha found it somewhat strange, though, that, despite the terrible blow she had suffered when the man she had promised to marry was arrested for a heinous crime almost at the very moment of their betrothal, despite her ensuing sickness, and the almost inevitable guilty verdict at the forthcoming trial, Grushenka had never lost her youthful gaiety. Her eyes, once so proud, now shone with a quiet glow, although, at times, the old hard and hostile fire still flickered in them. This was when an old anxiety stole into her heart, something she had never forgotten, something, indeed, that tormented her more than ever now. The object of this anxiety was Katerina, who had haunted Grushenka even in the feverish nightmares of her sickness. Alyosha understood that she was terribly jealous of her, although Katerina never once went to visit Mitya in prison, which she could have done easily enough had she chosen to. This had become a very difficult problem for Alyosha because he was the only person in whom Grushenka confided and whom she constantly asked for advice, and very often he was quite unable to tell her anything.

So he was full of misgivings as he entered her house now. She had been to visit Mitya and had been back home for half an hour. From the way she jumped up from the armchair by the table to come and meet him, Alyosha realized how impatiently she had been waiting for him. There were cards on the table and they seemed to have been dealt out for a game of Fools. On the other side of the table, a bed had been made up on the leather sofa, and in it Maximov, in a dressing gown and a cotton nightcap, lay propped up on pillows. He was obviously not feeling well and was very weak, but he was smiling happily. This homeless old man had stayed at Grushenka's ever since he had returned with her from Mokroye two months earlier. When they had arrived in rain and sleet, he had sat down on the sofa, wet through to the bone and frightened, and had looked at her with a beseeching smile. Grushenka, who was feeling miserable and was already in the first stages of a fever, almost completely forgot about his existence as she fussed about the house in the first half hour after their arrival. Then she suddenly noticed him and gave him a strange look, at which he gave a helpless little chuckle. She called Fenya and told her to give him something to eat. After that, he continued to sit in the same spot, hardly stirring. When it got dark and the shutters were closed, Fenya asked Grushenka:

"Why, madam, is the gentleman staying here for the night?"

"Yes, make up a bed for him on the sofa," Grushenka said.

When Grushenka had asked Maximov about his further plans, he had told her that he really had none for the moment and that, in fact, he had nowhere to go since "Mr. Kalganov, who has been putting me up until now, told me he couldn't have me anymore and gave me five rubles."

Filled as she was with her own grief, Grushenka felt sorry for poor old Maximov.

"Well, I guess you'd better stay here then," she said with a smile. That smile made Maximov's chin jerk and his lips tremble as he dissolved into tears of gratitude.

And so this nomadic sponger had remained with her ever since. Even when Grushenka became ill, he did not leave, and Fenya and her mother did not throw him out but continued to feed him and make up the bed on the sofa for him. Later, when Grushenka started visiting Mitya in prison (which she did as soon as she could go out, even before she had completely recovered), she would sit down upon her return with "Maximushka" and talk all kinds of nonsense to him, just to try and take her mind off her grief; and she became quite accustomed to him. Then she discovered that, on occasion, Maximov was quite good at telling stories, and gradually he became almost indispensable to her.

Otherwise, except for Alyosha, who did not come to see her every day and never stayed very long when he did come, Grushenka saw no one. Samsonov, Grushenka's old protector, was seriously ill at the time, "at his last gasp," they said in town, and, indeed, he was to die only a week after Mitya's trial. Three weeks before his death, he summoned his sons with their wives and children to his bedside and, feeling that his end was near, ordered them not to leave him. At the same time he ordered his servants not to admit Grushenka to the house and, if she came, to tell her that he wished her a long and happy life and many good times, and that he wanted her to forget him. Grushenka, however, sent someone every day to inquire about his health.

"Here you are at last," Grushenka cried, throwing down the cards and happily greeting Alyosha. "Maximushka kept frightening me by saying he didn't expect you'd come today. I wanted to see you so badly! Sit down here, at the table. Would you like some coffee?"

"That would be nice," Alyosha said, sitting down. "I'm rather hungry."

"Good. Fenya, Fenya! Bring us some coffee please! I've been keeping it hot for you, Alyosha. Fenya, bring some pies, too, and see that they're hot. I had a real row about those pies, Alyosha: I took them to Mitya in prison and, believe it or not, he wouldn't eat them. He even threw one pie on the floor and stepped on it. I said to him: 'I'll leave them with the guard and if you don't eat them before evening that'll show that it's your malicious spite that feeds you.' And I left. So we've quarreled again. You wouldn't believe it, Alyosha—every time I go to see him, we quarrel."

Grushenka fired all this off in one breath, in great excitement. Maximov seemed embarrassed. He lowered his eyes, still grinning.

"What did you two quarrel about this time?" Alyosha asked her.

"I never expected we could quarrel about this! Just imagine —now he's jealous of the Pole. 'Why are you keeping him?' he asks me, 'for I understand you're supporting him now!' He never stops being jealous. He's jealous while he eats, while he sleeps, all the time. Last week he even made a scene about Kuzma."

"But he knew about you and the Pole before, didn't he?"

"Go and try to understand him, though. He's known about it all the time, but today he suddenly jumped up and started reproaching me. I'm even ashamed to repeat the things he said. What a fool! Rakitin came to see him as I was leaving. Perhaps he's putting all these ideas into Mitya's head —do you think so?" she asked absentmindedly.

"He loves you so much—that's why he's like that. Besides, he's very much on edge just now."

"Well, it's quite natural that he should be on edge with the trial coming up tomorrow. In fact, I wanted to talk to him about it when I went there, for I'm afraid even to think of what will happen. Besides, do you think I'm not on edge too? And he finds nothing better to do than to worry about that Pole! Ah, the idiot! I hope he's not jealous of Maximushka, at least."

"My wife used to be very jealous too," Maximov said, putting in his word.

"That's really pretty hard to imagine." Grushenka laughed despite herself. "Who could she be possibly have been jealous of?"

"She was jealous of the young maids."

"Ah, keep quiet, Maximushka. I don't feel like laughing now. I'm too furious . . . And don't you look at the pies like that—you can't have any. And you can't have any liqueur either. As if I had nothing better to do now than look after you. This place has become a kind of alms house, really," she added with a laugh.

"I know I'm unworthy of your generosity," Maximov said

in a tearful voice; "perhaps you'd do better to be generous with people whom you need more than you need me . . ."

"Ah, Maximushka, every person is needed, and who can tell who is needed more and who less. Oh, Alyosha, I wish that Pole had never existed, for he, too, suddenly decided to fall ill today and I had to go and see him as well. Well, I'll send him some pies too. I hadn't sent him any before, but since Mitya has accused me of sending them to him, I'll send them now! Ah, here's Fenya with a letter . . . Yes, that's it, it's from the Poles again, and again they're asking me for money!"

Pan Musijalowicz had indeed sent Grushenka one of his long, florid letters, the gist of which was that he wanted her to send him three rubles. Enclosed in the letter was a signed IOU for that sum, payable within three months and counter-signed by Pan Wrublewski. Grushenka had already received many such letters and IOU's. They had started arriving two weeks before, when she had first recovered from her sickness. She also knew that, while she was still sick, the two Poles had come to inquire about her health. The first letter she had received was extremely long, filling a whole large sheet of notepaper. It had a huge family crest on the seal and was written in such a complicated, involved style that she gave up reading it when she got half way through because she could not follow. Besides, she had other things to worry about. The next day, she had received a second letter, in which Musijalowicz asked her to lend him two thousand rubles for a very short period. Grushenka had not answered that letter either. Then followed a whole series of letters, one a day, all just as pompous and florid as before and differing from each other only in the rapidly decreasing figure of the loan requested, until it became a mere one hundred rubles, then twenty-five, then ten, and then a letter came in which each Polish gentleman asked her for a loan of one ruble; it was accompanied by a receipt signed jointly by both.

Grushenka then felt sorry for her first love and in the evening went to pay the Poles a visit. She found them living in dire poverty, almost indigent, without food, heat, or to-bacco, and owing money to their landlady. The two hundred rubles they had won from Mitya in Mokroye had mysteri-ously disappeared. Grushenka was rather taken aback when the Poles met her with their usual pompous and aggressive airs of independence, when they insisted on maintaining a pretense of the same knightly etiquette and drowned her in their florid speeches. Grushenka just burst out laughing and gave ten rubles to her former seducer. The next day she laughingly recounted the incident to Mitya and, at that time, it had not made him feel jealous in the least. Since then, however, the Poles had never ceased bombarding Grushenka with letters asking her for money, and she had kept sending them small sums. And now, all of a sudden, Mitya had become jealous.

"Stupid as I am, I stopped over at the Pole's on my way to see Mitya. He had been taken ill, the Pole," Grushenka began again, speaking hurriedly and nervously. "Then, when I saw Mitya, I told him laughingly that the Pole had picked up his guitar and tried to sing me those old songs of his, hoping that I'd lose my head and go back to him. And as I was telling him, he all of a sudden jumped up and started swearing like a madman. Well, if that's the way it is, I'll just send those pies to the Poles. Fenya, did they send that girl again with the letter? All right, then, give her these three rubles and wrap up, say, ten pies, and tell her to take the package to them. And you, Alyosha, don't you forget to tell Mitya that I sent them those pies."

"I certainly won't tell him anything of the sort," Alyosha said, smiling.

"Why, do you think he's really suffering? No, he's just making himself jealous deliberately. He doesn't really care . . ." Grushenka said bitterly.

"What do you mean—deliberately?"

"You're very silly, Alyosha. You don't understand the first thing about it, although in other ways you're an intelligent man. What offends me is not that he's jealous of a woman like me—in fact, I would have been offended if he hadn't been jealous at all. The way I am, I don't mind jealousy. I myself can be pretty cruel when it comes down to it, and pretty jealous too. But what hurts me is that he doesn't really love me now, that he has deliberately worked himself up into that state. Why, you don't really think I'm so blind? He's suddenly started telling me about that Katya woman: she's so great and so marvelous and this and that, and she's sent for a doctor from Moscow and engaged the most eminent and learned lawyer, the very best there is, to save him, Mitya . . . Shows he must love her, if he praises her so unashamedly right to my face, looking at me with those shameless eyes of his! So he feels he's in the wrong and is just trying to put the blame on me instead, so he can say to me later: 'Well it was you who started by taking up with that Pole again, so it's all right for me to feel the way I do about Katya.' You see, that's the way it really is. He's trying to make himself believe that it's all my fault, so he's deliberately picking on the Pole now. I tell you, Alyosha! But I'll . . ."

Grushenka could not finish saying what she would do; she covered her face with a handkerchief and burst into sobs.

"He is not in love with Katerina," Alyosha said with assurance.

"I'll soon find out for myself whether he is or not," Grushenka said, a threatening note creeping into her voice as she removed the handkerchief from her face. Her face was contorted. Alyosha saw sadly that the face, which had so recently impressed him with its gentle serenity, had now become sullen and cruel.

"Enough of this nonsense," she said sharply. "This was certainly not why I asked you to come. Alyosha, my pet, tell me—what will happen tomorrow? I'm so terribly worried about it! But I look at the people here, and no one except me seems to care about it at all! Are you, at least, thinking about it, Alyosha? Why, they'll be judging him tomorrow! Tell me, how will they go about judging him? But that lackey is the murderer! My God, is it possible that they'll condemn him for something the lackey did and that no one will come to his defense? They haven't even bothered the flunkey, have they?"

"They did question Smerdyakov," Alyosha said thoughtfully, "quite thoroughly, but they concluded that he couldn't be the one. He's very ill now; in fact, he's been ill ever since then, after his epileptic fit. He's really ill, you know," Alyosha added.

"But won't you go and see that lawyer yourself and talk to him privately about the whole business. Why, I understand he was paid three thousand rubles to come here from Petersburg . . ."

"Katerina, Ivan, and I each gave one thousand to pay the three thousand for the lawyer, but she paid two thousand on her own to get that doctor here from Moscow. The lawyer, Fetyukovich, usually charges more, but this case has caused such a sensation across the country and received such detailed coverage in the newspapers and magazines that Fetyukovich has taken it on more for personal publicity than for any other reason. I saw him yesterday."

"So did you tell him?" Grushenka asked excitedly.

"He listened to me but made no comment. He just told me that he has his own ideas about it all. He promised, though, to take what I'd told him into consideration."

"What on earth does that mean—take it into consideration? Ah, the crooks! They'll make a mess of things and that'll be the end of Mitya! But what about the doctor? Why did she send for a doctor too?"

"She wants him as an expert. They plan to prove that Dmitry is insane and that he didn't know what he was doing when he killed," Alyosha said with a pale smile, "but Mitya won't accept that."

"But it would be true if he had killed him!" Grushenka cried. "He was insane then, completely insane, and it was all my fault, horrible creature that I am! But he didn't do it. He didn't kill him! And with all those people in town against him, constantly saying he's the murderer! Even Fenya, the way she testified, made it look as if he'd done it. And then that civil servant who was with him in the store, and all those people who heard him threaten to kill his father in the tavern—they're all against him, all screaming that he's guilty!"

"Yes, the evidence against him keeps mounting," Alyosha said mournfully.

"And Gregory too, Gregory keeps insisting that the door was open. He just won't budge from that statement. I went to see him myself—nothing doing. He even swore at me," Grushenka said helplessly.

"Yes, I think that's the strongest evidence against Dmitry," Alyosha said.

"As to Mitya being crazy—well, he's that all right, even now," Grushenka said anxiously in a peculiarly mysterious tone. "I've been wanting to tell you about it for a long time, Alyosha. I see him every day, and every time he surprises me. What do you think, for instance, he's been talking about now? He starts talking and talks on and on and I can't understand a word of what he's saying. Well, I thought it must be something very clever, quite over the head of a stupid woman like me. But when I listened, I noticed he was talking about what he called a 'babe.' It was some baby or other, and he kept repeating, 'Why is the babe so poor?' and 'It's because of the babe that I'll go to Siberia now. I didn't kill, but it's right that I should go!' What it was all about, and what 'babe' he was talking about, I could not make out at all. But he was talking so emotionally, with tears in his eyes, that I began crying myself; when he saw that, he suddenly kissed me and then made the sign of the cross over me. Now tell me, Alyosha, can you explain to me what he can have been talking about?"

"It could be Rakitin, who, for some reason, has been going to see him very often lately." Alyosha smiled. "Although, I don't think that comes from Rakitin. I didn't see Mitya yesterday, but I'm going today."

"No, it's not Rakitin. It's your brother Ivan who's getting him all confused; he's been seeing him regularly and . . ." Grushenka suddenly broke off as if something had snapped inside her.

Alyosha stared at her in amazement.

"You mean Ivan goes to see him, then? I didn't know he'd gone there. In fact, Mitya told me Ivan had never once been to see him."

"Ah, now what have I done? I've said something I wasn't supposed to say!" Grushenka blushed and looked embarrassed. "Wait, Alyosha, keep quiet. Since I've let the cat out of the bag, I'll tell you everything. Ivan went to see Mitya twice—the first time just after he arrived from Moscow. That was even before I was taken ill. The second time was about a week ago. And he told Mitya not to tell you about his coming, in fact, not to tell anybody. He said his visits had to be kept secret."

Alyosha was deep in thought, trying hard to work something out. He was obviously very much surprised by what he'd just heard.

"Ivan never talks to me about Dmitry's case," he said slowly. "And, in general, he hasn't talked to me very much during these past two months. Whenever I've been to see him, he has always seemed displeased that I'd come, so I haven't been for three weeks now. Hm . . . if he saw Mitya a week ago, that may really account for the change that has come over Mitya lately . . ."

"Yes, something has changed in him, hasn't it?" Grushenka interrupted eagerly. "There's a secret between the two of them. Mitya himself told me they had a secret, a secret that keeps him on edge all the time. Before that, he was quite gay and cheerful . . . Well, he's still quite cheerful, but now he's liable suddenly to start pacing the room, shaking his head, and twisting the hairs on his right temple with his finger. I can tell at once that something special is worrying him . . . Oh, I know him . . . He used to be gay, and even today he was gay!"

"But you told me he was irritable . . ."

"That's right, he was irritable, but he was also gay. One moment he's gay, then he becomes irritated, and then he's gay again. And you know—what strikes me as so strange is that, with all those frightening things he has ahead of him, he sometimes roars with laughter about all kinds of silly little things, just like a little child."

"And so he told you not to tell me about Ivan? How did he put it? Did he just say—'Don't tell him'?"

"That's right. That's just the way he said it—'Don't you tell him.' Because, he told me, 'it's a secret.' Please, Alyosha, go there and try to find out what's going on, what this secret is between them. And please come and tell me!" Grushenka suddenly cried beseechingly. "Tell me, so that I can know what to expect at least . . . That was what I wanted to ask you to do for me, Alyosha, when I sent for you today."

"What makes you think it's something that concerns you, though? If that were the case, he'd never have mentioned the secret to you, would he?"

"I don't know . . . Perhaps there's something he'd like to tell me but doesn't dare. Perhaps he's preparing me. 'I have a secret,' he says, but then he won't tell me what secret . . ."

"What do you think it could be?"

"What do I think? It's the end of me, that's what I think. They've been plotting how to get rid of me, the three of of them, since this Katerina woman is in on it, too. Indeed, it all comes from her in the first place. And when he stands there and tells me all about how wonderful she is, he also means that I'm no match for her. He says it to prepare me for what is to come. He's decided to break off with me, and that's what the secret's all about. The three of them have arranged it all—that fool Mitya, the Katerina woman, and your dear brother Ivan. Now, a week ago, Mitya suddenly tells me that Ivan is in love with that woman, because he keeps visiting her all the time. Can it be true? Tell me the truth, don't spare me!"

"I'll never lie to you. Ivan is not in love with Katerina. I don't think he is, at least."

"That's exactly what I thought! So he was lying to me shamelessly! And that's why he pretended to be jealous now. He wants to be able to say later that it was all my fault! But he's such a terrible fool. He has no idea how to make things sound likely. He's much too honest for that . . . But, wait, I'll show him, I'll show him yet. 'You,' he says to me, 'you think I killed him,' and he says that to me, of all people. He reproaches me with thinking that! I hope God will forgive him for it. But that Katya, I'll get her at the trial. I'll make her pay for it! There are a few things I'll tell them there. I'll tell them everything!"

Grushenka again began to weep bitterly.

"I can tell you this for certain, Grushenka," Alyosha said, getting up. "First of all, he loves you. He loves you more than anyone in the world, and only you—you must believe me. This is something I know, if I know anything. And the second thing I must tell you is that I won't try to worm any secret out of him; if he tells me of his own accord, I'll tell him that I've promised to tell you about it, and then I'll come here and tell you. But I don't believe Katerina has anything to do with it at all; I think their secret is about something completely different. I'm almost sure of it. And it doesn't seem at all likely that Katerina, as I know her, could be involved. And so good-by for now."

Alyosha pressed her hand. She was still crying. He realized that she didn't believe very much of what he had said and that the only good he had done her really was to give her an opportunity to get her bitter suspicions off her chest. He didn't like leaving her in that state, but he was in a hurry. There were so many things he had to to do that day.

CHAPTER 2

The Injured Foot

First, Alyosha had to go to Mrs. Khokhlakov's. He hurried over there, hoping to get the business out of the way quickly so that he wouldn't be late visiting Mitya in prison. Mrs. Khokhlakov had not been feeling well for the past three weeks: her foot had somehow become swollen and, although she was not actually in bed, she had to stay home, reclining in a very attractive, albeit most decorous, *déshabillé* on the sofa in her boudoir. Alyosha had once noted with innocent amusement that, despite her injured foot, Mrs. Khokhlakov was more careful than ever about what she wore, that she favored all sorts of new topknots, ribbons, and loose wrappers, and he had a pretty good explanation for this, although he dismissed such thoughts from his mind as frivolous. In the past two months, Peter Perkhotin had become one of the most frequent visitors to her house.

Alyosha had not been at the house for four days, and now, since he was in a hurry, he would have liked to go directly to Lise's room, for it was to see her that he had come. Lise had sent her maid to him the day before with a message saying that she had "something very important" to discuss with him, and this, for certain reasons of his own, aroused considerable interest in Alyosha. But while the maid was gone to announce him to Lise, Mrs. Khokhlakov, informed of his arrival, sent a servant to ask him "to come in for one minute" to see her. Alyosha decided that it would be better, under the circumstances, to see the lady first, for otherwise she would be sending someone to Lise's room every minute to remind him that she was waiting. Mrs. Khokhlakov was half lying on her sofa, looking particularly elegant, and was apparently very excited about something.

"It's been ages and ages since I've seen you! Do you know, it's been a whole week . . . although, when I come to think of it, I believe you were here only four days ago—on Wednesday. You've come to see Lise, haven't you? And I'm sure you intended to tiptoe in to her directly, so that I wouldn't even hear you! . . . My dear Alexei, I wish you knew how worried I am about Lise! But I'll come to that later, although it is what concerns me most of all. My dear Alexei, you know I trust you implicitly when it comes to Lise. Since the death of Father Zosima—may he rest in peace"—Mrs. Khokhlakov crossed herself—"I consider you a hermit, a hermit, although, I must say, you do look charming in that new suit. Where can you possibly have found such a tailor around here? . . . But that was not what I wanted to ask you about now. By the way, I hope you don't mind if I still call you Alyosha sometimes—I'm an old woman and I should really be allowed to," she said, smiling coquettishly. "But, we'll talk about that some other time, too. That's not the important thing I wanted to talk to you about now. The main thing is that I mustn't forget about the most important thing. I count on you to remind me of it when I get carried away by other things. But how can I know what the most important thing really is? . . . You know, ever since Lise took back that promise she made you, that childish promise to marry you, which, as you certainly must have realized, was nothing but the overwrought imaginings of a sick little girl who had been confined to her wheel-chair for so long . . . Ah, I'm so happy that now at last she can walk! . . . That new doctor, whom Katya brought from Moscow for your unhappy brother who is to go on trial tomorrow . . . But don't let's talk about tomorrow! The very thought of what will happen just kills me! I'm so incredibly curious to know! Well, as I was telling you, that doctor came here and examined Lise and I paid him fifty rubles for the visit, but, again, that's not what I wanted to tell you. I'm completely lost now, because I'm in such a hurry to tell you . . . Why am I in such a hurry, though? I really don't know. I can no longer see clearly. Everything has become lumped together. I'm afraid I'm boring you so horribly that you'll rush out of the room and I'll never see you again . . . But, good Lord, why are we just sitting here like this? First of all, let's have some coffee! Julia! Glafira! Coffee!"

Alyosha quickly assured her that he had just had some coffee.

"Where did you have coffee?"

"At Miss Svetlov's."

"At that woman's? That woman who's driven so many to their ruin! And yet, I don't know what to think of her anymore. Some people claim that she's turned into a saint. Seems to me, though, that it's a little late for that. She should have become a saint before; what's the use of her becoming a saint now? No, no, Alexei, please don't say anything, for I have so much to tell you . . . In fact, so much that I'm afraid I won't manage to say anything at all. That frightening trial! Oh, I'm getting ready, and I'll certainly attend it! I'll have them carry me into the courtroom in an armchair, for I'm quite capable of sitting up; besides, there will be somebody with me to assist me. And did you know they had listed me as a witness! Oh, I'm looking forward to testifying. Ah, I'll tell them. I'll tell them many things! I don't even know yet all the things I'll tell them . . . But they'll administer the oath to me, won't they?"

"I suppose they will. But I don't think you'll be well enough to appear in court."

"Oh, I can sit up very well . . . But you're confusing me by interrupting me this way! Ah, that beastly crime, then the trial, then they all leave for Siberia, while other people get married, and it all happens so quickly, so quickly, and everything changes and then everybody is old and there's only the grave before them. But good, who cares, I feel tired now.

You know, Katya, *cette charmante personne,* she's disappointed all my expectations. She's decided to follow your brother Dmitry to Siberia, while your other brother, Ivan, will follow her and live in some town not too far away, and so they'll go on tormenting one another. It all drives me nearly mad. And the worst of it all is the scandal: it has been in all the newspapers in Moscow and Petersburg. Millions of articles have been written about it. And do you know—they have even got me into it; one newspaper said that I was 'a very dear friend' of your brother's. Just imagine that, and I won't repeat the horrid phrase they used!"

"That's quite incredible! What did it say? What newspaper?"

"Wait, I'll show it to you. I received it yesterday. It's in that Petersburg paper called *Rumors.* It started coming out this year. I liked the idea of reading about all sorts of rumors and subscribed to it. But, my God, now I'm sorry I ever set eyes on that sheet; I never expected it would carry that sort of rumor! Here, you see the marked place—read it." And she handed Alyosha a newspaper which she had under her pillow.

She was not just upset. She seemed crushed and it is quite possible that everything had become entangled and mixed up in her head. The news item in question was quite typical of its kind and could, of course, have upset her considerably, had she been able to concentrate on anything at all. But in the state she was in, her mind could not rest longer than a second on any particular subject. The next moment it would skip to something completely different, and she would even forget about the newspaper altogether.

Alyosha was well aware that the news of the dreadful crime had spread all over Russia, carrying all sorts of rumors in its wake. He had read, during the past two months, true facts and the wildest inventions about Dmitry and about the other Karamazovs, even about himself. One report, for instance, said that, after his brother's crime, Alyosha was so horrified that he entered a monastery and became a hermit. Another newspaper disputed that report and explained that, in reality, almost the opposite was true: after the crime, Alyosha had "fled" the monastery in the company of the elder Zosima, the two of them having stolen the monastery's funds.

The item Mrs. Khokhlakov had handed Alyosha now bore the dateline of Skotoprigonievsk,* which, alas, is the name of

* "Cattletown." [A. MacA.]

our town (I have tried to avoid mentioning it all this time), and was entitled "Touching the Karamazov Affair." It was very brief and actually did not even mention Mrs. Khokhlakov or, for that matter, anyone else by name at all. It only said that the accused at the forthcoming scandalous trial was a former army captain, an impudent loafer, a reactionary who approved of the institution of serfdom and was mostly famous for his affairs with "bored and lonely ladies," and that one of these, "a pining widow who had convinced herself that she was still young" but who actually had "a grown-up daughter," had become so enamored of him that only two hours before the commission of the crime she had offered him three thousand rubles on condition that he leave with her at once for the gold mines. But the monster had thought he would rather kill his father than drag himself to the Siberian gold mines with a bored forty-year-old lady "of fading charms." And, as was to be expected, the playful report ended with an indignant moral indictment both of parricide in general and of the institution of serfdom, which had recently been abolished.

Alyosha read the report with curiosity, then folded the newspaper, and handed it back to Mrs. Khokhlakov.

"Well, who else could that be but me?" she started, prattling on again. "Why, didn't I suggest to him about an hour before the crime that he leave for the gold mines? But now, all of a sudden, they make me offer him my 'fading charms' as well! You don't imagine, do you, that that was why I suggested he go gold mining? It's a deliberate and vicious distortion! May the Almighty forgive that correspondent for those 'fading charms,' as I forgive him, for let me tell you, I know who that correspondent is! It's your friend Rakitin, of course!"

"That could well be," Alyosha said, "although I've heard nothing about it."

"It's not just that it could be he—it *is* he! Why, didn't you know that I turned him out of my house?"

"I think I heard that you'd asked him not to come to your house anymore, but I don't know what it was all about. I was never told—in any case you never told me . . ."

"So you must have heard it from him, right? Why, does he sound angry with me? Does he say bad things about me?"

"Yes, he does say bad things about you, but then he says bad things about everybody. But he never told me why you'd asked him not to come back. Besides, I see him very seldom now. And, you know, we're not friends."

"Well, in that case, I'll tell you everything and, since it can't be helped, I'll have to make a little confession, for it may be that I could be blamed for something, too. But that's only a very small point and I don't even know whether I could really be reproached for it. You see, Alyosha dear," she said, suddenly looking very playful, as a mysterious little smile appeared on her lips, "you see, I suspect, Alyosha, and I'm telling you this as if I were your mother . . . actually, no, just the contrary, as if you were my father, for my feeling like a mother toward you wouldn't fit very well here . . . Well, anyway, let's say that I feel as if I were confessing to the elder Zosima, and that's the truest comparison I can think of. It fits perfectly, and that's why I called you a hermit when you came in today . . . Well, then, that poor young man, that Rakitin—oh, Lord, I can't really hold it against him, and, although I'm angry and furious with him, I'm really not all that angry—in short, that rather thoughtless young man suddenly decided he had fallen in love with me. I noticed it only later, all of a sudden, but for about a month he'd been coming to see me almost every day, although I'd known him for quite a long time even before that. So I never gave it a thought when, to my great surprise, I began noticing certain signs . . . And perhaps you know, too, that for a couple of months now I've been receiving a very nice, well-mannered, serious young man who works here as a civil servant—Peter Perkhotin. I believe you've met him here yourself. Don't you think he's a charming, serious young man? Well, he comes to see me every other day—I wouldn't mind if it was every day—and he's always so nicely and neatly dressed. Oh, I love young people in general, Alyosha, young men like you, but Peter Perkhotin has the mind of a statesman almost and is so modest and unpresuming at the same time; I must, I must, put in a word for him with his superiors! He is a future member of the diplomatic corps, I'm certain! And you know, on that terrible night, when he came here, he practically saved my life! Your friend Rakitin, on the other hand, always wore those horribly ugly boots when he came to see me and he had the appalling habit of stretching his legs out in front of him when he sat down, over the carpet, you know . . . So, to make a long story short, he started making all kinds of hints about the way he felt and once, upon leaving, he gave my hand an awfully hard squeeze. But the moment he pressed my hand like that, my foot started to ache . . . Rakitin had, of course, met Peter Perkhotin in my house and he always tried to say

something unpleasant to him, to growl at him or something.
I watched them sometimes and I couldn't help being secretly
amused at the way they carried on with each other. Now, one
day I was alone at home. Mikhail Rakitin came in and he
showed me a short poem he'd written about my sore foot.
Wait a second—how did it go? It started, I believe,

> Little foot so nice and stout,
> Look, it's swollen, what a shame!

or something like that, for, you know, I have the most appalling memory for verse, but I have it somewhere and I'll show
it to you later. It was really charming and it was not just
about the foot; there was something edifying in it as well, a
really most enchanting thought, but I've forgotten right now
what it was—just the thing for an album! Of course, I thanked
him for the poem and he seemed very flattered. And just
then Mr. Perkhotin came in and Mr. Rakitin at once became
as gloomy as a stormy night. I saw clearly that Mr. Perkhotin
had interfered with his plans, for I think that Mr. Rakitin was
about to tell me something after he had read me his poem.
I felt it coming, but just then Peter Perkhotin came in. So I
showed Mr. Perkhotin the poem without, of course, telling
him who had written it. I'm sure he immediately guessed who
it was; he won't admit it to this day, but he's just pretending.
Well, when he'd read it, he laughed and started to criticize
the poem. 'This is an awful poem,' he said, 'sounds as if it
was written by a divinity student or someone like that.' And
you should have heard the way he went on, taking the poem
to pieces! And your friend Rakitin, instead of just laughing
it off, became absolutely livid with rage . . . I actually thought
the two of them would come to blows. 'I wrote that poem,' he
said. 'I wrote it as a joke, for I consider poetry writing a
despicable occupation. However, my poem is good. Your
Pushkin gets a whole monument just for writing about ladies'
feet, whereas my poem contains an ideological message as
well. As to you,' he said to Perkhotin, 'you're an advocate of
serfdom; there's not one single humanitarian impulse in you;
progress has never touched you; you're nothing but an official
and you accept graft!'

"At this point I began to shout, imploring them to stop it.
But Peter, who is not one to be easily intimidated as you
know, suddenly assumed a pose of outraged dignity, gave
Mr. Rakitin such a sarcastic look, and started to apologize:

'Oh, I had no idea you had written it! If I had known, I would never have said all those things. I would have praised your poem, for I have heard it said that poets are an irritable lot.' And he kept mocking him in that most dignified, apologetic way. He told me later himself that he was being sarcastic, but at the time I thought he meant what he was saying seriously . . .

"And as I was lying here on my sofa, just as I am now, Alexei, I suddenly thought to myself: 'Shouldn't I ask Mikhail Rakitin to leave my house immediately, because he is being insulting, shouting like this at my guest?' And would you believe it, I just closed my eyes and tried to make up my mind whether it would or would not be the right thing to do. I got all worked up about it and my heart was even palpitating, believe it or not, as I tried to decide whether to scream or not. One voice said to me: 'Interfere now. Raise your voice. Shout!' And another voice said: 'No, don't shout!' But the moment the second voice said that, I did scream, and then I fainted. That, of course, caused a terrible commotion. Suddenly I recovered, got up, and said to Mikhail Rakitin: 'It pains me greatly to tell you this, but I have decided I no longer wish to receive you in my house.'

"And that was how I threw him out, Alexei! Oh, I know very well, I ought not to have done it. For I was lying when I said I was angry with him. I wasn't really. It simply struck me that it would make such an effective scene, my telling him that . . . And, you know, it came off very naturally, because somehow I started to cry, and then I cried more during the next few days, until one day after dinner I suddenly completely forgot about the whole thing. And so he hasn't been to see me for two weeks now and I started wondering whether he'd ever come back. That was yesterday . . . But then in the evening I received that sheet, *Rumors*, read it, and gasped. Who else could have written it? I bet when he left here that day, he went directly home, sat down, wrote it and sent it off, and they printed it. You see, all this happened two weeks ago . . . But Alyosha dear, it's terrible—this isn't at all what I wanted to tell you about . . . But I can't help it, things just get said by themselves whether I want them to or not . . ."

"I'm afraid I have very little time. I must leave in time to visit my brother," Alyosha mumbled apologetically.

"Yes, yes, now you've reminded me of what I had to tell you. Listen, what does it mean—temporary insanity?"

"What temporary insanity?"

"Legal temporary insanity. The kind of insanity for which everything can be forgiven."

"I don't quite understand what it is you want to know."

"This is what I want to know: you know that Katya—ah, she's such a delightful, wonderful person, although I no longer know with whom she is in love . . . Recently she was sitting with me and I kept probing her about it, but it proved quite useless, especially since now she talks to me only about trivial matters. I mean, for instance, she inquires about such things as my health, and even her tone has become so . . . you know. So I said to myself, 'If that's the way she wants it, it's all right with me . . .' Ah yes, as I was telling you, that doctor, he came in connection with this temporary insanity business. You've heard about that doctor, haven't you? Ah yes, how could you help knowing about the doctor who can recognize when people are mad when you invited him here yourself? Although it wasn't you actually, was it? It was Katya. Katya does everything! Now, consider this: a man sits there, and he's not mad at all, but then suddenly he has this temporary insanity. He knows what's going on and remembers it later, but nevertheless he's temporarily insane. So that's the explanation: what happened to your brother Dmitry was just this temporary insanity. It was right after the judiciary reforms that they found out about temporary insanity, and this is one of the beneficial results of our new judicial system. That doctor came to see me and he questioned me at length about that evening, you know, about the gold mines . . . He wanted to know what Dmitry was like at the time. And how else could I describe his state but as temporary insanity? He came, he shouted, 'Give me three thousand rubles. I want three thousand right now!' And after that, he left and suddenly committed the murder. And for that very reason, they'll have to acquit him: he was resisting it, but he couldn't help himself and he killed."

"But he didn't kill anybody," Alyosha said a little sharply. He was growing impatient and was afraid to be late for his visit to Mitya.

"I know, it was that old man Gregory who murdered . . ."

"Gregory? What are you talking about?" Alyosha cried.

"Yes, yes, it was he. Your brother had hit him on the head, so he lay there for a while and then he got up, saw the door open, went in, and killed your father . . ."

"But why, why would he have done it?"

"Why, he was in a state of temporary insanity, of course, after your brother had struck him on the head. So when he came to, he went inside the house and killed Mr. Karamazov. As to his saying that he didn't kill him, he may simply not remember it. Only, you see, it would be much better if Dmitry was the murderer. Besides, he is the murderer; I may have just said it was Gregory, but it's really Dmitry and it's much better that way! And please don't imagine that I think it's better because I'd rather it was the son who murdered his father than anyone else! In fact, just the opposite, I feel children should show respect for their parents. But I still say it's much better if he did it, for in that case you really have nothing to worry about since he did it without being conscious of what he was doing or, to be more accurate, he was conscious and remembers it very well, but he has no idea what came over him. So let them acquit him—it would be so humane! And let everyone appreciate the benefits of our humanitarian reforms. Somehow, I know nothing about those changes, but they assure me that that's the way things have been now for a long time. When I heard of it, I was so amazed that I almost sent someone to call you . . .

"And after he's acquitted, I want him to come straight here from the courtroom, to dinner. I'll invite all my friends and we'll all drink to our new courts of justice! I don't think it would be dangerous to invite your brother to dinner, do you? Besides, there'll be many other guests, so they could always take him out if he started anything . . . And later he could go to some other town and become a justice of the peace or something of that sort, for I am convinced that people who have suffered themselves are the best qualified to judge others. But the most important thing is that one can no longer be sure nowadays who is and who is not in a state of temporary insanity—you may be now, I may be, we may all be . . . I can think of so many instances: Imagine a man sitting and singing a romantic song . . . Suddenly he gets annoyed at something or other, so he snatches up his pistol and kills the person nearest to him and eventually is acquitted. That's a case I read about recently and all the doctors agree that it was temporary insanity. This is really a blessing granted us by the judiciary reform.

"And you know what, my own Lise keeps lapsing into temporary insanity. Yesterday she reduced me to tears, and the day before too. But today at last I realized it was simply temporary insanity . . . Oh, I'm terribly worried about Lise, you know. I think she's gone quite mad lately. And, by the way, why did she send for you? Did she actually send for you or did you come of your own accord?"

"She sent for me and I must go and see her now," Alyosha said, getting up determinedly.

"Ah, my dear Alexei, this is perhaps the most important thing I wanted to tell you," Mrs. Khokhlakov exclaimed, unexpectedly bursting into tears. "As God is my witness, I trust you implicitly where Lise is concerned and I don't even mind that she asked you to come in secret from her mother. I cannot, however, entrust her so easily to your brother Ivan, although I want you to know that I consider him the most chivalrous young man . . . But, you know, he came to see Lise and I knew nothing about it!"

"Really? Ivan? When?" Alyosha was greatly surprised. He did not sit down again but remained standing, listening to her.

"Let me tell you about it. Actually, I think it was to talk to you about that that I asked you to come in and see me just now, although I'm no longer sure. Let me start by saying that Ivan has come to see me only twice since his return from Moscow: the first time was a courtesy visit and the second time, quite recently, he came in because he knew Katya was here. Of course, I have absolutely no right to reproach him for not visiting me more often because I know how busy he is now, *vous comprenez, cette affaire et la mort terrible de votre papa*, but then I suddenly found out that he had been received in my house after all, not by me but by Lise—six days ago: he came, stayed with her for five minutes, then left. And I didn't learn of it until three days later, when Glafira told me. It gave me quite a shock. So I called Lise, and do you know what she told me? She said: 'You were asleep when he came and he didn't want to disturb you. He just came to inquire after your health.' And when she said it, she laughed. Well, of course, I wouldn't think of doubting her word; but I'm so terribly upset about Lise! Imagine, one night —it was four days ago, after your last visit—she suddenly had a fit: crying, screaming, hysterics, everything! Now, why is it that I never have hysterics? The following day she had another fit, and another one the day after. And then yesterday, she had that temporary insanity, and during it she started shouting at me, 'I hate Ivan Karamazov and I demand that you forbid him to come to this house!' I was completely dumbfounded and told her that I wouldn't dream of closing

my door to a very distinguished young man, cultured and
well mannered, especially now, after the cruel blow he's suffered, when he's so unhappy—for after all that has happened
I must assume that he is more unhappy than happy, don't
you think? But all of a sudden Lise burst out laughing at my
words, and she laughed so insultingly, it was quite terrible.
Still, I was pleased. I thought that now that I'd made her
laugh she'd get over those fits, especially since I was planning
to tell your brother to stop paying her such strange visits, and
to ask him for an explanation.

"But this morning Lise awoke in one of those terrible
moods, and, imagine, she slapped Julia's face. I think that's
quite intolerable, because I myself always treat the maids as
equals. Now, one hour later, she threw herself at Julia's feet
and kissed them. But to me she sent a message that she would
not come to see me, that, in fact, she didn't think she wanted
to see me at all. So I, with my bad foot, dragged myself to her
room and when I got there, she threw herself on me, started
kissing me, and wept, and, still kissing me, pushed me out of
her room without a word of explanation, so that I never found
out anything.

"And now, my dear Alexei, all my hopes lie with you—
there's no need to tell you that my whole life is in your hands.
I simply beseech you to go and see Lise, find out everything
from her, as only you can do, and then come and tell me, her
mother, what's going on, for you must understand that it will
kill me, yes, actually kill me, if things continue like this. I will
have to flee this house. I cannot stand it any longer! I know
I have a great deal of patience, but I may lose it and then . . .
And then it will be really terrible! Ah Lord, here's Peter at
last!" Mrs. Khokhlakov cried, her face suddenly becoming
radiant at the sight of Perkhotin.

"Oh, you're so dreadfully late! Well, sit down then and tell
me the final word. What has the lawyer decided? Where are
you off to, Alexei?"

"I must go and see Lise."

"Oh, yes. And you won't forget what I asked you, will you?
It's most awfully important, you know!"

"I certainly won't forget and I'll do what I can . . . But I'm
very late as it is," Alyosha muttered, beating a hasty retreat.

"No, I don't want you to do what you can—you must come
and tell me. I'll die if you don't!" Mrs. Khokhlakov called
after him. But Alyosha was already gone.

CHAPTER 3

The Hell Kitten

When Alyosha entered Lise's room, she was reclining in her old wheel-chair, which she no longer needed since she was now able to walk. She did not move, but her sharp eyes were fixed searchingly on his face. Her eyes were slightly inflamed and her face was pale and sallow. Alyosha was struck by how much she had changed in the past three days; he thought she had even grown thinner. She did not offer him her hand and he stretched out his and touched the long slender fingers that lay motionless on her dress. Then, in silence, he sat down facing her.

"I know you're in a hurry to get to the prison," Lise said irritatedly, "and that my mother has kept you for two hours, telling you about me and Julia."

"How do you know what she told me?"

"I was eavesdropping. Why are you staring at me like that? If I want to eavesdrop, I'll eavesdrop; there's nothing wrong with it and I'm not going to apologize."

"Something is upsetting you, isn't it?"

"Nothing at all. Indeed, I was just thinking for the thirtieth time what a good thing it is that I broke off our engagement and decided not to become your wife. You wouldn't be much of a husband, you know. If I married you, I might some day give you a note to take to another man I'd fallen in love with and I'm sure you'd take it to him and bring me back his answer. And you'd still be carrying my little notes when you were forty."

She suddenly laughed.

"There's something spiteful and at the same time sincere about you," Alyosha said with a smile.

"I'm sincere simply because I'm shameless when I'm with you, because I don't even want to be ashamed of anything before you, yes, precisely before you. Why don't I have any respect for you, Alyosha? I'm terribly fond of you, you know, but I have no respect for you at all. For if I did respect you, I wouldn't be talking to you like this without feeling ashamed, would I?"

"No, you wouldn't."

"But do you believe that I feel no shame when I'm with you?"

"No, I don't."

Lise laughed nervously again. She was talking quickly, in staccato fashion.

"I sent some candy to your brother Dmitry in prison. Alyosha, do you know, you look awfully handsome! I'll always be terribly fond of you because you have allowed me so readily not to be in love with you!"

"Why did you send for me today, Lise?"

"Because I wanted to tell you something. I want someone to marry me, tear me to pieces, betray me, and then desert me. I don't want to be happy."

"Have you fallen in love with disorder?"

"Oh no, I don't want disorder. I keep yearning to set fire to this house. I keep imagining how I'd creep up quietly and start the fire. And I absolutely must do it quietly, on the sly. People will try to put the fire out, but it will go on burning. And I'll know but will say nothing. But this is all nonsense . . . Ah, it's such a bore."

She made a disgusted face and waved her hand.

"You live too comfortably. You're rich," Alyosha said quietly.

"Do you think I'd be better off if I were poor?"

"Yes, you would be."

"You got all these ideas from that monk who died recently, that friend of yours. And it's not true. I enjoy being rich, while everybody around me is poor. I'll stuff myself with candy and whipped cream and never offer any to other people. No, no, don't say anything!" she cried, waving her hands at Alyosha, although he hadn't even tried to open his mouth. "You've already told me everything you can tell me. I know it all by heart and I'm bored with it. If I were poor, I'd kill someone. As a matter of fact, I may still kill someone, even if I remain rich, for what use is it to just sit around doing nothing? You know what—I want to reap, to reap rye, so I'll marry you and you'll become a peasant, a real peasant, and we'll have a colt. Wouldn't you like that? Tell me, do you know Kalganov?"

"Yes, I do."

"He always goes around dreaming. He says: 'Why bother to live when it's much better to dream. It's always possible to dream up interesting things, while living is such a bore.' He says that, yet he'll get married soon. He even made a declaration of love to me. Do you know how to spin a top?"

"Yes."

"Well, he's just like a top: he could be wound up and set off and then all you'd have to do would be to keep whipping him. I may marry him and keep setting him off and whipping him all my life. Don't you feel ashamed to be sitting here with me?"

"No, I don't."

"I know you're furious with me because I won't talk to you about holy things. But I have no wish to be holy. What will they do, in the next world, to someone who has committed the greatest sin? I'm sure you know exactly what the penalty is."

"God will punish you," Alyosha said, watching her closely.

"And that's just what I want: I'd like to get there and be punished. I'd just laugh in their faces! I terribly want to set the house on fire, this house, our house . . . Don't you believe me?"

"Why shouldn't I believe you? There are even twelve-year-olds who feel a strong desire to set something on fire and who actually do so. It's some sort of sickness."

"It's not true. That's not the same thing! They're just children. That's not what I'm trying to tell you."

"You feel now that evil is good. This is just a momentary crisis. Perhaps it's the result of your former illness."

"I can see you still despise me. No, I simply don't want to do good—I want to do evil. It has nothing to do with any illness."

"But why do evil?"

"So that there should be nothing left anywhere. Ah, how nice it would be if there was nothing left! You know, I like to imagine sometimes that I've done a lot of evil, many, many horrible things, that I've worked at it quietly for a very long time, and then suddenly everybody finds out about it. They all crowd around me and point at me and I look back at them. That would be very pleasant. Why would it be so pleasant, Alyosha?"

"Just because you'd have satisfied your yearning to crush something that's good. Or, if you prefer, it's like setting fire to the house, as you told me yourself. That happens too."

"But I wasn't just saying that, you know. I'll really do it."

"I believe you."

"I love you so much because of the way you say, 'I believe

you.' And you're not lying either . . . Unless you think I've
told you all this just to tease you?"

"No, I don't think that. Although . . . there may be a little
of that in it too."

"Yes, there is a little of that. I can never lie to you," she
said with a strange glow in her eyes.

Alyosha was quite impressed by her seriousness: there was
no trace of playfulness or flippancy in her now, although
usually her gaiety and humor never left her, even in her
gravest moments.

"There are moments when people love crime," Alyosha
said thoughtfully.

"Yes, yes, I was just thinking that, but everybody loves it
and always, not just at some special moments. It's one of
those things that everybody seems to have agreed to lie about
and, since then, has always lied about. They all pretend they
detest evil, but secretly they all love it."

"I suppose you're still reading bad books?"

"I am. Mother reads them and hides them under her pillow,
and I steal them."

"Don't you think it's wrong to destroy yourself like this?"

"I want to destroy myself. There's a boy in town who lay
down on the railroad track and let the train pass over him.
How I envy him! And what do you think of this: they're
about to try your brother for killing his father and everybody
loves him now for having killed his father."

"You think they love him for killing his father?"

"Yes, they do. Everybody loves him a great deal, secretly,
although they all say that what he did is awful. I'm the first
to love him."

"There is a certain amount of truth in what you say about
people in general," Alyosha said in a very low voice.

"Oh, you have the right ideas about things!" Lise literally
shrieked with delight. "You of all people, you, the monk! You
can't possibly imagine how much I respect you, Alyosha, for
never lying. By the way, let me tell you about a funny dream
I had. It's night, I'm alone in my room, a candle is burning.
Suddenly the room is full of devils, in every corner, under the
table—they open the doors and outside, beyond the doors,
there's a whole crowd of them. They want to come in and
seize me. And they do get to me and are about to grab me
when I suddenly make the sign of the cross and they all reel
back. They are frightened, but they won't leave altogether;
they wait in the corners and by the door. Suddenly I get a

tremendous desire to say insulting things about God out loud and I begin to shout foul words. Immediately they are back at me. They laugh and are again about to seize me, but then I cross myself again and they reel back as before. I have a marvelous time. It takes my breath away!"

"I have that same dream sometimes, too," Alyosha said.

"I can't believe it! Tell me, Alyosha, and please don't laugh—what I'm going to ask you is very important: Do you really think it's possible for two different people to have the same dream?"

"Apparently it is."

"But it's so terribly important, don't you see?" Lise exclaimed in complete amazement. "It's not the dream that's important. It's the fact that you could have the same dream as I had. You never lie to me, so please don't lie now either —is it true? You're not making fun of me?"

"No, it's true."

Lise seemed dumbfounded and remained quiet for a whole minute.

"Alyosha, please come and see me again. Come more often, please," she said in an imploring voice.

"I'll always come and see you, as long as I live," Alyosha said firmly.

"You're the only person in the world to whom I can tell these things; I only admit them to myself and to you. In fact, I admit them more readily to you than to myself. And I don't feel at all ashamed when I tell them to you. Now, Alyosha, tell me this: is it true that Jews steal Christian children and slaughter them on Passover?"

"I don't know."

"I read in a book about the trial of a Jew, who first cut off all the fingers on both hands of a four-year-old boy and then nailed him to the wall, sort of crucifying him. After that, at the trial, the Jew said that the little boy died very quickly— it only took four hours, he said. That's what he called 'very quickly.' He said that the child moaned all the time while he stood there enjoying the spectacle. I think it must have been good!"

"Good?"

"Yes, good. Sometimes I imagine that I have crucified that child: the boy is nailed up there and moaning, while I sit facing him and eat stewed pineapple. I love stewed pineapple. Do you like it?"

Alyosha looked at her in silence. Her pale, sallow face was contorted, her eyes were afire.

"You know, when I first read about that Jew, I was shaken with sobs all night. I imagined that little boy crying and moaning, because, of course, a four-year-old would understand perfectly what was going on . . . But I still can't get that picture with the stewed pineapple and all out of my head. In the morning I sent a note to someone, asking him to come and see me without fail. He came and I told him everything, about the boy and the pineapple, *everything,* and I said: 'It's good!' He laughed and said, 'Yes, it's very good,' and left. He only stayed with me for five minutes. Do you think he despised me? Tell me, Alyosha, did he?"

She sat up and looked at Alyosha with fiery eyes.

"Tell me," Alyosha said, "are you sure it was you who asked him to come here?"

"Yes, it was me."

"Did you write him a letter?"

"Yes, I did."

"Just to ask him about . . . about that child?"

"No, it really had nothing to do with that. But the second he came in, I asked him about it. He laughed, answered me, and left."

"He acted honorably," Alyosha said quietly.

"But didn't he despise me and laugh at me?"

"No, because he himself believes in stewed pineapple. He's very sick too, Lise."

"Yes, he believes in it!" Lise said, her eyes flashing.

"He doesn't despise anyone. He simply doesn't believe in anyone. And it's only inasmuch as he doesn't believe in people that he despises them."

"Therefore he despises me too? Me?"

"Yes, you too."

"That's good too," Lise said with a strange quiver. "When he laughed and left, I enjoyed being despised. I found joy both in the little boy with his fingers cut off and in being despised myself . . ." And Lise let out a strangely shrill, wicked, unhealthy laugh, looking straight into Alyosha's face.

"You know, you know, I'd like . . . Save me, Alyosha!" she suddenly cried, rushing toward him. She flung her arms around him desperately. "Save me," she almost moaned, "for there is no one else in the world to whom I'd say the things I've just said to you. But what I said is the truth, you understand, the truth! I'll kill myself, because I find life so disgusting! Ah, Alyosha, you aren't in love with me at all, not in the least! Why aren't you?" she cried in exasperation.

"I do love you," Alyosha said with feeling.

"And will you cry for me?"

"Yes, I will."

"I mean not because I refuse to marry you, but simply cry because you're sorry for me."

"Yes, I will."

"Thank you. Yours are the only tears I want. As to the rest, let them torture me, crush me underfoot—I don't care about any of them, not a single one of them, do you understand, no one! Indeed, I hate them all! Now you'd better go, Alyosha —you must be in time to see your brother," she said, suddenly tearing herself away from him.

"How can I leave you like this, though?" Alyosha said in a worried tone.

"Hurry, go to the prison or it will be closed. Here, take your hat. Kiss Mitya for me. All right, go now!"

She almost pushed him out of the room. Alyosha was looking at her sadly puzzled, when he suddenly felt a letter in his hand. It was a small, folded, sealed sheet of paper. He looked at the address. It only said: "To Ivan Fyodorovich Karamazov." He glanced quickly at Lise. But her face was almost threatening now.

"Give it to him. Give it to him without fail!" she commanded frantically, her whole body shuddering. "Give it to him today or I'll poison myself! For this was why I sent for you!"

The door slammed and he heard the lock click. Alyosha put the letter in his pocket and went straight downstairs without stopping to see Mrs. Khokhlakov. In fact, he had completely forgotten about her.

And Lise, as soon as Alyosha had gone, unlocked the door, opened it a little, put her finger in the crack, and slammed the door as hard as she could. Ten seconds later she released her hand, went slowly to her chair, sat down, and looked intently at her blackened, swollen finger and the blood that was oozing out from under the nail. Her lips quivered.

"I'm a vile, vile, vile, despicable creature," she whispered

CHAPTER 4

A Hymn and a Secret

November days are short, and so it was already rather dark when Alyosha rang at the prison gate. He knew that they would let him in to see Mitya without making difficulties. Our town was just like anywhere else: at first, immediately following the preliminary investigation, Mitya's relatives and other people who wanted to visit him had to submit to certain regulations. Later, however, although the rules were not actually changed, they somehow were no longer applied to at least some of the people who went to see him. Often such visitors were allowed to spend a considerable time with him in the special room set aside for visits, for all practical purposes without supervision. There were, however, only three visitors who received this preferential treatment: Grushenka, Alyosha, and Rakitin. Grushenka stood high in the favor of Police Inspector Makarov. The old man was still trying to live down his insulting outburst against her at Mokroye, after which he had so radically changed his opinion of her. And strangely enough, although he was quite convinced that Mitya was the murderer, he had treated Mitya with ever-increasing sympathy since his imprisonment. "I'm sure that, deep down, he's a decent fellow," Makarov thought. "He's just been ruined by his drinking and his disorderly life." And his original horror of the crime was replaced by a deep pity for the criminal. As to Alyosha, the inspector had known him for a long time and had always been very fond of him. And Rakitin, who eventually became a very frequent visitor, happened to be on extremely friendly terms with "the inspector's young ladies," as he called them, because he gave lessons in the house of the kindly inspector, who was usually a fierce stickler for rules and regulations.

To go back to Alyosha, he was a special friend of the inspector's and the old man liked to discuss "abstruse" subjects with him. He would never have dared discuss these matters with Alyosha's brother Ivan, of whom he stood in great awe and in whose presence he felt himself too much of a "home-made" philosopher. Aside from his natural liking for Alyosha, in the last year Makarov had devoted much of his time to studying the Apocrypha, and he constantly discussed his ideas on this subject with his young friend. When Alyosha was still·in the monastery, the old police officer used to go and visit him there and discuss various texts with him and with the monks. So, even if Alyosha arrived at the prison after visiting hours, all he had to do was to ask for the inspector and everything would be arranged. Besides, all the wardens were used to Alyosha. As to the guards outside, they did not care one way or the other as long as Alyosha had permission from their superiors.

When he had visitors, Mitya was brought downstairs from his cell to the room especially reserved for visits; now, when he entered this room, Alyosha found Rakitin there, just about to leave Mitya. They had been talking loudly and Mitya, who had come all the way to the door with Rakitin, to see him off, was roaring with laughter. Rakitin was grumbling. Lately, Rakitin had seemed to dislike meeting Alyosha; he hardly spoke to him or even acknowledged his presence. And now, when he saw Alyosha come in, he knitted his brows and looked away, pretending to be absorbed in buttoning up his big heavy overcoat with its fur collar. After that he was busy looking for his umbrella.

"I hope I'm not forgetting anything of mine," he muttered, just to say something.

"And don't forget anything of anybody else's either!" Mitya said, roaring with laughter at his own witticism.

Rakitin at once flared up.

"You'd better keep that advice for one of you Karamazovs, you slave-owning breed! Don't tell it to a Rakitin!" he said, shaking with anger.

"Come on, calm down. I was just joking!" Mitya said. "Ah hell, they're all the same," he said, nodding to Alyosha at the door through which Rakitin had just vanished. "The fellow sat here, seeming to enjoy himself and laughing, and now all of a sudden he loses his temper and walks out on me. And he didn't even acknowledge your presence! Anything happen between you two? Have you quarreled or something? Why are you so late in coming, Alyosha? I can't even say I've been waiting for you——I've been yearning for you to come all morning. But never mind, we'll catch up."

"Why does he come to see you so often now? Have you become such great friends all of a sudden?" Alyosha asked, indicating with his head the door through which Rakitin had left.

"Great friends with him? No, we're no friends . . . The

swine thinks I'm some kind of a scheming crook. But the worst thing about his type is that they can't understand a joke. They never understand one. They're all dried up inside. Everything is bare and desolate in their souls; just like inside these prison walls, as they looked to me when I was brought here. But he's intelligent—yes, that he certainly is! Well, Alexei, looks like I'm done for, doesn't it!"

He sat down on the bench and made Alyosha sit next to him.

"Why do you feel it's so hopeless, Mitya?" Alyosha said apprehensively. "The trial only starts tomorrow, after all."

"What are you talking about?" Mitya gave him a vague look. "Ah, about the trial . . . Ah hell, ever since you've been coming to see me here, we talked about all sorts of nonsense, nothing but that trial, and I've never had a chance to talk to you about the most important things. I know the trial is tomorrow, but I wasn't thinking about it when I said I was done for . . . Hey, what is it? Why are you looking at me so disapprovingly?"

"What is it that's bothering you, then, Mitya?"

"It's ideas that are bothering me, ideas, ethics . . . What's ethics, Alyosha?"

"Ethics?" Alyosha asked in surprise.

"Yes. What is it—some kind of a science or what?"

"Yes, I suppose you could call it that, but I'm afraid I can't explain to you what it is exactly."

"But Rakitin knows. Ah, he knows so much, damn him! He won't become a monk. He's planning to go to Petersburg. He'll become a literary critic and he'll work for the betterment of mankind. Well, why not? He may do some useful work and make a career for himself. Ah, his kind are great at making careers! But ethics be damned—my goose is cooked, Alexei, you simple man of God! Let me tell you, it does something to my heart when I look at you, for I like you better than anyone. But now you tell me, was there somebody called Karl Bernard?"

"Karl Bernard?"

"No, wait, it wasn't Karl. I've got mixed up . . . Wasn't it Claude Bernard? Who's he? A chemist or something?"

"He's some sort of scientist, but I'm afraid I can't tell you much about him. I only know that he's a scientist. I don't know in what field."

"So to hell with him—I don't know either," Mitya said angrily. "I suppose he's one of those smart careerists, like the rest of them. And I'm sure Rakitin will make a career too. Rakitin will slip through a keyhole if he has to, but he'll get where he wants. Just like Bernard. Ah, all the Bernards! They're breeding all over the place these days!"

"But what's the matter with *you?*" Alyosha insisted.

"Rakitin wants to write an article about me, about my trial; he hopes to start on his journalistic career that way. He told me so himself. Oh, behind it will be the idea that I couldn't prevent myself from killing because I'm a victim of my environment, and so on and so forth—he explained it all to me. His piece will have socialist overtones, he told me. Well, what the hell do I care—if he wants it to have overtones, it can have them. I don't give a damn. You know, he hates Ivan and he doesn't like you too much either. The reason I don't chase him away is that, despite everything, he's so intelligent. He thinks a bit much of himself, though, and I said to him today: 'You can't despise the Karamazovs, because they're philosophers rather than scoundrels, just like all real Russian people. But you, with all your learning, you're no philosopher. You're just a low-down bastard.' That made him laugh. Kind of spitefully, though. So I said to him: '*De* "thinkabus" *non est disputandum.*' *De* thinkabus—don't you see that that's funny? At least I was taking a hand at classical quotations like a real scholar!" Mitya roared with laughter.

"But why did you say you were done for?" Alyosha interrupted him.

"Why am I done for? Hm . . . how shall I put it—well, all in all, I'm unhappy about God. That's why I'm lost."

"Unhappy about God—what do you mean?"

"Just imagine: there are those nerves in the head, I mean in the brain—damn them!—and those nerves have some kind of little tails which vibrate . . . And whenever I look at something with my eyes, those little tails vibrate and the image appears; it doesn't appear at once, though. It takes a while, a second maybe, and then there comes a moment, no, I don't mean a moment—damn the moment—I mean an image, that is, the object or the event or whatever it is. That's how I perceive things and how I think . . . So I think because of those little tails and not at all because I have a soul, or because I've been made in God's image, which is all nonsense. Rakitin explained all that to me yesterday and it really hit me hard. Science is wonderful, Alyosha—it will produce a new man. I understand all that very well. But I am unhappy about God—I miss Him!"

"That's something at least. I'm thankful for that," Alyosha said.

"You think it's good that I miss God? Why, if I feel like that, it's just chemistry. Yes, everything's chemistry! It's no use, my holy brother, you'll just have to move out of the way a bit, to make room for chemistry. Rakitin now—he doesn't like God, doesn't like Him at all. To people like him, God is a sore spot. But they hide it, they lie, they pretend. 'Will you,' I asked him, 'try to develop these ideas in your literary criticism?' 'They won't let me do it too openly,' he said, and laughed. 'But tell me,' I asked him, 'what will happen to men? If there's no God and no life beyond the grave, doesn't that mean that men will be allowed to do whatever they want?' 'Didn't you know that already?' he said and laughed again. 'An intelligent man can do anything he likes as long as he's clever enough to get away with it. But you, you got caught after you killed, so today you have to rot in prison.' He's a real swine to say that to my face; a few months ago I used to throw people like that out of the window. But now I just sit and listen to him. Because he says much that makes sense. And he can write well, too. A week ago he read me an article of his and I copied a sentence out of it. Here it is. Listen to it." Mitya hurriedly produced a piece of paper from his waistcoat pocket and read aloud: " 'To solve the problem, we must first conceive our individual I as distinct from the reality around us.' Do you grasp that, Alyosha?"

"No, I don't grasp it," Alyosha said, looking at Mitya with great curiosity.

"I don't either. It's obscure and involved, but it's also clever. 'Everybody writes like that these days,' Rakitin told me, 'because the environment demands it.' So I guess they're afraid of the environment . . . He also writes poetry, the animal. Ah, he wrote a poem about Mrs. Khokhlakov's foot, ha-ha-ha!" Mitya roared with laughter.

"I've heard about it."

"Did you hear the poem?"

"No."

"I have it and I'll read it to you. You don't know—there's a whole story behind it. Oh, he's such a fraud! About three weeks ago he came here and started teasing me. 'You

poor slob,' he said to me, 'you've got yourself into this mess
for a mere three thousand. Watch me now—I'll get myself
a hundred and fifty thousand by marrying a widow, and
I'll buy myself a mansion in Petersburg.' And he went on to
tell me how he was courting Mrs. Khokhlakov, who's never
been too bright and who now, at forty, has run out of what
little brains she had. 'She's very sentimental too, and that's
how I'll get her,' he said. 'I'll marry her, take her to Petersburg, and start publishing a newspaper there.' And I could
see he was drooling as he said it. Only, of course, it wasn't
Mrs. Khokhlakov's charms that made him drool like that
but the hundred and fifty thousand. And he convinced me
that he'd pull it off all right; every day he told me about the
progress he was making. 'She's biting at the bait!' he'd say,
beaming with joy. But then, all of a sudden, he was given the
boot! Turned out that good old Peter Perkhotin beat him to
it! Ah, I could have kissed that idiot woman for having
kicked Rakitin out!

"Well, it was while he was coming here to see me that he
composed that poem. And he felt he had to apologize. 'It's
the first time I've dirtied my hands with poetry! But I'm
doing it for a useful cause, for once I get hold of that
imbecile's capital I'll make it work for the public good.' That
kind always has the public good as a motive to justify every
abomination. And when he'd finished the poem, he said: 'It's
an improvement on Pushkin, whom you all admire so much,
because I at least have managed to show some concern for
intellectual ideas in this ridiculous piece, while Pushkin, who
was supposed to be such a talented man, just wrote about
ladies' legs and feet and nothing else and then was so terribly
proud of his poems!' Ah, the swollen heads these people have!
So here it is. He called it 'Wishes for the Recovery of the
Sore Little Foot of the Object of My Devotion.' He can be
quite funny sometimes. So here goes:

> Little foot so nice and stout,
> Look, it's swollen, what a shame!
> Doctors came and fussed about,
> Bandaged now, it's all aflame.

> But let Pushkin celebrate
> Ladies' feet instead of me.
> Heads that will not cerebrate,
> That's more worrying, you see!

Thoughts, though few, seemed on the way,
Now have fled from all this pain.
Help be soon at hand, I pray,
For fair lady's foot and brain.

"He's certainly a pig, but it comes off quite playfully, don't you think? And he did manage to put in a good word for 'thoughts' as well. But you should have seen how furious he was after she kicked him out! He was actually gnashing his teeth with rage!"

"He's already taken his revenge on her," Alyosha said. "He's sent a story about her to a newspaper."

And Alyosha told him briefly about the item that had appeared in *Rumors*.

"Yes, I'm sure it's his doing," Mitya said, frowning. "I know about that kind of news item. There's been so much dirt published already—about Grusha, for instance, and also about the other one, about Katya . . . hm . . ."

He walked up and down the room, looking worried.

"I can't stay long, Mitya," Alyosha said after a silence; "tomorrow is a terrible, crucial day—the judgment of God will be passed on you . . . You really amaze me, Mitya— how can you, under these circumstances, talk about all sorts of nonsense instead of the trial that you're about to face?"

"Why should you be amazed?" Mitya said heatedly. "Or do you expect me to keep talking about that reeking bastard, the murderer? Don't you think we've sufficiently covered the subject as it is? I don't want to talk about Reeking Lizaveta's son anymore! God will kill him, you'll see, so forget him now!"

In great agitation, Mitya walked over to Alyosha and unexpectedly kissed him. His eyes were burning.

"Rakitin could never understand this," he said with strange fervor, "but I know you'll understand it right away. And that's why I was longing for you to come today. You see, I've wanted to tell you many things since I've been behind these leprous walls, but I felt I couldn't bring up the most important thing; I felt the time hadn't come yet. And so I've waited until the very last moment to bare my soul before you. You know, in these past two months, it's as if I'd found a new man in myself, as if a new man had arisen in me! That man was locked inside me, but he would never have come out if it hadn't been for this terrible blow of fate. It's frightening! What does it matter if I spend the next twenty years in the mines, knocking out the ore with a hammer? That's not what I'm afraid of. What I'm terribly afraid of is that this new man within me may desert me! I'm sure I could find, underground in the mines there, a true human heart within another convict, a murderer working next to me, and I could befriend him, for in the mines, too, people can live and love and suffer! It would be possible to bring back to life a heart that had long been dead and frozen. I could work on it for years, and finally, out of that infernal den, a soul would emerge that was noble for having known suffering. Thus I might restore an angel to life and bring back a hero! There are many of them, and we all bear the responsibility for them! Otherwise, why should I have dreamt about that 'babe' at such a moment? And so I will go to Siberia because of that 'babe,' since every one of us is responsible for everyone else. We bear the guilt for all the 'babes,' because we are all children, small or grown-up, we are all 'babes.' I'll go and suffer for all of them, because someone, after all, has to pay for all the others. I didn't kill father, but I accept the guilt and I must suffer. I've understood all this here, behind these leprous walls . . . And just think, there are so many of them over there, under the ground, hammering away. Oh, I realize, we'll all be wearing chains and we'll be deprived of our freedom. But then, in our great misery, we shall arise again and know the joy without which a man cannot live and God cannot exist, because God gives us joy and giving it is His great privilege. Oh Lord, may man dissolve in prayer! But what would I do there, underground, without God? No, Rakitin is lying. And even if they succeed in banning God from the earth, we will meet Him under the earth. It is not possible for a convict to do without God, even less possible than it is for a free man. And we, the underground men, we shall sing from the entrails of the earth a tragic hymn to God, God in whom there is joy! So long live God and His joy! I love Him!"

Mitya delivered this wild speech almost breathlessly. He had turned pale, his lips were quivering, tears rolled down his cheeks.

"No," he began again, "there's so much in life and there's life underground, too. You cannot even imagine how much I want to live now, Alyosha, how much I long to exist and be conscious of my existence, and it has only dawned on me since I've been here behind these leprous walls. Rakitin cannot understand that. All he cares about is building a house and letting the tenants in. That's why I was longing for you to come. Besides, what is suffering, after all? I'm not afraid of it, however painful it may be. I used to be afraid of it, but I'm not any longer. And do you know what—I may not even defend myself at the trial . . . There's so much strength in me that I feel I will overcome everything. I'll bear every ordeal I must bear, as long as I can say to myself at any moment I choose: 'I am!' Through a thousand agonies, I am; writhing on the rack, I am! I'm locked in a cell, yes, but I am still alive. I can see the sun, and if I can't see the sun, I know there is the sun. And knowing there is the sun is already living. The trouble, though, Alyosha, my angel, is that all those philosophies of theirs just about kill me! Ah, damn those philosophies . . . And you know, Ivan, he . . ."

"What about Ivan?" Alyosha tried to interrupt, but Mitya didn't even hear him.

"You see, I never had any doubts before, but they were all hidden inside me. And perhaps it was because all those ideas were raging within me without my even being aware of their existence that I drank, behaved wildly, and beat people up; without knowing it, I was trying to drown out and silence those doubts. But Ivan is no Rakitin. There's an idea hidden inside Ivan. Our brother Ivan is a sphinx. He doesn't speak. He won't open up. But God torments me. And what if there is no God? What if Rakitin is really right and God is just a fiction created by men? Then, if there is no God, man becomes master of the earth and of the universe. That's great. But then, how can a man be virtuous without God? That's the snag, and I always come back to it. For whom will man love then? Whom will he be grateful to? Whom will he praise in his hymns? Rakitin just laughs and says that one can love mankind without God. But I feel you have to be a piece of slime to say that. I can't see it at all. Solving the problem of existence is easy for Rakitin: 'If you wanted to do something useful today, you could, for instance, fight for people's civil rights or even maintain the price of beef at a reasonable level; that would be a simpler and more direct way of manifesting your love for mankind than playing with all kinds of philosophical theories.' So I said to him: 'But if there's no God, you'd jerk up the price of beef yourself if you knew how to, and if you had a chance, if you could, you'd fleece people to make a ruble of profit on each kopek.' That made him angry. But what's virtue then? You tell me, Alexei. We, for instance, may think that virtue is one thing while the Chinese may believe it's something quite different. Isn't virtue something relative then? It's a pretty tricky question! I hope you won't laugh at me if I tell you that this question has prevented me from falling asleep for two nights in a row. You know, I'm surprised that some people can go through life without even wondering about these things. Ah, vanity! Well, Ivan has no God. He has an idea. His idea is too big for me to understand. And he won't talk. I suspect he's a Freemason. I asked him, but he wouldn't tell me. I was trying to slake my thirst for understanding at his spring, but he wouldn't talk. Only once did he say something."

"What did he say?" Alyosha said, jumping at the opportunity.

"I said to him: 'Therefore everything is allowed, if that is so.' He frowned and said: 'Fyodor Karamazov, our dear papa, was a pig, but he reasoned correctly.' That was quite an answer, wasn't it? That was all he said. But it goes a bit deeper than Rakitin, don't you think?"

"Yes, indeed," Alyosha agreed bitterly. "When did he come to see you?"

"I'll tell you about that later. I haven't told you anything about Ivan yet. I thought I'd leave that for the last. When we're through with all this comedy here, when they decide on the sentence, I'll tell you something then. There's some sinister business going on here . . . Well, you'll be my judge. But don't even ask me about it now—just forget it for the time being. You know, you were talking about the trial tomorrow—would you believe me if I told you that I have no idea at all what will happen there?"

"Haven't you spoken to that lawyer?"

"That lawyer! I told him everything. He's just one of those soft-spoken city fellows. Another Bernard! And he doesn't believe one word of what I say. He's convinced that I'm the murderer, I can see that. 'In that case,' I asked him, 'why did you come here to defend me?' To hell with the lot of them. They've also brought in a doctor to try and prove I'm mad. I won't let them, though. Katerina, of course, will do 'her duty to the bitter end,' as she sees it, and at whatever cost!" Mitya snorted bitterly. "She's a hard, cruel woman, who knows how to hate; she's a hell cat and I'm sure she knows what I said about her at the interrogation. They must have told her . . . And, you know, there are as many facts against me as there are grains of sand on a beach. Gregory

is sticking to his story. Gregory is honest, but he's stupid.
There are many people in the world who are honest just
because they are stupid. That's Rakitin's idea. Gregory is my
enemy. We're better off having some people as enemies than
as friends. In saying that, I'm thinking of Katerina. I'm very
much afraid of what she may say in court about the way she
bowed to me after I gave her that four-and-a-half thousand
rubles. She'll pay me back for that, for every kopek of it!
But I don't want any sacrifice from her! They'll shame me at
the trial for that. I don't know how I'll be able to stand it!
Please go and see her, Alyosha, and ask her not to say
anything about that in court. Or perhaps that's impossible?
Ah hell, I suppose I'll stand that too! But I'm not sorry for
her. She's sorry enough for herself. She's getting what she
deserves. I'll say what I have to say, Alexei, don't worry!"
Mitya snorted again. "But what about Grusha? Why should
she have to go through that ordeal, why should she?" Mitya
cried suddenly, tears appearing in his eyes. "It just kills me
when I think of Grusha, it just kills me . . . She was here
earlier today and . . ."

"She told me she had come. You made her very miserable
today."

"I know. Damn my lousy character! I was jealous. I felt
sorry when I kissed her as she was leaving, but I didn't ask
her to forgive me."

"Why not?" Alyosha cried in surprise.

Mitya laughed almost gaily.

"You're just a little boy, Alyosha, so here's a piece of
advice for you: never ask the woman you love for forgiveness! Especially if you really love her, however guilty you
may be before her. A woman is so peculiar, Alyosha. Damn
it, that's one subject I really know quite a bit about. I tell
you, the moment you admit to a woman that you've wronged
her and ask her to forgive you, she'll never stop showering
you with reproaches. No woman will ever just forgive you
for what you've done. First she'll humiliate you as much as
she can and remind you of all the mistakes you've ever made,
and even of those you never made; she will forget nothing
and add plenty, and only then will she forgive you. And
that's how the best, the nicest of them, act! She'll scrape the
bottom of the barrel and pour it over your head—it's an
instinct in those angels, without whom we cannot live. You
see, Alyosha, my boy, I'll tell you frankly—every self-
respecting man is bound to land under the heel of some

woman at one time or another. That's my conviction, or rather a feeling I have. A man should be forgiving—it will never degrade him. Forgiving will not stain even a hero, not even Caesar! And yet you must never ask a woman to forgive you—anything rather than that! I want you to remember this rule, taught you by your older brother Mitya, who perished because of women. No, I think I'd better make it up to Grusha in some other way, without asking her to forgive me. I stand in awe before her, Alexei. I worship her! She doesn't see it, though. She always thinks I don't love her enough. And she torments me, torments me all the time with love. My love for her before was nothing compared with the way I feel about her now. Before it was those infernal curves of hers that drove me crazy, while now it's her soul, her whole soul, which she has given me and which has made a new man out of me. Will they marry us, do you think? I'll die of jealousy if they don't. Every night I'm haunted by jealous dreams . . . What did she say to you about me?"

Alyosha told him what Grushenka had told him. Mitya listened attentively, asking him to repeat various things, and was pleased.

"So she's not angry with me for being jealous!" he cried. "There's a real woman for you. So she said that she can be hard and cruel herself—ah, I love cruel, strong women of that sort, although I cannot stand it when someone is jealous of me, I just can't stand it! Well, we'll fight then, but I'll love her, love her no end . . . I wonder whether they'll let a convict marry. Do you think they'll marry us, Alyosha? That's the question, for I cannot live without her."

Mitya frowned and started walking up and down the room. The room was almost completely dark now. Suddenly his face took on a terribly worried look.

"So she says I have a secret from her. That's what she says, does she? We're plotting, the three of us, against her, and 'that Katya woman' is in on it, she thinks. No, ma'am, you have that one upside down. You've twisted it all up in your silly woman's way, Grushenka, my girl! Ah hell, Alyosha, I'll tell you that secret of ours, after all."

He quickly looked all around him, went up very close to Alyosha, who was standing in front of him, and started whispering to him with an air of great mystery, although there was absolutely no danger of anyone's overhearing them. The old warden was dozing on a bench in the opposite corner of the room and the sentries outside were much too far away to hear, however loudly he spoke.

"I'll tell you our secret," Mitya whispered hurriedly. "I'd have told you later anyway, for how could I decide anything without you? You're everything to me. And although I believe Ivan is superior to both of us, to me you're a kind of angel. It will be just the way you decide. Perhaps you're the superior one and not Ivan, after all. It is, you understand, a matter of conscience, of the deepest moral concern, and that makes the secret too important for me to cope with alone, so I put off deciding until I'd talked it over with you. Still, the decision must await the verdict; as soon as it's announced, you'll decide my fate. Now I'll tell you all about it; listen to me, but don't decide yet—just stay still and say nothing. I'll tell you everything—the idea, that is, not the details—and I want you to keep quiet. Don't ask any questions or make any gestures, all right? But, my God, what can I do about your eyes? I'm afraid your eyes will tell me your decision even if you don't open your mouth. Oh, I'm so afraid of that!

"Listen to this, Alyosha: Ivan suggests that I *escape*. I won't go into the details—everything has been taken care of and it's sure to work. Be quiet—don't say anything! I'd go to America and Grusha would come with me. The thing is, I can't live without her. And if I don't escape, they won't let her follow me to Siberia unless we're married. Do they allow convicts to marry? Ivan says they don't. And without Grusha, how could I live there, underground, knocking out the ore with a hammer? I'd simply use the hammer to smash my head and that'd be that. But, on the other hand, what about my conscience? For if I ran away, it would be my ordeal that I'd be escaping! I have received the message and to run away would be to ignore it; I have found a road toward salvation, but, instead of taking it, I'd be turning to the left and trying to circle around it. Ivan says that 'a man of good will' can be of more use in America than in the Siberian mines. But then, what would become of that hymn to God rising up from underground? And what is America? Isn't it just another vanity of vanities? Somehow I believe that there is a great deal of corruption in America too. And I'd be the man who had run away from his crucifixion! I'm telling this to you, Alexei, because you're the only one who can understand it; to everyone else, what I just said about that hymn is stupid nonsense, sheer raving. They'll say that either I've gone off my head or I'm just stupid. But I haven't gone mad and

I'm not really that stupid either. Yes, Ivan too understands about the hymn—he certainly does—but he won't say what he thinks about it; no, Ivan won't talk. He doesn't believe in the hymn. No, no, don't say anything, Alyosha. I can see from your look that you've already decided! No, please don't decide. Take pity on me. I can't live without Grusha . . . Wait for the verdict!"

Mitya was frantic; he was holding Alyosha by the shoulders and his inflamed, searching eyes were riveted on his brother's.

"They don't allow convicts to marry, do they?" he repeated for the third time in an imploring voice.

Alyosha was visibly shaken. What Mitya had told him had taken him completely by surprise.

"Tell me one thing," Alyosha said. "Did Ivan insist very much? Whose idea was it in the first place?"

"It was his idea and he insists that I do it. He didn't come and see me at all until about a week ago and then he started talking about it right away. He's very determined: he doesn't suggest—he tells me to do it. And he has no doubt that I'll do as he says, although I've turned my heart inside out before him, just as I have before you, and told him about the hymn. He explained to me how he had planned it all and where he had got the necessary information, but I'll tell you about all that later. He's so completely set on it! And he told me about money: he says there'll be ten thousand to pay for my escape and another twenty thousand to start me off in America. For ten thousand, he says, we could organize a beautiful escape!"

"And he asked you not to say a word of this to me?" Alyosha asked again.

"Not to anybody, but above all not to you. He's probably afraid that you'll stand in my way, like my conscience. Please don't tell him I've told you. Oh, please don't!"

"You're right," Alyosha said. "It's impossible to decide before the verdict is known. And then, you'll decide for yourself. You'll find in yourself that new man you told me about, and he'll decide."

"That new man, or perhaps a Bernard, who may decide the way Bernard would have! Sometimes I think I'm just another despicable Bernard!"

Mitya grinned bitterly.

"But tell me, Mitya—why do you feel it's so hopeless to try to convince them of your innocence?"

Mitya's shoulders jerked upward spasmodically and he shook his head.

"Alyosha, my dear boy, you must go now," he said suddenly, in great haste. "I just heard the warden's voice outside in the courtyard and I'm sure he'll be here in a second. We're late and it's against their regulations. Here, quick—give me a hug, and make the sign of the cross over me, that will bless me for my crucifixion tomorrow . . ."

The brothers embraced and kissed.

"But Ivan," Mitya said, smiling bitterly, "wants me to run away when he himself believes I am the murderer."

"Have you ever asked him whether he believes that?"

"No, I haven't. I was about to once, but I couldn't do it. I didn't have the strength. But I don't have to really. I can see it in his eyes. All right, good-by then, Alyosha!"

They quickly embraced again and Alyosha was already at the door when Mitya called him back.

"Here, stand facing me . . . like this." And again he grasped him firmly by the shoulders.

Mitya's face had turned so white that Alyosha could see it clearly in the darkness. His mouth was contorted, his eyes fixed on Alyosha's.

"Alyosha, tell me the truth, as you would before God: do you believe I killed him? I want to know what you really think! Don't lie to me. Tell me the whole truth!" Mitya shouted insanely.

Alyosha swayed violently. He felt a sharp stab in his heart.

"What are you saying . . . stop it . . ." he mumbled vaguely.

"Don't lie. I want the truth!" Mitya repeated.

"I've never for one second believed that you were the murderer!" Alyosha suddenly heard his own quivering voice as he raised his right hand as though calling on God as a witness.

Mitya's whole face shone with bliss.

"Thank you," he drawled out slowly, as if letting out a sigh of relief. "You have given me a new lease on life. You know, I've been afraid to ask you that, you of all people, you! All right, go now, go! You've given me strength for tomorrow, Alyosha, God bless you! So go now, and love Ivan!"

The two last words gushed from Mitya's lips by themselves.

Alyosha left in tears. The depth of Mitya's lack of self-confidence and his uncertainty about everybody had suddenly been revealed to Alyosha and he realized now that he had never before understood his brother's abysmal unhappiness and despair. An infinite compassion overwhelmed Alyosha and twisted him in pain. His heart was hurting terribly from the stabbing sensation. "Love Ivan," he heard Mitya's voice ringing in his ears. Yes, he was on his way to see Ivan. He had been terribly anxious to see Ivan ever since the morning. Ivan worried him as much as Mitya, especially now, after what Mitya had told him.

CHAPTER 5

Not You, Not You!

On his way to Ivan's, Alyosha had to pass the house where Katerina had an apartment. He saw light in the windows, stopped, and decided to go in. He had not seen Katerina for more than a week. It occurred to him now that Ivan might very well be there, especially on the eve of the fateful day. He rang the bell below and started to walk up stairs that were dimly lighted by a Chinese lantern. Someone was coming down. When they met on the landing, Alyosha saw it was Ivan. He was obviously coming from Katerina's.

"Oh, it's you," Ivan said coldly. "Well, see you some other time—good-by. You going to see her?"

"Right."

"I wouldn't if I were you. She's in one of those emotional states, you know, and you'll only make her more irritated."

"No, no, Alexei, do come up!" a woman's voice called from upstairs, as a door was quickly flung open. "Have you just come from there?"

"Yes, I saw him."

"Did he give you a message for me? Do come in, Alexei, and you, Ivan, please come back . . . I want you to come back, Ivan, do you hear!"

Katerina's invitation sounded so imperious that, after a second's hesitation, Ivan decided to follow Alyosha upstairs.

"She was listening," he muttered angrily to himself, but Alyosha heard him.

"I hope you don't mind if I keep my coat on," Ivan said, stepping into Katerina's drawing room. "I won't even sit down, because I can't stay more than a minute really."

"Sit down, Alexei," Katerina said, although she herself remained standing.

She had not changed much during this time, but there was

a malevolent glow in her dark eyes. Alyosha remembered later how much he was struck by her beauty that evening.

"So what did he ask you to tell me?"

"Just this," Alyosha said, looking straight into her eyes. "He doesn't want you to say anything at the trial that would compromise you . . . You know . . ." Alyosha hesitated for a second. "Well, about what happened between you and him when you first met . . . in that other town, you know."

"You mean about my prostrating myself before him for the money?" Katerina laughed loudly. "I'd like to know, though, who he's afraid for—is it really for me or is it for himself? Whom doesn't he want me to compromise—him or myself? Do tell me, Alexei."

Alyosha was looking at her, trying hard to understand her.

"Yourself and him," he said quietly.

"I see," she said in a spiteful tone, suddenly turning red. "I'm afraid you don't know me very well," she said threateningly. "Indeed, I don't really know myself yet. It may be that you'll be longing to trample me to death after I'm through testifying tomorrow."

"I'm sure you'll testify honestly and that's all that's needed."

"A woman can often be dishonest," she said in cold fury. "Only an hour ago I thought I would not be able to bring myself to touch that monster, just as I can't touch reptiles. But I was wrong—he's still a human being for me. And it remains to be seen whether he's the killer. Was it he who killed him?" she cried hysterically, turning now to Ivan, and Alyosha understood at once that she had already asked Ivan that question, perhaps only a few minutes before, and probably for the hundredth time rather than the first, and that they had quarreled just before Ivan had left.

"I went to see Smerdyakov . . . It was you, Vanya, you who convinced me that he was the parricide, and I believed it only because you told me so!"

Ivan forced himself to grin. Alyosha started when he heard Katerina call him Vanya. He had never suspected that sort of relationship between them.

"Well, anyway, I must be going now," Ivan said coldly. "I'll come and see you tomorrow," And, without a moment's pause, he walked straight out of the room and downstairs. Katerina suddenly seized Alyosha by both hands and whispered peremptorily to him:

"Catch him! Run after him! Don't leave him alone for one second! He's insane. Don't you realize he's gone mad? He's feverish. It's a sort of nervous fever, a doctor told me. Please go—run after him!"

Alyosha jumped up and ran after Iavn. Ivan had not gone fifty yards when, hearing Alyosha running after him, he turned back.

"What do you want of me? I bet she told you to run after me because I'm crazy. I know her by heart," he said irritatedly.

"She's wrong about your being crazy, but she's right that you're not well," Alyosha said. "I was looking at you back there. You look very sick."

Ivan kept walking. Alyosha followed him.

"Do you have any idea, Alexei, how people go insane?" Ivan suddenly asked Alyosha in a voice that was no longer irritated but simply curious and amused.

"No, I don't really, but I suppose there are many different forms of madness."

"Do you think a man can watch himself go insane?"

"I don't suppose a person could make very clear observations under such circumstances," Alyosha said, surprised.

Ivan remained silent for a while.

"Listen, if there's something you'd like to talk to me about," he said suddenly, "please change the subject."

"Here, I have a letter for you. Take it now in case I forget about it later," Alyosha said timidly. He took Lise's letter out of his pocket and handed it to his brother just as they were passing a street light.

Ivan recognized her writing at once.

"Ah, this is from that hell kitten." Ivan laughed spitefully and, without opening the letter, tore it in several pieces and tossed them to the wind. "She's not yet sixteen and she's already offering herself," he said scornfully, walking quickly on again.

"What do you mean she's offering herself?" Alyosha cried.

"Why, don't you understand? The way a whore would, of course."

"What are you saying, Ivan? How can you!" Alyosha came bitterly and heatedly to Lise's defense. "She's just a little girl. You're hurting and insulting a child . . . She's sick too, very sick, and she, too, is going mad perhaps . . . I couldn't not give you her letter . . . In fact, I hoped you'd tell me about her . . . to try to save her."

"There's nothing I can tell you. She may be a small child, but I'm not her nanny. Don't keep on about it, Alexei. I don't even want to be bothered with thinking about it!"

They walked on in silence for another minute.

"Now she'll be praying all night to the Mother of God for guidance about what she should say in court tomorrow," Ivan said, breaking the silence in an abrupt and angry voice.

"You mean Katerina?"

"Yes. She'll be praying for light from above, to know whether she should save her dear Mitya or spell his doom. Because, you see, she hasn't had time to work it out for herself, so she's quite open-minded about it. She, too, thinks I'm a nanny and would like me to sing her lullabies to put her to sleep."

"Katerina loves you," Alyosha said sadly.

"Could be. Only I don't feel any inclination toward her."

"She's suffering . . . Why do you say things to her sometimes that . . . that give her hope?" Alyosha asked in timid reproach. "I know you've done so . . . I hope you'll forgive me for saying this."

"I can't act as I ought to toward her and tell her now that we're through," Ivan said irritably. "I must keep on pretending until they've decided who's the murderer. If I break with her right away, she'll ruin that miserable wretch in court tomorrow just to avenge herself on me, because she really hates him and she knows it. It's all lies, lies on top of more lies. But as long as I haven't broken with her yet, she still has hope and she won't spell the monster's doom because she knows how anxious I am to get him out of trouble. Ah, I can hardly wait for that damned verdict!"

The words "murderer" and "monster" echoed painfully in Alyosha's heart.

"But what can she do that would ruin Dmitry?" he asked, weighing Ivan's words. "What direct evidence can she possibly produce that would harm him so badly?"

"It's something you don't know about. She has a certain document written in our dear Mitya's own hand which proves mathematically that it was he who killed father."

"That's impossible!" Alyosha cried.

"What are you talking about? I've read it myself."

"Such a document cannot exist," Alyosha said heatedly, "for the very good reason that he's not the murderer. He didn't kill father. Not he!"

Ivan suddenly came to a halt.

"So who do you think is the murderer?" he said icily, a scornful note creeping into his voice.

"You know very well," Alyosha said in a low and penetrating voice.

"Who? Are you trying to drag in that cock and bull story about that crazy epileptic idiot, Smerdyakov?"

Alyosha suddenly realized that his whole body was shaking.

"You know who did it yourself." The words escaped him involuntarily. He was trying to control his breathing.

"But who, who?" Ivan shouted almost fiercely, dropping all restraint.

"I only know one thing," Alyosha said, still in almost a whisper. "It was *not you* who killed our father."

" 'Not you'! What does that mean?"

Ivan stood there dumbfounded.

"It was not you who killed father," Alyosha repeated firmly.

For half a minute neither of them spoke.

"I'm well aware that I didn't kill him. You must be raving really," Ivan said with a faint, twisted grin, his eyes fastened on Alyosha like tentacles. They were standing quite close to a street light now.

"No, Ivan, you said several times yourself that you were the murderer."

"When did I say that? I was in Moscow . . . When could I possibly have said that?" Ivan muttered, looking completely bewildered.

"You've said it many times when you were alone during these terrible two months," Alyosha said in the same low, quiet, clear voice, but he was no longer in control of what he was saying and the words came from his lips as if obeying some irresistible outside force. "You accused yourself and confessed that you were the murderer and no one else. But you are wrong, understand that—you're wrong. You are not the murderer. It was not you, not you! God has sent me to tell you this."

There was a silence, a silence that lasted for a whole minute. They stood there looking into each other's eyes. They were both pale. All of a sudden Ivan began to shake and seized Alyosha by the shoulder.

"You were in my room!" he said in a rasping whisper. "You were there the night he came . . . Admit it! You saw him, you saw him, didn't you?"

"Who are you talking about? Mitya?" Alyosha said, puzzled.

"Hell no, not that damned idiot monster!" Ivan shouted in furious impatience. "You know, he keeps coming to see me! How did you find out? You must tell me!"

"Who are you talking about? I have no idea what you mean . . ." Alyosha mumbled, becoming very worried.

"It's not true—you must know . . . Otherwise you wouldn't . . . It's impossible that you don't know . . ."

But suddenly Ivan seemed to recover his self-control. He stopped and stood there for a while, apparently deliberating. A wan smile twisted his lips.

"Ivan," Alyosha said in a quivering voice, "I told you this because I knew you would believe it if it came from me. I tell you again—it was *not you* and I want you to remember that for the rest of your life. You understand, you must remember it as long as you live. God has entrusted me to tell you this, even if you hate me forever afterward."

Obviously Ivan had now managed to regain complete control of his emotions.

"You know, Alexei," he said with an icy smile, "there are two things I cannot stand—prophets and epileptics, especially messengers from God, as I'm sure you're well aware. So, from now on, consider we don't know each other—and this is for good. I beg you to leave me at this corner. Besides, to get home you have to turn right here. And, above all, don't get it into your head to come and see me tonight. Is that clear?"

He turned away, walking off with a firm step without looking back.

"Ivan," Alyosha called after him, "if anything should happen to you tonight, think of me first!"

Ivan did not answer. Alyosha stood under the street light on the corner until Ivan had vanished into the darkness. Then he turned into the side street and walked slowly toward his lodgings.

Neither Alyosha nor Ivan had wanted to live in their father's house, which now stood empty, and each had his own lodgings. Alyosha had a furnished room that he rented from a family of tradespeople. In a different part of the town Ivan had a very comfortable apartment in the wing of a house belonging to the well-to-do widow of a civil servant. The only servant he had was a deaf and arthritic old woman who went to bed at six in the evening and got up at six in the morning. But Ivan had become strangely undemanding in the past two months; above all, he was anxious not to have anyone about him. He even made his own bed and cleaned the room himself; he practically never went into the other rooms of his apartment.

As he entered the gate of his house and was reaching out for the bell, his hand suddenly stopped in mid-air. He realized that he was trembling, vibrating with fury. He pulled back his hand, spat with rage, turned around, and walked quickly off to the other end of the town, a mile and a half away, to a small, sagging wooden house. This was where Maria Kondratiev now lived, old Fyodor Karamazov's former neighbor, who used to come to his kitchen for a bowl of soup, and to whom Smerdyakov used to sing songs to the accompaniment of his guitar. She had sold her house and now lived with her mother in an old, ramshackle cottage. With them also lived Smerdyakov, who had been very ill, close to death, ever since Fyodor Karamazov's death. It was to see him that Ivan was going now, on a sudden hunch that he felt impelled to follow up.

CHAPTER 6

The First Meeting with Smerdyakov

This was the third time, since his return from Moscow, that Ivan had been to see Smerdyakov. The first time after the murder that he had seen and spoken to him was on the very day of his arrival. Then he had paid him another visit two weeks later. But he had not returned after that second visit, so it was now over a month since he had seen Smerdyakov and, since that time, he had hardly heard anything about him.

Ivan had returned from Moscow on the fifth day after his father's death; he had even missed the funeral, which took place the day before his arrival. Ivan's delay was due to the fact that Alyosha, not knowing his brother's address in Moscow, had asked Katerina to send him a telegram. Not knowing his address herself, she had wired her sister and aunt, expecting that Ivan would call on them as soon as he arrived. But Ivan had not gone to see them until his fourth day in Moscow. Of course, as soon as he saw the telegram, he rushed back to our town. The first person he met in town was Alyosha. After talking to him, Ivan was amazed to find that Alyosha had never for a minute thought that Mitya could be the murderer and openly accused Smerdyakov—in complete disagreement with the opinion held by everyone else in town. Then Ivan had been to see, in turn, Inspector Makarov, the assistant public prosecutor, and the examining magistrate; when he learned about the available evidence and the circumstances surrounding the accused's arrest, he was even more surprised at Alyosha's stubborn stand and ascribed it to his unreasoning brotherly bias. Besides, Ivan knew how fond Alyosha was of their older brother.

It may be useful at this point to say a few words about Ivan's own feelings for his brother Dmitry. Ivan had never liked him; even when he felt sorry for him, the feeling of pity was always mixed with a contempt which at times bordered on outright revulsion. Dmitry's whole personality and even his appearance made Ivan cringe. Katerina's love for Mitya had filled Ivan with disgust and indignation. On the day of his return to town, however, Ivan had gone to see his brother in jail and that meeting, instead of shaking his belief in Dmitry's guilt, had, if anything, strengthened it. He found Dmitry in a strange state of agitation and nervous excitement: Dmitry spoke a great deal but seemed absentminded and distracted, kept skipping from one subject to another, was very cutting, accused Smerdyakov, and got entangled in his own sentences. And all the time he kept insisting on the three thousand that their late father was supposed to have "stolen" from him: "It was my money and, even if I had taken it, I'd have been in the right." He never tried to challenge the evidence against him and when he tried to explain certain facts that might be favorable to him, his explanations were incoherent and sometimes absurd, so that he gave the impression that he was not even bothering to try to convince Ivan or anybody else of his innocence; instead, he kept losing his temper, ignoring the incriminating evidence, and swearing. He just laughed disdainfully at Gregory's testimony that the door was open, repeated that it was the devil who had opened it, and was unable to suggest any sensible explanation of how it could have been open. During that first visit, he even managed to offend Ivan by telling him sharply that "people who believe that everything is permitted" were not really qualified to suspect and question him. In general, on that occasion, he behaved with considerable hostility toward Ivan.

It was right after that first visit to Dmitry in prison that Ivan went to see Smerdyakov. While in the train coming back from Moscow, Ivan had thought about Smerdyakov and their last conversation on the day before his departure. Much of it made him feel uneasy and aroused his suspicions. When he was questioned by the examining magistrate, however, Ivan decided not to mention that conversation for the time being. He thought he would postpone doing so until he had spoken to Smerdyakov, who was at that time at the city hospital. Both Dr. Herzenstube and Dr. Varvinsky, whom Ivan met at the hospital, agreed that there was no doubt about Smerdyakov's being an epileptic and they were extremely surprised at Ivan's insistent questioning as to whether it would not have been possible for Smerdyakov to have feigned an epileptic seizure on that occasion. They explained to him that this particular epileptic seizure was an exceptionally violent one; that, for several days afterward, it had kept recurring; that, indeed, the patient's life had been in considerable danger at first; and that only now, after intense medical care, could it be said that the danger had passed and the patient would live, although, Dr. Herzenstube added, it was possible that he would suffer from a mental disorder that might last for a very long time, "perhaps all his life." When Ivan had inquired impatiently whether that meant that Smerdyakov was insane now, he was told that he was "not yet insane in the actual, clinical sense" but that "certain symptoms of insanity had already been observed." Ivan had then decided to have a look at Smerdyakov's abnormalities for himself. At the hospital he was readily admitted. Smerdyakov was in a special ward. The bed next to his was occupied by a tradesman who was swollen with dropsy and was obviously not going to live more than two or three days, so he could hardly be a serious hindrance to their conversation.

When he saw Ivan, Smerdyakov grinned distrustfully, seeming at first rather taken aback. At least that was Ivan's impression. But it only lasted for a few seconds; after that and for the rest of the time, Ivan was, if anything, struck by Smerdyakov's composure. From the start, however, Ivan was completely convinced that the man was critically ill; he was extremely weak and spoke very slowly, moving his tongue with obvious difficulty; he had grown very thin and sallow and complained of headaches and pains throughout his whole body. His eunuch-like face seemed to have shrunk, the hair at his temples, brushed back so carefully before, was now tousled, and the wave that had formerly been plastered down on his forehead was now reduced to a thin tuft of hair stick-

ing up on the top of his head. But the slightly narrowed left
eye still seemed to be hinting at something and reminded Ivan
of the old Smerdyakov who had once remarked to him that
"it's always rewarding to talk to a clever man."

Ivan sat on a stool at the foot of the bed. Smerdyakov,
trying to turn his body, winced in pain. He did not speak. He
did not seem particularly interested.

"Can you talk?" Ivan asked. "It won't tire you too much?"

"Yes, I can. I'm all right . . ." Smerdyakov mumbled in
a weak voice. "When did you arrive, Mr. Ivan?" he added
somewhat condescendingly, as though to encourage his hesitant visitor.

"I just arrived today," Ivan said, "to clear up your mess
here."

Smerdyakov sighed.

"Why do you sigh? You knew very well what was coming."

Smerdyakov maintained a stolid silence for a few minutes.
Then he said:

"How could I help knowing what was coming, Mr. Ivan? It
was pretty clear, wasn't it? What I didn't know, though, was
that it would happen the way it did."

"What way? It's no use trying to turn around in circles
now! Why, you told me beforehand that you were going to
have that epileptic fit of yours as soon as you got down into
the cellar, didn't you? You told me—the cellar."

"Did you mention that in your deposition, Mr. Ivan?"
Smerdyakov asked calmly.

Ivan all of a sudden became very angry.

"No, I haven't mentioned it yet, but I certainly will. There
are quite a few things you'll have to explain to me, my good
fellow, and you'd better get out of your head, once and for
all, the notion that you can play games with me!"

"But why should I play games with you, Mr. Ivan, since
I've placed all my hopes in you, just like in Almighty God?"

Smerdyakov's voice was just as calm as before, but as he
spoke he closed his eyes for a second or two.

"In the first place, I know it's impossible to predict when
an epileptic fit is going to come on. I have made thorough
enough inquiries about it, so there's no point in your insisting
on it: no one can foretell the day and the hour. So how could
you tell me in advance exactly when you would fall down
those cellar stairs in an epileptic fit, unless you were planning
to sham it?"

"I knew I'd have to go to the cellar that day—more than

once even," Smerdyakov drawled unhurriedly. "And last year I fell in exactly the same way down the attic stairs. And while it's impossible to predict exactly the day and the time when the falling sickness will strike, one can still have a feeling when one is about to be hit by it."

"But you told me the day and the time, remember?"

"Why don't you ask the doctors about my sickness? They'll tell you whether it was genuine or not. I can tell you nothing more on the subject."

"And what about the cellar? How could you know that it would strike you just there?"

"The cellar, the cellar—why do you keep harping on the cellar, Mr. Ivan? When I went down into the cellar, I was frightened and worried about what might happen. And the reason I was so frightened was because, with you away, Mr. Ivan, there was no one left to come to my defense. And so, as I was going down those cellar stairs, I said to myself: 'What if it comes on now and strikes me—will I fall down or won't I?' And just from all that worry, the spasm seized me by the throat and I went flying through the air. All this, as well as the talk we had the evening before it all happened, I've told Dr. Herzenstube and also the examining magistrate, Mr. Nelyudov, and they took it all down and they have it all in writing. And the hospital doctor, Dr. Varvinsky, he even explained to the others that it hit me just because I was thinking and worrying, thinking to myself, 'What'll happen if I fall now?' And it was because of that that it seized me. And that's exactly what they wrote down: it was bound to happen, seeing how worried and frightened I was."

Having said this, Smerdyakov breathed deeply as if the effort had exhausted him.

"So you've told them about it already?" Ivan was caught by surprise. He had thought he would be able to put pressure on Smerdyakov by threatening to reveal their conversation, but suddenly it turned out that Smerdyakov had already reported it himself.

"I have nothing to fear," Smerdyakov said firmly. "Let them write down the whole truth."

"So you told them every word that we said during our talk by the gate?"

"No, I wouldn't say I told them every word of it, Mr. Ivan."

"Did you tell them that you knew how to sham an epileptic fit, as you boasted to me?"

"No, sir, I didn't tell them that."

"I want you to tell me now why you tried to send me off to Chermashnya."

"I didn't want you to go to Moscow, Mr. Ivan, because if you were in Chermashnya, you wouldn't be so far away."

"You're lying. It was you who suggested I should leave; you said I would be farther out of harm's way."

"I advised you to only because of my affection for you and my loyalty to you, Mr. Ivan. I felt there would be trouble in the house and I was concerned for you. Only I was even more concerned about myself, so while I was advising you to go farther away from trouble, I hoped you'd understand how dangerous things were in the house and that you'd stay with us to protect your father."

"Why couldn't you have said that plainly, you idiot?" Ivan said, suddenly flaring up.

"But how could I say it plainly? You knew I was being terrorized then, Mr. Ivan, and, besides, I was afraid to make you angry too. And, of course, I was afraid that Mr. Dmitry might come at any time to make trouble, because he looked on that money like it was his own. But how could I suspect that it would end up in murder? I thought Mr. Dmitry would just take the three thousand rubles in the envelope that your father kept under his mattress, but then he came and killed him too. You certainly wouldn't have guessed that either, Mr. Ivan, would you?"

"But since you say it was impossible to guess, why did you say before that you hoped I'd guess and decide to stay?" Ivan asked thoughtfully.

"You could have guessed because I was pleading with you to go to Chermashnya instead of Moscow, that's how."

"Who the hell could possibly guess from that?"

Smerdyakov seemed extremely tired and said nothing for a whole minute.

"You could have guessed because my begging you not to go all the way to Moscow but only to Chermashnya showed that I wanted you to be closer to us, and thought that, knowing that you weren't too far away, your brother, Mr. Dmitry, wouldn't dare be so bold. And, in case of need, you'd have been here sooner to protect me too, for I told you myself about Gregory being ill and also that I was afraid of an attack of falling sickness. When I explained to you about all those signals which, if you knocked them out on the door, would make your late father let you in, warning you that Mr. Dmitry knew them from me, I thought you wouldn't leave for Moscow, or even for Chermashnya for that matter, but stay here with us."

"He's damned coherent," Ivan thought, "and even if he mumbles a bit, I can't see how Herzenstube could find signs of impairment to his mental faculties . . ."

"You're putting on a whole act for my benefit, damn you!" Ivan cried angrily.

"But I must admit, Mr. Ivan, that I thought you'd guessed everything," Smerdyakov said in a completely innocent tone.

"If I had guessed, I'd have stayed, of course!" Ivan cried, flaring up again.

"But I thought it was just because you had guessed that you left in such a rush, that you wanted to be as far away as possible from trouble when it came, that you didn't really mind where you went since you were much too scared to stay."

"You imagine that everybody is a coward like you, don't you?"

"Forgive me, Mr. Ivan—I did think you were like me."

"Of course, I should have guessed," Ivan said worriedly, "and, in fact, it did occur to me that you were concocting some villainy or other . . . But, no, you're lying, you're lying again! I remember your coming up to the carriage when I was already in it and saying, 'It's always rewarding to talk to a clever man.' That shows you were pleased I was leaving, doesn't it, for why else would you've praised me like that?"

Smerdyakov sighed again and something like color appeared in his face.

"If I was pleased, it was only because you'd agreed to go to Chermashnya instead of to Moscow," he said somewhat haltingly. "After all, it was not so far. But when I said that to you about a clever man, I didn't mean it as praise—I meant it as a reproach."

"Why a reproach?"

"Because, although you sensed the danger, you were deserting your own father and refused to stay and protect us. And if anything happened, I could always be accused of having stolen that three thousand rubles."

"God damn you!" Ivan growled angrily. "But wait, did you tell the prosecutor about those signals, those knocks?"

"Yes, I told them all about the signals."

Ivan was puzzled again.

"If I imagined anything at that time," he started again, "it was that you, and you alone, were up to some villainy or other. I knew that Dmitry was capable of killing, but I never thought that he'd steal, while from you I could expect anything. Besides, you told me yourself then that you could always sham an epileptic fit. So why else would you have told me that?"

"Out of the trusting sincerity of my heart. But even so, I never shammed a fit either before or after that time, and I told you that just because I wanted to show you how clever I was. I admit, it was stupid of me. I'd become very attached to you, Mr. Ivan, and I had complete faith in you."

"Well, Dmitry accuses you openly: he says you killed our father and stole the money."

"But what else can he do now?" Smerdyakov grinned bitterly. "And who will believe him with all the evidence against him? Gregory even saw the door open after he'd done it. Well, I don't blame him really—he's afraid now and is trying to save his neck."

He remained quiet for a while, and then went on as if he'd just thought of something.

"You see, Mr. Ivan, it's like this. I've heard that Mr. Dmitry is trying to put the blame on me. Now, do you really imagine that if I had actually had any plans concerning your father before, I'd have boasted to you beforehand that I was good at shamming epileptic fits? If I was really preparing to murder him, would I be so stupid as to say something that would implicate me right away, and what's more, to say it to my victim's own son? Do you think that's likely, Mr. Ivan? I say, no one would ever do things that way. Now no one can hear me saying these things to you, except for what they call Providence. But suppose you went and repeated what I have just told you to the prosecutor or to Mr. Nelyudov, you know you'd clear me once and for all of any suspicion, because they'd say, 'How could a murderer be so simple-minded as to say such things beforehand?' Anybody can see that."

Ivan was impressed by Smerdyakov's last argument and he got up, putting an end to his visit.

"Listen," he said, "I don't really suspect you. In fact, I consider it absurd to suspect you and I'm grateful to you for having reassured me. I must be going now but I'll come to see you again. I hope you get better soon. Is there anything I can do for you in the meantime?"

"I thank you very kindly, Mr. Ivan, but Martha is so very

kind, she takes good care of me and sees to it that I get everything I need. And kind people come to see me every day."

"Good-by then. And, you know, I don't think I'll tell them about your ability to sham epileptic fits. And I wouldn't advise you to tell them of it either," Ivan added unexpectedly.

"I understand very well, Mr. Ivan, sir. And since you've decided not to report it, I won't report all the rest of our talk by the gate either."

After Ivan had left Smerdyakov and had gone ten steps or so, it suddenly occurred to him that Smerdyakov's last sentence contained a hint that was insulting to him. He was about to turn back but instead mumbled, "Nonsense!" and walked quickly away from the hospital. He actually felt reassured now that he was reasonably convinced that the murderer was his brother Dmitry rather than Smerdyakov, although it would seem more reasonable for him to have been more upset. Why he felt that way, he did not wish to analyze at the time. In fact, he felt an infinite reluctance to start digging into his own feelings. He was just anxious to forget about the whole business. In the next few days, after studying the depositions of the witnesses and the available evidence, Ivan became entirely convinced of Dmitry's guilt. Some of the evidence from secondary witnesses, such as Fenya and her mother, seemed to him quite sufficient, and as to Perkhotin, Dmitry's drinking companions, and the employees of the Plotnikov store, they seemed to make the case against Dmitry quite overwhelming. Both the prosecutor and the examining magistrate considered the information about the secret knocking signals almost as incriminating as Gregory's testimony about the open door. And Martha, too, told Ivan that Smerdyakov had spent that whole night in his bed, separated from hers and Gregory's by a mere partition, "no more than three steps away from us," she emphasized, and she said that, although she had slept rather deeply that night, she had woken up several times and each time had heard Smerdyakov moan: "He moaned and moaned, never stopped moaning," Martha said. And when Ivan told Dr. Herzenstube that Smerdyakov did not strike him as insane at all, the old doctor smiled ever so subtly.

"Just try and guess what the fellow spends his time on," he replied. "He's learning French words by heart. He has a notebook under his pillow in which someone has written French words down for him in Russian letters, and he's learning them by heart," the doctor concluded with a chuckle.

That was the end of Ivan's misgivings and the mere thought of his brother Dmitry became loathsome to him. There was only one thing that bothered him now, namely, that his other brother, Alexei, still stubbornly maintained that Dmitry had not killed their father and that "most probably it was Smerdyakov" who had done it. Ivan had always respected Alyosha's opinion and that was why he was so bewildered by it now. Ivan also felt it was rather strange that Alyosha never made any attempt to discuss their brother's trial, nor did he even mention Dmitry to him of his own accord, although he would answer any questions that Ivan asked about him. Ivan was very well aware of this, despite the fact that there was something quite unrelated weighing on him just then.

After he returned from Moscow, Ivan had given himself up entirely to his crazed passion for Katerina. This is not the proper place or time to speak of this passion of Ivan's, which marked him for life. It could make the subject of another novel, which I am not sure that I will ever embark upon. However, I will have to explain here that when Ivan had told Alyosha, after leaving Katerina's, that he didn't "feel any inclination toward her," he was lying, for at that moment he was terribly in love with her, although there were other moments when he hated her so much that he could have killed her. There were many reasons for this. Horribly shocked by Dmitry's arrest, she had thrown herself at Ivan as if he were her savior. She felt she had been insulted, hurt, and humiliated, but now the man who had loved her once (oh, she was well aware of it!) and whose intelligence and character she had always considered superior had reappeared on the scene. But this stern young woman never yielded to him completely, despite his unrestrained physical passion, so typical of a Karamazov, and despite the fact that she was very much under his spell. At the same time, she constantly suffered pangs of guilt for being disloyal to Dmitry and she told Ivan so during their innumerable violent squabbles. And it was this that Ivan had referred to as "lies on top of more lies" when he had spoken to Alyosha. Of course, there was much that was false in the whole business and it irritated Ivan terribly. But we shall come to that later. What matters here is that, because of his passion for Katerina, he forgot almost completely about Smerdyakov.

But a couple of weeks after his first visit to Smerdyakov, strange thoughts started to torment him again. Suffice it to say that he kept asking himself why, during his last night in his father's house, he had crept stealthily out of his room and listened like a thief, trying to hear what his father was doing downstairs. Why had he remembered this later with disgust? Why had he felt so despondent when he had left for Moscow the next morning and why, as the train was entering the outskirts of the capital, had he muttered under his breath, "I'm a low scoundrel!" He even imagined that all these painful thoughts might make him forget Katerina, so strong a hold did they have on him. It was soon after this had occurred to him that he met Alyosha in the street. He stopped and asked him:

"Do you remember, on the day when Dmitry broke into the house and beat up father, I said that I reserved to myself the *right to wish*. Tell me, did you think then that I was wishing father's death?"

"Yes, I did," Alyosha answered quietly.

"You were right. It wasn't so difficult to guess. But didn't you also think I wished that *one beast would devour the other,* that is, that Dmitry would kill father, and do so as soon as possible and . . . Well, and that I wouldn't mind making it easier for him?"

Alyosha turned very pale, staring without a word into his brother's eyes.

"Speak up, man! I absolutely must know what you were thinking then. I must know the truth!" Ivan was breathing noisily, glaring angrily at Alyosha as if anticipating what he would say.

"Forgive me, I did think that too," Alyosha whispered and fell silent, adding no "mitigating circumstances."

"Thanks," Ivan said and, leaving Alyosha, walked away.

Since that time, Alyosha noticed that Ivan had become more and more distant toward him and that he even seemed to have taken a violent dislike to him.

Actually, after he had left Alyosha that time, Ivan, who had been on his way home, went straight off, instead, to pay a second visit to Smerdyakov.

CHAPTER 7
The Second Meeting with Smerdyakov

By that time Smerdyakov had been discharged from the hospital. Ivan knew his new lodgings. They were in that sagging little wooden house that looked like two wooden shacks joined together and separated by a narrow covered passage. One of these shacks was occupied by Maria Kondratiev and her mother, the other by Smerdyakov. No one knew whether Smerdyakov lived there as a paying lodger or as a guest. Later, people assumed that he had gone to live there as Maria Kondratiev's fiancé and that she had not charged him rent. Both mother and daughter treated him with the respect due a superior person.

After knocking at the door for a considerable time, Ivan was let in and Maria Kondratiev showed him to the room on the left that was occupied by Smerdyakov. There was a tiled stove in the room and it was very hot. The walls were covered with bright blue wallpaper full of cracks, in which cockroaches swarmed in such amazing numbers that there was a continuous rustling. There was practically no furniture, just two benches along the walls and two chairs by the unpainted wooden · table that had on it, however, a white tablecloth with a pink design. There was a pot of geraniums in each window and a stand with icons in a corner. A battered copper samovar stood on the table next to a tray, on which there were two cups. But Smerdyakov had obviously finished his tea and the candle under the samovar had gone out. He was now sitting at the table copying something into his notebook in pen. The inkpot and a short iron candlestick with a tallow candle in it also stood in front of him on the table. Ivan saw at once from Smerdyakov's appearance that he had completely recovered from his illness: his face was much fresher and fuller, his forelock was carefully brushed up in the middle of his forehead, as in the old days, and the hair at his temples was neatly combed back. He wore a bright-colored, quilted dressing gown that was, however, very worn and stained. He had glasses on, which surprised Ivan, who had never seen him wearing glasses before. Somehow this particular detail doubled the irritation that was already seething within Ivan: "Why, the creature has taken to wearing glasses now, as well," he thought indignantly.

Smerdyakov slowly raised his head and looked at Ivan through the glasses. Then unhurriedly he removed them and raised himself slightly from his seat, apparently not particularly eager to make a great show of respect. As a matter of fact, he moved rather lackadaisically, like a man trying to observe the minimum requirements of civility. Ivan at once noticed and weighed all this; he was struck above all by the look the fellow gave him—a markedly displeased, hostile, and even contemptuous look that seemed to say something like, "Why the hell do you keep pestering me? Haven't we already agreed on everything once and for all? What do you want of me now?"

Ivan barely managed to control himself.

"It's too hot here," he said, still standing, and unbuttoned his overcoat.

"Take off your overcoat," Smerdyakov invited him.

Ivan removed his coat and threw it on the bench. His hands were trembling as he pulled a chair up to the table and sat down. Smerdyakov had already resumed his seat.

"First of all, are we alone here?" Ivan asked in a stern, business-like tone. "Can they hear us from the other room?"

"No one will hear us. You can see for yourself—there's a passage."

"Tell me, my good fellow, what did you mean the other day when, as I was leaving after visiting you in the hospital, you said that if I didn't mention your ability to sham epileptic fits, you, for your part, wouldn't tell the examining magistrate 'all the rest of our talk by the gate'? What can you possibly have meant by 'all the rest'? Were you trying to threaten me, by any chance? Or do you imagine that there's some kind of deal between us and that I'm afraid you may talk? Is that it?"

Ivan spoke with unconcealed anger, apparently deliberately showing Smerdyakov that he didn't want to bother to be diplomatic with him and had no need to put up any pretenses. An evil spark appeared in Smerdyakov's eyes and the left one began to twitch. And, as usual, he was ready with his answer and delivered it in his calm, restrained tone, while the expression on his face seemed to say, "All right, if you want to bring it out in the open, I'll meet you there too!"

"What I meant by that, and the reason I said it then," Smerdyakov said, "was that, although you knew your own father was about to be murdered, you left him there to be

killed so that later people wouldn't say wicked things about
your feelings for him, and perhaps a few other things as well.
That's what I promised you not to report to the examining
magistrate."

Smerdyakov said this unhurriedly, seemingly in perfect
possession of himself. Moreover, there was something stubborn, determined, hostile, and even challenging in his tone
now and his eyes were fixed on Ivan with such insolence that
Ivan had the dizzy impression that the room had begun to
sway.

"What! Have you gone mad? Have you lost your senses?"

"Not at all. I'm in full command of my senses."

"How the hell could I *know* then that he was going to be
murdered?" Ivan shouted, banging his fist on the table. "And
what are those other things you could tell them? Come on,
you lout, speak up!"

Smerdyakov remained silent, still looking at Ivan with the
same insolent expression on his face.

"Tell me, you reeking bastard, what are those 'other things
as well'?" Ivan screamed at the top of his voice.

"By 'other things as well,' I meant that you too were very
eager then that your father should die."

Ivan leaped to his feet, swung his fist back, and hit Smerdyakov. The blow landed on his shoulder and the man's back
was slammed against the wall. Within a second, Smerdyakov's
face was flooded with tears.

"Shame on you, sir, to hit a defenseless man," he muttered,
rubbing his eyes with his grimy, blue-checkered cotton handkerchief, and proceeding to whimper softly and tearfully. A
whole minute passed.

"Stop it. That's enough!" Ivan said peremptorily, sitting
down again. "Just don't push me to the limits of my patience."

Smerdyakov removed the rag from his eyes. Every feature
of his wrinkled little face expressed resentment for the indignity to which he had just been subjected.

"So I gather, then, that you assumed I was just like Dmitry
and wanted to kill my father, is that right?"

"I didn't know what you were thinking at the time,"
Smerdyakov said in a peeved tone, "and that's why I stopped
you by the gate—to try and find out what your thoughts
were."

"To find out what?"

"Just that: whether you wanted your father murdered or
not."

Smerdyakov's impudent tone, which he now maintained constantly, was driving Ivan frantic.

"It was you who killed him!" he shouted suddenly.

Smerdyakov smiled scornfully.

"You must know very well by now that I didn't kill him. I never thought that an intelligent man like you would want to talk about that anymore."

"But why, why, did you suspect me of such desires, then?"

"As you already know, it was fear that brought it on. I was so afraid that, in my state of terror, I sort of suspected everybody. So I decided to test even you. Because, I reasoned to myself, if you desired the same thing as your older brother, then that was the end of everything and I myself was lost, like a helpless fly."

"But you were talking quite differently two weeks ago. Why was that?"

"No, that was exactly what I meant when I spoke to you in the hospital. Only I hoped you would understand without my having to spell everything out, and I thought you didn't want things spelled out, because I thought you were the most intelligent of them all."

"You don't say! But I demand that you answer this now: What did I do to instill such a horrible suspicion into your vile mind?"

"To do the killing yourself—that was something you would never have been capable of. Nor did you have any desire to do it. But you did want someone else to do it—that, certainly, was something you wished."

"Listen to him! What calm, what assurance! But what would I want him dead for? What interest did I have in seeing him murdered?"

"What interest, Mr. Ivan? What about your share of the inheritance?" Smerdyakov said with venomous and vengeful glee. "Why, the share of each of you three Karamazov brothers should come to almost forty thousand rubles apiece, whereas if your late father had married that Miss Svetlov, she would soon enough have transferred all the money to her own name, for I understand she's a very smart lady. So there wouldn't have been even two rubles of your father's entire fortune to share between the three of you. And how much time was there left to you before he married her? It could have happened at any moment: all the lady had to do was to make him a tiny sign with her little finger and the next thing they'd have been in church and you three, you'd have been running around with your tongues hanging out."

Ivan contained himself with great effort.

"All right," he said after a long pause, "as you can see, I didn't leap up and give you a good beating or kill you. So keep talking: therefore, according to you I maneuvered my brother Dmitry into doing it, reckoning that he'd do it for me?"

"How could you help counting on Mr. Dmitry's doing it? Why, if he killed him for you, he would lose his civil rights and, along with them, his right to own property, and he'd be packed off to Siberia. Therefore, whatever was left from your papa would then be divided in half between you and Mr. Alexei and your shares would grow from forty to sixty thousand apiece. Yes, you were certainly counting on Mr. Dmitry."

"Ah, the things I put up with from you! Now let me tell you this, you dog: if I was counting on anyone at that time, it was certainly not Dmitry, but you, and, in fact, I swear I had a feeling that you were up to something loathsome . . . Yes, I remember that feeling clearly . . ."

"Yes, I also thought for a minute or two that you were counting on me too," Smerdyakov said with a mocking grin, "and by counting on me, you only gave yourself away even more. For if you felt I was likely to do it and nevertheless you left, that was just like saying to me: 'Go ahead, kill my father. I'm not stopping you.'"

"Ah, so that's the way you understood it, you low scoundrel!"

"Yes, and all because of Chermashnya. Good Lord, Mr. Ivan, just think for a moment: you decided to go to Moscow and wouldn't listen to your father, who was begging you to go to Chermashnya for him, but then, when I asked you to go there for some stupid reason, all of a sudden, you agreed. What possible reason could you have had for agreeing to go to Chermashnya then, instead of going to Moscow, just because I asked you to? There can only be one answer: you were expecting something of me."

"No, I swear it isn't true!" Ivan screamed, gritting his teeth.

"How could it not be true? Otherwise why, after what I'd told you, didn't you, Mr. Karamazov's own son, grab me by the collar and haul me off to the police, or at least give me a good beating then and there? But you were not a bit angry at what I said; you took my advice as if it came from a good friend, and left. You knew yourself that, unless you had something in mind, it would be the most stupid thing to do, because your duty was to stay here and protect your father's life. So how could I help drawing certain conclusions from your actions?"

Ivan sat scowling, leaning forward with his fists dug hard into his knees.

"Yes, it's a damned shame I didn't bash your face in for you then," he said, grinning bitterly. "Of course, it would have been impractical to drag you to the police station, because they couldn't just take my word for it and they'd have had nothing to go on. But I'm certainly sorry I didn't beat you up on that occasion, despite the fact that assaulting people is against the law; I wish I had beaten your ugly mug into a bloody pulp."

Smerdyakov was watching Ivan with close interest and seemed to be almost enjoying it all. Then he spoke in the smug, doctrinaire tone in which he used to argue with Gregory about religious matters in old Karamazov's presence.

"It is correct that, under ordinary circumstances, the law nowadays forbids punching citizens in the face and that practice has been stopped. But there are circumstances under which, not only in our Russia but also in all the rest of the world, including even the Republic of France, people continue beating people just as they did at the time of Adam and Eve, and they'll always do so. But you, you didn't dare to, under just such circumstances."

"What's that—are you learning French words now?" Ivan said, indicating with his head the notebook on the table.

"And why shouldn't I learn them, to improve my education? Who knows, it may be my fate some day to visit those happy places of Europe personally."

"Now I want you to understand this, you miserable freak," Ivan said, his eyes sparkling and his whole body beginning to shake. "I'm not afraid of your accusations and you can tell them whatever you like about me. And if I didn't beat you up just now it was because I suspect you of murder and I intend to see you tried for it. I'll see to it, believe me."

"Well, if you want my advice, you'd better keep quiet, because there's really nothing you can accuse me of for the good reason that I'm completely innocent, and, in any case, no one would believe you. Only, if you start, I'll have to tell them everything I know, for how else do you expect me to defend myself?"

"And do you imagine I'm afraid of that?"

"Yes, because even if the court doesn't believe what I've said to you today, the public will believe it and you'll feel ashamed."

"Does that mean again that it's always rewarding to talk to a clever man?" Ivan asked, gnashing his teeth.

"You've hit the bull's eye, Mr. Ivan, and I'm sure you'll act like the clever man you are."

Ivan stood up. He was trembling with rage. He put on his overcoat. He didn't say anything more to Smerdyakov; he didn't even look at him as he quickly walked out of the wooden house. The chilly evening air refreshed him. The moon was shining brightly. A nightmarish brew of thoughts and emotions was stewing inside him. "Should I go to the police and prefer charges against Smerdyakov?" he thought. "What could I tell them, though? For he's innocent, after all. In fact, he would accuse me. And it's true—why did I go to Chermashnya? What was the point of that? What? I did, indeed, expect something to happen. He's right." And for the hundredth time he remembered himself opening the door of his room on that last night in his father's house and listening for his father's movements downstairs. But this time the memory was so acutely painful that he stopped dead in the middle of the street. "Yes, that's just what I was expecting to happen—it's the truth! I wanted him to be killed, yes— killed, just that . . . Did I really want it, though, did I? I must kill Smerdyakov now. If I don't dare to kill Smerdyakov, there's no point in staying alive."

Instead of going home, Ivan went straight to Katerina's, frightening her by his appearance, for he looked like a madman. He repeated to her his entire conversation with Smerdyakov, every word of it, and was unable to relax despite all her efforts to calm him. He kept pacing the room and abruptly barking out rather strange things. At last he sat down at the table, leaned his elbows on it, rested his head on his hands, and delivered himself of the following peculiar pronouncement:

"If it was Smerdyakov rather than Dmitry who killed him, then, of course, I am an accomplice, because I incited him to do it. I must make sure, though, whether I really did incite him. But if he was the murderer and not Dmitry, then I am a murderer too."

Hearing this, Katerina got up without a word, went over to her desk, unlocked a box, took a piece of paper out of it, and placed it before Ivan. This was the document which Ivan had mentioned to Alyosha as "mathematical proof" that Dmitry was the killer. It was a letter that Dmitry had written to Katerina in a drunken state on the evening when he had talked to Alyosha, who was returning to the monastery, on the same day that Grushenka had insulted Katerina at tea.

After he had left Alyosha that night, Mitya had rushed off to Grushenka's. We don't know whether he found her at home or not, but he went straight from there to the Capital City Inn, where he got thoroughly drunk. In his drunken state he ordered them to bring him paper, pen, and ink, and produced a document that was to prove fatal to him. Actually, it was a mad, wordy, frantic, and incoherent letter, in fact, what one might call a "drunken letter." It sounded like the explanations of a man coming home drunk and, with tremendous excitement, telling his wife or other members of his family that he has just this minute been insulted by some scoundrel while he himself has behaved very nobly, that he will teach the scoundrel a lesson yet—he goes on and on about it, rambling incoherently, banging on the table, shedding drunken tears . . . The piece of paper they gave him in the inn was a sheet of cheap notepaper, none too clean, on the back of which somebody had calculated what was probably his bill. Obviously the small sheet was not large enough for Mitya's drunken prolixity, so he not only filled in all the margins but also scribbled the last lines across the top of what he had already written. The letter ran as follows:

Fateful Katya,
    I'll get money tomorrow and pay you back the three thousand and then it will be farewell, you woman of great wrath, but at the same time it will be farewell, my love! Tomorrow, I'll try to raise the money from everyone I can think of, but if I can't get it from them, I give you my word I'll go to see my father, smash his head in, and take the money from under his pillow, provided only that Ivan has left by then. I'll go to Siberia for it if I must, but I'll pay you back that money. And you yourself, good-by! I am prostrating myself before you because I know I have acted like a despicable wretch toward you. Forgive me. No, better not forgive me, because that would be easier for both you and me. Better Siberia than your love, Katya, for I love another woman, and I know that you got to know her only too well today, so I don't expect you can ever forgive us. I'll kill the man who's robbed me! And I'll go east, away from all of you, and I

don't want to know anybody at all. Not her either, because
you're not the only one who causes me to suffer, *she* does
too. So farewell then!

P.S. I curse you, but I adore you! I can hear it in my breast.
There's still one string there and it goes on jingling. I'd rather
break my heart in two! I'll kill myself, but before I do, I'll
kill that dog. And so, although I may have behaved like a pig
toward you, still I'm no thief. So wait for the three thousand.
The dog has a pink ribbon under his mattress. I'm no thief;
indeed, it is a thief that I'll kill. Don't you look at me with
such scorn, Katya: Dmitry Karamazov is not a thief—he's a
murderer. He has murdered his father and killed himself so
that he can hold up his head and not have to put up with
your scorn and pride. And he does not love you.
P.P.S. I kiss your feet! Farewell!
P.P.P.S. Katya, you'd better pray to God that somebody
lets me have the money, for then I won't have to cover myself with blood, but if no one does, there will be blood all
over me. Ah, kill me!

Your slave and enemy,
Dmitry Karamazov

After reading this letter, Ivan was completely convinced.
So it was Dmitry and not Smerdyakov. And if it wasn't
Smerdyakov, it wasn't Ivan either. This letter now became
for him a sort of mathematical demonstration of his innocence. He had no doubts left about Dmitry's guilt. And, by
the way, it never entered Ivan's mind that Dmitry and
Smerdyakov could have had a mutual understanding; besides,
that didn't seem to fit in with the known facts. Ivan felt
completely reassured.

The following morning he had nothing but contempt for
Smerdyakov and his sneers, and a few days later it struck
him as rather surprising that he should have been so painfully
hurt by Smerdyakov's suspicions. He decided to ignore him,
to forget him altogether. And so a month went by without
Ivan's even inquiring about Smerdyakov, although he vaguely
heard people say that the man was very sick and that he was
not in full possession of his mental faculties. "He will end up
insane," Dr. Varvinsky said of him, and Ivan took note of
that.

During the last week of that month, Ivan did not feel very
well himself and he even consulted the doctor whom Katerina
had summoned from Moscow for the trial. It was just at this
time that his relations with Katerina became extremely diffi-

cult. They were like two enemies desperately in love with each other. The short-lived but violent sparks of Katerina's former passion for Mitya drove Ivan frantic. It is strange that, until that last time at Katerina's, when Alyosha had come after seeing Dmitry in prison, Ivan had never once, during the whole month, heard Katerina express any doubt about Mitya's guilt, not even during those flare-ups of her old love that he so hated. It is also interesting that, while Ivan hated Dmitry more and more every day, he knew that it was not because of these "flare-ups" that he hated him, but *because it was he who had killed their father!* He was fully conscious of this. Nevertheless, ten days or so before the trial, he went to see Dmitry and offered to arrange his escape by an obviously carefully and thoroughly prepared plan. Aside from his main motive, he was also prompted by an unhealed scar on his pride caused by Smerdyakov's remark that it was to Ivan's advantage to see Mitya convicted because his own share of the inheritance would then increase from forty to sixty thousand rubles. So he decided to sacrifice thirty thousand rubles of his personal share to pay for Dmitry's escape. As he was coming back from his visit to the prison, Ivan felt sad and depressed, because he had suddenly become suspicious of himself—perhaps he was willing to give away that thirty thousand rubles, not to heal the scar on his conscience but for a quite different reason. "Isn't it really because, deep down, I feel I am just as much a murderer as he is?" Ivan wondered. A vague but stinging sensation lashed his heart. But the worst of it was that what made him suffer most during that month was his pride, but we shall return to that later.

When, after his talk with Alyosha, Ivan reached the house where he lived and, about to ring the bell at the gate, pulled his hand back and decided to go and see Smerdyakov instead, he was yielding to a sudden angry impulse.

The words Katerina had spoken in Alyosha's presence rang in his ears—that it was he, Ivan, and he alone who had convinced her that Mitya was the murderer. Thinking of it now, Ivan felt stunned: he had never tried to convince her that Mitya was the murderer; on the contrary, he had shared with her his suspicion that he himself was guilty of his father's death when he had returned from his visit to Smerdyakov. It was then that, in order to prove to him Dmitry's guilt, *she herself* had made him read that indicting "document." And on top of that, she had suddenly announced that she too had been to see Smerdyakov! When had she gone? Ivan had never heard of it. Didn't this show that she wasn't so very convinced of Mitya's guilt after all? And what could Smerdyakov have possibly told her? Yes, what had he actually told her? A great anger filled Ivan and he could not imagine how, only a half hour ago, he could have let her say those things without pouncing on her at once.

And so he pulled his hand back from the bell and rushed off to Smerdyakov's. "This time," he thought on his way, "I'll kill him perhaps."

CHAPTER 8

The Third and Last Meeting with Smerdyakov

Before Ivan had gone half way to Smerdyakov's house, the dry, nipping wind that had been blowing since morning became stronger and a fine, powdery snow started coming down heavily. It didn't stick on the ground; the wind kept whirling the snowflakes around and soon there was a real blizzard. There were practically no street lights in the part of town where Smerdyakov lived now and Ivan walked on in the dark, finding his way by instinct, without even noticing the blizzard. His head ached, there was a painful throbbing in his temples, and he felt his hands twitching convulsively. A little way before he reached Maria Kondratiev's house, Ivan met a short peasant wearing a warm but patched coat, who was zigzagging drunkenly, grumbling and swearing. The man kept starting a song, interrupting himself, swearing, and starting again in a hoarse, drunken voice:

> Vanya, Vanya went to town,
> I won't wait till he comes back . . .

But every time he reached this second line, he again interrupted his singing, swore at someone, and started the song over from the beginning. Ivan felt a terrible hatred for the man before he was really aware of his existence, then suddenly became conscious of him. He felt a violent impulse to hit the little peasant. And just at that second they came abreast of each other and the man, swaying from side to side, butted right into Ivan. Ivan pushed him violently and the peasant went flying and landed like a log on the frozen ground. He uttered one single plaintive "Oh-oh," and fell silent. Ivan took a step toward the prostrate body. The peasant lay there motionless, obviously unconscious. "He'll freeze to death," Ivan thought and walked on to Smerdyakov's.

Maria Kondratiev, who let him in, whispered that Paul Fyodorovich (that is, Smerdyakov) was very sick, although he was not in bed, but "he's acting strange-like" and had even told her to take away the tea she'd brought him, which he had not touched.

"Is he violent?" Ivan asked bluntly.

"Oh no, not at all. He's very quiet . . . Only I still think you shouldn't stay too long with him, please, sir," Maria Kondratiev said pleadingly.

Ivan opened the door and walked into Smerdyakov's room.

It was just as overheated as it had been on Ivan's previous visit, but there were certain changes in the room. One of the plain wooden benches by the wall had been replaced by a large leather and mahogany sofa, on which a bed with fairly clean white pillows and sheets was made up. Smerdyakov, still wearing the same dressing gown, was sitting on the bed. The table had been moved next to the sofa so that the room looked very cluttered now. A thick book in a yellow cover lay on the table, but Smerdyakov was not reading it and, in fact, seemed to have been just sitting there doing nothing. He met Ivan with a long, silent gaze and did not seem particularly surprised at his visit. He had changed considerably since the last time: he looked very pale and drawn; his skin was yellow; his eyes were sunken and the lids bluish.

"You must be really sick," Ivan said, stopping. "I won't keep you long; in fact, I won't bother to take my coat off."

He went to the opposite side of the table, pulled up a chair, and sat down.

"Why are you staring at me like that, saying nothing?" Ivan said. "I want to ask you only one question, but I swear I won't leave here until you've answered it. Tell me, has Miss Katerina Verkhovtsev been here to see you?"

For a while, Smerdyakov continued to look at Ivan without saying anything; then he shrugged and looked away.

"What's the matter with you?" Ivan cried.

"Nothing."

"What do you mean—nothing?"

"All right, she was here. But what's it to you? Leave me alone."

"No, I won't leave you alone. I want to know when she came."

"I hardly even remember her coming," Smerdyakov said, grinning scornfully, but then he turned toward Ivan again and started to stare at him with a strange, insane hatred in his eyes, just as he had looked at him during his previous visit.

"You look pretty sick yourself. Your face is real pinched," he said.

"Don't you worry about my health, just answer my questions."

"You know, the whites of your eyes have turned yellow now. You must be worrying a lot, no?" he said with a contemptuous snort and then, all of a sudden, began to laugh.

"Listen, as I said, I won't leave here until you've answered me," Ivan cried in a terrible rage.

"But why are you pestering me? Why must you come and torment me?" Smerdyakov said in a long-suffering tone.

"Ah hell, I don't give a damn about you, one way or the other. All I want is for you to answer me and, as soon as you've done so, I'll go."

"I have nothing to tell you," Smerdyakov said, lowering his eyes.

"I assure you, I'll make you answer me!"

"What is it that's worrying you so much?" Smerdyakov said, staring at Ivan again, this time not just with scorn but also with a strange and visible disgust. "Can it be that the trial is to start tomorrow? I assure you, nothing will happen to you. You needn't be afraid. Try to understand that finally! So go home, go to bed, and fear nothing."

"I don't even know what you're talking about. What is there for me to fear tomorrow?" Ivan said in surprise and suddenly felt a real wave of fear creep up his spine. Smerdyakov's eyes were watching him.

"You don't understand, do you?" he said in a reproachful tone. "And I don't understand why an intelligent man should want to go on playing such a comedy!"

Ivan looked at him in silence. The unexpected tone, quite unprecedentedly scornful, in which the former flunkey was speaking to him was in itself quite amazing. Even the last time Smerdyakov had not spoken to Ivan in that tone.

"So I'm telling you, you have nothing to fear from me. I won't make any statements about you and, in any case, there's no evidence that could incriminate you. Just look how your hands are trembling! Go on, go home—*it was not you who killed him!*"

Ivan shuddered. Alyosha's words earlier in the evening came to his mind.

"I know I didn't do it . . ." he muttered.

"So you do know?" Smerdyakov interrupted him, but Ivan jumped to his feet and caught him by the shoulder.

"Speak up then, you bastard! I want to know everything!"

Smerdyakov was not in the least frightened. He only riveted his eyes on Ivan's with infinite hatred.

"If that's the way it is—it was you who killed him all right," Smerdyakov hissed.

Ivan sank back into his chair. He seemed to have regained control over himself. A sarcastic smile played on his lips.

"Are you talking about the same thing as last time?"

"Why, you understood very well what I was saying the last time and you understand just as well now."

"The only thing I understand is that you are insane," Ivan said.

"Will you never get tired of this game?" Smerdyakov said. "Here we are sitting all alone, without anyone to hear us, so why must you insist on continuing with this comedy? Or are you trying to blame me alone for everything, to get me to believe it myself? It was you who murdered him. It is you who are the principal murderer, and I am only your accomplice, your faithful servant, who just carried out what you ordered me to do."

"Carried out? Why, did you kill him then?" Ivan cried, feeling himself grow cold.

Something snapped in his brain, an icy shiver shook his whole body. And now Smerdyakov looked at him in real surprise. The genuineness of Ivan's shock must have been quite unexpected to him.

"Do you mean you really didn't know?" he mumbled incredulously, grinning twistedly right into Ivan's face.

Ivan was still gaping at Smerdyakov in silence as if his tongue had become paralyzed. The two lines of the song

Vanya, Vanya went to town,
I won't wait till he comes back . . .

echoed in his head.

"I'm seeing all this in a dream . . . There's a ghost sitting in front of me . . . you're a ghost," Ivan muttered.

"There's no ghost around here, just the two of us and that other one sitting here between us."

"Who's that? Who else is here? Where?" Ivan said in alarm, looking quickly around the room, his eyes searching into every corner.

"That other one is Providence in person. It's right here, near us, but you might just as well give up looking for it—you won't find it."

"You lied to me when you said you killed him!" Ivan screamed madly. "Either you're insane or you're taunting me the way you did last time!"

Smerdyakov, quite unafraid, watched him intently. He found it incredible that Ivan "didn't know" and thought he was still trying to convince him, Smerdyakov, "shamelessly to my face," that he alone was guilty of everything.

"Just a minute," Smerdyakov said in a weak voice. He pulled his left leg out from under the table and started to roll up his trouser-leg. He had on long white socks and slippers. Unhurriedly he undid his garter and slipped his hand inside his sock, searching for something with his fingers.

Ivan stared at him and suddenly began to shake in convulsive terror.

"Madman!" he howled, leaping up. He reeled back, banging his back against the wall. Then he stood stiffly, as if glued to the wall, and stared at Smerdyakov in speechless terror.

Smerdyakov, not in the least disconcerted by Ivan's reaction, was still fumbling in the bottom of his sock, apparently trying to get hold of something with his fingers. At last he succeeded and began pulling it out. Ivan saw that it was papers of some sort, some bundle of documents. Smerdyakov pulled it out and put it on the table.

"Here, look," he said quietly.

"What?" Ivan was shaking.

"Go on, look at it," Smerdyakov repeated quietly.

Ivan stepped up to the table, took the bundle, and started to unwrap it, but suddenly he let it go and drew his fingers away in horror, as if he had touched something slimy and unbearably revolting.

"Your fingers are trembling so, you're liable to get a cramp in them," Smerdyakov commented and began unhurriedly unwrapping the bundle himself. When he removed the wrapping, Ivan saw that it contained three rolls of rainbow-colored, hundred-ruble bills.

"It's all here, the whole three thousand. You needn't bother to count it. You can take it." He nodded at the money.

Ivan sank back into his chair. He was livid.

"You frightened me with that sock of yours," he said, grinning strangely.

"Is it possible then, really possible, that you didn't know until now?" Smerdyakov asked again.

"I didn't . . . I thought it was Dmitry. Mitya, Mitya, oh, God!" He clutched his head with his hands. "Tell me now, tell me, did you do it alone, or was Dmitry in on it with you?"

"No, I did it only with you. It was you and me who killed him. Mr. Dmitry is completely innocent of it."

"All right, all right . . . We'll talk about me later . . . Why am I trembling like this? I can't even talk . . ."

"You used to be brave before and you used to say that everything is permitted, but you're certainly frightened now," Smerdyakov said in wonderment. "Would you like me to order some lemonade for you? It would refresh you perhaps. But we'd better hide this," he said, pointing to the money.

He got up to call Maria Kondratiev and ask her to prepare some lemonade, but first he tried to find something to cover the money with, so that she wouldn't see it. First he pulled a handkerchief out of his pocket, but it was all wet and slimy. Then he took the big book in the yellow cover that Ivan had noticed and put it on top of the bills. It was entitled *The Sayings of Father Isaac, the Syrian,* which fact Ivan took in without thinking.

"I don't want any lemonade," Ivan said, "and we'll talk about me later. Sit down now and tell me how you did it. Tell me everything . . ."

"You'd better take off your overcoat or you'll perspire too much . . ."

Ivan noticed only now that all this time he had been wearing his overcoat in the overheated room. Almost ripping it off, he threw it down on the bench.

"Go on, please—tell me."

He seemed calmer now. He was confident that now Smerdyakov would tell him *everything.*

"You mean, how I did it?" Smerdyakov sighed. "It was done in the most natural way. I just followed your words . . ."

"We'll discuss my words later," Ivan interrupted him, but this time in a firm, calm voice, apparently having regained full control over himself. "What I want now is a detailed account of how you did it, in proper order. Don't leave out anything. Above all, I want every little detail. Please."

"So when you left, I fell down the cellar stairs . . ."

"Was it a real epileptic fit or were you shamming it?"

"Of course I was shamming it. I shammed everything. I went down those stairs with no trouble at all, to the very bottom, then I lay down, and once I was lying down I started to scream and yell and writhe until they carried me out of there."

"Wait, wait! Tell me this: were you still putting it on when you were in the hospital too?"

"No sir, not there. The next morning, before they got me to the hospital, I had a genuine attack; it was the worst I'd had in years, and I don't remember anything of the next two days."

"Good, good. Please go on."

"So they put me in my bed, you know, behind that partition. I knew they'd put me there because whenever I was sick, Martha would make me spend the night next to their room, behind that partition. She's always been nice to me, ever since I was born. So at night I kept on moaning, quiet-like, as I was waiting for Mr. Dmitry to arrive."

"Waiting for him to come to see you?"

"Why to see me? No, just come to the house. I had no doubt whatsoever that he'd come that night, because with me not giving him any information about what was going on, he'd climb over the fence to find out for himself. I knew he could get over that fence and that he'd come."

"And what if he hadn't come?"

"Then nothing would have happened at all. I wouldn't have done it without him coming."

"All right, all right . . . Speak clearly, don't hurry and, above all, don't leave anything out."

"I expected he'd kill old Mr. Karamazov. I was just about sure he would because . . . well, I'd brought him to that point beforehand. And above all, I'd told him about those signals. With his suspiciousness and with the anger piled up inside him during the few days before, I was sure he'd use the signals to get inside the house. That looked pretty sure and I was reckoning on it."

"Just a moment," Ivan said, "do you realize that if he had killed him, he'd have taken the money too. I'm sure you must have thought of that. So I don't see what you would have got out of it."

"Ah, but he'd never have found the money. It was I, of course, who told him the money was under the mattress. But it wasn't true, see? Mr. Karamazov used to keep that money in a box on the table and that was where it was. But then I advised him to hide it in the corner behind the icons where no one would ever look for it, especially if they were in a hurry, and he took my advice, because I was the only person he really trusted in all the world. And so this package had been there behind those icons ever since. It would have been really stupid to keep the money under the mattress. It would have been less safe there than in the box, where at least it was locked. But in town everybody came to believe that he kept the money under his mattress, which is quite a stupid notion. So you see, if Mr. Dmitry had done the killing, he would have had to run away empty-handed, afraid of every noise and rustle, as murderers always are, or otherwise he'd have been arrested. So in that case, too, I could have got into Mr. Karamazov's bedroom the next morning, or even that same night, and picked up the money from behind the icons, and they would have accused Mr. Dmitry of stealing it too. I could at least hope that I'd be able to pull that one off."

"But what if he hadn't killed him but just beaten him up?"

"If he hadn't killed him, I wouldn't have dared to take the money, of course, and it would have stayed where it was. But even so, there was a chance that he'd beat him unconscious and that would give me enough time to pick up the money and then tell Mr. Karamazov that it was Mr. Dmitry who'd taken it after he'd beaten him up."

"Wait, I'm getting a bit mixed up. Couldn't Dmitry have killed him, then, while you only took the money?"

"No, it wasn't Mr. Dmitry who killed him. You see, I still could have told you that it was him, but I don't want to lie to you now because . . . well, because even if you really didn't understand until now—and I can see that you weren't just pretending that you didn't so as to blame me alone for everything, to my own face—you're still guilty in every way, because you knew about it and left me to take care of the killing while you left town, knowing very well what was going to happen. And that's why I want to prove it to you this evening: it is you who are the principal murderer and, although I did the killing, I'm not the principal one. Yes, you are the true and rightful murderer!"

"But why, why am I the murderer?" Ivan cried, unable to restrain himself any longer and forgetting that he had told Smerdyakov they would not discuss his own role in the murder until later. "Oh, God, is it because of the Chermashnya business? Wait! Tell me, then, why did you need

my consent if, to you, my departure for Chermashnya meant
consent anyway? What explanation do you have for that
now?"

"But I had to have full assurance of your consent because
that way I knew you'd never kick up a fuss about the missing
three thousand if something went wrong and they suspected
me, instead of Mr. Dmitry, or even just thought I was his
accomplice. On the contrary, you'd come to my defense that
way . . . And later, once you'd come into possession of your
inheritance, you'd have rewarded me for my services for
the rest of my life, because, after all, you wouldn't have
received anything if he'd married Miss Svetlov before dying.
You'd have inherited exactly zero rubles."

"I see, so you were planning to blackmail me later, too,
for the rest of my life," Ivan growled through his teeth. "But
what would have happened if, instead of leaving then, I'd
gone and reported you to the police?"

"What could you have told them, though? That I was
advising you to leave for Chermashnya, perhaps? That's just
silly. Besides, after I advised you to go, you could have
either left or stayed. Now, if you'd stayed, nothing would
have happened, for I'd have known then that you weren't interested in the business and I'd have dropped it. But by leaving, you were assuring me that you wouldn't dare be a
witness for the prosecution against me and that you'd allow
me to keep the three thousand. And you could never have
accused me in court, because if you had, I'd have told them
everything—oh, not that I killed him and stole the money,
that I certainly wouldn't have told them—but that you had
tried to incite me to kill and to rob and that I had refused.
So you see why I wanted your consent then? It was so you
couldn't push me around later. For what evidence do you
have against me now? I, on the other hand, had something
against you after I found out how badly you wanted your
father's death. And take my word for it: the public would
believe me and it'd mean shame and disgrace for you to the
end of your life."

"So you think I wanted it so very, very badly?" Ivan said
through his teeth.

"I'm sure you wanted it that badly, because it was by giving
me your consent that you made it possible for me to go
ahead," Smerdyakov said, looking with assurance straight into
Ivan's face.

Otherwise, he spoke in a low, tired voice and was in a very

weak state. But there was something inside him that was driving him on and inflaming him. Obviously he had something on his mind, and Ivan was aware of it.

"Go on," Ivan said. "Tell me what happened that night."

"Well, you know what happened. So I was lying there and suddenly I heard a voice, as if Mr. Karamazov had let out a shriek. Yes, before that, Gregory had got up and gone out, and then I'd heard him yell and after that there was nothing —just darkness and quiet. I lie there and wait, and my heart's beating and I just can't wait. So in the end I get up and go out. And I see, on my left, the window of the master's bedroom, which gives onto the garden, wide open. So I take a few steps in that direction and listen. I had to find out whether Mr. Karamazov was still there in his room, alive. Then I hear him moving around and moaning. Therefore he's still alive. 'Damn it,' I say to myself. I go up to the window and call out to him: 'It's me!' 'Ah,' he says to me, 'he was here, but he ran away.' He meant that Mr. Dmitry had been there. 'He's killed Gregory,' he says. 'Where?' I sort of whispered to him. 'In the garden, in that corner over there,' and now he's whispering too. 'Wait,' I said, and I went into the garden to have a look at Gregory. He was stretched out by the garden wall and, in fact, I stumbled against him. He was unconscious and all covered with blood. So it was a fact that Mr. Dmitry had been there, I thought to myself, and I decided to go through with the whole business then and there, what with Gregory lying there quite unconscious so he wouldn't know anything even if he did live. The only risk was that Martha might wake up. That occurred to me just then, but I was already so excited and eager to do it that it took my breath away.

"I returned to the master's bedroom window and I called out to him: 'Miss Svetlov's here, sir. She wants to be let in.' Ah, you should have seen the way he jumped when he heard that, just like a small boy. 'Is she here? Where?' and he gasps and moans but still can't believe she's there. 'She's over there, see. Open the door.' He looks at me through the window, he believes me and he doesn't believe me; looks like he's scared to open, even to me. You know, it's funny, I suddenly decided to bang that signal on the window frame, the one meaning, she's here. I did it right in front of his eyes, and although he didn't seem to believe me before, as soon as he heard the signal, he immediately ran to the door and opened it. I tried to walk in but he barred the way with his body and wouldn't let me pass. 'Where is she then?' He stares at me and I see he's trembling all over. 'Ah,' I say to myself, 'if he's so afraid even of me, it won't be too easy.' And my legs went all weak with fear that he wouldn't let me inside the house, or that he'd start shouting, or that Martha would come along, or whatever I thought might happen. I don't even remember all the things I feared then, but I must have been pretty pale as I stood there in front of him. So I whisper to him: 'Why, she's there, right under the window. I thought you saw her yourself.' 'So you bring her here,' he says. 'Bring her to the door.' 'She's scared,' I say. 'She was frightened by the shouting and hid herself in the bushes. Call her yourself from the window of your study.' So he ran in there, went to the window, put the candle on the window sill. 'Grushenka,' he shouted, 'are you there, Grushenka?' But although he's shouting like that, he won't lean out of the window. Nor will he move away from me, because all of a sudden he doesn't trust me anymore and is terribly frightened, and so he sticks close to me. 'There she is—can't you see?' I go to the window myself and lean very far out of it. 'She's behind that bush, see—she's laughing at you.' And now, all of a sudden he believes it. He begins to tremble something terrible and leans his whole body out of the window. He sure must have been in love with her, your father!

"So I got hold of that big iron paperweight, the one he had on his desk, remember—it must've weighed a good three pounds—and I let him have it from behind, with the edge of the thing, right on his crown. He didn't make a sound. He slumped down to the floor and I whacked him again and then once more. It was after I'd hit him the third time that I knew I'd cracked his skull. He fell backward then and lay there with his face turned toward the ceiling. And there was blood all over him. I examined myself: there was no blood on me at all. It never even splashed me. I wiped the paperweight clean and put it back. Then I went to the corner, took the money from behind the icons, and threw the empty packet on the floor and the pink ribbon next to it.

"I went out into the garden. I was trembling something terrible. I went straight to the apple tree that has a hollow in it—you know the one I mean—I'd kept a rag and some paper there for some time for just that purpose. I wrapped the money in the paper and the paper in the rag, and I stuffed it deep into the hollow, where it stayed for the whole two weeks I was in the hospital.

"So after I'd put the money in the hollow, I went back to the cottage and got into my bed, and then I started worrying: 'If Gregory dies,' I think to myself, 'there will be trouble for me. If he comes to, though, I'll be in the clear, for he'll be witness that Mr. Dmitry did come, so they'll be sure that it was he who did the killing and took the money too.' And I got myself all worked up, worrying about Gregory, and was so impatient to know that I started moaning louder and louder, to wake Martha up. Finally she did wake up. She got up and was about to rush in to me, but when she saw Gregory wasn't there, she ran out into the garden and then I heard her scream . . . Well, then the whole thing got going and I was no longer worried."

Smerdyakov finished talking. Ivan had been listening all the time in complete silence. He had hardly stirred or taken his eyes off him. Smerdyakov, on the other hand, had looked away most of the time, casting only occasional sidelong glances at Ivan. By the time he had come to the end of his account, he was obviously very agitated and was breathing with considerable difficulty. His face was sweating. It was impossible to tell, however, whether it was remorse or something else that had put him into that state.

"Wait," Ivan said slowly, trying to work something out. "What about that door? If father opened the door only to let you in, how could Gregory have seen it open before you even got there? Because he was there before you, wasn't he?"

It should be noted that Ivan asked this question in a very friendly tone that was quite different from the way he had spoken to Smerdyakov before; he no longer sounded in the least irritated, and if someone had noiselessly opened the door and watched them for a while unobserved, he would certainly have got the impression that these two men were having a friendly discussion about something quite usual, albeit extremely interesting.

"That door that Gregory saw open," Smerdyakov said with a contorted grin, "he just imagined it all. Let me tell you, he's not a man, that one, but a stubborn mule. He never saw it open, but he's convinced himself that he did and nothing will make him budge from that now. It was just a windfall for you and me that he invented that story, because that is what will pin Mr. Dmitry down for good."

"Listen," Ivan said, again looking as if he were groping for something and losing the thread, "there were many

things I wanted to ask you, but I've forgotten . . . I keep
forgetting things and getting mixed up somehow . . . Ah yes,
tell me this for one thing: Why did you open the package in
the room there and leave the wrapping on the floor? Why
didn't you take it wrapped up as it was? When you were
telling me about it, it sounded as though you considered that
the proper way to do things. But what was the point of it? I
don't see."

"Well, I had a good reason for that. You see, why should
someone who is in the know and is familiar with everything,
such as me, for instance, someone who has seen the money
before and who perhaps even helped put it into that envelope
and watched how it was sealed and addressed—why should
someone like that, if he happened to be the murderer, open
the envelope, especially if he was in a great hurry, when he
already knew for sure that the money was in there? So, if
the one who took it was in my position, for instance, he'd
just stuff the whole thing in his pocket and get out of there
as quick as he could. But it's not very likely that Mr. Dmitry
would act that way, is it? He only knew of that package from
what he'd been told. He'd never seen it himself and so,
when he took it from under the mattress, he'd be likely to
tear it open to check whether it really contained the money
he was after and then just toss the envelope away, in too
much of a rush to stop and think that the envelope could be
used as evidence against him later, seeing as he's no experi--
enced thief. Obviously, he'd never stolen anything like this
before, being a gentleman by birth, and if he decided to steal
now, he didn't think it was stealing but taking back something that was rightfully his, as he announced beforehand all
over town—he even bragged that he'd come and take away
from his father what was really his. When the prosecutor
questioned me, I didn't tell him that openly as I have just
now; I sort of brought it up by accident-like, as if I didn't
understand it myself, making as if he'd worked it out all by
himself without my suggesting it, and that prosecutor gentleman was really drooling when he caught my hint."

"Is it possible that you thought it all out so thoroughly at
that moment?" Ivan cried out in wide-eyed amazement, staring at Smerdyakov as if in awe.

"No, how could I think all that out in a hurry? It had all
been thought out in advance."

"Well, then . . . then the devil himself must have helped

you to pull it all off!" Ivan cried, still looking at him in amazement. "No, you aren't stupid at all—you're much, much more intelligent than I ever could have imagined."

He stood up, apparently intending to walk about the room for a while. He was filled with a dreadful anguish. But the table barred his way and, to get out, he'd have had to squeeze himself through the narrow gap between it and the wall, so he gave it up and sat down again. Perhaps it was the fact that he could not satisfy his impulse to stretch his legs that suddenly irritated him and brought back his rage.

"Listen to me, you miserable dog!" he screamed frantically. "Can't you understand that, if I haven't killed you yet, it's only because I want you alive in court tomorrow. May God be my witness," Ivan shouted, raising his hand, "that, although I may have secretly wished my father's death, I am nowhere near as guilty as you imagine and perhaps I didn't really mean to maneuver you into doing it. No, no, I didn't, I didn't! But never mind that. I'll bring it all up in court tomorrow. I have decided now! I'll tell them everything. I'll let them know that the two of us were involved in it together. And whatever you may say against me there, whatever you may bring up, I'll face up to it, and I want you to understand that I'm not afraid of anything you may tell them. I'll confirm it myself. But I want you, too, to confess everything in court; you must, you must—we shall go together, and that's how it's going to be!"

Ivan ended on a solemn, forceful note and it was obvious from his burning eyes that this was final.

"You're sick now, very sick, the whites of your eyes are completely yellow." There was no sarcasm in Smerdyakov's words; if anything there was even a note of sympathy.

"We'll go and tell them together!" Ivan said again. "And if you refuse, it won't make any difference—I'll confess anyway."

Smerdyakov seemed to think for a while in silence.

"Nothing like that will happen. You won't tell them," he declared with finality.

"You really don't understand me," Ivan cried reproachfully.

"You'll be too ashamed to admit everything. Besides, you'll be wasting your time, because I will certainly say that I never told you anything of the sort and that either you're very sick with one of those diseases—and you look it now—

or you've grown so sorry for your dear brother that you've decided to sacrifice yourself to save him and invented all these accusations against me, because, anyway, all your life you've always looked upon me as if I was some bug and not human at all. I ask you, then, who will ever believe you when you haven't got one single bit of evidence to prove it?"

"But that money you showed me just now. You did so to convince me, of course."

Smerdyakov took the book about Isaac the Syrian off the money and put it aside.

"You can take this money away with you," Smerdyakov said with a sigh.

"Of course I'll take it. But why are you giving it to me, since that was what you killed him for?"

Ivan looked at him greatly puzzled once more.

"I don't want it," Smerdyakov said in a quivering voice, waving his hand scornfully. "I did have an idea once that I'd use that money to start a new life in Moscow, or even better, abroad—it was just some kind of fancy I had—but I did it above all simply because 'everything is permitted.' And the truth is, I learned that from you; you taught me many things at that time, things like, since there is no infinite God, there's no such thing as virtue either and there's no need for it at all. You were right there. And that's the way I understood it."

"I see you worked it all out yourself," Ivan said with a crooked grin.

"Under your guidance."

"But now, have you decided to believe in God, after all, since you're giving me this money?"

"No, I don't believe in God," Smerdyakov whispered.

"So why are you giving it to me?"

"Ah, why don't you let that be?" Smerdyakov again dismissed the question with a wave of his hand. "You're the one who said that everything was permitted, so why are you so worried now? You even talk about going and accusing yourself! Ah, but nothing will come of it—you won't do it," Smerdyakov decided again with assurance.

"You'll see!"

"It's impossible. You're very, very intelligent. You love money, I know that. And you like people to honor and respect you, because you're very proud. You also like women too much. Yes, and what you like most of all is to live in comfort and security without having to bow to anyone for it. So it doesn't seem likely that you'll want to cover yourself with shame and disgrace by accusing yourself in court tomorrow. Of all his sons, you're the one who's most like the late Mr. Karamazov—your soul and his, they're just the same!"

"You *are* clever!" Ivan looked dumbfounded for a second, then the blood rushed to his face. "I used to think you were stupid. You meant that seriously just now," he said, looking at Smerdyakov with new eyes.

"It was your pride that made you think I was stupid. Here, take your money."

Ivan took the three bundles of bills and shoved them into his pocket without wrapping them in anything.

"I'll produce this money as evidence in court tomorrow."

"No one will believe you. You have enough money of your own now and they'll say you just took it out of your cash-box."

Ivan stood up.

"Let me repeat that the only reason I haven't killed you yet is that I'll need you in court tomorrow. Don't forget that!"

"I don't care. Go ahead—kill me, right now. Go ahead," Smerdyakov said in a strange voice. "Even that, you won't dare to do!" he snorted. "You dare do nothing—you, a man who talked so big!"

"See you tomorrow!" Ivan said, getting ready to leave.

"Wait, let me have one more look at it."

Ivan took the bills out of his pocket and showed them to Smerdyakov. Smerdyakov kept his eyes on them for ten seconds or so.

"All right, you can go," he said in a resigned tone. But before Ivan had taken three steps, he called out: "Mr. Ivan!"

"What is it now?"

"Farewell!"

"See you tomorrow then!" Ivan said and walked out.

The blizzard was still raging. Ivan started out energetically enough, but soon his steps became uncertain and he began to sway. "This is something physical," he thought with a grin. A strange happiness had come over him now. He felt full of determination: there would be no more wavering for him, wavering such as had caused him so much suffering lately. His mind was made up and he wasn't going to change it, he thought cheerfully. At that moment he stumbled against something and almost fell. He saw in the darkness that it was the little peasant, still lying there unconscious. By now almost his whole face was covered with snow. Ivan suddenly bent down, picked the man up, and, carrying him on his back, went on until he saw a house with a light inside. He knocked on the window and asked the man who answered to help him to carry the peasant to the police station, promising to give him three rubles for his help. The man put his coat on and came out.

I won't go into the details of how Ivan finally succeeded in getting the peasant to the police station, seeing that the man got properly taken care of and examined by a doctor, and generously providing "for possible expenses." I shall only say that it took almost a whole hour of his time, but Ivan felt that it was well worth his while.

His thoughts wandered as his mind worked intently. "If I hadn't made up my mind so definitely about tomorrow," he suddenly thought with delight, "I wouldn't have stopped and spent a whole hour looking after that peasant; I would have just gone on and not cared a damn if he froze to death . . . It's strange, though, that I can make all these observations about myself," he thought with even greater delight, "while those people there believe I'm going mad!"

When he reached his house and was about to go in, he stopped and asked himself: "Shouldn't I go and see the prosecutor right now and tell him everything without waiting?" But he answered his own question by entering the house. "Let it all be done tomorrow at the same time!" he whispered and at that very second all his joy and happiness vanished. When he got to his room, he felt as though icy fingers were clutching at his heart, a reminder of something painful and repulsive that was connected precisely with this room, that had been here, and that was here now at this very moment. He dropped exhausted onto the sofa. The old servant brought him the samovar, and Ivan poured himself tea, but he did not touch it and sent the old woman away for the night. As he sat on the sofa, the room began to sway before his eyes. He felt very weak and ill. He started to doze off but then nervously got up and walked up and down the room to shake off his drowsiness. At moments he thought he was delirious, but his illness had ceased to worry him. He sat down again, looking around him now and then as if expecting to find something. In the end his eyes rested on one particular point. He grinned, but then the blood rushed angrily to his head. He sat for a long time with his head resting heavily in his hands, his eyes focused on a certain spot in the middle of the sofa that stood against the opposite wall. There was obviously something there that made him nervous, some object that worried and tormented him.

CHAPTER 9

Ivan's Nightmare and the Devil

Although I am not a doctor, I feel that at this point I must give the reader at least some idea of the nature of Ivan's illness. I will anticipate somewhat and say that the following day Ivan was to succumb completely to the brain fever which he had been incubating for a long time, but which his organism had stubbornly resisted. Knowing very little about medicine, I will only risk the assumption that perhaps he had succeeded in delaying the sickness by a desperate effort of will, although of course he could not avoid it altogether. He knew he was not well but was horrified at the thought of falling ill just when he was faced with the most important moments of his life, when he had to be in full possession of his faculties in order to say bravely what he had to say and justify himself to himself. He had once consulted the Moscow doctor whom Katerina had invited to our town, following through on an idea I have already mentioned. The doctor examined him, sounded him with a stethoscope, and diagnosed that he was suffering from some sort of brain disorder, not seeming in the least surprised when Ivan reluctantly confessed to a certain symptom.

"Hallucinations are quite possible in your present condition," the doctor decided, "although we should really check on them . . . In general, I think you should undergo serious medical treatment without wasting a minute; otherwise it may become very serious."

Upon leaving the doctor, however, Ivan wisely ignored his advice and did not put himself in the doctor's hands. "As long as I'm strong enough to walk around, I'll do so; when I can no longer stand on my feet and have to stay in bed, let them give me any medical treatment they can think of," he decided, dismissing his illness with a shrug.

And so he sat now, realizing full well that he was delirious, with his eyes focused, as I've already mentioned, on that point on the sofa opposite him.

Now there was someone sitting in that spot. God knows how he'd got in, because he hadn't been in the room when Ivan first got home from Smerdyakov's. He was a Russian gentleman of a certain type, no longer young, *qui frisait la cinquantaine,* as the French would say, with dark, still-thick hair and pointed beard which were only slightly graying. He wore a brownish jacket which had obviously been made by a first-class tailor but a good three years earlier, for it was rather worn and was cut in a fashion that no wealthy man of the world would have been seen in for at least the past two years. His shirt and his wide tie were just the kind worn by elegant gentlemen, although if you looked closely you could see that the shirt was none too clean and the tie was slightly frayed. The visitor's checkered trousers fitted him perfectly, but again they were a bit too light and somewhat narrower than the present fashion. And his fluffy white felt hat was altogether out of season. In short, he looked like a very respectable gentleman somewhat down on his luck. He seemed to be the sort of idle landowner who prospered under serfdom, who once moved in high society and traveled, who used to have the right connections and perhaps had even kept them up but who, after a gay and lavish youth and after the recent abolition of serfdom, had little by little become impoverished and had turned into a well-bred parasite, sponging off his old acquaintances; they still received him because of his pleasant and sociable character, for he could be invited to dinner with anybody, although, of course, he would be seated at the far end of the table. Such pleasant, easy-going gentleman spongers, who, as a rule, know how to tell a good story and make up a fourth at cards, and are fiercely reluctant to run errands for anybody, are usually lonely men, bachelors or widowers; some of them even have children, but they are always being educated somewhere far away and being taken care of by an aunt, and the gentleman almost never mentions them in polite society, as if he were ashamed of them. And gradually such gentlemen became altogether estranged from their children, finally only hearing from them on their birthdays and at Christmas and occasionally acknowledging these greetings.

The unheralded visitor did not have a really kind appearance, but he looked pleasant enough and capable of assuming various amiable expressions to fit particular circumstances. He had no pocketwatch, but displayed a tortoise shell lorgnette on a black ribbon. On the middle finger of his right hand could be seen a massive gold signet ring set with a not very expensive opal.

Ivan maintained an annoyed silence, reluctant to be the one to start the conversation. The visitor sat there and waited, just as a parasite house guest does when he comes down from his room for tea but, seeing his host frowning and apparently preoccupied with something, waits patiently until he is addressed, always ready to start a pleasant tea-table conversation.

All of a sudden the visitor's face took on an expression of considerable worry.

"Listen," he said to Ivan, "forgive me, but I must remind you that you went to see Smerdyakov to find out about Katerina and you left without having found out anything at all about her. You probably forgot . . ."

"Ah yes, that's right!" Ivan cried, a very worried look appearing on his face. "I forgot all about it! But it doesn't make any difference now," he muttered to himself. "And you," he said to the visitor in annoyance, "I want you to know that I would have remembered it myself in a second, because that's what was bothering me now, but you rushed in ahead of me so I'd believe you had reminded me of it."

"Well, don't believe it," the gentleman said with an affable smile. "There's no point in trying to believe something against one's will. Besides, in matters of faith, proof, especially material proof, is pretty useless. Thomas believed, not because he saw that Christ had risen, but because he had the will to believe beforehand. Take the spiritualists, for example (I love them, by the way): would you believe it—they're sure they are helpful to the propagation of the faith just because the devils allow them to peek into the other world and have a glimpse at their horns, which is supposed to be material proof that the 'other world' exists. The 'world beyond' and material proof—a peculiar combination that only men would think up! And then, when you come to think of it, even if they have proved the existence of the devil, why should it follow that God exists too? I'd like to join one of their progressive philosophical discussion groups and take a stand as an anti-materialist realist." He chuckled.

"Listen," Ivan said, suddenly getting up. "I feel as if I were delirious. In fact, I'm sure I am . . . So you can go on talking drivel until you're blue in the face, you won't make me lose my temper as you did last time. I just feel ashamed of I don't know what . . . I want to pace the room . . . There are times when, unlike last time, I don't see you and don't even hear your voice, but I still know what nonsense you'll come up with, because, in actual fact, it is *I* myself and *not you* who says all that! I'm not sure of one thing, though: was I asleep and dreaming when I saw you last or was I awake? I'll try dipping a towel in cold water and holding it to my head to see whether that'll make you vanish."

Ivan went to the corner of the room, took a towel, dipped it in water, and, holding the wet towel against his head, went back to pacing the room.

"What I like about this," the visitor said, "is that from the very start we've addressed each other with complete familiarity."

"Idiot!" Ivan laughed. "How could I possibly treat you with conventional courtesy? You know, I'm really enjoying myself, except that I have a pain in my temples . . . Yes, and on top of my head too . . . Only, please, don't start again with your philosophizing, the way you did last time. If you won't make yourself scarce, at least let's talk about more cheerful things. And since you're an old parasite and rumor-monger, let's have some gossip, by all means! I know you're just one of those nightmarish visions that come and pester people, but then, you don't frighten me, you know. I'll get over it and they won't take me to a madhouse!"

"Parasite—*c'est charmant!* Well, I suppose that's just the right way for me to present myself, because what else can I be on earth but a parasite? And, by the way, as I listen to you, I notice, upon my word, that you're gradually beginning to accept me as someone real and not just a figment of your imagination, as you insisted on doing throughout my last visit."

"I've never for one second taken you as real," Ivan cried, strangely angry. "You're just a lie. You're my sickness. You're a phantom. I don't yet know, though, how to destroy you, so I'll have to put up with you for a while. You are my hallucination. You are an incarnation of myself, I mean of one aspect of me only, the personification of my worst and most stupid thoughts and feelings. From that point of view, I would be rather curious to have a look at you, if I had time to bother with it all now."

"Just a minute, just a minute, I've caught you now: remember, earlier this evening, when you became so angry with Alyosha, by that street light, you shouted: 'You must have got it from *him!* How did you find out that *he* was visiting me?' Why, I'm sure you were talking about me. Doesn't that show that, at least for a moment, be it ever so brief a moment, you did believe that I really exist—didn't you?" the gentleman said with a low chuckle.

"Yes, but it was just a passing aberration . . . But I still cannot believe in you. I don't even know whether I was asleep or awake last time, so perhaps I only saw you in my dream."

"But why, then, did you have to pounce on Alyosha the way you did then? He's such a sweet boy! You know, I feel rather guilty toward him, about the elder Zosima."

"Leave Alyosha alone! Don't you dare drag him into this, you miserable flunkey!"

Ivan laughed.

"You insult me and then you laugh. That's a good sign. In general, though, you're much more amiable with me than you were last time and I know very well why: it's because of that great resolution of yours."

"Don't you talk about my resolution!" Ivan cried fiercely.

"I understand, I understand—*c'est noble, c'est charmant!* Tomorrow, you'll go to the defense of your brother and make the sacrifice of your person . . . *c'est chevaleresque.*"

"Shut up or I'll kick you!"

"If you did, I'd be delighted in a way, because it would prove that you'd come to believe I really exist. For no one would think of kicking a phantom. But seriously, although I don't particularly mind your abuse, I still think you could be a bit more polite, even toward me. Why do you keep on using offensive words like 'idiot' and 'flunkey'?"

"Because by abusing you, I abuse myself." Ivan laughed again. "You're me with a different face; you keep telling me what I think and are unable to tell me anything new."

"If our thoughts happen to agree, that does me great honor," the gentleman replied tactfully.

"But they happen to be my worst and, above all, my most stupid and vulgar thoughts. Yes, you're awfully stupid really. No, after all, I can't stand you! But what can I do to get rid of you, what can I do?" Ivan said angrily through clenched teeth.

"In spite of all, my friend, I'll continue to behave like a gentleman, and I would greatly appreciate it if you treated me like one," the visitor said in a burst of mild, obviously flexible pride, typical of a sponger. "I am poor and, although

I cannot really claim to be very honest, it is usually an accepted convention in decent society that I am a fallen angel. Well, even if it is possible that I was once an angel, it must have been so long ago that I should not be blamed for having forgotten by now what it was like. So now I am just trying to maintain my reputation as a respectable man while trying to make a living somehow or other and being a congenial companion. I am sincerely fond of men and in many respects I've been slandered. When I stay among people for any length of time, I come to feel, after a while, as though I were really alive, and I enjoy that most of all. It's because, just like you, I suffer from that obsession with the fantastic, and that's why I appreciate your earthly realism so much. On your earth, everything is so clearly delineated, everything can be expressed in a neat formula, and your geometry is so precise, while where I come from everything is an indeterminate equation. While I walk about here on earth, I keep daydreaming. I love imagining things. And also, while on earth, I become superstitious. No, please don't laugh. Believe me, that is what I like most about being on earth—the fact that it makes me superstitious. And while I'm here, I adopt all your habits. For instance, I've become very fond of going to the public baths: I love to steam myself with your merchants and priests. My fondest wish is to be able to incarnate myself once and for all into some two-hundred-pound merchant's wife and to believe seriously in all those things that she believes in. My ideal is to go to church, light a candle, and offer up a prayer with the utmost sincerity. I swear this is true. That would be the end of my torments . . . And another thing I've come to like down here is taking care of my precious health. Last spring, for instance, there was a smallpox epidemic; well, I went to the Foundling Dispensary and had myself vaccinated. Ah, you cannot imagine how good it made me feel! That day I even donated ten rubles to the Rescue Fund for Our Slav Brothers Abroad . . . But you aren't even listening! You know, you don't seem to be quite yourself today." The visitor remained quiet for a moment and then added: "I know that you went to see that doctor yesterday . . . Well, how is your health? What did he tell you?"

"Idiot!" Ivan snapped.

"I know, I know, you yourself are so clever! You cannot manage without being offensive! I wasn't really worried for you; I just asked to be polite. So don't answer if you don't feel like it. You know, there's a lot of rheumatism going around . . ."

"Idiot!" Ivan snapped again.

"You just keep repeating that word again and again . . . But, you know, last year I had such a dreadful attack of rheumatism that I can't forget the misery it caused me . . ."

"What? A devil with rheumatism?"

"Why not? When I assume human form, I accept all the inconveniences connected therewith! *Satan sum et nihil humanum a me alienum puto.*"*

"What? *Satan sum et nihil humanum . . .* That's quite clever for the devil!"

"I'm delighted to have pleased you at last."

"Wait, you didn't get that from me!" Ivan suddenly stopped, struck by this fact. "It never even occurred to me . . . Strange!"

"C'est du nouveau, n'est-ce pas? Well, this time I'll be honest with you and let you in on it. Listen, in dreams and particularly in nightmares, caused perhaps by indigestion or whatever, a man may think up such artistic creations, such complex and realistic visions, events or even a whole world of events woven into a plot full of such astounding details that Leo Tolstoi himself could not invent them. And yet people who have such dreams don't have to be novelists but can be the most ordinary civil servants, newspapermen, priests, or anything . . . It creates, in fact, a most interesting problem: once, for instance, I heard a member of the government say that his best ideas came to him when he was asleep. Well, we are facing that problem now, too. I may be a hallucinations of yours, but, just as in a nightmare, I can say original things that have never even occurred to you and I don't necessarily have to repeat your old ideas, even if I am nothing but a nightmarish figment of your imagination."

"You're only trying to trick me now. Your aim is to convince me that you're an independent creature and not just a nightmarish vision, but now you suddenly say yourself that you're a phantom."

"My dear fellow, the line of approach I have adopted today is quite different, and I'll explain it to you later. Now, where

* A play on a famous verse by Terence: *Homo sum: humani nihil a me alienum puto* ("I am a man and I do not consider anything human alien to me"). [A. MacA.]

had I got to? Ah, yes, I caught a cold, but not here on earth. It was over there still . . ."

"Where is 'there'? Tell me, rather, how long will you stay here? Couldn't you leave now?" Ivan cried, almost in despair. He stopped walking, sat down on the sofa again, put his elbows on the table, and held his head tightly between his hands. He had tossed away the wet towel—apparently it had not done him any good.

"Your nerves are really upset," the visiting gentleman remarked in a casually familiar tone, but sounding quite friendly and concerned. "You even resent the fact that I could catch a cold, although really it happened in the most natural way. I was in a great hurry, that day, to get to a diplomatic reception given by a prominent Petersburg lady, who was trying to get a ministerial post for her husband. So I had to dress in white tie, tails, gloves, the whole lot, as you can well imagine, although I was God knows how far away at the time and had to cross quite a bit of outer space to get to your earth. Of course, it is just a matter of a moment, but you must remember that it takes eight whole minutes for a ray of light to travel from the sun to the earth, and I had to cross space in tails, which means an open waistcoat. I agree, of course, that spirits do not freeze, but I had already assumed human form. Well, I decided, 'Ah, let's go,' and I went whizzing through space, through the ether, the fluids up there, and really it was freezing! I don't even think that freezing describes it at all; just imagine, the temperature there was one hundred and fifty degrees below freezing, centigrade! You know the practical joke so loved by village girls: they dare a naive young boy to lick an axe at a temperature of thirty below, and, of course, the stupid fellow then takes the axe away along with the bleeding skin from his tongue. So at a hundred and fifty below, I bet that if you touched an axe, not even with your tongue but just with your finger, you'd never see that finger again, if, of course, you happened to come across such a thing as an axe in outer space."

"Could there be an axe there, though?" Ivan asked absent-mindedly, his face twisted in disgust. He was desperately trying not to succumb completely to his delirious visions.

"An axe?" the visitor asked him in a surprised tone.

"Yes, I want to know what would happen to an axe there?" Ivan cried, suddenly filled with fierce determination.

"What would happen to an axe in space? *Quelle idée!* If it

got far enough from the earth, I suppose it would start circling the earth without having any idea of why it was doing so—it would become a sort of satellite. Astronomers would calculate the hours of the axe-set and the axe-rise and Gatsuk would add the data to the calendar, and I suppose that would be that."

"You're too stupid, really, too hopelessly stupid," Ivan said cantankerously. "You'll have to invent something more intelligent to tell me or I won't listen to you. You're trying to overcome my disbelief in you and convince me that you exist by means of realism. But I don't want to believe, and there's nothing that will make me believe, in you!"

"But I wasn't even inventing anything; what I was telling you was the truth. It's simply unfortunate that the truth is hardly ever exciting. I can see clearly now that you're expecting something great, perhaps even something beautiful, of me. It's an awful shame, because I can't deliver more than there is in me."

"Ah, don't start philosophizing now, you fool!"

"I'm not philosophizing. How could I, anyway, when my whole right side is numb and I can't move without moaning and groaning? I have consulted every medical luminary and find they have no trouble in recognizing my complaint. They have every symptom at their finger tips, and they're absolutely incapable of curing it. Once I came across an enthusiastic young medical student. 'Even if you should die,' he told me, 'at least you'll know the disease that killed you!' And then they have that way, nowadays, of sending you off to a specialist: 'I can only diagnose your trouble,' a doctor will tell you, 'but if you go to see such and such a specialist, he'll know how to cure it.' I tell you, the old doctor who could cure you of every illness has all but vanished and you find nothing but specialists these days, and they even advertise in the newspapers. If you have something the matter with your nose, for instance, they'll send you to Paris where, they say, there is the foremost nose specialist in Europe. So you go to Paris. The specialist looks inside your nose and announces: 'Well, all right, I'll take care of your right nostril, but I really don't handle left nostrils; for that you'll have to go to Vienna where there's a great left-nostril specialist. He'll look into it when we've finished here.' So what can we do about it? Use home remedies like the one a German doctor recommended to me: to go to a public baths, rub myself with salt and honey, and steam myself. I followed his advice just because I'm so fond of steam-baths, but I just got myself sticky all over without the slightest benefit. In my despair I wrote to Count Mattei in Milan and he sent me a book and some drops—I can't even blame him for it! But then, you know what happened—Hoff's malt extract cured me! I bought a little bottle of the stuff by chance, drank half of it, and the complaint literally vanished—I could go and dance if I wanted to! So I decided to write a letter of appreciation to the newspapers—that's how grateful I felt! But then—and this is another curious story— not one single newspaper would punish my letter. 'It would sound too unenlightened,' the editors insisted. 'No one would believe it, since *le diable n'existe point!* You'd better,' they advised me, 'send it in anonymously.' But what sort of appreciation would it be, I ask you, if I sent it anonymously? So I tried pleading with those bureaucrats: 'What's unenlightened, nowadays, is to believe in God, but it's all right to believe in me, the devil!' 'We sympathize with you completely and agree that everybody really believes in the devil, but nevertheless it just cannot be done. Unless you want to do it in the form of a joke?' But I didn't think it would be a very funny joke, so I gave up. And, you know, I still feel depressed about it. The best feelings I'm capable of, such as gratitude, are forbidden to me, just because of my official social position."

"There you go philosophizing again!" Ivan said, with hatred.

"God forbid that I should philosophize, but how can I help complaining now and then? I have been slandered most awfully, you know. You, for instance, keep calling me stupid. That only shows how young you still are. My dear fellow, let me tell you—intelligence isn't everything. By nature, I'm a very kindly, cheerful person, you know, who can also enjoy all sorts of amusing social farces. You seem to have definitely taken me for a gray-haired version of Gogol's Khlestakov, but my function is a much more serious one. By some predestination that goes back to primeval times, by a decree that I could never make any sense of, I have been designated to be the Negator, despite my kindly nature and the fact that I'm really very poorly fitted for 'negation.' 'Never mind,' my protests were brushed aside, 'there must be negation, because without it there would be no criticism. You understand,' I was told, 'it would be just like having a magazine without a criticism section. It would be nothing but one uninterrupted hosannah. And in life, sheer hosannah is not enough, for things must be tested in the crucible of doubt, and so on and so forth.' I don't really have to go into all that, for I didn't create the world, and I'm not responsible for it. Anyway, they had to have a scapegoat, so they made me write my column of criticism and that made life possible. We understand this comedy. I, for instance, demand annihilation for myself. 'No,' they told me, 'you just have to live, because without you there would be nothing. For if everything on earth was reasonable, nothing would ever happen; there would be no happenings without you and we must have happenings.' And so here I am, serving under protest so as to make it possible for things to happen, and acting against reason on superior orders. And people take all this comedy seriously, even people endowed with indisputable intelligence. And that's their tragedy. Of course they suffer, but that still doesn't prevent them from living, and living a real, not an imaginary, life, because suffering *is* life. What joy would there be in life if there were no suffering? Everything would become one endless hymn of thanks to God, which would be very holy but rather dull too. Well, and what about me? I suffer, but I go on living. I am the x in an indeterminate equation. I am a phantom who has lost the beginning and the end and who has even forgotten his name. You're laughing . . . No, you aren't laughing, you're angry again. You're always angry, for all you're interested in is intelligence. So let me remind you again that I'd exchange all my life in starry space, all my titles and honors, to be incarnated into a two-hundred-pound merchant lady and light candles to God."

"Does that mean that even you don't believe in God?" Ivan asked with a grin of hatred.

"Well, how shall I put it . . . If you asked the question seriously . . ."

"Does God exist or not?" Ivan insisted fiercely.

"Oh, you meant it seriously then. Well, I really don't know. There, I have made a great revelation."

"You don't know? And you're supposed to have seen God! No, you're not an independent agent at all—you are *me* and nothing else. You are nonsense, a figment of my imagination!"

"Well, I'd rather put it this way: you and I, we have the same philosophy. That would be a much fairer statement. *Je pense, donc je suis,* that is something I know for certain. As for the rest—all those worlds, God, and even Satan himself— I'm not sure whether all that exists independently or is merely a passing and subjective emanation of myself . . . But I think I'd better stop there, because you look as if you were about to attack me."

"Oh, you'd better tell me an anecdote," Ivan said miserably.

"As a matter of fact, I have an anecdote in mind, one just on our theme, although it's really a legend rather than an anecdote. You accused me just now of disbelief, of seeing and still not believing. But you must understand, my dear fellow, that it's not just me; we're all rather confused over there, and all because of your sciences. As long as there were still atoms, the five senses, the four elements, well, it all fitted together somehow. For there were atoms in the ancient world too. But when we heard in our world beyond that you had discovered the 'chemical molecule,' 'protoplasm,' and God knows what, we all had our tails between our legs. There was terrible confusion among us and, above all, an upsurge of superstition and gossip (for there is as much gossip in our nether world as there is in yours, in fact a bit more) and also denunciations, because we, too, have an institution where denunciations of one's neighbors can be handed in. So here is the grim legend I started to tell you, that dates from the Middle Ages (our Middle Ages, not yours) and that no one believes except our equivalents of your two-hundred-pound merchants' wives. By the way, everything you have here, we have too. I reveal this to you out of friendship, because we aren't supposed to tell.

"This legend now, it's about heaven. Once there was on your earth a thinker and philosopher who rejected everything—laws, conscience, religion, and, above all, a future life. So when he died, he expected to plunge right into blackness and nothingness, but what did he find instead but future life. He was very surprised and quite outraged. 'This,' he said, 'is in complete disagreement with my convictions.' So they condemned him for that . . . I want you to understand that I'm telling you something that I was told myself, just a legend . . . So they sentenced him to walk a quadrillion kilometers on foot through the darkness (because we have the metric system now), and when he had finished walking that quadrillion kilometers, the gates of heaven would be opened to him and everything would be forgiven him . . ."

"And what other ordeals do you have in your world besides such quadrillion-kilometer walks?" Ivan asked with peculiar eagerness.

"What ordeals? Ah, I wish you hadn't asked me that. Before, we had all kinds, but nowadays they are mostly of a moral nature, like a guilty conscience and all that sort of nonsense. That, too, was influenced by your humanization of mores. Of course, the principal beneficiaries are those who have no conscience at all and so obviously cannot be tormented by guilt. On the other hand, the decent ones, who still have a conscience and a sense of honor, suffer the most . . . This, of course, is the result of adopting reforms when the ground is unprepared, especially when the reforms are copied from abroad and alien institutions are transplanted. Nothing but harm can result from such reforms. The good old hell fire was much better . . .

"To go back to our legend, the man who had been condemned to that long walk stood about for a while and then lay down in the road and said: 'No, I won't walk that far; it's against my principles!' Now, if you take the soul of an enlightened Russian atheist and mix it with the soul of the prophet Jonah, who sat pouting in the whale's belly for three days and nights, you'll understand the character of that thinker who lay down in the road."

"What did he lie on there?"

"I'm sure there was something to lie on. But aren't you trying to pull my leg?"

"I take my hat off to him!" Ivan cried with the same peculiar animation; he was listening eagerly to his visitor now. "Is he still lying there to this day, then?"

"No, he isn't, and that's what's so interesting about it. He lay there for a thousand years, but then he got up and started walking."

"What an ass!" Ivan laughed nervously. He thought intently for a moment. "But what's the difference—walk a quadrillion kilometers or lie there eternally? Why, it would take him a billion years to cover that distance anyway."

"Much longer than that even—I could calculate it for you if you gave me a pencil and a piece of paper. But, anyway, he finished his walk long ago, and that's really where the amusing story starts."

"How could he have finished? Where did he get the billion years to do it in?"

"You say that because you're thinking of our present earth. But you must understand that our present earth has repeated itself perhaps as many as a billion times: it died out, got covered with ice, cracked, broke to pieces, decomposed into its original component elements; and again there was just water above the firmament, then again a comet, again the sun, again the earth from the sun—the process can repeat itself infinitely and always in the same way, over and over again, to the minutest detail. It's all a huge, intolerable bore . . ."

"So what happened when he finally finished his walk?"

"No sooner had they opened the gates of heaven to him and he had stepped in, before he had spent two seconds there as timed by his watch (although I think his watch would have dissolved into its component elements ages before he got there), before, as I was saying, he had spent two seconds there, he declared that, for the sake of those two seconds, it would have been worth walking not just one quadrillion miles but a quadrillion quadrillions raised to the quadrillionth power! In other words, he sang his hosannah, and rather overdid it, for some people with a prouder way of thinking would not shake hands with him at first, feeling he had joined the conservative camp a bit too hurriedly. That's the Russian temperament for you! I repeat, it's just a legend and I tell it to you for what it's worth. It gives you an idea of the sort of notions we still have over there about all these matters."

"I've caught you now!" Ivan cried with a sort of childish glee, as though he had just remembered something that he had been trying hard to recall. "That story about the quadrillion—I invented it myself: I was seventeen at the time and a high school student in Moscow . . . I invented that story and told it to a classmate by the name of Korovkin . . . The story is peculiar enough that I couldn't have taken it from anywhere. I'd forgotten about it, but now it's come back to me unconsciously, so it was not really you who told it to me. It's just like the thousands of things that people who are being taken to be executed may unconsciously remember . . . I've remembered it in my dreams. So you are my dream. You're a dream and you don't really exist!"

"Judging by the vehemence with which you deny my existence, it would seem that, despite everything, you still believe in me," the gentleman said laughingly.

"Not in the slightest! I haven't the hundredth part of a grain of faith in you."

"Well, perhaps only a thousandth then. But, you know, homeopathic doses are the strongest perhaps. Admit that you believe at least to a ten-thousandth part . . ."

"Not for a moment!" Ivan cried furiously, but then added in a strange tone: "But, actually, I would really have liked to believe in you."

"Aha, that is quite an admission! But I'm a nice fellow and I'll help you out. Let me tell you this: it was I who caught you, not you me, just now! I deliberately told you your own story, that you had forgotten, to make you stop believing in me for good."

"You're lying now, since the goal of your appearing is to convince me that you exist."

"Precisely. But the hesitation, the worrying, the conflict between belief and disbelief—all that can cause such torment to a man with a conscience that at times he'd rather hang himself. Now, I lead you in turns between belief and disbelief and, in doing so, I'm pursuing a certain goal. It's a new method. For the moment you disbelieve in me completely, you'll start trying to convince me to my face that I'm not a dream, that I really exist. I already know you well enough —that is how I'll achieve my goal. And my goal is a noble one: I will cast into you just a tiny seed of belief and it will grow into an oak, and such an oak that, sitting on it, you will long to join 'the hermits in the wilderness and the immaculate virgins,' because that is what you are really secretly longing for: to wander in the desert, feed on locusts, and save your soul."

"Are you working so hard, then, to save my soul, you scoundrel?"

"Why not? Everyone must do good deeds once in a while. But I can see that you're furious."

"Ah, you buffoon! But tell me, have you ever tried to tempt those who feed on locusts, pray in the desert for seventeen years, and are overgrown with moss?"

"I've done practically nothing but that, my friend. One can forget this and all the other worlds when one works on such a person, because he is really a gold mine: in some cases his soul may be worth a whole constellation, that is, of course, in our special accounting system. A victory in such a case is priceless! And some of those fellows, I assure you, are in no way less sophisticated than you are and, although you may not believe it, they're capable of visualizing such depths of belief and disbelief at the same time that there are moments when it looks as if the fellow is within a hair's breadth of plunging head over heels into the abyss."

"And what happened? Did you always leave empty-handed with your nose in the air?"

"My friend," the visitor said in a sententious tone, "it is better to leave empty-handed with your nose in the air than to lose your nose, as was observed recently by an ailing marquis (he must have been treated by a specialist) to his confessor, a Jesuit father. I witnessed the confession and found it absolutely enchanting. 'Give me back my nose!' the marquis said, smiting his breast. 'My son,' the Jesuit said, dodging the issue, 'in its inscrutable way, Providence sees to it that everything is compensated for and an apparent disaster may result in a great, albeit hidden, benefit. And if stern fate has deprived you of your nose now, then, for one thing, no one will be able to tell you in the future that you've had your nose pulled!' 'But, Holy Father, that's no comfort to me!' the marquis cried in despair. 'I would be delighted to have my nose pulled every day if necessary, as long as it was in its proper place!' 'My son,' the Jesuit father sighed, 'you may not claim all benefits at the same time, because that is murmuring against Providence, which has not forgotten you even in this case. For if you repine, as you were repining just now, and declare that you would be glad to have your nose pulled every day of your life, your wish has indirectly been fulfilled because, having lost your nose, you have had it permanently pulled off, as it were . . .'"

"Ah, how stupid can you be!"

"I only wanted to make you laugh, but I swear that that is authentic Jesuit casuistry and that it happened exactly as I told you. It happened quite recently and it gave me a great deal of trouble. The unhappy young man went home and shot himself that very night. I was there with him up to the very last moment . . . As to the Jesuit confessional, it is, indeed, one of my sweetest distractions in the sad moments of my existence. Let me tell you of another instance that occurred only a few days ago. A blonde, twenty-year-old Norman girl comes to an old Jesuit father. A buxom, natural beauty—makes you drool just to look at her. She bends down and whispers her sins to the priest through that little grill. 'What are you saying, my daughter—already? You've fallen again?' the Jesuit exclaims. 'Oh, Sancta Maria, and not even with the same man! How long will this continue, tell me? Aren't you ashamed of yourself?' *'Ah, mon père,'* the sinner answered him, the tears flowing down her cheeks, *'ça lui fait tant de plaisir et à moi si peu de peine!'* What do

you think of that answer! Well, I gave up on her: that was
a true cry of nature, purer, if you will, than innocence itself!
And so I absolved her sin and was about to leave when I
heard the old Jesuit arranging, through that little grill of
the confessional, to meet her later. Just think—that old man,
hard as flint, and there he fell in the twinkling of an eye!
The truth is, though, that nature took its due! Why are you
screwing up your nose again—are you still angry? Well, I
am really at a loss how to please you . . ."

"Leave me alone. You're just hammering on my brain like
a persistent nightmare," Ivan moaned in pain, feeling helpless before his apparition. "You bore me. You bore me mercilessly, unbearably! I would give anything to get rid of
you."

"I repeat: all you have to do is to moderate your demands,
stop expecting great and sublime things of me, and you'll
see how nicely we'll get along," the visitor said admonish-
ingly. "In reality, you resent my not having come to you
surrounded by a red glow, in thunder and lightning and with
scorched wings, but appearing, instead, in such modest attire.
First, your esthetic feelings are offended and, secondly, your
pride is hurt. You feel that a great and brilliant fellow like
you was entitled to something better than such a trite, vulgar
devil. Yes, I see you have that romantic streak that Belinsky
was already ridiculing quite a while ago. Well, young man,
I cannot help you really. When I was about to come to
you, I first thought of coming, as a joke, in the guise of a
retired high government official, who had served in the
Caucasus, wearing the star of the Lion and of the Sun on
my frock-coat. But then I thought you might assault me
for having put on only the Lion and the Sun and not the
North Star and Sirius as well. And then, you keep telling
me I'm stupid. But, good God, I have absolutely no preten-
sions to being your equal in intelligence. When Mephistopheles appeared to Faust, he introduced himself as one who
wished evil but did only good. Well, that's his business, but
in my case it's just the opposite. I am perhaps the only one
in all creation who loves truth and wishes good.

"I was there when the Word who died on the cross as-
cended into heaven bearing on His bosom the soul of the
penitent thief. I heard the joyful cries of the cherubim
singing and shouting hosannah and the thunderous, rapturous
shouts of the seraphim that shook heaven and all creation.
And I swear to you by all that is holy that I longed to join

the choir and shout, 'Hosannah' with the rest! The word
was forming in my throat and almost escaped from my lips,
for, as you may well know, I'm very sensitive and artistically
receptive. But then my common sense, which is my most
unhappy feature, kept me within my assigned limits and I
missed the opportune moment. Because, I thought, what
would happen after I shouted, 'Hosannah'? Everything in
the world would be extinguished and there would be no more
happenings. And so it was only out of my sense of duty
and in deference to my public image that I stifled the good
impulses within me and remained in my assigned position, to
take care of the dirty work. Somebody claims all the honor
for good works, leaving me nothing but the foul play. But
I did not covet the honor of living a life of deceit, for I
am not vainglorious. So why must I be the only creature
in the world condemned to the curses of all decent people,
even to be kicked by them, for when I assume human form
I must face all the consequences of it too? Why, I know
for sure that there is a secret there, a secret they'll never reveal to me, for if I found out what it was all about, I might
very well start shouting, 'Hosannah!' and the indispensable
minus sign would disappear, reasonableness would rule the
world, and it would be the end of everything, including the
newspapers and magazines, for who would think of subscribing to them then? I know, though, that in the end I'll reconcile myself, complete my quadrillion too, and learn the
secret. But until that happens, I'll have to go on sulking and
continue, very much against my own grain, to spell the
doom of thousands so that one may be saved. How many
souls, for instance, had to be destroyed, how many reputations ruined for the sake of the righteous Job, over whom
I was so utterly swindled long ago! As long as I do not
know the secret, though, two truths exist for me: one truth
is theirs over there, of which I still know nothing, and the
other truth is my own. And I am still not sure which of the
two is worse . . . Have you fallen asleep?"

"How could I help it?" Ivan moaned in pain. "All that
is stupid in me, everything that I have outgrown, that I have
rehashed in my brain over and over again, all those rotting
rejects—you're offering it all to me as if it were something
new!"

"So again I've failed to please you! And I was hoping
even my artistic presentation would charm you: don't you
think the cries of hosannah in heaven lend quite a literary

touch? And after that, without transition, I switched to a sarcastic tone *à la* Heine. Don't you think that rather effective?"

"No, I've never been such a flunkey! So how could my soul have begotten a flunkey like you?"

"My dear friend, I know a sweet, charming young Russian gentleman, a thinker and a great lover of literature and the elegant arts, the promising author of a poem called 'The Grand Inquisitor' . . . Well, he's the one I had in mind."

"I forbid you to mention 'The Grand Inquisitor'!" Ivan cried, blushing violently in shame.

"Well, and what about 'The Geological Upheaval'? That's quite a poem, I must say!"

"Shut up or I'll kill you!"

"*You*—kill *me?* Oh no, you'll just have to excuse me and hear me out. This is a treat for me and that's why I came. Oh, I love the aspirations of my ardent young friends, trembling with eagerness to live! When you were about to come here last spring, you thought to yourself: 'There are new people there who plan to destroy everything and start once again with cannibalism. Ah, the stupid fools, they ought to consult me first, for I don't believe they have to destroy anything, except man's idea of God—that would be the way to start. Then the blind fools would achieve their goal! Once every member of the human race discards the idea of God (and I believe that such an era will come, like some new geological age), the old world-view will collapse by itself without recourse to cannibalism. And the first thing to disintegrate will be the old morality, for everything will be new and different. Men will unite their efforts to get everything out of life that it can offer them, but only for joy and happiness in this world. Man will be exalted spiritually with a divine, titanic pride and the man-god will come into being. Extending his conquest over nature beyond all bounds through his will and his science, man will constantly experience such great joy that it will replace for him his former anticipation of the pleasures that await him in heaven. Everyone will know that he is mortal, that there is no resurrection for him, and will accept his death with calm and dignity, like a god. He will understand, out of sheer pride, that there is no point in protesting that life lasts only a fleeting moment and he will love his brother man without expecting any reward for it. Love will satisfy only a moment in life, but the very awareness of its momentary nature will concentrate its flames, which before were diffused and made pale by the anticipation of eternal life beyond the grave . . .' And so on and so forth. Very sweet!"

Ivan sat there with his hands pressed over his ears, his eyes downcast. He was trembling all over. The visitor went on.

"The whole question, my thinker thought, was whether such a time would ever come. If it did come, then everything would be solved and mankind would be all right. But since, because human stupidity is so deeply ingrained, it could not come to pass for at least a thousand years, every thinking man who already recognized the truth could arrange his life as he pleased in accordance with the new principles, without waiting. In that sense, 'everything was permitted' to him. Furthermore, even if such a time never did come, since God and immortality still would not exist, the new man might become the man-god, even if he were the only one in the whole world, and, of course, in that new capacity, he might, if the need arose, jump without scruple over every barrier of the old moral code devised for the man-slave. There is no law for God, for whatever stand God takes is right. Wherever I stand thereby becomes the most important spot . . . So everything is permitted and that's all there is to it! That is all very nice. But if you have made up your mind to break the rules, why do you still need the stamp of righteousness? But our modern Russian man is so constituted that he wouldn't dare cheat, even if he were allowed to, because he has come to love truth so much . . ."

The visitor had obviously been carried away by his eloquence, his voice rising higher and higher as he glanced ironically at his host. But he did not have a chance to finish his speech as Ivan suddenly seized a glass from the table and hurled it at the speaker.

"*Ah, mais c'est bête enfin!*" the visitor exclaimed, jumping up from his seat and flicking drops of tea from his clothes. "What's come over you? Did you suddenly remember Luther's inkpot? You say I am your dream and then you proceed to throw glasses at your dream! That's more like a woman's logic! And, you know, I suspected as much: you were just pretending to stop up your ears—you were listening . . ."

There was a sudden loud knocking at the window. Ivan leapt up from the sofa.

"You'd better open it," the visitor said. "It's your brother

Alyosha and he has a most unexpected piece of news for you—I can guarantee you that!"

"Shut up, you fake. I knew it was Alyosha before you opened your mouth. I felt he'd come and obviously he wouldn't come for nothing, so he must have some news for me!"

Ivan was in a state of frenzy.

"So let him in. Go and let him in! There's a blizzard outside and he's your brother. *Monsieur sait-il le temps qu'il fait? C'est à ne pas mettre un chien dehors . . .*"

The knocking continued. Ivan wanted to rush to the window but it was as if his legs and arms had suddenly been fettered. He tried desperately to break those fetters, but in vain. The knocking grew louder and louder. Finally the fetters broke and Ivan leaped up. He looked wildly around him. The two candles were almost burnt out. The glass he had just tossed at his visitor was standing before him and there was no one sitting opposite him on the sofa. The knocking at the window continued, but it was not at all as loud as it had seemed to him through his dream; in fact, it was a rather subdued, although insistent, knocking.

"It was not a dream. I swear it was not a dream. It all really happened!" Ivan cried, rushing to the window and opening it.

"Alyosha, what are you doing here? Didn't I tell you not to come here again!" he shouted angrily at his brother. "Tell me in two words what you want of me, just two words, do you understand!"

"An hour ago Smerdyakov hanged himself," Alyosha said from outside.

"Go to the door. I'll let you in," Ivan said, and went to open the door.

CHAPTER 10

It Was He Who Said That

Alyosha told Ivan that, a little more than an hour before, Maria Kondratievna had come running over to his lodgings to tell him that Smerdyakov had killed himself. "I went into his room to clear away the tea things," she had told Alyosha, "and there he was, hanging from a nail on the wall." When Alyosha asked her if she had told the police, she said she had not because she had hurried directly to him and "had run all the way." She was trembling like a leaf and seemed completely out of her mind. Alyosha had then gone back to her house with her and found Smerdyakov still hanging from the wall. There was a note on the table saying: "I am putting an end to my life of my own free will and no one should be blamed for it." Alyosha, leaving the note on the table, went straight to the police inspector and told him all he knew, and from there, "I came straight here to tell you," he said, looking intently into Ivan's face. And all the while he had been telling Ivan about Smerdyakov, he had never taken his eyes off him, so struck was he by Ivan's strange expression.

"Ivan," he cried suddenly, "you must be terribly ill— you're staring at me as if you didn't understand what I was saying."

"It's a good thing you came," Ivan said dreamily, as if he hadn't heard Alyosha's last exclamation. "But, you know, I knew that he'd hanged himself."

"From whom?"

"I don't know from whom. But I did know about it. Did I really know? Yes, he told me. He was telling me just now, in fact . . ."

Ivan was standing in the middle of the room, still talking in the same dreamy voice, his eyes downcast.

"Who is *he?*" Alyosha asked, instinctively looking around.

"He just slipped away." Ivan raised his eyes and smiled. "He was scared of you, the gentle dove, the pure cherub . . . You know, Dmitry calls you 'the cherub.' The cherub . . . The thunderous shout of rapture of the seraphim . . . What is a seraph? Perhaps a whole constellation . . . But, on the other hand, a whole constellation may be a mere chemical molecule . . . Do you know if there's a constellation of the Lion and the Sun? Is there such a constellation?"

"Sit down, Ivan, please, here on the sofa," Alyosha said, frightened. "You're feverish. Lie down. Put your head on the pillow. Right. Would you like a wet towel on your head? It might help."

"Give me that towel over there . . . I threw it on that chair, see?"

"There's nothing there, but don't worry, I'll find it. Here it is." He found the clean, folded, untouched towel by the wash basin in the far corner of the room. Ivan looked at the towel in surprise. Memory was apparently returning to him.

"Wait," he said, sitting up on the sofa, "about an hour ago I took that towel from over there, wet it, and held it against my head. Then I threw it down over here . . . How could it possibly be dry already? I know there was no other towel here."

"You wet the towel and held it to your head, you say?"

"Yes, and I was pacing the room with it on my head, about an hour ago . . . Why are these candles burnt down so low? What time is it?"

"It's almost twelve."

"No, no, no! It was not a dream!" Ivan shouted suddenly. "He was here and he sat over there, on that other sofa. When you knocked on the window, I threw the glass at him . . . Here, this glass here. Wait, I did sleep before that, but this was not a dream. It has happened to me before. I have dreams now, Alyosha, but I'm not asleep when I dream them; I'm awake, I walk around and talk and can see everything, but I'm asleep. But he was here and he sat on that sofa . . . He's terribly stupid, Alyosha, unbelievably stupid."

Ivan laughed. He suddenly stood up and started pacing the room.

"Who's stupid? Who is it you're talking about, Ivan?" Alyosha asked in anguish.

"The devil. He has started coming here. He's visited me twice, maybe even three times. He teased me, saying I resented his being such a lowly devil and not Satan in person with scorched wings, surrounded by thunder and lightning. But he's no Satan—he just talks nonsense. He's just a fraud, a petty devil. He goes to the public baths. If you undressed him you'd find a yard-long, smooth brown tail, like a Great Dane's . . . You must be cold, Alyosha, with all that snow outside. Would you like some tea, perhaps? What? It's cold? Shall I order some boiling water? *C'est à ne pas mettre un chien dehors . . .*"

Alyosha went over to the wash basin and wet the towel. He persuaded Ivan to sit down, and wrapped the wet towel around his head. Then he sat down next to him.

"What was it you were telling me about Lise earlier this evening?" Ivan began again, now feeling very talkative. "I like Lise. I believe I said something nasty about her to you. I lied to you—I like her . . . But I'm more worried about Katya tomorrow than anything else. I'm afraid for the future. She'll throw me over tomorrow and trample me underfoot. She imagines that I'm trying to ruin Mitya because I'm jealous over her. Yes, that's what she thinks! But that's not true. And tomorrow I will face my ordeal, but I won't hang myself. No, I shan't hang myself, Alyosha, because, you know, I could never deprive myself of life. Perhaps it's because I'm too contemptible. I'm not a coward, though. It's because I'm too eager to live. But how did I know that Smerdyakov had hanged himself? Yes, it was *he* who told me."

"So you're absolutely convinced that someone was here with you?"

"Yes, he sat over there, on that sofa in the corner. It was you who chased him away. He vanished as soon as you came. I like your face, Alyosha. Did you know that I liked your face? And *he*, Alyosha, is me, he is really me myself, everything that is base, wicked, and despicable in me. Yes, he noticed that I'm a 'romantic,' although of course that's slander. He's extremely stupid, but that's how he gets around people. And he's cunning, with an animal cunning. He knows so well how to drive me into a rage! It was by taunting me and telling me I believed in him that he forced me to listen to him. He fooled me, as if I were a little boy. But he also told me much that was true. I would never have told myself those things without him. And you know, Alyosha," Ivan said, his tone suddenly very grave and confidential, "I would like it so very much if he really were *him* and not me."

"He has exhausted you!" Alyosha said, looking compassionately at his brother.

"He taunted me, and, you know, he was rather clever at it. Conscience! What is conscience? I manufacture it myself. So why am I tormenting myself? Out of habit, a seven-thousand-year-old habit, shared by all mankind. All right, so we'll overcome that habit and become gods . . . It was he who said that, Alyosha."

"Are you sure it wasn't you?" Alyosha couldn't prevent himself from crying out, looking at Ivan with clear eyes. "Well, forget about him. Leave him alone! Let him go and take away with him everything that you loathe now, and may he never come back again."

"Yes, but he's vicious. He was laughing at me. You cannot imagine how impudent he was, Alyosha. But in many things, he slandered me. He accused me falsely to my face: 'You will go and do a noble deed, accusing yourself of killing your father, announcing that the lackey killed him at your instigation!' "

"Ivan," Alyosha interrupted him, "stop it. You didn't kill him. It is not true!"

"He says that and he knows. 'You're going to perform a virtuous deed, although you don't believe in virtue, and that's what annoys and torments you and makes you so vengeful'— that's what he said about me and he knows . . ."

"It's you who's saying that, not he!" Alyosha cried sadly. "And you say it because you are ill, delirious, tormenting yourself!"

"No, he knows what he's talking about. He says that it's out of pride that I'll go before them and say to them: 'It was I who did it. Why do you look so horrified? You're lying! I despise your opinion and your horror.' He says I'll say that and then he says to me: 'But you know, you're longing for their appreciation. You want them to think: "He may be a criminal and a murderer, but what nobility of soul—he's confessing to save his brother!"' But that, Alyosha, is a damned lie!" Ivan shouted, his eyes aflame. "I don't want any praise from that stinking mob! He was lying, I swear! I threw a glass at him and it smashed against his ugly mug!"

"Calm down, Ivan. Stop it."

"But he knows how to torment people. He's very cruel," Ivan went on, without hearing Alyosha. "I always felt I knew why he came here. 'While you are going before them out of pride,' he says, 'you still hope that they'll get enough evidence against Smerdyakov and pack him off to Siberia, that they'll acquit Mitya, and condemn you only *morally,* while some will even praise you.' And he laughed, saying that, do you hear—he laughed! 'But now,' he says, 'with Smerdyakov dead, who will believe your story when you tell it in court? But you're still going to tell them. You are, because you've made up your mind that you'll speak up. But what's the point of it now?' That's frightening, Alyosha. I cannot stand those questions. How dare he ask me those questions?"

"Ivan," Alyosha said, cold with fear but still hoping to bring Ivan to his senses, "how could he possibly have told you about Smerdyakov's death before I came here, when no one else knew about it or could possibly have had time to find out about it?"

"He did tell me about it," Ivan said in a tone that left no room for doubt. "As a matter of fact, he spoke of practically nothing else. 'It would be all right,' he said, 'if you believed in virtue at least, and said: "Let them not believe me, I must still tell them as a matter of principle!" But you are just as

much of a pig as your papa and you don't give a damn about
virtue! So what would be the point of your going through
with it now, when your sacrifice would be quite useless? The
answer is that you don't know yourself why you want to do
it. And it's not at all that you've made up your mind, because
you haven't made it up yet. You'll sit up all night trying to
decide whether you should go or not. But in the end you'll
go and you know you'll go, because you know that, whatever
you decide, it no longer depends on you. You'll go because
you don't dare not to. And why don't you dare? Well, take a
guess—it's your problem!' And when he said that, he got up
and left. You came—he left. He called me a coward, Alyosha.
Le mot de l'énigme is that I'm a coward. 'You're no eagle
who soars above the earth,' he added. Yes, he added that, and
Smerdyakov said that too. He ought to be killed. Katya has
despised me for months—I've been aware of it. And Lise too
will start despising me soon. He says, 'You're going to do it
because you want to be praised.' That's a filthy lie! And you
too, Alyosha, you despise me. Now I'll hate you again. And
I hate the monster, I hate him! I don't want to save the
monster. Let him rot in prison! Now he's started singing that
hymn of his! Oh, I'll go tomorrow, face them, and spit in
their eye!"

He leapt up frantically, threw away the wet towel, and
again began to walk up and down the room. Alyosha thought
of what Ivan had told him about sleeping while awake, about
walking about, seeing, and talking, and yet sleeping at the
same time. And that was happening right now. For a moment
he thought of rushing out to get a doctor, but he was afraid
to leave Ivan alone, since there would be no one to look after
him while he was gone.

Gradually Ivan began to lose consciousness altogether. He
was still talking constantly, but quite incoherently now. His
very words were becoming blurred and unclear. Suddenly he
staggered violently. Alyosha ran to him, to prevent him from
collapsing, and led him over to the bed. He undressed him,
put him to bed, and sat there for a couple of hours watching
over him. Ivan slept deeply, without stirring, breathing quietly
and regularly. Alyosha took a pillow and, without undressing,
lay down on the sofa. Before he fell asleep, he prayed for
Mitya and for Ivan. He was beginning to understand the
nature of Ivan's sickness—the agony caused by his proud
resolution and deep-seated feeling of responsibility. God, in
whom Ivan did not believe, and His truth were beginning to

overcome the heart, which still refused to submit. "Yes," Alyosha thought, his head already on the pillow, "with Smerdyakov dead, Ivan's testimony will not be believed; nevertheless he'll go and testify!" Alyosha smiled gently. "God will triumph," he thought. "And Ivan will either rise in the light of truth or . . . or he will perish in hate, punishing himself and all the others for having served something in which he does not believe," Alyosha added sadly and once again prayed for Ivan.

BOOK XII

MISCARRIAGE OF JUSTICE

CHAPTER 1

The Fatal Day

At ten in the morning of the day following the events just described, the trial of Dmitry Karamazov opened in district court.

I must make it clear from the outset that I feel unable to give a really complete account of all that happened during the trial or, for that matter, to report the events in their proper sequence. I believe that to bring it all up and explain it properly would take a whole volume of its own, and a big volume at that. So I hope it will not be held against me if I report only what particularly struck me and then stuck in my mind. I may very well have mistaken points of secondary importance for crucial developments and have omitted altogether some essential facts. Now that I have said this, I regret having embarked upon explanations. I'll do my best and the reader will see for himself that that is all I can do.

And now, before we enter the courtroom, I will mention the thing that surprised me most that day. Actually, as it turned out later, it surprised not only me, but everyone else as well. Everybody knew that the trial had aroused great interest among the general public, that people could hardly wait for it to begin, that everyone in town had been talking, conjecturing, exclaiming, and making surmises about the trial for the past two months. Yet, although they were all aware that the case stirred up curiosity all across the country, they never expected it to produce such violent excitement all over Russia as was evidenced on the opening day.

The town was full of visitors from other parts of the country, including many people from Moscow and Petersburg. Among the visitors were many jurists, quite a few famous public figures, and also a number of society ladies. All the admission tickets had been snatched up. For the most prominent and illustrious visiting gentlemen, special armchairs had been installed behind the judges' table, something that had never been done in our courtroom before.

At least half the audience was made up of women, local or visiting ladies. And the number of jurists who wanted to attend the trial was so large that fitting them into the courtroom was a serious problem, for all the tickets had long since been requested, even begged for, and distributed. I myself saw them hurriedly put up a special enclosure at the end of the courtroom, behind the dais, from which they removed all the chairs so as to be able to pack as many of the visiting jurists as possible into the space; and those who managed to get in there considered themselves very lucky, even though they were packed in tight and had to stand up throughout the whole trial. Some of the ladies, especially the out-of-towners, appeared in the gallery in the most sumptuous attire, but most of the women gave no thought to elegance. Their faces reflected a hysterical, greedy, almost morbid curiosity. A remarkable fact about the ladies was that the overwhelming majority of them, it turned out later, were on Mitya's side and wanted to see him acquitted. The main reason for this may have been his reputation as a conqueror of women's hearts. They knew that the two women contending for his love would appear at the trial. Katerina was an object of particular interest. All sorts of extraordinary stories circulated about her passionate love for Mitya, even after he had committed the crime. A great deal was said about her pride—"She practically never visits anyone in town"—and her "aristocratic connections." It was rumored that she was planning to request permission from the authorities to accompany Mitya to Siberia and marry him there, somewhere in the mines, underground. There was also great curiosity about Katerina's rival, Grushenka. People were eagerly anticipating the confrontation in court between the two rivals—the proud, aristocratic young lady and the "hetaera." Our local ladies, however, knew more about Grushenka than about Katerina. They had seen "that woman who spelled the doom of Fyodor Karamazov and his unhappy son," and they were quite puzzled to know "how such a plain, or in any case, by no means beautiful, low-class woman could have inspired such violent love in both the father and the son." In short, there was a lot of talk going around. I even heard from unimpeachable sources that several serious family quarrels had broken out on Mitya's account. Many ladies could not tolerate their husbands' disagreement with their sympathy for the accused, which naturally caused

those husbands, by the time they appeared in court, not only
to be unsympathetic toward Mitya but even to feel personally
irritated against him. But then we may say that, by and large,
men were as unfavorably disposed toward the accused as
women were favorable to him. There were many stern and
frowning faces, some of them outright hostile. It is true that
Mitya had managed to offend some of these gentlemen since
he had come to our town. Of course, some of the men in the
audience appeared to be perfectly cheerful and quite indifferent to what would happen to Mitya personally, although
they were extremely interested in the trial itself. As we said
before, the majority of the men wanted to see the accused
convicted. The jurists, however, were not interested in the
moral aspects of the case and viewed the whole business from
the point of view of the legal technicalities involved as a result
of the recent judicial reforms.

Everybody was excited by the presence of the famous
defense counsel, Fetyukovich. His talent was acclaimed all
over Russia and this was not the first time that he had
appeared in a sensational criminal case in the provinces. With
such appearances, the trials became famous and were remembered for a long time. There were also some amusing stories
about our public prosecutor and our presiding judge. It was
said that our prosecutor, Ippolit Kirillovich, was terrified of
Fetyukovich and that they had been old enemies since the
days in Petersburg when they were starting out on their
careers. It was said that our conceited prosecutor, who always
considered his talents so unfairly undervalued, had at first seen
in the Karamazov case an unexpected chance to restore his
hopes for recognition and that it was only the prospect of
facing Fetyukovich that frightened him. But the stories of
his fear of Fetyukovich were not quite fair. Our prosecutor
was not one of those men who become dispirited in the face
of danger, but rather one whose pride grows and who may
become inspired as the danger grows. It must be noted, in
general, that he was a hot-tempered and rather erratic man.
In some instances he would put his whole soul into a case
and act as though his entire career and his very life depended
on it. This caused many members of the legal profession to
laugh at him and gave him a greater notoriety than his
modest position would otherwise have afforded him. It was,
above all, his passion for the psychological approach that
made him the butt of jokes. I feel they were wrong to find
him so ridiculous, because he was much more serious and

determined, as a lawyer and as a man, than they suspected. But from the very outset of his legal career, this sickly man had been unable to command the respect due his talents, and he never managed to close this gap later.

As to the presiding judge, it can only be said of him that he was well educated and humane, a competent jurist, and a man with the most modern views. He was rather proud, but was not overly concerned with his career. His main aim in life was to be considered as "progressive" as possible. With all that, he was a wealthy man with good connections. He was, it turned out later, extremely interested in the Karamazov case from "the social point of view." He was interested in it as a social manifestation and was anxious to classify the accused and his outlook as the product of his social background, as a typically Russian phenomenon, etc., etc. As to the specific case, the tragedy itself and the individuals involved, from the accused on down—the presiding judge felt quite indifferent and detached about it all, as perhaps, indeed, he should have.

Long before the appearance of the judges, the court was packed to overflowing. Our courtroom is the best hall in town: it is spacious, has high ceilings and excellent acoustics. To the right of the members of the court, who were seated on a dais, a table and two rows of chairs had been reserved for the jury. On the left sat the accused and his counsel. In the middle was the table for the material exhibits; the bloodstained white silk dressing gown that had belonged to Fyodor Karamazov; what was assumed to be the murder weapon, the brass pestle; Mitya's shirt with its bloodstained sleeve; his jacket covered with bloodstains in the back over the pocket, where he had put his blood-soaked handkerchief; the handkerchief itself, all caked with blood and by now quite yellow; the pistol that Mitya had loaded at Perkhotin's so that he could shoot himself but that had later been secretly taken out of its box by Trifon in Mokroye; the envelope Fyodor Karamazov had inscribed to Grushenka, from which the three thousand rubles had been removed; the narrow pink ribbon that had been tied around it; and various other items that I cannot remember offhand. Farther down, there were the seats for the public, but before the balustrade there were a few chairs for the witnesses, who were required to remain in court after they had testified.

The three judges marched in at ten o'clock—the presiding judge, the associate judge, and the honorary justice of the peace—and they were at once followed by the public prosecutor. The presiding judge was a squat, thick-set man of about fifty, with a hemorrhoidal complexion and dark, graying, close-cropped hair, and the red ribbon of some order, I no longer know which. The striking thing about the prosecutor was his pallor; indeed, his face was almost green and he seemed to have grown even thinner, perhaps in a single night —for I had seen him only two days before and then he had still looked quite his former self. The presiding judge opened the session by asking the bailiff whether all the jurors had reported . . .

But I realize I cannot continue like this, because there were quite a few things I didn't catch, other things whose meaning escaped me, still other things that I have forgotten to mention, and, above all, as I said before, if I try to record everything that happened and was said, I will soon run out of both time and space. I can only say that neither the counsel for the defense nor the prosecutor challenged many jurors. I remember the final composition of the jury: of the twelve, four were government officials, two were merchants, and six were artisans and laborers. Well before the trial, I recall hearing members of the more elegant society of our town, ladies especially, saying something like: "How is it possible to entrust such a subtle, complex psychological case to the judgment of some obscure minor civil servants, and even laborers? What can a petty official and, still less, a peasant understand about these things?" And, indeed, the four officials were very minor, three of them already gray-haired (and the fourth only somewhat younger), none of them known in our society, people who probably eked out a living on a small salary, were married to elderly and unpresentable wives, and had many children who probably ran around barefoot. The only diversion of such officials was an occasional game of cards and it seemed certain that none of them would ever have been caught reading a book. The two merchants looked respectable enough, but they seemed strangely quiet and slow-moving. One of them was clean-shaven and dressed in the European style, while the other had a graying beard and wore some medal or other on a red ribbon around his neck. I need hardly speak of the artisans and laborers, because in our agricultural town such people are quite indistinguishable from peasants, and artisans often even till the soil. Two of these people were also dressed in European-style clothes, which perhaps only made them look shabbier and less tidy than the other four. So it was

quite natural that, looking at them, one should start to wonder, as I did among others, what these people could understand in a business such as this one. Nevertheless, frowning
and stern, their faces were strangely impressive, even awe-
inspiring.

At last the presiding judge declared the case concerning the
murder of Fyodor Pavlovich Karamazov open—I don't remember the exact wording of the declaration. The bailiff was
ordered to bring in the accused, and Mitya was brought in.
The courtroom became so utterly quiet that one could have
heard the buzzing of a fly. I cannot speak for the others but,
on me personally, Mitya made a most unpleasant impression.
The worst of it was that he came into court dressed up like
a regular dandy in a new, perfectly fitted frock-coat. I found
out later that he had ordered that frock-coat especially for the
trial from his Moscow tailor, who had his measurements. His
linen was immaculate and exquisite. He was also wearing
brand new kid gloves. He marched in with his long stride,
looking straight ahead of him, and sat down, looking completely detached. Right behind him came his celebrated defense counsel, Fetyukovich, and a subdued hum rose from
the audience. He was a tall, spare man with very long, lean
legs and very long, pale fingers. He was clean-shaven and
wore his soberly brushed hair rather short. His thin lips
would curve now and then into what could be interpreted
either as a sneering grin or as a smile. He was about forty
and his face might have been described as pleasant, had it
not been for his eyes. These eyes, themselves rather small and
unexpressive, were set exceptionally close together, divided
only by the very thin bone of his long, slender nose. On the
whole, there was something strikingly bird-like in the face of
this jurist, who was dressed in a frock-coat and a white tie.

I remember that the presiding judge asked Mitya the routine preliminary questions—his name, occupation, etc. Mitya
answered smartly and clearly, but somehow in an unexpectedly loud voice that made the presiding judge sit up slightly,
looking almost surprised. Then they read the list of names
of the people who were to take part in the court proceedings,
that is, the witnesses and the special experts. It was a long
list; four of the witnesses did not appear: Miusov, who was
at that time in Paris but whose deposition was available in
the records of the preliminary investigation; Mrs. Khokhlakov
and Mr. Maximov, both unavailable because of illness; and
Smerdyakov, because of his sudden death, the certificate of

which had been presented by the police. The news of Smerd-yakov's suicide caused considerable commotion and whisper-ing among the audience, for, clearly, many of those present could not have known so soon about that sudden develop-ment. But what really caused a sensation was Mitya's unex-pected outburst.

As soon as the reason for Smerdyakov's absence was an-nounced publicly, Mitya leapt to his feet and shouted in a voice that resounded throughout the courtroom:

"A dog's death for a dog!"

I can still see his defense counsel seizing him and hear the presiding judge threatening him that he'd have to take appro-priate measures if he behaved in such an unseemly way once more. Mitya nodded his head, repeating in an undertone to his counsel, "All right, all right, I won't do it again. I just couldn't control myself. I won't do it again . . ." but without looking in the least regretful.

I am quite convinced that this brief incident did not help him gain the sympathy of either the jury or the public: he was revealing his true face. It was after that incident that the act of indictment was read out by the clerk of the court. It was brief and to the point; it listed the main reasons why Dmitry Karamazov had been arrested and brought to trial, etc. Nevertheless, it made a great impression. The clerk read it in a clear, loud, firm voice. The whole tragedy gained sub-stance and came to life, appearing in a new, harsh light.

I remember how, immediately after the reading of the act of indictment, the presiding judge asked Mitya in a stern, admonishing tone:

"Do you plead guilty or not guilty?"

Mitya quickly jumped to his feet.

"I plead guilty to drunkenness and disorderly behavior," he said, again in an unexpectedly excited, almost frantic tone, "I plead guilty to laziness and debauchery. But I had resolved to become a decent man for the rest of my life when I was struck down by this blow of fate . . . And I am not guilty of the death of the old man who was my enemy and my father, no, I am not guilty of that! And I am not guilty of robbing him—no, no, how could I be guilty of that? Dmitry Kara-mazov is a despicable scoundrel, but he is not a thief!"

After shouting this, he sat down all atremble. The presiding judge again warned him that he should just answer the ques-tions and not indulge in frenzied and irrelevant exclamations, and then he ordered the proceedings resumed.

Next, all the witnesses were brought forward and sworn in. That was when I saw them all at the same time. The brothers of the accused, however, were not sworn in. After a few words from the priest and brief instructions from the presiding judge, the witnesses were led away and seated as far as possible from one another. Then they proceeded to call them back, one at a time.

CHAPTER 2

Dangerous Witnesses

I am not sure whether the presiding judge somehow separated the witnesses for the prosecution from those for the defense (I expect he did), or in what order they were supposed to be called. All I know is that the first to be called were witnesses for the prosecution. I repeat, I have no intention of reporting the entire questioning of the witnesses, step by step. Besides, such an account would be partly repetitive, for the remarkable speeches of the prosecutor and the defense counsel presented all the facts of the case and summed up all the testimony, focusing it clearly and, in each instance, presenting the case characteristically from a different angle. These I took down verbatim, at least in part, and I will quote from them in due course. I shall also report at length on an extraordinary and quite unexpected incident which occurred before the summing up by the two attorneys and which certainly influenced, to some extent, the harsh and fateful outcome of the trial.

It must be pointed out that, from the very beginning, everyone was aware of the lopsidedness of the case, that is, of the strength of the prosecution's position as compared with the means of refutation at the disposal of the defense. And this became more and more obvious as, in the grim courtroom atmosphere, evidence from various angles and unrelated facts all seemed to point in the same direction and the outlines of the horrible, gory murder became more and more distinct. Perhaps it was even clear to everybody from the outset that there was no room for a difference of opinion at this trial, no real need for legal argument, that the whole trial had been staged merely for form's sake, and that the accused was guilty without a shadow of a doubt. I think that even the ladies, who, almost without exception, wished the handsome and

interesting accused man to be acquitted, had, at the same
time, not the slightest doubt about his guilt. Moreover, I
believe they would have been rather disappointed if his guilt
could not have been definitely established, because that would
have spoiled the dramatic effect of his acquittal. For, strange
as it may seem, all the ladies were absolutely convinced, up
to the very last second, that he would be acquitted. "He is
guilty," they thought, "but he will be acquitted out of humane
considerations, under the impact of the new ideas and the new
feelings about these matters," etc., etc. And that was why
they had all rushed to the trial with such tremendous impatience. The men were mainly interested in the duel between
our prosecutor and the celebrated Fetyukovich. They were
very curious to see what a talented lawyer like Fetyukovich
could do with such a hopeless case and so they followed his
every move with tremendous interest and concentration. But
Fetyukovich remained a puzzle to them all until the very end,
until his final summation to the jury. People with experience
felt that he had a plan, that he had already established something or other, and that he was progressing toward a certain
goal, although they could not yet see what that goal was. His
poise and self-assurance, however, were quite striking. Also,
it was noted approvingly that, although he had been in town
only a very short time, a mere three days in fact, he seemed
to have studied the case thoroughly and acquainted himself
with all its finest points. Later, they delightedly told and
retold how he had succeeded in catching the prosecution witnesses off balance and confusing them at the right moment
and, above all, how clever he was at casting doubt on their
moral reputation, and thus, of course, discrediting their testimony. There were some who thought, however, that he did
this just as part of the game, to display his virtuosity, and to
prove that not one of the accepted legal methods had been neglected. For everyone was convinced that all this discrediting
of witnesses could not really make much difference to the
outcome and that Fetyukovich himself must realize this better
than anyone else, but that he still had some idea in reserve,
some secret weapon that he would use when he decided the
time was right. But, in the meantime, he seemed to be just
having a little fun, well aware of his strength. For instance,
during the cross-examination of the victim's former servant
Gregory, who had, under direct examination, repeated his
testimony that he had seen the door leading from the garden
into the house open, Fetyukovich literally pounced on him.

It must be pointed out that, when Gregory made his appearance in court, he was not in the least awed by the solemnity of the occasion or the size of the audience. He looked calm, almost majestic. He answered the questions in the self-assured tone that he used in talking to his wife Martha when they were alone, although, of course, with rather more deference. It was quite impossible to trip him up. First, he was questioned by the prosecutor, who asked him about the Karamazov family. It was obvious from Gregory's tone and countenance that he was an honest and impartial witness. Despite his profound respect for his former master, Gregory, for instance, did not hesitate to say that he had been unfair to Mitya and that he had not brought up his children as he ought to have.

"If it had not been for me," Gregory said, speaking of Mitya, "he would have been devoured by lice when he was little." And later he added: "And also, it wasn't right for a father to do his son out of his own mother's family estate."

When, then, the prosecutor asked him what grounds he had for asserting that Fyodor Karamazov had acted dishonestly toward his son with regard to that estate, Gregory, to everyone's surprise, was unable to offer any support for his statement but simply insisted that the settlement was "unfair" and that the father ought to have paid the son "a few thousand more." (Let me point out here that the prosecutor asked that question of every witness who might know anything about it, including Alyosha and Ivan, but none of them could give him any positive facts, although they all agreed that Mitya had been wronged.)

After that, Gregory described the scene when Dmitry had broken into the house, beaten his father, and threatened to come back and kill him. The story made a very grim impression on the audience and the effect was strengthened by the calm way in which the old servant told it, without any superfluous words and in his own language. As to Mitya's striking him in the face and knocking him down, Gregory said that he held no grudge for that and had forgiven him long ago. When questioned about Smerdyakov, Gregory crossed himself and said that "he was an able fellow, but stupid and pestered by his sickness and, worst of all, he was a godless man, and it was Mr. Karamazov and Mr. Ivan who taught him his godlessness." But he emphatically, indeed almost heatedly, attested to Smerdyakov's honesty, and told them about the time when Smerdyakov had found some money his master had dropped and had returned it, and how Fyodor Karamazov had given him a ten-ruble gold piece as a reward and had trusted him completely ever after.

And once again Gregory repeated with stubborn insistence that he had seen the door leading into the garden open. But he was asked so many questions in the direct examination that I cannot remember them all.

At last it was time for the defense counsel to cross-examine him, and the first thing Fetyukovich wanted to know was about "the envelope that allegedly contained three thousand rubles intended for a certain person."

"Did you see it with your own eyes, you who were for so many years your master's most trusted servant?"

Gregory replied that he had not seen it with his own eyes and that, in fact, he had not even heard about that money "until just now when everybody was talking about it." (By the way, Fetyukovich asked that question about the envelope with the money in it of every witness who was at all likely to know about it, just as persistently as the prosecutor asked about the settlement of the estate left by Mitya's mother, and he received a series of similar answers to the effect that they had all heard of the envelope with the money in it, but that none of them had actually seen it. The defense counsel's insistence on that question was noted from the very beginning.)

"And now may I ask you this, if you don't mind," Fetyukovich said, unexpectedly changing his line of questioning, "what were the ingredients in the preparation, or shall we call it the brew, with which, as appears from the preliminary investigation, your wife rubbed your back that evening, in an attempt to relieve your pain?"

Gregory looked blankly at the lawyer and after a moment of silence mumbled that "there was some sage in it . . ."

"Only sage? You don't recollect anything else?"

"There was plantain in it too."

"Perhaps it contained pepper as well?"

"That's right, sir, it had pepper in it too."

"And so on, and so forth, and all these things were mixed up in good old vodka, weren't they?"

"In alcohol, sir."

There was scattered laughter among the audience.

"You don't say—so it was even alcohol! Well then, after your back had been rubbed with that concoction, did you or did you not drink what remained in the bottle while your wife recited a certain pious prayer known only to her?"

"I did."

"How much of that stuff would you say you drank? Approximately. Was it the equivalent of one glass, two glasses? What would you say?"

"I'd say one glass."

"A whole glassful! Might it have been, say, a glass and a half?"

Gregory did not answer. He didn't seem to understand the question.

"So let's say you gulped down a glass and a half of pure alcohol—that's not bad, is it? With that, you might have seen even the gates of heaven wide open, to say nothing of a door leading into the garden!"

Gregory still said nothing. There was some more laughter among the audience and the presiding judge stirred disapprovingly in his seat.

"Are you absolutely certain that you were not asleep when you saw that door open?" Fetyukovich pursued his attack relentlessly.

"I was on my feet."

"That still doesn't convince me that you were wide awake," Fetyukovich snapped sarcastically, and there was more subdued laughter. "Could you, for instance, have said what year it was if someone had asked you?"

"I don't know about that."

"And, by the way, what year, anno domini, is it now?"

Gregory, looking completely confused, stared blankly at his tormentor. It did seem rather strange that he did not know what year it was.

"Perhaps you can tell me, though, how many fingers you have on your hand?"

"I have no choice now," Gregory said suddenly, in a loud, clear voice, "and if the authorities wish to make a fool of me, I'll just have to bear it."

Fetyukovich seemed slightly taken aback. On top of that, the presiding judge interfered and warned him in an admonishing tone to limit himself to more relevant questions. Fetyukovich made a dignified bow and declared that he had finished with the witness. Of course, he may have implanted a small worm of doubt in the jury and the public as to the value of the testimony of a man who was in a state in which he could have seen even "the gates of heaven wide open," and who, moreover, still did not know what year it was. So, in a way, the defense counsel may have achieved his objective.

But another incident occurred before Gregory left. The presiding judge addressed himself directly to the accused, asking him whether he had any comments in connection with Gregory's testimony.

"Except for that door, everything else he said was true," Mitya said in a loud voice. "And I'm grateful to him for combing the lice out of my head when I was little and for forgiving me for hitting him. The old man has been honest all his life and was as faithful to my father as seven hundred poodles."

"I warn the accused to be more careful in his choice of words," the presiding judge said sternly.

"I'm no poodle," Gregory grumbled.

"All right, it's I who am the poodle then!" Mitya cried. "If I have insulted him, I take the insult on myself: I was a brute and I was horrible to him! And I was also horrible to old Aesop . . ."

"Who is Aesop?" the presiding judge asked sternly.

"Well, Pierrot . . . I mean my father, Fyodor Karamazov."

The presiding judge again admonished Mitya to choose his words more carefully.

"You are harming yourself in the opinion of your judges," he said.

The defense counsel was just as nimble in dealing with Rakitin. It must be said that Rakitin was one of the witnesses the prosecutor considered extremely important and on whose testimony he reckoned greatly. It sounded as if Rakitin knew a great deal, as if he had seen everything, been everywhere, spoken to everybody, was familiar with every detail of Fyodor Karamazov's life story and, indeed, of the life stories of all the Karamazovs. It is true, though, that it was only from the accused that he had heard about the envelope with the three thousand rubles in it. He made up for this by describing at great length Mitya's various exploits at the Capital City Inn, repeating all Mitya's compromising statements and threats, and telling of the incident between Mitya and Captain Snegirev, whom the accused had dragged out of the tavern by his "back-scrubber."

But not even Rakitin could shed any light on whether the father still owed the son something in the settlement of Mitya's mother's estate and contented himself with a few general scornful remarks to the effect that it was impossible to tell who had cheated whom "in all that Karamazov mess." He presented the whole tragedy of the accused and of the crime as a product of outdated mores surviving from the days of serfdom and of the chaos prevailing in Russia because of the lack of proper social organization and adequate public services. In short, he was given a chance to say his piece. Indeed, it was as a witness at this trial that Mr. Mikhail Rakitin attracted public attention to himself and was given the opportunity to show the world the stuff he was made of. The prosecutor knew that Rakitin was preparing a magazine article on the true causes behind this crime and later, in his summation, mentioned, as we shall see, some of the ideas contained in that article, which shows that he was already familiar with it. The picture drawn by Rakitin was grim and tragic and it seemed to further strengthen the position of the prosecution. In general, Rakitin's account seduced the public through the independence of its ideas and the loftiness of its vision. There were even two or three spontaneous bursts of applause at passages in which he denounced serfdom and the chaos Russia was now experiencing in its wake. However, Rakitin, being still very young, made one small slip, on which Fetyukovich at once capitalized. Well aware of his success with the audience and somewhat dazzled by the noble and idealized position he had attained on the wings of his eloquence, he allowed himself to use a rather scornful tone concerning Grushenka, referring to her as "Samsonov's kept woman." He would have given anything to take the words back afterward, for it was on them that Fetyukovich caught him. And it all happened because Rakitin had never imagined that the defense counsel could have become so quickly acquainted with the subtlest detail of the situation.

"May I ask you this," Fetyukovich said with a most amiable and even respectful smile, when his turn came to cross-examine this hostile witness, "you, of course, are the same Mr. Rakitin who wrote the pamphlet *Life of the Deceased Elder, Father Zosima,* that was published by the ecclesiastical authorities. I read it quite recently and I found many profound, religious thoughts in it. I enjoyed particularly your pious introduction dedicated to the Bishop. I was really impressed."

"It wasn't meant for publication . . . They decided to publish it later . . ." Rakitin muttered, somewhat taken aback. He sounded rather apologetic, almost ashamed.

"Oh, I think it's wonderful! I'm sure that a thinker of your caliber must approach every social phenomenon with a perfectly open mind and have a very unprejudiced view of things.

Thanks to the patronage of the Bishop, your very useful pamphlet was widely circulated and thus has been even more beneficial . . . But what I really meant to ask you was this: you stated in your deposition that you were very well acquainted with Miss Svetlov. Is that correct?"

(It was at the trial, by the way, that I heard Grushenka's last name for the first time—I had not been aware of it until then.)

"I cannot be held answerable for every person I know . . ." Rakitin replied, at once flushing all over. "You don't really expect a young man to be responsible for all the people he comes across, do you?"

"Of course not, of course not, I understand that perfectly!" Fetyukovich exclaimed with feigned embarrassment, as if he were trying to apologize for his grossness. "It is quite natural that you, just like any other young man, might be interested in knowing a young and beautiful woman who readily entertained the local young élite . . . However, I would like you to clear up the following point for me: we know that a couple of months ago Miss Svetlov was anxious to meet the youngest of the Karamazovs and that she had promised to pay you twenty-five rubles if you brought him to her in his monastic attire. We also know that the meeting in question took place on the very day that was to end in the catastrophe which led to the present trial. So, on that same day, you took Alexei Karamazov to Miss Svetlov's house—and received twenty-five rubles from her for that service? I would like to hear what you have to say about it."

"It was a kind of joke . . . I don't see, though, why it should concern you . . . I took the money, planning to give it back to her later."

"So you did take the money? But you still haven't returned it, have you?"

"That is nonsense," Rakitin muttered. "I can't answer that sort of question . . . Besides, of course, I'll give it back."

The presiding judge intervened, but the defense counsel announced that he was through with Mr. Rakitin, and Mr. Rakitin stepped down from the witness box rather deflated. The impression created by his lofty, altruistic flights was spoiled and, as he was leaving, Fetyukovich accompanied him with a gaze that seemed to say: "Well, well, well, so that's how high-minded the witnesses for the prosecution are!"

I remember that here, too, Mitya could not keep quiet. Enraged by Rakitin's tone when he spoke of Grushenka,

Mitya suddenly cried out from his place: "You Bernard!" Then, after Rakitin had been excused, the presiding judge asked the accused whether he wished to comment on his testimony. Mitya shouted in a resounding voice:

"He's been borrowing money from me while I've been in prison, and he's a contemptible Bernard and a careerist who doesn't believe in God and who has deceived the Bishop!"

Obviously Mitya was called to order again, but that took care of Rakitin completely.

Captain Snegirev did not fare any better as a witness, but for quite a different reason. He appeared in dirty, tattered clothes and muddy shoes and, despite all precautions and a preliminary examination by medical experts, he turned out to be quite seriously drunk. When asked about the insult he had suffered at Mitya's hands, he refused to answer.

"May God forgive him," Snegirev said. "Ilyusha didn't want me to complain. God will make it up to me some time . . ."

"Who told you that? Who are you referring to?"

"To my son, to Ilyusha. He said to me: 'Papa, papa, ah, the way he treated you!' He said that by the stone. And now he's dying."

Snegirev began to sob and all of a sudden threw himself at the feet of the presiding judge. He was quickly led out amidst the laughter of the audience. The effect the prosecutor had hoped to achieve by his testimony was completely lost.

The defense counsel continued to use every possible trick and he astounded everybody by his intimate knowledge of the minutest detail of the case.

For instance, under direct examination, the testimony of the innkeeper at Mokroye, Trifon, created an impression extremely unfavorable to Mitya. He almost proved by counting on his fingers that, during his first wild party at Mokroye, Mitya *must* have spent "three thousand rubles, or just short of that figure but something very close to it." He dwelt on the sums Mitya had squandered on the gypsy girls, and, as to "our lousy" peasants, he didn't toss them each just half-ruble pieces, but twenty-five-ruble bills! And all the money they stole from him—they didn't give him receipts for it, so we'd never know how much it was.

"The villagers are all thieves," Trifon said. "They don't care about saving their souls . . . And you should have seen the money the village women got out of him! They're rich now, believe me. They'll never go hungry no more!"

In short, Trifon claimed to remember every item of Mitya's expenses and to have added them up in his mind, "like on my abacus." And so Mitya's claim that he had spent only fifteen hundred rubles that night and sewed the rest up in the rag appeared quite untenable. "I saw the three thousand in his hands with my own eyes. I'm pretty used to handling money and can tell!" the innkeeper insisted, trying hard to please "the authorities."

But when the witness was handed over to Fetyukovich for cross-examination, the lawyer made only a token attempt to refute his testimony and, instead, brought up another incident from Mitya's first wild party at Mokroye a month before his arrest: at that time Timofei the coachman and another man named Akim had found in the passage a hundred-ruble bill that Mitya had dropped when he was drunk, and had given it to the innkeeper, who had given them one ruble each.

"Well," Fetyukovich wanted to know, "did you return the hundred rubles to Mr. Karamazov?"

Trifon tried hard to deny the story, but after the two men had been called in to repeat their account, he finally admitted it, although he insisted that he had at once given the hundred rubles back to Mr. Karamazov, who of course, he remarked, could not possibly remember it, "on account of the state he was in at that time." However, since the witness had first repeatedly denied an incident which he later admitted to, his whole testimony lost much of its credibility and the innkeeper's honesty was put very much in question.

The same discrediting technique was applied to the Poles, who came in with haughty and arrogant airs, declared that they were "servants of the Crown," that the accused "had tried to buy their honor for three thousand rubles," and that they themselves had seen him holding in his hands "large sums of money." Pan Musijalowicz used a number of Polish words and expressions, and when he saw that this seemed to impress the presiding judge and the prosecutor, he was inspired to switch to Polish almost entirely. But Fetyukovich made short shrift of their reputations too. He had the innkeeper recalled to the stand and, despite the man's obvious ill-will, made him testify to Pan Wrublewski's substituting a deck of marked cards for the one Trifon had given him and Pan Musijalowicz's cheating when dealing. And this was also confirmed by Kalganov when he was called, so the Poles left disgraced, accompanied by laughter.

And the same pattern was maintained with all the more

dangerous witnesses. In every case, Fetyukovich succeeded in casting aspersions on their reputations and they looked a bit ridiculous when he was through with them. The jurists and the connoisseurs admired his nimbleness, although, as I said before, they were not sure how it could change the situation for, despite everything, the case for the prosecution seemed more and more clear cut. But the self-confidence and calm of that "great magician" made them wonder: a lawyer of his caliber would never have bothered to come all the way from Petersburg, to return with nothing to show for his efforts. He certainly did not seem to be that sort of a man.

CHAPTER 3

The Medical Experts and a Pound of Nuts

The testimony of the medical experts was of little help to the accused. Actually, as became obvious later, Fetyukovich had never expected much from it. Primarily, it had been Katerina's idea and it was she who had insisted on bringing in the Moscow luminary. The defense, of course, could lose nothing by it and with luck might even derive some advantage from it. As it turned out, it contributed a touch of comedy because of the differences in the experts' opinions. The three medical experts were the famous Moscow practitioner, our old Dr. Herzenstube, and Varvinsky, a young doctor who had moved to our town quite recently. The latter two had also appeared as ordinary witnesses for the prosecution.

The first expert to testify was seventy-year-old Dr. Herzenstube, a sturdily built old man of medium height with a gray crown of hair surrounding a bald dome. He was greatly liked and esteemed in our town. He was a conscientious physician, a kindly, pious man, a member either of the Herrnhuter Society or the Moravian Brethren, I'm not sure which. He had lived in our town for many years and had always behaved with great dignity. He was a good and humane man, who gave his medical services free to the poor, visiting them in their huts and hovels, and even leaving them money to buy the medicines he prescribed. But, for all his kindness, he was as stubborn as a mule. Once he had got an idea into his head, it was quite hopeless to try and make him change his mind. By the way, everybody in town knew that, within two or three days of his arrival in town, the famous Moscow doctor had indulged in some extremely disparaging remarks about Dr. Herzenstube's professional competence. This came about because, although the Moscow luminary charged at least twenty-five rubles a visit, people were anxious to take advantage of his presence in town and rushed to consult him. Otherwise, of course, they were all Dr. Herzenstube's regular patients. But the Moscow doctor turned out to be sharply critical of Herzenstube's treatments, and after a few days, when he saw a patient for the first time, the doctor would begin by saying something like: "Well, well, hm . . . looks as if Dr. Herzenstube has been trying one of those treatments of his own on you? Ha-ha!" Obviously, it wasn't long before Dr. Herzenstube heard about this.

And now these two doctors, along with a third, were scheduled to appear in court, each in turn, as medical experts.

Dr. Herzenstube declared unhesitatingly that "the abnormality of the patient's mental processes is self-evident." He then proceeded to give his reasons for his statement, which I shall omit, and added that mental disturbance in the accused could be deduced both from his former acts and from his present behavior. When he was asked to explain this last statement, the old doctor, in his direct, simple-hearted way, mentioned, as an illustration of his point, the manner in which the accused had entered the courtroom:

"His behavior was unusual and peculiar under the circumstances. He marched straight in like a soldier with his eyes fixed in front of him, stubbornly, whereas his normal way would have been to look to his left where most of the ladies are seated, because he is a great admirer of the fair sex and must have been thinking about what the ladies would say of him."

It must be noted here that, although Dr. Herzenstube spoke Russian with zest and volubility, his sentences somehow made one think of German sentences. This, however, never bothered him, for he had always considered his mastery of the Russian language "exemplary" and his use of it more correct than that of native Russians. He also loved to quote Russian sayings and proverbs, which he considered the best in the world. It should also be noted that, from absentmindedness or some other cause, the most usual words, words that he knew perfectly well, would every now and then slip his mind. This happened to him whether he was speaking Russian or German, and, on such occasions, he would wave one hand in front of his face as if trying to catch the word that had escaped him, and no one could make him continue what he was trying to say until he had finally recaptured the slippery word. Dr. Herzenstube's remark that the accused would normally have looked at the ladies when entering the courtroom stirred up some playful whispering in the audience. The ladies liked the old fellow very much and they were aware that this old, pious, and most proper bachelor had looked upon women as superior beings all his life. It was in view of this that his remark struck everybody as most unexpected.

The Moscow doctor was the next to give his expert opinion. He confirmed in a sharp and incontrovertible tone that he considered the accused's mental condition "abnormal, and abnormal to the highest degree." He expounded learnedly and at great length on manias and different forms of temporary insanity, and declared that it could be deduced from the available facts that the accused had been in a state of temporary insanity for several days before his arrest and that, even if he had known what he was doing when he committed his crime, he was absolutely helpless to resist the mental obsession that held him in its grip. But aside from this temporary insanity, the doctor also found that Mitya was afflicted with a mania which, according to him, would unfailingly lead to full-fledged insanity. I have translated all this into my own words, because the doctor, of course, expressed it in his specialized and learned language.

"All his actions are contrary to common sense," the doctor went on, "and, of course, I am not speaking of what I have not seen, that is, the crime itself and the catastrophic events that preceded it. But just two days ago, he wore a quite unaccountable fixed stare when we were talking. And he would burst out laughing when there was absolutely no reason for it. Then he used words like 'Bernard' and 'ethics' that were either incomprehensible or meaningless in their context."

But the accused's mania manifested itself most clearly, according to the doctor, in the fact that he was unable to speak about the three thousand rubles of which he considered he had been cheated without an anger and emotion that were out of all proportion, whereas he could dwell calmly on his other failures and frustrations. And finally, the doctor said, the accused, who became almost frantic at the mention of the three thousand, was, according to all the witnesses, a man very little interested in money matters and anything but avaricious.

"As to the opinion of my learned colleague," the Moscow doctor added ironically at the end of his speech, "that the accused should have looked at the ladies rather than in front of him, I would simply say that, aside from the flippancy of such a statement, it also happens to be radically wrong. For, although I agree with him that, when entering the courtroom, the stiffness of the accused's bearing and the fixity of his stare could be considered symptoms of his disturbed mental state at that particular moment, I submit that he should have looked not to his left at the ladies, as my colleague claims, but to the right, where he should have been seeking with his eyes the counsel for the defense, who is his only hope and on whom his future now depends." The Moscow doctor ended his statement most emphatically.

The comic disagreement among the experts became even more evident with the statement of Dr. Varvinsky, the last expert called to testify. His conclusions came as a complete surprise. According to him, the accused was now, and had always been, perfectly normal and, although before his arrest he had been in a nervous and highly excited state, that state could easily be accounted for by many quite obvious reasons: jealousy, anger, constant inebriation, etc. And there was no need at all, Dr. Varvinsky said, to drag in what had been referred to as "temporary insanity." As to whether the accused "should" have looked to the left or to the right when he entered the courtroom, in Dr. Varvinsky's "humble opinion," Dmitry Karamazov had done just the right thing in looking straight ahead of him, for right in front of him sat the presiding judge and the two associate judges on whom his fate really depended, and, by looking in that direction, "he established his sanity at that particular moment."

"Bravo, doctor, you tell 'em!" Mitya shouted approvingly from his seat.

It goes without saying that he was again admonished, but the opinion of the young doctor had, as was proved later, a decisive effect on the judges, the jury, and the public in general.

Later, however, Dr. Herzenstube, when recalled to the stand, this time as an ordinary witness for the prosecution, quite unexpectedly came up with some evidence in Mitya's favor. As an inhabitant of the town, who had known the Karamazov family for many years, he was recounting various facts that the prosecutor wanted on record when, all of a sudden, he seemed to think of something and added:

"However, this poor young man deserved infinitely better of life, for he had a good heart when he was a child and even when he was no longer a child. I can say that because I know him well. There is a Russian proverb that teaches us that if a person has a clever head, it is good, but if someone clever comes to see him, it is even better, because two good heads . . ."

"Are better than one," the prosecutor prompted him impatiently, for he was familiar with the old man's slow and long-winded way of speaking and knew that the doctor was quite unperturbed by the idea that he might be boring his audience, that, indeed, he liked to make them wait, trusting fully to his heavy, humorless German wit.

"Right, right, and, as I was saying, one head is good, but two is much, much better," Dr. Herzenstube went on stubbornly. "So no one with a good head came to join him, and later he allowed his own head out . . . How do you say it? He let it out . . . Ah, what's the word? . . ." the doctor waved his hand impatiently in front of his face. "He let it out . . . ah, yes, he let it out *spazieren.*"

"For a walk?"

"Right, he let it out for a walk—that's just what I was trying to say. And so his head went for a walk and found itself in such a dark place that it lost itself there. But he was a very sensitive boy who was always grateful to anyone who did anything for him. Ah, I remember when he was just a baby thrown out into the backyard by his father, where I saw him trotting around barefoot, his little trousers held up by a single button . . ."

A tender, even sentimental, note suddenly crept into the old man's voice. Fetyukovich suddenly started, as if sensing something in the air, and perked up his ears.

"Oh yes, I was still a young man myself then . . . I must have been perhaps forty-five or so—it wasn't long after I had moved here. I was sorry for the little boy and I asked myself, why shouldn't I buy him a pound of . . . a pound of . . . Ah, I've forgotten the word—children usually like them very much. What are they called?" and he began to wave his hands in front of his face. "They grow on trees, you know, they pick them and give them to people . . ."

"Apples?"

"No, no, apples are sold by the dozen, the things I mean are sold by the pound—there are too many of them . . .

They're small, children put them in their mouths, and crra-ck, crrr—ack!"

"Nuts?"

"Right, nuts, that's what I wanted to say," the doctor said imperturbably, as though he had never forgotten the word but been interrupted. "So I brought the boy a pound of nuts and it was the first pound of nuts anyone had ever given him. So I raised my finger and I said to him: 'My boy,' I said, '*Gott der Vater.*' And he laughed and said '*Gott der Vater.*' Then I said '*Gott der Sohn,*' and he babbled in his tiny voice, '*Gott der Sohn,*' and laughed again. Then I said '*Gott der heilige Geist,*' and he tried to repeat as much of it as he could, laughing all the time. Two days later, as I was passing their house, I heard the little boy calling out to me, 'Hey, uncle, *Gott der Vater, Gott der Sohn!*' He had only forgotten *Gott der heilige Geist,* but I reminded him of it and I again felt very sorry for him. But later they took him away and I didn't see him for a long time. And so twenty-three years go by, and one morning I'm sitting in my study—my hair is completely white now—and suddenly a blooming young man comes in. I don't recognize him, but he lifts his finger, laughs, and says to me: '*Gott der Vater, Gott der Sohn, und Gott der heilige Geist!* I've just come to town,' he says, 'and I want to thank you now for the pound of nuts you once gave me, because you're the only person who has ever given me a pound of nuts in my whole life!' And then I remembered my happy young years and that poor little boy playing barefoot in the backyard, and my heart was stirred and I said, 'You're a grateful young man, for in all this time you've never forgotten that pound of nuts I brought you when you were a little child.' And I embraced him and gave him my blessing and I started to cry. He laughed, but later he wept too. But Russians often laugh when it would be more appropriate to cry. But he wept too, I saw it . . . And now, alas . . ."

"I weep even now, German, even now, you dear old man!" Mitya suddenly shouted from his seat.

Be that as it may, Dr. Herzenstube's little story produced a wave of sympathy for Mitya among the public.

A much more important impression, favorable to Mitya, was produced by Katerina's evidence, which I am about to describe. In general, when they started calling in the witnesses for the defense, fortune suddenly seemed to smile on Mitya, remarkably enough, to the surprise of the defense counsel himself. But even before Katerina was called to the stand, Alyosha was questioned and reported a fact that seemed to deal a crushing blow to one of the most important points raised by the prosecution.

CHAPTER 4

Things Look Up for Mitya

It all happened quite unexpectedly, even for Alyosha. He did not testify under oath, and I remember very well the sympathy and consideration with which both sides treated him. It was obvious that his good reputation had preceded him. Alyosha testified modestly and with restraint, but his anxious concern for his unhappy brother was obvious throughout. From his answers to the various questions that were asked him, a picture gradually emerged of his older brother as a man swayed by passions, a man of a violent temperament, but at the same time honorable, proud, and generous, prepared even to sacrifice himself if the circumstances demanded it. He conceded that, in the days just preceding the crime, his brother had been in an unbearable state of tension because of his passion for Grushenka and his rivalry with his father. But Alyosha indignantly rejected the suggestion that Mitya could have killed for the sake of the money, although he readily conceded that the three thousand rubles had become an obsession with him, that he regarded the sum as rightfully his, as part of his inheritance from his mother that his father had misappropriated, and that, while not in the least avaricious, Mitya could not hear the three thousand mentioned without flying into a completely disproportionate rage. As to the rivalry between "the two ladies," as the prosecutor referred to Grushenka and Katerina, Alyosha answered very evasively and even left a couple of questions unanswered altogether.

"Did your brother tell you that he planned to kill his father?" the prosecutor asked him at one point, adding: "You needn't answer this question if you don't wish to."

"Not directly," Alyosha said.

"Did he tell you indirectly then?"

"He told me about his deep-seated hatred for his father and he said he was afraid that . . . that he might find it unendurable at some moment . . . that his loathing would perhaps get the better of him, and then he could kill him . . ."

"And did you believe him when he told you that?"

"I'm afraid I did. But I was always convinced that, if such a critical moment did come, he would be saved from doing it by the nobler side of his character. And that is exactly what happened, for it was *not he* who killed my father," Alyosha declared in a loud, firm voice that resounded throughout the hall.

The counsel for the defense started like a battle-horse at the sound of a trumpet.

"Let me assure you, first of all, that I have implicit faith in your sincerity and I am sure that it is not impaired or affected by your love for your unfortunate brother. We are already aware of your personal opinion about the tragic event from your deposition during the preliminary investigation. I may tell you that it is an extremely personal opinion that goes against all the evidence gathered by the prosecution. And because of this, I feel I will have to insist that you answer the following question: 'What is the basis for your absolute belief in your brother's innocence and in the guilt of another person, whom you named at the preliminary investigation?' "

"At the preliminary investigation I answered the questions that were put to me," Alyosha said in a quiet, calm tone, "but I never volunteered an accusation against Smerdyakov spontaneously."

"Nevertheless, you did accuse him, didn't you?"

"I was basing myself on what Dmitry had told me. Even before I was questioned then, I had been told what had happened when he was arrested and how he had accused Smerdyakov. I am absolutely convinced that my brother is innocent. And since he didn't do it, it must have been . . ."

"Smerdyakov, right? But why precisely Smerdyakov? And what makes you so convinced of your brother's innocence?"

"I couldn't not believe Dmitry. I knew he wouldn't lie to me. I could tell by his face that he was telling the truth."

"You could tell by his face! Is that all you have to go on, then?"

"I have no other proof."

"And your accusation against Smerdyakov is also based only on what your brother told you and on his facial expression while telling you."

"That's right—I have no other proof."

At this point the prosecutor declared that he was through

with the witness. Alyosha's answers seemed to have disappointed the expectations of the public. People in town had been talking about Smerdyakov even before the trial; there were all sorts of rumors about him, various hints at the role he might have played in the sordid story, and some people believed that Alyosha had gathered facts that would point to the lackey's involvement and thus help Dmitry. But now they saw he had nothing to go on except his own private conviction of the accused's innocence, quite a common feeling for a brother.

But then the witness was taken over by Fetyukovich. He started by asking Alyosha when exactly the accused had told him about his hatred for his father and his intention to kill him, and whether he had repeated it again during their last meeting before the catastrophe. As he started to answer, Alyosha suddenly gave a start, as though he had just remembered and understood something.

"I've just remembered something that had quite slipped my mind," he said, "but then, at the time, I didn't grasp its meaning and it is only now that . . ."

And Alyosha told, very excitedly, like someone who unexpectedly sees clearly something that has been obscure to him until then, how during their last meeting Mitya had struck his breast—"the upper part of his breast"—saying that he had there what was necessary for him to restore his honor.

"At the time I thought that he was talking about his heart," Alyosha said, "that he could find in his heart enough strength to escape some horrible disgrace of which he could not tell even me. I must admit that, at the time, I thought his gesture indicated his horror at the thought that he might do violence to his father, but I realize now that he was indicating something he had on his chest. I recall how it struck me that it was not at all in the area of the heart that he was striking himself, it was considerably higher and more in the middle, in fact, just under his neck. Again and again he pointed at that spot. I dismissed my observation as silly and irrelevant, but now I think he may really have been pointing at the fifteen hundred rubles sewn in the rag that he carried around his neck!"

"Right!" Mitya shouted from his place. "It's true, Alyosha, it was the money that I was smiting with my fist!"

Fetyukovich hurried back to his client, begging him to calm down, and then at once latched on to what Alyosha had just said. Alyosha, excited by his recollection, expressed the opinion that the disgrace Mitya had had in mind lay in the fact that, although he had the fifteen hundred rubles on him and could give it back to Katerina, nevertheless he had decided not to return it and, instead, to use the money to take Grushenka away, if she was willing to go with him.

"That's it! That's exactly what it was!" Alyosha cried in tremendous excitement. "My brother said that half of the disgrace—he repeated the word 'half' several times—could be removed at once, but that he didn't do it because of his wretched weakness of character, and he knew in advance that it would be beyond his strength to do it later . . ."

"And you remember clearly that it was on that spot on his breast that the accused struck himself?" Fetyukovich continued to press him.

"Absolutely clearly and unmistakably, because I remember wondering why he was striking himself so high, when the heart was much lower. But I thought I was being stupid . . . so the question just flashed through my mind . . . In fact, I can't understand why I didn't think of it until now! He was indicating that rag, to show that, although he had the fifteen hundred rubles, he wouldn't give it back. And after that, when they arrested him in Mokroye, I understand he declared that he considered the most disgraceful thing in his life the fact that, while he had the money to pay Katerina back one half of what he owed her—he specified 'one half'— and thus not to be an outright thief in her eyes, he preferred to become just that rather than to part with the money. And ah, how that debt weighed on him!" Alyosha exclaimed finally.

Obviously, the prosecutor insisted on re-examining the witness and he asked Alyosha to describe the scene to him again and made him repeat several times that the accused was actually indicating something definite on his chest, rather than just pounding himself with his fist.

"Not just with his fist, he pointed at it with his finger too, here, very high up . . . I don't understand how it could have slipped my mind until this minute!"

When the presiding judge asked the accused to comment on this latest testimony, Mitya confirmed everything, said that he had, indeed, been pointing at the fifteen hundred rubles he had hidden under his shirt, that he had felt disgraced by it, "a disgrace I will not deny now, the most contemptible act of my whole life."

"I could have returned that money, but I didn't do it," Mitya cried. "I preferred to remain a thief in her eyes. And the worst of it is that I knew in advance that I wouldn't pay her back! Alyosha has everything right! Thank you, Alyosha!"

And that was the end of Alyosha's testimony. The most important point made was that, at long last, there was at least something that indicated, something that could be considered as a kind of proof, that the fifteen hundred rubles sewn in a rag, which the accused claimed to have carried around his neck, had really existed and that he had not just invented it during the preliminary investigation in Mokroye. Alyosha was pleased; very flushed, he went back to the place assigned to him, repeating to himself: "How could I have forgotten that! It's really incredible that it should have come back to me only now!"

Then it was Katerina's turn to testify. Her very appearance caused a great stir. The ladies turned their lorgnettes and opera glasses on her; some of the men leaped to their feet to get a better look at her. Later, everybody agreed that Mitya turned as white as a sheet as soon as she appeared. Dressed in black, she stepped forward modestly, almost shyly, to the witness stand. Her inner emotions were not reflected in her expression, although her dark, sultry eyes glowed with determination. Many agreed later that she was stunningly beautiful at that moment. She spoke in a quiet but very clear voice and her words could be understood in every corner of the courtroom. She expressed herself with great calm, or at least forced herself to sound calm and detached. The presiding judge started to question her very cautiously, showing great consideration for the witness's feelings and trying to avoid touching "certain chords" that might be particularly painful to her in her great unhappiness. But she herself declared, in the process of answering one of the first questions, that she had been engaged to the accused until the time when he had broken their engagement. And when asked about the three thousand rubles she had given Mitya to send to her relatives in Moscow, she said that she had not asked him to send the money right away, but, that, being aware that he needed money, she had given it to him, telling him that he could send it off any time within a month . . .

"There was really no reason for him to reproach himself and feel so miserable about that debt later . . ."

I won't go into all the questions that were asked her or all the answers she gave, but will content myself with conveying the gist of her testimony.

"I was always convinced that he would send my relatives the three thousand rubles as soon as he got that money from his father," she testified further. "There was never any doubt in my mind about his being completely disinterested and honorable . . . He is a man of scrupulous honesty . . . in money matters. He felt certain that he would receive three thousand rubles from his father and he told me so repeatedly. I knew that he had serious differences with his father and I always believed that his father had taken undue advantage of him. I cannot recall his ever making any threatening remarks about his father. In my presence, at least, he never made any such threats concerning his father's life. If he had come to me then, I would certainly have put his mind at rest about that wretched three thousand, but he never came to see me anymore. And I myself, I—I was not in a position to take the initiative and ask him to come. Besides, I had no right whatsoever to be so demanding of him about that debt because, once," she said with a determined note in her voice, "I had borrowed money from him myself and it was more than three thousand, and I did so although I was not sure at the time when I would be able to pay him back . . ."

There was a strange challenge in her tone when she had said this. Just at that juncture Fetyukovich's turn to question her came.

"That sum you borrowed from my client—you didn't borrow it here in this town. It happened elsewhere, when you first met him. Is that right?" Fetyukovich started cautiously, sensing that there was something in his favor here that he could explore.

It must be noted here parenthetically that, although Katerina was partly responsible for Fetyukovich's coming all the way from Petersburg to defend Mitya, she had never told him about the five thousand rubles Mitya had lent her once and about her "prostrating" herself before him. She had hidden that fact from him, and the strangest thing about it was that, up to the very last second, she herself did not know whether she would or would not recount that episode in court, as if uncertain whether she would be in a state to do so.

Oh, I shall never be able to forget those moments! She started to tell the story, and she told *everything*, the whole story that Mitya had told Alyosha, including her deep grati-

tude and her "prostration" before him; in explaining why she
had needed the money, she told of her father's troubles and
of her going to Mitya's lodgings . . . But she never even
hinted that it had been on Mitya's initiative that she had
gone and that he had suggested to her sister that, if Katerina
wanted the money, she should come for it in person. Concealing all that, she said that it was on her own impulse that
she ran to the young officer's lodgings, hoping somehow that
she would be able to convince him to lend her the money.

It was an absolutely stunning spectacle! Cold shivers ran
down my spine as I listened to her. The courtroom was completely quiet. Everyone was anxious to catch every word she
uttered. This was something unprecedented, something absolutely astounding, even for a strong-willed, proud, and
haughty person like her, for who could have expected such
a complete confession and self-indictment! And in the name
of what did she do it? Simply to help the man who had
betrayed her and wronged her, only to try to create a
favorable impression of his character! And, indeed, she did
create the image of a young officer who readily gave away his
last five thousand and who then refused to take advantage
of an innocent young girl. Yes, it showed Mitya as a warm
and decent man but . . . but my heart contracted when I
heard her tell it! I felt that it could have awful consequences
later, such as slander, and, alas, that is indeed what eventually
came out of it!

Later, some people remarked with malicious chuckles that
Katerina's story might not be quite accurate, particularly the
part where the army officer was supposed to have let the
young girl go home with the money and a respectful bow.
Some felt that something had been left out at that point.
And some of our most respectable ladies remarked that,
"even if nothing was left out," they were still none too
certain that this was the proper way for a nice young lady
to act, even if saving her father depended on it. I don't see
how Katerina, with her intelligence and her almost morbid
sensitivity, could have failed to foresee that people would
say just such things. Indeed, I'm certain she did foresee it but
decided to go ahead anyway!

It is true that all the mud slinging started only much later,
for, at first, everyone was immensely impressed by her reve-
lations. As to the members of the court, they listened to
Katerina's deposition in an awed, almost self-conscious silence. The prosecutor did not allow himself to press her any

further on the subject and Fetyukovich bowed deeply to her. Oh, he felt quite exultant internally, so much had been gained by that testimony! It would obviously be inconsistent for a man who was capable of making a generous gesture and giving away his last five thousand rubles on the spur of the moment to kill his own father in the middle of the night in order to rob him of three thousand! Fetyukovich felt that now, at least, he could dispose of the charge of theft against Mitya. The "case" now appeared in quite a new light. There was a sudden wave of sympathy for Mitya.

As to Mitya himself, they say that two or three times during Katerina's testimony, he leapt to his feet, then sank back into his chair again, and sat listening to her with his face buried in his hands; when she had finished, he cried out in a quivering voice, his arms stretched out toward her:

"Why have you done this to me, Katya. You've ruined me!" And for a few seconds his sobs resounded throughout the whole courtroom. But he quickly regained possession of himself and shouted: "Now I am doomed!"

Then he sort of froze in his seat, with his teeth clenched and his arms folded tightly across his chest.

Katerina remained in the courtroom, sitting in the chair that had been assigned to her. She was pale and sat with her eyes cast down. Those sitting near her said later that she trembled all the time, as if in a bout of fever.

After her, it was Grushenka's turn to testify.

I am now coming to the catastrophe that struck suddenly and may actually have sealed Mitya's doom. For I am certain, and so are all the jurists, that, without this, the accused would at least have been given the benefit of mitigating circumstances. But we shall come to that a little later, for first we must say a couple of words about Grushenka.

She, too, came dressed all in black, with her magnificent shawl on her shoulders. She walked in with her gliding, noiseless step, swaying slightly, as statuesque women sometimes do. As she approached the witness stand, she kept her eyes fixed on the presiding judge and glanced neither right nor left. I thought she looked strikingly beautiful and that she was not in the least pale, as some ladies claimed later. People also said that her expression was strained and malicious. I can only assume that she was irritated by the insulting curiosity with which she was stared at by all those people, so eager for gossip and scandal. She had a proud nature, and was one of those who, as soon as they become aware of anybody's lack of respect, flare up in anger and are eager to strike back. And, on top of that, there was also a certain shyness about her, of which she was ashamed. So it is hardly surprising that her tone was uneven—one moment angry, the next scornful or deliberately rude, and then suddenly showing a sincere, heartfelt note of self-accusation and self-condemnation. At other moments, she spoke as if she felt she were plunging into an abyss, as if she had made up her mind to speak her piece, whatever the consequences. When asked about her relations with Fyodor Karamazov, she answered impatiently: "It was nothing at all. And, anyway, what could I do if he kept badgering me?" But a minute or so later she declared: "It is all my fault, because I was leading them on, both of them, the old man and him, and it was I who put them in that state. So I'm really the one to be blamed for what happened." When Samsonov's name came up, she snapped with arrogant defiance: "That's nobody's business! He was good to me and took me in when my own family had kicked me out of the house and I was running about barefoot." And when the presiding judge reminded her, as courteously as he could, that she was just to answer the questions without going into unnecessary details, Grushenka blushed and her eyes flashed.

When asked about the money Fyodor Karamazov had prepared for her, she said she had never seen it and had only heard from "the murderer" that there was an envelope with three thousand rubles in it. "But I just laughed, because I had no intention whatsoever of going there, in any case . . ."

"You used the word 'murderer' just now. I would like to know who you were referring to?" the prosecutor asked her.

"To the lackey who killed his master and who hanged himself yesterday—to Smerdyakov," Grushenka explained.

Obviously, she was at once asked what grounds she had for such a categorical accusation and, of course, she had no grounds.

"Dmitry Karamazov told me that, and you must believe him. It was that woman who ruined him. She brought it all on, and that's the truth!" Grushenka added in a voice filled with hatred.

She was again asked to whom she was referring.

"To that young lady, Katerina Verkhovtsev, who once invited me to visit her and tried to win me over by offering me a cup of chocolate. The trouble with her is that she's so shameless . . ."

The presiding judge interrupted her with a stern warning to moderate her language, but Grushenka's jealousy was ablaze now and she no longer cared what the consequence of her words might be—she was ready for the plunge.

"When the accused was arrested in Mokroye," the prosecutor said, "many witnesses saw you run out of the other room and cry out that you were to blame for everything and that you would go to Siberia with the accused. Does this not indicate that, at that moment, you, too, were convinced that he had killed his father?"

"I don't remember what I thought then," Grushenka replied. "Everyone was shouting that he was the murderer and I felt that, if he had killed his father, he must have done it because of me. But the moment he said he hadn't done it, I believed him at once, and I still believe him, because he isn't the kind of man who would lie about it."

When Fetyukovich's turn came to question her, I remember his asking her about Rakitin and about her paying him twenty-five rubles "to bring Alexei Karamazov to your house."

"There was nothing so unusual in his taking money from me," Grushenka said, smiling in contemptuous disgust. "He often came to ask me for money. Many times I would give him as much as thirty rubles in the course of a month, and he'd spend it on all sorts of fancies, because he had enough for his board and lodging without what he got from me."

"But why were you so generous to Mr. Rakitin?" Fetyukovich pursued this line of questioning, although the presiding judge was stirring disapprovingly in his chair.

"Why, he's my first cousin, of course—our mothers are sisters. Only he asked me not to tell that to anyone around here. He was much too ashamed of it."

This revelation came as a complete surprise to everybody, for no one in the town or in the monastery had ever heard of it, not even Mitya. I was later told that Rakitin's face turned almost purple with shame. Before her arrival at the courthouse, Grushenka had somehow heard that Rakitin's testimony had been highly unfavorable to Mitya and she had become furious. And so the impression created by Rakitin's whole noble speech, with its indignant attacks on the institution of serfdom and the present lack of civil rights in Russia, was now completely spoiled in the eyes of the public. Fetyukovich was very pleased—his luck seemed to be holding out. Grushenka was not kept long on the witness stand because she obviously had nothing particular to add to the available evidence. The impression she had made on the public was a quite unpleasant one. Hundreds of scornful glances accompanied her to the seat assigned to her, which was quite far from Katerina's. While she was being questioned, Mitya kept silent, his eyes fixed on the ground, as if he had been turned to stone.

The next witness to be called was Ivan Karamazov.

CHAPTER 5

Sudden Disaster

Originally Ivan had been scheduled to testify before Alyosha. But the bailiff had informed the presiding judge that, owing to a sudden illness or an attack of some sort, the witness could not appear in court at that time but would be at the disposal of the judge as soon as his state of health permitted. Somehow, however, no one in the audience seems to have heard this announcement when it was made and they learned of Ivan's illness only later. When he did appear, nobody noticed him at first. The most important witnesses, it was generally felt, had already been questioned and the public's curiosity was, for the time being, satisfied. As a matter of fact, the public seemed a little tired: they still had to hear several witnesses, who probably would be unable to add any new information since everything seemed to have been pretty well covered already, and time was passing.

Ivan came in very, very slowly, his head down, and not looking at anyone, as though he were trying hard to work something out. His brow was knit in concentration. He was immaculately groomed and dressed, but his face made me, at least, think he looked sick; it was grayish, rather like the face of a dying man. When he finally raised his eyes and his look slowly swept the courtroom, I was struck by the opaque dullness of those eyes, and I remember that Alyosha, making as if to jump up, let out a moan: "Ah!" I remember it clearly, but I don't think many other people noticed it.

The presiding judge reminded Ivan that he was not testifying under oath and was free to answer or not to answer questions, but that, of course, whatever he said must be true to the best of his knowledge, etc., etc. Ivan listened, staring at the presiding judge with his lusterless eyes. But gradually his face began to relax into a smile and, as the face of the magistrate, who was still talking, expressed considerable surprise, Ivan suddenly burst out laughing.

"Well, what else?" he asked in a loud voice.

The room grew completely quiet. Something seemed to be in the air. The presiding judge was obviously worried.

"Perhaps you still don't feel very well?" he inquired and started searching with his eyes for the bailiff.

"Please don't worry, Your Honor. I feel quite well and I believe I have something quite interesting to tell you," Ivan answered, now very calm and deferent.

"Do you have something special to say?"

The presiding judge still sounded distrustful. Ivan lowered his eyes, waited for a few moments, and then looked up again and said with a sort of stammer:

"No-o . . . n-nothing special, n-nothing . . ."

They started questioning him then and he answered with apparent reluctance, with exaggerated brevity and unconcealed distaste that seemed to increase as the questioning went on, although his answers were clear and to the point. There were also a number of questions to which he said he could not give the answers because he did not know them. He knew nothing, for instance, about the accounts between his father and Dmitry. "I wasn't interested," he said. He had heard the accused threaten to kill his father, and he had heard from Smerdyakov about the money.

"It's the same thing all over again," he suddenly said, looking very tired. "There's nothing new that I can tell the court."

"I can see that you're not well and I understand your feelings . . ." the presiding judge said and then, turning to the prosecutor and the counsel for the defense, he asked them to examine the witness only if they thought it might be really helpful. But Ivan said in an exhausted voice:

"Please allow me to be excused, Your Honor. I feel very ill."

Having said this, Ivan, without waiting for the judge's permission, got up and started to walk away from the witness stand. But after a few steps, he stopped, seemed to think for a second, smiled quietly, and returned to the witness stand.

"I suppose I'm just like that peasant lass in the song, Your Honor, who says, 'If I fancy—I get up; if I don't fancy, I don't get up.' They follow her about with her wedding dress, to take her to the church to get married. But she just keeps repeating, 'If I fancy, I get up; if I don't . . .' I don't remember which part of the country that song comes from but . . ."

"What are you trying to say by that?" the presiding judge asked sternly.

"This is what," Ivan said and suddenly took a bundle of bills out of his pocket. "Here's the money . . . I mean the money that was in that envelope over there." He motioned with his head to the table on which the exhibits lay. "It was for the sake of this money that my father was killed. What shall I do with it? Here, bailiff, would you take care of it, please?"

The bailiff went over to Ivan, took the money, and handed it to the presiding judge.

"How do you come to have this money, if, indeed, it is the same money?" the presiding judge asked in great surprise.

"It was given to me yesterday by Smerdyakov, the murderer," Ivan said. "I saw him just before he hanged himself. It was he who killed my father, and not Dmitry. Smerdyakov killed him on my instructions . . . Why, is there anyone who doesn't wish his father's death?"

"Are you in your right mind?" The question slipped from the judge's lips.

"Yes, I am very much in my right mind, and that's the trouble, because my right mind is just as vile as yours and anyone else's—because just look at all those mugs!" Ivan cried, glaring around at the public. "A father has been killed and they pretend they're shocked!" he snarled with immense loathing. "They're putting it all on for each other's benefit. The liars! They all long for their father's death, because one beast devours another . . . If it were proved here that no parricide had been committed, they would be angry and would leave terribly disappointed . . . A circus! That's what they want, bread and circuses! But I myself, I haven't got so much to brag about either! Do you have any water here? Give me a drink, for heaven's sake!"

Ivan suddenly seized his head in his hands.

The bailiff moved quickly toward him and Alyosha shouted, "Don't believe what he's saying. He's sick and feverish!" Katerina rose from her seat, staring at Ivan in horror. Mitya stood up, looking intently at his brother with a strange, wild, contorted smile.

"Don't worry, I'm not a madman. I'm just an ordinary murderer!" Ivan said. "And you have no right, really, to demand eloquence from a murderer," he added unexpectedly, his mouth twisting as he laughed.

The prosecutor, who was obviously at a loss, hurried over to the presiding judge and stood there whispering something to him. The three judges started a sort of whispered conference. Fetyukovich listened intently, ready to act. The entire courtroom waited in dead silence.

Within seconds, though, the presiding judge seemed to come to himself. He said to Ivan:

"Your words are inadmissible in court and quite incomprehensible. So please calm down and try to explain what you have on your mind, if you really have anything to tell us. What do you have to offer as proof of the confession you have just made? Assuming, of course, that you were not raving when you made that confession."

"Well, that's just the trouble—I have no witnesses. That dog Smerdyakov won't send you his corroboration from the other world . . . in an envelope. No, I have no witnesses, except for one, perhaps," Ivan added with a dreamy smile.

"Who is that witness?"

"He has a tail, Your Honor, and I'm afraid you won't consider him acceptable in court. *Le diable n'existe point!* Don't pay any attention, he's nothing but an ordinary, petty devil." Ivan suddenly stopped grinning and spoke in a confidential tone. "He's probably somewhere around, perhaps under that table with the exhibits on it, for where else could he be sitting, if not there? You know, when I told him that I refused to remain silent, he tried to switch the conversation to geological upheavals and all that sort of nonsense! Well, go ahead, free the monster. He has started singing his hymn now, because he feels so elated about it! He's just like that drunken pig, hollering at the top of his voice, 'Vanya, Vanya went to town . . .' but I, for my part, would give a quadrillion quadrillions for two seconds of happiness . . . You don't know me! Oh, how stupidly you have arranged everything: go ahead then, take me instead of him! For, otherwise, what was the point of my coming here? But why, why must everything be so stupid?"

And again he looked around the room slowly and dreamily. But the whole place was in a commotion now. Alyosha had jumped up and was trying to get to him, but the bailiff had already seized Ivan by the arm.

"What's going on?" Ivan shouted, staring into the bailiff's face, and all of a sudden he seized the man by the shoulders and, full of rage, hurled him to the floor. The guards were all over him and held on to him tightly. Ivan let out a terrifying scream, and he continued to scream, inhumanly and inarticulately, as he was carried out.

Utter confusion followed. I cannot remember in proper order what happened then, because I myself was terribly agitated and was in no state to observe developments properly. I can only say that later, when order had been restored and everyone, calming down, realized what had happened, the presiding judge reprimanded the bailiff, despite the man's assurances that, before appearing on the stand, the witness had been in a completely normal state, that he had been seen by the doctor an hour earlier, when he had felt slightly nauseated, that, before appearing in court, he had spoken quite coherently, so that it had been really quite impossible to anticipate that he would behave in such a manner in court, especially since he himself had been very anxious to testify.

But before order had been completely restored and the public had recovered from this scene, it was followed by another no less dramatic one: Katerina in hysterics. She shrieked shrilly, burst into sobs, refused to leave, pushed away the guards who tried to seize her, implored them not to remove her, and then, turning to the presiding judge, cried out:

"I have one more thing to tell, I must tell it, I must! Here's a document, a letter—take it, read it at once! Hurry, it's a letter from that monster," she pointed at Mitya. "It was he who killed his father and in this letter he writes me that he's about to kill him! But the other one, his brother, he's sick, he's delirious. I know he's been delirious for three days now!"

And she kept shrieking, beside herself, until the bailiff took the letter from her and gave it to the presiding judge. Then she sank into her chair, buried her face in her hands, and sobbed noiselessly and convulsively, suppressing the moans that tried to escape her, so that they would not make her leave the courtroom. The letter she had handed in was the one Mitya had written her from the Capital City Inn, which Ivan had referred to as the "mathematical" proof of Mitya's guilt. And, alas, this letter was recognized as such by Mitya's judges too; it is very likely that, without it, Mitya would have escaped his doom, or at least that the verdict would not have been so crushing. I repeat, it was very hard for me to follow all the developments in order, and, even today, the whole scene is still very confused in my mind. I believe the presiding judge at once communicated this new piece of evidence to the associate judges, to the prosecutor and the defense counsel, and then to the jurors. I remember, though, that Katerina was called back to the stand and the first question the presiding judge asked her, in a very gentle voice, was: "Are you feeling all right now?" Her impulsive answer was, "I'm ready, I'm ready! I'm perfectly capable of answering your questions!" Her tone showed that she was still terribly afraid that, for some reason or other, they might refuse to listen to her. Then she was asked to explain in greater detail the circumstances under which that letter had been written and received.

"I received it the day before the crime was committed, and it was written the previous day in a tavern. You can see for yourself that it was written on somebody's bill!" she cried, almost out of breath. "He hated me at that moment, because he himself had acted outrageously, running after that creature . . . and because he owed me that three thousand rubles . . . Oh, he felt insulted by the fact that he owed me the three thousand, because it made him realize how contemptible he was himself! I'll tell you the story behind that money now, and I beg you, I beseech you, to hear me out to the end! One morning—it was three weeks before he killed his father—he came to see me. I knew he needed money and I knew what he needed it for: it was to entice that creature to go away with him. Even then, I was well aware that he had betrayed me and was planning to break with me altogether. Knowing all that, I offered him the money under the pretext that I wanted to send it to my sister in Moscow. As I handed it to him, I looked into his eyes and told him that he could send it at any time that was convenient for him, even in a month if he wanted to. He cannot possibly not have understood that; it was just as if I were telling him straight to his face: 'So you need money to betray me with that creature? All right, here's some. I'm giving it to you myself. Take it, if you're so completely without honor!' I wanted him to see for himself what sort of person he was, and, indeed, he took the money and spent it with that creature in that place, in one single night . . . But, believe me, he realized very well that I knew everything, and also that I was testing him by offering him that money—to see whether he so completely lacked any sense of honor as to accept it. I looked into his eyes and he looked into mine, and I saw he understood everything and took it nevertheless. He pocketed the money and left!"

"That's right, Katya!" Mitya suddenly screamed. "I looked into your eyes and knew you were trying to disgrace me, but I still took the money! Despise me, everybody. I have deserved your scorn!"

"One more word and I'll have you removed!" the presiding judge warned Mitya in a loud voice.

"That money kept weighing on him," Katerina continued anxiously. "He would have liked to pay it back to me, but he needed it too badly, for that creature. And then he killed his father, but still didn't pay me the money back. Instead, he left with her for Mokroye, where he was arrested. And once again he squandered the money there that he had stolen from his father after he killed him. And the day before he killed his father, he wrote me that letter, wrote it in a drunken state, as I at once realized, wrote it out of sheer viciousness, because he knew I would never show it to anyone, whether he went through with the murder or not. If he had thought I would show it, he wouldn't have written it. He knew I wouldn't want to avenge myself on him and ruin him! But please, please, read it slowly and carefully and you'll see that he describes everything in advance—how he'll kill his father and where he'll find the money his father was hiding. And I want you to note the sentence where he writes: 'I'll kill him provided Ivan leaves.' Doesn't that prove he'd worked out in advance how he'd go about the murder?" Katerina pleaded maliciously with the court, and it was plain that she had studied and knew every word, every implication, of that fateful letter. "If he hadn't been so drunk, he wouldn't have written it!" she cried. "But look, see for yourselves, it tells you everything in advance, and when he actually did kill his father, he followed it point by point—it contains his whole program!"

It was obvious that she no longer cared what consequences her testimony might have for herself, although she must have visualized them earlier, for during the previous month she had often asked herself whether she should not, after all, reveal the letter at the trial, and she had shuddered with rage as she imagined the scene. And now she felt as if she had leaped into an abyss. I remember that it was at that juncture that the letter was read aloud in court by the clerk; the public was horribly shocked.

Mitya was then asked whether he recognized the letter.

"Yes, I wrote it, I wrote it. I was drunk, otherwise I wouldn't have written it! There were many things that made us hate each other, Katya, but I swear to you, I loved you while I hated you, but you did not love me!"

He collapsed back into his chair, wringing his hands in despair.

The prosecutor and the defense counsel questioned Katerina, mostly in an attempt to find out why she had concealed such an important piece of evidence until then and why her attitude toward the accused had been so different during her previous testimony.

"Yes, yes, I lied before. I lied, ignoring conscience and honor, trying to save him at any cost, because he hated and despised me!" Katya cried hysterically. "Oh yes, he despised me horribly. He always had, ever since the time I prostrated myself at his feet to thank him for that money, at the very beginning . . . I saw it . . . I felt it as soon as I did it, but I didn't want to believe it was true. So many times I have read in his eyes: 'Remember, it was you who came to me first, on your own initiative, after all.' Ah, he never, never understood then what had made me come to him, for a man like that can only suspect the most despicable motives in other people! He judged others by himself; he thought everyone was like him!" Katerina screamed furiously, losing all control of herself. "And he only became engaged to me because of the money I inherited. Yes, that's all, and I always suspected as much! Oh, he's an animal! He was convinced that all my life I'd be ashamed to look him in the face, because I had come to him that time, and that that would make it possible for him to despise me and dominate me for the rest of his life! And that's why he wanted to marry me! Yes, that's true, absolutely true, and although I tried to win him over by my love, my limitless love—I was even willing to forgive him his betrayal—he didn't understand anything at all! Besides, how could he understand anything? He's a monster! I only received the letter the next evening, when they brought it to me from the Capital City Inn, but on the morning of the day they brought it to me, I was still prepared to forgive him everything, even his betrayal!"

Of course, the presiding judge and the prosecutor tried to calm her, and I'm sure they felt rather embarrassed at taking advantage of her hysterical outburst to hear her confession. I remember them saying something like, "We appreciate how painful this is for you," and, "Please believe us—we understand how you feel." Nevertheless, they extracted all the statements they needed, from a woman in hysterics. And in the end she described, with the great clarity that often appears at moments of highest nervous tension, how Ivan Karamazov had almost driven himself insane during the past two months, in his desire to save "that monster and murderer who happens to be his brother."

"He kept tormenting himself terribly," she said. "He tried to reduce his brother's guilt by admitting to me that he himself disliked his father and that he, too, probably wished for his death. Oh, he is a man of deep, deep scruples! His conscience makes him suffer atrociously! He confided all these thoughts to me when he came to see me, for he came to my house every day, as I was his only friend. Yes, I am proud and greatly honored to be his only friend!" she shouted challengingly, her eyes flashing. "He did go to see Smerdyakov twice. He told me: 'If Dmitry did not kill him, it must have been Smerdyakov'—for somehow a stupid story had got around that Smerdyakov had done it—'and if it was Smerdyakov,' Ivan Karamazov told me, 'then I am really the one to blame, because Smerdyakov knew I didn't like father, and he may have decided I wanted him killed.' It was then that I showed him this letter, and it convinced him altogether that it was his brother who had done it, and it drove him completely out of his mind. He couldn't bear the idea that his own brother was a parricide! A week ago I saw that the thought was oppressing him so much that it had made him ill. During the past few days he would suddenly start raving while he was sitting and talking to me at my house. I saw he was going out of his mind. He raved even as he walked through the streets. I asked the doctor who came here from Moscow for the trial to examine him, and he did so, two days ago. He told me that Ivan was on the verge of a breakdown, and all because of that monster, that horrible brother of his! Yesterday, when he learned of Smerdyakov's death, he was so shocked by the news that it did, in fact, drive him insane . . . And to think that it was all the fault of the monster he was so desperately anxious to save!"

Obviously, it is possible to speak and to confess in this way only once in a lifetime, when facing death, for instance, when mounting the scaffold. But then, such an explosion was very much in character for Katerina; this is how she spontaneously reacted at such a dramatic moment. This was the same

impulsive Katya who had hurried to the lodgings of the
young rake to save her father's honor, the same young woman
who, proud and chaste, had earlier been willing to forget
her feminine modesty before the public, in order to tell of
Mitya's generosity, because it would, she hoped then, help
him with the jury. And, in the same way now, she was
willing to sacrifice herself and everything else for another
man, perhaps for the first time realizing how precious that
other man had become to her! She sacrificed herself because she thought he would ruin himself by claiming that he,
rather than his brother, was guilty of his father's death, and
she was prepared to do anything to save his name and his
reputation!

And yet there was a horrible possibility: Wasn't she lying
now, in describing her former relations with Mitya? That
was the question. No, no, she was not slandering him deliberately when she said he despised her for having prostrated
herself at his feet once upon a time! She believed it herself;
ever since then, she had been convinced that the simple-hearted
Mitya, who adored her at the time, actually despised her. And
it was only out of pride that she responded to his feelings
for her with love, a hysterical, twisted love made up of
offended pride, a love that resembled revenge more than love.
It is quite possible that, eventually, her twisted love would
have turned into a real love; perhaps there was nothing in
the world Katya wanted more, but then Mitya insulted her
deeply by preferring another woman to her, and she could
never forgive him that. Suddenly she was overwhelmed by a
longing for revenge. It had been accumulating for a long
time, pressing painfully on her, and now, all of a sudden, it
exploded and she immolated both Mitya and herself!

As might have been expected, no sooner had she spoken
out than the pressure broke and she was crushed by shame.
She had another fit of hysterics: she fell to the ground,
sobbing and screaming. They carried her out of the courtroom. While Katerina was being carried out, Grushenka
jumped to her feet and, with a shout of agony, rushed to
Mitya so impetuously that they could not stop her in time.

"Mitya!" Grushenka shouted at the top of her voice. "She's
ruined you, that viper of yours! Ah, she's finally shown her
true face!" she shrieked, shaking with fury and glaring at
the judges.

The presiding judge made a sign. The guards seized Grushenka and attempted to lead her out. She fought them off, trying to get back to Mitya. Mitya roared wildly and tried to rush to her, but the guards overpowered him.

I feel pretty certain that the spectators, the ladies especially, were quite satisfied with the spectacle: it was, indeed, a choice one.

After that, I remember the Moscow doctor being called back to the stand. I believe that, even before that, the presiding judge had given instructions that Ivan Karamazov was to receive the necessary medical help. The doctor declared that Ivan was suffering from an extremely critical attack of brain fever and that he ought to be taken home at once. When pressed both by the prosecutor and the defense counsel, the doctor confirmed that Ivan Karamazov had come to consult him two days previously, that he had warned him that the threat of a brain fever attack was imminent, but that the patient had refused to be treated.

"Even then, he was definitely not in full possession of his mental faculties, for he admitted to me that he had hallucinations while walking about, that he met various persons who were dead in the street, and that Satan came to visit him every evening."

Having completed his testimony, the celebrated doctor left. The letter presented by Katerina was added to the exhibits.

After a brief conference among the judges, they ordered that Ivan's testimony, as well as Katerina's unscheduled additional evidence, be entered in the record and that the trial be resumed.

But I shall not describe the questioning of the rest of the witnesses. Anyway, their testimony merely confirmed that of those who had preceded them on the stand, although each witness presented his evidence from his own characteristic point of view. But, as I have said before, all these views will be combined and arranged in the prosecutor's summation, to which we shall now come. The audience was excited, electrified by the scenes and the outbursts that had just taken place, and they were anxiously awaiting the conclusion of the show—the summations of the prosecutor and the defense counsel, and then the verdict.

Fetyukovich had been visibly shaken by Katerina's second appearance on the witness stand. The prosecutor, on the other hand, was exultant. After the last witness had testified, the court was adjourned for an hour and then, at last, the presiding judge called upon the prosecutor and the counsel for the defense to present their summations.

I believe it was exactly 8 p.m. when our prosecutor began his speech.

CHAPTER 6

The Public Prosecutor's Speech. Psychological Portrayals

As he began his speech, the prosecutor was trembling nervously. A cold and sickly sweat broke out on his forehead and on his temples. Hot and cold waves flooded his body in turns. He admitted it himself later. He expected this speech to be his chef d'oeuvre, the masterpiece of his whole life, and also his swan song. And indeed, since he was to die of galloping consumption within nine months, he would have had the right to liken his speech to a swan song had he really known how close his death was. He put all his heart and intelligence into that oration, and he proved to the world that he had in him an unexpected awareness of civic problems and of the great philosophical issues, at least insofar as our poor public prosecutor could cope with these matters. The main strength of his speech, though, lay in its sincerity. He was absolutely convinced of the guilt of the accused and was not simply trying to prove him guilty because that was his role and function; since he felt he was pleading for the just punishment of a culprit, he was eager to "protect society." Even the ladies in the audience, who were on the whole hostile to the prosecutor, had to concede that he made his point most impressively. He began in a cracked, faltering voice, which became firmer and firmer as he went on, until soon it resounded throughout the courtroom, filling it, to the end of the speech. But the moment he had finished, he almost fainted.

"Gentlemen of the jury," the prosecutor began, "this case has created a sensation throughout Russia. But why? What is there so special about it? Why should it stir up such amazement and horror in us, who have seen everything and have become used to everything? Well, that is just what is so terrible about it: such horrible things have ceased to horrify us today. And what we must fear above all is our growing general tolerance of crime, rather than this or that criminal act committed by an individual. What is the reason for our indifference, for our strangely mild reaction to certain crimes that are the signs of the times and that promise us an extremely unenviable future? Are we to look for it in our cynicism or in the premature exhaustion of the intellect and the imagination of our still very young, yet already decrepit, society? Does it lie in the weakening of our moral principles or simply, perhaps, in a lack of such principles? I cannot answer these questions, disturbing though they are. I can only say that every citizen ought to—indeed, must—concern himself with them. Our newspapers, though still inexperienced, have already rendered a considerable service to society, for, without them, we would never have learned so fully about the horrors of unbridled license and moral degradation; instances of such behavior are reported in their pages, and are read by everyone, not only those who attend the public trials that have been instituted in our country by the judicial reform of the current regime. What sort of things do we read almost every day now? Well, there are many crimes beside which the crime we are concerned with here pales and begins to look like something quite usual. But the worst of it is that many of our Russian criminal cases indicate a certain state of mind in our society, a sort of general calamity that has taken root among us and that we find more and more difficult to resist as it becomes an omnipresent evil.

"In one case, a dashing young army officer, belonging to our highest society, a young man just setting out on his life and career, cuts the throats of some minor official and of a maid-servant who just happens to be there. He commits these heinous, cowardly crimes in cold blood, without scruple or hesitation, in order to steal back his own IOU's from the man, who had been helping him, and, while he is at it, he steals some ready cash as well. Why, the young officer feels that the money might come in useful for social occasions and in promoting his career. And he leaves the scene of the crime after placing a pillow under the head of each of his victims . . . Or take the case of a young hero, decorated many times for bravery, who kills the mother of his benefactor in a highway robbery, after having assured his accomplices that 'she loves me as if I were her own son, so she'll follow my advice and take no precautions for her safety.' Granted, this man is a monster, but I no longer dare assert that his is an exceptional case nowadays. And there are many who, although they have not actually murdered anyone, still think and feel in the same way and, deep down, are just as dishonest. Perhaps, when alone with their consciences, they may ask themselves: 'What does honor really mean? Isn't the idea that shedding blood is wrong just another prejudice?'

"Some may cry out in indignation at what I have just said and say that I am a sick and hysterical person, that I am exaggerating monstrously, slandering our people, and raving. I wish I were. I would be only too happy if it were so! Oh, do not believe me, think that I am sick, but please remember this: even if only one tenth or one twentieth of what I say is true, even that is dreadful enough! And also, gentlemen, consider the ease with which young people shoot themselves these days. Oh, unlike Hamlet, they do not worry about 'the dread of something after death,' as if the entire preoccupation with the soul and what will happen to it after death had long since been erased from their minds and covered over with sand.

"And now, look at the debauchery among us, at our sensualists. Fyodor Karamazov, the unhappy victim in this murder trial, is an innocent babe compared with some. And yet we all knew him—'for among us he lived,' as the poet said . . . Yes, perhaps some day the greatest intellects in this country and in Europe will devote themselves to the study of Russian criminal psychology, for the subject is certainly worth while. But such a study will be conducted later, at leisure, seen with greater detachment, and analyzed more intelligently than I can do today, for instance. But now we are either horrified at what we see or we pretend we are horrified, while in reality we relish the spectacle, as connoisseurs of strong and eccentric sensations that rouse us from our cynical and lazy apathy; or else we are like little children who wave off frightening apparitions, bury their faces in their pillows, and wait until the frightening phantoms are gone, so that they can quickly forget them in their games and cheerful laughter. But there comes a moment when we, too, must face our reality soberly and thoughtfully, examine both ourselves and our society, and try to understand the problems facing this society of ours, or at least come to grips with those problems. A great writer of the preceding generation, Gogol, in the finale to his greatest work, *Dead Souls,* compares Russia to a galloping troika streaking toward an unknown destination, and exclaims: 'Oh troika, oh bird-like troika! Who invented you?' and then he proudly adds that other nations, filled with awe, step out of the way of the Russian troika, as it gallops ahead at a mad rate. Well, it is true, gentlemen, so let them get out of the way, either with or without awe, but in my humble opinion the great writer finished his novel in that way, either in a fit of childish sentimentality or simply to placate the censors of his time, for, if his own heroes Sobakevich, Nozdrev, and Chichikov had been harnessed to his troika, such horses would not get anywhere, whoever held the reins! And bad as those horses were, those of our generation are infinitely worse!"

At this point applause interrupted the prosecutor. His "liberal" views on Gogol's troika had a wide appeal. It is true that the clapping was very brief, so that the presiding judge did not even have to threaten "to clear the courtroom" and only glared sternly at those who had applauded. The prosecutor, however, felt greatly heartened, for he had never been applauded before. They had refused to listen to him for so many years, and it was only now that, for the first time, he was being given the opportunity to speak his mind before the whole of Russia.

"Indeed," he went on, "let us have a look, now, at the Karamazov family, whose sad fame has suddenly spread through all Russia. I may be exaggerating, but I believe I can recognize certain of the basic elements in our contemporary educated classes, in the picture that emerges from the close study we have had to make of this charming family. Oh, not all the elements, by any means, but a few, and in a microscopic view, like a picture of the sun in a droplet of water . . . Let us first glance at the hapless, licentious, and depraved old man, that *pater familias* who ended his life so lamentably. He, a hereditary member of the gentry, started his career as a ragged hanger-on, then, by an unexpected piece of luck, married a wife with a dowry, and thus got hold of a little capital with which to operate. And so this petty crook, this servile buffoon, despite the fact that he was born with quite considerable intellectual endowments, became, primarily, a usurer. With the years, his capital grew and he became more and more self-assured. His humility and servility vanished, and what was left was a sneering cynic and sensualist. Those spiritual needs he may have had evaporated completely, while his appetite for life expanded. It became so great that he saw nothing in life except the pleasures of the flesh, and that is how he brought up his sons. He never felt any of the moral duties of a father: his children were brought up in his backyard, and he was delighted when someone was willing to take them away. And soon he forgot about them altogether. His whole mentality can be summed up in the words: '*Après moi le déluge.*' All this is just the opposite of what a citizen should be; it is total isolation—I would even say a deliberately hostile isolation—from society, an attitude that may be summed up thus: 'Let the rest of the world go up in flames as long as I am fine.' And he does feel fine and is eager to go on living for another twenty or thirty years. He cheats his own son of his mother's inheritance and uses the money to seduce that son's mistress. No, I have no intention of leaving to the talented defense counsel from Petersburg the defense of the accused; I will speak the whole truth myself, for I understand fully the resentment that the father had sown in the heart of the accused. But that is enough about that wretched old man, who has received his just deserts. Let us only bear in mind that he was one of our contemporary fathers, and I hope the public will not be too offended if I suggest that there are many such fathers today. For there are many like him, alas, although they do not express themselves as cynically as he did, because they are better bred and more polished. But deep down, their philosophy of life is very much like his. All right, let us assume that I am overpessimistic; we have already agreed that you will make allowances for that. So let us make a further agreement: you don't have to believe me. I will keep talking, but there is no need for you to take my word for anything. Nevertheless, allow me to have my say, for it is possible that you may remember some of my words.

"And now let us have a look at the children of this 'head of a family.' One of them is before you, in the dock, the accused, and I will speak of him at greater length later, but first I would like to say a few words about the others. The elder of the two is a modern young gentleman, highly educated and endowed with a fairly powerful intelligence, but he already believes in nothing, and, just like his father, has discarded too much in life, and sneers at it. We have all heard him speak. When he came here, he was well received in our society. He did not try to hide his views, just the contrary, and this enables me to speak boldly of him, not as a private individual, of course, but as a member of the Karamazov family.

"Yesterday, on the outskirts of this town, a sick, epileptic idiot died by his own hand. He was Smerdyakov, a former servant of Fyodor Karamazov's and perhaps his illegitimate son, who had also been strongly implicated in the murder.

Well, during the preliminary investigation, this Smerdyakov told me, in hysterical tears, how much Ivan Karamazov had frightened him with his talk of the absence of moral restraints. 'Mr. Ivan says,' he told me, 'that everything is permitted in the world, that from now on nothing is forbidden—yes, that's what Mr. Ivan told me.' It would appear, therefore, that this poor idiot was driven out of his senses by that thesis, although I admit that both his falling sickness and the terrible catastrophe in the house also played a part in his breakdown. But this idiot somehow made a very curious observation, one that would have done honor to an infinitely more intelligent observer, and that is why I have brought him in now: 'Of all the sons,' he said, 'the one who is the most like my master is Mr. Ivan.' And with this observation, I will conclude this character sketch, for I feel it would be tactless in me to pursue it any further. Oh, I have no wish to draw final conclusions and prophesy disaster for that young man. That would be to croak like a raven. We all saw this morning, in court, that the spontaneous force of truth is still alive in his young heart, that the feeling of brotherly attachment has not been smothered by his skepticism and moral cynicism, which he acquired more from his father than from working things out for himself by painful searching.

"Then there is the youngest son, who is still a youth, a pious and humble young man, whose views are just the opposite of his brother's gloomy vision of decay. This young man is trying to latch on to the 'national principle,' or whatever is meant by that obscure phrase in the dark recesses of our theorizing intelligentsia. He, you see, tied himself to the monastery and almost became a monk. I believe that, unconsciously and very early in life, he felt a meek despair, such as is experienced by many among us, who, fearing the cynicism and depravity that they mistakenly consider a European influence, look for salvation in 'their native soil,' like small children rushing into the arms of their ailing mother, where they hope to be able to sleep, perhaps sleep throughout their entire lives, just so as not to see the sights that horrify them! As far as I am concerned, I wish all the best to that good and talented young man. I hope that his youthful idealism and his fascination with the fundamental beliefs of the uneducated Russian masses will not turn some day, as it so often does, into a gloomy mysticism in his moral outlook and an obtuse chauvinism in his political stand—two positions that present an even greater threat to our nation than the precocious corruption, resulting from overfeeding on the unearned and misinterpreted fruits of European enlightenment, that afflicts his elder brother."

The words "mysticism" and "chauvinism" again elicited some applause for the prosecutor, although he had obviously, in his excitement, strayed a bit far afield from the case at hand. But then, this embittered and consumptive man had felt an irresistible urge to have his say, at least once in his life. People said later that, in his portrayal of Ivan, the prosecutor was motivated, to some extent, by personal resentment, which was quite improper in the present circumstances. They said that Ivan had bested him in a couple of arguments in front of many witnesses, and now the prosecutor was avenging himself. I am not sure whether such an accusation is entirely fair. In any case, thus far, what he had said was simply an introduction. Only after this did his speech deal with the business at hand.

"Now we come to the eldest son of this modern family," the prosecutor went on, "who is here, sitting in the dock, before you. We know about his life and we know what he did, since it has now all been opened up to public scrutiny. Unlike his brothers, one of whom represents the 'Western' and the other the 'Russian national' principle, Dmitry Karamazov represents Russia directly, as it is today, although he certainly does not represent all of modern Russia—God forbid that he should! Nevertheless, she is all there, our old mother Russia; we can smell her! Oh, like him, we are such a spontaneous, sincere people; we are such an amazing mixture of good and evil; we love enlightenment and Schiller, but we also love to rage and storm in taverns and to tear out the beards of our drunken drinking companions. Oh, we can behave in a 'beautiful and sublime' way, provided we are in the right mood! Indeed, we are even obsessed—yes, obsessed—with the most noble ideals, if, that is, we happen to stumble on such ideals by chance, if they fall into our laps from the sky, and as long as we don't have to pay for them. In general, we hate to pay for anything and we love to receive things for nothing—that goes for everything. Oh, just give us everything, everything that is good in life—for we won't settle for less—and, above all, do not interfere in any way with our habits, our way of life, and our impulses, and then we shall prove to you that we can be good and beautiful and sublime. We are not avaricious, no, but you must give us lots and lots of money, and then you will see how generous we are, and you will be able to admire the scorn with which we scatter the despicable metal to the winds in wild, unrestrained revelry! And if you don't give us money, we'll show you that we can get it anyhow, if we want it badly enough . . .

"But I shall come to that later, for I want the events to unfold before you step by step, in proper order. First, we have before us a poor little boy, abandoned in the backyard, without shoes, as we were told by a shocked witness, a highly esteemed townsman of ours, a man, alas, of foreign extraction. I repeat again: I yield to no one the right to defend the accused, for I am both accuser and defender! Yes, we, too, are human beings, and we, too, can appreciate the effect the first memories and impressions in the family 'nest' can have upon the formation of a man's character . . .

"Next, we see the little boy grown into a youth, then into a young officer and gentleman. For his wild behavior and his dueling, they send him off to a regiment stationed in a remote garrison town on one of the borders of our vast Russia. There he serves his country and there he leads an even wilder and more extravagant life. And, of course, the wilder the life, the higher the cost. And so he needs money, more and more of it. Well, after lengthy haggling with his father, they reach an agreement that he is entitled to six thousand rubles more, as a final settlement of the inheritance left him by his mother, and he receives that sum. Please note that there exists a document in which he practically renounces all further claims and, with this six thousand rubles, his argument with his father over the inheritance ends. At this moment, the young officer meets a young lady of high intelligence and high moral standards. Oh, I do not wish to go into the details of their relations. You have heard them here; they involve honor and self-sacrifice, and I won't say any more. We had a glimpse of that irresponsible and wayward young man subdued by true nobility of feeling and higher ideals, and a spark of sympathy for him was lighted in our hearts. But shortly after that, in this same courtroom, we were also shown the other side of the coin. Again, I do not feel I have the right to make guesses and assumptions or to offer my analysis of how such a reversal of testimony took place. But there certainly were good reasons for it. The same young lady, her eyes now filled with the tears of indignation that had been suppressed for so long, told us that he was the first to despise her for her spontaneous, perhaps reckless, but certainly high-minded and generous, impulse. He was the first on whose face she detected that sarcastic little smile, and he, the man she was to marry, was the only person on whose face she could not bear to see it. Although she was well aware that he was deceiving her (being fully convinced that now she would have to bear everything, including even his faithlessness), she nevertheless put three thousand rubles at his disposal, letting him understand quite clearly that she was offering him this money to betray her with. 'Will you be so cynical as to accept it?' her intent, scrutinizing eyes asked him. He met her look and understood perfectly what she was thinking (why, he admitted here in court that he had understood everything), but he went on and took that three thousand and squandered it all in two days, on a wild spree with his new mistress. So what are we to believe? The first legend about the impulse of this noble man who gives away his last penny and who admires the young lady's virtue? Or the obverse side of the coin, that is so revolting? Usually, in life, the truth lies between the two extremes. But, in this case, this rule definitely does not apply. Most probably, he was absolutely sincere in his generous impulse in the first instance, and just as sincere in his villainy in the second. And why is this so? Well, precisely because we are in the presence of one of these wide-ranging natures, the Karamazov nature, that can accommodate simultaneously the most contradictory traits and the two infinities—the infinite heights of the most noble ideals and the infinite depths of the lowest festering degradation. And that is what I am leading up to. Let me remind you of a brilliant thought expressed here earlier by Mr. Rakitin, a young observer who had observed the Karamazov family at very close quarters: 'The feeling of degradation is as indispensable to these unbridled and unrestrained natures as the sense of supreme nobility.' And this is very true; what they need is that unnatural combination, and they need it all the time, unceasingly. The two infinities, gentlemen, they need the two infinities at the very same moment, and without them they are unhappy and frustrated, they feel that their life is not complete. Ah, the breadth of our natures is as wide as our mother Russia, and it can contain everything; everything can coexist within us!

"Since the three thousand rubles has been mentioned now, I will allow myself to anticipate a little at this point. Can you conceive, gentlemen, that, having obtained money in such a shameful, degrading, and humiliating way, a man like the accused could, on the very day he had got hold of the money, set half the sum aside and sew it up in a rag, and then have the firmness of character to carry it around his neck for a whole month, despite all temptations to spend it and despite his urgent need for money? Neither during his drunken orgies nor when he had to rush out of town to look, God knows where, for the money he needed to take his beloved away from the temptations of his rival, his own father, could he bring himself to touch the little bag he carried around his neck! If only not to let his beloved succumb to the old man of whom he was so madly jealous, he would have ripped open the rag, stayed home, and guarded his lady love unceasingly until she finally told him, 'I'm all yours!' and then run away with her, as far as possible from this sinister setting. But no, he would not touch the little bag. And what reasons does he give? His original reason was that, when she finally said to him, 'I'm all yours, take me away from here, wherever you want,' he wanted to have the money to take her away with. But, according to the accused's own admission, he had an even more important reason for not tearing open the rag: 'As long as I have that money on me,' he says he felt, 'I may be a scoundrel but I'm not a thief, because I can always go to the woman I have betrayed, lay the remaining half of the misappropriated sum before her, and say to her, "See, I may have spent half your money and thus shown my weakness and lack of firm principles, shown myself to be, if you wish, a scoundrel" '—I am using the accused's own language—' "but I am, nevertheless, not a thief, for if I were, I would not have returned the remaining half of the money to you, but would have kept it and used it as I had the first half." ' This is the amazing explanation he offers us! We are asked to believe that this violent but weak man, a man who could not resist the temptation of accepting so dishonorably that three thousand rubles, would suddenly become so stoical as to carry fifteen hundred rubles around his neck without allowing himself to touch it! Is this the slightest bit consistent with what we have learned of his character? It is not, and I will take the liberty of telling you what Dmitry Karamazov would really have done if he had somehow decided to sew the money up in that little bag and carry it around his neck. Well, at the very first temptation, for instance, to entertain his new lady love, on whom he had already squandered fifteen hundred rubles, he would have ripped open the rag and taken out, let's say, just one hundred rubles, for why should he return exactly half the original sum—fifteen hundred rubles—to its rightful owner? Wouldn't fourteen hundred do as well? For, couldn't he still tell her: 'See, here I am bringing you back fourteen hundred rubles, so I am a scoundrel but not a thief, for a thief would have kept this too.' Then, a bit later, he would have taken another hundred, then a third and a fourth and so on, and by the end of the month it would be the last hundred but one. He could still reason that, if he brought back even one single hundred-ruble bill, it would be the same thing and he could still tell her, 'Here is your hundred rubles. I have spent twenty-nine hundred of your money, but this one I have brought back to you, because I am no thief, just a scoundrel.' But finally, after the last but one hundred had been spent, he would look at the very last bill and he'd say to himself: 'What's the use of hanging on to this last hundred? I guess I might just as well spend it like the rest!' Yes, that is how the real Dmitry Karamazov, whom we know, would have acted. The whole fiction about the little bag with the hundred-ruble bills in it is as incompatible with the facts as it could be. We could assume anything rather than that. But we shall come back to it."

The prosecutor then summed up the known facts about the financial disputes between Fyodor Karamazov and his son Dmitry and about the personal relations between them, once again pointing out that it was impossible to determine who had been wronged and who had gained in the settlement of the inheritance left by Dmitry's mother. After that, the prosecutor turned to the accused's *idée fixe* about the three thousand rubles he considered his father owed him, and then he spoke of the testimony of the medical experts.

CHAPTER 7

A Chronological Survey

"The medical experts have tried to establish here that the accused is not in his right mind, that he is a maniac. I submit that he *is* in his right mind, but that this only makes things worse. If he were not in his right mind, he might have acted much more intelligently. As to his being a maniac, I would accept this notion, but only in one particular aspect—namely, when it comes to the three thousand rubles that his father allegedly still owed him, just as the medical experts pointed out. It may be possible, however, to find a much more obvious explanation for the accused's excessively emotional attitude toward that money than a predisposition to insanity. Personally, I fully agree with the opinion of the young doctor, who believes that the accused is in complete possession of his mental faculties and that he was simply in a state of excessive resentment and irritation. And this is just the point: the constant frantic irritation of the accused was not actually caused by the three thousand rubles; something else triggered his anger. And that was jealousy!"

Here the prosecutor discussed at great length the accused's fatal passion for Grushenka. He started from the point when the accused went to the lady's house with the intention of "giving her a beating" (the prosecutor said he was using the accused's own words), "but, instead of hitting her, he remained at her feet, and that was the beginning of his love." But, at the same time, the accused's father also noticed the young lady, and it was an amazing and fatal coincidence that these two hearts should have been set afire simultaneously, for although they had both met and known this person before, not until then were they seized by that violent, typically Karamazov passion.

"By her own admission," the prosecutor went on, "she was laughing at both of them. Yes, she suddenly decided to have a bit of fun at their expense—she had not thought of it before, but now she did—and soon she had both of them conquered and lying at her feet. The old man, a money-worshipper, immediately set aside three thousand rubles, which would be hers if she simply paid him a visit at his house, but soon she brought him to a point where he would have been happy to give her his name and all his possessions if only she would agree to become his wife. We have irrefutable evidence on this point.

"As to the accused, his tragic fate is here before our eyes. It was not part of her game to give him any hope, and hope, real hope, was given him only at the last moment when, kneeling before his tormentress, he stretched out his hands to her, covered with the blood of his father and rival. And it was in that posture that he was arrested. 'It was all my fault. I have brought him to this. I am the guiltiest of all. Send me to Siberia with him!' the young woman cried out in sincere repentance when he was arrested. That talented young man, Mr. Rakitin, whom I have already mentioned, characterized that fatal woman in the following few phrases: 'Early disappointment, betrayal, and fall, desertion by the man who seduced her. Then angry eviction by her respectable family, poverty, and finally a rich old protector, whom she still regards as her benefactor. Her young heart, which had perhaps once contained much that was good, was thus very early in life filled with angry resentment. She became calculating, money-hoarding. She became sarcastic and full of vengeful, anti-social feelings.' If you accept this characterization, you will easily understand how she could enjoy herself by wickedly playing the two men against each other.

"And so, in that month of hopeless passion, of moral degradation, of betrayal of the woman to whom he was engaged, after misappropriating the money that had been entrusted to his honor, the accused finds himself on the verge of a frantic explosion provoked by his constant jealousy. And of whom is he jealous? He is jealous of his own father! And what makes it even worse is that the crazy old man is trying to tempt the object of their common passion with the very three thousand rubles that somehow or other the son considers his own rightful inheritance from his mother's estate, out of which, he is convinced, his father has cheated him.

"Yes, I agree, it was a difficult situation to bear and it could have turned the accused into a maniac. But it is not the sum of money itself that matters here—it is the fact that this sum was being used with disgusting cynicism to shatter his dream!"

From here, the prosecutor went on to explain how the idea of parricide gradually gained ground in the mind of the accused, and he retraced it step by step.

"At first, he only shouted about it in taverns and inns. That went on for a month. Oh, he likes company and likes to say out loud anything that comes to his mind, including the most monstrous thoughts, and for some reason, he expects everyone to respond to it all with spontaneous sympathy, to be concerned with his worries and fears, to become furious and tear the tavern to pieces." At this point the prosecutor recounted the incident with retired Captain Snegirev. "Those who saw and heard the accused during that month," he went on, "finally came to realize that there might be more than shouting and empty threats to kill his father here, that, in the frantic state the man was in, his threats could very well be turned to action at any moment."

The prosecutor then related the family meeting at the monastery, mentioned Dmitry's conversation with Alyosha, and told of the ugly scene in the victim's house, when the accused broke in and beat up his father. Then he continued:

"I believe that, until that scene, the accused had not made up his mind to get his father out of his way by killing him. But the idea had occurred to him several times and he had given it some thought; we have evidence on this point both from witnesses' testimony and his own confession. I will admit, however, that, until today, I have hesitated to think that this was a planned and premeditated murder. Although I was fully convinced that he had had a vision of the fatal moment many times before, I thought it was just a vision, just a possibility, but that he had not determined on a definite time or place or means of carrying it out. But that was only until I saw today the fateful piece of evidence presented by Miss Katerina Verkhovtsev. That letter gave, indeed, a full program of the crime. And that is just how she described it, that letter written by the accused while he was in a drunken state. Indeed, the letter proves that the accused had a 'program,' and this stamps his crime as premeditated murder! This letter was written forty-eight hours before the terrible plan was carried out, for in it the accused swore that, if he failed to find the sum he needed the next day, he would kill his father and take the money in the envelope tied with a red ribbon that the old man kept under his pillow, 'provided,' he added, 'Ivan has left town.' Please note that Ivan had to be away, which means that everything had been worked out. And, to be sure, he carried it all out, exactly as planned and described in this letter! Therefore, there can be no doubt about planning and premeditation: he had decided to kill in order to steal the money and we have his written and signed statement to this effect. The accused does not even try to contest his signature. Some may object that he was drunk when he wrote it, but that changes nothing; if anything, it makes it more important: when drunk he wrote something that he had decided when he was sober, for if he had not conceived the idea when he was sober, he would not have written it down when he was drunk. I suppose people may also ask why he went around the taverns shouting his threats, for a man who is premeditating a murder usually keeps it to himself and keeps his affairs a secret. That is true, but when he was shouting it about, he had not yet made any plan or thought it out; it was just wishful thinking then. The idea was maturing in his mind. Later, though, he talked less about it. The evening he wrote that letter, after drinking at the

Capital City Inn, he was unusually quiet, did not play billiards, sat alone without talking to anyone, and only made a local shopkeeper move out of his seat, and that he did almost unthinkingly, out of habit, because when he was in a drinking place, he felt something was missing if he hadn't succeeded in picking a quarrel. It is also a fact that, once he had made up his mind, it must have occurred to the accused that he had been shouting about it all over town far too much and that that might make him look like the perpetrator if he now actually went through with the crime. But what could he do about it? It was too late. He could not undo what he had done. And besides, he had often been in tight spots before and had somehow managed to get out of them, so he hoped it would be the same this time. He was, in fact, just trusting to his luck, gentlemen of the jury! I must also concede that he tried hard to find some other way out, to avoid the gory situation. 'I shall beg everybody to give me three thousand,' he writes in his peculiar language, 'but if people do not give it to me, blood will be shed.' And this again was written when he was drunk but carried out when he was sober."

The prosecutor then described in great detail Mitya's efforts to obtain the money he needed and thus avoid killing his father. He described his offer to Samsonov, his trip out of town in search of the Hound, and documented everything.

"Finally he returns to town, exhausted, hungry, feeling that he has been made a fool of. To go on that fool's errand he had to sell his watch, although allegedly—oh, allegedly!—he had fifteen hundred rubles on him. And, mind you, he left town worried to death that the object of his love would, in his absence, rush to his father. But, thank God, he finds that she has not gone to his father's. Then he sees her off to her protector's house, for, strangely enough, he is not jealous of Samsonov—a very characteristic psychological feature of his affair. After that he returns to his observation post in the back garden, and there he learns that Smerdyakov has had an epileptic seizure and that the other man-servant is sick too. So the field is clear for action and he knows the agreed knocking signals. This is quite a temptation! Nevertheless, he still resists it and goes first to see Mrs. Khokhlakov, one of the most respected citizens in our town. Mrs. Khokhlakov had long felt sorry for him and now she offered him an extremely sensible piece of advice—namely, to quit his debauchery, leave his ugly passion, stop wasting his youthful energy in taverns, and, instead, to go gold-mining in Siberia where, she said, he would find an application for his turbulent energies and his romantic character which so longed for adventure."

After describing the result of the accused's conversation with Mrs. Khokhlakov, the prosecutor recounted how Mitya had learned that Grushenka had not really stayed at Samsonov's and how this exasperated, nervous man had grown frantic at the thought that, since she had deceived him, she might be with his father at that very moment. The prosecutor emphasized the important part played by chance:

"If the maid-servant of his lady love had told him right off that her mistress was in Mokroye with her 'first and rightful' lover, nothing would have happened. But she lost her head in her fear and swore ignorance; she believes that if the accused did not kill her then and there, it was only because he was in too much of a hurry to catch up with her mistress, who had deceived him. But I want you to note this: frantic as he was at that moment, he still snatched up that brass pestle and took it along with him. And why did he choose that pestle rather than any other weapon? For a whole month he had been visualizing the scene of the crime and preparing himself for it, so as soon as he caught sight of something that could be used as a weapon, he picked it up. He had been thinking during the whole month that such an object could be used as a weapon, so he recognized and accepted it as such the very second he saw it! Hence, it cannot be said that he picked up the fatal pestle unconsciously and involuntarily.

"The next thing, he is in his father's garden. The field is clear. There are no witnesses about. It is late at night, it is dark, and he is mad with jealousy. The suspicion that she may be there with his father, in his rival's arms, perhaps laughing at him at this moment, takes his breath away. Besides, he feels this is no longer a matter of mere suspicion. He is now sure she has deceived him and is in there, behind the lighted window, in his father's room, behind the screen. And the wretched man steals up to the window and peers in . . .

"And then he leaves. Quietly and reasonably he hurries away from possible trouble, afraid that something dangerous and immoral might take place . . . This is what they want us to believe, we who understand so well the character of the accused and the state in which he was at that moment, a state clearly revealed by the evidence at our disposal, and, above all, who know that, being aware of the secret knocks, the accused could at any moment have the door opened and be let into the house!"

Here, in connection with the knocking signals, the prosecutor felt he had to leave aside for the moment his account of the crime to dwell at some length on the character of Smerdyakov, in order to put an end once and for all to the unfounded speculations about Smerdyakov's possible role in the murder. He did it very circumstantially and thoroughly. Evidently, despite his professed scorn for the theory of Smerdyakov's guilt, he must have considered it sufficiently important, since he went to such great lengths to dismiss it.

CHAPTER 8

A Treatise on Smerdyakov

"In the first place," the prosecutor began, "what is the origin of this suspicion? The first to accuse Smerdyakov of the murder was the accused himself, the moment he was arrested, and, since that first accusation, to this very minute, he has never been able to offer us a single fact to corroborate his statement, or, indeed, anything that could be humanly considered as a hint of a fact. Now we have only three other persons who agree with this accusation: the accused's two brothers and Miss Svetlov. And even then, the older of the two brothers, Ivan, did not express his suspicion of Smerdyakov until today, when he was obviously feverish and in a state of nervous disorder, for during the past two months we know for fact that he shared the general conviction of his brother's guilt and he never even tried to argue against it. We shall return to this later. As to the youngest brother of the accused, Alexei, he conceded here, earlier today, that he had no facts to back up his hunch concerning Smerdyakov's guilt and was basing himself solely on the accused's words and his facial expression. Yes, that impressive proof was all that the brother of the accused could offer us! As to Miss Svetlov, her argument was perhaps even more impressive: 'It is true,' she assured us, 'since the accused says so, for he is not the sort of man who would tell lies!' This is all the proof we have against Smerdyakov, and it so happens that these accusations all come from persons directly interested in what happens to the accused. Nevertheless, rumors of Smerdyakov's guilt have been circulating and are still in the air, hardly believable or imaginable though that may be!"

Here the prosecutor decided to outline the character of the

late Smerdyakov, who, according to him, had "put an end to
his life in a fit of violent madness." He described Smerdyakov
as a feeble-minded man with some rudiments of education,
confused by certain philosophical ideas that were too much
for his intelligence and frightened by some of the modern
theories about the concept of duty and of one's obligations,
which he had had considerable opportunity to observe in his
master—probably also his father—who openly led a highly
irresponsible life. Smerdyakov had heard of these theories
from his master's son, Ivan Karamazov, with whom he had
had some rather strange conversations on various philosophical subjects. Ivan indulged in these talks, either because he
was bored or because he had a need to make fun of people
and had no better subject than Smerdyakov at hand at the
time. "Smerdyakov himself told me of his mental confusion
during his last days in his master's house," the prosecutor
explained, "but others also testify to it: the accused himself,
Ivan Karamazov, and even the servant Gregory, that is, all
those who knew him closely. And, besides being afflicted with
the falling sickness, Smerdyakov was about as brave as a
chicken, according to the accused. 'He would drag himself to
my feet and kiss them,' the accused told us, before he realized
that such information might be to his disadvantage. 'A chicken
suffering from falling sickness' is how the accused actually
described Smerdyakov, in his own characteristic language.
And the accused himself testified that he had forced Smerdyakov to be his spy and informer by terrorizing him. And in
his capacity as the accused's 'eye,' Smerdyakov betrayed his
master and told the accused of the existence of the envelope
with the money in it and also of the knocking signals that
would enable him to get into the house. But Smerdyakov had
no choice: 'He'd have killed me if I hadn't told him. I could
see right away he'd have killed me!' he declared at the preliminary hearing and he was still trembling all over as he spoke
to us, although by then the man who had terrorized him was
safely under lock and key and could no longer harm him.
'Mr. Dmitry suspected me at every moment and I was trembling with fear all the time; just so he wouldn't be so angry
with me, I hurried to tell him every single thing I knew, so
he'd believe I was being straightforward with him and would
let me stay alive.' Those are Smerdyakov's own words. I have
them written down. 'When he starts shouting at me, I just
drop to my knees before him.' Being a naturally honest young
man and having gained the trust of his master, who had

discerned that honesty when Smerdyakov returned some money he had lost, Smerdyakov, we must assume, was very unhappy at being forced to betray his master, whom he loved as his benefactor. According to psychiatrists of the highest standing, epileptics are inclined to constant, morbid self-condemnation; they are tormented by a feeling of guilt, which is often, of course, quite unfounded, and sometimes go as far as inventing sins and crimes for themselves. Such an individual acts like a really guilty man just out of fear, or because he has been intimidated. Besides, he felt strongly that something evil would result from what was going on before his eyes. When Ivan Karamazov decided to leave for Moscow, Smerdyakov beseeched him to stay, without, however, having the courage to state clearly and precisely what he was afraid of—he was much too timorous for that. He contented himself with hints, but his hints were not understood. I must point out that, in Ivan Karamazov, Smerdyakov saw a defender; he felt sure that, as long as Ivan was there, nothing evil would happen. And please consider this together with what Dmitry Karamazov wrote in his 'drunken' letter, namely, that he would kill the old man provided Ivan had left. So Ivan's presence seemed to be a guarantee of peace and order in the house. Nevertheless, Ivan decides to leave, and almost at once, actually within an hour, Smerdyakov has an epileptic seizure. But this is quite understandable. It should be mentioned that, weighed down by his fears and by a sort of despair, Smerdyakov had, during the last few days, felt himself threatened by an approaching epileptic seizure, for he usually had them when he was in a state of mental strain and shock. It is, of course, impossible to predict exactly the day and time of a fit, but any epileptic will tell you that he can feel when a fit is coming on. This is borne out by medical experience.

"And so, after Ivan's departure, Smerdyakov, who was feeling abandoned and oppressed by his helplessness, had to go down to the cellar for some reason or other; as he descends the steep, narrow stairs, he thinks to himself: 'Will my sickness strike me now or not? And what will happen if it hits me right now?' And then, because of this very fear of a seizure, because he is asking himself these questions, he feels the spasm in his throat that always precedes an attack, and the next thing he knows, he is flying head downward to the bottom of the cellar. And it is on this perfectly natural sequence of events that some people have managed to base their suspicions and to find indications that Smerdyakov *shammed* his seizure! But assuming that he shammed it, what was his motive? What was he hoping to gain by it? Without even bringing in the doctors' depositions—because people may say medicine is often wrong and doctors make mistakes—all right, fine, but I still want to know what Smerdyakov would have gained by feigning an epileptic fit? If he had planned the murder, would he then stage the attack so as to attract everybody's attention to himself?

"Think of this, gentlemen of the jury—on the night of the crime, five persons were present at one time or another in Fyodor Karamazov's house. First, Fyodor Karamazov, but he obviously did not kill himself. Second, his servant Gregory, who himself was almost killed. Third, Gregory's wife Martha, but I would be ashamed even to discuss the possibility of her being the murderer. So that leaves us two people: the accused and Smerdyakov. Now, since the accused assures us that he is not the murderer, it must be Smerdyakov, for there was no one else about who could have done it. And this is where that 'clever' and colossally absurd suspicion of the poor idiot originates! The only reason they suspect him is that they have been unable to unearth anyone else! If there were a shadow of a possibility that someone else—some sixth person—might have been there, I am sure that they would have suspected him instead, for even the accused realizes how utterly absurd it is to suspect Smerdyakov of the murder.

"But let us leave psychology now, let us leave medicine, let us leave even logic itself, and let us turn to the facts, to the facts alone, and see what they have to tell us. Assuming that Smerdyakov killed his master, how did he kill him? Did he do it alone or was the accused his accomplice? Let us first examine the possibility that Smerdyakov did it on his own. But, of course, if he killed his master, he must have had a motive. Now, since Smerdyakov, unlike the accused, had no motives such as hatred, jealousy, and so on, for murdering Fyodor Karamazov, he could have conceivably done it for money, namely, to take the three thousand rubles that he had seen his master put into the envelope. And so, having decided to commit the crime, he goes and reveals all the details about the money to another person—the accused—who, he knows, is extremely interested in that money, and he initiates him into every secret: where the money is hidden, what is written on the envelope, how to knock on the door to be let in—the secret knocking code that would enable him to get inside the house, which is the most important. Why did he tell him all that? Was it to give him in advance the clues as to who committed the crime? Or did Smerdyakov want to have some competition from a man who was very likely to want to appropriate the money himself? You may object that he told him all this out of fear. But that makes no sense, because a man capable of conceiving and then carrying out such a daring and brutal murder would never tell anyone secrets that he alone in the world knew and that no one would ever guess if he just held his tongue. No, cowardly as that man may have been, once he had conceived such a plan, he would never have said a word to anyone, at least about the envelope with the money in it and the knocking signals, because that was tantamount to betraying himself. He would have thought up something or other, if the man had absolutely insisted on having some information, but he would certainly have kept those things to himself! Indeed, had he kept quiet, if only about the money, and then killed his master and taken the money, no one in the world could ever have accused him of murdering for money, because no one but him had seen that money or knew there was such a sum of money in the house. So even if he were suspected of murder, they would look for another motive. But no one would have been able to establish any motive, for everybody knew that he was liked by his master and felt honored by the trust his master had in him. So he would have been the last to be suspected. Instead of falling on him, suspicion would have fallen first on someone who had all the motives, who never concealed them, who went around publicly proclaiming them—in a word, suspicion would have fallen directly on Dmitry Karamazov. So Smerdyakov could have killed and stolen the money, and Dmitry would have been suspected. And this, of course, would have been to Smerdyakov's advantage, too. So why, may I ask, did Smerdyakov have to tell Dmitry Karamazov beforehand both about the money and the secret knocking signals? What was he thinking when he told him that? What was his logic?

"And now comes the day on which Smerdyakov has planned to commit his crime and he throws himself down the cellar stairs and *pretends* he is having an epileptic fit. Why does he do it? Is it so that old Gregory, who intended to take his wife's 'cure,' will postpone it when he sees there is no one to guard the premises and, instead of taking the 'cure,' will stay awake and keep watch? Or did he sham his seizure to put his master even more on his guard and make him even more careful and distrustful, realizing that there was no one to watch out for his son Dmitry, whose coming he so openly feared? Finally, and this is, of course, the most important, was he trying to make them transfer him from the kitchen, where he usually slept, far from anyone else, where there was a door leading into the yard that he could use unnoticed by anyone—transfer him from there to the other end of the servants' quarters and put him into the bed separated from Gregory's and Martha's by a mere partition, only three paces away from them, where they always put him, on their master's orders, when he was disabled by his sickness, so that the kind-hearted couple could look after him? And lying behind that partition, Smerdyakov proceeds, deliberately, to moan loud enough to keep waking up Martha and Gregory—we have their statement to that effect—and he does all this so that he can at some moment get up and quietly kill his master?

"Some may say that he feigned the fit precisely to avoid being suspected of the murder himself, having told the accused about the money and the signals to lure him to come and kill Fyodor Karamazov and hoping to beat him to the money. Was he hoping that Dmitry Karamazov would make enough noise, wake up witnesses, and bring them to the scene of the murder, and then he, Smerdyakov, would get up and follow them (well, he would have to get up then, that couldn't be helped!), go and kill his master for a second time, and steal the money that had already been stolen!

"I see you are laughing, gentlemen of the jury. Believe me, I feel quite embarrassed at voicing such preposterous ideas. But the accused claims this is just what happened. He suggests that, after he had left the house, after he had knocked Gregory out and had alarmed the whole neighborhood, Smerdyakov got out of his bed, walked over to his master's house, killed him, and took the money. To start with, it is really amazing that Smerdyakov could have calculated in advance at exactly what time the crazed, exasperated son of the victim would come, just in order to peer discreetly into the window and then, although he knew the signals that would let him in, quietly withdraw, leaving the prey and the loot to Smerdyakov! But, gentlemen, I ask you seriously now: At what moment is Smerdyakov supposed to have committed the crime? Tell me that first, for if you don't, you have no right to accuse him!

"So let us assume that the epileptic seizure was a genuine one after all. Well, the sick man suddenly regained his senses, heard the shouting, went out, and what? Did he look around and then say to himself: 'Why shouldn't I go and kill the master now?' But how could he know what had been going on in the house while he was lying there unconscious? But I believe, gentlemen, that there should be a limit even to people's fantasies!

"Very good, some subtle observers may object, and what if the two of them acted in concert, what if they murdered him together and shared the money afterward?

"Yes, that sounds like a serious possibility and there seems to be quite an impressive array of facts to support it. We then have a situation in which one of the accomplices does all the work while the other lies in bed feigning an epileptic fit, just so as to arouse everybody's suspicions and put both Gregory and the master on the alert. I would be very curious to know what logic could have guided the two accomplices in thinking up such a crazy plan. It may be objected again that possibly Smerdyakov was not an active, willing accomplice, but a passive and involuntary one; perhaps, under the threats of the accused, he agreed not to interfere with his plans to kill his father and, foreseeing that he would be suspect himself in allowing Dmitry Karamazov to kill his master without calling for help or trying to stop him, Smerdyakov persuaded the accused to allow him to simulate an epileptic fit, while, 'You yourself,' he told him, 'go ahead. Kill him if you wish. It has nothing to do with me!' But if that were the case, the epileptic seizure was bound to cause a commotion in the house and Dmitry Karamazov would never have allowed him to indulge in one! But even if it had happened that way, even so, Dmitry Karamazov would be the murderer and the direct instigator of the crime, while Smerdyakov would be merely an accomplice, and indeed, an involuntary one, since he would have been forced to agree through terror, and that difference would certainly have been taken into account by the court. And what do we find in reality? No sooner was the accused arrested than he tried to put *the whole* blame on Smerdyakov. He never accused him of being merely his accomplice. No, he at once claimed that Smerdyakov had done it all by himself— that he had both killed and taken the money. Where have you ever seen accomplices accusing one another like that? I have never seen such a thing. Now think of this: Karamazov was running a great risk. He was the actual murderer, while Smerdyakov merely connived in it by lying there behind his partition. But then Karamazov tries to blame a man who was lying in bed at the time, knowing full well that he may anger him and make him immediately tell the truth, if only to protect himself—make him reveal that both of them were in on it, but that he himself was not the killer and had simply been too frightened to prevent the other from killing. Smerdyakov would have readily grasped that the court would differentiate between the two of them and that, even if he were to be punished, his punishment would be quite minor compared with that of the main culprit, who was now trying to put all the blame on him. In that case, he would have confessed, because he would have had to. But that is not what happened. Smerdyakov never even hinted at the possibility of such complicity, despite the fact that the accused kept insisting that Smerdyakov was the real and the sole murderer. And, on top of that, Smerdyakov told us during the preliminary investigation that *he* was the one who had informed the accused about the envelope with the money and about the knocking signals and that, otherwise, the accused would not have known anything at all. If he had been an accomplice to the crime, do you imagine that he would have so readily admitted, at the investigation, that the accused had obtained from him all the information he later used to commit the crime? He would certainly have tried to avoid answering those questions and would at least have tried to distort and play down the importance of the information he had given the accused. But he never tried to distort anything or play down its importance. Only a man who is completely innocent and is not afraid of being accused of complicity could act this way. Then, in a fit of morbid depression, caused by the combination of his epilepsy and the terrible disaster that had struck his house, Smerdyakov hanged himself. Before hanging himself, he left a note, which was rather strangely worded: 'I am putting an end to my life of my own free will and no one should be blamed for it.' What would it have cost him to add to that note the words, 'I am the murderer, not Karamazov.' But he did not. If he had sufficient scruples to worry that someone might be blamed for his own death, did he then run out of scruples so completely as to allow an innocent man to be blamed for the death of his former master?

"And what happens next? A short while ago, a witness produced three thousand rubles in cash, claiming that these bills had once been enclosed in the envelope that is one of the exhibits on that table there and that he received the money yesterday from Smerdyakov. But I am sure, gentlemen of the jury, that you can remember for yourselves the sad scene that

followed. And even though I know I do not have to refresh
your memories, I will point out two or three very minor
things, which, just because they are minor, some of you may
not have noticed or, if you did, may have already forgotten.
To start with, the implication is that, yesterday, Smerdyakov,
seized by remorse, returned the money he had stolen and
then hanged himself, because, of course, if he had not been
remorseful he would not have returned the money. And, of
course, it was not until last night that he admitted his guilt to
Ivan Karamazov, as Ivan Karamazov testified himself, for
obviously Ivan would have announced it before, had he
known it. But if he admitted it to the brother of the accused,
why didn't he confirm it in the note he left behind, knowing
that an unjustly accused man was to face a terrible trial on
the following day? For, obviously, money by itself is not a
proof of anything. A week or so ago, for instance, it came to
my notice, and to a couple of other people's as well, that Ivan
Karamazov had sent two five per cent bonds of five thousand
rubles each—which makes ten thousand—to the capital of our
province, to be cashed there. I mention this only to show that
there may be all sorts of reasons for a person to have so much
cash in his possession at one time and that, by producing
three thousand rubles in court, the witness has not convinced
us that they are necessarily the bills from that particular
envelope.

"And finally, last night, after having learned the identity
of the true murderer, Ivan Karamazov calmly went home,
instead of hurrying off at once to report it to the proper
authorities. Why did he put it off until morning? I believe I
have the right to conjecture why: he had been ill for over a
week and had admitted that he was suffering from hallucinations both to the doctor and to persons close to him, telling
them he was seeing the ghosts of dead people. He was on the
verge of the brain fever to which he succumbed completely
after the shock of Smerdyakov's death. And then he suddenly
conceived the following idea: 'The man is dead and now I can
save my brother by shifting the blame for the murder onto
Smerdyakov. Since I have cash at home, I'll take three thousand rubles with me and tell them that Smerdyakov gave me
the money.' You may say that it is dishonorable to slander a
dead man, even in order to save one's brother. You are right,
but then he may have lied without knowing he was lying; he
may have imagined that this really happened, when his mind
became confused under the impact of the news of Smerdya-

kov's death. You witnessed the scene that took place when he was testifying; you could see for yourselves the state in which he was. He could stand on his feet, he could speak, but who knows what was going on inside him?

"And then, following the testimony of this feverish man, we were handed a document—a letter from the accused to Miss Katerina Verkhovtsev, a letter written two days before the murder, a letter containing a detailed program of the forthcoming crime. So what need have we to look any further afield, since we now have the plan underlying the crime and know who its author is? Yes, gentlemen of the jury, everything was carried out 'according to plan,' as they say. The accused did not really hurry dutifully and fearfully away from his father's window, especially as he was convinced his lady love was in there. No, that would be most unlikely and, in this case, completely impossible. He went in and did what he had come to do. Probably he killed in an outburst of rage, his passion inflamed at the mere sight of the face of his hated rival, but after killing him—which he may have done with a single powerful blow of the pestle—and after convincing himself that she was not there, he still did not forget to thrust his hand under the pillow, pull out the envelope with the money in it, and tear it open. And you can see that torn envelope here on the table with the other exhibits.

"I have described all this in the hope that you would notice a fact that I consider extremely revealing. If this were a calculating criminal—someone killing coldly for money—would he have left the torn envelope near the body of the victim where it was found later? Let us assume, for instance, that Smerdyakov had killed his master to rob him, wouldn't he have calmly put the whole envelope in his pocket without bothering to open it while standing over his victim? He certainly would have, because *he knew* the money was there, since it was put there in his presence. And if he had taken the whole envelope, no one would have known that a theft as well as a murder had been committed. Now decide for yourselves, gentlemen of the jury—if Smerdyakov were the murderer, would he have left the envelope lying on the floor when he left? No, the presence of that envelope there indicates that the murderer was a frantic man, a man who was no longer reasoning clearly, a man who might be a killer but who was not a thief, a man who had never stolen before, who now reached for the money that was under the pillow, not as a thief would, but as a man who considered it rightfully his, indeed, was convinced that he was taking it back from the thief who had stolen it from him in the first place—for we know how Dmitry Karamazov felt on this subject and that this money had become a mania with him. When he had hold of the envelope, which he had never seen before, he tore it open to see whether the money was really there, and then rushed off with the money stuffed in his pockets, without giving a thought to the torn envelope. And he acted in that way because he was Dmitry Karamazov and not Smerdyakov, because he did not calculate, and was certainly not in a state to think clearly: he was in too much of a hurry to get away from there!

"So he ran off and climbed the fence, pursued by the screaming Gregory, who managed to catch his foot as he sat astride the fence. So he hit the old man with the brass pestle, knocked him out, and then jumped down from the fence, filled with pity for the old servant. Just imagine, he assured us that he jumped down from the wall because he was sorry for Gregory and wanted to see whether he could not do something for him! A strange moment for a man to show such compassion, wasn't it? No, he jumped down to make sure that the only witness to his crime was dead. Any other concern, any other motivation, on his part, at that particular moment, would have been quite unnatural. Now note this: as he examined Gregory, he wiped away the man's blood with his handkerchief and, once convinced that the old man was dead, he rushed off like a madman, still covered with blood, back to the house of his lady love, apparently without worrying that he would at once attract attention and be arrested. But then the accused told us himself that he hadn't even noticed he was covered with blood, and this we can readily believe, because it is what usually happens with criminals. So, in some respects, he was diabolically calculating, while in others, his mind seems to have been completely blank. At that particular moment, the only thought in his mind was, 'Where is she now?' He had to know at once. That's why he rushed so impatiently to her place, where a most shattering piece of news awaited him: she had left for Mokroye with her first lover, the man to whom, the accused had felt all along, she 'rightfully belonged.'"

CHAPTER 9

Full Steam Ahead into Psychology.
A Galloping Troika.
The Finale of the Prosecutor's Speech

Like many nervous speakers who have to restrain their impatience and a tendency to wander off the subject, our prosecutor favored a chronological method of exposition that offered him a solid framework in which to contain his flights into the irrelevant. But when he reached the point where Grushenka's "first and rightful" lover had to be introduced, the prosecutor indulged in several interesting comments.

"Karamazov, who was madly jealous of everyone else," he said, "all of a sudden bows and yields to the claims on his lady love of this 'first and rightful' lover of hers. And what makes this attitude even stranger is that, until then, he had hardly paid any attention to the threat the new rival presented to his own aspirations. But he had imagined that it was only a far-off, remote threat, and Dmitry Karamazov is, above all, a man who lives entirely in the present. Possibly he even viewed that 'first lover' as a sort of fictional character. Now, however, his aching heart suddenly understood that his lady love had been concealing this new rival from him, had lied to him earlier that day, because the new rival was all too real for her, was not at all a fictional character or a figment of her imagination, but a man in whom she had invested all her hopes. And the moment he understood that, Karamazov resigned himself.

"I cannot pass over in silence, gentlemen of the jury, this sudden change of heart that took place in the accused, a change of which he seemed quite incapable, a sudden hankering after justice, a sudden recognition of the right of this woman to follow her feelings—all these feelings appearing in him just as he stood there, his hands still dripping with his father's blood, that he had shed because of her! It is also true that, at the same moment, the spilt blood was crying out for vengeance, for he was now a man who had lost his soul and his right to live on earth; and he knew that, as of this moment, he was just nothing to the being he loved more than his soul, now that her 'first and rightful' one had come back to her and was prepared to make up to her the harm he had done her and offer her a new and happy life! So what could Karamazov offer her now? He realized this, and he also realized that his crime had closed all roads to him and that he was no longer a man looking forward to life, but a hunted criminal facing punishment. That idea crushed him completely. He at once conceived a mad plan which, with his character, he could not fail to view as the only possible and the fatal way out. His solution was suicide. So the next thing he did was to rush to Mr. Perkhotin, with whom he had left his pistols as security, and, as he ran, he pulled out of his pockets the bills for the sake of which he had stained his hands with his father's blood. Oh, it was money he needed now more than anything else! For Karamazov was about to die, about to shoot himself, and he wanted to mark the occasion, so that everybody would remember it. Why, wasn't he a poet? Wasn't he a man who always burnt his candle at both ends? To see her once more, and to have a feast wilder than anything anyone had ever seen! A crazy party with mad noise, gypsy songs, and wild dances, during which he, Mitya Karamazov, would toast with champagne the newly found happiness of his lady love. And after that, at her feet, he would smash his skull with a bullet and rid himself of his life. Yes, they'd remember Mitya Karamazov, and they would all see how much he loved her!

"There is a great deal of showing off in this, many wild romantic notions, a lot of the typical Karamazov lack of restraint, much sentimentality . . . But there is *something else* in it too, gentlemen of the jury, something that weighs on him, something that nags at his heart and drips deadly poison into it, something that is called *conscience*, gentlemen, a terrible remorse! But he reckoned that a loaded pistol would take care of everything for him. That was the only solution, but it was a solution. I do not know whether Karamazov ever worried about *what would happen in the other world*, or whether this poet and would-be Hamlet was capable of worrying about such things as the *beyond*. No, gentlemen of the jury, in the West they may have their Hamlets, but as yet we have nothing but Karamazovs!"

The prosecutor then dwelt in great detail on Mitya's preparations for the party, first at Perkhotin's, then at the store, and then with the drivers. He quoted many of Mitya's words and phrases, described many of his gestures, all attested to by witnesses, and the picture he drew impressed his audience greatly. What impressed them most was the accumulation of facts. The guilt of this madly agitated man, who was beyond caring what might happen to him, appeared beyond all doubt.

"He no longer had any reason to try to save himself," the prosecutor said; "two or three times he was on the verge of admitting everything; he almost hinted that it was he who had done it without, however, quite saying so," and the prosecutor quoted from the testimony of two or three witnesses. "He even shouted to his driver on the way there: 'You know, you're driving a murderer!' But he couldn't, of course, admit it outright, because he first wanted to get to Mokroye, for it was there that he planned to put an end to his personal poem!

"But what did the unhappy man find in Mokroye? From the very first look he understood that his 'rightful' and undisputed rival might not be so undisputed after all, and perhaps not even rightful either, and that no one expected him to toast them in champagne or to hear his best wishes for new life and happiness. But you already know the facts from the examination of the witnesses, gentlemen of the jury. Karamazov's triumph over his rival was overwhelming. And here began a new phase in his soul, oh, the most painful of all the phases his soul had been through! We may certainly say that outraged nature and the criminal heart were wreaking their own revenge more fully than any man-devised justice could!" the prosecutor exclaimed. "And what's more, man-made justice and punishment really alleviate nature's punishment and are even indispensable for the criminal's soul at such a moment, to save him from despair. For I cannot even imagine the full horror of the mental torments that Karamazov was subjected to when he learned that she really loved him, that she would reject her 'first and rightful' lover for him, that it was with him, Dmitry Karamazov, that she now wanted to start on a new life of happiness, and all this at a moment when everything was ruined and nothing was possible any longer!

"I want to note here something that may be very important to an understanding of the accused's situation at that time. The woman he loved had, up until the very last moment, right up to his very arrest, been inaccessible to him and, although he desired her passionately, she had always been out of his reach. But why, why didn't he shoot himself then? Why did he abandon his decision and even forget where his pistol was? The answer is that he was held back by his ardent yearning for love and his hope to satisfy it then and there. Through the drunken mist of revelry, he clung to his beloved, who was also taking an active part in the feast and who was in his eyes more beautiful and more desirable than ever before. He never left her side; he admired only her; the rest of the world did not exist for him. And this passionate man succeeded in drowning out for a moment, not only his fear of arrest, but even his pangs of guilt. Oh, only for a moment, only for a brief moment! I can imagine the mental state in which the accused was at that time, under the sway of three influences: first, the wild party, with its cries, songs, and dances, reaching him through a drunken mist, and she, next to him, flushed with wine, singing, and dancing, tipsy, laughing and looking at him; second, his wishful thinking that the fatal consequences were still far away, at least that the danger was not yet immediate, that it might take them a day or two yet to catch up with him, and that they certainly would not come to take him until morning, which left him several hours of safety—and that was lots and lots of time! One can think up so many things in a few hours, so many ways out! I imagine that he felt like a man who is being driven to the place of execution and knows that he has to go down a very, very long street and that it will take quite a while, since he is being driven at a slow walking pace past thousands of people. And after that, they will have to turn into still another street and go all the way to the very end of it, for it is only there that the terrible square is where they have erected the gallows! I imagine that, at the beginning, when the procession first starts off, the condemned man, sitting in his cart, must feel that he still has all eternity before him. But then he passes one house after another, his cart moves on and on . . . Oh, never mind, it is still very far to that corner where they will turn into the second street, and, reassured by this thought, the condemned man looks cheerfully to his right and to his left, at all those thousands of curious people who are so unconcerned with what is about to happen to him, and under their fixed stares, he still has the delusion that he is one of them, just another human being. Oh, but here is that corner . . . They turn into the second street, oh! Ah, that's nothing, there's still all the length of that street. And as they again pass house after house, the condemned man keeps thinking that there are still very, very many houses ahead. And this goes on all the time, until they reach the square where the execution is to take place.

"This is how I imagine Karamazov must have felt. 'They can't have found out anything yet, and by the time they do, I'll manage to think up something . . . But now, now . . . ah, she's so beautiful!' Deep down, he feels frightened and bewildered, but he still manages to count off half the sum he has on him and hide it somewhere—for I can find no other explanation of what happened to half the three thousand rubles he had taken a few hours earlier from under his father's pillow.

"It was not the first time the accused had been in Mokroye; he had been there once before and had reveled for two days and nights. He knew that big wooden inn very well, with all its barns, sheds, and verandahs. For I believe he hid a part of the money there shortly before his arrest, stuffed it into some hole, some chink under the floorboards, or in a little corner under the roof. And why did he hide it? That's obvious: disaster could descend on him at any moment after all, and he still hadn't had time to think up a plan of defense, because his head was throbbing and he could not think of anything but *her*. But money, he would need money in any case, for, in order to feel like a man, a man must have money. You may think that it is unlikely that a man like that would be so calculating at such a moment. But let me remind you that he himself tried to assure us that he had, a month earlier, at another moment of crisis, divided three thousand rubles in two and sewn up half the sum in a little bag. And although that is untrue, as we shall prove, it shows that the idea was not alien to Karamazov and that, indeed, it had occurred to him. I would suggest, moreover, that when he later tried to assure the examining magistrate that he had sewn fifteen hundred rubles up in a bag a month before, he was able to invent that story about the little bag so quickly—the little bag that never really existed—precisely because a couple of hours earlier he had taken half the money he had on him and hidden it somewhere in the Mokroye inn until morning, so as not to have it on him, because he had suddenly had a feeling that something might happen after all. Two abysses, gentlemen of the jury, you must remember that Karamazov was capable of contemplating two abysses at the same time! We have searched the house, but have found nothing. Perhaps the money is still there. Perhaps it vanished from there the next day and is now again in the possession of the accused. In any case, when arrested, he was with his lady love; actually he was kneeling before her with his hands stretched out to her, as she lay on the bed, and he was so oblivious of everything else at that moment that he did not even hear those who had come to arrest him. And he had no ready answers—both he and his reason had been taken by surprise.

"Now he is facing his judges, facing the men who will determine his fate. There are moments, gentlemen of the jury, when our duty terrifies us, when we are frightened to face the man whose fate we must decide, when we are afraid for that man! These are the moments when we recognize in the accused the animal terror that seizes him when he realizes that all is lost, although he continues to fight back because his instinct for self-preservation has been aroused. As he is trying to save himself, he looks at you so intently, with such questioning and suffering eyes; he studies your faces and expressions; he tries to guess your thoughts; he tries to anticipate from which side the blow will fall and forms thousands of plans in his throbbing brain, but he is still afraid to talk, afraid to give himself away . . . These are humiliating moments for a man to experience; it is a calvary, it is an animal yearning to escape—it is all so horrible that it makes you shudder and fills you with compassion, for there is compassion for the criminal, even in the investigating magistrate! And, in this case, we all felt it.

"At first he was dumbfounded, terror-stricken, and in his panic he blurted out some highly compromising words and phrases like, 'Blood!' and, 'Serves me right!' But he soon managed to take hold of himself. He had not yet thought out what to say, how to answer our questions, but he was ready for us with his stubborn denial: 'I did not kill my father!' This was his first line of defense, his first barricade, and behind that barricade he hoped to be able to build another where he could make a stand. He started by explaining that his first compromising outcries had referred to Gregory, because he believed he was guilty of Gregory's death—'That, I admit, I am responsible for. But who could have killed father, *since it was not me?* Who could it possibly have been?' You understand, he is asking this of us, of us who have come to ask him that very question! And I want you to note the form of his question, in which the assumption, *'Since* it was not me,' is taken for granted. Note the animal cunning of it, combined with the naivety and the impulsiveness characteristic of a Karamazov. He is telling us he did not kill his father and we should not for a second think that he could have done such a thing, although he goes on to admit that the idea of killing his father had occurred to him and had tempted him. Yes, he admits that at once, urgently, but then adds: 'Although I wanted to kill him, it was not I who killed him.' So he makes a concession to us: he felt like killing his father. This, he believes, will make him seem sincere and make us believe he is telling the truth when he assures us that, nevertheless, he did not do it.

"Oh, in these instances, a criminal often becomes very credulous and thoughtless. And so, as if by chance, he was asked, in the simplest and most direct way, whether it might not have been Smerdyakov. His reaction was just what we had anticipated: he was very annoyed that we should have brought Smerdyakov up before he had and thus caught him off balance. For he had been waiting to bring in Smerdyakov at the moment he felt would be most effective for his defense. And, in keeping with his temperament, he at once went to the opposite extreme and started assuring us that Smerdyakov could not have possibly killed his father, that, indeed, a man like that would be quite incapable of ever killing anyone. But don't believe he was sincere—it was just a trick on his part. He had not given up his plans for implicating Smerdyakov: he would still use him, for there was no one else he could use, but he would do it later, because for the time being that move had been spoiled for him. He might wait to bring in Smerdyakov for a day or two and, when the right moment came, he would exclaim: 'You see, I rejected the possibility of Smerdyakov being the murderer even more strongly than you did, but now I have come around and am convinced that he did it and no one else!' And in the meantime, Karamazov denies with gloomy irritation all involvement in the crime, becomes angry and impatient, and, in his anger, offers us a completely incredible story of how he looked into his father's window and then, quietly and discreetly, withdrew. It is important to note that, at this point, he still knew nothing about Gregory's recovery and about how damaging the old servant's testimony would be.

"He was then searched and examined. The search angered him but also gave him courage, because, with what money there was on him, it was possible to account for only fifteen hundred rubles, and not for the whole three thousand. And it was certainly at this point that he first conceived the story of how the fifteen hundred rubles came out of the little bag in which he had sewn it a month earlier and which he had worn around his neck. Obviously, he was well aware that his story was incredible, for he tried desperately to make it more credible and devised a whole complicated account that seemed, at least to him, quite plausible. In such cases, the main job of the investigators is not to give the suspect a chance to prepare himself, to try and catch him napping, to make him blurt out his most intimate thoughts, which will be revealing in their naivety, improbability, and inconsistency. The way to make a suspect talk is by revealing to him, accidentally as it were, some new fact that is very important in the case, but that he had not suspected until then and could not possibly have foreseen. And we had such a fact ready for him, a fact we had been keeping to ourselves until then. It was Gregory's deposition to the effect that he had noticed that the door of the house leading into the garden was open, the door out of which the accused must have come. He had completely forgotten about that door and it had never occurred to him that Gregory could have seen it. The revelation about the door produced a colossal effect on him. He leaped to his feet and shouted: 'It was Smerdyakov who killed him, it was Smerdyakov!' And so he played his secret card; he produced his basic argument in his defense in its most improbable form, for Smerdyakov could have killed the victim *only after* Karamazov had felled Gregory and escaped over the fence. When we told the accused that Gregory had seen the door open *before* he had been knocked out, indeed, immediately after he had left his room and had heard Smerdyakov moaning behind the partition, the accused appeared to be utterly crushed. My able colleague, the talented examining magistrate Nelyudov, told me later that, at that moment, he felt so immensely sorry for Karamazov that he was almost moved to tears.

"And it was at this juncture that the accused, trying desperately to mend his fences, hurriedly told us about that little bag around his neck, as if to say: 'All right, then, if that's how it is, I'll have to tell you the whole truth now!' I have already explained, gentlemen of the jury, why I consider this story about the money sewn up in the rag a month before to be not only a fabrication, but the most unlikely fabrication that a man could have come up with under the circumstances. I would even bet that no one could have invented anything more incredible if he had tried deliberately. Even a triumphant novelist can be confounded and reduced to ashes by the infinity of details in real life; but people who are forced to make up stories under duress never even think of little, seemingly irrelevant details. They cannot be bothered about these things at such moments, their minds are completely absorbed in creating an overall story and they cannot bear to be interrupted and asked about ins... they get caught.

"You may ask the suspect, where he got the material, or th... was supposedly sewn, and who d... sewed it myself.' 'But what about the... offended at being asked such a trivial... genuinely angry. 'I tore it off an old sh...' Now he gets 'Very good, then, tomorrow I will find am...and becomes with a piece torn off it.' And, of course, ge...,' he says. found such a shirt among his clothes or in his...irts one how could we fail to find it if it existed?—it wou...d we of evidence, something tangible that would have co...for suspect's words. But then he changes his statement:... sure, he now thinks he used an old bonnet of his lan... rather than a piece torn off his own shirt. 'What sort... bonnet was it?' 'I don't know, some piece of old cal... junk . . .' 'Are you sure?' 'No, I'm not sure,' and he loses h... temper. But, I ask you, how could he have forgotten some thing like that, if it had been true? It is the most terrible moments of their lives that people remember best. A man is likely to remember the tiniest details when, for instance, he is being taken to the place of execution: he may forget every thing else, but he will always remember a green roof on which his eyes fell, or a jackdaw sitting on the cross of a tombstone. If he had really sewn up that little bag himself, he would have clearly remembered his humiliating fear that he might be sur prised by someone in the house with the needle in his hands; he would have remembered how, when he heard someone outside the door of his room, he had hurried behind the screen, for there happens to be a screen in his room.

"But why do you think, gentlemen of the jury, that I am bothering to tell you about all sorts of details the accused would have remembered if his story had been true?" the prosecutor suddenly asked in a loud voice. "Well, I'll tell you. It is because, up to this very moment, the accused still main tains that this preposterous explanation of his is true! And now that two months have passed since the fateful night, he still has not been able to offer us one single explanation; he has not added one single fact that would support his fantastic stories; he merely snaps impatiently at us for pestering him with irrelevant and petty details, and demands that we take his word for whatever he wishes to tell us! Oh, we would be only too happy to believe him, we are longing to believe him

...ecause we are not jackals
on nothing but his word of hor... want is one fact, one single
thirsting for human blood! A...used's innocence; we would
fact, that would suggest t...al, tangible fact, not a conclu-
welcome it. But it must ...rtion that when the accused was
sion based on the exp... actually pointing at his little bag
by his brother, or ...sertion made by that same brother—
smiting his breast ...at breast-smiting is supposed to have
with the bills in...rk. As soon as we are given one fact, we
and, mind y...nd will withdraw our accusations; indeed,
taken plac...nce. But as of this moment, justice cries out
will be ...d and we cannot withdraw anything at all."
we will...ator reached the finale of his peroration here.
for ...ever, he demanded dramatically that the son be
...ay for shedding his father's blood "with the base
...f robbery." He pointed to the tragic coincidence of
...lable facts.

...nd whatever you may now hear from the celebrated
...nse counsel, so justly famed for his talents," the prosecutor was unable to refrain from adding, "whatever eloquent
and heartbreaking words are aimed at your emotions, you
must never for a moment forget that you are performing the
sacred duty of administering justice, that you are champions
of the truth and defenders of our holy Russia, of her foundations, of her institution of the family, and of everything that
she holds sacred! Yes, you represent Russia now, and your
verdict will be heard not only in this courtroom, but all over
the country, and all Russia will be either strengthened or let
down by this verdict of yours! So do not let Russia down, do
not disappoint her expectations, for the troika of our fate may
be carrying us headlong to our doom! For many years now,
people in Russia have been wringing their hands beseechingly
and begging us to stop this madly galloping troika. And if
other nations are still getting out of the way of our onrushing
troika, it is not at all out of awe, as the poet would like us
to believe, but simply out of fear, and I want you to note
that. Yes, people draw back because they are afraid, or perhaps because they are horrified and disgusted. Even so, we
are very lucky that they do draw back, for they could decide
to stand their ground and face this streaking apparition like a
solid wall. They would then force the crazy gallop of our
unbridled passions to a stop in the name of their own salvation, in the name of enlightenment and civilization! An

alarmed rumbling of voices has, indeed, already reached us from Europe. And it is growing louder. So do not provoke them, do not cause their hatred for us to grow by acquitting a son who has killed his father!"

In short, although our public prosecutor had let his enthusiasm get the better of him, he did finish his speech with a dramatic flourish which had a tremendous effect on the audience. When he finished, he hurriedly left the courtroom, and as I said earlier, he almost fainted once he was safely out of sight. There was no applause, but the responsible citizens present were very satisfied. The ladies were less pleased with the prosecutor's summation, but even they were duly impressed by his eloquence, especially since they were not in the least worried about the outcome and had complete confidence in Defense Counsel Fetyukovich, who was to speak at last and would, they felt, crush all opposition. Everybody kept glancing at Mitya who, throughout the prosecutor's speech, had sat in silence, his hands tightly clasped, his teeth clenched, his eyes fixed on the ground, only now and then raising his head and listening intently. This he did when the prosecutor mentioned Grushenka and what Rakitin thought of her. At that point, a scornful, disgusted grin twisted Mitya's lips and he muttered quite audibly, "The Bernards!" When the prosecutor described his methods of interrogation and of putting suspects under pressure, which he had applied to Mitya in Mokroye, Mitya looked up, listening to him with great curiosity. Once he seemed about to leap up and shout something, but, making an obvious effort to control himself, he remained seated and merely shrugged scornfully, as if dismissing his accuser. Later, those closing parts of the speech in which the prosecutor related the brilliant stratagems he had used in Mokroye became the target of various jokes in our society: "He couldn't restrain himself," they said. "He had to call people's attention to his talents; he was afraid they would fail to notice them!"

The court was recessed, but only for fifteen or twenty minutes. Some of the spectators engaged in excited discussions interspersed with exclamations. Some of these I still remember.

"A business-like speech," a gentleman in one group said.

"All that psychology—he really drove it in a bit hard!" someone else said.

"But he is right. Everything he said is irrefutably true!"

"He certainly is a past master at that!"

"He summed up the case perfectly."

"And he brought us all into it, too, while summing up!" another voice butted in. "Do you remember his starting off by saying that everybody is just like the late Fyodor Karamazov?"

"But then again, the things he said in the end! He did get rather carried away."

"Yes, and it was not always too clear what he was trying to say."

"Well, so he got carried away, as you say."

"You're being very unfair, sir."

"But no. I admit that it was all very well done. The fellow had waited for this opportunity for such a long time, and now he certainly got it all off his chest. Ha-ha-ha!"

"I wonder what the defense counsel will say now?"

And in another group I heard:

"I don't think it was too smart of him to provoke that Petersburg lawyer by saying that he'd try to appeal to the jury's emotions, do you remember?"

"Yes, it was a rather clumsy move."

"He said it without thinking."

"He's too tense, I think."

"You know, here we are laughing, but just think how the accused must feel about it."

"Yes, I wonder how dear Mitya-boy feels?"

"Let's see what the defense counsel has to say now."

And in a third group:

"Who's that fat lady with the lorgnette? The one sitting over there, at the end of the row?"

"She used to be married to a general. She's divorced now. I know her."

"Oh, so that's why she keeps looking around with her lorgnette!"

"That won't help her!"

"Don't say that, there's a lot to her!"

"Look two seats away from her—you see that little blonde? I'd rather go for that!"

"Say, don't you think it was very clever, the way they caught up with him in Mokroye?"

"Yes, certainly, it was pretty clever, but he told the story all over again. Why, I've heard him tell it in every house I've seen him in!"

"So he couldn't restrain himself here either! The vanity of it!"

"He's an embittered man!"

"And so touchy too . . . Also, he goes in for rhetoric too much, and those long sentences . . ."

"And he keeps trying to scare us. Remember what he said about that troika? And then about their having their Hamlets while we still have only our Karamazovs? That was rather clever, I must say!"

"He's trying to get on good terms with the liberals—he's afraid of them."

"He's afraid of the defense counsel too!"

"Yes, I wonder what Mr. Fetyukovich will have to say?"

"Whatever he says, there's no danger that he'll get through to those thick-headed peasants!"

In a fourth group:

"About that troika—he put it nicely, didn't he, when he said that about the other nations?"

"Yes, and it's true that the other nations won't stand for it."

"Why, what makes you say that?"

"Don't you remember, last week, that member of Parliament in England asking the Foreign Secretary whether the time hadn't come for them to do something about our nihilists, whether they shouldn't teach a lesson to that nation of barbarians—meaning us. That's what the prosecutor was referring to, I know, because I heard him talking about it last week."

"Nonsense, why should we care what those English fools think of us?"

"Why are they fools? And what makes you think they can't do anything?"

"Because all we have to do is to seal off Kronstadt and not let them have any wheat. Where would they get it from then?"

"From America. That's where they get it now."

"Now you're talking nonsense . . ."

The bell rang. Everyone hurried to his seat. Fetyukovich mounted the rostrum.

CHAPTER 10

The Summation of the Defense.
An Argument That Cuts Both Ways

Everything grew completely quiet as the famous orator's first words resounded. The eyes of all the spectators were fastened on him. He started simply, directly, with an air of sincere conviction and without a trace of conceit. He made no attempt at eloquence, at emotional modulations, at pathos, or at dramatic phrasemaking. He sounded like a man trying to explain something to intimate friends. His voice was beautiful—warm and powerful—and in itself conveyed sincerity and frankness. Nevertheless, everyone present felt that if he chose to, the speaker could suddenly raise himself to the summits of true pathos and strike at their hearts with uncanny power. His language was perhaps more colloquial than the prosecutor's, but it was also more precise, and he avoided long and involved sentences. There was one thing in his manner, however, of which the ladies did not approve—that was the way he bent his back. At the beginning of his speech, in particular, it looked as if he were not just bowing to the spectators, but preparing to rush or fly toward them. He obtained that effect by folding his long, thin back roughly in the middle, as if he had a hinge in it that enabled him to keep it bent almost at right angles.

At first, he seemed to skip from one subject to another, as though stumbling on topics at random, without any system. Eventually, however, everything fell neatly into its proper place. His speech can be roughly divided into two parts: first, the refutation of the accusation, during which he sometimes used sarcasm and sometimes malice; and the second part, in which he suddenly changed both his tone and his manner and quickly raised himself to the summits of pathos, and when this happened, the audience responded at once with a quiver of delight, as if they had all been waiting for just that.

He went straight to the point by announcing that, although he usually practiced in Petersburg, he sometimes agreed to go to other towns to defend people of whose innocence he was either certain or at least instinctively convinced.

"And this is just such as case," he said, "for the very first newspaper reports suggested something to me that was very much in favor of the accused. There was a certain legal problem that interested me here, and, although similar problems occur quite often in legal practice, I believe I have never seen this one appear so fully, with all its characteristic aspects, as here. I should really have kept this point for the end of my speech, for my final summation, but I will explain my idea now, at the outset, because I have a weakness for going straight to the point, without trying to save any possible effect for later, without economizing my ammunition. I may be accused of improvidence, but at least no one can say that I am not straightforward. This idea of mine is that, while I concede that the sum total of facts does point to the guilt of the accused, there is not one single fact that could be considered unassailable if taken individually. The more I read and heard about this case, the more this impression was confirmed. And then one day the family of the accused approached me and asked me to handle his defense. I accepted immediately and now I am completely convinced that my first impressions were absolutely correct. I accepted the case in order to destroy that frightening collection of facts by exposing them, one by one, as unproven and far-fetched."

After this introduction, Fetyukovich suddenly exclaimed:

"Gentlemen of the jury, you must remember that I am a stranger here! I have no preconceived ideas, for everything is new to me. The accused, who, I understand, is a violent and unrestrained man, has never had the occasion to offend me, as he may perhaps have offended as many as a hundred people living in this town, thus prejudicing them against him. Of course, I won't argue that the moral indignation against the accused here is not quite justified, because of his reprehensible behavior. I know, nevertheless, that he was received in the houses of members of local society and that, indeed, he was very warmly received in the house of the highly talented prosecutor."

At these words two or three laughs came from among the spectators and, however muffled and quickly suppressed, they were noticed by everyone. It must be pointed out that, although the prosecutor had received Mitya, he had done so against his own wishes. This had been the doing of the prosecutor's wife, a highly respectable but somewhat eccentric and stubborn lady, who had taken an unaccountable interest in Mitya and who liked in some instances, usually quite unimportant ones, to oppose her husband's wishes. Mitya, incidentally, visited their house rather seldom.

"Nevertheless," Fetyukovich went on, "I can conceive that even a man whose judgment is as fair and as detached as that of my distinguished opponent's could conceivably have formed a mistaken and prejudiced opinion of my unfortunate client. Oh, that is quite natural: the poor man deserved to have people prejudiced against him. An offended moral and, even worse, esthetic feeling often produces a most unappeasable resentment. Of course, the brilliant summation of the prosecutor—which gave us a severe analysis of the accused's character and behavior, painted for us a grim picture of the whole situation, and, above all, took us down into such psychological depths, where we could understand for ourselves the essence of the case—could not have been delivered by someone who was in the slightest degree maliciously prejudiced, personally, against the accused, for, in that case, he would have been quite incapable of all those profound insights. But there are certain things that, in such cases, are even worse and even more lethal than a deliberately hostile bias. One such thing, for instance, is what we may describe as an irresistible urge for artistic self-expression, a desire to invent one's own novel, especially, as in this case, when nature has lavished on the speaker such a talent for psychological insight. While I was still in Petersburg, preparing to come here, I was warned—although I was already aware of it myself and didn't need the warning—that I would have to deal with an opponent who had earned a reputation for himself among our young jurists for his profound and subtle psychological insights.

"But, gentlemen, although I acknowledge that psychology is a very profound science, at the same time, I submit that it is a knife that cuts both ways."

At this point there were a few chuckles among the audience.

"I hope you will forgive me this trivial simile," Fetyukovich went on, "because I am not very good at elegant phrasemaking. But let me illustrate what I mean. I will take the first statement from the prosecutor's speech that comes to my mind. It came up during the scene when, in the middle of the night, the accused flees across the garden, climbs the fence, and with a brass pestle knocks down the man-servant, who has caught him by the foot. Then he climbs down again and, for five minutes, fusses over the man he has felled, trying to see whether he has killed him or not. Now the prosecutor absolutely refuses to believe that the accused could have jumped back into the garden out of compassion for old

Gregory. 'No,' the prosecutor declares, and then proceeds to claim something to the effect that such a sentimental impulse must be ruled out at such a moment because it would be unnatural; that he jumped down precisely to find out whether the only witness to the crime was dead or alive; and that this proves that he did commit the crime, because there was no other possible reason why he should jump back into the garden. That is psychology for you! But let us apply the same psychological reasoning in another way and we will find an explanation that is no less convincing. So we have the murderer jumping down from the fence as a precaution, to make sure that the only witness to his crime is dead, although he is a murderer who has left next to the body of his father, whom he has just killed, what the prosecutor himself described as a fatal piece of incriminating evidence, in the form of the envelope that had contained the money. Why, all he had to do, according to the prosecutor, was to take the envelope with him, and no one would ever have known of the existence of that money and, therefore, no one would ever have suspected him of stealing it. This, I repeat, is the prosecutor's own conclusion. So we have here a criminal who does not have enough sense to take the proper precautions and who runs away from the scene of the crime, leaving behind evidence that is bound to incriminate him, but two minutes later, after he has struck and felled another victim, he suddenly is supposed to have become the coolest, the most calculating criminal, just because it suits the argument. But let us assume that everything happened exactly as my opponent described it, for the intricacy of psychology is such that at one moment a man can be as perspicacious and murderous as an eagle in the mountains of the Caucasus, and the next moment become as blind and meek as a poor mole. But then if, murderous, cold, and calculating, a man jumps down from the fence to see whether the only witness is dead or alive, what need is there for him to waste five minutes examining his new victim and thus risk having five more witnesses to his crimes? And why should he soak his handkerchief in the blood of this new victim, thus leaving one more clue that may lead to him? No, if the accused was so ruthless and calculating at that moment, why, once he had jumped down into the garden, didn't he smash the old man's skull with that same pestle and make really sure that the old man was well and truly dead, so that he would have nothing more to worry about on that score? What's more, instead of doing so, the cunning murderer leaves his murder weapon, his pestle, there on the path, the pestle that he had picked up in the presence of two women who would obviously recognize it and testify that he had it! And he didn't just drop it, forget about it; no, he must have actually tossed it away, because it was found on the path about fifteen yards from the spot where Gregory had been felled.

"Well, the question of why he jumped down must be answered precisely as the accused answered it—namely, that he was sorry for the old servant he thought he had killed, and that is why, angry with himself, he tossed away the pestle, cursing in disgust, for otherwise, why would he have thrown it away so violently? And if we have here a man who feels so sorry for having killed someone, that man certainly could not have killed his father. For if he had killed his father, he would not have felt any pity for his second victim. He would have had other things on his mind. He would have been too preoccupied with self-preservation, and there is absolutely no doubt about that. Indeed, the murderer would have made sure that the old man's skull was smashed and certainly would not have spent five whole minutes fussing over him. But as it is, there was room in him for pity and kindness, because my client's conscience was quite clear.

"And now we have a different conclusion based on psychology. But I want you to understand, gentlemen of the jury, that the only reason I have dabbled in psychology here is to demonstrate to you that you can use it to arrive at whatever conclusions suit you best. It all depends on who uses it. Psychology tempts even the most responsible and serious people to create fictions, and they cannot really be blamed for that. Actually I am talking about the extravagant use of psychology, gentlemen of the jury, of its misuse, to be precise."

Again there was approving laughter in the audience, obviously at the expense of the prosecutor.

I shall not reproduce here the entire speech of the counsel for the defense, but shall quote only certain passages, in which he made his most important points.

CHAPTER 11

There Was No Money and No Robbery

One point in the defense counsel's speech surprised everyone, and that was his categorical denial of the very existence of the fatal three thousand rubles, and hence of the possibility of their having been stolen.

"Any unprejudiced outsider," Fetyukovich started his argument, "will be struck by the fact that, besides murder, the accused in this case is also charged with robbery, although it could never be proved exactly what was stolen. It has been said that money was stolen, namely, three thousand rubles, but no one knows for a fact that the money actually existed. Just consider the following. In the first place, how did we find out that there was three thousand rubles there, and who saw the money? Smerdyakov was the only one who claimed to have seen it being placed in an envelope and, before the crime, he told the accused and his brother Ivan about it. The other person informed of the existence of the three thousand rubles was Miss Svetlov. But none of the latter three had ever laid eyes on the money. So, again, Smerdyakov was the only one who had seen it. But we may ask this now: Assuming that the money did exist and that Smerdyakov had seen it, when did he last see it? What if his master had taken the envelope from under his bedding and put it back in his money-box without telling Smerdyakov? Mind you, according to Smerdyakov, the money was under the mattress, and the accused is supposed to have pulled it out from under the mattress. But the bed was not disturbed in any way, a fact that was carefully recorded. How could the accused have managed to leave the bed quite undisturbed, especially since his hands were covered with blood at the time? Why weren't there any bloodstains on the fine, white linen sheets that had been specially changed that day? You may object: 'But what about the torn envelope that was found on the floor?' Well, I believe it would be worth our while to discuss that envelope for a few minutes. I must say I was rather surprised when the highly talented prosecutor, having brought up that envelope, suddenly and of his own accord—I repeat, of his own accord—declared, in the very passage of his speech in which he dismissed as preposterous the suggestion that Smerdyakov could be the murderer, that, *if that envelope had not been left lying on the floor as a clue, if the thief had taken it with him, no one in the whole world would have known that there had been an envelope with money in it and that the money had been stolen by the accused.* And so now we find out, by the admission of the prosecutor himself, that the entire accusation of robbery against my client is based on that torn envelope with its inscription, because, as he said himself, *without it no one would have even known of the existence of the money, let alone that it had been stolen.* But if you come to think of it, is a torn piece of paper lying on the floor really proof that there once was money in it and that the money was stolen? 'But Smerdyakov saw that money inside the envelope!' some will answer. Fine, but what I want to know is, when was the last time he saw it? I asked Smerdyakov that question and he told me it was two days before the murder. But what is there to prevent me from imagining, for instance, that, while sitting locked up inside his house, waiting nervously and anxiously for his beloved to come, old Fyodor Karamazov might, just to while away the time, have torn open the envelope, reasoning thus: 'She may not believe me if I just tell her what this envelope contains; it might be better to show her a bundle of thirty rainbow-colored, hundred-ruble bills in my hand; that would certainly impress her very much more! I bet her mouth would even begin to water!' And so he tore open the envelope, took out the money, and then tossed the torn envelope on the floor, because he was the master of the house and certainly did not have to worry about leaving clues. What, gentlemen of the jury, could be more plausible than that? Why couldn't it have actually happened? And if this, or something of the sort, could have happened, doesn't that make the whole charge of theft quite unfounded? For, if there was no money there in the first place, there could not be any theft either. And if the discarded envelope was lying on the floor, why can't we come to just the opposite conclusion—namely, that the fact that the torn envelope was found on the floor shows that its owner had thrown it away after removing the money from it? 'But what happened to the money then,' you may ask me, 'since no money was found when the house was searched later?' First of all, some money was found in his cash-box and, in the second place, he could have opened the envelope that morning or even the previous day, disposed of the money in some other way, paid it out, sent it away, or he could have changed his mind and modified his plan of action altogether, without feeling that he had to keep Smerdyakov informed of his latest intentions. And as long as there is the barest possibility that any of these alternatives may be true, how can anyone assert categorically that robbery was the motive for the murder, or even that robbery was involved at all? In insisting on it, we are crossing into the realm of fiction. For, in order to assert that something has been stolen, that something must first be identified, or it must at least be proven that it existed. And in our case, nobody has even seen it.

"Recently, a young street-hawker—he was only eighteen—entered a Petersburg money-changer's shop in broad daylight and, with a boldness typical of youth, killed the owner with an axe he had brought with him, and left with fifteen hundred rubles in cash. He was arrested four or five hours later and they found all the money on him, except for fifteen rubles that he had managed to spend in the meantime. Moreover, the shop-assistant, who had been out of the shop during the murder, not only told the police the exact sum missing, but also described the bills and the coins, that is, the number of rainbow-colored bills, blue, ten-ruble bills, red, five-ruble bills, how many gold coins and of what denominations. And the bills and coins found on the murderer corresponded very closely to that description. On top of all that, the youth confessed that he had killed the shop owner and that the money he now had on him had been stolen from the shop. Well, that is what I would describe as incriminating evidence, gentlemen of the jury! In that case, I could see and touch the money, and I could not deny its existence, which is very different from the case at hand.

"But I must remind you that, here too, you are faced with a matter of life and death for a man! 'Right,' you may say, 'but he was having a wild time the night he was arrested and they found fifteen hundred rubles on him too, and where can he have got that fifteen hundred rubles?' To that I answer that precisely the fact that, with what they found on him, they could only account for fifteen hundred rubles, not for the three thousand he was supposed to have stolen, suggests that the money had come from somewhere else, that it had never been sealed in that envelope. According to the most rigorous schedule of the accused's movements, established during the preliminary investigation, we know that, after leaving Miss Svetlov's maid, he went straight to Mr. Perkhotin's without stopping at home, or anywhere else for that matter, and that, after that, he was never alone, so he never had an opportunity to count off half of three thousand rubles and hide it somewhere in town. And it was just this fact that caused the prosecutor to assume that the money must be hidden in some crevice in Mokroye. But why not in a dungeon of the Castle of Udolpho while we're at it? Isn't such an assumption a flight of pure imagination straight from a Gothic novel? And I want you to note that, since the whole thing is based on the one assumption that the money is hidden in Mokroye, the moment that that assumption is discarded, the whole accusation of murder motivated by robbery dissolves into thin air, for then we still do not know whether the allegedly missing fifteen hundred rubles ever really existed. By what miracle can it have vanished, since it is established that the accused was never anywhere else where he could have hidden it? And with such fictions we are willing to ruin a human life! Again, some may object that he is unable to explain convincingly where he had got the fifteen hundred rubles that he did have, when everybody in town knew he didn't have any money until that night. My answer to that is: 'Who were the people who knew he didn't have any money?' Besides, the accused accounted clearly and without equivocation for the origin of that money, and his explanation, I submit, is very much in keeping with the accused's personality and character. The prosecutor seemed to be very satisfied with his own piece of fiction about the accused being a weak-willed man who so shamefully accepted the three thousand rubles offered him, under such humiliating circumstances, by his fiancée, a man too spineless to keep the money sewn in that little bag of his, a man who, even if he had sewn the money up in that bag originally, would have been unsewing it every second day to fish out one hundred-ruble bill after another, until after a month or so, he had gone through the whole sum. And, if you remember, we were told all this in a tone that brooked no dissent.

"But what if, in reality, things were entirely different, and what if the accused is not at all like the character in the novel made up by the prosecutor? And that is just what is wrong with his novel—he has created a character who bears no resemblance to the accused whatsoever.

"Of course, there are witnesses who will tell you that he had spent all of the three thousand rubles he had taken from Miss Verkhovtsev a month before, spent all of it like a kopek, and that he therefore could not possibly have tucked away half that sum. Fine, but who are those witnesses? Their doubtful credibility was exposed during the cross-examination in court here. Besides, as we all know, a bundle of bills in someone else's hand always seems bigger than it really is! And none of those witnesses ever counted that money; each one gave an estimate based on the size of the bundle. Why, didn't witness Maximov estimate the bundle in the accused's hand to be worth twenty thousand rubles? And now, gentlemen of the jury, since you have understood that psychology is a blade that cuts both ways, allow me to do a little cutting of my own with the other edge of it, and let's see what we get.

"About a month before the disaster, Miss Verkhovtsev gave the accused three thousand rubles to mail for her. But is it correct to suggest that she entrusted that money to him in the humiliating and insulting manner implied here? In Miss Verkhovtsev's first testimony, this hardly seemed to have been the case. As to her second appearance on the stand, we all heard her voice shrill with resentment, spite, and hatred. Besides, the assumption that the witness lied under oath in her first testimony creates a serious possibility that she lied under oath again in her second testimony. The prosecutor said he did not 'wish' or 'dare'—those are his own words—to touch upon that romance. All right, I won't go into it either, but I will allow myself to remark that if a person as respectable and honorable as Miss Verkhovtsev suddenly decides to change her testimony, as she did with the obvious intention of ruining the accused, she cannot be considered a cool, impartial, and detached witness. Will they really maintain that I have no right to suggest that a woman in such a vengeful mood might exaggerate? Yes, exaggerate the shame and the humiliation that accepting the money inflicted upon the accused. I say that, on the contrary, the way she succeeded in making him take that money was precisely the likeliest way an unthinking and irresponsible man like him would accept it. Moreover, at the time, he reckoned that he would soon get from his father the three thousand that he considered was owed to him. Of course, his assurance was quite unfounded and irresponsible, but it was because of this thoughtlessness and irresponsibility that he felt sure his father would pay him the money and then he would be able to refund the sum to Miss Verkhovtsev by mailing the three thousand rubles to her relatives. But the prosecutor categorically rejects the possibility that the accused could, on that day, have set aside half the money and sewn it up in a rag, because, he says, 'This is not the sort of man Karamazov is, and he cannot possibly feel that way about things.' I wonder why he says that, though, for he himself earlier declaimed about the wide range of feelings contained simultaneously in Karamazov's nature, including even, he said, two abysses. Well, precisely, with such a wide-ranging nature, that covers two abysses, Karamazov is capable of stopping dead in the middle of the wildest revelry, if the vision of that opposite abyss occurs to him. And I submit that that opposite abyss was, in this instance, his love, a love that flared up like gunpowder; it was for this love that he had to have money, had to have it for more important things even than spending it all on a wild spree with his new love. Why, if she said to him: 'I want nothing to do with your father. I am yours. Take me away from here!' he would take her away at once . . . That is, if he had the money to take her away with. And that, of course, was more important than spending the money on wild parties; Karamazov certainly felt that, knew it. Why, he was worrying himself sick about not having any money for such an eventuality! So what is so extraordinary about his dividing the money and putting half of it aside for that purpose?

"But then, days pass and my client's father does not pay him the three thousand rubles. Indeed, instead of paying it back to him, he apparently decides to use that money to seduce the woman his son loves. And so my client says to himself: 'If father doesn't give me that money, it'll be as if I'd stolen Katerina's money.' And he decides to take the fifteen hundred rubles sewn in the rag, hand it to Miss Verkhovtsev, and say to her: 'I may be a scoundrel, but a thief I am not!' So we have here a second reason impelling him to hold on jealously to the money sewn in the bag, not to open the bag, and certainly not to fish out one hundred-ruble bill after another. Why should you, gentlemen, refuse to recognize that my client has a sense of honor? Because he certainly has a sense of honor. Perhaps it is a distorted and a misguided one, but it is undoubtedly a sense of honor, a passionate sense of honor, and he has demonstrated it! Then, however, things become more complicated. His pangs of jealousy reach their highest pitch and the same two questions arise more and more tauntingly in the fevered brain of the accused, namely: 'Should I give that money back to Katerina, and, if I do, where will I find the money to take Grushenka away from here?' And if he drank so much and raged so violently in the taverns during that month, it was probably because he himself felt the dilemma so unbearable. And it was those two questions that, in the end, were to drive him to despair. At one point, he sent his youngest brother to ask their father, for the last time, to give him that three thousand, but he couldn't wait for the answer, broke into the house, and gave his father a beating in the presence of witnesses. And then the hope of getting the three thousand was gone, for he knew his father would never give it to him after the beating. Later that evening, my client pounded the upper part of his chest—where the bag with the bills was hanging—in the presence of his brother, swearing to him that he still had the means to save himself from being a despicable blackguard, but admitting that he would remain a blackguard, because he lacked the strength and determination to use that means. And why, may I ask you, does the prosecutor choose to disbelieve Alexei Karamazov's testimony, which sounded so honest, sincere, and straightforward? Why, instead of that, does he ask us to believe in some money concealed in a crevice in a dungeon of the Castle of Udolpho?

"Then, on that same evening, after his conversation with his brother, my client wrote that fatal letter, which is, indeed, the main, the most damning, evidence that he is guilty of premeditated murder and robbery! He writes in it: 'I will beg everybody for the money and if they turn me down, I'll kill father and take the envelope tied with a pink ribbon that he keeps under his mattress. Provided Ivan has left!' Well then, this is a complete program of the crime, so how can he not be the murderer? And everything was later carried out according to this plan offered to us in writing, the prosecution claims.

"But, in the first place, this letter was written by someone who was very drunk and in a state of great nervous tension. In the second place, I repeat once again, what he writes here about the envelope he knows only from what Smerdyakov has told him, because he himself has never set eyes on it. And in the third place, while it is an indisputable fact that he wrote this letter, it is not at all an indisputable fact that everything happened just as the letter says it will, because my client did not rush to his father's place to commit a coldly premeditated robbery; he was spontaneously driven there by insane jealousy.

" 'Fine, fine,' they may object to this, 'but still, when he got there, he killed his father and took the money.'

"But I would like to question this too: was it really he who killed his father? As for the charge of robbery, I can only dismiss it with indignation, because no one has the right to prefer such a charge without having shown us exactly what was stolen. That goes without saying! Furthermore, I would like to study the question of whether my client killed his father without robbing him. Has this really been proven? Or is it nothing but a piece of fiction, like all the rest?"

CHAPTER 12

No Murder Either

"You must be very careful, gentlemen of the jury," Fetyu-kovich went on; "a human life is at stake here, and we must all be very careful. We have heard the prosecutor admit that, up to the very last moment, until this very day in fact, he hesitated about whether he should charge my client with cold-blooded, premeditated murder. In fact, he continued to hesitate until that 'drunken' letter was produced in court, which made him decide, 'It all happened just as described there!'

"So let me say, once again, that the accused rushed off to try to find out where *she* was. This is an absolutely indisputable fact. If she had been at home, he would have stayed with her and certainly would not have carried out the 'program' outlined in his 'drunken' letter. But as it happened, he dashed off to his father's place, unexpectedly, spontaneously, and the chances are that he did not even remember about his 'drunken' letter at all. On his way, he snatched up that pestle. Yes, you have heard a whole psychological theory constructed around that brass pestle: why the accused was bound to view the pestle as a weapon, what prompted him to snatch it up as one snatches up a weapon, and so on and so forth. Now, I wonder what would have happened if that pestle had not been lying there in full sight, but had been put away in the cupboard? Then it would not have caught the eye of the accused and he would have rushed off to his father's unarmed and, perhaps, would not have killed anyone at all. So, how can the pestle be considered proof that there was premeditation, that is, that my client armed himself with it in order to kill his father? Certainly, argues the prosecution, but this man, who had been shouting in every tavern that he wanted to kill his father, two days before the murder, when he wrote that letter, behaved in an unusually quiet manner and picked only one quarrel with some shop-assistant, because, we are told, 'Karamazov could not help picking a quarrel with someone.'

"To this, I would like to answer that a person contemplating committing a murder, especially a murder that is to follow a carefully prepared plan, would certainly not pick quarrels even with shop-assistants, and would probably stay out of taverns altogether, for a man who is about to carry out such a plan, as a rule, tries to be as inconspicuous and quiet as possible; he wishes to be neither seen nor heard; his attitude is, 'Forget me altogether,' and this is more a matter of instinct than calculation. Yes, gentlemen of the jury, psychology does cut both ways, and we, too, know how to interpret psychology!

"As to all those drunken threats during that month, well, every one of you must have heard children and drunks threaten each other often enough, saying, 'I'll kill you!'—a threat that is not usually carried out. As a matter of fact, the 'drunken' letter itself could be just a written form of that same angry, drunken outcry: 'I'll kill you all, the whole lot of you!' Why couldn't it be just that? Why should you think of it as 'the fatal letter,' rather than as 'the ridiculous letter'? The only reason I can see is that the body of my client's murdered father was found in his house, while a witness saw my client fleeing, armed, through the garden and then was struck down by him himself. And that is supposed to prove that everything took place exactly according to the plan explained in the letter, so that it is a fatal and not a ridiculous letter.

"And now, thank God, we have come to the real point. 'He was in the garden,' we are told, 'hence he is the murderer.' It is on this proposition, 'He *was* there, hence he *is*,' that the whole case of the prosecution rests. But what if I decide to challenge their 'hence'? What if I say: even if he were there, *hence nothing*. Oh, I readily concede that the accumulation of facts and the collection of coincidences is quite impressive, but I suggest you examine each fact separately, without being influenced by their combined implications. Let us examine, for instance, the prosecution's refusal to conceive the possibility that the accused may simply have run away from

under his father's window. Do you remember the sarcasm in
which the prosecution indulged, about the filial 'respect' and
'discretion' that are supposed to have suddenly come over
the accused? And what if my client did feel something of
that sort, although what he felt could be described more
aptly as a wave of pious decency. 'It was as if my mother
had interceded for me with God,' was the way the accused
described it, and so, the moment he was satisfied that Miss
Svetlov was not there, he just ran away.

"'But he couldn't be sure of it, just by looking in the
window!' the prosecutor replies, and to this, in turn, I answer,
'Why couldn't he?' Fyodor Karamazov opened the window
when he heard the agreed signal and he may very well have
let out an exclamation, a cry that would have fully convinced the accused that Miss Svetlov was not there. Why
must you believe that everything happened exactly as the
prosecution suggests it happened, as it stubbornly wishes to
believe? In real life, thousands of things may have happened
that would have escaped the scrutiny of the subtlest fiction
writer.

"'But Gregory saw that the door was open; therefore the
accused must have been inside the house, and therefore he
must be the murderer . . .' Now let us talk about that door
a little, gentlemen of the jury. I want you to note that only
one witness has testified here that the door was open, a witness who was at the time in a state that renders the reliability
of his testimony very questionable . . . But, all right, let us
assume that it was open and that the accused denied it and
lied, claiming that it was closed out of an instinct of self-
preservation, which would be be quite understandable under
the circumstances. Let us also assume that he had been inside the house. Well, what of that? It still would not necessarily follow that he had killed his father. He could break
into the house, dash through the rooms, push his father out
of his way, even hit him. But once he saw that Miss Svetlov
was not there, he could flee, happy that he had not committed murder. The prosecutor has painted a grim and horri-
fying picture of the state the accused was in, in Mokroye,
when he discovered that she loved him, when a new life was
beckoning to him, while he knew that he could no longer
aspire to love, because his father's bloodstained body was
now in his way, and beyond that body lay, not his happiness,
but his ordeal. The prosecutor, however, allowed my client
love and then proceeded, in his usual way, to give us a

psychological description of the mental state of the accused: he was drunk, we were told, he was like a criminal who is being taken to his execution but feels he still has a lot of time ahead of him, etc., etc. But didn't you, Mr. Prosecutor, create, for your purposes, a fictional character who is quite unlike the accused? Is my client really so callous and inhuman as to think only of love and of avoiding justice, if he is really guilty of his father's murder? My answer to that is no, no, and no! I feel absolutely convinced that, the moment she had revealed her love to him, asked him to go away with her and live in a new happiness, the body of the murdered father behind him would have doubled, trebled, his urge to kill himself, and he would certainly have killed himself if he had been his father's murderer! Oh, he certainly would not have forgotten where he had left his pistols! I know the accused well enough to say that he is not the wooden, heartless creature the prosecutor is trying to portray him as! He would certainly have killed himself if he had killed his father. However, he had not killed him, precisely because 'his mother had interceded for him,' and so he was not guilty of spilling his father's blood. That night in Mokroye, he was unhappy and worried about the old servant Gregory; he was praying that the old man would regain his senses and live, that the blow he had struck him would not prove fatal, and that he—my client—would not be held responsible for that death. And why shouldn't we accept that explanation of what happened? What proof do we have that the accused did not tell us the truth?

" 'But there is the corpse,' they will remind us. 'If the accused rushed out of the house without killing his father, who did kill him?'

"As I have said before, the whole argument of the prosecution is based on this: 'If not he, then who? We see no one else who could have done it, except him.' After that, the prosecutor counted off on his fingers the five persons who had been on the premises during the night. I will agree with him that, of the five, three can be eliminated from the start: the victim himself, Gregory, and his wife Martha. That leaves us with my client and Smerdyakov. And at this point the prosecutor exclaims dramatically that my client only accused Smerdyakov because there was not a sixth person about, for had there been a sixth person, or even only the ghost of a sixth person, Karamazov would have dropped his accusations against Smerdyakov and accused the ghost, because he was ashamed of suggesting that Smerdyakov might have been the murderer . . . But what is there to prevent me, gentlemen of the jury, from reversing that argument and saying that, with only the two of them as possible suspects, the only reason my client is accused of the crime is that, except for Smerdyakov, they have not found anyone who could be accused of it? And I submit that the prosecutor can find no one else to suspect only because he had, from the start, arbitrarily decided not to suspect Smerdyakov. It is a fact that, besides the accused, his two brothers, and Miss Svetlov, no one else has declared openly that he believes Smerdyakov to be the murderer. Isn't it a fact, though, that there is a certain vague feeling among the people of your town, a certain dissatisfaction with the results of the investigation, some sort of expectation of further developments and discoveries? And then there is a certain peculiar combination of circumstances which, however, I must admit, does not enable me to draw any clear conclusions. First, there was that epileptic seizure that took place on the very day of the murder, a fit whose genuineness the prosecutor felt impelled to defend so strongly, for reasons that are best known to him alone. Then there was Smerdyakov's sudden suicide, just on the eve of the trial. And lastly, there was the equally unexpected testimony of the accused's brother Ivan, who, until then, had believed the accused guilty, but who now produced that money in court, and who accused Smerdyakov of being the murderer. Oh, I agree with the court and the prosecution that Ivan Karamazov was feverish and that his testimony could have been a desperate attempt, perhaps conceived in a feverish state, to save his brother by blaming a dead man for the crime. But still, once again Smerdyakov's name has been brought in, and I find something rather suspicious about this. I have the impression that something has remained unsaid here, something is still unfinished. And perhaps there will be something more to be said about it. But let us leave it for the time being.

"Although the court has decided to get the case over with as quickly as possible, I would still like to make a few comments, for instance, concerning the public prosecutor's brilliant character sketch of the late Smerdyakov. While I admire the talent of the author of the sketch, I cannot possibly go along with the essence of the portrayal. I met Smerdyakov. I went to see him and spoke to him, but the impression he made on me was altogether different. I agree that he was weak physically and that his health was poor. But in character, in spirit, he was no weakling, as the prosecutor wishes us to believe. Particularly, I found none of that peculiar timidity in him that the prosecutor so vividly described. Nor was there anything open about him; indeed, I found a tremendous distrust, concealed behind a mask of open-hearted simplicity; and I also found in him an intelligence capable of seeing through a great many things. I submit that the prosecutor was rather naive in concluding that Smerdyakov was feeble-minded. I left him with the definite conviction that he was a malicious, morbidly vain, vengeful, and spitefully envious creature. And after some investigation, I discovered that he hated the story of his parentage, that he was ashamed of it, and would gnash his teeth when reminded that he was the son of Reeking Lizaveta. He never treated Gregory and Martha, who had looked after him throughout his childhood, with respect. He hated and cursed Russia, and his dream was to go to France and become a Frenchman. Many people heard him say so and, also, that one day he would find enough money to carry out his plan. I don't believe he loved anyone but himself, and he also had a very inflated opinion of his own talents. To him, the symbols of enlightenment were good clothes, clean linen, and polished boots. Knowing he was an illegitimate son of Fyodor Karamazov—and we have evidence that he knew it—Smerdyakov was bitter about his position as compared with that of Fyodor Karamazov's legitimate sons, who, he felt, had everything while he had nothing, who would inherit their father's money while he, Smerdyakov, was doomed to remain a cook all his life. He also told me that he had helped Fyodor Karamazov put the hundred-ruble bills into that envelope. It stands to reason that he hated the thought of where the money was to go, a sum that would have been enough to change his own future. Furthermore, he saw the three thousand rubles in brand new, bright, rainbow-colored bills (I deliberately asked him about that). Oh, if you want a piece of good advice, never allow a conceited, envious man to see a large sum of money in your hand! It was the first time in his life that Smerdyakov had seen a large sum in Fyodor Karamazov's hand! The many rainbow-colored bills must have made a violent impression on his imagination, although, at that point, without disastrous consequences. My talented friend the prosecutor drew up for us a list of all the pros and cons of the possibility of Smerdyakov's guilt and, among other things, asked: What possible reason could Smerdyakov have for shamming an epileptic seizure? Why, perhaps he didn't sham it at all; the attack could have occurred naturally. But after it, the sick man could have regained consciousness. He needn't have recovered completely. He could just have come to, as patients afflicted with the falling sickness usually do. The prosecutor asks us: At what moment could Smerdyakov have committed the crime? It would be very easy to answer that question for him. Smerdyakov could have woken from his deep sleep—because he was actually simply asleep, for epileptic seizures are usually followed by a deep sleep—woken just at the second that old Gregory seized Dmitry Karamazov's foot, as it dangled from the garden fence, and screamed, 'Father-killer!' at the top of his voice. That cry resounded deafeningly through the stillness of the night and could very well have awakened Smerdyakov, whose sleep, by that time, was not necessarily all that deep, for he could have been coming gradually to for an hour or so by then. So Smerdyakov could have gotten up and almost unthinkingly, without anything precise in mind, gone to see what was happening. He's still feeling very vague and confused in the head, but, without noticing what he is doing, he crosses the garden, walks over to the lighted windows, and hears from his master—who, of course, is very pleased to see him—what has just happened. All at once, the idea flashes through his head. His frightened master tells him everything in great detail, and gradually a plan of action appears in Smerdyakov's aching, throbbing head—a dangerous but very tempting opportunity, one that logic tells him is the best and safest opportunity he will ever have: he could kill his master, take the three thousand rubles, and have the master's son take the blame for it all, because, obviously, no one other than that son would be suspected, with all the evidence of his presence. His tremendous yearning for that money could have taken his breath away, and it was strengthened by his deep conviction that now he could do it with complete impunity. Oh, such sudden, irresistible impulses often occur at the right moment to potential murderers who, a few seconds previously, would never have thought that they would want to kill! And so Smerdyakov was in a position to get into the house and to carry out his plan. As to the weapon—well, it could have been, for instance, a rock, as long as it was heavy enough; he could have picked it up in the garden before going in. And what was his motive? Why, three thousand rubles would take care of his entire future career. Oh, I am not really contradicting myself, for that money could have existed, after all. And it is possible that no one except Smerdyakov knew where Fyodor Karamazov had hidden it. And as for the torn envelope on the floor, let me go back to what the prosecutor had to say on that subject: he developed a very subtle theory to the effect that only an inexperienced thief such as my client would have left it there, but that never would a man like Smerdyakov think of leaving behind such a piece of incriminating evidence against himself. Well, gentlemen of the jury, when I heard him say that, it somehow sounded awfully familiar to me, and just imagine—I had heard that same assumption, that Dmitry Karamazov would do precisely that with the envelope, from none other than Smerdyakov himself. I was even struck by the falsely naive tone in which he tried to implant that idea in my head, trying to get me to say it without realizing that he had put it in my mind in the first place. Now, I just wonder whether he didn't quietly intimate that theory to the talented prosecutor during the preliminary investigation. In other words, I wonder whether the whole idea did not originate with him.

"There is still the old woman Martha, who is supposed to have heard Smerdyakov moaning all night behind the partition. Well, she may have heard him, but even so, the reliability of her testimony remains very questionable. I once knew a lady who complained that she couldn't sleep at night because of the barking of a neighbor's lap-dog. But it was later established that the poor little beast yelped only two or three times in the course of the whole night. And this is quite natural. For a person could be asleep, then suddenly hear a moan, wake up furious at being awakened, and then at once fall asleep again. Two hours later, he is woken up by another moan, and again goes to sleep. And once more, two hours later, his sleep is interrupted for the third time. In the morning the sleeper will complain that someone's moaning prevented him from sleeping all night. But that is a very natural reaction, for since he slept through the two-hour periods, he forgets about them, but he remembers clearly the brief spells when he was awake.

" 'But why,' the prosecution cries, 'didn't Smerdyakov confess his guilt in his suicide note? Why did he have sufficient scruples to be concerned that no one should be accused of his death, but not enough to stop an innocent man from being accused of his crime?' But isn't there a confusion of issues here? Scruples involve repentance, and Smerdyakov never felt repentant—he was filled with despair. Repentance and despair are two very different things. Despair may be combined with irreconcilable resentment, and, at the moment of perishing by his own hand, a suicide may find his hatred doubled for those he envied during his life.

"Gentlemen of the jury, do not allow justice to miscarry in this case. There is absolutely nothing in what I have told you that could not have happened. Just try and find any absurdity in the versions I have suggested, try and prove them wrong or impossible! And as long as there is a shadow of a possibility that things might have happened the way I have suggested, you may not declare my client guilty as charged! I swear to you, by everything I hold sacred, that I sincerely believe what I have just told you about the murder. And more than anything else, I am disturbed and outraged by the thought that, out of all the mass of facts piled up by the prosecution, there is not a single one that is unanswerable and final, and that my unhappy client is threatened only by the accumulation of those facts. Yes, the total weight of the facts is terrifying: there is that blood dripping from his fingers, staining his linen; there is that dark night interrupted by the piercing cry of 'Father-killer!' as the man crying out those words is felled, his skull broken; and then there is a stream of phrases, statements, gestures, and exclamations, all of which could bias people's opinions, sway their feelings. But should you, gentlemen of the jury, allow your feelings and opinions to be swayed like this? Remember, you have been entrusted with a tremendous power, the power to decide. But, as you must know, the greater the power, the more frightening is the responsibility of wielding it! I won't retreat one inch from what I have said here, but even if I did, for one second, agree that my client's hands had really been covered with his father's blood—again, it would be only an assumption, for I have no doubt whatever of his innocence—but if, for argument's sake, I went along with the prosecution and agreed that my client was guilty of parricide, even so I beg you to hear what I have to say. I feel very strongly impelled to say something more to you, because I can see the great inner struggle taking place in your hearts and minds . . . Please forgive me for mentioning your hearts and minds, gentlemen of the jury, but I want to be truthful and sincere to the very end. So let us be sincere, all of us! . . ."

Considerable applause interrupted the counsel for the defense. Indeed, he had uttered the last words with such sincerity that the audience felt he was really about to say something of the greatest importance. But, hearing the clapping, the presiding judge loudly called the spectators to order, threatening to "clear the courtroom" if such an "incident" occurred again. Everything was quiet after that, and Fetyukovich began in a new, penetrating voice, quite different from the one in which he had spoken up till then.

CHAPTER 13

Corrupters of Thought

"It is not just the accumulation of facts that is crushing my client," Fetyukovich announced, "there is actually one single fact that dooms him—the fact that the dead body is that of his father! Had this been an ordinary murder case, with the shaky evidence, sweeping assumptions, and lack of positive proof, when every available fact is considered in turn, you would have refused, gentlemen of the jury, to ruin a man's life, just because of biased feelings against him, which may well, alas, have been justified. But this is not just murder that we are dealing with here, it is parricide! The idea of it shocks and impresses us so much that the inadequate proof ceases to appear inadequate and the questionable facts cease to appear questionable, even to the least prejudiced persons! How could such a man be acquitted, for suppose he did kill his father? How could such a monster be allowed to go unpunished? Yes, that is what everyone must feel deep down, instinctively as it were. Yes, it is the most terrible thing there is, to shed the blood of one's father, the blood of the man who gave you life, who loved you, who would have given his life for you when you were a small child, who suffered through all your misery, who was unhappy through your unhappiness, and who rejoiced only in your joy and success! Oh, it is impossible to conceive what it would mean to kill such a father! Gentlemen of the jury, what is a father, a real father? What does that word mean? What great thought is contained in that name—'father'? What I have just said is only part of what a true father ought to be. But in the case we are now faced with, that has shocked us so painfully, the father—Fyodor Karamazov—bore no resemblance whatever to the type of father we have just described. He was a disgrace. Indeed, such a father was a complete disgrace, and I suggest we examine this more closely. You must not shirk anything, gentlemen of the jury, because you will have to make a decision of the utmost importance. Above all, we have no right, now, to be afraid of certain ideas, to brush them aside, as if we were coy women or little children, as my talented opponent put it so eloquently.

"But in his ardent plea my highly esteemed opponent—who disagreed with me before I had even uttered a word—declared several times that he refused to yield the right of defending the accused to anyone, particularly to the counsel who had come all the way from Petersburg to defend him, because, he exclaimed, 'I am both accuser and defender!' But, after several such exclamations, he somehow forgot to make the point that, if an abominable man like the accused was capable of remembering with gratitude, for twenty-three years, the pound of nuts given to him by the only person who ever treated him with kindness while he lived in his father's house, it stands to reason that this same accused could not have forgotten that twenty-three years ago he was running about loose in his father's backyard, barefoot and with his trousers held up by one remaining button, as the kind Dr. Herzenstube described the scene to us.

"Ah, gentlemen of the jury, is there any need to go more deeply into the disgrace that such a father represents? Must I repeat again things that everyone already knows? Must I describe the sort of welcome my client received when he came to this town to see his father? What need was there, I ask you, to represent my client as an insensitive monster? I grant you that he is impulsive, wild, and violent—that is why he is in the dock at this moment. But whose responsibility is it that he became like that? Whose fault is it that this man, with his naturally good inclinations and his responsive and sensitive heart, was brought up in such a preposterous way? Did anyone ever teach him to behave sensibly? Did anyone concern himself with his education? Did anyone love him, even a little, while he was a small child? My client grew up under no one's protection but God's, which means he grew up as wild animals do. Perhaps, after his long absence, he was anxious to see his father; perhaps, before he came, he recalled his childhood many, many times, seeing it like a distant dream, dismissing the ugly ghosts of his early years and longing to rehabilitate his father's image in his own eyes and to embrace the old man. But what did he find? He was met with cynical sneers, suspicious glares, and evasive quibbling about money that he considered his. He sees his father leading a life that revolts him; every day he hears the disgusting conversation his father indulges in, while sipping his brandy; and finally he realizes that this man, his own father, is trying to take away from him the woman he loves and money he feels is his own! Isn't this both cruel and unspeakably revolting, gentlemen of the jury? And on top of that, the old man goes about complaining that his son is unkind and fails to show him proper respect, slanders him in society, and buys up his son's IOU's in order to have him put in debtor's prison!

"I submit that some people, who may appear hard, violent, and unrestrained, such as my client, are really very tender-hearted underneath, incredible though that may seem. Please, do not laugh when I say that; do not do as the able prosecutor did when he so mercilessly mocked my client, sneering at him because he loves Schiller and all that is beautiful and sublime! Yes, I want to speak up for people like him, people so often maligned and misunderstood. I want to tell you that they often long for justice, tenderness, and beauty, precisely in contrast to their violence and ruthlessness. I want to tell you that they are capable of great love and that, when they fall in love with a woman, they will love her with an idealistic, spiritual love. Again, I beg you not to laugh at what I say, because this is just what happens with people like my client. In his case, he was unable to hide his passions, which at times appeared in very crude form and were noticed by everyone, whereas the delicate feelings within him remained undetected. But whereas all these passions are very quickly satisfied, contact with a noble woman leads such a seemingly crude and insensitive man to make an effort to change and become a better man, a more honorable and more understanding man; he reaches out for 'the beautiful and the sublime,' and I am not afraid to use this phrase, although so many have tried to ridicule it.

"I said earlier that I would not allow myself to go into my client's romance with Miss Verkhovtsev. I feel, however, that I should be allowed to say this much. What we heard during her last appearance on the witness stand was not testimony, but the frantic outcry of a resentful and vengeful woman. But, in reality, she has no right to accuse my client of betraying her, because it was she who betrayed him! I say that, if she had given herself a little time to think, she would never have allowed herself to say what she did. You must not believe her, for my client is not a 'monster,' as she called him. He who accepted the cross out of His love for man said: 'I am the good shepherd and I lay down my life for the sheep so that no one of them might be lost.' So let us not allow this human soul to be lost, gentlemen of the jury!

"Remember, I asked you what the word 'father' meant, and I said that it was a word with great meaning to it. But I believe we must use words honestly and call things by their proper names. A man like the murdered Fyodor Karamazov is not worthy to be called a father. Love for a father that the father has not deserved is inconceivable and absurd. It is impossible to create love out of nothing, for God alone can create something out of nothing. 'Fathers, do not provoke your children to anger,' the Apostle wrote from the depth of his heart, filled with ardent love. And it is not just for the sake of my client that I quote these sacred words, but rather as a reminder to all fathers. What entitles me, any more than anyone else, to preach to fathers? Nothing at all, but I appeal to them all—*vivos voco*—as a human being and a citizen. Our stay on earth is not a long one, but, in the course of it, we do and say much that is wicked. So we must avail ourselves of every opportunity to say something good. And, while I stand here, I will avail myself of this opportunity. By divine will, words said in this courtroom will be heard all over Russia and so I am not addressing myself just to the fathers of this town, but to the fathers of all Russia: 'Fathers, do not provoke your children to anger!' Let us obey Christ's precept ourselves, before we demand that our children follow it. Otherwise we are not the fathers of our children, but their enemies, and they are our enemies, not our children, and we are to blame, for we have made them our enemies! 'With what ye mete, it shall be measured to you again.' It is not I who say this, it is an injunction of the Gospel.

"Recently in Finland, a young housemaid was suspected of having secretly given birth to a baby. They watched her and eventually they found in a trunk they had never seen before, hidden behind a screen of bricks in the corner of a loft, the tiny body of the new-born baby, whom she had killed. And next to that body were two more skeletons of new-born babies, whom she had also killed as soon as they were born, as she finally admitted herself. Now, let me ask you this, gentlemen of the jury, would you describe that woman as the mother of those children? Of course, she was the woman who brought them into the world, but does she deserve to be called their mother? Is there anyone here who would dare to bestow upon her the sacred title of mother? Let us be bold, let us even be ruthless, gentlemen of the jury, for it is our duty on this occasion; we must not be afraid of words and ideas, like those characters in Ostrovsky's comedy, who are terrorized by words whose meaning they do not understand. Let us show the world at large that the progress of the past few years has reached us too and that, today, the word 'father' designates not merely the man who has begotten you, but rather the man who has both begotten you and then deserved your love. Oh, I know there is another concept of fatherhood, and, according to that interpretation, a father may be a monster who treats his children viciously, but who must nevertheless always be respected as a father, because he has conceived his children. But that is a mystical attitude that my reason does not understand, that I can accept only *on faith,* so to speak, just as we are asked to accept so many things that we do not understand, but that our religion orders us to believe. But in that case, let it stay outside the sphere of everyday life, a life that has its own rights and also imposes on us certain duties, for in this sphere we must behave in a humane, Christian fashion and we have the obligation to act on our beliefs based on reason, tested by experience and the analysis of that experience; we have the duty to behave sanely, and not insanely, as we do in our dreams or when we are delirious, and we must see to it that we harm no one, inflict no suffering upon others, and send no man to his doom. Only then will we act like true Christians, not like mystics, but like reasonable and truly humane beings . . ."

Loud applause greeted these words but Fetyukovich waved his hands, as if beseeching the spectators to be quiet and allow him to finish. Everything grew quiet again, and then he went on.

"Do you believe, gentlemen of the jury, that our children will be spared these problems, that is, those of them who are old enough to reason? No, they most certainly will not be spared them, and we have no right to demand that they abstain from asking such questions. The sight of an unworthy father inevitably arouses painful questions in a boy's mind, especially if he compares his behavior with that of the worthy fathers of his contemporaries. And to these questions he receives the stereotyped answer: 'He gave you life, you are his flesh and blood, and therefore you must love him.' The boy is bound to ask himself: 'Did he love me when he begot me?' And gradually he will find more and more things that puzzle him: 'He could not have begotten me for my own sake, because he did not even know whether I'd turn out to be a boy or a girl at the moment of his passion, which may have been kindled by liquor in the first place, for all he has given me is my propensity to drunkenness. That is all the benefit I have derived from him. So why should I love him? Just for having conceived me and then not cared about my existence?'

"You may feel that such questions are crude and unfeeling, but you cannot demand of a young mind that it stop asking questions. That would be hopeless anyway, for, as they say, you may throw nature out the door, but it will come back through the window. And, above all, let us not be afraid of words we cannot understand like Ostrovsky's ignorant characters; let us face our problems as reason dictates, rather than having our decisions dictated by obscure, mystical concepts.

"And how are we to answer our son, who asks us such questions? Well, let the son face his father and ask him: 'Tell me, why should I love you? Prove to me that it is my duty to love you.' If the father manages to give him a satisfactory answer, it is a normal family, a family not based on some mystical prejudice, but founded on reasonable, responsible, and strictly humane premises. But if, on the other hand, the father fails to prove to his son that he is worthy of his love, he does not deserve to be his father and the son is free to consider his father as a stranger or even as his enemy. Our position, gentlemen of the jury, must be a school of true and sound concepts!"

Now Fetyukovich was interrupted by uncontrollable, almost frenzied applause. Of course, not all the spectators applauded, but a good half of them did. Fathers and mothers clapped. And from the galleries, where many ladies were seated, came enthusiastic shrieks and cries. Some people even waved their handkerchiefs. The presiding judge rang his bell with all his might. He was visibly outraged by this unseemly display but did not dare carry out his threat to clear the courtroom, because even the eminent old gentlemen with important decorations and stars on their frock-coats, who sat in specially reserved armchairs, were clapping the orator or waving their handkerchiefs in homage to him. And so the presiding judge had to content himself with simply repeating his threat to clear the room, as the excited and triumphant Fetyukovich resumed his speech.

"Gentlemen of the jury, think of that terrible night, of which so much has been said today, the night the son climbed over the fence, entered his father's house, and confronted his enemy and tormentor, who had begotten him. I want to emphasize this as strongly as I can: he had not come for money! To accuse him of robbery is completely absurd, as I have already explained. And neither did he break into the house to kill him. Certainly not, for if it had been a premeditated murder, he would have prepared a weapon well in advance and not arrived with a brass pestle that he had picked up instinctively, without even knowing why. Let us assume that he deceived his father by knocking the secret signal, let us even assume that he entered the house—although, as I have already told you, I don't believe it for one second—but I am willing to assume it. Gentlemen of the jury, I swear to you by everything I hold sacred that, if that man had not been his father, if it had been an outsider who had caused him all that suffering, my client would have dashed through the rooms and, having assured himself that the woman was not in the house, would have left hurriedly, without harming his rival; he might have pushed him out of his way or, at most, hit him, but that is all, for he was in too much of a hurry to bother with the would-be seducer. But his father, his father—at the sight of his father, whom he had hated since childhood, his enemy, his tormentor, and now, of all things, his monstrous rival—the feeling of hatred might have seized him, despite himself, and overwhelmed him. In that case he would have been the victim of temporary insanity; he would have simply been subject to a natural law, irresistibly and unconsciously, like everything in nature. But even so, I claim and proclaim, even so he would not have killed deliberately; he would have swung his brass pestle in loathing and disgust, without realizing that he might kill, without any intention of killing! And if he had not had that unfortunate pestle, he might or might not have struck his father, but he certainly would not have killed him. And he would have dashed off without knowing whether the old man was alive or dead. That sort of murder is not murder. And that sort of murder is not parricide either. No, killing such a father under such circumstances cannot be called parricide; it could be classified as such only if we blindly accept an old prejudice!

"But did such a murder occur? No, gentlemen of the jury, I beg you, from the very bottom of my heart, to believe me when I say that he did not kill the victim, not even in that manner! If you condemn him now, he will think: 'These people have never done anything for me—they never helped me to grow up, to become a decent, educated man; they never fed me or gave me to drink; they never visited me in jail, and now they are sending me off to the penitentiary in Siberia. Well, so we are even now. I owe them nothing. Since they are spiteful, I will be spiteful too; since they are heartless, I will also be heartless.' Yes, this is what he will say to himself, gentlemen of the jury. And I swear that, if you condemn him, you will only make it easier for his conscience, for he will end by cursing the man whose blood was spilled, instead of weeping for him! At the same time, you will destroy the man he could have been, because you will doom him to remain blind and embittered for the rest of his life. On the other hand, wouldn't you rather punish him sternly and painfully, indeed, inflict upon him the worst punishment imaginable, but a punishment that will save his soul and regenerate him? If so, then smother him with your mercy! Then you will see and hear him flinch and shudder in awe: 'How am I to endure this mercy? What have I done to deserve so much love? Can I ever become worthy of it?' Yes, this is what his heart will cry out. Oh, I know so well that wild heart—wild, yes, but also noble and generous! And he will bow before your great act of mercy, because he is yearning for an act of love, and his heart will catch fire and he will be saved forever and ever! There are men whose narrow horizons cause them to blame the rest of the world rather than themselves for everything. But, believe me, smother this man in mercy and love, and he will curse his wayward past, for there is so much that is promising in him! His soul will grow and will see how infinite is the mercy of God and how good men can be! And it will be weighed down by remorse and by the debt he will feel, from now on, he owes his fellow men. Instead of saying, 'All right, we are even now,' he will say, 'I am guilty before all men and I am unworthy of them.' And with tears of penitence and with fervor, he will cry out: 'My fellow men are better than I am, because, instead of destroying me, they want to save me!'

"Oh, it is very easy for you to perform this act of mercy because, with nothing but circumstantial evidence, it will be too painful for you to pronounce him guilty. And, as you know, it is infinitely better to allow ten guilty men to go free than to punish one innocent man. Hear, hear that great voice of the past century of our country's glorious history! Who am I, an insignificant lawyer, to remind you that the idea of Russian justice is not only just punishment, but also the rehabilitation of our lost fellow men! Let other nations stick to the letter of the law; for us, the most important thing is its spirit, its meaning, and the rehabilitation of the wayward! And if that is so, if Russia and her justice are really what I know they are, may Russia forge ahead, ahead, and let no one try to frighten us with stories about madly galloping troikas, from which foreign nations pull back in disgust! It is not a mad troika but the majestic Russian chariot that is rolling calmly and solemnly toward its goal.

"And now the life of my client is in your hands, and also in your hands is the future of Russian justice! You must save it, defend it. You must prove to the world at large that there are men ready to uphold it, and that it is in good hands!"

CHAPTER 14

Our Good Old Peasants Stand Their Ground

Fetyukovich ended his speech and this time the enthusiasm of the audience broke all bounds and burst forth in an uncontrollable storm. It would have been unthinkable to try to interfere with it: the women were in tears, so were many men. Even two of the important old dignitaries shed a few tears. The presiding judge gave in and put off ringing his little bell as long as he could, for he may have felt, as our ladies later insisted, that "interfering with such enthusiasm would have been tantamount to interfering with something sacred." The orator himself was genuinely moved.

And it was during this moment of exaltation that our prosecutor rose to his feet to "object to some points brought up by the defense." He was met with cold glares of hatred. "What does he want now? What is he up to? Who does he think he is?" the ladies protested in whispers. But even if the ladies of the entire world had joined their protest, even if they had been headed by the prosecutor's own wife, even then they would have failed to stop him at that moment. He was so pale, tense, and trembling that his first words were quite unintelligible: he gasped for breath, mispronouncing and misplacing words. Soon enough, however, he took hold of himself.

I would like to quote only a few brief passages of that second speech of his.

". . . I have been accused here of making up a whole novel. And what about the defense? What has it offered us if not a romance based on another romance? There was everything in it, short of verse. Awaiting his mistress, Fyodor Karamazov tears open the envelope and throws it on the floor. We are even told the words he mutters as he does so. Isn't that a poem in itself? But what proof is there that he took that money out of the envelope? And who heard him mutter those words? And then we have that feeble-minded idiot Smerdyakov presented to us as a Byronic hero out to avenge himself on society for his illegitimate birth—isn't that a poem in the Byronic style? And then there is the son breaking into his father's house, killing him and, at the same time, not killing him. No, this is no longer a novel; this is a riddle of the sphinx, a riddle that he himself cannot possibly solve. One would think that, if he killed him, he did it. But not here: he killed him, but he didn't do it! Just try to make sense out of that! And after that, having announced that this courtroom must be a platform for justice, for a sound, rational approach, we hear the counsel for the defense announce under oath that parricide is nothing but an obsolete prejudice. But just imagine what would happen to the family, the mainstay of our society, if, as he suggests, every child started by asking his father, 'Tell me why I should love you'? The word 'parricide' is simply one of those words that frighten us because we have not grasped its meaning and so find ourselves in the position of Ostrovsky's ignorant characters.

"The defense presents the most sacred and treasured precepts of Russian justice, which guide it today and will do so in its future development, irresponsibly in a completely distorted way, just to serve his immediate purpose—to obtain the acquittal of a criminal who has no right to be acquitted. 'Oh, please, smother him with mercy!' the defense counsel exclaims; 'this is all the murderer needs, and he will show you soon enough how smothered he is!' Perhaps the defense counsel is even too modest when he asks you simply to acquit his client? Couldn't he, for instance, suggest the creation of a scholarship grant bearing the name of this parricide, so that his fine deed would be properly remembered by our young and our descendants?

"And the counsel goes on to put straight the Gospels and established religion as a whole. 'It's all mysticism,' he tells us, 'for it is I who possess the secret of true Christianity; I have subjected it to the analysis of my reason and verified it against sound rational concepts.' So a false picture of Christ is waved before our eyes. 'With what measure ye mete, it shall be measured to you again!' the defense counsel exclaims and, without blinking an eye, goes on to conclude that Christ teaches us to mete out to others as others mete out to us, and he does so from what he himself describes as a platform for justice and for sane, healthy ideas! I can see him glancing at the Gospels as he prepares one of his speeches—oh, only then —for it may be quite useful to show off his knowledge of this work, which is quite original and contains many passages likely to produce an effect on the audience, whenever such an effect is required. But here his interpretation is just the opposite of Christ's commandment: Christ commands us precisely not to mete out to others as is meted out to us, which is the way of the wicked world. He wants us to forgive and to offer the other cheek. That is what our Lord taught us, and He did not teach us that it is only a prejudice to believe that children should not kill their parents! Let us not presume to correct, from this platform of justice and sanity, the precepts given us in the Gospels by our Lord, to whom the counsel condescendingly refers as 'the crucified humanitarian,' whereas to our Russian Orthodox Church He is 'the Lord, our God'!"

The presiding judge interfered at this point, warning the prosecutor that he was going rather too far, that he must remain within the bounds of the argument, and so on and so forth—the usual things that presiding magistrates say in these cases. Besides, the spectators were growing restive. Fetyukovich did not bother to answer the objections. He merely stood up, placed his hand on his heart, and said a few words in a tone of offended dignity. He made a few more ironic comments on the prosecutor's "romances" and his "psychological approach," and managed to slip in the saying, "Jupiter, thou art irate, this shows thou art wrong," which evoked some laughter, for no one could be more unlike Jupiter than our prosecutor. Then, with great dignity, Fetyukovich declared that he would not honor with a comment the remark that he was encouraging members of the young generation to kill their fathers. As to the accusation that he had distorted the image of Christ and referred to Him as 'the crucified humanitarian,' which allegedly clashed with the view of Russia's official church and therefore should not have been uttered in a Russian court, which was a platform of justice and sane beliefs, Fetyukovich considered it 'a hostile insinuation'; he said that when he had decided to come to this town, he had felt confident that the court would offer him protection from "slurs on my reputation as a good citizen and a loyal subject of His Majesty the Tsar." At this point, the presiding judge called him to order too. Fetyukovich bowed, said he had finished, and went back to his seat, accompanied by an approving hum from the spectators. At that moment, every woman among them had no doubt whatever that our prosecutor had been crushed so thoroughly that he would never recover.

The accused was asked if he had anything to say to the jurors, and Mitya stood up. But he did not say much. He was terribly tired, both physically and mentally. The air of strength and self-reliance he had had in the morning, when he had first entered the courtroom, had evaporated. It was as though what he had experienced that day had made him understand something of the utmost importance that would stay with him for the rest of his life, something that had been quite beyond him until then. He no longer spoke loudly as he had before; his voice was weak now; there was defeat and resignation in it, and also a new kind of understanding.

"What can I tell you, gentlemen? My hour of judgment has come and I am now in the hands of God. This is the end of the wayward man I used to be. But, confessing as if to God, I say to you: 'No, I am not guilty of my father's blood!' For the last time, I tell you: 'I did not kill him!' I was dissolute, but I loved goodness. I wanted to mend my ways all the time, but I continued to live like a wild animal. I want to thank the prosecutor for telling me many things about myself that I did not know, but when he says I killed my father, the prosecutor is wrong! I want to thank my defender, too. I wept as he was speaking. But he did not have to assume that I killed my father, since I did not kill him—he shouldn't even have assumed it. And you must not believe the doctors: I am completely normal; I just feel a terrible weight on my heart. If you show mercy and acquit me, I will pray for you, and I will become a better man than I was before. I give you my word that I will, as God is my witness. If you condemn me, I will break my sword over my head with my own hands and kiss the two halves. But have mercy, gentlemen. Please, do not deprive me of my God now, for knowing myself, I am afraid I will rise against him. I feel deeply unhappy, gentlemen of the jury, spare me . . ."

He almost fell as he sank back into his chair. His voice faltered and he hardly managed to articulate the last words.

The presiding judge then read off the questions that the jurors were to answer and asked both sides to make their final statements. I will pass over all these details. At last the jurors rose, ready to retire. The presiding judge was very tired by now, so his address to the jury was quite weak; it contained all the usual exhortations, such as, "Be impartial," "Don't allow yourselves to be swayed by the eloquence of the defense counsel," "Remember, however, the great burden of responsibility you bear," etc., etc. The jurors retired and the court was adjourned.

People could now stand up, stretch their legs, have a snack at the buffet, exchange impressions. It was very late, well past 1 a.m., but no one even thought of going home. They were all much too tense and excited to think of sleep. Some people's hearts pounded wildly as they waited, while the hearts of others continued beating quite calmly. The ladies were hysterically impatient, but they were not actually worried about the verdict: "There is not the slightest doubt—he will be acquitted!" They were all waiting for the dramatic announcement. I must say that, by then, many of the men were also convinced that the accused would be acquitted; some of them were pleased about it, while others frowned gloomily. Indeed, some looked quite sad and despondent. An acquittal, they felt, would be scandalous! Fetyukovich himself was sure of success. He was surrounded by people, congratulating him and showering him with flattery. Later I was told that he said to those around him:

"Certain invisible ties must be established between the defender and the jurors during the defender's speech. I felt that the contact was made. I don't think you need worry—we've won."

"I wonder what our good peasants will say now?" said a fat, pockmarked local landowner, joining one of the groups discussing the trial.

"But they aren't actually peasants, are they? Four of them are civil servants."

"Some civil servants!" remarked a member of the local agricultural board, coming up.

"Tell me, Prokhor Nazaryev, do you know that big merchant on the jury, the one with the medal?"

"Yes. Why do you ask?"

"He has plenty of brains. Let me tell you that."

"He never says much though."

"True, he doesn't say much, but that's lucky for that Petersburg fellow, because if he opened his mouth he could teach that lawyer and all his Petersburg friends a lesson. Just think, he's the father of twelve children!"

"What are you talking about? How can they fail to acquit him!" cried someone in a group of young civil servants.

"I'm certain they'll acquit him," a voice answered him, brooking no contradiction.

"It would be a real shame and a disgrace if they didn't!" the first civil servant cried. "Even if he did kill him—there are fathers and fathers. Besides, he was in such a frantic state when it happened and, as the defender said, it could be that he simply swung the pestle and the other just fell. It's a shame they felt they had to drag that flunkey into it. It's just too ridiculous. If I were the defender, I would have said straight out, he killed him but he is not guilty, and the hell with all the rest!"

"That's exactly what he did, except for saying, 'The hell with all the rest.'"

"And he almost said that," a third voice butted in.

"But listen, after all, they acquitted that actress, during Lent, who cut the throat of her lover's legitimate wife, didn't they?"

"But she didn't cut it all the way . . ."

"What's the difference? She had a good go at it!"

"Don't you think it was marvelous what he said about fathers and children?"

"Yes, it was really great!"

"And the way he spoke about mysticism. What did you think of that?"

"Ah, forget about mystics and think of our prosecutor! Why, I bet you his wife will scratch his eyes out tomorrow for the things he said about dear Mitya-boy!"

"Isn't she here now?"

"Of course not. If she'd been here, she'd have scratched his eyes out right now! No, she's at home with a toothache, ha-ha-ha!"

"He-he-he!"

In a third group:

"Why, looks like Mitya-boy will get away with it."

"I bet he'll tear the Capital City Inn to pieces tomorrow, and he'll go on a drunken binge for at least ten days!"

"Ah, the devil!"

"You're right there—the devil must be in on it too. He'd never have been able to carry it off without the devil's help, and that's the devil's proper place!"

"All right, gentlemen, eloquence is a great thing, but I ask you now—should people really be encouraged to bash their fathers' heads in with blunt implements?"

"Speaking of eloquence, do you remember how he brought that chariot in?"

"Yes, he managed to make a chariot out of a cart!"

"But tomorrow he'll make a cart out of the chariot, if it'll help him win his case. It just depends on what's needed!"

"There are so many clever people about these days! Makes me wonder whether there is still such a thing as justice left in Russia."

The bell rang. The jurors had been out for exactly an hour, no more, no less. As soon as the public was seated, there was complete silence. I remember the jurors filing back into the courtroom. At last! I will skip the formal questions and answers on the various points—they have slipped my memory. But I remember clearly the first answer to the crucial question asked by the presiding judge: "Is the accused guilty or not guilty of the charge of premeditated murder with robbery?" (I have forgotten the exact wording.) A dead silence followed, after which the foreman of the jury—the youngest of the four civil servants—spoke out loudly and clearly in the stillness of the courtroom:

"We find the accused guilty as charged!"

And then, to the remaining questions, one after another, the answer was always the same—guilty, guilty, guilty—and always without extenuating circumstances, without recommendation for leniency. Everyone was stunned, for nearly everybody had been certain that, whatever happened, at least leniency would be recommended. The spectators were still dead silent; every single person seemed truly stunned, both those who had been hoping for an acquittal and those who had wanted a verdict of guilty. But that lasted only a few moments, and then there was a general commotion. Many men appeared to be very pleased and some of them actually rubbed their hands with joy, without bothering to conceal their delight. Those who were displeased looked depressed, shrugged in disgust, exchanged whispers, still not seeming to have realized what had happened. But the ladies, my Lord, what happened to our ladies! I thought they were going to start a riot. At first they seemed unable to believe their ears. Then cries rose from among the spectators: "What's going on here?" "What is all this?" They leapt to their feet. They apparently were under the impression that what had happened could still be changed and undone.

At that moment Mitya stood up and in a bloodcurdling voice shouted:

"I swear by God and by His last judgment that I am innocent of my father's blood! I forgive you, Katya! Brothers, friends, take care of Grusha!"

He could not go on and started to sob in a loud, frightening voice that was completely unlike him and that resounded throughout the courtroom. Then, from the farthest corner of the gallery, came the piercing shriek of a woman. It was Grushenka. She had succeeded in convincing someone or other to let her into the courtroom again before the prosecutor and the defense counsel made their speeches.

Mitya was led away. The sentencing was to take place the next day. Everyone was on his feet now. The public was in great turmoil. But I did not wait any longer or listen to what was said. I remember, though, a few exclamations I heard as I was going down the steps outside the court building:

"He'll have his noseful of the smell of mines in the next twenty years!"

"That's the least of what he'll have!"

"I must say, our good old peasants certainly stood their ground!"

"Yes, they've put dear Mitya-boy right out of the way!"

EPILOGUE

CHAPTER 1

Plans to Save Mitya

Early on the morning of the fifth day following Mitya's trial, Alyosha went to Katerina's house to settle a matter of great importance to both of them. He also had a message for her. She received him in the room where she had once received Grushenka. In the next room lay Alyosha's brother Ivan, unconscious and with a high fever. Immediately after the scene in the courtroom, Katerina had had the sick and unconscious Ivan moved to her house without bothering about the inevitable gossip that would result and the general disapproval of our town's society. One of the two relatives who had been living with her left for Moscow after the trial, while the other stayed on. But even if they had both left, Katerina would have done the same, and would have nursed Ivan night and day. Ivan was attended by Dr. Varvinsky and Dr. Herzenstube, since the Moscow doctor had returned to Moscow, refusing to commit himself on the probable outcome of the illness. The other two doctors tried to reassure Katerina and Alyosha as much as they could, but it was obvious that they could not hold out any definite hope for Ivan's recovery. Alyosha went to visit Ivan twice a day, but this time he had something special and rather unpleasant to discuss with Katerina and he knew how difficult it was going to be for him to bring up the subject. Also, he had very little time: he had other business to attend to elsewhere that same morning, so he had to be very quick about it.

They had been talking for about fifteen minutes. Katerina was very pale and tired and Alyosha could feel the nervous tension in her. She, for her part, knew what he had come to see her about now.

"You needn't worry about what he decides," she said with firm assurance. "One way or another he is bound to come to the conclusion that he must escape. That unhappy man, that man of honor and conscience—I am not speaking of Dmitry, of course, but of this one, lying sick beyond that door, who has sacrificed himself for his brother—" Katerina added with flashing eyes, "he told me long ago about the plan of escape. He had already taken steps . . . I have mentioned this to you before . . . You see, it will probably be at the third stop in the

913

convoy of convicts to Siberia. But it's still a long way off. Ivan has already been to see the commandant of the place where the party will stop after the third lap of the trip. We still don't know, though, who will be in charge of the escort, but, anyway, that's quite impossible to find out in advance. Perhaps tomorrow I'll show you the detailed plan Ivan left with me, 'just in case.' He gave it to me that evening when you came . . . We had just had a quarrel then; if you remember, he walked out and was going downstairs when he met you and I insisted that he come back. You do remember, don't you? And do you know what we quarreled about then?"

"No, I don't," Alyosha said.

"Well, of course, he couldn't tell you then, but it was precisely about that plan of escape. He had told me three days before about the idea of an escape and, for the three days that followed, we kept quarreling. Our quarrels started because Ivan announced that, if sentenced, Dmitry was to escape abroad in the company of that horrible creature, and that made me furious. Why it made me so furious I couldn't explain to you, because I don't know myself . . . Although, of course, the mere mention of that creature made me angry, and precisely because he wanted to send her abroad with Dmitry!" Katerina suddenly cried out, her lips beginning to quiver. "And when Ivan saw I was so angry about the creature, he at once decided I was jealous of her and, therefore, that I was still in love with Dmitry. That was how we first quarreled. I felt I owed him no explanations or apologies, for I resented the fact that someone like Ivan should suspect me of still being in love with that . . . after I had told him myself that I no longer loved Dmitry and loved only him! In fact, it was because of my loathing for that creature that I was angry with him. Then, three days later, which was the day you came, he handed me a sealed envelope and asked me to open it at once if anything should happen to him. Oh, I'm sure he felt that sickness of his coming on. He explained that the envelope contained a detailed plan for Dmitry's escape and that, should he fall sick or die, I would have to save Dmitry myself. And he left almost ten thousand rubles here too, the money the prosecutor, having somehow found out that Ivan had sent somebody to cash it for him, mentioned in his speech. I was suddenly very struck by the fact that, while he was jealous of Dmitry and was convinced I still loved him, he was so determined to save his brother that, seeing no other way, he asked me, of all people, to save him! Oh, that was a terribly painful decision for him to make and I'm sure, Alexei, you cannot fully appreciate the self-sacrifice it represented for him! I felt like throwing myself at his feet in admiration of such selflessness, but it occurred to me that he would interpret my doing so as joy that Mitya was to be saved—and I'm sure that is just how he would have interpreted it!—so then I was terribly irritated at the thought of his being so unfair and, instead of falling at his feet, I made another scene! Oh, I am so unhappy because of this miserable, terrible character of mine! You'll see—I'll make life so impossible for him that he, too, will leave me for some other woman, as Dmitry did, but then . . . No, that I could never bear—I'll kill myself if he does that! And when you came that time, when I called out to you to come in and asked Ivan to come back with you, he gave me a look so full of scorn and hatred that I was seized by a terrible fury and shouted that it was *he, he alone*, who had convinced me that Dmitry was the murderer. It was not true. I said it deliberately, to offend him, for he had never, never once, tried to convince me that Dmitry was the murderer; on the contrary, it was I who kept telling him that! Oh, it's all the fault of my frenzied temperament! It was I who drove him to make that horrible appearance on the witness stand, because he felt he had to prove to me how noble he was and that, even though I loved his brother, he would never allow him to perish out of jealousy or to avenge himself. And that's why he said those things in court . . . It's all my fault. I'm the one to blame for everything!"

Never before had Katerina made such admissions to Alyosha. He felt she had reached that degree of suffering when the proudest people painfully cast away their pride and collapse under the weight of their unhappiness. Alyosha knew that there was still another terrible reason for her to suffer, which she would not admit to him, and which had been tormenting her since Mitya's conviction. But it would have been very painful to him if she had decided to throw away all restraint now and tell him about it, too. Yes, she was suffering because of her "betrayal" at the trial, and Alyosha knew that her conscience was urging her to talk about it, to express all those feelings, and that it was before him, Alyosha, that she longed to let herself go, to have hysterics, scream, and writhe on the floor. He dreaded that moment and wanted to spare this unhappy woman. And that made it all the more difficult for him to give her the message he had for her. He again spoke of Mitya.

"Don't worry, don't worry about him!" she again answered stubbornly and impatiently. "That won't last—I know him only too well. Take my word for it—he'll go along with the escape plan. Besides, he has plenty of time to change his mind and, by then, Ivan will have recovered and will take charge of everything, and I'll be out of it altogether. There's nothing for you to worry about: he'll escape. In fact, I'm sure he's made up his mind already, for you don't really think, do you, that he'd be willing to be separated from that creature? And since they won't let her go to the penitentiary with him, there's no other way out for him but to escape. What makes him hesitate is the fear of your moral disapproval, Alexei. He's afraid that you'll think his fleeing is morally wrong. So all you have to do is generously give him your blessing, since he seems to need your permission so badly," she added stingingly, and then, after a brief pause, went on: "He was babbling on about hymns, about a cross, that sort of stuff—Ivan told me about it, and you should have heard the tone in which he told me about it!" she cried again with uncontrollable emotion. "I cannot convey to you how much he loved that wretched brother of his at that moment and how, at that moment too, he loathed him! And I stood there with a sarcastic smile, listening to his words and looking at the tears in his eyes! Ah, horrible creature! I am speaking of myself now, for if he is lying there in a high fever, it's all my fault! As to the convict, do you by any chance imagine that he is prepared to accept his ordeal?" Katerina asked in great irritation. "Do you think that a man like him is capable of suffering? Let me tell you that men like him never suffer at all!"

There was hatred, scorn, and loathing in the voice of this woman for the man whom she had betrayed. "It is because she feels guilty toward him that she hates him so at certain moments," Alyosha decided. And he wanted very badly for it to be only "at certain moments"! He had detected a challenge in Katerina's last words, but he ignored it.

"The reason I wanted to talk to you today was to ask you to convince him yourself to agree right now. Unless you, too, believe that running away would be dishonorable, unheroic, or what have you—perhaps un-Christian?"

She looked at him even more challengingly.

"No, no, nothing of the sort . . . I'll tell him everything . . ." Alyosha mumbled. "He would like you to come and see him today," he suddenly blurted out, looking straight into her eyes.

She gave a start and pulled back, away from him, on the sofa.

"Me? How is that possible?"

"It is both possible and necessary!" Alyosha said with warmth. "He needs you very much, especially now. I would not hurt you by bringing it up if it hadn't been urgent. He is sick, almost out of his mind, and he's asking for you. You needn't go there to make up with him: all you have to do is show yourself at the door . . . Much has changed in him since that day. He understands how infinitely guilty he is before you. He does not ask you to forgive him: 'I am unpardonable,' he says, 'I'd just like to see her at the door . . .'"

"Now you've suddenly . . ." Katerina muttered. "All these days I've known that it would come to this . . . I was certain he'd send for me . . . It's impossible though . . ."

"Impossible or not, just go there. You must understand that it's the first time he has understood how much he has hurt you. He never realized it so fully and so deeply before. He says that, if you refuse to come and see him now, he'll be unhappy for the rest of his life. So there's a man facing twenty years of hard labor but who still aspires to happiness! Isn't that moving? Just think: you will pay a visit to an unjustly condemned, innocent man!" Alyosha cried challengingly, despite himself. "His hands are clean—there is no blood on them! In the name of the long ordeal ahead of him, please go and see him now! Come, see him off as he is about to vanish into the darkness. Just show yourself in his doorway. That's all he is asking of you. And you must, you must do it," Alyosha said, emphasizing the word "must."

"I must, but I cannot . . ." Katerina moaned. "I won't be able to stand his looking at me . . . I can't . . ."

"Your eyes will have to meet. For how could you live the rest of your life if you lack the courage to face him now?"

"I'd rather suffer all my life than that."

"But you must go, understand, *you must*," Alyosha insisted, still mercilessly emphasizing the "must."

"But why must I go today, at once? . . . I cannot leave Ivan, sick as he is . . ."

"You can. You'll go there for just one minute. And if you don't go, he'll be in a fever by tonight. You know I wouldn't lie to you. So please, have mercy on him!"

"And you, have mercy on me!" Katerina said reproachfully, bursting into tears.

"So I take it you're coming," Alyosha said firmly, seeing her tears. "I'll go and tell him now that you're coming."

"No, no, you mustn't tell him that, not for anything!" she cried in terror. "I'll go there, but don't tell him anything, because I might not go in . . . I don't know yet . . ."

Her voice faltered. She was out of breath. Alyosha stood up, ready to leave.

"And what if I should meet somebody there?" she said in a quiet voice, turning completely white.

"Well, that's why I think you should go right away, for you won't meet anyone at this hour. I'm quite certain that there'll be no one else with him now. We'll be waiting for you," he concluded firmly, and left the house.

CHAPTER 2

A Lie Temporarily Becomes the Truth

Alyosha hurried to the municipal hospital, to which they had transferred Mitya the day after the trial, when he became ill with a nervous fever. He was in the prison ward. But, yielding to the pleas of Alyosha and many others, including Mrs. Khokhlakov and Lise, Dr. Varvinsky had Mitya kept away from the other prison inmates and put into a small, separate room, the one, in fact, that had previously been occupied by Smerdyakov. Still, there were bars on the window and a guard stood in the passage outside the door, so Dr. Varvinsky did not have to worry—he had allowed a slight irregularity, but he was a kind and compassionate young doctor. He understood that it would be too painful for someone like Mitya to find himself suddenly surrounded by thieves, swindlers, and murderers, and that he ought to be given a chance to get used to them. As to the visits of relatives and close friends, they were allowed not only by the doctor but also by the chief warden of the prison and by the police inspector, although that was also not strictly according to the regulations. But, thus far, the only two persons to visit Mitya had been Alyosha and Grushenka. A couple of times Rakitin had tried to see him, but Mitya had firmly asked Dr. Varvinsky not to admit him.

When Alyosha arrived, Mitya was sitting on his bed in a

hospital gown. He was running a temperature and his head was wrapped in a towel soaked in water and vinegar. He first glanced absently at Alyosha, but soon a frightened look appeared on his face.

In general, Mitya had become strangely absentminded since the trial. There were times when he would remain for half an hour without saying a word, so deeply absorbed in his own thoughts that he forgot all about his visitor. And even when he came out of his thoughts and addressed his visitor, it was always suddenly, unexpectedly, and he always sounded as though he had said something other than what he had intended to say. Now and then, Alyosha caught Mitya looking at him with deep compassion. With Grushenka, he felt easier than with Alyosha, although he spoke very little to her. But every time she came, his face would light up with joy.

Alyosha sat down on a stool next to his cot. This time, Dmitry had been awaiting Alyosha's arrival with great apprehension, but he waited for Alyosha to speak first, for he did not dare ask him what had happened. He was sure that Katerina would refuse to come and, at the same time, he felt that, if she did not come, he would be unable to face his future. Alyosha knew exactly what was going on inside his brother.

"What do you think about Trifon?" Mitya began breathlessly. "I understand he's pulling out the floorboards, tearing up the planks, taking his whole inn to pieces, looking for that treasure, for that fifteen hundred rubles the prosecutor said I hid there! I understand that he started searching for the money as soon as he got home. Let him work for nothing then, and I hope it teaches the swindler a lesson! The guard here told me—he comes from Mokroye, you know . . ."

"Listen," Alyosha said, "she's coming. I don't know exactly when. It may be today or any of these days, but she definitely is coming, that's sure."

Mitya started. He was about to say something but changed his mind. The news had a violent effect on him. He was obviously longing to know more of what Katerina had said to Alyosha, but again he was afraid to ask: anything scornful or cruel on Katya's part would have felt like the slash of a knife to him at that moment.

"She asked me, by the way, to reassure you about the escape, to tell you that you can do it with a clear conscience.

You know that, if Ivan hasn't recovered by that time, she will take care of everything herself."

"You've told me that already," Mitya said musingly.

"And you have already repeated it to Grushenka."

"Yes," Mitya admitted. "She won't come until the evening today," he said, looking shyly at Alyosha. "When I told her that Katya was arranging things, her lips twisted, but she said nothing at first. Later she whispered only: 'Let her.' She knows it's important. I couldn't keep her in ignorance any longer. I'm sure that, by now, she must have understood that Katya no longer loves me, that she loves Ivan."

"But is that the truth?" Alyosha could not help asking.

"Maybe it isn't. In any case, she won't come this morning," Mitya said hurriedly, to make it clear. "I've asked her to do an errand for me . . . Listen, Alyosha, Ivan will surpass everybody. If anybody must live, it is him more than us. He'll recover."

"Strangely enough, Katya, who is terribly worried about him, also has no doubt that he'll pull through," Alyosha said.

"That means she's convinced he will die. It's because she's so afraid of it that she's sure he'll recover."

"Ivan has a strong constitution," Alyosha said worriedly, "and I am very, very hopeful that he will recover."

"He will recover, but Katya is convinced he'll die. There is so much unhappiness in her . . ."

They fell silent. Something very important was tormenting Mitya.

"Alyosha, I love Grusha terribly," Mitya said suddenly in a quivering voice.

"They won't allow her to follow you *there*," Alyosha put in quickly.

"And this is what I wanted to tell you," Mitya said in a voice that had suddenly acquired a strange ringing quality, "if anyone ever raises a hand to me, whether on the way or *there*, I won't stand for it; I'll kill him and they'll shoot me. And I'm supposed to bear it for twenty years! They're already addressing me as, 'Hey you!' here, before we've even left. Last night I lay here and I decided that I'm not ready for it. I have no strength to bear it! I thought before that I'd sing that 'hymn,' but I see now that I can't even get over being pushed around by the guards. I'm willing to bear anything for Grusha's sake . . . no, not the beatings. But, anyway, they won't allow her to follow me *there*."

Alyosha listened to him with a gentle smile.

"Let me tell you once and for all what I think a...
Mitya. And you know very well that I'd never lie to you...
listen: you're not ready for it and that ordeal is not for you.
And since you're not ready for it, there's no need for you to
go through such a martyrdom. If you had killed father, I
would be sad to see you trying to evade your cross. But you
are innocent, and that cross would be too much for you. You
want to regenerate yourself and become a new man through
suffering. But I think it will be enough for you if you remember all your life that new man you want to be, wherever you
are after you have escaped from here. And indeed, by escaping the great ordeal, you will become even more acutely
aware of your debt, for the rest of your life, and that will
help your regeneration perhaps even more than if you went
there. For if you went *there*, you wouldn't be able to bear it,
and you'd rebel, and perhaps you'd really say to yourself, 'We
are even now!' The defense counsel was right about that. Not
every man can bear the same burden; for some, it may prove
to be beyond their strength . . . Well, that is what I think, if it
really interests you. If others had to be made responsible for
your escape—officers or soldiers of the escort, or whoever—I
would not have 'allowed' you to go through with it," Alyosha
said with a smile. "But I understand, they assured me—the
commandant even told Ivan—that if it's done cleverly, there
won't be much trouble for anyone, and they could get off
with practically nothing. I know, of course, that bribery is
dishonest, even under these circumstances, but I really have
no right to judge, for if Ivan and Katya had wanted me to
handle it for you, I'd have paid the bribes myself, and that's
the truth. So I cannot judge you if you do it, but I want you
to know that I will never condemn you for doing it. Besides,
when you think of it—how could I possibly be your judge?
Well, I think that's just about it for now."

"You may never condemn me, but I'll condemn myself!"
Mitya cried. "I'll escape. It was settled without you, for how
could old Mitya Karamazov turn down an offer to escape?
And then I'll condemn myself and, wherever I find myself,
I'll keep praying that my sins be forgiven me! Isn't that the
way the Jesuits talk? That's what we've come to, is it?"

"Right." Alyosha smiled gently.

"You always tell the whole truth, never hold back anything,
and I love you for it!" Mitya said with a joyful laugh. "So
now I've caught my little brother Alyosha behaving like a
Jesuit! I feel like giving you a huge hug for it! Listen to the

rest of it then; let me bare the other half of my soul. Here is what I have been thinking about and what I have decided: if I were to escape, and even if it were with money and a passport, and I managed to get as far away as America, what cheers me is the thought that what I'd find there would not be joy and happiness, but something that might be even worse than hard labor in Siberia. Yes, worse, Alexei, believe me. I know what I'm saying! That America, God damn it, I hate it already! Even if Grusha is with me, for look at her, what kind of an American woman is she? Every little bone in her body is Russian, that's how Russian she is, and in no time she'll be missing her old Russia terribly, and I'll have to watch her being miserable and homesick, and I'll know that it was because of me that she accepted that awful ordeal, she who has really done nothing to deserve it! And I myself, do you imagine I'll be able to live there among those completely strange natives, even though every one of them may be a much better man than I am. I hate America already, from here! And even if every one of those fellows was the greatest of engineers or the greatest anything, I still say the hell with them, they aren't my kind of people, and I don't want to have anything to do with them. It's Russia I love, Alexei, and I love the Russian God, although I myself am no good. I'll die there like a dog," Dmitry suddenly cried with flashing eyes, his voice quivering with suppressed sobs.

"So here is what I have decided, Alexei," he went on, overcoming his emotion. "As soon as Grusha and I get there, we'll move somewhere far out of the way, where there is nothing but wild bears, and we'll settle on the land, and till the soil. Because there certainly must be such wild places there too. I understand that there are still some Redskins about, somewhere on the frontier, on the horizon, the last of the Mohicans or something—well, that's where I want to go, to the frontier, to those Mohicans . . . And right away, we'll start learning English, both Grusha and I, and we'll keep at it for three years; it will be nothing but tilling the land and grammar all that time. Well, after those three years, we'll know English like genuine English people and, as soon as we do, that will be the end of America! We'll return to Russia as American citizens. Ah, you needn't worry, we won't come back to this lousy town. We'll hide ourselves somewhere far away, in the north or in the south, I don't know, and I'll look different by then, and she will too. Some doctor over there in America will graft a wart or something onto my face, for they're great technicians, those Americans, after all. And if they can't manage that, I'll take out one of my eyes and grow a yard-long, gray beard—for my hair will have turned gray from homesickness by then—and I hope they'll never recognize me. If they do, let them pack me off to Siberia then; that'll just prove it was my fate, after all, to end up there . . . So if they don't find me out, we'll settle here, somewhere out of the way too, and work the land, and I'll just have to pretend I'm an American as long as I live. But at least we'll die in our own country. That is my plan and it is final. So what do you say to it? Do you approve?"

"I approve all right," Alyosha said, not wanting to contradict him.

Mitya remained silent for a moment, then suddenly said:

"And what do you say about the trial? It was all fixed in advance, wasn't it?"

"Whether it was or not, you would have been convicted anyway," Alyosha said with a sigh.

"Yes, I suppose people around here got tired of seeing my face. Well, that's just the way they feel, I suppose, but it does hurt!"

They remained silent for a moment and then Mitya burst out:

"Alyosha, hit me with it right now: is she coming now or not? What did she actually say to you? How did she say it?"

"She said she'd come, but she didn't know whether she'd come today. You must understand that it isn't easy for her," Alyosha said, looking timidly at his brother.

"Oh, I'm sure it isn't easy for her. I know that! It's driving me mad, Alyosha! And the way Grusha keeps looking at me —she understands everything. O God, punish me! What is it I want? I want Katya! Do I know myself what I'm after? It's that same, unrestrained, unholy Karamazov urge! No, I'm not ready for the ordeal—I'm just a low scoundrel and nothing more!"

"Here she is!" Alyosha said.

Katerina appeared in the doorway. She stopped for a second, looking forlorn, her eyes on Mitya. He turned pale and leapt to his feet. He looked very frightened at first, but within a second, a shy, beseeching smile appeared on his lips and he stretched out his arms toward Katerina. When she saw it, she flew to him impetuously, seized him by the hands, almost forced him to sit down on his cot, and sat down close by him, never letting go of his hands and pressing them spasmodically. Several times she tried to say something but apparently could not, and they kept looking into each other's eyes, smiling strangely. It was as if they were shackled together. Two minutes passed in that way.

"Have you forgiven me?" Mitya muttered at last and then, turning toward Alyosha, his face beaming with joy, he cried out to him: "Did you hear? Did you hear what I asked her?"

"That is why I loved you!" Katya cried emotionally. "I loved you because you are so generous. Besides, you have no need of my forgiveness and I have no need of yours. For whether you forgive me or not, you'll always remain an open wound in my conscience, just as I will be in yours. And this is as it should be." She stopped to catch her breath, then continued very quickly, in a fervent, exalted tone. "I've come to embrace your feet, to press your hands so hard that it hurts you, just as I did in Moscow, remember. I've come to tell you again that you are my god, my joy, to tell you that I love you, love you terribly . . ." A moan of pain escaped her lips. She suddenly pressed them violently to Dmitry's hand, as tears gushed from her eyes. Alyosha stood there in speechless embarrassment; he had never expected anything of this sort.

"Love is gone, Mitya," she began again, "but what is gone is so dear to me that it hurts. I want you to know it always. But now, for a brief moment only, let there be something that could have been," she said with a twisted smile, looking happily into his eyes. "I know you are now in love with another woman, and I myself am in love with another man, but nevertheless I'll always love you and you'll always love me. Didn't you know that? You must always love me, as long as you live, do you hear me?" she said with a quiver in her voice that sounded almost like a threat.

"I shall love you, you know that, Katya," Dmitry said, breathing heavily between words. "You know, that evening, five days ago, when you fainted there and they carried you away . . . I loved you. And all my life it will be like that, always . . ."

And they went on murmuring wild, almost incoherent things to each other, things that were perhaps not even really true. But at that second they were true, and the two of them believed them unquestioningly.

"Katya," Mitya suddenly asked her, "did you believe I killed him? I know you don't believe it now, but did you believe it then . . . when you were on the witness stand? . . . Did you really believe it?"

"I didn't believe it then either! I never believed it! I hated you then and I just managed to convince myself for one second . . . Just when I was testifying . . . Yes, I believed it . . . But as soon as I had finished testifying—I no longer did. You must know all that. Ah, I forgot that I came here to punish myself," she added, her expression changing abruptly from what it had been when they were murmuring lovingly to each other.

"It's hard on you, woman." The words came quite unexpectedly from Mitya's lips.

"Let me go now," she whispered. "I'll come again; it's too painful now."

She stood up. But all of a sudden she let out a piercing cry and reeled back.

Grushenka had entered the room. She had come in with her light, noiseless step and none of them had heard her. They had not expected her then. Katerina took a couple of quick, determined steps toward the door, but when she reached Grushenka, she stopped. Her face was completely bloodless. In a whisper reminiscent of a sigh, she said to her:

"Forgive me . . ."

Grushenka looked straight into her eyes for a few seconds and then, in a voice distorted with fury, answered:

"We are too vicious, my good woman, both of us, and we're both past the niceties of forgiveness. But all you have to do now is to save him, and if you do, I promise I'll pray for you as long as I live."

"You refused to forgive her!" Mitya shouted at Grushenka in a crazily reproachful voice.

"You needn't worry, I'll save him for you!" Katerina said in a quick whisper, and hurried out of the room.

"How could you not forgive her after she said to you herself, 'Forgive me'?" Mitya persisted bitterly.

"You have no right to make such reproaches to Grushenka!" Alyosha told him heatedly.

"It was just that insolent mouth of hers that asked for forgiveness, it wasn't her heart," Grushenka said in a strangely disgusted tone. "But if she gets you out of trouble, I'll forgive her for everything anyway."

She fell silent, as if suppressing something within her. She still had not quite taken hold of herself. It turned out later that she had just come to see Mitya on the spur of the moment, without any suspicion of whom she might find with him.

"Run after her, Alyosha," Mitya cried agitatedly. "Tell her . . . I don't know what you should tell her. Just don't let her go away like that . . ."

"I'll come back in the evening," Alyosha cried as he rushed out to catch Katerina. When he caught up with her, she had already left the hospital grounds. She was walking very fast, but when she saw Alyosha she turned toward him and said:

"No, I cannot prostrate myself before that woman! I asked her to forgive me, because I wanted to punish myself completely. She didn't forgive me. I like her for that!" Katerina added in an unrecognizable voice, her eyes flashing with a wild hatred.

"Mitya was not expecting her to come. He was sure she wouldn't come," Alyosha muttered lamely.

"I'm sure of that, but let's forget it," she snapped. "Listen, I can't go to that funeral with you now. I've already had flowers sent. I think they must still have enough money left. And tell them that if they need some later, I'll never abandon them. And now leave me, please. Besides, you'll never get there in time—the bells are ringing for late mass . . . Oh, leave me, please . . ."

CHAPTER 3

Ilyusha's Funeral. The Speech by the Stone

As Katerina had thought, Alyosha did not get there in time. They had waited for him and had finally decided to carry the pretty little coffin, all bedecked with flowers, to the church without him. It was Ilyusha's coffin. The poor child had died two days after Mitya had been sentenced. When Ilyusha's young friends saw Alyosha at the gate, they called out to him: they were greatly relieved to see he had come at last. There were twelve schoolboys there and they had all come with their schoolbags slung across their shoulders.

"Papa will cry," Ilyusha had told them before he died. "Please stay with him." And now the boys wanted to do as he had asked them. Kolya Krasotkin was at the head of the group.

"I'm so glad to see you!" Kolya exclaimed, shaking Alyosha's hand. "It's so awfully depressing here, really painful

to watch. We know for certain that Snegirev hasn't had anything to drink all day, but he's acting just as if he were
drunk . . . I've always been able to control my feelings, but
what's happening here today is really horrible! But before
you go in, Karamazov, may I ask just one thing, if it's all
right with you?"

"What is it, Kolya?" Alyosha said, stopping.

"Is your brother really guilty or is he innocent? Was it he
or the lackey who killed your father? I'll believe whatever you
tell me. I've spent four sleepless nights trying to work it out."

"My brother didn't do it. It was the lackey."

"That's what I said all along!" young Smurov suddenly
cried out.

"And so your brother will perish, an innocent victim, for
the truth!" Kolya cried. "He is a happy man, although he has
been condemned. Indeed, I envy him!"

"What are you talking about? What do you mean by that?"
Alyosha said in surprise.

"Oh, if only I knew that one day I would be given the
chance to sacrifice myself for truth and justice," Kolya said
enthusiastically.

"But you certainly can't mean like that, not with the terrible disgrace and horror it involved!" Alyosha cried.

"Of course, what I want is to die in the service of mankind
as a whole. As for the disgrace, what difference does it make?
Let our names be disgraced if they must! I respect your
brother!"

"And so do I!" the boy who had once announced that he
knew who had founded Troy cried out quite unexpectedly.
And now, as then, having made his announcement, he turned
red as a peony.

Alyosha entered the room. Ilyusha, with his hands folded
on his chest, lay in a blue coffin edged with a white frill. The
emaciated face had hardly changed and, strangely enough,
almost no smell came from the boy's body. His face wore a
stern expression, as if he were deep in thought. The crossed
hands were particularly beautiful; they looked as if they had
been carved out of marble. There were flowers in Ilyusha's
hands, and the whole coffin was covered with flowers. They
had been brought in early in the morning, having been
ordered by Lise Khokhlakov. There were flowers from Katerina too, and when Alyosha went in, Snegirev had a bunch
of flowers in his shaking hands and was scattering them over

his dear boy. As Alyosha entered, Snegirev hardly glanced at
him. In fact, he hardly paid any attention to anyone, not even
to his weeping, crazy wife, who kept trying to get up on her
crippled legs to have a closer look at her dead son. The
schoolboys had brought Ilyusha's sister Nina close to the coffin in her chair, and now she was sitting there right next to
it, her head pressed against the wood, crying quietly. Snegirev
looked agitated and bewildered, and also evidenced a certain
frantic exasperation. There was something insane in his gestures and in the words that escaped him now and then. "Old
man, ah, dear old man!" he kept exclaiming, looking at
Ilyusha, for he used to call him "old man" as a term of affection, when the boy was still alive.

"Papa, I want some flowers too!" crazy Mrs. Snegirev
whimpered. "Take that white one out of his hand and give it
to me!"

Either because the little white rose fascinated her or because she wanted the flower as a keepsake, since it had been
in her boy's hands, she became very excited and stretched out
her hands toward the flower.

"Nobody can have it! They are his flowers, not yours!"
Snegirev snapped at her mercilessly.

"Papa, please, give the flower to mamma," Nina said, raising her tearstained face to her father.

"I won't give anything to anyone, and to her least of all!
She never loved him! That time she took the little cannon
away from him—and he let her have it . . ." Snegirev suddenly cried in a sobbing voice, remembering how the boy had
yielded the cannon to his mother.

The poor madwoman burst into tears, hiding her face in
her hands.

The time came to carry the coffin out, but Snegirev would
not budge from it. The schoolboys surrounded it and started
to lift it.

"I don't want him to be buried in the churchyard!" Snegirev screamed; "he must be buried by our big stone. The way
Ilyusha wanted it. I won't let you take him away!"

Long before, he had said that he wanted the boy buried by
the stone, but now everybody intervened—Alyosha, Kolya,
the old landlady, Nina, and all the boys.

"What are you thinking of—wanting the child buried by
that unholy stone?" the landlady said severely. "That's where
they'd bury someone who'd hanged himself or something. He
must be buried in the churchyard, which is holy ground, under

a cross. They'll pray for him there. The singing and the deacon's reading can be heard clearly from the church there, so it's as if they were reading right over his grave."

Finally Snegirev waved his arms in helpless despair, as if saying, "All right, do whatever you want."

The boys picked up the coffin, but as they carried it past Ilyusha's mother, they lowered it to allow her to say a last good-by to her son. And now that she saw the child's face so close to her, after having looked at it for three days at a distance, she suddenly started to shake all over and toss her gray head back and forth.

"Mother, make the sign of the cross over him. Give him your blessing, and kiss him," Nina prompted her.

But Mrs. Snegirev went on jerking her head like an automaton, her face contorted with pain, and, without saying a word, suddenly started pounding her breast with her fist.

The boys picked up the coffin, and when they lowered it beside Nina, she kissed her brother's lips for the last time.

As he was leaving the house, Alyosha asked the landlady to look after Ilyusha's mother and his sister who, of course, had to stay behind. But she did not even give him a chance to finish.

"I know, I know, I'm a Christian too. I'll look after them," she said. She was weeping too.

It wasn't far to the church, three hundred yards or so. It was a clear, windless day and the temperature was only slightly below freezing. The bells were still ringing. Snegirev followed the coffin with a worried, forlorn look. He wore his short summer overcoat and his head was bare; he carried his wide-brimmed felt hat in his hand. He seemed to be trying to cope with some insurmountable difficulty: he would suddenly dash up in front of the coffin and hold out his hand to support it, getting in the way of those were carrying it, and then he would come at it from the side and look for a spot there. And when a flower fell into the snow, he hurried to pick it up with an expression so tense that it seemed as if everything depended on his retrieving that flower.

"What about the piece of bread? We forgot the bread!" he suddenly cried out in panic.

The boys reminded him that he had taken a piece of bread and put it in his pocket earlier. He took it out to make sure it was there and then grew calmer.

"Ilyusha wanted it," he explained. "As I sat by his bed one night, he said to me: 'Papa, when they fill my grave, I want

you to scatter some bread crumbs on top of it, so the sparrows will come and I'll have company there and it will be
fun!' "

"That's a good idea," Alyosha said. "You should scatter
crumbs on his grave often."

"Every day, every single day!" Snegirev said quickly, visibly
cheered.

They reached the church, placing the coffin in the middle
of it. The boys stood around it and remained standing reverently throughout the service. The church was old and poor
and many of the icons had no settings, but somehow one
prays better in such churches. Snegirev seemed to have calmed
down somewhat, although, from time to time, that perplexed,
worried look would reappear on his face, and then he would
approach the coffin to set the cover or a wreath straight, and
when a candle fell out of its candlestick, he rushed up and
busied himself for a very long time with putting it back. When
he had finally done it, he stood still by the head of the coffin
with a dumbly worried and bewildered expression. After the
epistle, he suddenly whispered into Alyosha's ear that "they
hadn't read it quite right," but he did not elaborate further.
During the hymn "Like the Cherubim," he tried to join in the
singing but soon gave up, knelt down, put his forehead on the
stone floor, and remained in that position for a long time.

Then they distributed candles and started the requiem
chant. The poor father was again overwhelmed with misery
and started to fidget. But the moving chants brought him back
to reality with a shock. He suddenly seemed to have shrunk
and started to shake in short sobs, at first silent but soon
uncontrolled and noisy. When the time came for him to take
leave of his dead son and to close the coffin, he put his arms
around the casket, as if trying to prevent them from covering
his little Ilyusha, and kissed the dead boy's lips eagerly and
lengthily. They finally succeeded in making him step down,
but he suddenly rushed back to the coffin, put his hand inside
it, and snatched up a few flowers. As he stared at those
flowers, some new idea must have come to him and he seemed
to have forgotten for the moment where he was and what was
going on around him. He was now as if in a dream and
offered no resistance when they picked up the coffin and carried it to the open grave. It was an expensive grave, very close
to the church. It had been paid for by Katerina. After the
customary rites, the coffin was lowered into the ground.
Snegirev went so close to the open grave and bent so far over

it, still holding the flowers in his hand, that the boys, afraid that he would fall in, seized him by the skirts of his coat and pulled him back. But he obviously no longer realized what was happening around him. When they started to fill the grave, he pointed anxiously to the falling earth, said something that no one understood, and then gave up and fell silent. Then they reminded him about the bread crumbs, and, becoming very agitated, he took the piece of bread from his pocket and started tearing small bits off it and throwing them on the grave:

"Come down, little birdies, come, little sparrows," he muttered.

One of the boys pointed out to him that it would be easier for him if he allowed someone to hold the flowers while he scattered the crumbs, but Snegirev refused, even looking frightened, as if they wanted to take the flowers away from him. He looked at the grave to make sure that everything was in order and that the crumbs were in place, and then, to everybody's surprise, he turned away and slowly started walking home. Gradually his steps became faster and faster and soon he was almost running. Alyosha and the boys followed close behind him.

"Flowers for mamma, for mamma! We've not been nice to her!" he suddenly cried out, and then repeated it again and again.

Somebody suggested he put on his hat, for it was growing very cold. Somehow that seemed to anger him and he flung his hat into the snow muttering, "I don't want the hat, I don't want it . . ." Young Smurov picked it up and carried it after him. All the boys were crying, and the two who cried the hardest were Kolya and the boy who knew who had founded Troy. And although Smurov, who was carrying the hat, was weeping too, he nevertheless managed to snatch up, almost on the run, a piece of brick that looked very red in the snow and to throw it at a flock of sparrows that was flying by. Of course, he missed and continued to trot along, the tears running down his cheeks. Half way home, Snegirev suddenly stopped, stood still for half a minute, then briskly turning back as if he had remembered something, set off toward the grave they had left. The boys quickly caught up with him, surrounding him on all sides. He fell helplessly into the snow, as if someone had pushed him down, and started to wail and sob, writhing on the ground and crying out: "Ilyusha! Old

man! Ilyusha!" Alyosha and Kolya tried to reason with him
and make him get up.

"Captain, Captain Snegirev, you must bear it—you are a
brave man," Kolya said.

"You'll spoil the flowers!" Alyosha said. "Mrs. Snegirev
is crying. She is waiting for these flowers—you didn't give
her any of Ilyusha's flowers . . . And Ilyusha's bed is still
there . . ."

"Yes, yes, let's go back to mamma," Snegirev said, suddenly
remembering her. "Ah, and they will take the bed away! They
will, they will take it away!" he cried worriedly, and then got
to his feet and started running, toward the house now.

They got there very quickly, all of them together. Snegirev
opened the door and shouted to his wife, at whom he had
snapped so sharply about the flowers before:

"Here, mamma dear, Ilyusha has sent you some flowers.
Ah, you poor dear with your sore legs!"

And he handed her the little bunch of frozen flowers. Many
of them had been broken while he was writhing in the snow.

But in that same second he caught sight of Ilyusha's little
boots by the boy's bed. They had been put neatly together
there by the landlady, who had come in and tidied the room.
Snegirev looked at Ilyusha's old, patched, ragged, and discol-
ored boots for a second; then he quickly knelt beside them,
picked them up, and kissed them ardently, crying out: "Ah,
Ilyusha, old man, my Ilyusha, ah, and where are your poor
little feet now? . . ."

"Where did you take him, where?" the crazy woman
screamed at him in a bloodcurdling voice.

Now Nina began to sob too. Kolya rushed out of the room
and the boys started to file out behind him. Alyosha was the
last to come out.

"Let them cry in peace," Alyosha said. "There's nothing
we can do now to make them feel better. Let's wait here for
a while and then go back in."

"Yes, indeed, we can do nothing, and that's the worst of
it," Kolya said. "You know, Karamazov," he said, lowering
his voice so as not to be overheard by the others, "I feel so
awful about it. I would give anything in the world to bring
him back to life!"

"So would I," Alyosha said.

"Do you really think we should come back here this evening, Karamazov? Why, he's sure to have got himself drunk
by then."

"He may very well do precisely that. Let's just the two of us come back and spend an hour with Mrs. Snegirev and Nina. I think it would be better if the others didn't come, for all of us together here would bring it all back to them," Alyosha suggested.

"The landlady is laying the table in there now. They'll have a funeral repast, I suppose, and the priest is coming back too. Do you think we have to go back there right now?"

"I certainly do think so."

"Doesn't it strike you as peculiar, though, when you stop to think of it? There's such terrible grief there and now they're supposed to eat those pancakes . . . All these religious things are so unnatural!"

"They'll have smoked salmon too," the expert on Troy put in unexpectedly in a loud voice.

"I'd greatly appreciate it, Kartashov, if you'd spare us your asinine remarks when no one has asked for your opinion or, for that matter, is even aware that you exist!" Kolya snapped at the boy, who turned beet-red but did not dare to answer.

In the meantime, they had walked quite a distance down the path and suddenly Smurov cried:

"Here's Ilyusha's stone, under which he wanted to be buried!"

They stopped silently by the big stone. Alyosha visualized the whole scene that had taken place there, that Snegirev had described to him. He saw the boy hugging his father and saying: "Papa, papa, it's terrible what he did to you, the way he insulted you!" Something happened within Alyosha and, looking at all those bright young faces around him, he said:

"Boys, there's something I'd like to tell you here, by this stone."

They crowded around him in a semi-circle, looking at him in expectation.

"Boys, you and I will have to part quite soon. I'll have to stay here for some time, though, with my two brothers. One of them is waiting to be sent off to Siberia. The other is very ill, and his life is in danger. But I'll leave this town soon enough and may be gone for a very long time. And so we shall part. So let us agree, here by this stone, that we shall never forget, first, Ilyusha and, second, one another. And whatever happens to us later in life, even if we do not meet again for the next twenty years, let us always remember this day when we buried the poor little boy whom we previously pelted with stones—remember, by that bridge?—and to whom,

later, we all became so attached. He was a nice, kind, brave
boy, very conscious of his father's dignity and very sensitive
to the cruel insults showered on his father. And it was against
those insults that he revolted. And so let us, each one of us,
remember him as long as we live. And whether you are
absorbed in the most important pursuits, reaching out for the
highest honors, or struck down by the cruelest griefs, always
remember how good it felt when we were all here together,
united by a good and decent feeling, which made us, while
we all loved this boy, better people, probably, than we would
otherwise have been.

"You look to me at this moment like so many little doves,
and that's what I'd like to call you, 'my little doves,' for you
look like those pretty, gray-blue birds, your faces are so nice
and kind. My dear boys, possibly you won't even understand
what I'm saying now, for I often speak very unclearly, but I
think you'll remember it, nevertheless, and some day you may
agree with my words.

"I want you to understand, then, that there is nothing
nobler, stronger, healthier, and more helpful in life than a
good remembrance, particularly a remembrance from our
childhood, when we still lived in our parents' house. You
often hear people speak about upbringing and education, but
I feel that a beautiful, holy memory preserved from early
childhood can be the most important single thing in our
development. And if a person succeeds, in the course of his
life, in collecting many such memories, he will be saved for
the rest of his life. And even if we have only one such memory, it is possible that it will be enough to save us some day.
Perhaps some of us will even turn evil one day; perhaps we
will be unable to resist wicked temptations, will sneer at other
people's tears, and will laugh spitefully at those who exclaim,
as Kolya did today, that they would like to suffer for all men.
But bad and wicked though we may become—which God
forbid should happen to us—whenever we remember Ilyusha,
how he died, how we loved him, how united we all were by
this big stone, the cruelest and the most sarcastic of us, if that
is what he has become, will still never dare, deep inside, to
laugh at the good, kind boy he was at this moment! More
than that—perhaps this memory will protect him from suc-
cumbing to the temptation to commit a mortal sin and he will
think better of it, saying to himself: 'Yes, there was a moment
when I was good and kind and brave!' Let him grin ironically
at himself then, it doesn't matter, for a man often laughs at

what is good and kind—it is only part of his thoughtlessness. But as soon as he grins in that way, he will feel deep down, 'No, it's not right for me to laugh at it, because this is a thing at which we must never laugh.' "

"I understand very well what you mean, Karamazov, and I'm sure it's the absolute truth!" Kolya cried with flashing eyes.

The younger boys were moved and wanted to voice their approval too, but restrained themselves, looking at Alyosha with warmth and admiration.

"I say this in case any of us should turn wicked," Alyosha said, "but there is no need for us to become wicked, don't you agree, boys? Let us be first of all kind and then honest, and finally let us never forget one another. Let me give you my word that, for my part, I will never forget any of you. Even in thirty years, I will remember each face that is turned toward me at this second. A few minutes ago, for instance, Kolya said to Kartashov that he didn't care whether Kartashov existed or not. But how could I ever forget that Kartashov exists and that, at this second, he is not blushing as he did after he had founded Troy, but is simply looking at me out of his nice, kind, cheerful eyes? Let us, my dear boys, be as brave and generous as Ilyusha, as intelligent, bold, and generous as Kolya—and he will become still more intelligent when he grows up—and as shy, intelligent, and sweet as Kartashov! But there was no special reason for me to mention Krasotkin and Kartashov rather than anyone else, for, from today on, I shall carry you all in my heart and I beg you, every one of you, to accept me also in yours! And the one who will unite us all in this noble feeling, the one whom we shall and are determined always to remember is our kind, sweet little Ilyusha, the boy whom we shall cherish forever and ever! So let us never forget him, let us always treasure his memory in our hearts, now and always!"

"Yes, yes, now and always! Forever and ever!" the boys cried out in their ringing young voices, all looking at Alyosha with great emotion.

"We shall remember his face and his dress, his poor little boots, and his little coffin; and also, his unhappy, sinful father, in defense of whom Ilyusha so bravely challenged his whole class!"

"Yes, we shall remember him; he was brave and he was kind!" the boys cried again.

"Oh, I loved him so!" Kolya exclaimed.

"You know, boys," Alyosha said, "you needn't be afraid of life! Life is so good when you do something that is good and just."

"Yes, yes, right!" some of the boys cried enthusiastically.

"We like you, Karamazov!" cried a voice that could very well have been Kartashov's.

"We all like you, love you!" all the boys joined in, and tears glistened in their eyes.

"Three cheers for Karamazov!" Kolya shouted solemnly.

"May the memory of the dead boy live forever!" Alyosha said.

"May it live forever!" the boys echoed.

"Karamazov," Kolya said suddenly, "can it be true, as our religion claims, that we shall all rise from the dead, come back to life, and meet again, Ilyusha too?"

"We shall certainly rise and we shall certainly all meet again and tell each other happily and joyfully everything that has happened to us," Alyosha said laughingly but, at the same time, fervently.

"Ah, won't that be good!" Kolya cried spontaneously.

"But now, enough talking, for it's time to go to the funeral repast. And don't feel embarrassed when you eat those pancakes. Since it's an ancient, eternal custom, there must be something that's right about it!" Alyosha laughed. "Well, let's go then, hand in hand!"

"And let's always go like this, hand in hand, throughout our lives, and three cheers for Karamazov!" Kolya shouted ecstatically, and again the boys cheered Alyosha.

ABOUT THE TRANSLATOR

ANDREW R. MACANDREW, the translator of *THE BROTHERS KARAMAZOV*, is a teacher of literature at the University of Virginia. He has translated over forty books, French as well as Russian, and has written numerous articles for national magazines, HARPER'S Magazine, THE REPORTER, NEW REPUBLIC and COMMENTARY among them. Mr. MacAndrew has translated three books for Bantam: *Three Short Novels* and *The Gambler* by Dostoevsky and *Great Russian Short Novels*.

THE NAMES THAT SPELL GREAT LITERATURE

Choose from today's most renowned world authors—every one an important addition to your personal library.

Hermann Hesse

☐	2906	KNULP	—$1.95
☐	2645	MAGISTER LUDI	—$1.75
☐	2944	DEMIAN	—$1.75
☐	10060	GERTRUDE	—$1.95
☐	10136	THE JOURNEY TO THE EAST	—$1.75
☐	10266	SIDDHARTHA	—$1.75
☐	10352	BENEATH THE WHEEL	—$1.95
☐	10466	NARCISSUS AND GOLDMUND	—$1.95
☐	11289	STEPPENWOLF	—$1.95
☐	11510	ROSSHALDE	—$1.95

Alexander Solzhenitsyn

☐	11712	ONE DAY IN THE LIFE OF IVAN DENISOVICH	—$1.95
☐	2997	AUGUST 1914	—$2.50
☐	7409	STORIES AND PROSE POEMS	—$1.50
☐	10246	THE LOVE-GIRL AND THE INNOCENT	—$1.50
☐	11300	CANCER WARD	—$2.50

Jerzy Kosinski

☐	10625	BEING THERE	—$1.75
☐	11100	STEPS	—$1.75
☐	11407	THE PAINTED BIRD	—$1.95
☐	2613	COCKPIT	—$2.25

Doris Lessing

☐	2640	THE SUMMER BEFORE THE DARK	—$1.95
☐	10425	THE GOLDEN NOTEBOOK	—$2.25
☐	7937	THE FOUR-GATED CITY	—$1.95
☐	11717	BRIEFING FOR A DESCENT INTO HELL	—$2.25

André Schwarz-Bart

☐	10469	THE LAST OF THE JUST	—$1.95

Buy them at your local bookstore or use this handy coupon for ordering:

Bantam Book Catalog

Here's your up-to-the-minute listing of every book currently available from Bantam.

This easy-to-use catalog is divided into categories and contains over 1400 titles by your favorite authors.

So don't delay—take advantage of this special opportunity to increase your reading pleasure.

Just send us your name and address and 25¢ (to help defray postage and handling costs).